Men may cry peace, but there is no peace.

Jeremiah

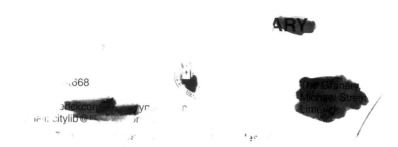

CRY PEACE

By the same author

FICTION

China and the West:
Manchu (1624–1652)
Mandarin (1854–1875)
Dynasty (1900–1970)
White Sun, Red Star (1921–1952)

A Kind of Treason
The Seeking
Bianca
The Everlasting Sorrow
The Big Brown Bears
Last Year in Hong Kong

NON-FICTION

China's Red Leaders
The Dragon's Seed
The Centre of the World
Mao's Great Revolution
Mao versus Chiang
The Great Cities: Hong Kong
Pacific Destiny: Inside Asia Today

CRY PEACE

Robert Elegant

ROBERT HALE · LONDON

© Robert Elegant 2005
First published in Great Britain 2005

ISBN 0 7090 7828 5

Robert Hale Limited
Clerkenwell House
Clerkenwell Green
London EC1R 0HT

2 4 6 8 10 9 7 5 3 1

Typeset in 10/12 Dante
Printed in Great Britain by St Edmundsbury Press
Bury St Edmunds, Suffolk.
Bound by Woolnough Bookbinding Ltd

Prologue

The enemy soldiers glared at each other across the barbed-wired barricades. Their hatred was as palpable as the low, dark clouds scudding across the ashen sky before the biting Korean wind. Their armament was grossly unequal.

A few of the Chinese People's Volunteers carried homemade firearms or makeshift grenades. Like a peasant host of the Middle Ages, most were armed with spears, swords, or chain-maces. If the need arose, they were prepared to engage their enemies hand-to-hand, since they could command no supporting firepower – not so much as a light field-piece, certainly no heavy artillery, not even trench mortars, or a single machine-gun.

The chief American weapon was the deadly quad-fifty, which was designed to bring down aircraft. Four fifty-caliber machines-guns mounted on a half-track fired thousands of shots in seconds. A single bullet, big as a man's thumb, would knock a soldier down if it so much as brushed him – and the shock could kill him. Struck squarely, he would all but explode into bloody fragments. The Americans could, besides, call in tanks and artillery.

Though the Chinese showed no fear, the Americans glanced apprehensively at each other. Despite their enemies' overwhelming firepower, the People's Volunteers were massed behind their officers in straight-line regular formations like the troops of Wellington or Napoleon. Responding to high-pitched commands, they marched without a visible tremor towards the barbed-wire that hedged their positions. Their calloused feet slapped the ochre–red earth in straw sandals, in worn-out tennis shoes, or in cut-down leather boots trampled flat in back.

As if mesmerized, the Americans stood stock-still beneath the pale-blue flag of the United Nations, while reinforcements straggled from the prisoners-of-war barracks. Some had only one arm; some leaned on walking-sticks; some swung themselves on improvised wooden crutches. Undaunted, they screamed defiance in Chinese – and the Americans flinched.

Thrust against the high barbed-wire fence by the comrades behind them, the front-ranks did not flinch. Their sallow faces contorted with rage, their short-cropped hair bristling as if in indignation, they taunted the GIs in broken English larded with profanity and obscenity.

The Americans recoiled instinctively when the *Internationale* soared loud and defiant in Chinese, ending: 'The International Soviet will be the human race!' The POWs then chanted the anthem of their own revolution *Chi Lai*: 'Arise, all ye who refuse to be bond slaves ... with our flesh and blood, we will build a new Great Wall!'

A submachine-gun coughed in the distance. The Chinese Volunteers did not turn their heads, but single-mindedly – all too single minded, wholly unthinking – chanted in unison the slogans their officers shouted. They were respectfully silent when a tall, slightly stooped, and painfully thin – all but emaciated – man of middle years mounted an improvised platform in their midst.

'Comrades!' he declaimed in the formal falsetto of Chinese oratory. 'Comrades, our struggle goes forward. Day by day the imperialists quail under our hammer blows. We shall triumph!

'We must not weaken. We must ignore the siren calls of the imperialists' propaganda. Only keep your hearts pure, your resolution unwavering – and we will triumph.

'Some among you, though I know it cannot be more than a few, may not be able to call to mind immediately the immortal and immutable counsel the great commander of hosts, the conqueror of many states, Marquis Wu Chi, gave to his generals about four hundred years before the so-called Christian Era: "By and large on the battlefield – soon to become a graveyard – if soldiers are committed to fight to the death for the cause, they will live! If they strive above all to remain alive, they will die. A good general will act as if all are adrift in a sinking ship or trapped in a burning building, so that there is not a spare instant for the wise to devise new tactics or even the bravest to rise to full anger. Only engaging the enemy without a moment's hesitation will serve."

' "Thus", it is said with profound truth, "the greatest harm to an army's purposes stems from hesitation, while disasters that can destroy a host arise from hesitation!"

'Only an immediate, all-out assault on the enemy will do!

'Only thus can we triumph, when no man fights to live, but only to serve the people ... to press onward with the great proletarian revolution.

'All hail to People's China! Ten thousand years! Ten thousand times ten thousand years to Chairman Mao Zedong! All hail to our great ally in the camp of peace, the Socialist, fraternal People's Democratic Republic of North Korea!'

Major-General Li Mao bowed his head to acknowledge the waves of applause that flowed from the packed ranks of his troops. His narrow face radiant, he applauded in return. His smile fading, he nodded to the four POWs standing nearby. Instantly obedient, they dragged forward a sagging, limp figure with a battered face and forced him to his knees on the rickety platform.

'You all know this dog's turd called Cheng,' General Li Mao spoke out again.

'You all took part in the trial that condemned him. Now he pays the price – as will all the wretched traitors who exploit and savage the people!'

He nodded again, and a sword flashed in the dull afternoon light. A feathery fountain spurted crimson from the culprit's neck, and his head dropped to the platform. The round object rolled and tumbled softly for a few seconds on the uneven surface – and then lay still, the torn lips drawn back, grinning as if in thanks. A hundred blood-red banners flaunting golden stars blossomed from the massed formations to challenge the blue-and-white world flag of the United Nations. The sharp breezes blowing off the Yellow Sea onto Koje-do tossed the flag of the People's Republic of China, which its enemies called Red China. Behind the barbed-wire barricades of other compounds, their allies unfurled a hundred flags of the People's Democratic Republic of Korea, which the same enemies called simply North Korea: a black star superimposed on broad white and red stripes.

Thirty miles away on the mainland of the long peninsula, a motorcade trailed through the drab, battered, filthy, reeking port-city of Pusan, the provisional capital of the Republic of Korea. Communist flags streamed defiantly from the olive-drab trucks driven by pale American soldiers.

A cruel and barbarous war had been waged up and down the peninsula of Korea for two years, devastating countryside and town, decimating the civilian populace, which had already lost almost all its property, even to the porcelain wine-cups prized by hard-drinking males from fifteen to eighty. Now the tautly disciplined enemy soldiers flaunted their flags 300 miles behind the front lines – while American and South Korean soldiers looked on helpless, as if themselves prisoners.

Chapter I

My entire life has been a continual retraining program ranging in severity from the outward tenderness of psychotherapy to the candid brutality of a reform through labor camp run by disciples of Mao Zedong, Kim Il Sung, or Ho Chi Minh. Having already gone astray as a small boy, I have since then been the object of constant efforts to remake my character. Grandparents and neighbors, parents and teachers, wives and mistresses, friends and employers, even my own children have sought to expunge my many faults through biting criticism.

All their efforts have failed. The faulty raw material has defeated every last reformer by its intrinsic shoddiness, which simply cannot be overcome.

Still, before I get into the tale, which is *not* my own, which is emphatically *not* the story of my own life, I suppose I should introduce myself. I shall try to tell you who or – perhaps better, *what*, I am – that is, more distinctively and more usefully just what kind of human animal I am: the essential character of the man behind the voice, so to speak.

My name is Harland Birch. Being as rich in hope as they were poor in cash or valuables, my parents rather grandiloquently christened me: Harland Ulysses Lee, surnamed Birch. Harland was my mother's maiden name. Ulysses for General Ulysees S. Grant and Lee for General Robert E. Lee, respectively the paladin of the Union North and the paladin of the Secessionist South in the Civil War, otherwise the War Between the [Disunited American] States, which was fought in the mid-1800s, just about a century before the conflict between North and South Korea.

In the West Virginia hills, where my father scratched a marginal living from miserable land, most of the inhabitants were not really neutral. When I was growing up, most were as passionately committed as their grandfathers had been. Southern in sympathy, by conscious choice and by natural inclination, as well as in their courtly manner, the poor whites had, however, owned no slaves, but had themselves worked their own land. Instinctively kin to the embattled South, many nonetheless believed with fervid, burning conviction that the Union must be preserved.

A border state or a straddler state? Hard to say! But, anyway, an ambiguous state.

The North–South conflict was still hotly refought in words when I was born. My oxymoronic name was another gesture towards reconciling the quarrel within my own family. It was damned pretentious, that name. It would have made a ridiculous byline. I shortened it to Harland Birch over my first front-page story, and so it has remained. Incidentally, everyone who doesn't call me Mr Birch or Birch-san calls me Harland. Never Hal or even Harry. Above all, the Good Lord forfend, not Harley.

In the winter 1951–52, I was thirty-seven years old, and I was employed as the Far East Correspondent of the *Richmond Daily Courier*. You can work out how old I am today, if you care to – and the mental exercise isn't too great a strain. I was based in Tokyo and in theory covered all Asia from Sakhalin to the Persian Gulf. In 1952, I spent almost all my time in Korea reporting the war that had begun in June 1950 when the North invaded the South, thus oddly evoking the War Between the States almost a century earlier. I was then, as I fear I am at the present time, as you've already gathered by now, considered a difficult character : normally cantankerous, often ornery or just plain nasty, and always damned mean. Altogether I was then – as they say I still am – a very imperfect human being.

But this tale is *not* about me, except for what may slip out between the twin barriers of garrulousness and evasiveness. It's about the lieutenant I ran into late one afternoon in February 1952 on the reverse slope, that is our side, of a position on the main line of resistance, otherwise, the front line. We called that hill Old Baldy; it had been so thoroughly swept, so totally cleansed, by shells and bombs that it displayed not a single blade of grass. A long, loud firefight was rattling the heavy air, as the Third Division of the Eighth United States Army fought to deny possession of Old Baldy to units of the 220th Army of the so-called Chinese People's Volunteers.

Those troops were manifestly *not* volunteers at all. It was blatantly obvious that they had not entered the conflict of their own free will, that is, not voluntarily. They had, rather, been herded across the Yalu River from China's Manchurian provinces into Korea after their units, almost all of which had originally been opposed to the Communists in the Chinese civil war, were sucked into Peking's so-called People's Liberation Army.

That winter afternoon when we met again, the 27-year-old first lieutenant was totally unlike me – as he so strikingly still is. In contrast to the great sum of my faults, he was just about as perfect a young American man can be. Therefore, he offered no attraction, no challenge at all, to the flock of eager reformers who swarm around me like fleas on a hedgehog. He was – on the surface at least, and maybe deep down as well – perfectly poised and indomitably well adjusted. Open and affable to all, whether total strangers or mere acquaintances, as well as to a few close friends, he was clearly not in need of succour. He was not a problem child, as I was and, it appears, always will be, even if, by the inexplicable whim of an inscrutable God, I should attain the age of ninety. It had been evident from the time he was very small that he needed little improvement – perhaps, indeed, all but certainly – none at all. He needed only to be allowed to develop freely and naturally. Thus he would inevitably develop for the better – not to say the best.

His manner was courteous, indeed courtly, almost, you could say, stately, but not pompous. His features were regular, that is, prepossessing without being pretty! He was always ready to help others who were less fortunate, which patently meant almost everyone else in the entire world. He was a model citizen, a copybook Eagle Scout, though hardly a prig or a goody-goody.

He was redeemed from tepid perfection by his single gravest fault: his compulsive idealism could on occasion render him dangerously naïve. He had committed some very stupid acts with the best of intentions, indeed, with sterling purposes, with all the good will in the world.

Furthermore, his all but unvarying good humor was not assumed, but quite spontaneous. Quite effortlessly, as it seemed, he charmed all the girls – young women, I suppose I should say nowadays. But he did not arouse jealousy among the big boys. Young men of his own age, as well as older men, thought him a damned good guy, a great pal.

I saw early on in our friendship, that his total self-confidence was an illusion, a misleading outward show he did nothing to foster. He did not try to impress others; the invariably favorable impression came, as I've said, naturally. Yet, as was by no means evident, he was hypersensitive and extremely vulnerable. His high opinion of mankind could make him a fall guy, though only the blackest villain would set out to take advantage of such a good fellow.

The lieutenant was *almost* too good to be true, though perhaps not quite. Even his name was near perfection, substantial and impressive, but not assertive: John Luxborough Maynell.

Everyone called him Luke. The trumpet flourish of Luxborough did not fit a young man who was so amiable and so unassuming. But he was distinctly *not* just plain Jack. Only one person called him Jack: his favorite girl for a time, she was, nonetheless, one among many. She called him Jack, because, she said, she was always afraid he would fall down and break his crown. That overblown idealism again!

Life had unrolled a red carpet before Luke Maynell. His father was a fourth generation San Francisco banker, the kind who send their sons – and now their daughters – to Ivy League colleges, rather than to Stanford. His mother, a New York debutante, brought a good chunk of the Luxborough fortune to the marriage. Luke himself had actually been an Eagle Scout before coming East to finish his secondary schooling at Choate and then go on to Yale.

Luke also possessed – and vigorously exercised – the upper middle-class virtues that in those days, which now seem so long ago, came with his extensive upper middle-class privileges and his staunch upper middle-class view of the world. Most such virtues are nowadays, need I say it, considered failings or, at least, weaknesses. He was a stalwart, though soft-spoken patriot, and he was democratic by nature, indeed virtually selfless.

Driven by such American *noblesse oblige*, Luke Maynell had enlisted in 1943, disdaining to await the draft. He had chosen the army because it offered the *least* glory and the *greatest* hardship. As ever, he had to make big sacrifices to make up for his slew of advantages. Besides, whether he knew it or not, he wanted, as ever, the one thing he could never attain – to be like everyone else.

He told me once, when he had a snootful of Scotch, that he had not joined the Marine Corps, which promised even greater danger and worse hardship, because it was *too* glamorous. He didn't want to be distinctive, but to be 'ordinary, like the army.' He damned the US Marines as *elitist* long before that shibboleth became a pejorative catchword of liberal intellectuals.

(Watch those superlatives, Harland, knock off the fancy language.)

When I met Luke for the first time early in 1945, he was a staff sergeant, the senior non-com in a thirty-six-man platoon of the 32nd Infantry Regiment of General Simon Bolivar Buckner's 6th Army fighting the defenders of the Japanese homeland on Okinawa. He should have been at least one step up, a technical sergeant or even a master sergeant. But he'd refused higher non-commissioned rank. His company commander told me further that Luke had turned down a battlefield commission.

He just didn't want to be different.

Nonetheless, having somehow acquired some basic Japanese, in good part not by trying, but just by listening, he was, thereby, distinctive. He was used, when necessary, as a frontline interpreter with the prisoners-of-war we were finally taking in respectable numbers toward the end of the War in the Pacific. I can't help repeating: he tried hard to be down to earth. Despite his own inclination and his earnest efforts, he simply could not help being different.

As for myself, Harland Birch was already a well known byline by 1945. I wasn't as famous as Ernie Pyle or Ernest Hemingway. They had a head start on me. But, anyway, I wasn't doing badly for a guy who'd never finished high school. I had fought my way up in the newspaper business, becoming the senior police reporter for the *Honolulu Advertiser* in 1940, a year before Pearl Harbor. Afterwards I made the Tarawa landing as a gunny sergeant in a Marine Corps line regiment. Then I was assigned as a combat correspondent. The job with the *Richmond Daily Courier* of course came much later.

I next saw Luke Maynell in the summer of 1948. Being between wives, as well as between assignments, I was greatly enjoying my year as a Tutwell Scholar at Yale when I ran into him under the plane trees fronting the Taft Hotel. I had already spent a year in London with the United Press and had decided Europe was not for me – too easy, too decadent. When the Tutwell offer came up, I grabbed it. I knew by then that I wanted to work in Asia. I also knew that I didn't know beans about Asia, except for its battlefields.

Both Luke and I sat in a graduate seminar on modern Chinese history, and we spent a lot of time together. Now, Chinese was hardly a mainstream choice for a young man who was graduating *summa cum laude*, junior Phi Bete, too. But Luke disdained the normal choices that were wide open for him: law, medicine, banking, business, or government service. He wanted to be more like everyone else, though, of course, not like his over-privileged classmates at Choate and Yale. So he took Chinese, and he polished his basic Japanese – thus becoming even less like the idealized 'everyone else' he courted unbeknownst.

When we met on the reverse slope of Old Baldy in February 1952, I naturally wondered how in the world Luke had come to be in Korea, and as a lieutenant. He had, as I've already indicated, never been entranced by the military life, but rather the opposite. Yet he had felt unable to resist enlisting, that is, serving voluntarily, not waiting to be drafted, as I've also said. That was, of course, at a time so unlike our times, when so-called idealists have evaded service by any means, however vile, and have boasted about it. During World War II *no* able-bodied young man could consider himself truly a man if he were *not* in uniform.

But that first day I couldn't ask Luke why he was in Korea and why as a lieutenant. We only had time to say hello.

Guided by a pimply young rifleman, Luke was clambering up the steep slopes toward our main line of resistance, the trenches and the bunkers strung along ridges where not even a jeep could go. He could only tell me in haste that he was reporting to a Military Intelligence prisoner-of-war interrogation team.

Anyway, incoming trench-mortar fire was getting uncomfortably close. I told him to look me up at the Press Billets when he came to Seoul. He said something about getting to the front before the early dusk fell and the Chinese artillery really opened up, all but immune to counter-battery fire in the dark.

For a minute or so I watched him trudge up the hill, a tall figure with heavy shoulders, yet supple beside the gawky stringbean of a teenage private who was his escort. I liked Luke Maynell, always had, even when, sometimes, his bouncy optimism and his unrelenting idealism set my teeth on edge. Even sometimes when he very briefly sank into near depression.

The mid-twentieth century was no time for a Don Quixote, but neither was Miguel Cervantes's late-sixteenth century. That, of course, was Cervantes's point. It could turn out to be the old point in this new tale.

Anyway, it was time for me to get going before nightfall made it even tougher to drive back to Seoul to write and file my piece. The faint yellowish rays thrown by the cat's-eye headlights of my rattletrap jeep dimly lit the rutted and cratered dirt road, very dimly and never more than ten feet ahead.

That spring the relatively static war was a lot less dramatic and less dangerous than the wild dashes up and down the Korean peninsula in 1950 and 1951. Battle had yo-yoed north and south before a UN counter-offensive finally stabilized a line roughly along the 38th parallel, which had divided North from South before the invasion.

The new kind of war was, however, also a hell of a lot harder to cover. A reporter had to go to the story, rather than just letting the action come to him – and then, he could hope, get out with his skin and his story intact. It was also a hell of a lot more complicated, and it took a damn sight better writing to make it clear, not to speak of grabbing the reader's attention in the first place.

The fighting on Old Baldy that day was the latest link in a chain of action and counter-action that had begun a week earlier. The Chinese had assaulted the so-called mountain, which was really a biggish sort of hill that overlooked their positions, in order to gain a tad more security. The attack followed a brutal pounding by the artillery pieces the Chinese ran out of tunnels cut right through the hills. They'd fire a round or two, then pull back into the tunnel before counter-battery fire could zero on their position. Maybe a third of their guns, no more, were Russian. The rest were American, captured either from Generalissimo Chiang Kai-shek's defeated Nationalists during the Chinese Civil War, or taken from retreating American troops in Korea itself. Regardless of the kind of gun, they were brilliant artillerymen – crack shots.

We retook Old Baldy from the Chinese, held it for a couple of days, and were thrown off again. That day, when I saw Luke Maynell, we were well on our way to retaking the big hill for the second time – and, this time, keeping it. Even the callous Chinese high command was apparently getting tired of pouring out so much blood to seize terrain whose possession did hardly more than tidy up the lines.On the forward slopes of Old Baldy you could trickle the earth between your fingers. Constant shelling had pounded the topsoil into pale-yellow powder a foot deep.

I took a last look at the stick-figures of Luke Maynell and his gawky guide trudging up the steep slope before pelting downhill to my jeep. We were still taking mortar fire, and, from time to time, a Chinese field-piece blindly dropped a shell nearby. Not so much for effect, it was clear, as to annoy. Nonetheless, such random harassing and interdiction fire could kill.

The play my story got in the papers would depend more on the mood of editors in the United States than on the fierceness of the combat or how well I put it over. The American public, too, was a little tired, bored with the inconclusive war, so editors were playing Korea differently from day to day, almost by whim, as it seemed to us reporters in the field. Some would run the ferocious battles for Old Baldy as just more skirmishes in a war of position, which they were in a way. Other editors would play up the blood-and-guts. My young colleagues of the wire serv-ices, particularly the United Press and the International News Service, were getting orders ('Requests' they delicately called them) from New York for gory reporting, the gorier the better.

Also, of course, for the heroics! We needed heroes.

They didn't have to look hard. There were plenty of heroes to go around, real heroes – true authentic heroes. Also plenty of blood-and-guts – and plenty of killed and wounded.

One foot already in my jeep, I watched the American dead begin their long journey home. They were coming down the corkscrew paths of the slope on litters carried by the stocky middle-aged men of the Korean Service Corps. A little earlier, the same litter-bearers had scrabbled up the slopes with artillery shells, ration–boxes, and kerosene-tins strapped to their backs. The KSCs had clung with their fingertips to the steep hillside, digging the heels of their rubber boots into the loose soil. They now came slipping and sliding downhill, time after time all but losing their footing and their burdens.

Every so often a wounded man stumbled down the hill on faltering feet or was carried on a stretcher by American medics. The most seriously wounded had been taken off earlier by little bubble-top Bell helicopters. The journey on a stretcher strapped to a landing skid was cold and terrifying. Yet such occasional helicopter rescue was the precursor of the nearly miraculous 'medevac' by bigger choppers like the all purpose HUEY that saved thousands of lives in Vietnam by night and by day – the lives of Vietnamese as well as Americans, civilians as well as soldiers.

There was no need to hurry the dead off Old Baldy. The ragged, dusty procession came down slowly through gray twilight fringed with a pale-violet aura. The dead lay on litters improvised by slipping rifles through dark-green GI ponchos. Most were half naked, their filthy fatigues having been cut away by battlefield medics to get at their wounds. The arms of the slain soldiers dangled over the sides of those litters, flopping crazily with each step of their bearers, and their hands trailed in the dust. Most had had so much blood drained away that their bodies were almost the color of the earth: a pallid waxy yellow.

Winding down the hillside, they might have been a frieze on a Greek temple, some with high arched chests not yet collapsed, others with great pale-red wounds gouged in their sides. Some were untouched. They could have been asleep, except for their terrible parchment pallor.

I've heard soldiers joking with bravado learned from gangster movies: 'If I do die young, I'll make a good-looking corpse.' The dead were all young, but they were not good looking. More like macabre wax works.

Well, I'd seen dead soldiers before – and would undoubtedly see many more. Right now, I had to get back to Seoul to file, but my jeep was mired in a muddy ditch. One of the many charms of the Korean climate is its ability to let go torrents of rain, near floods, one minute and to produce a dust storm the next.

A little way down the dirt road that twisted around the hill, a Sherman tank was firing its long cannon at three-minute intervals. I knocked on the side with my canteen, and a tanker's helmet pooped out of the turret.

'I'm stuck in the mud,' I shouted. 'Can you pull me out?'

'Just a minute, buddy,' he replied. 'Got to make smoke first. The Chinks're looking down our throats.'

As I should already have seen, the angle of the gun showed that we were under direct enemy observation. Hardly elevated, it was firing in a virtually straight line. Aside from napalm dropped by fighter-bombers, which, contrary to canards, did *not* repeat *not* seek out schools and orphanages, tanks' flat-trajectory fire was the only way to hit the mouths of the tunnels where the Chinese field-pieces lurked.

Driving through the blackout towards Seoul, I thought about Luke Maynell, who was spending his first night in the front-line of a kind of war new to him. Later, he told me about the scene he'd walked into.

(I'm telling you now just how I know about Luke's initiation. But don't expect me to tell you every time how I know what happened. Even though some think I'm in my dotage, when I'm only seventy-seven, just now entering my second childhood, you can from here on in just assume my facts are right.)

Anyway, that night, Luke began to grow up. He was already 27, and he'd already been through a lot of rough combat, but he finally grew up in Korea. The Korean War wasn't just boom-boom and rat-a-tat-tat, not just blood-and-guts and heroics – and terror. It was an intricate fabric woven of many historical, cultural, social, and political threads. It was a very complicated war, and Luke was to play a complex part in it.

Chapter II

West Central Front
Main Line of Resistance
February 1952

Dusk outlined the crags and the ridges with pure crystal light, and the battered hills loomed closer in that preternatural clarity. The floors of the narrow valleys, which largely ran north and south, already brimmed with the gloom of night. The hills that overtopped and girded those valleys glowed pale in the last rays of the sun, which was retreating westward across the Yellow Sea towards China.

Through a loophole in the parapet of a trench, First Lieutenant John Luxborough Maynell looked on an illusorily peaceful landscape. Though snow still sprinkled distant mountain peaks, the nearby hills were already bright with golden forsythia. Spring–green grass twined around the gray rock faces that cropped through the sparse soil.

The slopes nearby were pitted with shell craters, scarred as well by long, serpentine trenches behind massive tangles of barbed wire. Patches of ground were scorched black by incendiary bombs filled with jellied gasoline, which was called napalm.

In that no man's land Luke saw abandoned Chinese rifles with very long barrels and rusting Chinese burp-guns with perforated cooling jackets around their stubby barrels amid heaps of green US Army ration cans. He also saw a great number of Chinese killed-in-action. Clad coarsely in heavy dirt-brown field uniforms that were quilted horizontally like the Michelin man's, they looked like dolls who had been lovingly dressed, but were soon discarded by bored children. He could not count all the dead that lay in rough piles or were strung singly across the slopes. At least 200, he guessed, perhaps 300 or even 400. Those corpses were a terminal moraine, the high-water mark of the last vain attack by an insanely belligerent enemy.

The jagged landscape, which stretched over the hills and the valleys to the far horizon, was brilliantly lit for a few minutes just before dusk fell. Across that expanse nothing moved, neither man nor beast, not even a vagrant bird. True, a lark trilled somewhere unseen, but the battleground was deserted as far as the eye could tell. Not even a single wisp of smoke signalled the presence of living human beings.

A hand tugged at his sleeve, and his guide urged: 'Let's go, Lieutenant. We gotta be back before dark. Captain's got his bowels in an uproar. You shoulda been here a week ago ... sir.'

Luke smiled at the casual ways of the modern Army of the US. The 'sir', almost forgotten, was hastily added to the last sentence like a caboose tacked at the last possible moment onto a freight-train.

He expected no more. Except for the ramrod-stiff Marines, who were a rule unto themselves, American soldiers, the closer they came to the enemy, the more off-hand they were towards their officers. Their breezy ways did not mean that they were less effective or less disciplined. The self-confidence in self-worth that lay behind their airy manner did, however, assure that non-commissioned officers, even privates, could successfully improvise winning tactics if cut off from their commissioned officers.

'All right, let's go,' Luke replied. 'I've seen enough for now.'

'Don't overdo it, Lieutenant. You'll be damned sick of the frigging scenery before long.'

Luke resettled his heavy steel helmet on his head and turned to follow his guide. The front-line trenches, eight to ten feet deep, clung to the contours of the hill, twisting, rising, and falling as the land itself did. The two sidled from an apparent dead end into a trench that veered away at a right angle; they reversed direction, apparently heading backwards for a minute or two; they slipped downwards, then trudged with difficulty up steep inclines.

Reinforced bunkers, hardly more than dugouts, strung like lumpy beads on the tangled string of trenches, were the strongpoints of the main line of resistance. He would live for weeks, even a month or longer at a single stretch, like a caveman – eating, shaving, defecating, working, and sleeping under ten feet of earth to emerge from time to time through observation bunkers covered with corrugated-iron roofs heaped with sandbags. He would share those cramped quarters with twenty or so others — and he would look after himself. Unlike hierarchical Britain, the egalitarian United States did not provide junior officers with batmen, otherwise known as orderlies. Each army then reflected its own society, as both still do.

In the Military Intelligence bunker, Luke would only splash his face and hands to keep from being totally filthy; he would not even attempt to launder his green-cotton field fatigues. There was no room to wash himself except cursorily, even if water could be spared from the scant supplies back-carried up the hills in jerrycans filled from jeep-towed trailer-tanks by the bent gnomes of the Korean Service Corps.

Luke's new home stank like a heavily used locker-room: cigarette butts, Coca Cola, dirty socks, pungent male sweat, moldering jockstraps, rotting leftover rations, putrid hunks of hotdogs, and bite-scarred chocolate bars, casually discarded, half-eaten, by men accustomed to the abundance the Army of the US provided even in the frontlines to troops who expected – and got – freshly roasted turkey followed by fresh fruit and many flavored ice cream for Thanksgiving and Christmas.

The stench of an old-fashioned privy underlay those acrid odors: excrement, urine, damp mould, and rotting wood. Beneath all, an ancient aboriginal scent, a whiff from a Neanderthal cavern: burnt-out wood-fires, decaying meat, running wounds, and new-turned earth.

The reek of the man-made cave was uncannily familiar. Luke had been assailed by the rank, feral stench that was, somehow, black with primeval menace, once before – in the reptile house of the Long Beach Zoo.

His olfactory nerves were shutting down in self-defense, while his eyes were rather slowly becoming accustomed to the perpetual twilight in the bunker. His ears, though, were heavily engaged.

In the background thumped the raucous beat of an Elvis Presley number. It did not, however, drown out all other noise, as had the stereo hi-fi in the transient officers quarters at Tachikawa Air Base. He could, somehow, catch the burbling of water steaming in a tin basin on the flat top of the potbellied kerosene stove, lest it freeze solid. He could even make out the hissing of an acetylene lantern set precariously on a ledge out into the raw earth.

A tableau had been frozen by his entrance. Three men were crouched around a captured Chinese who lay on a stretcher set on the packed-earth floor. Two of the three were heavy-set Americans, the third a tall, thin Asian. A burly Chinese in that ragletaggle quilted, dirt-brown uniform sat propped against the earthen wall. He was guarded by an American soldier armed with a carbine, which, as I hardly need say, is a short-barreled rifle with a narrower wooden stock, which shoots a shorter-range bullet.

'About time you got your ass up here, Lieutenant Maynell!' The deep voice was heavy with authority. 'Finally get tired of dipping your wick in Japan? Or couldn't get it up anymore?'

'Sorry, sir!' Although blameless, having spent all his twenty hours in Japan at Tachikawa waiting for a much delayed and diverted flight to Seoul, Luke placated the stocky man with the long cigar in his mouth and the twin silver bars on his collar. 'You're Captain de Marco?'

'Who else? Welcome to the Korea Waldorf-Astoria, Maynell. Now let's get to work.'

'Yes, sir.'

'Lieutenant, we have here two heroic fighters of the Chinese People's Volunteers. Captured no more'n two hours ago. One's very sensible ... couldn't wait to drop his burp-gun and raise his hands. The other's got a hunk of shrapnel in his leg. We wanna know the obvious to start with: unit numbers, unit strengths, time of arrival in Korea and at the front ... tactical stuff.'

'What've they already said, Captain?'

'How the hell should I know?'

'Well, sir, it sure looks as if you're interrogating them.'

'I am. But Mr. Kim here's not getting diddly-squat out of 'em.'

'Mr. Kim?'

'This beanpole here. Korean civilian attached to my language team. Maybe his Chinese is OK, but his English is damned near unintelligible.... Good you're here now, Maynell. I speak Spanish, Italian, and French ... German at a pinch. And Lieutenant Simons here ...'

Luke nodded to the short lieutenant, whose wispy blond hair shone like a halo in the blue-white glare of the acetylene lanterns.

'... his Russian 'n Polish are terrific. His Hebrew 'n his Arabic're fine, too. But not one of us speaks a word of Chinese, or even Japanese.'

'An Intelligence Prisoner Interrogation Team?'

'You know the army! A miracle they didn't send *you* to Iceland.' The stocky captain champed on his panatella and regarded Luke with suspicion. 'You do speak Chinese, don't you? Not Swedish and Bantu?'

'Yes, sir. That is, no, sir, I don't know a word of Swedish or Swahili. But I'm not bad in Chinese. Some Japanese too.'

'*Deo gratias*! Now I can ship Mr. Kim out. He's shit-scared of the big, bad Chinese ... nervous as a virgin in a cat house.'

Captain Anthony de Marco reached into the knapsack hanging from a spike driven into the earth wall and pulled out a squat bottle. He poured cognac generously into the tin canteen-cup and the three thick china mugs that stood on the ledge beside the acetylene lantern.

'Courvoisier VSOP, Lieutenant. I get it from the Brits. Nothing but three point two beer and rotgut like Four Roses from the US Commissary. Let's drink to your arrival. Also to Kim's leaving.' He handed the canteen cup to the tall Korean. 'He loves this firewater ... *Salute*, Mr. Kim, *arrivederci!* brave ally – and good riddance.'

'*Shen-mo ta show?*' the Korean asked in broken Mandarin. 'What'd he say? I can't understand a word of his English.'

'Just wishing you a safe departure,' Luke lied. 'How far'd you get with the POWs?'

'I was just starting,' the Korean replied. 'Not much. Really nothing.'

'Well, then, I guess I know where to begin.'

Kneeling beside the stretcher, Luke raised the wounded POW's head and lifted a mug of brandy to his mouth. The Chinese captive's black eyes gleamed. His face was so dark with grime that only his slanted eyes reflected the lantern's glare. His tongue darted in and out, nervously licking his lips.

The POW gulped the brandy greedily, convulsively. Luke steeled himself not to shy away from his stench, which overwhelmed the manifold inherent stenches of the bunker. There are, after all, degrees of filth. The POW smelled as if he had never washed in his entire life, not even the obligatory baths at birth and marriage required for even the poorest Chinese peasant, preceding that last obligatory bath required after his death.

'*My* brandy, Lieutenant!' de Marco objected. 'Why the hell are you throwing it around like tapwater?'

Luke ignored the captain's question, since his wish to please the POW was obvious. Instead, he asked the POW with heavy old fashioned courtesy. '*Nin guei-hsing*? ... Your noble name, good sir?'

'Lu ... Lu Pei-an,' the Chinese replied with a thick Manchurian accent.

'I am called Lu Kuh. The same surname. We might almost be kinsmen.'

'Your Honor is too kind to a miserable peasant!' The formula slid easily off the captive's tongue. How often had he flattered powerful men to turn their displeasure aside? 'You are far too kind.'

'*Shen-mo shr-hoe, Lu Hsien–sheng* ... And when, Mr. Lu, did you come to Korea?'

'Not Mr. Lu, just Old Lu,' the prisoner protested. 'What is this Korea?'

Luke tried the other common Chinese term for Korea, not *Chao Hsien* but *Han Kuo* – and was rewarded by no recognition whatever. The soldier called Lu Pei-an had no concept of a nation, much less a nation called Korea. Nor did he know what a division was, much less the number of his own division.

Questions put in succession regarding the nature and the designation of his regiment, battalion, and company drew no response, not even a sign of comprehension, much less recognition, from the wounded Chinese. He did, however, know the term for squad, and he declared confidently, 'Old Li, my squad leader, he'll be waiting for me when I go back. He's a good old stick.'

Luke concluded that Lu Pei-an was not a fool, a little slow and deathly ignorant, but not a fool.

'This could do it.' The POW was quite unexpectedly, not to say unprecedentedly, shrewd about what affected him directly. 'This wound could get me out of the army. They say you American imperialists have good doctors and you even treat prisoners who're hurt.'

Luke assured him that his injuries would be given the best possible care, just like a wounded American. But, he warned, the captive would be confined in a prisoner-of-war camp until the war was over. Lu Pei-an waved that obstacle aside, asking, 'My leg? When it's fixed, I can plough again, can't I?'

Although he could not by any means know the answer to that life or death question, Luke assured the POW that he would soon be on his feet again. Lu Pei-an declared with profound satisfaction, 'That's all right then. I know Little Lao's looking after my half-acre so the landlord won't take it back. Also keeping an eye on my wife. He promised he would.... And Little Lao never lies!'

Curiosity piqued by such stalwart confidence, Luke ignored Captain de Marco's mounting impatience and asked a further personal question. The answer staggered him. Not for a decade and a half had Lu Pei-an seen his small plot, which lay some seventy miles from the metropolis and rail center of Mukden in Manchuria.

The POW confided that he had, fifteen years earlier, been pressed into the army nominally commanded by the prince who had been the last emperor of China, deposed at the beginning of the twentieth century. Pu Yi had been enthroned by the Japanese occupation forces as their puppet sovereign of Manchukuo, which means in colloquial northern Chinese simply the Nation of the Manchus. Pu Yi's forebears had invaded China from their native Manchuria, and had reigned as emperors for three and a half centuries.

That hardly very complicated history was totally unknown to Lu Pei-an, the POW. He did, however, just recognize the name Pu Yi, and he did just recall that his unit of the puppet army had been incorporated into the forces of Nationalist Generalissimo Chiang Kai-shek. The troops, of course, never consulted, had subsequently been absorbed by Communist Chairman Mao Zedong's People's Liberation Army. Inspired by the Chairman's 'Resist America and Aid Korea Campaign', a political commissar had, by a swirl of his ballpoint, enrolled, naturally of their own volition, Lu Pei-an's regiment in the Chinese People's Volunteers. That force was created simply by renaming regular Liberation Army units.

All through those turbulent times, Lu Pei-an had served with the same comrades. All but himself and two others among his thirteen-man squad had already been killed in action on the battlefield, say five in all, while the rest had either died from neglected wounds or from disease untreated because it was undiagnosed. The Chinese People's Volunteers, who had few doctors, *never* discharged individual soldiers. The cavalcade of great events in which he marched for so long had, aside from the loss of his comrades, not touched the peasant.

Lu Pei-an clung, however, to the promise made half a generation ago by his neighbor, Little Lao, to tend his pitiful half-acre plot and to look after his wife, who was just sixteen when they were parted. It was more than likely that both Little Lao and Lu Pei-an's wife were dead, probably his rapacious landlord as well. But Lu Pei-an had no way of knowing.

Following the banners of history across Manchuria for almost two decades, he had passed close to his native village many times. But he had never been allowed leave to visit his native village. Nor had he dared defy authority and break away, even for a day or two. His chief duty was, after all, his responsibility to his parents. His duty was to live as long as he possibly could and honor their memory, while thus also keeping alive his hope of giving them grandchildren to carry on the sacred line of the family.

So Lu Pei-an unblushingly affirmed to Luke, who poured him another brandy. Captain Anthony de Marco frowned. Insouciantly, Luke rinsed the mug under the conical green-canvas water-bag that hung, not yet frozen stiff, from a tripod of poles and poured himself another slug, a hefty slug.

'It's thirsty work, sir,' he told de Marco. 'Anyway, I've got a source in Seoul, an old friend. He'll get us all the cognac we can drink.'

His putative supplier was myself, Harland Birch, for he knew no one else in Seoul. He hoped, indeed simply assumed, that I would be amenable – just as he confidently assumed that I would be able to provide. We knew each other well.

Luke's insouciance was hardly dented when the second prisoner demanded without polite preliminary, '*Gei waw baw-lah-dee!*.... Gimme brandy!'

De Marco shrugged, 'Sure, Maynell, give him a slug. Go out and invite a couple of his friends, too. Never thought I'd be running a gin-mill for Chink POWs!'

The second prisoner gulped the Courvoisier, sighed windily, and belched. Luke offered him a Lucky Strike from a battered white packet and lit the cigarette with his shiny steel Zippo.

In the fierce light of the acetylene lantern, the second POW was almost as filthy as Lu Pei-an. Yet the layers of plain accumulated filth, the mud, and the ashes of gunpowder that caked his face and hands was not as deeply ingrained. It would wash off. The cropped hair bristling above his broad forehead was gray with dust. His nose, rather high in the bridge for a Chinese, was almost covered by a blood-speckled bandage. His big canny eyes shifted constantly, without a halt assessing his enemies. When he rose with studied politeness to hand back the mug, Luke estimated his height at five foot eight, tall for a common Chinese soldier.

'*Waw bi-hsing* ... My worthless name ... ' The prisoner offered the polite formula without consideration, certainly without prompting, for the antique courtesy was the only way to offer one's own name.

'My worthless name is Huang, Huang Hsi-wu. I am a junior sergeant, a squad leader in the 106th division of the 220th Army of the Chinese People's Volunteers. My unit took two weeks by train to get to Antung in Manchuria, starting from Chengdu in Szechwan. We crossed into Korea over the Yalu River bridge on 23 December, 1950. We crossed on foot. We've been marching and fighting ever since ... with hardly a moment's rest and not too much food. Always on foot because there's little transport, none at all for the infantry. Not nearly enough trucks even to move supplies. Lately, even ammunition's been getting short.'

Captain de Marco rubbed his hands together and burbled, 'He's singing like a little bird, isn't he? More bullshit? Or are we finally hitting pay dirt?'

'Pay dirt, I think, Captain,' Luke replied, and then asked, 'Tell me more about your unit, Mr. Huang.'

The second POW, like the first POW, looked startled at being addressed as *Hsien-sheng*, Mister, literally One Borne Earlier [than myself]. The second was accustomed to being called Comrade or Squad Leader, never Mister.

'When we came into Korea,' he, nonetheless, responded promptly and specifically, 'the Division was over-strength, maybe ten thousand men. Even though reinforcements've been trickling in, the division's now down to five thousand. Total casualties've been nearly a hundred per cent.'

'You're awfully helpful, Mr. Huang.' Luke was discomforted by the POW's eagerness, disquieted by his precise revelations. 'Just hold on a minute.'

Luke turned to de Marco. 'Captain, he's just bursting with information. Do they all talk so freely?'

'Some. Once they see we're not going to barbecue 'em for supper. This Chink, though, looks like he wants to be teacher's pet. What've you got so far?'

Luke told de Marco briefly and turned again to Sergeant Huang, whose service in the Chinese Communist armed forces was now over. Luke would not imperil the flow of information by questioning the POW's motives, however gently.

'You're wondering why I am talking so freely, aren't you?' Huang Hsi-wu anticipated the unasked question. 'Because I am anti-Communist. That's why I let myself be captured. I never want to go back to the hell Mao Zedong's made of China.'

He flourished a flimsy, much folded sheet of paper that bore the flags of the United Nations and the United States. 'Your safe-conduct pass ... I saw it dropped from an airplane. It says I won't have to go back.'

'Tell 'im that's definite,' de Marco directed. 'He can go anywhere he wants.'

'Are we sure about that now, sir?'

'Don't give me that shit, Maynell. Just tell 'im!'

'I've no experience with Chinese POWs,' Luke said. 'But he seems *very* eager. I wonder—'

'Not our problem, Maynell. We're interested in tactical info, not really the big picture, not at this level. But I'll shove a note into his file, let the rear echelon boys worry about him ... Anyway, tell him he doesn't have to go back. He can even go to Taiwan to see Generalissimo Chiang Kai-shek, if he wants.'

Chapter III

I saw Luke again in Seoul a few weeks later, say late February 1952. He was fairly drunk and very loud, drawing hard looks from the few senior officers present. But they were only a couple of majors and a lieutenant-colonel, a light-colonel as the troops called that ambiguous rank.

Anyway, the Temple Bar was full of noisy junior officers. Loudest of all the drinkers, though, were a couple of young war correspondents who'd been shot over pretty thoroughly that day. A third correspondent, who had gone with them to visit the British Commonwealth Division, was now on a hospital plane bound for Japan with a shred of shrapnel in his shoulder. No use in telling these greenhorns it was practically a phoney war nowadays, not like the summer of 1950, when we were losing correspondents by the dozen – and soldiers by the hundreds.

Luke was shouting and guffawing, nothing like his usual soft-spoken, poised, and effortlessly controlled self. Still, he would have to make a lot more noise to get himself thrown out. The Temple Bar was a sanctuary where junior officers could blow off steam. You *could* get thrown out if you took a bayonet to the furniture or to your drinking buddy, but hardly for anything less.

The regular army master-sergeants who ran the place worried more about the furniture than about the patrons. If you slugged your drinking companion, they'd politely ask you to stop. If you began breaking up the chairs and tables, which were made from old beer kegs marked Asahi or Kirin, they'd heave you out so hard you bounced.

Even so, if they liked you, they might let you stay. But only if you came up with a damned good explanation – and enough military scrip, which looked like Monopoly money, to more than cover the damage. Greenbacks were also acceptable, though they had been declared illegal tender in Korea in the hope of starving the black market. The old master-sergeants were pillars of the black market.

We all called it the Temple Bar because the Eighth United States Army, Korea, the high command of our action, had taken over an old shrine for a junior officers' club. A bar stacked with bottles now stretched along the back wall of the long, narrow room, where the altar had once been surrounded by sacred images. The ceiling, what you could see of the ceiling through the smoke-hazed gloom, was supported by upswept eaves, their once brilliant scarlet now a faded red, an almost transparent pinkish shade.

Sacrilege? Maybe, but the city was bare of the civilians who might have worshipped there. Having fled south before the Communist invaders, they were not permitted to return. Besides, making it a club preserved the traditional structure with its wavelike gray-tiled roof and its gaudy lacquer-red pillars, the shiny surface of which was for some reason not faded. Shrines and schoolhouses had suffered badly as Seoul changed hands five times. Most had gone up in smoke.

Officers liked their spaciousness, for they could accommodate lots of troops. The troops were careless with kerosene heaters, as they were with the extremely effective under-floor heating that Koreans were already enjoying when America had not been discovered and Europeans were still shivering around open fires or hoping to wring a little warmth from draughty fireplaces.

A few months later, the Temple Bar was to go the same way. But it was a very comfortable refuge that rainy night.

When, despite the distance across the room, I recognized Luke's distinctive Yaley drawl with the rising inflection at the end of sentences, I said goodbye to the very young, very self-pitying tyro war correspondents. Their self-dramatization was hard to take. Nothing is more boring than another correspondent's war stories.

The candles on the beer-keg tables were burning low behind the dinky little red shades that the old master-sergeants thought gave class to the joint. Those shades were a tad too cute, but they were better than the fluorescent glare of most other clubs. Korea wasn't a chic war, not like Vietnam later.

I couldn't see much by the intentionally dim lighting, which was further obscured by tobacco smoke. Cigarettes were our great consolation, an apparently unbreakable habit no one even thought of breaking in those golden days before the great nicotine scare. I couldn't see all that much, but I could hear Luke six tables away.

When he rather grandly waved me to an empty chair, I saw that he was drinking with a couple of lieutenants who wore impossibly crisp fatigues with the globe-and-anchor logo of the US Marines stencilled in black on their breast pockets. The two were virtually identical: snub-nosed and blue-eyed, darkish blond hair cut so short their scalps shone white between the bristles, both were pumpkin yellow from the atabrin their medical corpsmen loaded them with to ward off malaria.

'That's bullshit ... and you know it,' Luke declared, slapping the table so hard the glasses rattled. 'You're not a suicide squad. Leave the *kamikaze* act to the Nipponese.'

'Look, you've got me wrong. I don't *want* to die!' one lieutenant insisted. 'But, I ask you, what're the chances? Statistically ...'

'Chuck, why'd you sign on for a second tour? Maybe you do want to die!' the other interjected. 'They've been talking peace at Panmunjom for a year now. But only God knows how much longer before we get an armistice that'll save our asses. Anyway you look at it, the United States Marines're still fighting. And we're still dying.'

'Irregardless, Billy, you're right. Chances of my surviving're damned low statistically,' Chuck stated, with the stilted precision of a man sliding into drunkenness. 'Only a damned fool wouldn't prepare himself … get ready to die.'

'Suppose you're ready to die, all ready. But … but if it doesn't happen, what then? You're relieved, of course, Goddamned relieved. But maybe a little disappointed, too!'

'You really *do* want to die, don't you?' Luke marveled. 'What's eating you Marines? Why're you so suicidal?'

'Not suicidal,' Billy protested. 'It's what Chuck says. We've got to be ready … all set to die. Otherwise we couldn't do our job. And the Corps wouldn't be the Corps.'

'I've got to be alive to do my job,' Luke responded drily.

'Sure thing, Captain. But *you're* not a Marine.'

I noticed then that the collar of Luke's stained fatigues bore the twin silver bars of a captain, rather than the single silver bar of a first lieutenant. That was quick promotion, but he was 27, pretty old for a lieutenant in Korea.

'Congratulations, Luke,' I said. 'Is that why you didn't look me up? Too high and mighty now that you've got rank?'

'I was going to call you tomorrow, Harland. I've only been in town a few hours … and they only hung these railroad tracks on me this morning.'

'What're you up to in Seoul?'

'I'm on TDY to Eighth Army, working in Psywar for a month or so. What do I know about psychological warfare? Practically nothing. Still TDY, supposedly temporary duty, has a way of turning into a permanent change station.'

'That's great. It must be pretty shitty cooped up in a dugout on the line … a tad dangerous, too, even now. You ought to be pleased.'

'Thass jus' the trouble.' His words were slightly slurred. 'I'm not pleased. For some reason, I'm not pleased 'tall … not happy about it!'

I nodded to the US Marine lieutenants, who were rising from their beer-keg chairs with ponderous alcoholic dignity. The conversation was becoming personal and, even worse, serious. They hadn't come to Seoul for heavy conversation.

The one called Chuck leaned over, all but breathing into my ear, and asked, 'Say, buddy, can you tell me where …?'

'Down near the main PX,' I told him. 'You'll find the girls in the back streets around the PX. But watch out for MPs … and transvestites.'

'No, Harland, my friend,' Luke repeated when the Marines had left, 'I'm not 'tall pleased.'

'What the hell does that mean?'

'Not muchsh. Only that I felt alive up on th' line … really alive for th' first time since Okinawa!'

'You still get a kick out of getting shot at? Haven't you had enough? Are you addicted to danger? The adrenalin?'

'Hell no!' he broke in. 'I'm shure sure as hell not ad … addic … addicted to gettin' shot at. Not 'tall.'

'Don't kid yourself, Luke. I know how you feel. Myself, when this war started, it was like being charged with electricity, high-voltage current. Action again! That gets to you too, doesn't it?'

'Hell no, Harland! Anyway, there'sh not so mush … not so much action. We hold Old Baldy 'n' Chinese're not all that so eager to boot ush off. Last heavy contact was that day I met you. Mostly we jusht sit around the dugout, may fire a few rounds to break the monotony, and play a lot of poker.'

'Do you get a charge out of that? What about wringing out POWs?'

'Not that many POWs, either. For a while, none 'tall. But a new Chicom division then moved into the line. Very security minded, really committed to the cause. Nothin' like the old retread Nationalist troops we used to be up against.'

'What'd you do?'

'Had to get some prisoners. So I took out a few patrols … a couple were hairy … pretty hairy. Mosht o' the time we'd hit a Chinese outpost and scurry away with any warm body we could grab.'

'And you still say you're *not* addicted to danger?'

'I've told you no, Harland. Of coursh, I'm not. Shtands to reason. One funny thing, though. I thought I'd never get used to that stinking dugout. But coming back from a patrol was like checking into the Presidential Suite at the Mark Hopkins. Some fun!'

Luke Maynell did not look as if he'd been enjoying himself much. His long face was haggard, his light beard now a darkish shadow under his pallid skin. Such prison pallor was normal for a frontline soldier who lived in his dugout like a mole in a burrow, emerging only after nightfall. Luke was normally the embodiment of health and vigor, the All American boy, his fair skin lightly tanned. But tonight Luke looked ill.

'Life was a hell of a lot simpler than it was in New Haven or San Francisco,' he remarked. 'Simpler, I suspect, than it'll be in Seoul.'

'Did you find your real self in a trench on the MLR?' Needling isn't the worst way to set a man talking. 'Saved you a trip to India to join an ashram to seek truth?'

'Not really, Harland.'

He did not take offense. But his light-brown eyes looked through me as if he were indeed gazing across a great distance at newly revealed truth.

'They were just ordinary fellows,' he resumed, as if I had not said a word. 'Nothing special: little Lieutenant Karl Simons, his family came to the States from Nuremberg, refugees, in the early '30s. A PFC from Fresno called Harris, willing, but, by God, stupid. And my boss, a cocky New Yorker, Captain Anthony de Marco, who normally teaches law at NYU and practices a little … mostly negligence cases … '

'All in all a mixed bag,' I interjected. 'But sounds normal for the Army of the US.'

'As you say, Harland. Exshept we were all working together … putting our lives on the line. And I was one of them.'

'Luke, you're hardly just another GI!'

'Well, maybe not. I was a little different, even in that crew, I suppose. Who in his right mind would've learned not only some Chinese, but a little Japanese? Any rate, they didn't hold it against me. G² teams're used to oddballs.'

This new Luke Maynell was different from the easy assumptions I'd made. More complicated, less obviously the golden boy, not nearly so much fortune's favorite son.

He had, I remembered, years earlier, protested over a highball at Mori's: 'Harland, you've got me wrong. I'm not the golden boy you think. It's not all effortless attainment, sure success, whatever I do. I'm not destiny's tot.'

I must be careful in this account, though nobody ever called Harland Birch fortune's favorite. Anyway, I want to draw an honest picture of a young man of whom I'd become very fond. I did not, of course, know at the time how deeply he was to be mired in the moral quicksands lying just under the surface violence of the Korean War. I could hardly guess that he was almost to be pulled under or that he was to face problems that were largely insoluble. Nor could I foresee that almost every harsh decision thrust upon him would lead him to a new dilemma.

To do Luke justice, I must be very careful.

Anyway, it *was* more than forty years ago. Memory is tricky: one moment sharp, showing me everything in minute detail, the next moment selective, choosing what it wants me to know, at the same time painstakingly precise and grandly deceptive. Like the light you see as you come to the end of a long tunnel, my memories glow with illusory clarity. The scene within the bright circle is *too* tightly focused, *too* well defined. It is an image of reality, not reality itself.

If only I could look backward down the tunnel to where I've been, rather than forward to where I am going. Yet, that is, somehow, the way I remember Korea. Through the fog of time. Incidents long past and individuals all but forgotten now loom, at first distant and dim, then preternaturally precise, far too clear, almost terrifying in their intensity. And utterly real, *too* real.

I can still see Luke Maynell exactly as he looked that late-February night at the Temple Bar, exhausted and half-drunk, bereft at being transferred from the unit where he had, quite unexpectedly and quite incongruously, found himself at home. His green fatigues were ineradicably stained. Glittering new captain's bars gleamed on one side of the collar; tarnished old infantry rifles were dull on the other. The oversize blouse hung loose on his lean six-foot-one frame. The baggy trousers, torn at the knee, were tucked clumsily into calf-high combat boots with mud caked thick on their heavy soles and their worn-down heels.

Even in that bedraggled, half-inebriated state, somehow he still appeared confident, despite his expressed unhappiness. It was partly the way he lounged so casually in the barrel-chair, he was extremely restless that evening, restless and loud, but evidently in command of himself. Such self-confidence – apparently impervious to fatigue, unaffected by setbacks, staring down humiliation, stoutly overcoming defeat to fight again harder – such self-confidence, such total assurance is bred by many generations of forebears who possess secure wealth and unshakeable social standing. So, anyway, it seemed to me that night. Maybe that was my mistake, arising from my own deprived background.

But that is another story, a story that some of my self-appointed reformers charge obsesses me. Relax! I won't parade my King Charles's head just now.

That night I believed I read Luke's invincible security in his features, oddly, perhaps shortly after having assessed his discouragement and his exhaustion from that outward appearance. Beneath the skin that was taut and pale, the bones were assertive: the long jaw, strong and sculpted; the pronounced cheekbones, which expressed determination even when he smiled; and the high forehead, which, as was to be expected, signalled a powerful intellect. Under his finely arched nose with its minutely flared nostrils, his mouth was full, yet firm. When he was very tired as he was that night, his lower lip drooped slightly. His light-brown eyes were changeable as the April weather: one moment serene and the next wary, one moment assertive and the next relaxed.

Though self-possessed, he was that evening visibly alert: like a stag safe in his own secure corner of the forest, but still vigilant against hunters; like a tiger, arrogant in his strength and his speed, yet always listening for the rustle of his prey or the footsteps of the only predator that would attack him. I mean man, of course.

Luke's dark-brown eyebrows, which were set straight across his face in a bold bar, looked black in the dimness. So, too did his crisp, wiry hair, which was longer than most officers would allow themselves, or many commanding officers tolerate. His was the kind of hair that women love to tousle, as a number of young women had told him, archly and provocatively.

Many young women had run their fingers through his hair playfully, amorously, or covetously. He was a magnet to their iron-filings, a honeycomb to their bees. So many had been charmed by his assured air and his easy manner – also attracted, however contrary that might appear, by his boyish vulnerability when his lower lip drooped slightly.

Luke, I had earlier concluded not without a smidgen of envy, could have almost any woman he wanted. But he could not keep any of them – not one. He had consistently bad luck with women.

The old flame who had catalogued Luke's attractions for me was an intern at Columbia Presbyterian Medical Center called Mary Kaye Sommers. She had mused softly over highballs at a small table near the bar of the refuge in upper Manhattan called the Carousel. Even though we, that is, she and I, Harland Birch, had just gotten out of bed, she took Luke more seriously at that intimate moment than she did me. The old flame still burnt high, although she thought it had gone out or, at least, said so.

'You're completely different, Harley.' Her tongue lingered lasciviously over the diminutive I detest, signalling to me that our brief affair was all but over. 'You're fun. You're exciting ... good for a quick roll in the hay. But a girl'd be a fool to take you seriously. I bet you always have good luck with women: love 'em and leave 'em crying. But, as for Luke now ...'

Mary Kaye sipped her fourth Scotch and water. She preferred Justerini & Brooks. She was apparently unaware that it was making her excessively loquacious, not to say dangerously indiscreet – as she would have been were she talking to a rival who disliked Luke and wanted to harm him, rather than to a good friend who could not truly be jealous of him and wanted only what would please him. She really went in a big way for J & B, which is deceptively light in color and gentle, even bland in flavor, but packs the same wallop as any Scotch whisky. Probably a harder punch, because its apparent mildness encouraged her to drink more.

Her voice soft and husky, Mary Kaye resumed: 'Luke's always had bad luck with women, as he says. Maybe that's because he's so serious way down deep. Even though he's funny and light-hearted, and entertaining, less inhibited than you, my dear Harley, in bed ...'

I knew then that our affair was definitely over. If she didn't end it, I would. Harley, she called me! And inhibited in bed! *Me*, inhibited! For God's sake!

'Even so, even when he's in his lightest mood, even when he's chortling at trivial things, he's always serious. And his intentions are always honorable. He looks like a great catch, every girl's dream of the man she wants when the time come to stop playing and settle down.'

'So then, where's this bad luck you're talking up?' I prodded. 'What's all this guff about what a great guy Luke is, not to speak of being a demon lover! But, still you say, he's abused by fortune ... unlucky. I see him as one of the luckiest guys in the world.'

Mary Kaye smiled, obviously delighted at having provoked that outburst. She smiled spitefully, and I was absolutely sure that I never wanted to see her again after this. Then she went on extolling Luke and bemoaning his misfortunes.

'Every girl he's truly involved with sooner or later senses that way down deep, at rock bottom, he's *not* serious, *not* really good husband and father material at all. He'd always be haring off, chasing maybe, though not necessarily, another woman. More likely, chasing a cause: an intellectual or political ideal, the Platonic ideal of the perfect world – even if he can't find the perfect woman.

'So he's had a whole procession of girlfriends, some even lasting a few years. He's so full of fun and joy and unforced affection that all those girls are eager and loving in the beginning – until they realize that he's not reliable, not in the long run. But Luke's not interested in the kind of girl who's not interested in the long run.'

Her tone lightened, and she began to talk about us, 'our own lovely relationship', as she said with light malice that was almost negligent. Only a little crestfallen by this time, I joined in a verbal *pas de deux* that I sensed was the ritual prelude to our parting. This particular broad, at least, I wouldn't leave crying. She was too tough.

In another bar far away from Manhattan, drinking amid the perpetual smoke-screen that hung over the Temple Bar, I learned that Luke was clearly in Korea by choice. Others, whether officers or correspondents, were also there by choice, but few would admit it. I, for one, was not inclined to tell anyone who was less close to me than Luke that the war had an electric effect on me. I could always say that my assignment, my work itself, required me to attend this war. An Asia correspondent who didn't cover the biggest story on his beat would be a sorry specimen.

But Luke had done his time in the army, so they couldn't draft him. Yet he had obviously volunteered for the Korean imbroglio. Why, I wondered, was he really here?

'You remember Mary Kaye Sommers, don't you, Harland?' he asked abruptly. 'I almost married that girl!'

'Yes, I remember Mary Kaye, remember her well,' I said slowly. 'I was just thinking about her.'

'You know, Harland, I almosht ... almosht ma ... mar ... married her,' he repeated, his words even more slurred. 'I was all set to ask her to marry me, but she began sending out negative signals. So I didn't. But I never returned the ring to Tiffany's. My mother's holding it now. Goddamned ring.'

His voice rose stertorously, and his left hand slammed down to the table. The glasses arrayed on the round top bounced and jangled. One fell, crashing on the flagstones.

Luke was holding a big, delicate, double-martini goblet with a long stem, cradled in his right hand. Very deliberately, virtually in slow motion, his fingers closed like a vize, and the goblet shattered. Blood trickling between his fingers, he dusted the glass shards from his palm with a not very white handkerchief, which he then wrapped awkwardly around the cuts. Mesmerized, I watched him struggle to tie a knot with his left hand and his teeth.

He snarled incomprehensibly when I made a move to help, and finally he got the ends knotted together.

'Another drink?' he suggested calmly. 'It's on me. With my new rank, I can afford it.'

'At ten cents a throw it's pretty pricey,' I laughed. 'But why not, if you're buying?'

Momentarily sober, as it appeared, Luke asked dispassionately, 'Did you know Mary Kaye ran away with a surgeon who was twenty years older? One of her professors. They just upped and took off one evening. Obviously, she didn't give a damn about her reputation – or her career. Just ran off with this horny old geezer, without a thought to her future – or his wife and four kids.'

When I nodded, he said plaintively, 'She can't get away with that kind of stuff, Harland. Where in the world they can practice medicine, God alone knows. Maybe in some banana republic, but nowhere else.'

'Luke?' I asked abruptly. 'What brought you to Korea?'

'Circumstance, Harland, just circumstance. You know I got tied up ... fascinated by ... the Orient, mostly the Far East: the culture and the languages, the art, the religions, and the history.

'I never thought what I'd do with the knowledge I was acquiring. It drove my old man up the wall. He kept saying: 'Then, if you must, get a PhD. At least, you'll be able to teach or get some kind of government boondoggle.'

'I flat refused ... wouldn't take the PhD. The course was too rigid, too mechanical. The old man was damned sore at me. Of course, that was nothing new.

'Finally, partly to make him happy, I applied to the Foreign Service. They took one look and rolled out the red carpet. I can be so damned Yaley when it suits. My first assignment was the US Information Service in Chungking. I was supposed to sail in the summer of 1949. Right then the Communists took Chungking. So that was that. No diplomatic relations between Washington and Peking. No USIS post in Chungking – and no job for me!'

'And then?'

'I went back to school ... almost got that PhD. Then came this War in Korea. I was feeling patriotic again. Damned fool! So I talked to the army. They offered me my old rank back: staff sergeant, maybe even tech sergeant. I figured they weren't really serious ... wouldn't use me properly, not as a sergeant. But, at my age, it would all the same've been juvenile to insist on being an enlisted man. So, my old man wangled me a commission.'

His head drooped, and he murmured, 'At first, they didn't want me. The old colonels said there was no conceivable use for a Chinese or Japanese-language officer in Korea. After all, there were no Japs there any more – and all the Chinks were running restaurants. When I told them all adult Koreans spoke Japanese, they looked at me as if I were nuts. But, soon enough, even the G² colonels realized there were lots of Chinks in Korea – lots of tough Chinks carrying guns.'

Luke's head drooped again, almost touching the table as he slid down his chair. Since I didn't know where he was billeted, I hauled him back to the Correspondents' Quarters and let him sleep it off on a vacant bunk.

Chapter IV

The Psychological Warfare Section, Eighth US Army, Korea, had an apparently straightforward mission: to savage the enemy's morale and thus undermine his will to fight, so that he would surrender or, at the least, be put out of action. A demoralized soldier could be wounded or killed more easily.

Most Chinese and North Koreans were inherently receptive to Psywar's message: 'Surrender! Come over to the UN side and be well looked after.'

Their day-to-day life was bitter, and they were in constant peril of death. Besides, their loyalties were confused, not only by being forced into totalitarian armies. Further, because the historical, social, and political roots of the conflict were intricately entangled – simply beyond their understanding.

Nonetheless, Psywar still had to communicate with the enemy to get its message across and, it hoped, to thus shatter his fighting morale. The Psywar Section of the Eighth Army was a little better off for Chinese linguists than Captain Anthony de Marco's Intelligence Team. But not much!

Lieutenant-Colonel Lesward Murray Howse, who commanded the Section, was, therefore, much pleased by the arrival of Captain John Luxborough Maynell: a gifted Chinese linguist, and Japanese thrown in. The colonel was so pleased that he almost threw a party, but his inherent caution, petrified by twenty-two years in the military, forestalled such a rash act.

His cardinal principle was: *Never take any decisive action, however minor. If possible, do nothing at all, and you will be promoted regularly!*

His ingrained shrinking from action was reinforced by his inborn Scottish disinclination to spend money, even the twenty or thirty dollars at the low commissary prices that would have provided a lavish spread for the entire Psywar Section of thirty-seven men and two women.

Howse had been transferred from a snug berth as academic director of the Army Language School at the Presidio of Monterey to command a line battalion in Korea. His fitness for that assignment was certified by the crossed rifles of the infantry and the silver oak leaf of his rank on his collar. He was relieved after two disastrous weeks during which his battalion suffered the highest casualties in Eighth Army. Yet Colonel Howse had many friends, as well as many debtors. He was, therefore, not court-martialed for scandalous negligence and dereliction of duty.

Besides, a trial would have made public his manifest incompetence as an infantry officer, which the army preferred to forget.

He was, instead, assigned to Psywar, where he could do little good, but, equally, little harm. Settling into Eighth Army Headquarters in the big red-brick building that housed Ehwa Women's College before the invasion, the 'light-colonel', as the troops ironically called his rank, had found he had only one Chinese linguist in uniform.

More specifically, he had two half-linguists. When he was sent to Korea, Second-Lieutenant George Miner had just begun to learn Mandarin, the most widely spoken form of Chinese. Major Benjamin Gam spoke passable Toisan, the Cantonese dialect of his forefathers – as long as the conversation didn't become too abstract. But he was, he would confess with a rueful grimace, 'a little weak on reading and writing.' He really meant he was functionally illiterate.

His talent for scrounging everything from cognac and mattresses to loud-speakers and jeeps was, however, invaluable, while his good humor oiled the psychological machinery. Otherwise he was little use to the Psywar Section, which was required to produce propaganda leaflets in Chinese ideograms and propaganda broadcasts in Mandarin.

Colonel Howse's own 201 file certified him as a Japanese linguist, as well as an infantry commander. Sadly, he was no more adept as a linguist than he had proved as a commanding officer in the field. If he rehearsed twice or thrice beforehand, he could stumble through a speech in Japanese that had been ghostwritten for him and then typed on foolscap paper in outsize Roman letters. He would be lost if the text were, as it would normally be, written in *kanji*, the Chinese-originated ideograms the Japanese used, intermixed with *kana*, the Japanese syllabic alphabet. Although he knew nothing of the language of China, he resented as a personal affront Eighth Army's appointing him to command a unit that lacked the language skills essential to its task.

In truth, he could not really acknowledge that he was fortunate not to have been reduced in rank or summarily retired after the débâcle of his first combat command. Nor could he acknowledge that he would never wear the silver eagles of a full colonel. He would, however, he reflected dismally, be cruelly handicapped in the race for promotion to full colonel because he had not been assigned the specialist officers necessary to Psywar's performance.

'Glad to have you, Maynell!' he said, automatically concealing his pleasure in Luke's capability. 'Took your time getting here, didn't you?'

Alternating mild enthusiasm and bleak reproach in language alternately down to earth and pretentiously refined, Howse welcomed a viciously hung-over Luke Maynell with black coffee from the Pyrex pot bubbling in a corner of the former lecture hall that housed the Psywar Section. Charts and posters were arrayed with military precision on the drab brown walls; aligned in ruler-straight line were tables and chairs scarred by long use though protected by sickly yellow shellac. Howse sat behind a blackwood desk, which was inlaid with iridescent mother-of-pearl patterns. From the lecturer's dais, he looked down on his subordinates.

At 46, rather old in grade, the light-colonel was bulky in his woolen olive drab uniform, bulky yet flabby. His watery blue eyes, set in a face unhealthily flushed, were magnified by his square rimless glasses. Thinning gray hair combed straight back, he looked like an assistant professor denied tenure, who had, therefore, shifted to administration.

In military terms, too, he was exactly that. He had been commissioned as a specialist on Japan in 1942, glad to be shot of the cow college in Wyoming where he was teaching a scratch course in Far Eastern civilization. Transferring to the Regular Army after World War II, he had ensured his promotion by heavy obsequiousness to his superiors and by avoiding any positive action. He had been happily ensconced in the Army Language School at picturesque Monterey, California, happily anticipating advancement to commandant and the insignia of a full colonel, often called a bird colonel because its insignia was a silver eagle. His transfer to a combat command in Korea ruined everything

'You really speak Chinese, don't you?' he asked abruptly. 'Mandarin?'

'Yes, Colonel.' Luke ardently wished that the insipid coffee in the chipped mug were Asahi beer in a frost-pearled glass. 'Most of the time.'

'Most of the time? What's that supposed to mean?' Howse demanded. 'Either you do, or you don't!'

'Yes, sir, I do!'

'You're out of line, Captain. Too damned facetious! Drop it!'

'Sorry, sir. I wasn't thinking.'

'Do so. There's no place in my command for an officer who doesn't think. You read Chinese, your 201 file says. You write it, too?'

'Yes, sir, naturally. It's a basic skill, isn't it?'

'Never mind that wise guy stuff, Maynell. You're not the first Phi Beta Kappa I've had under my command. Most of 'em turned out bad.'

'I'll try to do better.'

As long as Luke was on TDY, temporary duty, not permanently assigned to Psywar, he was not technically under the command of this neurotically insecure light-colonel. Still, it was wise to be wary of Howse.

'Do so and you'll get along fine. As you'll see, I've been handed an impossible job. Major Gam's a crackerjack exec-officer. But he's about as much use to my primary mission as tits on wild boar. I wonder what's become of all the Chinese-language officers we trained in Monterey … there's only Lieutenant Miner, who had six months there. Not enough by a long shot, but a start, at least.'

Luke nodded to the lanky, dark-haired lieutenant, who looked more like a basketball player than a Chinese scholar.

'… and there's also Mr. Kim,' Howse said,

Luke all but expected to see again the cadaverously thin civilian with a smattering of Mandarin who had fled from the frontline with Captain Anthony de

Marco's blessing. Instead, he saw a plump Korean with a wispy white beard and eyes so narrow that, when he smiled, they were all but invisible slits in his apple-red face. Rising from his chair, Luke greeted the older man in respectful Mandarin. He was rewarded with words of old-fashioned, self-abnegating courtesy, which were remarkably pure in both accent and diction.

'His spoken English, it's not so hot,' the colonel observed. 'Hell, it's practically non-existent, though I've seen him reading Chaucer in the original. You'll be a big help with Kim. Of course, I could speak Japanese to him, but time's so short …'

Luke registered automatically that he would be required to interpret between Mr. Kim and Colonel Howse. He had heard the colonel's Japanese described by a skilled interpreter as 'pretty good – for a parakeet!'

'Our focus … our target … our bull's eye … is the Chinese,' Howse continued. 'Mostly we leave the North Koreans to their southern brethren to seduce. That's just natural when you think of the balance of the enemy's forces: more than half a million Chinks and no more'n fifty, sixty thousand *Han-gook-in*, as the Koreans say, that is, men of the country called Han.

'Mr. Kim does a little liaison work, but our official liaison officer is Miss Suja Chae. She's an odd duck.'

Looking around the room, Luke saw a mousy Korean woman at the back of the hall pasting photographs into a scrapbook. He turned interrogatively to his superior.

'No, that's not her,' the colonel laughed. 'Little Mrs. Pak just does some odd jobs. Altogether, I've got thirty-nine under my command here plus three field teams. Talent and skill enough to run a brigade – all under my command. Helluva lot more real power and, naturally, more problems than a line battalion.'

'What's so odd about Suja Chae?' Luke asked, remembering to add with overblown respect, 'Do tell me, sir?'

'Nifty little number, if you like slant eyes.' Luke wondered at a nominal Japanese-language officer who was a racist. 'Seconded from the ROK Ministry of Education. Young slip of a thing, only twenty-six. American educated at some Eastern college.

'But Counter Intelligence is sniffing around Miss Chae. Her mother's half-Chinese. They lived in Shanghai in the '30s, mixing with Chink commies. Suja speaks Mandarin, as well as Shanghainese, and she reads *kanji*, that is, ideograms. Most Koreans her age can read Japanese *kanji*, but how many speak perfect English?'

With a strained smile Luke nodded at the instruction in a fundamental reality: all education in Korea had been conducted in the language of the overlords during forty years of Japanese occupation. He dismissed the absent Miss Chae from his thoughts when Howse held out a sheet of paper.

'We drop this to the Chinks. Safe-conduct pass for those surrendering.'

'Good enough.' Initially noncommittal, Luke added, 'There are some grammatical errors. And it refers to the League of Nations. Nobody tell your translator we're fighting under the United Nations banner, sir?'

'You can start here by rewriting it,' Howse directed. 'Give me a new safe-conduct pass. Stress they don't have to go back to Red China when the war ends. Not ever!'

Lieutenant-Colonel Lesward Murray Howse beamed, and Luke wondered if beneath his egotistical bombast he was truly dedicated to his mission. Or was he simply happy that his unit would in the future make fewer glaring errors, maybe even rack up a few visible triumphs? Perhaps he was still dreaming of silver eagles.

'She'll be in this afternoon, our Miss Chae,' Howse said. 'I can't keep her away, no matter what Counter Intelligence says. I couldn't even if I wanted to. The ROKs, that is, the government of the Republic of Korea, have assigned her to me. I can't afford to offend them, our hosts and allies. And I don't really think she's a spy. Maybe her mother, but not her.'

Luke wondered what possible secrets could attract a spy to Psywar, which by its nature, *wanted* information passed to the enemy. He did not, however, tread on the colonel's sensitive toes by raising the question. They were returning from the Senior Officers' Mess, where Howse had expansively invited Luke to lunch. The hot dogs and beans were no better than they would have been at the junior officers' Consolidated Mess, but it was pleasant to be served by a middle-aged Korean clad in a crude replica of an American waitress's uniform.

Luke would have known that the pert young woman was Suja Chae, even if she has not been sitting at the writing-table beside the colonel's dais chatting cosily with Major Ben Gam. Who else would be so relaxed in an alien setting amid alien soldiers? Besides, she had emulated the practice of the US Army, wearing a shiny black-plastic badge that bore her name in not only the Roman alphabet, but in Korean script and Chinese ideograms. Her given name, he saw, meant Fresh and Keen, that is, fresh as in unsullied and bright, not as in nasty and insolent.

Somehow, this Miss Chae seemed vaguely familiar, almost as if he had already met her. But that was hardly likely. Besides, she was very much like a number of the Asian girls who had attracted him at one time or another.

Sitting at her ease, Miss Chae looked Luke over carefully, indeed with ostentatious thoroughness, before extending her hand. Her hand was very small, almost as tiny as a child's, though the nails gleamed with blood-red polish. Her firm mouth was generously lipsticked the same color, which matched the very small pumps with very high heels on her very dainty feet. Her *chipao*, which, as Luke, of course, knew meant 'riding coat', was derived from the equestrian costume the nomadic Manchus had worn before they conquered China. Now a typical Shanghai-style dress, it was made of silk damask with a stand-up collar, was slit to just above her knees for ease of movement, and was padded with raw silk fiber against the chill of late February.

He could well believe that she had been at college in the United States when she said 'Hello!' in a husky drawl like Katherine Hepburn's. Only the vestige of a lilt hinted that she was not a native-born American

'Well, my dear, will he do?' the colonel asked archly. 'Do you like what you see?'

'I'm not sure, Colonel.' She was assertively detached. 'After all, I've *just* met him.'

Why, Luke wondered, did she stress the word *just*? Probably no more than a quirk of her speech.

Suja Chae lowered her eyelids, revealing long curled lashes. She was still studying Luke, as if cataloguing a new variety of microbe she had just discovered. Why, he wondered, such intense interest? He was genuinely puzzled. Luke did not flatter himself. He simply refused to acknowledge the reality that others saw as obvious: most women, young or old, were immediately interested in him.

'We should've met before, Miss Chae, even though we haven't.' He was instinctively charming. 'We're both very much interested in things Asian.'

'Speak for yourself, Captain,' she rejoined. 'I know I *look* Asian. I *am* Asian. But I'm not obsessed with that accidental fact. I didn't choose my race.'

'Of course, not!' Luke tried again. 'But you *are* still Asian ... heiress to a treasure trove of literature and art ... heiress to Asian culture.'

'So much flattery ... much enthusiasm!' she replied. 'I really do wonder. Is the captain another phoney Asia expert? Is he full of wind and opinions, but really as ignorant as a newborn puppy? I can't tell just by looking.'

Luke was startled by her pugnacity. He was amused, as well. He could not take offense at such a sweeping, unprovoked attack by a girl he'd just met. It would have been ridiculous to be that sensitive.

Now, Lieutenant-Colonel Howse was manifestly a 'phoney Asia expert' by Suja Chae's definition. But the colonel evidently could not imagine that a slip of a girl would dare mock him.

'Captain Maynell will be a great help to all of us,' he remarked jovially. 'He's taking over Chinese propaganda. Reads and writes the lingo. Also speaks perfect Mandarin, I'm told.'

Slowly and distinctly, as if talking to a small child or to an imbecile, Miss Chae asked in Mandarin with a slight Shanghai accent: '*Ni hao ma, Shang-wei Hsien-sheng? Wo-men dou hen gao-hsing nin lai* ... How are you, Captain, sir? We are all very glad that Your Honor has arrived.'

'I am in excellent health, by far the better for your gracious enquiry.' Luke replied elaborately in the furry accent of Peking, which snobs consider the most cultivated spoken Chinese. For good measure, he added in rudimentary Shanghai dialect, '*Ala fu hsiu-deh Sanghai eeow* ... I don't know any Shanghainese.'

She looked at him warily beneath the glossy black bangs that fringed her porcelain forehead. Her contempt for outsiders who pretended to knowledge of Asia evidently somewhat allayed, she said in English, 'I hear and believe. The captain speaks Chinese like a mandarin.'

'And the lady speaks English like an aristocrat.'

'American, Captain! I speak American, not English. And they called me Sue when I was at Vassar.'

Vassar? Luke wondered if he might have met her on his visits to nearby Vassar when he was at Yale. Perhaps! More than likely, but there were a number of girls from Asia at the women's college. He could hardly remember them all.

'Quite, Miss Chae,' he finally replied, determined to be pleasant. 'By the way, everyone calls me Luke.'

'Well, Luke,' she said, still grudgingly, 'I guess we have to work together, but don't expect me to carry your share of the load. If you can't deal with it, well ...'

Luke stifled the ungallant retort that came to his lips. A certain degree of defensiveness he could understand and, understanding, pardon. There came to him unsought a vivid recollection of the atmosphere on the Vassar campus shortly after World War II, when she must have been there. He could easily imagine her being treated on occasion like an exotic prize cat and on other occasions like an unfamiliar, indeed unknown, and therefore dangerous beast: one day patronized and the next shunned.

Still, her antagonism toward a stranger who happened to be white went beyond natural resentment. She might almost have muttered that he was a crude barbarian who stank disgustingly of butter and beef – a virtually unlettered barbarian who misread every text in classical Chinese on which his eyes lighted. Such defensive contempt one could often encounter, almost routinely, among agéd Chinese Confucian scholars. They, of course, feared that the props of their livelihood, even more critically, the props sustaining their battered self-esteem would be broken by foreigners penetrating the sacred mysteries of their ancient culture. But such contempt was not normally to be expected on the part of an attractive American-educated young woman.

Attractive? Yes, she was beyond question extremely attractive, although definitely not his type.

Sitting close to her, the old safe-conduct passes heaped on his small table, Luke lit a Lucky Strike. He meditatively studied Suja Chae through the haze of smoke.

Her eyes had sparkled with glee when she sparred with him. They were, nonetheless, like all Korean eyes, secretive. Eskimo blood maybe, the viciously cold winter perhaps, squeezed the black eyes of Koreans tight. But Suja Chae's eyes were a shade wider. Just barely tinged with green and gold flecks, they were set at only a slight angle to her delicate cheekbones.

Her face was a perfect oval from its shining black crown to its rounded chin with a minute dimple. It was by no means the perfectly round 'moon-face' beloved of Chinese and Korean poets and painters. Her features were sharply defined: not a flat blob of a nose, but, rather, aquiline like a Japanese *noh* mask; not a tiny red mouth like a Cupid, but generous, yet firm lips now set in a wry smile. Women, Luke imagined, would notice first her perfect skin, which was the color of old ivory. The faces of most Korean women were chafed, splotched red by wind and cold. As far as he could tell, her complexion was not enhanced by make-up, though mascara and eyeliner, as well as faint green eyeshadow, enlarged her eyes. And she wore that vivid scarlet lipstick.

'You two work on it together!' Colonel Howse broke into Luke's reverie. 'You'll have an advantage, the clash of different viewpoints: American and Oriental.'

Suja flushed in irritation, proving that her complexion was not enhanced by make-up. Luke was equally irritated by Howse's smug implication that there was a single Oriental mind, as if Chinese, Koreans, Japanese, even Vietnamese were virtually the same race with the same culture. In reality, even the Confucian heritage that linked them found remarkably different expression in each race.

Howse went on, 'No harm going over the background. Even though you think you've got it down perfect. Good to clarify your thinking.'

Howse would always state the obvious, Luke noted. Howse would state and restate the obvious as if it were his own unique discovery. An instant later, Luke acknowledged, rebuking his own impetuous judgement, that the colonel was in this matter right to do so. The issue was momentous, in truth crucial, elusive as well as perplexing: *Was the US-controlled United Nations Command to force unwilling POWs to return to the tyranny of Mao Zedong's China or Kim Il Sung's North Korea when an armistice was finally attained?*

It could be stated simply, but neither international law nor any general practice made the issue clear. The issue stood in urgent need of severe re-examination, starting with Eighth Army's Psywar Section at a relatively low level. The issue required stringent rethinking, at the highest level – not only by generals, but by the men at the very highest level, the men who formulated policy.

'For the first time in any war, any conflict I know of, we're guaranteeing captive enemy soldiers a free choice.' Howse portentously restated the essential background. 'We've told those POWs ... we've deeply impressed upon them ... that those who come over to us, exercising their own free will, that they will not be required to return to Communist oppression. No involuntary repatriation is now *the* fundamental issue of international affairs.'

Howse cleared his throat with a glutinous rumble and addressed anew his audience of two with a grandiloquent oratorical manner. 'We have, over and over again, assured them they need not go back to endure severe punishment for desertion ... likely executed without even the pretext of a hearing, murdered.

'You both should know! You'd better know! The armistice talks at a deserted village called Panmunjom between the lines have been hung up, totally stalled, on this crucial issue for more than a year now. Everything else is pretty much settled. If it weren't for the elemental human rights of the men we've captured or, better still, induced to come over, we could have a cease-fire tomorrow or, at the latest, the day after tomorrow.

'Naturally, the Commie dogs won't go along with voluntary repatriation. They're stuck on getting *all* their troops back, no matter what those poor bastards really want. Definitely ... absolutely ... no free choice. No question of their agreeing to only voluntary repatriation. They've got too much at stake: a break in their power, an enormous loss of face at home and abroad, if a lot of their captive troops don't go back. Say ten to twenty per cent. It won't go higher than that!'

Once launched into full flow, the light-colonel, quite clearly, could not possibly come to a halt of his own volition. The ship of his eloquence could neither heave to nor drop anchor.

'But what a victory for us!' he rhapsodized. 'What a triumph for Psywar! An imperial triumph for us ... for our ... for my strategy!'

He paused in smug self-satisfaction, noted Luke, in virtual self-adoration. Before Howse could resume, Luke spoke, at length, spinning his thoughts out in similarly high-flown language, before concluding: 'It is exceedingly clear that Peking and Pyongyang do not ... cannot possibly ... credit our promise to give POWs a free choice ... Why should they? What cause've we given them to ...

'Of course, they themselves, they lie all the time ... for their cause, they say, never for personal advantage,' Luke continued. 'They exalt such lying as "principled discourse", because it advances their crusade. They seek no less than perfection of humanity under a *perfectly* motivated "dictatorship of the proletariat" exercised by *perfect* commissars under *perfect* conditions.

'The Communists do not ... cannot possibly ... believe any Chinese or North Korea POW could freely decide not to return home. They *know* that those POWs will be intimidated by violence and by threats, by brain-washing and by mind-twisting ... will be forced to declare they don't want to go home. The commissars know exactly how they would deal with such POWs in their hands. So they know we are lying, but *not* telling principled lies.

'That's all the commissars can believe. Or is it really? How can we convince them they must agree – to make peace?'

'I can't, even I cannot say for sure!' Howse restated his unprecedented confession to a degree of ignorance in more dignified terms: 'Of course, it is extremely difficult ... arduous and, I fear, imprecise, to ascertain what the utterly unprincipled commissars truly believe. But the bastards ... scoundrels, I suppose I should say ... are taking no chances. Theirs not to take the slightest risk, but rather to avoid any possible danger.

'Our first hasty screening turned up a much larger number of non-repats than we'd considered remotely possible. Many more than we had imagined declared flatly their right not to be transported back to a Marxist-Leninist hell.

'No question whatsoever, it's a great victory, a magnificent psychological victory for Psywar. But, looked at from another point of view, it's a God-awful mess!'

Howse paused to allow his audience to savor that paradox.

'Too many taxpayers are protesting because so many American boys are dying. At the taxpayers' expense, they say, then rush to add that expense is not the significant element. Money lost can be found again. But the loss of our boys ... our brave soldier boys, they say ... that is truly unbearable.

'"And why are our boys dying?" They ask that crucial question and they answer themselves: So Oriental peasants can lounge around comfortable ... practically luxurious ... prison camps making up their primitive Oriental minds what country they want to belong to ... where they can best live in peace and security – and idleness. So a bunch of Oriental hicks ... yokels with no education and no ambition ... can be given every possible privilege – at America's expense ... at a brutal cost in American lives!'

The pitch of Suja's normally tempered voice rose high in her anger at those racist slurs. 'It's more complicated, Colonel Howse, a lot more complicated than you seem able to understand. Obviously you can't see the complexity ... all the ramifications! Your mind, such as it is, and your so-called thinking, they're both far too simple.'

Her fury unabated, she smiled all but sadistically, when the colonel winced. He dared not vent his ire on her by retorting in the same terms. Obviously, he feared the retaliation that, as he would say, a sneaky, duplistic, twisted Oriental brain could devise. Besides, she was the representative of the ROK government, even when she gave way to personal vehemence.

Howse's thought process took some time, its slow progress revealed by the rapid blinking of his watery-blue eyes, which were enormous behind his square-lensed rimless glasses. Suja, however, pre-empted the defensive reply that Howse's parted lips showed he was finally prepared to venture.

'Thank Heaven, there are good Americans who aren't racist ignoramuses.' Her tone was still fierce, despite her partially conciliatory words. 'They're fighting for just such free choice! Not only Americans, but sixteen other countries, are fighting to ensure the God-given right of the people of Korea to refuse to be oppressed by totalitarian despots.'

Sue paused, but the colonel had either forgotten his carefully prepared reply or was simply not ready to contest what she said. She thereupon resumed, her plaint as poignant, though her tone was softer.

'You Americans tend to forget about us Koreans. You Americans are sot [cq] in your own ways ... barricaded by your own prejudices. You won't acknowledge, not even to yourselves, that the majority of those fighting ... and dying ... in this civil war are Koreans.'

Suja continued on her new tack, veering away from the question of solely voluntary repatriation. Having endured his lengthy oration, she was apparently determined to make a peroration as lengthy – and even more spirited.

'We are grateful ... very grateful ... for American help, for the other nations' help. Still, we Koreans are just as brave as the others. We are extremely courageous, sometimes even foolhardy. We are fighting fiercely ... fighting for our country and for our future.

'We are making the greatest sacrifices of all to stem the red tide, which for a time appeared irresistible. King Canute could not stem the tide, but we are winning ... albeit slowly ... amid great pain ... in anguish.

'Our land has been ravaged; our cities and countryside laid waste; our lives blighted, perhaps irrevocably! Blighted as they would *not* have been had we meekly chosen not to resist the invasion.'

Suja's rhetoric rose to greater heights on the flood tide of her eloquence.

'Hundreds of thousands of brave Koreans have died. Whether in uniform or not. Not only men. Also a multitude of women and children, even infants. Most likely a million dead. And the end is not yet.'

Even Luke, who knew Asia as Colonel Howse never could, Luke, who truly admired Asians, was deeply impressed, as if struck anew by the glory of Asia itself. Suja's spirited comments were penetrating and incisive, as well as highly emotional, he was later to confide to me, Harland Birch, your itinerant storyteller.

I, in turn explained when Luke read this, my tale, that [cq] is the equivalent of [sic] in a more formal document. [Cq] means a newspaperman telling his type-setter: 'That word is correct, not an error as it may appear, so let it stand.'

Moreover, Suja's using the uncommon word 'sot' further evidenced her intimate familiarity with the English language. Besides, her tone was lofty; her diction, that is, her selection of words and allusions, was learnéd. In her fury Suja's discourse verged on the florid. It was all the more moving for that presumed fault. So Luke judged in his virtually verbatim account of her subduing Howse, who had finally ventured: 'Nobody ... not me, not I, that is ... ever said Koreans weren't ... '

Suja's contemptuous glance silenced the light-colonel. She concluded hotly, 'Anyway, no forcible repatriation isn't just a presumably selfless moral principle: it's very practical. As you've admitted, it's another inducement to the helots of Peking and Pyongyang, the bond slaves of Mao Zedong and Kim Il Sung, to come over ... to desert and surrender.

'Besides, it's obvious you slap-dash Americans didn't know what you were getting up to. Obvious that you didn't even begin to think through that impromptu policy beforehand ... didn't ever consider the consequences. Now you're stuck with that policy and with its bleak consequences. Bleak, at least, to you, who want an armistice so you can run away. You're trapped by your own expedience!'

'Expedience?' Luke hoped to ameliorate their hostility by a measured comment. 'Maybe expedient at first. But, Suja, you should ... you must ... understand that the decision was hardly casual, however hasty it may have been. It has deep roots, moral and political, also spiritual roots. The Yanks and the Brits, both are now fighting for Korea, fighting on the same side as we did in World War II. Both the Yanks and the Brits, though, still feel guilty ... about the way we acted just after that war ended.

'We betrayed hundreds of thousands of soldiers who'd been fighting beside us. Not only the soldiers. But the families of soldiers on our side. We forced them back to their presumed homeland. We drove them back at gunpoint to the Soviet Union after World War II. They were slaughtered, as they had feared. Slaughtered by kindly old Uncle Joe Stalin.

'We won't ... we cannot ... allow that to happen again.'

'So you don't agree with me, Luke?' she flared. 'You saying it's not expediency that later froze into a moral position ... not primarily an ethical pretext?'

'It's definitely not that clear, Suja, not that simple. You've already said it's a complex issue. Now what're you saying?'

He did not wish to provoke her further. Even less did he wish to appear to stand in agreement with Lieutenant-Colonel Lesward Murray Howse, whom he was rapidly learning to despise. Yet he could not twist and distort his own principles in

order to placate Suja Chae. He would not ... could not ... compromise the fundamental convictions that underlay the surface charm of his easy manner.

Luke knew that he normally tried to please. He knew that he felt instinctive
sympathy, fellow feeling, with most others he encountered. Regardless, he could
not deny his deep-rooted principles. Ultimately he could not dissemble.

'There has to be some consistency ... some legal axiom behind our stand,' he
continued. 'We're fighting to repel a blatant invasion. We're also fighting for the
rule of law. Yet the Geneva Conventions on prisoners of war don't even mention
involuntary repatriation. The issue never came up. The men who drafted the
Geneva Conventions didn't ever dream that POWs would not yearn for their homeland.'

Suja retorted inconsistently, 'We're talking about my brothers and my cousins,
Koreans and Chinese. You may know I've some Chinese in my own bloodline.
They're not ink on paper, not abstract legal principles, but living, breathing,
suffering men, some women, too. They're real human beings of bone and flesh and
blood. They bleed! They bleed – and they die!'

She leaned forward, her shining black pageboy in close contrast to Luke's
tousled dark-brown hair. Her eyes narrowed, her lips drawn tight, she was,
somehow, even more attractive physically. She was, however, far less pleasing,
somehow much less attractive overall.

Luke knew he would have to work closely with Suja. He would, therefore, be
polite, as he would be polite in any event. He would be extremely courteous, so
courteous that he might, despite himself, appear stilted.

Nonetheless, superficial amiability would do. He need try no harder. He need
not be affable nor seek to charm her. Of course he had to acknowledge that her
anger was well founded, her indignation wholly justified. He was nonetheless, glad
that he definitely did *not* have to see that harridan for even an instant outside the
office.

A pity! A great pity in a way! Suja could have been an interesting diversion were
it not for her dogmatism, her ferocious temper, her illogical assertions, and her own
racist xenophobia.

'That'll do, you two!' Colonel Howse instructed. 'No matter what you may
think or you may feel, Captain Maynell and Miss Chae, just make sure you follow
my orders. See to it that you obey me! Right now just sit right there, the two of you,
and draw up a new safe-conduct pass. Tell 'em loud and clear ... tell 'em over and
over again ... that men who come to us of their own free will won't ... not ever, not
under any circumstances ... have to go back to the Commies!'

Chapter V

I've had a bad day recalling events almost five decades past. Even I, Harland Birch, don't have a flawless memory now that I'm approaching eighty. This freezing raw weather gets into my bones. Anyway, my back aches when I sit at the typewriter too long. Standing only helps the pain a little

The blizzards sweeping upper New York State this January are, I suppose, evocative reminders of Arctic winters in Korea. They're also a Goddamn pain in the butt. What, I wonder, am I doing trapped here in these God-forsaken woods?

The storms cut me off from the world. I have no telephone, no electricity, and only a few gallons of water in the tank in the attic. Without electricity, there's no heat except a flicker from the fireplace. Without electricity, I can't pump water from the well, since there's no hand-pump in this ultra-modern shack. Anyway, the pipe from the well is frozen solid. Thank God for the tank in the attic and for the fact that gravity still works … hasn't frozen up.

When I tried to get the electricity fixed, before the telephone conked out, the idiot on the other end of the line had never heard of Harland Birch. Fair enough! There've been other wars since Korea, even since Vietnam.

Also, he'd never heard of the Pulitzer Prize or the *Boston Globe*, a damned influential newspaper. I did my farewell tour in Asia for the *Globe* after reluctantly consenting to retire from the *Richmond Courier* twelve years ago. The idiot working for the electricity company had never heard of the *Globe* or the *Courier*. In fact, he hardly knew that newspapers existed, or had ever existed. If it wasn't on television, it didn't exist for him!

Despite the miserable climate, memories are flowing fast, and I'm pinning them down with the faithful Smith-Corona portable I carried through six wars. Old it is, very old, practically an antique, truly an antique. One thing, it folds for compactness, the keyboard flipping over on the top of the letter-bars. Smith-Corona once told me they made their last folding model in 1938. But it works fine: facts and thoughts pour onto the paper.

Thank God I never shifted to a word processor with a flashy screen and flashing lights. A computer would be as much use in this snow-bound cottage as the television set whose blank face glowers darkly at me. Since I used up the batteries for my little radio, I'm totally isolated.

Maybe that's why memories are truly flowing, practically a deluge. Yet I sometimes wonder if it's worth the strain of writing by the light of a kerosene lantern – or worth the strain of writing at all.

Still, that's what I do. I write.

It doesn't seem to matter very much how many readers actually see my words, even though naturally I want them in print. As long as I can get the words down on paper, though, I'm all right. Is my writing then fundamentally therapeutic, as they say nowadays, 'cathartic', as we used to say? Or as I might still ask: 'Does it really let off steam? Does it get the troubles off my chest?' That's what I would've said before I picked up the psychological jargon at Yale as a Tutwell Fellow.

My God, it's strange! Very odd indeed! After all these years of earning my living with a typewriter, how can I still think of writing as a therapeutic exercise?

Anyway, the memories are flowing. Yet it all seems so long ago, even longer than the forty years that have passed so quickly. I might be remembering Henry VII's courtiers watching the wooden battleship *Mary Rose* sink off Southsea in the mid-1500s. I might almost be resurrecting painful memories of the Continental Army of General George Washington camped in the misery at Valley Forge during the brutal winter of 1777–1778. So long ago, so ancient does the War in Korea sometimes appear to me. Somebody remarked the other day, before I was cut off by the ice curtain, that that conflict was almost as long ago as was the Boer War when the Korean War began in 1950.

Yet, in a way, I'm more at ease with leisurely meandering into historical events than I am with today's miraculous technology. Just think of it! When we fought in Korea, we did *not* have: jet airliners, television networks, photocopiers, or fax machines, not even portable tape-recorders. And, of course, we did not yet have the silicon chip that is at the heart of the computers that dominate the present era.

No wonder it seems so very long ago. Epochs! So anachronistic even to myself are my own thoughts and reactions when I dwell on those days. So dated are the sights and the sounds of that virtually antique age. So far removed from our preoccupations today, so etiolated and attenuated are even the basic emotions of those times. Once again, I can all but feel with my fingertips the texture of a wholly diverse age, as different from the slick present era as is fine broadcloth from shoddy polyester.

A half-century ago, most Americans felt secure in themselves and their beliefs. They were confident of the integrity of their property and of their own immunity to physical assault. The nuclear age was only five years old in 1950 when the Korean War began. The attitudes, the certainties, of an earlier day still held true. As I've been remembering, young men actually volunteered for military service – even young women, but overwhelmingly men, who were, as always, more emotional and less realistic than women. And they served for material rewards which were even then derisory, $21 a month for a private! Not like so many today who are, in actual fact, bribed to wear a uniform.

Then many still almost contended for the privilege of getting shot at. Men felt diminished if they had not served in uniform. Once having put on a uniform, many felt themselves worth less if they had not seen combat. They competed even for danger, since they believed there were values worth defending – as well as splendid aspirations and noble goals worth striving for.

Things were changing fast even then. Nonetheless, Korea was our last old-fashioned war, morally as well as technologically. Many felt it was worth fighting, a challenge to our creeds and our virtues. Technologically it was a continuation of World War II against a different enemy. Our weapons and our equipment were all of that vintage, almost everything the ground forces used, except Mickey Mouse thermal boots and the new slightly improved jeeps.

Most warplanes were propeller-driven. Our strategic bomber was the B-29 Superfortress, which had ravaged Japanese supply lines and incinerated Japanese cities. Our tactical bombers were mostly B-26s, while the prop-driven F-51, the Mustang, was still a better close support airplane than any jet. Fighters were the main exception. Jet fighters had actually flown in World War II, though they saw day-in-day-out action for the first time over Korea. American-made F-86 Sabrejets and Soviet-made MiG-15s jousted along the Yalu River, which divides North Korea from China's Manchurian provinces. Helicopters were rather tentatively used in the early 1950s for liaison and medical evacuation; they were not yet deployed as weapons' platforms in actual combat.

We could never fight another old-fashioned war like Korea. Who could get Americans to do it again? The spirit's gone out of the American fighting man, unless it's a quick hi-tech turkey shoot like the one in the Persian Gulf a year ago.[1]

I saw great courage and great dedication, readiness to sacrifice personal interests, even life. Maybe those men were naïve. But, by God, they were motivated.

Hell, they were wildly quixotic by the standards of our cynical self-seeking age. What a contrast to the war in Vietnam! But I'll come to that later.

Americans just don't believe any more. At the time of Korea, only professional outsiders like correspondents asked such insidious questions as: 'Should we be here at all?' Of course, I, too, quite naturally asked such questions. That was my job, and it was important. But we didn't ask too often or too insistently.

Anyway, the facts were clear. So was the purpose of the first major armed conflict against the Stalinist bloc. Assisted vitally by Moscow and Peking, North Korea threw against the under-manned, under-equipped, and greatly outnumbered Constabulary of the Republic of Korea columns of Soviet-made tanks, whose field commanders and crews had been painstakingly trained by Soviet officers. There was no nonsense, no real expectation of victory in 'people's wars' mounted by guerrillas, although Pyongyang, like Hanoi later, hoped for an uprising that never materialized. Instead there was a swift invasion by conventional forces along a broad front, adhering closely to the strategic plans drafted by Soviet staffs.

---

[1] Editor's Note: Please remember that Harland Birch was setting down these reflections in 1992, just after the 1990-1991 Gulf War but years before George W. Bush's so badly managed occupation of Iraq. Clearly, bad management was not a late development, as is demonstrated by the little we have already learned of the handling of POWs in Korea.

Washington had invited that attack twice over. First the US had failed to sponsor an effective armed force for the ROK, allowing only a feeble constabulary, which possessed neither artillery nor tanks, not even trench mortars, lest, it was feared, Syngman Rhee should invade the north to unify the country. (Some irony there!) Secondly, a senior official of the State Department had publicly declared that the Korean Peninsula did *not* lie within the realm of primary American interests in Asia.

However, when the US decided to oppose the invasion, Washington did succeed in getting the United Nations to endorse that resistance. As I've noted earlier, I believe, the Soviet Union could not exercise its veto, for one simple reason: it was not around. Stalin was boycotting the UN Security Council in protest against the American refusal to transfer China's seat from the Nationalists to the Communists.

In all, twenty-four nations were engaged on the UN side in the war that followed. The fifteen that sent troops to fight beside the South Koreans and the Americans under the blue-and-white UN flag, ranged from Colombia, Australia, and Ethiopia through Britain, France, and Belgium all the way to Turkey, Thailand, and South Africa. Five sent medical units: Italy, India, Denmark, Sweden, and Norway.

When the invasion mounted by North Korea was hurled back by General of the Army Douglas MacArthur, whose forces were surging towards the Yalu River, China cobbled together the Chinese People's Volunteers. The Soviet Union had no overt presence. Nonetheless, as I've indicated, Moscow provided almost all of Pyongyang's supplies and weapons, as well as fighter pilots and, of course, warplanes.

Korea was the first major international conflict after World War II, the first and, in fact, the epitome of wholly united defense of the principle: *No compromise with aggression*! True, the 1991 Gulf War carried on that purpose, thrusting back the troops of Saddam Hussein who had invaded Kuwait. But that coalition was the last gasp: nor was it fought under the United Nations' banner. Of course, that effort also guaranteed a continuing flow of oil, which went largely to Japan and Western Europe, although the US organized and commanded the expeditionary force, as it had in Korea.

Of course, the War in Korea also served our self-interest. It kept a Marxist-Leninist military invasion from seizing one territory and then, inspired by such successful aggression, going on to seize other territories, like, say, West Berlin. Nonetheless, UN intervention in Korea was inspired as much by principle as by self-protection. The War in Korea was the last Great Crusade!

I saw the whole show there. Later, I was in and out of Vietnam, mostly *in*, over a stretch of more than twenty years from 1955-1975. I was, thus, in country before the American commitment; during the major American effort, which deployed many more US troops than we had in Korea; and then for the débâcle that followed American withdrawal. Vietnam was rough, very rough at times, and it was always heartbreaking. But it wasn't all that rough compared to what we and our allies saw of not only military casualties, but civilian casualties in Korea. Material destruction was also much greater in Korea.

Yet nobody was scragged in Korea, not the way the GIs shot officers in Vietnam, and most soldiers weren't on drugs. A few officers and non-coms might've got shot in the back. Some do in every war. Otherwise, booze and the pursuit of nooky on rest and recreation leave in Japan kept soldiers going, those who survived.

Of course, Vietnam cost more in American blood, as well as American treasure. Still the figures show the difference in intensity. About 35,000 American dead in Korea in three years against 58,000 American dead in Vietnam over twelve years: about 11,000 a year in Korea compared to somewhat less than 5,000 a year in Vietnam.

Of course there were public doubts about Korea, as well as Vietnam. There were bound to be. Doubt was even healthy up to a point. There wasn't much cheering for Korea, or much protest, but mostly silence.

Americans want banners flying, bands playing, and the press trumpeting encouragement. They don't march well to a quavering trumpet in a war they're constantly told is, at best, second-rate and, regardless, essentially evil as they were told about Vietnam.

A lineal continuation of World War II on the ground and in the air, Korea was, above all, a political war, a new phenomenon for most Americans. On our side, it was fought to impress certain realities upon the minds of potential foes, so that they would not make the same mistake elsewhere. The ultimate goal was neither to take ground nor to destroy the enemy forces – as some few American generals finally learned. The Communist objective was winning the hearts of ordinary folks thousands of miles away – conquering public opinion in the US and throughout the world. That strategy inhibited the US in Korea, and won them a great political victory in Vietnam.

Few Americans, however, were aware of the epoch-making change in the nature of war. Neither were their self-important tribunes, the Press, nor their often insolent servants, civilian and military bureaucrats. Even those Americans who understood intellectually did not necessarily feel the difference in their guts. Some understood cerebrally, but hardly any understood viscerally the new era that had just begun – and was to close in 1989. Nonetheless, Korea was the start of a Forty Years' War against Marxist-Leninist tyranny, which ended with total victory in Europe.

The Communists knew precisely what kind of war they were fighting. Mao Zedong's tacticians had done it before. They had conquered China by psychological warfare, which the UN Command in Korea still treated as an embarrassing stepchild.

Still that war was on-the-job training. The Communists were still *makee-learnees*, as tyros are called in Hong Kong. They were still learning just how to overcome a foreign enemy by undermining his morale in the field and destroying his support at home, so that academics, the media, politicians, and in the end many ordinary folks demanded withdrawal. By Vietnam, the Communists were masters of that art – and decent Americans spat at the veterans of that war.

Yet America fielded to Vietnam what were quite likely the most professional ground forces it ever mustered. From the initial commitment in 1966 through the great allied victory at Tet in 1968 those forces fought tenaciously and victoriously – before the insidiously implanted virus of self-doubt really got to work. But that is another story, as Rudyard Kipling would have said.

In Korea, *makee-learnees* though they were, the Communists were effective psychological warriors, and they grew more skilful every day. 'Learn revolution by revolting,' Chairman Mao Zedong exhorted them. Whip-smart, they also learned subversion by subverting.

The Chicoms and their cadres taught themselves well. Don't you believe that an autodidact, a self-taught man, *always* has a fool for a teacher. I didn't. But that, too, is another story.

Chapter VI

Luke Maynell would not address Suja Chae as Sue, although all the other Americans did – and she had asked him to specifically, even if somewhat perfunctorily. Since Miss Chae would have been too pointed between contemporaries, he called her Suja. When they spoke in Chinese, he called her *Hsiaojieh*, Miss.

No profound insight was required, to see that his refusal, which bordered on the churlish, maintained a marked distance between them. I could not at the time quite fathom why he felt not just casual distaste, but positive dislike for Sue. I, Harland Birch, no mean judge of women, found her charming and attractive. She was vivacious and intelligent, as well as extremely good looking, indeed almost beautiful in her own subtle way. Yet Luke disliked her intensely.

I did not, of course, allow his weird quirk to interfere with either my pleasure or my business. Unfortunately, it was all business with Sue Chae.

I had already let her know that I admired her – and that I was available at any time for whatever she might wish. She had signalled unmistakably that she was not available to me – and that she never would be. I wondered if my loose-lipped colleagues, who were not exactly good friends, had been telling her weird tales of my three star-crossed marriages or, even worse, entertaining her with horror stories about my drinking. Either topic invariably led to vastly exaggerated accounts of my penchant for beating-up my women.

Actually, that sort of thing only happened a few times, four or so, maybe five or six, at most – and I had good reason every time. Of course, I regret those brief incidents. Anyway, I very soon learned that fragile-looking Oriental women are not so fragile at all. I also learned that they won't put up with such robust expressions of affection.

Funny though! Some of those big, wholesome American women just love a caress with the fist. Nothing perverted, you understand, no sadism or masochism about it. Well, maybe a little, but certainly no blood. Mainly to show them who's boss. One rangy brunette told me it made her feel small and delicate and feminine to be knocked about by a wiry fellow like me. God knows, I'm no giant!

Anyway, it was strictly business between Sue Chae and me, more's the pity. I wasn't going to risk losing a first class news source by making a crude play for her. It's always a pain for a correspondent to be forced to choose: a woman or a source.

Most of the time, though, there's no need to choose. Some of my best sources have been some of my best women. But Sue Chae just wouldn't play, even though she knew I liked her enormously.

Hell, I like most women – and they seem to like me well enough. My friends say they're baffled as to what the ladies see in a grizzled, balding guy no more that five foot seven who wears big Harold Lloyd specs. But I know damned well what they like.

God knows, I'm no oil painting, and I'm definitely no weight lifter. But I am available. I'm also tough and menacing – therefore exciting. Above all, however, the ladies know I really care deeply about them as fellow human beings. They know I'm interested in more than a quick lay or, even, a succession of slow lays.

By the way, you'd be surprised at the number of ladies who are themselves only interested in a quick lay. Thank God for the great institution of marriage. It's kept my bed full of wives, mostly other people's wives.

My secret? What'll I say in the unlikely event that someone wants to write the story of my life and asks me the secret of my success with women? Very simple. It's what I am *not*, rather than what I am or what I may be. I may be a cad, as an Englishwoman once called me, reverting to her Victorian roots. But I'm *not* a lout, and I *do* care.

Few of my so-called friends give more than a casual damn about women. Just listen to them talk about their sexual exploits. I remember a wire-service photographer's bragging in the Tokyo Correspondents' Club with wives and girl friends well within earshot: 'You know Mary Ellen. She *never* stops talking. So I shoved it into her mouth – and she went to work with gusto. But she never stopped talking … talked around it.'

Even though it may detract from my image as a rough, tough character, you'll never hear me talk that way. In part, I suppose, because I don't want to queer my chances. No question, the ladies can sense the usual male contempt for females. Well, maybe not usual, but certainly widespread contempt, although maybe not contempt, but certainly lack of regard.

Maybe not *every* day is ladies' day with me. Yet, above all, I *never* condescend to them. In good part, I suppose, the ladies respond to me because I genuinely value them highly. Hell, let me put it straight: I admire and esteem women.

Nonetheless, Sue Chae acted like a nun with me, although a very modern nun wearing green eyeshadow and showing her perfect ankles in the sheerest nylon stockings. A nun not only with me. Half of the correspondents in Seoul were after her – and none got anywhere. But everyone went to the parties she gave in her little house with its little garden near Namzan, that is, South Mountain, behind the palace the US Embassy reclaimed when it finally moved back to Seoul from Pusan. Her parties were a delightful break from the squalor of war.

If you'll pardon or, at least, put up with the scrambled metaphor, let me say Sue was, besides, a pipeline to the Korean government and a mirror of the Korean people. She held some vague position in the ROK Ministry of Information and

Education, but she was, it seemed, on indefinite temporary duty with Syngman Rhee's Presidential Office, as well as with Psywar, Eighth Army.

Her penetrating insight into her own country was, however, her greatest value, even more valuable than the inside information she rationed to myself, as well as two or three other serious political reporters. I mean those few foreign correspondents who were working hard to report on the Republic of Korea, on civilian as well as military affairs, those who also filed stories on ROK troops in combat, not limiting our coverage to action by US and other foreign troops.

Sue could look deep into the mind of Korea; for she knew her countrymen's psychology intimately, yet with a degree of objectivity bred by her long residence abroad. She helped me understand her people's plight. She offered skilled guidance on Korean reactions, as well as Korean hopes and aspirations – individual as well as general, private as well as public, personal as well as bureaucratic.

Nor did she seek to mislead me, although she was a senior official of the ROK Ministry of Information, which, naturally, sought not only to provide information, but to convince the Press that the administration always acted correctly. Sue never parroted the government line without signaling clearly that she was doing so.

Although I did not, of course, always take on board all her views, I depended heavily on Sue Chae.

I and the few others who reported on Korea as a nation, not just a battleground, *had* to depend on her. Who the hell spoke Korean? Not even the army or the embassy had more than a couple of Americans who were Korean speakers.

The best speakers ended up at the truce talks at that ruined village of Panmunjon between the lines. US negotiators could not depend on young ROK lieutenants who wore the disdained interpreter's parrot insignia on their collars. The other US officials asked in crude self-exculpation: 'Who ever dreamed we'd be fighting in Korea before Harry Truman hustled us into war?' So the US didn't bother to train a whole lot of Korean language officers, military or diplomats – and most of those few seemed to be assigned to France or Brazil. So we relied on Sue for insights, as well as hard facts, except for two or three correspondents who spoke Japanese, as did, of course, all adult Koreans.

Some other correspondents envied those who spoke Japanese, envied even my smattering of Japanese, but not enough to do anything about it. After all, this war wouldn't last forever, and there were better things to do than grinding away at Korean or even Japanese. Besides, as I've said, the UN forces, especially the Americans, were the big story, definitely not the Koreans. After all, it was only their country.

Getting back to Luke and Sue.

I didn't ask him. I just told him we were having dinner that night with Sue Chae and an American friend of hers somewhat curiously name Bartleby Howard, but called Betsie. I told him Sue was important to me professionally. So he couldn't really say no.

Besides, Luke could not snub his own colleague, even if he had promised himself he would not see her except on duty. He might have snubbed her outright if she had been an American woman he disliked. He had weird likes and dislikes, but he was too tender to snub a Korean, too sensitive to Asian sensitivity.

We planned to start the evening with drinks at Sue's house and go on to the Chinese restaurant called Shantung Palace, which was one of two, maybe at most three decent restaurants in Seoul. I liked the globular red paper lanterns with silvered tassels hanging from the outside eaves. Besides, it was the best food in Seoul, unless you could wangle an invitation to the French liaison mission.

Still, if you did, you had to listen to screwy analyses of the present condition of Korea, not to speak of the unsatisfactory state of the world from the Gallic point of view. Anyway, I got tired of impassioned lectures on the eternal glory of France.

Chapter VII

'You are taking her!' Luke directed peremptorily. 'Miss Suja Chae's *your* date. Miss Betsie Howard's mine.'

The two girls had just set off together for the bathroom of Sue's little house. Instinctively, it seemed, one would not go off without the other. That female ritual probably arose for mutual protection during the Middle Ages. A girl alone could easily get herself raped by a drunken man-at-arms in the stone corridors that wound from the castle's banqueting-hall to the little wooden cabin over the moat.

I say girl, because Suja Chae and Bartleby Howard called themselves girls, not young women, as our latter-day convention has it. They also called themselves ladies from time to time, usually half-joking. Nor did they see anything amiss in the word ladylike, despite its ramifications regarding social class, faith, morals, and manners.

But 'girls' they said most often. Just entering their later twenties, when youth is suddenly seen clearly to be fleeting, they liked that youthful description best. Besides they were in 1952 under no pressure from the strictures of a new cult of feminism to consider themselves earnest young women, rather than frivolous girls, nor, to describe themselves so. I shall call them girls or women as the word comes to me, suspended as I am between those two incompatible decades, the 1950s and the 1990s.

'Sue's all yours,' Luke insisted.

'Unfortunately,' I replied, 'it's strictly Platonic between Sue and me.'

'You're damned lucky!' He was uncharacteristically vehement. 'She'd chew you up and spit out the bones. She's a harpy, a first class ball-buster!'

I looked at Luke surprised. One of his endearing quirks was his dislike of profanity. Though, I had been told, he swore like a Shansi mule-driver in Chinese, only very strong feeling could drive him to use even a mild obscenity in English.

'What've you got against Sue?' I persisted. 'She can have me any time she crooks her little finger. But you—'

'That's the way the cookie crumbles!' Luke evaded my question with the new GI catch-phrase, then grinned mockingly, and added another cliché, 'But this Bartleby dame can park her slippers under my bed anytime.'

'She'll be delighted to hear that. Now can we knock off this imitation of tough locker-room banter?'

Luke smiled affably at my rebuke. Although he would not tell me what irked him so about Sue, he took no offense at my probing. Even when he was acting odd, just a little weird, you couldn't help liking Luke.

High heels clattered in the flagstone corridor. Sue's Kelly-green pumps were assertively occidental in style, as was her green eyeshadow, and also her lipstick and her nail polish, both bright scarlet. But her festive Korean costume harked back to the twelfth century: a bell-skirt of heavy tangerine silk skimmed her ankles, and an aquamarine bolero was fastened with a great bow over a cream-silk blouse.

Her hair shone glossy black, as always, and a chunky silver bracelet set with amethysts encircled her slender wrist. When she sat down to draw on fur-lined suede boots, the stiff skirt billowed, incongruously revealing sheer black stockings.

Why, I wondered, that assertively ethnic get up, rather than the tartan skirts and cashmere sweaters, or the more formal *chipao* she normally wore? Then I saw why. The finery was for Luke's benefit, not mine.

Was that finery intended to win his attention? Or was she taunting him?

Regardless, tension all but visible arced between them, alternately attracting and repelling. That force, it struck me somehow, was as much intellectual, that is, cerebral, as it was emotional or, putting it plainly, sexual.

Sue and Luke personified antipathetic civilizations, yet each partook substantially of the other's, she the West and he the Orient. They were like the interlocked red and blue half circles of the *yin-yang* disc on the Korean flag symbolizing darkness-and-light, female-and-male, earth-and-heaven. The mutual interpenetration of those opposites is represented by the red spot in the blue half and the blue spot in the red half.

Alongside the complex high-voltage tension between those two complex personalities Sue and Luke, Bartleby Howard appeared delightfully simple and untroubled: direct, straightforward, and sincere.

Perhaps she truly was! Perhaps not!

I sensed from Luke's thoughtful expression that he was pondering the same question. As was obvious to me who knew him so well, his amber eyes were turned inward in puzzled meditation. He, too, was evidently wondering about Betsie Howard, perhaps speculating as to who she really was, that is, her essential character.

He was also, as he later told me, wondering why she intrigued him so, aroused such curiosity – even aside from her physical attractions and her sprightly manner. Why did she, somehow, appear so familiar to him?

Perhaps, I sensed, he was already finding some answers to those questions. Perhaps he was already remembering Betsie and why he felt he knew her, although it appeared that they had just met. Regardless, he was not yet prepared to put that question to her. Luke realized that he was for some reason wary of her.

I, too, had a vague feeling that I had seen Betsie Howard somewhere some time ago, just as Luke had felt on first encountering Sue Chae at the Psywar Section. Still, Betsie, like Sue, was a familiar type, though each was definitely at the head of her class.

I wondered, further, what had lured that hale and wholesome lass to Korea — to wear a Red Cross uniform and to serve, as the Japanese say, as a comfort girl.

Of course, Betsie comforted the troops in a chaste American way, not a lewd Japanese way. She listened to the troubles of the young airmen at Suwon Airbase, which was some thirty miles south of Seoul, and she championed them with their superiors.

She also dished out coffee and donuts at three in the morning to B-26 crews just back from bombing the North. Seeing an American girl, she said, meant much more to the fliers that the watery coffee or the stale donuts.

She was apparently not disturbed by her largely ornamental function. As I recall, the term 'sex object' had not yet been coined in 1952. It had certainly not come into wide usage. Regardless, Bartleby Howard would even then have happily agreed that she was a sex object – symbolically of course.

Yet, I still wondered, why was she really here in Korea at war? Clearly not for kicks!

She had already made it explicitly clear that she loathed the universal squalor and that she agonized over the fearful suffering. She had already revealed by her passing remarks that no boyfriend or husband, present or future, was serving in country. Unattached she was, and she intended to remain unattached. She had, as far as I could tell from what she let slip, come to Korea to get away from her loving, but smothering family – and she was exhilarated by her first experience of true independence.

'I had to get away,' she'd said. 'Mom and Dad kept me on a tight rein, even at twenty-five. I've got to admit Bartleby's an old family name. But I just know they called me Bartleby so I'd have to live up to all those dignified syllables. But every-body calls me Betsie.'

Luke had glowed with pleasure when the meandering conversation revealed that she, too, had more than a passing interest in Asian art – in particular, much more than an amateur's acquaintance with Korean celadon-ware and Chinese carved jade. He had then volunteered, as if it were the natural sequel to her remarks, that his own nickname derived from Luxborough, which was at least as pretentious as Bartleby.

'Luxborough…. It's damned showy: flamboyant, and affected!' he'd added, as if set on belittling himself. Warm, confiding, and self-deprecating to a young woman he had, as far as he knew, met only half an hour earlier, he had wondered aloud if Luke, which everyone called him, really suited.

Betsie fitted her perfectly. She looked like the all-American girl of the 1950s. She was very much like Doris Day and the blondes in the Coca Cola ads, though her hair was a dark ruddy-brown, almost mahogany. When she smiled happily, even cheerily, she showed perfect white teeth. Her eyes, which were wide under peaked eyebrows, glowed a luminous blue; her mouth was sensuous, her lower lip almost too full and perhaps, a shade *too* vulnerable.

Whatever that wholesome, guileless appearance might lead one to expect, she was anything but vapid. Not the absolute contrary, but close. She was beyond question very intelligent, though, evidently, not quite brilliant. Her perception was quick, as were her reactions, but her judgement did not impress me as penetrating.

Her figure, too, was at odds with the innocent *ingénue* impression she conveyed at first. Some five foot four, Betsie was reasonably slender in a plain black A-line dress worn with a strand of pearls and a parrot-shaped brooch of semi-precious stones. Her long legs were spectacular. But her bosom was too generous and her hips too rounded for the virginal purity of an all-American girl. She was beguilingly voluptuous, and she was, whether by design or by nature, extremely provocative.

The girls bundled themselves into fur-lined boots and fur coats. Beaver or sheared lamb, I believe, nothing very fancy. I opened the front door a crack, and the wind stormed into the tiny vestibule. Already shivering, we drew scarves over our mouths before we climbed onto my open jeep for a jolting ride through pitch-black Seoul. The cratered roads, clogged by snow where not slick with ice, carried no other traffic that night except an occasional Military Police jeep.

The red-paper lanterns that trailed silvery-silk tassels before the restaurant's boarded-up windows had been battered by the blizzard, leaving them lopsided. Inside, vermilion pillars twined with faded gilt dragons stood sentry before painted scrolls that depicted fierce tigers, shy beauties, and idyllic villages. The tiny parquet dance-floor, now scuffed and scarred, testified to past glories, as did the low bandstand.

Neither the coarse tablecloths, which were newly washed but still dingy, nor the clouded glasses with bubble-like flaws were in harmony with the restaurant's pretentious name, the Shantung Palace. Wartime austerity, indeed the deprivation of the civilian economy, was evident in bowls filled not with pearly white rice, but with lumpy, half-hulled grains that were heavily mixed with barley. Yet the food was very good, remarkably for Seoul. The Peking duck, the butterfly fried shrimp, the fish slices in a thick vinegar-wine sauce, and the steamed dumplings – all were excellent. So was the Asahi beer and the Seigetsu *sake*.

Regardless, a festive night out in Seoul could hardly equal any night out in Tokyo. We did our best. Where else could we take two young ladies who swore they never wanted to see another officers' club?

Sue and I sparred verbally. But she would not be drawn on the ROK Government's response to the imminent resumption of the Panmunjom peace talks, which President Syngman Rhee repetitiously denounced. She only smiled and rolled another wrapper pancake around crisp duck-skin, scallions, and plum sauce.

The Communists and the UN were on the point of declaring the present frontline to be the *de facto* frontier between the Republic of (South) Korea and the Democratic People's Republic of (North) Korea. Syngman Rhee objected strenuously. Such an agreement, he maintained, would be a major defeat for the UN Command, as well for the Republic of Korea, virtual surrender to the Communist aggressors, who respectively called themselves the Democratic People's Republic of Korea and the People's Republic of China.

The US had joined battle to preserve the existing boundary between the ROK and the DPRK. Rhee now demanded that the United Nations reunite the entire Korean peninsula under his aegis. As clear legal justification, he cited the heady, ambitious resolutions the Security Council had passed at the fleeting and illusory moment of apparent total victory in 1950. Having twice driven the invaders out of Seoul, by and large back to the original dividing line between North and South, the 38th parallel of latitude, Rhee insisted, the UN must now win the war – by marching north to the Manchurian border again.

That advance had provoked Chinese intervention, which was intended not only to avert the threat to Manchuria, but, even more vitally, to prevent ... co-opt ... the extension of hostilities to China proper. That grave peril Peking discerned in the rapid advance to the Yalu River of the UN forces under General of the Army Douglas MacArthur – not entirely without cause.

General MacArthur had not minced words. He had let it be known that he saw a great opportunity to overthrow the Communist regime of Chairman Mao Zedong and to restore to power over China his friend Generalissimo Chiang Kai-shek. If necessary, he had further declared, he would use nuclear bombs to hasten an all-out victory – and thus drastically lessen the cost in his soldiers' lives. Although no racist, MacArthur had not mentioned the cost in civilians' lives, Korean or Chinese.

Syngman Rhee, however implicitly, welcomed the extension of the Chinese civil war to Korea. He pooh-poohed Washington's fear of provoking a second Chinese incursion even more powerful than the first, perhaps provoking overt Soviet inter-vention. He simply ignored the American Embassy's reiterated advice that Washington would not under any circumstances reinforce the Eighth Army by the four or five divisions required for such a victory. Washington would not, perhaps could not, thus more than double the number of American fighting men committed to Korea.

Syngman Rhee absolutely rejected the American Ambassador's further caution, which was really a flat warning, that Washington absolutely would *not* meet the cost in blood and treasure, that is, soldiers' lives and gold ingots, necessary for such a victory – regardless of the mounting diplomatic and media pressure Rhee was applying. Nor, indeed, despite the moral blackmail he was constantly intensifying.

I knew that Sue Chae agreed in principle that Korea must be reunited. But she hated Syngman Rhee for his rapacity and his venality, for his brutality and his government's swingeing inefficiency. She hated Rhee, almost as fiercely as she hated the dictator Kim Il Sung, who had imposed a gray, barbarous tyranny on the northern half of her country. Where precisely that left her, I could not fathom.

At that moment I only wanted Sue to give me some indication as to how Rhee and his gang would react to an armistice. I hoped that she would, even in her own delicate position, perhaps offer at least an oblique hint as to how the ROK would behave when the negotiations were resumed. Rhee, who was in his mid-seventies, had already threatened that he would defy any armistice. He would, he had declared reclaim his armed forces from the UN command and fight on alone. Was he making any preparations for such a military move, I wondered, or only talking, as he so often talked, in empty words?

Sue was normally kept very well informed of the government's thinking, largely because of her influence with the foreign Press. As Rhee knew so well after spending decades in Princeton, NJ, the Press would greatly influence Washington's decision. Perhaps Sue did not want to appear to endorse Rhee's latest threats by repeating them. Inevitably, her official role and her personal feelings sometimes conflicted. Whatever the reason, she would not comment.

Nonetheless, she glowered when Luke lifted his *sake* cup and offered a deliberately provocative toast, perhaps to help me smoke her out.

'To a speedy armistice and speedy American withdrawal from Korea – regardless of pampered POWs and megalomaniacal presidents.'

Sue scowled, set her cup down, and crossed her arms beneath her pert breasts. She addressed not another word to Luke that evening, but simply turned her back when he spoke.

Why, I wondered, was Luke so damned rough? What had happened to his vaunted sensitivity to Asian feelings? He could have made his point differently, much less offensively, however strongly he had come to believe in US disengagement.

He had already expounded his reasoning to me at some length. Quirky, as idiosyncratic as ever, it was certainly worthy of thought.

The US, Luke argued, was losing not only affection, but also respect throughout Asia by relentlessly slaughtering Asians, both Korean and Chinese. The US was, in truth, well on the way to becoming grossly unpopular in Asia. That setback, he contended, would outweigh any advantage, psychological or material, we might gain by fighting on. Besides, he concluded, the continuing war was pinching the home front economically – at the same time building up Japan as a likely industrial and commercial rival.

I'd told him he was shortsighted, that he was overlooking the consequences of giving in to Moscow and Peking: more blackmail and more invasions elsewhere on the globe. But he was wholly committed to an Asian view that somehow excluded the South Korean view.

He could not see the flaws in his argument, largely because of his overheated emotional commitment to what he called the Asian viewpoint. I concluded, that he did *not* want to see those flaws. He dismissed as inconsequential exceptions Thailand and the Philippines, those undeniably Asian nations that had sent their troops to fight in Korea.

Luke's newfound dogma was, I further suspected, a major reason, though clearly not the *only* reason, for his intense antipathy towards Sue, who had, please remember, baited him before he turned on her. I believe he *wanted* to offend her;

that he deliberately aroused her anger. In good part, I sensed, to avoid being seduced into a personal commitment as his country had been seduced into a military commitment.

Still, it was even then extremely difficult, perhaps impossible, to parse the nuances of Luke's feelings towards Sue and his feelings towards Betsie or their feelings towards Luke. It was apparently only a few days since he had met either girl. Yet the relationship, alternating attraction and revulsion, was already twisted and snarled, already confused and confusing, thus foreshadowing the form it was soon to take: an intricate, inextricable tangle.

Betsie daintily removed a shrimp-tail from her mouth with the small silvered chopsticks and said softly, 'You still feel the same way about chasing peace, don't you, Luke? You really haven't changed since those days in Poughkeepsie.'

Luke mimed astonishment and demonstratively glanced down at the nametag pinned over the breast pocket of his green Eisenhower jacket as if to verify his own identity. He lifted his hands, palms upturned to signal incomprehension.

'You *really* don't remember, do you?' Betsie's tone was edged. 'That's hardly flattering!'

Sue Chae looked down the coarse tablecloth, now strewn with bits of food and stained with sauces. She then looked into Betsie's eyes, which were clouded by emotion and shrugged, as if to say: 'I told you so!' A lightning flash of memory told me where I had met Betsie Howard before. Sue, too, though Asian women were a dime a dozen in my life. But Luke anticipated me.

'My God!' he exploded. 'You ... *that* Betsie! Of course I remember. What you must think of me ... '

Sue smiled derisively, but did not speak. Betsie studied the portrait of Generalissimo Chiang Kai-shek hanging on the damp-stained wall.

'I swear, Betsie, it was amnesia ... temporary amnesia,' Luke expostulated, 'I've often thought of you ... what might've been. But I never expected to see you here. So I didn't connect ... '

I could see why Luke would not reveal earlier that he had begun to recognize Betsie. Better a total failure of memory than a partial lapse. Somehow, less offensive to her. Clearly, he had *not* wanted to remember her. Was it shame, regret, or contrition regarding his actions the last time around? Or, even more poignant, sudden recognition of what he ... they ... had missed?

Betsie smiled faintly at his too earnest effort to extricate himself from embarrassment. She smiled with some restraint, but she did not relent and forgive him.

Her eyes were, however, no longer clouded, but clear and shining. They were, in fact, suspiciously shiny, for she had been matching Luke and me drink for drink, both *sake* and beer. Sue was more careful, only sipping her *sake* and turning her half-full beer-glass round and round. Nonetheless, her cheeks were very pink, and her expression was less guarded.

Luke leaned towards Sue so that she could not turn away. Grudgingly making amends, he said, 'And Suja, too. How could I forget? I'm an idiot.'

The waiters rescued Luke, killing all conversation with the clatter of dishes. The duck's carcass, already picked bare, would return in the soup that closed the meal. While clearing up, the waiters chatted across our heads in Shantung-accented Mandarin, speculating imaginatively and anatomically on our relations with each other.

Sue turned pink, and Luke visibly smothered his irritation. They had ordered in Mandarin, but the waiters evidently believed no non-Chinese could understand their patois.

Grimy hands darted out of the gray sleeves of their once white jackets to set tumblers and a plain-glass bottle on the table. The older enunciated in broken English with painful distinctness: 'House compliments. No charge. Please drink deep. Best *baigar*, ancient old *baigar*. Very cold … frozening … this night.'

It *was* damned cold! In such gale-blown, sub-freezing weather, the mercury could drop to 20 below Fahrenheit in Seoul. The temperature was often even lower in the countryside, I could get through a bottle and a half of cognac a day when I was driving an open jeep, its windshield folded down so that it would not glint and attract the enemy artillery's forward observers. A bottle and a half, almost two fifths of a gallon, and I would only feel a little warmer, by no means befuddled.

It was also very cold in the restaurant. Four charcoal-burning hibachis produced noxious fumes aplenty, but little heat.

So we drank the powerful spirit called *baigar* which was normally made from sorghum – otherwise with whatever else was handy. Smelling worse than Limburger cheese, the clouded liquor belied its name: *baigar* means clear and dry. Still we drank it to warm ourselves.

That was a mistake. Tempers already high mounted higher; tongues barely curbed clapped vehemently.

'Why shouldn't you forget me, Luke?' Sue jabbed. 'We only talked politics, didn't we? We've only ever talked politics. But Betsie and you … '

Betsie watched Luke with her extraordinary eyes, their luminous sky-blue intensity now soft and liquid. Beyond embarrassment, she advised, 'Forget it, Sue. It's not important. Forget it. Whatever you say, he just forgot us!'

'Damn it all, I didn't, ' Luke protested. 'Only I didn't recognize you immediately. Tonight's the first time we've seen each other in four years.'

'Whose fault is that?' Betsie asked. 'What about Sue? You've been working together for more than a month – and you *never* said a word.'

'Damn it, Betsie, *she* could've said something. She's not a deaf mute. I certainly noticed *that*. Hard not to.'

Voices raised and faces flushed, they squabbled fiercely, yet, somehow, intimately, excluding Sue and me. The memory of their brief romance then came to me entire.

I remembered New Haven, Connecticut, a dull depressing town sodden with rain in the spring of 1948 except when the sun briefly emerged to gild the leaves of the plane trees on College Green. Above all, though, I remembered Vassar College in Poughkeepsie, NY.

Over the neo-Gothic campus hung a powerful female miasma: the dusty fragrance of the red-tipped Deb cigarettes all the girls were smoking that year; the powdery nutmeg-and-roses scent of their cosmetics; the floral and musk of the perfumes they favored, Mitsuoko and Fleur de Rocaille; a saline whiff of blood; the floury white polish of the saddle-shoes still in vogue; and, over all, the light powerful aroma of young female perspiration – sweet, yet fresh and ripe,

The aroma was at once springlike and innocent, yet enticing and alluring, above all, feral and sexually laden.

The miasma lured the white-shoe boys – as preppies were called then – from Yale and Columbia, as well, of course, as the boys from nearby cow colleges. The Vassar girls attracted the boys as if in heat.

Dorothy Parker is supposed to have cracked wise: 'If all the girls at the Vassar Freshman Prom were laid end to end, I wouldn't be a bit surprised!'

I would've been surprised, but only a little. Of course, some were willing, enthusiastic, and experimental. But not *that* eager!

Some were willing way back in 1952. But most were saving themselves for marriage, which was their favored career. They were not squandering their assets on horny, hot-handed college boys who had years to go before they could even think of proposing.

There were, however, a number of glorious exceptions. The hot ticket that year was the 'progressive' political movement, a crusade for the well-being of a proletariat that was already virtually invisible in the US. That cause offered many benefits.

If you were progressive, you got a warm 'fraternal welcome' at Vassar. You also enjoyed the ineffable pleasure of feeling superior because you were, like a secular St Jerome, prepared to sacrifice all for the cause.

You were also pretty sure to get laid! Who cared if the girls sacrificed their chastity for the cause, not primarily for your manly charm?

Hormones were spouting like geysers in a thousand youthful bloodstreams in Poughkeepsie that spring, just like every other spring. The progressive cause gave ardent young women the excuse they needed. Brassières were unhooked, and skirts were lifted for the betterment of the working class and the protection of the 'workers motherland', the Union of Soviet Socialist Republics.

If you were progressive, there was always a keg of beer, always plenty of hard liquor, and someone always had a guitar. The progressives sang uproariously, uncertain tenors and untrained baritones mingling with tender altos and sure sopranos. Somehow, the girls always sang better than the boys. But there were always a few – males, as well as females, mostly graduate students – who were practised singers, practically professionals. One of that crew always had a guitar.

The progressives sang of despair and suffering, also of hope and promise. They loved folk songs and workers' songs, spirituals and laments, ballads of class warfare and the Spanish Civil War. Ledbelly, Woody Guthrie, and Pete Seegar were their mentors. Also Kurt Weil, Bertold Brecht, and anonymous bards of the movement.

Paul Robeson was their idol: the stunningly handsome, many talented black Phi Beta Kappa and star running back at Rutgers. Paul Robeson, as all progressives knew and resented, was treated brutally. He was denied his due by the white ruling class because of his capability and his courage and his devotion to the progressive crusade.

Vassar progressives chorused the songs that white racists had rioted to keep Paul Robeson from singing in Poughkeepsie: *The Peatbog Soldiers* and *Die Thaelmann Brigade*; *Joe Hill* and *The Four Insurgent Generals*. Also *A Union Maid* to the tune of bawdy *Redwing*, as well, particularly as *Chi Lai!*, the anthem of the Chinese Communists, who stood that spring on the verge of victory.

I had spent one weekend with Luke among the progressives at Vassar. I didn't go back for a second helping. It was all a little *jéjune* for my taste. It was also a little frightening after what I had recently seen in Europe and Asia.

To be progressive meant to embrace the many faceted doctrine its detractors called Stalinism. Joseph Stalin then ruled the USSR brutally and ruthlessly. His oppressive, exploitive, relentlessly cruel regime was hailed by American progressives for its 'revolutionary rigor'. He was rapidly expanding the Soviet empire by taking over Eastern Europe, because, the progressives explained, those countries, lately terrorized by the Nazis, were now 'essential buffers' for the Soviet Union against imperialist aggression. Czechoslovakia, the latest buffer, had been taken at no greater cost by blood than that shed when Foreign Minister Jan Masaryk hurled himself from the window of his office – or was hurled by helpful Czech progressives.

The Cold War had just begun. It was only eighteen months since Winston Churchill had warned in Fulton, Missouri, of the Iron Curtain descending across Europe. President Harry Truman and General of the Army George Marshall were striving to rebuild Europe for democracy and moderate capitalism. The progressives ritually denounced the Marshall Plan as 'imperialistic aggression'.

Henry Wallace was running for president on the ticket of the newly formed Progressive Party. Wallace was supremely idealistic – and extremely bitter. Having served during one four-year term as Franklin Delano Roosevelt's vice-president, he had been dumped in favor of Harry Truman, who succeeded to the presidency on FDR's death in 1945.

Progressives drank a lot of beer, sang a lot of songs, and fornicated a lot. They also stuffed envelopes, canvassed voters, and demonstrated forcefully for the Progressive Party.

Electing Henry Wallace, they preached, would mean a great victory for peace and democracy. They conceded privately that electing Wallace was all but impossible against the entrenched power of the 'bourgeois parties', above all, the Democrats and the Republicans. Nonetheless, a strong tally for Henry Wallace would demonstrate the people's power and would rally opposition to imperialism. At the very least, the Progressive Party would draw votes away from the liberal Democrat, Harry S. Truman – and thus ensure the election of his Republican opponent, the reactionary Thomas E. Dewey.

'Why,' I asked, 'is a reactionary victory so desirable?'

An earnest brunette with heavy glasses and a stunningly beautiful mouth explained. 'The reactionaries will make such a mess because of their greed and their incompetence that the people's victory will be assured next time.'

Luke laughed when I repeated that conversation. He was beyond such simplistic notions, for he knew that the reactionaries were by no means incompetent. He also knew that the reactionaries were rapacious, corrupt, and brutal. Although he was not enthusiastic about the Progressive Party, he was idealistic, even then in my eyes at least, quixotic.

He therefore worked wholeheartedly for the progressive cause. Having been a platoon sergeant in combat, he hated war. He deeply distrusted the generals and the munitions makers who wielded enormous influence. Having seen war inflict such suffering on Asians, whom he found so attractive, he feared that hot war would erupt from the cold war. He hoped the Progressive Party would lessen that danger by rallying popular opposition to war – opposition to any war and to all war.

During that weekend at Vassar, I now recalled, I had met both Sue and Betsie – among dozens of damsels bubbling with enthusiasm. The long weekend had been a blur of booze, girls, and singsong, which wasn't so bad at all. But for a while afterwards I'd had to listen to Luke carrying on about Betsie Howard. She was, he had rhapsodized, perfect, except that she would not sleep with him. Yet her reserve was also a form of perfection. Sue he had never mentioned.

Yet he did not recognize Betsie the moment he saw her that evening in Seoul, but only a little later. Well, their romance, though intense, had lasted hardly a month before the spring semester ended. Luke had then gone on to other girls, as always looking for the absolute perfection that, as always, eluded him. He must have had four or five serious girlfriends during the four years from 1948 to 1952 – and twice as many casual girlfriends. He was as indefatigable in loving as he thought himself unlucky in love.

It was time to call it a night. Despite my cajoling, Sue refused to discuss Syngman Rhee's plans. And there was nothing else doing with her.

I'd had my eye on Betsie although Luke insisted that Sue was my date. But Luke and Betsie, having greatly enjoyed squabbling, were now recalling with fond nostalgia their brief encounter that hectic spring four years ago. Nothing doing for me there either.

Luke later recalled that I had subsided into silence, which was an exceptional occurrence in itself.

'You looked aggrieved,' he said, 'just like a balding monkey deprived of peanuts. You sulked, playing with your specs and darting impatient looks at the waiter, who was painfully totting up a bill that would not come to even four dollars in *hwan*.'

We left the restaurant at midnight, very late for war-blighted Seoul. No one spoke during the ride to Sue's house; the icy gusts would have blown our words away. After she kissed us all on the cheek, even Luke, we saw Sue safe through her door. We left when the multiple locks and bolts had clicked into place, transforming the small brick house into a miniature fortress.

Betsie was staying at the Chosun Hotel, one of no more than four substantial buildings still standing, though badly scarred, in the razed wilderness that was Seoul. The 'frozen Chosun,' we called it, for the heating worked intermittently, if at all. Betsie could not stay with Sue, although she missed the long gossip they might have had in a warm bedroom.

'American personnel are not authorized to subsist on the economy,' Eighth Army instructed, 'lest they deprive Koreans of scarce food and scant housing.'

That justification was, I suppose, valid. Still, the directive was not without further intent. It kept Americans from getting too close to 'indigenous personnel'. The brass were suspicious of foreigners, all foreigners, even the foreigners they'd come 10,000 miles to defend.

The MPs at the entrance of the frozen Chosun, one ROK and one US, waved me through.

'Hi, Mr. Birch,' the American said. 'Hot story tonight?'

Betsie they scrutinized, carefully checking her ID card before smiling and saluting. Luke they held up, calling for their commanding officer, a first lieutenant, who had cannily chosen to make the hotel his headquarters.

Most uncharacteristically, Luke showed his irritation when the lieutenant declared officiously, 'You're breaking curfew, Captain. I hope you've got a good reason ... sir.'

Luke took the lieutenant aside before displaying an ID card that identified him as an intelligence officer.

'There's no excuse for impertinence, Lieutenant,' he said tartly. 'I'd advise you not to be a wise guy!'

He then turned towards the small barroom. But Betsie demurred, saying: 'I have to be up early. Time to say goodnight.'

'I'll walk you up to your room,' Luke offered. 'Birch is too old to climb the stairs. He can wait in the bar.'

He capped that genial insult by smiling broadly. His message was clear: *Don't wait, buddy. I won't be down for hours ... maybe all night.*

Nonetheless, I ordered a double Black Jack Daniel's on the rocks. Just five minutes later, Luke clumped disconsolately down the stairs. I smiled broadly as we left the frozen Chosun.

'No need to grin like a shit-eating possum,' he said. 'Doesn't improve your looks. You're a fine pair, you and that microcephalic MP lieutenant.'

'What's the matter, boy? She turn you down?'

'She sure did.' He could at least laugh at his own discomfiture. 'I tried hard ... said there was unfinished business between us. I told her I was overjoyed to see her, which is God's own truth. I reminded her God gave us our bodies to enjoy. I got a long passionate kiss and a big hug. But she wasn't having any more.'

'Well, boy, that's the way the cookie crumbles.'

He laughed loudly at the jibe. As I've said before, you just couldn't help liking Luke, even when he was testy.

'Anyway, I'm seeing her tomorrow,' he said, clambering into my jeep. 'You know, Harland, I'm a little sorry I volunteered for the front again. Sure, the good Colonel Howse is impossible. Besides, I can't preach peace while myself sticking to the safe rear areas. Got to prove it's not my own safety that worries me.

'But, with Betsie here now, I'm just a little sorry that I'll be leaving Seoul.'

Chapter VIII

C aptain John Luxborough Maynell was lured by the simplicities of the frontline – that outlandish amalgam of boredom, danger, and camaraderie. He was, somehow, captivated by the paucity of nuance in speech or deed. Having lived so long as a self-conscious intellectual, he was, somehow soothed by the dearth of cerebral, emotional, or spiritual contention. He was pleased that the only serious contention was the death-dealing confrontation with the enemy. In that respect, Luke was not much touched by fear. He had as a lowly sergeant led an infantry platoon in savage combat against a fanatical, suicidally courageous foe on Okinawa long before he was commissioned as an intelligence officer.

A request such as his to return to a combat assignment was infrequent, though not remarkable. Such a request was normally granted speedily, all but automatically. Yet Lieutenant-Colonel Lesward Murray Howse would not release him, and he could not push the issue, regardless of how strongly he now felt he should. The Psywar Section was acquiring greater authority as the character of the war changed.

Seeing Betsie Howard quite frequently, whether she came to Seoul, or he chose to make the thirty-mile journey to airfield K-9 at Suwon, in good part reconciled Luke to remaining in the rear area. So, too, did the metamorphosis the war was undergoing in the first several months of the year 1952, the fundamental mutation that gave the Psywar Section its high priority on the service of the officers it required.

Hostile patrols might clash, enduring some blood-letting, capturing some prisoners or losing some of their own men to the enemy when they encountered each other, deliberately or by chance, in the no man's land between the UN's main line of resistance and the linked chain of Communist strongholds. Either side might from time to time launch an assault, albeit on a relatively small scale, ostensibly to harass the enemy and to tidy up the lines by taking a hill that dangerously overlooked its own positions, actually to demonstrate to superiors the strength, the initiative, and the courage of the commanding officers of the smaller units.

Nonetheless, the conflict was by early 1952 unmistakably a *political* war. Its chief battlefield was the minds and the sensibilities of millions of influential men and women in the US, as well as throughout the world. Psychological warfare was becoming a major strategic force, potentially, indeed quite likely, *the* decisive force. Naturally, the UN Command, which was dominated by orthodox, conventionally-minded mud-and-gore generals, was characteristically slow to comprehend the transformation. The Command was by no means eager to acknowledge, much less to respond to the new reality: this was now a wholly distinct, significantly divergent, newly minted manner of fighting a major war.

Successful attacks on the psychological front were, however, already mounted by a Communist sixth column in South Korea. That new fighting force meshed with a conventional fifth column made up of a swarm of agents, who were themselves loosely linked with a few thousand guerrillas in the remote south-west. Some agents exercised great influence in powerful circles in the ROK; others were primarily engaged in espionage, a few at a lofty strategic height, most at the nuts-and-bolts level. Altogether, they were an extremely effective force. The sixth column that served Peking and Pyongyang was to prove at least as effective as that fifth column. It was made up of a good number among the not quite 200,000 prisoners of war held by the UN Command on Koje-do, a large island shaped rather like an amoeba in spasm, which lay off the port of Pusan at the south-eastern tip of the peninsula of Korea.

The pro-Communist POWs, who apparently predominated, could do almost anything they wished. They could even break out *en masse* from the barbed-wire compounds that accommodated their crude barracks and their makeshift shacks. But they had *not* broken out. Nor would they break out.

Their battlefield was right there in the enclosures of the prison camp. Their enemy was now not only (*ex officio*, so as to say) the camp administration and its troops, who were their long-term, strategic opponents and their chief ultimate objective. Their immediate enemy, their mid-term, tactical target, was the perhaps smaller, but, nonetheless, well organized and generously supplied anti-Communist forces in the compounds.

Neither Eighth Army Headquarters in Seoul and the UN Supreme Command in Tokyo nor the POW camp's administration on Koje-do itself realized for some time – if they ever fully understood – that they faced a fierce attack from their own prisoners. The high command definitely did not grasp until it was far too late the plain fact that the precisely planned assault by the POWs could go far towards determining the outcome of this new kind of war. Starting with the particularly dim-witted brigadier-general who was the commandant on Koje-do, almost all the generals all the way up the chain of command still believed they were fighting a traditional war.

General Mark Wayne Clark, who succeeded General Matthew B. Ridgeway, who had succeeded General of the Army Douglas A. MacArthur as Supreme Commander, Far East, had never heard of Koje-do when he landed in Tokyo in early May 1952. Matt Ridgeway handed Wayne Clark that political grenade, which was already ticking, its firing-pin already extracted, shortly before taking off for

Paris to take command of the North Atlantic Treaty Organization's armed forces.

Before that eerie month of May, the brass had simply assumed that Asian Communists would be docile POWs. Other prisoners in other wars might have plagued their guards, but POWs had not been a major force in any previous war. Despite a drumfire of incidents in the compounds, American officers clung to the comforting delusion that these POWs would be no different. When their attention was forcefully drawn to the danger, the generals laughed at the absurd warning that POWs could be a serious threat.

Two correspondents visited Koje Island in November 1951, one from powerful *Time* Magazine, the other from the Overseas News Agency, a small feature outfit. A Chinese-speaking political analyst of the US Embassy in Pusan had put the correspondents on the trail because the army consistently ignored his confidential reports. The ONA man, a friend of Luke Maynell at Yale, also spoke Chinese, which helped. One way or another, the two reporters got around the obstruction of the plodding Military Police lieutenant-colonels who ran the camps – and discovered a minefield.

The military were inherently antipathetic to the Press, which they viewed with much justification as a challenge to their accustomed, comfortable way of waging war. Many senior officers were quite frankly and openly hostile in public to the reporters, who, they believed, knew so little about fighting a war. By and large, they were probably right, although a number of the correspondents had served in the military in one capacity or another. Most correspondents were, however, genuinely puzzled by the generals' complacency.

Their own military experience could have inclined them to skepticism just as it might have inclined them to sympathy with the high brass. Not only the generals, but the MP light-colonels on Koje, having ignored the Embassy's confidential warnings, now ignored the correspondents' public reports on the grave danger impending. All was well in the POW camp, they declared, and Supreme Headquarters in Tokyo, which wanted to believe, of course, believed them. The colonels told the generals, in truth all but swore on the Bible: 'As usual, the Press is sensational and alarmist. Correspondents are interested only in headlines that will give them publicity and gain circulation for their papers.'

There was, though I hate to confess it, *no* premonitory report on Koje-do under the byline Harland Birch. I simply missed the opening scenes. Yet I soon caught up with the big story, greatly assisted by Luke's advice and information, as well as by leaked intelligence reports.

It was a hell of a big story. The threat was personified by Chang Hsi-lo, who called himself Huang Hsi-wu, the Chinese POW who had coolly demanded cigarettes and brandy from the interrogating officer on Luke's first night in the G^2 bunker on the main line of resistance.

'*Waw bi-hsing, Huang,*' the captive had stated without being asked. 'My worthless name is Huang ... Huang Hsi-wu. I am a junior sergeant, a squad leader in the 220th Division of the 106th Army of the Chinese People's Volunteers.

'I am also an anti–Communist. That's why I let myself be captured.'

Luke was intrigued when he sighted that same young man leading *pro-*Communist Chinese POWs on Koje. Luke was, as he put it wryly, doing market research. He was getting a sharper picture of Psywar's customers, since the POWs were, he said, a cross section, a representative sample of the men to whom Psywar's propaganda was addressed.

After recognizing Huang Hsi-wu, Luke reconstructed the man's history with the co-operation of anti-Communist Chinese prisoners. As Huang himself had admitted, his desertion and his surrender to the enemy were deliberate acts, planned long in advance. Yet Luke could, initially at least, only speculate as to the specific purpose that had brought the young Chinese from the frontlines to the POW camp.

'Every single fact in the so-called Huang's first apparently spontaneous declaration was false – all except one.' Luke told me. 'He did indeed allow himself to be captured.'

His name, however, was not really Huang Hsi-wu, but Chang Hsi-lo, pronounced, if it matters to you, good reader, Johng See-woo. His father was a senior general of the People's Liberation Army and, equally important, a member of the Standing Commission of the Central Executive Committee of the Chinese Communist Party. The son, Chang Hsi-lo himself, was definitely *not* an anti-Communist. He was actually a dedicated Marxist-Leninist revolutionary, an apostle of the canonical Thought of Mao Zedong. Nor was he a junior sergeant and a squad leader, as he had declared, but a major and a political commissar. His primary mission was to see that the instructions of the Communist Party Center vigorously directed China's professional soldiers, the regular officers of the People's Liberation Army, who were now the senior officers of the so-called Chinese People's Volunteers.

Chang held high rank for a stripling of twenty-three, and he bore grave responsibilities. He was, however, his father's son, and his father had stood beside Chairman Mao Zedong since the Autumn Crop Uprising of 1927. Such a distinguished lineage in the Communist Party's collective judgement attested that young Chang was not only utterly dependable, a 'hard bone' of the Maoist movement, but also highly capable.

Major Chang Hsi-lo's father, who was a four-star general, would, of course, see that the sons of the men who had seen to his son's advancement were, in their turn, rewarded with promotion and privilege. Whatever else Maoism might mean, that secular creed certainly did not mean abandoning the courtesies that had oiled the working of traditional Chinese civilization. Nepotism was, naturally, paramount among those self-lubricating public courtesies, just as were such backhanded deals, which benefited both the bribed and the bribe-donor.

But why, Luke wondered in March 1952, had Commissar/Major Chang Hsi-lo allowed himself to be captured? What was his mission? Why was the son of such a powerful father required to risk his life in the cauldron of the prison camp? Why was he ordered to retire from the fray at the frontline to enter a backwater, as the Koje-do camp still appeared to be?

Chairman Mao Zedong had himself lost his son to an American air raid on Pyongyang in 1950. Perhaps the godlike Chairman Mao required his henchmen to prove their readiness to make the same sacrifice for the cause by sending their sons into peril. Had Jehovah, the God of another stiff-necked people, not demanded the same proof of fealty from Abraham, that he show himself ready to slay his son Isaac?

But why send young Chang to the prison camp, where one able body was much like another? Why not the son of a lesser personage? Did the mission assigned to Political Commissar/Major Chang Hsi-lo require the familial prestige that enwreathed him?

What had been a tantalizing mystery in February became transparently clear by the brilliant light of hindsight in March. By the middle of that fateful month, Luke even had access to transcripts of the Chinese POW leaders' strategy conferences. Treachery was as readily sold and bought as any other commodity in the camp – only cheaper than most commodities because it was abundant and easily purchased. After a time, Luke, therefore, knew almost as much about the POWs as they knew about us. Our own intelligence was far from being as adept as theirs. It was in general barely adequate. And it was grossly deficient in a number of key aspects. No wonder few responsible officers read those intelligence reports – and even fewer took them seriously.

Yet I myself only a little later read a verbatim record of the first conversation between newly arrived Political Commissar/Major Chang Hsi-lo and the man the POW Command's sketchy, confused records carried as Li Mao, age between 52 and 55, private soldier in the 55th Division, Chinese Communist Forces, captured May 6, 1951. Their conversation had been taken down surreptitiously by a pro-Nationalist infiltrator in Compound 7 of the Koje Prison Camp. Compound 7 was a Communist stronghold, a red fortress that American guards did not enter.

The ingenious infiltrator had concealed an antiquated telephone earpiece in one of the big plaited-bamboo rice sacks that patched the wall of the rickety bamboo-and-straw shelter where Li Mao slept. The American MP colonels did not provide more sophisticated equipment than that earpiece, which was linked to its candle-stick base by a long cable buried in the ruddy-yellow soil. For those light-colonels, bugging was still an underdeveloped art.

The Communist masters of Compound 7 conferred behind barriers contrived from the sacks containing the raw rice that was a major source of their power. They dominated their fellow prisoners primarily by threats, violence, and conspiracy. Also, however, because they dominated the supply of rice. Control of that most basic staple foodstuff was secured by bribes. Most ROK guards were older men who had families to support. They were hardly as well off as the POW leaders, who regularly received smuggled funds. But, for once, the rice-sacks were proving an impediment to the communists, rather than a source of power, because they hid the bugging earpiece.

Curiously, the major addressed the private as *Hsien-sheng*. Yet that respectful salutation, which is even more deferential than 'sir', the Communists officially discouraged in favor of *Tung-jr*, Comrade. *Hsien-sheng*, which literally means 'born before [me]', is a verbal obeisance, a bow inspired by traditional China's veneration of age. Such veneration the Communists further discouraged because it encouraged retention of the evil ways of the past. Yet Major Chang obviously did not call Private Li *Hsien-sheng* simply or even primarily because the presumed private was so much older than himself.

The Communist conspirators believed themselves secure in their improvised safehouse. They were always within sight of a number of other prisoners, for it was impossible to isolate oneself entirely from the swarm of humanity in the compound. Being Chinese, besides, they had never known true privacy. Not once in his entire life had either man been completely alone, out of sight, as well as beyond earshot of all others.

'… can see recent converts are best.' The transcript opened in the middle of Li Mao's cryptic statement, for the hidden telephone had malfunctioned until the infiltrator replaced the batteries in the base-unit with trembling hands. Crouched in a half-covered ditch behind the open air latrines, he was deathly afraid the telephone's screeching and crackling would give him away. Once discovered, he would be dead within minutes. Vengeance was sure, swift, and brutal in Compound 7.

'The new ones are far the best,' Li Mao repeated with relish. 'True converts, I mean. Not frauds like that fellow Hu!'

'Sergeant-Major Hu Ah-kwang?' Major Chang Hsi-lo asked.

'Has his fame reached Peking?'

'Sadly, yes, *Hsien-sheng*.'

'My mistake, that one,' the older man acknowledged. 'He's as bent as a dog's leg, a crook and a lickspittle. A turtle's egg and a total lackey of the imperialists. I misjudged badly there.'

Major Chang responded to that extraordinary admission only after a prolonged pause. In his milieu, which was the heights of the Chinese Communist Party, the stuff of everyday existence was intrigue and betrayal, exercised by backbiting and backstabbing. Men scrambled upward over the broken careers and broken lives – not infrequently over the broken bodies – of yesterday's friends. Living amid constant treachery no man in power freely acknowledged a mistake, since his enemies – and his temporary allies – would inevitably use his candor to bring him down. Only a man already broken, a man who knew he would soon be discarded, would admit to error – either such a failed careerist, or a senior commissar who was absolutely secure. Li Mao was evidently so sure of his power that he could openly acknowledge a grave lapse of judgement.

'And nothing's to be done about him, *Hsien-sheng*? The mistake cannot be remedied?'

Major Chang Hsi-lo leaned forward, his lean body bent sharply at the waist. His large eyes glittered, and his sharply chiselled, high-peaked nose appeared as rapacious as an eagle's beak.

Amusement colored Li Mao's tone when he riposted, 'Why so eager to confirm my error, young Chang? Are you after my job? I warn you, it's not an easy one.'

'Of course not, *Shih-chang!*'

The badly typed transcript in English used the Chinese term *Shih-chang* as it did *Hsien-sheng*, as if the original translator were not sure of the English equivalents. Luke had explained to me, Harland Birch, your narrator, that the Chinese military was divided into formal ranks equivalent to ours: lieutenant, captain, colonel, and so on. But, he had added, they were normally called by their function: a major was addressed as 'battalion commander', a colonel as 'regimental commander'. And Luke had pencilled in his neat script: *Shih-chang*, literally 'division commander': a major-general in our terms – no less than a major-general to command our motley lot of POWs.

'Young Chang, I'm not in love with this assignment,' the general observed testily. 'But that's another matter. We were discussing conversion and converts. Thought reform, I see from the imperialists' propaganda, is called "Chinese brain-washing" in the West. Disgusting!'

'Disgusting!' Major Chang agreed promptly. 'Change the name – and you can change everything.'

'As Chairman Mao learned from the Confucians' doctrine of rectification of names,' the General interjected softly. 'Do go on.'

'Obviously, the imperialists're slandering us. They want to defame our techniques of "thought reform." They want to cast doubt on the means we use to help counter-revolutionaries recognize their errors, so that they can then reform their thinking and serve the people.'

'Don't parrot slogans to me, young Chang. I knew them all when you were wearing pants without seats ... even before that. Don't forget your father and I were comrades on the Long March ... reached Yenan before Mao Zedong himself did. Yenan was the great slogan factory. Yenan produced slogans and dissension above all.

'Anyway, conditions are different here. The tried and true techniques you've studied don't always work.'

The expression Major-General Li Mao's face then wore was later to become familiar to Luke. Under the short-cropped white hair, his wide, though not lofty, forehead crinkled skeptically. The quizzical smile on the thin, liverish lips bared yellowed teeth to reveal a broken right canine. His eyes were clear and inquisitive, the irises light in color ... almost hazel ... with minute emerald specks.

'The Party Center recognizes that techniques must change with circumstances ... with local conditions. As long, of course, as their essence does not alter,' Major Chang offered. 'I must apologize for repeating that motto. I was sent to you to pass on that message, as well as to help, as far as my limited capability permits, to co-ordinate the coming offensive here. I have come to Koje-do only to assist ... to be your obedient right arm, *Hsien-sheng*.'

The outward respect Major Chang Hsi-lo tendered Major-General Li Mao was profound, in truth abject. Even the most submissive American officer would not be so obsequious to his commanding general. Hell, the major made the studied deference British officers paid to a superior appear casual. His self-abasement rivalled the heel-clicking subservience of the German staff officer. Was this the egalitarianism the Chicoms so loudly proclaimed?

I would have shivered at this point if I were Major General Li Mao. [Luke had pencilled in the margin.] *There is definite menace in Chang's slavering respect. But Li Mao hardly seems worried. Perhaps he doesn't care.*

'An interesting convert here is a nineteen-year-old called Wang, Wang En-su.' The major-general was unabashed. 'His mother was the fourth concubine of a filthy rich landlord-usurer in a big market town in my native Hunan Province.'

The whip flicked, reminding the presumptuous young officer that Li Mao and Mao Zedong were fellow Hunanese, bound to each other by particularly strong and long enduring loyalty because they sprang from the same province. That bond did not take in Major Chang's father. He had been a lieutenant in the army of a marauding warlord from Yunnan Province in the remote south-west when he deserted to join Mao Zedong after the Hunan Autumn Crop Rising.

'Naturally, this Wang's father was an opium addict,' the general continued. 'Also very cruel, even for an old fashioned landlord who took eighty per cent of his tenants' crop. When drinking with his henchman, he would round up the share-croppers' young wives and virgin daughters. But he knew the value of a virgin … what he could sell them for. He usually kept them unscathed.

'Wang's father would strip the wives bare and line them up at one end of his courtyard. The husbands he would blindfold and spin round and round until they were dizzy. He would then hand each husband a pistol with one round in the chamber – and make them fire or be shot themselves. He roared with laughter at the anxious gyrations of men who knew they *must* shoot, but didn't know where their wives stood. Innocent amusement, he called that game, sheer lenience! Why, those wives who survived were not *always* raped.

'He stirred up vicious disputes and dissension within families and clans. Everyone's hand was against his brother; so they couldn't unite against the land-lord.'

'I see your point, *Hsien-sheng.*'

'Do you now? That's fine. Young Wang's mother, the fourth concubine, died of exposure after a complicated sex game in the snow one December evening. Young Wang killed his father in a rage. He was then remorseful, not primarily for killing his father, though there was no greater sin in old China! But chiefly because of his own sins against the people. He volunteered, *really* volunteered, for Korea. Not like most Chinese People's Volunteers, eh?'

'To get away from everything? Maybe hoping to be killed?'

'Precisely! He was running away from his past and from himself. He was all at sea, a whirligig on the waves. His confusion and his guilt made him prime material.'

'I guess, *Hsien-sheng*, you then broke down whatever residual beliefs he still held. You threw him into total despair ... into the abyss.'

'Right out of the text books, young Chang. When we offered him the joy and glory of serving the people, he reacted classically ... leaped at the chance to obey the party selflessly and unquestioningly.

'Little Wang is now one of my most faithful lieutenants. You'd think he *invented* "proletarian dictatorship under the guidance of the Communist Party!"'

'A classic case, as you said, General.'

'Even with its many abnormal factors. For the rest, all the POWs wonder how long they'll be penned up here ... fear they'll never be released. Most of all, though, they fear punishment for being captured when they are all sent back. They worry even more what may have become of their families without their own protection. They feel weak, unmanned, almost emasculated before their jailers ... .The ground is very favourable. Regardless, we still need quick conversions, mass conversions that stick.'

'Especially with our big push coming so soon!'

'Truly! I plan to ...'

The conversation fell ... perhaps I should say soared ... into the rarefied terms of Marxist-Leninist-Maoist Thought, virtually a different language that was extremely difficult to follow. The young major and the white-haired major-general did not speak like combat commanders planning their next attack, though they were doing just that. They sounded, rather, like junior officers drafting a theoretical study at a war college. Perhaps, though, even more like woolly academics discussing arcane theories of no immediate relevance. Not one among the American light-colonels who in theory controlled the POW camp would have understood a word. Anyway, the literal transcript of that conversation took a while to translate from that esoteric Chinese into comprehensible English. The copies were not circulated soon enough to have been useful – *if* those officers had bothered to read them or could make any sense of them.

Sheer ignorance was at the heart of the POW Command's failure to move against Major-General Li Mao. The MP colonels were actually unaware of his existence until far too late. Anyway, the compounds, which were surrounded by two or three barbed-wire fences, one within the other, appeared to be run well by the inmate officers. Those men, about whom the American officers by and large hadn't a clue, the same Americans in unaware condescension called *honchos*, which is Japanese for squad leaders, that is, corporals. The light-colonels were, however, not dealing with corporals.

Why, the colonels asked, interfere when all was orderly, even if it was virtually impossible for UN troops to enter some compounds? The GIs could, of course, bull their way into those enclosures supported by tanks and quad-fifties. But how could you justify deploying such weapons in force, much less using them against POWs armed only with sticks and home-made spears, when all was calm? Careers had foundered on lesser initiatives. Besides, such bold action could just possibly be costly in American lives. Such losses, apparently incurred for no particular reason with little justification, would scandalize US public opinion. Better to leave the compounds in the hands of their efficient inmate officers.

'Now, young Chang, I'm assigning you to Compound 4,' Li Mao said. 'I need a man of your caliber there. Power in Compound 4 is divided between ourselves and the Chiang Kai-shek Nationalist remnant clique. Actually, they claim more followers, and they're just about right. I expect you to turn Compound 4 around.'

'Yes, General, I will. Have no doubt! But you say *you* are assigning me? You, *Hsien-sheng*? What about the American imperialists?'

'True, my young friend.' Major-General Li Mao chuckled complacently. 'Here on Koje, *I* make the assignments. I, *not* the Americans.'

Chapter IX

Seoul
Betsie and Luke
March 1952

'I didn't come out here to talk politics,' Luke Maynell declared fretfully. 'Not on a glorious day like this.'

'I don't see what the weather has to do with politics ... or with anything else,' Betsie Howard responded primly. 'We came out here to talk. Nothing else! Remember?'

'What else?' He grinned and swept his arm grandly across the vista. 'Just look at that.'

Their world was deserted, eerily empty of other human beings only a few miles south of Seoul that early March afternoon in the year 1952. Still, forsythia flared golden yellow along the Han River, while the scrub grass of that verdant spring was rapidly covering the scars that battle had left on the face of the earth. Aside from the distant rumble of invisible trucks plying the main supply route from Pusan, the only sound that deceptively tranquil afternoon was the melodies of the birds. They sang loud, unafraid evidently, aware that they were quite safe because their human hunters were hunting each other. Moorfowl piped shrill in the reeds along the river-banks; somewhere a robin chirped; a little closer a thrush sang his heart out; and the wild geese honked, flying low in a great V-formation.

Snow still lay on the jagged gray-stone peaks that palisaded the bowl-like valley. The wind whistled dolefully through the boughs of the trees that had somehow survived the shelling and the fuel-hungry refugees. But the sun was bright and warm with the promise of spring's bounty.

It might almost have been peacetime, when thousands had streamed out of the smoke-fetid city to hail the rebirth of the land, which had been almost beyond imagining during the frigid winter. Yet the peasants who worked the land in peace-time had fled from the repeated battles. Few, if any, had returned. The two Americans who were celebrating the annual miracle so far from home were alone on the gray blanket stencilled in black, *US Army Medical Corps*, which was spread in the bulbous shadow of Luke's new jeep.

'Isn't that beautiful?' he repeated. 'What a view!'

'It's very beautiful … in a harsh, rugged way,' Betsie agreed. 'But we can't sit staring at each other in silence like plaster Buddhas.'

'Just to talk?'

'Certainly! What else?'

Luke grinned, but did not respond. Instead he sipped beer from a handleless white cup. Betsie looked at him with mock severity, her mouth drawn tight and her wonderful aquamarine eyes cold.

'All right, let's talk,' he agreed. 'Let's talk about anything but politics.'

'What else is there to talk about in Korea?'

'You! Me! You and me and the future!'

'Not that!' Her severity was now genuine. 'It's really not a good idea.'

'And why not? Do we have to wait till the war's over and we're both safe?'

'Just not that useless subject,' she reiterated with a narrow smile. 'And don't get all pathetic. I've heard the same line from half the flyboys at Suwon. Eat, drink, and be merry, for tomorrow we may buy the farm … prang … flame out. And you know very well their idea of being merry!'

'Betsie, this is different. We didn't meet yesterday morning. Anyway, I'm not looking for a quick roll in the hay. Naturally, I want … but not until you … '

'John Luxborough Maynell, I must warn you.' She was no longer severe, but she was still grave, her luminous blue eyes shadowed by her thick black-mascaraed lashes. 'We mustn't go any further … for your sake.'

'*My* sake?'

'Yes, yours! If it happens between us … I'm not talking only about going to bed, though I'm not ready for even that. If love happens and then grows … first the spark, then the flame … you'd better beware.'

'Betsie, my nutty darling, you're making a big fuss about nothing. Every day boys and girls, men and women, fall in love. If *we* do, what's to fear? Why should we—'

'Because this time, *if* we do, I *won't* let go, Luke. Once I get my talons into you, I won't let you go … ever.'

'I'll take the chance. One way or another, it doesn't seem the worst thing in the world … definitely not the worst.'

'You're joking, Luke. But I'm serious … dead serious. Now, for goodness sake, try the fried chicken – and stop looking at me as if I were the next course.'

'You could be, Bets.'

'Not damned likely!' She laughed, mocking his antics. 'Down boy!'

She was, Betsie assured herself, serious in warning him off – absolutely serious. She did not want to fall in love with Luke. She knew very well that she should not. She was determined not to. But *if* she did, this time it would be no charade. This time, *if* it happened, she would hang on to him with all her might.

She shouldn't, of course. She shouldn't fall in love with him now in Korea as she had begun to fall in love four years ago in Poughkeepsie. But if she did …

Yet, why shouldn't she?

She had met a lot of boys before Luke. She had met a lot of boys ... and men ... since Luke. But none had moved her so deeply. None could make her laugh so happily – or weep so miserably. No one else had ever made her feel such exhilaration or such despair, lifting her to stratospheric heights, then casting her into primeval depths. The possibilities of life with Luke were limitless, myriad, almost infinite.

She had laughed and soared with Luke four years ago. She had also cried a lot that forlorn spring. But, she swore to herself, he would not do that again to her.

'You know, Luke,' she said slowly. 'I don't understand you.'

'I'll explain all, ma'am,' he promised jocularly. 'Do I sense a personal question? You *are* interested? I'm not pining in vain?'

'When did you ever pine?' she laughed. 'You've never lacked for female company. Five minutes after breaking up, you'd be with someone new.'

'I don't know that's true at all now. Only, maybe, because I couldn't bear the deprivation, Bets. I couldn't bear losing you!' He defended himself against that unfair accusation, first lightly, then seriously. 'How could I lose all the sweet joy you'd shown me? It would be agony ... .But, do tell me! How do you know all about my evil ways?'

'I have my spies,' she replied just as lightly. 'Any rate, there's a personal question I'd like to ask.'

'Ask away.'

'Well, it's sort of personal. Luke, I'd really like to know. You remember at Vassar, we were all for peace on earth, for democracy and equality ... against war and fascism. All that burning idealism!'

'So we were. But you said a personal question. This one sounds like a political question.'

'Maybe it is. Please, Luke, just bear with me. You're now here fighting in this war *voluntarily*. Of your own choice.' Betsie pressed on. 'As for myself, I suspected even then. Even at Vassar in those early days I was a little suspicious. I suspected that it was all just as substantial as moonbeams and fairy dew – all the brave talk and the stirring songs and the ecstatic promises.

'When the Communists invaded the ROK, I knew we'd been duped. I knew we'd been played for fools by Uncle Joe Stalin. But, Luke, you seem to be turning around again. You now contend we shouldn't be here at all, we Americans. So why are you in Korea voluntarily?'

Luke replied without hesitation, touching almost lightly on a subject he has obviously pondered for a long time.

'Maybe we were duped by the highfalutin talk and the high-flown ideals. But Old Cornpone Henry Wallace made some good points, some valid points: the US, Wallace said, was provoking hostility ... inviting counter-attacks. Just look at us Americans here in Korea right this minute. We're not just involved. We really invited the invasion. I didn't say provoked, mark you, but definitely invited. After all, it takes two to tango ... two sides to fight a war.'

'So all we had to do was give in?'

'We should just've stayed out. It wasn't our quarrel in the beginning. And it's not now. Worse still, we look like butchers. After all, who dropped atomic bombs on Asians? And now we're making it all worse!'

'If you believe that, then, I'll ask again, why *are* you here?'

'I couldn't stay away. Had to see for myself if I was right. Now that I've seen this war, I know I'm right.'

'Well, *I* think you're wrong, dead wrong.' Betsie's emphasis was heavy. 'Way down deep, you just hate to commit yourself … to another person … or to a position or a principle, either political or philosophical. You're doing it now. You're not just ducking any commitment. Besides, you're making everything far too complicated.'

'Life *is* complicated, dear Betsie. I'll show you.'

He leaned over, put an arm around her waist, and forced her down on the blanket. She lay unmoving when his mouth came down on hers. For a moment, she responded in spite of herself. She finally turned her head away, but only after a time.

'You see now?' His laughter was forced. 'That was a sneak attack. But you didn't resist very hard, did you? No resistance, so no fighting, no war.'

'Are you saying everyone should just give in: countries, ladies, everyone?'

'Well, not everyone … not always. But in this case … '

He smiled slowly, lazily. But his light-brown eyes narrowed, and his lips were drawn taut. Almost against her will, Betsie touched his crisp, tousled hair with her fingertips, then slowly drew her hand away. He did not move, but lay watching her, his face four inches from hers. She shivered involuntarily when his breath caressed her cheek.

'I wonder …' he said softly. 'I just wonder …'

'Yes, Luke. What do you wonder?'

'Oh, nothing portentous. In fact, nothing worth mentioning.'

A vagrant doubt had slipped into his thoughts: was it automatic lust that made him want Betsie so? Was it no more than a reflex reaction to her nearness and her attractions? Or was it more? She was far from his own image of the woman he had been seeking for years – too light-hearted, even frivolous, emotionally; too shallow intellectually; almost too attractive physically. Still, right here and right now, did it matter why he wanted her?

'Anyway,' he resumed, 'you didn't resist a moment ago.'

'Well, no, I didn't,' she agreed softly. 'Do stop talking, Luke. Try another sneak attack.'

Her arms went around his neck and she pulled him down to her. Languor made her limbs heavy and her nipples hard.

'Just give in,' he murmured, his mouth against her ear. 'It's so—'

'No! I'm not giving in!' She pushed him away. 'You'll have to fight.'

Betsie pummelled his chest with her fists. Luke laughed and caught her hands, imprisoning them both in his right hand, and kissed her again. When his free hand stole under her green tunic, she pulled away again.

Yet, Betsie wondered, why not? It was a long time since she had been with a man. Not that she had been with many men. Still, why not let herself go? Even if she did, even if they did sleep together again, that didn't – wouldn't necessarily – mean she was falling in love with Luke.

Moving slowly, almost meditatively, she rose to a sitting position and let him unbutton her tunic. When his hand slipped under her silk blouse, she smiled dreamily. She stared unfocused into the distance, feeling his hands on her.

Abruptly, with no warning even to herself, she stiffened and sat up straight. Regardless of what she might have wanted an instant earlier, she pushed Luke away. She was no longer provocative, but almost prim. And now, as she had not when she rejected Luke, Betsie saw three figures in white just across the valley, just a hundred or so yards away.

'We've got an audience.' She was glad of the excuse. 'Farmers maybe. I'm sorry, Luke. I'm very sorry! The game's called on account of rain. No hits, no runs, no errors. We'll never know how it would've come out ... the score.'

'Do I get a rain-check? You're not calling off the game forever. You can't. I won't let you!'

'Who knows?' Once more in control, Betsie smiled mischievously. 'Let's get going. I don't want to be caught out after dark.'

Bouncing on the jeep's seat cushion, which was marginally softer and margin-ally thicker then the earlier World War II model's, Betsie congratulated herself on a narrow escape. Another moment and she would have surrendered totally.

Yet would that have been so terrible? The cult of virginity she had already repu-diated. She was still inexperienced, though she was not a virgin. You couldn't be a little bit virginal, could you? No more then you could be a little bit pregnant.

Why, then, should she still worship the cult of impenetrability? Why did American females make a fetish of being untouchable? Why should she so zeal-ously guard the citadel between her thighs? No wonder foreigners said American women were neurotic, fixated on resisting regardless of their own feelings!

Betsie chuckled at that absurdity. Luke turned his head, his dark eyebrows raised questioningly. She did not respond. Let him wonder!

She had also been amused by the terrible time he would have had fighting his way through the thickets that guarded her: the cashmere long johns under her green-wool slacks, the tight girdle, and the snug panties. The long johns were a lovely pale mauve, Abercrombie and Fitch's best, soft as a cloud. Yet they would have been a serious deterrent to his passion, maybe to her own, too.

Clutching the seat, she squirmed into a more relaxed position. She felt an uncomfortable tightness in her breasts and across her belly.

'What's that new slang?' Betsie asked, in a small voice the next day. 'What the GIs call someone who's not all there?'

'*Sukoshi* nobody home upstairs,' Luke laughed. 'A little bit vacant.'

'Well, maybe, there's *sukoshi* nobody home in my upstairs,' she observed complacently. 'Maybe I've been foolish. But my downstairs, it's very happy ... glad to have a boarder.'

He leaned over gently, careful not to dislodge her head from his arm and stared into her eyes. Her pupils were deep violet, almost indigo, in the half-light of the hotel room at dusk. She grasped his earlobes between her thumbs and her index fingers – and gently pulled his mouth down to hers.

That much I, Harland Birch, know about the first time Betsie and Luke made love. I know because she later told Sue Chae in some detail, in wounding detail, how she finally went to bed with him the afternoon before her five-day pass was up and she had to return to her Red Cross duties at Suwon Airbase. Betsie told Sue because she was very angry at her closest friend, and Sue told me when she was furious with Betsie. Later Luke told me a little in exasperation at all women. But he was circumspect, since he disliked sexual gossip as much as he disliked obscenities.

In a way, it was my fault. I'd been up with the French battalion, who really knew how to live. Two of the six bottles of Pommery champagne the commandant gave me I had in turn given to Luke to drink a farewell toast with Betsie.

Well, they did. Naturally, her room at the frozen Chosun was the only place they could drink their toast in privacy. Where else was there? The Temple Bar? The mess hall? The room he shared in the Bachelor Officers' Quarters?

So they toasted each other in champagne in her room at the Chosun. And the inevitable happened, as they both had suspected it would.

Luke smiled at me gingerly and added bitterly, 'Of course, I heard a peal of trumpets. Doesn't everyone? But the earth only moved a little.

'If I'd only known where that was leading, I wouldn't have touched her. I wondered a little when I left her early that morning. I wondered just where we were headed. It had to be more than a one-night stand, a lot more. I wondered about the future. The possibility didn't seem bad at all. Quite the opposite!'

Luke had left Betsie tousled and sleepy, warm and fragrant among the tumbled bedclothes to go out into the cold, gray streets of Seoul before the dawn. She had slept late, almost missing the ration truck in which she had arranged to ride back to the Airbase. Her euphoria was almost unclouded by guilt for the past or unease for the future.

Almost! Betsie was not quite that insouciant. Later she told me, much later, when it was all over, 'I left a big tip for the Korean chambermaid, a pretty girl a little older than myself. I left her twenty-five dollars and a bottle of perfume. I think I was trying to buy her approval. I couldn't stand the way she looked at me that morning. She made me feel like a whore, a wanton woman, an easy lay ... like so many of her countrywomen with the GIs.

'Only they had no choice if they were to survive. I did.

'A moment later, I was glad again, bubbling over with delight. The future ... our future ... was not only bright and rosy. It was golden!'

Chapter X

Harland Birch
Hunting Lodge
Upper New York State
Near Plattsburgh
February 1992

After lowering for a week, alternating grim ashen days of threat with sunny promises of remission, the blizzard had finally blustered in the day before yesterday. Blowing out twenty hours later, it left me totally isolated, truly imprisoned, in this so-called Hunting Lodge twenty-nine miles from Plattsburgh.

I couldn't even get out of the house. Both front and back doors were blocked shut by snow heaped well above their lintels, and, anyway, their brass deadlocks were frozen shut. The doors wouldn't budge. Not a squeak out of them, though I heated the key, somehow thinking I might be able to push aside the high-piled snow.

I caught myself just in time before siphoning boiling water into those balky deadlocks. It was so cold that even boiling water would have frozen in the locks. Anyway, I still had hot food and fitful light. Thank God for bottled gas for cooking – and for kerosene lanterns.

Nonetheless, it was a strange jail for a man who so loved tropical climes. I knew full well there would be no more reports from the tropics bylined Harland Birch. I was firmly retired this time. No chance of going back to regular reporting. Although I wondered if I really wanted to return to that daily grind, there was absolutely no chance.

Anyway, I still had this account of Luke and Betsie and Sue and the Koje melodrama to write. Plenty to keep me busy.

I finally came to my senses and stopped trying to get out. Why hurl myself against the invisible bars of my jail like a wasp trapped between a window and a screen? If I did break out, how far would I get through twelve-foot snowdrifts? Anyway, what was my hurry?

There was no particular place I wanted to be more than where I was, no need for me to be anywhere else. It was just habit, my frantic busyness. I had lived since the age of eighteen with a deadline constantly hanging over me. Some assignments had required my being 200 – or even 2000 – miles away before tomorrow's breakfast. I was as conditioned to movement as I was to breathing. *Anything*, rather than sit still and do nothing – or just write.

The world outside the storm windows, which were also frozen shut, was, as far as I could see through some cracks in their integument, smothered by snow where it was not sheeted with ice. All the visible world looked like the snow-white, ice-edged Akasaka Prince Hotel in Tokyo.

Yet there was one big difference. The Akasaka Prince is jagged and ugly, as well as sterile and menacing. But the ice-sheathed boughs of the leaf-bare trees surrounding the cabin glittered with crystal sequins. The hills were heaped with snow feathers, which somehow looked as if they were warm inside, so warm, with the certainty of rebirth beneath their cold carapace.

Since the thaw was on the way, I would just sit still. There was plenty of water, as well as heat, since the electricity had miraculously come back to life. I could now hear on the TV's speakers the voices of others, as well as see on its screen the images of the world beyond this endless whiteness.

When I saw what I was missing, I wondered why I had been so eager to get back in touch.

The latest darling of the piffle machine called television was a Korean author who had written two novels, both recently translated. The first described the war he had seen as a small boy; the second was based on his time as a soldier of the Republic of Korea in Vietnam. Both were strung on the same theme: *Everything is America's fault!*

The first novel centered on a rape committed by an American soldier. His own mother, the novelist declared, had blackened her face to make herself unattractive, so that she would not be raped by the barbarous American soldiery. Most GIs, it seemed, spent most of their time chasing terrified Korean virgins or matrons, whoever was handy, perhaps firing a shot or two in the general direction of the enemy between those chases.

The reality, as I had seen it, was just a tad different. There were certainly rapes – and some rapists were Americans. Not as many American rapists, though, as the rapists among North Korean or South Korean troops. The Chinese? Who knows?

Rape is an absolute evil, an atrocity, an outrage, a vicious, vile crime. What more can I say? But heaping the onus on the poor GI is a bit hard.

Not because the GIs were all virtuous. They were just about as dedicated to doing good as the British common soldiers a century or more ago of whom Rudyard Kipling observed: 'Single men in barracks don't grow into plaster saints.'

Nor that the GIs weren't horny. How many 17 to 20-year-old lads aren't horny , even if they're not cooped up in barracks, but stuck in holes scooped out of the ground? It was simply just that most GIs were not anywhere near anyone *to* rape.

The GIs on the line were far away from Korean civilians, female or male, matrons or virgins. Besides, most GIs, no matter how horny, were repelled by the ragged, dirty, diseased mass of Korean women.

So there was little need for women to blacken their faces to fend off GI rapists. That precaution came from a tale of Korean folklore brought up to date.

Anyway, who needed to rape? There were plenty of Korean whores, more than enough to go round.

Sure, there were a lot of GIs in the rear areas, a long way from deserted Seoul. Remember the ridiculously numerous 'division tail' of the American military establishment, although these 'logistic personnel' were also supplying a lot of ROK civilians' needs as well.

In cities way behind the line, like Pusan and, say, Taegu, an occasional rape might be down to a stupid GI. But that was nothing like the rape the egregious novelist described as an everyday occurrence.

To the contrary. Much more frequent, almost commonplace, was the association the military establishment distastefully called cohabitation, and the GIs called shacking up. You could tell a GI's girlfriend by finery straight from the Sears Roebuck or the Monkey Ward catalogue. The sling-back pumps, the sheer black nylon stockings, and the bouffant petticoats in vogue in the States in the complacent, self-satisfied, occasionally frivolous 1950s were just the thing for the broken pavements, the mud-slimed streets, and the stony dirt roads.

Soon, of course, began to arrive the Amerasian kids whom Pearl Buck later made such a fuss about. Quite rightly!

But rape? Hardly universal, not even general, but, in truth, infrequent. That first novel by the much touted South Korean tyro author was neither fair nor a true portrait of the time. It was actually a gross distortion of the reality.

The second novel, I gathered, did not attack Koreans vigorously for fighting in Vietnam. Why blame Koreans when you can blame Americans?

The ROKs, the novelist insisted, were simply going through a rite of passage. They were emulating American policy, behaving as badly as Americans because they were, for some inexplicable reason, grateful for America's preventing reunification by keeping the Democratic People's Republic of (North) Korea from imposing Communist rule on the entire peninsula. Now the ROK was glad to help the Americans oppress another Asian people. Still, the second novel did not wholly absolve the Koreans of guilt, certainly not that harsh and effective dictator Park Chung Hee, who sent those ROK soldiers to Vietnam.

Just like his American counterparts, the novelist was pandering to the masochistic streak so pronounced in modern intellectuals, whether American, Asian, or European. He it was who was aping Western behavior. When he thought himself emancipated and daring, he was actually plumb in the mainstream of a self-flagellating society.

Funny about judgements that are either exuberantly adulatory or severely condemnatory. Such opinions rarely alter. Americans love Jack Kennedy despite his satyriasis and his failure to deliver in the brief time he had. Even though Jack Kennedy got us into Vietnam, he is exalted by those who consider Korea a failure and Vietnam an abomination.

Most intractable are abstract issues that can neither be proved nor disproved, since they exist primarily in our minds, rather then the material realm. But even those erroneous judgements that can be – even are – disproved on the ground, yield very slowly to reality.

Poor old Ignaz Semmelweiss had a terrible time. He dared suggest that doctors coming straight from autopsies should wash their hands before they delivered babies. Outraged at the view that *they* carried the infection, his colleagues exiled him from Vienna, all but read him out of the medical profession.

Never rehabilitated in his own lifetime, his great contribution to medical knowledge not even acknowledged while he still lived, Semmelweiss proved conclusively that doctors spread childbed fever – and thus he saved innumerable mothers and babies.

Childbed fever is a physical phenomenon. It exists in the material world, and its cause could be proved; but an abstract concept that cannot be so proved becomes truth if many believe it – or even a vocal minority.

A large group, to which I once belonged, believes Korea was a defeat for the United States. Actually, it was a qualified triumph.

The Korean novelist who set me off on this tack, however, believes implicitly that American intervention was an imposition on the Korean people. Inevitably, he also believes Vietnam was scandalous American aggression criminally abetted by a quasi-Fascist Korean government.

I think he is wrong. The South Korean government saw the insurgency in Vietnam as a continuation of the aggression their country had suffered and a direct threat to themselves, to all non-communist Asia.

Nonetheless, he raised a valid question: *Was it right for South Korea to send troops to Vietnam? Was it wise, regardless of the immediate payoff in American goodwill?*

A Korean political figure whom I know well insisted at the time: 'No ROK soldiers, not a single infantryman, should be sent to Vietnam! It's wrong morally. And it's a mistake politically!'

He said so in public – and suffered for it. Yet, despite his convictions and his courage, I think he was wrong.

But, by God, he had guts, even for a Korean. And most Koreans are so gutsy and so ornery they frighten even me. His name was also Chae, Chae Byongyup.

When I first met him, he was dressed in heavily worn, beautifully pressed fatigues with the silver parrot of an interpreter on the collar and the two brass chrysanthemums of a first lieutenant pinned over the breast pocket. Slender, he was tall for a Korean, about five ten. In the afternoon sunlight his longish hair glinted with chestnut highlights. His mouth was wide and generous, but also very stubborn, and his voice was like the roll of a pipe-organ, deep and sonorous. He spoke slowly, savoring every syllable he uttered.

We got on fine almost, though not quite, from the moment Sue Chae introduced us. Chae Byongyup was innately cantankerous and compulsively outspoken.

He still is. Some say I'm much the same. Surprisingly for two men presumably so prickly, we got on fine after a brief clash. We still do.

First, though, we tangled fiercely. I didn't appreciate his questioning American motives in Korea or his sneering at our military performance. Naturally, I hit back. I passed some pretty harsh remarks about the piss-poor performance of the ROK troops I'd been watching in action for two years.

'Most don't want to fight,' I exaggerated. 'Won't fight … can't fight.'

'Who taught us Koreans about modern war?' Lieutenant Chae asked aggressively. 'Only you Americans! A poor teacher turns out poor students. Who commands and trains our troops? Who kept us so short … of warplanes or artillery that our weakness was an invitation to the Communist invasion? Who, even now, in the midst of a war, doles us out a miser's ration of ammunition and supplies?'

I was impressed by Lieutenant Chae; and by the issues he raised, although I argued against them. Grudging as it might be, all that American babying would not be necessary if the Koreans could get their own act together. Naturally, of course, I did not patronize Chae by saying how impressed I was by his eloquence. I was, however, not surprised when he asked: 'Do you wonder that a humble Oriental can express himself reasonably well in English? I was at Harrow and briefly at Cambridge. That was just before World War II, when the English still spoke their language well.'

I snapped that some Americans managed to get out a sentence or two that wasn't mangled, but I added to ease the tension, 'A friend of mine called Matsumoto spoke the best English I've ever heard. He said the *Tale of Genji* read far better in Arthur Waley's translation than in the original – because twentieth-century English is a far more expressive medium than eleventh-century Japanese.'

When Chae Byongyup raised an eyebrow at that digression, I returned to the subject. 'Anyway, the US is fighting with one hand tied behind its back. We're not striking at Chinese bases in Manchuria. We can't bring in Generalissimo Chiang Kai-shek's Nationalist troops. Other hand, we're carrying you ROKs. You can't cut the mustard on your own.'

'My dear chap, that's rubbish. And you know it. Do you *really* want to extend the Chinese Civil War to the Korean peninsula?'

I didn't, of course. Besides, the Gimo's battered, demoralized troops were even less use than the ROKs. Chae countered, 'And who is responsible for the coming disaster in the POW camp? Not we inefficient Orientals!'

I resented his superior manner, but I was interested. I had heard talk of troubles in the POW camp – troubles that could just possibly be a good story. Naturally, I'd also heard that a lot of POWs didn't want to go back home.

'Our fault? That'll be a change.' I goaded him. 'If it'd been up to you ROKs, there'd be no POWs to worry about.'

'And if it were up to you Yanks, they'd all be shipped back to the Communists … to the tender mercies of Kim Il Sung and Mao Zedong: As is—'

'As is, most, the overwhelming majority, will freely choose to go back.' I interjected. 'How many will abandon home and family for a political notion? You're fussing about a few thousand non-repatriates.'

'A few thousand? More like tens of thousands, even, perhaps, more than a hundred thousand.'

'Never *hachi tomodachi!*' The Japanesey GI slang would annoy him. 'It'll never happen, friend. Not in a million years.'

'Not a million years, Mr. Birch, *this* year. The non-repatriates will be multitudinous. That's why the Communist POWs are campaigning *en masse* to prevent the UN's screening out the non-repatriates. There could be a pitched battle with the American warders. A political disaster, as well as a bloodbath!'

'Well, I'll look into it!'

'Mr. Birch, I'm glad you do not wholly share Captain Maynell's Polyanna views. He burns with incandescent *naïveté*.'

'If Americans weren't naïve, we wouldn't be here at all. You Koreans aren't very big on gratitude, are you?'

It was not for such bruising encounters that Sue had brought us together that Sunday afternoon in March when the jonquils were in full bloom. She had asked a dozen or so men, Americans and Koreans, to a reception in the interests of ROK-US amity.

Her ultimate boss, President Syngman Rhee, liked to score off the US, when he wasn't wooing its support. He believed he knew us well, having spent most of his life in the States, even taking a PhD at Princeton. He knew he *had* to keep the American people on his side – or he was lost. He reckoned he could make a good start by plying the Press with food and drink.

Of course, nobody could buy the fearless, dedicated American Press – certainly not that cheap. Still, Rhee never looked back after he discovered how easy it was to lead television by the nose. The future 800-pound gorilla, then a mewling infant, was delighted by any attention at all. The print media too, responded like automata when Rhee pressed the right buttons: 'exclusive' interviews that put his case with moral indignation and with just-manufactured news that refuted charges of ROK recalcitrance.

I had been introduced to Chae Byongyup at a literary and cultural salon that was a significant factor in Syngman Rhee's seduction of the Press.

Sue Chae and her mother, who was always Madame Chae to us, ran that salon. Seoul was an impossible venue, since it was devastated, depopulated, and too close to the front. Pusan in the south-east had, however, not been directly battered by battle. Though harshly scarred by war and bursting with refugees, Pusan offered the closest approximation to normal life in South Korea.

I was making one of my regular calls on government ministries and foreign embassies, which had moved to Pusan during the first retreat from Seoul – and had not returned. It wasn't enough just to cover the combat, as did almost all my colleagues. Not if you wanted to convey the full reality of Korea at war – and, with a little luck, the reality, the meaning behind the headlines.

Now, Luke had recently been transferred to the Information and Education Section of the Prisoner of War Command on indefinite TDY. He had been ordered to accompany Lesward Murray Howse, who was assigned to head that section. Howse now wore the silver eagles of a full colonel, an extraordinary promotion for an infantry officer who had failed spectacularly as a battalion commander. Self-important in a Class A green tunic that bulged over his paunch, Howse was ringed by his satellites: Major Benjamin Gam, the ace scrounger; lanky George Miner, automatically a first lieutenant after ninety days in the theatre of war; and Mr. Kim Number Two, the *good* Mr. Kim.

Promotions had been falling like stars on Alabama. Luke Maynell's captain's bars were still very new. I also saw in Pusan former Captain, now Major, Anthony de Marco, commanding officer of the Military Intelligence Language Team with which Luke had served. He was accompanied by his satellite, Lieutenant Simons, but, fortunately, not by his former interpreter, Mr. Kim Number One, the *bad* Mr. Kim.

I also saw a one-star ROK general I knew, but I did not speak to him then. I had no stomach that day for a chat with Syngman Rhee's chief hatchetman, no wish to shake his manicured hand, though the blood on it did not show. Other sightings: a smooth civilian in a lustrous tan gabardine suit of exquisite cut, who did not quite look Korean, and was introduced as Raymond Wu, a civilian Chinese interpreter from Taiwan assigned to the POW command; as well as a diplomat attached to the American Embassy; a couple of Korean stringers for the wire services; and two visiting correspondents from Washington. All in all, a mixed bag of mid-level types.

A pair of shabby maids passed around green celadon platters heaped high with Korean delicacies. Not only *manchou,* that is, steamed dumplings, but chunks of dried octopus and white *daikon* radish flavoured with soy sauce mixed with *kimchi,* that pungent blend of cabbage and hot peppers preserved for prolonged storage with vinegar. *Kimchi* had been invented by the Koreans long before Napoleon demanded tin cans to keep food edible for his army. Also Chinese-style small chow: *hsiao loong bao,* Shanghai dumplings with a dipping sauce of shredded ginger in black vinegar; small roasted spareribs with a Sichuan hot sauce, big steamed prawns, crunchy spring-rolls, and mini-tepees of crisp-fried eel strips. All in all, that was a veritable feast at the time, not just casual cocktail party tidbits. Also, however, hunks of canned tuna topped with mayonnaise, as well as cubes of soapy yellow cheese crowned with pearl onions, both served on sodden Saltines. The US Commissary provided the raw material for those triumphs of the American culinary art.

It was a genteel little reception. Occasionally voices rose a few decibels, but we were all on our best behavior. The ROK brigadier-general and Raymond Wu oozed good fellowship. Colonel Howse, the ranking American officer, was heavily and condescendingly avuncular. Informality was virtually compulsory, for all the guests had left their shoes outside in deference to the well-worn straw mats, the *tatami* of the Japanese-style room. It was also a rather dull little reception.

The only excitement was generated by one of the hot-shot visiting correspondents. Full of bonhomie and booze, he was helping himself from the bottles set on a table in front of the *shoji,* those now familiar Japanese paper-paned sliding screens. To kill the germs he knew lurked everywhere, lethal and relentless, he was drinking bourbon, cut just a little with water, which was provided in Gordon's Gin bottles. The visitor lit a cigarette, took a swig of his highball – and spluttered. Flushed crimson, he spat out the liquid. The spray was ignited in midair by his still burning Zippo lighter. This time, the clear fluid in the Gordon's Gin bottle really was gin.

Neither of those hot-shot correspondents, by the way, was to get any closer to the fighting than the standard guided tour to the devastated village of Panmunjom between the lines where the start-and-stop truce talks had been sputtering for a year. Yet, both were to write profound analyses, declaring, as had previously a newly arrived chief of the Tokyo Bureau of the International News Service, Marvin Stone, after visiting Panmunjom, where no combat occurred, and after deploring the failings of his green staff in Korea: 'Now that I've been to the front, I can see the strategic and tactical problems of Korea clearly.'

Both the visitors that day had avoided the fighting front, although both were pretty combative – tough-talking right-wing. Their pieces, as you can imagine, hewed to the Eighth Army line on military matters. Their political judgements, however, hewed to the hard line of President Syngman Rhee. They demanded that at least four more American divisions be sent to Korea to support a march to the north.

That emphasis was, it appeared, a triumph for Sue Chae, whatever her personal views. As the crackerjack liaison officer of the Ministry of Information, she had accompanied those crackerjack non-war correspondents to demonstrate most forcefully and graphically her country's plight at its most heart-wringing.

Of course, I never asked Sue – though I was personally frustrated, exasperated by her nunlike behavior, not even on those professionally frustrating occasions when she simply refused to give me information or guidance. I didn't ask, but I'm certain her liaison work stopped at that, no matter how her bosses pressed her to be 'nice' to such plenipotentiaries of the media. Sue would not be nice. She simply turned a blind eye when her male colleagues found Korean ladies who were happy to offer visitors a more intimate introduction to Korean ways.

Sue actually detested the Neanderthal views of such out-of-town correspondents who were so enthusiastic about Syngman Rhee. Sue had, somehow, let it be known that she was not a prude, not a virgin in love with her own chastity. Nonetheless, it was obvious that she felt cheapened by her colleagues' pimping for those visiting firemen. She would after a few Scotches even concede that beside such visitors some of the resident correspondents were intelligent and enlightened, some few even well-mannered, as well as, remarkably, slightly less obsessed with sex.

Although holding herself aloof, she dressed the part of a temptress. That afternoon she wore a *chipao* of fine apple-green jade wool that provocatively showed off her slender figure. Although discreetly slit no more than two inches above the knee, the clinging dress showcased her beautiful legs. Even moderately shapely ankles were a rare attribute among Korean girls in those days of cheap, starchy food. Sue was thus a gorgeous vision of the stunning, mysterious Orient for impressionable newcomers.

But she spoke good wholesome American, which delighted them even more. Nothing like intrepidly adventuring abroad – and meeting home folks!

Madame Chae, 48 that year, was cast as the supporting actress to her 25-year-old daughter. She almost outshone the star.

Three inches taller than Sue's five foot two, Madame Chae was striking. There was something gypsyish, something beguilingly operatic, about her dark features, which were periodically obscured by the smoke of the acrid Gauloise in her six-inch ivory cigarette-holder.

Her oval face was alluring. Her features were at once distinguished and seductive within the frame of gleaming jet hair, its splendour enhanced by a few silver threads, that was drawn sleekly over her ears. She was attired in the age-old costume of a lady of the high nobility: a bolero of shimmering lavender moiré silk worn over a cream-damask blouse trailed its silver ribbons across a bell-skirt of indigo satin. A long necklace of topaz and amber picked out with coral fell on her voluptuous bosom, and a bracelet of shining sea-green jade set with giant pearls hung on her left wrist.

The jewelry was Mongol and Tibetan, Sue told me. She was amused at my interest in such a trivial matter. She was also suspicious, perhaps wondering if I planned to contrast such *haute couture* grandeur with the suffering the multitude of refugees endured in the squalid provisional capital of the Republic of Korea. Of course the thought had occurred to me, but I had already decided it would be petty to strike that obvious note. Anyway, Sue talked of her mother's spectacular jewelry with no more than a hint of daughterly derision.

Madame Chae was not as charitable. The darts of her light malice were, however, not directed at Sue, but at other targets. Her dramatic features grew viper-sharp when she derided with a knowing half-smile both the effectiveness and the honesty of the ROK Government. She said little about the North Koreans, except to deplore the ease with which their tanks had overrun ROK forces at the start of the war. She smiled thinly when she sniped at the *naïveté* and the ineptitude of 'Yankee-style good Samaritans'.

'Americans don't belong here, Mr. Birch.' She fixed me with glittering eyes. 'You'll be sorry you interfered. You'll be very sorry!'

'What do you mean, Madame Chae?'

I was genuinely puzzled. This was definitely not the kind of talk we had been invited to hear. Quite the contrary.

Syngman Rhee would throw a fit if he knew he was paying for a public relations shindig whose hostess was talking virtual treason. Madame Chae continued, clearly unafraid, 'You're interfering in affairs you don't understand. It's just like Shanghai in '46. You Americans are backing the wrong horse again, the certain loser.'

'Loser?' I said. 'Maybe Rhee won't bring the whole country under his control. But Kim Il Sung sure as hell won't reconquer the South. Rhee's the winner, though it's a limited victory.'

'Mr. Birch, in the end the people's wishes will prevail, just as they did in China. The people will create an efficient, honest, fair-dealing government of their own, after they overthrow Syngman Rhee's quasi-Fascist dictatorship. The people will also expel Yankee imperialism.'

She paused, drew on her Gauloise, blew out a dark cloud of pungent smoke and beamed in on me. 'Mr. Birch, you've been given a second chance. You Americans can make up for your mistakes in China ... for backing the wrong horse, supporting the Chiang Kai-shek remnant dictatorial clique. I remember Madame Sun Yat-sen telling me about the foreign Press ... about you in particular.'

Madame Chae clearly disdained concealment. She openly opposed Syngman Rhee's authoritarian government, as did almost all South Korean intellectuals, despite the war. But those others would not parade their disdain so publicly, above all not when Rhee's chief enforcer was sipping a gin and tonic in the same room.

Madame Chae had further revealed her sympathies, indeed her unshakeable loyalty and her immutable creed. Recalling Madame Sun Yat-sen, the widow of the Founding Father of the Chinese Republic, precisely identified her fundamental allegiance.

Madame Sun Yat-sen had during the '30s and the '40s enjoyed international acclaim as the personification of a 'third way' for China, neither Nationalist nor Communist. After Mao Zedong's victory in 1949, she had joined the new regime, which initially paraded under the cloak of 'coalition government'. Manifestly, beyond any question, Madame Sun had been serving the Communists all those years.

After the war, she and Anna Wong, the Austrian wife of a senior Chinese Communist, ran a political salon in Shanghai. Although that metropolis was no longer foreign-ruled, it was still foreign-oriented. In cosmopolitan Shanghai, they could speak their minds, despite its Nationalist mayoralty. That meant they could spread thinly veiled Communist propaganda without fear of stern reprisals that would arouse the wrath of foreign power. Moreover, Madame Sun was sacrosanct, a secular icon that could not be touched.

Madame Sun's favorite guests were foreign correspondents, above all Americans. Her crucial message, delivered in American English with a southern accent, had run like this: 'Generalissimo Chiang Kai-shek is my brother-in-law. I love my little sister, his wife Mei-ling. Nonetheless, I must tell you that the Chiang regime is bankrupt: corrupt and ineffective. It cannot survive. The only hope for China is Chairman Mao Zedong. He is utterly trustworthy, and his word is unbreakable. Chairman Mao has sworn not to impose dictatorship, but to rule with the participation of other political parties.'

Although preoccupied for a moment with my memories of Shanghai just after World War II ended in the Pacific, I nonetheless wondered how Madame Chae dared speak so freely in Pusan just a few years later. She evidently enjoyed secure, impenetrable protection, even, perhaps, high-level patronage. But, I wondered, solely because of her daughter's services to the regime? Was there not some other reason as well?

I glanced in puzzlement at Luke and Sue, who had joined us while her mother spoke. Sue, naturally, said not a word, although she clearly knew what I was thinking. Such instant grasp, particularly comprehension of the thinking of foreigners, Americans above all, was her business, a good part of her stock in trade.

Luke looked quizzical and said softly, 'Ma'am, I can't agree with everything you say. But mostly you're talking good sense.'

'The Americans must withdraw,' Madame Chae pronounced, 'before they do themselves ... and us ... irreparable harm.'

Sue looked pained, incapable of wholly concealing her concern at such maternal imprudence. As the tide of the party swept us apart, she threw a worried look at her mother. Or was it reproachful?

I attempted to fill the awkward pause by observing that Madame Chae's English was almost as fluent as Sue's own, almost as eloquent as the enigmatic Lieutenant Chae's. Sue smiled distractedly and said vaguely, 'She ... we ... lived in Shanghai, the International Settlement, for a while.'

I got no more out of Sue that day beyond that restatement of what I already knew. Uncharacteristically coquettish, she threaded her arm through Luke's and drew him onto the narrow wood-board walkway that ran around the outside of the house. The glass-panes in the sliding windows outside the *shoji* were filmed with dust. Several panes, evidently broken, had been replaced with coarse gunny-sacking that still bore the black half-moon with which the Quartermaster Corps labelled foodstuffs.

Tanuki-san, a time-hallowed Japanese stone badger, crouched in the small court-yard beside a ceremonial stone lantern. The badger was missing a paw, and the lantern was tilted crazily on its pedestal.

The texture of that day was gritty, as coarse and prickly as the jute-sacking. Regardless of the weather, I usually felt grubby in wartime Korea, never really clean. A half-hour after lathering under a hot shower on the gleaming white hospital ship *Hope*, which was always tied up at a Pusan dock, I always felt shop-soiled again.

The Chae house, once the residence of a senior Japanese official, looked down on the port city of Pusan 200 feet below. Under a smoke-blue haze that veiled the filth and the misery, its gray-tile roofs were a sea of wintry waves momentarily stilled. The hooting of horns, the grinding of engines, and the swish of tires on streets never entirely dry were a modern mechanical serenade to the traditional grim majesty of the granite mountains beyond the city.

I glanced again at the two figures spotlighted by the declining sun. Sue's small breasts jutted against her tight *chipao*. For once wearing a dark-green class A dress-uniform tunic, Luke stooped to hear her better. Though their words were inaudible, the pair looked strained, their features and their gestures stiff. The tension between them was in full view, and I assumed that they were quarrelling again.

*

They were *not* quarrelling.

'I swear, Harland, the attraction was so strong we could've ripped off our clothes and made love right there in the courtyard.' Luke, who rarely talked about sex, later told me. 'It was that powerful! That violent! ... But it can't go any farther. It wouldn't be fair to Betsie ... or to Sue.'

His eyes were remote, staring into the distance as if seeing that moment again. 'It was weird!' he recalled. 'Not a word spoken. But the feeling ... the urgency ... wanting each other desperately ... arced between us like a bolt of lightning.'

'What *did* you talk about?'

'She wanted to talk about her past life.'

'She's angling for your understanding, boy, for your sympathy. You're getting in deeper than you think.'

'I never thought I'd hear hard-nosed old Harland Birch spouting psychobabble,' Luke laughed ostentatiously. 'I'm not getting into *anything*. Just that Suja felt like talking. And I was handy, someone who could understand both aspects of her life ... in Asia and in America.'

'If you say so.' I shrugged. 'But it sounds dangerous to me.'

'The trouble with you, Birch, is you're sex mad. You just can't conceive of a man and a woman having a conversation that isn't flirtatious, that isn't really foreplay, can you?'

'Not in this case, Luke. Definitely not! You're much too susceptible. And what did you just say about sexual lightning?'

He grinned at that thrust, when anyone less self-confident or less good tempered would have blustered defensively. He grinned and told me the gist of their conversation. Luke simply had to talk that very instant, right then and there, just as Sue had felt compelled to speak out in the small garden – had to spill out her heart.

'You're wondering about my mother?' she had asked Luke, looking down at the smoke-wreathed turmoil of Pusan. 'Why she talks that way?'

'Obviously she's not so far off base,' Luke replied. 'She knows what she's doing. But, tell me, how does she get away with murder? How come she dares to talk that way? Men've been thrown in jail ... shot ... for less.'

'Or been beaten to death in back alleys. But, you ask, why is she a tolerated gadfly? For a number of reasons, complex reasons. The Rhee gang doesn't take her seriously, and they believe no one else will take her seriously. Anyway, she's a living refutation when outsiders, mostly Americans, complain about lack of freedom in the Republic of Korea. Besides, the Rhee gang needs me. Especially, they feel, because I'm so good at dealing with Americans. Mother's liberty is my price for working for them.'

'Could you work so hard for Rhee if you didn't believe the cause was ultimately good?'

'I don't know, Luke. How idealistic can I afford to be? Do *you* believe Rhee's cause is just?'

'That's hard for me to say right now. But no, not really. As you know, I think

America should ... must ... get out of Korea. Reunification may be a just goal, but it's unattainable now. As to whether Syngman Rhee will ever succeed ... '

'I believe in reunification ... passionately. We *must* unify the country. My father fought all his life for an independent, united Korea.

'You never mentioned your father before, Suja.'

'How many of my relatives have I ever mentioned ... wanted ... to tell you about?' Her smile was balm to the sting of that retort. 'None I think.'

Luke ignored the oblique rebuke. He was intrigued, for she had never before that afternoon spoken so personally.

'Your father?' he asked. 'What were you saying?'

'Another reason Mother is almost immune to Syngman Rhee's thought police. Her husband's a martyr. Rhee had my father shot as a leftist three years ago. Mother is walking, breathing, and, above all, talking evidence. She *proves* that Syngman Rhee doesn't persecute the families of his political enemies, not even a Communist agitator executed for treason. It's almost funny ... in a macabre way. Father was really a rightist, to the right of even Rhee.'

'A rightist?'

'I better explain. I come from a mixed-up family. And I've led a mixed-up life. That's why I'm such a crazy mixed-up kid.'

'I wouldn't say that. Do tell me about your father.'

'I have to start at the beginning. Tell me when you get bored.'

'How could I?' Luke's murmured denial was not just politesse, for he was fascinated. 'Do go on. Please.'

'It started for me in Shanghai. We lived in Shanghai from the mid-30's till 1945. That's how I picked up English ... American English at the American school. Father came from a landowning family with a strong conservative Confucian bias. Anything but leftist!'

Sue smiled nostalgically, floating somewhere between her fond memories of the past and her distress at present-day Korea.

'He was also violently anti-Japanese,' she continued. 'The Chae family had lost most of its land to Japanese scallywags and carpetbaggers. All of them crooks and speculators in cahoots with the vile, vicious Japanese Kwantung Army and its hyper-ambitious generals. All those scoundrels ... bribing the greedy colonial governor and his thieving bureaucrats, the whole gang of avaricious—'

'Did you have to flee to the International Settlement?'

'Anything but! The Japanese sent Father to Shanghai. He believed he could help bring the Japanese down by pretending to work for them. The thought police, the Kempei-tai, needed a reliable Korean agent in Shanghai. The International Settlement and the French Concession were a refuge for all sorts of political dissidents, as well as for criminals. Chinese law didn't apply there.'

'Don't teach your grandmother to suck eggs, Suja! That much I know.'

'Sorry.' She flushed at his remonstrance. 'Anyhow, Father was ordered to infiltrate the Korean refugees' resistance movement. But he really worked for the resistance, deliberately confusing the Japs. And he kept the resistance informed of Jap plans. Jap plans in Shanghai, also Jap plans in Korea.'

'And the Japanese never caught on?'

'They got close at times. Life was very exciting … too exciting. In 1946, when Korea was free of the Japs, we came home. A few months later, I went to the States … to Vassar. There was enough money for that. Father was getting our land back.'

'Wasn't he labelled pro-Japanese?'

'He took a lot of flak. They said he was a collaborator, a Jap stooge. Even after Syngman Rhee gave him a medal, there were still whispers. If he wasn't a Jap stooge, people said, he was a Communist! One or the other, maybe both.'

'How come?'

'If you'll stop interrupting … '

'Sorry.'

'Rhee's secret police were confused. They mixed up Father's politics with Mother's politics. Mother was … is … way to the left. You heard how she talks.

'Hers is a family of intellectuals … they were scholar-mandarins a century ago. But they fell on hard times, lapsed into shabby gentility. High thinking and plain living,' Emerson said. More like not thinking and barely living. Wanting to help the common people, it was natural for them to move to the left.

'In Shanghai, Mother not only worked with the Korean resistance, but with Madame Sun Yat-sen … with the Chinese Communist underground. Naturally, I was—'

'Should you be telling me all this?' Luke interposed.

'It's nothing that Rhee's secret police don't know. Anyway, I was indoctrinated early in Shanghai and again at Vassar. Educated, I should say.'

'Yes?'

'You know about the Yosu and Chirisan revolt, mostly in the south-west, in 1948, don't you?' She looked at him challengingly. 'The big armed rising that was supposed to carry the Communists to power in the South.'

'Along with a half-dozen other risings at the same time all across Asia.'

'The secret police said Father was involved. They shot him out of hand. Execution for treason, they said. Really, though, Rhee ordered the murder. He was afraid of Father's challenge … from the right, not the left. So that's how it happened.'

'Your poor mother!'

'Oh, they didn't get on, my parents. I don't think she mourned much. Now she plays the virtuous widow. I hope she has a lover or two.'

Sue's gaze returned to the valley below, where the oncoming darkness of dusk joined the low-lying smoke to further obscure the squalor of Pusan. The incessant clatter of traffic overlaid the incessant buzzing of the millions packed into the city. The headlights of long convoys glowed through the smog like an endless string of tarnished luminescent beads.

Sue looked away, abashed at having touched on such a delicate matter with a man, a foreigner to boot. She fell silent for a few moments, the discreet Korean and the straightforward American sides of her divided psyche clawing at each other.

Luke prompted, 'And?'

'And ... what? Oh, yes. You see, Mother was a second wife, almost a concubine. Actually she was a legal ... a legitimate wife, but second fiddle. He only married her formally, made her the first violin, in the late '30s. It took him six years after the death of his first wife, who was the mother of Chae Byongyup.'

'The lieutenant I was talking to? The interpreter? I wondered.'

'Yes, Byongyup is my half-brother. He's ... let me count ... ten, no eleven years older. We've never seen much of each other.'

'Naturally, with such a difference in age.'

Luke did not really think it natural that brother and sister should see so little of each other. Not at all natural in family-oriented Korea. Daily life was still, as it had been for millennia, directed by the precepts of the Sage Confucius, who taught that the family was the foundation of all human affairs, the keystone of man's existence, the coping-stone of government, morality, and proper behavior.

'We Westerners,' Luke reflected aloud in rather formal language to me, Harland Birch, your storyteller, late the same night. 'We are far too deeply involved with ourselves. We're far too concerned with our individual lives and our personal ambitions. We glory in assertion of self. We hail our self-centeredness ... and our selfishness as 'creative individualism'.

'We're so damned individualistic that we've lost sight of the continuity of the generations through the millennia. We are, therefore, only tangentially aware of the immortality of mankind itself. That immortality should be the chief consolation for our individual mortality.'

Luke shaped his ornate sentences with great care. 'Suja Chae is a self-aware, self-conscious individual, although the daughter of a collective Confucian society. How could she be otherwise, having grown up amid the anarchic individualism of foreign Shanghai before moving to hyper-individualistic Vassar? Yet Sue has her being at least as much, perhaps even more, in her forebears and in her future progeny, as she does in her selfhood.'

Luke finally came to the end of his musing and looked at me for approval.

'Very deep, kid!' I said. 'Profound!'

'Come on, Harland,' he retorted. 'Try to use your head as more than a parking place for your thinning hair.'

'You'll be the first to know if I ever do. Say, have you heard? Betsie Howard's coming to Pusan hubba-hubba? Got herself transferred to the repple-depple here.'

Chuckling at my exaggerated GI slang, Luke replied, 'Of course I've heard. Betsie'll keep me out of trouble ... with anyone else. Harland, I don't know what to do about Betsie. Sometimes I think I should ask her to ... But sometimes she's so overwhelming.'

'She can overwhelm me any time she wants, pal.'

Chapter XI

Koje-do, the dung-colored island some thirty miles south-west of Pusan, that bloated, festering ulcer of a metropolis that is the provisional capital of the Republic of Korea in the spring of 1952.

Koje-do, thrusting out jagged pseudopods like an amoeba in spasm, a scant twenty miles east of Kobak Bay, where Admiral Yi Sun-sin defeated successive Japanese invasion fleets, proving the supremacy of his tortoise-like, iron-clad warships two and a half centuries before the *Monitor* and the *Merrimac* hurled shells against each other's armor.

Koje-do, the Devil's Island of North Asia, at two in the morning, when the tall guard towers with jutting machine-guns are gaunt black silhouettes balanced on long, spindly legs against a pale crescent moon.

Koje-do, where kerosene lanterns flash momentarily in the barbed-wire compounds in which hundreds of thousands of prisoners-of-war are packed into tattered canvas tents, cardboard with corrugated iron hovels, and makeshift barracks.

As always, Compound 4 stinks of urine, excrement, and sour rice, also harsh half-cured tobacco, powerful *baigar* moonshine, and, above all, the rank exhalation of long unwashed male bodies. As always, most of the 4000-odd Chinese confined in that cramped compound sleep fitfully, some dreaming of their homes and their women, others dreaming of revenge on the men who have tormented them.

Not all those fantasies of revenge are directed at their South Korean and American jailers. Not even most. Many see in their uneasy sleep the faces of military officers, civilian bureaucrats, landlords, and commissars who scourged them in their homeland. Others, more sanguine, dream of escaping from this seemingly endless captivity, escaping to freedom anywhere else.

The war rolls on month by interminable month, year after unending year, and the POWs fear they will never be released. Ironically, the war is prolonged by haggling over their fate: the only issue not basically resolved by United Nations and Communist negotiators: whether *all* prisoners must be repatriated, even against their will.

All the men crammed side-by-side on canvas cots, straw pallets, or the bare ground are relieved at simply having survived. Hundreds of thousands did not emerge from the meat-grinder into which their Communist rulers fed them: war against the overwhelming firepower of the industrial colossus that is the United States of America in the second half of the twentieth century. By day POWs shout so-called 'patriotic and anti-imperialist slogans', thus reaffirming their present allegiance to the totalitarian masters of North Korea and China. Others conceal beneath that forced enthusiasm their relief at surviving – and their detestation of their former masters.

Yet they are not safe even now. Many POWs toss restlessly, troubled by real fears. Some jerk awake, terrified by the terror that stalks the night on Koje-do.

It might have been any night on the prison island. But this night the terrifying hours between midnight and dawn were burdened by an extraordinary weight of menace. Boy POWs, 12 to 14 years old, cowered in the arms of their protectors. Grown men in their twenties and their thirties covered their ears and screwed their eyes shut against the fearful noises heard faintly and the cruel sights glimpsed briefly in the night.

The intense blue-white rays of an acetylene lantern hanging on a tent-pole cast a cone of brightness within the darkness of the oblong tent. Five men sat at a rough-planed table just outside the tepee of light. They were lit fleetingly each time the tent-pole swayed under the wind's buffeting – and the lantern with it.

The faces revealed by those lightning flickers were set hard, determinedly impassive. The oblique eyes were narrowed slits; their lips were clamped tight. Who would look to those faces for compassion? Certainly not for mercy! Justice those hard-faced men might on occasion dispense, but always punishment, unquestionably and unquestioningly.

The five were a court of last appeal, but a midnight court, a clandestine court. Nonetheless, they possessed the trappings of authority – and the power too. The tent was encircled by a platoon of POW military police. Beyond those MPs, sentries stood watch among the neighboring tents. Spies among their enemies would raise the alarm if there were any move to attack.

Forward scouts watched the outer perimeter, the twelve-foot barbed-wire fences that enclosed the compound. There was, however, no reason to fear interference from outside. The legal authorities, the American and ROK officers of the United Nations Prisoner of War Command, were naturally complacent – and many were bribed to quiescence.

Two men in great pain squatted on the earthen floor within the cone of light. They were huddled, drawn into themselves, at a brief glance two bulky shapes that might have been gunny-sacks. A second look revealed that they were men, their wrists and ankles tethered with barbed-wire that tore the flesh under their tattered cotton fatigues.

When they looked up fearfully, their sallow faces were momentarily visible, blotched with purple-and-black bruises. The high-bridged nose of one prisoner was splayed across his battered face. The other, who was just as battered, kept his eyes shut against glare.

A hand reached into the cone of light to pull his head back, and a deep voice commanded, '*Siang fa-ting kan-chyu!* ... Look at the court!'

The prisoner looked up slowly, blinking at the harsh blue-white glare. His left eye was red with blood; his right eye-socket was empty, oozing pus, its edges torn and raw.

'*Han-jyen!* Traitors!' the deep voice declared. 'Selling out the Motherland to the foreign imperialists.'

'I never ... ' protested the man with the broken nose, his words whistling through his shattered teeth. 'I have fought the imperialists. I fight for the Motherland!'

'*You* are the traitors,' the POW with the ravaged eye-socket retorted. 'You have collaborated ... still collaborate ... with the blood enemies of China. You are all running dogs of the imperialists!'

The disembodied hand clutching the one-eyed man's hair shook his battered head like a child's rattle, and the deep voice commanded, 'Silence! Do not insult the court!'

'Court? What court?' the man with the broken nose demanded. 'Who gave you the right to try us? You're only rotten renegades ... foreigners' lackeys. We do not recognize the authority of this so-called court.'

'You will!' The older man in the middle of the panel of judges spoke, his voice dry and distant as a breeze rustling across desert sands. 'You most assuredly will!'

The judge on the extreme right declared in a high-pitched formal tone, 'The charges are: first, treason; second, murder; third, conspiracy against the Chinese people; fourth, grand larceny, that is, stealing public property; fifth, refusing to obey lawful instructions; and sixth, inciting others to similar defiance.'

'How plead you?' The chief judge might have been enquiring whether they preferred green tea or black tea, so totally lacking in emphasis was his voice. 'You may plead separately to each count. Sincere repentance will lead to lenient treatment. But defiance will certainly—'

'We do not recognize your authority,' the prisoner with the broken nose reiterated. 'This is no court. It's a sham ... a kangaroo court!'

The chief judge asked, 'You refuse to plead?'

'We have nothing to say to you.'

'So be it. Let the record show ...'

The setting was bizarre, dark as a secret society den. The prosecutor's behavior was grotesque. He slowly disentangled his fingers from the hair of the one-eyed man and read the particulars of the indictment, the specific acts allegedly committed by the defendants. After each particular, he paused to allow them to reply. But neither accused spoke during the half-hour it took to read all the charges.

'This is your last chance to reply,' the chief judge told them, when the prosecution had completed its case, which was supported by neither witnesses nor physical evidence. 'If you have nothing to say, I shall call on your defense attorney.'

The prisoner with the broken nose stared in silence at the rippling shadow that was, to his glare dazzled eyes, the chief judge. The one-eyed prisoner turned slowly as if his bleary gaze could penetrate the curtain of light to see the defense counsel rise from his seat beside the judges.

The defendants could not respond, for they could not thus acknowledge the authority of the court.

Yet, despite their silent defiance, someone would plead their case.

The defense counsel shifted in embarrassment from foot to foot. He cleared his throat, groped with his right hand for the tea cup on the rough board table before him, and nervously crinkled the single sheet of paper in his left hand.

'Comrades, truth is far mightier than falsehood,' the defense counsel finally croaked. 'Why should I fly in the face of truth? I acknowledge freely that the defendants have committed all the acts specified, as well as other undiscovered crimes. Nonetheless, I plead with the court to show mercy, little as they deserve mercy either by their past behavior or their demeanor here in this court today.'

'Thank you, Counsellor, for discharging a thankless task so gracefully.' The chief judge's gaze flickered across his colleagues . 'There is no disagreement among the judges, I see. Neither regarding the evidence nor the verdict.'

He addressed the accused. 'Prisoners, you are found guilty on all counts. But the court will be merciful … lenient, despite your defiance. You will endure no more than fifty strokes of the bamboo on your bare backs, rather than the hundred I should order. You will then be hanged. And your bodies will be displayed to admonish others against your crimes.'

When the sun rose at 4:43 that morning, the ROK guards on the main gate of the compound saw two corpses dangling from an improvised gallows. Hammered together from boards supplied for carpentry classes, it rested on a base made of bricks provided to train masons. The sergeant of the guard easily read the Chinese characters on the placards nailed to their chests: *Traitors to the Chinese People Die!*

A squad of ROK guards marched unmolested into the compound to cut the bodies down. The one-eyed corpse appeared to stare at them accusingly. The sergeant groaned, calculating the cost of the incense and rice he would have to offer at Buddha's shrine to placate the vengeful spirits of the dead men.

Chapter XII

Luke Maynell was edgy as he waited with mounting impatience – and some apprehension – for that day's train from Seoul to puff into Pusan Station.

He tried to ignore the alternately pathetic and threatening demands for 'tea money' from the urchins, whose faces and scalps were bruised and scabby, twin green tracks of mucous running unwiped from their noses. But his resistance cracked after no more than half a minute. Smiling wryly at his own weakness, he reached into his trench-coat pocket for a handful of the silver-foiled Hershey's Kisses he always carried nowadays.

They said you only made it worse by giving. They said you always brought down a swarm of child-beggars who'd pick your pockets with one hand while accepting your charity with the other. *They* were the old Pusan hands, American as well as Korean, and they were probably right.

But what did they expect him to do, box their ears? How could he ignore the kids? How pretend they didn't exist?

A girl who looked to be nine or ten, carrying an infant in a sling on her back, grabbed a half-dozen of the conical chocolates. A smile of sheer delight lit her grimy face, and she called out: *'Kansan hamnida!'* On his first day in the country Luke had effortlessly learned that meant 'Thank you!' (Effortlessly because the first word was so close to *gan-hsieh*, Chinese for 'express gratitude', from which it was obviously derived.) The girl scurried away, clutching her treasure to her chest to keep it from the other children.

A one-legged boy clumping along on a rough-hewn crutch asked hopefully, 'Hava chewn' gum, Joe?'

'Sorry, kid,' Luke responded. 'Hava no!'

The one-legged boy snatched the remaining Hershey Kisses from Luke's palm and backed away, muttering balefully, 'Numbah ten! You no fuckin' use, Capt'n!'

Three youths evidently in their mid-to-late teens edged closer, their pinched faces and their cropped hair incongruous above olive-green Army Nurse Corps overcoats. The metal taps on the soles of their heavily worn, clumsily repaired combat boots rang on the broken pavement, cocky and menacing.

Luke faced them, a little sheepish at feeling threatened although he was a head taller than they. He was also robust, well nourished on the bounty of the farms of America, as the youths were certainly not. He wondered how they had escaped the press gangs, which did not hesitate to pull in underage conscripts. Neither, though, did those ROK MPs hesitate to take bribes.

'Luckies.' The foremost youth did not make a request, but demanded. 'I give good price: five hundred *won* one pack.'

Determined for some reason he did not analyse not to be outfaced, Luke dug into the breast-pocket of his tunic under the trench-coat, found a pack with four cigarettes remaining, and lit one. The youths frowned in disapproval. For them tailor-made cigarettes were a medium of exchange, not to be wasted in worthless smoke solely for pleasure.

They smoked Rizlas filled with burnt-out tobacco from the butts they picked up in the street. Even a single pristine tailor-made cigarette was valuable, though not worth a twentieth as much as an unopened pack. A carton of ten packs was wealth, the basic unit of currency in the black market, which dominated consumer trading. Some cartons, even some packs, went the rounds for months before getting so dirty and so scuffed, they were only fit to smoke.

One of the youths snatched the crumpled pack from Luke's fingers, and all three demonstratively lit up with a battered Zippo. That was sheer Korean bravado. They thus proved they could be just as profligate as Luke, even if they were not born as wasteful Americans.

'Howza green?' the leading youth asked. 'Hava green-backs, Capt'n? Nine hundred twenty *won* for one dollah.'

That free market rate valued the dollar as worth five times more than the official price at which the Korean government sold the US Army the *won* required for local payments. Yet 920 was twenty per cent below today's realistic, that is, open-market price for the dollar. Luke had to follow the daily fluctuations, for the POWs ran their own sophisticated black market, as well as doing a brisk barter trade. Besides, they usually found it convenient to bribe their ROK guards with cash, rather than sophisticated handicraft products or foodstuffs. Besides, Korean functionaries and politicians openly manipulated both the official and the black market exchange rates for their own profit.

'Hava Em Pee Shee?' The youth enquired when Luke shook his head. 'One dollah Em Pee Shee ... give five hundred *won*.'

MPC were Military Payment Certificates, the only legal US tender for UN personnel in Korea. They brought a lower price than greenbacks on the open market, since MPC could not be deposited in American or Swiss bank accounts. When Luke shrugged, the youths encircled him, their menace no longer disguised.

'What th' fuck hava, Joe?' their leader demanded. 'You no fuckin' good. Numbah eleven.'

Jaunty in his glossy varnished helmet-liner and broad white pistol-belt, an American MP sergeant strode down the platform twirling his nightstick. The teenage entrepreneurs did not move until he was almost upon them. They then scampered away behind a Parthian barrage of obscenities that surprised even the hard-case MP sergeant.

'*Karrah!*' he barked. '*Karrah*! Get the hell outa here.'

Luke solemnly returned the MP's salute as the railroad tracks began to hum irrythmically.

Silver on top, rusty on their sides, the rails flexed noisily as the spikes that secured them worked in and out on the virtually antique, split and buckled wooden sleepers. The shiny steel strips vibrated in rough syncopation with the pounding of steel wheels around the bend. Puffs of smoke further polluted the air, when the locomotive whooped cheerfully twice and then twice again.

No melancholy whistle, but exuberant whoops heralded the EUSAK Express, which ran from Seoul to Pusan by way of Yongdong Po, Taejon, and Taegu. EUSAK was, as you'll doubtless recall, good reader, the official acronym for Eighth United States Army, Korea. All traffic on the peninsula's main rail line was controlled by the American military. Koreans, whether military or civilian, travelled at the pleasure of the Army of the United States.

Yet most of the passengers, at least three-quarters, were Korean. Any American with any rank at all could hitch a ride on the military transport planes that constantly crisscrossed South Korea. Those who could not, largely privates and corporals, travelled with their units on troop trains, although even those lowly enlisted men flew directly from Seoul to Japan on individual furloughs.

Knowing the EUSAK Express was anything but a luxurious Pullman, Betsie Howard had nonetheless insisted against all advice on taking the overnight train, which rattled at twenty miles an hour along its bumpy roadbed. The craters left by artillery shells and guerrillas' mines were refilled hastily and carelessly, more often than not leaving dangerous cavities in the ground. Black grime caked the once crimson sleeping cars, and gouges in the paint shone a metallic patchy silver. In the filthy interior, open bed-platforms rose in three tiers to the cobwebbed gray ceiling.

Betsie was pale, and her mahogany hair was tangled, 'a mess', as she put it. Yet her marvellous light-blue eyes shone with delight at finally arriving.

She carried a square, alligator-hide train-case and a vermilion-leather purse as big as a saddle-bag. Her coat was the beaver Luke remembered, and her mid-calf leather boots were trimmed with the same fur. Hardly regulation gear even for the lenient Red Cross, whose olive-green jacket and skirt were revealed when her coat swung open. Behind her, a pair of Korean lieutenants, both smiling broadly, lugged three alligator-hide suitcases and a cylindrical hatbox.

Luke's breath caught, and elation bubbled through his veins. He was, almost against his will, possessed by joy that was much greater than his expectation.

'You remembered me this time, Luke,' Betsie said softly. 'I'm so glad.' She kissed him, her lips soft against his, and she clung to him for a long instant.

Despite himself, Luke wondered, 'Why that proprietary gesture? And why remind him right now, immediately upon her arrival, of his earlier failure to remember her? Nonetheless, delighted by her arrival, he closed his arms around the soft bulk of her beaver coat and kissed her hard.

When he took Betsie's train-case, she tucked her arm through his. Followed by the ROK lieutenants like an honor guard, they strolled towards his jeep. Betsie thanked the young officers while Luke's heavy-set driver bundled her bags into the jeep.

'Betsie, this is Private First Class Hanrahan,' Luke said. 'Hanrahan, Miss Howard. I'm taking her to the Open Mess for a bite.'

'Why's he toting a carbine?' Betsie asked. 'Is it really necessary so far behind the lines?'

'Regulations. Anyway, he needs his carbine to guard your stuff. Otherwise, they'd steal him blind. They'd take the jeep, too.'

A flimsy note worth a quarter of a dollar bought a transient all he could eat at the Open Mess, which had been originally the waiting room of Pusan Main Station. After selecting their food from a long counter cafeteria style, Betsie and Luke sat at one of the wood-plank tables that were aligned in precise ranks. Betsie ate with gusto, evidently not put off by the flaccid bacon or the cheese omelette that the steam-table kept warm and rubbery. She appeared to relish even the limp toast smeared with anaemic grape jelly.

'I like a girl who likes her food,' Luke laughed.

'I wouldn't say I *like* it. But I need it ... need nourishment.'

'Didn't you take something with you on the train?'

'Yes. They gave me a big basket: enough for two or three ... maybe four. But the Korean lady with her three little girls in the next bunk and those two lieutenants, somehow, they got almost all the food. I told them I wasn't hungry.

'Some kind soul had also slipped in a big bottle of bourbon. So we had a party, the whole car.'

'One bottle? Hardly enough for a car full ... and you, too.'

'Whatever you think, Luke, I'm not an alcoholic. I'm not a drunk, though I do like a nip or two. Anyway, it was a good party ... Amazing how you can communicate with only a few words in common.

'They don't get much to eat, Korean civilians, not even Korean officers. Americans and Koreans live in different worlds, in the same place at the same time.'

Luke lifted the heavy white mug and sipped coffee laced with condensed milk. The combination was just palatable, though condensed milk on its own was even more disgusting than GI coffee on its own.

'How long are you staying?' he asked.

'Indefinitely! I'm assigned to the repple-depple, the replacement depot here. Why ask me so soon, when I've just got here? Are you that eager to get rid of me?'

'Hardly, Betsie, hardly! Anything but! Honestly, I'm delighted to see you.' He paused, afraid of going too far too fast. 'Sue will be, too.'

'You and Sue both delighted? The same way?'

'Well, not *quite* the same.' He fell easily into the banter that did not entirely mask emotion. 'Sue needs someone to talk to: a good girlfriend.'

'And you, Luke? What do you need?'

'I guess,' he said lightly, 'the same.'

'Well, I'm here now. A good girlfriend for you, too – as long as you want. Indefinitely, if you want!'

'You don't fool around, do you? No ladylike appetite and no ladylike reticence.'

'I didn't say forever, may I note? Anyway, why not? Should I hold back?'

'I guess not.'

'You only guess?' she persisted. 'You're not sure?'

'Betsie, give me a break! I didn't know ... wasn't sure you'd be on the train ... wasn't at all sure you were really coming to Pusan!' he evaded clumsily. 'Then, seeing you, when you got down from that train, you were so ... It was wonderful ... marvellous ... a true miracle: springtime and rainbows and birds singing their hearts out and all the flowers in the world.'

'Well, Captain, so eloquent! So romantic! Starry-eyed! Any rate, Luke, that'll do for now. Not a bad start, though, compliments for brunch. You know, Luke, you're ...'

'Yes?'

'... you're not so bad yourself. In fact, you're a great relief after the dashing fly boys.'

He wrestled an unopened pack of Luckies from his pocket, lit two, and handed her one. Neither that smokescreen nor their badinage could entirely veil their intense pleasure at being together again.

'I'm glad you didn't get tripped up by some fathead with wings on his chest. You belong here ... with me.'

'I like the company here.' She laid her hand on his. 'I think I'll stay awhile.'

She knew, absolutely knew, from his momentary possessiveness that he was hers to do with as she pleased. Her strawberry-red lips parted, but she did not speak. Only her luminous aquamarine eyes darkened for an instant in triumph and in joy, then glowed brighter.

'That'll be great,' Luke replied in haste, once again clumsily evasive. 'Stay as long as you wish.'

Betsie half-smiled in relief, glad that she had not gone too far in her delight at being with him again.

Not so fast! she cautioned herself.

During the protracted silence that followed, Luke, too, was busy with his own thoughts. 'A long while', she'd said. Just *how long* did she mean? How long could it be? Not even a year ... at the very most ... not even that! Events moved too fast in wartime, though sometimes they drag. Let's say a year. I can live happily with that ... very happily. But no longer!

'The Pusan repple-depple's slowing down,' he finally said aloud. 'Most replacements now fly direct. Not many come by ship. It's the POWs who're the growth industry around here. But we don't provide them with compassionate Red Cross girls. Not yet at least.'

He then surprised himself, by suggesting, 'Why not get hooked up with the International Red Cross delegation to the POW command? They're going to be very busy checking all the complaints about the way we're running things. The Switzers'll need an American Girl Friday.'

'Where can I find them?'

'I'll take you round tomorrow.'

Why, Luke wondered for a moment, was he was being so helpful? Why so eager to keep Betsie beside him for a longish time, though he had no intention of making it a permanent relationship? And there would undoubtedly be other girls for companionship and for whatever else – as there always had been.

'Just as soon,' he added, nonetheless, making it a firm promise, 'as I can get away from Colonel Lesward Murray Howse.'

Betsie was delighted by the implicit commitment she discerned behind that offer, which, she knew with total confidence, she could readily transform into a long-term commitment. She wondered again whether she was going too fast. She could not truly gauge the force of Luke's feelings for her. She certainly could not gauge his intentions, whether short-term or long-term. Why, for that matter, she was not even completely sure of her own feelings.

No question about it, she was strongly attracted to Luke. Not just physically! But was her feeling for Luke so powerful. Was her great affection truly love? Could she seriously think of a permanent relationship? She did not really know.

Betsie banished her introspection and her uncertainties to the back of her mind. She banished her self-searching, her practical deliberation, and her cool, as she hoped, calculation. When they rose from the table, she slipped her arm again through Luke's.

The Open Mess was familiar and comfortable. It was really a part of the USA.

They entered another country, a misery-stricken Korea at war, as they strolled toward Luke's jeep, which was parked under the red-brick clock-tower of the Japanese built Edwardian-style terminal. The heavily cracked flagstones were gritty beneath their feet, yet slippery with nameless slime. Ashen clouds blanketed the sky, only an occasional watery ray of sun lit the leaden afternoon. Yet a loud murmur swelled in the dank chill air. It was very much like the keening of a multitude of querulous katydids, a million unhappy locusts.

The solemn chant was wrung from souls mired in desperation beyond hope. That endless chorus, which voiced sorrow and misery, rose from the hundreds of refugees who edged the station square like a filth-soiled fringe on a dirt-ingrained carpet. Some squatted on the slimy flagstones. Others, more fortunate, had found just enough room to recline or to stretch out. The most fortunate lay on tattered straw-mats.

They were wretchedly clad in the cast-offs of war: patched fatigues and green tunics rent by jagged rips. Some huddled in traditional Korean formal robes, once snow-white, but now black with filth. Also trousers or skirts run up from discarded flour-sacks branded Pillsbury and General Mills. Most common were makeshift garments with many holes that had been cobbled from GI blankets of olive drab.

'Brueghel ,' Luke observed. 'Brueghel the Younger! You know, he was obsessive.'

He painted the deformed and the maimed. Also the poverty-stricken, the starving, and the dying.'

A legless veteran wearing a heavily stained and much torn field-jacket bearing the tiger-head shoulder patch of the ROK Capital Division swung towards them on two sticks to which bark still clung. A knotted scar twisted scarlet and yellow across his grime-tattooed forehead like a fiery serpent. An able-bodied man wrapped in a blanket followed, his hand on the cripple's shoulder. A greasy, bloodstained bandage covered his eyes.

'The POWs get first-class medical attention from us,' Luke said. 'But our allies, disabled ROK veterans like these, get nothing. There's nothing for them, not even rudimentary medical care. In the entire country there's not one hospital a tenth as good as the US hospital for POWs in Pusan! Not one, military or civilian!'

Luke fished out of the capacious pocket of his trench-coat a loaf of bread he had taken from the Open Mess. He handed it to the cripple, murmuring something that sounded like *Mian Hamnida!* No need to guess that meant 'I'm so sorry!'

'You know, I feel guilty,' Betsie said. 'I feel very guilty, just for being decently fed.'

She took five purloined oranges from her saddle-bag of a purse. Smiling apologetically, she handed them to a woman who squatted on an unravelling straw-mat, eyes dull in cheeks chafed red-raw by wind. An extremely pretty, small girl, cute as a Korean doll, clutched the woman's arm. Behind his mother and his sister, a boy no older then ten squinted at the Americans. His single remaining eye was half-closed by the scarlet scars that covered his face, a terrible shiny cicatrix that twisted his features out of all but a distant semblance to humanity. Only his lips and his chin were unmarred.

'Napalm?' Betsie asked softly.

'Not this case. It's smallpox. We're not responsible for *every* horror in the Korean peninsula.'

'Is there any hope for them? I don't mean just for survival,' she asked, and Luke warmed to her compassion. 'Is there any real hope for their future … as ordinary human beings … as Koreans?'

'Not much, I'm afraid. Very little hope for the future for a country that's been fought over again and again … been by and large devastated! Yet Koreans're a tough breed. Many will survive somehow. Every orange, every hunk of bread, helps. Uncle Sam can afford it, thank God!'

The International Committee of the Red Cross was founded in the mid-nineteenth century by those well-meaning busybodies, the Swiss, better to interfere in the lives of others. The ICRC had also fulfilled very well its avowed purpose: To relieve the suffering of humanity. Mankind – and, as I suppose even I, unreconstructed Harland Birch, must now say – womankind, too, have benefited greatly. All because of the profound boredom Switzerland inflicts on its livelier sons and daughters.

Your average Switzer is orderly and dull, iron-bound by laws and regulations, brought up to pettifogging and nit-picking. Even the more sprightly Switzers, those

who join the ICRC, they don't … can't … wholly shed those traits when they
venture abroad. They are the pre-eminent bureaucrats of that bureaucrats' paradise, the realm of international philanthropy.[1]

The ICRC delegation deputed to look into the treatment of POWs, among
other concerns, confronted a grave problem at the time Luke Maynell presented
Betsie Howard to the administrative officer. The delegates were all certifiably
neutral Swiss. All were, moreover, extremely conscientious – and all were
profoundly perturbed because they could not fully execute their assigned mission
in wartime Korea. They had been directed to inspect the camps where the belligerents confined the enemy soldiers they had taken prisoner, the camps in the North,
as well as those in the South. They were charged to report the treatment of POWs
by both sides – and to ameliorate their condition if necessary.

The UN Command was generally co-operative, that is, no more than normally
evasive. The MP light-colonels, who not only executed, but in practice *made* policy,
were less antagonistic towards the Swiss than they were towards the Press. The
International Committee of the Red Cross was, after all, an *official authority,* and
they had been trained, whether initially as military or as civil police officers, to
respect authority.

The Communists did *not* welcome the Swiss. They flatly refused to allow the
ICRC into their POW camps, although the Geneva Conventions on Treatment of
Prisoners of War obliged belligerents to submit to such inspection. Neither the so-
called People's Democratic Republic of Korea nor the so-called People's Republic of
China, which deployed the miscalled Chinese People's Volunteers, had signed those
agreements. Nonetheless, the North Koreans and the Chinese went out of their way
to declare – as they maintained they were *not* required to certify – that their treatment of the POWs they held was far better than the Geneva Conventions required
regarding such fundamental needs as: shelter, food, clothing, and recreation.

Nonetheless, they stressed, they would submit to *no* outside inspection. Nor,
they stressed again, were they bound to do so under international law, since they
had not adhered to the Conventions.

They did *not* hasten to add that they would admit no outsiders *except* those
outsiders who were their henchman or their accomplices. In truth, those men were
Communist employees, well compensated for the services they rendered. Most
prominent were a Briton and an Australian, both nominally journalists, who had
for some time been propagandists for the Stalinist line. They were charged to cajole
American and British Commonwealth captives and thus to persuade them to
denounce their own countries. Almost invariably, the inquisitors had to resort to
threats and violence, to scourging and to torture, psychological as well as physical,
in the attempt to compel POWs to confess, as one or two did, that they themselves
had committed war crimes.

---

[1] Editor's note: Here, as elsewhere, Harland Birch is a man of strong opinions, assertively
expressed.

Chief among those imagined crimes was the UN's waging 'germ warfare', which was clearly an invention of the Communists. I, Harland Birch, your teller of tales, *know* beyond any possible doubt or question that the UN Command, as always under American control, did *not* indulge in germ warfare. It would have been impossible for the Eighth Army and its Air Force or for the Seventh Fleet to have done so on the scale the Communists charged without a flock of perniciously inquisitive correspondents of a dozen nations learning of that atrocity – as we learned about super-secret operations in North Korea. It is all but impossible for a democracy to conduct major operations in a theater of war without a democratic free Press's learning about them – flatly impossible for a democracy to do so over a long period of time, as was alleged.

The Communists, however, had no difficulty in finding presumably objective worthies to endorse their allegations. Among them were: Joseph Needham, who was greatly and justly acclaimed as the pioneering investigator of Chinese technology over the ages, who apparently let his political sympathies and his near reverence for Chinese civilization prevail over his scientific detachment; as well as Bertrand Russell, the brilliant and erratic mathematician and philosopher, who was by nature contrarian, and who was admired, when not reviled, for his irreverence by even such as I.

No, my friends, such wholly false political testimony did not originate in Vietnam, where it was, according to North Vietnamese generals' unsolicited revelations, decisive in their final victory on the ground. Needham and Russell were the predecessors of such creatures as: opportunistic, self-publicizing 'Hanoi Jane' Fonda; sometime Attorney General Ramsey Clark, who implacably opposed any decisive American action abroad; and the self-promoting, incessantly grandstanding Noam Chomsky, who is neither an original thinker nor was ever a critic of the Marxist-Leninist-Stalinist organized left, as his admirers assert, but a persistent apologist for that dictatorial doctrine.

At any rate, the ardently bureaucratic administrative officer of the bloated delegation of the International Commission of the Red Cross in Pusan was reluctant to take Betsie on his staff. To safeguard the appearance, as well as the reality of Swiss neutrality, ties between the ICRC and national organizations like the American Red Cross were deliberately tenuous. It would, therefore, be far better for a delegation concerned with an essentially American war if Betsie were not attached to the American Red Cross, better still if she were not an American.

Employing Betsie would be an irregularity, albeit a minor irregularity. The administrative officer's tidy Swiss soul initially rejected such an anomaly. However, his frugal Swiss soul soon thrilled to securing at no more cost than her living quarters a go-between who could understand the normally incomprehensible American colonels.

It did not take long for the advantages to overcame his scruples, though he stressed, 'Unfortunately, we cannot pay you.'

The director of the American Red Cross for Korea was resigned to the vagaries of her flock. She had sanctioned without a qualm Betsie's transfer to Pusan, although that young lady was obviously in pursuit of Luke. She feared that Betsie would otherwise quit the voluntary service, finding some other pretext to remain in country. The director did not know that Betsie would not – would never – abandon an obligation she had freely assumed. The repple-depple, the Replacement Depot, didn't really need another Red Cross girl, but Betsie could do good work that would satisfy her need to assist others by performing useful service for the ICRC.

Sue Chae offered to put Betsie up in the villa on the hill, but Eighth Army regulations forbade that simple expedient. No American was permitted to 'live on the economy', not even a civilian volunteer.

The prohibition could, however, only to a limited degree prevent Americans' getting too close to the distressing realities of daily life, as well as the enfeebling privations and the vicious political struggle. The Republic of Korea was more democratic than the Stalinist dictatorship that ruled the People's Democratic Republic of Korea in the North. More democratic, but not much more. Syngman Rhee's regime in the South was an attempted dictatorship, though far less efficient than the totalitarian rigor Kim Il Sung imposed in the North. The generals didn't want that reality to impinge closely on individual Americans, lest it undermine the overall American commitment to the war.

Nonetheless, Betsie spent very little time in her politically chaste room above the ICRC offices, but she spent many hours in the Chae villa perched above the putrid ferment of Pusan. When Sue was for a moment free of her many tasks, they gossiped and giggled as if they were still giddy undergraduates. Inevitably, Betsie became deeply involved with Korea emotionally, as well as intellectually.

Still, Sue was often absent, drawn into the maelstrom of the POW problem. As the turmoil in the camp intensified, Luke, too, was caught up, spending long hours on duty at Koje-do.

Betsie had made no bones about having to come to Pusan to be with Luke. Her normal common sense and her cheery good humor temporarily in abeyance, she was now indignant at the war's interfering with her plans.

Betsie often found herself with Sue's half-brother. Senior Lieutenant Chae Byongyup seemed to have all the time in the world at his disposal, although he, too, was attached to the POW command. It was Betsie who pinned on his chest the three brass chrysanthemums of a captain and toasted his promotion in champagne from the American Commissary.

Although she was a civilian, her Red Cross uniform admitted her to the commissary. Although he was a soldier, a commissioned officer, his uniform did not admit him, for it was Korean. Otherwise, the commissary and the PX would have been swamped with Korean soldiers – and the black market would have overflowed with PX goods. The exclusion rankled.

Chae Byongyup was undeniably attractive, Betsie conceded to herself. Yet, she insisted, there was nothing romantic about their burgeoning friendship. She was no butterfly flitting from man to man. A girl could have men friends who did not interest her romantically. She was, she assured herself, interested in his mind: he was opening not only Korea, but the entire Orient to her.

Of course Chae Byongyup was fascinating: old world, sophisticated, and dashing. But he was already thirty-seven, way too old for her. Also, when you came right down to it, he was a Korean, a man of another race, as well as another culture.

Not that she had anything against Koreans. To the contrary, she found the country and its people more appealing every day – as she learned more of Asia's history, above all, Asia's supernal artistic achievement. Besides, Sue was her best friend ... had been for years. All that proved she had no racial prejudice.

Still, it was clear. A girl *might* have an affair with a Korean. But she would *not* marry a Korean.

Not that she had the slightest inclination towards an affair with Captain Chae Byongyup!

That settled, Betsie allowed herself to enjoy his company unworried about consequences. She particularly liked his English accent and greatly enjoyed his occasional odd turn of phrase.

'They called me Tommy when I was up at Downing.' Byongyup poured the last of their second bottle of champagne. 'Downing College of the University of Cambridge. An Oxbridge university is rather like an aircraft carrier. The ship is far bigger, but the individual colleges, like the warplanes, are the striking force.'

Betsie admired his grace. He was squatting stockstill on the fringed orange silk floor-cushion with no support and no apparent strain. She leaned gratefully against the sliding *shoji*, and her legs were stretched out before her, sheathed in slim olive-green slacks that did not conceal their spectacular beauty.

When Byongyup rose, his feet in khaki socks were silent on the worn *tatami*. He moved easily, as if no effort were worth making and none was necessary. His manner was casual, but his meticulously pressed fatigues fitted as if tailored to his lean body. As they had been.

A few freckles lay lightly across his arched nose, for his complexion was fair. A hint of ruddy-brown glinted in his black hair, which swirled around his ears in a most unmilitary manner, and the double-fold of his eyelids was slight. Yet he did not look Western, but, rather, like a narrow-faced, intellectually inclined aristocrat, a traditional scholar official wearing two swords in an old Japanese print.

'They called me Tommy,' he repeated, opening another bottle. 'God knows why. But I got to like it. Could you bring yourself to call me Tommy?'

She hesitated. Because of his age? Not that he was that much older than she. Eleven years was hardly an eternity!

'It was about time you were promoted ... Tommy,' she finally ventured. 'How long've you been in the army?'

'Only since the war started. Actually, captain is the highest rank for an inter-preter. As you know, our insignia is a parrot ... hardly a mark of respect. The generals reckon we're over-educated and effete because we speak English and have foreign friends. Funny that! A Confucian society's meant to revere learning.'

'But interpreters're indispensable,' she protested. 'How could you fight along-side Americans if you couldn't talk to them?'

'Maybe better to know Chinese ... for the future. Like your friend Captain Maynell.'

'Perhaps,' she answered coolly, not wanting to think about Luke just now. 'But how many parrots make captain?'

'I wasn't promoted for meritorious service, or for outstanding ability, or great promise.' Even when he mocked himself, Tommy Chae's voice was deep, dark velvet. 'Syngman Rhee hated my father. But he wants me on his side. By accepting promotion, I've given him a promissory note. I couldn't reject the promotion. Too pointed ... too political to say *No!* But that promissory note, he'll call it some day soon – certainly to my discomfiture.'

'Why would the president want a promissory note from a mere captain?'

'I have certain influence, a good following in the Chollas, the two south-western provinces. As you know, the Chollas are independently minded ... not subservient to Seoul.

'Rhee's in trouble. He needs all the support he can gather, particularly in the breakaway Chollas. The ROK constitution provides for the National Assembly to choose the president. That election is due ... is overdue. But Rhee wants a direct popular ballot, election by the people.'

'Why, that's fine. I didn't know Syngman Rhee was so democratic. From what I've heard ...'

'Rhee has too many enemies, too many rivals in the National Assembly. The Assembly'd never elect him again. But the people ...'

'Regardless, he wants to move towards the democratic way ... popular election. Anyway, it looks that way to me.'

Tommy Chae bowed his head as if imploring God to grant him patience and demanded, 'Does democracy mean stuffing ballot boxes, a trick he couldn't pull in the Assembly? Does democracy mean buying votes? What about beating and jailing opposition supporters? What about murdering opposition candidates?'

'That *is* a funny kind of democracy,' Betsie conceded. 'But direct election by the people is the best way in the long run.'

'You Americans!' Tommy Chae shrugged. 'Everything has to be done your way – as if you were supermen! You want to run the whole world like that town in New York State called Syracuse. [He pronounced it Sigh-rah-kews.] Funny name for a town like that when you think what went on in Syracuse in Sicily: Plato's protégé Alcibiades, not even to begin to think about Frederic Stupor Mundi, the great emperor with a thousand intellectual passions.

'Sorry I've got carried away. Still, I must say it right out: we are not fighting to become little slant-eyed Americans.'

'What *are* you fighting for?' Betsie snapped. 'Your enemy is the Communists. Remember? And we Americans are your best allies.'

'I *am* sorry.' Tommy recovered his poise. 'I shouldn't have blown up. We do appreciate deeply, profoundly what the US is doing.'

'I'm sorry, too, Tommy, very sorry.' Betsie's eyes, wide in contrition, shone the pale blue of a robin's egg in the morning dew. 'I misunderstood. You see, I ...'

This, Betsie suddenly realized, was one of those rare moments when the course of a lifetime can be *seen* to be decided. *If* she said no more than another word, no matter what ... *If* she simply smiled in a certain way ...

Treasuring the moment, knowing in her very bones how precious it was, she leaned forward and smiled tentatively. She did not speak, for she was overcome by shyness.

Marking Betsie's confusion, Tommy was moved by instinctive sympathy. With the utmost affection, he placed his hand on hers. When her fingers curled around his, he said in wonder, 'Who would have thought? My dear ... '

'*Yabaseo!*' Sue's contralto called from the vestibule. 'Anyone home?'

Betsie released Tommy's hand and leaned back against the *shoji*. He sighed almost imperceptibly, acknowledging that the moment and the mood were fleeting: too fragile to preserve, perhaps too fragile ever to recreate. Betsie realized even then, at that instant of deprivation that she was almost as relieved as she was disappointed. She had escaped complications that could have overwhelmed her. Although relieved, she felt bereft.

'Let me tell you about my brother Byongyup,' Sue said. 'I'm sure you're calling him Tommy now.'

'He did ask me ...'

'He always does.'

'What *are* you talking about?' Betsie demanded. 'Tommy's no sooner out the door than you're bad-mouthing him!'

'I see he's been hard at work. And he's a fast worker.' Sue's laugh was tinny. 'Did I interrupt something? Were you billing and cooing?'

'Certainly not!' Betsie said indignantly, then added softly, 'That is, not exactly ... well, almost.'

Sue laughed and resumed. 'I'll explain Tommy to you, though he's something of a mystery to me, too. First, he's a terrible philanderer: maidens' delight and maidens' despair. Wives, too ... other men's wives. Also he's ruthless, aggressive and ruthless.'

'Don't be ridiculous, Sue! He's anything but aggressive. He's tender, almost shy.'

'That, too, my girl. He's a ruthless womanizer, but thin-skinned, vulnerable. A porcupine with a tissue-paper skin.'

'You're being ridiculous! Talking fanciful nonsense!'

'Did he tell you he was married?'

'Why should he? It's none of my business anyway, nothing to do with me. Things ... we ... didn't go that far. And we won't.'

'Relax, Bets. His wife died three years ago. Constant disappointment and constant betrayal … sheer heartbreak. Though Korean wives should be used to—'

'Why did you try to make me believe he's still married?' Betsie was happy to be indignant, rather than sheepish. She was, nevertheless, disturbed by the relief, close to joy, she felt on learning that Tommy was no longer a married man. 'Not that it's anything to me.'

'I hope not. Anyway, Bets, be careful.'

'Sue dear, you haven't even begun to explain Tommy. He's a lot more besides a Lothario … much more!' Betsie now diverted the issue. 'What's all this about his political influence? And Syngman Rhee's needing him?'

'True enough! The Chaes, my family, come from Kwangju, deep in South Cholla Province.'

'So what makes the Chaes so important? Tommy started to tell me, but …'

'North Cholla and South Cholla lie beside each other. But they're isolated, back-ward, tucked away behind mountains in the remote south-west. They're remnants psychologically, even geographically, leftovers, still loyal to the old Yi Dynasty. The Japanese never got the Chollas completely under control. Certainly Syngman Rhee hasn't. The Chollas are feudal. They hate the government of the Republic of Korea.'

'I see it a little better now, Sue. You know, he … Luke … told me there're still strong Communist guerrilla units in South Cholla. And they're in touch with the POWs. But how can the Chollans be feudal *and* pro-Communist at the same time?'

'The people sympathize with the guerrillas' plight. The people are opposed to *any* central government. They would hate *anyone* who ruled from Seoul.'

'Where does Tommy come into it?'

'He has a big following in the Chollas. Not just because we Chaes have a valid claim to the throne as descendants of the paramount nobility, the Dukes of Kwangju.'

Sue sighed, quite evidently moved by deep sadness, as if mourning.

'The Chollans never believed my father was a traitor, a collaborator,' she went on slowly. 'They knew he was anti-Japanese, a true patriot. Anyway, Tommy can swing a lot of votes in the Chollas, votes Syngman Rhee needs to win a popular election.'

'I see,' Betsie mused aloud. 'So that's why Tommy's so poised, so sure of himself. It's his hereditary authority. According to you, he also believes he has the *droit de seigneur*. That hereditary, too?'

'I never said that, Betsie.'

'I've never heard stronger innuendo!' Betsie's restraint had been dissolved by the plentiful champagne. 'I still don't understand: There's a big Red guerrilla force in South Cholla, isn't there?'

'Rooted in the Chirisan mountain range.'

'And the Chaes are powerful in South Cholla, especially Tommy?'

'I've already said so. Tell me, dear, when do you get out the rubber hose? Where's this third degree leading?'

'Exactly what is your connection with the Communists? If the Chaes are that strong, they must've made a deal with the Reds.'

'That's what Syngman Rhee said when he shot my father.' Sue looked into her earthenware teacup. 'But it's not true. It's a *reductio ad absurdum* from a flawed premise. We have no connection with Communists, north or south. How could we possibly be *for* them?'

'Why not? You are virulently anti-Rhee. Your mother is an ardent fellow traveller, maybe a member of the Communist Party. Your family's anti-American, hardly bothers to hide it. I ask you again, Sue: tell me exactly what is your connection with the Reds?'

Sue sipped her tea, relishing the bitter barley flavor. But she could not hide behind social ritual indefinitely. She had to decide what else to tell her friend. If it was really worthwhile continuing this galling conversation.

Betsie had learned a little about Korea; she had seen a tiny part of its roiled surface. Betsie was, further, becoming a super-patriot. She was sternly applying American standards to a situation that was as confusing and misleading, as knotted and ingrown as a nest of newly hatched, black-hooded cobras incessantly intertwining and untwining, already deadly poisonous.

Sue's temper rose. Was it worth the effort, she wondered, the humiliation of answering those sharp yet naïve questions?

Yet Betsie was her closest friend. Betsie had now come to share the Korean side of her life, having already shared the American side. How could she not, at least, try to make Betsie understand? Besides, it could be dangerous to allow her to remain in ignorance.

The ROK secret police knew the Chaes intimately – and discounted her mother's diatribes. But some things the secret police did not know. A nudge from American Counter Intelligence could impel them to investigate again and to make new discoveries. Could even impel the police to make an example of her mother to please the Americans. Perhaps to make a dire example of Tommy and herself as well.

Would her closest friend inform on them?

Betsie was now inflamed by American patriotism, as she had a few years ago been inflamed by solidarity with the international working class under the leadership of the Soviet Union. She was, therefore, capable of informing the US Army's Counter Intelligence Corps.

Only after agonizing over her conflicting loyalties would Betsie turn informer. But, in the end, she would talk to the CIC.

Betsie was too certain in her beliefs, absolutely convinced she was right. She was, besides, too idealistic to put friendship before the anti-Communist crusade. An Occidental idealist would usually choose abstract principle over flesh-and-blood human beings. An Oriental idealist would hardly ever do so, for principles were too varied, as well as too distant, while human beings were too near.

Sue concluded wearily that she had no choice but to unveil the true circum-

stance to Betsie. Yet the Gordian intricacies of Korean politics, the endless elabora-
tions of ambitions and rivalries, were too much to explain in one afternoon.
Perhaps too much at any time for a straightforward, literal-minded American girl,
however intelligent. A simpler approach was required.

'Did I ever tell you how we left Seoul the second time? No? Then I'll show you
how absurd are your suspicions. Let's go back to the beginning. Just imagine how
I felt then! You can easily … you know me so well!'

Sue refilled their earthenware cups with dark barley tea.

'Sunday, June 25, 1950, the North invaded,' Sue continued, 'Mother was still in
the hospital after surgery, a hysterectomy. But she had to make way for the war
wounded. Luckily, my uncle, her elder brother, is a doctor. Uncle could look after
her.

'Nobody told us what was happening. Nobody even suggested what we should
do. The government radio was confusing, at first in its own confusion. I mean unintentionally. But not much later it was deliberately confusing. The regime didn't
want to take responsibility for its own people.

'The only bridge across the Han River was crammed with refugees: a few cars,
many ox-carts, but most just walking … trudging along with treasured belongings
on their backs. President Syngman Rhee was now telling us over and over again to
stay in Seoul. *He* was already far away.'

Betsie interjected, 'Wasn't Syngman Rhee forced to leave? I heard that our
ambassador suggested that Rhee leave Seoul … get out immediately. The ambassador said the US couldn't possibly get there with enough force in time to hold
Seoul. So Rhee had to leave or there would be no government of the ROK. If
President Rhee were killed or captured, the war would be over almost before it
began. And the Communists would be undisputed victors. The Republic of Korea
would be finished.'

'I've heard that story, too, Betsie. But I'm telling you how it was then for us …
how we felt at the time. How we suffered!

'The Communists took Seoul after a few days, as you know. They held Seoul for
almost three months. Those were the months that put the iron in our souls. The
Communists searched every house … over and over again … by night and by day.
They took every grain of rice, also every drop of *kimchi* they could glom on to.
They took silverware and bedding, any valuables, anything that caught their eye.
They'd already been deprived … on short rations … for five years. Fortunately, we'd
hidden our radio.

'Worse than the looting was the ceaseless search for young men, never pausing
for an instant! Soon, there wasn't a single male from fourteen to fifty left in Seoul.
They were all marching north under the guns of the Korean People's Army. Most
were to be cannon-fodder. Forced to soldier for the Communists. Some *People's*
Army!

'Tommy had left the very first day, gone to Kwangju where he could help most.
We didn't, after a few hours, believe the government's promise to hold Seoul. But I

had to be with Mother. She just couldn't travel ... far too weak, just recovering. Uncle stayed because he believed the Communists wouldn't ... couldn't ... touch him. He was over sixty and a doctor.'

'Then you were liberated?'

'Yes, you could call it liberation. General MacArthur's forces landed at Inchon in mid-September and, two weeks later, drove the North Koreans out of Seoul.

'Then began the second witchhunt.

'The North had staged a witchhunt for ROK supporters. Now Syngman Rhee mounted his own witchhunt ... looking high and low for Communists and Communist sympathizers. There was a lot of shooting, a lot of killing, beginning the very first days after liberation. And all Communists? Hardly!'

'Sue, I know you don't like Syngman Rhee.' Betsie sought reassurance. 'But it was better than the Communists, wasn't it? Much better?'

'I guess so. Most important, the UN Command ... the Americans ... brought us rice.

'But then, in mid-December it started all over again! The Korean Communists were now supported by the Chinese. They struck again at Seoul.

'The government didn't order us to leave, but the neighbors began disappearing. So Mother decided it was time for us to leave, before the ROK pulled out and the People's Army marched into Seoul again.

'Uncle had already been evacuated. Doctors were badly need for the refugees. Mother and I took with us a group of women and children, eight in all. We walked to the Han River, got across the temporary bridge, somehow, on foot. Then we walked to the railroad station at Yongdongpo. Sometimes it felt like crawling.

'We carried everything we could. I wore three layers of clothes – to keep warm and to save them. Then we struggled ... bribed ... our way onto a freight train going to Pusan. It took two days in a boxcar with the doors wide open to the driving wind, the hail big as golfballs, and, all the time, the icy frozen sleet. The children never stopped crying. Their hands and feet were freezing – hurt terribly.

'We could hardly move. We were packed together so tight. But we were better off ... much better off than those riding on top of the cars. They were brushed off in the tunnels. Some just let go when their fingers froze.'

'Sue, dear, it must've been terrible – appalling and horrifying. I understand now. I'm so sorry I made you tell me.'

'Betsie, it's better for me to remember than to suppress it. You really do see now, don't you? Tommy and I, the whole family, we don't like Rhee, but we hate the Communists much more. And we're afraid of the Communists ... we loathe and fear them dreadfully.'

Sue paused again, so moved she could hardly speak for a time. She then drove home the crucial point that she had to make Betsie understand. 'Tommy could never work with the Communists. He knows them too well. Always has.

'Between 1945 and 1950, when controls were slack, he used to flit back and forth across the border. No problem! He'd stay a while in the North, teaching the classics to make a living and to keep Korean learning alive. As you know, our classics are the Chinese classics the way yours are Latin and Greek. Only ours are harder, much harder to understand fully. Also only a little different later, moving a little with the times. Tommy taught the classics … to keep learning, the soul of Korea, alive.

'He finally settled in the South. It's not wonderful here, but it is better.'

Chapter XIII

'The big brass figure it's our baby now, Luke,' Colonel Howse confided. 'The kangaroo court *and* the necktie party!'

Luke Maynell gazed at his mud-spattered combat-boots to hide his grin. Nowadays Howse's speech was chockablock with slightly outmoded slang, especially when he talked tough.

'I don't want my balls caught in a wringer. So I shipped out the stiffs toot sweet – before more shit hit the fan.'

Howse then directed, 'Get your ass over to Pusan hubba-hubba. Get ahold of Rosenstein, the little Hebe second john who *honchos* administration at the POW Hospital. Get him to take you to the icehouse, so you can take a gander at the corpuses delicti.'

'The ice-house?' Luke asked innocently. 'I'm sorry sir. My military terminology's not so hot.'

'The mortuary, Captain. They're doing a post mortem, an autopsy, carving up our late friends to have a look at them from the inside.'

'You want me to go over to the mainland just to look at the bodies, sir?'

'That's right, Luke. Eyeball them. Never know what'll crawl out of the woodwork.'

The colonel had been transformed by his assignment to run the sputtering Information and Education Program for the POWs on Koje-do. At the very least, he was expected to make them into good little democrats – or maybe republicans.

The Army did not classify Howse's new operation as Psychological Warfare, since the POWs were supposed to be out of the war. But the objective was the same: to alter the prisoners' convictions, destroying any loyalty to Marxism-Leninism or its commissars, and then induce them to co-operate gladly with the POW Command. That meant in plain language: Kick them in the butt hard to kick out of them whatever they presently believed, then kicking them, even harder if necessary, into working with the anti-Communist hardliners.

The effect on the prisoners was negligible, as far as anyone outside the barbed wire could really tell. But the assignment had radically altered Lesward Murray Howse.

He had craved the approbation of his peers all his life. He had yearned to be as popular socially as he knew he was superior intellectually. Yet he had remained an outsider, never wholly accepted by his community, whether academic or military.

He was, however, welcomed heartily by his new brothers-in-arms, the MP light-colonels. Elated by that reception, he emulated their manners and their speech – practically mimicked them, Luke felt.

They were an odd lot.

Brigadier-General Francis Xavier Dodd, who was a Regular Army officer, commanded the POW camp. Most of his senior officers had, however, been commissioned into the Corps of Military Police during World War II because they were policemen in civilian life. Still essentially small-town cops, a dozen over-age lieutenant-colonels were the warders of Koje-do. They were steeped in ignorance. The mentality and the culture of some 200,000 inmates, their languages and their customs, were totally unknown to the colonels.

The POWs could have been Martians for all the fellow feeling the colonels could muster for their common humanity.

The jailers did not even know the identity of most of the prisoners. Since the Americans could not distinguish one Oriental from the other, the prisoners confused their warders further by trading names and changing barracks, even compounds, at will. Fingerprint records were few, and most of those few were attached to another's name and a misleading description.

Counting heads was no use at all. The light-colonels fumed because they arrived at a total that differed by hundreds each time they counted inmates of a compound.

When the MP officers were off duty, there was nothing to do except drink. Aside from the ramshackle brothels – obviously thick with contagion – the POWs and the ROKs frequented, Koje offered no diversion whatsoever for the light-colonels.

Those officers therefore suffered professional frustration and endured mortal boredom, as well as the affliction of the mammoth hangovers bestowed by rye whiskey at ten cents a double-slug. Mock candlelight strained through pink rayon shades shone on the joyless cavorting in the dreary atmosphere of Koje's tawdry officer's club. They indulged in interminable games of liars' dice punctuated by victors' whoops and losers' groans. Their Indian arm-wrestling almost ended in blows. They told endlessly tedious tales of their past triumphs, and they bellowed off-key renditions of mildly obscene songs.

Little Redwing to the melody of a trade union anthem was a little too subtle, though not too raunchy, for them. A favorite was *The Good Ship Venus*, whose 'mast was an elephant's penis'. They rejoiced in *Cigarettes and Whiskey and Wild, Wild Women*, with its triumphal chorus: 'They'll drive you crazy, they'll drive you insane!'

Those immortal lyrics they bawled out with ferocious slapping of thighs and staccato stamping of combat boots.

In the beginning, Howse was, therefore, repelled by his new brothers-in-arms. Their crude language and their simplistic opinions inflamed his intellectual arrogance, which derived equally from his long servitude in second-rate colleges and from his Lowland Scots ancestors.

The MPs' unreserved welcome won him over. His bald forehead pink with sincerity, his long nose sweat-dewed, his rimless glasses sparkling, he confided to his satellite, Lieutenant George Miner, 'It's great to be among real people, son. I've had a bellyful of puffed-up professors and stuffed shirt brasshats!'

Howse had acquired his new vocabulary from those failed policemen, who called themselves cops or harness bulls or dicks, but never flat-feet. Their anti-quated slang was straight out of an Edward G. Robinson gangster movie.

That rain-shrouded afternoon, Colonel Howse was wrung by perplexity and troubled by fear. A single misstep – amid the constant envy of less able men – could cost him the brigadier-general's star he now believed to be well within his reach, if not yet his grasp.

The quasi-judicial – or, rather, mock-judicial – murder of two Chinese POWs had provided Peking with a quiverful of denunciations. Radio Peking was, as usual, well informed, its broadcasts chockablock with the latest news from Koje, all that news reporting constant outrages, indeed atrocities, perpetrated by the Americans. Colonel Howse was now required, indeed flatly ordered, to provide 'facts' to counter those attacks.

The POW Command had initially ignored the bold defiance flung at them by the two battered corpses of Chinese prisoners hanging from the makeshift gallows in Compound 4. The Nationalist slogans pinned to their chests were a political embarrassment to the regime of Generalissimo Chiang Kai-shek, which was known to be co-operating with the UN.

Why, in that case, were the same Nationalists staging kangaroo courts and hanging their adversaries? How explain the blatant breach of discipline to Supreme Headquarters in Tokyo? Above all, however, Peking's allegation of American brutality urgently required refutation. Correspondents were asking embarrassing questions in Seoul and Tokyo, as were editors from London and Sydney to Los Angeles and Lisbon.

'You and I know it's the Commies,' Howse assured Luke. 'Slippery bastards strung up two anti-Communists – and tried to pin the blame on the Nationalists.... And on us.

'We've gotta show up the Reds' tricks, Luke. Even if you bust a ball trying. Open the whole can of worms. Dig down to the bottom of the barrel and *prove* it's all Commie lies. You gotta prove *they* did it.'

'I'll see what I can do, Colonel.' Luke replied equivocally. 'When do I leave?'

'Yesterday! Get your ass in motion right now!'

The unspoken portion of Howse's message was as clear as were his instructions to find – if necessary, manufacture – evidence that the Communist underground had murdered two anti-Communists and blamed the Nationalists. Luke would suffer severely should he fail to do so!

'If I get a handle on this mess, some important people'll owe me big favors!' The colonel had signalled his desperation. 'If you muff it, I can kiss my star goodbye.'

★

Either his ambitions or his fears, perhaps both, drove the colonel to Pusan the next day. Luke was commanded by telephone to meet Howse at the officers' club beside the beach that afternoon.

'Well, my boy, what've you got for me?' Howse rubbed his plump hands together in anxiety. 'I know you've found the proof I need!'

'Proof, Colonel?' Luke stalled.

'Proof the Coms did it … hung those two bozos sky high. Spit it out, Maynell.'

'Colonel, it's not so easy.' Luke equivocated. 'I need a little more time.'

'Don't wanta press you. Take all the time you need. But, remember, I gotta have it yesterday. At least, tell me you're beginning to crack it. I've got an awful lot going on this one.'

'Fucking-A, Colonel, you're on. I'll bull it through anyhow!'

Howse did not react to that blatant parody of his new conversational style, if indeed he noticed it. He bore Luke's temerity, rather than risk alienating the officer on whose ability and endeavors now rested his hopes of promotion.

Having thus so easily averted a showdown, Luke went on, 'I want to hit the bull's eye. I know we've got to drop this bombshell right in the pickle barrel.'

Howse nodded in thanks, ignoring the further provocation. His avowed contempt for a wiseass Phi Beta Kappa was diluted by his grudging respect for Luke's language skills. Besides, why take the chance of a serious confrontation with a junior officer whose father was president of California's second largest bank?

'Then get your ass in gear – and get me what I need,' he riposted. 'Don't hang around here.'

Luke threw the colonel a stiff salute that was not too obviously irreverent and made for the door. A bellow halted him.

'Not so fast, Luke. I need your help on something else.'

'What's that, sir?'

'I promised a couple of the boys I'd show 'em a good time. Two new MP lieutenant-colonels: McNamara and Ghurkin. And you know Pusan better'n I do.'

'Pusan's got no good restaurants or bars. Nothing even as fancy as this O Club. Pusan's not Paris. It's not even San Francisco.'

'Only in a *certain* way, my boy.' Howse's tone was ingratiating and insinuating. 'The girls, Maynell! *Les Girls* … all over the place … just like Paris.'

'Not quite, Colonel. But I can point you in the right direction. I can easily find a Korean who'll know where to look.'

Luke's tone was aggressively matter-of-fact. He was not going to sound like a prig by declaring self-righteously that he would not pimp for anyone, particularly not for his boss. But he learned that he could not push the task of pandering off on someone else.

'No, Maynell. I want you to come along. I need you with me.'

'Need me with you, sir?' When in doubt, echo the last command. 'Need me?'

'To do the talking, my boy.' The eager colonel forgot his new slang. 'You know my Japanese is rusty.'

'I'm sorry, Colonel, but I don't understand what you need me for.' Luke's distaste for playing the role of a go-between for prostitute and customer, as he was now virtually ordered to, overcame his prudence. Besides, discretion was never his strongest point. 'Do you want me to screw them? Or to translate a speech you make to the defenceless whores?'

Lesward Murray Howse's turkey-wattle jowls flushed crimson, and his small eyes narrowed behind his rimless glasses. But his tone remained oleaginous. 'Neither, Maynell, neither. The boys want to see an *exhibition*.'

No discretion could this time allow Luke to pretend not to grasp his colonel's meaning. Howse's exaggerated French nasality made it very clear what he wanted: an *ex ... hi ... bi ... shun*. Was it, Luke wondered, marginally less distasteful to act as an impresario for a sex show than to act as a pimp?

He shrugged. He could not openly defy Howse again, no matter how badly the colonel might need him. Besides, the delay while the new light-colonels gaped at an exhibition would be helpful. Howse would patently not relent in his demand for manufactured evidence of Communist guilt, but the fulfilment Luke had decided *not* to provide would be put off for another day. So, thus, would any direct confrontation with Howse.

Better still, after performing that unorthodox service he would have a moral advantage, you might just say. He would on Howse's command have performed a service Howse would very much want the brass hats *not* to know he had demanded.

Luke was, moreover, seriously disturbed by the little he had already learned about the kangaroo court and the execution. He needed time to ponder his own best course of action.

'Yes, sir!' He did not allow his disgust to tinge his voice. 'Does the colonel wish to go right now?'

The anteroom was cramped and claustrophobic. The sugar-and-acid reek of cheap perfume did not mask either the stench of a blocked toilet or the musty smell of mold. Despite the warmth of the afternoon, the single window was shut tight. Two of its six panes were cracked. Glass had been replaced by corrugated cardboard in a third.

The half-light filtering through the grimy mauve curtains was presumably meant to be seductive. But the lieutenant-colonels shifted uneasily on the shabby, stained mauve cushions of a flimsy wooden bench. Looming enormous in starched green fatigues, they made the room appear even smaller, hardly more than a vestibule in a dilapidated doll's house.

The two MP officers twisted their billed caps in their rawboned hands and warily watched the by-play. His glasses greasy and his forehead sweaty, Colonel Lesward Howse prompted a reluctant Captain Luke Maynell.

Luke laughed when he told me, Harland Birch, of the incident. He wasn't laughing at the time, but penduluming between disgust and anger. Besides, it wasn't at all easy to get the colonel's message through to the slight Korean girl.

Her schooling had evidently been scanty. She could speak only a few words of Japanese, which had been the language of instruction in all schools throughout occupied Korea until the end of the War in the Pacific. Still, it was a full seven years since the Japanese had scarpered. She might not have been of school age then, since she was, quite possibly, no more than fourteen, though she looked, perhaps, seventeen.

The young girl was the image of innocent depravity. Defiantly, she straddled the unpainted three-legged stool in front of the threadbare scarlet curtain on the doorway leading to the rear. Her immature breasts were half-exposed by a loose halter-top that was checkered green-and-orange. Monkey Ward catalogue's best.

Her knees were spread to keep her balance astride the stool. Her short skirt of flimsy pink rayon rode up over her narrow thighs to show the crotch of peach panties trimmed with soiled lace. From time to time, she jerked the hem down with automatic coquetry. But the skirt soon rode up again.

Her mouth, which was now twisted in her effort to understand Luke, would have become a Raphael cherub. Beneath caked cherry-red lipstick, her lips were a perfect Cupid's bow. Her face was thin and unlined, yet somehow rapacious, the petal-smooth cinnamon skin marred by a small brown scar below her left nostril. Her iodine-black eyes were expressionless, yet somehow moving, as if appealing for help. At once vicious and vulnerable, predatory and defenceless, she was unmistakably predestined for tragedy.

She ignored the colonels' lecherous stare. Forehead wrinkled in concentration, she struggled to comprehend the mixture of basic Japanese and GI English to which Luke had resorted. She understood most of the individual words, he sensed, but not the meaning they sought to convey.

'*Futatsu … tabun mitsu musume,*' Luke repeated. 'Colonel-san want see two, maybe three, girlsans make jig-jig … pom-pom.'

'Hava 'nother two-piece *musume,*' she piped in a schoolgirl treble. 'You wait. *Toshiyori-san* go numbah one. Very quick over!'

She grinned derisively and in spite of his revulsion, Luke could not quite avoid a sympathetic smile. He did not tell his superior officer that the little whore had called him elderly and, by clear implication, hardly still virile.

'No … no want jig-jig *musume.*' He, instead, tried again. '*Toshiyori-san* want see *musume* jig-jig other *musume. Futastu* maybe *mitsu … pom-pom* together … two piece maybe three girlsans.'

Luke's self-esteem shrivelled at his own complicity. The child whore was beginning to understand what the colonels wanted. Finally realization broke upon her.

Her perfect mouth twisting in her virginal, corrupt, sensuous face, she replied, 'Look, Mac, ex'bee shun hava-no! You speak one way or other: fuck or suck!'

Chapter XIV

I believe it was Kipling who wrote: 'Four things greater than all things are, horses and something and women and war.'

I'm not certain it was Rudyard the Bard. My early schooling was short and sketchy. I only came to love Kipling much later. Anyway, where would I get a volume of his poetry or even a dictionary of quotations buried up here in the north woods?

The thaw's begun all right. But it's a very slow thaw, and I'm not risking my neck on the icy roads just yet.

Anyway, it hardly matters what Kipling believed the other thing was. For me, the last two say it all: women and war have dominated my life. Not just easy sex and quick fights, which you can find any day anywhere in Asia, but real women and real war.

Naturally, I can't write about war without writing about raw sex. You can smell the lust when a halfway attractive female comes into the view of men who haven't seen a woman for months. In Korea, even a dog of a non-Korean female got a great big reception simply because she had round eyes. That's one reason I can't stand female so-called war correspondents. They confuse the issue and drive the troops crazy. Besides, they don't do a very good job.

I'm not blaming them. They can't help not understanding what's going on. God made women incapable of comprehending war. A female war correspondent, like a male wet nurse, is a contradiction in terms, an impossibility.[1]

Except for Maggie, of course. Maggie Higgins was a great war correspondent, far better than most men. Maggie was a phenomenon, the kind that turns up once in a thousand years, a force of nature like Helen of Troy or Joan of Arc. But even Maggie wasn't above using her little girl's smile and her big girl's body to get the jump on her competition.

Why should she have been?

Women are normally more single minded and more ruthless than men, but they differ in what they believe is truly important. A woman like Maggie, who believed that brilliantly reporting a war was all important, could, therefore, get the jump on almost any man.

---

[1] Editor's note: It should be clear here that Harland Birch is expressing a highly personal view, which he implicitly contradicts in the following paragraphs. It is *his* view, not necessarily the view of the editor whose name appears on the dustjacket and the spine of this volume.

But I digress. I was talking about sex and combat, as well as women and war.

Sex was rampant even on Koje. A few POWs even wormed their way into the compound that held a few hundred North Korean women. Thousands visited the cat-houses in civilian villages not far from their compounds. They just walked through holes cut in the fence while well-bribed ROK guards looked the other way.

Not only outside, but *inside* the compounds, sex was rampant. You could practically see the welling of lust when an attractive youth, a smooth-cheeked boy, walked past. He didn't have to wear a sign saying, *I am a girl!*, though many did. Lust was virtually automatic, even if he didn't waggle his hips, as most did. What other choice did the boys have if they were to survive?

The Chinese prisoners' *honchos*, whether Communist or Nationalist, treated homosexual attachments the same way their home armies did. They just ignored it, denied even to themselves that it existed. *Don't ask, don't tell!* wasn't invented by Bill Clinton.

But I digress again. The Greek vice was never my vice. Instead, two grand themes have shaped my days, two swelling organ chords: mortal danger and compulsive coupling. You can call it fornication if you like and be done with it. But it was never only the physical sensations, glorious and addictive as they are. There's always been a strong emotional bond between me and my women, numerous as they've been.

Death and birth. Those extremes meet and blend, since everything is circular in life. It's all in those three syllables. What else is there to say? When men daily face death or mutilation, normal desire becomes monstrously enlarged.[2] So it was for the troops manning the main line of resistance, those few who were lucky enough to get to Seoul. Best of all, most gloriously tumescent, was their one-and-only leave to Japan for rest and recreation, as precious as rubies and gold dust.

R&R, rum and rape, the troops called it, in clear contradiction to Winston Churchill's description of the Royal Navy as 'rum, sodomy, and the lash'. R&R was the smartest move the UN Command ever made.

Tokyo could've been designed to comfort battle-weary warriors. It certainly was in the olden days when the city was called Edo. Like the counterfeit paradise the Old Man of the Mountain created for his assassins, Tokyo provided an amplitude of women, as well as both narcotics and stimulants, in this case, mostly booze rather than hash. Still, marijuana was readily available, although not the heroin from the Golden Triangle that ravaged the US Army in Vietnam after 1968, albeit, not anywhere to the extent the censorious media described. I must note, not nearly to the extent of seriously inhibiting the most professional ground forces the US ever deployed. As for R&R in Japan, men returned to the main line of resistance almost happily to recover from the exhaustion of their debauchery.

---

[2] I know the thought's not original. I'm not trying to be original. I don't know if I can. I'm just trying to tell you how it was in Korea in the early '50s.

Naturally, many rear-area characters used the danger to which they were not exposed as a reason, an excuse, for their concupiscence. How many soldiers, after all, were really in contact with the enemy? Half? Not that many, given the American way of war with its swollen logistical and administrative tail. At most a quarter, more realistically a fifth.

Take First Lieutenant George Miner, that faithful satellite of Colonel Lesward Murray Howse. Miner was a showy rear-echelon commando. He carried a big Colt .45 in a shoulder holster like a movie gangster. He'd wave the .45 around to the peril of everyone within fifty feet, but chiefly to his own peril.

Miner was tall, rawboned, and gawky. His big red Adam's apple sprouted a couple of sandy-blond hairs; his big, soft, pale nose looked like one of those fat white veal sausages called *Weisswurst* they love in Munich. That big Adam's apple and that big nose, he boasted, showed how well hung he was, the size of his penis being in direct proportion. So much for the science of anatometrics as practiced by Lieutenant George Miner.

He had another funny tick. Given any encouragement, sometime none at all, he would whip out a deck of dogeared photographs. All, he would brag, taken by himself, some in Memphis, some in Seoul or Pusan.

Some were conventionally sickening. Fat white women wearing only high-heeled shoes and a string of pearls were sodomized by little guys with hairline mustaches. In other photos, the same ample ladies or their sisters munched on the same dudes' improbably enormous organs.

I hate such raw pornography, though a good Japanese or Chinese pillow book is a work of art. Pornography is not really about sex, but about degradation.

Miner's dirty pictures taken in Korea were just pathetic, even less suggestive, not erotic at all. Most showed Korean whores with pendulous breasts and legs opened wide to display startlingly bushy pubic hair. In some, the whores, grinning with bravado, spread the lips of their clefts with their fingers. Somehow, the grainy black-and-white realism of those photos made them even more revolting

Regardless of that kind of stuff, you can't write honestly about young men at war without writing a lot about sex. It just wouldn't be true.

In war, sex is everywhere. It tinges every sight and echoes in every sound, a compulsion beyond individual will. Sex is a virulent virus in the blood, a raging fever in the nerves. Sex seethes in every brain, a fury heightened not so much by constant danger as by the uprooted lives soldiers endure. Soldiers are tossed around, driven by the shifting winds, repeatedly torn loose from whatever feeble emotional roots they may put down in their temporary billets.

And the women? As always, the women respond to the needs of men, as always giving too much and receiving too little. That was true of the Korean whores in their Monkey Ward finery, as it was of that greatest of all camp followers, the chaste Saint Joan.

★

Luke Maynell thought himself above such raw compulsion. At 27, he was older than most junior officers and, of course, older than the corporals and privates, older even than most sergeants. He felt he was fully mature, intellectually as well as emotionally.

Intellectually he just about was, perhaps. But emotionally? Hardly, for he could never commit himself fully, much less unreservedly, to any other human being. So it came about that Luke, who was attracted when at a distance, repelled when close, later swung, rather like a malfunctioning pendulum between Betsie Howard and Sue Chae.

That is a sorry tale. The two had been like sisters. More than sisters because not bound by birth, but because they themselves had chosen each other. And they had complemented each other perfectly. Unwitting in his naïve egotism and his genuine good will, Luke all but destroyed that loving friendship.

He was drawn to Sue when upon occasion he felt Betsie's love for him become too great, repressive, even stifling. He was drawn to Sue because she was unattainable – or at least appeared to be unattainable. She was attractive because she was safe: she could never become possessive.

Even at that early stage, when Betsie had just come to Pusan, I wondered whether she was not a little doubtful about Luke. My feeling had little to justify it, except an old reporter's instinct. Yet, even so early, I felt a certain strain — an unhealthy tension – between them. Betsie may have … she just may have already sensed she wasn't necessarily going to get the handsome hero to keep. She may also have sensed that she might, perhaps definitely would in the end *not* really want him.

Luke naturally put great store by physical love between men and women. Though a dedicated scholar, he was no bloodless bookworm, but was as the Edwardians used to say, 'full blooded'. So was Betsie, tastefully sensual, provocatively voluptuous Betsie.

Neither had a truly private refuge. So they spent the few free hours they could manage in the bijou Mijin Hotel, which had just opened, planning to accommodate the businessmen Syngman Rhee hoped to attract once the war was over. Such was the old man's foresight, which was compounded by the strictly commercial foresight of his Austrian wife Francesca, who, everyone said, owned the Mijin. Anyway, the Mijin was the first hotel to open in Pusan during the war, indeed at the time the only hotel.

I had no idea *exactly* what went on during those stolen hours in the Mijin. Nor did I want to know. I'm not the reporter who's under the bed when the assignation takes place. Just as long as things were going well between them, precisely what they did in bed or on the floor or in the shower didn't matter.

It's not a spectator sport, sex. The anatomical details are thoroughly banal, although not, perhaps, to the participants, even though sexual activity is the most thoroughly analysed aspect of human life. That analysis should, however, be much more concerned with the head and the heart than with the genitalia.

*

Betsie was already seeing a lot of Sue's half-brother, Captain Chae Byongyup, in good part because Luke could now steal very few hours to be with her. Really, Luke hardly had time enough to even think of her.

There was, Betsie assured herself, nothing physical between her and Tommy Chae. No more than an occasional extemporary exchange of glances or a chance brushing of fingertips. The man who was, his sister said, an incorrigible rake behaved as respectfully, as chastely, as an Eagle Scout. Rather than a lover, Tommy Chae became a guru, Betsie's guide to the Orient.

Luke was hardly concerned with Betsie at all the day after the humiliating scene at the brothel, which his self-esteem was already covering with the scar tissue of forgetfulness. Before that débâcle, he had already told his superior that his investigation of the hanging of the two Chinese prisoners was making progress. That was true. However, Colonel Howse would have been horrified if he had known the direction that investigation was taking.

Luke had a pretty good idea where he was heading. The evidence was convincing, if not yet conclusive. No court would credit his tentative judgement, since what information he possessed was manifestly far from complete.

He had been struck with a sudden revelation while he was shepherding the sheepish MP lieutenant-colonels back to their billet. In order to test that insight he returned to the mortuary of the POW General Hospital.

Second-Lieutenant Sidney Rosenstein, the hospital's administrative officer, led Luke through the maze of Quonset huts with good grace, although he disliked visiting the charnel house that some days 'processed,' as the army put it, a half-dozen post-mortems. Blond, compact, and muscular, Sid spoke with a Georgia drawl that had survived four years at the University of Pennsylvania. The second son of the proprietor of the largest department store in Atlanta, he was determined to make a life as a man of letters. He chafed at the triviality of his duties, but nonetheless performed them with brusque efficiency.

'If I'd only taken Latin in high school,' he told Luke, 'I wouldn't be walking into this particular shambles now. I'd be as happy as a shit-eating possum up a tree doing my time as a private on the main line of resistance.'

'How come?' Luke enjoyed Sid's comic routine. 'Since when do you need a classical education to be a rifleman?'

'Because I'd never taken Latin, Penn gave me a Bachelor of Science degree, not a Bachelor of Arts. I majored in English, largely Elizabethan drama, nothing to do with science. But the army insisted on commissioning me in the Medical Administrative Corps. My B.S. was the qualification. They had a quota to fill ... wouldn't take no for an answer.'

'Par for the course.' Luke nodded in sympathetic understanding. 'I practically had to hit the adjutant general on the head to get sent here. The army never dreamed it might need a Chinese speaker in Korea, or even a Japanese speaker. Though I was qualified in part because I knew very little about Korea, not like China or Japan where I have a smattering ...'

The normally irrepressible cheerfulness of Sid Rosenstein was subdued when he opened the outer door of the Quonset hut, which, curved in a half hoop, could be cut to length like a Liberty Ship. They saw double wooden doors with chromium handles, which opened into an immense walk-in refrigerator like that of a really big meat wholesaler. They did not enter the fridge. Nonetheless, the air inside the Quonset itself was marginally cooler than outside, despite the morning sun beating on the hut's corrugated-iron skin.

They inhaled the sickly sweet smell of putrefaction, which was not quite masked by the harsh odors of formaldehyde and carbolic acid. A fecal stench wafted from the far end of the hut. Sid Rosenstein blew his breath out through pursed lips in revulsion.

Luke and Sid saw at the same moment behind a half-drawn green curtain two men whose surgeons' half-masks and skin-tight rubber gloves contrasted oddly with their olive-drab singlets and bloodstained fatigue trousers. One wielded a stubby, big-toothed saw; the other clutched huge shiny steel shears. A disjointed form that might once have been human lay on an outsize stainless-steel drainboard.

The overwhelming fecal stench billowed sickeningly, and Sid gagged.

'Yes, sir, Lieutenant!' A tall black medical corpsman wearing a long white coat splotched brown-and-red came around a corner. 'Can I help you gentlemen?'

'We've come to see those two Chinese,' Rosenstein said. 'Roll them out for me.'

'Lieutenant, sir, we got lots of Chinks,' the medic replied. 'Sorta specialize in 'em.'

The pathologists behind the curtain guffawed. A saw grated on bone; an electric drill whirred; and some soft object squished into the pail under the drainboard.

'All right, Jefferson,' Sid Rosenstein rasped. 'Quit the clowning. And roll them out pronto. I'm not going to spend the day trading wisecracks with you ghouls.'

'Yes, sir! Right now, Lieutenant, sir.'

Rosenstein ignored the levity. His face pale, his blond hair drenched with sweat, he helped the medic trundle a stretcher on wheels out of the walk-in meat refrigerator.

'That's one,' he said. 'Though why you want to see *that* again ... '

'I don't want to, Sid,' Luke replied softly. 'I *have* to.'

Luke clenched his teeth and looked down at the naked corpse. It was curiously flattened, somehow diminished in size in death. Where the bruised skin was neither torn by wounds nor sliced by the pathologist's knife, it was the pale greasy yellow of the fat on a lamb's carcase. Black-tarred twine roughly stitched together the lips of the incision that split the corpse from the chin to the sparse pubic hair above the shrivelled penis.

Luke gulped down the copper bile that rose in the back of his throat. He was not merely queasy, but close to vomiting. He had seen battle-dead many times, but had never seen a body quite so widely lacerated, so battered and broken. The mock-clinical atmosphere, the pitiless fluorescent lights, the reek of the mortuary left him aghast, all but horrified him. He forced himself to study the face, what he could see beneath a carapace of incisions and scabs.

'Yo, Captain, you interested in this poor bozo?' A pathologist spoke around the green curtain. 'Never in all my days have I seen a corpse as beat up as this miserable Chinaman. Nearly every bone in his body broken. He was half-dead when they strung him up. But he suffered the torments of hell on the way.'

'Thanks, Doctor,' Luke answered softly. 'That makes it clearer.'

The victim's features emerged gradually through the screen of purple bruises and black lipped wounds. Now visibly stamped with a snarl of agony, the face was somehow familiar. It was, Luke realized, the face of the enemy, the first living enemy he had seen in Korea. It was unmistakably Political Commissar/Major Chang Hsi-lo, who had identified himself as Junior Sergeant Huang Hsi-wu in the intelligence bunker months earlier.

Somehow, the curved bridge of the nose, now brutally crushed, the broad forehead, now bruise-mottled, and the tight thin lips, now viciously ripped apart, were once again in Luke's mind, debonair and defiant. Despite the empty eye-socket and the shattered cheekbones, Major Chang Hsi-lo was still casually insolent, as if on the point of again demanding a cigarette and a brandy.

Sid Rosenstein was a vertiginous green, and the black medic was a chalky gray. Luke's head drooped, suddenly too heavy for his neck, and the fluorescent lights flickered blindingly.

'Let's get out of here!' he demanded. 'I've seen it all … everything I came to see.'

The air outside was sweet in their nostrils, although tainted by the exhalations of hundreds of unwashed bodies, by the sour stench of fermenting rice, and by the sickening smell of rancid cooking-oil. The sunlight no longer glared but fell softly and kindly on the ruddy yellow earth. Green shoots among the faded brownish wisps of grass on hills stripped bare for firewood, promised new life.

Luke had been deeply disturbed, revolted yet pitying, when he saw the corpse a day earlier. Now, driven by a sense of a duty not yet fulfilled, he saw the same face, which had been roughly cleansed. And he was certain, despite the awesome wounds, that it was the face of the cocky Chinese political commissar who had originally sworn that he was an anti-Communist deserter.

Not so long after that encounter, Luke had come to Koje-do for the first time. He had then seen that same face contorted with hatred, the thin lips screaming anti-American slogans. The massed ranks of Chinese prisoners had roared the same slogans, no less raucously. Yet some POWs had only one leg or one arm, many were heavily bandaged, and a few were naked except for the olive-drab blankets draped around them.

Luke had thereafter been on the lookout for the man he had soon identified as a field grade officer in the Chinese People's Volunteers, an impassioned Communist agitator, the son of Mao Zedong's close henchman. He had thereafter seen Major Chang Hsi-lo in the front rank of two demonstrations. He had once seen Chang Hsi-lo in earnest, respectful conversation with the middle-aged pseudo-private who was, as Luke learned, the senior officer of the paramilitary Communist force in the camp.

Beyond any doubt, the dead man had been a dedicated Maoist, a fanatical and indefatigable agitator, an irreconcilable foe of the 'Chiang Kai-shek remnant clique' and 'Yankee imperialism'. It was, therefore, highly unlikely to say the very least, in fact, just about impossible to believe that Political Commissar Chang Hsi-lo had been tried by a *Communist* kangaroo court and then executed by *Communist* goons.

Luke, of course, knew very well that fierce fanatical rivalries divided the Communists. Mao's satrap in Manchuria had only a month or so earlier been deposed for 'plotting to establish a separatist regime' there. Yet who would dare murder the son of Senior General Chang Wen-to, member of the Standing Commission that controlled the Central Executive Committee of the Communist Party of China and deputy chief of the powerful Political Department of the People's Liberation Army? No sane Communist would dare.

Yet the two corpses had been clumsily placarded with Communist slogans, in addition to the stern warning that all traitors to China faced the same deadly punishment. They had, further, been draped with a flag so ill stitched together that it might have been intentionally made crude to mislead all others regarding the identity of those who had sewed it.

Dyed red with mercurochrome from a first-aid kit, it bore the five stars of the People's Republic of China, amateurishly cut from the gold paper the drama class used for making costumes. All in all, it was a self-evidently maladroit spectacle, which I, Harland Birch, your narrator, did not describe in full earlier in this account because, as I now see so clearly, it would have confused you, my esteemed readers.

Anyway Raymond Wu, the interpreter from Nationalist Taiwan, had unhesitatingly affirmed that the Communists were responsible for the outrage.

Luke had felt even then that that immediate confirmation was suspect. He had wondered why Raymond Wu had not bothered to look at the scanty evidence, much less look deeper into the matter, whatever collateral information might then appear. But the Nationalist agent had no desire to uncover the truth. Raymond Wu's mission was to malign his enemies regardless of the realities – to discredit the Communists in every possible way.

The UN Command had been angry at the Communists' outrageous breach of discipline. But the generals in Tokyo had not been alarmed. They were not alarmed until Radio Peking trumpeted grave charges.

'A reign of white terror stalks the torture camp on Koje Island, where the heroic fighters of the Chinese People's Volunteers are penned like wild beasts,' Peking claimed. 'Unchecked by the American authorities, provocateurs of the discredited Chiang Kai-shek remnant clique are running wild, tormenting and murdering the brave People's Volunteers. Two patriots were this week tried by an illegal court and hanged. The American imperialists are colluding with the so-called Nationalists to weaken the will of those courageous Chinese patriots and to force them to go to Taiwan, rather than return to their Motherland!'

The UN Command thereupon demanded concrete proof that it was indeed the Communists who had executed the two men. The generals wanted unassailable evidence to refute Radio Peking's lies.

Gulping fresh air, Luke pondered his own position. He was well on the way to concluding, though not precisely proving, that the Nationalists had murdered two Communist stalwarts – and then faked both the leftist slogans on the placards and the red flag to lay the blame on the Communists. His evidence was not unassailable, but it was fairly solid.

Was it, however, wise to pursue his investigation in that direction? Colonel Howse expected Luke to confirm Communist responsibility for the crime. Howse would never allow Luke to condemn the Nationalists, who were enthusiastically co-operating with Howse's indoctrination campaign. Why assist the enemy by revealing such a damaging truth?

Luke knew he was all but beyond reach of the vengeance of his superiors. No general would further publicize Luke's unwanted conclusions by court-martialling him. At the worst, he could be transferred to an unpleasant post in the Aleutians or the Arizona desert. After a few weeks, his father's friends in Washington would correct that injustice. He would not suffer if he did his duty.

But what exactly was his duty? Simply to reveal the truth, as he knew it? Even if that truth damaged the US – and assisted the Communists? He simply did not know.

He would have prayed for guidance had he not forgotten how to pray. He did not quite know at that dire moment whether he still believed in God. But, on the whole, he doubted it just then. He was, as he soon acknowledged, too vain of his powerful independent intellect.

God, Luke mused wryly, suffers the same paradoxical dilemma that afflicted British and American colonial governments. The better the education they gave a man, the more likely he was to rise against them. The more intelligent God makes His children, the more likely they are to be dazzled by their own gifts — and to deny His existence.

Chapter XV

'Radish?' Luke twirled the handle of the field telephone that had been installed in his room in the Pusan Bachelor Officers' Quarters just an hour earlier. 'Is that Radish?'

He owed both the instrument in its oil-stained green canvas case and the singular privacy of a private one-man room with its metal-framed cot and its plywood dresser to the pressure Colonel Lesward Murray Howse had exerted so that Luke could continue his investigation from a base in Pusan. The Colonel owed his much increased power to the pressure Supreme Headquarters in Tokyo was exerting on the POW Command. Tokyo required a prompt and conclusive rebuttal to Peking Radio's charge that Nationalist agents had murdered two patriotic Chinese POWs – and had framed blameless Socialist patriots who only wished to return to their Motherland unimpeded.

Tokyo Headquarters was in turn under great pressure from Washington, which was being pressed hard to refute the accusation by allied governments in London, Paris, and Bogota, among a half-dozen others. Those governments were, for their part, facing awkward questions from men and women of genuine good will; as well as from perennial *bien pensants,* who could not bear to think ill of any dictator who called himself a man of the left, however bloody his hands, who indeed thought all the better of such a dictator, the more blood he had on his hands. That lot, who idolized Joseph Stalin and Mao Zedong, further respected Kim Il Sung greatly.

The acknowledged lackeys of Moscow and Peking in local Communist Parties, as well as the outright 'non-Communist' protégés of the so-called Socialist bloc, were mounting demonstrations in New Delhi, Stockholm, and Wellington, as well as in London and Paris. A number of those 'peaceful demonstrations' had turned into violent riots, claiming the lives of police as well as protestors and inflicting damage on property.

American diplomatic missions throughout the world, above all, the vulnerable libraries of the United States Information Service, always the first to burn, were putting up their shutters and reinforcing their guard of US Marines and local police. Legislators were asking discomfiting questions in the Capitol in Washington, in the Palace of Westminster in London, in Parliament House in Canberra, and in the Chamber of Deputies in Paris.[1]

---

[1] Remarkably enough, the French were still our allies in Korea, a long way from home. As remarkably, they were fighting with a will.

Quite naturally, indeed properly, the Press of forty countries had seized on the issue. So far, the mood of the Press was honestly enquiring, rather than adversarial or vengeful. The sixteen-nation alliance that defended South Korea was hardly on the point of unravelling. Nonetheless, the fabric was under strain.

The focus of all those diverse pressures was a 27-year-old temporary captain in the Army of the United States who had been trying for twenty-five minutes to put through a local telephone call. Pusan was less than forty miles from Koje-do. But the rickety military telephone network, its oddly named exchanges manned by inept operators, considerably lengthened that distance.

'Yah, suh, hyeah's Radish.' Why, Luke wondered, did most of the operators speak with the virtually unintelligible red-neck accents? 'Kin Ah he'p yuh?'

'Thanks, Radish.' Luke had flipped the butterfly switch on the instrument to *TALK* and half-shouted, 'Can you get me Redpath, please?'

'Redpath, suh!' The instantaneous response was clear, emboldening Luke to ask in a normal tone, 'Redpath, please give me Robust.'

Loud crackling like bacon frying was followed by metallic crashes like hail on a tin roof. And then a prolonged silence. Luke twirled the handle again.

'Radish, hyeah's Radish, suh. Kindly stop crankin' yo' handle. Yo'ah makin' me deef.'

'Sorry, Radish. I got cut off. Could you get me Redpath again?'

Silence for a full minute, then a distant voice speaking unintelligible words.

'Redpath? Is that Redpath?' Luke called out. 'I can hardly hear you. I say again: is that Redpath?'

'Yes, suh, Redpath.' The distant voice suddenly boomed in Luke's ear. 'Numbah, please.'

'Redpath, I want Robust. This is a priority call.'

'Yoah rank, suh?'

'Colonel.' Captains rated hardly any priority. 'Lieutenant-Colonel Schmidt.'

'Yes, suh. Givin' yuh Robust.'

The long pause that ensued was filled by the remote tinkle of radio music and tinny echoes of other conversations. Though the voice of the Redpath operator was faint, Luke heard him pass on the priority claimed as a lieutenant-colonel.

'Robust, give me six. Priority.'

'The lyen is busy, Colonel, sirrr.' A Midwest trilling of the final *r*.

'Break in then. This is a priority call.'

'I'm sorry, Colonel. I can interrupt Colonel Howse only for a call from the commandant or a major-general. New orders.'

'I'll wait.' No point in blustering at that cool Midwest voice. 'Just keep an eye on the line.'

Luke regretted not having promoted himself to major-general. While he waited, the doubts he thought he had overcome orbited his brain.

Should he simply tell Howse the truth – insofar as he knew the truth? Or should he provide the evidence of Communist culpability that so many senior officers so desperately wanted? He was not, after all, absolutely certain that Political Commissar/Major Chang Hsi-lo had been the victim of a *Nationalist* conspiracy. It could conceivably, even plausibly if stretched, have been a *Communist* conspiracy, a violent episode in an internal leftist struggle.

Luke could easily enough turn the evidence on its head. He could even plausibly identify the corpse as a *Nationalist* ringleader. He could initially cite his own memory and then without any trouble find whatever 'proof' he needed in the disorderly files of the POW Command. If the hanged Chinese were indeed Nationalist stalwarts, then they would, logically at least, appear to have been murdered by Communist activists.

No one would even question the evidence, much less challenge so satisfactory a conclusion. He himself would then be off the hook – as would so many powerful men in so many distant capitals.

'I'll wait,' he repeated. 'Please don't lose my call.'

From time to time, I, Harland Birch, your storyteller, found it necessary to tell Luke Maynell that he was a hopeless romantic, a naïve idealist. He usually reacted with indignation, sometimes with feigned anger. But he would, after another drink, acknowledge that I was not entirely wrong.

Waiting to speak to Colonel Howse, Luke mused on my comment. He might indeed be a romantic and an idealist. But he was not suicidal. He would, of course, consider his own interests before committing himself to a dangerous course of action. He prized his practical streak, of which I saw little sign. Only the previous evening, he reassured himself, he had demonstrated his keen instinct for self-preservation.

A visit to Madame Chae's mansion on the heights over looking Pusan had been necessary. Although Luke had in good part prolonged his stay in Pusan in hopes of seeing more of Betsie, she had for a couple of days, he believed, been immured in the International Red Cross's little house on Koje itself. At any rate, he could not find her.

Yet he needed a break from Howse's constant pressure, as well as a respite from the even greater pressure of the decision he must very soon take. Besides, he had to keep in touch with the world outside the involuted and increasingly paranoid Prisoner of War Command.

It was, however, an off night at the house on the heights. Neither senior officers' jeeps nor diplomats and generals' sedans were parked outside. Luke wrestled off his combat boots in the vestibule in deference to the *tatami* mats within and padded into the lobby on the thick cushion soles of his GI socks.

In deference to the unseasonable warmth of the evening, Sue was attired informally, as she might be to greet a member of the family. She wore a blue-and-white-cotton *yukata* printed with the crests of Japanese noble families. Spying Betsie wearing a similar *yukata*, Luke was instantly delighted, though a moment later he felt sheepish. He had, he told himself severely, not really tried hard to get in touch with her since coming to Pusan two days earlier. At that same moment, he was by no means pleased to see Captain Chae Byongyup, who was, as always, dapper in his worn but perfectly fitting fatigues.

Fortunately, Chae Byongyup, whom they all called Tommy now, was on his way out. Luke was again pleased, for he could not talk openly in Tommy's presence. He had, of course, he further realized, come to the house on the heights to discuss his dilemma circumspectly with Sue, who could be extremely hardheaded. Betsie would now provide another viewpoint, one that he took very seriously.

Sue gave her half-brother a quick hug and a kiss on the cheek, as she would not have done had they not both been Westernized, but instead practiced traditional Korean manners. Luke was not pleased when Betsie, voluptuous in her thin cotton, tight-belted *yukata,* offered Tommy the same sisterly goodbye.

He did not, of course, comment on that over-fond farewell, though he was hurt by Betsie's casual welcome. She dutifully tilted her face for his kiss, but her lips were cool and unresponsive. Unquestionably straightforward and seemingly uncomplicated as ever, Betsie left him no doubt as to her displeasure.

'I'm absolutely *delighted* to see you, Luke!' she said, with heavy sarcasm. 'Glad you finally got around to me ... even if by accident. I heard you've been in Pusan for three days.'

'Only *two* days, Bets,' he answered awkwardly. 'I've been run off my feet ... under diabolical pressure. I just couldn't get to a telephone.'

'For two days? And then you come *here* first? Before looking for me?'

'You don't *know* that's so, Bets, do you? I reckoned I'd find you here ... at least Suja would know where you were. And it's absolutely true about the phone. First, I was dancing attendance on the worthy Colonel Howse. Then I was trapped at the POW Hospital. I couldn't phone from the mortuary.'

'It's hard to believe that for two days you—'

'All right, children, let's not quarrel!' Sue was commanding, although, just five foot two in her flat-heeled red slippers. 'Why the mortuary, Luke? What's up?'

Luke had not quite decided how he would answer that inevitable question, but he made up his mind on the instant. He would not overdo his candor. Nor would he dwell on either the historical significance of his assignment or the immediate risk of his provoking a bitter confrontation between the US and its allies. All in all, though, he assured himself, he could hardly find a more responsive audience than the two girls, who would undoubtedly be helpful and judicious. Nor, he could at least hope, find an audience more discreet.

Yet he was a little uncomfortable. Not about Suja, but, of all persons, Betsie, to whom he was already half-pledged. She had become a tough-talking militant patriot behind her delightful façade of amethyst-eyed *naïveté.* She had attacked him fiercely when he asserted his now even stronger conviction that the US should withdraw from Korea just as soon as it could.

They were in sharp disagreement. Betsie would, however, not utter a single word that might divert what was in her eyes the entirely righteous American endeavor from its present course. She would, therefore, not necessarily pass on his own hardening belief that the executions were a Nationalist plot.

However oddly, Sue was no more likely to do so. Despite her contempt for Syngman Rhee's corrupt regime, she, too, was a staunch patriot, a Korean patriot who hated the dictatorship in the North. A clash between Chinese and American propagandists might appear remote from her own immediate concerns. His search for the actual killers of the two Chinese POWs might appear irrelevant. Nonetheless, she would never say a word that could imperil United Nations' support for the Republic of Korea.

Sue poured Scotch from her apparently inexhaustible supply as Luke began to speak. Slowly at first, he outlined his dilemma, growing fluent as his own words defined the problem more clearly for himself.

Should he temporize to please his superiors – and to avoid unpleasant consequences for the US, perhaps for himself as well? Or should he tell the truth as he saw it – and damn the consequences? Where lay his true duty, Luke wondered, to the truth, an abstraction that might prove harmful, or to the gaggle of incompetent MP lieutenant-colonels and to slippery politicians around the world?

Betsie and Sue heard him through, intently considering the issue in silence. When he stopped, Betsie stubbed out her cigarette, took a pull on her highball, and spoke decisively.

'You may think I'm inconsistent. You may, probably do, think I'd advise whatever's best for our cause. But I'd say: *Tell the truth and be damned to the Nationalists.* Also, let the POWs make up their own minds, without that kind of pressure.

'It's an unpleasant dilemma, but I don't see that it's such a big problem! Not when you think it through. Our ... America's ... whole purpose collapses if you *don't* tell the truth, Luke. There goes our whole reason for being in Korea. Maybe I'm oversimplifying, but lying makes us as bad as *they* are. Anyway, as a practical matter, I can't see you living a lie. You're not the type.'

Regarding him with fond concern, she added, 'Luke, dear, I can see you're so worried. Why don't you see what Harland thinks? He's coming down tomorrow.'

'Are you nuts, Betsie, clean out of your mind?' Sue's topaz eyes glinted, and she set her drink, hardly touched, on the black-lacquer coffee-table. 'You might as well take full page ads in the *Richmond Daily Courier* and the *New York Times* as ask a newsman to keep quiet about something this big!'

'That's not fair, Suja,' Luke responded. 'Harland's sat on even bigger stories until he was ready to break them ... Anyway, I know what he'd say: *Tell the truth and shame the Devil!* He's conditioned to print the facts, just as surely as Pavlov's dogs were conditioned to salivate when they heard the bell. And, Suja, I think I know what you'll say.'

'It's a matter of life and death, Luke!' Sue rejoined. 'The battle for Korea's being fought in Washington and London and Canberra and Paris ... not just on the main line of resistance. We're struggling hard to hold onto worldwide support for the Republic of Korea.

'You're an officer of the United States Army and the United Nations Command. There's no question! It's your plain bounden duty – and the right thing to do. You *must* find what you've been ordered to find. You *must* come up with the right evidence.'

'We're beginning to sound like a freshman ethics class,' Luke rejoined with rather feeble humor. 'Sue, why should I take the lie on my conscience? Why should I lie on Howse's command? Why shouldn't I report the truth as I've found it – and let them, the brass, do the lying?'

Sue laid her hand on Luke's for emphasis and declared, 'There's no easy way out. Suppose you tell Howse what you think is the truth, could you really let the brass get away with lying about it afterward? Besides, you know damned well they'd order you to testify – their way. You can't unload the responsibility on Howse and the generals. They won't let you.'

Betsie was glowering at the hands on the table, Sue's resting on Luke's. He hurriedly withdrew to light two cigarettes, one of which he offered to Betsie, who took it with a strained smile.

'Either way, it'll be a *cause célèbre*,' she pointed out. 'Do you really want to be the point man for a lying campaign? You know damned well you'd be publicly leading the charge against Radio Peking. You're bound to be pushed forward in the Psywar battle. And all for a lie?'

'It's not only a question of ethics, Betsie,' Luke pointed out. 'This is real! It's not a moot case. I've got to make up my mind what to do in a crucial matter. Not just submit a term paper in a philosophy class.'

'Suppose it comes out later, as it's practically sure to?' Betsie asked. 'Suppose in ten years or so. You're a respected scholar and writer, perhaps a distinguished diplomat or, God forbid, a prominent banker. Then the truth comes out – and everyone knows you lied. Nobody would ever trust your word again. You'd be ruined.'

'Don't kid yourself, Luke,' Sue insisted. 'The problem is now, not in the unforeseeable future. Howse would murder his mother to get his star. If you don't knuckle under, he'll ruin you! He'll find a half-dozen different ways to destroy you. You're not fireproof, my friend. No one is. They could even kill you. They could easily get Syngman Rhee's hatchetmen to do the job.'

Luke smiled at that melodramatic warning, but Betsie looked grave and advised, 'All the more reason to tell the truth … very publicly. Then you'll be safe. Once you've spoken out, they wouldn't dare.'

'Don't be so sure!' Sue retorted. '*Accidents* do happen. Luke, do you really *want* to be a traitor … to break your oath of allegiance? That's your choice. Be a traitor who can't keep his mouth shut – and suffer for it right now. Or do your duty, hard as it is. Then you might, only *might*, get hurt ten years later! Anything else is wildly unrealistic.'

Betsie said softly, 'I never thought Sue and I would be so far apart. It's a nightmare, your being trapped this way. I'm so sorry, dear, but in the end it's got to be up to you.'

Luke forced a half-smile and said, 'It's clear. I've got to make up my own mind by myself. God knows what I would've done if you two had agreed – either way. As is, you're leaving it up to me with a vengeance!'

The young women hung on his words as if he were a judge on the point of delivering a crucial verdict that could shake the earth. They regarded him as intently as if he were a small boy whom they had to protect.

Luke laughed hollowly, only sipped his drink, deliberately lit another Lucky, and finally spoke. 'Getting right down to brass tacks, there is another question, just as Betsie says. How good a liar am I? Could I carry it off if I decide to lie?'

Somehow he now looked carefree, as if wholly in command of his life. The illusion of natural authority was strengthened by his long, lean jawline, his clean-cut, slightly arched nose, and his thinker's brow.

For a time, he actually succeeded in putting the dilemma out of his mind, giving himself over to the girls' deliberately diversionary chatter. He saw, nonetheless, that Betsie's eyes were fixed on him with grave concern and, evidently, deep affection. She had, it appeared, forgiven his not coming to her first of all. He wondered *what* he was to do about Betsie, whose ardent emotion, perhaps love, gave her a powerful claim on him.

The lamplight was dim, and Sue's eyes were secretive, in any event. He caught a hint of pity in her glance, perhaps something more than pity.

The atmosphere in the villa on the heights was charged with sensuality. The luckiest American in Pusan, perhaps in all Korea that night, he was sitting with two very attractive young women, both of whom were, at the very least, very fond of him.

Yet nothing could come of the desire that charged the air. He could take Betsie back to her billet, but she could not ask him in because of her Swiss bosses' Puritanism. The Mijin Hotel was out of the question at that hour. Besides, she had agreed to spend the night at Sue's villa on the heights.

As for Sue? Nothing doing there, now or any other night! Not that he expected anything. Not that he really wanted Sue, but only that his mind was moving that way of its own volition. He had never seriously considered Sue as a likely bedfellow, not for any length of time, not even when the lightning of lust had arced between them in the small garden.

Luke was abashed by his own lickerishness, though, he excused himself, danger was a great aphrodisiac. Not just the physical danger of war, but the moral threat that now hung above him. At any rate, regardless of what he might wish, regardless of his fantasies, he was tonight destined to be frustrated.

Sue went off to her bedroom after unrolling a sleeping bag for him in the living-room. Betsie lingered to kiss him goodnight in the darkened room.

When his hands became insistent, she slipped out of his grasp, whispering, 'Darling, I want you, too. I want you just as much … maybe even more. But with Sue here, what …'

He lay down alone on the *tatami* floor. It was some time before he fell asleep.

'I can connect you now, sir.' The Midwest twang of the operator of the Robust exchange jerked Luke out of his reverie. 'I'm ringing Colonel Howse.'

'Yo!' The unmistakable tones of Lieutenant George Miner squawked. 'Colonel Howse's line'

'Hello, George. Luke Maynell in Pusan. Let me speak to the colonel.'

'He stepped out for a moment, Captain. But I know he's anxious to talk with you. Can I get back to you in ten minutes?'

'No, George, I'm afraid not. Something's come up. I can't wait even a minute. I'll try later to—'

'Hold on, Luke. What should I tell the Old Man? He'll skin me alive if I tell him you called, but didn't leave a message.'

'Tell him? Why, tell him there's some interesting developments, very interesting. I hope to—'

Now faint and distant, Miner's voice interrupted. 'Can I at least tell him it's looking hopeful? I gotta tell him something. Tokyo's been driving us ape … The Commandant, no less than Brigadier-General Francis X. Dodd himself, he's talking about calling in the CID and the CIC. So far, the Old Man's stalled him … told him it's not that kind of case.

'Irregardless, you don't have much more time, Luke. Can I tell him it's looking hopeful?'

'George, then just tell him I should have a result very soon. Tell him it's looking interesting … hopeful.'

'Luke, you gotta give him more than that. Something specific.'

'What's that?' Luke shouted. 'What's that you said? You're fading … fading badly. By all means tell him that—'

Luke's thumb released the butterfly switch, cutting himself off. He was not going to be cross-examined by George Miner before he'd made up his mind what conclusion to report. Besides, he did, truly, have one more lead to follow.

'*Nin wei-shen-mo jyao wo, Shr-jang*? … Why did you send for me, General?' Luke was perched precariously on an orange-plastic stool. 'Why the note and this meeting? Why help your enemy?'

'Captain Lu Kuh, I have no intention of aiding my enemy, but even enemies should talk from time to time,' responded the middle-aged Chinese wearing the blue-striped robe of a hospital patient who was seated in a wheelchair. 'You must know our old saying: *Da da! Tan tan!*'

'Fight a little and then talk a little!' Luke translated in his mind. Winston Churchill, who had said most things better, had said this, too, better: 'Jaw jaw is better than war war!' However, the Chinese maxim did not imply a preference for talking over fighting. It meant that enemies could talk a while, then fight a while, then talk again, and then fight again *ad infinitum*. As Clausewitz could have said,

'Negotiation is a continuation of war by other means!'

'Why did I ask you to meet me?' the white-haired patient continued. 'Not solely because you speak good Chinese. Not only because you're investigating the abominable murder of my second-in-command, Major Chang Hsi-lo. You and I, we would have had to meet anyway.'

'General Li Mao, I'm glad to talk with you. But please don't flatter me. I have only a poor grasp of Chinese. And please do not think you can sway my loyalties. You can't win my co-operation so easily – now or ever!'

'Your loyalty wouldn't be worth much if I could. As I've already said, Captain Lu Kuh, we would have met in any event. It was inevitable! Think of yourself as a liaison officer, a go-between to your enemy.'

Luke was accustomed to charming, even dominating others, with his eclectic knowledge, his quick mind, his relaxed manner, and his authoritative air. His good looks – handsome enough, though definitely not pretty – touched women, but did not alienate men. So, too, his patent self-assurance.

He was not nearly as confident as he appeared. Who is? Regardless, he felt like a schoolboy when he talked for the first time with Major-General Li Mao, commanding officer of the secret Communist army in the Koje-do POW camp.

Li Mao was sucking greedily on a cigarette. He would, while they talked, go through two and a half packs from the ten-pack carton Luke had given him. Evidently the Chinese general, too, was not quite as self-assured as he appeared.

Little distinguished Li Mao from tens of millions of his countrymen; he could have been one of hundreds of thousands on the streets of Peking or Shanghai. He was spare, though tall for a Chinese of his generation at five foot eight. His thin lips were brownish-purple. His teeth were stained yellow by nicotine, the stub of his broken right canine almost brown. He looked commonplace, like a third-rank bureaucrat or a small-time merchant, except for the height of the forehead under his brush of white hair and the intensity of his luminous hazel eyes.

Luke felt the same power emanate from Li Mao that he had felt once in the presence of General of the Army Douglas MacArthur – just as strong, even without MacArthur's melodramatic props, his well worn, gold-strewn military impresario's peaked cap, his deliberately homely corncob pipe, and his dramatic dark sunglasses. No subordinate could fail to obey Li Mao implicitly. No one would dare flout his instructions as Luke was at that moment explicitly flouting the instructions of Colonel Lesward Murray Howse.

Luke warned himself that he must be careful, very careful, with this formidable antagonist. He had actually wondered for a minute or two whether to keep this clandestine meeting, which, the Communist general insisted, must be kept secret from all others. Luke had rapidly concluded that duty required him to meet the enemy leader – to draw from him all possible information regarding the murder investigation, as well as other matters.

Luke had found the note when he returned to the Bachelors Officers' quarters from Sue Chae's villa to shave and shower. He was conscientiously ruffling the bedclothes of his cot to conceal his overnight absence when he saw the envelope under his pillow. A Korean housegirl had probably been bribed to leave it there, but that was not his concern. The brief message in hand-written Chinese characters read:

Captain Lu Kuh
Information & Education Section
Prisoner of War Command, Koje-do

Esteemed Captain Lu,

I believe a meeting between us will be mutually useful.
*   I believe the former X-ray room is the best place to meet. I leave it to you to make the arrangements and to fix the time, which you will note on the reverse of this sheet.*
*   I shall be at the POW General Hospital for the next three days. Please leave this note crumpled on your dresser to signify agreement.*

Li Mao
Major-General
Chinese People's Volunteers

The eleven black pen-strokes of the signature were assertive. This was not a petition from a prisoner to his jailor, but a communication between equals. In truth, the peremptory tone implied that the Chinese considered himself the superior, as he was truly senior in both age and rank. It was further apparent that Major-General Li Mao enjoyed substantial freedom of movement. He could be where he wished when he wished, although his warders thought him securely confined within Compound 9 on Koje.

Li Mao had even designated the meeting place. Feeling himself summoned to a summit meeting with the enemy, Luke had lifted the cumbersome handset of his field telephone to call Second-Lieutenant Sidney Rosenstein at the POW Hospital.

Having been ordered to 'give immediate attention and total co-operation to all requests of Captain J.L. Maynell', Sid Rosenstein had been happy to assign the old X-ray room to Luke. Sid had himself driven in the nails that fixed to the door the sign that warned: *Off Limits to All Personnel. Radiation Danger!*

There they were now ensconced, secure against discovery or interruption. Luke replied to Mao's overture. 'General, you say even enemies should talk. What's to talk about?'

'Esteemed Captain, it is quite plainly appropriate for intelligent men to meet and to exchange ideas or simply to chat. Please do not make me doubt my judgement of your intelligence by feigning not to understand the reason.'

Luke smiled at those formal remarks, but did not reply. He entertained no illusion that he could manipulate, much less deceive, the Chinese general. Still, he would learn more by saying as little as he could and letting his antagonist speak out. Li Mao had called this meeting, and Li Mao could set the pace.

'I shall speak with candor,' the prisoner-general said at length. 'Not total candor, which is impossible to any man. However, I shall be as candid as is humanly possible. Nor shall I lie to you, Captain Lu.'

'Not lie in *your* terms?' Luke pounced. 'Or in *mine*?'

'In yours, my friend. I shall not deviate from facts as I know them.' An ironic smile illuminated Li Mao's narrow face. 'Not even when, in *my* terms, deviation is justified, nay required, for the greater good of the masses.'

'General Li, I believe you, though some would think me a fool to do so. Do, please, tell me *why*. Why not twist the facts? Why such candor?'

'Because the strict truth ... what you can call truth ... serves my purpose. Why pretend that the Chinese People's Volunteers are not, on the instructions of the Communist Party, waging a military campaign against the imperialists and their puppets *inside* the POW camp?'

Luke smiled wryly and replied, deliberately not quite straightforwardly, but circuitously: 'I am on my guard automatically when somebody promises spontaneously that he won't do something I never thought he would. From a man: "Luke, old pal, I'd never cheat you. Just trust me!" Or from a woman: "Luke, darling, I'll never leave you. I'll never give you a moment's worry!"'

'And each very soon does precisely what he's promised not to do.' Li Mao chuckled. 'However, your suspicion does not apply in this case.'

'Just what I'd expect you to say, General.' Luke too, was enjoying the clash. 'Do tell me why suspicion isn't on.'

'Simply, esteemed Captain, because you *expect* me to lie.'

'Of course!'

'When lies are expected, the best strategy is to tell the truth. In this case, as the bourgeoisie define truth. Candor can also be a powerful weapon. Stupid men who think themselves clever are easily deceived by the truth as spoken by men like myself whom they believe incapable of being truthful. Even easier to deceive are clever men who have learned, quite correctly, that truth to Communists is that which serves our cause. And I shall tell you the truth in *your* terms.'

'I'll try hard to believe you.'

'I see your difficulty. For you, of course, "principled behavior" means moral behavior. But sometimes it is necessary to deviate from apparent reality.

'You'll recall, of course, that the sage Confucius described as the natural rulers of mankind, the small number of princely men of great learning. Those virtuous savants are, as you know, the equivalent in our terms of Plato's philosopher-kings. Any rate, Confucius advised that those men need not believe in heaven or in gods. Indeed most would not. But those princely men *must* behave as if they did believe – in order to set an example for the people ... to lead them along the proper path.'

'Am I to take it that Confucius is *your* mentor?'

'I am Chinese, as well as Marxist-Leninist.

'That far more recent doctrine, Marxism-Leninism, dictates that restating reality to serve the great cause ... our ever continuing, unending revolution ... is a *principled* action!'

'And today?'

'Why should I try to deceive you when it is not necessary? I tell you candidly that I want to inflame your bourgeois conscience. You believe murder can never be justified. How then can you ignore the murder of two of my people? How can you let the murderers walk free? Unless, that is, you are, like myself, concerned primarily with political effect, rather than abstract justice.'

'You assume Chang Hsi-lo was murdered by the Nationalists?'

'Of course, Captain. Don't you?'

'Maybe so,' Luke smiled thinly and brushed back his wiry hair with his fingers. 'But you've got to prove it – in spades.'

'I'll do just that. I further tell you candidly that I *want* you to dissent from the official version. I *want* you to inspire widespread dissension within the POW Command. I *want* the scandal and also the publicity that will further my cause.'

'What makes you think I'll oblige?'

'Because you must!'

'Must? That's a strong word, General!'

'You must because you indulge your conscience.'

'And your crowd? Seems to me you've got *no* conscience at all.'

'That's a bourgeois lie. Marxism-Leninism and Mao Zedong Thought can justify ... often demand ... harsh decisions. We must cut deep to cure the patient. We must injure some who have done no wrong in order to save the masses. History sometimes requires what you may call lies or murder. Such deeds are actually revolutionary ruthlessness. Absolutely necessary, they are therefore moral ... principled ... actions.'

'General, that sounds like a lecture to freshmen just learning your ideology. What's it to do with me?'

'A great deal, although you march to a different drummer ... a drummer who beats a false measure. You are doomed by the inexorable march of history. Defending a rotten, hopeless *status quo*, you have only your bourgeois individualism to cling to ... your so-called conscience. And your conscience, Captain, requires you to tell the truth as you see it. Otherwise, you're a hypocrite and a liar, betraying your inner self.'

'Harsh words, General.' Luke leaned casually against the X-ray table. 'But why meet with me? I don't fully understand your motives, maybe not at all.'

'You're too intelligent not to understand. You're trying to draw me out – and I shall let myself be drawn.'

Luke regretted not having brought one of those new miniature wire-recorders. But they were too big to be hidden in a pocket. He could, otherwise, have had the X-ray room bugged to record this remarkable conversation. But that would have involved too many others – and would have left a paper trail of requisitions. His gut feeling told him to keep this meeting secret. Even Sid Rosenstein did not know who he was seeing.

'We're not fighting for land, you see, Captain Lu. Not after repulsing the American assault aimed at Manchuria. World public opinion is now our primary objective. By winning the fervent support of world opinion, we will force you imperialists to withdraw from Korea.'

'That's all very interesting, General Li,' Luke said. 'But I still haven't heard from you the facts about the executions.'

'I shall give you proof – and you will then be trapped. We'll then see whether you dare to act as your principles require.'

'Try me!' Luke did not know what he would do. 'Just give me the evidence.'

'Very well, Captain Lu. You are, of course, aware that Major Chang Hsi-lo was ordered to surrender to your side by his superiors in Peking. Are you also aware that he was assigned as my second-in-command?'

'I recognized him, saw he was a Communist activist. But there's no hard evidence.'

'Will this do to start?'

Li Mao leaned forward in his wheelchair and pulled a large brown-paper envelope from under his cushion. He extracted one piece from a sheaf of documents and without comment handed Luke a flimsy, much folded sheet of paper covered with small Chinese characters.

'Not the easiest reading.' Luke squinted at the scrawled characters. 'It'll take me a while.'

'By all means, Captain. I've put off all my appointments to the day after tomorrow. Take as much time as you need.'

Slowly mastering the spiky handwriting and the military-bureaucratic jargon, Luke finally said, 'A movement order from the Political Department of the People's Liberation Army, I make it. Political Commissar Chang Hsi-lo to make his way to Koje and report to you, the camp commander! Camp commander are you now, General?'

'In *our* terms, of course. Am I convincing you?'

'You could've forged this yesterday.'

'I could, though it's not my handwriting. Yes, I could have forged it. But, in truth, young Chang brought the document with him to prove his bona fides. Sewn into the lining of his jacket.'

'We can't turn every prisoner inside out … search every one to the skin. There are too many!' Luke replied defensively. 'But this is not enough. Even assuming it's genuine, which is a big assumption, it's still not definitive.'

'What of this? Definitely *not* carried by Major Chang.'

Dated 2 January, 1952, the letter written on coarse tan paper flecked with wood-chips was addressed to Comrade Major-General Li Mao. It advised him in terse officialese that Comrade Major Chang Hsi-lo would within ten weeks arrive in Koje-do under the name Huang Hsi-wu with the ostensible rank of junior sergeant.

Major Chang, whose thumbprint at the bottom of the sheet would confirm his identity, would bring vital new instructions from Peking.

'And how,' Luke asked casually, 'did you get this?'

'Nice try, Captain.' Li Mao grinned derisively. 'That information's classified. And don't bother asking what are those important new instructions. But you can take this with you to confirm Chang's identity by his thumbprint. That is, the corpse's identity. Are you convinced?'

'It's beginning to look—'

Li Mao slipped from the envelope a glossy five-by-four-inch black-and-white photograph of two men standing side by side on the balcony of the Tiananmen, the Gate of Heavenly Peace, in Peking.

'Chairman Mao Zedong, you will, of course, recognize. The other is—'

'Senior General Chang Wen-to, father of Major Chang Hsi-lo. We do sometimes do our homework, General. But why did Peking send you the photo?'

'Proof positive of both young Chang's identity and the validity of the vital instructions he carried. We are not slapdash ... I can also give you the culprits, the murderers, along with further evidence ... when next we talk.'

'I've got to think about it. I'm almost convinced. I'm sure the thumbprint'll match ... prove that the man they hanged was Chang Hsi-lo. But, I wonder, will the further evidence you've dangled before my nose also be convincing? Convince others?'

'Don't be obtuse, Captain. What else is bothering you now, aside from your tender bourgeois conscience, at keeping this meeting secret? Is it not reporting to your superiors?'

Luke winced at that sally, which had hit home. He rose and crossed the X-ray room, speaking again only as he turned the doorknob to let himself out.

'How do I know our talk won't be reported on Radio Peking?'

'You don't! No more than I can be certain that you haven't made a recording. We're forced to behave as if we trust each other.'

'That's where we started.' Luke laughed in spite of his unease. 'Tell me again, General. Why should we even pretend to trust each other?'

'Simply because this matter, even the quasi-judicial Chang Hsi-lo murder ... grave as it is ... is not as vital as our burgeoning relationship. I shall not sacrifice that relationship ... the long-term advantage ... for *any* other purpose.

'For your part, you will undoubtedly want to talk with me again as time goes by. Sooner rather than later, I believe. Now as for myself, I need someone I can talk with ... perhaps even trust, with prudent reservations, of course ... in the POW Command. Not one of those idiotic dunderhead colonels, those broken-down, fifth-rate flatfeet. *You!*'

Chapter XVI

It was in his genes. Major Anthony de Marco was music-mad – anything from Palestrina to Hindemith by way of such great composers as Scarlatti, Mozart, Verdi, Gershwin, Cole Porter, Richard Rogers, and a multitude of other music-makers. He had put up with the whiney ballads his men played endlessly in the bunker at the front. He had from time to time even caught himself enjoying the bald rhythms and the threadbare lyrics. Music was music.

On the main line of resistance, de Marco had to content himself with a hand-cranked phonograph that played only cumbersome old records, not even the new long playing discs. In his new billet near Pusan, only the best would do. He prized with almost religious devotion the sophisticated lash-up he had paid an Air Force radar technician $25 to put together from components bought at the big Tokyo PX: a Gerrard turntable, a Marantz amplifier, and a pair of three-foot-high Leak speakers.

The year 1952 was, of course, the beginning of the end of the electronic Ice Age. That was just before the Japanese relieved us of the bother of manufacturing such equipment – and got ready to put a hi-fi stereo set-up into every hooch in Vietnam with tape-deck, short-wave radio, and versatile player that could take a stack of discs: $33\frac{1}{3}$, 45 r.p.m., as well as old fashioned 78 r.p.m. Those stereos were probably responsible for more deaths than land-mines. The pounding drums and the screeching saxophones, their constant undertone, the grumbling diesel generators, drowned out any noise made by approaching Viet Cong assailants. By that time, too, Honda and Suzuki motorbikes were taking a heavy toll of South Vietnamese, soldiers as well as civilians.

I never wondered which side the Japanese were on. I knew! *Their own* – and be damned to everyone else! But what do you expect?

The giant Leaks were blaring 'The Oldest Established Permanent Floating Crap Game in New York' when Luke Maynell lifted the flap of the tent Tony de Marco used as both bedroom and office in preference to the crowded and cramped Pusan Headquarters in a deserted schoolhouse. *Guys and Dolls* sung by the Broadway cast on $33\frac{1}{3}$ r.p.m. long-playing records was the theme music for the discussion between de Marco and Luke, who had come directly from his conversation with Major-General Li Mao.

For decades thereafter, whenever Luke heard the refrain of the title song, 'The guy's only doing it for some doll!' he was to recall that moment. He was to smell again the sun baking the green-canvas tent; and he was to see again de Marco's neat Sicilian features gilded by the sunlight that kindled Lieutenant Karl Simon's fine blond hair. He was then to always remember with horror the deadly menace that lay just over the horizon on the sullen prison island of Koje-do.

Luke had stalled both his commanding officer, Colonel Lesward Murray Howse, and his self-appointed collaborator, Major-General Li Mao, by asserting that he needed more time. He was truly dissatisfied with the progress of his investigation. Besides, he felt he would have to know a lot more about Li Mao before he could properly assess the further information the Chinese general had promised to provide. Better informed, he might also understand better the complex game the general was playing with him – and with the POW Command.

Major Anthony de Marco, Luke's former commanding officer, was a possible key to the information Luke needed. Though a reservist, de Marco nurtured a host of friends, contacts, and informants along the military intelligence network from Seoul and Tokyo all the way to Washington and Brussels.

'Whaddya want, Maynell?' De Marco removed the cigar from his pursed lips and scowled. 'Can't you see I'm shit busy?'

Karl Simons smiled behind his superior's back and mimed, empty palms extended, that they had little to do.

Luke saluted snappily and replied, 'Well, Major, in that case I'll take myself off.'

'For Chris' sake siddown, Luke,' de Marco rumbled. 'What's this *Major* shit? You'd think we were in the army or something. What's up?'

'I've got a problem. And I need some answers fast.'

'Just spit it all out in Daddy's hand. Two heads're better'n one, especially if that one is your dumb head.'

'Thanks, Tony, thanks a lot.' Luke laughed. 'As always, gross flattery delivered with your world renowned finesse.

'Thing is, though, you'll be better off if you don't know the problem. It's very tricky, a loose cannon as the swabbies say at sea, a grenade with the safety pin pulled out.'

'Luke, my boy, you're asking me an awful lot. You're getting me involved willy-nilly, but you're not telling me diddley-squat. The risk? A quick, sharp pain like a blind date? Or is it life and death like Russian roulette? I wanna know: am I going to get my balls caught in a wringer?'

'Could be! I hope not. But, yes, you could.'

'Well, kid, tell me only as much as I need to know to help you out. But don't expect such blind faith ever again.'

'To hell with it, Tony,' Luke decided, 'I'll lay it all out for you and Karl. If I can't trust you two, who can I? But don't blame me if—'

'Sounds good to me.' Karl Simon's faintly guttural accent was a remote echo of the Black Forest. 'We're dying of boredom here.'

'Don't give away trade secrets, *Oberleutnant*,' de Marco scolded and then to Luke, 'Of course we'll blame you. Who else?'

He listened in intent silence while Luke described his investigation of the death of two Chinese prisoners of war, barely fudging over the identity of his own high-level POW contact.

'You didn't ask me for advice!' de Marco said, at the close of the tale. 'But I'll give you my advice anyway: *Tell Bird Colonel Howse, Commandant Francis X. Dodd, and the Supreme Commander Allied Powers in Tokyo to go fuck themselves! You've gotta play it straight! Shit or get off the pot! If you can't hack it, quit right now.*'

'They won't let me quit.'

'Then play it straight, kid. You're a lousy liar. Now whaddya want me to do?'

'I want to know everything you can possibly find out about Major-General Li Mao, the POW I'm talking with. Everything from his taste in women ... or boys ... to his hat size and his first-grade teacher's dental chart.'

'I suppose you want it yesterday?'

'Day before yesterday, Tony.'

The time difference between Pusan and Washington is fourteen hours, if you forget the extra day on the Asian side of the international dateline. Owing in part to that substantial time difference, it took thirty-six hours for de Marco to get the information Luke had requested – and, even then, it was not the full information Luke needed. Little more than name, rank, and a few posh assignments, it provided tantalizing clues as to Li Mao's authority and his likely purposes, but nothing remotely conclusive.

'If we knew that much about this guy,' de Marco had pointed out, 'you wouldn't be sniffing along his trail. There'd be no need to.'

Stalling the impatient Colonel Howse with increasing difficulty, Luke squeezed his informants among the POWs at the General Hospital and on Koje itself. Captain Chae Byongyup, pressed by Betsie, discreetly searched the files of ROK Intelligence. Although Sue was still urging Luke to manufacture the appropriate evidence and give his superiors the Communist scapegoats they wanted, she telephoned several ROK generals who had served with the Chinese Communists' Eighth Route Army against the Japanese. She also spoke to her mother.

A good deal of partial information on Li Mao was available, surprisingly quite a lot of new information in Korea. But no one had put the pieces together to form a coherent portrait – neither the US Central Intelligence Agency nor the Korean CIA and the ROK secret security police, neither the US Army's Intelligence Service nor the new Defense Intelligence Agency.

The contributions of de Marco's cronies were useful, but not central. The recollections of the ROK generals were valuable. Madame Chae's memory was invaluable, assisted as she was by the recollections of two Korean ladies she had known in Shanghai.

Luke let me see the assessment afterward, when it was all over. It was essentially a few good hard facts seasoned with a reasonable amount of conjecture. Taken altogether, it painted a partial portrait of an extremely complex and greatly gifted man, a multi-talented, much experienced, and highly capable officer.

Eye witnesses among the POWs commented that Li Mao had either been very clumsy or had deliberately allowed himself to be swept up in May 1951 by the high tide of the American advance. And he was *not* clumsy. It took no great leap of intuition to conclude that Peking had ordered Li Mao to let himself be captured. Presumably, Chairman Mao Zedong and Premier Zhou Enlai had foreseen that the thousands of People's Volunteers who were being captured, some actually surrendering of their own free will, could be for 'People's China' either a fearful problem or a powerful weapon. Therefore, it was surmised, the Chairman and/or the Premier had chosen Li Mao to sidestep the problem and to wield the weapon.

The man they chose was immediately available in a front-line division in Korea. He was a faithful crony, a deeply trusted, highly competent henchman, adroit and agile in action, ideologically staunch and politically sophisticated. He was also well acquainted with foreigners and their vagaries, as were very few of the senior leaders of Communist China. Moreover, he spoke adequate Korean as well as fluent English, a revelation that made Luke Maynell feel sheepish.

Li Mao had been born in 1905 in a village near Changsha, the capital of Hunan Province. Not far away lies the village of Shaoshan, where Mao Zedong was born in 1893.

The two were not only fellow provincials, but virtually from the same county, a strong tie in China, after 'liberation,' as well as before 'liberation'. That fact underlay the profound trust the Chairman reposed in Li Mao. Of course the Chairman never gave *all* his trust to anyone.

Li Mao's father was a grandee of the new commercial age that had burgeoned with large numbers of foreigners coming to China to trade, bringing with them foreign capital and foreign technology. (Mao Zedong's father was, by the way, a yokel, a minor landowner and a small-time money lender.) The elder Li, having resigned from the mandarinate, became the agent for Standard Oil in Hunan Province. Prospering amid the turmoil of the Warlord Era that followed the overthrow of the Manchu Dynasty in 1911, he sent his own son to St. John's University, which was run by American missionaries, in the International Settlement of Shanghai.

Through the even greater turmoil of the latter 1920s and the early 1930s, when Communists and Nationalists fought viciously for mastery of China, Li Mao himself prospered. He became a highly successful lawyer who often represented Chinese before the non-Chinese judges and the Chinese judges of the Settlement's Mixed Court. He occasionally represented a company that was in conflict with an individual, but his eloquence normally served the underdog. Despite the Settlement's conservatism, his crusading endeared him to the younger set, both Chinese and foreign, as did the American-accented colloquial English he had picked up at St. John's and had polished in the law courts.

Madame Kim Okcha, a Korean leftist who had worked for Li Mao and briefly been his mistress, remembered his joining Chinese Communist Party in 1929. The newly established Nationalist regime of Generalissimo Chiang Kai-shek was already showing distressing sycophancy to the wealthy and the privileged. Li Mao believed the Communist Party was the only hope of the oppressed. He was, moreover, not just idealistic, but quixotic: he joined the CCP when its fortunes were at a low ebb.

He was, however, clear sighted enough to recognize his own faults. He knew that he tended to act hastily on matters of principle and to seize, perhaps too quickly, opportunities as they arose, without necessarily allowing himself sufficient time for reflection. He had repeatedly assured Madame Kim Okcha that he had completely overcome such rashness. She was not convinced.

Li Mao was by that time an agent under deep cover of the illegal Communist Party's underground apparatus, and the CCP still, formally at least, maintained its headquarters in Shanghai. He was instructed to lead the life of a bourgeois lawyer who was something of a playboy. Whether in the law courts, at the racecourse, or on the tennis court, his function was twofold: to ferret out police plans in order to give early warning of raids against the underground; and to pass on tips regarding Chinese or foreigners who might readily be recruited to the service of the revolution. He was *not* employed in active operations.

Li Mao was happy in that essentially passive role. He even allowed himself to fall in love, thus confirming his Communist masters' view that he suffered from bourgeois weakness. Within a span of just three years, he married the daughter of a minor gold merchant, fathered a doll-pretty girl baby, and became a childless widower. A police sweep through the Chinese Nationalist-ruled northern districts of cosmopolitan Shanghai caught up his wife and daughter, who were visiting friends in a house that was suspected of being a Communist hideout, but was actually not. They both died in prison that same night.

Not all the official explanations could explain why two gentle, helpless females had been beaten to death. Nor could any forthcoming apologies or offers of monetary compensation assuage Li Mao's overwhelming grief. He suspected that his wife had been tortured to force her to reveal his underground activities – and that his daughter had been tortured to induce her mother to talk. Since his wife knew nothing of his clandestine life, she could offer her Nationalist captors nothing in exchange for the lives of her baby or herself.

Li Mao did not wait for the underground to confirm his suspicions. Neither, did he wait for the Nationalist Secret Service to advise the International Settlement Police of their suspicions regarding himself.

He fled Shanghai disguised as a crewman on a Yangtze River cargo-junk. Landing at Kiukiang, he worked his way through the cordon of tens of thousands of troops that the Nationalists' Extermination Campaign had thrown around Mao Zedong's Kiangsi Soviet Area. Awkward in the countryside, the city-bred lawyer of 34 was challenged four times and shot at twice. Once he blundered into a Nationalist sentry and, after a desperate struggle, bludgeoned the spindly soldier to death with the man's own rifle.

When he arrived in Juichin, the capital of the Kiangsi Soviet Area, his clothing was in shreds, and his wounds were oozing blood. The worst injuries had been inflicted by the rocks he fell upon and the brush that tore at him, rather than the all but expended bullet that struck his shoulder.

Limping and sore, Li Mao reported to the Committee for the White Areas, which, although so far away, sought to direct underground activities in the Nationalist-held cities. He found no one who was actively in charge, only a junior clerk who lacked the authority even to record his arrival, much less grant him permission to stay. Juichin may not have been in a total panic, but it was certainly in a hectic state of alarm as the Nationalist noose tightened.

No one was, therefore, even slightly interested in Li Mao's report on the situation in Shanghai, where other rival commissars contended. He was however, finally well received by the headquarters of the First Area Army of the Workers' and Peasants' Red Army, commanded by Mao Zedong's alter ego, General Chu Teh. After proving his bona fides to suspicious officers who were wary of enemy infiltration, he was given a position equivalent to second-lieutenant. The Red Army was packing up in order to break through the Nationalist cordon, abandoning Kiangsi Province.

Li Mao began the great escape from Juichin in the south-east to Yenan in the north-west as a platoon leader in a ragtaggle militia company. His own, personal Long March ended a year and a half later as a company commander in the bodyguard of Mao Zedong. Mao had recently been given the title 'Chairman' by a rump session of the Party's Central Executive Committee. All but one or two of the few present were Mao's utterly committed followers. Their careers, indeed their lives, depended on his patronage and his protection. Mao had warmed to Li as a fellow Hunanese, and Li Mao had delighted in intimidating the odd one or two recalcitrant members of the Central Committee to plump for Mao.

For the next ten years he was to fight the Nationalists often and the Japanese invaders occasionally usually as a line commander, but alternately as a political commissar. When the War in the Pacific ended in 1945, the Communists concentrated their forces against their true enemy, Chiang Kai-shek. Colonel Li Mao was sent to Shanghai to pose as a civilian refugee who had sat out the war in a remote village in the south-west. He resumed old contacts under his own name. During that time, he met Madame Chae, Sue's mother, through her friend Madame Kim Okcha, who was again his mistress.

The foreign-ruled International Settlement no longer existed. It had been returned to Chinese rule during the war, when the great powers voluntarily surrendered their privilege of governing foreign concessions under foreign law on Chinese territory. The Nationalist Secret Service proving somewhat more effective in running down Communist agents in Shanghai than the foreign-officered police had been, Li Mao was prudently reassigned to troop duty in 1947. He thus fought in the final battles of the Chinese Civil War as a commander in the field.

When Chairman Mao Zedong proclaimed the People's Republic of China from the balcony of the Tiananmen, the Gate of Heavenly Peace, in Peking on October, 1949, Li Mao was a brigadier-general commanding a division of the Communists' Fourth Field Army. A year later, when the Chinese People's Volunteers entered Korea to counter the American offensive that, as Peking was utterly convinced, aimed at invading China across the Manchurian border, Li Mao was a deceptively lowly sergeant-major in a former Nationalist division.

That unit had surrendered *en masse* when its commanding general was convinced of the justice of the Communists cause by gold bars worth $100,000. It had then been taken into the Fourth Field Army. Informed early one morning that they were no longer a unit of the People's Liberation Army, but were now serving as Chinese People's Volunteers, the troops had marched across the bridge from Antung into Korea that same night.

Li Mao's responsibility was in a sense global, that is, to assess the capability and the effectiveness of that new expeditionary force of the Liberation Army, the Chinese People's Volunteers. His immediate assignment was to test the loyalty of the former Nationalist division and to assess the performance of its green young Communist officers. He found both qualities barely satisfactory even for a unit that was hardly more than cannon-fodder, deployed to sop up the enemy's fire-power before more politically reliable, better trained divisions were committed.

Having already taken a great step downward in his apparent rank, he reverted to the rank of private in order to infiltrate the POW camp on Koje-do. He was to take command of the Chinese prisoners, who had apparently been neutralized by capture. He was charged to transform those POWs into an aggressive army that would mount a major campaign of psychological warfare.

I, Harland Birch, your narrator, know from Luke's extensive reminiscing about the surprisingly candid talks he had with the Chinese General that Li Mao accepted his nominal demotion and his taxing assignment with only minor misgivings. Li Mao had, after all, a remarkably varied career – as fraught with danger as it was rich with opportunity for advancement.

Luke and he had forged a strange relationship. Though they began as avowed enemies – and ended their confidential discussion still enemies – certain sensitive subjects they dared discuss only with each other.

Beyond the normal restraints of caution because they were both by and large acting independently, both recognized that they were bound to each other, above all, by enmity. Their ideals and their principles, as well as their immediate interests, were in conflict. Their unblinking acknowledgement that they were enemies and, barring a miracle, would remain enemies somehow made their long talks cordial.

Relieved of pretense, they were frank. Li Mao chuckled when he told Luke that Chairman Mao Zedong had observed to Premier Zhou Enlai: 'Being a POW ... it'll take old Li Mao down a peg or two ... keep him out of trouble. At least, it'll force him to control his weakness for women.'

Li Mao protested mock-indignantly. 'What a pair to censure me for womanizing! Mao's had four wives and God knows how many concubines, practically a new virgin every night. Zhou's been a lifelong monogamist, largely because his wife is the brains of the pair. But, while she's out doing Marxist-Leninist good works, he revels in the affection he inspires in the ladies, especially his pretty secretaries and interpreters.'

Li Mao puffed contentedly on a Lucky and said, 'A few months after I took up my duties here, they made me a major-general. Of course, it was a secret promotion, like the Pope's naming a cardinal *in petto*. I may be the only major-general who's ever had word of his promotion while he was sewing the soles back on his only pair of shoes.'

General Li Mao was the veteran of a hundred battles and a thousand intrigues, a merciless political infighter, a master of subversion and propaganda. The UN was represented by a callow temporary captain half Li Mao's age. It was hardly an equal contest.

Li Mao is austere, dedicated, and incorruptible. [So read the final report made by Luke Maynell and ignored by his superiors.] *He is deeply compassionate when he allows himself to be, but never at the expense of his duty. He has repeatedly feigned spontaneous indiscretion in order to make me sympathetic – and thus draw me to indiscretion.*

He is, as a human being, altogether admirable, possessing humor and wit leached of malice. His passionate nature hates injustice.

As a political animal he is the unswervable agent of a conspiracy that would stamp out all such admirable qualities in all men and women in order to transform them into robotic fighters for the Marxist-Leninist Maoist revolution.

Li Mao is, further, untouchable. He is beyond influencing or intimidating by any means available to the UN Command, not even prolonged solitary confinement or threat of execution.

The danger he poses to the UN war effort through the resurgent POWs would not end if he were replaced by a new underground commander. The threat might well become more damaging.

Aside from his confrontations with his enemies, ROK and US, Li Mao employs only as much force as is necessary to control his troops. A successor who lacked Li Mao's integrity and personal prestige could not enforce stringent discipline so lightly. The present orchestrated campaign could turn into a permanent riot – anarchy behind barbed wire.

I have just heard [Luke had added a last-minute footnote] *that Li Mao has a brother considerably younger than himself who is also a prisoner.*

Chapter XVII

Captain John Luxborough Maynell regarded Colonel Lesward Howse as a comic figure: blustering, ineffectual, clumsily ambitious. His mental portrait of his commanding officer was a crude caricature: sawn-off legs ending in enormous, flap-soled combat boots; pendulous paunch waggling to a fat man's awkward strut; a long, sharp nose colored bright red – by alcohol as much as by nature.

Howse was to Luke an unwitting clown, an unintentional humorist, a figure of fun. But definitely not a court jester. He was not shrewd or quick-witted enough for that role, and he was, besides, too much of a lickspittle.

Luke was forced to re-examine that assessment when he was summoned by the colonel to return to Koje a week after the fiasco at the brothel. While Luke stood braced at attention, Howse took up on his desk a model tank made by POWs from old beer cans, which normally perched beside his mother-of-pearl-inlaid nameplate. He swivelled the shiny brass turret, pointing the long cannon at Luke's head and barked jovially, 'Boom, boom! You're dead!' Luke realized at that moment that he had walked into an ambush, had, perhaps, ambushed himself.

The colonel was actually anything but jovial. He was actually in a cold rage, judging by the reptilian flatness of his pale-blue eyes behind his rimless lenses and the flush that crimsoned his cheeks and his wattles. Howse was evidently not only outraged by Luke's tedious, step-by-step report of his investigation and his still tentative conclusion that the Nationalists were responsible for the kangaroo court and the quasi-judicial murder of two Communist *honchos*. With a sickening lurch into self-blame, Luke realized that he had baited a trap for himself by underrating his boss.

Colonel Howse was today no figure of fun. He was nothing like the laughable incompetent booby Luke had lampooned at Madame Chae's parties, laughing at his own wit, unable to resist the dangerous temptation to be clever. Today, Colonel Lesward Murray Howse was quite shrewd enough, *too* shrewd. And all his guns were trained on Captain John Luxborough Maynell.

Whatever Howse was by nature – Pagliacci or Figaro, Falstaff or King Lear, perhaps Charlie Chaplin – his so recently enhanced power, though still hardly huge, had transformed him. His accrued authority since his reassignment to Koje, had altered him significantly, though not by anywhere the same measure as the vast power, the inherent authority, and, above all, the absolute responsibility of the presidency had transformed Harry S-for-nothing Truman. Still, Lesward Howse, too, had grown into the role assigned him. Fear that his ambition would be thwarted edging his voice, rage glittering in his watery eyes, he was formidable.

'I've been hearing some peculiar reports about your activities, Captain,' Howse barked. 'I want one thing fully understood: I am running this operation here, *not* you ... *I* ... *I* ... not *you* and your slant-eyed friends. *I* am in charge, *not* a raggedy-ass temporary captain with his gook stooges. *I I I* ... not *you!* Is that clear?'

'Yes, sir.'

'Another thing, Maynell. It seems you're not only a frequenter of low brothels ...' Luke winced at the shameless charge 'but also a menace to respectable God-fearing ladies.'

'Colonel?' Luke managed to inject an interrogatory yet indignant note into that single word before a glare silenced him.

'Be quiet until I've finished!' Howse ordered. 'And stand at attention. Nobody gave you an at ease. Brace it, Captain.'

'Yes, sir.'

Luke swallowed his anger at that bizarre accusation and stood to rigid attention. It would be unpardonably stupid, even foolhardy, truly dangerous to show his contempt for his overblown, unspeakable commanding officer.

His father's powerful friends could protect him from any grave charge that the colonel might dream up, but no one could protect him from lesser charges or from the day-to-day harassment that could make his life miserable.

By the letter of the Code of Uniform Military Justice he was undeniably insubordinate. A scornful word just now, even a disdainful glance, could entangle him in the gears of the ponderous machinery of military justice. Once drawn into that mincing machine, he could not struggle free without suffering some wounds and, worse, wasting aeons of time.

'The commandant called me, General Dodd himself.' Awe deepened the Colonel's squeaky voice. 'He's had a complaint from a lady ... one Madame Chae who's close to the ROK Government. She says you're pursuing her daughter, her *innocent* daughter with *indecent* proposals. You're insulting ... outraging ... Korean womanhood.'

To Luke's astonishment, one glacial, yet glaring eye was momentarily veiled by an eyelid. Revelling in the sadistic exercise the GIs called 'chewing ass,' the colonel had nonetheless winked at him.

'Now, Luke, you and I know what that means.' Howse's tone was deeper, almost warm. 'It's a crock, a load of horseshit. Who ever heard of an *innocent* Korean dame over eight? They're all whores, natural whores.'

He pronounced the word *hoors,* as did the ex-cops who were his cronies. He was now resuming his new, racy diction with the apparent cooling of the fury that had initially led him to speak to Luke with stiff, pretentious formality that was professionally pompous, anything but colloquial.

'All gook broads're born hoors. But we gotta keep the ROKs sweet. So I'm bawling you out ... formally reprimanding you. Y'get me?'

'Yes, sir.' Luke had heard his brother officers discourse on Korean morals too often to feel more than a flicker of irritation. 'Is that all, sir?'

'It's damned well not, Captain. Just the beginning. I'm keepin' it out of your 201 file, keepin' it off the record, for your sake. I'm covering your fuckin' ass. But I'll tell you straight from the shoulder, I personally am *very* pissed off at you. With me you stand lower'n a snake's belly. You're a fuckin' traitor ... a Commie-loving pimp.'

Luke stood at attention through the tirade, which Howse closed by demanding, 'Well, Captain, nothing to say for yourself?'

Luke was silent, overwhelmingly humiliated by a man he considered a buffoon, until Howse, after a long expectant silence, exploded in vintage MP-speak. 'If you got nothin' to say, I got lots! This fancy report of yours, this fairy-tale, I'll junk it ... shove it into the circular file. Like I said, I'll cover your ass. But you gotta catch me them Commie murderers toot sweet. Yesterday's not soon enough.'

'Sir, I'm very sorry, but I can't invent evidence.'

Luke knew he was expected to express his gratitude for Howse's protecting him. He was, moreover, expected to shelve his preliminary report, since it would undoubtedly arouse wrath in high places if it were sent through normal channels. Clearly, Howse was covering his own ass first. But Luke could not placate his commanding officer by promising to co-operate – and to fabricate evidence proving the guilt of non-existent Communist criminals. He deserved no credit for rectitude and courage. He simply could not lie convincingly.

'There's no evidence,' he reiterated, 'and I can't make it up.'

'Whadda ya mean, Captain? I don't get your drift.'

'Just that I can find no Communist involvement in—'

'Couple or three dead ones'll do ... I'm not looking for living sacrifices.' The colonel returned to his original formal diction. 'Nonetheless, I *must* have the names of the culprits immediately.'

'I'm very sorry, Colonel. But it looks like the Nationalists—'

'Don't even breathe it!' Howse was horrified. 'It *has* to be the Commies. It *cannot*, I repeat for your sluggish, tardy comprehension, *cannot* in any wise be the Nationalists. How can I possibly report that my protégés ... the star pupils of my Information and Education Program ... How in the name of all that's holy can I report they've taken up murder as an extracurricular activity?'

Howse halted in mid-tirade and then asked in his assertively GI mode, 'Ya gone ape, Captain? Gone bananas, have ya? Or do you figure I'm loco?'

Anything Luke could say would bring down even greater wrath on his head. Besides, he was bound to sound prissy and prim, a prude and a prig. He took refuge in silence again.

'How'd you like to be a major, Luke, my boy?' The honeyed bribe dripped into the air drop by drop. 'There's a slot in my table of organization I could justify you're filling.'

'Too much honor, sir.'

Howse's eyes popped like ripe blueberries, and his purpled lips parted in amazement. He stared at Luke, frankly suspicious of his subordinate's motives. He, who lived for promotion, could not believe that any sane officer, even a temporary officer, would not grab an offer of advancement to field grade. And all Luke had to do was apply a little bit of butter, a smidgen of polish, simply put a different gloss on a few paltry words.

At last, the enpurpled lips snapped shut, the red-mottled eyelids again drooped, and the rimless glasses were lifted off the long pointed nose. Needlessly polishing the square lenses with his stiff-starched olive-drab handkerchief, the colonel spoke meditatively, as if to himself.

'In that case, you leave me no choice.' The formal diction revealed intense agitation. 'If it were not for your ... ah ... other duties, it would be different: *I'd make your life totally, irredeemably, irreversibly miserable. I'd break you to corporal!* As is, I'll—'

'Yes, sir?' With a characteristically Yaley interrogatory rising inflection, Luke broke the Colonel's prolonged pause, which was clearly intended to be the ultimate threat that would compel compliance. 'Yes, sir?'

'You know I don't have the time to brush up my Japanese. Otherwise I wouldn't need you, Captain Maynell. But one thing I know damned well: The Japs ... the Chinks ... they don't trust any roundeye who learns their language well. Figure he's too slick ... bound to be a shifty character. The Japs and the Chinks're damned well right. Just look at yourself.'

The colonel was recovering his equanimity and resuming his outmoded slang. 'Well, anyhow, ol' buddy, that's another story. Right now, Maynell, I'm shipping your sorry ass to Seoul on TDY. Your spook pals wanna talk to ya. Get your miserable carcase on the next airyplane. I don't wanna see your skinny ass around here a single, sorry second longer. If I do, I'll whup it good. Get the God-damned hell outta here!'

So ended the encounter – neither with a bang nor a whimper, but with a soft whoosh like the air escaping from a child's balloon.

Colonel Howse did not push the issue farther. Captain Maynell did not swear to tell the world the truth as he saw it regardless of personal consequences. Yet each had stood his ground: Howse would not drop his demand that Luke falsify the facts or, at least, promise to remain silent if another officer invented evidence to frame Communist culprits. He was still astonished that Luke had without a second's hesitation turned down a promotion at which most junior officers would have jumped.

It would have pleased Luke's father to see him a major at twenty-seven. But, he pondered, did he really want to please his father that much?

Anyway, there were no heroics. The antagonists had reached an accommodation, a tacit understanding to stop sniping at each other. It was, however, at best an armistice, a temporary ceasefire rather than a permanent cessation of hostilities.

*

Luke told me, Harland Birch, about that bitter exchange when he turned up in Seoul the same night and demanded a bed in the Press Billets. Usurping my function as chronicler and arbiter, he analysed the impasse with surprising objectivity.

'You know, Harland, the score's zero-zero. Look's like a draw, but we both lost. Looks as if Howse's afraid to buck me. Maybe thinks I've got a lot of drag in Washington. Maybe he thinks I'll help push his promotion if he scares me rigid and then lets me off the hook. It'll be a cold day in Hell when I push a promotion for Colonel Howse.'

'You think you've got him stymied?'

'Not really. He's not getting the frame-up he wants ... needs ... desperately ... to feed his dream of a star. And me? I fumbled the chance to make a big stink ... just let it go by.'

'Do you really want to spill the beans about Howse's framing some pro-Communist POWs?'

'For Chris' sake, Harland, don't write a word now. I haven't got all my ducks lined up yet. Can't really prove it. That's why I didn't defy Howse ... didn't threaten to take it higher myself. Anyway, it's the last thing in the world the brass wants to hear right now.'

'You *are* worried about pleasing the generals?'

'Hardly! Well no, not really! But the evidence isn't all in ... sure as hell isn't conclusive. I'd look like a prime jerk if I blew the whistle and then couldn't prove my case. Besides, I *cannot* speak to the Press. It's a court-martial offense in my present job.'

'No need to quote you ...'

'Don't be an idiot, Harland. Who else could it come from? Anyway, if *you* file that story, everybody'd know exactly where you got it.'

'True enough,' I conceded. 'What're you going to do?'

'I'll worry about that later. I'm in deep shit already, thanks to Bird-Colonel Howse, who couldn't command a platoon, much less a regiment ... Then this business with Suja, the nonsense Madame Chae made up. Chae Byongyup's going to come at me with a samurai sword. Betsie's so sore she's not speaking to me. Also ...'

'Any truth in it?'

'Goddamn, Harland, what do you think? Of course, not! Though Suja's no vestal virgin.'

I didn't ask Luke how he knew.

'Well, we, Sue and I, are a little closer now,' he conceded, evidently unaware that he had for the first time called her by the name she preferred. 'Sue's a great girl ... tough and brainy. But that's all. No hanky-panky!'

Luke was not wholly candid. Sue and he had not slept with each other. Not yet! But they didn't have to bed down together to become intimates, the closest friends – as Betsie knew well and was, therefore, very worried.

Madame Chae's evident fear that Luke would ruin her daughter's life was, nonetheless, rather fanciful. For an ardent Stalinist and a strong egalitarian,

Madame Chae took an old fashioned view of the consequences of a Korean girl of good family becoming the mistress of an American officer. But Madame Chae was also a Maoist and thus, *ipso facto,* a racist. She was, however, an unreconstructed bourgeois in her present views on sexual morality, certainly at the very least as they applied to her own daughter.

In her mother's eyes, Sue was already suspect because of the years she had spent in the United States with no respectable Korean matron to keep a wary eye on her. Madame Chae was, however, also a realist. She knew that the GI's blatant racism was only a pale-faced version of a Korean's bone-deep racism. Even worse than marrying a Japanese, the worst transgression a respectable decent Korean woman could commit was cohabiting with an *American.*

Naturally, the more we did for the Koreans, the more they despised us. They wouldn't have been human if they hadn't. How else could they repay our benevolence except with resentment, scorn, and hatred? Of course, American benevolence was frequently accompanied by hectoring, sometimes by unreasonable demands, even occasionally by impossible demands.

Of course, the GIs did some terrible things—like any soldiers fighting a nasty war a long way from home. But mass atrocities were virtually unknown, maybe one or two altogether. The war of attrition simply did not offer the combat troops many opportunities to be beastly to civilians.

Besides, the rear-echelon GIs made their own arrangements for home comforts 10,000 miles away from home. Violence was hardly necessary when a Monkey Ward catalogue was such a potent force.

When Luke turned up in Seoul in disgrace I sensed something missing from his story. He was uncharacteristically mum, keeping quiet about some major element in the imbroglio. I was not to learn what he was concealing until some years later.

Luke's passivity in the face of his colonel's bullying just didn't ring true. The Luke Maynell I'd known so well at Yale would not have accepted such a tacit compromise, however temporary. That Luke would have charged the barricades.

The Luke Maynell I knew in Korea was at heart the same idealistic firebrand, careless of his own welfare in his passion for truth and justice. Yet he now appeared content simply to distance himself from the colonel's plot. He could not spike the colonel's guns. He could not stymie the conspiracy to railroad a few innocent POWs, Communists' tools though they might be, for a double murder committed by pro-Nationalist POWs, who were, he knew but could not prove, goaded by Nationalist agents from Taiwan.

Luke was obviously leery of offending Colonel Lesward Murray Howse further. If he goaded Howse, he would not long remain in Pusan to carry on his complicated amours with Betsie Howard and, now, for all I knew, with Sue Chae as well. But Luke was still the same knight errant I had known in New Haven. Personal convenience, even personal passion, would not deter him from duty.

'He just doesn't care that much about people,' his old flame, Mary Kaye

Sommers, had told me bitterly. 'Not the way he cares about ideas. He'll always sacrifice an individual or a relationship to an abstract ideal. He'll sacrifice himself, too. Ruthlessly!'

No, Luke wasn't wholly candid when he turned up in Seoul. He certainly wasn't candid about the 'other duties' to which, he let it slip, Howse had alluded in passing. In fact, he didn't say another word about those duties.

No point in pressing him. Not that he'd lie. He'd just go silent or talk of other things.

I wondered particularly why he'd said it was a court martial offense to talk to the Press 'in my job'.

Of course, the Army didn't like soldiers' talking to trouble-making correspondents without clearance, whether those soldiers were PFCs or colonels. But the army couldn't keep free-wheeling Americans from exercising their constitutional right to make fools of themselves if they pleased. No more could the army ensure that outspoken Americans spouted the official line. It could not court martial every man who stepped over that line.

What, I wondered, was biting Luke?

He finally told me a few years ago about the 'special duties' he had shared with Lieutenant Sidney Rosenstein, whom the ineffable Colonel Howse called 'the little Hebe who *honchos* the POW Hospital'.

Both had been doing chores for the Central Intelligence Agency, though neither had received a penny more than his regular pay. Both had, however, enjoyed the privilege inherent in that duty: far greater freedom than other junior officers, a license to make their own duty schedules.

Lesward Howse was thoroughly frustrated, unable to lean heavily on his subordinate. Howse had been ordered to tolerate Luke's erratic movements. Howse had also been ordered – to his fury – not to press Luke for his refusal to fake evidence. Nothing was to interfere with Luke's other assignment.

In those days, when few if any Americans recoiled from working with the CIA, its influence was far greater than it is today. Even the brass hats yielded without too much fuss to a request, not really even pressure, from the CIA. The agency and the army were allies in Korea, not the bitter rivals they were to become in Vietnam. A good word from the spooks might even give Lesward Murray Howse a boost toward his star.

Luke Maynell and Sid Rosenstein were recruiting officers for the CIA.

Luke was on the lookout for likely men to be trained in espionage and sent back to mainland China as agents. Potential agents had to disappear without a trace, lest such busybodies as the International Committee of the Red Cross, unwittingly assisted by guileless Betsie Howard, raise questions about their fate.

It was not only prisoner *honchos* who could make men vanish as if they had never existed.

Rosenstein in turn expunged those men from the records of the POW Hospital, where they were ostensibly sent to die. They died only on paper.

Decades later, when Luke told me about his 'special assignment', he still could not understand why the POW Command had not used the same cunning to plant their own spies among the POWs. If they had, the subsequent disasters might have been averted.

At any rate, the operation Luke and Sid Rosenstein ran was called Lazarus. The CIA was confident that Peking's counter-espionage service would get no clue from that code name. Communist spy catchers, the Americans believed, did not read the Bible. I rather suspect they did.

Luke was happy to turn his hand to recruiting agents. Espionage was not, even in those simpler days, a way of life Luke wished to pursue indefinitely. He was, however, confident at the time that he was thus serving both the American people and the Chinese people.

Above all, he wished for peace through mutual understanding between the United States and the People's Republic. Better knowledge of each other was a prerequisite for such understanding. Yet both were zealously cutting off their remaining lines of communication, each sealing itself to prevent the other's infecting it with subversive ideas. The Sino-American relationship was then, as it is now, intensely emotional – and essentially irrational.

The Americans had to recruit their own agents – or remain dependent on the Nationalists for detailed information on China from the golden rooftops of the Forbidden City to the rice-roots in distant provinces like Shansi and Yunnan. Unfortunately, the Nationalists were dedicated to 'reconquering the mainland'. Their intelligence assessments were blighted by wishful thinking or were deliberately distorted for American consumption.

Only five agents out of several score planted by Operation Lazarus in mainland China ever reported back to their handlers. And the others? Some were undoubtedly caught. The Central People's Broadcasting Station, otherwise Radio Peking, often trumpeted the good news of the arrest and execution of 'agents of the American imperialists and the remnant Chiang Kai-shek Fascist clique.'

Luke never knew if it was he who had recruited those unfortunates, since he was not privy to their cover names. Nor was he ever to know whether the efforts of Operation Lazarus ever produced useful information. He allowed himself to assume, however, that Lazarus, like most such operations, had from time to time found a nugget among the rubble.

Luke's 'special duties', as I learned later, also justified the hours he spent fencing verbally with Major General Li Mao, the commanding officer of Mao Zedong's sixth column, the underground Chinese army, on Koje-do. Luke never truly believed that he would in time turn Li Mao around. How could he even hope to transform the intimate confidant of Chairman Mao Zedong into an American agent of influence?

Luke did not delude himself. But he was not loath to delude the camp command, whom he all but convinced that Li Mao was on the verge of turning.

Luke's individualism was tolerated by the collectivist army with gritted teeth. Luke was not merely valuable. If he were, the generals would not have so long overlooked his continual insubordination. He was invaluable, the only American officer available with both the language ability and the political sophistication to recruit agents to spy in China. He was, therefore, for a time that rarest of creature, that all but non-existent being, the truly indispensable man.

After an hour-long search, Luke finally found in the tangle of backstreets behind Namzahmon, the old South Gate of Seoul, the particular small, gray-tile roofed houses miraculously still standing in the gutted city. Unimaginatively, the slip of unpainted wood on the doorpost bore the most common Korean surname of all: Kim, meaning Gold.

'Just call me Mr. Gold,' directed the tubby, middle-aged man lounging in an orange-tufted easy chair, its horsehair stuffing escaping from a half dozen holes. 'Or, if you prefer, Colonel Gold.'

The invitation was delivered in a Central European accent by a man who was certainly not a colonel in the US Army or any other army, despite the shiny new eagle on his collar. His brand new olive-drab shirt, two sizes too big, still bore the creases of its original packing, but displayed neither medal-ribbons nor unit patches. Besides, his features were somehow unmilitary; the bulbous nose and the full lips might pass, but not the habitual expression of benevolent though intrusive inquisitiveness.

Beside the synthetic colonel, Luke saw a figure he had last seen on Koje-do a week earlier. Raymond Wu, seated on an equally dilapidated foot-stool, was a civilian interpreter from Taiwan.

Luke had known Raymond's father in China. He was called Speedy Wu for the bulky Speed Graphic press camera he carried everywhere. China's most famous news photographer in peace, as well as war, Speedy Wu was straightforward and fair. He was also scrupulously honest, except when he was snapping propaganda pictures like the infant weeping on railroad tracks the Japanese had just bombed. Speedy had slapped the symbolic orphan to make him cry. His son Raymond, who now wore impeccable tailored fatigues, had evidently inherited his father's less admirable traits.

Luke came to rigid attention and snapped a salute all but Prussian in its stiff angularity. Colonel/Mr. Gold stared in surprise. His soft brown eyes widened in astonishment when Luke turned on his heel and left the house. Although inured to the antics of his temperamental agents, Gold did not expect quite such eccentric behavior from a captain in uniform. Resignedly, he pursued the maverick through the muddy puddles of the broken road and steered him into the house's minuscule backyard.

'Sir, I resign,' Luke said. 'Please send me back to troop duty.'

'Don't be ridiculous, Captain Maynell, You can't resign. And I can't send you back to troop duty. You don't think I'm a real colonel, do you?'

'No danger, Mr. Gold!' Luke grinned. 'Nobody could make that mistake.'

'Thanks, my friend. I'm deeply relieved. Now, tell me, what's all this nonsense?'

'How can we discuss my assignment in front of Raymond Wu? He may not be an enemy agent, but he's certainly not one of us.'

'Mr … ah … Captain Maynell, Mr. Wu is going with you.'

'Not with me, he's not. If he's going anywhere, he's going alone.'

'Why so recalcitrant?'

'I don't trust young Master Wu. His priorities … his bosses' priorities … are different from ours. He's working for Taiwan, not for us.'

'He's supposed to assist you … take some of the burden off your shoulders.'

'You're sending me to the front to look for likely agents among the just captured Chinese POWs, sir?'

The man called Gold nodded and explained further: 'Before they get into the POW works. So no one knows what's become of them, except that they're missing or dead. Your friend General Li Mao's pipeline to Peking is too good. Most of your recruits from Koje've been blown before they got anywhere near the mainland of China.'

'I can do the job alone far better … without compromising security. Just give me a jeep-driver and a half-dozen cases of booze to oil the boys at the front.'

'Done, Mr. Maynell. I like a man who knows what he wants, even if his tastes are strange, as the prima donna Lola Montez said to mad King Ludwig of Bavaria. Come back tomorrow, and I'll have everything you want. Also more specific guidance … instructions. For now just go away and let me explain to Mr. Wu that signals've changed … that neither you nor he is going anywhere.'

The next afternoon Luke Maynell and a chatty corporal called Harry Jackson left Seoul for Chorwon on the west central front. Luke yawned and lit a Lucky, happy to let a driver wrestle with the slippery plastic steering-wheel as the jeep bucked and skittered on the deep-rutted, occasionally shell-pocked dirt road. The poppies, he noticed idly, were opening in the deserted fields on either side of the road, tiny blood-crimson drops against the scarred dun earth.

He was mulling over the detailed shopping-list of human beings handed to him in parting. It was intimidating.

Men were wanted to operate on their home ground: the metropolises of Peking, Shanghai, and Canton, also most specifically the provinces of Sichwan, Yunnan, and Lioaning. To cap the list, agents were needed who were natives of Sinkiang Province, whether themselves Uighur or Han Chinese by race and culture. Badly needed were such natives of the 'autonomous Uighur region' of Sinkiang in the remote north-west where nuclear weapons research at Lop Nor was the chief priority in this third year of the People's Republic. Also, men who were qualified by their occupation, rather than by their family or their locality: former sailors, longshoremen, metal-workers, mechanical engineers, masons, even civil servants.

Fat hope of finding any such, much less all of them! Unless officers were captured in large numbers, where could he possibly find former engineers and civil servants? The educated usually managed to evade the nets of conscription that emptied into the Chinese People's Volunteers. And officers were *never* captured *en masse*.

At least, the assignment kept him at a good distance from the intrigues of Pusan and Koje for a time. The assignment also kept him away from Betsie and Sue. Since he honestly didn't know which of the girls he missed more sorely, that was probably a good thing.

Chapter XVIII

It was no contest, the brief skirmish between Luke's sense of duty and his own wishes, which conveniently masqueraded as the dictates of conscience. His counterfeit conscience won hands down – and he did as he wished.

No question about it, Luke knew that he should not have snapped up Stanley Kamen's invitation to see the bunker on the main line of resistance that was the command post of Company B of the Third Battalion of the US 32nd Infantry Regiment. He had no business putting himself again in harm's way – looking into the guns of the 128th Division of the Chinese People's Volunteers. His duty was to stay away from danger and to carry on his search for likely agents among POWs who had just been captured and were on their way to be confined in holding pens before shipment to Koje.

Against that counsel of prudence, he knew that the 128th Division of the Chinese Volunteers, recently arrived in Korea, was still cocky and aggressive. Its troops from time to time probed the UN's main line of resistance itself, striking towards those deeply entrenched and heavily sandbagged bunkers. The men of the 128th regularly attacked – and sometimes overwhelmed – American outposts in no man's land, which stretched some 300 yards wide to the north-east from the tangled coils of barbed wire protecting the zig-zag main line of resistance. However, it would not be long before these newly-arrived Chinese troops learned the reality of constant mortal peril; they would then be much more cautious, less gung-ho.

Luke was therefore commanded by his convenient conscience to go up to the main line of resistance. There was in truth a very good chance that Company B's patrols in no man's land would take a prisoner or two, a far better chance than there would be after the enemy had learned prudence.

And it was his duty, his urgent assignment, to talk with the POWs. The closer to the moment of his capture, the more likely a prisoner was to reveal his true character, as well as whatever tactical knowledge he might possess. A fresh caught People's Volunteer, almost certainly resentful at having been drafted into the front line, could be a first class source of immediate information. Critically to Luke's secret mission, such a newly captured Chinese was a more likely prospect for recruiting as an agent of espionage in mainland China itself.

In part at least, Luke's deference to duty was, nonetheless, a pretext. He had longed to be back in the firing line, where he would no longer endure the reproaches of his wayward conscience at having landed a safe billet far behind the lines. Although he had come to detest the war, he felt that he could not preach withdrawal unless he had experienced immediate danger once again. Besides, he missed the camaraderie of the trenches and the sure purpose that transcended the spider-web perplexities of everyday life, whether military or civilian.

He had run into Captain Stanley Kamen at the Command Post of the 28th Regiment. Luke was talking with the regiment's G², arranging to interrogate two Chinese taken a day earlier in his own disguise of a staff officer seeking fresh strategic intelligence. Stan Kamen had, rather unusually, come back to regimental headquarters to check with the staff and to collect a dozen-odd fresh infantrymen for his casualty-depleted company. About half of those replacements were Americans, the others KATUSAs, Koreans Attached to the US Army. But they're another story, the KATUSAs. I'll get to them later.

Luke had met Stan Kamen several months earlier when Kamen visited Eighth Army Headquarters in Seoul. Kamen was one of the few front-line company commanders who was truly interested in the endeavours of the Psywar Section and was, moreover, eager to co-operate.

A Flatbush boy, he had finished a semester at Brooklyn College before he was drafted for the big one, World War II. Two years later he had jumped from staff-sergeant to second-lieutenant, commissioned on the battlefield. Discharged in 1946 as a first-lieutenant, he had taken his BA in psychology before he was recalled for duty in Korea. He had made captain a few months later, when he was given a company command.

Stan was small, dark, and intense – in marked contrast to Luke's lean height and casual manner. His neat features were genial and open, but his incisive mind was just as quick and agile as Luke's, perhaps even a shade quicker. Stan Kamen was not shy about showing his intellectual superiority, unlike Luke, who tried to maintain the pretense that he was just one of the boys.

Despite that difference, they got on very well. Besides, Kamen, unlike ninety-nine per cent of the troops, was attracted by the glories of Far Eastern culture, which he had no more than glimpsed amid the chaos of war. Luke was pleased to meet a fellow enthusiast – even better, an enthusiast who welcomed his guidance.

In the half-darkness of the command bunker, Stan Kamen was for once relaxed. His wiry body was sprawled on a bedroll raised a few inches above the ever damp packed-earth floor on a crude board pallet. His dark-blue eyes flickered in the silvery beams of the acetylene lantern swaying on one of the timber pit-props that held up the roof of the dugout. He raised himself on one elbow in response to the faint tinkle of the green canvas-encased field-telephone. But no one was on the line.

The corporal who was Company B's signalman picked up the handset when the bell tinkled again, although even fainter. There was no response to his repeatedly shouted 'Hello!'

'All modern conveniences, this war,' Kamen said. 'Sabrejets, napalm, and Mickey Mouse boots. But, as for communications …'

The brilliance of an illuminating flare fired by a nervous sentry shone around the edge of the khaki blanket that screened the entrance. Startled by that sudden half-brightness, Luke and Stan looked at each other warily. Something was wrong. The next instant they realized as one that they could hear no sound outside: no artillery, no mortars, not even sporadic machine-gun and rifle fire. An uncanny, unnatural silence had submerged the normal din of the main line of resistance.

Kamen shrugged eloquently, his gesture expressing at the same time resignation, alarm, and decision. The two captains picked up loaded carbines and buckled webbing belts from which ponderous Colt .45 pistols hung in canvas holsters. A .45 was fine for hand-to-hand combat, for intimidating a captive, or for hitting a target no more than ten paces away. It was virtually useless otherwise.

Luke followed Kamen up the earthen ramp to the entrance and into the trenches. The deep, glutinous mud clung tenaciously to their combat boots; each step was a brief struggle followed by a prolonged sucking noise.

That was the only sound to be heard. Silence lay palpable over the front lines, so thick it enveloped the soldiers. In the lingering light of the flare, the troops manning the trench instinctively looked upward; their faces were white blobs glimmering in the dark frames of their coal-scuttle helmets. They searched for the source of the silence as if it were tangible, an entity in itself, not the mere absence of sound. They were extremely fearful, frightened by the suspension of the clamor to which they had become habituated.

'Beats the shit out of me,' Stan Kamen said. 'I've never heard *nothing* before! But you can be damned sure it's *not* a good omen.'

Luke peered over the parapet at the scarred and pitted man-made wilderness of no man's land. He saw no moving object, no man, no bird, not even one of the foxes and rabbits that thrived in the gap between the armies where no hunter could venture. He was oppressed not only by the eerie, ominous silence, but as much by the complete absence of movement or life. No man's land was absolutely deserted – as sterile, lifeless, and frozen as the reverse face of the moon, where men had not yet walked.

Luke turned towards Kamen to speak. His words were lost in an eruption of sound. The sudden din sounded like regiments of giants fighting with spears, swords, and maces. Artillery rumbled, abrupt and fierce as a tropical thunderstorm, and shells ploughed the earth around the trenches. Mortar bombs fell in phalanxes, an orderly avalanche of death. Small arms fire quickened, staccato bursts melting into a single unbroken clamor, the individual reports of machine-guns, grease-guns, and rifles indistinguishable.

The clangor was incongruous, indeed bizarre. It sounded like an enormous impromptu celebration. Brilliant fireworks reinforced the illusion: red-and-yellow flashes of exploding shells; strings of fiery tracers arching against the dark sky; searchlights probing enemy positions; red, green, and blue flares soaring high; and again and again, the searing brilliance of star shells flaming in mid-air with intensely inflammable white phosphorous, as well as the incendiary sky-rockets that burst into illuminating flares.

Luke slid the barrel of his carbine between two of the sandbags that crowned the trench's parapet and aimed bursts of automatic fire at the Chinese in horizontally quilted green-brown uniforms who were springing from the earth like dragon's seed.

Bugles blared! Gongs roared! Drums pounded! Shouted political slogans spurred on the heaving mass of men, shrill and piercing as Mohawk war whoops, blood-chilling as the Confederates' rebel yell. Close packed as a swarm of killer bees, the teeming Chinese attack all but hid the ground itself.

Luke was again swept up in the slaughter of war. He was caught up by the killing, immersed in that chaos which he abhorred – except when his blood ran hot and his heart pounded in his throat. In that fierce elation all his senses were preter-naturally sharp. Through the silver glow that now undulated over the battlefield, he could see a gnat's eyes or an enemy's eyes a hundred yards away.

The tumult abated as Chinese artillery fire slowed and then stopped to keep from slaughtering its own infantrymen. The waves of sound rose high again as American artillery, mortars, and small arms scythed the enemy troops who were pushing through gaps blown in the tangled concertinas of needle-sharp barbed-wire stacked high in front of the fortified trenches of the main line of resistance. Harrowed by leaden shot and by exploding shells, the green-brown mass rolled forward, spontaneously closing up the furrows blasted in its tight-packed ranks.

A stream of Chinese poured over the parapet into the trench. Individuals were distinguishable as they drew closer. They were, somehow, all alike, all but identical: automated robots in the same slovenly, quilted uniforms that were apparently molting, the coarse greyish lining spilling out of manifold rips. Some carried the American M1 rifles they had been issued when their division was part of Chiang Kai-shek's Nationalist armies. Some carried Russian-made Kalashnikovs with fixed bayonets, and a number flourished old fashioned Chinese-made submachine-guns with perforated metal guards around their barrels fed by circular magazines like those of the infamous tommygun.

The Chinese mass had simply rolled over Company B's outposts in no man's land, hardly losing momentum when they slaughtered a dozen American soldiers. The faint tinkle of the field telephone, immediately suppressed, had been the only requiem for those men. That last message, which was never received, would have warned that invisible Chinese multitudes were creeping on their bellies towards the main line of resistance, their metal accoutrements padded so that no clink would betray their advance.

Luke was cut off by swirling enemy troops from Stan Kamen, who, twenty or so feet away, was leading a dozen men in a counter-attack. Luke's carbine barrel was so hot from rapid firing it burnt his palm when he fell back to the bunker's entrance to protect the company's communications. The signalman must be reporting their predicament to regimental headquarters by telephone, if the landline were still intact. More likely by field radio.

Luke leaned into the bunker and shouted to the signalman. 'Tell regiment we need artillery and mortars. Just forward of our own trenches. Shave it as close as they can.'

That command risked their own troops being felled by friendly fire. The danger was acute, as Luke knew full well, but his decision was, nonetheless, justified. Since the main line of resistance had hardly shifted for months, the artillery was precisely zeroed on every possible target.

Luke heard the cough of a Chinese submachine-gun, and flung himself face down in the mud. Sputtering, he levelled his carbine and took deliberate aim at the panicky enemy soldier, who was firing wildly, not pausing to aim at the hordes of enraged red-haired demons he saw everywhere around him. The heavy-set Chinese tottered, dropped very slowly to one knee, then crumpled, fell slowly and toppled over gradually, as if engaged in a gymnastic exercise. Luke dropped the carbine. Its ammunition-clip was exhausted, and no more loaded magazines were anywhere within reach.

He wrestled with a ponderous Browning automatic rifle abandoned on the parapet when the Chinese tide swept away its two-man crew. Though an awkward weapon for one man, ammunition was plentiful, the long belts of ammunition strewn on the sandbags. The deadly stream of heavy bullets chopped down the Chinese troops who stood between Kamen and himself.

No clarity was possible in the hectic turmoil. Not primarily because of the so-called fog of war. Primarily because the light was uncertain, wavering into darkness, then flashing bright for an instant, dimming and then glowing under a starless sky. The three-quarter moon shone intermittently through rifts in the heavy cloud cover, disappearing for minutes at a time.

One instant Luke saw both enemy and friendly troops sharply outlined. The next instant those figures were obscured by the recurring darkness and by drifting smoke, which stank of pungent gunpowder. It might have been a scene from an arty-crafty movie filmed in half-light to simulate night – and to keep down costs.

Afraid of hitting his own men, Luke stopped firing. He no longer heard the shrieks and the explosions. But he knew his request for supporting fire had been answered when the earth trembled. He could not but hear the regular crump-crump-crump of the big 4.2 mortar bombs walking up and down the strip of scarred earth directly in front of the trench.

The bombardment was extraordinarily accurate and acutely co-ordinated. Chinese reinforcements could not pierce that waterfall of jagged metal. The enemy soldiers already in the trench were cut off from any reinforcement, effectively isolated behind a curtain of shrapnel.

The moon emerged for half a minute, and a white phosphorous star shell lit the trench with a hundred floodlights, far brighter than daylight. Luke could now see clearly. The Chinese were no longer attacking, but those in the trench were doggedly defending themselves.

Some fifteen feet away, he saw Stan Kamen drop his empty pistol and raise his carbine. The Colt .45 had done much slaughter at close quarters, but he had no more magazines for it. Only inches from the enemy, his carbine spat bursts of metal-jacketed slugs, all but cutting two Chinese in half. Slamming magazine after magazine into the weapon, Kamen forced the enemy soldiers back.

When the carbine at length clicked empty, Kamen reversed it. He whirled the weapon around his head like a Judean warrior fighting beside Joshua at the siege of Jericho. The carbine flailed the enemy soldiers, its scarred wooden stock dripping blood. Furious and fighting mad, Kamen hacked a path through the Chinese.

Returning darkness threw into panic the now cowed and purposeless Chinese People's Volunteers. They retreated helter-skelter before the savage attack of the American captain, who was now backed by only three men, his other followers having fallen.

But the enemy had nowhere to go. Trapped between the ferocious American officer and a sharp bend in the trench, they threw up their hands. In the half-light, Kamen did not take in that gesture for ten to twenty seconds. Then, he finally lowered his bludgeon, his shoulders drooping in exhaustion.

The heat and the rage of battle cooled in the gentle light of a misshapen moon, which shone for some time free of obscuring clouds. Luke breathed deep to calm himself and coughed on the gunpowder fumes. Only then could he assess the scene.

Stan Kamen's right arm was dripping blood from a bayonet slash. Three enlisted men held under the muzzles of their rifles thirty-odd Chinese. The captives smiled broadly, apparently delighted to surrender. Above all, it was clear, they also smiled in relief at having survived the berserk fury of the American officer.

Luke now had the prisoners he had been seeking. His game plan had worked splendidly – by the fluke of an unanticipated Chinese attack.

Captain Stanley Kamen had himself broken the overwhelming attack on Company B's position. Luke had all but forgotten that he himself had called in the murderous artillery barrage that threatened friendly troops, while cutting off any possible reinforcements for the Chinese in Company B's trenches. He had seen raw courage in combat, but rarely such blazing courage. He laughed uproariously, laughed in sharp relief, when Kamen said sheepishly, 'I guess I lost my temper.'

Dazzled by Stan Kamen's prowess, Luke urged the regimental commander to recommend him for a Congressional Medal of Honor, the highest American decoration for valor. He later heard that Kamen had been awarded a Distinguished Service Cross, the second highest decoration for valor, as well as a Purple Heart to add to the two Purple Hearts that honoured his previous wounds.

We took over, we Americans. And what we didn't do to Korea and the Koreans!

Now hold on a second! I guess I'd better explain, throw in a station identification before rushing on pell-mell with the tale.

This is Harland Birch amid the torrents of melting snow lapping at the cabin vaingloriously called a hunting lodge in the woods of upper New York State. I've

been thinking hard, pondering again the political aspects of the largely unremem-
bered war in Korea, which ended more than four decades earlier.

Significant new factors had entered the complex equation of armistice talks and
armed combat, Churchill's 'Jaw! Jaw! – War! War!', as Luke Maynell trekked east-
ward along the front toward the Sea of Japan. He had bid farewell to Stan Kamen,
having already talked at length with the four among the newly captured POWs
who showed promise for training as American agents.

A major new factor in the equation was a strikingly different mood among
Chinese when they were captured. One way or another, the changing attitudes of
POWs were a counterpoint to the travels of the young American officer.

The largest number had previously been resigned to incarceration, while generally indifferent to the contending ideologies. A few, ashamed at falling into the
enemy's hands, had been determined to resist the enemy's wishes at any cost. A
small number had rejoiced and thus shown themselves ripe for conversion to anti-
Communism.

By the early summer of 1952 the ratio had changed radically. Most newly
captured POWs were delighted to be out of the war, no longer in danger of being
maimed or killed. Only a few were openly hostile. Many were, however, deeply
resentful – incipiently hostile – to the Communist regime that had ruled their
homeland for almost three years.

Chairman Mao Zedong and his henchmen had shown themselves to be harsh
and blood-thirsty, as well as oppressive, dogmatic, vicious, and capricious.
Chairman Mao's first sweeping measure to remake China's society and economy
was called land reform. It was ostensibly intended to distribute cropland to the
peasants equably, but was primarily concerned to impose the relentless control of
the Communist Party on the people of China.

The process of land reform forced the peasants to play a militant part in raucous
public trials that condemned landlords to death – thus breaking the power of the
'class enemy'. The most vocal supporters of the new tyranny got the best land. The
less enthusiastic – or less hypocritical – got the leavings.

Far worse, the peasants suspected that the land they were allotted would not
long be theirs, for they were given no title to that land. They already saw the spectre
of collective farms, which were to be lightly camouflaged as 'co-operatives', arising
a few years thereafter.

Another new factor was the rapidly evolving – you could also say deteriorating
– relationship between the two chief allies, the USA and the ROK. That reality was
brought home to Luke when he was asked to a late evening party given by ROK
generals in a tent at ROK II Corps headquarters, not far from the trenches of the
main line.

I'll get to the generals' shindig very soon. Meanwhile, let's go back a little to illu-
minate the political scene. 'We took over!' as I remarked a few paragraphs earlier.
'As usual, we Americans took over the whole shebang. And what we did to the
Koreans!'

We ran the war just as we pleased. After all, if the Americans hadn't come in, there would be no war. There would only be South Korea prostrate beneath the heel of North Korea and the Soviet Union. We ran not only the war; we practically ran South Korea, what was left to run after the armies had battled up and down the peninsula several times.

As always, we kidded ourselves. Americans in the war zone and those at home truly believed that democracy could be implanted in Korea – and, what's more, that democracy would work. What greater blessing could be bestowed by the USA, which had waxed prosperous and powerful under democracy? What was good for San Francisco was bound to be good for Pusan, too.

Having actually learned something from the Korean experience, American policy makers were to be slightly more realistic in Vietnam. Whatever President Lyndon Johnson is reported to have said about an election's being the best birthday present he could imagine, the men who shaped American policy day by day warned Saigon *not* to hold a nationwide election in the late 1960s. But the Saigon government insisted, largely because it hoped thus to charm the fickle American public, which venerated democracy.

But no working democracy stemmed from that dubious election. It only weakened Saigon's power.

More plausibly, President Syngman Rhee of the ROK went through all the democratic motions – even to creating political parties. Not surprisingly, no working democracy emerged. How could democracy burgeon in the midst of total war in a country that had never known popular rule, a country that had for millennia known only despotism and foreign oppression?

Anyway, Rhee, unlike the men of Saigon, had no wish to nurture democracy. His pseudo-democracy was a device to enable him to retain power indefinitely. It worked for more than a decade.

Syngman Rhee truly believed that he was the only hope for Korea, North as well as South. Because his personal interests were identical with the national interest, exactly the same, he knew he was inherently incapable of any self-serving action. He saw nothing wrong with keeping his power by bribery and intimidation. After all, everything he did was for the benefit of the nation!

Rhee was, of course, not the only despot who sincerely believed that only he could save his country. The century has seen: Benito Mussolini, the wicked buffoon; Adolf Hitler, the fanatical butcher; Josef Stalin, who imposed his will on everything from genetics to music by fear and slaughter; Chiang Kai-shek, who just wasn't up to the job; and Mao Zedong, the megalomaniacal visionary responsible for at least sixty million deaths, whose undiscriminating sexual athleticism made John F. Kennedy look like a repressed puritan.

Another new factor in the equation in Korea in mid-1952 was illusory.

The US was finally considering how to make the Republic of Korea fit to survive largely on its own – with only a token American force left in country as a tripwire. That same strategy was later to be called Vietnamization, and it was hotly discussed. Nonetheless, the US was able to take no firm, purposeful action to make either, initially the Republic of Korea or ultimately, the Republic of Vietnam fully capable of standing on its own feet.

But the US was already standing on Korean feet here and there. (Please excuse the lame metaphor). That balance of dominance and dependence was so common-place that no one remarked that one of the three infantrymen who fought beside Captain Stanley Kamen to the end was a Korean. Two years after the outbreak of the war, hardly a squad in the Eighth US Army, aside from the Marines, but counted two or three Koreans in its ranks. They were, as I wrote earlier, called KATUSAs, Koreans Attached to the United States Army.

Despite the slaughter of the previous two years, the Republic of Korea still possessed surplus manpower, in part because the USA still kept the ROK short of the full quota of supplies and weapons necessary to equip all its potential soldiers. Some of those men, the older and the less fit, were pressed into the Korean Service Corps. They worked as coolies for the Americans, hardly more than beasts of burden. For the US Army, chronically short of manpower despite the creaky mech-anism of the draft, the KATUSAs were a very welcome, in truth, an essential addition to American combat units.

Arbitrarily given *noms de guerre* like Frank, Joe, and Charlie, they fought side by side with American GIs. Not remarkably, they fought better in US units than they did in ROK units. KATUSAs were better fed than ROK soldiers, better equipped, better clothed, and enjoyed much stronger fire-support, as well as more even handed discipline.

Naturally, therefore, the KATUSAs' morale was higher than the ROKs'. Americans did not condescend to KATUSAs, as many Americans condescended even to ROK generals. KATUSAs were treated as equals by their squad-mates, whose lives depended on every man, including the KATUSAs, fighting as one.

President Harry Truman instinctively understood the demoralizing effect of segregation on US soldiers themselves. Overruling the hidebound military bureau-cracy, he ordered the dissolution of two US regiments in Korea. The 65th, composed entirely of Puerto Ricans, had a lacklustre combat record. The 24th, its enlisted men all Negroes, as blacks were then called, was famous for running away. 'When you hear the pitter-patter of little feet,' ran the parody song, 'it's the old Deuce Four in full retreat, We're bugging out ... 'cause they're getting too close to our MLR.' Distributed among other units, both Puerto Ricans and Afro-Americans fought just as well as the next man.

Harry Truman was eminently practical. Too damned practical, Luke still contends, in dropping atomic bombs on Hiroshima and Nagasaki when he already knew the Japanese were looking to surrender.

To me, though, the A-bombing was a practical move when I, like Luke, was girding myself psychologically for the slaughter that was bound to accompany an invasion of Japan's home islands. Let's leave the controversial, indeed explosive, issue of the A-bombs aside. Regardless, when the hard hand of racial and religious prejudice pressed heavily upon *all* Americans, victims and perpetrators alike, in the early 1950s, Harry Truman for practical reasons initiated in the military the deseg-regation of American society that was to flower in the 1970s and the 1980s.

Now for that ROK generals' party. Finally getting back to the story, you may say, after all that deep thinking. Such double-doming is the self-indulgence few corre-spondents can long resist, although they are hired to report, definitely *not* employed to think.

The setting was just right for the mood, as was the atmosphere. No stage designer could have improved on the scenery or the lighting for that little drama of Korea at war. The big mess tent appeared to extend forever into the distance from the flaring light of the bonfire in its center, as seen by the wavering light of dozens of candles and a few kerosene lamps broadly distributed around its expanse. The rumble of distant artillery and the faint rattle of not-too-distant small arms were a somber undertone to the clatter of tableware and the tinkling of glasses. The soft candlelight picked out the officers' insignia, lingering on the generals' constella-tions of stars.

The brassy firelight kindled the rich silks of the few ladies who mingled easily with the men. Actually, they were not ladies at all, but gilded prostitutes, no different morally from the whores who flocked around the big PX in Seoul. Still, these impeccably made-up whores were polished and accomplished. They were truly courtesans, quite distinct from street-walkers, and they were the heiresses of a great tradition. For centuries social gatherings of Korean gentleman had been enlivened by *kisang*, who were as adept in conversation, poetry, music, and bois-terous games as the more celebrated *geisha* of Japan.

Like the patricians of Periclean Athens, who so highly valued their own courte-sans, the *hetaerae*, the Korean gentry excluded respectable ladies from their revels. Ill-educated and inept except in household matters, their wives and daughters were by and large bores. The *kisang* were enchanting.

'Bullshit!' Luke Maynell murmured just audibly. He was sourly amused by the workings of his own mind in that glittering company. The historical analogies bubbled up spontaneously. Yet, were he to speak his thoughts aloud, he would sound like a pretentious pedant.

'Bullshit!' he murmured again.

Nowadays the *kisang*'s real distinction from the street whores was they cost more, much more. The generals of ROK II Corps, which held the central front, would pay an exorbitant price for their company tonight. Still, the rapacious Korean generals could well afford the *kisang*, for they extorted every last penny in graft they possibly could.

Such was the Confucian custom, the inevitable consequence of giving great power to officials, civilian or military, while paying them poorly. The West calls it corruption, somehow considering it is even more heinous if the officials actually deliver the favors they sell so expensively. The practise was, however, universal in East Asia, as it still is, hallowed by custom for millennia. The generals took graft for granted, much as they did the brutality that enforced their harsh discipline on their troops.

Despite such unlovely traits, most ROK officers engendered loyalty, even affection, in most of the Americans who worked closely with them under the aegis of KMAG, the Korea Military Advisory Group. Rough men in a rough land, they were also gallant, humorous, and straightforward in a most un-Oriental way. Brave as well, they were stoic, never whining, though like all soldiers often grousing. The ROKs were seen through a romantic haze by many American officers who had never seen a people or a way of life so different from their own.

Colonel Waylin Harvey Rowlands Jr., Infantry, US Army, the senior military advisor to the major-general commanding ROK II Corps, likened himself to a nine-teenth-century British officer serving with native troops. Having read too much Kipling, he had earlier that evening rhapsodized to Luke:

'They're like Gurkhas, the ROKS. Courageous, loyal, and just plain tough, hard-ball tough. Nothing can match them when they're good. The Japs never understood their potential ... used them as prison camp guards or labor detachments. But we're making them very good, very professional soldiers. Just give them intelligent leadership and the weapons. Then get out of the way – and let them rip and roar!'

Despite such camaraderie, untainted by condescension, relations between ROK and USA officers could be strained.

The ROKs considered most Americans a bit dim. Not very bright, yet arrogant and imperious. Besides, the American officers were, so the ROK generals judged, incapable of altering their preconceptions to fit the reality of a new war in a country of which they knew little. Nonetheless, one had to be kind to the Americans. They provided, albeit meagerly, the weapons and munitions to hold off the Communists.

For their part, many Americans saw ROK officers as pigheaded, rejecting out of hand tactics that were new to them although already proved in World War II. In exasperation, the Americans called the ROKs *Gooks*, which they believed was a term of abuse. Actually it derived from one name for Korea: *Han Gook*, the Land of Han.[1]

Tonight, however, all was bonhomie fostered by the trilling *kisang* and the fifteen-man brass band playing in a corner. The generals sat at a long table near the bonfire, which slightly warmed the frigid night air. Chief among them was Major-General Park Chung Hee, deputy commander of ROK II Corps. A trim figure with an authoritative manner, Park was later to take command of the nation itself by a

---

[1] As Luke told me in detail: *Gook* simply means 'country' in Korean, just as does *kuo* in modern Mandarin, both based on the same original ideogram. Chung-*kuo*, pronounced joong gwo, the Chinese call their country, literally 'the country at the center [of all things], therefore *the* most important country in existence, otherwise often translated as 'the center of the world'. Incidentaly, the same ideogram, i.e, Chinese character, is pronounced *gwok* in Cantonese, an older form of the language and, therefore, an older pronunciation, to which the Korean *Gook* is obviously much closer.

coup d'etat and to set the ROK despotically on the road to industrialization and pros-
perity, from which true democracy was in time to flow.

Opposite Park sat muscular, ebullient Brigadier-General Song Il Chong, who
was called Tiger. He commanded the Capital Division, which was by general
acclaim the ROK's best unit. A corpulent officer beside Tiger Song sported the two
stars of a major-general, but not the US Army-style name tag the other generals
wore. His identity was intended to remain a mystery.

That guest of honor was dark, unsmiling Won Yong Duk, whose function in II
Corps had been obscure, although Luke had divined his role in the nation itself
shortly after meeting him at Sue Chae's villa on the hill above Pusan.

Won Yon Dok's role was now unmistakable. Just promoted to major-general, he
had just been given command of the ROK's security apparatus. His authority now
took in all organs of espionage and counter-espionage, as well as the military
police, the civilian police, and the secret police. He was to use that immense power
to enrich himself enormously, as well as to protect his patron, President Syngman
Rhee.

The reception was intended to say farewell to Won Yong Duk and to wish him
good luck in his new office. The fighting ROK generals were not fond of the security man. In fact, most detested him. Indeed, the commanding general of ROK II
Corps was in Seoul 'for consultations,' thus deliberately absenting himself. But no
other ROK general felt secure enough to stay away tonight.

Luke Maynell, who was the lowest ranking officer present as a guest, sat beside
Tiger Song, to whom he spoke in Chinese. Song, who had served with the Chinese
Red Army against the Japanese, was now strongly anti-Communist. But he automatically referred to his American ally as *Mei-ti*, pronounced for those who may
care *May-dee*, the contemptuous Communist term meaning 'American imperialism'.

A number of ROK colonels crowded the table, as did American colonels and
lieutenant-colonels who were advisers to various ROK units. Behind them hovered
ROK lieutenants wearing the parrot insignia. Luke was glad that he was not
dependent on those erratic interpreters, some very good and some abysmal. There
was no ROK officer present with whom he could not communicate in either
Chinese or Japanese.

The American colonels were obviously on easy terms with their counterparts,
the commanding officers of the ROK units to whom they were assigned. Their
relaxed manner owed something to the bottles of bourbon, scotch, brandy, and *sake*
on the table. Japanese beer was chilling in the GI garbage-cans, while waiters
poured gingerly from bottles of cloudy *shochu*. That Korean home brew distilled
from rice wine rivals Kentucky white lightning for sheer ornery ferocity; it is even
more potent than Chinese *baigar*.

Luke heard a distant whistle over the tinkling laughter of the *kisang*, over the
baritone buzzing and the whooping guffaws of uninhibited masculine talk, over the
band's valiant effort to play the overture to *Guys and Dolls*. During the ten to twenty

seconds before that prolonged whistle ended in a muffled crump, conversation ceased. Even the *kisang* fell silent. The next whistle was closer, but still comfortably distant. Five more shells fell no more than a few hundred yards away, as shown by the volume of their explosion.

Luke waited for the counter-battery fire that would reply to those enemy shells. There was no counter-battery fire. The incoming artillery ranged as it pleased, unhampered by return shelling. Yet not only division, but corps artillery should have already targeted the enemy guns, whose positions were precisely marked on their maps.

Luke felt tension rise. He saw several ROK officers scowl. They were evidently not afraid, but angry. The animated talk did not resume, for, it seemed, everyone was listening for the next shell to fall.

'Only H & I, General Park,' Colonel Waylin Harvey Rowlands Jr. dismissed the shelling with the acronym for harassing and interdiction fire, which was employed primarily for its nuisance effect. 'Doesn't mean a thing. They're just trying to rile us.'

He lifted his glass, which was half-full of Scotch and water, saying, 'Bottoms up, General.'

The convivial reception was, however, veering out of control. The acting commander of ROK II Corps did not wait for the interpreter, since the American's meaning was clear from his tone and his dismissive gesture. Major General Park Chung Hee slammed his glass down on the table. The interpreter's voice trembled as he rendered the general's outburst into barely intelligible English.

'Maybe it doesn't bother you, Colonel,' General Park Chung Hee had said. 'It sure as hell bothers me. Here we sit, defenceless targets, like dummies, like ducks in a shooting gallery, while the Chinese drop whatever shit they please on our heads.'

'Now hold on, General,' Rowlands objected. 'You know damned well it takes a while for the Fifth Artillery Group to get on target. Can't be helped ... language and distance problems ...'

As if cued by that remark, the crump of outgoing artillery sounded in the distance, followed by a long diminishing whoosh abruptly cut off when the shell landed in enemy territory. A dozen or so shots sounded before the supporting artillery shut down.

'Just so, Rowlands. It takes five to ten minutes for counter-battery fire. By that time it's too late.'

Four more incoming shells punctuated the general's retort. He had not been placated, but had been further irritated by the American colonel's protest. The resumed Chinese shelling aroused his anger.

'Always this way ... from the beginning,' he said hotly. 'The Communists marched in because we were so weak in 1950. We didn't even have an army, only the so-called Korean Constabulary. No artillery, no tanks, and of course, no warplanes. All because you Yanks believed Syngman Rhee would invade the North if he had the force. Pity he didn't ...

'After all this time ... two years of war ... my corps ... it's still got no organic artillery. Not our own artillery. Only your US Fifth Support Group, which takes the devil's own time to get into action. We've got nothing ... not even those big 4.2 mortars. Are you Yanks still afraid we'll invade the North if we're properly equipped?

'The big trouble with you Yanks is you think you're supermen ... that only you can fire modern artillery or fly jet planes! I tell you this: *You Yanks are not a super-race!*'

Colonel Waylin Harvey Rowlands Jr., born in Atlanta, did not like being called a Yank. Regardless, he could muster no rebuttal to General Park Chung Hee's furious denunciation of US policy. But he never again likened himself to a Gurkha officer.

Rowlands returned to duty in the Pentagon early the following year. He did not see the final humiliation of ROK II Corps in June 1953.

All the terms of an armistice had been agreed in outline by the UN delegation and the Communist delegation at Panmunjom, even to the handling of non-repatriate prisoners of war. The few minor details still at issue would obviously be ironed out very soon. The Communists wanted peace as eagerly as did the UN. Perhaps more eagerly, for they were desperate.

President Syngman Rhee was, however, an unmoving obstacle to an armistice. On Rhee's orders ROK representatives were boycotting the negotiations. He would not, he declared, accept an armistice on any conceivable terms. Regardless of the outcome at Panmunjom, he warned, his forces would march north. The ROK Army would unify the nation on its own if his allies deserted him.

The Chinese command decided to teach Rhee a lesson. In June 1953 the People's Volunteers attacked ROK II Corps in overwhelming force. After holding for a day or so, the South Koreans broke and ran. It was not an orderly retreat, but a rout. The bugout took the ROKs thirty miles southward. When the over-extended Chinese supply lines broke down, the 'People's Volunteers' could not continue the punishing pursuit. In any event, they did not want the territory, but only wanted a crushing defeat that would humiliate the ROKs and show them who was boss. They pulled back, allowing the ROKs to re-occupy their original main line of resistance.

The lesson was clear: *The ROKs could not possibly march north alone!* Whatever the terms of the armistice, Syngman Rhee had learned that his forces were still relatively feeble. They could not hold a fortified trench line against the Chinese, much less conquer the North. He finally yielded to reality, his humiliation salved by an American undertaking to fund a billion dollar super-highway linking Seoul and Pusan.

When ROK II Corps broke and ran, it had still possessed no organic artillery. Only the dilatory US Fifth Artillery Group provided some desultory covering fire support before it, too, packed up and moved out of the way of the Chinese juggernaut.

The US was a little less miserly the next time around. The much derided Army of the Republic of Vietnam was, therefore, a far better fighting force in 1968 at the time of the Tet Offensive than the much touted Republic of Korea Army had been in 1953. US policy-makers had finally learned some of the lessons of US military parsimony in Korea. But by no means all.

Chapter XIX

Spring had laid her soft hands on Seoul, covering the scars on the war-weary earth with grass and shrubs, yet leaving bare the conical hill that reared north of the Press Billets, granite-laced and barren. After two weeks' trekking along the front, Luke Maynell returned gratefully to that haven. He asked for any messages left for him and nodded somberly when I said there were none. Then he slumped into the one battered easy chair in my room, which was furnished with cast-offs wheedled or lifted from Koreans.

He was, he said, sore of foot and butt. His skin was ingrained with black particles and he was very tired. He was, in truth, bone weary, incapable of talking any more to gung ho soldiers over firewater like Four Roses and Three Feathers. He wanted in this order: a very dry martini; a long, steamy shower; and a long night's sleep unbroken by shellfire. A really good meal at the Billets was, of course, beyond his reach – or anyone's.

I was stirring the martini to disperse the trace of vermouth before decanting it into an Old Fashioned tumbler after rubbing the rim with lemon peel. And I was thanking the fates for the refrigerator 'liberated' from some diplomat's abandoned residence. ('Liberated', meaning 'taken without a request or a thought of recompense', we had learned to say from the catchword of Chairman Mao Zedong, who was ever promising new benefits, ever cynical, ever confiscating others' property.

Luke was sprawled in the chair, a monstrosity with urine-yellow wooden arms and gray velour upholstery that had once been white. His combat boots lay beside the chair, his cushion-soled socks draped across their buckled uppers. He gazed with distaste at his bare feet, which were striated with dirt.

'Good trip?' I asked.

'Middling. Not much doing on the MLR.'

'Did you do any good? Learn anything new and startling about Red China? Or our friendly neighborhood enemies, the Chinese People's Volunteers?'

'Not much, except that surrenders now outnumber captures. Chairman Mao's boys aren't exactly wild about his cause.'

'That's all you've got for me?'

'There's not much more to tell, Harland. I did a lot of interrogation. Let's leave it at that for now.'

'Come on, kid. That's no way to treat the buddy who's giving you a bed – and hiding you from the MPs.'

'No need. They can't touch me. Anyway, I'm beat ... pulverized. Let's just say I did the best I could.'

'Those are the most pernicious words of tongue or pen.' I filled the awkward silence with an old truism I had just invented. 'My biggest mistake's been doing my best ... doing my job up to the limit of my ability.'

Luke smiled at that remark, amused despite his weariness, and asked, 'Just what's that supposed to mean, Harland?'

'Just what I said: the biggest mistake I've ever made – and that repeatedly over and over again — is putting everything I've got into my reporting. It only makes enemies: first, for being right, and, second, for showing them up. It's a mistake keeping your eye on the ball, never taking time to go sightseeing or whoring. The smart ones, the boys and girls who get ahead in this business, they coast on the job.'

'Harland, the high-fliers never take their eyes off the ball.'

'Sure, but their particular ball's *not* their assignment. It's their climb up the ladder. They keep an unblinking eye on their own advancement. They're not much interested in whatever story they happen to be covering. But *only* in getting ahead.'

'You're hard on your colleagues.'

'Maybe,' I conceded. 'The human heart's not exactly an open book to me. I've got to go by visible outward behavior ... . I can't tell what else they're up to.'

Luke did not answer, for he was snoring softly. I told myself that his exhaustion, rather than my anodyne conversation had sent him to sleep.

Maybe I *was* a little hard on my colleagues. I've known dozens of honest reporters who worked their hearts out to get to the truth. Most war correspondents in Korea did an honest job. But, later in Vietnam, the story was too often secondary, even tertiary. Only sluggards who'd never be anchormen – oops, anchor*persons* – cared, above all, about the story. The others set out to make a name for themselves with big stories sure to get big play even though they had to present them just like a great play, a gripping drama: invent the plot, write the script, set the stage, and direct the actors.

The Buddhist riots against President Ngo Dinh Diem were stage-managed by the Press, right down to the monks' fiery self-immolation. 'Buddhist barbecues', they were called by the staunchly Roman Catholic President Diem's fiery sister-in-law, Madame Ngo Dinh Nhu, the Dragon Lady of Vietnam. Of course, that flaming self-sacrifice was not an original idea of the correspondent. Mahayana Buddhism, the Big Carriage-Wheel Sect practiced in East Asia, among other nations by China, Japan, and Vietnam, has a strong tradition of suicide for a transcendent cause. Setting one's self on fire is a favored way of suicide under pressure, since it bestows much greater suffering for the cause than almost any other way – and rallies public support against the oppressor.

Anyway, let's get back to the vexed question of honest reporting. Or, really, the ever more widespread practice of lying, often in chorus with other self-seeking so-called reporters, to advance one's self.

You know, TV's that way naturally. It all but automatically distorts, forces misrepresentation on even conscientious reporters. The picture on the screen must be dramatic and striking – not necessarily what's important or significant, even what makes for clearer understanding. And the voice-over follows the image. Yet for one TV reporter the story wasn't even tertiary. Facts, reality itself, were only raw material to him, clay to be molded as he pleased.

A Vietnamese cameraman had shot some great film of one Buddhist demonstration, but without sound. Our boy viewed the film and then did a voice-over. Sitting in the Caravelle Hotel, he opened a window to let in the street noises, and he talked as if he were right in the middle of the riot. Even on a normal day Saigon sounded like a riot. Then he'd cough and mutter, 'The tear gas is really getting thick now. It's choking me!'

But I'm getting carried away from the subject. I was telling you about Luke Maynell's return to Seoul after a couple of weeks trawling the front for likely agents for the CIA. Although he only told me about that mission years later. At the time, listening to Luke snoring in the big easy chair oblivious to my typing, I could only wonder what he'd been up to – and try to guess why he wouldn't talk about it.

Luke slept for several hours. It was late afternoon when he was awakened by the big, blond, brash, brilliant, crop-haired *Time-Life* bureau chief Duane Morton, who made the glass door rattle when he strode into my small room.

'I don't want you, Harland,' Morton boomed. 'I want your buddy with the forked-tongue, the speaker of many languages. We're doing one of those socially significant pieces my brain-damaged editors in New York love: *The life of ordinary Koreans amid the devastation of war.*'

Luke opened one amber eye and glanced at the ebullient *Time* man.

'I've got a hot prospect across the street, a real tear-jerker,' the irrepressible Morton rolled on. 'We found this old boy who's very, very sick. Diseased as a rotting leper … and half-starved. Just lying in a deserted house waiting to die.

'I think I'll pop him over to the Nethersole Hospital. The military won't take him, but the missionaries will. How else justify their existence? First, though, I want a little talk with papa-san – and I need you, Luke Maynell, the man of many tongues.'

Luke grimaced at being awakened from his first deep slumber in two weeks. He rose stiffly, his legs cramped by his awkward position. He amiably agreed to interpret for Duane Morton just as soon as he'd had a cup of coffee and a cigarette.

'An old farmer, a real old-fashioned papa-san in baggy pants and a long, once-white coat, even a birdcage hat,' Luke told me when he returned. 'Boy, was his Japanese rusty. He crept into the city hoping to find someone from his family to help him. But his son was gone, totally vanished. So he crawled into the gutted house to die.

'They said at the Nethersole he had typhus – and a bellyful of lesser complaints like dehydration, acute malnutrition, and a touch of pneumonia. At least we've all had our shots ... even the Koreans who work for us.'

Although I knew I'd sound unfeeling, even harsh, I asked, 'What's the prognosis?'

I was trying hard to feel empathy, so that my pieces would touch the hearts of my readers. I was also trying hard to avoid getting involved with such pathetic cases. You could see a dozen every day: wounded soldiers, many missing legs or arms; little kids burned by napalm or blinded by smallpox, sometimes hard to tell the difference; women crippled by accident or maimed by men.

My skin was supposed to get thicker the longer I lived in Asia, but it was getting thinner. Hard cases were getting harder to take. I had to keep telling myself that I was there to report, not to agonize.

Luke turned both thumbs down and said softly: 'Not a hope. He's too far gone. But they'll make him comfortable till he goes. Duane's houseboy Paik is swearing a blue streak about the blood and pus stains on the upholstery of the *Time-Life* sedan.'

Li interjected: 'Paik really loves that Chevy *Time* got from the Fortieth Division. Paik knows he's getting it when the war's over.'

'No wonder he looks so pained seeing the big, fat fleas crawling over the seats.' Luke paused. 'Funny, though, Paik's acting as if Duane and I were saints, practically demigods. Just because we took the trouble to get the old man to the hospital. And the wise men of the West, those deep thinkers of ours, say Orientals have no respect for life ... no use for kindness!'

He lit another cigarette and asked, 'Any coffee left?'

When I handed him a chipped mug, he looked into the muddy liquid dubiously, set the mug down hard, and said, 'To hell with this muck. I need something a lot stronger. I think I'll get drunk.'

'Not with me you won't, buster. Not tonight. I've got a long think-piece to finish. Go find your playmate Duane. He's always ready for a bender or an orgy.'

It was, I suppose, inevitable once Luke Maynell and Duane Morton got together in the tiny bar at the rear of the Press Billets. It was inevitable that a quiet little drinking match should end up as a spree.

Both were two-fisted drinkers when the mood was on them. Both were young men who had been without female company or female comfort for several weeks. Unlike many other American males in Korea, neither was inured to that deprivation.

Luke was feeling battered by life: the long hard journey along the MLR; the unresolved confrontation with Colonel Lesward Murray Howse; and, now, the pointed silence of both Betsie Howard and Sue Chae. In his stained fatigues, he looked worn, as if a film of cobwebs lay over his strong features. Grit was caked in new lines on his forehead; shadows dented the skin beneath his bloodshot eyes; and his right index finger was stained yellow by nicotine. It was well past time for him to let go of his inhibitions.

Duane was, as I'd warned Luke, a wild man once he began drinking. His normal resolution petrified into obstinacy, and his normally orotund sentences soared into virtual blank verse. The *Time* man naturally preferred the silken *geisha* houses of Tokyo: their polished wood, floral perfumes, fragrant *onsen* baths, tinkling *samisen*, and the cultured chatter of the girls themselves. So much preferable to the sordid streets behind the Seoul PX, where you never knew what kind of contaminated whore you might draw. But he was a big man with a big sexual appetite to feed, no matter how.

Duane called for two more double-martinis. For the second time that evening he explained at needless length to the Korean bartender in the white monkey-jacket, who already knew the technique full well, exactly how to tincture precisely a quarter drop of Noilly Prat into the Beefeater Gin that swirled limpid around the ice cubes in the double Old Fashioned tumbler. Whatever the corre-spondents' bar lacked in décor, it was bountifully equipped with glassware. A lot got broken.

The pair had, somehow, forgotten the mess hall and the evening meal, which Duane vociferously refused to dignify by calling it dinner. Peanuts and pretzels were the only sustenance available. Both were absentmindedly cramming their mouths between sips of the high-powered martinis.

'Luke, my good man, it may be true,' Duane said solemnly, 'but I reckon it's a rumor deliberately put out by the medics. Tuberculosis of the penis, no less. Started in Yongdongpo, just a tad south of the River Han. They say it's spread by blow-jobs. Your tool swells up at the end, looks something like a mushroom. Whadda ya say we test the theory?'

Somehow that proposal struck Luke as ineffably funny. Chuckling cheerily, he pushed back the metal chair. His movements were lithe, easy as if the martinis had restored his flagging vitality, but had not otherwise affected him. The two merry men climbed into the *Time-Life* jeep, taking a thermos of martinis along.

'For emergencies like snakebite. Korean vipers are virulent, not to speak of Korean ladies of the night.' Duane explained solemnly, tucking into his pocket the wad of greenbacks he had found in a desk-drawer in the *Time-Life* room.

'For bait,' he added. 'Can't catch fat fish without bait.'

Trawling the half-darkness of the late dusk, they easily caught two tasty fish. One, who wore the traditional bolero and full bell-skirt, both glaring purple, was tall and slender. The other was short and well rounded in a plaid skirt and a tight organdie blouse, courtesy of Monkey Ward. Luke had his eye on the tall one, but she was appropriated by Duane. Telling himself that she had a sulky mouth, he contented himself with her friend.

He was also content with silence after the women's standard greeting: 'Hello, GI! Makee pom-pom?'

That courtesy was followed by the standard response when Duane offered them $5 each. 'Whassa matta, you kurazy, GI? You makee joke? Ten dollas bottom. My friend make pom-pom very good.'

Luke decided to speak no Japanese to the women, though both, at, say, seventeen or eighteen, must have had at least scraps of schooling under the Japanese colonial masters. Tonight he would remain silent, although Duane Morton was stumbling along in pidgin Japanese, drawing responses in Japanese almost as rudimentary as his own. Pidgin English would've been better.

'Now let's just see exactly what we've got here,' Duane declaimed, when they entered the spacious room in the rear wing of the Press Billets, which he was taking over without permission from several absent British correspondents. He switched on the big overhead light, which glared on the shiny metal frames of the camp beds placed in the corners, and examined the teenage prostitutes critically.

The small one cowered, frightened by his loud voice and his sweeping gestures. The tall one appeared more irritated than frightened, angrily brushing away Duane's hand when he lifted her chin to examine her features. Nonetheless, Luke saw that her eyes were blank as if to deny herself full knowledge of her degradation. Her mouth, Luke further saw, was not only sulky, but hard.

'A tad moldy, both of them,' Duane pronounced. 'We'll have to clean them up to render them fit for our attentions. You could use a wash yourself, my good man.'

He slipped off the tall girl's bolero and then her blouse. She submitted casually yet disdainfully, as if he were no more than a lady's maid undressing her for the night. Her small unfettered breasts stood free as he loosened the waist-cord of her threadbare bell-skirt and slipped it over her narrow hips. Anticipating him, she tucked her thumbs into the elastic band of her aniline-blue panties and discarded them to stand naked and challenging. Her vulva was almost hairless.

Luke turned to his lady for the night, fumbling as he peeled off her clothes. His fingers were clumsy, not, he told himself, because of all those martinis, but because of the public display. Somehow, as in the Pusan bordello where the *exhibition* had *not* taken place, there was no decent privacy for sex in Korea. Removed, the black-silk bra revealed a bountiful bosom with large brown areolae and nipples. The matching black-silk panties slid off to reveal the perfect triangle of a thick black bush.

Flicking their buttocks with a towel, Duane Morton drove the two girls across the hall into the big shower-room. He turned on all the hot taps, and water streamed from the six shower-heads set high on the walls. Steam softened the glare of the fluorescent ceiling light and wreathed the four naked bodies.

'No, not that!' Duane said sternly, when the tall girl, her sulky expression unchanged, reached out to grasp his half-erect penis. 'None of that nonsense now, my lady. First, we must get you squeaky clean.'

Luke attacked his own cumulative filthiness with a wash-cloth, leaving his companion to wash herself. She was plying a sponge with vigor when the door opened. A milk-pale, mortally thin, middle-aged man entered, a towel around his loins. He blinked at the steam-filled room and began to untie his towel. An instant later, he blinked again in evident astonishment and hastily retied his towel.

'Good evening, Father!' Duane deftly turned his woman so that she faced the wall and continued to scrub her back. 'It's Saturday night bath time. Won't you join us?'

The girls giggled loudly. The thin man flushed crimson from head to waist and scuttled out of the shower-room.

'Father Paddy McDonagh of the Catholic News Service.' Duane chuckled. 'He's going to be sore as a boil at me for a while. But he'll get over it. It's not the first time … and Paddy's a good egg.'

Luke was still hesitant. He was slightly abashed at the communal sex party, which was rather unusual, not the common practice, in those unenlightened days forty-odd years ago, quite unlike our jolly exercise today, our happy casting off of inhibition. But he was aroused and eager by the time Duane had completed the bathing ritual that was obviously not new to him.

First the girls had to be dried very carefully, not missing a nook or a cranny. Then they had to perform the same service for the two men. Finally, the girls were patted with fragrant Ponds talcum powder and led ceremoniously to two beds in the far corners of the big room.

'Lights out, brother Luke,' Duane intoned, flicking a switch. 'Sleep tight – or otherwise as the case may be. Anyway: Enjoy! Enjoy!'

The big room was now lit only by the feeble moonbeams that sneaked between the hopsack curtains. The touch of the virtually anonymous hands on Luke's flanks was gentle, yet exhilarating. All awareness of Duane and the woman in the other corner passed from his consciousness. He bent over the bed where the little Korean whore lay in the moonlight like Goya's portrait of the Nude Maja. Yet he realized with a start of guilt, that he had not thought of either Betsie or Sue for hours. His reflexive self-blame was spontaneously dispersed as he lowered himself onto the receptive form.

They coupled once eagerly and quickly, too quickly. The deft fingers and soft lips having restored desire and vigor, he slid again into her soft moistness slowly. Deliberately detached to prolong the pleasure, he heard from the other bed a high voice commanding, '*Ima! Ima!* … Now! Now!' Gently, tantalizingly, he withdrew slightly, and she rose to his movement.

'Ah,' she sighed wordlessly. 'Ah … ah.'

Her sigh turned into a shriek, and she drew him to her, her hands on his back.

A ghostly beam of blue light raced around the walls at head height, momentarily illuminating the stark black-and-white photographs that hung on the walls. There followed a string of smaller lights, some red, some yellow, some green.

Luke heard the rattle of an express train. Was he hallucinating? Yet an instant later a locomotive whistle whooped peremptorily, then wailed long and mournful.

'Hope it didn't startle you too much, brother Luke, didn't catch you in midstroke.' Duane's sonorous voice bubbled with suppressed laughter. 'Electric trains run from the next room, courtesy of Dick Cottor. Realistic, no? Dick's a great photographer, but that leaves him lots of free time. Since he never cracks a book, he builds model trains – and runs them, as you've seen.'

A peremptory rustle recalled Luke to his pleasure. A minute later the room was silent except for rustling, sighs, and grunts. But from time to time that febrile demi-silence was broken by the rattling of rails, the recorded announcements of a conductor, and the lonely wail of a distant train racing through the night.

Chapter XX

Everyone in the Press Billets knew that Luke Maynell and Duane Morton had been out on the tiles the night before, although their Cinderellas of the night had with very professional finesse vanished before first light. The roomgirls, plying their mops and rattling their buckets, grinned conspiratorially when Luke and Duane finally awoke that afternoon. Correspondents shouted ribald congratulations. They might have been star running backs after a dramatic victory on the gridiron.

Everyone had heard the orgasmic whooping of the model train as it raced around the walls, its model passengers craning voyeurlike from the windows. Everyone had also heard the post-coital wailing as the train chugged wearily around the walls, its blue-white headlight flashing on the stark black-and-white photographs of war and riots. At the end of each run, just before plunging into the tunnel to the adjoining room, the Cyclopean headlight had illuminated the six-by-three-foot enlargement of the famous calendar picture of Marilyn Monroe stretched on a red velvet coverlet wearing only a come hither smile and, presumably, Chanel No. 5.

A lamp burned before that picture, as if in constant homage before a shrine. Even without the votive lamp, the picture would have been curiously unerotic. Not salacious at all, but somehow chaste and innocent, wholly untainted by sensuality or earthly desire, as pure as a Bellini Madonna cloaked in heavenly blue.

That calendar art encapsulated the American ideal of sex: as wholesome as the sunlit smile of a Coca-Cola girl, far removed from the sweaty raptures and the feral reek of the secretions of the night. No hint of flesh and bone and blood, only the shiny porcelain prettiness of a Meissen shepherdess. Yet that unsullied girl-woman was to be tortured by her men. She was to be adored and then discarded by two successive celebrity husbands, Joe di Maggio and Arthur Miller, who saw in her the embodiment of all their illusions of fair ladies. Until she was last used and discarded for eternity by Jack Kennedy and Bobby Kennedy, who had *no* illusions whatsoever.

Luke settled proprietorially into the easy chair with the wooden arms shellacked urine yellow. He grimaced when I suggested an Asahi beer and a bowl of *misoshiro*, that authoritative essence of soya-bean soup that Miss Kim, our roomgirl, conjured up on an electric hotplate. It was my favorite hangover breakfast, but, Luke said only thinking about it made him want to throw up. He would settle for a large mug of black coffee and six aspirins.

'Well that separates the boys from the men, Luke,' I said. 'If you can't take a hearty breakfast afterwards ...'

'This boy did a man's job pretty damned well last night, Harland!'

'Go ahead, blow your own trumpet! Although I assume you had it blown for you last night! But what's so splendid about unruly hormones? You've only proved you're competent in the activity at which, as John Calhoun once said, buck niggers and billy goats excel.'

'I knew you were a Fascist, Harland. Didn't know you were a racist, too.'

'I only quote.'

'Please don't.' Luke bantered, though I knew he was half-serious. 'I can't take that kind of stuff with a raging hangover.'

'No regrets?'

'What do you think? Of course regrets. What d'you call it, picking up some miserable girl who's got to do it to live? Do you call it love? Instant attraction? Elective affinities?'

'I call it a necessity,' I responded soothingly. 'Maybe regrettable, but a necessity from time to time. Even though you were only deprived for a couple of weeks ... Anyway, if you didn't, she wouldn't.'

'Wouldn't what? Pick up someone else? Now, Harland ... Oh, survive, you mean? Like the rickshaw coolie? If nobody hires him because everybody feels sorry for him ... can't bear to be pulled by a human being like a draft animal. So, he can't buy food – and he dies!'

Luke grinned suddenly and boasted, 'Anyway, she certainly seemed to enjoy herself.'

'What d'you expect her to do? Spit in your eye? Say you disgusted her? Like any businesswoman she's got to think of return trade. Are you going back?'

'Shit no!' Luke's vehemence broke the light mood. 'I'm fed up with women, *all* women, not just sad Korean whores.'

'With *all* women, even the lovely, serene Bartleby Howard? I thought you two ...'

'I thought so, too. But serene she's not. Definitely not. I only said a few friendly words to Suja ... Sue Chae ... and all the fires of Hell erupted.'

'Well, that proves she cares for you, doesn't it? Still, no word from either of them in almost three weeks. Of course, military mail's slow as molasses in January flowing uphill.'

'She could've called. She knew I'd be here. And some last word I had from Betsie! Just before I left Pusan, she sent me a record ... a song with the refrain: *When I'm not near the girl that I cling to, I cling to the girl that I'm near.* Across the jacket she'd written: "Your theme song!" '

'She does have a point,' I needled him.

'I'll have that beer now,' he said. 'God knows what Betsie's up to with Sue's half-brother. You know him, the terribly, terribly Anglicized Captain Chae Byongyup.'

'And Sue?'

'Nothing doing there, Harland. She's not my type. But she has an interesting mind. That's what ... that's all that interests me, her mind.'

'I see. With that figure ... that come-to-me smile ... you're only interested in her mind. So why're you also fed up with poor little Sue?'

'She could've dropped a line, just a few words. Anyway, it's not just Sue. I'm fed up with all Koreans. I'm fed up with Korea ... this everlasting war. We could go on talking and dying forever.'

'What's become of the Oriental patience you always say I should learn? What really happened to you the past two weeks? The front's been quiet enough.'

'Nothing really. Oh, hell, Harland, you see ... ' Evidently on the verge of a revelation, Luke stopped abruptly. 'No, nothing really. Nothing to talk about. Anyway, I wasn't at the front all two weeks. There's a limit to the time you can spend ...'

He paused, then resumed more temperately, 'A limit to the time anyone can spend interrogating fresh captured Chinese, while also doing a consumer survey to improve propaganda.'

Patently, Luke had not originally intended to say what he finally did say, but something quite different. I did not press him. He would, I knew, tell me in time. I did not know quite how long a time that would be.

'Anyway, I stopped by the apple orchard at Munsan to see the boys of the truce talks staff,' he went on. 'Spent a day at Panmunjom, too. I'm not happy about the way we're handling the POW issue in the talks. You know, it's now officially the *only* issue that stands between us and a truce.'

I couldn't let that one go by. Normally, I didn't bother much with spot news. But the likelihood of an early armistice was, of course, too big a story to pass up.

Luke was happy to talk, so happy I wondered for a moment if he'd been told to plant the story. But he would have told me if that were the case. His quirky code of honor commanded him to clam up, however obviously or even revealingly, rather than intentionally mislead a friend. He certainly wouldn't play the stooge for the generals with a close friend like me.

Yes, he told me in essence, the UN and the Chinese-North Korean sides would soon announce a recess so that the UN could do a recount, check again the number of POWs it held and survey their wishes again. The Communists quite honestly could not believe that some, more than a hundred thousand out of, the estimated 170 thousand Korean and Chinese prisoners in UN hands had flatly refused to he repatriated to North Korea or to mainland China. The Communists were sincerely convinced those figures were a massive subterfuge, another great big lie in the UN's propaganda campaign.

It was also an implicit violation of the Geneva Conventions to ask POWs whether they wanted to go home, rather than just shipping them home. Implicit because that likelihood was not treated explicitly in the Conventions, neither sanctioned nor prohibited, indeed not even mentioned. It had never occurred to the men who drafted the Conventions that any prisoner of war would *not* want to go home as soon as he possibly could.

'You know I am not a super-patriot like Betsie,' Luke told me. 'But there is a time to kick up a fuss and a time to go along.'

'And now?'

'The war could go on forever. We could go on talking eternally while men die. I used to think the UN could just hang on to the very few POWs who genuinely didn't want to go home. I was sure there'd be only a few. But the large number is legitimate ... too damned legitimate. Of course, it'll drop in the recount, but how much?'

'What's to be done?'

'Damned if I know. We certainly don't want to hang on to them. We're doing everything except lighting fires under the non-repats to get them to go home.'

Luke Maynell did not, of course, bear the responsibility for deciding what was to be done with the recalcitrant POWs. He was much too low on the totem pole.

Nonetheless, he was one of the few Americans available who spoke good Chinese. And he had been in close contact with the POWs for some time. He was, further, the only American with access to Major-General Li Mao, commander of the militant legion of captive Chinese.

Luke knew that, at the least, his judgement would be heard. So, instead of shrugging his shoulders, he pondered the issue, worried the question in his mind. He really wanted to advise: *Just send them all home regardless of their own wishes – and bring the war to an end. Save a lot of lives and spare a lot of suffering!*

But his conscience would not let him take that easy way out. Conscience can be a damnable nuisance for an army officer or for a war correspondent, a nuisance better done without. My conscience had gnawed at me over another matter.

'Birch, I've read your stuff on the red guerrillas in the south-west.' An officious 'public information' colonel prefixed an accusation. 'You sure blew up a little matter we had nicely under wraps. Are you a Commie stooge or a good American reporter? Whose side are you on anyway, ours or theirs?'

'On the side of truth, Colonel.' I naturally replied. 'Of course not theirs. I only want to be an honest reporter – not a propagandist!'

That sickly reply bothered me later. My conscience, which is, thank God, not hyperactive, finally told me I had done the right thing in filing fully on the Communist guerillas deep inside the Republic of Korea. Why cover up an ulcer that will keep bleeding anyway? Because I had blown the cover, the ROK forces would move more forcefully against the threat.

Clearly, that approach had not worked with the POW problem. The army had blithely ignored both State Department and Press warnings that Koje could blow up any time.

Yet the fundamental issues bothered few consciences. Few doubted that the US should be in Korea. Most Americans agreed without enthusiasm that the US had been forced by the North Korean invasion to enter the conflict. A small group in the States had other ideas, but its influence was negligible. Most Americans didn't care strongly about Korea one way or the other, though they did vote in 1952 for Dwight Eisenhower – and for the peace he promised. But they would've voted for the amiable, down-to-earth general over egghead Adlai Stevenson even if Eisenhower had sworn that he would obliterate Peking with nuclear rockets to force the Chinese People's Volunteers to pull out of Korea.

Korea was different from Vietnam. It was not the subject of hot dispute. Even at the time, it was a largely ignored, half-forgotten war.

Korea is now an almost entirely forgotten war. Obviously, I believe its significance should be reviewed to teach us a thing or two. Just so, of course, as I am trying to reawaken interest here and now. Korea was seen differently from Vietnam, although the Communists were already refining the strategy and the tactics of the Psywar assault they were to mount in Vietnam, where the intense campaign of propaganda aimed at world public opinion won them that engagement.

Vietnam was, of course, to be a bitter issue – in good part because of that decisive campaign. By that time, that is, the '60s and the '70s, even those who were convinced that we should defend South Vietnam kept searching their consciences. They kept scratching away at their convictions, because everyone else was doing just that. Also because they heard virtually nothing but denunciation of Washington's actions from the media and from academia.

It was virtually only the government that tried to justify our involvement. And who could possibly believe the government?

Now, a personal note that may surprise you: I was opposed to our getting involved in Vietnam in the early '60s, when the Kennedys and Arthur Schlesinger Jr were hot to trot. I thought we had no primary national interest in Vietnam and that any peripheral interest would be hard to defend. Of course, I was at a disadvantage: I didn't know much about Vietnam, but I did know a little, which was a lot more than ninety-five per cent of my colleagues knew.

I remember, just after we jumped into Vietnam with both combat boots, a television producer, of all people, a TV big thinker, pronouncing: 'Right or wrong, Vietnam's virtually unknown to the rest of the world, except, maybe, the French. Anyway, Vietnam's very complicated ... much too complicated for the American people to understand. So they won't support our involvement! So we have no business being there!'

Short, sweet, simplistic – and largely true!

His colleagues in television went along. By this time TV was a gorilla, though not yet, perhaps, 800 pounds of muscle. At any rate, those colleagues and competitors agreed viscerally with his recommendation. I say 'viscerally', since few, if any, reasoned cerebrally – and virtually none reasoned objectively or reported impartially. Instead, they discovered – or made up, just invented – simple, readily understandable reasons why we should *not* be in Vietnam! And the sheeplike public followed, baaing righteously.

The media with TV in the lead presented those facts and those opinions that would buttress the dovecotes, the lofts where the doves congregated and reinforced each other's prejudices by constant repetition of their views and other misjudge-ments. Presented with copious evidence in glorious technicolor, the public forthwith judged Vietnam a 'dirty war' that we had no business fighting. Yet the media – with TV almost always in the lead – somehow appeared to be more honest, more thoughtful, and more accurate than the government. The media were igno-rant, biased, and dishonest, but they could make themselves look detached, authoritative, and scrupulous.

The authorities couldn't even *look* plausible, neither in Washington nor in Saigon, which by the way had quite different appreciations of the facts and greatly varying agendas. They couldn't look plausible because they just weren't.

Most of the men in authority, including notably such a self-serving, self-impor-tant, sexually rampant ambassador as Henry Cabot Lodge, who sent his wife to Bangkok, stumbled unknowing from crisis to crisis. Lodge, of course, collaborated happily in the *coup d'état* that deposed Ngo Dinh Diem, that dynamic and difficult ally. Lodge not only endorsed, but ensured the cold-blooded murder of Diem, to which, as he understood with good reason, no objection was felt by the adminis-tration of John Fitzgerald Kennedy, who was to be murdered shortly afterward.

A significant number of those woefully uninformed so-called diplomats could not get beyond their absolute confidence in the inevitability of an American victory in this, as in every other war. That conviction made Vietnam itself a secondary consideration. Those pathetic envoys blundered along in a state of half-ignorance, lying even to themselves. They had little idea of real conditions in the Republic of Vietnam or the thinking of the Saigon government – and they cared less.

In time, the redoubtable Ellsworth Bunker was appointed ambassador. He strove mightily to work hard with the Vietnamese, whom he admired and largely understood. But it was then too late. The home-front had been fatally, under-mined.

Most Americans had by that time been convinced that the US was in Vietnam for selfish reasons, impelled by the military-industrial complex of which Dwight Eisenhower had so strongly warned a decade earlier. Most of the world believed the US was fighting in Vietnam for economic gain, as well as to expand the power and enlarge the scope of the mighty, arrogant, self-serving American empire, which in reality did not exist.

In plain truth, rarely has an epoch-making action stemmed *less* from economic self-interest. The US gained no wealth in Vietnam, but spilled out treasure and blood.

To the contrary, Japan, above all others, benefited. Without the war in Korea, the war I'm trying to demarcate for you, Japan would not have taken off economi-cally. Without its immense profits from Vietnam, Japan would not have gone into orbit economically. The US got almost nothing from Vietnam except domestic divi-sions leading to social turmoil, except inflation and increased national debt, as well, of course, as international opprobrium.

Just compare that over-idealistic commitment to Vietnam with the 1941-1945

War in the Pacific. That war was hailed as a crusade, the Press heartily concurring that it was an unselfish endeavor to block Japanese expansion to the detriment of other Asians. Yet, in truth, that war was primarily economic – a classic imperialist war in the Marxist-Leninist sense. Japan wanted access to the assets of East Asia, to its raw materials like tin, oil, and rubber, access also to the people of East Asia as labor and as customers in a huge single market. The United States would not cede those assets. Therefore Pearl Harbor!

But let's return to Vietnam for another moment, if you'll bear with me.

Ironically, half a generation after US withdrawal, the largely idealistic American objectives in Vietnam have largely been attained. Similarly, so, by and large, have the objectives we sought in Korea. Who said war was always futile? Who asserted that war never accomplished anything positive? Both those wars bought time and provided security for the peaceful development of the nations of the Far East and South-east Asia, including memorably, the People's Republic of China itself.

North Korea is still a harsh, oppressive, exploitive, dunder-headed military dicta-torship, which deprives its people of necessities and leaves them to live – if survive they can – amid gross deprivation, not only material, but intellectual. Besides, North Korea continues to pose a great threat to peace and stability. Still, we did not go into Korea to reunite the country, but to repulse Pyongyang's aggression.

Nonetheless, even more crucially, China is no longer messianically dedicated to remaking Asia and the world by violence. The Maoists preached world revolution through 'people's wars' waged by guerrillas, which would 'drive the capitalists and imperialists back to their lairs, where they would in time be destroyed. The Chairman truly believed that the Thought of Mao Zedong would thus become the paramount doctrine of an entire world ruled by himself under the guise of the 'dictatorship of the proletariat.' He believed in that victory as devoutly as he also believed in the creation of a perfect new society modeled on the Paris Commune of 1871, which he endeavored to recreate through his own Great People's Communes.

The dedication of the Maoist clique to 'people's war' and the conviction that it must prevail were both undermined by the US commitment to Vietnam. The demonstration that the decadent capitalists would fight cast grave doubts upon 'the inevitable victory of the masses through people's wars waged by guerrillas.' Maoism tottered when it became clear, a year or two before the Chairman's death in 1976 at the age of eighty-three, that only massed conventional forces could hope to overcome the imperialists and their lackeys.

The second pillar of Maoism was also badly shaken, not only in part by Vietnam, but in larger part by the demonstration that the Chairman's obsessive dogmatic policies could not create a functioning productive economy, much less the 'perfect society composed of perfected men and women' he envisioned. China was in 1979, only three years after the Chairman's departure, to be the first nation obviously to begin to dismantle the 'command economy' decreed by V.I. Lenin. Chinese thus repudiated the gospel holding that the state, which meant in practise the bureaucrats guided by the commissars, always knew best. That repudiation led to the collapse of Marxism-Leninism elsewhere, giving the other 'fraternal Socialist republics' a good, hard shove towards realism.

Finally, look at Vietnam itself. Communist hierarchs even more stubborn and more corrupt than the Chinese, which is saying something, are very slowly and very painfully adapting their economic practises to the realities of the outside world. They are thus inescapably weakening their own hold on power. By God, the Chinese and the Vietnamese are competing for investment by foreign capitalists.

Luke Maynell had for years derided my strong stand on the Vietnam venture, for I became a hawk when US power was committed. Of course, Vietnam was, as I have said, disastrous for the US in the short run, but pretty damned beneficial for the Vietnamese or, at the least, is proving so in the long run.

The last time we talked about it, a year ago, Luke commented wryly, 'When the Vietnamese get the foreign investment, chaos follows! No doubt now about who won the war! We did! And with that victory we won the right to corrupt the people with our baubles and gadgets even more sickeningly than their ascetic Communist rulers had made them suffer under the dead hand of Marxism-Leninism.

'American and European capitalists, also, of course, the omnipresent Japanese, are bringing the benighted Vietnamese the blessings of the modern world. Golf courses grab big swatches of arable land. Hanoi is wooing the volatile, undependable, and degrading tourist dollar. Also the sex trade, the sale of adolescent virgins to fat, beer-swilling Germans and lean, predatory Japanese executives. Substituting those glorious enterprises for that unexciting staple crop – rice.'

Actually, as I did not bother to point out at that time, peace with its adjustment of the economic burden, had increased the rice crop. More rubber was garnered, as well, when tappers no longer had to duck bullets. For the first time in decades, Vietnam was actually exporting rice, even rubber. But Luke was launched on a broad denunciation that brooked no such emendation.

'Delightful Hanoi, dreaming amid its placid lakes, is being transformed into another Bangkok,' he lectured. 'Traffic jams that stink of gasoline fumes and, also, the sickly sweet fumes of hash everywhere. Glossy new hotels built on the dikes that protect the city. Those dikes are, not so gradually, sinking under the weight of those dollar catchers … opening the city to flooding by the Red River. Many of those new hotels are nothing but glorified brothels.

'Sex tours from Europe and Asia are luring young women into prostitution, rather transparently disguised as escort services or personal assistance to harried businessmen. That commerce in flesh started a few years back, when the word went out that the sinuous, childlike virgins of Vietnam were *not* infected by AIDS. They are now, though few females over thirteen are still virgins. Nymphets instead. The stakes are too high: more *dong* or, better, dollars to be earned in one night than a senior civil servant makes in six months. Saigon and Hanoi now compete with Manila and Bangkok in the AIDS stakes.'

Luke halted his tirade abruptly, when he took in my deprecating smile. He resumed softly after a long pause.

'We've also raised the stakes on corruption. Once you could buy a clerk in a key ministry for a hundred dollars and know he'd stay bought – at least for that entire transaction. Now it costs thousands of dollars – and there's no certainty he'll stay bought. Also—'

'At least that's some improvement,' I put in. 'Rise in purchasing power for crooked cadres. And how can there be any cadres who're not crooked?'

'Harland, I know it sounds glib, even rehearsed,' Luke rejoined, rather defensively. 'But I've been thinking about the underside of the blessings of capitalism a lot lately … .Well, at least, the Vietnamese can afford to buy Sukhoi fighters from the Russians to guard them against their eternal enemies, the Chinese.'

I didn't take issue with Luke directly. Most of his strictures were essentially accurate, though overstated. Besides, none of those events, good or evil, would have occurred if the United States had not fought – and at first apparently lost – in Vietnam. Nothing much would have occurred in Hanoi's realm except continuing gray misery and heavy-handed oppression under the loom of an aggressive Maoist China.

Some of my enemies, even many of my friends, say I'm obsessive about Vietnam, even more fixated then I am on Korea. They call Vietnam my King Charles's head.

Regardless, it's now clear that we lost politically after all but winning militarily, because, as that TV producer said decades ago, the American people won't support a war they can't understand. So we withdrew after a figleaf of an agreement that won Henry Kissinger and Le Duc Tho a joint Nobel Peace Prize.

Neither thought the peace would last. Le Duc Tho because he was already planning the invasion of the South with his generals. Kissinger because he did not know that the retribution he threatened for such an invasion was to be pre-empted by a shameful US Congress, which would not even provide Saigon with the minimal military material sanctioned by that agreement. It's an ironic delight to look at Vietnam today and see that we have at least won economically and that we shall soon win politically. Further, Vietnam will remain an obstacle to Chinese hegemony.

Yet complexity remains an American bugbear. What's happening in Vietnam is still hard to understand, so for millions, including most of our media gurus, it simply doesn't exist. The Lord may temper the wind to the shorn lamb. He will not oversimplify complex reality for a light-minded people. He leaves that to the media with TV indubitably in the lead.

Chapter XXI

Two days after his little Bacchanalia with Duane Morton, Luke was shaken awake in mid-morning.

'Your girlfriend's on the horn,' I told him. 'Eager to talk to you.'

'Betsie, darling. How—' Embarrassed, Luke broke off. 'Yes, I see. It's great to hear from you, Sue. How are you?'

Her static-ridden voice came through the loudspeaker I'd had rigged so I could keep both hands on the keyboard while on the phone: 'I'm fine. But you won't be so fine if you don't get back here hubba-hubba.'

Luke grunted, and she continued, 'I didn't want to tell Howse where you were. He'd have kittens if he knew you were staying with a newsman. So I said I'd call, though it would be a chore finding you. That made him happy. Old Uncle Lesward doesn't like doing anything involving effort.'

'Of course, Sue. I almost forgot you're still attached to the I and E unit. We don't see you that often.'

'You seem to spend more time away than here. Luke, the final screening starts in seventy-two hours. And dear Colonel Howse says, and I quote: "Tell your fancy man to get his bony ass back here to Poo-city, doll. I need his many lingoed forked tongue. If he's not here toot-sweet, I'll tear his tongue out with my bare mitts."'

Luke grimaced, but said coolly, 'I don't have much choice, do I?'

'Doesn't sound like it.' Sue laughed. 'I'll tell the big cheese you'll be on the next plane.'

'Sue, be a honey. Tell Tony de Marco I need to talk to him before I go over to Koje. And ... and ... would you mind terribly telling Betsie I'm looking forward to seeing her? If it's humanly possible, I'll stop off and look for her at the ICRC. You don't mind telling her, Sue, do you?'

Sue's laugh was theatrical, but her tone was light when she replied, 'Mind? Why should I mind? If you really want to see Betsie, you'd better look for my brother, Tommy, Captain Chae Byongyup.'

Luke slipped into Chinese, obviously to exclude me from the further conversation. Before Sue could reply, a nasal American voice broke in, 'You're not allowed to speak anything but English on military lines. I'm cutting you off ... '

*

The nightly EUSAK Express was in theory the most convenient and the fastest scheduled land route between Seoul and Pusan, a steel-rail hypotenuse running north-west to south-east to link the extreme angles of South Korea. It was in reality a very uncomfortable way to get from the abandoned capital to the provisional capital, as Betsie Howard had learned a while ago. It was also an uncertain way. Its hard seats and its three-decker bunks were usually booked out long in advance by Korean friends of the American sergeants who allotted the space. Naturally, those close friends expressed their gratitude with gifts of jewelry or greenbacks. Colonels and generals could normally get reservations on the spot without waiting, but none was foolish enough to travel by train when he could whistle up air-borne transport.

Impressed by the urgency of his boss's summons, Luke didn't even consider the EUSAK Express. He asked me to drive him fifteen miles or so to K-16, the chief airfield serving Seoul. There were, of course, no civil flights, only military.

He soon found an accommodating pilot. The last I saw of Luke was a figure in a borrowed fleece-lined flight-jacket strapped into the bombardier's seat in the plexiglass nose of a twin-engined B-26 bound for Taejon to pick up 'emergency supplies.' Ten to one those urgently needed supplies were booze for the officers' club.

'I was way out in front, way forward of the engines' noise on the wings,' Luke later recalled. 'I couldn't see any part of the bomber except my own perch. It was like sitting on a cloud. I was all alone in the sky, lifted high, it seemed, by some kind of supernatural force.

'The B-26 landed at Taejon shortly after dusk. For me strapped into the transparent nose right up front it was like diving naked into a pool of solid blackness. I expected to scrape the tarmac any moment. Then the runway lights flashed on either side for maybe twenty seconds to guide us in. It was utterly terrifying to see the runway suddenly appear just twenty feet below.'

He shook his head in wonder at that memory. He was still capable of childlike awe at such a transcendent phenomenon. That was one of the odd traits that made me fond of him. He then answered the question that I had asked without my saying a word, asked just by raising an eyebrow.

'Was it exhilarating? Yes, of course! It was also unearthly, literally, of course, as well as figuratively. A supernal experience, as if I lay in the palm of God.

'It was sublime. And it was absolutely terrifying! No more magic carpets for me.'

After that landing at Taejon, which lies just about equidistant from Seoul and from Pusan, Luke picked up a more conventional flight, though he had a long wait. A twin-engined C-46 transport was taking off unladen for Pusan at 2.30 in the morning, the co-pilot's seat unoccupied behind the shiny glass panes like a small greenhouse that enclosed the flight deck. The pilot said he needed 'somebody to help push and pull levers', but he really wanted company on the lonely night flight.

Luke was ever afterward to delight in that memory: the detached, all but disembodied joy of the two-hour flight through the empty night sky over the warring peninsula. He felt himself suspended under an immense inverted bowl whose intense blackness was, rather infrequently, broken by the glitter of a star or the dim red-and-green navigation lights of an otherwise invisible aircraft. Like their landing fields, airplanes blacked out all other lighting so as not to offer illuminated targets for the virtually non-existent North Korean Air Force. Besides, the Russian and Chinese pilots of MIG fighter planes hardly ever ventured farther than twenty, at most, thirty miles south of the Yalu River, a long way from Taejon. Still, it would have been hellishly embarrassing for the mighty US Air Force to be caught with its lights on and its defenses down.

The minuscule red flare of a cooking-fire or the dim glow of slitted cat's eye headlights appeared from time to time far below and then quickly vanished. The countryside closed down at night, locked itself behind barred doors and windows when darkness fell, hoping thus to gain a little more security from guerrillas and bandits.

South Korea was moving very fast, almost literally at breakneck speed, but it was in some respects progressing backwards. A web of wires spun by the Japanese had formerly carried electricity to the most remote hamlets. Now there were only the lonely fires, the vagrant headlights, and the encompassing silence.

But the chatter in Luke's breakfast-coffee-cup-sized earphones never stopped. Voices without substance spoke across the ether in Chinese, Korean, and Japanese, as well as English. He hung fascinated on a conversation between a corps commander and a division commander of the Chinese People's Volunteers. Animatedly humorous, they discussed the evidently ceaseless Chinese checkers match they were playing at a distance.

Abruptly the enemy was as human as the Americans or the prisoners with whom he worked. Too human!

The pilot abruptly switched channels, and Luke heard again the deliberately toneless, under-emphasized, unstressed voices of air traffic controllers at airfields scattered through the peninsula.

'Peter Yoke zero niner, this is K-14 Control again. I repeat: You are clear to land. Runway lights will illuminate for twenty seconds half a minute from now. Emergency vehicles standing by. Say your condition, please?'

The accent of the invisible pilot in the invisible aircraft a hundred miles away was flat nasal Bostonian, but his bass voice was crackling with tension. 'Roger, K-14 Control. Gear's now wound down, but all hydraulics're out. That last burst of m-g fire must've cut the line. My co-pilot's bleeding bad. My gunner does not answer the intercom. Blood's getting into my eyes, but I can cope.'

'B-26 out of Suwon,' Luke's pilot commented laconically. 'Poor bastard!'

A minute or two of near silence dragged out at seemingly interminable length, broken by involuntary gasps from the B-26 pilot and the controller's laconic directions: 'Little higher.... Come starboard two degrees.... On the path!'

Three minutes later, the controller's voice rang out jubilantly, his professional detachment abandoned in his relief. 'Terrific landing, buddy. Ambulance and fire-trucks're rolling right next to you!'

Luke's pilot moved his gloved fingers on the knurled tuning knob, and the staccato *dit ... dah ... .dit ... dah* of an approach beacon supplanted the emotional outbreak of the ground-to-air controller. Drawn by the electronic string, the C-46 landed at the airfield designated K-2 near Pusan shortly before dawn.

Having hurried back, Luke tarried over a breakfast of dried eggs and fried spam at the airbase. Suddenly overcome by revulsion for Koje-do, he was in no hurry to immure himself again among the foul smells and the hideous sights of the drab prisoner island.

At any rate, he told himself, it was too late. He could not catch the despatch boat that regularly left Pusan at dawn for Koje. Regardless, he would have an excellent chance finding a supply boat later, a near certainty. He caught a lift to Pusan in a jeep temporarily assigned to a captain called Elfenbein, a Jewish chaplain off a C-54 from Tokyo.

The habitual illogic of the army was in high gear in four-wheel drive, pulling briskly away from realism and from reality itself. Its purpose was, as so often, utterly unfathomable! The rabbi had been assigned to the prisoner command, where there might be a few Jews, perhaps a half dozen or even at most a dozen, other than Lieutenant Sid Rosenstein, who was in any event quartered at the big POW Hospital on the mainland, not on Koje Island.

Himself not strong on realism, Chaplain Elfenbein was looking forward to learning from Chinese prisoners about the ancient Jewish settlement at Kaifeng in Hupei Province.

Rather than disillusion the hopeful chaplain, Luke prevaricated. He did not tell Rabbi Elfenbein that most POWs hardly knew their own birthplaces, much less the attenuated lore of a community of Chinese Jews that was now almost extinct. He resolved to keep an eye on the endearingly naïve rabbi, who must have offended the two-star chief of chaplains seriously to be sent to Koje. He further resolved to press Sid Rosenstein to scrape up some kind of Jewish congregation.

When the chaplain dropped him off at the G² tent, Luke found Major Tony de Marco and First Lieutenant Karl Simons listening raptly to a Bach cantata that was resoundingly yet subtly rendered by the massive Leak speakers. Seated under an awning before their tent, they were breakfasting leisurely on fresh eggs scrambled with fresh mushrooms and Bayonne ham accompanied by toasted French bread spread with Chivers bitter English marmalade.

'Hi, Luke!' Simons was assertively American despite his *Bratwurst* accent. 'Howsa boy? Howya doing?'

'Karl, Tony, good to see you,' Luke replied. 'Is the coffee as good as the chow?'

'At least as good.' de Marco assured him. 'Fresh beans flown in every week from Lohmeyer's in Tokyo. Not the GI shit. And our Miss Oh's a virtuosa of the pots and pans.'

Luke happily accepted a brimming blue-and-pink Royal Crown Derby cup. The jet-black coffee gave off a delicious Continental aroma, as far from GI coffee cut with condensed milk as Paris is from Duluth. The food was ambrosia.

He marvelled at de Marco's ability to find almost anywhere almost everything needed for comfort. The stocky lawyer, was, somewhat surprisingly, for the moment without the real Havana cigar that normally protruded from his fleshy mouth. Major Tony de Marco was almost in the same class as that acknowledged maestro of scroungers, Major Bennie Gam, Colonel Lesward Murray Howse's nominal second-in-command.

If challenged, really put on his mettle, Bennie Gam could assuredly conjure up a Georgian silver service for twelve and a classic 1935 Mercedes K-120 roadster from the war-devastated wastes of Korea. Tony de Marco, although just as shrewd and almost as plausible, was not as wholly dedicated to the fine craft of scrounging as was Bennie Gam.

Tony was a gifted amateur. Bennie was a professional.

'Majuh Gan, he's a artist. He'd do anything, anything at all, to get what he wants.' Lieutenant George Miner had once summed up, his mind running in its usual groove. 'He'd even screw Francesca, Madame Syngman Rhee herself, if he needed her recipe for apple strudel: pointy, drippy little Austrian nose, fat Austrian cheeks, bad breath and all!'

'Well shithead, what can we do for you?' de Marco was in normal form. 'You're surely not here for our charm alone.'

'Your charm would make a pig vomit, Tony. But I've got perverted tastes. Dr. Johnson, Samuel Johnson, liked rancid butter and putrid meat. Same way, somehow I like you.'

'Terribly, terribly lit'ry, aren't we today, Captain Maynell? Must be sniffing around for information again.'

'The hot poop is what you want?' Karl Simons asked. 'Well, you've come to the wrong place. We don't know nothing from nothing.'

'What've you heard about the rescreening from the big brass, from Washington, or from your low-life contacts?' Luke demanded. 'Up in the apple orchard at Munsan the negotiators're throwing fits. They're scared stiff the count won't come out right ... deadly afraid there'll be too many non-repats! But they're even more afraid to monkey with the figures. They're telling Koje the tally has to be strictly on the up and up.'

'Hell, Luke, I don't know a damned thing, only that the brass are desperate,' de Marco replied. 'Shit scared of screwing up. They've assigned me to supervise a section of interrogators. *Me!* What'm I supposed to do? Talk high Castillian to the Chinks? You gotta tell me what *you* know.'

Luke briefed the intelligence officers. He passed on all he had learned about the peace talks and the morale of both enemy and friendly troops. Summing up his three weeks' absence, he concluded that he had learned little.

'Not a hell of a lot, is it, Luke?' de Marco agreed. 'I *can* tell you one thing, though. The brass've put your enquiry on ice. They won't put any more pressure on you to fake evidence that the two Commies were killed by their own people. They're too antsy about repatriation to worry about a little thing like a double murder.'

'For the time being, anyway.' Luke was not convinced. 'And my buddy Major-General Li Mao? What's he been up to?'

'Disappeared, Luke, *spurlos verschwunden*. Not a peep out of him for a month. Not even a sighting.'

'That's a little ominous, isn't it?'

'You'd better look around. See if you can run him down.'

'Fat chance, but I'll try. Anything else I ought to know?'

'Well ... ' de Marco paused and glanced at Simons, who shrugged his shoulders and rolled his blue eyes, looking like a roguish cherub under his halo of wispy golden hair. 'OK, Karl, *you* tell him.'

'Well, Luke, it's nothing really. Nothing to disturb you, I'm sure. It's only that your ... Bets ... Miss Howard is often seen with this Captain Chae Byongyup.'

'Is that all, Karl?' Luke responded defensively. 'Why the fuss? For God's sake, she's supposed to be with him ... as liaison for the Switzers, for the Red Cross.'

'The question, young man,' de Marco interjected, 'is exactly *what* kind of liaison work she's doing.'

'Tony, you can damn well lay off the innuendos. You don't really *know* anything.'

'I'd be a piss poor G² officer if I didn't. They're all over the place together.'

'Just cut it out, Tony!'

Luke dampened his show of anger with a shower of bonhomie, even though shrewd Tony de Marco was not to be taken in by such a specious display of good humor. Lest he appear to be leaving in wrath, Luke chatted with the under-employed intelligence officers for another ten minutes, until he could reasonably ask de Marco to lend him a jeep and driver.

The boxy little vehicle skidded insouciantly around the potholes in the slippery coastal road, narrowly missing ox-drawn 'honey carts' redolent of the human manure liberally applied to fertilize the rice-fields. The driver did not draw aside or even slacken his speed to cut down the amount of liquefied shit slopping over the sides. Rather than yield the road, he preferred to endure being constantly spattered with mud thrown up by convoys of heavy six-by-six army trucks with canvas tops like prairie schooners. Prairie schooners, that is, covered wagons to you of the latest semi-literate generation.

Unpainted fishing boats were drawn high up the beaches, half-anchored by the heavy stones lashed to their bulwarks. Their patched sails were furled, and their oars were bound down tight against the raging wind. That half-gale hurled salt spume into the eyes of the women and children gleaning driftwood from the coarse brown sand. The branches of the few surviving fir trees were blown so hard they streamed horizontal.

Luke remembered Betsie's only half-comical complaint. ICRC headquarters, she joked, was not just a long way from the city of Pusan, but practically in China! Not simply hard to find, but virtually inaccessible.

'Anyone who makes the trip must be serious about me.' He could all but hear her say it again with that throaty chuckle that made the fine hairs on the back of his neck tingle. 'A girl's a fool if she expects strictly honorable intentions in the middle of this war. But any man who gets all the way out here and doesn't complain must, at the least, be making a very serious assault on my so-called virtue.'

As so often, Betsie had talked provocatively while behaving circumspectly — and subtly deprecating herself. For all her buxom perfection, the All American Girl suffered from a slight deficiency that no miracle drug could cure. She was – or at least pretended to be – unsure of her own charms. Nothing could assuage her slight failure of self-assurance. That was the way she was.

It was, however, no joke at all, the sheer difficulty of finding her at the IRCR headquarters. Luke knew the way from his own dealings with the International Red Cross team. He had, after all, taken Betsie there to introduce her to the ICRC. Yet he felt he was making an interminable journey through the gritty Korean rain towards an elusive destination that almost seemed to move further away. Anyway, she would probably be out when he finally got there.

Kurt Schuler, the ICRC administrative officer, greeted Luke warmly. The staid Swiss had grown fond of the unpredictable American officer who sometimes acted like an irresponsible 12-year old, but was at other times resembled a venerable, imperturbable graybeard steeped in the wisdom of the East.

Schuler looked pained for a moment, perhaps fearful of Betsie Howard's returning arm-in-arm with Captain Chae Byongyup. The next instant, blandly noncommittal unconcern smoothed his blunt features. He was neutral, and he was diplomatic.

All in all, he was very Swiss. He spoke rather like a headwaiter explaining airily, yet in deep concern, why a table reservation has gone astray. Not quite, however, like an undertaker oozing antiseptic professional sympathy.

'Miss ... ah ... Bartleby is unfortunately not present, Captain,' he said in his precise English, which was only a shade *too* precise. 'But it was her intention to return at eleven. Given the vicissitudes of travel in this country, I cannot guarantee that she will arrive on time. I cannot offer full assurance, however ... '

'Thanks a lot, Herr Schuler,' Luke responded. 'We both know she's never on time. But I'll wait if I may.'

'Certainly, Captain. In the library, perhaps?'

The Swiss were proud of their library, which was hung with tourist posters boasting snowcapped peaks and well nourished dairymaids in low-cut dirndls, as well as the stately Palais des Nations in Geneva. If they had been Americans, the library, frankly called a bar, would have reeked of old cigarettes' low lying smoke and of stale beer. Instead, the wood-panelled room in the former Japanese prefecturate smelled slightly of some mild disinfectant, but was aromatic with beeswax furniture-polish, as well as a whiff of pear brandy.

Luke settled down to wait with yesterday's *Stars and Stripes*. In the next hour and a half, he consumed a full week's file of the GI newspaper. He was progressively more annoyed by the mealy-mouthed coverage of the POW issue, and he was progressively less amused at the cartoons depicting the misadventures of American soldiers in Japan and Korea.

Still, Americans could poke fun at themselves, even in an officially unofficial newspaper like *Stars and Stripes*. Wondering if Mao Zedong and his commissars would ever feel secure enough to laugh at themselves, Luke inconsequentially recalled a manual on humor issued by the German Army during World War I. It instructed the Kaiser's soldiers that they must learn to laugh, even at themselves. With the German thoroughness, it taught them exactly *how* to laugh by clinically analysing British soldiers' humor.

Luke remembered his favorite line from that earnest handbook of humor. A cartoon showed Old Bill, the British GI Joe of that war, sheltering with a young recruit in a hut with walls pierced by large round holes.

'What made them 'oles, Bill?' the recruit asks.

'Mice, son, mice,' Old Bill replies.

A footnote in the German manual explained: *It was not mice. It was shells.*

A jeep skidded to a halt in the driveway, invisible behind the opaque *shoji* shielding the windows. The screech of rubber tires and the shower of gravel were, nonetheless, a giveaway. No Swiss would drive with such reckless panache. Unless some unknown American or ROK officer had business with the ICRC, Betsie had indubitably arrived, either driving herself in her normal flashy way or chauffeured by Captain Chae Byongyup with equal dash.

Luke was jolted by that familiar sound. He realized that he was apprehensive. He was actually a little nervous at the prospect of seeing Betsie the next minute. That sensation was odd, very strange, indeed unprecedented.

He was no more than realistic in recognizing that he was known for his *savoir faire*: his unshakeable good temper and his calm response to any challenge, however dire. He was also, he acknowledged, all but famous, perhaps notorious for his polite, total self-possession, for his utter, unshakeable self-assurance in dealing with women. Who wouldn't be when the little darlings flocked to him unbidden?

But he was now edgy at the prospect of meeting the girl he had, quite unconcerned, left behind like a doll on a shelf. He had, he recalled unhappily, been wholly confident of Betsie. If he had thought about it, if he had considered the question at all, he would have told himself that she would still be exactly there, where he wanted her, when he returned. After all, she was entirely his, as he wished when he wished.

Is she really? he now wondered.

Luke lit another Lucky Strike to ease his unwonted fears. Having been told, perhaps warned, by Schuler of his presence, Betsie might be dismissing Chae Byongyup or she might be primping. In any event, she was clearly not eager to rush into his arms. He was stubbing out his third butt when the click of high heels on the hard teak floor heralded her arrival.

Unabashedly theatrical, Betsie made a grand entrance. She stalked into the library trailing a gorgeous coat of golden Siberian mink as if it were an empress's train. Her shoes were scarlet, and her stockings were smoky gray. Her cowl-necked dress of soft burgundy jersey flared into a full skirt that swirled around her slender calves. Pinned to the tight bodice that molded her full breasts and her taut ribcage she wore the parrot brooch of semi-precious stones Luke remembered from their first meeting in Seoul.

Nothing to do with Chae Byongyup and his interpreter's parrot insignia, Luke assured himself. An old family heirloom, she had once explained.

When Betsie smiled thinly, he saw that two of her upper front teeth were faintly smudged with the tangerine lipstick she had evidently just applied. Her long ruddy-mahogany hair was twisted into a chignon; the fine wisps that escaped gave her an enticingly dishevelled air. She was flushed as if she had just come out of the wind, and her turquoise eyes shone bright.

Luke's heart leaped. He felt the physical impact: his heart jumped in his chest and his breath caught in his throat like a 16-year-old on his first date. He was overcome, all but overwhelmed, by the sweet, agonizing uncertainty: by the fanciful fears and the flight of self-assurance, possessed by the desperate ardor of adolescence. He was swept once more, as he had not been for at least a decade, by delicious terror before the unknown. He trembled, actually trembled for an instant, before the glorious mystery of the feminine. Miss Bartleby Howard might have been the first girl he had ever dated.

Luke now saw with sharp, prickly clarity that she was a woman, not a cuddly plush animal. She was herself, a complete human being, not a pretty plaything lent to amuse him. He knew then that he loved Betsie as he had never loved any of her dozens of forerunners. He repented of the attentions he had paid all those girls and young women; he bitterly regretted having wasted time and emotion on them. Quite consciously, with deliberate resolution, he banished them forever from his thoughts.

Luke's censorious conscience reproached him with the voluptuous Korean prostitute he had used only two nights earlier. Still, he *had* been drunk! And it was in truth only the second time in his life he had paid a bed partner, not since he was actually sixteen. Still, the memory was distasteful, extremely distasteful.

Betsie was the only woman for him, Luke saw in the intense clarity of the moment, the only woman for him forever. He was exhilarated, his head whirling. The next moment, he was also indignant and afraid.

He had before this moment not even thought about monogamy. What he had to do he could do far better unencumbered. Besides, he had, until this morning, delighted in the opportunities, sexual and emotional, that his freedom provided. Yet, he realized with a shock that was almost physical, he was now determined to marry Betsie. How else could he keep her beside him forever?

Luke reeled under the violent gusts of his own deepest feelings. He had until a minute or so earlier complacently believed his life was wholly under his own control. Even now his intractable intellect fought back.

The scant moments since Betsie made her dramatic entrance had revealed that she was beyond any doubt the only woman for him. But to tie himself to one woman for life? At just 27 years of age to tie himself down for all the years to come?

Luke Maynell reproached himself. *I must stop inventing difficulties!*

The pattern of his reactions was familiar, far too familiar. Every one of his earlier love affairs had reached the beginning of its ending when such prudent, such eminently reasonable objections bubbled into his mind. This blessed love must not end the same way when it had only just begun. This was a wholly new, radiant experience in a newly discovered, enchanted realm.

'Hello, Luke,' Betsie smiled coolly. 'It's good to see you after all this time.'

She tilted her head back for his kiss. The gesture was, somehow, at once peremptory and tentative, as if she wondered whether she could – or even wished to – assert her proprietary right over Luke. Her lips were cool and soft, tasting of that new tangerine lipstick. She drew back after a few seconds and looked hard at him, her minute smile still in place.

Luke flared into anger. He had just made the most important decision of his life. He had overridden his misgivings, and he had committed himself for life to this woman. But she was frosty, almost ice cold.

'That was a nice kiss, Bets,' he said lightly. 'A nice *sisterly* kiss.'

'I don't know about your sisters, Luke.' Her husky laugh taunted him. 'But I wouldn't advise them to scatter kisses like that around. They could be misunderstood.'

'I hope to God I haven't misunderstood you, Bartleby Howard,' Luke said softly.

Betsie hardly heard that remark. Rocking slightly on her toes, she gazed at the man whom she now knew she still wanted, wanted badly. But *not* just for a quick fling amid the supercharged atmosphere and the perils of war. She wanted him desperately at that moment, feeling herself moisten to receive him. But above all, she wanted him for *all* her life. As coolly as she could, her own roiled emotions barely under control, Betsie Howard assessed Luke Maynell.

His normally crisp, shining chestnut hair was lank and dust-filmed. His amber eyes were red-rimmed, and the soft skin beneath them was a livid violet. The dark stubble on his cheeks made him appear even more unkempt and debilitated, in fact, totally exhausted.

Disheveled and dirty, he was nonetheless attractive. The firm cheekbones, the finely arched nose, and the sensitive mouth were unaltered. The grimy fingernails and the abraded knuckles barely detracted from the grace of his long-fingered hands. His quick smile, like the first rays of the sun at dawn, still had the power to warm her – and to inflame her. The quicksilver play of his mind could still bewitch her, making her forget prudence.

She had warned Luke at their new beginning in Seoul. She had warned him that, when … if … they came together again, she would never let go. Once she got her talons into him, she would clutch him to herself all of his life. That conviction was still powerful, all the more powerful for what had grown between them during the past few months.

But did she, even now, truly *want* to lock her talons in Luke?

Betsie reviewed her misgivings. Above all, Luke was erratic, perhaps, indeed probably, too erratic to make a life-long husband and an ever dependable father. He was everyone's friend and every woman's knight errant.

How could he possibly be wholly faithful to one woman? His attention and his affection would be repeatedly diverted by his overriding concern for others, just as in Robert Browning's lyric the unhappy Duke judged his 'Last Duchess' to be *too* kind because *too* compassionate. Luke's dedication to his ideals and his fascination with most abstract ideas would make him a mercurial, volatile, disturbing life-partner.

When dishes needed drying, he would be discussing the finer points of Thomas Aquinas or, more likely, Mencius. When the baby needed changing or snowdrifts needed shoveling, he would be crusading for the rights of Asian immigrants. When an influential man or woman needed a little flattery, he would on principle with-hold that lubricant. Chances were he would sometimes forget to pay the mortgage, although, in fairness and rather comfortingly, they would need no mortgage. Still, over all, chances were even greater that he would be in Japan or China when she needed him most.

Nonetheless, Betsie Howard told herself again, one fact was absolutely clear: she would dearly love to have Luke Maynell beside her all her life. He was exciting and sensual, yet, somehow, reassuring. He was stirring and disturbing, yet she felt secure when she was with him. The wealth he would some day inherit, she acknowledged, did not detract from his glamour. Neither did the power of his family.

Her own family was quite stalwart in itself. Their belongings, their valuables, their real estate, even their bric-a-brac, certainly their bank accounts and their shares, were quite adequate to relieve her of any suspicion of greed. What she was likely to inherit in time, much time, she hoped, was more than sufficient to sustain her own state and to assure her reputation for integrity. Although the Maynells, as well as the Luxboroughs, were seriously rich, many times over multi-millionaires, she would never feel remotely like a gold-digger or ever be looked upon as a gold-digger.

She could never be censured as a harpy preying on his wealth. How could she, when she had all she could ever need or want.

Nonetheless, the likely price of a lifetime with Luke – if a lifetime were possibly attainable – could be too high. The inherent risk could be too great. The security she felt when with him was probably an illusion, although his allure was for her very real – the physical, intellectual, and emotional fascination. Yet, even if they lived in Asia, as she, too, might wish, he would always be drifting away somewhere.

Besides, there was Tommy – Captain Chae Byongyup. She must, at the very least, think of Tommy. He was a sophisticated grown-up of great charm, while Luke sometimes appeared still to be an unsure adolescent, although at other times, she had to admit, he shone as the epitome of mature wisdom.

She had, Betsie acknowledged to herself, started with Tommy to get back at Luke – to make Luke jealous. That old ploy! Nevertheless, Sue's half-brother was himself very attractive. Yet Tommy was, of course, quite plainly *not* to be taken seriously! There could quite definitely be no future with him. Tommy Chae was a blithe diversion, a passing amusement. In the end, however sublime in himself, he was no more than a charming plaything for herself.

'I hope I haven't misunderstood you,' Luke reiterated softly.

'Misunderstood?' Betsie rose to the challenge. 'How could you misunderstand me? I've always been open and direct ... completely honest with you, Luke.'

'In everything, Betsie?'

Feeling vulnerable in regard to Tommy Chae, Betsie defended herself with a vigorous attack. 'Yes of course. And I'll be honest and direct now. Luke, I'm annoyed at you, very annoyed. I'm annoyed and disappointed.'

'Disappointed? How come? I haven't been around to disappoint you lately, have I?'

'That's it! You disappeared ... just disappeared ... for three whole weeks. I didn't have the vaguest idea where you were. Luke, if I didn't care—'

'Some of the time, nobody knew where I was,' he interrupted. 'They weren't supposed to. But you knew you could always reach me through Harland Birch – and you didn't try. Only Sue finally called me. Where were you when—'

'I tried ... five times. There was never an answer. For all I knew, you'd given me a phony number. But Sue got an answer the very first time. Funny, isn't it?'

'Why in the name of God would I do that?'

'I don't know. But who wouldn't be suspicious? You and Sue are awfully cosy lately.'

'Now, Bets, you know there's nothing to that. We work together. And I have a lot of regard ... high regard for her. But that's all. It's not like you and me.'

Almost against her own will, Betsie was relieved. She had drawn back from the brink of the precipice that she had unwittingly approached by questioning Luke's relations with Sue. He could have snapped back at her, demanding to know what she was up to with Tommy. It appeared that Luke was either unaware of her dangerous flirtation or, more likely, had quite sensibly, in truth shrewdly, decided not to raise that issue just now. Despite the fuss he was kicking up, she was suddenly struck by worry – perhaps he didn't care enough about her to bother.

'How could I find you?' she demanded. 'Do you think I've got second sight?'

'Betsie, I expect nothing more than you're willing to give ... want to give.' Luke deliberately misunderstood her question. 'If you feel half as much as I do, you'll want to ... to be with me ... want to be together all the time we can.'

'I see,' she acknowledged almost inaudibly. 'And then?'

'And then? You know, there *is* a future. There is a life after Korea, and I thought ...'

He paused.

'Just let me get through the next week or two, the damned rescreening. Then we can really talk. It's not fair to you now. Nor to me!'

Betsie had worked herself up to towering indignation in self-defense. She was certainly distressed because Luke had been so remote, so distant. He had, after all, failed to say a word, not even sent her a brief message, no word for three weeks. She was, however, almost equally disturbed by nagging guilt over her essentially innocent, in reality quite harmless, relationship with Tommy Chae. Besides, she wondered, she was truly in doubt whether Luke could ever be tamed.

Yet she melted at his soft words. Their implicit promise was the closest he had ever come to expressing or even suggesting, hope that they could have a future together. She cautioned herself to hold him off, certainly not to yield so easily. Despising her weak female submission to a dominant male, she took Luke's hand and gently touched his shoulder with her other hand.

When he let her go, her ribs ached and her lips tingled. Yet she was relaxed and confident.

'So you've come back for the rescreening,' she teased. 'And I thought it was to see me.'

'Unofficially, personally, I only wanted to see you. Officially, I was ordered to come back for the recount.'

'Well, my dear, don't work too hard at it.'

'What do you mean?'

'Luke, don't send even a single POW back. Why should we help out the Communists, after everything they've done? The sneak attacks! The atrocities! All the trouble they've caused in the camps!'

'Do you know what you're saying?' he asked. 'How else can we end the war?'

'I think so many POWs don't want repatriation … not enough POWs want to go back to end the war. The Communists'll lose face anyway, not enough. So why shouldn't they lose *all* their face? Anyway, when Korea's united, the repatriation issue won't matter. Just a little push now – and the Chinese'll pull out. All it needs is a couple of American divisions more.'

'More US troops? Impossible, I'd say. Washington won't send another platoon. Anyway, what about the Chinese who do want to go home?'

'The Chinese?' She wondered how he could be so impractical, still so idealistic. 'There's plenty of Chinese in China already. In fact, far too many!'

Luke was no longer simply suspicious. He knew the words were Chae Byongyup's, though the voice was Betsie's. Although bitterly opposed to Syngman Rhee, Chae, too, was inherently anti-Chinese. Chae, too, wanted his country reunified at virtually any cost.

Still, Luke had neither time nor stomach for a confrontation with Betsie at that moment. To examine the divisive political issues seriously would take hours. To avoid the divisive personal issue of Chae Byongyup would be impossible.

He simply lacked the courage. Having thrown over so many girls, having rarely, hardly ever, taken any girl seriously for any length of time, Luke was now virtually paralyzed by fear of losing one particular girl. It would be nothing less than tragic! It would be bitter and ironic, a profound tragedy to lose Betsie so soon after discovering just how much he needed her.

Luke did not reveal his inner turmoil. His temper was now under normal tight control behind his normal surface amiability. He retreated behind a smokescreen of bonhomie, he assured himself, in order to fight another day.

If he were serious about Betsie, as he most certainly was serious, deeply serious in his hopes and his plans, he would work it all out with her another day very soon. They could work it all out after the rescreening.

That new interrogation, designed to definitively separate all the non-repatriates from the willing returnees, was becoming a benchmark in his life, as it was in the lives of almost 200,000 captives. A benchmark, yet, in reality, far more than a point delineating the scope of a policy! It was now, above all, a great endeavor that could determine the duration of the war.

'My God, I've got to get on my horse,' he said. 'Howse'll have a screaming fit if I don't report today.'

He kissed her hard and was out the door before she could say another word. Hearing his jeep kicking up gravel, Betsie touched her lips with her fingertips and wondered.

Chapter XXII

George Miner, First-Lieutenant, Infantry, Army of the United States, diploma'd Chinese linguist, was adjutant, confidant, and, above all, toady to Colonel Lesward Murray Howse. His rangy frame, sandy hair, generous features, and drawling voice reminded the impressionable of Gary Cooper, the sensitive he-man actor, who was always independent, who was, despite intense social pressures, always his own man.

That parallel was wildly misleading. Whatever independence Miner might once have possessed had been shaken by his induction, scythed by officer training, and, finally, crushed by his blustering superior. He was now happiest within range of Howse's squeaky, yet hectoring voice, since no initiative would then be required of him. All individual judgement, which was in theory encouraged by the army in all ranks from private to five-star general, was in practise forbidden by this lately promoted bird-colonel.

At the very moment, right now, George Miner felt himself perilously isolated – with no hope of appealing to higher authority. He could not pass on to the colonel any decision that might be required of him. He knew, deeply feared, that he might be forced to make a decision on an important issue. But he was on his own, marooned alone behind a rickety green-baize table in one of the squad tents erected a short distance from the compounds of the POW camp.

Lieutenant Miner shivered. Though late-April, it was chilly and dank an hour before dawn on Koje-do when the wind blew from the sea. He lit a Camel with the Zippo lighter his elder brother had brought home from serving in the Army of Occupation in Germany. The engraved inscription literally translated was, perhaps, characteristic: *With every passing day there grows the number of those who can just kiss my ass!*

George Miner liked that sentiment. It precisely expressed the devil-may-care individualism he believed he embodied. He reached into the pocket of his field jacket for the sheaf of glossy prints he called his 'art studies'. He had assiduously photographed dozens of exhibitionist Korean prostitutes during his six months in the country. He drew comfort from looking them over – comfort and renewed confidence. The masterly photographs proved that he was not only a dashing soldier, but a gifted artist.

'Fuck!' he said without vehemence, when his hand encountered no photographs. 'Fucking son of a bitch stupid shitass!'

217

Like a prayer, that mild expression of dissatisfaction restored Miner's equanimity. Forbidding him to bring the art studies into the interrogation tent, Luke Maynell had asked, 'What are you thinking of, George? Were you planning to show your treasures to the POWs? We don't need Peking charging us with corrupting pure young warriors with pornography.'

'It's not pornography, Luke. It's art. Anyway, I always carry them. Gives me a warm feeling.'

'Not tonight, Josephine,' Luke had concluded briskly, before assigning him to the tent where he now sat alone. 'No pornography for you, buster!'

Despite his irritation, George Miner was glad when the tent-flap was pushed aside to admit a cloud of pre-dawn mist and Captain Luke Maynell. Luke, too, was obviously nervous. He ground out a half-smoked Lucky Strike beneath his boot on the plank floor and immediately lit another.

'Just checking,' he said. 'They should be here any minute. Relax, George. There's nothing to be jumpy about.'

'That's fine for you, pal. But not for me. I only had six lousy months of Chinese at Monterey. And I've hardly used it since I came to Korea. Too busy being chief cook, dog-robber, bottle-washer, and driver for His Honor Colonel Lesward Murray Howse. But you expect me to—'

'I've told you over and over again, George. It's orders! I've got no choice! You know the score. We've got to use whoever we can.

'And how do you think Bennie Gam feels? Worse than you, I'd bet. He *looks* Chinese. But he can hardly speak a word of Mandarin, not even with the drilling I've given you both the past few days.'

'Thanks, Luke. It was a big help. But ... aw shit, political questions! Why can't we use the boys from Taiwan? Ray Wu could do the job standing on his head.'

'You friggin' well do know why ... you just don't want to accept it.' The half-euphemism for the Army's favorite word, which he disliked using, betrayed Luke's irritation. 'But I'll go through it again ... just once more. We can*not*, I repeat can*not*, use your pal Raymond Wu and his boys because they'd try to talk every last POW into *not* going back to mainland China.

'Chiang Kai-shek doesn't want this war to end soon. The longer it lasts, the better for him. He does want the propaganda victory: thousands of Chinese POWs deciding to go to Taiwan.'

'What about ROK civilian interpreters? I know eight, maybe more, who speak pretty good Chinese.'

'The same reason ... only more so. As you know full well, Syngman Rhee doesn't want an armistice. He wants to march north – with US backing. All ROK interrogators, civilian or military, are under orders to finagle ... to find a majority of non-repats. We can't help using ROKs with the Korean POWs. But definitely not with the Chinese.'

'Hard to say, Luke, isn't it, exactly whose side our own brass is on – ours or the Commies'. Practically forcing prisoners to go home! It stinks!'

'Maybe, but those're our orders. The brass is deathly afraid the numbers'll come out wrong. Too many non-repats could prolong the war indefinitely.'

'OK, Luke, I'll do my best. But please don't get too far away. I could need help.'

'Don't worry, George. Won't be that many who refuse to go back. It's not natural.'

Luke patted the apprehensive lieutenant on the shoulder. George Miner would need all the self-confidence he could muster today.

As for Major Bennie Gam, what, short of divine intercession, could help him? The Chinese-American was impressive mentally, as well as physically. An instinctive political thinker, a consummate procurer of scarce goods ranging from whiskey to jeeps, a brilliant manipulator of the military bureaucracy, he was, sadly, no linguist. With his benevolent features, which were generously proportioned, but finely cut, he looked like a benign Buddha. Only the Great Buddha of Hope, to whom he prayed, could help him today.

Bennie Gam could now just get a few words of China's 'national' tongue off his own tongue. But his ragged Toisan dialect, basically peasant Cantonese from China's south-east adulterated by a New York accent, would be gibberish to almost all the POWs, who came from the north and the west. They all could, though, just understand each other, although they spoke quite distinct varieties of the 'national' or 'common tongue', which we outsiders call Mandarin, because it was spoken by the officials of imperial China, the officials we call Mandarins.

Presumably any prisoner who complained of being misunderstood after this rescreening could be re-examined. But how many would dare complain? Anyone who did complain would be slaughtered or, at the least, maimed by the merciless enforcers of either the Communist or the Nationalist compound to which he had in error been consigned.

A hell of a way to run an exercise that would determine the fate of so many human beings! Out of more than 170,000 prisoners of war, some 38,000 South Koreans who had been press-ganged by the Communists were already eliminated. They were to remain in the ROK without further examination – to the Communists' voluble fury. The remainder, 100,000 from North Korea and 22,000 from China, were to be questioned again. They could, as we've already noted a dozen times, elect either to go home or to be released after an armistice in South Korea or Taiwan. A few might avail themselves of the further privilege Psywar had promised – and choose refuge in other non-Communist nations. But only a very few!

It is well worth noting that ROK and US instructions to interrogators diverged diametrically. ROK interrogators would strive to persuade POWs that they did *not* want to be repatriated. Most US interrogators would urge them, however sublimi-nally, however unintentionally, to choose repatriation. Beside some interrogators, like George Miner and Bennie Gam, could barely speak the language of the POWs.

Dicing thus with tens of thousands of lives was diabolical, though the purpose was noble: to end a war. Still, combat could kill hundreds of thousands if it continued indefinitely.

When would President Harry S-for-nothing Truman tire of holding his hand and send half-a-dozen additional American divisions to Korea? If he considered such massive reinforcement too costly or, more likely, they were simply not available, when would he lose his famous temper and drop an atomic bomb or two on the Chinese People's Volunteers or, even, on China itself, as he had already dropped A-bombs on two Japanese cities?

That danger was, however, slight to virtually non-existent. Harry Truman was not a patient man, but he had learned wisdom on the job.

Luke leaned against his jeep, which was parked beside the row of green tents erected for the rescreening. With deliberate calm, he slipped a cigarette out of its white packet and lit it with a blue-lacquered Dunhill lighter bought at the PX. Awaiting the trials of the coming day, he was tense, though hardly as tense as George Miner.

Who *was* as tense as George Miner? Only thousands of POWs!

Luke rubbed his knotted neck muscles and cartwheeled his arms. In vain, for his neck and shoulders remained tensed. His sixth cigarette before dawn was not calming, but actually making him even more jittery.

As the morning mist slowly dispersed, it unveiled the bleak contours of the harsh prison island. Wherever trees or bushes had once stood, everywhere grass had once grown or wild flowers had bloomed, the earth was savaged by bulldozers. The laterite soil displaced from that widespread digging ranged from a matte ruddy ochre to glistening blood-red, enormous wounds in the island's dreary face. The paddyfields where rice had once thrust through silvery water in spear-straight rows were now greasy ash-brownish morasses pocked with stones.

Clumps of packed-mud houses with mangy gray-thatched roofs stood close to the jagged shadows cast by the twelve-foot-high barbed-wire fences. All those dwellings were deserted. The camp authorities had finally realized that those villages were not only seedbeds of venereal disease and emporiums of the black market, but communication centers. Their rather sophisticated facilities not only relayed messages, between compounds, but connected POW *honchos* to their far away commanding generals.

Yet communication between different compounds, even communication from Koje to Pyongyang or Peking had only been slightly hampered by evacuating those villages. Pro-Communist compounds now used smuggled two-way radios to speak to headquarters that were hundreds of miles distant. Many Korean radio messages were relayed to Pyongyang by Communist guerrillas who were harrying the southwest, not so far away at all. The Chinese so-called Volunteers could, of course, use the same route, although some of their powerful hidden wireless sets spoke directly to Peking.

No UN officer wanted to be responsible for the pitched battle that would undoubtedly be provoked by a shack-by-shack search of the compounds for hidden transceivers. Still, pro-Communist POW *honchos* feared direction finders could triangulate their radios' exact positions. Communication between compounds was, therefore, now usually airborne. Koreans, who are wizards at taming dragonflies, sent those miniaturized carrier pigeons aloft with flimsy paper messages tied around their abdomens.

'The damned Koreans are like their own pet dragonflies,' General Li Mao had remarked to Luke. 'You know the old saying *Chingting Dien Shui!* The dragonfly only skims the surface of the pond! Senior Colonel Lee Hak Koo, who commands my Korean allies, is just the same. He skims the surface, never penetrating to the deeper ramifications of a policy or a decision. He is superficial, superficiality incarnate. So he makes fundamental mistake after fundamental mistake. Just like the dragonfly.'

Shades of Dr. Doolittle! Luke smiled at the contrast between the mid-twentieth-century horrors of Koje and the kindly Edwardian Englishman who could speak with every kind of animal, but was misunderstood by his fellow humans.

That smile did not lighten Luke's foreboding as dawn crept across the prisoner island. The scene thus revealed graphically recalled a stark 1920s woodcut of social protest, particularly a Käthe Kollwitz or a George Grosz, spiky black shapes against a grim gray background.

The elongated silhouettes of watchtowers brooded like predatory dinosaurs over the compound fences; every strand of barbed-wire sharply outlined in the sudden dawn clarity. The helmets of the guards on the towers glistened shiny black with dew, and their soaked ponchos sprouted long rifle-barrels. The sour stench of tens of thousands of penned human beings was spread by the dawn wind as the shadows grew pale.

Luke heard hoarse singing from Compound 76 a half-mile away. He recognized the tune of that paean to 'Our Beloved Leader, Comrade Kim Il Sung'. Compound 76 would not be coming out for rescreening. Its Communist rulers would slaughter any man who stepped forward. Whatever they might individually wish, *all* the POWs in Compound 76 were going north – with the UN Command's fervent blessing.

A strange alliance of expediency between enemies!

From Compound 27, which was much closer, he could distinguish the rival stations of two Chinese songs: '*Chi Lai!*', the Communist anthem opposed to '*San Min Chu Yi!*', the Nationalist anthem. Over the singing rose the falsetto chanting of political slogans. The battle between the two Chinese factions was now met openly on Koje-do. The winners would decide the inmates' fate: the Nationalists determined to choose Taiwan, the Communists determined not to submit to questioning at all.

No way, Luke reflected glumly, could most POWs choose freely. The pressure on them was too great. Perhaps a stubborn handful would hold out courageously. Most, however, would go where they were told to go by their *honchos*.

Luke promised himself that no POW that he or his interrogators saw would be bullied into choosing Taiwan. It was, after all, only natural that most would want to go home. Ideology made a cold bedmate! Alien Taiwan and its alien people would be poor substitutes for prisoners' native places and the clansmen among whom they had grown up. Whatever his own disconcerting previous experience of the first screening, Luke concluded, the great majority would ... must ... inevitably choose repatriation. And the damnable war would finally come to an end!

Formerly a hero to those Americans, who cared, now a black villain, Syngman Rhee wanted POWs to choose *not* to be repatriated. Having been re-elected by blatant ballot-box stuffing, the president of South Korea now appeared to be a blood-thirsty old man who was eager to sacrifice tens of thousands, even hundreds of thousands, to his ambition. Rhee now wanted his allies against aggression to win for him the prize he could not win for himself: control of the entire peninsula. Yet some Americans – and many Koreans – saw him still as an embattled hero gallantly carrying on his lifelong fight for an independent, unified, nation.

'You know, Luke, it's all working out for the best.' Lesward Murray Howse had been mellow, his movie tough guy's talk forgotten, when Luke returned from Seoul to report to him. 'Good thing our indoctrination didn't convince many POWs to turn their coats. That first screening, the cards were stacked for repatriation. This time, we'll get an honest reading – and they'll go home where they belong.'

'Let's hope so, Colonel.'

'Did you hear Raymond Wu and his Taiwan thugs raised holy hell ... kicked up a Godawful fuss? Even threatened *me!* If I didn't let them keep working on the POWs, they'd tell the world the US was forcing POWs to choose repatriation.'

'It's a tough call, sir!'

Facing that dilemma, Luke was a man of many minds. He knew that a prompt armistice would serve both American and Asian interests, the sooner the better. Yet he abhorred the intimidation of helpless prisoners to attain that armistice. And he hated working so closely with Lesward Murray Howse, whom he despised.

'What'd you do, Colonel?' he asked.

'Go ahead and blab, young Raymond, I told him. You just blab – and I'll put out the truth about your part in the murders of those two poor bozos the Communists hung. Your evidence was decisive, Luke. No trouble from brother Wu after that! He's afraid of a court martial – or a knife in the back.'

Howse toyed with the beer-can battle-tank on his desk; meditatively rotating the shiny turret.

'Damned good thing we couldn't turn around so many pro-Communist prisoners,' he confided. 'If we'd won a majority, the fat would really be in the fire now. Sure, it could look like we – Information and Education – we failed. But this time the shit's *not* going to hit the fan.'

Luke sat silent. He was by no means surprised by his superior officer's cynicism. He was, however, somewhat startled by its frank expression. He should, he told himself wryly, have expected nothing less.

Depending on your viewpoint, Howse was the very best kind of officer – or the very worst. He felt no compunction in totally reversing his course in an instant, making a 180 degree turn. He felt neither guilt nor shame at turning his back on his original grand purpose, which had been to win over large numbers of non-repats. He was now strenuously striving to conjure up a grand majority of repats.

Howse was perfectly flexible in his perfect obedience to the perhaps imperfect instructions of his superiors, all of them generals. It clearly did not bother him at all that those new orders might be – indeed were in this matter – diametrically opposite their previous orders. The Nuremberg Tribunal might never have ruled that, regardless of their superiors' instructions, soldiers were personally responsible for any individual action that violated the rules of war or outraged human decency. Howse obeyed orders, whatever they were!

Even more reprehensible was the reason for Howse's extreme pliability. He was hardly driven by fear of severe retribution, perhaps execution, for rejecting an order, as the Nazi defendants had claimed at Nuremburg they were. The US Army would not, could not, punish him for refusing to coerce POWs into returning home, although the instructions to Howse might be only implicitly expressed, since to so coerce them was itself illegal. Howse was driven by ambition. He would do anything, commit any sin, happily violate any law, to get that elusive star.

Yet, Luke reflected unhappily, he was himself engaged in the same endeavor he found revolting on Howse's part. They both wanted to induce POWs to choose repatriation. Was there any difference between Howse and himself?

Yes, there was, he assured himself, a great moral distinction.

Howse did not care what the prisoners wanted. It meant nothing to him whether they yearned for home or desperately wanted to go elsewhere. Howse wanted only what his chiefs wanted. He had previously labored to convert all POWs into good little anti-Communists. He was now laboring just as hard to transform the same POWs into good little Communists who were eager to go home. To that end he would indiscriminately use fair means or foul.

Yet, perhaps it only appeared that Howse preferred foul means. Quite likely, his conscience, such as it might be, made no distinction between fair and foul.

I'm different, Luke assured himself, only half-attending to Howse's unwitting confession. I'm not all over the place depending on the last order I get. I try to think for myself, make my own decisions. I'm not just a tool in the hands of the brass.

Besides, I have made a clear moral judgement. Intellectually, as well as emotionally, I despise the tyranny they miscall Communism! I hate its oppression and its slaughter! I detest the way it suppresses independent thinking and distorts truth! I hate and fear totalitarianism, whether it is red or brown, Stalin and Mao, or Hitler and Mussolini.

I also despise Senator Joe McCarthy and his three-ring circus. Morally, his anti-Communist demagoguery is virtually indistinguishable from Stalin's Communism.

Luke recalled his meandering thoughts to the rescreening. In his heart he believed that POWs should be given a free choice as to their fate, although it had not occurred to the drafters of the Geneva Conventions to underwrite that freedom. Still, there should ... would ... be no conflict between his conscience and his duty. Although the preliminary partial screening had been botched, the large majority of POWs unquestionably wanted to go home. When they said so, made that clear in this rescreening, the war would end – and the healing process could begin.

Chapter XXIII

From its opening glory, the day turned abruptly into a miser's dawn, a few rays of tarnished gold grudgingly trickled into a pallid sky. A few minutes later, the sky was leaden above an ashen landscape that would undoubtedly remain dank and cheerless until nightfall. The meager dawn was an unpromising start to an unpromising operation reluctantly undertaken.

All the prisoners of war who were finally emerging from the barbed-wire compounds of Koje-do had been harangued and threatened. Many had been bullied and beaten. Some had been sadistically tortured. A few had not survived that ordeal. They had died in agony as a bracing demonstration of the dire consequences of disobedience or, even, non-conformism, no more than failure to comply immediately with their *honchos'* orders.

Chairman Mao Zedong was, unlike those POWs, snug in the Jongnanhai, the area called Central South Lake, where were set the most senior commissars' all but imperial mansions beside the Imperial City of the Confucian Dynasties. He described the frequent Communist practise of forcible intimidation as 'teaching by negative example'.

Not *all* such stringent negative examples were, however, the work of Communist *honchos*. The Nationalists did not openly exalt the practise, but they, too, often followed that violent pedagogical principle.

Captain John Luxborough Maynell was still worrying about unqualified interrogators like George Miner and Bennie Gam as he watched the long shabby green caterpillars of POWs guarded by indifferent GIs shuffling along the muddy roads in broken-backed shoes. Of course, he reminded himself, a large majority of the Chinese prisoners would freely choose to go to Mao Zedong's People's Republic of China on the mainland, rather than to Chiang Kai-shek's Republic of China on Taiwan.

Assuredly, even the majority of POWs from Nationalist controlled compounds would make that natural choice once free of their *honchos'* intimidation. There was simply no question about Communist-controlled compounds, whose *honchos* flatly refused to let their inmates emerge for rescreening. All those POWs would, naturally, return to mainland China. Doubtless, at least seventy-five per cent of Chinese POWs, the same percentage of the Koreans as well, would go home – and the war would be over.

Luke was naturally concerned – deeply concerned – by the *honchos'* vicious intimidation of their fellow prisoners. Yet, whether it was Nationalist brutality or Communist brutality, he could do little to mitigate either. The POW *honchos* were in control. Almost equally disturbing, the political issues were intertwined with his own life.

He glowed with happiness when he recalled, all but word for word, Betsie Howard's declaration of love. Nevertheless, he was uneasy, much worried by her infatuation with Tommy Chae and by her contending that not a single POW, Korean or Chinese, should be sent back home. It appeared that Betsie actually wanted to see the extremely bloody renewed hostilities that would be crowned by the South's conquering the North. Luke was perturbed by her perverse views, even more perturbed because those views demonstrated just how strong was her infatuation with Captain Tommy Chae Byongyup.

Betsie was no fool. But she was just now profoundly influenced by a more powerful – at least, more resolute and less compassionate – mind. Tommy Chae's sway over her intellect and therefore over her emotions was frightening.

Luke feared she might change her mind about himself, dazzled as she was by the Korean. Rather paradoxically, as I must say, he was also uneasy because he had inextricably, as it appeared, committed himself to Betsie. Thus, he felt uneasily, he had trapped himself, so that the decision henceforth lay in her hands, not his own. One moment he feared he would not win Betsie, and the next he feared that he had already won her.

His revulsion from what appeared to him Betsie's casual brutality on the great politico-military issue underlay that schism in his emotions. In any event he discerned in her a wholly uncharacteristic lack of compassion for fellow human beings, she who agonized over the suffering of the Koreans she met. Above all, it appeared to him, she saw the POWs as political pawns, rather then fellow human beings. She was apparently not much concerned about the personal fate of so many unhappy captives – as long as their disposition, what became of them, served the end she championed.

Such harshness sat strangely on the All American Girl. It struck me, Harland Birch, as if the scrubbed Coca-Cola blonde were to say 'Fuck!' every third word. They didn't then!

The times were *truly* different more than forty years ago. Even those few strange hybrid creatures, female war correspondents, rarely blasphemed and almost never swore. They mostly said 'Heck!' instead of 'Hell!', and 'Shoot!' was just about their strongest expletive.

Luke had been diverted from such worries on the day of his return from Seoul by Suja Chae, who was encased in the khaki trousers and green field jacket of a Korean Women's Army Corps officer. He had encountered Sue on the rust-stained deck of the Japanese tug just casting off for Koje, which he had found by scouting around the filthy docks of Pusan. The docks were jammed with supply ships carrying equipment and munitions from Japan, as well as ships with war material brought directly from the US. She was perched on a bollard, looking small and disconsolate.

'I hoped I'd run into you, Luke,' she had said without coyness. 'There's lots to talk about.'

They had then gone below to the small saloon, where they were sheltered from the gust of rain hurled by the rising wind. Rabbi Elfenbein, who had missed the dawn boat because he diverted to take Luke to the G² tent, regarded them with undisguised curiosity when they sat chatting in Japanese with two crewmen, sharing *sashimi*, that is, slices of raw tuna, and powerful *misoshiro*, essence of soya bean soup. The rabbi looked hard, but did not intrude. To his eyes they were clearly lovers reunited after a long separation.

Sue and Luke climbed back to the afterdeck later, when they had finished that scratch meal. Although the shallow-draft tug was rolling and pitching like a log in a millrace, it was better outside. The cramped saloon was humid and hot, fetid with cooking odors, as well as the characteristically Japanese rank vinegar-sour urine stench from the toilets. Even in the raw afternoon weather, the afterdeck was shielded from the wind by the bridgehouse.

Sue laid her hand, tiny in its pigskin glove, on Luke's arm. Korean WACs might wear ungainly brown-woollen gloves, but not she, not the daughter of the great landowner Chae Paik Chung, a descendant of the old high nobility and himself a martyred patriot. Sue regarded Luke anxiously through her green-tinged pupils, which were wider than most Koreans' eyes, but were, nonetheless, secretive, even mysterious. Her full mouth was parted slightly in the perfect oval of her face, whether in anticipation or in fear, it was impossible to say. Regardless, her inherent dignity made her appear to be a beautiful actress who was costumed as a WAC, rather than the real thing, which Sue was, after all, not quite.

'Luke, I'm worried,' she said. 'I wonder if we're doing the right thing.'

'The rescreening, you mean?'

'Of course! Is there another topic now?'

'What's bothering you, Suja?'

'Remember? When we met again for the first time in Seoul, I told you I had my doubts about non-repatriation. I'm more worried now. Of course we shouldn't send them back against their will. But I do wonder!'

The articulate Miss Chae paused as if to marshal her thoughts before continuing awkwardly, 'I suppose we have no choice now. But is it really worth the suffering … all that killing still going on? Maybe you were right that first day, maybe the whole thing is a mistake.

'What a choice for them: exile or slavery! I'm thinking of individuals, not numbers, but individuals – and their families. I've got two cousins in Compound 76.'

'Suja, the negotiators're saying at Munsan: "If we can deliver a minimum of a hundred thousand POWs, the Communists'll be satisfied. They want peace as much as … even more than … we do." So it's in the bag.'

'A hundred thousand? You think that many will go back?'

'Easily!' he replied without hesitation. 'Most will go back happily. The problem will solve itself. Don't worry about it too much, dear.'

The endearment slipped out unwished, startling Luke himself. Most Americans were free with words like *dear* and *darling*. He was not normally. Besides, he had been careful not to toss such casual endearments at Suja Chae. Beneath her brittle American carapace, she was a Korean patrician who could well be offended. Why then now?

He was, of course, relieved. He was, in truth, warmed by Sue's worrying about the POWs as individual human beings, especially when Betsie virtually dismissed them as no more than insensate pieces on the strategic chessboard. Betsie supported the position of Syngman Rhee, who was a ruthless quasi-Fascist dictator. Betsie hardly differed in essence from the Communist dictators in Pyongyang and Peking, who looked on the POWs as suicide battalions to be sacrificed as became advantageous. Sue was different.

Yet more than relief lay behind that apparently casual *dear*. Luke was lanced again by the intense physical desire that had arced between Sue and himself that first afternoon in the garden of the villa overlooking Pusan. He wondered what she really felt beneath her forbidding uniform.

Perhaps she felt bound by some arcane female non-poaching agreement. He was in her eyes presumably Betsie's property. Yet she had told him she had hoped to find him on the tug. That was the oldest female come-on of all: telling a reluctant or obtuse male that she wanted to be with him.

Still, the mystery of Sue's motives was perhaps no mystery at all. Most likely, she simply wanted to discuss the rescreening, although he doubted that he had truly reassured her regarding the outcome.

The mystery then was not only her feelings, but also his own. It was perverse for him to desire Sue so urgently at this moment. He had just left Betsie, having told her that he loved her to the exclusion of all others and, further, that he wanted to be with her all his life. Yet he now felt not only the exquisite agony of desire, but a welling of tenderness for Sue. Was he deluding himself about his feelings for Betsie or was he an emotional monster?

Luke laughed years later when he told me of that conflict of his emotions and his self-scarification. It was the indulgent, yet ironic laughter of a man belittling the foolish peccadilloes of his youth. He laughed in retrospective self-exculpation, and he said that his ridiculously sensitive conscience had, once again, been acting up. But it was no laughing matter to Luke that stormy afternoon on the pitching and yawing tugboat shortly before the agony of rescreening began.

Waiting in the dismal dawn for the prisoners to enter the interrogation enclosure, Luke spent a half-hour in such retrospection. Normally careful to stay clear of even the brink of depression, he deliberately did not cultivate the habit of introspection. But he could not today avoid a glum conclusion: his own life was becoming tangled, as vexatious and as morally ambiguous as was the perplexing issue of repatriation.

To escape from the maze of his thoughts Luke went over the procedure of the day again. It was simple, quite straightforward by design.

Chinese prisoners would one by one enter a tent where an interrogator waited. Those who declared that they wanted to return to mainland China, which meant Communist rule, would be taken out one exit and placed in a holding enclosure. Those who wanted to go to Taiwan would leave the tent by another exit, bound for a separate holding enclosure. Although Luke thought the gesture unrealistic given the certain imbalance in favor of repatriation, the two enclosures were the same size.

He himself would now, seated in one of those tents, ask exactly the same questions in exactly the same sequence he had drilled into the five interrogators in other tents.

He looked up and smiled. Violating his own instructions, he offered a cigarette to the first Chinese to come through the tent's flap. The POW, who wore ragged, flimsy cotton trousers and a much ripped dun-colored jacket that was leaking its quilted padding, was followed by an American guard, a carbine slung over his shoulder and a shiny lacquered MP helmet-liner on his head.

Neither the pungent gasoline odor of Luke's lighter, which he had for convenience dipped into the gas-tank of his jeep, nor the fragrance of the cigarette's smoke covered the POW's stench. Sucking on the Lucky Strike with wet lips, the man who was called Wang Mei-nao, reeked of privies, sour rice, and sweat. Tall and very thin, almost emaciated, unlike most of his short, surprisingly well-fed fellows, he obviously found the interrogation hard to grasp.

'Ni hsiang hui-dao Jung-guo chyu?' Luke duly put the prescribed opening question: 'Wouldn't you like to go back to China?'

It was almost, but not quite even-handed, only marginally unfair: no direct pressure, but a gentle invitation to return home.

When Private Wang gaped, cigarette smoke seeping from his open mouth, Luke repeated the question. Wang pondered for a moment and then nodded his head violently.

'Shr-di!' he said emphatically. 'Yes!'

Luke sighed and gestured towards the left-hand exit at the back of the tent. If this Wang Mei-nao were a reliable omen, all would go smoothly – just as he anticipated. Although he came from a Nationalist-dominated compound, Private Wang, when given a free choice, had said he wished to go home. So it would probably go all day.

Luke assured himself that he was well pleased. Yet he felt vaguely sad. Exposure to a different way of life, however, fleeting, and all the heavy indoctrination, had clearly made little or no impression on Private Wang. Democracy and freedom were no more than utterly incomprehensible abstractions to men like Wang, who could not possibly grasp any abstraction. So much for the crusade against tyranny. Well, at least, the war would soon be over.

The next prisoner made the same quick choice, and Luke felt himself settling into the routine. Yet he would before long have to check the other tents to see that the same procedure was followed exactly. Besides, he would from now on offer a cigarette only to men who looked downcast or appeared to be in pain. Theirs was a simple choice, but these men had not made a free choice in many years, if ever.

The next prisoner was very young, no more than 15, Luke guessed, and he was clearly depressed. He thanked Luke for the cigarette softly, almost diffidently.

'Wouldn't you like to go back to China?' Luke encouraged him, but the youth shook his head and replied, '*Bu-yao! Yao hui Taiwan!*'

Naturally, some would swim against the tide. The youth had actually said: 'No! I want to return to Taiwan!' How could he return to a place he'd never been? But the issue today was not semantics. Regardless, the mandatory follow-up questions would clarify any misunderstanding.

'Would you forcibly resist repatriation?' Luke asked.

The youth nodded and replied, 'With all my strength.'

He had evidently been well drilled by the Nationalist *honchos*, for the set questions were no secret. There were very few secrets on cram-packed Koje.

Luke lit a cigarette for himself before asking the next stilted question. 'Have you carefully considered the grave effect of your decision on your family?'

That appeal to Chinese family solidarity should have been the clincher. Luke had been overruled by Colonel Lesward Howse when he suggested that it should be 'the *possible* effect.' Howse had directed flatly, 'The Chinks all know their old man'll have his balls cut off if they stay away. And their wife'll have her tits cut off. Why screw around with nuances?'

The youth replied softly to that crucial question, 'I know. But I can't help it.'

So much for family loyalty!

Luke continued doggedly: 'Do you understand that you could remain on Koje for a long time after those who choose repatriation go home?'

A quick nod replied. The next two questions applied further not so gentle pressure. 'Do you clearly understand that the United Nations Command does not promise to send you to any particular place? Do you still insist on forcibly resisting repatriation?'

The youth nodded.

Disgusted by the slanted questions, Luke asked the final one. 'If the UN should send you back to mainland China despite your decision, what would you do?'

That was the trickiest of all, the very nastiest. A man had to say he would commit suicide or resist to the death, at least that he would brave retaliation by death to avoid repatriation. Death had to come into it – or he would be shipped back.

'*Wo yao hui Taiwan! Wo gan sse!*' the young POW shouted. 'I want to go to Taiwan! I'm not afraid to die!'

Well, that was clear enough. Luke gestured to the right-hand exit and said softly: '*Hao tsai!* ... Good luck!' That wish was probably a violation of the strict neutrality enjoined on interrogators, although the youth had already made his choice. Besides, the questions themselves were hardly neutral.

Three more non-repatriates followed. The first bared his chest to show a tattooed map of the tobacco leaf-shaped island of Taiwan under the slogan *Chiang Chung-cheng wan sui!* ... Long live Chiang Kai-shek!

He answered all the questions by repeating monotonously, '*Hui Taiwan!*' All except the last question, to which he declared, 'I'll die before I go back to Communism!'

The next man was also low key. His successor sprang into the tent as if it were a stage and shouted before a question was asked, 'Taiwan! Taiwan! Long live Taiwan! Mao Zedong is a son of a bitch!'

Breaking for a general inspection after that performance, Luke found the ratio was running one to ten in the other tents: one repatriate to ten who declared vehemently that they would die rather than live under Communist rule. Though all those already questioned came from a Nationalist-ruled compound, Luke was surprised at the near unanimity of their replies to the loaded questions.

As the day wore on he was astonished that so few chose to go home to China. Even with POWs from a mixed compound, the ratio shifted to no less than half and half: five choosing repatriation and five choosing Taiwan.

'I'll have thirty non-repats back,' he told the lieutenant commanding the MPs. 'Men who've gone through other tents ... men I haven't seen.'

Luke could not fault his ill-qualified interrogators. Out of thirty POWs selected at random from the non-repats, twenty-nine reaffirmed that decision. One, who was obviously a little retarded, said he would go where Old Chou was going. The MPs took a half-hour to find Old Chou. Luke took a minute to determine that Old Chou was set upon going to Taiwan.

Luke had been given no instruction to interrogate the repatriates again. If he had requested permission, he would have been told to leave the repats alone with their decision. Therefore, he did not ask, but ordered thirty who had chosen to go to China brought back for a second re-examination.

Most performed as he had expected. They screamed abuse at him as a blood-sucking American imperialist, and they threatened him with the vengeance of Chairman Mao Zedong and the Chinese people. One whipped out a shrivelled penis and trained a robust yellow stream at Luke's feet before a scandalized MP yanked him out by the collar. Beyond question, those men truly wanted to go home – as far away as they could possibly go from the demonic Americans.

Yet nine out of those thirty repats now declared they wanted to go to Taiwan. Four said they had changed their minds on finding themselves in the dangerous company of fanatical Communists in the repatriates' enclosure. Three claimed they had been misunderstood and bustled out of the tent after the first question. One seemed bemused, but determined.

Luke felt that he should in justice question all the repats again. But he knew he could not. It would be physically impossible to comb through them all again. Not that there were so many. The final ratio on the first day of rescreening worked out at seven non-repats to three repats.

Luke was astonished by that figure – astonished and troubled. This hasty refer-
endum would definitely *not* end the war. Too many POWs had defied the
Communist rulers of China. Fighting would certainly continue if the ratio among
the Chinese did not shift radically. And what if the same large majority of non-
repats were found among the North Korean POWs, as was not unlikely?

Well, the diehard pro-Communists had still not emerged. The Communist
honchos, like their distant masters, contended that the original screening and this
rescreening were both illegal – by the terms of the Geneva Conventions they did
not recognize. But the Communist *honchos* would almost certainly in good time
order their men to undergo interrogation. How else than by going along under
protest could they muster a respectable number of declared repats? How else could
they avoid a stunning propaganda defeat?

Luke was, against his own inclination, appalled by the intimidation in which he
had participated. The questions were not merely loaded: in totality, they were
bludgeoning the non-repats to change their minds. Yet the bludgeoning had not
prevailed.

The UN Command was in a sense fighting itself. Its indoctrination had initially
sought to make prisoners anti-Communist. Beyond defending the ROK, the aim of
the war was, after all, to discredit the Communist regimes in Peking and
Pyongyang. Then the emphasis had changed abruptly. The UN Command was now
striving to persuade, to all but force POWs to go home so that the Communists
would sign an armistice.

Neither the right hand nor the left hand knew what the other was doing. The US
was Indian arm-wrestling itself, its right forearm desperately striving to overcome
its left. Wrestling against one's self, one could not win.

Chapter XXIV

Here I am, totally alone in Upper New York State four decades later, and everything is sopping wet. The thaw that was so long in coming is now weeping down the inside walls of the cabin, so that it's practically impossible to get anything dry. Outside all is water and slush. I can hear the icy torrents of the flood pouring into the streams over their banks.

Spring is finally on her way! The earth is soon to be reborn! And I'm totally fed up with this climate, first freezing hard and now sopping wet.

Give me the tropics anytime. A little rain occasionally – and that's it. All right then. A tropical downpour almost every day. But only a short, brisk downpour, except in the rainy season, when there may be two or three such downpours a day. Anyway, the rainy season is nowhere as long or as drenched as it sounds. Somerset Maugham was himself all wet with his unending *Rain*, though I've always been fond of Sadie Thompson, who was like no whore ever seen in this world.

After the tropical downpour, the sun comes out and blesses the world, and splendid vegetation springs out of the earth: pale-green rice shoots piercing the silver surface of flooded paddy fields; clusters of fruit, red, pink, blue, most like none you've ever seen before; and so many succulent vegetables, they're all but impossible to describe, but a delicious surprise to consume.

Obviously this has nothing to do with Korea, which has a climate that, even now, can make Plattsburgh seem mild. I just want to remind you where it is I'm setting down this account of certain events in the middle of the twentieth century. Those events are, I'm afraid, practically as far distant both psychologically and, if you'll allow me the coinage, informationally, as the Middle Ages are to many today, who are not only sodding ignorant, but don't give a damn for anything that happened before yesterday.

It is late winter in the early 1990s in upper New York State, but my mental picture depicts South Korea in early May of 1952. The winter wheat was already reaped, and the earth was ripening again. But no one was singing, 'With a hey nonny nonny and a ho ho ho!' – certainly not in English, and, of course, not even in Korean or Chinese.

On the grisly island called Koje late spring brought little or nothing that was in any way pleasant to Luke Maynell. Nor even anything that was particularly new, in truth hardly more than a bumper crop of weeds in the fallow fields. For the POWs

it meant masterfully orchestrated restiveness that verged on open and public, virtually unrestricted warfare against the Camp Command. The 'fighters', as Radio
Peking and Radio Pyongyang invariably described the POWs, were about to launch
their May Offensive.

For Luke the season further meant pressing personal troubles. In a particularly
high-soaring flight of fancy he complained that his life was like a loom on which
two groups of rival weavers were working frantically, one by day, the other by
night. No wonder the pattern was chaotic, and the colors clashed.

He liked that simile. If nothing else, it was at least more original than likening
his existence to a bowl of ice-cold noodles, all tangled and knotted.

Since we're indulging in high-flown metaphor, may I say that not just Luke's
troubles, but the entire disgusting situation, looked to me far more gruesome, not
to say macabre. Like thousands of maggots burrowing in a chunk of rotten meat:
the slick-white little worms constantly growing bigger, ceaselessly changing shape,
endlessly slipping around each other in their continual blind feeding.

If you, dear putative reader, find that simile nauseating, please do remember
that maggots are no more then incipient baby flies.

Not, though, that flies are so attractive! Not that Luke's circumstances were not
somewhat revolting! I'll come back to that.

Revolving around ROK President Syngman Rhee's re-election, the entire
politico-military situation – the fighting, the electioneering, and the peace talks –
was endlessly complex, though rather easy to describe. Syngman Rhee had
dreamed during his decades in exile that he would be the president of Korea – all
Korea, not merely a rump republic in the south. Believing he knew the US intimately from long residence, he was convinced that the Americans, would, if the
war continued, finally lose their patience and thereupon march north to liberate
the entire peninsula.

In early May 1952, it looked as if he would be proved right. It looked as if the
war would go on indefinitely – and President Harry Truman was not noted for his
patience.

Syngman Rhee deliberately frayed the patience and the temper of both
Harry Truman and the American public. He skilfully manipulated the media,
which were sceptical regarding his motivations and his purposes, suspicious as
well of his peculation. He adroitly marshalled his arguments, his misrepresentation, and his misleading variations from the truth. He came very close to
equalling the bravura dexterity the Communists were to deploy a decade or so
later in manipulating the media, which were not sceptical but sympathetic to
Hanoi and to the presumed popular enthusiasm and the presumed spontaneous
support for the Viet Cong in South Vietnam. Notably, Rhee was the first of
America's recalcitrant allies to strive to turn the mighty current of public
opinion against an administration's policies. He was certainly the first to explore
the power of television, although those idiot boxes with their black-and-white
screens had hardly begun to dominate the American living-room and the

American psyche as their technicolor successors were to dominate the entire country a decade or so later.

The staff in his official residence, the Blue House, invited not only the note-books of print reporters and the tape-recorders of radio reporters, but the still rather primitive Aireflex cameras of CBS, NBC, and ABC. Granting the networks 'exclusive interviews' one by one, Rhee gave each an 'exclusive' fact or interpreta-tion that differed slightly from the 'exclusives' he gave their competitors. Anyway, he played with devilish skill on the rivalry of the newspaper special correspondents and on the competition among the young men of the five wire-services, three American, one British and one French, who were generally known as 'the boy war correspondents'.

The most ingenious drama he directed was played out by the young ladies in the dust.

Through the open windows of the Press Billets one somnolent afternoon the high-pitched slogan sounded in surprisingly youthful trebles : 'Pukchin Tungi ... March north to unity!'

Bug-eyed correspondents looked out to see rank upon rank of young ladies in their teens, girls wearing the gray boleros, white blouses, and dark bell-skirts that were the uniform garb of the newly reopened elite girls' schools. They carried plac-ards demanding that the US support the ROK in reunifying Korea. They responded in emphatic tones each time their leaders, who were only a little older, shouted the catchwords of the moment.

When a whistle shrilled, more than 200 schoolgirls plumped themselves down on the dusty roadway as one. A second whistle – and they all burst into tears.

Dozens of war correspondents, for once nonplussed, watched the girls sob for minutes as if their hearts were breaking. When the girls departed, still sobbing as they trailed away, the lads sat down to excel themselves in writing the tale. It made a pleasant light feature for a dull news day, as Rhee's public relations advisers had reckoned.

We didn't call them spin-doctors in those days. Still, the public relations advisers of Kim Il Sung, the rival dictator, undoubtedly reckoned they would get big play in the press for another gambit aimed at the correspondents. They sent two or three of the North's light airplanes, which were like underpowered Piper Cubs, to lob a few bombs at the Press Billets. Pyongyang did get the play, but not precisely as it would have liked.

Granted the pursuit planes of the Eighth US Air Force were too fast to deal with such gadflies, nobody thought of slow-flying helicopters till it was too late. Anyway, those little choppers were at a premium, since we had so few. So there wasn't much anyone could do, except try to stay out of the way of the light bombs that dribbled down on the Billets. A couple of correspondents were actually wounded, very slightly. I escaped a direct hit only because the key of the padlock that secured my jeep was balky.

Still, the mini-raids did not come through the editorial wringers very impressively. They did not strike readers as a strong show of force, but, rather, as a some-what ludicrous demonstration of the weakness of North Korea.

All the while, Syngman Rhee and Kim Il Sung were staging such stunts to move the war correspondents, only the question of voluntary repatriation prevented an armistice. Neither Rhee nor Kim wanted an end to hostilities, as did their senior partners: the USA and the People's Republic of China.

The peace talks at Panmunjom, you'll recall, had recessed in early April 1952 to allow time for the recount. When the talks resumed in late April, the American delegates presented the new figures with no great hope. Some 70,000, less than half the POWs, had chosen to return to Communist rule.

In late April, the Communists declared that it was 'completely impossible' for them to accept that figure. At the end of April they summarily rejected a UN compromise offer, because it did not, as it *could* not, alter the number of repatriates. We were back to where we'd started.

The armistice talks were to continue intermittently thereafter, as both sides prepared for limited counter-offensives. The crucial battle in the Psywar campaign was still met on the propaganda front, although the battle on the ground became a little more lively. Notwithstanding what either side may have wished, the Communists *could* not mount a full-scale offensive on the ground, and the UN *would* not – regardless of Syngman Rhee's diatribes and complaints, whatever his warnings of the consequences of 'defeat' and his calculation of American suscepti-bility to his pleas for sympathy with his pathetic plight.

The passage of time and, perhaps, a touch of senility have led me to rethink many of my views of the time. I wonder if Syngman Rhee and his political foe, but fellow Korean patriot, Captain Chae Byongyup, were not right in their dedication to total victory. At the time, I wasn't quite sure where I stood, though I had talked myself into accepting a limited war that sought limited objectives.

Even after catastrophic Chinese entry into the conflict in the fall of 1950, Truman continued to describe the war as a 'police action', which was thus implic-itly limited in scope, rather than a war. Despite the strategic arguments and the pleas of the Supreme Commander Douglas MacArthur that striking directly at the enemy would save many lives, Truman forbade attacks against Chinese territory. Not even a single raid at the sacrosanct refuge that was the Manchurian bases of MiG-15 fighter-bombers, most piloted by Russians, some by Chinese, one or two by Koreans. That restraint, I told myself then, was an act of courage in itself. Refusing to be drawn into the wider conflict that such attacks might provoke was, I argued, the epitome of political and military sophistication.

The hell it was!

Unlike Luke, who seemed at times almost to relish the prospect of a limited defeat in a limited war, I really could not stomach our not winning outright. I then believed that we could have won with just a little more effort. That may have been a correct assessment, or it may have been dead wrong. For one thing I had at that time not taken on board the absolute determination of the Chinese to maintain for their own security the buffer of a 'Socialist' North Korea.

Regardless, it is just not – absolutely not – the American way to stop short of total victory. Besides, our chief ally, the ROKs, were gutsy, although they were ill-trained and under-equipped. Since the US was responsible for both training and equipment, those deficiencies could easily have been remedied – and we could have marched north together with the ROKs.

And the Russians? Would they not have joined battle if we'd marched north again?

We now know, as many then surmised, that there was never any danger of Joe Stalin's pouring Soviet troops into Korea. The risk was too high: perhaps getting beaten up in limited combat in Europe, maybe even getting atom-bombed by Harry S-for-nothing Truman, the only man who'd ever ordered nuclear weapons used in earnest. The Russians weren't coming, no more than the Chinese later had any idea of intervening directly in Vietnam!

Not, definitely not, against the Americans, although, ironically, the Chinese did move later against the Vietnamese, the *Communist* Vietnamese!

Luke Maynell's world was not quite shattered by the decision of a majority of the prisoners not to go home. His self-confidence was, however, severely bruised. He was credited with deep understanding of Asian prisoners of war – particularly the Chinese, of whom he was believed to possess intimate, instinctive, all but total, comprehension. Yet he had committed a massive misassessment – a portentous misjudgement of their intentions regarding the vital issue of repatriation.

Luke's acuity regarding Asians was not only vital to his present assignment, but was the core of his life. His psychological sensitivity and his political astuteness were his personal pride, as well as his professional credentials. If he did not really understand Asians, if he did not know them intimately, why all those years of academic study? And, further, what was his subsequent practical experience really worth?

Yet his projection prior to the rescreening had been totally wrong. He had predicted that a large majority would choose repatriation, even allowing for intimidation by both sides, which just about balanced out. Yet he could not question the rough accuracy of the rescreening, which he had watched keenly. Besides, the questions had been monstrously loaded for repatriation.

Luke was, to say the least, chastened. He was, in truth, severely taken aback. His verve was gravely depleted, and his self-assurance was on the ropes, albeit temporarily.

Colonel Lesward Murray Howse and his myrmidons reverted to their old ways with sighs of relief and smiles of triumph. The POWs' stinging rejection of the dictators who ruled their homelands was, he declared with pride, a great psychological and propaganda victory for the UN. Having failed to make peace by coercing the prisoners, the military gloried in the victory by default thus plucked from the yawning jaws of defeat. Having failed to induce a majority to go home to

Communist rule, Colonel Howse was again ordered to make militant anti-Communists of all POWs.

The cock-a-hoop American command even ordered Luke Maynell to turn Major-General Li Mao around – to transform the commander of the underground Communist army into an American agent. I'll come back to that near lunacy later.

Appalled by his massive error of judgement, Luke's faith in himself was roughly shaken. He consequently questioned his assessment of the entire Asian scene. Would the best interests of all concerned truly have been served by a now impossible immediate armistice? Was he right in advocating *rapprochement* with Peking? Or were the hardliners right in demanding attacks on China itself? Could China and the US ever be reconciled?

Those were anything but abstract political questions to Luke. The answers, if answers there were, must determine both his immediate actions and his future course. If his judgements on Asia were badly flawed, what could he accomplish there? If he were not engaged with Asia, what was he to do with himself?

Although afflicted by such questions, Luke was working eighteen hours a day to contain the strife that was sweeping Koje. That conflict and his self-doubts further unnerved him when his deepest personal emotions were torn and tattered.

He had seen both Betsie and Sue repeatedly since his return from Seoul. Their work, too, required them to spend much time on Koje: Betsie bird-dogging for the International Committee of the Red Cross; Sue carrying out mysterious errands for the Rhee regime, as well as executing her shadowy duties for Colonel Howse.

He could, however, never be alone with either on the island. Koje, as always, swarmed with bedraggled prisoners in dust-laden, filth-splotched brown-and-green rags, just as numerous and, it appeared, as purposeless, as directionless, as the winged drones that swarm from a giant anthill kicked over by an elephant. Consequently, Luke had spoken to neither in privacy nor for more than a stolen minute or two. And, of course, the atmosphere on that Devil's Island of Asia, Koje-do, was hardly conducive to delicate or subtle emotional interplay.

Betsie was volatile, sometimes affectionate, sometimes distant, quite inconsistently without any apparent reason alternately cool and then warm. Sometimes she would lay her hand on his sleeve, and her wonderful luminous eyes would gaze lovingly at him. Sometimes she appeared to wish to linger with him; sometimes she would be abrupt, as if impatient to get away.

It was unmistakably evident that Betsie was deeply disturbed. Something was distressing her greatly. Something was dismaying her usual cheery imperturbability. Whatever was distressing her was not primarily the POW issue, although that issue obsessed them all. The highly personal something, Luke felt, by no means flattering himself, could be doubts regarding their future together. She might well be intrigued by the thought of a future spent with Chae Byongyup, rather than with Luke.

Luke could not simply reassure Betsie that she could count on his unswerving affection, even if he could make a chance to talk seriously with her. He could not by any means tell her so in their briefly snatched, unavoidably banal conversations. How could he possibly make her understand that she was the center of his being and that he wanted nothing more than to prove his faithfulness to her all his life. Always under a hundred eyes, he could not embrace her and tell her that he loved her profoundly, loved her alone and would love her alone forever.

Besides, he wondered against his own will, was that wholly true? When he saw Sue, now tricked out in the uniform of a captain in the Korean WACs, he felt a stab of desire. Sue was invariably warm, if often hurried. Sometimes, she was very warm. But what did she really mean to him? What did he mean to her?

Was Sue sorry for him because her friend Betsie was stepping out with her half-brother Tommy? Was it no more than sympathy? Or did she feel something more, something quite different from – though allied to – the overwhelming physical attraction that had swept them both in the garden of the villa?

Luke simply did not know. He really did not know what either girl really felt about or, for that matter, precisely what he felt about either.

He had always been the one to make or break a relationship. For the first time in his life, he was flustered and uncertain, at the mercy of females, rather than the dominant male.

Luke was torn by the deep affection he felt for both Betsie and Sue. Yet he was mystified as to their true feelings. He grinned ruefully at being in the same fix as most of the Eighth Army. Not only was he not getting any feminine affection; he wasn't even getting laid. Resorting to prostitutes was unthinkable in his new contrite mood. It had, besides, never been his way.

Not that he wanted to. He told me sententiously that 'the lack of the quick spasm of release' was definitely not what was bothering him.

Well, maybe not!

Chapter XXV

Aquasi-catastrophe that was actually rather ludicrous capered impatiently in the wings of that demoniacal playhouse of the tragic/absurd called Koje-do, while Thespis, the impish muse of theatre, and her wicked sister Cleo, the muse of history, rubbed their hands in glee that was no less malicious for their girlish giggles. For several days that bizarre episode reduced to broad farce the Grand Guignol melodrama of Koje-do. It was the crowning absurdity of the absurd decision to prolong the conflict in Korea indefinitely for the sake of a few tens of thousands of former enemy soldiers. It began on 7 May, 1952, a day that should, paraphrasing Franklin Delano Roosevelt, live in ridicule.

Today, a good four decades later, myself, Harland Birch, your narrator, finally released from the iron grip of winter in upper New York State, I cannot quite believe it really happened. I've spent a lifetime coming to terms with that flat, final, and wholly veracious statement: *The ridiculous is far more common in human affairs than the logical or the heroic!* Yet the tragicomic drama of those four days still bemuses me. I am appalled, indignant, and, at the same time, vastly amused. Luke Maynell, who watched the crude slapstick gig unfold, later confessed that he did not really believe it was happening even while he was watching it happen.

Still, it fits our times today, as well as it did yesteryear. Our era is even more lunatic than any that has gone before.

It is as wickedly self-indulgent as the Rome of Caligula and Petronius, just as obsessed with trivia and entertainment. It is as wantonly self-destructive as the Europe of the Hundred Years War with its ridiculous hair-splitting of cult and creed. It is even more foolish, though just as preposterous as the Confucian/Maoist conviction that men and women can transform the world by exerting their own will – the absolute certainty that human beings can make reality itself conform to their own vision of the ideal by altering their society's outward aspect and calling their milieu by a different name.

I do not believe that I must necessarily enlarge on that statement. I see no great need, faithful reader, to explicate my perhaps somewhat elided meaning to you. Nevertheless, I shall do so, paraphrasing Chairman Mao Zedong's most bizarre assertions.

That massive fallacy, the perfectibility of mankind, is most sharply visible to us in the Chairman's Great People's Communes, which, he declared, 'instantly created

240

an entirely new administrative and social unit, the foundation of a society of perfected men and women.' That glorious misapprehension is the legacy handed down from the ancients that has during four millennia sustained in practise as well as in principle the authoritarian rigor exerted upon the Chinese people to fix their beliefs as well as their behavior. Confucius, himself inspired by the lucubration of the Yellow Emperor, asserted that human beings could be made perfect, as did his disciples, even unto Kang Yu-wei and Liang Chi-chao, who thus strove to preserve the imperial system at the turn of the twentieth century. Mao Zedong seized upon that extraordinary – extraordinary to many Judaeo-Christian Occidentals, at least – assertion of the supremacy of mankind over not only the natural, but the supernatural. He liberally applied Marxist illogic – and, presto, the Great Leap Forward and the Great People's Communes with their *perfect* denizens.

Perfectibility? Rather the contrary!

We are, of course, inferior in our behavior to those who came before us. We are even lower on the totem pole of the ages, even more degraded morally. Our technological mastery compresses and distorts not only space, but time itself. Evils that might once have unfolded over the course of a century now occur in a decade; absurdities, whether ludicrous or blasphemous, conquer the entire world in the course of no more than a year or two.

We have elevated greed to a moral imperative. We have sanctified avarice as the prime virtue, if not quite the only virtue, because it services our material needs and it fuels our constantly expanding self-indulgence. Too many human beings believe that any given act is not only desirable, but is ethical, if it feeds their gluttony and/or provides instant gratification.

Most ridiculous, is the nearly universal belief that we have mastered Nature herself. Humankind is swollen with a conviction of omniscience, close even to omnipotence, as well, which is more grandiose than the nearly total self-assurance that inspired the builders of the Tower of Babel. In our own era, Hitler and Stalin, above all Mao Zedong and Pol Pot, believed they could remake mankind by slaughtering millions. Today essentially passive academics and fervent activists truly believe they can remake mankind by instantly remaking the social and cultural institutions, as well as the linguistic and intellectual institutions that have evolved over many centuries.

Inciting to murder is now virtually sacrosanct, unpunishable because we must not interfere with the self-expression of oppressed minorities, particularly when such murderous self-expression brings large profits to big corporations. Abortion, which, I must freely confess, I have not only encouraged as a libertarian right, but have funded on several occasions, is not merely the natural privilege, but virtually the moral obligation of every right-thinking woman. How else prove her transcendence of the physiological burden of perpetuating the human race laid upon her by men, not to speak of Nature? Yet at the same time, women's costumes have become more revealing, thus more provocative, recalling the virtual nudity of high fashion gowns of transparent Chinese silks in the latter days of the Republic of Rome or the age of Napoleon.

More recently, a promiscuous bulimic married into the royal House of Windsor becomes a media star. She is virtually canonized by a sentimental public manipulated by publicity-obsessed politicians, by trade union mavens, and by assertive entertainers, as well as by posturing celebrities and avid do-gooders. All that lot, of course, have a great deal to gain by their participation in that rite. If you will further tolerate for another moment this observation, tacked by the editor's kind consent, to a reprinting of my original tale, I should like to note: A volume of childish sexual innuendoes littered with photographs in mildly obscene poses of a chunky, dyed-blonde singer who calls herself Madonna by sacrilegious intent becomes one of the best-selling books of our times.

My feelings about this era may be due to the decline with age of my capacity to be deceived or, above all, my ability to deceive myself. In 1952 I wept for the defeat of Adlai Stevenson by that obvious Babbit, Dwight Eisenhower. I did not cry in 1963, but I was profoundly moved when Jack Kennedy's Camelot was shattered by a bullet in his brain, although I knew that he was a male chauvinist wild boar who contemptuously over-exercised his *droit de seigneur*. My own ire at our present times certainly derives in part from a decline in my capacity for enjoyment, while my ability to hope oozes away.

In the early 1950s, we wondered just when the Communists and the Americans would abate their manic rivalry. Meanwhile men died in combat so that former combatants, now prisoners, would decide at their leisure whether they wished to go home or to be resettled elsewhere.

Once when I was particularly downcast, Luke observed mockingly, 'All ages are pretty much the same. Contemporary commentators a thousand years ago felt just as you do now. The human condition bewilders human beings – always has. Other animals live by logical behavior, either inborn or taught by their mothers. We humans live by illogic, constantly flouting all sensible standards of behavior.'

He paused as if in appreciation of his own eloquence, and finally said, 'Like the Bourbons, we never forget. Like the Bourbons, we don't learn anything new, nothing truly new that is truly fundamental. We bipeds who are in awe of our own cerebellums are the only animal that does not learn from the experience of its elders.'

By May 1952, the armistice talks at Panmunjom had deteriorated from solemn farce into antic slapstick.

American Admiral Turner Joy had proposed that the Communists accept 70,000 out of some 170,000 POWs held by the UN and return some 12,000 UN POWs. An armistice would follow – and everybody could go home.

North Korean General Nam Il declared the proposal unacceptable but offered, he said, 'a major concession … a final proposal.' Some 40,000 captured ROK soldiers had been impressed into the North Korean People's Army and had subsequently been retaken by the UN forces. The Communists magnanimously would not demand their 'return' if the UN returned *all* other POWs, so that not a single Chinese remained in the UN hands.

Nam Il thus affirmed that POW repatriation was now the *only* issue blocking an armistice. Turner Joy asked for time, though he knew the proposal was unacceptable. Doughty Harry Truman in the White House, independent and stubborn as always, responded personally. 'We will not buy an armistice by turning over human beings for slaughter or slavery.'

On Koje-do, the Communists deployed about 70,000 troops, equivalent in manpower to seven of their combat divisions. Almost all those men wielded handmade weapons that were as effective as conventional firearms in the renewed struggle on Koje. After all, the battlefield was psychological, rather than territorial. Even the MP light-colonels had learned to say that the objective was the minds and hearts of the people of the world, above all the Americans. The thrust of the Communist counter-attack was already obvious, though the POW Command, consistent to the last in its self-delusion, ignored the signals.

One morning early in May, Lieutenant-Colonel Wilbur Raven meandered alone into Compound 76, which confined the most fervently doctrinaire and most stringently disciplined North Korean prisoners. Befitting his name, Raven was black-browed and dark-visaged. But he lacked that canny bird's suspicious nature.

He was responding to a message fixing a meeting with the POW *honcho,* the actual Compound Commander, North Korean Senior Colonel Lee Hak Koo. An invitation, at worst a request in the eyes of Colonel Raven, the message was a summons, a virtual command in the eyes of Colonel Lee, who was accustomed to manipulating his wardens.

As we have seen, the MP light-colonels were easy going. Some, dare I say it, were even a little lazy. Many had been relegated to undemanding duty with the POW Command by superior officers who would not trust them in combat. Not exactly the pattern set by the assignment of Colonel Howse, but it was very close. All those colonels wished, above all, to prevent any untoward incident they might have to explain. Almost all chose to avoid trouble by getting along with their prisoners, indeed by going along with the prisoners, although that meant in practise ceding control of compounds to the *honchos,* the officers set over the POWs by higher authority in Peking or Pyongyang.

Wilbur Raven was definitely one of the light-colonels who got along by going along. He casually returned the salute of the American MPs on the gate and strolled into Compound 76, as he had often done before. He was immediately surrounded by a mob of POWs who were chanting provocative slogans. When the mob dispersed, he had vanished. Three hours later, a spluttering Raven was bustled out of the compound, his fatigues stained by the excrement and the hot soup flung at him while he was harangued by Communist agitators.

The MPs on the gate had watched his abduction passive and bewildered. They had not dared attempt a rescue, since they, too, would have been swallowed by the sea of prisoners. In any event, they had received no orders from complacent POW

Command Headquarters to intervene or even to observe and report on the affairs of Compound 76. Neither before nor after that affront to Colonel Raven had they received either orders or guidance as to their behavior *vis-à-vis* the POWs.

Only to stand guard at the gate. To guard against *what?* No one had said. No one evidently thought any such instruction was necessary. Perhaps, then, to guard against a mass breakout! As if a mass breakout were contemplated, or even necessary, to the *honchos'* purposes. After all, most prisoners came and went as they pleased, either individually or in small groups.

Shaken by his ordeal, Raven needed a couple of hours at the bar of the Officers' Club to recover. His accustomed equanimity, his habitual lethargy indeed, was hardly touched. Neither was his faith in his POWs' good faith. Senior Colonel Lee Hak Koo had assured him that it was all a mistake.

Such was the first incident, melodramatic, slightly comic, somehow inconclusive. Captain Luke Maynell, however, gave warning of a second planned incident to his commanding officer, Colonel Lesward Murray Howse, who was in high spirits that day.

Wilbur Raven, his chief rival for the favor of the Commandant, Brigadier General Francis Xavier Dodd, was not wholly discredited. Yet Raven was, to say the least, out of favor, although his brief captivity by his own captives had, fortunately, not leaked to the Press. Besides, Howse congratulated himself, his own brilliant direction of the miscalled *Civil*, but patently *Military*, Information and Education program could no longer be ignored.

Every non-repat was a brand snatched from the burning, a precious soul saved, an immortal spirit redeemed from the secular heresy of Communism and pledged to the true faith, Democracy. If not all had also been won for Christianity, that was, perhaps, a pity, but I & E was not committed to that purpose. That ultimate conversion was not – could not be – an official objective of the USA, which was predicated on separation of church and state.

Nonetheless, our lot was also preferable on sectarian grounds. If Syngman Rhee and Chiang Kai-shek were not perfect democrats, they were unquestionably superior, morally as well as politically, to the Godless dictators who ruled the other parts of their divided countries. Actually it happened that they were both Christians, although Chiang's devotion was, perhaps, just a little more practically motivated than it was necessarily spiritual.

His instant conversion had won him glamorous, intelligent, American-educated Soong Mei-ling as his last wife, and highly skilled public relations counsellor and brilliant adviser on international affairs. Conversion had also won him the political and commercial backing of the wealthy and influential clan founded by Charlie Soong, who had grown up in the States before returning to China to create one of the greatest fortunes of wealthy Shanghai, initially by publishing the Bible. Soong Mei-ling's elder sister Ching-ling had, you'll recall, married Dr. Sun Yat-sen the American-educated father of the Chinese Republic.

Be that as it may, Chiang Kai-shek, like the Princeton PhD Syngman Rhee, was seen as a staunch ally of the United States. Both Chiang and Rhee were also detested in many quarters as ruthless sons of bitches. Regardless, they were *our* sons of bitches.

'I figure we've immobilized more enemy soldiers than an entire army corps at the front.' Colonel Howse twirled the turret of his beer-can tank and genially waved his maverick subordinate, Captain Maynell, to the chair the prisoners' work-shop had upholstered for him in Hunting Stewart tartan. 'A job well done!'

Having heard so much liturgical self-praise recently, Luke hesitated, but finally asked, 'By locking them up, Colonel? *We* didn't capture them!'

'No, Luke. By keeping them from going back and fighting against us in another war!'

'The way Colonel Raven tied up a couple of hundred POWs to stand guard over him?'

'Something like that, Luke.' Howse's wattles glowed pink with pleasure at that sally against his rival.

'Everything's looking good ... very good. Truman's finally lost his patience. Now he'll give us another half-dozen US divisions – and we'll smash the Gooks.'

'I haven't heard about a horde of reinforcements, Colonel. Is that the latest poop from Tokyo?'

'Well, there's nothing official. Not yet, at least. But it stands to reason ...'

'Yes, sir!' Luke retreated into the subordinate's refuge, the negative-affirmative. 'Meanwhile, Colonel, there is something else ... a problem that could come up.'

'This is no day to dump problems on me, Maynell.' Colonel Howse sighed. 'But, if you gotta', let's have it.'

'Sir, that business with Raven, it's only the beginning. I've heard Compound 76 is planning something *really* big real soon.'

'Your source, Luke? Li Mao, is it?'

Luke could not retreat into the newsman's refuge – confidentiality. He could not refuse to compromise his source by revealing its name. Howse had, after all, conveyed to him the instructions to win over the Chinese major-general. Luke had, however, discreetly suppressed certain portions of his protracted conversations with Li Mao. He had *not* reported that Li Mao was fully aware of the reason for Luke's repeated visits. If Brigadier-General Francis Dodd and the CIA wanted to believe the underground commander of the prison camp was a fool, let them.

'Yes sir, it's Li Mao,' Luke replied. 'He won't tell me exactly what's coming up. He says he doesn't know—'

'Bullshit! If *he* doesn't know who the hell does?'

'Could be, Colonel. Anyway, he won't say much else. Only says it'll be big ... very big. Says we've got to be super-alert!'

'*Why* tell you? He hasn't switched sides, has he?'

'No, sir, not yet!' Luke did *not* add: 'Or ever!'

'Why then? A feud with the Koreans? Is he out to get Lee Hak Koo?'

'Could be, sir.'

Luke feared Howse would not act if he repeated the candid explanation the Chinese general had proffered when asked why he was betraying his Korean ally.

'Luke, if you weren't still very naïve politically, you wouldn't ask.' Li Mao had replied paternally. 'I want you to be alert for my own sake ... for my inevitable final victory. Lee Hak Koo is planning some tomfoolery. I'm not sure exactly what. I do know it's adventurism ... romantic leftist adventurism that can only injure the cause.

'Lee Hak Koo is arrogant ... arrogant even for a Korean. He's a muscular Communist with little understanding of the strategy of Marxism-Lenism.'

'You mean, General, you're having troubles with your Korean allies?' Luke had interposed. 'Just like us naïve Americans.'

'Draw your own conclusion, Captain. But drive my warning home! Otherwise, I shall face a major defeat. Lee Hak Koo's provocation is certain to bring retribution. An American crackdown that'll cost many loyal lives – and delay my inevitable victory. Even the soft hearted Americans will have to react if Lee pulls this one off.'

'My chief'll know this comes from you, General. It could leak.'

'I know that. Don't worry about protecting your enemy, Luke.' Li Mao closed the conversation: 'Just get the message across.'

Luke now saw that he was not getting Li Mao's message across. Howse's eyes were half-closed. He had already concluded that the information he was being given could do him little good. If it were correct, well, nobody loves a Cassandra. In fact, the more incisive she was, the more significant her revelation, the more she's hated. If the information were false, well, everyone detests the boy who cries wolf.

'I'll buck it up to the big brass ... make it crystal clear it comes from you.' Howse would not risk blocking vital intelligence, certainly not when he could shift the blame to his subordinate if necessary. 'Hell, Luke, why not write it up yourself? Why should I grab all the glory?'

Luke compressed Li Mao's warning into two brief paragraphs with no attribution. Anyone who read it could make a shrewd guess as to its source. As to the specific action the North Koreans planned, he just did not know. But what G² report was perfect?

To his surprise, Luke was not asked for further information. Nor was he pressed to reveal his source. But he had at least alerted the POW Command. Compound 76, the kettle that had already boiled over several times, was set to boil over again, perhaps to explode if the heat continued to mount.

Surely, he mused, someone somewhere along the chain of command must have reacted and ordered appropriate counter-measures. He saw no sign of such precautions, but that might be all to the good. If he were not forewarned, neither would the conspirators be forewarned.

Luke believed he was inured to the US Army's absurdities. He could no longer be surprised by anything his superiors did – or failed to do. Caring nothing for promotion, for commendation, or for decorations, he was free to buck the system. He was free as well to taunt his immediate superior, that obsessive careerist,

Colonel Lesward Murray Howse. Yet, despite Luke's smug self-approval, he was shaken when he heard from Lieutenant George Miner exactly what reception his warning had received.

'Better hightail it outta here, Luke, ol' buddy,' the irrepressible Miner snorted through his pale trumpet of a nose. 'The ol' man's got a cob up his ass. He's gunnin' for you, pal. Go on down to that little ol' hooch by the side gate. Sweetest pussy in the world, 'cept for a Memphis high yaller. But get outta here 'fore the boss catches up with you.'

'What's eating his colonelship?' Luke was irritated, rather than alarmed. 'Won't they give him his pretty little star?'

'Hell, way he's talkin' you'd think he was gonna be busted to PFC – and all account a' you. Brigadier-General Francis Dodd, the big rooster hisself, tossed back your little report. Said, near as I can learn, it was a crock of shit he's not gonna have stinkin' up his office. And why for fuck's sake did Howse buck it up?'

'Thanks, George,' Luke sighed. 'I'll keep out of Howse's way for now. A long trip to Pusan, maybe Seoul, sounds just about right. Anyway, I'll look forward to seeing the bomb blow up in Dodd's face.'

The bomb went off the next day. Luke was so close to the explosion he was almost singed.

Luke was returning the long way round from a long talk in the backroom of the Koje infirmary with Li Mao. He was counting on Colonel Howse's having vanished from the office for an after-lunch nap. Howse would call it 'a siesta after curry tiffin', grandiosely equating himself with a proconsul set by the British Empire over the lesser breeds. But, unlike those sometimes choleric magistrates, Lesward Howse shied away from public confrontation. He would not utter a reprimand with others present. He feared Luke's scoring off him with a response just short of open insolence.

Luke was mulling over his conversation with the Chinese major-general while simultaneously wondering at another level of his mind how he could justify a trip to Pusan.

Who, he asked himself, was persuading whom?

He was supposed to be winning Li Mao over to the UN side. At the least, he was supposed to neutralize the commanding general of the Chinese underground army on Koje. Li Mao was also a higher ranking consultant to Senior Colonel Lee Hak Koo, who commanded the more numerous North Korean underground army. Ideally, Luke was supposed to convince the veteran of the Long March that the future lay with the non-Communist nations, that is, the free world. Chairman Mao Zedong's comrade-in-arms was to be recruited as an American agent.

Such a transformation was spectacularly unlikely. But at 27, Luke was still imbued with the undiscriminating optimism of youth, no matter how hard-headed, hard-nosed, and cynical he thought himself. Although his objective appeared unobtainable, he persevered.

He was buoyed by the conviction that the non-Communist cause was not only just in itself, but was best for mankind. He maintained that belief despite his irritation, sometimes rising to fury, at the idiocies, the brutalities, even the crimes, committed in the name of the United Nations. Besides, he enjoyed the interplay with General Li Mao. The Chinese general possessed the most supple, the quickest, the best stocked mind he had encountered since the Yale professor under whom he had studied symbolic logic – none too brilliantly.

'Come now, Luke,' Liu Mao had opened their discussion that morning. 'You don't *really* think I'm unaware of your purpose, do you?'

'Purpose, sir?' Luke grinned, ostentatiously disingenuous. 'I guess my superiors think I could stumble on some useful information ...'

'Which they will then ignore!'

'I'm sorry. It's beyond me, General, why they've ignored your warning. Anyway, they reckon you can't get up to any mischief while you're chatting harmlessly with me.'

'Next, I imagine, you'll tell me what an honor it is to talk with me.'

'I won't tell you again, General. Though it's true. At any rate, at some point you're bound to realize that I'm right and you're ... ah ... misguided.'

'You award yourself much credit, don't you?'

'Not personally. Only because I stand on the shoulders of the great thinkers of Asia and Europe: Confucius, Mencius, and the Buddha, Chu Hsi as well. Also Socrates, Plato, Chuang-tzu, and William James, among others.'

'And, you'd say, Captain, that I've abandoned my own Chinese heritage. All for the lucubrations of a couple of unhappy, unbelieving German Jews who thought Hegel was an inspired prophet.'

'You said it, sir, not I. But, if I *were* to say that, I'd add: *Marx and Engel's teachings, which are really high-falutin' speculation, have been utterly distorted by their self-serving disciples, Lenin, Stalin, and of course Mao Zedong.*'

'You dare question the Chairman's unique wisdom?' Li Mao's thin, liverish lips parted in a vulpine smile, and his dark-hazel eyes narrowed in amusement. 'Well, lad, you're not the only one, though old Mao *was* magnificent as a revolutionary leader. We shall see where he leads us now, and, if necessary ...'

'A great general for the conquest of power. But as a political leader, a nation builder? Mao is too ruthless. He invites counter-attack. The intellectuals, the professionals, the managers, even the common people, they won't put up with ... '

'We shall see what the Chinese people will or will not put up with. But it's clear that your gang will put up with just about anything from its servants: stupidity. Your generals, your political leaders, will put up with self-promotion, with outright theft, with constant unremitting error. Not to speak of tolerating defiance from your corrupt lackeys, Syngman Rhee and Chiang Kai-shek.

'Yours is, moreover, also the *only* nation ever to incinerate more than a hundred thousand civilian non-combatants with a single explosion. But the victims were *only* Asiatics. And everyone knows an Asiatic doesn't give a tinker's dam – to seal a hole in a pot about life – his own life or anyone else's – so unlike you pious Westerners.'

'The Japanese made a good stab at mass murder in Nanking, sir! Two or three hundred thousand dead!'

'For which they will be punished in our own good time,' the Chinese murmured. 'Above all, I detest American passivity. Asians are supposed to be fatalistic, always resigned. But you Americans, events dictate your actions. You react, rather than act first, because you cannot read the will of history.'

'Back to your old chestnut, General? Your *infallible* Marxist-Leninist prophets who know beyond any possible doubt the *inevitable* course of history!'

'Not infallible, Luke!' Li Mao took a long pull on his cigarette. 'Unlike the so-tolerant Roman Catholic Church, nobody has made that claim. Simply more enlightened ... more systematic.'

Luke felt he was making progress. The Chinese general would a few weeks earlier have snorted at any criticism of Mao Zedong or the holy Red trinity of Marx, Engels, and Lenin.

By their very nature Luke's own loose, liberal democratic beliefs lacked precision. He made no claim to the perfectibility of mankind, certainly no claim to personal infallibility. Nonetheless, Luke felt he had gained an edge.

Li Mao's Marxism-Leninism was nothing if it were not absolutely infallible. That hard-edged doctrine claimed to be an invariably correct guide to the future, a minutely accurate chart of the tracks on which raced the locomotive of history. Even Li Mao's glancing admission that Marxism-Leninism was *not* seamlessly perfect was, therefore, a significant victory for Luke Maynell – and for the truth as he saw it. Unlike the bamboo, the Chinese general could not bow before the wind, in this case the force of reason, without in the end cracking.

Luke was pleased by that minute victory, although he was no more optimistic about converting Li Mao. This war, the next war, too, and just maybe the war after that would be long over before an inquisitor not yet thirty could win the soul of a grizzled guerrilla general in his fifties. His mission, Luke chided himself once again, was essentially stupid. It was as pointless as it was hopeless, just another instance of the determination of the Army of the US to jam square pegs into round holes.

Still, Luke liked that assignment. Intellectual stimulation was not readily available either on bleak Koje-do or at the barren front. Yet he nonetheless felt guilt at enjoying his disputation with the enemy general while other men were living amid filth and danger in the trenches.

Luke was now approaching Compound 76, where Senior Colonel Lee Hak Koo and his dour myrmidons spun a web of deception and violence. Four American soldiers lounged beside the big wood-framed barbed-wire gate. Their green-lacquered helmet-liners bore the letters MP for Military Police. Armed with semi-automatic carbines and Colt .45 automatic pistols, they were the regular guards on the gate. Just now, as ever, they hardly glanced into the compound.

Luke sniffed involuntarily when his nostrils were assailed with the fecal stench of the wooden honey-buckets carried on shoulder yokes by about twenty North Korean POWs. Civilians, who farmed close to the camp's perimeter, paid the POWs for their excrement, which fertilized the crops. The American private shepherding the detail was looking into the distance, probably counting the days until he was to leave Koje for the US, the land that was the big PX.

Luke was himself looking for a plausible pretext for getting off the island, though only for a few days and only as far as Pusan. Sue Chae, he recalled, had retreated to the mainland, her work for Syngman Rhee on Koje apparently in abeyance.

With no portent whatsoever, no warning or premonition at all, Luke was transfixed by yearning so sharp it was all but a physical pain. He knew that he ached to see Sue.

He abruptly realized that he had not seen Betsie Howard for days. Surprised, he realized further that he had made no effort to see Betsie, though she was buzzing around the island prying into the screening in the name of the International Committee of the Red Cross. How, he wondered, did she reconcile that pursuit with her hundred and ten per cent patriotism, her contention that *no* POW be repatriated?

Luke smiled fondly at her ostentatious busyness. He would not mind seeing Betsie, even if she were still blowing hot and cold. She was always amusing. But he felt no great need to see her. *Rather strange that was*, the thought only flitted like a dragonfly across the surface of his mind. It was, however, very strange indeed, when only a week or two earlier he had been desperate to win her love and to bind her to him for all his life!

His detachment, he reflected now that his attention had been deflected to Betsie, was not due solely to her blatant flirtation with Captain Chae Byongyup, which could not possibly be innocent. He simply felt no excitement, no thrill of anticipation, when he thought of her. Their brief affair was dying, perhaps had already died of its own weight. Really, it was finished, lifeless, stone-cold dead!

Perhaps perversely, he was just a tad thankful to Chae Byongyup. He was even more thankful for Betsie's waywardness, which he would normally have resented. He was grateful, rather than smarting from wounded male pride. If Betsie had simply drifted away, rather than gravitating to the Korean, he would have had to chalk up another name in the long list of his failures with women. But this time, *she*, rather than he, would effectively have broken the relationship and for another man.

Not until much later was Luke to acknowledge to himself that he had driven Betsie away. Not until much later was he to acknowledge that he had driven almost all his women away, almost invariably by convincing them, without intending to do so, that he was incapable of sustaining a lasting relationship.

But that comes logically just a little later in this story, which is now moving towards its end. So I'll get back to where I was.

Yes, Luke was walking past the gate of Compound 76 with the stink of Korean shit in his nostrils, and he was looking for a solid pretext for going to Pusan. He had just decided that the obvious was, as usual, the best resort. Li Mao was a long-term project. Meanwhile he really should have a look at a couple of Chinese prisoners Lieutenant Sid Rosenstein had put on ice for him at the POW General Hospital. He might even turn up a prospective agent.

Luke felt the afternoon sunlight hot on his back through his green-twill fatigue jacket, and sweat trickled between his shoulder-blades. For a moment he stood stock still, giving himself entirely to the pleasure of a new sensation that was almost unknown on Koje-do: virtual isolation, illusory privacy. No more than a half-dozen other figures were visible on the dirt road that wound among the barbed wire enclosures. The only vehicle was a motionless olive drab half-track, its quad-fifty machine-guns unmanned. No one, prisoner or warder, was ever wholly alone on the crammed island, but Luke allowed himself to enjoy feeling a great distance from his fellow men.

He smiled dreamily. He was filled with excitement when he thought of seeing Sue tomorrow or, at worst, the following day. He had once been told by an angry woman that he could not exist without a woman, but that *any* woman – or almost any woman – would do. Somehow, that was no longer true.

He had no idea what he might expect of Sue or, for that matter, what he might expect of himself when they met again. Perhaps nothing, no sensation at all. Perhaps bitter disappointment. Yet they might feel a rush of mutual tenderness, perhaps a resurgence of the sensual electricity that had once arced between them. Perhaps!

Two officers wearing not the usual fatigues, but suntan summer uniforms starched board-stiff drifted into the field of his vision from behind the drab metallic bulk of the half-track. Intent on their conversation, they strode purposefully towards Compound 76. The shorter officer wore square rimless glasses on the aquiline nose that bisected his square face. Bushy eyebrows joined into a single black bar made his heavy-set companion appear to be scowling.

Even before Luke saw the silver star on the collar of the first officer and the silver oak leaf on the other's collar he knew they were the Commandant, Brigadier-General Francis Dodd, and his faithful follower, Lieutenant-Colonel Wilbur Raven. Neither was armed, although standing orders required American officers to carry side-arms at all times. When he saluted, Luke felt the pull of the heavy Colt .45 hanging from his webbing belt. General Dodd's cold glare and tight-clamped lips showed that Captain Maynell was still in high disfavor for his disquieting warning that North Korea Senior Colonel Lee Kak Koo was planning a new assault on the authority of the POW Command.

Idly, Luke watched Dodd and Raven approach the gate, which stood open to admit the night-soil detail returning with empty honey-buckets. The American MPs on the gate stiffened to attention and saluted. General Dodd casually raised his right hand to his cap, his eyes fixed on the half-dozen POWs waiting just inside the gate. He nodded to the MPs, and the POWs came forward to greet him.

Prisoners and wardens met as the stately sun descended into the cloudbanks in the west. A shaft of brilliant light pierced the clouds to illuminate the group with sudden radiance. Captives and keepers, the North Koreans in rumpled olive drab bearing the big black letters **PW** and the Americans in crisp suntans, both glowed like Apostles in a medieval Italian painting.

Struck by the theatrical tableau, Luke heard voices raised in anger. Though he could not make out the words, he saw that arms were waving in indignation and that faces were contorted with rage. He could quite easily imagine what they were saying after his own confrontations with hard-core Chinese prisoners.

The burden of the prisoners' accusations would be similar, whatever the specific complaint the exalted commandant had injudiciously come to Senior Colonel Lee Hak Koo to hear, instead of having Lee brought to him. The hard-core Communist POWs would be demanding better food, new clothing, additional medical supplies, and more charcoal. They would also be protesting against 'forced screening' and the Soviet Union's exclusion from the peace process.

It was all quite routine. Yet it was an extraordinary spectacle: Koje's commandant negotiating with POWs as equals. Luke yawned and turned to leave, but halted in mid-stride.

The returning honey-bucket detail was swirling around the group, obscuring his view of the two American officers. An instant later, Luke saw Lieutenant-Colonel Raven clinging to the gate-post and shouting for help. Three prisoners were prying him loose. General Dodd was nowhere in sight.

Unslinging their carbines the MPs trotted to the light-colonel's rescue. The POWs broke away, retreating from the threat of those weapons. The guards had never fired a shot, but you could never tell what the mad Americans might do.

Thus released, Wilbur Raven stumbled through the open gate to safety. Luke ran forward, cocking his Colt .45.

For an instant, General Dodd was partially visible among the crush of prisoners who were frog-marching him into the compound. The MPs leveled their carbines, and Luke aimed his pistol at the prisoners. Index fingers took up the slack of triggers.

General Dodd hurled himself against the arms that held him, struggling to free himself. He could not entirely break away to race for liberty. Nor did he try to escape during the few seconds he was free of his captors' grip. Instead, he cupped his hands around his mouth and shouted an order to Luke and the MPs.

'Don't shoot!' The general's command rang over the tumult. 'I'll court martial any man who fires his weapon!'

Chapter XXVI

The Supreme Commander Allied Powers was all but incoherent with astonishment and rage in his headquarters in Tokyo. The new Supreme Commander, General Mark Wayne Clark, who had just arrived from Washington, could wring little enlightenment from his staff.

Almost any officer could explain, as the Pentagon had not bothered to explain to General Clark in full, how the POWs had become *the* crucial roadblock to an armistice. Any officer could tell General Clark of the disorder, intermittently verging on open revolt, which had for months roiled the POW camp. That devastating matter the Pentagon had failed to mention at all. But no staff officer, for all that, no officer assigned to Koje camp could essentially explain why the commandant of the POW island had been so spectacularly foolhardy as to allow his prisoners to take him prisoner.

On Koje itself, the Prisoner of War Command was no further disorganized, no more ineffective for the loss of its commandant – no less disorganized or ineffective either. Much as usual, the officers of the Command were rushing back and forth madly without any discernible effect. Yet, panic now tinged the MP light-colonels' accustomed ineptitude, standard maladroitness, and just plain normal stupidity. The emotional atmosphere, which crackled with fear, yet was soggy with frustration, prevented any action whatsoever except the baffling and humiliating negotiations with North Korean Senior Colonel Lee Hak Koo for the release of Brigadier-General Francis Xavier Dodd. Otherwise, the POW Command staggered along like a drunk under its own momentum, as it usually did, as if this immensely, monstrously mortifying and humbling, this utterly shameful eighth day of May 1952 were no different from any other day.

In the midst of the most humiliating crisis the crisis-prone POW Command had ever faced, Compound 78 was staging a gala reception for the International Committee of the Red Cross. Compound 78 accommodated a thousand-odd largely pro-Nationalist and, therefore, non-repatriate Chinese.

The Command, insofar as it had any conscious purpose at all, was eager to show the entire world what was truly the case. Those staff officers who still functioned, however feebly, were anxious to prove by that serene anti-Communist demonstration that the imprisonment of the commanding general by his own prisoners had not disrupted the smooth operation of the camp. *Presumed* smooth operation, Luke Maynell observed.

In reality, Koje had never operated smoothly at all, for its atmosphere had always been roiled. It was always violently disrupted by internal rivalry, by the pressure of presumed allies like the Nationalists' Republic of China and Syngman Rhee's Republic of Korea, above all, of course, by the assault of the prisoners themselves.

Tyro delegates of International Committee of the Red Cross, newly arrived in Korea, were to see the inside of a prisoner compound for the first time. Betsie Howard shepherded the stiff Switzers in their stiff new combat boots and their warehouse-creased field jackets.

Her own Burberry raincoat was unbuttoned in the crisp morning sunshine. Under her coat Betsie wore her neat olive-green American Red Cross uniform, rather than her accustomed slacks and sweater. An official inspection by the ICRC merited a certain formality. Still, the knee-high red-rubber boots she had drawn on against the compound's mud and muck lent an informal touch, a hint of light gaiety, to the drab scene.

Betsie's official assignment was to smooth over any misunderstanding between the ICRC delegates and the American officers of the POW Command. Unofficially, she strove to impress on the delegates not only the benevolent treatment afforded the prisoners, but the grave crime against humanity it would be if a single prisoner were shipped (she actually said 'Shanghaied') to North Korea or to Red China against his will. Betsie had been transformed into a super-patriot by the sorcery of war, but she had lost none of her charm or her quirky humor.

Luke had assigned himself to observe the ICRC inspection primarily because he knew that Betsie would accompany the Swiss. He had found her elusive for the past two weeks, whether by chance or by intent he could not tell. On the other hand, he had not really tried hard to find her, but had planned to take himself off to Pusan for a few days. Although that diversion had been thwarted by the capture of the commandant, he was now obviously free to pursue her as he had not been when he was snared by the rescreening.

Yet, he was not entirely sure, even now, that there was not today an element of duty, rather than spontaneous eagerness, in his desire to be with her. That doubt, too, was not entirely unfamiliar to Luke, who had not too infrequently known the same puzzlement regarding other girls.

Nor was he wholly unburdened by additional, rather irregular responsibilities. He had been ordered to intensify his hunt for the activists of the kangaroo court that had hanged two pro-Communist Chinese prisoners.

Luke could by and large do as he pleased, as long as he did not affront Colonel Lesward Murray Howse directly. The radical change in the POW Command's strategy and, therefore, the change in its tactics following the rescreening had made him invaluable again – invaluable and therefore indulged.

Supreme Headquarters in Tokyo no longer believed that the great majority of POWs wanted to go home. Nor did Supreme Commander Allied Powers in Tokyo any longer believe that a prompt armistice could be assured by hurling tens of thousands of unwilling prisoners into the claws of the Marxist-Leninist dictators who ruled their homelands. Whatever the SCAP believed, President Harry Truman himself had ruled against such a surrender.

The POW Command was, therefore, now determined to win even greater propaganda victories by encouraging even greater numbers to reject repatriation. Howse had earlier told Luke to forget about finding Communist scapegoats for the quasi-judicial murder of the two Chinese POWs. But he was now under pressure to identify the pro-Nationalist POWs whom he had tentatively identified as the culprits.

Luke had no idea what was in store for those men once found, whether they would be acclaimed or condemned. He had asked Howse flatly, but had elicited no intelligible answer. He suspected that Howse himself did not fully understand his superiors' renewed anxiety to pin those culprits down. Howse could himself certainly not hang medals on them, but neither could he now prosecute them. Beyond the manifest impact on the Psywar front of a demonstration of anti-Communist vileness at the present time, the colonel's dilemma, rather let us say the colonel's dream-world illogic was unfathomable when he was evidently powerless to act, much less dictate a new policy. Regardless, Luke was in no hurry to track down the culprits. It suited him to take his time.

Betsie cheerfully watched the pro-Nationalist prisoners of Compound 78 radiate light to order and inspire joy on demand. Among the spectators of that forced show were a half-dozen correspondents who had nothing better to do at the moment than await developments. The staff officers would not talk, and the correspondents could not talk to the POWs. Like carrion crows, as the MP light-colonels said bitterly, the Press had been drawn by the sensational and comical story of the commandant's kidnapping. Luke chuckled ruefully at the satirical couplet he'd heard from one of the correspondents who descended on Koje: 'How odd of God, said General Dodd, they've got *me* in quod.'

Standing between Luke and the six ICRC delegates, Betsie asked softly, 'What's the big joke?'

'Tell you later,' he replied, and turned his gaze to the ceremony.

The visitors had been welcomed at the gate by the two senior officers among the pro-Taiwan POWs, a lieutenant and a sergeant-major. Both carried themselves with assured authority. Both wore snappy peaked caps bearing the Nationalists' white-sun emblem, as well as snappily tailored approximations of Nationalist dress uniforms, complete to shiny metal insignia and gaudy-ribboned medals.

The Swiss showed themselves initially startled and then embarrassed when those officers slipped many colored-paper leis over their heads.

'Is this Hawaii?' one jested heavily. 'I thought we were in Korea.'

The Swiss were even more embarrassed when they realized that their leis were made of toilet paper cunningly shaped and colored to be all but indistinguishable from real flowers.

Luke marvelled anew that the POWs were supplied with toilet-paper at all. Presumably, toilet-paper was identified with the American way of life and, therefore, with democracy and freedom by the *Reader's Digest* mentality of the MP light-colonels. Yet, Luke wondered idly, how many of the peasants, who were the great majority among the Chinese POWs, had even heard of toilet-paper before being captured? How many now actually used it as it was meant to be used?

Precious few, if any, he answered himself. Toilet-paper was too valuable for public relations.

Dyed bright red and blue with ink, green with sap pressed from grass, white with blackboard chalk, and black with soot, the toilet-paper blossoms made nosegays and wreaths, as well as leis. Since all vegetation except scrub grass and weeds had been crushed out of existence, pastel-flowered toilet-paper vines twined around the bamboo-and-board columns of the impromptu bandstand, which had been improvised from a tattered canvas tarpaulin stretched over packing-cases.

The musicians as well as the prisoner officers wore peaked caps improvised from the cardboard and leather provided for prisoners' theatricals. Those caps were red and gold, reminiscent of the finery of the brass bands that had played for funerals in Shanghai, Peking, and Chungking, as well as hundreds of smaller towns, before Mao Zedong came to power. The Communists banned such practises as superstitious, regardless of how comforting and distracting to the bereaved might be tunes like *Dixie*, *Clementine*, and *Alexander's Ragtime Band*.

The musicians, too, wore mock uniforms, though they were hardly as natty as the Nationalist officers. Most of the inmates of Compound 78 wore khaki and green garments that were markedly superior to the scraps and rags of the pro-Communist prisoners. The pro-Communists had originally been issued stout, serviceable clothing, no different from that of the pro-Nationalists. The Communists had ripped and torn their clothing to make themselves look ragged and neglected in order to demonstrate their jailers' discrimination and inhumanity.

The band played the Swiss national anthem and then the catchy *San Min Chu Yi*, rather like a quick two-step, which is the anthem of the Nationalist government of the Republic of China 'provisionally' situated on Taiwan. The ICRC delegates were again embarrassed. Whether as international philanthropists or as representatives of the Swiss Federation, they were required to be seen as neutral politically. The American officers were, however, proudly proprietorial when the POW band blared the sprightly melody of *Three Principles of the People*, the national hymn of the Republic of China, which played no formal role in the war.

Luke and Betsie were not surprised by the brass band's favorite melodies. Neither *Marching Through Georgia* nor *The Battle Hymn of the Republic* now sounded bizarre swelling over the barbed wire. The incongruity no longer struck them, no more than did the stench of excrement, long unwashed male bodies, and rotting food that hung over the compound despite the inmates' strenuous efforts to cleanse it. As for the POWs, they did not know that most of the MP officers hailed from south of the Mason-Dixon line and were not greatly pleased to hear Union marches. The POWs did, however, know damned well that their jailers, like themselves, wanted the Swiss inspectors to find everything in good order so as to demonstrate the discipline and the enthusiasm of the pro-Nationalists.

Why should they rock the lifeboat that would in time carry them to Taiwan? Of course, they did not really know what life was like on the big Nationalist-ruled island. But they *did* know what life was in Mao Zedong's China.

'Hurrah, hurrah, we'll beat the jubilee. We'll sing it as we used to sing it as we marched along from Atlanta to the sea.'

Luke laughed exuberantly, while Betsie smiled tentatively. They were both softly singing the incendiary words. Encouraged by each other, they sang out loudly: 'When we were marching through Georgia!'

That rollicking refrain was pumped out by the prisoner's home-made instruments: cigar-box violins, both four-string Western violins and two-string Chinese violins, both strung with nylon and copper-wire; also zithers and *pi-pa*, that is, Chinese lutes, made largely from packing cases. The prisoners had hammered fifes and bugles out of the ubiquitous beer cans. They had carved wooden flutes like the Japanese *shakuhachi,* and they had cobbled four kinds of drums from the jerry cans and the hides provided for theatrical performances. The cymbals, whose triumphal clash dominated the rendition, were forged from brass supplied to metal-working classes.

Neither Chinese nor American wished to call attention to the deadly weapons made chiefly from that brass, from the metal bands girdling packing-cases, and from the lead pipes meant to train inmates as plumbers. All these weapons were unmentionable, the swords and the spears, the maces and the daggers that had won the pro-Nationalists control of the compound. Superficially, at least, all was now harmony, for the non-repatriate POWs were in cahoots with their jailers.

Luke could, however, not put out of his thoughts the monstrous sight he had seen less than an hour earlier in that same compound. He had noticed a scar on the packed reddish soil behind an open-air communal latrine, which was no more than a long ditch barely concealed behind canvas screens. The earth had apparently been recently dug out and a little later filled in again. When he walked across that narrow patch, the earth moved beneath his feet. It was like walking on jelly.

It took hardly more than a minute or two for a couple of prisoners with shovels to reveal what lay under that fresh scar. The naked Chinese corpse lay twisted on its side, a distorted, indeed maimed shape aping a fetal posture. The broken head had been thrust between raised knees that were dotted black with blood.

Luke thought himself inured to gruesome sights after the horrors he had seen in two wars. Nonetheless, he was severely pained by this latest atrocity.

The face was battered almost beyond recognition as human, he saw, when the diggers levered the corpse onto its back with their shovels. Bruised, lacerated, and ripped, the body lolled like a half-filled sack when it was thus moved. Obviously, almost every bone had been broken, if not indeed all the bones.

The lips were hideously blistered and torn. The man might have drunk caustic soda, perhaps thus agonizingly committing suicide. But where would he have found caustic soda? More likely, acid, perhaps hydrochloride from the metal-working shop, had been forced down his throat.

Presumably, the body had been buried to avoid explanations to the authorities. Yet why buried so shallowly that the grave was certain to be found? Perhaps the grave-diggers had hurried, fearing discovery. More likely, the tortured corpse was meant to be found – as a warning to any other independent-minded POWs.

Luke tried without much success to shrug away his pain. He was already resigned to never learning the reality, the true facts. The fate of the anonymous victim would remain among the manifold mysteries of Koje, impenetrable to the authorities, but immediately and profoundly significant to the inmates. Suddenly he yearned to make love to Betsie, symbolically at least thus creating new life to replace the tormented Chinese prisoner.

Betsie and he turned to each other when *Marching Through Georgia* ended. She felt she should properly accompany the Swiss to inspect the barracks and the kitchens. But the English-speaking Chinese teachers of crafts and, *sotto voce*, of politics from Taiwan could interpret, as she could not. Anyway, someone would call her if she were needed.

Someone would undoubtedly call Luke if he were needed. The American officers were on cozy terms with those dual-purpose teachers, but in critical matters they depended on Luke's command of the Chinese language and on his American common sense.

Luke was relaxed yet energetic after a week's rest. He was suddenly very attractive in Betsie's eyes. Although wary of him because of his very nature, as well as her own behavior, she could not belie her spontaneous reactions.

His light-brown eyes glowed like amber in the morning light. The affection and the need Betsie discerned in their depths all but overwhelmed her determination to resist his attraction. His lips were firm against his tanned cheeks, yet their slight fullness was vulnerable and appealing. His crisp dark-brown hair seemed to crackle with vitality. Luke was vigorous and forceful once again, after the rescreening that had totally preoccupied him – and had virtually excluded her from his life.

Betsie sensed that Luke was deeply moved by seeing her. Yet she further sensed that he, like herself, had believed their brief fling was over. His indifference had evidently matched her own. She had therefore not bothered to call him either in Seoul or when he returned to Koje. Better to let the affair perish of its own dead weight, rather than try to revive it.

Luke reflected wryly how Betsie had said his behavior was summed up in the chorus of a new popular song: 'When I'm not near the girl that I yearn for, I yearn for the girl I'm near.' Lately, Sue Chae had been that girl.

Yet Sue was not up to Betsie in a number of ways, though she was at least as attractive in her own manner. No Asian girl could match Betsie's luminous light-blue eyes, which were set off by the soft fall of her hair across her cheek, hair not coarse and black, but soft and scented, glowing deep mahogany. Accentuated by the tight-waisted Red Cross uniform, her bosom and her hips were seductive. He remembered the perfection of her long legs, now hidden by her delightfully frivolous red boots.

Yes, Luke concluded, Betsie Howard was damned provocative, but she was not only provocative.

She had changed greatly since coming to Korea. In part, it was undeniable, because of her association, as Luke put it primly to himself, with Captain Chae Byongyup, however far that had gone. He shied away from the thought of Betsie and Chae coming together physically. That was as painful as purposely probing a sore tooth.

Whatever Chae Byongyup might or might not have contributed, Betsie had grown up in the midst of the war. She had attained a maturity he had once thought beyond her. Though he had believed he already knew her well, she now conveyed a whisper of mystery a hint of secret thoughts and secret feelings, perhaps a secret wisdom, too.

'Well, Betsie,' he smiled. 'It's been a long time ... too damned long.'

'So what?' she retorted. 'You don't care how long!'

'Betsie, I—'

'Forget it, Luke. It's a pity in a way. But it's all water over the dam now. Of that I'm sure. Damned sure!'

'You don't sound so sure. Seems to me—'

'I don't care. I don't care how it seems to you. You had your chance: Twice! And you blew it twice. I'm not fool enough to stand still for three strikes.'

'Three strikes and out? Maybe. But you could hit a home run.'

'With you? Don't make me laugh! You're no use ... none at all to me, even if ...'

'Even if what?' he prompted.

'I was about to say ... ' Betsie paused indecisively, as if looking for the right word, but finally said, 'Oh, nothing. Just leave it alone, Luke.'

'Even if what?' Luke insisted. 'What were you going to say?'

Betsie looked away, as if fascinated by the man-made vines twining around the makeshift columns of the bandstand. Her face averted, she blurted out, 'Even ... even if I didn't still ... still care for you!'

'You *do*, Betsie?' He was oddly tentative, almost disbelieving; he was not triumphant, but palpably relieved. 'You really do?'

'For what it's worth.' She recovered her poise briskly. 'I'm afraid it's not worth much. Anyway, I'll get over it.'

'You may, but will I?' he asked. 'It's wonderful, but hard to believe.'

'Oh, Luke!' Her tone was fond despite herself. 'Why so hard to believe? Of course, I do.'

'You've got a funny way of showing it,' he mused aloud, by no means assertive, but manifestly puzzled. 'Skipping out on me ... avoiding me.'

'Who avoided who, Luke?'

'Yes, I can see how you'd think that. And what about Tommy, Captain Chae Byongyup? You haven't been avoiding *him*, have you?'

'Why should I? He's fascinating. And there's no danger there.'

'He is not dangerous, but *I* am?'

'You know what exactly I mean, Luke. He's not dangerous because there's no possibility of an ongoing relationship. It just can't happen. But you, you're different.'

'How's that? I don't get this feminine subtlety. What do you mean?'

'It's simple. You won't … maybe can't … commit yourself. I'm not talking about husband material. Obviously, you're not husband material. Anyway, I'm not looking for a husband. Not yet, anyway.'

'Bets, I can think of far worse prospects than—'

'Don't play with me, Luke, please. Forget about husband material or wife material. I just can't count on you.'

She paused, evidently not so much to marshal the words to express her feelings as to assess her feelings themselves. She was quite evidently not sure of how she really felt, much less sure of what she really wanted of Luke or herself.

'I'm afraid you're not even long-term lover material,' she finally essayed, still defining her meaning as she uttered those words. 'One minute you're here, and the next you're far away.

'I don't mean that you're called away on duty. I don't even mean that you're away in another place. I mean your feelings … your behavior toward me. I mean shying away when it … things get intense. There's no … no emotional stability. Nothing to hang on to.'

'You *must* know that I really care for you,' Luke said. 'Really deeply. Now I've said it – finally. And I mean it totally. Betsie, I'll try hard … be what you want, if—'

'If nothing, Luke. No matter how much I care for you, I'm not going through it again. The uncertainty … the hope and the despair. The terrible loneliness.'

'And Chae Byongyup? He's solid as a rock, no doubt.'

'Tommy's no rock. Hardly! But I don't expect him to … If … he … Anyway, he … it doesn't matter.'

'Then what's his fatal attraction? Obviously something I lack.'

'He's fascinating. I'm learning a lot from him. So much.'

Luke glared at her, his lips clamped shut. Betsie simply could not resist puncturing the balloon of his unaccustomed earnestness, when she felt their exchange becoming too intense. She rolled her eyes in a travesty of lust, affected a roguish leer, and forced a lewd chuckle deep in her throat.

'Maybe *that*, too!' she teased. 'Also about life in Asia. How it is for a sensitive, intelligent human being with a profound classical education in two cultures, not only the East, but the West? A man of refined aesthetic taste. How it is for him in a rough, crude country like Korea. Especially, of course, during a war, a horrible all destroying war.

'I'm also learning how Koreans *really* think and feel, how they *really* react. I'm getting an insider's look at their society, at their deepest emotions, and, naturally, at their politics.'

'That's quite something. But, you say, that is all!'

'No, it isn't, not quite. Sometimes he says we could be together permanently. But he doesn't mean it ... couldn't. I don't take it seriously. Anyway ... Luke, I hate to admit it ... but I don't care for him. I mean I do care for him ... a lot. But not *that* way, not really. Not as much as I—'

'Bets, darling, you know how I feel about you. I want ... I could ... '

'Can't you say it, Luke? Try!'

'Betsie, I do love you. And I want to be with you forever. Can't we start again? This time, I promise ... '

She hesitated then asked sharply, 'Don't you really mean you want to make love again?'

'Yes, of course,' Luke replied without hesitation. 'That, too, naturally. But not only that. Just to sit and talk and have a quiet drink together ... forget the misery and squalor and fear. Also maybe it'd help change your mind about me ... as a long term prospect.'

'It won't, Luke, I know it won't. But it would be nice, wouldn't it? Just this time. I'm probably a fool, but ...'

Chapter XXVII

The infirmary reeked of iodoform and carbolic acid. The ineradicable, sweet, revolting stench of vomit and feces lingered in the background. Those old fashioned odors had been all but banished from modern hospitals by the mid-twentieth century miracles of DDT and antibiotics, also by sheer elbow-grease, that is rigorous hygiene. The infirmary on Koje was a throwback to an earlier age. The farthest outpost of Lieutenant Sid Rosenstein's empire, which centered on the General Hospital for Prisoners of War at Pusan, the infirmary on Koje Island provided only the simplest treatment.

The infirmary was all but medieval. No antibiotics or soporifics, certainly no narcotics, were stocked lest the few POWs who wandered so freely by night break into the insecure Quonset hut. This way, they knew there was nothing worth stealing.

If you were really in bad shape, seriously ill, you got sent to the POW General Hospital, which was the largest single facility providing medical treatment, military or civilian, in all Korea. If you were truly ill, but not seriously, you got a few days' rest in one of the beds in the infirmary, which offered a brief refuge from the horrors of the compounds. If you were only slightly ill, you got sent back to your compound, clutching a handful of virtually anodyne APC[1] pills and musing, puzzling out in bewilderment the doctor's instruction to avoid stress and get plenty of rest.

The US Army doctors on rotating duty at the infirmary of course knew that it was virtually impossible to avoid stress amid the foul tumult of Koje – and totally impossible to rest undisturbed. Yet what else could they tell their patients? The doctors had also found that a good third or so of their patients would be healed spontaneously – not so much by the rudimentary drugs, but by that glancing contact with the magic of Western medicine. Confidence was all.

The remaining two-thirds knew beyond question that Western medicine was a lot of superstitious mumbo jumbo cluttered with a lot of useless paraphernalia such as hypodermics, stethoscopes, and X-rays. Only millennia-proven traditional Chinese medicine could cure them. Its potions were all natural. All were 'organic', as we would say today. Those medications were compounded of vegetable and plants, as well as animal parts, by herbal doctors who had spent twenty years

[1] Asprin, phenacetin, codeine.

learning their art. Had Chinese savants not published the world's first pharma-copoeia, the original scientific analysis of medicinal substances, 3000 years ago? Sadly, there were no fully qualified herbal doctors in the camp, only a few quasi-interns who had still been learning when pressed into the ranks.

Yet even the sceptics, who were committed to the traditional herbal medicine of the Orient and regarded Occidental medicine as flimflammery, went along to the Western-style infirmary for the ride. They revelled in spending time outside their pestilential compounds, just a few hours beyond the barbed-wire fences that were *not* devoted to in labor gangs.

The middle-aged Chinese who lay listlessly on a cot behind khaki-canvas screens belonged to neither group. He was not interested in that synthetic controversy between the different schools of care. He was neither a believer nor a sceptic. He had, however, for more than a year used the infirmary as a communications center where his couriers exchanged messages with couriers from other compounds. He had ruled the pro-Communist Chinese compounds by those commands. And he had conferred in the infirmary with the North Korean leaders, who were not neces-sarily responsive to his instructions.

The Koreans agreed that communication through the infirmary was more effi-cient than releasing captured dragonflies with notes on onionskin paper wrapped around their abdomens. But they continued to use dragonflies as well. The insects' iridescent splendor recalled the joys of childhood play with dragonflies.

On the second day of Brigadier-General Francis Xavier Dodd's captivity, a Chinese representative and an American representative met in secret at the infir-mary. Theirs was the only discussion between the two sides that was not subject to the pressures generated by General Dodd's captivity.

His captors allowed, nay encouraged, General Dodd to speak by telephone to Brigadier-General Charles Colson, his second-in-command, who was now acting commandant of Koje. Dodd was still pleading with his alternate to hasten his release by granting every last concession the POWs demanded. Dodd even wanted to allow them to set up their own prisoner headquarters staffed by executives, secretaries, and clerks. Those functionaries were to be provided with desks, swivel chairs, and filing cabinets in partitioned offices. They also demanded up-to-date communications equipment, that is, telephone lines connecting all Koje's compounds as well as long-range transceivers that could reach Pyongyang, even Peking, which, quite significantly in the broader strategic and political context, was hardly farther distant from the POW island than was the embattled capital of North Korea.

Only a single channel of communication between prisoners and jailers, however tortuous, was free of such demands: the seriatim conversations between Major-General Li Mao of the Chinese People's Volunteers and Captain John Luxborough Maynell of the Army of the US.

Had the duty doctor not been ordered to admit the Chinese officer, he would have done so anyway. Had he not been instructed to keep Li Mao in the infirmary, the doctor would have sent him to the POW General Hospital at Pusan. The doctor found it almost as hard as would a layman to believe that Li Mao was *not* seriously ill. Regardless of any likely physical ailment, the doctor diagnosed acute emotional shock.

Li Mao's virtually fleshless face was parchment gray. His eyes, sunk in their bone sockets, were flat and dull. They were, further, apathetic and withdrawn, their so-called whites, where not bloodshot, were sickly brown around the hazel-dark pupils. Luke was struck by Li Mao's apparent lethargy. For the first time, the Chinese general was not domineering. Not dominating, certainly not assertive; he was simply no longer forceful.

Li Mao had previously exuded calm assurance, confident that his every order would be obeyed without question. That assurance had evaporated into the muggy air. He now looked very old, agéd and feeble. He appeared actually to be grateful for the meager comfort of the steel-framed camp bed, though it was supposed to be no more than a prop in the charade of illness that enabled him to meet Luke in secret at the infirmary.

'Lu Kuh, I'll tell you today what you've been after so long!' His voice rasped, and his fuzzy Hunan accent slurred his words. 'I shouldn't even now … .But I'll give you names and details.'

Li Mao was finally assuring Luke that he would identify the pro-Taiwan POWs who had hanged the pro-Peking POWs and nailed Communist slogans to their bodies. Lesward Howse would like that! Or would he? Regardless, Howse was now pressing Luke to discover the names and, more important, to secure accurate descriptions of the culprits. Without such detail and, ideally, if most unlikely, finger-prints as well, they could hide under false names indefinitely.

But how would Li Mao react if, as Luke feared, Howse somehow rewarded the pro-Taiwan prisoners for the murder? Just now the Chinese general appeared to be sunk in grief or despair, perhaps both. For the moment, he was quiescent, no longer a potent force in the camp.

Yet he was remarkably resilient! He would assuredly revive and resume his great power. When this farcical crisis ended with either General Dodd's release or General Dodd's death, the struggle between Nationalists and Communists would of course go on. Assuredly, Li Mao would once again be a major factor, perhaps *the* decisive factor in that struggle.

Luke had to stay in touch with him.

The link between them was forged of mutual respect and mutual trust, albeit both attributes were constrained by mutual suspicion, as well by as their antipa-thetic purposes. Both respect and trust would be destroyed if Howse made heroes of the murderers.

'I'll tell you, if you really want to know.' Li Mao repeated. 'But first, a word or two of advice regarding your own future. Objective advice, if you wish it.'

Luke only nodded, having learned not to press his antagonist.

'Above all, my young friend, distrust all absolutes and everyone who embraces an absolute belief. Distrust all dogmas, whether Communist or Socialist, Fascist or

Monarchist. Distrust, above all, so-called free enterprise and so-called liberal democracy. Although the latter has some safeguards inbuilt against extremism, it can often work far too freely ... too loosely.

'Further, as you already sense, you should beware of anyone who is dedicated to any cause without any reservation. Such persons are dangerous. Absolutely dangerous!'

After a pause that was evidently occasioned as much by fatigue as by introspection, Li Mao went on wearily. Wholly uncharacteristically, he rambled. He was tentative, almost diffident.

'I should ... really, I should wait and take my own vengeance myself, though they're well protected. Regardless, I should take vengeance myself ... and be seen to take vengeance. Only way to keep on top in the struggle ... essential to maintain control!'

Li Mao's voice dwindled to resume sluggishly after nearly half a minute, his manner resigned, quite unlike his words: 'To hell with that! To hell with the struggle!'

Shocked at that volte face, Luke was spontaneously censorious in spite of himself, so much of the general's philosophy had he absorbed, so much sympathy with the general's motivations had he embraced. It was traumatic to hear Li Mao damn the struggle for China's independence of action and China's Socialist development, the purposes to which he had given his life.

This man, who had trudged beside Mao Zedong on the fabled, in truth mythologized, Long March, was repudiating not only his previous heartfelt beliefs, but his previous heroic deeds. Luke had striven to convince the Iron Bolshevik, this imperturbable Communist paladin, that he was worshipping a false god, marching to the wrong drummer. Luke had never for an instant expected to succeed.

Li Mao was steely – austere, dedicated, and incorruptible. He was, quite remarkably, even genuinely, compassionate when compassion was possible for a wholly committed 'class warrior'. The general was admirable, imbued even with humor and humanity. His love of birds, which were surprisingly numerous in the manmade wilderness of Koje, lent him even greater personal appeal. Yet he had never before this moment directly rejected or even obliquely questioned, much less repudiated, the ruthlessness demanded by his lifelong battle for the Marxist, Leninist cause.

'That ... that body you found yesterday, it was ...'

Luke was no longer surprised by Li Mao's extensive knowledge of events on Koje. His intelligence network was far more effective than the POW Command's intelligence service, which relied on Taiwan and ROK sources whose purposes were often in conflict with American purposes. It did not occur to Luke to ask how Li Mao knew that he had found the corpse of a tortured Chinese POW. He could hardly expect a coherent reply from the general, who observed *omerta*, silence on critical issues, as strictly as any Mafia *capo*.

'*Not* a suicide, *not* at all!'

The general's voice rasped. His cultivated impassivity, which was so much at odds with his actual character, crumbled in that instant. His professional reserve gave way entirely, and he expressed vividly the emotional anguish, even the self-evident physical pain, it cost him to speak at all.

'*They* killed him. *They* also killed my brother Hung-hsien. He never did them ... never did anyone ... any harm at all. They killed him for their own good reasons ... to enable them to seize greater power. Above all, though, to get at me ... to erode my power ... to destroy me. I ... I alone, no other ... was designated by Mao Zedong himself to command the war in the POW camp. But they want to seize power ... *my* power.'

All but blinding revulsion flared behind Luke's eyes, an incandescent scorching revelation. By that intense light, he saw very clearly that he was disgusted with his assignment – and with himself.

Why in the name of God was he perched on the edge of a camp bed in the half-darkness behind a canvas screen, his newly laundered, knife-edge pressed fatigues permeated – inescapably, irredeemably, ineradicably – by the perpetual fecal, putre-fying stench of Koje? Why was he compelled to look on the agony of this man in prisoner's rags whom he had, almost despite himself, leaned to respect highly?

Luke had not wished it at all, never. Quite the contrary. Indeed, he still struggled painfully against his strong emotional attachment to the prisoner general. That involuntary personal commitment went far beyond his military duty, extended much farther than even his inborn sense of obligation to all his fellow humans. Li Mao was not merely a worthy antagonist, but a sterling human being for whom Luke had, against his own conscious will, developed strong affection, as well as profound respect.

'Hung-hsien was two decades younger,' the general said softly. 'He always followed me ... did as I did ... did as I said. I was his hero. And I killed him. They killed him to get at me. So I might just as well have killed him myself.

'And all for power. Just as I have killed ... killed hundreds, even thousands ... for power.'

Li Mao's hands gripped each other fiercely, left against right, his short spatulate fingers writhing as if striving to break each other. The compulsive flow of his words, he who had always been tautly controlled, demonstrated how abysmally he was shaken!

His spontaneous confession, the base revelations that he could not control, indi-cated that he was shattered. In truth, he was utterly devastated. His entire being was wrenched apart. He mourned his brother obsessively, yielding to the ingrained devotion to family, above all else, that has been the chief moving force among Chinese for millennia. His fundamental belief, that is, his secular political creed, as well as his personal loyalty, had been radically transformed. The tender, home-and-hearth-centered Confucian doctrine of his ancestors had triumphed over the cold, rigid-and-mechanical Marx-Engels dogma to which he had given all his own life.

'He was a Communist,' Li Mao continued compulsively. 'Of course, Hung-hsien was a Communist … .Not because he truly understood or strongly believed, but because *I* was a Communist.

'I'll never know what he really believed. I only know that he changed here in this hellhole.'

Li Mao's voice sank so low that his words were virtually inaudible for a moment or two.

'When you Americans captured him, Hung-hsien was severely wounded. But your doctors nursed him back to full health in the earthly heaven of the great Pusan hospital. Then they tossed him into this hell of Koje-do.

'I had my hand over him … kept him safe. But when my guard slipped, when my attention strayed for an instant … they slaughtered him … sacrificed him like a stray lamb.'

The general closed his eyes as if to shut out the irrevocable reality of the death of his brother, whom he had failed to protect. Crimson patches blotted his sunken cheeks, and his voice rose in pitch as well as in volume, not only much louder, but shrill.

'We've created a monster, Lu Kuh. A monster that feeds on its own children. And on itself. My little brother Hung-hsien was faithful and loyal. He was, I must confess, unthinking on great matters, but he was always obedient – just what Mao Zedong wants in his followers. Hung-hsien was utterly obedient and utterly devoted. So the monster ate him. To the Red monster he was no more than *another* tidbit among the tens of millions it has devoured.'

'What can I do, General?' Luke was not happy in the role of confessor in which Li Mao had cast him, but he had to offer his help. 'What do you want of me?'

'I have no stomach for revenge, Lu Kuh, I cannot do it myself, not any more. I have already killed too many, far too many – with my own hands and with my orders. No more killing for me.

'But this … this … is different.

'In this envelope are their names, all five who sat on the kangaroo court that condemned Hung-hsien, along with my subordinate, my Political Commissar Major Chang-lo, those monsters tortured both men, then tortured Hung-hsien fearfully before killing him. All of those demons are fanatical Maoists. Here, then, are descriptions, photographs, and fingerprints. Do as you will with them!'

'As you wish, Li Mao. And the Nationalists … the other murderers, those in Compound 78? You said so … said you knew that I found the corpse. You must know who did that deed.'

'He was only an impediment … an agent of the Maoists in the Nationalist camp. In this second envelope are their names, photos, and prints. His murderers. Render impartial justice to both groups, Lu Kuh. You must!'

Li Mao was obviously exhausted, wracked, as well, by anger and remorse. Luke wanted to halt the interrogation. He wished only to console his antagonist who had become his mentor. But he could not desist. He could not leave off questioning the prisoner general.

'Li Mao, what about Dodd, the commandant?' he asked urgently. 'What can you tell me?'

'I didn't want them to take Dodd, if only because of the inexorable, the wholly predictable certainty of repercussions. Even you sheep-patient Americans won't swallow this insult. I told Senior Colonel Lee Hak Koo it was an error. A clear case of left-wing adventurism, Lenin would've called it. But I could do nothing with the mad Koreans. So, we shall see ...'

'Will they release Dodd?'

'I'm surprised you ask, my friend.' Li Mao looked up sharply. 'It's obvious! Of course they'll let him go. Sooner, rather than later. Even that fool Lee Hak Koo knows it's better to free Dodd than to kill him. Far better tactically. Far better to wring scandalous admissions from Dodd and his successor, this Colson. Far better than bearing the odium of executing Dodd, however much he may deserve it.

'The North Koreans will believe they've won a great propaganda victory, though hundreds of prisoners will die in retribution. Truly a great victory, so it is. But it is an evanescent victory. American tanks will roll ... quad-fifties open up if there is any significant resistance. That inevitability, Senior Colonel Lee Hak Koo can not grasp!'

Luke rose to leave, for he could say no more. How could he console that inconsolable general, whose life work lay in shreds about him? Worse yet, even more culpably, by his own decision! But Li Mao gestured him to stay and then spoke with evident effort in a neutral tone leached of emotion. The complexity and the precision of his sentences, which were couched in formal semi-archaic Chinese, showed that he had pondered long on the forbidden judgements he now revealed – and that he had polished them to gleaming eloquence.

'Lu Kuh, we have all been wounded. *All* men have been wounded. We finger our scars with reminiscent pride. Not only with chagrin and with regret, but with pride. Our scars define us! Those who are unscarred – if they exist – are not human. Our scars are inflicted by our defeats, both large and small. We seek to forget our defeats, but we are condemned to remember every single one.

'To all men and all women – except megalomaniacs and self-anointed messiahs – life is a series of débâcles. In our hearts, our souls, we are all defeated in the end.

'It is much more difficult for us human beings to remember our triumphs, much more knotty, more thorny than to remember our failures. The glow of victory must be deliberately summoned to return to us ... to emerge from our memories. The ghosts of our defeats arise unsummoned to mock us and deride us.'

'Why is that?' Luke asked, responding in the main to alleviate, however slightly, the anguish Li Mao felt in those extremely painful, indeed, agonizing, truths.

'Why do we relish our defeats? you ask. Perhaps because our victories, our major victories, perfuse through us. They become integrated throughout our being. Therefore, we do not remember them individually, except with great effort. Obviously, no one wishes his defeats to become an integral part of himself. So they do not! But we recall them spontaneously ... individually ... always.

'Every last defeat, every shameful rout, retains its distinct, galling identity. Every single defeat unmistakably leaves its distinct scar. All ache like fury when the emotional weather changes.'

Li Mao sat up with a muffled groan, wincing at the movement that wrenched his back. Li Mao had never complained, but Luke knew from Sid Rosenstein's summary of his doctors' reports that the Chinese general's body was a patchwork of painful scars left by wounds and operations. Li Mao braced his shoulders awkwardly against the curved, faded moss-green wall and gazed over Luke's shoulder at some point that was forever receding into the ever more remote distance.

'We were all there was left ... we two ... only we two of all our family!' His words came now in clusters. 'As blood family we had only each other. All the rest ... all ... every single one was wiped out: mother, father, three brothers, and our lovely sister.

'They died chiefly by the political struggle. Also by hunger and disease. And by malign chance: a stray bullet, the random arrow of a mountain tribesman, a fall from a cliff.'

The seasoned Chinese general sighed deeply. 'The veteran of a hundred battles, tempered to rock hardness in the armed struggle', as his official biography asserted, was utterly disconsolate. Inconsolable, as well!

'I love my wife Mei-lu,' he said. 'I esteem her as a woman, as a companion, and as a friend. Guide and mentor, too, with her wisdom and her sharp eye. Not to dwell on her sometimes sharper tongue. Wonderful through all our life together, twenty-six years. Yet we've been so often apart that our time together totals less than half those years.

'I've depended on her dedication and also on her *you-maw*. I say *you-maw*, which is simply transliterating into Chinese the sounds of the English word 'humor'. As you know, there is no native Chinese word for 'humor'. Gentle or self-deprecating humor is not a Chinese trait. Though I know sixteen native words for betray, plot, double cross, sell out, deceive, intrigue, distrust, conspire, and the like.'

Luke broke in, 'English is also pretty rich in words like those.'

'That only shows English-speakers are human, too: treacherous, avaricious, self-seeking, deceitful, and self-deluding!' Li Mao smiled woefully. 'My friend, you must forgive my bleak talk.'

He declared: 'Luke, I do not expect to see Mei-lu again. Not in this life. Is there another life, as the Jews, Muslims, and Christians preach, as some of the Sages of China have promised?

'I fear I shall soon know. I grow weary ... and mischance is never far from my footsteps. The murderers stalk me, too.

'I was speaking of Mei-lu. She is ... has always been ... to me perfection. Only one thing amiss: she could not give me sons, not even daughters. No descendants! Perhaps I was foolish. But I could not ... not ever ... take another as wife or concubine. Not for me one woman and then another and another and still another, as is the way of *the invincible leader, the great helmsman and the saving star of the people,* Chairman Mao.'

Irony springing from hatred tinged Li Mao's voice, italicizing in mid-air the extravagant, outrageous titles Mao Zedong's profligate legions of sycophants had bestowed upon him.

'Not for me four wives. That is no more than serial concubinage, though Maoists denounce concubinage for enslaving women. No Marxist endorses multiple marriages. But Mao was not a Marxist, never. He is a god to himself and to his worshippers.

'Every other night, sometimes every night for show, he takes an awe-struck virgin from the deep countryside onto the enormous platform of his bed. Or he takes from the corrupt bourgeoisie an ardent, breathless girl student who is profoundly honoured, dazzled beyond all comprehension, to give herself to the peerless leader. Sometimes the brief union is consummated. As often, it is not! Often he only plays with them like a curious, perverse child.

'Such nonsense was not for me. I go childless to the grave. Now they have killed my brother. They tortured him and murdered him, leaving only his tormented corpse. At least they did not mutilate Hung-hsien. He has gone to Heaven whole in body as in soul.'

Troubled as he was, Luke smiled behind his hand. How utterly Confucian it was, this valedictory of a Marxist-Leninist who had since the age of sixteen obsessively devoted himself to the class struggle, which was, philosophically, above all, anti-Confucian.

This man, the greatest man Luke had ever known, had often in the past ritually denounced the Confucian state-ideology as the particularly Chinese opiate of the people. He had fought compulsively to extirpate Confucianism, its temples and its shrines, its classic literature, and its indelible stamp upon manners and thought.

Yet Li Mao was now reverting, a Confucian once more, like his ancestors for two millennia. He grieved because he had no offspring to honor his memory and to bow low before hallowed family tablets, where his name should have been emblazoned with scores of generations before him. He grieved for his brother. But he rejoiced, however meagerly, that his brother had not been maimed and could therefore enter the hazy Heaven prescribed by Confucius a whole man, as he could not if any part of his body were missing.

How utterly Confucian was Li Mao's instinctive use of the word Heaven! As Luke reminded me, Confucius himself had said that the wise man, the philosopher-king, did not necessarily know whether Heaven existed, but behaved as if it did in order to set an example for the lower orders.

'Of course, I do not know the answer: Is there Heaven or not? Yet I can all but see Hung-hsien standing before the Jade Emperor of Heaven. Anyway Lu Kuh, I'll know soon enough!'

Luke only nodded, not trusting himself to speak.

'As I am now transformed, so will China be transformed some day. This vicious lunacy of Mao Zedong. Thought which is addled like a rotten egg by Marxist-Leninism ... it cannot endure.'

Thus, as Luke later observed with some satisfaction, did Major-General Li Mao predict and himself prefigure the future of China, its spiritual resurrection, as well as its economic and political transfiguration.

The following day Luke intermittently escaped from the pain of his harrowing conversation with Li Mao and from the infernal embarrassment of a commandant held captive by his own prisoners. Neither the surface nor the depths of his mind were roiled for some time by such painful recollections. Sheer pleasure drove out every disagreeable thought.

The small bedroom in the Mijin Hotel was a momentary refuge from the gritty realities of war-worn Pusan. No more than passably comfortable by the standards of Tokyo or San Francisco, the furnishings were the utmost in luxury for Korea. The pale-violet light passing through the mauve shades of the bedside lamps would at another time in another place have seemed self-consciously romanticist, not to say common or just plain vulgar. But that light was glorious at this moment. So was the king-size playground created by pushing twin beds together. The pink sheets were rumpled and creased, also damp in places, but he could not imagine a more splendid couch.

Luke's cheek lay on Betsie's bare belly, and his fingers toyed with her nipple. Mock-wary Betsie watched him beneath lowered eyelids. She, too, was sated and content, just now wholly quiescent. In Luke's nostrils the mingled fragrance of Sortilège perfume and sweet female sweat was at once calming and exhilarating. The small room was redolent of sex: a pungent, saline, oystery odor reminiscent of the sea from which all life came.

'Stop that!' Betsie directed peremptorily, stilling with her own palm his hand on her breast. 'I can't concentrate.'

'Concentrate on this,' he suggested, licking her navel.

Despite herself, Betsie responded, revelling in the sensation as his tongue traced a path downward. She smiled dreamily and for a few moments yielded entirely. Then she stiffened and pulled his head away abruptly, her fingers entwined in his hair.

'I really mean it, Luke! I want to concentrate … I want to think what I'm saying.'

Betsie sat up among the plentitude of pillows, drawing the sheet over her firm breasts. She spoke in semi-formal terms, in part in curiosity, in part in accusation.

'Luke, I've been thinking … in my spare time, what little you leave me to think, you sex maniac … .Anyway, I've been thinking about what you told me. Luke, your Li Mao brought it on himself, didn't he? If it weren't for his evil doctrine, Marxism-Leninism, he would not have suffered so … He would not be mourning his brother.

'It's noble of you, very compassionate, to worry so about him. I can see how you feel … how you honor him, even love him. But it makes my skin crawl when you talk about him as if he reached beyond most human beings, somehow transcended humanity.

'You revere him, your Red Chinese general. Don't you, Luke? You practically worship him. But he *did* bring it on himself!'

Luke was delighted to engage her mind again, as delighted as he was to engage her body. He considered her words, turning her meaning round and round in his mind, before replying, 'The times were all awry, Betsie. They still are for that matter.

'Tell me, what choice did he have! Tell me, if you can, what else he could have done! There was nothing else!

'Not if he was a man ... a decent human being. He had to join the people's struggle. He had to follow Mao Zedong. You know that was a strange note, when he spoke of Mao.'

'Not just strange, Luke, the way you tell it. Bizarre ... grotesque. I also remember it was Li Mao only a couple months ago. It was definitely Li Mao in person who ordered that unfortunate prisoner beheaded as a warning to the others.'

'Bets, you've struck a spark about Mao. You're a Sybil, an inspired prophetess. But this time you're misreading the entrails of the sacrificial lamb. That was only *one* man. Other generals, our generals, too, slaughter *thousands*, ten of thousands, hundreds of thousands in the long run.'

Luke continued meditatively, as if thinking aloud, 'I *do* honor Li Mao. But it's nonsense to say I revere him. I certainly don't worship him. I honor his suffering, and I treasure the lessons he's taught me. But that's it. That's all there is at a personal level.

'You know, Betsie, maybe I would've been a better man if I'd thrown myself into such an honorable ... such a noble struggle. Fighting for the dignity of all men and women. Instead, I'm an intellectual dilettante, fooling around with the vestiges of an exotic, ancient, and far-away civilization. Really I'm a parasite on society. So many years I didn't earn a penny myself, but I was nonetheless coddled and spoiled.'

'Now, that's really nonsense!' she declared hotly. 'You're worth ten of him any day. He's a twisted, self-deluding murderer. A modern Torquemada, killing others to save their souls.

'So now he repents! That's easy. Very easy to save his own soul by repenting now ... recanting, when it's too late to help others. It's only himself he's helping now at the eleventh hour! Your selfless, noble hero cares only about himself, nobody else!'

'Betsie, you're dead wrong!' Luke's voice was edged. 'I'm worth very little compared to General Li Mao. He's learned wisdom through struggle all his long life. And I've been drinking in that wisdom.'

'So I see, Luke. It's easy to see you've practically gone over to the Chicoms in your thinking. God knows, it's just luck, pure dumb luck, you haven't ...'

'Haven't what, Betsie? What are you getting at? Stop hinting ... insinuating ... and tell me.'

Feeling the sheet slipping down, she yanked it up over her breasts with an abrupt annoyed gesture.

'It's pure dumb luck you haven't gone all the way ... and helped your precious Chinese general in his struggle here. His noble struggle to undermine good men like General Francis Xavier Dodd! I'm not blind, Luke, though maybe I'm dumb. I've seen what the Communists do here.

'Really, Luke, *what* has got into you?'

'Watch it, Betsie. You're talking utter nonsense ... you've gone ape, the GIs'd say, bananas. My darling girl, why don't you just drop it? This super-patriotism of yours! Where did you pick it up? Where did you learn all those nationalistic, imperialistic, jingoist buzzwords? From Captain Chae Byongyup?'

'Leave Tommy out of it, Luke! Some ways he's a better man than you, really in many ways. He's certainly a far better man than your sanctified Li Mao.'

Seeking a respite, hoping that a deliberate pause would allow her anger to cool, Betsie lit a Chesterfield with a silvery Zippo. After her first puff, she blew out the smoke forcefully as if to subdue her fury – to blow it out. She undertook a firm resolution. Feeling nervy, she made a strained decision not to provoke a further confrontation – regardless of the stress.

Nonetheless, Luke's forced smile was unmistakably complacent in her eyes. Her anger inflamed again, she could no longer refrain from demanding, 'What's more, don't patronize me! Don't "darling girl" me! I'm not a fluffy little sexpot with nothing in her head but clothes and sports cars and having a good time. Luke, I, too ... I also think. You're not the only one who thinks! So just be good enough to ... Anyway, what's wrong with patriotism?'

'I know you think, Betsie! Of course you do, deep thinking, if you'll allow me to say so absolutely without irony. Absolutely sincerely let me say: your mind is half of your charm, maybe more!. Though sometimes ... only sometimes, of course it strikes me it's like a little dog walking.'

'Of course, there's nothing wrong with patriotism – in proportion,' Luke knew immediately that he had gone too far. That image was condescending. He nevertheless persisted. 'But, God help us, this ranting super-patriotism of yours! The United States of America can do no wrong! Harry Truman is infallible, practically God's vicar on earth! Now come on, Betsie!'

'I told you not to patronize me!'

Still speaking, Betsie threw off the sheet and rose to stand naked in the narrow aisle beside the bed. She stooped to gather up her garments, which were strewn on the floor, and Luke felt himself stir just looking at her. Her movements jerky and angular, she began to dress, drawing the wisps of silk around her sensuous provocative body.

'A dog walking on its hind legs!' Her voice was muffled by the black slip she was pulling over her head. 'You do believe I'm a fool, don't you? Do you think I don't know what Dr. Johnson said? *A woman preaching is like a dog walking on its hind legs. Don't ask whether it's well done. Just marvel that it's done at all!*'

Luke was staggered by the sudden recrudescence of Betsie's fury while he was still hoping to persuade her to relent. He could at that instant say nothing at all, stunned as he was by the pain he felt at her evident determination to cast him off. Overwhelmed by an emotional turmoil, he was for a moment incapable of speaking.

He could, besides, find no words to placate her. Worse yet, he dared not speak. She, too, was caught in a vortex, a whirlpool of anger at her evident rejection by himself. In truth, of course, she was rejecting him. Yet whatever he might find it possible to say, would do no good! Any words at all would only make it worse!

'What's more, Luke my darling boy, don't tell me I've got the quotation wrong. So what? In fact, don't tell me anything more. I'm not going to spend the rest of my life with you bullying me and condescending to me! Not even the rest of today! You'll never correct me again! You'll never patronize me again!'

Still doing up the gilt buttons of her olive-green tunic, Betsie strode out of the room. She did not slam the door. Nor did she look back.

Surprised by her rage, Luke was astounded by that abrupt dismissal.

'What the devil was all that about?' he asked himself aloud. 'The dog walking? Did she really think I would seriously talk that way? Why couldn't she see I was kidding her?'

When no answer came to mind, he put on an uneasy half-smile and assured himself, 'She'll be back!'

Chapter XXVIII

On May 10, 1952, it was all over – except for the shooting.

After holding Brigadier-General Francis Xavier Dodd in close captivity for more than fifty-five hours, Senior Colonel Lee Hak Koo released the commandant on the instruction of his distant masters. His orders were broadcast in code from Pyongyang, the North Korean capital; relayed by the transmitters of Communist guerrillas entrenched in Chirisan, the mountain range deep in disaffected South Cholla Province in the south-west of the Republic of Korea; received by a concealed radio in Compound 73, rather than the infirmary, since the North Koreans did not repose full trust and confidence in their Chinese allies, who controlled that message center. It was forwarded by couriers, as well as by dragonflies, to Senior Colonel Lee Hak Koo in Compound 76.

Pyongyang had received Colonel Lee's reports on his negotiations with the Acting Commandant, Brigadier-General Charles Colson, by the same route in reverse. Pyongyang had then concluded that all possible propaganda advantage had already been wrung from the incident. Not only General Dodd, but his deputy and his acting successor, General Colson, had quite publicly made severely damaging admissions regarding the American treatment of POWs. Dodd had whined and pleaded with Colson to confirm any Communist accusation at all, however vicious. Dodd had instructed Colson to confess to any conceivable misdeed, whether a crime or a sin, in order to secure his own prompt release.

Convinced that Tokyo would never agree, Colson had stopped short of allowing the prisoners to set up their own structured parallel administration of the camp. Yet he had signed a formal document implicitly acknowledging most of the pro-Communists' complaints. He had specifically promised there would be 'no more mistreatment of prisoners' and 'no more forced screening' to separate repatriates from non-repatriates. Undertaking that there would be 'no more' misdeeds acknowledged that there had already been widespread misdeeds.

The victory of the Communists and the humiliation of the UN Command was all but absolute – and not a drop of blood had been shed in this battle. The outside world had learned that the US Army was both tyrannical and weak. The army could not control the prisoners, despite the harsh treatment to which Coulson had confessed.

Yet in reality the army had erred grievously on the side of leniency or, as the light-colonels called it, proud of their command of that tag from the French, *laissez faire*.

The other nations fighting in Korea distanced themselves from the mutinous camp on Koje-do. Ottawa objected strenuously when the Eighth Army transferred a Canadian company from the main line of resistance to the island. Regardless of the dismay of the government, the troops preferred Koje to the front. Far less chance of being killed or wounded and far more comfortable living.

The Supreme Allied Commander, four-star General Mark Wayne Clark in Tokyo, seized the nettle his predecessor had barely noticed. He reduced both Dodd and Colson to the rank of colonel. He promoted Brigadier-General Hayden Boatner to major-general. Boatner, who had been a deputy division commander at the front, was a tough disciplinarian. He was also a China specialist, having studied the language before World War II. Rather remarkably, he could still get along in Mandarin.

But he would not be talking to the prisoners. Forewarned by the demotion of Dodd and Colson, Boatner had other plans.

Correspondents once again descended in swarms on Koje to report the stand-off between UN troops who dared not enter the prison compounds and defiant POWs who, nonetheless, dared not break out. Quad-fifties and armored vehicles faced prisoners armed with clubs, swords, spears, maces and a few home-made firearms. My own byline, Harland Birch, once again appeared on stories about that face-to-face confrontation.

I was not particularly happy to be back in Koje, although the story was hot, and I had an inside track through Luke Maynell and Sue Chae. I've never liked group coverage, no matter how good the story. Besides, the bleak island was as depressing as ever.

This gory hullabaloo was all due to a slip of the pen. As you'll remember, US psychological warriors had created the imbroglio by casually promising that enemy soldiers who surrendered would not be sent back to their native lands if they did not want to go back.

Anyway, I was annoyed with Luke, and he knew it. He had for all intents and purposes taken Betsie Howard away from me and then practically tossed her aside. What a waste of talent!

Although my mood was sour, the drama of the confrontation was stirring. Extremely confident, Major-General Hayden Boatner fought his battle to regain control of the POWs under the eyes of as many reporters as could be enticed to Koje. Having lost so much face in public, the UN Command was determined to regain face in public. A host of print reporters and still photographers, as well as a sprinkling of newsreel and television cameramen, were hauled around the camp in big khaki buses, as if they were rubber-necking tourists. However, no tourist guide, but an officer of Colonel Lesward Murray Howse's Civil Information and Education Section offered a running commentary as the bus trundled through corridors palisaded by twelve-foot-high barbed-wire fences.

Luke hated that assignment, which required him to spout the official line. When he did so, he further explained that the prisoners had got out of hand because they were treated far too leniently. Besides, he prefaced almost every sentence with the self-denying formula: 'The Command states that ...'

Not even Colonel Howse objected to that evasion of personal responsibility. Even Howse knew it was now no longer possible to mislead the Press, which had for so long not only been roundly deceived by the UN command, but had roundly deceived itself. Not even the dullest wire service reporter could fail to see that a critical battle of the Korean War was being fought on Koje-do, a battle that was very soon likely to be at least as bloody as the skirmishing at the front.

That unpalatable assignment did at least give Luke a chance to talk with Sue Chae. He hoped Sue would carry a conciliatory message to Betsie Howard, who flatly refused to talk with him or even to acknowledge his existence when, as was unavoidable, they all but bumped into each other on Koje-do.

Sue talked about the North Korean POWs to the Press. She did not dare distance herself from the official line of the ROK regime. In any event on the verge of proclaiming martial law, the government was cracking down hard on dissidents. Not only her mother's safety depended on Sue's retaining her privileged position by forcefully carrying out her propaganda duties. Her half-brother Chae Byongyup's dignity and freedom, even perhaps his life, also depended upon Sue's personal influence. Therefore, she spouted the Rhee line without qualification, even when canny correspondents smiled at her orthodoxy.

Not that Chae Byongyup appeared concerned. He was, it seemed, wholly taken up with his successful pursuit of Betsie Howard. Off duty, one never appeared without the other.

Sue was not pleased by the renewed intimacy between her brother and her closest friend. One or the other, perhaps both, would be badly hurt when their unnatural affair broke up, as it must inevitably. Betsie and Byongyup were so far apart in so many ways, not only in age, experience, and outlook, but in their fundamental nature.

Betsie took for granted the freedom of thought and action that was normal for a young American woman. She could never fit herself into the bleak poverty of war-ravaged Korea. Nor could she even submit to the suppression inflicted on Korean women, although they were, oddly enough, among the more emancipated women of Asia. Nor could she in the long run possibly adapt herself to Byongyup's tortured personality, which had been shaped by domestic and public tyranny, by *folie de grandeur* and exalted expectations, by popular acclaim and personal renown, by persecution and oppression, as well as by constant political frustration.

Still it was very odd. Despite Sue Chae's many misgivings, the intimacy between Betsie Howard and Chae Byongyup somewhat paradoxically jibed with Sue's own inclinations. Sue would follow her own independent course. She would carry no conciliatory message from Luke to Betsie, for she had her own fish to fry.

Sue was appalled by the prospect of remaining indefinitely in a Korea not only maimed by civil war, but ground down by a callous, corrupt dictatorship masquerading as a democracy. Yet where could she go as matters presently stood? Certainly not to America!

Although America would be ideal, it was virtually impossible for her to obtain a long term visa. However, there *was* Luke Maynell, who was no longer Betsie Howard's private property. Sue was intrigued by Luke, and, God knew, the physical attraction between them was potent.

Luke caught himself humming a catchy little tune, his fingers tapping out the beat on the steering-wheel of his jeep. Amused at his vagrant thoughts, he sang the silly words under his breath: 'My girl's from Vassar. None can surpass her. She got a pair of hips just like two battleships.'

What did battleships have to do with hips, except that they rhymed? He couldn't quite recall the next line. Maybe it was: 'I buy her ... *something* ... clothes to keep her ... *can't remember* ... knows. Oh God, that's where my money goes.'

His wayward thoughts then strayed to Sue Chae, who had asked him to dinner at the old Japanese villa on the hill overlooking Pusan. She had not told him who else was coming, but Sue's dinner parties usually netted a half-dozen men who could be useful to the Republic of Korea. He assumed that Harland Birch would be among her guests tonight, as well as some of the other correspondents who were still in town even though the pace of General Boatner's campaign to regain control of Koje had slackened during the past few days.

Pity in a way, that Sue's dinners were so big. But did it really matter? He certainly had no designs on her. He was still committed to Betsie, although she would now not even nod to him.

Yet why not use the oldest ploy in the book? Why not make Betsie jealous by flaunting a close relationship with Sue, her best friend?

Still, that ploy might not work. Betsie's anger could well require days, maybe weeks, to cool.

Regardless, the ploy was too naïve. Both young women were sophisticated when it came to the war between the sexes.

The Vassar class of '48 was proud of its emancipation from conventional bourgeois restraints. A fair number of the girls had demonstrated that they would go all the way, hopping into bed with potential recruits for the 'progressive' cause. That cause covered everything from touting Paul Robeson's concerts and acclaiming Henry Wallace's toadying to the Soviet Union all the way to the Leninist dictum that sex was no more important than a glass of water.

You drink when you're thirsty, don't you? Then why not screw when you're randy? It's the same thing!

As far as Luke knew, Sue had not succumbed to that facile counsel. He would certainly know if she had, for he'd spent some time with the progressives of Vassar. If Sue had experimented with sex at all, she had done so discreetly and infrequently. Although he did not believe that she was a virgin after living for several years in the United States, Luke did believe that her experience with men was limited. Something not readily definable in her demeanor told him so. She was sometimes forward, even brash when her duties required brashness. But he sensed shyness and uncertainty beneath her professional boldness. Sometimes she was even diffident.

Sue was innately a strictly reared upper-class Korean young lady instilled with strict Confucian standards. Regardless of her intellectual repudiation of Confucian values, regardless of her mother's progressive politics, regardless of new values acquired at Vassar, her moral and aesthetic touchstones were Confucian. That definitely meant no sleeping around.

Well, time would tell!

Still, the last thing on his mind, Luke reminded himself sternly, was seducing Sue Chae. For one thing, he was not really attracted by the thin willowy type with no more than budding breasts. Despite the lightning flash, that electric shock of desire that had arced between them that one time, he told himself that he preferred a more explicit display of the female form. Not too obvious, of course, not blatant, but rather like Betsie's restrained voluptuousness.

Another thing, there was Betsie herself. She might think their affair was over, but he did not, *definitely* not. Spurred by the unfamiliar thrill of the chase, the man into whose arms so many women had tumbled solemnly promised himself that he would win Betsie back the hard way.

Yet he wondered as the old jeep wheezed up the winding road to the villa, its engine pinging in protest at the climb: *Why then the sexual electricity between Sue and himself?*

Emerging abruptly from the smog that blanketed Pusan in the warm June dusk, Luke was struck by the sudden beauty displayed by the little wooden houses that lined the road helter-skelter. All were lit by the declining sun. He might have been entering an enchanted realm, one of the many Taoist-Buddhist Heavens. The nearly horizontal sunrays gilded the unpainted, weathered boards of the houses and turned the wavelike roof tiles silver. The small windows sparkled like sequins.

Bemused by that vision, Luke smiled to himself as he drove through the open wrought-iron gates of the villa. The police sentry saluted casually. Sue had said seven, but it was already half past. Yet Luke saw no other vehicles, except the battered ancient jeep that she drove.

Alerted by the grinding of his engine, Sue welcomed Luke at the door. She wore a scarlet-silk *chipao*. Her only jewelry was a green jade ring incised deeply with the Chinese character for long life. Her make-up was light, no more than a dash of lipstick and a hint of eye-shadow.

'I'm sorry,' she said. 'You'll have to put up with me alone. There's a political flap on, and the others had to beg off.'

'I can think of nothing better,' Luke responded with automatic gallantry. 'But tell me, what's up?'

'Some spat ... infighting in the Rhee faction. Thank God, nothing to do with you or me.'

'How come the correspondents, Harland, maybe, couldn't—'

Luke cut off the embarrassing question with a forced cough. Any infighting among Syngman Rhee's clique that was important enough to draw the interest of war correspondents who normally shunned the confusion of Korean politics would assuredly require Sue Chae to interpret and to explain. If she wanted to be alone with him, but didn't want to say so, that was fine with him.

A small table and two camp chairs stood on the small terrace in front of the open *shoji* wall screens. Four bottles, their necks covered with gilt foil, protruded from a silver wine-cooler beside the table.

'Champagne,' Luke said appreciatively. 'What's the occasion? Are congratulations in order?'

'A present from the French Press attaché. No occasion and no congratulations. I just felt like champagne. Would you prefer something else?'

'Certainly not. I never refuse champagne.'

'Well that's settled.'

'I'm glad we've got that tough decision over with.'

Luke selected a bottle, noting with appreciation that it was Pol Roger, famously Winston Churchill's favorite marque. He removed the gilt foil and twirled the cork, his fingers sheathed in a handkerchief to give him a purchase on the slick surface. He poured the bubbling wine into broad shallow goblets with hollow stems; the conical champagne flute had not yet made it to Korea. Despite that easy target, he spilled a few drops, for his eyes were drawn to the sight below.

If the approach to the villa were the road to a Taoist-Buddhist Heaven, then the glorious floor of Heaven itself now lay below them. The noxious amalgam of fog, smoke, and exhaust fumes that covered fetid Pusan was transformed by the retreating sun into a luminous canopy that concealed the squalid city. Nor did Pusan's raucous din penetrate that canopy to mar the tranquil evening, while the radiance reflected from the canopy flooded the air with gold.

Sue herself could have been a rather saucy, perhaps even rebellious, denizen of that other worldly realm. The perfect oval of her flawless ivory face was set off by the red-glints in her jet-black bangs, while her shoulder-length page-boy hairdo somehow for the moment made her appear more Western then Asian. Her green-tinged eyes sparkled with humor and, as he already knew from her own words, with skepticism toward the official line she sometimes parroted. Still, she smiled in genuine welcome, and her husky voice was intriguing, not to say seductive.

It was hard to keep a clear head while gazing at Sue against the overwhelming radiance. When Luke opened the second bottle of Pol Roger, he realized that Sue was drinking one goblet to his two. Apparently determined to keep her head, she could do as she wished. He was already enjoying the golden glow of the bubbles in his bloodstream, sinking joyously into the totally carefree, utterly relaxed mood that champagne bestowed upon him.

'I suppose we should eat some time,' he nevertheless ventured.

'All in good time, Luke. No need to rush.'

They chatted for a time. Their banter was unmemorable, simply reflecting their light-hearted, festive mood. The tone of voice, the tinkle of laughter, were, somehow, momentous, though trivial, far more meaningful than the words themselves.

This was one of those blessed occasions. Luke's euphoria attained a high plateau where it would remain for some time, whether he drank more champagne or not. He sensed that Sue felt the same way from her intimate smile, from the light touch of her hand on his arm, from her perfumed breath playing on his face. He felt desire rise in response.

He knew he should draw back, at least delay, lest they be swept again by the overwhelming flood of mutual passion they had once before felt on this same terrace. Neither needed to further complicate a life already too complex.

'What're we doing, Sue?' he asked jovially. 'What're we up to?'

'I'm not sure what you're up to, Luke.' Her soft breath in his ear made him shiver. 'But I'm trying to seduce you.'

Her avowal loosed the whirlwind. The tide of desire lifted them to the heights again, and they reached frantically for each other. Between desperation and ecstasy, they fumbled and clawed at each other's garments. Luke lifted her slight weight and carried Sue into the room with the yielding tatami floor. Clad only in wisps of silk, Sue reached for his last remaining garment.

The next instant, she froze as if lanced, and Luke froze with her. At the same moment, both retreated from the encounter, retreated psychologically and physically. Both were confounded and abashed. They recoiled as from an act of incest.

'It's not right!' Luke spoke for them both. 'What's between us is strong ... devilish strong. But it's not that kind of tie, not physical ... not that way. It's ... '

'... much more like brother and sister.' Sue could laugh again, if weakly. 'More's the pity!'

Major-General Hayden Boatner's mammoth bulldozer made up of heavily armed troops was studded with guns as a porcupine is studded with quills. It was composed of thousands of infantrymen, military policemen, tanks, quad-fifties, and scout cars. That armoured bulldozer was poised before the gates of Compound 76 just before dawn on 9 June, 1952. When their machines rumbled forward, the final battle to suppress the protracted POW military mutiny would begin.

North Korean Senior Colonel Lee Hak Koo still skulked in Compound 76, still digesting the bitter realization that seizing Commandant Francis Dodd had been a catastrophic error. The Chinese General Li Mao had warned that swift retaliation would follow, but Lee Hak Koo had ignored that counsel. Pyongyang's interests did not always run parallel with Peking's.

Armed forces had already wrested control of other compounds from the prisoner *honchos*. There had inevitably been casualties, both dead and injured, though a surprisingly small number. Most prisoners were already confined in temporary compounds that held no more than 500 men. The POWs were now incapable of mustering sufficient force to defy the Koje Command, as compounds that held thousands had done so spectacularly. Besides, the North Korean pro-Communist *honchos* had been specifically identified, primarily by Captain Chae Byongyup, the Chinese primarily by Captain John Luxborough Maynell.

To ensure that no further mutiny could occur, Koje itself was to be abandoned. A stream of Landing Craft Tanks, which looked like sea-going baking pans, would evacuate miserably seasick POWs to their new places of confinement.

All Chinese POWs were to be sent to the rugged island called Cheju off Korea's south-west coast, which traditionally boasted that it possessed 'many women and many winds'. All the Koreans were to be resettled on the mainland, in small camps widely dispersed so that there could no further collusion among rebellious POWs.

Luke heartily welcomed those moves. He was exhausted by the incessant struggle with the POWs, the interminable palavering, the ruthless haggling, and the cruel violence, above all, the constant jockeying for advantage between jailers and prisoners. The most formidable battle, that between pro-Communist POWs and anti-Communist POWs, had ceased now that the power of all pro-Communist *honchos* had been broken and all the POWs were penned in small compounds. Then, thank God, no more invidious negotiating.

Li Mao was, of course, a sterling exception. He could not be allowed to disappear into the antheap of unidentifiable and untraceable POWs. Luke had already sent a memo to Major-General Hayden Boatner urging that Li Mao be detached from the mass of prisoners. Li Mao merited such special treatment now more than ever, since he had explicitly repudiated both Mao Zedong and Marxism-Leninism.

Why not move him to Tokyo? It was not likely that he would submit to a rigorous intelligence debriefing, but, he could provide valuable insights into the behavior of a regime he knew intimately because he had served it so long at such a high level – a regime that he now despised.

Luke also welcomed the reorganization of the bureaucratic chain of command. The POW camps were no longer administered by the Eighth Army, but were directly under the Supreme Commander Allied Powers in Tokyo, his instructions channelled through the independent Korea Logistical Command. Rumors of uncertain origin were afloat that Luke himself was to be reassigned to SCAP in Tokyo. That wide open, neon-lit epicentre of hedonism in Asia would be a stunning contrast to brutal, stinking Koje and squalid, miserable Pusan.

What was there to keep him in Korea now that his assignment was no longer demanding? Not Betsie, who was virtually dead to him, try as he might to win her back.

And Sue? She was a challenge and an enigma. But he felt no great need to unwind the riddles and the mysteries that swathed that enigma, not just now at any rate. His relationship with Sue was comfortably settled. She made no urgent demands upon him.

Luke was ambivalent, not quite sure whether he was pleased or disappointed that his request to return to troop duty at the front had been summarily turned down. His talents, SCAP declared, were too valuable to be wasted in combat. Besides, he knew too many secrets to be exposed to possible capture.

He feared the brass were deciding at their leisure whether to decorate him for his services on Koje or to reprimand him, perhaps court martial him, for persistently defying authority. He knew that Colonel Lesward Murray Howse had recommended that he be charged with gross insubordination. Howse was as vindictive as he was incompetent.

The sun rose reluctantly, slowly, very slowly, dispelling the night fog – and General Boatner's armoured bulldozer began to roll. The POW guards inside the gates of Senior Colonel Lee Hak Koo's Compound 76 vanished when those gates were thrown open and American infantrymen trotted warily into the toughest enclosure on Koje. Tanks and quad-fifties pressed against the fences of barbed wire. Those killing machines would knock down the fences and race to assist the infantry if the foot soldiers ran into any significant resistance.

The men in the vanguard knew that artillery was lined up to support them if necessary: six field guns deployed out of sight behind a hillock. The newly minted Major-General Boatner was taking no chances. Neither the POW Command nor he himself would be humiliated this day.

There was, however, no truth in the rumor that a squadron of F-84 fighter-bombers had been assigned to support Boatner's armoured bulldozer. No hotshot pilots were alert in their cockpits ready to scramble. No air support had been laid on, in part because US and enemy forces were too close to each other to allow effective air support. Besides, Hayden Boatner hardly wanted the gaggle of correspondents to report that he had used bombs or napalm to subdue lightly armed POWs.

The battle for Compound 76 was tactically frustrating, since the actual conflict was all but impossible for the bystanders to observe. The reinforced swarm of correspondents, initially at least, found it supremely frustrating, because no discernible pattern of action emerged. Yet the operation, although clearly necessary, had been staged in part to satisfy that audience, the Press. It was for all the world meant to be like a fight to the death by gladiators before the Roman public in the Colosseum.

Bayonets fixed, the American vanguard poured into the corridors between the rows of barracks – and disappeared. The next rank took up blocking positions. A half-dozen POWs here, a dozen there, one or two elsewhere, broke into the open, scurrying as if their lives depended on their fleetness. Actually, their lives depended on their not moving at all. They halted after warning shots were fired over their heads. They stood stockstill and meekly surrendered to the GIs.

An invisible rifle barked somewhere among the rows of barracks that had swallowed the US vanguard. Submachine-guns rattled once or twice in the distance. A shrill scream arced over the tin roofs, then another and another. The

backup force formed a tight line to net the scores of Korean POWs hurtling out
of the corridors between the barracks to escape hand-to-hand combat deep in
the compound.

A dull explosion rumbled, telling Luke that at least a few POWs were resisting
strenuously. Red dust billowed into the air from the center of the compound. The
Americans carried only concussion grenades, which stunned in an enclosed space
and disoriented in the open. That full throated explosion was assuredly a mine
improvised by the POWs.

The tanks and armored quad-fifty half-tracks along the perimeter stirred like
restive rhinos gathering themselves to charge. Their radios crackled, and they
resumed their fixed positions.

A stretcher borne between a pair of medics emerged from the nearest corridor.
On the taut canvas lay an American infantrymen whose hands trailed ominously
along the earth. Dead or severely wounded? Who knew?

Then two more stretchers, their burdens identical: wounded Americans with
gashes in their exposed abdomens. The spears and swords run up in metal-working
classes had been proved in action.

No POWs, however, neither wounded nor dead. Not, Luke knew, because there
were no North Korean casualties. Only because the GIs had been ordered not to
stop to succor wounded enemies. That would come later.

Whirlwinds of red dust rising from the crumbling laterite soil enveloped the
compound, obscuring the shapes of the few GIs still in sight. It was impossible to
see with any clarity. Only indistinct, wavering figures were visible, a slightly deeper
red among the billows of red dust.

The inevitable was, of course, occurring. Despite their zeal and their courage,
half-trained POWs with improvised weapons were hardly a match for heavily
armed, combat-tempered troops.

Luke glimpsed a man who resembled Senior Colonel Lee Hak Koo being
dragged by a pair of MPs through the clouds of dust toward the open gate.
Although he could not be sure that the bedraggled, humbled figure was indeed the
North Korean *honcho*, Luke knew then that the tragic epic of Koje was over. The
plight of the POWs would endure until an armistice was signed, a drawn-out
epilogue to the high drama of the Korean Devil's Island.

The epilogue closed with another attempt at deception that was inevitably in
vain. The Koje Command declared that no firearms had been used in the
assault, although correspondents had seen the armed assault and had heard
some shots. Yet the Command acknowledged that one American and thirty-one
North Koreans had been killed. So many POWs killed, but not by firearms?
Ridiculous!

Koje-do was now finally done with the POWs and their brilliant campaign
against their jailers. Moreover, Luke was finally done with Koje-do. Also, he hoped,
he was finally through with the prisoners, yet he could not quite believe that was
so.

★

'Jeeow dzo, Siao Mai, dzo yi dzo. Ni jen mafan waw ... ' Grizzled Major-General Hayden Boatner waved Luke Maynell to a chair, speaking first in American accented Mandarin, then dropping with relief into English. 'Sit down, young man. You're a damned nuisance. But I'm prepared to put up with you ... up to a point. It's not every day I run into an American officer who's the confidant of a Chicom major-general. That's part of the trouble, of course.'

'Trouble, sir?'

'Bu gei waw chr doufu, Shang-wei.' Boatner showed off his Chinese slang. 'Don't feed me tofu, Captain,' he said, meaning: 'Don't kid me!'

'You know damned well you're in deep trouble with your boss, Colonel Howse.'

General Boatner lifted a thick manila file and said, 'It's all in here, complaint after complaint from the day you joined his unit. Insubordination, insolence, failure to carry out express orders, sticking to your own opinion when your superiors've told you it's wrong, protracted absences from duty on slim pretexts. Trafficking with the enemy ... assisting the enemy. And so on and so on. The charges get heavier as Howse gets up steam. Take trafficking with the enemy and assisting the enemy. Upheld, those crimes would bring the death penalty.'

Luke dropped his head into his hands, only in part in shock. Even more to hide his triumph in learning how gravely he had offended his bumbling superior. Besides, the death penalty was not merely unlikely, but just about impossible. Yet he could possibly draw a long prison term. Twenty-odd years in Leavenworth, would be sheer purgatory for a former officer among criminals who were former enlisted men.

He looked up to see the major-general grinning at him with malicious glee, and his heart plummeted. He could all but feel the thud as it hit his diaphragm.

'But also rave after rave from de Marco of G², ' Boatner continued. 'Not to speak of heartfelt gratitude from the spooks. Big question is: should you be on my shit list? I considered promoting you and making you my aide. But that won't wash. You're too plumb ornery, too damned pig-headed. The army's no place for mavericks.'

'Then I *am* on your shit list, sir? You're going to court martial me?'

'Not so fast, young man. There's gotta be more palaver before I make up my mind what to do with you.'

A surge of relief swept Luke. He could feel his heart rise to its accustomed place. Even his father's influence would be of little use if his commanding general were determined to ram through guilty verdicts on a dozen different charges. Boatner did not sound as if he were planning a court martial. Yet his next words again aroused apprehension.

'You know, Captain, you're up shit creek. You're damned vulnerable. De Marco's commendations are all to the good, but you only served under him for a few weeks. And the love notes ... appreciation from the spooks? Sure we work together, but the army's not wild about the CIA. Neither am I, to be brutally honest. So how much good ...'

Boatner turned over the documents in the manila file, looked up at Luke, and said accusingly, 'Also a charge of suspected homosexuality. Active homosexual practices.'

Luke gulped, then grinned at the general in derisive incredulity. '*Me*, sir? Homosexuality? Of all the screwy ... .Whatever else, I may ... probably be a simple, damned quixotic fool, I'm definitely heterosexual ... very heterosexual. Just ask—'

'All that time alone with Major-General Li Mao in the infirmary with convenient beds all around. Everybody knows a middle-aged Chinaman'll settle for a good-looking young man if he can't get a nubile virgin. And why did he talk so freely, if ... ? And all those fresh-faced, juicy Chinese lads running around with signs on their caps: *I am a girl!* You recommended to Howse that we ignore that perversion.'

'Getting involved would've raised havoc, sir. We'd have been tarred.... We couldn't win.'

'That figures. We'll see about that. Phew! Howse also intimates you're too close to Korean civilians, violating the unwritten understood rules against fraternization. Also ... this is a good one ... too close to the POWs, the Chinese, of course.'

'That was my job, sir,' Luke interjected. 'The Chinese!'

'Good reason, it says here, *to suspect Communist leanings ... a sympathizer and a fellow traveler at the least*. This bozo, Howse, he's really a big fan of yours!'

'That's all bullshit, sir. He's using a shotgun, sir. Shooting everything he can dream up ... hoping something'll stick.'

'Looks like it. You've heard of Senator Joe McCarthy, Captain? Tailgunner Joe?'

'Yes, sir. Vaguely.'

'Nothing vague about Joe McCarthy. He's using the biggest shotgun in the world. Finding Communists in the government and the army. He's loading up for General George Marshall now. Marshall, by God! Might as well indict Abe Lincoln for Communism! After all, he freed the slaves ... took away the plantation-owner's property. Anyway, a young captain who's been hanging around the Chinese for years would be just Joe McCarthy's meat. If he ever saw this file ... '

'But it's all bullshit, sir. Total nonsense!'

'Maybe, Maynell, maybe! That wouldn't matter if Tailgunner Joe got hold of this file. He's got stooges in the Pentagon. And all Howse's charges are still on the record!'

'Yes, sir!' Fear chilled Luke's backbone. 'What can I do?'

'Not much, Maynell. The accusations're on the record. And there they'll stay until someone in authority decides to press charges or to strike them all.'

'Then it's all up to you, sir?'

'That's right, lad. Nothing's gone into your permanent file yet. Maybe won't. It's all my baby ... I wish they'd dropped it into somebody else's lap, but I've got to decide. Strikes me you're either guilty of everything or it's a lot of malicious gossip by a lot of old women in uniform. Specially Colonel Lesward Murray Howse, who might just revert very soon to his permanent rank of captain. It's him or you, Maynell!'

'Then I'm all right, sir? That's what you're saying, isn't it? *Ding gua gua!*'

'*Juehdway bu shrla, siao Mai!*' The general reverted to Chinese. 'Absolutely not, young man! … .And leave off that *Ding gua gua!* stuff! Everything's not copacetic, not by a long shot. Anyway, I've had a bellyful of fractured Chinese. 'Just don't get cocky. You're not out of the woods yet. Not by a long shot. You're up shit creek till I throw you a paddle.'

'Are you going to, General?'

'Might. Haven't made up my mind yet.'

Boatner picked up the toy tank made of beer cans that still graced the desk occupied for some time by former Brigadier-General Dodd and so briefly by former Brigadier-General Colson. He swivelled the turret, evidently weighing the problem Luke presented. Abruptly, he hurled the tank at the wall. The impact sheered off the turret and the tracks, leaving a pathetic little metal carcase on the green rug.

'You know, Luke,' Boatner said expressionless, 'Howse is right about one thing. You *are* too damned soft on the Chinese. When you've been dealing with them as long as I have, you'll know you've got to be tough. Polite, of course, but very firm.'

Luke smiled. He almost laughed with relief. Boatner's using his first name thus casually signalled that, at the very least there was a very strong likelihood that he would quash the charges.

'Tough wouldn't have done me much good with Li Mao, sir!' Luke rejoined. 'He's twice as tough as I am – intellectually and morally. May be as tough as you, General.'

'Year and a half as a stinking POW, eh? Don't know if I could take it. Not as a prisoner of the Chinks, for sure … Anyway, that's clear. You'd've got beans out of Li Mao if you tried to tough him out. And your information was right on the nose, even if the idiots here didn't act on it … All right, Captain, I'll think about it.'

'Thank you, sir.' Relieved, but by no means entirely off the hook, Luke took those words as his dismissal and began to rise.

'Sit down, son, sit down,' the general commanded. 'There's one more item of business, isn't there?'

'Sure is, General. But nobody else's shown any interest.' Luke brightened even further and said, 'I've got two files here, complete with descriptions, real names, pictures, and fingerprints …'

'From old Li?'

'Yes, sir. One lot, these five, are the deep-dyed, fanatical Maoists who strung up those two moderate Communists a couple of months ago. Tacked a crude Communist flag and some garbled Mao sayings all over the bodies to make it look like a Nationalist plot to put the blame on the Coms … It was actually an action against Li Mao, killing his deputy and his brother.'

'Some time ago, wasn't it?'

'You could say so, General. Still it was a grave crime … could've ended in a general rising if Li Mao hadn't quashed it.'

'Well, even if it was a while ago, murder is murder ... And the others ... your other file?'

'These three are the pro-Nationalists who killed a lukewarm follower to put the fear of Chiang Kai-shek into the others. That body I found.'

'Fine, Captain, well done! We'll try those five murderers. We'll make our own example!'

'And the pro-Nats, sir?'

'Why in the name of God? Of course not! I'll turn a blind eye like Nelson. My problem is the Chicoms, not the Chinats.'

'But justice, sir? Plain, simple justice?'

'What's the problem, Captain? If those three Chicoms're innocent, they'll be acquitted.'

'Are you saying your colonels would acquit men you obviously want them to find guilty ... as an example?'

Grizzled General Boatner grinned and cheerfully admitted: 'I guess not. But I've got to make an example. Only thing the Chicoms understand is force. *Power grows out of the barrel of the gun!* Old Mao Zedong's said it a hundred times.'

'So we just forget about justice?'

Luke persisted most unwisely. Really, though, it wasn't just unwise, but downright foolhardy to bait Boatner, who held Luke's future in his hard hands. Even though Boatner had definitely *not* entirely let him off the hook, Luke persisted.

'Young man, I'm astonished, plumb astonished,' General Boatner replied equably. 'This isn't about justice. My job's not to dispense justice. My job's to make the POWs behave themselves. No more riots ... no more kangaroo courts ... no more murders.'

'Just like the way we deal with Syngman Rhee, General?' The hotheaded Luke was in the saddle, ignoring the counsels of caution as Don Quixote had ignored Sancho Panza. 'The same way we put up with Rhee and his rotten gang ... .Put up with Rhee's corruption ... with his infiltrating the ROK divisions ... politicizing the army and undermining combat efficiency. Anything goes?'

'Precisely, Captain. Not because it's the *best* way, but because it's the *only* way. Rhee's a brutal, conniving, thieving, son of a bitch. But he's *our* son of a bitch.'

'And we forget about justice, General? Completely forget?'

'For the time being, yes. Right now, I've got to make damned sure the POWs don't create an even bigger obstacle ... which Syngman Rhee would dearly love. We've stopped the Coms on the 38th parallel and that's it.'

Major-General Hayden Boatner paused for effect. His tone deepened, for he had clearly learned a good deal more than pretty good basic Mandarin in Peking before World War II. He had learned to make his words ring, not by assuming a higher pitch as the Chinese would, but by letting his powerful voice sink to the bass depths.

'That's winning, Luke. My job's not dispensing justice. My job's winning!'

Epilogue

Well, that's about it, everything except the last act of the play, the denouement, I suppose I should call it. The final score I'd say if it were a ball game – except that it was no ball game and there would even in that event be *no* final score anyway. The presumed game still goes on, even after the collapse of the 'fraternal Socialist bloc' in Europe. At the very least, North Korea and mainland China are still in contention. The first somehow continues to exist under the schizophrenic 'great leader' Kim Il Sung, while the latter is still a Marxist-Leninist, if no longer a Maoist dictatorship, and still eying Taiwan.

At any rate, the hectic political and personal drama originally set on Koje-do was pretty much played out when all the POWs were distributed to compounds, each securely confining no more than 500 prisoners. After that, it was routine moving them piecemeal to separate locations, preferably some distance from each other.

Mark you, I am not saying it was *all* over, the immediate drama in Korea. Nor am I saying that it was no more than a protracted anticlimax thereafter. Anything but!

The intense political engagement of the POWs did not simply dissipate when Major-General Hayden Boatner's armored hedgehog took control of Compound 76 away from roundly defeated Senior Colonel Lee Hak Koo. There was no close out, not even a pause, much less a reduction in the high tension of the complex relations among the chief individual characters in what, I supposed, I might even call a melodrama when General Boatner closed down Koje-do.

Really, I suppose, I should tell you first what happened *after* the denouement before I depict that climactic episode.

As you know, I've already given you the highlights of a major engagement of the war in Korea. That conflict, as I've tried to impress upon you, my highly prized readers, was not fully appreciated while it was fought. The Korean War, its significance, its vital affect on the future, was not really comprehended at the time – and it is now hardly remembered at all. Yet, during the third and last year of that war, the battle on Koje-do with its manifold ramifications, shaped the future not only the future of Korea, but all Asia, more effectively than did the constant skirmishing and the occasional limited battles along the all but static frontlines. In all truth, that war itself, its final crucial battles joined on Koje-do, most positively decided the shape of the twentieth century throughout the world.

That fact has, I trust, already been foreshadowed in the course of this account.

But what, you will ask, being no more than human, became of the chief players in the drama?

I shall try to carry out my own assignment to myself to tell the full story.

First, though, I'd like to say that I've learned it's not easy to write a book. After decades of daily reporting, it's damned hard to work on the same story day upon day, week upon week, month upon month. Journalism, to use that pretentious word, is nothing like such a long servitude, ploughing the same furrow for a year or even more. Journalists report on different matters every successive day or at least, report a continuing development as it unfolds, from a different angle day by day.

Sure, journalism is demanding. Reporters need agility to swivel away from yesterday's story and concentrate on today's story.

In return, however, journalism offers the stimulus of constant variety and the ease of inescapable superficiality. There's little danger of getting fed up with one story before you're covering a new one. There is obviously little need for what Goethe called *Sitzfleisch*, literally 'sitting flesh', a term that can be rendered in English almost as inelegantly as 'applying the seat of the trousers to the seat of the chair for a long, long time.'

That's why so many reporters, even some television hacks, have dog-eared, unfinished manuscripts of novels in their desk drawers. They aspire to dilate on profound matters at length. They aspire to fascinate readers by brilliantly deploying incident; by writing intriguingly and allusively to capture the reader's unflagging attention, as well as writing subtly to convey the finest nuance of human behavior; by writing penetratingly, so that the intricate nooks and crannies of existence are fully explored; above all, by writing with soaring imagination. Yet, somehow, they just can't find time to complete their manuscripts.

Of course, you gentle reader, like myself, your narrator, Harland Birch, know they cannot do it because they lack the essential patience. They lack, as well, perhaps, the dedication that is absolutely necessary, indeed indispensable, to set one's self aside and concentrate on the needs and moods of your characters for a prolonged period, almost an epoch in one's own short life. Also they cannot muster the intense concentration and the overweening self-confidence to carry through the task they've set themselves.

No deadline forces completion. It is nothing like handing in a story about events occurring today that will be printed tomorrow and forgotten the day after. It is nothing like working for an editor who has to have something, sometimes almost anything, to put into the paper

Those would-be authors are, therefore, fearful, sometimes almost to the point of panic. They dread submitting to a book publisher's critical judgement the opus they have conceived with blood, tears, and, above all, sweat. So they simply can't find the time to finish the job.

I have now done it! I've written a book, even though it's a true story, not a made-up epic. I guess I just don't possess the creative imagination to write a novel.

Nonetheless, I feel wonderful, triumphant, since I've accomplished the virtually impossible.

There lies now on my desk a big fat manuscript, which will surely someday appear as a bound book with the author's name, Harland Birch, on the spine. No longer will I have to punish my 'sitting flesh' by applying the seat of my trousers to the seat of my chair hour after hour, day after day, week after week, month after month. Unlike those damned POWs, I am now free. I am no longer bound by the steel links of conscience to my self-assigned task. I am at liberty now that the arctic New York winter has passed beyond the sopping wet thaw. Now that the buds of spring are bursting forth: snowdrops and purple crocuses already flowering , yellow daffodils and pastel primroses on the way.

Now that I'm nearly done I'll just recall briefly some past events before relating the events that followed the dispersal of the POWs, both the pro-Communists and the non-Communists, or, I suppose I could say, the anti-Communists. Obviously, I cannot say pro-Communist and pro-Democratic or even pro-Free World. Syngman Rhee's Korea and Chiang Kai-shek's Taiwan were hardly exemplars of democracy or freedom. Happily for themselves, as well as for those who fought in Korea for justice, both countries have during subsequent decades made bounding economic strides, even moved away from political tyranny.

Still, that progress is beyond my self-assigned scope. I am herein not concerned with the distant future. I am concerned with what lay immediately ahead of us then, although I am writing almost half a century after the events. Please bear with me if I touch on ground already trodden.

The last fifteen months of the war in Korea, roughly, say, from April 1952 to July 1953, were a protracted purgatory, obviously not peace, yet not all-out war. During that period, the two sides clashed intermittently on the battlefield, the troops of seventeen countries fighting under the United Nations banner. Against them stood the troops fielded by Pyongyang and Peking – chiefly Peking's troops, indeed overwhelmingly Peking's – which were loosely amalgamated under Soviet auspices. All that time the UN delegates and the Communist delegates haggled over the terms of an armistice at the gutted village of Panmunjom in a so-called 'demilitarized enclave' between the front-lines that was policed by MPs, but cleared of combatant soldiers.

Panmunjom, as I had learned early on, means the Inn with the Wooden Door. In the shattered remains of that inn, which were neither windproof nor rainproof, correspondents from the opposing sides drank coffee and brandy, smoked innumerable cigarettes, fenced with each other, and from time to time co-operated minimally.

Most prominent on the other side were: Chu Chi-ping of *Ta Kung Pao*, which still ran under its logo the French slogan, *l'Impartial*; waspish Alan Winnington of the London *Daily Worker*; and Wilfred Burchett, an outwardly amiable Australian nominally employed by the Communist organ *L'Unita* of Rome, if I recall correctly.

Burchett was the most adroit propagandist of the trio, as well as the most ruthless henchmen serving his masters in Moscow.

Chu Chi-ping was 'conflicted,' so as to say in present-day psycho-babble. He was in deep conflict with himself, his hopes of the future and his assessments of the present waging a constant struggle against each other. His ideals were wilting under the blasts of the winds of reality only three years after the proclamation of the People's Republic, when his paper still entertained vestigial hopes of reporting honestly. Driven by conscience and by patriotism, rather than by any expectation of any material reward, Chu Chi-ping was soon to become an agent of the British Secret Intelligence Service. As I may have noted earlier, Winnington and, above all, Burchett aggressively intimidated Americans, Australians, and British POWs in North Korea, regularly interrogating them under torture in order to extract confessions to non-existent crimes like germ warfare.

Burchett, an engaging personality who was remarkably candid off stage, would, years later in Moscow, tell me plaintively of his subsequent troubles with the dilatory paymasters of the Labor (Communist) Party of Vietnam. Most interestingly, Burchett has been hailed as a paragon of courageous, objective, investigative reporting – by a flock of ostensibly objective investigative reporters who are in reality neither objective nor reporters and not so hot at investigation.

All the while the armistice talks sputtered at Panmunjon, some young men died in trench warfare that recalled in a minor key the bloody stalemate in France from 1915 to 1918. Women, children, and older men died of starvation, disease, and guerrilla action, as well as accidents and quarrels. Yet the armistice negotiators, as you'll recall, had effectively settled all major issues except the question of repatriating UN-held prisoners of war who did not want to go home. In makeshift meeting-rooms at Panmunjom, generals talked of peace, while the people of Korea endured apparently unending war.

Syngman Rhee had been re-elected president of the Republic of Korea by a popular vote that was suborned, intimidated, sold outright, or delivered in job lots by men like Captain Chae Byongyup, for whom the alternative was either imprisonment or, as likely, death. Rhee's delegates stood absolutely firm at Panmunjom, despite pressure from the UN, which of course meant the US. The ROKs insisted that there could be no forced repatriation of POWs, for they were adamantly opposed to any armistice that would keep Rhee's regime from 'uniting' the country under its aegis – uniting Korea by an all out offensive with the Army of the US and the US Marines as its spearhead.

On 3 March, 1953, Joseph Stalin died, precipitating a battle for supreme power that was accompanied by the usual Marxist-Leninist grace notes: bribery, collusion, intimidation, beatings, scourging, and just plain old-fashioned murder. All that was, of course, nothing new in the USSR, except perhaps that the murders tended to be individual, rather than *en masse*. The effect of that death and the consequent struggle for power on the War in Korea was, however, benign. Not solely, perhaps, because kindly old Uncle Joe Stalin had been the architect of that aggressive enterprise.

In June 1950, Ambassador Jakov Malik, the chief representative of the Soviet Union to the United Nations, had been boycotting the Security Council. He had refused to attend its sessions as a protest, he declared, against its refusal under American pressure to invite the Peking regime to take the permanent seat allotted to China. That seat was occupied by the Nationalist regime of Generalissimo Chiang Kai-shek, which had retreated to the big offshore island of Taiwan, but continued to assert that it was the legal government of the entire Republic of China. If Malik had been present to impose the Soviet veto, the US would not have been able to secure the UN's endorsement of its defense of the Republic of Korea.

On the heels of Stalin's departure, Jakov Malik, sitting again in the Security Council alongside Taiwan, urged both sides to strike a compromise at Panmunjom. Having initiated the invasion in June 1950, the Soviet Union had fostered the consequent conflict. Having made war by its belligerent strategy, its combative counseling, its shipments of arms, above all, by Soviet advisers' detailed planning of the initial invasion and occasional leadership in action, Moscow declared for peace, in May 1953.

At that moment, Chinese armies again attacked ROK II Corps. The People's Volunteers were acclaimed as an 'independent force' by Peking and Peking's toadies. Their intervention in Korea 'on their own accord' was described as a forward defense of China's own territory in Manchuria, not without some justification. Those 'Volunteers' had then mounted an offensive that drove the UN forces back to where they started. The Chinese were impelled by their own momentum, as well as by the need to contain the enemy and to demonstrate that the Americans no longer had a free hand in Korea.

Those presumably defensive Volunteers, who had presumably entered Korea on their own accord, now moved in undeniable conjunction with Moscow's wishes, as interpreted and directed by Peking. The Volunteers mounted a new offensive in support of Moscow's new policy of peace.

They once again knifed into ROK II Corps, putting to flight all those skittish, unreliable ROK divisions, which preferred to run, rather than stand and fight. The Chinese then halted in their tracks, although there had been no repeat no effective, indeed no visible, ROK resistance.

The ROK's self-justification blamed the UN Command. – with some justification, may I again note – for the lack of artillery support, the shortage of weapons, and the faulty co-ordination of the two forces. The ROKs attacked the US on the field of public opinion, as they would not counter-attack the Chinese in the narrow, hill-girt, stony valleys of the battleground. The ROKs would not stand because they were afraid. They were, anyway, not very good soldiers. The troops Seoul deployed were then, even in the last days of that war, inferior in spirit and in effectiveness to the forces Saigon deployed in the early days of that resistance to a Communist attack.

Enough of that nay saying! Let me only recall that the Chinese halted abruptly when no man stood against them. They halted abruptly before withdrawing to their starting line and allowing the ROKs to crawl back to their undamaged trenches.

In the meantime, however, the Chinese made a great show of force. Their artillery concentrations and their trench-mortar bombardment were particularly heavy. The sky above the abandoned trenches was blotched scarlet with air bursts, that is, shells exploding a hundred or so feet above the ground to shower the front-line with shrapnel. The Chinese were still engaged in education: they were teaching the ROKs to be afraid, although the ROKs stood in no need of such pedagoguery.

Peking thus acted in accord with Moscow, as it had from the beginning of the war. Peking adhered to the strategy laid down millennia earlier in Chinese manuals on warfare: *Da! Da!* ... *Tan! Tan!* ... *Da! Da!* Fight! Fight! ... Talk! Talk! ... Fight! Fight!

I may have said some of this earlier. Indeed I believe I did. I hope you'll bear with me, that you'll excuse the repetition. I warned you that I might again tread on familiar ground.

Let me then note again that the second defeat on the same ground as the first defeat a month or two earlier was obviously intended to plant terror of Chinese troops even deeper in the hearts of all South Koreans. The ROK was, therefore, expected to return to the armistice talks. The ROK was, further, expected by both the Communists and the UN to declare for peace, having learned that its best troops could not even stand up to Chinese attacks, much less mount an offensive that would drive the Volunteers back to Manchuria.

Seoul was manifestly incapable of implementing Syngman Rhee's formidable policy: *Pukchin! Tungil!* ... March North and Unify Korea!

A number of minor issues that had still been hanging fire were then resolved at Panmunjom. The exact boundary between North and South was promptly agreed by conciliatory North Korea and Chinese representatives: along the 38th parallel of latitude, where it had lain before the war, with local adjustments to preserve salients south of the line held by Pyongyang and salients north of the line held by the UN. Thus the interntional boundary was basically to be the present frontlines, which would be separated by a 'demilitarized zone,' roughly the existing no man's land extended some way both north and south.

There was, nevertheless, still no agreement on the vital issue of repatriation. However, in practise the Communists' hard line on POWs was softening. In the spring of 1953, a number of 'sick and wounded' POWs were exchanged in an operation designated Little Switch. Even those seriously ill prisoners were returned to their original armies *only* if they so wished. British and American, Thai and Filipino, Australian and South African POWs, as well as POWs of other nationalities returned to the UN were all emaciated. All were, further, either crippled or gravely ill.

The Chinese and North Korean prisoners returned by the UN were generally in much better condition. That striking contrast would have embarrassed the Communists – if they had allowed themselves to be embarrassed or, indeed, if they had been capable of such a spontaneous reaction. That big POW hospital run by Sid Rosenstein in Pusan was the chief reason for the contrast. The US Army Medical Corps made little distinction between friendly and enemy patients, treating them with the same care, except in combat when urgent treatment to save life was given first to the UN wounded. The field hospitals dispatched by five other nations, including India and Norway, made no such distinction at all.

That shameful contrast between the POWs was another black eye the Communists tried to ignore. They had less success than they were to have later in Vietnam in obfuscating the discrepancy between their pretensions and their actions.

As you'll recall, Peking and Pyongyang had insisted that their POW camps met all the stipulations of the Geneva Conventions. Yet they would permit no inspection by the International Committee of the Red Cross because they were *not* parties to those Conventions. However, the truth emerged at Little Switch, most obtrusively in the physical condition of the POWs the Communists returned, most detailed and shaming in the accounts the UN returnees gave of their treatment.

That stark physical contrast was recorded by the ballpoints of print reporters. It was captured by the clicking shutters of still photographers for *Life Magazine, Paris Match*, and the *London Illustrated News*, and as well by the whirring motors of a few newsreel and television cameras. The UN returnees, who were as a matter of course produced for Press interviews, told heart-rending tales of neglect, abuse, and vicious mistreatment at the hands of both North Koreans and Chinese. Those tales rang true because they were spontaneous, clearly not manufactured. They further rang true because they were so much alike, although the prisoners had no opportunity to concoct joint tales.

The North Koreans were far worse than the Chinese. They were casually brutal, and fiercely cruel for cruelty's own sake. They were viciously sadistic, clearly enjoying with all but sensual satisfaction the suffering they inflicted. What possible justification in noting that the ferocious behavior of Koreans, North or South, was a generalized retribution for their vile maltreatment by the Japanese!

The Chinese, on the other hand, often had a political reason for starving, beating, or burying to the neck living men to be set on by biting insects. They, too, had suffered at the hands of the Japanese and the Western powers. But they did not overtly appear to be seeking revenge. Directed by their political commissars, who had been well trained by their mentors in the security services and the departments of public order, they were generally 'principled' in their deeds, however painful. 'Principled', of course, meant to them any action that 'advances the people's cause', ie, strengthens the dictatorship of the proletariat exercised by the Communist Party.

I see that I must again apologize for digressing, however pertinent to the moral of this tale that digression may be. Let us now return to the contrast between the UN and the Communist custody of the POWs as viewed in Little Switch, which was supposed to involve seriously ill or wounded men.

The North Korean and Chinese returnees, were, as we've noted, distressingly healthy beside those returned to the UN. Although they were manifestly *not* carrying infectious organisms, they were ostentatiously disinfected and deloused. They were liberally squirted with antiseptics and insecticide by medics wearing hospital medic's long white coats and surgeons' face-masks with clinical mob-caps, as well as spiffy white-rubber boots. The Communist POWs now contemptuously cast away the few garments they had not already thrown from the trains that carried them north. Thus clad only in GI khaki underpants or improvised breech-clouts, they inadvertently revealed that they were all well nourished, unlike the ill-fed POWs returned to the UN Command by the Chinese and the North Koreans.

The final breakthrough at Panmunjom came in late June 1953. It had, as we've just seen, been heralded by a second, even more devastating Chinese attack on ROK II Corps, which was still bereft of organic artillery. Again, the ROKs had broken and run away. Again, the Chinese had halted when more than twenty miles separated them from the fleeing ROKs. The Volunteers had then once again withdrawn, allowing the ROKs to reoccupy their former positions.

Syngman Rhee's government was at that point boycotting[1] the truce talks to protest those terms that had already been accepted by both the UN and the Communists – as well as to cast doubt upon any terms that might soon be agreed upon. Nonetheless, the ROK was fully informed of the progress of the negotiations. On a sultry evening towards the end of June, the ROKs learned that the last and most difficult obstacle had been surmounted. That was, of course, the issue of repatriation. Very soon after a ceasefire, a group of 'neutral nations' would supervise 'explanations' to non-repatriates in the demilitarized zone. 'Explanations' meant the non-repats would be lectured and hectored by Communist political commissars.

The Communists were manifestly not only eager for peace, but evidently desperate. In any event, they were convinced that the great majority of the non-repats would freely choose to go home, once free of American, ROK, and Taiwan pressure.

Acting Prime Minister Pyun Yong-tai was told at two in the morning by Robert Elegant of the International News Service that its correspondents had learned of that final agreement, which had previously been kept secret. Pyun conceded that the agreement meant an armistice was imminent. Asked what the ROK would do, he replied: 'We'll fight on alone!'

And fight the South Korean regime did!

Battle intensified on the crucial Psywar front. President Syngman Rhee, his cabinet ministers, and his generals strove even harder to convince the American public that their cause was just. They contended that the terms agreed at Panmunjom 'betrayed' the UN cause, that those terms actually meant 'surrendering' to the Communists. Sue Chae worked arduously to make that case to such

---

[1] Shades of Jakov Malik boycotting the Security Council!

correspondents as might be susceptible to those arguments. So did the Blue House, where Syngman Rhee himself was the point man of that campaign.

Newspaper and radio correspondents, even those few who also fed nascent television newscasts, were granted unprecedented access to the president. Mass demonstrations drove home the ROK argument, stressing the slogan: *Pukchin! Tungil!* ... March North and Unify Korea!

Most poignant, you may recall, were the well drilled schoolgirls who sat themselves down in the dust before the Press Billets and wept on command. Most demonstrations were less subtle, if we can call that performance subtle. All were much rougher, some overtly menacing the outsiders who were 'selling out' the Republic of Korea.

Aside from that propaganda effort, President Syngman Rhee concluded with rigid and, he believed, irrefutable logic that there could be no armistice if there were no prisoners to undergo 'explanations' in the demilitarized zone. Rhee simply released all non-repatriate Korean POWs who were under ROK control, which meant almost all.

Where American guards might interfere with that orderly release, the prisoners swarmed over the barbed-wire fences of their enclosures. No more than ROK guards would the Americans aim bullets at those men who were fleeing even the possibility that they would be compelled to return and to live under Communist tyranny. Neither would the Americans fire their weapons into the air in admonition. Like the ROKs, they feared they might inadvertently hit an escapee.

They had no specific orders because, once again, no one had thought of the eventuality. Who could have foreseen that Rhee would let those men go in a deliberate provocation to his allies? The Americans had, in any event, been instructed to take no action that could offend their ROK allies or lead to any public display of tensions between the two.

Rhee had not ordered the gates opened. That would have been too obvious and too pointed a defiance of the UN Command. Instead the POWs were encouraged to make a 'mass escape'.

The after effects of that licensed break-out were painfully apparent the same evening at the POW compound near Inchon some twenty miles west of Seoul. The cost of that escape had been high, a public sacrifice to support Rhee's thrust.

Under the glare of searchlights the sharp points of the barbed-wire fence were visibly festooned with the damage inflicted upon the men clambering over that barrier. I saw jagged swatches of GI blankets and rags torn from khaki garments. I also saw strips of skin and shreds of flesh. Getting out had been rough.

The prisoners who had taken that painful route unquestionably wanted to stay in the South. Their overwhelmingly anti-Communist countrymen naturally took them in. The wire services, above all, were eager to talk with those non-repats who had escaped. The ROK administration was, of course, keen to help those correspondents. Sympathetic feature stories could have a strong impact on warmhearted Americans.

My favorite wire-service story began: 'I asked the chief of police of Ulsan where I could find an escaped POW, and he introduced me to three.'

Strangely perhaps, the disappearance of tens of thousands of non-repatriate Korean POWs had little impact on the armistice negotiations. After ritual denunciation of the UN for violating settled terms, the Communists went on to the agenda already set for the day.

What more striking demonstration could there be that the Soviets had the whip-hand? Pyongyang was instructed by Moscow to ignore the episode —and Pyongyang evidently had no choice but to obey.[2]

Syngman Rhee still threatened to fight on alone. His rhetoric was not affected by the repeated demonstration that the ROK Army could not face up to the Chinese, much less march north. The new American administration of President Dwight D. Eisenhower was advised by Robert Murphy, its senior diplomat on the spot, in the same words he confided to me: 'Syngman Rhee's not going out into the backyard to cut his throat with a rusty razor!' Nevertheless, the Eisenhower Administration feared suicidal action by the ROK and strove to placate Rhee.

For placate, read also: bribe. A stream of senior American officials poured into Seoul. Finally, no less a figure than Secretary of State John Foster Dulles alighted at K-16. As usual looking like a disheveled gray parrot in a fit of anger, Dulles had not come to practice the new art of brinksmanship he had just espoused, but to engage in old-fashioned checkbook diplomacy.

Not at all placated, but truly bought, Syngman Rhee finally gave in. He agreed not to disrupt the armistice after he had been promised several billion additional dollars in economic aid, as well as American backing for the billion-dollar super-highway from Seoul to Pusan of which he had dreamed so long. Please do remember that was in the days when a billion dollars was really a billion dollars.

The formal signing of the armistice agreement was delayed by haggling. The UN Command would not sign in a newly erected hall on whose façade were hung the doves of peace drawn by Pablo Picasso, because they were a Communist propaganda trademark. The Republic of Korea would not sign at all. Neither the Democratic People's Republic of Korea, nor the People's Republic of China would sign in their national character.

The chief signatories were: the Commander-in-Chief of the Chinese People's Volunteers, General Peng Teh-huai, who was soon as a field marshal to be Peking's Minister of Defence, and the Supreme Commander Allied Powers, Far East, General Mark Wayne Clark, who was soon to deplore in a volume ghost-written for his signature the odium of Washington having consented to an armistice that fell short of total victory.

---

[2] Soviet military aid enabled the Democratic People's Republic of (North) Korea to wage war. Subsequently Soviet economic aid enabled the DPRK to survive. Only a few years after the disintegration of the Soviet Union, the regime and the economy of North Korea were collapsing, sustained for a time only by Chinese aid.

Neither Peng Teh-huai nor Mark Clark was present when the truce documents were formally signed at Panmunjom. Both had put their signatures to those documents in private at some distance from the lines, rather then do so in public.

This armistice was no *rapprochement*, no prelude to better relations between the United States and China or North Korea. The ceasefire, rather, institutionalized the antagonism between Washington and Peking that was to endure until Richard Nixon and Henry Kissinger, initiated a reconciliation two decades later. Pyongyang was to remain hostile forty years afterwards.[3]

Like Mark Clark, hardliners in both chief belligerents deplored a settlement without decisive victory.

Chinese hardliners had a slightly more difficult case to make. Their surprise intervention had driven the Americans back from the border between North Korea and China's three north-easternmost provinces which were together called Manchuria and were exceedingly vulnerably to assault. But the 'Chinese People's Volunteers' could march no further south than the 38th parallel in the teeth of massive American superiority in weapons, above all the tanks and the warplanes that dominated the battlefield.

The American hardliners' complaint was the mirror image of the Chinese hardliners' complaint. The US had achieved Harry Truman's original purpose by driving the North Korean army and the Chinese invaders out of the South. Neither Truman nor Eisenhower after him would commit the substantial reinforcements necessary to drive North to the frontier again. Not only that cost, but the hazards were too high: the certainty of much stronger Chinese opposition, even the possibility of direct Soviet intervention. The US would not attempt to roll back the bamboo curtain.

Both sides could claim victory, for each had achieved its defensive war aims. But neither truly believed in its victory.

Yet both had learned much from the experience. The Chinese were never again to challenge American troups face to face, nor even American-backed forces. They were instead to seek victory by what Mao Zedong called 'people's war' fought by guerrillas. That strategy, of course, leaves open the question of a conventional Communist attack on Taiwan, the quasi-independent island that is still backed by the US. My own assessment, for what it may be worth on a question of Chinese psychology, is that Peking no more wants to assault Taiwan than Taipei would welcome a closer connection with Peking.

Total victory with the complete subjugation of the enemy was the American way of war. At least, it had been the American way of war until Korea. You'll recall that Harry Truman presciently refused to consider declaring war, but had decided our intervention as a 'police action', thus implicitly confining its scope.

---

[3] And to flourish a claimed nuclear arsenal well into the next decade. Selling missiles and, presumably nuclear technology as well.

When that undeclared war finally ended, sophisticated American thinkers had learned the chief lesson of Korea. They understood that a new approach to warfare was necessary to contain the Soviet Union and its lackeys of the 'Socialist bloc', not to speak of 'People's China' itself.

Any attempt to subjugate the Soviet Union could have destroyed civilization by triggering a nuclear exchange. Such a conflict, its course largely unpredictable, could have incalculable consequences. Why, moreover, be so foolish as to repeat the disastrous error committed by both Napoleon Bonaparte and Adolph Hitler in invading the enormous territory under Russia's sway? That devastating blunder had brought down both the creative genius from Corsica and the megalomaniacal butcher from Austria.

American strategic thinkers had reached the conclusion that 'limited war' was the way of the future, that is, conflict without full commitment of the American military potential. Unless the US came under direct threat, they advised, we should go to war only to attain specific political or economic ends, whose scope was itself confined.

Such a limited war was, in theory at least, the conflict in Vietnam. True, American troops were deployed in strength, some 550,000 men, significantly more than in Korea. Those troops were, however, committed over a period of several years, not all at once. They were committed to preserve a non-Communist regime from an armed attack that initially appeared to be mounted by native guerrillas. That force was, however, soon to be seen as composed almost entirely of the regular soldiers of the People's Army of (North) Vietnam. The remaining guerrillas had been crushed in the striking victory won by the troops of the Republic of Vietnam and the US against the Tet Offensive, which was mounted throughout the country by the Communists in February 1968 and on.

Unlike Korea, the Vietnam conflict was not decided on the battlefield, where, contrary to the impression that the media conveyed, our forces generally prevailed. Vietnam was decided in the worldwide arena of psychological warfare.

The Communists acknowledged that they had been defeated two or three weeks after Tet, yet the American Press insisted that they had won a great victory.

When agreeing to withdraw our troops in 1973, Secretary of State Henry Kissinger had promised Saigon, as he had warned Hanoi, that the US would intervene in great force if the North seriously violated the terms of that agreement by major military action. The Communists, please remember, were deathly afraid of American air power, although attacks by our bombers on the territory of the North had been stringently limited. Misled public opinion had prevailed totally after President Richard Nixon committed a series of legal malfeasances made even more heinous by his political misdeeds. The Congress of the United States would not authorize even the extremely limited resupply and reweaponing of Saigon's forces that was sanctioned by the agreement between Kissinger and the Hanoi's Le Duc Tho. Moreover, massive intervention by US air power was no longer possible.

As a direct consequence, Saigon fell to Hanoi's forces, although the conflict continued for almost three years after the American troops were out of country. Besides, Hanoi had to mount a full-scale conventional attack spearheaded by some 400 tanks backed by heavy artillery in order to overthrow the Saigon government.

Hanoi had consistently failed to inspire the people of the South to mount the 'general uprising' that the Tet Offensive and its aftermath had sought. Hanoi failed not only because so many Catholics lived in the South, but because the Vietnamese were far too well acquainted with the Communists' brutality throughout the entire country. A chilling example: 'land reform' had to be abandoned after 50,000 so-called landlords died. Despite the myth-makers, the people of South Vietnam signally did *not* support the Communists in their hearts or by their actions. Despite another myth, Vietnam was not a 'quagmire', and the war was not unwinnable. That catchword appeared only after 1975, when Hanoi's oppression and exploitation of the conquered South made it clear that the American effort had not been 'unjust'.

Misreporting on both undeclared wars had resulted in wrenching clashes with our allies, as well as within the US itself. The clashes over Vietnam were more grievous, in good part because the media's coverage of that conflict was so biased and so spectacularly inaccurate.

However, British Prime Minister Clement Atlee, who had committed troops to Korea, was alarmed by hyped Press reports that the US was considering using nuclear weapons there. He flew pell-mell to Washington to persuade President Harry Truman not to do what Truman had no intention of doing.

A reporter had put to Truman a pointed question regarding the possible use of nuclear weapons in Korea, a question that was in no way untoward, but justified. Truman had replied equably, as he was bound to do, that the US always had under consideration the use of all the weapons in its arsenal.

In reality, the US was quite restrained in both conflicts. We did actually fight limited wars. We did not bomb the dams that controlled North Korea's Yalu River. No more did we subsequently bomb the dikes that constrained North Vietnam's Red River. Strategists did consider thus catastrophically flooding the enemies' homebases, just as they considered using nuclear weapons. It was their job to study all possible courses of action. Both the deluge and the atomic holocaust were flatly rejected as too extreme, which meant, of course, too widely lethal.

When withdrawing from Indo-China in 1955, the French confided to a few newsmen whom they considered serious reporters, myself among them, that they were infuriated by American restraint. President Dwight Eisenhower supported Secretary of State John Foster Dulles's flat refusal even to consider dropping A-bombs on the Viet Minh regulars of Ho Chi Minh and General Vo Nguyen Giap that were besieging the last remaining French garrison in Vietnam at Dien Bien Phu. Cargo planes of Air America, the CIA's own airline, had regularly dropped supplies and armament to that garrison. The French did not consider that support adequate.

By the way, the last French commanding general told me that his predecessor had selected Dien Bien Phu for that last stand because it was the junction of the opium routes. That bland narcotic had filled the personal need for solace felt by many French officers, military or civilian. It had, further, made a number of them extremely rich. Not the CIA, as was charged in error, but the French high command was in the narcotics business.

Although Hanoi and its sycophants were claiming that US bombers deliberately struck at schools, orphanages, hospitals, hospices, and similar humane institutions, the US was, again, restrained. The US Air Force and the US Navy lost many aircraft and pilots because they were determined to limit 'collateral' damage, above all, to minimize casualties among non-combatants.

The Daumier Bridge spanning the Red River at Hanoi was a prime strategic target. Yet US bombers approached that target by flying along the winding river, facing heavy anti-aircraft fire. They would undoubtedly have risked inflicting civilian casualties if they had taken the direct route over heavily inhabited areas, which was less fiercely defended. That bridge was finally destroyed by just two bombs – the first time the wireless-guided 'smart bomb' was used in combat.

Longer lasting and more divisive than clashes with allies or with public opinion was the inherent conflict between Western and Asian manners of thought and ways of life. Americans were deeply impressed by the capacity they discerned in Asians to endure great hardship and to tolerate grievous inequity, as well as great iniquity. Such stalwart endurance conflicted with the confident American passion for rapid, virtually perfect solutions – not only in great political affairs, but in the private lives of individual men and women.

That inherent conflict rose almost every time that Koreans or Vietnamese dealt with Americans. Still, they worked together. Not always harmoniously, in fact rarely; not always successfully, rather often ending in failure. Not always with one mind, but quite often pulling in different directions. Nonetheless, they did work together to attain common goals.

The war in Korea was not an immaculate crusade by the UN forces, although there was no question in the minds of most observers that North Korea was the aggressor. Neither was that war futile, despite the assertively promoted belief by unthinking, self-styled intellectuals that all war is futile because war accomplishes nothing. In the real world, the conflict in Korea initiated the series of social, political, military, and economic events that culminated in 1989 with the collapse of expansionist Marxism-Leninism in Europe, as well as in Asia.

A clumsy, stupid, awkward and circuitous process? Yes, it was! Still, that is the way human beings behave and the way the story of mankind unfolds.

Lesward Murray Howse got his silver star, the insignia of a brigadier-general. But he was never afforded the opportunity to wear it day in and day out. He could put up that star, only on ceremonial occasions, which he sought eagerly. It was a retirement promotion, a final pat on the back, for a mediocre player, not a step up while he was still on active service.

I wanted that succinct statement to begin my account of the lives of the chief characters after the drama of Koje-do closed. Unfortunately, that statement is not true.

Wafted upward like a hot-air balloon on the success of his Civil Information and Education Section, Howse actually got his star shortly after the armistice. Individually, none of his superiors would have retained him in grade as anything more than a captain. His failings and his failures were too blatant, his sycophancy far too brazen. Yet, as a group, his superiors could not deny him that promotion. It was strategically necessary to reward him promptly for his contribution to the stunning Psywar victory demonstrated when the mass of POWs, particularly the Chinese, rejected repatriation.

Indoctrination of those POWs had not ceased with the armistice. Indoctrination had actually redoubled. Howse was at the forefront of that campaign, no longer hampered by the hypersensitive conscience of Luke Maynell, who had been assigned to Supreme Headquarters, Far East, in Tokyo.

The UN still controlled the compounds of non-repatriate POWs in the demilitarized zone, although they were nominally again under the aegis of 'neutral nations'. Ninety-eight per cent of those prisoners again rejected repatriation when exposed to Communist 'explanations', this time in full public view. The Press duly reported that slap in the face to the entire world, except, of course, for the sealed off 'fraternal Socialist camp'.

I'm not saying the choice would have been different if indoctrination had not continued. It would probably have varied little. But that is how it actually happened.

Proudly displaying not only his brigadier-general's silver star, but the ribbon of the Distinguished Service Cross, Lesward Murray Howse was assigned as deputy commander of the United States Military Advice and Assistance Group on Taiwan. Some outsiders derided the big island as the defeated Nationalists' last refuge, while others saw it as a base for reclaiming the mainland of China from the Communists.

Regardless, Washington's directive to the Military Group was clear as rock crystal: MAAG, Taiwan, was to do its very best to rebuild Chiang Kai-shek's shattered military force. However, MAAG was, above all, *never* to antagonize its hosts in any way, not even to make those forces more effective.

Before China's intervention in Korea, Harry Truman had set in motion his plan to recognize Peking, which would have meant derecognizing Taiwan. If Dwight Eisenhower and John Foster Dulles had wished to do so – as they emphatically did not – they still could *not* have revived Truman's plan. The Nationalist propaganda machine in the US, the so-called China Lobby, was too effective. Placating the Nationalists was the highly political priority of the Military Advice and Assistance Group on Taiwan.

No American general was better suited to that task then Lesward Murray Howse, whatever his other failings. Beyond doubt, he knew the Chinese well, and he possessed profound insight into their psychology. So he had proved in Korea.

Howse was in effect detached from the normal duties of the deputy-commander of the Military Advice and Assistance Group. His sole duty was to soothe the roiled egos of Nationalist bigwigs, civilian as well as military, when that was necessary – and to flatter them all incessantly. The major-general commanding MAAG was delighted thus to be relieved of his military incompetent deputy. Brigadier-General Howse was, in turn, delighted by what he grandly described as 'my diplomatic politico-military mission', which was really no more than high-level toadying.

Besides, he was no longer sexually deprived. His glittering star attracted beautiful Chinese ladies, who were not deterred by either his gross appearance or his crude manners. Those ladies were vigorously encouraged by senior Nationalist officials to pay their attentions to the brigadier-general. Mutual flattery and generalized prevarication, as well as indirect bribery, were the currency of diplomacy. Howse was so successful at such diplomacy that he dreamed of a second star that would make him a major-general. Although that was not to be, his four years on Taiwan were the best time of his life.

Shortly before his tour ended, he gave up his extensive sexual peregrinations to marry a striking Chinese girl less than half his age. Discharged with the permanent rank and the generous pension of a brigadier-general, Howse settled with his wife in San Francisco. His ego was bolstered by constant requests from think tanks, from corporations, and from academia for his advice on Chinese affairs, indeed on all Asian questions. The much-acclaimed China expert was astonished when his beautiful young wife sued for divorce a week after she was naturalized as an American citizen.

Aside from that bumbling failure Colonel (former Brigadier-General) Francis Xavier Dodd and that resolute victor Major-General Hayden L. Boatner, another general played a decisive role in that drama of Koje. He was, you'll recall, Major-General Li Mao of the Chinese People's Liberation Army. He had been seconded, nominally as a private, to the miscalled Chinese People's Volunteers, which were actually units of the regular People's Liberation Army. He was subsequently commander-in-chief of the initially secret Chinese sixth column in the prison camp which developed into a fighting force of high visibility. The Chinese general was also the senior adviser, Peking's ambassador plenipotentiary in the camp, to North Korean Senior Colonel Lee Hak Koo, who spurned his counsel.

Li Mao in defeat, even in despair, was far more impressive than Lesward Murray Howse in triumph, altogether a more substantial human being. As Luke Maynell urged, Li Mao was sent to Tokyo when the POW camp on Koje-do was broken up. He was, of course, to be allowed a free choice to return to China or to resettle in Taiwan.

Luke was more concerned to save Li Mao's life than to win whatever information the general might still yield. Dispirited and isolated, bereft of all his followers, Li Mao would undoubtedly have been murdered if he had been allowed to remain among fanatically pro-Communist POWs who wanted a new leader.

Li Mao spoke more candidly to Luke in Tokyo than he had when they were adversaries on Koje. Not that they were allies now, but, rather, tentative friends. Even Li Mao's casual observations on the men who ruled China were, besides, extremely valuable. He had worked closely with those men for decades.

He would, however, neither submit to a structured intelligence debriefing nor, indeed, speak to any American other than Luke. Above all, he would not utter a single word that he believed could injure China or the Chinese people. However, he spoke with much freedom about the dogmatic tyrants who, he believed, were the grossest oppressors China had known for centuries. He had, you'll recall, broken decisively with those tyrants, as he had with their rigid, illusory doctrines and their fanatical, cruel actions.

Luke was not disturbed by Li Mao's self-censorship, not even when it appeared to him to be excessively cautious. Neither did Luke wish to injure China or the Chinese people.

Anyway, he was resigned to his own reports of their conversations being consigned to the files. Someday perhaps someone would look up those memoranda, perhaps even draw useful insights from the recollections of a man whose life had been devoted to the service of the Communist Party of China. Yet, Luke believed, that day was a long way off, far into the future, if indeed, it was ever to come. Even the Central Intelligence Agency, which had been his principal employer, was now more interested in dirty tricks than in grade A information.

The Army of the US, flush with its Psywar victory on Koje, was most definitely *not* interested in either tortuous ideological discussions or even in tidbits of intelligence. As for insight into the mind of China, Brigadier-General Howse could provide all that was needed. He would, quite obviously, not have made brigadier if he were not an authentic expert.

Major-General Hayden Boatner was infuriated by Howse's advancement, which he had tried in vain to block. To compensate, at least in part, for that atrocious promotion, he had made a gesture that Luke Maynell welcomed warmly. He had transferred Li Mao to Tokyo, as Luke had suggested. He had also handed out some baubles that Luke did not value highly – the gold oak leaf of a major and a Bronze Star.

Boatner reckoned that the man who had kept the Chinese POW compounds from exploding deserved recognition, particularly since Howse, the man who had all but lit the fuse, was so liberally rewarded. The official record of the incidents on Koje, which were supplemented by Luke's own notes on those incidents and his discussions with Li Mao had convinced Boatner. He believed that Luke had strongly influenced the captive Communist General, above all, by opening a window on the outside world. At the very least, yet crucially, their conversations had moved the commander-in-chief of the Chinese underground army to put off an all-out uprising. He had delayed until it was too late the mass assault on the POW Command that Peking had ordered.

Hayden Boatner had also read with intense, if strained attention, Lesward Murray Howse's war diary. He knew exactly why the director of the misnamed

Civil Information and Education Section had pressed Luke so hard to find the judges of the Nationalist, as he believed it to be, kangaroo court that had executed two pro-Communists and tried to pin the blame on the Communists. Howse had planned to use those anti-Communist stalwarts to provoke violent disturbances that would purge one particular compound of all pro-Communists, while their shock waves fostered bloody rioting in other compounds. Thus had Howse planned to manufacture a pretext for US troops' marching in force into every single compound and wiping out thousands of pro-Communist POWs. Senior Colonel Lee Hak Koo's detention of Brigadier-General Dodd had provided the necessity for such action. But there had been no mass slaughter.

Yet why use Luke, rather than the Taiwan teacher-agitators with whom Howse was so thick? This once, though, Howse had wanted to be free of any possible Taiwan interference. He did not know whether the Nationalists' emissaries would favor his plan or disapprove – and obviously he could not ask them. Luke might demur, but Howse knew he could make Luke do as he was told.

General Boatner could do no better for Luke than a Bronze Star, which ranked way below Howse's Distinguished Service Cross. Anyway, Luke didn't really care one way or the other, except that it made his father happy.

When Li Mao was asked to choose repatriation to Peking or a new life in Taiwan, he confounded everyone by opting for the United States. He hardly wished, he said, to return to face the wrath of his former comrades in Peking – and he could hardly expect to be welcomed warmly by his vindictive former antagonists on Taiwan. Li Mao's choice set off a two-year struggle between the Army of the US on one side and the Immigration and Naturalization Service on the other.

Fully committed, the Eighth Army noted that the US had fought for more than a year in order to enforce the principle first enunciated casually by its Psychological Warfare Section and later ringingly endorsed by President Harry Truman: no repatriation of unwilling prisoners of war, but, rather, resettlement in a place of their own choice. The Immigration and Naturalization Service argued rather feebly that immigration law prohibited the entry of even a former member of a Communist Party, however powerful his sponsorship. The Army of the US replied that Li Mao's admission was vital to national security.

When his visa was finally granted, Li Mao further surprised all those who dealt with the case by choosing to go to Los Angeles. That was, after all, his right, as he argued in a lawyerly fashion.

He could in the first instance count on the financial support that Luke wangled from Washington as a condition for his talking at all. He was, however, not worried about making a living, although he was in his late fifties and had no visible means of support. Even Luke had slighted the fact that Li Mao's education at St. John's University in Shanghai had given him command of English, as well as a law degree. He had actually practiced in the courts of the International Settlement, which applied both American and British law. After two months of intensive study, the former Communist general passed the California bar examination with little diffi-culty. His practise now concentrated on would-be Chinese immigrants and the varied problems they faced.

Li Mao had been profoundly depressed only a few years earlier. He now appeared to be depressed no longer – nor to be disturbed by the behavior of his wife Mei-lu, whom he had married in 1936. She had at first neither said a word in public nor communicated with him, as she could have through clandestine chan-nels. Evidently the Party Center had imposed total silence on Mei-lu, whom it also suspected of treasonous heresy.

A year or so later, she had roundly denounced the United States in public. Failing to repatriate her husband as he had undoubtedly wished, she charged, the American authorities had kidnapped him and transported him to Los Angeles, where he was now held under duress. Li Mao only smiled vaguely at the charges his wife threw about so wildly.

Three years later, evidently once again trusted by the Party, Mei-lu was sent with a cultural mission to Mexico. She defected to the US Embassy her first night in Mexico City. Although she was still a convinced Communist, love conquered ideology. There were, thankfully, no children to be held hostage in China. Anyway, she was curious about life in the US, which was the hated, despised, and envied foe of People's China.

She could, she told Li Mao, always redefect if she wished, for the US authorities would interpose no obstacle. She never did, although the gross abundance and the profligate wastefulness of the American way of life was loathsome to her. It was truly obscene when she recalled the meager, niggardly life of China.

Mei-lu never became a great admirer of the United States. How could she when she was never entirely free of guilt for abandoning the Chinese people and the Maoists' presumed endeavor to improve their lot? Nonetheless, she was reasonably happy to be living again with her husband, even in a nation that was, as she saw so clearly, presumably idealistic, even benevolent, but actually brutal.

Nor did Li Mao himself ever become a great advocate of either the free market economy or liberal democracy, though both worked well in California. Neither, he felt, would ever do for China. Not the *largely* free market because decades would pass before there were enough goods to go round, and because Chinese traders were inherently grasping. They had to be grasping to survive in a realm of scarcity.

'Not liberal democracy!' he further insisted. 'Not ever! My people, the Chinese, have hardly changed at all in four thousand years. They are too anarchic, too regionalized, too provincial for representative democracy. Worse, they are much too individualistic.'

Now, as to Sue Chae, who felt she had been cast adrift on the capricious tides of chance after Luke's rushed departure for Tokyo. There were others. There were always other men, but it was not the same.

He had promised to come back if only to see her. But how often did Luke honor such a promise to a girl? Not that he didn't intend to! Not that he didn't want to! But something always came up, usually another girl.

Sue had never counted on his return. She knew him too well. Anyway, theirs was not a romantic relationship, however close they had grown. There had not been, perhaps never could be, a physical relationship between them. Yet she realized after his hasty farewell how much she had come to depend on his just being there, how highly she valued his laughter and his sometimes sardonic wit. Also, how stirred she was by his amber eyes and his slow, appraising smile.

There had been no physical relationship. But with Betsie totally out of the picture, who could say there never would be? Luke had telephoned her several times on the American military circuit from Tokyo, as ever warmly and deeply concerned about her. But who could say anything more with the ears of a half-dozen GI operators flapping?

Still, she had no real claim on him. Sue cursed her inhibitions and her sense of fair play. If it had not been for Betsie, would she have made love to Luke that night when she plied him with champagne? Probably, almost certainly! She had, as she told Luke candidly, set out to seduce him.

Yet perhaps not. The incident had been too methodically planned, too cunning and too devious, on her part. Worst of all, too sharply calculating, too much out of character, for her to retain her self-respect.

Curiously, he, too, had pulled back at the last moment. Luke Maynell was not as easy to seduce as she had thought him. And everyone knew how hard he was to keep!

Sue did not much like the cool, scheming streak in her character, which she tried hard to deny. She had acquired that distaste in America, where forthrightness and warm-heartedness were prized above all. At least, those traits were greatly praised on the surface of American life. She had nonetheless, known many Americans who notably lacked spontaneity or warmth; who never took an important step without shrewdly weighing the consequences beforehand: dyed in the wool Americans who unabashedly manipulated others. Such calculation was, however, not essential to survival in trusting, open-hearted, forgiving, abundant America, not the *sine qua non* it was in tightly structured, authoritarian, niggardly Korea.

Putting aside all that introspection, she concluded that there was truly no one but herself to look out for her future.

Her half-brother Tommy, nowadays always Chae Byongyup, was deeply immersed in his own ambitions, which led him even farther into peril under the ever more oppressive elected dictatorship of Syngman Rhee. Her mother had actually been a burden most of their life together. She had never been a bulwark, but always a vulnerable plank, a rib that could easily snap. Madame Chae was at once too flighty and too confident, therefore certain to run afoul of the political police of General Won Yong Duk before too long. Sue could still protect her mother because of her value to the Rhee regime, although she was with the end of the war finding her work increasingly distasteful. She could no longer justify tolerating, even at times taking part in shady deals under duress. She simply did not know just how long she could keep it up.

Korea itself was becoming onerous to Sue, almost unbearable. She detested the hordes of venal politicians and corrupt capitalists, the scalawags and carpet-baggers of South Korea. No longer scheming to attack the North, if he had ever done so seriously, Syngman Rhee was now utterly certain that anything whatsoever he did for himself he did as least as much for the nation. He was convinced that he *was* the nation – and he was looting its sparse wealth. Misery and deprivation had been spreading, rather then lessening after the armistice. American aid was being stolen outright. But the US Embassy believed it could do little to prevent such wholesale theft – and did not try very hard.

Who except the Press could show up Syngman Rhee, the saviour of Korea, as a megalomaniacal monster? But who took the Press seriously?

In 1955, two years after the armistice, Sue *knew* she was desperate. She could perhaps appeal to Luke, who was now 10,000 miles away. To her surprise, he had actually returned to Korea shortly before the armistice, making the journey only to see her. Yet he, as well as she, had tacitly agreed that there could be nothing lasting between them.

She could still appeal to Luke, who would do all he could for her. But what exactly *could* he do now?

Above all, she had to get out of Korea, taking her foolhardy mother with her. Yet she could not get an immigrant visa to the United States, not, at least, without waiting several years. Perhaps not even then. Yet where else was there for her? Where else could she hope to make a living by one means or another?

Now unabashedly calculating, Sue Chae set out to marry Kenny Lowe, a Chinese-American captain in the substantial US force that had remained in South Korea and was to remain for decades. She truly liked Kenny, who was virtually the archetype of a straightforward, warm-hearted, honorable American. Characteristically, he spoke not a word of any Asian language except pidgin Cantonese. She knew that Kenny admired her wholeheartedly, and she felt certain that his admiration would soon turn to love.

His immigrant parents, who were pressing him to marry, were quite fortunately vague about geography. To those offspring of peasants of Toisan County in southerly Kwangtung (Guandong), a Korean was hardly different from, say, a Manchurian. Both came from way up north, where it was cold, icy, and snowy, unlike Santa Barbara, where they were now well settled.

A year or so after Sue married Kenny in California, she was delighted to find that her fondness for him had turned into devotion. It might not be passionate, romantic love, but it would do. It would do very well. She had found a haven that was wholly agreeable, and she was much more than simply grateful to the man who provided that haven. She was very happy, if not ecstatic, in her marriage of convenience.

Since Kenny was doing well in real estate, she had no need to earn money. That was a great relief after years of being not only the sole shield, but the sole support of her family. Her mother, too, was well settled in the tight Korean community of Los Angeles. Madame Chae was just close enough to keep in touch, just far enough not to be a pain. Sue's life was almost idyllic.

Nonetheless, she was restless after giving Kenny the boy and girl he wanted. Not that she did not love her children. Kenny teased her for doting on them. But she grew tired and bored of talking largely, if not solely, to people under three feet tall. Fortunately, a local lecture agent set up talks for her about Korea and China to local women's clubs, to church suppers, to Rotary Clubs, and to similar groups. To her surprise, Sue found herself in growing demand as Americans' eyes turned towards Asia or, at least, the eyes of West Coast Americans.

'It doesn't,' Kenny observed smugly, 'hurt that you're such a damned attractive lady.'

Sue's deep knowledge of Korea and China attracted the interest of nearby universities, as well as RAND, the think tank sponsored by the US Air Force. She did not want a full-time job, which would leave her little time for the kids and Kenny. Still, she was happy to be engaged in the world's work again, lecturing to college classes and writing research papers for RAND. She had feared that her mind was rusting away.

So she told Betsie Howard, when her oldest friend popped up in Los Angeles. After a long estrangement, they had again grown close. Betsie now popped up frequently, while Sue made occasional trips to New York and Washington for RAND.

Visiting Korea on assignment from time to time, she was astonished and delighted by the rapid economic strides her war-ravaged country was making under a military regime dedicated to material progress. That regime could at least bring some order to the fissiparous ROK and impose some discipline on its almost pathologically independent people. Syngman Rhee had been deposed by General Park Chung Hee, once the hapless deputy-commander of ROK II Corps. In principle, Sue detested military rule, but the generals at least sought to move the country forward, not solely to loot it.

Sue Chae Lowe's nearest and dearest were the last to desert her sad country. Theirs was a drawn-out, painful, and for one of them, at least, a guilt-ridden withdrawal. Betsie Howard had told Luke Maynell that she cared for Tommy, Captain Chae Byongyup, but not with the forlorn, incurable passion she felt for Luke himself. It had, however, not even occurred to her to pursue Luke to Tokyo, as she had pursued him to Pusan. Whoever was responsible, that part of her life was finished. Yet she acknowledged mournfully to herself that she might never get over her addiction to Luke, which had endured since their first meeting in the spring of 1948. Betsie nevertheless turned with longing to Tommy Chae after the grudging armistice lent a gloss of normalcy to their lives.

She had earlier told herself, although not really in jest, that a girl like herself might take a Korean as a lover, but would never marry him. She had already granted Byongyup the privileges of a lover, if not her heart entire. She was, however, now even more firmly convinced that marriage, for which he pressed, would be a disaster.

He was besotted with her, far more committed than she was to him. Yet she would, she knew, lose all her independence, almost all initiative in thought or deed, if she married him. She would be no more than an exotic adornment to the great nobleman, the heir presumptive to the throne of the Chollas.

Betsie knew that she possessed neither the stamina nor, perhaps, the masochism to be the wife of a Korean. She had nowhere else to go just now, and she had no wish to leave. But she could not seriously contemplate living permanently in a country that was not only paupered by the depredation of war, but was profoundly xenophobic. The Americans, who were the saviors of the Republic of Korea, were, naturally, disliked most fiercely and denounced most vehemently by Korean intellectuals. Only the ingrained, ritual hatred for the former colonial overlords, the Japanese, was more impassioned.

Betsie therefore clung to her lifeline, keeping her tie to the American Red Cross when the Swiss of the International Committee of the Red Cross departed, their mission superceded, even if never wholly accomplished. She was thus not totally dependent on Tommy. Besides her parents would immediately supply anything for which she asked, though she did not like to ask. The Red Cross, however, provided a small stipend, as well as the PX and Commissary privileges that were worth much more in the impoverished country.

That connection was secure. There was still a real need for the ministrations of the Red Cross among the tens of thousands of GIs who remained in Korea and were to remain for decades. The demands on the remaining volunteers like Betsie were, however, necessarily light, lest they simply leave.

For two years the pleasant, occasionally frenzied, relationship between Betsie and Tommy flowed onward without encountering any great obstacles. She was constantly learning more about Asia, about Europe, as well, from the cultivated man who stood between those two worlds. Nor was he lacking in passion or tenderness.

Chae Byongyup, the quintessential restrained Confucian, was entranced by the candor with which she conveyed her emotional variations, as well as by her intellectual peregrinations. He was from time to time lifted to euphoria by her blithe presence, and he was captivated by her uninhibited ardor, which was sometimes even savage. He could certainly not have found the same encompassing joy – emotional, intellectual, and physical – with any Korean woman, certainly not with a woman of his own class. All pleasure would invariably be constrained. They would be bound hand, foot, and heart by the severe inhibitions imposed by their austere traditional culture.

Betsie and Byongyup were often apart. Betsie could not ignore her obligations to the tolerant Red Cross. Byongyup was heavily involved in politics, as well as in reclaiming and regenerating his land holdings in South Cholla. Still, such separation spiced their pleasure when they came together.

They spent much time in Kwangju, the provincial capital. After her first delight at discovering a fragment of times long past that was preserved virtually intact, Betsie was bored and dismayed by the isolation and the provincialism of that stronghold of the seventeenth century. Her growing fluency in Korean only made it worse. She could now generally understand the banality and the triviality of conversation in that remote corner of the peninsula.

Even Byongyup, to whom Kwanjgu was home, was harried by the demands it made upon him. He was, further, apprehensive of the dangers it posed to him. In Kwanjgu, even more than in Pusan or Seoul, he was living too close to the edge. In South Cholla Province he had no choice but to behave as the rightful heir to many acres and the natural claimant to legitimate authority. That role was hazardous. Syngman Rhee's central government despised the Chollas, and the Chollas detested Seoul.

Byongyup was repeatedly warned by friends in the regime that General Won Yong Duk's security apparatus was seeking to find – if necessary to create – a sensational transgression on his part so as to arrest him. It was not only that imminent danger, but the constant frustration that confounded him. If he were too cautious, he would accomplish nothing. If he were bold, too fiery, arousing militant opposition to Seoul, he would be seized and condemned out of hand. And he would, almost without question, be executed by Syngman Rhee's secret police, legally murdered as his father had been.

Byongyup cracked first, though only a day before Betsie had planned to tell him she could not go on living on the slopes of a smoking volcano. Giving her no time to pack, he bundled Betsie into a motorized fishing boat that sailed for the Tsushima Islands in the straits between Korea and Japan. They escaped only by a fluke. Heavy mist had been succeeded by dense fog that veiled the straits, but they heard the whooping and the sirens of the small craft pursuing them.

'You can always go back and get your things,' he told her. 'Of course, Won Yong Duk's Gestapo would dearly love to grab you ... to get back at me through you. But they wouldn't dare. Not an American lady. Not yet, at least!'

'What now, Tommy ... Byongyup?' she asked softly. 'Where do you go from here?'

He heard the tremor in her voice, as well as the ominous 'you', rather than the normal 'we', but he answered equably, 'I've been thinking ... as you know.'

'Yes, we have been kicking it around. What to do if you had to get away. But we never seemed to decide ... nothing definite anyway. There's always the States ... '

'Won't do!' he declared sharply. 'I've got no foothold there ... no friends or connections.'

'What then?'

'The UK, London. I've all the friends and connections there in the world. Also the funds I've been moving out – enough to get along very well. London'll make a good base for an anti-Rhee movement, maybe even a government in exile. Our message *shall* get through. Rhee can't drop a bamboo curtain around the entire country.

'I feel rotten ... guilty ... for running away. But what choice is there? Anyway, you'll like London. I know.'

'I wonder, Tommy, I really do. There's everything for you in England, but precious little for me. I'll think about it. But it's probably time for me to go back to the States.'

'Please God, don't go back! Marry me then!' he offered for the twentieth time. 'It won't be like living in the ROK. As my wife you wouldn't be hemmed in ... not in London.'

'Let me think about it, dear. It's not that I don't love you. You know I do. It's just that I ... '

Bartleby Howard, whom everyone called Betsie, knew she loved Chae Byongyup, whom she called Tommy. She loved him after a fashion. She did not know if she loved him deeply and enduringly. Besides, it would be a very different matter living with him in London than it had been in ever mysterious and therefore fascinating Korea.

He would strive to rally support for a political movement opposed to the Seoul regime. But he would, she feared, strive in vain to displace Syngman Rhee. Tommy had often enough said the only force capable of deposing the dictator was the ROK Army. He was, of course, to be proved right, although not for several more years.

Betsie finally decided to return to the US for a time before, presumably, joining him in London. This lengthier separation would tell her whether she truly loved Tommy, loved him so much that she would give up for him all hope of a normal life. It would always be chopping and changing with Tommy, always chasing the dragon of a democratic government for Korea, and, if that fantastically elusive beast were captured, there would be that other dragon, reunification.

She was, Betsie told herself sternly, not by any means Tommy Chae's first priority or even his second. Nor would she ever be! Korea and his career would always come first: the nation and his obligations as the rightful heir to the leadership, if no longer now the non-existent monarchy of the Chollas.

Nonetheless, she was filled with compassion for Tommy, as well as with ardor. His course was bound to be a rough one, perilous and storm-tossed. She could, she knew, be a great solace to him. She could give him comfort as well as joy. She would, Betsie admonished herself, have to be very careful of Tommy's feelings, particularly since, as she had reluctantly recognized, his devotion to her was still greater than her devotion to him.

Still, she assured herself, she might well find that she missed Tommy profoundly – deeply and madly. Well, if she learned through a prolonged separation that she really, truly, could not live without him, she could easily shift to England.

Besides, she'd been away for years. She missed America.

She also wanted to see Luke again, if only, she told herself righteously, to test the strength of her love for Tommy. She really did not want Luke any longer, although she had almost absentmindedly kept up with his doings.

He had only been released from the service late in 1954, since the US Army had with unintended irony belatedly decided it badly needed Chinese and Japanese linguists. Luke had only escaped transfer to Taiwan when Brigadier-General Lesward Murray Howse energetically vetoed that assignment.

A civilian again, Luke faced an impasse, which he finally resolved by enrolling in the University of Chicago for a PhD in ancient Chinese philosophy – of all the esoteric and impractical fields. In part that was a delaying action. Yet the subject truly fascinated him. It was the taproot of all present-day East Asian civilization. It had, moreover, very strongly, though subliminally, influenced the development of European-American culture.

Luke was, he told himself, only thirty, not yet ready to decide what to do with the rest of his life, though his father was pressing him to make a 'sensible decision'. He was not drawn to academia with its tedium, its small mindedness, and its sheep-herd-like compulsion to intellectual conformism. He was not enamored of either banking or business, which his father insisted were the logical choice. Nor was he eager to undertake the drudgery of law school, which would invariably be followed by the wearing, yet trivial tasks of starting a practice, even if he were to join a glamorous international law firm that concentrated on East Asia, particularly Japan. At that time, China was still out of bounds to Americans.

Luke had witnessed too much corruption in government, not only, though primarily, on the part of self-seeking politicians, but also among both appointed officials and tenured bureaucrats. He would not even consider that approach to power. Anyway, why should he want power?

Journalism, then, which was detached by its very nature, just about as objective and independent as one can get?

No, not journalism! Not at all! He had seen too much of the dark side of journalism, not to speak of the silly side. Besides, he was himself in a sense too frivolous for journalism, too prone to see that comic aspect of matters that had to be treated with utmost earnestness. Yet he was also too serious, too quixotic for journalism as I, Harland Birch, had told him.

He could not, anyway, conscientiously undertake always to remain uninvolved and unbiased. I had also told him that such detachment and objectivity was no longer a requisite. I had told him that championing a cause would now ensure fast advancement – so long, of course, as it was the *right* cause, the popular cause.

The answer, Luke concluded roundly and inconclusively, was to dip into all those fields, but at this point to commit himself to none of them. He would, he assured himself, of course, make a more definite choice once he had completed his doctoral dissertation on Mo Tzu, the moral philosopher and political theorist. That great champion of democratic impartiality and rule by law, was, curiously enough, also the pre-eminent advocate of authoritarian rigor enforced by strict punishments, as well as made attractive by lavish rewards. Although his inspiration was never acknowledged by orthodox Confucian historians, Mo Tzu's thinking had shaped the great imperial dynasties at least as much, possibly even more, than had Confucius's own doctrines.

Of course, there wasn't a lot of money in such butterflying. Or was it, Luke wondered, on his part the superficial dragonflying that Li Mao had comically denounced as a Korean addiction, flitting back and forth among several vocations, sipping at one flower and then another. Besides nectar was a little thin as a steady diet.

Still, he did not need much money, and those moderate sums were readily available. His father disapproved of his indecisiveness, but was happy to support him for as long as the PhD might take. Professoring didn't carry the weight of banking or lawyering, but it was respectable and respected.

His mother encouraged him to find his own way. She was 'comically doting' on her son, as his father said. She was also independently well-to-do. Money was not the problem.

Yet Luke's life looked haphazard, even helter-skelter, to others.

'What are you trying to prove?' I, Harland Birch, demanded at one point. 'That you're a renaissance man? That you can master anything and everything?'

Still, it somehow made sense to Luke himself. Besides, a pattern was slowly emerging. He served a tour with the US Information Service on Taiwan long after Brigadier-General Lesward Murray Howse had departed. He taught for a year at the University of Pennsylvania, lecturing chiefly on Japan, since he found the pre-eminent professor of Chinese dauntingly pro-Communist. And he spent some time with the American Universities Field Service in Asia, studying and writing about South-east Asian nations, primarily Indonesia and Malaysia.

He wrote primarily for serious periodicals like *The Reporter, Commentary,* and *Harpers,* as well as for a few learned journals. He also published several serious, but entertaining books on Asia, their emphasis ranging from philosophy to cock-fighting. He dabbled in raising enterprise capital in Hong Kong, Taiwan, and Singapore, impressing overseas Chinese associates with his grasp of Mandarin, the national language, a grasp that was far better than their own. But he rapidly concluded that investing venture capital was not his forte. He was bored, and he was lucky to escape with only his fingertips singed.

He was a happy man, Luke told himself, except for one thing. Although he was moving into his third decade, he still attracted women, but he still could hold on to none of them. In truth, he found, he did *not* want to hold on to any of them.

Of course, you, gentle reader, can now see it coming.

Luke had taken only three women seriously in his entire life. One was Mary Kaye Sommers, who complained that he would never settle down with her or anyone else and had then eloped with a surgeon decades older than herself. Another was Sue Chae, whom he saw whenever he passed through Los Angeles or whenever she appeared in New York, Washington, or Seoul, when he happened to be there. That relationship, too, was long settled. She was happily married. Although he had once been drawn to her as if galvanized, he had not really wanted to follow through. Too much like incest, somehow!

No question, reader, that you can really see it coming now.

Betsie Howard was the only woman who had dumped him instead of his dumping her. She was cataloged in his mind under Unfinished Business when she called him in Philadelphia one Sunday afternoon.

Betsie had not immediately looked up Luke after parting with Tommy Chae. That would have been too cold-blooded. Besides, she had learned on her own without any need to see Luke for comparison just how she felt about Tommy. Her feeling for him – love, fondness, affection, whatever she might call it – was strong, but not really profound, neither transcendent nor enduring.

It had been great fun. No, much more than fun! It had been a deeply moving experience. But it had no future.

When she finally telephoned Luke, Betsie had already made up her mind. She had years earlier warned him that he would never shake her once she got her talons into him. He could not shake her now, nor did he try too hard. After a year or two of her unrelenting pursuit, he finally stopped running away.

To their astonishment they were very happy together. Even blissful from time to time, although they had not expected to experience again the moments of ecstasy they had known in the beginning. It had all taken so long, their muddled, passionate, madcap courtship, that they could not expect bliss.

They married almost without conscious decision. It was just the natural thing to do. And they found great happiness, indeed joy.

They were indispensable to each other: Betsie's strong convictions, now tempered by experience; her incisive judgement of people, her trenchant humor, her instinctive grasp of complex matters, and her restraint of his wilder notions; Luke's finally settling down with the one woman from whom he couldn't bear to part; his meticulous scholarship, his flashes of brilliance, and his compassion. Also her complete devotion and his unswerving faithfulness. After all their youthful, virtually adolescent, toing and froing, after the indecision, the bitterness, and the rejection, theirs was a grown-up union.

Korea had brought them together and had then forced them apart. The war had been the critical factor in their lives, as for so many others. The war had formed their character and had forged their future.

Of all the moments in that war, the boring and the terrifying, the simply wearying and the excruciatingly intense, I, Harland Birch, your storyteller, remember best a half-hour or so at the tail end. It was at once grotesque and profound, virtually inexplicable, totally unexpected, extremely poignant, and deeply inspiring.

The ceasefire, the close of more than three years of shooting, was scheduled for 11:30 in the evening of July 27, 1953. The armistice agreement had been signed a few hours earlier. There was to be no more killing after midnight of that same day.

I decided to spend the moment with the First Marine Division, which held the main line of resistance north of Seoul. Luke Maynell drove to the front with me. He was exhausted and shaken.

He had for the past six weeks been making what he called 'my goodbye trawl', his final effort to find potential agents among newly captured Chinese prisoners. His last journey along the main line of resistance had been his most dangerous, far more dangerous than, say, the life of a company commander sitting snug in his own bunker. He had been caught up by the last major Chinese offensive in June 1953, when ROK II Corps broke again.

'Air bursts!' he recalled. 'They look like ripe tomatoes smashing on a glass skylight. This time, dozens bursting scarlet all at once. I stayed behind with a redheaded American major who scorned a steel helmet. And the trenches hastily improvised, were, maybe waist high. It would've been damned ironic … getting killed in the last gasp of the war. Thank God that's over. I won't have to do it again, not ever!'

As the ceasefire approached, at half-past eleven on a middling dark night, the trenches were filled with US Marines eager to see what, if anything, would happen at the precise moment. In the distance, sporadic harassing and interdicting artillery fire rumbled. From time to time small-arms rattled. They were like noises off stage, as if the soldiers were obediently playing out their appointed role to the very end.

Then it just stopped. Precisely at half-past eleven, the fitful shooting stopped. The silence was strange, but it was still not extraordinary. There had been long pauses between shooting all that evening.

The shooting did not resume. Tentatively, almost fearfully, only half-believing, deathly afraid that it was an illusion, all of us in the front-line trench began to feel the ceasefire might be real. That was hard to believe after more than three years of deathly strife, but it might just last.

I saw by the half-light of a crescent moon that Luke was fiddling with his Zippo lighter, flipping it open and closed. It had for years been the height of folly to light a cigarette in sight of the enemy in the foremost trenches of the main line of resistance. You might as well have put up an illuminated sign reading: *Here I am! Come shoot me!*

The Marines, too, were playing with cigarettes. But none lit up.

Suddenly, alarmingly, searchlights, rockets, flares, and starshells brilliantly illuminated the hills across the valley, which were deeply scarred by the heavily fortified enemy frontline. The enemy, the Chinese People's Volunteers, were climbing out of their trenches, first by the dozen, then by the hundreds. They stood still, blinking at the glare, for a few moments. They then began dancing.

Cavorting and pirouetting, prancing and gamboling, hundreds of Chinese soldiers were celebrating the ceasefire with antic gaiety.

It was eerie. We had rarely seen individual enemy soldiers unless met in close combat. Mostly, they had been invisible to us, as we were presumably to them. Yet here they were, dancing in the brightly lit night, showing themselves without fear.

'They trust us a hell of a lot more than we do them,' someone said. 'But what the hell!'

As if on cue, lighters flared, and dozens of cigarettes glowed in the half-darkness.

There was silence again in the trench. We might all have been struck dumb, awed by the realization that the war was truly over.

I heard a few murmurs that were too faint to understand, half choked. Then I heard Luke Maynell say aloud in wonder the words we'd all been thinking: 'I've survived! By God I've survived!'

Perspectives in Exercise Science
and Sports Medicine: Volume 12

The Metabolic Basis of Performance in Exercise and Sport

Edited by

David R. Lamb
The Ohio State University

Robert Murray
The Gatorade Company

COOPER
Publishing
Group

Library of Congress Cataloging in Publication Data:
LAMB, DAVID R., 1939-
PERSPECTIVES IN EXERCISE SCIENCE AND SPORTS MEDICINE
VOLUME 12: THE METABOLIC BASIS OF PERFORMANCE IN EXERCISE AND SPORT

Cover Design: Gary Schmitt

Library of Congress Catalog Card number: 98-74105

ISBN: 1-884125-73-5

Printed in the United States of America by Cooper Publishing Group LLC, P.O. Box 562, Carmel, IN 46082

10 9 8 7 6 5 4 3 2 1

Contents

Contributors

Luis F. Aragon-Vargas, Ph.D.
75m Sur Productors de Conreto
San Francisco de Dos Rios
San Jose, COSTA RICA

Wink Barnette, A.D.
Florida Athletic Coaches Assoc.
Ocala, FL 34470

Oded Bar-Or, M.D.
Children's Exercise & Nutrition Ctr.
Chedoke Hospital Division
Hamilton, Ontario L8N 3Z5
CANADA

Jidi Chen, M.D.
Institute of Sports Medicine
Beijing Medical University
Beijing 100083
CHINA

Priscilla M. Clarkson, Ph.D.
Department of Exercise Science
University of Massachusetts
Amherst, MA 01003

Andrew Coggin, Ph.D.
University of Maryland School of
Medicine
Division of Gerontology
Baltimore VA Medical Center
Baltimore, MD 21201

Edward F. Coyle, Ph.D
Human Performance Lab
University of Texas
Austin,TX 78712

J. Mark Davis, Ph.D.
Department of Exercise Science
University of South Carolina
Columbia, SC 29208

E. Randy Eichner, M.D.
Section of Hematology
University of Oklahoma
Health Sciences Center
Oklahoma City, OK 73190

Mark Febbraio, Ph.D.
Department of Physiology
University of Melbourne
Parkville, Victoria 3050
AUSTRALIA

Ed Frey, Ed.D.
Phillips Exeter Academy
Exeter, NH 03833

Carl V. Gisolfi, Ph.D.
Dept. of Exercise Science
University of Iowa
Iowa City, IA 52242

Mark Hargreaves, Ph.D.
School of Health Sciences
Deakin University
Burwood, Victoria 3125
AUSTRALIA

George J.F. Heigenhouser, Ph.D.
Department of Medicine
McMaster University
Hamilton, Ontario L8N 3Z5
CANADA

Bradley J. Hodgkinson, M.A.
Human Performance Lab
University of Texas
Austin, TX 78712

Craig A. Horswill, Ph.D.
Gatorade Exercise Physiology
Laboratory
The Gatorade Company
Barrington, IL 60010

Richard A. Howlett, Ph.D.
Human Biology and Nutritional
Sciences
University of Guelph
Guelph, Ontario N1G 2WI
CANADA

W. Larry Kenney, Ph.D.
Noll Physiological Research Center
Pennyslvania State University
University Park, PA 16802

Tom Koto, A.T.C.
Idaho Sports Institute
Boise, ID 83706

David Lamb, Ph.D.
School of Physical Activity and
Educational Services
The Ohio State University
Columbus, OH 43210

Florian Lang, M.D.
Physiology Institute
Eberhard-Karls-University, Tubingen
D-72076 Tubingen
GERMANY

Henry K. Lukaski, Ph.D.
Human Nutrition Research Center
U.S.D.A - A.R.S.
Grand Forks, ND 58202

Ron J. Maughan, Ph.D.
Dept. of Environmental/
Occupational Medicine
University of Aberdeen
Forresterhill, Aberdeen AB9 2ZD
SCOTLAND

Robert Murray, Ph.D.
Gatorade Exercise Physiology
Laboratory
The Gatorade Company
Barrington, IL 60010

Ethan R. Nadel, Ph.D.
John B. Pierce Foundation Laboratory
New Haven, CT 06519

Suzanne Nelson-Steen, D.Sc., R.D.
1125 Aqua Vista Dr. NW
Gig Harbor, WA 98335
Boise, ID 83725

Linda Petlichkoff, Ph.D.
Department HPER
Boise State University
Boise, ID 83725

Bill Prentice, Ph.D., P.T., A.T.C.
University of North Carolina
Chapel Hill, NC 28599

Delphis Richardson, M.D.
Mesa Pediatrics Professional Assoc.
Mesa, AZ 85202

Yvonne Satterwhite, M.D., C.S.C.S.
Kentucky Sports Medicine Clinic, PSC
Lexington, KY 40517

W. Michael Sherman, Ph.D.
School of Physical Activity and
Educational Services
The Ohio State University
Columbus, OH 43210

Xiaocai Shi, Ph.D.
Gatorade Exercise Physiology
Laboratory
The Gatorade Company
Barrington, IL 60010

Lawrence L. Spriet, Ph.D.
Human Biology & Nutritional
Sciences
University of Guelph
Guelph, Ontario N1G 2WI
CANADA

Dixie Stanforth, M.S.
Department of Kinesiology
The University of Texas at Austin
Austin, TX 87831

Mark Tarnopolsky, M.D., Ph.D.
Depts. of Kinesiology and Pediatrics
McMaster University Medical Center
Hamilton, Ontario L8N 3Z5
CANADA

Anton J.M. Wagenmakers, Ph.D.
Department of Human Biology
University of Limburg
Maastricht, 6200 MD
THE NETHERLANDS

Janet Walberg-Rankin, Ph.D.
Dept. of Human Nutrition,
Foods and Exercise
Virginia Polytechnic Institute
and State University
Blacksburg, VA 24061

Clyde Williams, Ph.D.
Dept. Physical Education, Sports
Science & Recreation Management
Loughborough University
Loughborough,
Leicestershire LE11 3TU
ENGLAND

Wayne T. Willis, Ph.D.
Dept. of Exercise Science & Physical
Education
Arizona State University
Tempe, AZ 85287

Dedication

Ethan R. Nadel

This volume is dedicated to the memory of Ethan R. Nadel, Ph.D., who died on December 26, 1998, at 57 years of age. Ethan was among our most highly respected colleagues and was recognized internationally for his expertise in fluid homeostasis, exercise science, and temperature regulation. He was an author or reviewer for each of the 12 volumes of *Perspectives in Exercise Science and Sports Medicine,* and was a charter member of the Sports Medicine Review Board of the Gatorade Sports Science Institute. The articles he contributed to the Perspectives series and to Sports Science Exchange were representative of his remarkable ability to transmit complex ideas in a simple and understandable fashion.

Professor Nadel was a dedicated teacher and superb scholar who had spent most of his professional life at the John B. Pierce Foundation Laboratory affiliated with Yale University. He had recently been elected to a second term as Director of the Pierce Laboratory. His stature in the field is also exemplified by his recent election to the office of Councillor of the American Physiological Society (APS) and his selection by the Exercise and Environmental Physiology Section of the APS to deliver the 1999 Edward F. Adolph Lecture, one of the most prestigious honors of the APS.

The Daedalus project, a study of human-powered flight that Dr. Nadel was planning to present as part of his Adolph lecture, is a prime example of his ability to combine basic and applied science in a meaningful way. Dr. Nadel was distinguished in the scientific community by his mechanistic approach to physiological problems and especially by his scientific integrity. He was a participant in every major international conference on fluid balance and temperature regulation in the last two decades.

As a mentor at the undergraduate, graduate, and postdoctoral levels, Ethan was outstanding, not only because of his broad knowledge base, but more importantly because of his wisdom and ability to communicate in a friendly and sincere manner. Although he never said very much about his athletic abilities, he was a sub 3-hour marathon runner. He also loved the outdoors and was an accomplished sailor.

Ethan was more than a colleague, he was a dear friend to many. As stated by one of us, "Ethan was a mentor-away-from-home, always willing to advise me on career decisions, scientific questions, people decisions, or just to talk about stuff."

Ethan Nadel will be missed by the scientific community, but much more by those of us who were fortunate enough to have a personal relationship with him. We will always remember his self-effacing sense of humor and his genuine warmth, acceptance and sincere caring for others.

Carl V. Gisolfi
David R. Lamb
Larry Kenney

Acknowledgement

The Metabolic Basis of Performance in Exercise and Sport is the twelfth text in the series, *Perspectives in Exercise Science and Sports Medicine*. The Gatorade Company has been proud to sponsor each of the scientific meetings that have resulted in the publication of a Perspectives text. The 1998 meeting was held in Durango, Colorado and the authors and reviewers worked diligently to critically review each chapter to make certain that the information contained in this text reflects the latest and most accurate scientific knowledge available on this topic. An enormous amount of work went into producing this book and we hope you find it to be a useful addition to your professional library.

Susan D. Wellington
President, Gatorade—U.S.
The Quaker Oats Company
Chicago, IL

Preface

The purpose of this volume is to present critical and expert reviews of recent literature on the interaction between metabolism and performance in exercise and sport. The authors were charged with producing chapters that present not only the scientific background essential to understanding the various topics but also the potential practical applications of that science. The first chapter by Lawrence Spriet establishes a framework for the rest of the book by summarizing the mechanisms by which metabolism is regulated during exercise. In this second chapter, Florian Lang describes evidence that changes in cell volume can markedly affect the rates of synthesis and degradation of cellular proteins. This phenomenon may eventually prove to be responsible for some of the muscle hypertrophy that occurs as an adaptation to resistance training and perhaps to nutritional manipulations.

The next three chapters by Mark Hargreaves, Mark Tarnopolsky, and Edward Coyle explain how changing the relative proportions of carbohydrate, fat, and protein in the diet can affect metabolism and exercise performance. Chapters 6 and 7, by Anton Wagenmakers and Henry Lukaski describe the responses of metabolism and performance to the ingestion of vitamins, minerals, and other popular dietary supplements. Finally, Mark Febbraio and Andrew Coggan discuss how metabolism and performance are affected by environmental temperature, age, and gender.

I thank these authors for contributing to what I believe will be a highly acclaimed volume. I also appreciate the efforts of those scientists and practitioners who reviewed the manuscripts and participated in the conference at which the chapters were discussed and fine tuned. In particular, Mark Hargreaves and Lawrence Spriet conceived the theme for this book, identified the chapters and authors, and played a major role in the organization of the conference. Bob Murray of the Gatorade Exercise Physiology Laboratory also deserves kudos for his indefatigable efforts in seeing to it that every detail of the conference, from conception to the final banquet, was executed superbly.

Cozette Lamb was a wonderful associate editor for this volume, and I thank her for her excellent work without which several deadlines would have been missed. All of the participants are grateful to Paula Darr and her colleagues at McCord Travel Management, who did their usual fine job of managing the conference logistics. Thanks also to Joan Seye and Betty Dye, the conference secretaries from the University of Iowa, who did a magnificent job of transcribing the conference discussions.

Finally, I recognize the wonderful sponsorship of the Gatorade Company, which has backed these scientific conferences in a superb manner for the last 12 years. This *Perspectives* series could not have been sustained for this long without the loyal support of Gatorade. I sincerely appreciate their understanding of the importance of a strong relationship between science and the corporate world, especially when dealing with the health, safety, and performance of athletes and other active people.

David R. Lamb

1

Metabolic Control of Energy Production During Physical Activity

LAWRENCE L. SPRIET, PH.D
RICHARD A. HOWLETT, PH.D.

INTRODUCTION

The ability of skeletal muscle to convert chemical energy to mechanical energy for physical activity makes it a most remarkable organ. The immediate source of chemical energy in muscle is adenosine triphosphate (ATP). The muscle store of ATP is not large and would be consumed in only a few seconds of maximal contractions if it were not quickly replenished. Therefore, the metabolic pathways that synthesize ATP must be able to rapidly respond to an increased demand for ATP, which can increase more than 100-fold when moving from rest to strenuous physical activity. In most exercise situations, a precise matching of ATP demand and ATP provision is accomplished because the muscle ATP store is maintained. Even during maximal sprinting or electrical stimulation, muscle ATP levels only decrease by 25–40% (McCartney et al., 1986; Spriet et al., 1987a).

The purpose of this chapter is to examine the metabolic control of energy production in human skeletal muscle during physical activity. We have attempted to identify the signals that are believed to communicate the need for ATP production to the pathways that synthesize the required ATP. The chapter begins with general metabolic concepts, definitions, and paradigms, then examines the regulation of ATP production in specific pathways, and ends with a discussion of factors that presently limit the study of muscle metabolism. The reader is also encouraged to consult other textbooks and edited books for more detail in certain areas of the control of energy metabolism (Hargreaves, 1995; Hargreaves & Thompson, 1998; Maughan & Shirreffs, 1996; Maughan et al., 1997; Newsholme & Leech, 1983; Nicholls & Ferguson, 1992; Richter et al., 1998). Of special note is the volume of the *Handbook of Physiology* entitled *"Exercise: Regulation and Integration of Multiple Systems,"* edited by Rowell and Shepherd (1996), which has several chapters that provide excellent reviews of metabolism-related topics. In addition, many review articles on specific metabolic topics have been cited throughout the chapter.

ATP UTILIZATION DURING PHYSICAL ACTIVITY

It is important to start the discussion of metabolic control in skeletal muscle with the realization that the enzymes that degrade ATP during exercise will determine the magnitude of the challenge facing the ATP-producing pathways. The major enzymes that degrade ATP during exercise are those associated with the contraction-relaxation cycle in skeletal muscle, including the actomyosin, Ca^+-transport, and Na^+-K^+-transport adenosine triphosphatases (ATPases). During exercise, the release of Ca^+ from the sarcoplasmic reticulum activates the actomyosin and Ca^+ ATPases, and they account for ~70% and 25–30% of the ATP consumed, respectively (Kushmerick, 1983; Rall, 1985). The Na^+-K^+-transport ATPase is also active to maintain the ionic status of the cell, and other ATPases involved in maintenance of the cell may be active. However, the ATP consumed by these enzymes appears to be quantitatively insignificant. Therefore, the intensity of the exercise (rate of ATP utilization) is the independent variable that determines the rate of ATP synthesis. If cellular homeostasis (a constant ATP concentration) is to be maintained within an acceptable range during exercise, ATP synthesis must match the rate of ATP utilization, and the dependent variables become the factors that regulate the energy producing pathways (Meyer & Foley, 1996).

THE STUDY OF ENERGY PRODUCTION IN HUMANS

Exercise Intensity

The intensity of physical activity or exercise is most often characterized on a relative basis as the percentage of the power output that can be sustained by oxidative ATP production. The relationship between power output and O_2 uptake ($\dot{V}O_2$) is linear until the maximal O_2 uptake ($\dot{V}O_2max$) is reached. Power outputs above $\dot{V}O_2max$ can be sustained for short periods of time by synthesizing additional ATP anaerobically. These high power outputs can be expressed as a percentage of $\dot{V}O_2max$. For example, if $\dot{V}O_2max$ in an individual is reached at 250 W, exercise at an average power output of 250% $\dot{V}O_2max$ or 625 W can be sustained for 30 s during sprinting in well-motivated individuals (McCartney et al., 1986; Spriet et al., 1989). Exercise at 85–100, 165, and 215–230 W would therefore constitute intensities of 35–40%, 65%, and 85–90% $\dot{V}O_2max$ (Table 1-1). While it is common to refer to exercise intensities below $\dot{V}O_2max$ as submaximal and those above $\dot{V}O_2max$ as supramaximal, this classification refers only to the ability to provide aerobic ATP. All aerobic exercise (0–100% $\dot{V}O_2max$) occurs at power outputs that are less than 50% of the power output that can be sustained during maximal sprint situations in most individuals.

TABLE 1-1. *Hypothetical power outputs at various intensities of exercise (%$\dot{V}O_2$max)for a 70 kg person whose $\dot{V}O_2$max is 3200 ml/min.*

Percent $\dot{V}O_2$max	Power output, W	O_2 uptake, ml/min
35–40%	85–100	1120–1280
65%	165	2080
85–90%	215–230	2720–2880
250%	625	~2250[1]

Based on an average.

[1]$\dot{V}O_2$ increases from rest values to ~70% $\dot{V}O_2$max in 30 s of sprinting at a power output representing 250% $\dot{V}O_2$max.

Sources of Metabolic Fuel

The ability of skeletal muscle to synthesize ATP during exercise and during recovery following exercise is dependent on foodstuffs consumed in the diet. Fat and carbohydrate (CHO) provide the vast majority of the metabolic fuel, with protein, ketone bodies, and acetate contributing small amounts of ATP in certain situations. Both fat and CHO are stored in skeletal muscle (intramuscular) and in other sites in the body (extramuscular). The extramuscular storage site for fat is adipose tissue, found in many locations throughout the body, while extramuscular CHO is stored in the liver. Both fuels are also present in small amounts in the blood.

Signals inherent to the muscle regulate the utilization of intramuscular fuels. Mobilization of extramuscular fuels into the blood for delivery to the working skeletal muscles is controlled by various physiological systems, including the neural, endocrine, and cardiovascular systems, and will not be discussed in this chapter. However, the ability of skeletal muscle to regulate the uptake and use of these extramuscular fuels will be examined.

Rates of ATP Production in Metabolic Pathways

Most exercise situations involve a combination of fat and CHO metabolism to provide the required ATP through aerobic pathways (Figure 1-1). However, it is important to remember that the maximal rate of ATP synthesis from fat can provide only enough ATP to sustain exercise at 55–75% $\dot{V}O_2$max, depending on the aerobic training status of the individual (Putman et al., 1993). On the other hand, CHO can sustain aerobic exercise up to 100% $\dot{V}O_2$max in untrained or trained individuals (Bergstrom et al., 1969).

Anaerobic ATP production, or substrate phosphorylation, is required when aerobic metabolism (oxidative phosphorylation) cannot

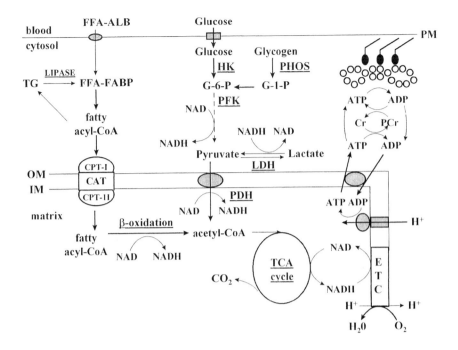

FIGURE 1-1. *Schematic overview of energy production in skeletal muscle.* Abbreviations: PM, plasma membrane; OM, IM, outer and inner mitochondrial membranes; FFA, free fatty acid; ALB, albumin; FABP, fatty acid binding protein; CoA, coenzyme A; CPT I, II, carnitine palmitoyltransferase I and II; CAT, carnitine-acylcarnitine translocase; NAD, NADH, oxidized and reduced nicotinamide adenine dinucleotide; HK, hexokinase; PFK, phosphofructokinase; PHOS, glycogen phosphorylase; LDH, lactate dehydrogenase; PDH, pyruvate dehydrogenase; G-6-P, G-1-P, glucose 6- and 1-phosphate; PCr, phosphocreatine; Cr, creatine; TCA, tricarboxylic acid; ETC, electron transport chain.

provide all the required ATP to sustain exercise. This occurs during exercise at intensities of about 85–100% V̇O₂max and certainly at power outputs above 100% V̇O₂max. The main sources of anaerobic ATP synthesis are via the degradation of phosphocreatine (PCr) and from the glycolytic pathway with the production of lactate and H+ ("anaerobic glycolysis"). A major advantage of the two anaerobic pathways acting together is the high rate of ATP synthesis they provide compared to aerobic ATP production (up to 5–6 times higher). These systems allow us to engage in physical activities like sprinting, jumping, and weight lifting that require high power outputs and high rates of ATP production. However, the major limitation is the very short period of time that these high rates of ATP production can be maintained, due to the depletion of PCr and the accumulation of byproducts of anaerobic glycolysis.

It is important to remember that CHO is a fuel for both aerobic and anaerobic ATP synthesis. Aerobic use of CHO yields a large amount of energy, providing ~38–39 millimoles (mmol) ATP for each mmol of glucose or glycogen consumed. Anaerobic use of CHO yields much less energy, providing only 3 mmol ATP per mmol of glucose derived from muscle glycogen. However, the rate of ATP provision is ~2-fold greater when derived anaerobically. A consequence of the rapid anaerobic metabolism of CHO in a sprint situation is the very low energy yield of muscle glycogen use.

Methods For Studying Human Skeletal Muscle Metabolism

Most of what is known regarding the control of energy production in human skeletal muscle has been derived from chemical measurements of fuels, enzymes, metabolites, and byproducts in fresh or frozen needle biopsies of the vastus lateralis muscle of the thigh. Muscle biopsies take 3-8 s to perform and are then plunged into liquid N_2, requiring a few additional seconds for complete freezing. There has been concern expressed regarding the delay in the freezing of the muscle and the possibility that Ca^{2+} is released during the cutting of the muscle. The concern over the freezing is difficult to test in an intact human, but does not appear to be a problem for sensitive metabolites like PCr (Soderlund & Hultman, 1986). The Ca^{2+} concern appears important at rest for enzymes that are Ca^{2+} sensitive and exist in active and less-active forms (e.g., glycogen phosphorylase), but this is less of a factor during exercise, when Ca^{2+} concentrations are already higher due to the contractions (Chesley et al., 1998; Ren & Hultman, 1988).

Another concern with biopsies is that measurements provide only average responses for the fiber-type population that exists in a given muscle. For example, in human vastus lateralis muscles, the fiber-type distribution is heterogeneous, ~50% slow-twitch and ~50% fast-twitch, with the fast-twitch fibers further subdivided into ~35–40% type IIa and 10–15% IIb (Schantz et al. 1983), although significant variations can exist in certain individuals (McCartney et al., 1983). An additional problem with the "average muscle" approach occurs during low intensity exercise, when all motor units have not been recruited. In this case, the average response of the muscle underestimates the response of the active motor units. This is less of a problem at higher power outputs when all motor units are recruited and further increases in force occur by increasing the frequency of motor unit firing (Henneman, 1957). The problems associated with interpreting average fiber-type responses in human skeletal muscle are somewhat reduced by the fact that the differences between type I and II measurements and responses to exercise are much less than those reported in rodent slow, oxidative fibers vs. fast, glycolytic fibers (Casey et al., 1996; Greenhaff et al., 1991; Meyer & Foley, 1996; Saltin & Gollnick, 1983). This problem has also been addressed in studies that have separated muscle fibers and examined enzymes and responses of compounds that can be measured in groups of type I and II fibers (Casey et al., 1996; Greenhaff et al., 1991; Lowry et al., 1978).

^{31}P nuclear magnetic resonance (NMR) spectroscopy has also been used to study changes in phosphorus compounds related to metabolism in human skeletal muscle. This method has the distinct advantage of being non-invasive, but it remains a rather insensitive research tool (qualitative), is expensive and technically demanding to operate, and shares the muscle heterogeneity problem discussed above with the biopsy technique (Meyer & Foley, 1996).

Metabolic Control of Enzymes and Pathways

Metabolic pathways are designed with two general types of enzymes, non-equilibrium and near-equilibrium. The non-equilibrium enzymes catalyze reactions that can be regulated by factors other than substrate and product concentrations and generally have lower maximal activities than do the near-equilibrium enzymes in a pathway. During exercise, they are covalently and allosterically regulated by factors related to the intensity of the muscle contraction (hormones and Ca^{2+}) and the severity of the demand for ATP. Allosteric regulation occurs when a compound binds to an enzyme at a site other than the active sites (where substrates bind) and increases or decreases the activity of the enzyme. Covalent regulation involves enzymes that exist in two forms, a less or non-active *b* form and a more active *a* form. Usually, a kinase phosphorylates the enzyme to one form and a phosphatase dephosphorylates the enzyme to the other form, with either being the more active form, depending on the enzyme (e.g., pyruvate dehydrogenase vs. glycogen phosphorylase). The kinase and phosphatase enzymes are sensitive to allosteric regulators, and in some cases both the *a* and *b* forms of the covalently regulated enzyme (e.g., phosphorylase) are also sensitive to allosteric regulators. Lastly, non-equilibrium enzymes can also be influenced by substrate concentrations, and they play a very important role in certain situations. Near-equilibrium enzymes, on the other hand, are regulated solely by the concentrations of their substrates and products. In other words, they are sensitive to what occurs in other reactions in the pathway. When the substrate concentrations are increased, flux through the near-equilibrium enzyme-catalyzed reactions increases. Therefore, the contraction-related signals that turn on metabolism during exercise target the non-equilibrium, regulatory enzymes, and the increased flux through these reactions provides substrates that activate the near-equilibrium enzymes.

THE SIGNALS THAT MATCH ATP SYNTHESIS
WITH THE DEMAND FOR ATP

The metabolic signals that are believed to play major roles in activating the various energy-producing pathways can be classified into three categories: Ca^{2+}, metabolites related to the cytoplasmic phosphorylation potential, and the mitochondrial reduction/oxidation (redox) state of nicotinamide adenine dinucleotide (NAD/NADH) (Meyer & Foley, 1996). All three signals are important in up-regulating enzymes that are important for ATP production in the mitochondrial and cytoplasmic compartments during physical activity. Ca^{2+} release plays an important role in initiating muscle contraction and in turning on metabolism in a feed-forward or "early warning" manner (Figure 1-2). The cytoplasmic phosphorylation potential of the muscle cells is a function of the concentrations of ATP, free adenosine diphosphate (ADP), and free inorganic phosphate (P_i) and is usually expressed as [ATP]/[ADP][P_i]. The concentrations of free adenosine monophosphate (AMP) and H^+ are related compounds that also have important regulatory functions in metabolism. As soon as ATP is degraded during physical activity, accumulations of adenine nucleotides (ADP, AMP) and metabolites (P_i) activate the enzymes and pathways that resynthesize ATP in a feedback manner (Figure 1-2). In sprint situations, ammonium (NH_4^+) and inosine monophosphate (IMP) may also be important in activating enzymes, whereas H^+ may do the opposite later in the sprint (Spriet, 1991; 1992). The redox state of the muscle is usually expressed as the ratio of NAD in its oxidized and reduced forms (NAD/NADH). NADH is an important substrate for the electron transport chain, and the redox couple (NAD/NADH) is involved in numerous reactions in substrate/product or activator/inhibitor capacities (Figure 1-2) (Newsholme & Leech, 1983).

Muscle contractions occur as the result of depolarization of the muscle membrane and t-tubules, which ultimately leads to the release of Ca^{2+} from the sarcoplasmic reticulum into the cytoplasm. The Ca^{2+} activates the actomyosin ATPases to degrade ATP (equation 1), which provides the energy for mechanical movement of crossbridges and muscle force production:

$$ATP \rightarrow ADP + P_i + H^+ \qquad (1)$$

At the same time, Ca^{2+} activates several key regulatory enzymes in pathways that lead to the resynthesis of ATP. The breakdown of ATP to its byproducts also provides metabolic signals that activate key enzymes of energy metabolism to resynthesize ATP in several reactions and pathways.

Aerobic metabolism of CHO and fat involves the production of reducing equivalents (NADH + H^+ and $FADH_2$) and acetyl-CoA in the gly-

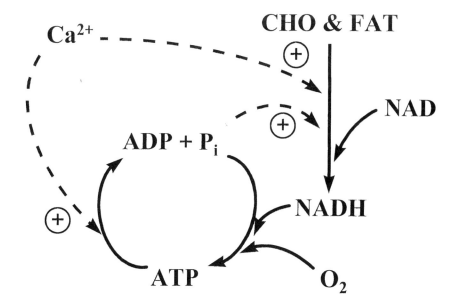

FIGURE 1-2. *Schematic diagram demonstrating the importance of Ca^{2+}, byproducts associated with the energy state of the cell ($ADP + P_i$), and the redox couple ($NAD/NADH$) in the activation of the pathways that synthesize ATP.*

colytic and beta-oxidation pathways, respectively (Figure 1-1). The acetyl-CoA is further metabolized in the tricarboxylic (TCA) cycle, producing more reducing equivalents. Ultimately, the availability of ADP, P_i, NADH + H^+, $FADH_2$, and O_2 stimulates the mitochondrial production of ATP in the processes of electron transport and oxidative phosphorylation. The production of energy from the complete aerobic combustion of 1 mmol of glucose from muscle glycogen is 39 mmol ATP (equation 2):

$$C_6H_{12}O_6 + 6\ O_2 + 39\ ADP + 39\ P_i \rightarrow 6\ CO_2 + 6\ H_2O + 39\ ATP \qquad (2)$$

and for 1 mmol of an 18-carbon fatty acid (e.g., stearic acid) is 146 mmol ATP (equation 3):

$$CH_3(CH_2)_{16}COOH + 26\ O_2 + 146\ ADP + 146\ P_i$$
$$\rightarrow 18\ CO_2 + 52\ H_2O + 146\ ATP \qquad (3)$$

When aerobic metabolism is unable to provide ATP at the required rate, anaerobic ATP pathways are used to provide the remaining ATP. These include the degradation of PCr in the creatine kinase (CK) reaction (equation 4) plus the glycogenolytic/glycolytic pathway, which results in the production of lactate (equation 5):

$$PCr + ADP + H^+ \rightarrow ATP + Creatine\ (Cr) \qquad (4)$$

$$\text{Glycogen} + 3 \text{ ADP} + 3 \text{ P}_i \rightarrow 3 \text{ ATP} + 2 \text{ lactate} + 2 \text{ H}^+ \tag{5}$$

During sprint exercise, ATP can also be synthesized anaerobically in the adenylate kinase reaction (equation 6). The subsequent AMP production stimulates AMP removal in the AMP deaminase reaction with the production of NH_4^+ (equation 7):

$$2 \text{ ADP} \rightarrow \text{ATP} + \text{AMP} \tag{6}$$

$$\text{AMP} + \text{H}^+ \rightarrow \text{IMP} + \text{NH}_4^+ \tag{7}$$

The amount of ATP generated in reaction 6 appears to be quantitatively insignificant in human skeletal muscle, even during sprint situations, possibly because reactions 6 and 7 reduce the total adenine nucleotide pool (ATP + ADP + AMP) and increase the time taken for the muscle to recover following exercise (Bangsbo et al., 1992; Spriet et al., 1987a).

REGULATION OF MITOCHONDRIAL RESPIRATION

The mitochondrial processes responsible for setting the rate of cellular oxidative ATP provision and O_2 utilization are oxidative phosphorylation and electron transport. The electron transport chain (ETC) is a series of four enzyme complexes (I–IV) that oxidize mitochondrial NADH and $FADH_2$, transferring electrons to reduce O_2 to H_2O (Figure 1-3). During oxidative phosphorylation, an enzyme complex (F_1F_0 ATPase) converts its substrates, ADP and P_i, to ATP. The overall reaction for the process of oxidative phosphorylation is commonly written (equation 8):

$$3 \text{ ADP} + 3 \text{ P}_i + \text{NADH} + \tfrac{1}{2} O_2 + \text{H}^+ \rightarrow 3 \text{ ATP} + \text{NAD}^+ + \text{H}_2\text{O} \tag{8}$$

It is apparent from this equation that there is input from three factors: ADP and P_i, NADH ($FADH_2$), and O_2. Because of the near-equilibrium nature of the ETC and oxidative phosphorylation processes, the substrates and products of this reaction will determine the rate of ATP production (Newsholme & Leech, 1983; Nicholls & Ferguson, 1992). Therefore, the ETC and oxidative phosphorylation processes are not sites of regulation, but the pathways that supply their substrates are.

To maintain skeletal muscle function and contractile activity, ATPases located in the cytoplasm break down ATP and produce ADP and P_i. Cytoplasmic ADP is transported into the matrix of the mitochondria via the adenine nucleotide translocase in exchange for ATP released into the cytoplasm (Figure 1-3). Likewise, the free P_i is transported into the mitochondria via a P_i/H^+ symport (Nicholls & Ferguson, 1992). To keep the ATPases supplied with required substrate, skeletal muscle mitochondria must convert the ADP and P_i back to ATP via oxidative phosphorylation. Inside the mitochondrial matrix, the ADP and P_i are converted to ATP by the F_1F_0 ATPase, which is driven by the influx of protons (H^+), generated by the proton electrochemical gradient (Nicholls & Ferguson, 1992). As electrons are transferred down the ETC from NADH and $FADH_2$ to O_2, protons are pumped from the matrix to the intermembrane space of the mitochondria, setting up an electrochemical or membrane potential (Figure 1-3). The exact mechanism responsible for the proton extrusion is currently unknown.

At rest, when the muscle cell breaks down ATP at low rates, a high rate of oxidative phosphorylation is not required, and it is easy for the mitochondria to maintain the membrane potential. However, during exercise, ATP turnover can increase by greater than 100–fold in skeletal muscle. There has been debate as to which cellular signals permit the increase in oxidative phosphorylation that occurs with the onset of contraction. For an explanation of current models of mitochondrial respiratory control, consult the review papers of Brand & Murphy, 1987; Erecinska & Wilson, 1982; and Wilson, 1994.

Two common theories are that the control of respiration is regulated kinetically by the concentrations of ADP, ATP, and P_i, or some combination of the three, or by a near-equilibrium thermodynamic model involving the free energy of the cytoplasmic phosphorylation potential, the mitochondrial redox potential, and the mitochondrial membrane potential. Regardless of the model that most accurately predicts mitochondrial respiration, the process is the same. When muscle contractions begin, the increases in ADP and P_i cause a fall in the cytoplasmic phosphorylation potential. This fall is signaled to the mitochondria via the adenine translocase, and ADP and P_i accumulate. As these substrates are converted to ATP to maintain the cellular ATP concentration, proton flux occurs through the F_1F_0ATPase, causing a fall in the membrane poten-

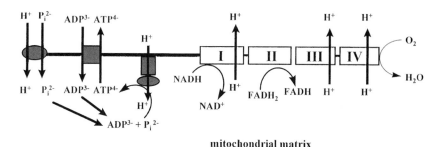

FIGURE 1-3. *Schematic diagram of the electron transport chain and the process of oxidative phosphorylation.* FADH, $FADH_2$, oxidized and reduced forms of flavin adenine dinucleotide.

tial. In trying to defend the membrane potential, electron transport is stimulated, facilitating proton pumping, but at the expense of the redox potential, as NADH is utilized as a substrate for the ETC. Finally, to produce the required NADH to defend the redox potential, the TCA cycle must be stimulated

Because the ETC behaves as a redox couple with NADH and NAD at one end and O_2 and H_2O at the other, the relative concentrations of these species are important in regulating ETC flux. It is important to examine how O_2 and NADH concentrations affect the ETC. Experiments by Chance and Quistorff (1978) demonstrated that the critical mitochondrial O_2, i.e., the lowest partial pressure of O_2 (PO_2) that will support maximal turnover of cytochrome a,a^3 (complex IV of the ETC) in isolated mitochondria, is extremely low, about 0.1 mm Hg. However, in intact cells it has been largely problematic to determine what the intracellular PO_2 actually is, especially during contraction. Likewise, it has been suggested that although mitochondria can function at very low O_2 levels, they are sensitive to PO_2 at a much higher level and adjust to O_2 levels through changes in the mitochondrial redox potential, the membrane potential, and the cytoplasmic phosphorylation potential, thus affecting the respiratory rate. Put simply, as O_2 levels fall below a critical in-vivo PO_2, the mitochondria can maintain a given respiration rate (and ATP production) by adjusting the redox potential or NAD/NADH ratio. To do this, the mitochondria must stimulate TCA cycle flux, requiring a fall in the membrane potential and in the ability to rephosphorylate ATP, causing a reduction in the phosphorylation potential. Therefore, the ATP turnover rate can be maintained at a lower PO_2, but at the cost of a reduced cellular energy state. The cellular consequences of this lowered energy state are many and will be examined in later sections.

To maintain ATP levels, the mitochondria must rephosphorylate ADP at tremendous rates, requiring a large flux of protons through the $F_1F_0ATPase$ at the expense of the membrane potential. In order to buffer this fall in membrane potential, mitochondrial electron transport must begin. Substrate for electron transport, or NADH and $FADH_2$, is mainly provided in the mitochondria from the TCA cycle. Therefore, it is necessary for flux through the TCA cycle to increase once ATP turnover increases. Previously it was mentioned that TCA cycle flux is activated by changes in the events occurring in the ETC, and the following section outlines how this may occur.

REGULATION OF THE TRICARBOXYLIC ACID CYCLE

Regulation of NADH production by the TCA cycle is believed to occur on several fronts. The two TCA cycle enzymes believed to be crucial in regulating flux rate are isocitrate dehydrogenase (IDH) and 2-ox-oglutarate dehydrogenase (2-OGDH) (Figure 1-4)(Newsholme & Leech, 1983). The activities of these enzymes are much lower than those of the rest of the cycle, and they are also non-equilibrium, allosterically regulated enzymes. Both enzymes are stimulated by Ca^{2+}, ADP, and various cations, especially Mg^{2+}, and by increases in the substrate/product ratio of NAD/NADH. This allosteric regulation favors very low activity during resting conditions and much greater activities when the concentrations of modulators increase with exercise. Mitochondria take up Ca^{2+} as contractions begin, causing increased activation of these enzymes (McCormack & Denton, 1986). Also, as ATP is broken down by muscle, the fall in mitochondrial phosphorylation potential results in increased ADP concentrations, stimulating IDH and 2-OGDH. It has been hypothesized that an increase in the NAD/NADH ratio is important in stimulating IDH and 2-OGDH (Newsholme & Leech, 1983), and this is consistent with a fall in the redox potential at the start of exercise. However, as discussed later, estimating the mitochondrial redox state in human skeletal muscle has proved problematic.

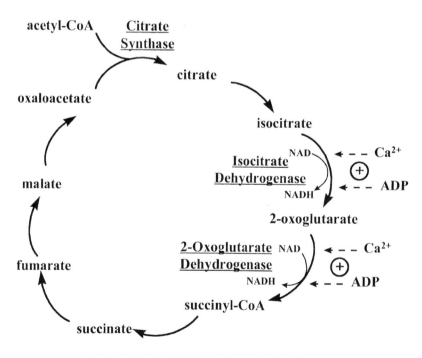

FIGURE 1-4. *Tricarboxylic acid cycle, highlighting the regulation of key enzymes.*

The increased flux through the TCA cycle has also been hypothesized to be dependent on increases in the concentrations of TCA intermediates with exercise (Gibala et al., 1997b; Sahlin et al., 1990). TCA cycle flux increases up to 100-fold at the start of exercise, suggesting that an increase in TCA intermediates is necessary to support the increased flux. Studies have demonstrated that TCA intermediates increase at the start of exercise, but whether or not this increase is absolutely required for the increase in flux is currently debated. An early study demonstrated that the muscle content of some TCA intermediates fell at exhaustion, suggesting that increased TCA intermediates were needed to maintain oxidative metabolism during exercise (Sahlin et al., 1990). However, a more recent study indicated that although TCA intermediates increased with exercise and then declined to a small degree, they remained significantly elevated above rest values at exhaustion (Gibala et al., 1997b). It has also been suggested that the availability of pyruvate at the onset of exercise is important for the increase in TCA intermediates (Gibala et al., 1997a). The authors proposed that the TCA intermediate increases are dependent on the alanine aminotransferase reaction that converts glutamate and pyruvate to alanine and 2-oxoglutarate (Figure 1-5). The 2-oxoglutarate is transferred into the mitochondria to support the increase in TCA intermediates.

Finally, the enzyme citrate synthase, which catalyzes the first step in the TCA cycle, has also been reported to be regulatory in nature (Figure 1-4) (Newsholme & Leech, 1983). The activity of citrate synthase is potentially activated by both of its substrates, oxaloacetate and acetyl-CoA, and inhibited by its product, citrate. As a TCA intermediate, oxaloacetate increases during exercise and provides one substrate for the reaction. Increases in the mitochondrial NAD/NADH ratio would favor the production of oxaloacetate because this redox couple is involved in the malate dehydrogenase reaction, which produces oxaloacetate. Possibly just as important is the availability of acetyl-CoA, as it increases as a function of power output during exercise (Constantin-Teodosiu et al., 1991; Howlett et al., 1998). Acetyl-CoA may also be important because it can be derived both from CHO (via pyruvate dehydrogenase) and fat (via beta-oxidation), and its provision is crucial in the selection of fuel that the mitochondria oxidize during exercise. Therefore, the pathways that are responsible for providing acetyl-CoA from fat and CHO sources are also important in both NADH production in the mitochondria and in determining which fuels are used during rest and exercise. Lastly, it appears that the potential inhibitory effect of increasing citrate concentration on citrate synthase activity during exercise is overridden by other factors because the flux through citrate synthase and the TCA cycle increases several fold.

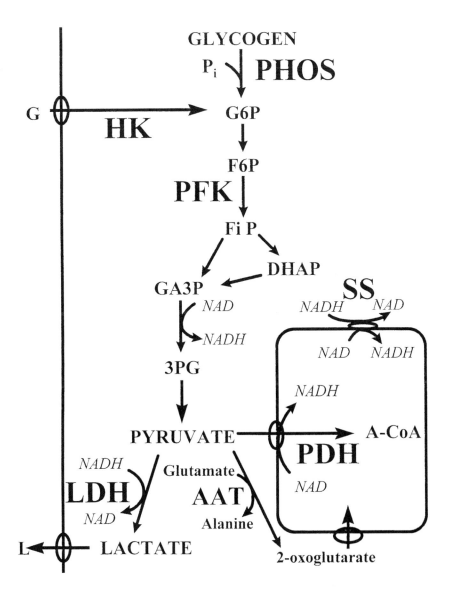

FIGURE 1-5. *Schematic of the glycogenolytic/glycolytic pathways, highlighting key enzymes and major fates of pyruvate.* Vertical line indicates muscle membrane separating blood and muscle cytoplasm; the rectangle depicts the mitochondrion; the ellipses indicate a transport process; and the arrows indicate the direction of net flux. G, glucose; L, lactate; A-CoA, acetyl-Coenzyme A; PHOS, glycogen phosphorylase; HK, hexokinase; PFK, phosphofructokinase; SS, malate-aspartate shuttle system; LDH, lactate dehydrogenase; G6P and F6P, glucose and fructose 6-phosphate; FbiP, fructose 1,6 bisphosphate; DHAP, dihydroxyacetone phosphate; GA3P, glyceraldehyde 3-phosphate; 3PG, 3-phosphoglycerol phosphate; AAT, alanine amino transferase; PDH, pyruvate dehydrogenase.

REGULATION OF AEROBIC CARBOHYDRATE METABOLISM

Unlike the almost unlimited stores of fat in the body, the amount of energy stored as CHO is relatively small. For skeletal muscle, the two sources of CHO for physical activity are liver glycogen (delivered in the form of blood glucose) and muscle glycogen. Blood glucose concentrations, controlled by hepatic glucose output, can play a role in glucose utilization, but this will not be discussed. However, regulation of the processes involved in the uptake and oxidative disposal of blood glucose by glycolysis and the degradation of muscle glycogen via glycogenolysis in skeletal muscle during exercise will be examined (Figure 1-5).

Glucose Transport

Glucose diffuses into the intercellular space from the blood and is moved into skeletal muscle cells by facilitated transport via specific glucose transporters. It is generally accepted that glucose transport is rate limiting for glucose utilization under normal conditions (Richter, 1996). Currently, six different glucose transporters (GLUT) have been identified throughout the body, with skeletal muscle expressing the ubiquitous GLUT1 isoform and the GLUT4 isoform (James, 1995; Mueckler, 1995; Richter, 1996).

GLUT1 is expressed in every tissue of the body and is believed to be responsible for basal glucose uptake. In skeletal muscle, no intracellular pool of GLUT1 has been found, suggesting that GLUT1 concentrations at the plasma membrane do not change acutely in response to either insulin or contraction. However, the GLUT1 content in the plasma membranes does appear to increase with training, facilitating greater basal glucose disposal (Phillips et al., 1996).

In contrast to GLUT1, GLUT4 is found on the surface of the sarcolemma and inside the skeletal muscle cell, associated with the Golgi apparatus. The cytoplasmic pool of GLUT4 represents the transporters that are readily available for translocation to the cell membrane in response to insulin and/or muscle contraction (James, 1995; Mueckler, 1995). The exact mechanisms responsible for the translocation of GLUT4 to the sarcolemma are presently unknown and currently under intense investigation. However, an increase in blood insulin concentration and/or increases in muscle contraction cause a very rapid increase in both the number and, possibly, the activity of GLUT4 protein associated with the plasma membrane (James, 1995; Mueckler, 1995). This increase in GLUT4 allows skeletal muscle to rapidly take up glucose for oxidation via glycolysis. Endurance training increases the GLUT4 content of skeletal muscle and the magnitude of the insulin and contraction responses (Dela et al., 1993; Phillips et al., 1996). Trained individuals are also more sensitive to insulin, allowing them to translocate more GLUT4 to the cell surface in response to a given insulin dose. This increased responsiveness due to training allows for a greater absolute glucose uptake by trained individuals, even though these individuals tend to use less glucose at the same absolute power output after training.

Glycolysis

When glucose is transported into the cytoplasm of the skeletal muscle during exercise, its primary fate is oxidation (Figure 1-5). To enter the glycolytic pathway, free glucose is first phosphorylated by hexokinase to glucose 6-phosphate (G-6-P). Hexokinase is a non-equilibrium enzyme, stimulated by insulin and the free glucose concentration, which allows greater glucose utilization when transport of glucose into the cell is high. Hexokinase is also inhibited by its product, G-6-P, which in situations when the G-6-P concentration is high may decrease glucose uptake at rest and during contractions (Randle et al., 1963). The maximal activity of hexokinase is similar to the maximal rate of glucose uptake by skeletal muscle and is increased with training, which also increases glucose uptake, implying that hexokinase may become limiting at high rates of glucose uptake (Bloomstrand et al., 1986; Katz et al. 1986).

Once glucose is phosphorylated, the main regulatory enzyme in the glycolytic pathway is phosphofructokinase (PFK), which converts ATP and fructose 6-phosphate (F-6-P) to fructose 1,6-diphosphate, and ADP. PFK is a non-equilibrium enzyme that is regulated by a number of allosteric modulators (Figure 1-6). While ATP is a substrate for the enzyme, it is also the most powerful allosteric regulator of PFK. High concentrations of ATP at rest allow ATP to bind at its allosteric or regulatory site and decrease the binding of F-6-P to its active site, thereby inhibiting PFK (Bock & Frieden, 1976). Citrate and H^+ potentiate the inhibition by strengthening the binding of ATP at its allosteric site (Bock & Frieden, 1976). During exercise, when ATP is degraded, the rise in ADP, P_i, and AMP stimulate PFK activity by reducing ATP binding to its regulatory site on the enzyme, in spite of increases in citrate and also H^+ at the higher aerobic power outputs (Spriet, 1991; Spriet et al., 1987b). At the same time, glycogen phosphorylase is activated higher up in the pathway, providing a higher rate of F-6-P production for the PFK reaction. Thus, the initial fall in the cellular energy state caused by muscle contractions increases the glycolytic rate by activating glycogen phosphorylase and relieving PFK inhibition.

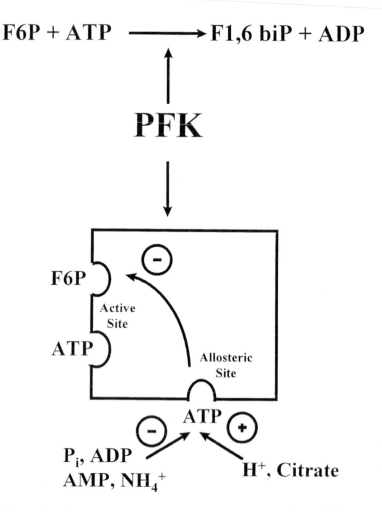

FIGURE 1-6. *Schematic diagram of proposed regulation of phosphofructokinase.* PFK, phosphofructokinase; F6P, fructose 6-phosphate; F1,6 biP, fructose 1,6 bisphosphate.

Glycogenolysis

During exercise at power outputs above ~50% $\dot{V}O_2$max, muscle glycogen becomes quantitatively the most important fuel during exercise, with the rate of glycogen breakdown increasing exponentially above 75% $\dot{V}O_2$max (Saltin & Karlsson, 1971). The first step in glycogen degradation, the cleavage and phosphorylation of one glucose residue from glycogen to form glucose-1-phosphate (G-1-P), is controlled by the rate-limiting enzyme, glycogen phosphorylase (PHOS). PHOS exists as a less active *b* form and more active *a* form (Figure 1-7). PHOS *b* is phosphorylated to the *a* form by phosphorylase kinase and returned to the *b* form by phosphorylase phosphatase. The transformation from the less active *b* to more active *a* form occurs with the onset of exercise, due to a stimulation of phosphorylase kinase, primarily by Ca^{2+} and to a lesser extent by epinephrine (Chasiotis et al., 1982; Ren & Hultman, 1989; 1990). A second stage of control, which serves as a mechanism to "fine-tune" the flux through PHOS (both *a* and *b* forms), is related to the energy status of the cell. During the transition from rest to exercise, the temporary mismatch between ATP demand and aerobic ATP synthesis causes accumulations of free ADP, AMP, and P_i. These accumulations increase PHOS flux because free P_i is a substrate for the reaction and free AMP is an allosteric regulator of both forms of the enzyme (Figure 1-7). The flux through the PHOS reaction will be dominated by the *a* form, especially at the onset of intense aerobic exercise. However, the *b* form may become more important later in exercise, when the *a* form has decreased. Very little is presently known regarding the activity of the phosphatase responsible for returning PHOS back to the *b* form. Studies using short-term and long-term training (Green et al., 1992, 1995), fat infusion (Dyck et al., 1996), and caffeine ingestion (Chesley et al., 1998) have demonstrated that the exercise-induced accumulations of free

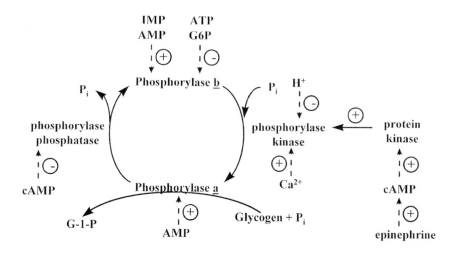

FIGURE 1-7. *Schematic diagram of proposed regulation of glycogen phosphorylase.* cAMP, cyclic AMP; G-1-P, glucose 1-phosphate.

AMP and P_i are blunted during exercise when glycogen sparing occurs. These changes appear to be related to increased fat oxidation and the interaction between fat and CHO fuel use, as discussed later.

PHOS transformation does not necessarily correlate with flux through the PHOS reaction during aerobic exercise (Chesley et al., 1995; Howlett et al., 1998; Ren & Hultman, 1990). It is important to note, however, that the catalytic activity of the transformed enzyme (PHOS a) is very large; as a result, potential flux through the PHOS reaction is almost always well in excess of the actual flux through the enzyme. In other words, the initial transformation of PHOS to the a form at the onset of exercise is in excess of what is needed. The accumulations of P_i and free AMP then "fine-tune" the actual flux to the demand for ATP. This apparent overshoot in PHOS transformation during aerobic exercise occurs because the flux rates required at these aerobic power outputs are less than 10% of that required during the high power outputs associated with maximal sprint exercise. In the sprint situation, the high flux through the PHOS reaction is required because anaerobic metabolism, i.e., substrate phosphorylation, provides a large portion of the consumed ATP. The processes involved in anaerobic ATP production are examined later in the chapter.

Pyruvate Dehydrogenase

In contracting muscle, glycolysis and glycogenolysis set the rates of glucose and glycogen utilization. However, the rate of CHO entry into the mitochondria and its subsequent oxidative metabolism are primarily regulated by the mitochondrial pyruvate dehydrogenase (PDH) complex, consisting of several enzymes. PDH, the regulated enzyme in the complex, exists in a non-active b form and an active a form (Figure 1-8). However, as opposed to PHOS, the inactive form of PDH is phosphorylated. The transformation of PDH is regulated by the balance between the activities of PDH kinase (deactivating) and PDH phosphatase (activating). PDH kinase is inhibited by pyruvate and high ratios of coenzyme A/acetyl-CoA and NAD/NADH and is stimulated by a high ATP/ADP ratio, whereas PDH phosphatase is stimulated by Ca^{2+} (Pettit et al., 1975; Reed, 1981; Wieland, 1983).

At rest, the high ratio of ATP/ADP and low ratio of coenzyme A/acetyl-CoA and low pyruvate concentration keep PDH kinase activated, and the low concentration of Ca^{2+} at rest keeps PDH phosphatase relatively inactive, resulting in a small amount of PDH in the a form. During exercise, increases in concentrations of Ca^{2+}, pyruvate, and ADP all work to increase the amount of PDH in the a form (Hultman, 1996). Ca^{2+} increases during muscle contraction to activate PDH phosphatase.

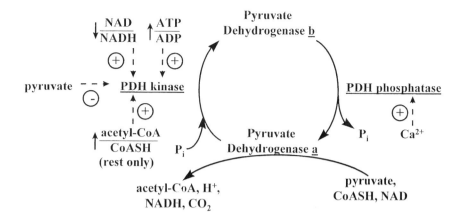

FIGURE 1-8. *Schematic diagram of proposed regulation of pyruvate dehydrogenase.*

The decrease in the ATP/ADP ratio during the transition from rest to exercise will inhibit PDH kinase. The increase in glycogenolysis, mediated by a fall in cellular energy state, increases pyruvate delivery. Because pyruvate is both an inhibitor of PDH kinase and a substrate for PDH, it increases PDH transformation and flux of pyruvate through the reaction (Figure 1-8). The rise in acetyl-CoA during exercise should oppose the transformation of PDH, but this rise appears to be largely overridden during exercise (Constantin-Teodosiu et al., 1991; Howlett et al., 1998). Finally, the relationship between the NAD/NADH ratio and PDH transformation is difficult to quantify due to the difficulty in measuring the mitochondrial redox state during exercise. Studies utilizing different methodologies have reported qualitatively different results for the redox state of exercising human skeletal muscle (Graham & Saltin, 1989; Sahlin et al., 1987). This problem will be discussed in a later section.

The activity of PDH *a* has been shown to be quantitatively similar to estimates of PDH flux under many conditions, including exercise at different power outputs (Howlett et al., 1998; Putman et al., 1995). Therefore, it is apparent that PDH transformation is synonymous with flux in most exercise situations. As contraction begins, Ca^{2+} increases PHOS transformation and flux and also stimulates PDH transformation and flux. The increase in PHOS flux increases the pyruvate concentration, further stimulating PDH, and increasing PDH flux. The exercise-induced fall in the energy state of the cell will then set the steady-state rate of glycogenolysis, and therefore pyruvate delivery, determining the rate of PDH flux and the rate of oxidative CHO metabolism.

REGULATION OF FAT METABOLISM

Fat is an important substrate for the production of ATP during most exercise situations. It provides reducing equivalents and acetyl-CoA in the beta-oxidation pathway and additional reducing equivalents when the acetyl-CoA is further metabolized in the TCA cycle. Fat is a very energy-dense fuel and is stored in large quantities in the body. During exercise, the predominant source of usable fat is in the form of long-chain, free fatty acids (FFA). Skeletal muscle does not have the ability to synthesize FFA de novo, either during exercise or in recovery following exercise. Therefore, during exercise, FFA are delivered to the muscle bound to albumin and are taken up from the blood into the cytoplasm (Vander Vusse & Reneman, 1996). FFA may also be released from the cytoplasmic store of muscle triacylglycerol (TGm) during exercise. The FFA are then delivered to the mitochondria, transported across the mitochondrial membranes and made available for beta-oxidation (Figure 1-1).

In resting situations, when there is a need to replenish the muscle TG store, i.e., following exercise and/or to remove fat from the circulation, i.e., following a meal, FFA appear to be derived mainly from TG that are present in the blood in the form of chylomicrons and very low-density lipoproteins (VLDL)(Vander Vusse & Reneman, 1996). The enzyme lipoprotein lipase (LPL) degrades the TG, and the muscle takes up the released FFA. Therefore, the majority of the FFA taken up during exercise are derived from albumin-bound FFA and during rest are from circulating TG via the action of LPL.

A common theme in skeletal muscle fat metabolism is the need to chaperon FFA molecules by binding them to proteins, as they are not soluble in aqueous media and can interfere with enzyme functioning and electrical conductance at high concentrations. Whereas the free fatty acids discussed in muscle metabolism are free in the sense that they are not bound to a glycerol backbone to form TG, only a very small proportion of the FFA in the blood and in the cells are actually "free" and not bound to some protein. To avoid this confusion, FFA are often referred to as non-esterified fatty acids. The regulation of FFA release from adipose tissue will not be covered in this chapter. However, recent reviews have examined the regulation of both FFA release from adipose tissue and fat metabolism in skeletal muscle (Richter et al., 1998;Turcotte et al., 1995; Vander Vusse & Reneman, 1996).

Fat Uptake by Muscle

It was once believed that FFA moved across the muscle membrane by simple diffusion. However, evidence now suggests that the majority of the FFA are transported across the muscle membrane by a carrier protein, like those for glucose and lactate transport (Kiens et al., 1993; Turcotte et al., 1991). The remainder of FFA movement into the cell is still believed to occur via diffusion into the muscles due to the lipophilic nature of FFA. The presence of a fat carrier protein in the muscle membrane that transports most of the FFA into muscle suggests that this is a potential site of regulation for fat metabolism. Proteins that are related to fat transport have been identified in rat skeletal muscle, and the transport of fat into muscle appears to be a saturable process (Bonen et al., 1998; Turcotte et al., 1991). However, physiological FFA concentrations (< 1 mM) are normally well below the level required (~1.5–2 mM) for saturation to occur. At present, very little is known regarding the regulation of this process in human skeletal muscle during certain exercise situations, and it is not known if movement of FFA into the cell limits fat oxidation.

Fat Transfer in the Cytoplasm

Once inside the cell, FFA are bound to a fatty acid binding protein (FABP), which appears responsible for transferring FFA to either the cytoplasmic (for storage as TGm) or mitochondrial (for oxidation) sites for further processing (Figure 1-1). FABP is present in almost all tissues, including human skeletal muscle. FABP increases in response to aerobic training, and its content is related to the oxidative capacity of the muscle (Peeters et al., 1989; 1991).

Regulation of Muscle Triacylglycerol Metabolism

A significant amount of fat is stored as TG in the cytoplasm of human skeletal muscle and usually has about the same total energetic value as stored glycogen. FFA can also be released from this source and made available to the mitochondria during exercise (Figure 1-1). Very little is known about the regulation of the muscle version of the enzyme TG lipase, which is responsible for TGm degradation. It is often assumed that the enzyme is covalently modulated between more and less active forms and regulated mainly via beta-adrenergic stimulation from outside the muscle (Langfort et al., 1998; Oscai et al., 1990). However, much of the known information comes from adipose tissue, in which a related enzyme, hormone sensitive lipase (HSL), is responsible for TG degradation. This external regulation would be atypical of key enzymes involved in providing substrate for ATP synthesis in muscle, as they are predominately regulated by intracellular signals, with external influences playing smaller roles. It would be expected that Ca^{2+} and metabolites related to the energy status of the cell would be involved in the activation of muscle TG lipase during exercise. However, this has not been demonstrated to date.

Much of the confusion regarding the control of muscle TG lipase during exercise stems from the uncertainty over when this enzyme is active. Some researchers have estimated substantial TGm use during 90 min of exercise at 60–65% $\dot{V}O_2$max in untrained and trained subjects (Hurley et al., 1986; Romijn et al., 1993). Others have been unable to measure net TGm degradation during exercise of similar duration and intensity (Kiens et al., 1993; Kiens & Richter, 1998; Starling et al., 1997; Wendling et al., 1996). A second problem involves isolating muscle TG lipase and studying its effects, as it is present in small amounts in muscle. Skeletal muscle also contains significant amounts of LPL and may have some adipose tissue between sections of the muscle. Therefore, TG lipase and LPL from muscle and LPL and HSL from adipose tissue may all be present in a given muscle tissue sample. The activity of TG lipase in rat skeletal muscle represents less than 5% of the HSL activity found in rat adipose tissue (Holm et al., 1987; Peters et al., 1998).

Fat Transport into the Mitochondria

All long-chain FFA, whether they originate from outside the cell or from TGm, are delivered to the mitochondria. They are then bound to coenzyme A through the action of a fatty acyl-CoA synthetase, which is also bound to the cytoplasmic side of the outer mitochondrial membrane (Figure 1-9). This process is called "activation" and puts the FFA into a form that can be transported into the mitochondria. Transport across the mitochondrial membranes is believed to be a highly regulated and rate-limiting step in the oxidation of long-chain FFA (McGarry & Brown, 1997).

The transport is L-carnitine dependent and catalyzed by the carnitine palmitoyltransferase (CPT) enzyme system, which consists of CPT I, carnitine-acylcarnitine translocase, and a mitochondrial form of CPT (CPT II). CPT I is located in the outer mitochondrial membrane and catalyzes the conversion of fatty acyl-CoA to acylcarnitine, which is then transported across the inner mitochondrial membrane via the carnitine-acylcarnitine translocase (Figure 1-9). The translocase acts as an antiport, allowing the simultaneous export of L-carnitine from the mitochondrial matrix. The acylcarnitine is reconverted into fatty acyl-CoA via CPT II on the matrix side of the inner mitochondrial membrane.

It has been well established, using test tube assays in a variety of tissues, that the activity of CPT I can be reversibly inhibited by malonyl-CoA (M-CoA), whereas CPT II is unaffected (Berthon et al., 1998; McGarry et al., 1983; Saggerson & Carpenter, 1981). In tissues that synthesize FFA de novo (e.g., adipose tissue), high glucose availability increases the M-CoA content because M-CoA is the first committed intermediate in this process. The high M-CoA concentration inhibits CPT I

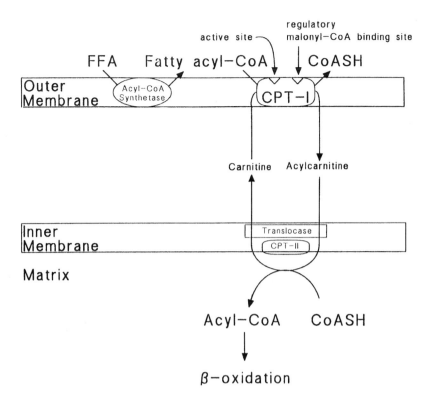

FIGURE 1-9. *Schematic diagram of proposed regulation of long-chain free fatty acid transport into the mitochondria.* CPT I and II, carnitine palmitoyltransferase I and II.

activity and FFA transport into the mitochondria. Therefore, when fat is being synthesized from CHO, fat use in the mitochondria is inhibited. The M-CoA inhibition of CPT I has also been hypothesized to be an important regulatory mechanism in skeletal muscle. At rest, M-CoA levels may be high enough to limit FFA transport into the mitochondria. During exercise, decreased M-CoA contents have been observed in rat skeletal muscle, suggesting that the decrease contributes to increased FFA transport and oxidation (Winder, et al., 1989, 1990). However, the importance of M-CoA in the regulation of CPT I activity in humans has been recently questioned because no consistent decreases in M-CoA contents were found in human skeletal muscle during cycling at 35% and 65% $\dot{V}O_2$max (Odland et al., 1996, 1998b). Respiratory exchange ratio and $\dot{V}O_2$ data suggested that fat oxidation increased several fold from rest to exercise at both power outputs.

Future experiments with intact mitochondria isolated from human skeletal muscle may be able to identify if regulators other than M-CoA are involved in the activation of CPT I during exercise (Berthon et al., 1998). It would be expected that the same "exercise" signals that activate other enzymes might be involved at this important regulatory site. Alternately, increases in substrate or molecular mechanisms that interfere with the ability of M-CoA to inhibit CPT I may explain the increased CPT I activity during exercise (Figure 1-9).

Beta-Oxidation

Once inside the mitochondria, fatty acyl CoA is degraded in the beta-oxidation pathway in a step-wise manner. Each pass through the four reactions of the beta-oxidation pathway produces a two-carbon acetyl-CoA molecule from the long-chain FFA with the production of one $FADH_2$ and one NADH. An 18 carbon FFA (e.g., stearic) provides 9 acetyl-CoA molecules for the TCA cycle, 8 $FADH_2$, and 8 NADH. Since each acetyl-CoA then provides 3 NADH and 1 $FADH_2$ in the TCA cycle, it is clear why one FFA ultimately provides so much ATP. It appears that all of the beta-oxidation enzymes are near-equilibrium in nature and are regulated only by the availability of their substrates, fatty acyl-CoA, FAD, NAD and coenzyme A (Newsholme & Leech, 1983). In other words, if fatty acyl-CoA is delivered to the mitochondrial matrix, beta-oxidation will proceed. This is why the regulation of fatty acyl-CoA delivery via CPT I is a key regulatory site for fat oxidation. The most commonly measured enzyme in the beta-oxidation pathway is 3-hydroxyacyl CoA dehydrogenase (HAD). An increase in HAD following aerobic training indicates an increased mitochondrial volume in the form of larger mitochondria and/or new mitochondria. Assuming that this enzyme is representative of the others in the beta-oxidation pathway implies that all enzymes in the pathway are increased following aerobic training.

COORDINATE REGULATION OF FAT AND CARBOHYDRATE METABOLISM

Fat and CHO combine to provide the fuel required for ATP production in human skeletal muscle during most intensities of aerobic exercise. The relative proportions of fat and CHO use during exercise vary and depend on the exercise intensity and duration, aerobic training status, dietary habits (CHO, fat and caffeine), ingestion of CHO prior to and during exercise, and, possibly, age and gender of the subject. For example, increasing the availability of fat during exercise increases fat oxidation and reduces CHO oxidation (Costill et al., 1977; Dyck et al., 1993; Hargreaves et al., 1991; Romijn et al., 1995), whereas increasing CHO availability increases CHO utilization and reduces fat oxidation (Coyle et al., 1997; Horowitz et al., 1997). Recent reviews have focused on the biochemical mechanisms that explain these shifts in fuel selection in exercising humans (Spriet & Dyck, 1996; Spriet & Odland, 1998).

As discussed above, two of the key regulatory enzymes responsible for substrate choice are PDH and CPT I, which control the entry of CHO and FFA into the mitochondria, respectively (Figure 1-1). Glycogen PHOS also plays an important role during moderate and intense exercise. The interaction between CHO and fat metabolism during exercise is believed to depend both on the availability of substrate and on the balance between the activities of these, and possibly other, key enzymes.

Glucose-Fatty Acid Cycle

Randle et al. (1963, 1964) provided the first information regarding the regulation of fat/CHO interaction in perfused, contracting heart muscle and incubated, resting diaphragm muscle. Using the findings from their isolated muscle experiments and test tube enzyme studies, they proposed a theory to explain the reciprocal relationship between fat and CHO metabolism, the glucose-fatty acid cycle (Figure 1-10). Briefly, increasing the availability of FFA to the muscle increased the delivery of FFA to the mitochondria and the rate of beta-oxidation, producing measurable increases in muscle acetyl-CoA and citrate contents.

Test tube studies demonstrated that acetyl-CoA inhibited PDH activity by activating PDH kinase, the enzyme that phosphorylates PDH to its less active form. Similar work identified citrate as a potent inhibitor of the cytoplasmic enzyme PFK, suggesting that citrate could inhibit PFK activity following transport into the cytoplasm. The combined effects of decreased PFK and PDH activities and, therefore, reduced flux through the glycolytic pathway, were an accumulation of the glycolytic intermediate G-6-P. The elevated G-6-P level was believed to inhibit hexokinase and ultimately decrease the uptake of glucose in some unexplained manner. Later work in contracting rodent skeletal muscle supported aspects of this theory (Rennie et al., 1976; Rennie & Holloszy, 1977).

Human Studies of Increased Fat Availability

In humans, increasing the availability of FFA to the working skeletal muscle demonstrated that CHO utilization was down-regulated primarily at the level of glycogen PHOS during exercise at 65% and 85% $\dot{V}O_2$max (Dyck et al., 1993; 1996; Odland et al., 1998a). Muscle glycogen use was decreased at these power outputs, whereas exogenous glucose uptake was unaffected at 40% and 65% $\dot{V}O_2$max (Odland et al., 1998a). The decreased glycogenolysis appeared to be mediated through reductions in the accumulations of free P_i and AMP, post-transformational regulators of the active form of PHOS. It is not understood how in-

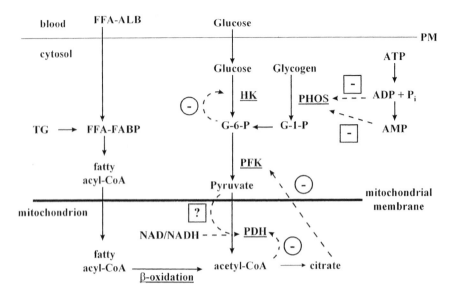

FIGURE 1-10. *Schematic of fat/carbohydrate interaction in skeletal muscle.* Circles depict control points of the classic glucose-fatty acid cycle. Squares represent proposed control points in human skeletal muscle. PM, plasma membrane; FFA, free fatty acid; ALB, albumin; FABP, fatty acid binding protein; HK, hexokinase; PFK, phosphofructokinase; PHOS, glycogen phosphorylase; PDH, pyruvate dehydrogenase; G-6-P and G-1-P, glucose 6- and 1-phosphate.

creased fat availability produces these changes (Figure 1-10). However, they may be due to a greater accumulation or availability of mitochondrial NADH in the presence of extra fat, which permits a better matching of ATP demand and aerobic ATP provision in the muscle cells during the transition from rest to exercise (Chesley et al., 1998; From et al., 1990). Consequently, less PCr degradation is required, and the signals that activate PHOS *a* in the muscle cell are less pronounced. Coordinate down-regulation of PDH transformation to PDH *a* also occurred at 40% and 65% $\dot{V}O_2$max, but not during intense aerobic exercise. Because concentrations of Ca^{2+}, acetyl-CoA, and ATP could not account for the reduction in PDH transformation, the factors that are responsible are presently unknown. Decreases in pyruvate and increases in NADH at the onset of exercise in the presence of extra fat may be responsible for greater PDH kinase activity and lower PDH *a* levels (Figure 1-10), but this will require further study.

Human Studies of Skeletal Muscle Malonyl-CoA

The transport of long-chain FFA into the mitochondria via CPT I appears to be another site controlling the interaction between fat and CHO metabolism in human skeletal muscle (Figure 1-9). M-CoA is a well-established inhibitor of CPT I activity and fatty acid oxidation in lipogenic tissues such as adipose tissue and liver and is produced in the cytoplasm by acetyl-CoA carboxylase (McGarry et al., 1983). When CHO supply is abundant and lipid is synthesized in these tissues, high levels of M-CoA inhibit CPT I activity and the transport of fat into the mitochondria. It also appears that M-CoA is a regulator of fatty acid oxidation in perfused working heart muscle (Saddik et al., 1993).

However, because skeletal muscle is not a lipogenic tissue, the role that M-CoA plays in regulating the entry of FFA into mitochondria during exercise is not clear. The unique aspect of skeletal muscle is that exercise requires a simultaneous increase in both fat and CHO oxidation to meet the large increase in energy demand. This is quite different than the reciprocal changes in CHO and fat oxidation that occur in other tissues and in resting skeletal muscle when the demand for ATP is constant.

In rodent skeletal muscle it has been suggested that resting M-CoA levels are high enough to inhibit excessive entry of FFA into the mitochondria. During treadmill running, when the demand for energy from both fat and CHO oxidation increased, M-CoA content decreased (Winder et al., 1989, 1990). This lead to the suggestion that the decreased M-CoA released CPT I inhibition and increased both FFA transport into the mitochondria and FFA oxidation during exercise. However, as discussed above, measurements of M-CoA in human skeletal muscle during exercise demonstrated that M-CoA was largely unaffected by exercise at all power outputs (Odland et al., 1996, 1998b). These results do not support the suggestion that decreases in the concentration of M-CoA are required to permit an increase in FFA transport and FFA oxidation during exercise. In addition, the human results also demonstrated that the decrease in fat oxidation at intense aerobic power outputs is not due to increases in M-CoA (Odland et al., 1998b). These findings suggest that the regulation of CPT I is more complex than control by a single regulator and/or that M-CoA may be an important regulator at rest, but not during exercise (Figure 1-9).

Human Studies of Increased Carbohydrate Availability

It should also be mentioned that many whole-body physiological studies have examined the effects of glucose ingestion prior to exercise on CHO and fat metabolism during exercise. Unfortunately, virtually no invasive biochemical work has been done in human skeletal muscle to explain the down-regulation of fat metabolism that occurs in these exercise situations. However, existing work suggests that major sites of control involve the release of FFA from adipose tissue and transport of FFA across the muscle and mitochondrial membranes (Coyle et al., 1997; Horowitz et al., 1997; Sidossis et al., 1997).

REGULATION OF ANAEROBIC ATP PRODUCTION

Aerobic metabolism provides the vast majority of ATP in most exercise situations. However, when aerobic metabolism is unable to provide ATP at the required rate, anaerobic ATP pathways are used to provide the remaining energy. The most common situations in which anaerobic ATP is required include the transition from rest to exercise, the transition from one power output to a higher power output, and exercise at power outputs that are greater than can be sustained with oxidative phosphorylation (i.e., > 100% $\dot{V}O_2$max). Anaerobic production of ATP (substrate phosphorylation) occurs via the degradation of PCr and by the glycogenolytic/glycolytic pathway with the production of lactate as described above in equations 4 and 5.

Phosphocreatine Degradation

Creatine kinase catalyzes the conversion of PCr and ADP to produce ATP (equation 4). It is an equilibrium enzyme and is present in the cytoplasm of human skeletal muscle in great amounts (Connett & Sahlin, 1996; Newsholme & Leech, 1983). This is consistent with its role as an ATP buffer (Figure 1-1). When ATP is degraded in the cytoplasm at the onset of exercise, increases in free ADP and decreases in ATP force the reaction in the direction of ATP production. The net reaction of ATP utilization and PCr breakdown is outlined in equation 9:

$$PCr + H^+ \rightarrow Cr + P_i \qquad (9)$$

Therefore, the buildup of P_i is directly related to the breakdown of PCr (minus the P_i that is bound to glycolytic intermediates). The PCr store in muscle is limited; normal resting levels are ~70–90 mmol/kg dry muscle (dm)(Dyck et al., 1996; Howlett et al., 1998). In the first minute of exercise at 35% $\dot{V}O_2$max, the mismatch between ATP demand and ATP provision from oxidative sources is small, and PCr decreases by ~10 mmol/kg dm (Figure 1-11). At higher aerobic power outputs of 65% and 90% $\dot{V}O_2$max, the decreases are ~30 and 45 mmol/kg dm (Howlett et al., 1998). As aerobic ATP production increases towards a steady state in the initial seconds and minutes of aerobic exercise, the magnitudes of the changes in ATP and free ADP are reduced, and PCr degradation is reduced or stops (Figures 1-11, 1-12 and 1-13). During exercise at power outputs above 100% $\dot{V}O_2$ max, the increase in free ADP and decrease in ATP are maintained, and PCr continues to be degraded until very little remains (McCartney et al., 1986; Putman et al., 1995). In maximal sprinting, the demand for ATP is so severe that PCr stores are nearly completely depleted, yet the muscle ATP concentrations decrease by only 25–40% (Figures 1-11 and 1-13). The large increases in free ADP and AMP activate the adenylate kinase and AMP deaminase reactions (equations 6 and 7), with the resultant production of NH_4^+ and IMP.

Lactate Production

The metabolism of CHO in the glycogenolytic/glycolytic pathway results in the production of pyruvate (Figure 1-5). The pyruvate is then metabolized in the cytoplasm or transported across the inner mitochondrial membrane and metabolized inside the mitochondria. The most important mitochondrial pathway of pyruvate metabolism is conversion to acetyl-CoA by PDH as discussed above. The acetyl-CoA is then available to enter the TCA cycle, resulting in the production of NADH and $FADH_2$ and ultimately ATP via oxidative phosphorylation. The oxidative use of 1 mmol glucose yields a large amount of energy, resulting in the production of ~39 mmol ATP. The most important cytoplasmic fate of pyruvate is conversion to lactate with the oxidation of NADH to NAD in the lactate dehydrogenase (LDH) reaction. This "anaerobic" use of CHO yields much less energy, as 1 mmol glucose provides only 2 (extramuscular glucose) or 3 mmol (muscle glycogen) of ATP.

Pyruvate can also combine with glutamate to form 2-oxoglutarate and alanine in the alanine aminotransferase reaction in the cytoplasm and to a minor extent in the mitochondria (Figure 1-5). This reaction appears to be important in the early stages of exercise to increase the content of the TCA cycle intermediates, but it accounts for only ~2–5% of pyruvate disposal (Gibala et al. 1997a, 1997a). Pyruvate carboxylase and malic enzyme are also present in the cytoplasm and compete for pyruvate but do not appear to be quantitatively important (Mole et al., 1973), although they have not been studied in human muscle. NADH, the other substrate for LDH, can also be reconverted to NAD in the cytoplasm via the near-equilibrium malate-aspartate and alpha-glycerophosphate shuttle systems (SS), which transfer reducing equivalents to the mitochondria (Figure 1-5). The malate-aspartate shuttle appears to be the quantitatively important system (Newsholme & Leech, 1983; Schantz et al., 1986).

Skeletal muscle LDH is present in two isoforms, a muscle form and a heart form, both of which favor the production of lactate. As a near-equilibrium enzyme, LDH is not under covalent or allosteric control, but is sensitive to the concentrations of its substrates and products. Therefore, increases in pyruvate and NADH increase the flux through LDH in human skeletal muscle.

Lactate is generally produced and accumulated in human skeletal

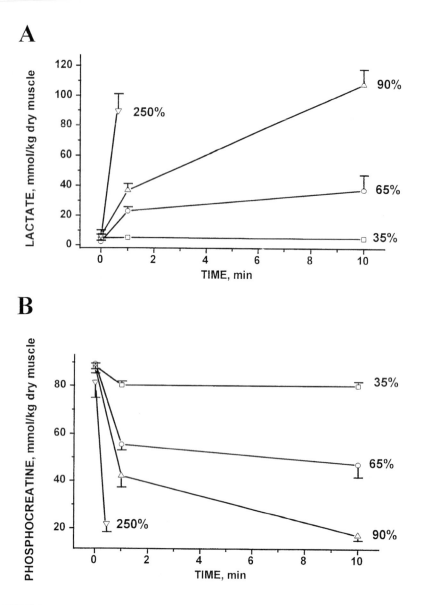

FIGURE 1-11. *Human skeletal muscle contents of lactate (A) and phosphocreatine (B) during cycling for 10 min at varying power outputs (35–90% VO₂max) and 30s at 250% VO₂max.* Data are means ± SE and were redrawn from Howlett et al., 1988; Putman et al., 1995, and Spriet et al., 1989.

A

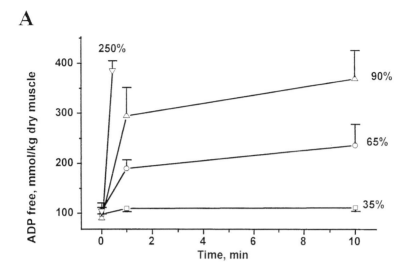

B

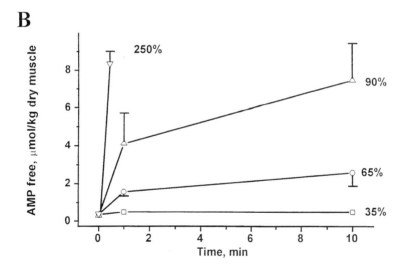

FIGURE 1-12. *Human skeletal muscle contents of free ADP (A) and free AMP (B) during cycling for 10 min at varying power outputs (35–90% V̇O₂max) and 30s at 250% V̇O₂max.* Data are means ± SE and were redrawn from Howlett et al., 1988; Putman et al., 1995, and Spriet et al., 1989. Free ADP and AMP were calculated as described by Dudley et al., 1987.

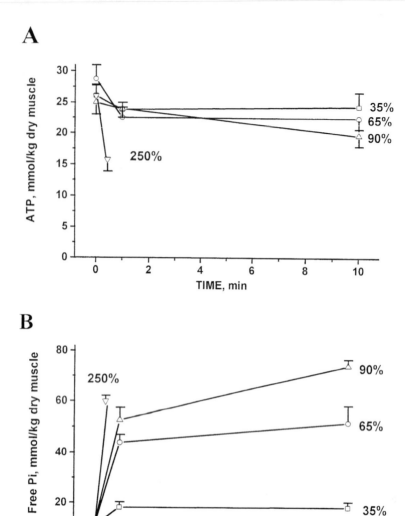

FIGURE 1-13. *Human skeletal muscle contents of ATP (A) and free inorganic phosphate (P$_i$) (B) during cycling for 10 min at varying power outputs (35–90% V̇O$_2$max) and 30s at 250% V̇O$_2$max. Data are means ± SE and were redrawn from Howlett et al., 1988; Putman et al., 1995, and Spriet et al., 1989.*

muscle as a function of increasing exercise power output (Figure 1-11). The rate of lactate production in skeletal muscle at any power output will depend mainly on the flux of substrate through the glycogenolytic/glycolytic pathway and on the relative activities of the SS and the PDH and LDH pathways of pyruvate metabolism (Figure 1-5). Generally, the greater the demand for ATP, the greater the increase in free Pi and AMP and the greater the activation of the enzymes that regulate glycogenolytic/glycolytic flux (Figures 1-12 and 1-13). During exercise at low power outputs, the demand for ATP, the glycolytic flux, and the rate of pyruvate production are all low, and most of the pyruvate is converted to acetyl-CoA in the mitochondria in the PDH reaction. The reducing equivalents (NADH) produced in the glycolytic pathway are also transferred across the mitochondrial membrane via the SS. Therefore, with both substrates of the LDH reaction low, the production of lactate is minimal (Figure 1-11).

At higher aerobic power outputs, with a higher demand for ATP, activation of the glycolytic pathway increases due to Ca^{2+} release and accumulations of ADP, AMP and P_i (Figures 1-12 and 1-13). As the rates of pyruvate and NADH production exceed the ability of PDH to metabolize pyruvate and/or the ability of SS to transfer reducing equivalents into the mitochondria, lactate will be produced (Figure 1-11). However, the situation during power outputs above 100% $\dot{V}O_2$max is very different. These power outputs cannot be sustained solely by aerobic ATP production. The ATP that cannot be provided aerobically must be generated anaerobically via substrate phosphorylation from the degradation of PCr and in the glycolytic pathway with the conversion of glycogen to lactate. Therefore, the demand on the glycogenolytic/glycolytic pathway is not only to produce pyruvate for aerobic ATP production but also for anaerobic ATP provision.

Although the yield of anaerobic ATP production from the conversion of stored glycogen to lactate is low, the rate of ATP production that can be achieved is much higher than that of CHO-derived aerobic ATP production. For this to be true, the flux through the glycogenolytic/glycolytic pathway must be substantially higher than during aerobic exercise. This results in pyruvate and NADH production rates that are much higher than can be handled in the PDH and SS reactions, respectively, and lactate and NAD must be produced by LDH. Because the sum of cytoplasmic NAD and NADH is fixed, the regeneration of NAD is important for sustained high glycolytic flux; the NAD is reutilized higher up in the pathway (glyceraldehyde phosphate dehydrogenase reaction) (Figure 1-5). The produced lactate accumulates in the muscle, and some is transported out of the cell.

The examples above show how the glycogenolytic/glycolytic pathway must be sensitive to extremes in demand, i.e., the low flux of aerobic exercise and the very high flux of sprint exercise. The maximal activities of PHOS and PFK measured in the test tube are very high, and flux through these reactions approaches the maximal activities of PHOS and PFK during maximal sprint exercise. Conversely, since the test tube maximal activities of the enzymes involved only in aerobic metabolism (SS and PDH) are much lower, flux rates approach the maximal activities of SS and PDH during exercise at high aerobic power outputs.

It has been argued that lactate production occurs only in response to situations where the muscle cell lacks sufficient O_2 to metabolize pyruvate and fat in the mitochondria (Katz & Sahlin, 1988). Others have maintained that lactate production at the onset of intense aerobic exercise (65–100% $\dot{V}O_2$max) is not related to the availability of O_2 but to slow activation of the metabolic pathways (e.g., PDH activation, TCA cycle, beta-oxidation) that provide substrate for aerobic ATP production (Howlett et al., 1998; Timmons et al., 1998). An additional interpretation is that lactate production is unrelated to O_2 availability and is simply a required by-product of glycolytic flux (Connett et al., 1984). A portion of the produced pyruvate would always be converted to lactate via LDH, regardless of the rate of pyruvate production in a mass action manner. At low intensities and glycolytic flux, lactate production would be hard to detect. At higher power outputs with higher glycolytic flux, the lactate production would be substantial. In these situations, it is important to remember that lactate production may result from more than one of these causes, especially when muscle fiber-type differences are considered.

It must also be remembered that although lactate production is ultimately related to the activities of the various enzymes in the glycolytic pathway and in the SS and the PDH complexes, events in the mitochondria at all power outputs determine how active the glycolytic pathway needs to be to assist in meeting the demand for energy (Figure 1-1). Some evidence indicates that following aerobic training (with or without increased mitochondrial density), lactate production at a given submaximal power output is reduced (Chesley et al., 1996; Green et al., 1992; Holloszy & Coyle, 1984; Spina et al., 1996). In other words, the increase in glycolytic flux and resulting lactate production at the onset of exercise and during sustained aerobic exercise at a given submaximal power output is reduced. PCr degradation, glycogen utilization, and the accumulations of the byproducts of ATP breakdown are reduced consequent to an increased ability to oxidize fat and/or provide O_2 to the mitochondria following short-term and prolonged aerobic training with increased mitochondrial density (Chesley et al., 1996; Holloszy & Coyle, 1984; Spina et al., 1996). These same metabolic changes are present during intense aerobic exercise following acute perturbations (short-term training, increased fat availability, caffeine ingestion) that appear to increase fat metabolism and/or NADH provision, when no changes in mitochondrial density have occurred (Chesley et al., 1998; Dyck et al., 1996; Green et al., 1992).

FACTORS LIMITING THE STUDY OF MUSCLE METABOLISM: DIRECTIONS FOR FUTURE RESEARCH

It was mentioned at the outset of this chapter that there are several limitations that must be kept in mind when studying human skeletal muscle metabolism. These are associated with the needle biopsy and NMR techniques for examining metabolism. However, there are other, more global concerns or limitations that are related to the study of metabolism in general, especially regarding the signals that govern ATP supply and demand. These include the assumptions associated with estimating free ADP and AMP concentrations, the difficulty in estimating the mitochondrial redox state, the inability to differentiate between mitochondrial and cytoplasmic metabolite levels, the difficulty in explaining why metabolic processes stop when exercise ceases, and the use of enzyme kinetic information from test tube studies to predict enzyme and pathway behavior in the intact cell. Each of these issues should prove to be a fertile area of future research.

Estimation of Free ADP and AMP

The concentrations of total muscle ADP and AMP are sufficiently high to permit biochemical measurement. However, it appears that the majority of ADP and AMP is bound to proteins in the muscle cell, leaving the actual free concentrations difficult to measure. Therefore, the free, and metabolically active, cytoplasmic levels are normally calculated. The near-equilibrium nature of CK and adenylate kinase permits the use of these reactions to calculate free ADP and AMP concentrations in the intact cell (Dudley et al., 1987; Lawson & Veech, 1979). Typically, muscle levels of PCr, ATP, and Cr are measured, and H^+ concentration is predicted from the regression equation of muscle lactate and H^+ (Sahlin et al., 1976). These values and the equilibrium constant (1.66×10^{-9}) are used in the CK reaction (equation 4) to calculate the free ADP concentration. The free AMP can then be estimated using the calculated free ADP, the measured ATP concentration, and the equilibrium constant (1.05) in the adenylate kinase reaction (equation 6). Even with these calculations, no specific information exists regarding the exact location of free ADP and AMP in muscle. Future research should be directed toward obtaining this information.

Compartmentalization of Metabolites

A serious limitation to understanding metabolic control in skeletal muscle is the lack of information regarding the mitochondrial and cytoplasmic concentrations of many metabolites, and more research effort is warranted to address this problem. Certain enzymes and metabolites are believed to be specific to one compartment, but many exist in both major compartments. If these compounds are regulatory, we have no idea what the correct concentration is in either compartment as measured levels simply represent averages of both compartments. Examples of this problem are acetyl-CoA, free CoA, malonyl-CoA, citrate, and the other TCA cycle metabolites, many of which are believed to exist in both the mitochondrial and cytoplasmic compartments.

Mitochondrial NAD/NADH

Perhaps the greatest concern associated with the compartment problem is an inability to measure the compartment concentrations of NAD and NADH and, therefore, the inability to establish the NAD/NADH ratio in the mitochondria. Several approaches have been used to estimate the mitochondrial NAD/NADH ratio, with very little agreement, even with respect to qualitative changes during exercise. The glutamate dehydrogenase reaction, which is confined to the mitochondrial space and is assumed to be in equilibrium, has been used to estimate the muscle NAD/NADH ratio. A substantial increase in the NAD/NADH ratio was reported in human skeletal muscle during cycling (75% and 100% $\dot{V}O_2$max) (Graham & Saltin, 1989). In contrast, Duhaylongsod et al. (1993) monitored redox state in stimulated canine gracilis muscle using near-infrared spectroscopy and reported a decreased NAD/NADH ratio at all power outputs. Furthermore, NADH measured in human muscle has been shown to decrease at 45% $\dot{V}O_2$max and to increase at higher power outputs (Sahlin et al., 1987). Therefore, until an accepted method for measuring or estimating mitochondrial NAD/NADH ratio is developed through future research, the exact importance of these compounds in regulating energy metabolism will remain unclear.

SUMMARY

Human skeletal muscle is capable of producing energy (ATP) at very high rates to support physical activity over a wide range of intensities. The intensity of the exercise determines the rate of ATP utilization that is required to support movement. If cellular homeostasis is to be maintained within an acceptable range during exercise (constant ATP concentration), ATP synthesis must quickly match the rate of ATP utilization. In most exercise situations, a precise matching of ATP demand and synthesis is accomplished. Even during maximal sprint exercise, muscle ATP levels decrease by only 25–40%.

Fat and carbohydrate provide the vast majority of the metabolic fuel used to resynthesize ATP during physical activity. Both fat and carbohydrate are stored in human skeletal muscle and in other locations in the body. Ultimately, these fuels provide substrate for the electron transport process, which combines with the process of oxidative phosphorylation to synthesize ATP in the mitochondria. Carbohydrate plus muscle stores of phosphocreatine can also provide energy without the use of oxygen through substrate phosphorylation (anaerobic ATP synthesis).

Three classes of signals appear to play the major roles in activating the energy producing pathways in human skeletal muscle. They are Ca^{2+}, metabolites related to the energy status or phosphorylation potential of the cell, and the reduction/oxidation (redox) state of the cell (NADH/NAD). Ca^{2+} release initiates muscle contraction and activates metabolism in a feed-forward or "early warning" manner. The energy status of the muscle cell (ATP, free ADP, free AMP, and Pi) is altered as soon as muscle contractions begin. ATP is degraded, and the accumulations of these metabolites activate the enzymes and pathways that resynthesize the ATP in a feedback manner. The redox state of the muscle is also important for energy metabolism as NADH is a required substrate for the electron transport chain and the redox couple is involved in numerous reactions in substrate/product or activator/inhibitor capacities. These contraction-related signals that activate metabolism during exercise target the non-equilibrium, regulatory enzymes in the various pathways of energy metabolism, and the increased flux through these enzymes provides substrates which activate the near-equilibrium enzymes in the pathways.

The metabolic events occurring in the mitochondria of skeletal muscle cells not only provide the majority of the required ATP for physical activity but also determine when the anaerobic pathways of ATP synthesis are activated. Whenever mitochondrial ATP synthesis is less than the rate of ATP utilization, signals related to the energy status of the cell will activate creatine kinase to provide ATP from phosphocreatine and activate the glycogenolytic pathway to produce ATP. These "anaerobic processes" can provide ATP at very high rates for exercise at high power outputs, but only for very short periods of time. Most commonly, anaerobic ATP is needed at the onset of exercise and during exercise at power outputs above that required to elicit 100% $\dot{V}O_2$max.

The present state of knowledge in the field of human skeletal muscle metabolism is limited by the inability to make critical measurements during exercise. Numerous technical advancements will be required to obtain new insights into the control of energy production. These include direct measurements of the free forms of metabolically active compounds and measurements of metabolic compounds in the cytoplasmic and mitochondrial compartments of the entire muscle and in individual fibers.

BIBLIOGRAPHY

Bangsbo, J., T. Graham, L. Johansen, S, Strange, C. Christensen, and B. Saltin (1992). Elevated muscle acidity and energy production during exhaustive exercise in humans. *Amer. J. Physiol.* 263: R891–R899.

Bergstrom, J., E. Hultman, L. Jorfeldt, B. Pernow, and J. Wahren (1969). Effect of nicotinic acid on physical working capacity and on metabolism of muscle glycogen in man. *J. Appl. Physiol.* 26:170–176.

Berthon, P.M., R.A. Howlett, G.J.F. Heigenhauser, and L.L. Spriet (1998). Human skeletal muscle carnitine palmitoyltransferase I activity determined in isolated intact mitochondria. *J. Appl. Physiol.* 85: 148–153.

Bloomstrand, E., B. Ekblom, and E.A. Newsholme (1986). Maximal activities of key glycolytic and oxidative enzymes in human skeletal muscle from differently trained individuals. *J. Physiol.* 381: 111–118.

Bock, P.E., and C. Frieden (1976). Phosphofructokinase I: Mechanism of the pH-dependent inactivation and reactivation of the rabbit skeletal muscle enzyme. *J. Biol. Chem.* 251: 5630–5636.

Bonen, A., S. Liu, D.J. Dyck, B. Kiens, S. Kristiansen, J.J.F.P. Luiken, G.J. Vander Vusse, and J.F.C. Glatz (1998). Palmitate transport and fatty acid transporters in red and white muscles. *Amer. J. Physiol.* 275: E471–E478.

Brand, M.D., and M.P. Murphy (1987). Control of electron flux through the respiratory chain in mitochondria and cells. *Biol. Rev.* 62: 141–193.

Casey, A., D. Constantin-Teodosiu, S. Howell, E. Hultman, and P.L. Greenhaff (1996). Metabolic response of type I and II muscle fibers during repeated bouts of maximal exercise in humans. *Amer. J. Physiol.* 271: E38–E43.

Chance, B., and B. Quistorff (1978). Study of tissue oxygen gradients by single and multiple indicators. *Adv. Exp. Med. Biol.* 94: 331–338.

Chasiotis, D., K. Sahlin, and E. Hultman (1982). Regulation of glycogenolysis in human skeletal muscle at rest and during exercise. *J. Appl. Physiol.* 53: 708–715.

Chesley, A., G.J.F. Heigenhauser, and L.L. Spriet (1996). Regulation of muscle glycogen phosphorylase activity following short-term endurance training. *Amer. J. Physiol.* 270: E328–E335.

Chesley, A., R.A. Howlett, G.J.F. Heigenhauser, E. Hultman, and L.L. Spriet (1998). Regulation of muscle glycogenolytic flux during intense aerobic exercise following caffeine ingestion. *Amer. J. Physiol.* 275:R596–R603.

Chesley, A., E. Hultman, and L.L. Spriet (1995). Effects of epinephrine infusion on muscle glycogenolysis during intense aerobic exercise. *Amer. J. Physiol.* 268: E127–E134.

Connett, R.J, and K. Sahlin (1996). Control of glycolysis and glycogen metabolism. In: L.B. Rowell and J.T. Shepherd (eds.) *Handbook of Physiology, Section 12, Exercise: Regulation and Integration of Multiple Systems.* New York: Oxford University Press, pp. 870–911.

Connett, R.J., T.E. Gayeski, and C.R. Honig (1984). Lactate accumulation in fully aerobic, working, dog gracilis muscle. *Amer. J. Physiol.* 246: H120–H128.

Constantin-Teodosiu, D., G. Cederblad, and E. Hultman (1991). Acetyl group accumulation and pyruvate dehydrogenase activity in human muscle during incremental exercise. *Acta Physiol. Scand.* 143: 367–372.

Costill, D.L., E. Coyle, G. Dalsky, W. Evans, W. Fink, and D. Hoops (1977). Effects of elevated plasma FFA and insulin on muscle glycogen usage during exercise. *J. Appl. Physiol.* 43: 695–699.

Coyle, E.F., A.E. Jeukendrup, A.J.M. Wagenmakers, and W.H.M. Saris (1997). Fatty acid oxidation is directly regulated by carbohydrate metabolism during exercise. *Amer. J. Physiol.* 273: E268–E275.

Dela, F., A. Handberg, K.J. Mikines, J. Vinten, and H. Galbo (1993). GLUT 4 and insulin receptor binding and kinase activity in trained human muscle. *J. Physiol.* 469: 615–624.

Dudley, G.A., P.C. Tullson, and R.L. Terjung (1987). Influence of mitochondrial content on the sensitivity of respiratory control. *J. Biol. Chem.* 262: 9109–9114.

Duhaylongsod, F.G., J.A. Griebel, D.S. Bacon, W.G. Wolfe, and A. Piantadosi (1993). Effects of muscle contraction on cytochrome a,a^3 redox state. *J. Appl. Physiol.* 75: 790–797.

Dyck, D.J., S.J. Peters, P.S. Wendling, A. Chesley, E. Hultman, and L.L. Spriet (1996). Regulation of muscle glycogen phosphorylase activity during intense aerobic cycling with elevated FFA. *Amer. J. Physiol.* 270: E116–E125.

Dyck, D.J., C.T. Putman, G.J.F. Heigenhauser, E. Hultman, and L.L. Spriet (1993). Regulation of fat-carbohydrate interaction in skeletal muscle during intense aerobic cycling. *Amer. J. Physiol.* 265: E852–E859.

Erecinska, M., and D.F. Wilson (1982). Regulation of cellular energy metabolism. *J. Memb. Biol.* 70: 1–14.

From, A.H.L., S.D. Zimmer, S.P. Michurski, P. Mohanakrishnan, V.K. Ulstad, W.J. Thoma, and K. Ugurbil (1990). Regulation of the oxidative phosphorylation rate in the intact cell. *Biochem.* 29: 3731–3743.

Gibala, M.J., D.A. MacLean, T.E. Graham, and B. Saltin (1997a). Anaplerotic processes in human skeletal muscle during brief dynamic exercise. *J. Physiol.* 502.3: 703–713.

Gibala, M.J., M.A. Tarnopolsky, and T.E. Graham (1997b). Tricarboxylic acid cycle intermediates in human skeletal muscle at rest and during prolonged cycling. *Amer. J. Physiol.* 272: E239–E344.

Graham, T.E., and B. Saltin (1989). Estimation of mitochondrial redox state in human skeletal muscle during exercise. *J. Appl. Physiol.* 66: 561–566.

Green, H.J., R. Helyar, M. Ball-Burnett, B. Farrance, and D. Ranney (1992). Metabolic adaptations to training precede changes in muscle mitochondrial capacity. *J. Appl. Physiol.* 72: 484–491.

Green, H.J., S. Jones, M. Ball-Burnett, B. Farrance, and D. Ranney (1995). Adaptations in muscle metabolism to prolonged voluntary exercise and training. *J. Appl. Physiol.* 78: 138–145.

Greenhaff, P.L., J.-M. Ren, K. Soderlund, and E. Hultman (1991). Energy metabolism in single human muscle fibers during contraction without and with epinephrine infusion. *Amer. J. Physiol.* 260: E713–E718.

Hargreaves, M. (ed.) (1995). *Exercise Metabolism.* Windsor: Human Kinetics.

Hargreaves, M., and M. Thompson (eds.) (1988). *Biochemistry of Exercise X.* Windsor: Human Kinetics.

Hargreaves, M., B. Kiens, and E.A. Richter (1991). Effect of plasma free fatty acid concentration on muscle metabolism in exercising men. *J. Appl. Physiol.* 70: 194–210.

Henneman, E. (1957). Relation between size of neurons and their susceptibility to discharge. *Science* 126: 1345–1347.

Holloszy, J.O., and E.F. Coyle (1984). Adaptations of skeletal muscle to endurance exercise and their metabolic consequences. *J. Appl. Physiol.* 56: 831–838.

Holm, C., P. Belfrage, and G. Fredrikson (1987). Immunological evidence for the presence of hormone sensitive lipase in rat tissues other than adipose tissue. *Biochem. Biophys. Res. Commun.* 148: 99–105.

Horowitz, J.F., R. Mora-Rodriguez, L.O. Byerley, and E.F. Coyle (1997). Lipolytic suppression following carbohydrate ingestion limits fat oxidation during exercise. *Amer. J. Physiol.* 273: E768–E775.

Howlett, R.A., M.L. Parolin, D.J. Dyck, E. Hultman, N.L. Jones, G.J.F. Heigenhauser, and L.L. Spriet (1998). Regulation of skeletal muscle glycogen phosphorylase and pyruvate dehydrogenase at varying power outputs. *Am. J. Physiol.* 275: R418–R425.

Hultman, E. (1996). Pyruvate dehydrogenase as a regulator of substrate utilization in skeletal muscle. In: R.J. Maughan and S.M. Shirreffs (eds.) *Biochemistry of Exercise IX* Windsor: Human Kinetics, pp. 157–172.

Hurley, B.F., P.M. Nemeth, W.H. Martin, J.M. Hagberg, G.P. Dalsky, and J.O. Holloszy (1993). Muscle triglyceride utilization during exercise: effect of training. *J. Appl. Physiol.* 60: 562–567.

James, D.E. (1995). The mammalian facilitative glucose transporter family. *News Physiol. Sci.* 10: 67–71.

Katz, A., and K. Sahlin (1988). Regulation of lactic acid production during exercise. *J. Appl. Physiol.* 65: 509–518.

Katz, A., S. Broberg, K. Sahlin, and J. Wahren (1986). Leg glucose uptake during maximal dynamic exercise in humans. *Amer. J. Physiol.* 251: E65–E70.

Kiens, B., and E.A Richter (1998). Utilization of skeletal muscle triacylglycerol during postexercise recovery in humans. *Amer. J. Physiol.* 275: E332–E337.

Kiens, B., B. Essen-Gustavsson, N.J. Christensen, and B. Saltin (1993). Skeletal muscle substrate utilization during submaximal exercise in man. Effect of training. *J. Physiol.* 469: 459–478.

Kushmerick, M.J. (1983). Energetics of muscle contraction. In: L.D. Peachey, R.H. Adrian, and S.R. Geiger (eds.) *Handbook of Physiology, Skeletal Muscle* Bethesda: American Physiological Society, pp. 315–353.

Langfort, J., T. Ploug, J. Ihlemann, L.H. Enevoldsen, B. Stallknecht, M. Saldo, M. Kjaer, C. Holm, and H. Galbo (1998). Hormone-sensitive lipase (HSL) expression and regulation in skeletal muscle. In: Richter, E.A., B. Kiens, H. Galbo and B. Saltin (eds.) *Skeletal Muscle Metabolism in Exercise and Diabetes* New York: Plenum, pp. 219–228.

Lawson, J.W.R., and R.L. Veech (1979). Effects of pH and free Mg^{2+} on the Keq of the creatine kinase and other phosphate hydrolyses and phosphate transferases. *J. Biol. Chem.* 254:6528–6537.

Lowry, C.V., J.S. Kimmey, S. Felder, M. M.-Y. Chi, K.K. Kaiser, P.N. Passonneau, K.A. Kirk, and O.H. Lowry (1978). Enzyme patterns in single muscle fibers. *J. Biol. Chem.* 253: 8269–8277.

McCormack, J.G., and R.M. Denton (1986). Ca^{2+} as a second messenger within mitochondria. *Trends in Biochem. Sci.* 11: 258–262.

METABOLIC CONTROL OF ENERGY **41**

Maughan, R., and S.M. Shirreffs (eds.) (1996). *Biochemistry of Exercise IX.* Windsor: Human Kinetics.

Maughan, R., M. Gleeson, and P.L. Greenhaff (1997). *Biochemistry of Exercise and Training.* New York: Oxford University Press.

McCartney, N., G.J.F. Heigenhauser, and N.L. Jones (1983). Power output and fatigue of human muscle in maximal cycling exercise. *J. Appl. Physiol.* 55:218–224.

McCartney, N., L.L. Spriet, G.J.F. Heigenhauser, J.M. Kowalchuk, J. R. Sutton, and N.L. Jones (1986). Muscle power and metabolism in maximal intermittent exercise. *J. Appl. Physiol.* 60: 1164–1169.

McGarry, J.D., and N.F. Brown (1997). The mitochondrial carnitine palmitoyltransferase system. From concept to molecular analysis. *Eur. J. Biochem.* 244: 1–14.

McGarry, J.D., S.E. Mills, C.S. Long, and D.W. Foster (1983). Observations on the affinity for carnitine, and malonyl-CoA sensitivity, of carnitine palmitoyltransferase-I in animal and human tissues. *Biochem. J.* 214: 21–28.

Meyer, R.A, and J.M. Foley (1996). Cellular processes integrating the metabolic response to exercise. In: L.B. Rowell, and J.T. Shepherd (eds.) *Handbook of Physiology, Section 12, Exercise: Regulation and Integration of Multiple Systems.* New York: Oxford University Press, pp. 841–869.

Mole, P.A., K.M. Baldwin, R.L. Terjung, and J.O. Holloszy (1973). Enzymatic pathways of pyruvate metabolism in skeletal muscle: adaptations to exercise. *Amer. J. Physiol.* 224: 50–54.

Mueckler, M.M. (1995). Glucose transport and glucose homeostasis: Insights from transgenic mice. *News Physiol. Sci.* 10: 22–29.

Newsholme, E.A., and A.R. Leech (1983) *Biochemistry for the Medical Sciences* Toronto: Wiley.

Nicholls, D.G., and S.J. Ferguson (1992). *Bioenergetics 2.* Toronto: Academic Press.

Odland, L.M., G.J.F. Heigenhauser, G.D. Lopaschuk, and L.L. Spriet (1996). Human skeletal muscle malonyl-CoA at rest and during prolonged submaximal exercise. *Amer. J. Physiol.* 270: E541–E544.

Odland, L.M., G.J.F. Heigenhauser, D. Wong, M. G. Hollidge-Horvat, and L.L. Spriet (1998a). Effects of increased fat availability on fat-carbohydrate interaction during prolonged exercise in men. *Amer. J. Physiol.* 275: R894–R902.

Odland, L.M., R.A. Howlett, G.J.F. Heigenhauser, E. Hultman, and L.L. Spriet (1998b). Skeletal muscle malonyl-CoA content at the onset of exercise at varying power outputs in humans. *Amer. J. Physiol.* 274: E1080–E1085.

Oscai, L.B., D.A. Essig, and W.K. Palmer (1990). Lipase regulation of muscle triglyceride hydrolysis. *J. Appl. Physiol.* 60: 562– 567.

Peeters, R.A., M.A. In't Groen, and J.H. Veerkamp (1989). The fatty acid-binding protein from human skeletal muscle. *Arch. Biochem. Biophys.* 274:556–563.

Peeters, R.A., J.H. Veerkamp, A.J. Van Kessel, T. Kanda, and T. Ono (1991). Cloning of the cDNA encoding human skeletal- muscle fatty-acid binding protein, its peptide sequence and chromosomal localization. *Biochem. J.* 276: 203–207.

Peters, S.J., D.J. Dyck, A. Bonen, and L.L. Spriet (1998). Effects of epinephrine on lipid metabolism in resting skeletal muscle. *Amer. J. Physiol.* 275: E300–E309.

Pettit, F.H., J.W. Pelley, and L.J. Reed (1975). Regulation of pyruvate dehydrogenase kinase and phosphatase by acetyl-CoA/CoA and NADH/NAD+ ratios. *Biochem. Biophys. Res. Commun.* 65: 575–582.

Phillips, S.M., X.-X. Han, H.J. Green, and A. Bonen (1996). Increments in skeletal muscle GLUT-1 and GLUT-4 after endurance training in humans. *Amer. J. Physiol.* 270: E456–E462.

Putman, C.T., N.L. Jones, L.C. Lands, T.M. Bragg, M.G. Hollidge-Horvat, and G.J.F. Heigenhauser (1995). Skeletal muscle pyruvate dehydrogenase activity during maximal exercise in humans. *Amer. J. Physiol.* 269: E458–E468.

Putman, C.T., L.L. Spriet, E. Hultman, M.I. Lindinger, L.C. Lands, R.S. McKelvie, G, Cederblad, N.L. Jones, and G,J. F. Heigenhauser (1993). Pyruvate dehydrogenase activity and acetyl group accumulation during exercise after different diets. *Amer. J. Physiol.* 265: E752–E760.

Rall, J.A. (1985). Energetic aspects of skeletal muscle contraction: implication of fiber types. *Exerc. Sport Sci. Rev.* 13: 33–74.

Randle, P.J., C.N. Hales, P.B. Garland, and E.A. Newsholme (1963). The glucose fatty-acid cycle. Its role in insulin sensitivity and the metabolic disturbances of diabetes mellitus. *Lancet* I: 785–789.

Randle, P.J., E.A. Newsholme, and P.B. Garland (1964). Regulation of glucose uptake by muscle. 8. Effects of fatty acids, ketone bodies and pyruvate, and of alloxan-diabetes and starvation, on the uptake and metabolic fate of glucose in rat heart and diaphragm muscles. *Biochem. J.* 93: 652–665.

Reed, L.J. (1981). Regulation of pyruvate dehydrogenase complex by a phosphorylation-dephosphorylation cycle. *Curr. Top. Cell. Reg.* 8: 95–106.

Ren, J.M., and E. Hultman (1988). Phosphorylase activity in needle biopsy samples—factors influencing transformation. *Acta Physiol. Scand.* 133:109–144.

Ren, J.M., and E. Hultman (1989). Regulation of glycogenolysis in human skeletal muscle. *J. Appl. Physiol.* 67: 2243–2248.

Ren, J.M., and E. Hultman (1990). Regulation of phosphorylase-a activity in human skeletal muscle. *J. Appl. Physiol.* 69: 919–923.

Rennie, M.J., and J.O. Holloszy (1997). Inhibition of glucose uptake and glycogenolysis by availability of oleate in well-oxygenated perfused skeletal muscle. *Biochem. J.* 168: 161–170.

Rennie, M.J., W.W. Winder, and J.O. Holloszy (1976). A sparing effect of increased plasma fatty acids on muscle and liver glycogen content in the exercising rat. *Biochem. J.* 156: 647–655.

Richter, E.A. (1996). Glucose Utilization. In: L.B. Rowell and J.T. Shepherd (eds.) *Handbook of Physiology, Section 12, Exercise: Regulation and Integration of Multiple Systems.* New York: Oxford University Press, pp. 912–951.

Richter, E.A., B. Kiens, H, Galbo, and B. Saltin (eds.) (1998). *Skeletal Muscle Metabolism in Exercise and Diabetes.* New York: Plenum.

Romijn, J.A., E.F. Coyle, L.S. Sidossis, A. Gastaldelli, J.F. Horowitz, and R.R. Wolfe (1993). Regulation of endogenous fat and carbohydrate metabolism in relation to exercise intensity and duration. *Amer. J. Physiol.* 265: E380–E391.

Romijn, J.A., E.F. Coyle, L.S. Sidossis, X.-J. Zhang, and R.R. Wolfe (1995). Relationship between fatty acid delivery and fatty acid oxidation during strenuous exercise. *J. Appl. Physiol.* 79: 1939–1945.

Rowell, L.B., and J.T. Shepherd (eds.) (1996). *Handbook of Physiology, Section 12, Exercise: Regulation and Integration of Multiple Systems.* New York: Oxford University Press.

Saddik, M., J. Gamble, L.A. Witters, and G.D. Lopaschuk (1993). Acetyl-CoA carboxylase regulation of fatty acid oxidation in the heart. *J. Biol. Chem.* 268: 25836–25845.

Saggerson, E.D., and C.A. Carpenter (1981). Carnitine palmitoyltransferase and carnitine octanoyl-transferase activities in liver, kidney cortex, adipocyte, lactating mammary gland, skeletal muscle and heart. *FEBS Lett.* 129: 229–232.

Sahlin, K., R.C. Harris, B. Nylind, and E. Hultman (1976). Lactate content and pH in muscle samples obtained after dynamic exercise. *Pfluegers Arch.* 367: 143–149.

Sahlin, K., A. Katz, and S. Broberg (1990). Tricarboxylic cycle intermediates in human muscle during prolonged exercise. *Amer. J. Physiol.* 259: C834–C841.

Sahlin, K., A. Katz, and J. Henriksson (1987). Redox state and lactate accumulation in human skeletal muscle during dynamic exercise. *Biochem. J.* 245 551–556.

Saltin, B., and P. Gollnick (1983). Skeletal muscle adaptability: significance for metabolism and performance. In: L.D. Peachey, R.H. Adrian, and S.R. Geiger (eds.) *Handbook of Physiology, Skeletal Muscle.* Bethesda: American Physiological Society, pp. 555–631.

Saltin, B., and J. Karlsson (1971). Muscle glycogen utilization during work of different intensities. In: B. Pernow and B. Saltin (eds.) *Muscle Metabolism During Exercise* New York: Plenum, pp. 289–299.

Schantz, P., E. Randall-Fox, W. Hutchison, A. Tyden, and P-O. Astrand (1983). Muscle fibre type distribution, muscle cross-sectional area and maximal voluntary strength in humans. *Acta Physiol. Scand.* 117: 219–226.

Schantz, P.G., B. Sjoberg, and J. Svedenhag (1986). Malate-aspartate and alpha-glycerophosphate shuttle enzyme levels in human skeletal muscle: methodological considerations and effect of endurance training. *Acta Physiol. Scand.* 128: 397–407.

Sidossis, L.S., A. Gastaldelli, S. Klein, and R.R. Wolfe (1997). Regulation of plasma fatty acid oxidation during low- and high-intensity exercise. *Amer. J. Physiol.* 272: E1065–E1070.

Soderlund, K., and E. Hultman (1986). Effects of delayed freezing on content of phosphagens in human skeletal muscle biopsy samples. *J. Appl. Physiol.* 61: 832–835.

Spina, R.J., M. M.-Y. Chi, M.G. Hopkins, P.M. Nemeth, O.H. Lowry, and J.O. Holloszy (1996). Mitochondrial enzymes increase in muscle in response to 7–10 days of cycle exercise. *J. Appl. Physiol.* 80: 2250–2254.

Spriet, L.L. (1992). Anaerobic metabolism in human skeletal muscle during short-term intense activity. *Can. J. Physiol. Pharmacol.* 70:157–165.

Spriet, L.L. (1991). Phosphofructokinase activity and acidosis during short-term tetanic contractions. *Can. J. Physiol. Pharmacol.* 69: 298–304.

Spriet, L.L., and D.J. Dyck (1996). The glucose-fatty acid cycle in skeletal muscle at rest and during exercise. In R. Maughan, and S.M. Shirreffs (eds.). *Biochemistry of Exercise IX* Windsor: Human Kinetics. pp. 127–155.

Spriet, L.L., and L.M. Odland (1998). Biochemical regulation of carbohydrate-lipid interaction in skeletal muscle during low and moderate intensity exercise. In: M. Hargreaves and M. Thompson (eds.) *Biochemistry of Exercise X.* Windsor: Human Kinetics, pp. 263–274.

Spriet, L.L., M.I. Lindinger, R.S. McKelvie, G.J.F. Heigenhauser, and N.L. Jones (1989). Muscle glycogenolysis and hydrogen ion concentration during maximal intermittent cycling. *J. Appl. Physiol.* 66: 8–13.

Spriet, L.L., K. Soderlund, M. Bergstrom, and E. Hultman (1987a). Anaerobic energy release in skeletal muscle during electrical stimulation in man. *J. Appl. Physiol.* 62:611–615.

Spriet, L.L., K. Soderlund, M. Bergstrom, and E. Hultman (1987b). Skeletal muscle glycogenolysis, glycolysis and pH during electrical stimulation in man. *J. Appl. Physiol.* 62:616–621.

Starling, R.D., T.A. Trappe, A.C. Parcell, C.G. Kerr, W.J. Fink, and D.L. Costill (1997). Effects of diet on muscle triglyceride and endurance performance. *J. Appl. Physiol.* 82: 1185–1189.

Timmons, J.A., T. Gustafsson, C.J. Sundberg, E. Jansson, and P.L. Greenhaff (1998). Muscle acetyl group availability is a major determinant of oxygen deficit in humans during submaximal exercise. *Amer J. Physiol.* 274: E377–E380.

Turcotte, L.P., B. Kiens, and E.A. Richter (1991). Saturation kinetics of palmitate uptake in perfused skeletal muscle. *FEBS Lett.* 279: 327–329.

Turcotte, L.P., E.A. Richter, and B. Kiens (1995). Lipid metabolism during exercise. In: M. Hargreaves, (ed.) *Exercise Metabolism* Windsor: Human Kinetics, pp. 99–130.

Vander Vusse, G.J., and R.S. Reneman (1996). Lipid metabolism in muscle. In: *Handbook of Physiology: Exercise: Regulation and integration of multiple systems.* (Section 12). New York: Oxford Press, pp. 952–994.

Wendling, P.S., S.J. Peters, G.J.F. Heigenhauser, and L.L. Spriet (1996). Variability of triacylglycerol content in human skeletal muscle biopsy samples. *J. Appl. Physiol.* 81:1150–1155.

Wieland, O.H. (1983). The mammalian pyruvate dehydrogenase complex: structure and regulation. *Rev. Physiol. Biochem. Pharmacol.* 96: 123–170.

Wilson, D.F. (1994). Factors affecting the rate and energetics of mitochondrial oxidative phosphorylation. *Med. Sci. Sports Exerc.* 26: 37–43.

Winder, W.W., J. Arogyasami, R.J. Barton, I.M. Elayan, and P.B. Vehrs (1989). Muscle malonyl-CoA decreases during exercise. *J. Appl. Physiol.* 67: 2230–2233.

Winder, W.W., J. Arogyasami, I.M. Elayan, and D. Cartmill. (1990). Time course of the exercise–induced decline in malonyl-CoA in different muscle types. *Amer J. Physiol.* 259: E266–E271.

DISCUSSION

MAUGHAN: The Randall theory said that citrate was a major factor in regulating the interplay between fat and carbohydrate metabolism in heart muscle. A lot of people spent a great deal of time and effort unsuccessfully trying to show that citrate was important in human skeletal muscle during exercise. The two explanations for these discrepancies were that the metabolic rate of the skeletal muscle studied in the negative reports was not sufficiently high (these were often studies using resting muscle) and that the oxidative capacity of skeletal muscle was much lower than that of the isolated contracting rat heart, in which the Randall effect was originally shown to be important. Now you seem to be suggesting that citrate is important in skeletal muscle at rest, but not during exercise.

SPRIET: The evidence has swung away from citrate being a major metabolic regulator of PFK, but there are other putative roles of citrate. Eric Newsholme suggests that citrate is a powerful regulator of citrate synthesis, i.e., at least in insect flight muscle, citrate accumulation reduces the activity of citrate synthase by allosteric inhibition. If this were important, given the known increase in citrate synthase activity during exercise, what should happen when you start to exercise is that citrate content should decrease to stimulate the enzyme activity. But we know that in human muscle during aerobic exercise, citrate concentration increases. Clearly, something else must be happening at the level of the citrate synthase enzyme to explain the increase in its activity during exercise.

We have some evidence from studies of the interaction of fat and carbohydrate that citrate might play a role in down-regulating PFK during low-to-moderate power outputs. However, our in-vitro studies of citrate—with physiological concentrations of substrates and regulators in the test tube—suggest that it is not a very big player. In other words, when you mimic the conditions that occur during exercise, citrate's inhibitory effect on PFK is minimal.

MAUGHAN: Are those differences maintained if you make fiber-specific measurements of citrate concentrations rather than looking at whole muscle?

SPRIET: I can't answer that from the in-vitro work because it is done with purified PFK, but the implication from the classic in-vitro work is that citrate and hydrogen ions are the most powerful inhibitors of PFK. However, if that were true, how do we explain the tremendous flux through PFK and the glycolytic pathway during sprinting, when the citrate and hydrogen ion levels are increasing? Clearly something doesn't add up. When we try to mimic exercise-like situations in the test tube, we see that the activators of PFK, i.e., ADP, AMP, and P_i, can override the effects of the inhibition of PFK by citrate and hydrogen ions. However, it is difficult to prove this experimentally in human muscle in-vivo.

WAGENMAKERS: The difference between heart and skeletal muscle in the role of citrate may be that only cardiac muscle has a mitochondrial citrate transporter. How sure are we that the cytosolic citrate concentration is increasing in skeletal muscle during exercise?

SPRIET: We have precious little evidence to answer that question, but there are two studies that show that the release of citrate from muscle increases during exercise, which strongly suggests that citrate is moving from the mitochondria to the cytoplasm and that some is actually moving outside the muscle. Clearly, if I could accurately measure the two compartments (mitochondrial and cytoplasmic), it would be very useful. The people that study the transporters that might exist in the mitochondrial membrane seem quite convinced that citrate should be able to move across relatively easily. However, until we make the proper measurements, we are simply assuming that when citrate increases in the muscle, it is going to be distributed equally between the two compartments.

COYLE: It is difficult with current techniques to study the fluxes through various pathways. What are some of your ideas for the direction of future research on how the AMP kinase reaction and other metabolic reactions might control substrate flux? For example, AMP kinase can have a big effect on increasing muscle glucose uptake. I think a more dynamic approach to energy metabolism, focusing on integration of flux regulation, is where we are headed, as your work is leading us.

SPRIET: I don't agree that recent data are any different from what has been reported before because there are several examples of measuring flux through pathways, or at least trying to match the enzymatic measurements to the actual flux through the pathways. For instance, in sprinting, muscle measurements can be used to measure flux. Also, when you measure the amount of PDH in its active form, in most normal situations it matches very well with the actual flux through that reaction.

FEBBRAIO: During maximal sprinting there is decreasing power output but increasing rates of oxidative phosphorylation and glycolysis as sprinting progresses. Why do you think that ATP stores decline in these situations by only about 40%?

SPRIET: Fatigue after about 10 s of maximal sprinting could be a function of ATP limitation. At that time phosphocreatine is nearly depleted, and the ability of the glycolytic system to provide ATP is starting to wane. I agree that the oxidative processes are still increasing, but they contribute very little of the total required ATP. Many people would argue that most fatigue is an electrical or contractile phenomenon and that it doesn't make sense to have metabolism as the limiting factor for performance. But when glycogen depletion occurs, metabolism is limiting, and maximal sprinting might be another case in which ATP provision limits performance. At the onset of sprinting, both of the anaerobic energy expansion systems are working together at high rates, and as their capacities and rates start to decrease, the force the muscle produces has to decrease.

Why doesn't the ATP content decrease? When fish swim fast, they decrease their ATP contents to zero because it appears from an evolutionary point of view that it is important to get every last bit of ATP out of those muscles to escape predators and stay alive. For some reason, mammalian skeletal muscle has evolved to the point where it has decided it is not worth letting ATP content drop more than 25–40% of resting levels because there are very serious consequences, the major one being that it takes several hours to replenish the adenine nucleotide store, during which time the mammal is less able to exercise. It seems as if mammalian muscle has decided it is not worth getting a few extra seconds activity out of the ATP store, considering how long it is going to take to recover. As to why we have evolved that way, it may have something to do with the way we existed. We didn't have to sprint away from predators but rather moved away at fairly high rates, stopped to recover, and then moved again. I think that something else during sprinting, perhaps the hydrogen ion concentration and/or inorganic phosphate accumulation, is shutting down the contractile system upstream from metabolism to prevent further contractions and ATP loss. We did an experiment in which we tried to drive the muscle ATP store to zero by electrically stimulating the muscle and removing the brain as the driving force for contractions. Even when we bypassed the brain, the muscles would not let ATP levels drop more than 25–40% of resting levels.

NADEL: I tell medical students that in humans, when ATP concentrations reach zero in skeletal muscle, the muscle goes into rigor, which is irreversible. Clearly, powerful evolutionary strategies have evolved to prevent this from happening.

SPRIET: I agree with you, but ATP in species such as fish can go right to zero, and after 6–12 h of rest, they will replenish their ATP stores.

FEBBRAIO: Do you think it is possible that there is no massive fall in the intracellular ATP pool because this would result in a stoichiometric rise in the IMP concentration, which could have some dire consequences?

SPRIET: That is possible, but it seems highly unlikely that IMP would be a major player when you consider the large increases in hydrogen ions and in P_i that occur. It seems very likely that they are exerting an inhibitory effect upstream from metabolism at several sites to slow down the contractile process. However, the trouble with the experiments, of course, is that everything changes at once, and one can't figure out what is cause and what is effect. Maybe they are all important. Possibly it is a redundant system in which several factors are inhibiting contraction. One additional point is that in many studies the IMP does not increase to a large extent.

FEBBRAIO: In high-intensity exercise you can get the IMP up to 10 $mmol \cdot kg^{-1}$ dry weight.

SPRIET: Yes. We have used electrical stimulation to produce IMP values of 10–15 $mmol \cdot kg^{-1}$ dry muscle. However, you really have to drive the subjects hard to get IMP up to that level; at such high levels it could be a fatigue factor.

HARGREAVES: Perhaps even though the ATP concentration in a whole muscle is not dramatically reduced, localized ATP depletion in the area of the important cellular ATPases may be limiting. A good example is David Allen's work with caged ATP. They estimated that an increase in ATP concentration as small as 93 µmol/L resulted in increases in single fiber force output. So, it may be something linked to the potential compartmentalization of ATP within the muscle.

SPRIET: I agree with you. We are led to believe in our traditional schooling that transduction of the energy occurs easily between the mitochondria and the cytoplasm and that normally it is not a concern. However, if the overall ATP concentration drops by 25–40%, the compartmental changes you suggest are entirely possible. Unfortunately, this hypothesis is very difficult to test experimentally.

TARNOPOLSKY: Edwards and his group differentiated high frequency fatigue from low frequency fatigue. When we stimulate skeletal muscle at a high frequency of 50 Hz, which is fairly analogous to the frequency of contraction during sprinting, the M-wave drops dramatically, presumably because the accumulation of potassium in the transverse tubules causes a physiologic conduction block. That occurs even before metabolism is activated. With low frequency fatigue, on the other hand, there may be a several sensitive factors related to compartmentalization of ATP. The dihydropyridine receptor, which is the so-called voltage sensor, is linked, probably through a protein called triadin, to the ryanodine receptor that initiates contraction. This process may be ATP dependent through inositol triphosphate, which is re-phosphorylated by ATP. Thus, a local ATP depletion may down-regulate inositol triphosphate, which we have shown to be a modulator of calcium release from the sarcoplasmic reticulum.

SPRIET: I agree. It makes a lot of sense to regulate the system upstream from metabolism. If one were designing the system and wanted to turn it off when the situation dictated, it would make sense to turn it off at the very top. Some of the metabolic by-products might be quite important in targeting multiple sites upstream to inhibit contractions.

WAGENMAKERS: You seem to exclude IMP as a major regulator of the glycolytic flux. How sure are you that ammonia is an allosteric regulator and has functional significance?

SPRIET: The in-vitro experiments suggest that it allosterically regulates the enzyme in the test tube at high concentrations. The pertinent question is whether or not it increases sufficiently during sprinting to have an effect. My opinion is that ammonia is not a big player and that the ADP, AMP, the P_i are the major activators, but I can't entirely rule it out.

WAGENMAKERS: As far as I know there are no experiments to positively confirm that ammonia is an allosteric regulator.

SPRIET: There is at least one study that has shown this. There are always questions about the medium in which the enzyme was examined. Another factor that I haven't talked about with respect to PFK is that it is one of the few enzymes that, when diluted in a test tube, changes its structure and therefore its kinetic activity. When we did our recent in-vitro PFK studies, we used a crowding agent to keep PFK in its tetrameric structure and more closely mimic the cellular environment. However, your point is well taken. It is very difficult to know exactly where ammonia should be on that list and in which situations it would be important.

WILLIS: At least in the case of ion pumps, it has been shown that flows and forces are linearly related so that as the driving force decreases, the flux falls and, therefore, the ATP-splitting rate should fall. For the data concerning contractile ATPase, that relationship is perhaps more tenuous, but that may offer a direct mechanism to explain why, as the free energy of ATP hydrolysis falls, the cell would be protected against depleting its adenylate pool. As the creatine kinase reaction dried up due to the depletion of phosphocreatine, that would usher in Connett's energetic depleting phase. The free energy of ATP hydrolysis would fall steeply, and that would automatically slow down the ATP breakdown rate.

SPRIET: Yes, I agree that this is a possibility.

WALBERG-RANKIN: I have a very practical methodological question. You brought up the fact that interpretation of data from muscle biopsies might be limited by changes that occur due to acquisition of the biopsy. For example, you mentioned an increase in muscle calcium might result from the biopsy and affect enzyme activity or substrate levels. I am curious whether this affects the later biopsy samples done in an experiment that includes repeated biopsies. For example, after obtaining a biopsy, have you observed changes in blood epinephrine that could influence muscle glycogen or changes in cytokine levels that might influence protein metabolism? Are you aware of any biopsy-associated systemic or localized changes in the muscle that could confound interpretation of the biochemical analyses?

SPRIET: Yes, there are some minor residual effects of repeated biopsies. The best defense would be to take repeated biopsies at rest and examine resting metabolite concentrations. We have done that and don't see any changes in the resting cell, especially with the sensitive metabolites like phosphocreatine. Another way to prevent this is to avoid taking too many biopsies from one leg during one experiment. One practical aspect is the size of the muscle that you are using. If you get a volunteer who has a small muscle, there is no question that there is a higher risk of one biopsy affecting the next. It is difficult to prove that the cutting of the muscle and/or increases in calcium don't have an effect, but it seems to be more of a concern for enzymes that are activated by calcium at rest. We would expect that the calcium levels at rest would be very low and that cutting the muscle might increase the concentration, whereas during exercise, when the calcium levels are much higher, it is likely that the cutting isn't going to affect the calcium concentration.

COGGAN: Another methodological issue might be the amount of anesthesia that is used and whether or not epinephrine is a component of the anesthetic. There are large differences in people's approaches to doing biopsies, and I've seen some investigators do them in a way likely to affect the quality of the data.

SPRIET: My advice is to avoid using epinephrine in the anesthetic and to make sure that when making the incision through the skin and fascia to minimize any cutting of the muscle itself. This way, the needle has easy access through the outer layers, but the anesthetic and incision have not affected the muscle.

HEIGENHAUSER: When do we get "anaerobic metabolism," or does it really exist, or should we be calling it "substrate phosphorylation" when we are talking about lactate production in the glycolytic pathway?

SPRIET: I have no problem using the terms "substrate phosphorylation," "anaerobic ATP production," or "non-oxidative ATP production." I agree that even during steady-state exercise some of the pyruvate is converted to lactate and that this isn't necessarily because we want to generate ATP in that pathway. I stayed away from the contentious issue of why lactate is produced and whether it is caused by an oxygen limitation or is a metabolic limitation.

WILLIS: The term "anaerobic" has the historical context of being a state of oxygen lack. Perhaps "nonoxidative ATP production" would be a better term. In addition, I think there may be danger in equating non-oxidative or anaerobic phosphorylation with substrate level phosphorylation, given that the succinyl-CoA thiokinase reaction is also a substrate level phosphorylation.

SPRIET: Yes, I agree that "non-oxidative ATP production" is the most accurate expression.

TARNOPOLSKY: It has been shown that free creatine can up-regulate PFK. Thus, as phosphocreatine breaks down to free creatine, the free creatine can then stimulate PFK to activate glycolysis. Additionally, Wallimam has shown that creatine may be as potent a stimulator of state-3 respiration as is ADP.

SPRIET: I believe the information suggesting either phosphocreatine or free creatine stimulates PFK is wrong. In those experiments the chemicals were contaminated with ADP, so it appears that it was the ADP that actually had the effect. However, it is quite possible that the breakdown in creatine can play some role in metabolic regulation. I stayed away from a detailed discussion regarding the movement of ATP into the cytoplasm and ADP and P_i into the mitochondria. There are very differing opinions on how important the adenosine nucleotide translocases are versus the so-called "phosphocreatine shuttle." Clearly there is a lot of work that has to be done.

WILLIAMS: Do you think that there is an advantage to inhibiting fat metabolism during high-intensity exercise to allow glycolysis to continue to produce a high ATP turnover that allows the sprint to continue?

SPRIET: The speed with which the carbohydrate pathway is activated seems to far exceed that of fat metabolism. In addition, even when you turn on fat metabolism to its maximum, it has a much lower maximum ATP production rate than does carbohydrate metabolism. It is as if the system has evolved to have only one rapid system of energy provision. There isn't much information linking the common metabolic regulators to activation of the fat pathway. Why are we not able to use triglyceride through the muscle lipase reaction very quickly during exercise? We know very little about the regulation of this enzyme, so it could be that it is not activated with the same signals that the carbohydrate side is, and, therefore, it is automatically at a disadvantage and will not be a player in these very short-term activities.

WILLIAMS: Yes, I think we have generally accepted the idea that the slower rate of fat metabolism is the reason for the smaller contribution to ATP production during heavy exercise. It is interesting to consider whether or not there is positive inhibition of fat metabolism.

SPRIET: Yes, it is puzzling if you look at Ed Coyle's study with very well-trained people. When increasing power output from 65% to 85% $\dot{V}O_2$max, the fat contribution decreased, whereas other species that have to work at very high power outputs seem to be able to use fat at much higher rates than do humans. Is it something to do with inhibition of TG lipase or perhaps a limitation in the transfer of fat across the mitochondrial membrane? What are the inhibitors? We simply don't know. We used to think that if fatty acids were provided to the cell, fat would be used, but now we understand that there is the potential for regulation at several sites in fat metabolism. Perhaps we are designed to exercise at 50% $\dot{V}O_2$max for hours and hours and fat is a big player at this intensity. On the other hand, we are not designed to run for an hour and half at 80–85% $\dot{V}O_2$max.

CLARKSON: Is there any evidence that there could be a mechanical factor contributing to the activation and deactivation of key pathways to turn ATP production on and off? These enzymes are sitting in a complex cytoskeletal network that would be very sensitive to movement.

SPRIET: I am not aware of literature linking mechanical factors and metabolism, but I would be surprised if there was no link.

NADEL: Tarbell, a bioengineer from Penn State, has shown that mechanical deformation of skeletal muscle cells causes activation of second messenger systems, thereby contributing to appropriate metabolic adjustments.

SPRIET: That would make a lot of sense if one were designing a muscle cell. I think that most of the things we see with metabolic control surprise us because there appears to be redundant control in all systems.

2

Metabolic Responses to Changes in Cellular Hydration

FLORIAN LANG, M.D.

INTRODUCTION

The integrity of cells critically depends on the constancy of cell volume. In view of their delicate subcellular structure, it is obvious that cells cannot tolerate gross changes of their volume without destruction of their architecture. Moreover, dilution or concentration of cellular constituents during alterations of cell volume is expected to substantially alter cell metabolism. As a matter of fact, it has been convincingly shown that the properties of macromolecules such as enzymes are highly sensitive to alterations of cellular hydration. Also, changes in cell volume of only a few percent have profound effects on cellular function. Thus, survival of cells relies on their ability to keep their volumes within narrow limits.

With only a few exceptions, animal cell membranes are highly permeable to water and cannot resist significant pressure gradients. In the absence of hydraulic pressure gradients, water will follow osmotic gradients, i.e., any difference between intracellular and extracellular osmolarity will result in the respective movement of water and a change of cell volume (Figure 2-1).

The cellular accumulation of osmotically active substrates creates an imbalance of osmolarity across the cell membrane that is to be counterbalanced by asymmetrical ion distribution; the Na^+/K^+ ATPase extrudes Na^+ in exchange for K^+. The cell membrane is usually highly permeable to K^+ but only poorly to Na^+. Following its chemical gradient, K^+ then leaves the cells and thus creates a cell-negative electrical potential

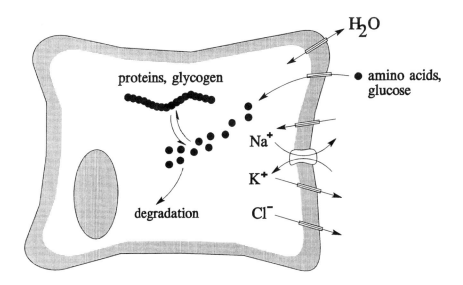

FIGURE 2-1. *Challenges of cell volume constancy.* Since the cell membrane does not resist significant pressure gradients, the movement of water across the cell membrane is governed solely by osmotic forces, i.e., the difference of osmolarity between cytosol and extracellular space. Besides alterations of extracellular osmolarity, any transport of osmotically active matter across the cell membrane, cellular degradation and formation of macromolecules, or metabolic formation or breakdown of osmotically active substances all lead to the respective alterations of osmotic gradient and the respective water movements.

difference across the cell membrane. It is this potential difference that drives Cl^- out of the cell. The low intracellular Cl^- concentration compensates for the high intracellular concentration of organic substances (Figure 2-2).

Obviously, the osmotic equilibrium across the cell membrane is challenged by alterations of extracellular osmolarity. An increase of extracellular osmolarity will create an osmotic gradient from cell to extracellular fluid and thus abstract cellular water and lead to cell shrinkage. Conversely, following a decrease of extracellular osmolarity, water will enter the cells following the osmotic gradient and thus lead to cell swelling.

In the human organism extracellular osmolarity is tightly regulated by the kidney, and most cells are bathed in fluid that undergoes little change of osmolarity. Thus, at times it was believed that alterations of cell volume were not relevant for their function. However, in the past few years it has become obvious that the alterations of extracellular osmolarity encountered in physiological and pathophysiological conditions are large enough to substantially alter cellular function.

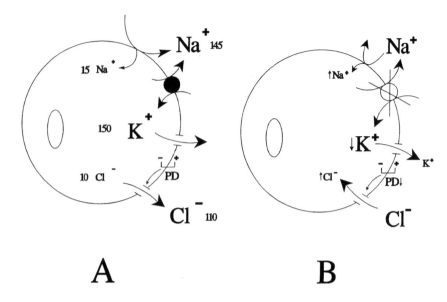

FIGURE 2-2. *Cell swelling by energy depletion:* The Na^+/K^+ ATPase maintains a low intracellular Na^+ and high intracellular K^+. K^+ diffusion along the chemical gradient establishes a cell membrane potential (PD) which drives Cl^- out of the cells (A). Energy depletion compromises the function of the Na^+/K^+ ATPase, and thus leads to dissipation of the Na^+ and K^+ gradients, depolarization, entry of Cl^-, and subsequent cell swelling (B).

Even at constant extracellular osmolarity, cell volume constancy may be challenged by altered transport across the cell membrane, leading to uptake or release of osmotically active substances. Moreover, the metabolic generation or disposal of osmotically active substances alters cellular osmolarity and thus cell volume. Again, the extent of cell swelling or shrinkage during metabolic or transport function is large enough to profoundly modify cell function.

Given the high sensitivity of cell function to cell volume on the one hand and the many challenges of cell volume constancy on the other, it is not surprising that virtually all cells express cell-volume regulatory mechanisms, comprising transport across the cell membrane and metabolism. Following cell swelling, the cells release ions and organic osmolytes by triggering the respective transport systems; following cell shrinkage, the cells accumulate ions and organic osmolytes, again triggering the appropriate transport systems. Beyond that, cell swelling inhibits the degradation of macromolecules such as glycogen and proteins to the osmotically more active monomers glucose phosphate and amino acids, and cell shrinkage stimulates glycogenolysis and proteolysis as well as metabolic pathways leading to cellular accumulation of organic osmolytes. Due to the effect of cell volume on protein and glycogen metabolism, cell swelling is a strong anabolic, and cell shrinkage a strong catabolic, stimulus. The volume regulatory mechanisms are exploited by hormones to influence cellular function through alterations of cell volume. Thus, cell volume is an integral element in the machinery governing cellular performance.

In this chapter a discussion of factors modifying cell volume will be followed by review of the many cell-volume regulatory mechanisms, and the influence of cell volume on cellular metabolism and gene expression. Finally, some thoughts will be added on the putative role of altered cell volume in physical performance. Clearly, this last part of the chapter must remain speculative because little is known about the effect of cell volume on physical or mental performance. However, it is hoped that this chapter will stimulate efforts to determine the interaction of cell volume and performance and thus add new complexity to this exciting area of research.

CHALLENGES OF CELL VOLUME CONSTANCY

A wide variety of mechanisms leads to cell swelling or shrinkage. They do so by modifying osmolarity or composition of extracellular fluid, by influencing transport across the cell membrane, and by triggering metabolic generation or disposal of osmotically active substances.

Extracellular Fluid Osmolarity

Extracellular osmolarity may exceed isotonicity by 300% in the kidney medulla (Beck et al., 1988). Intestinal cells may be exposed to hypertonic or hypotonic luminal fluid, and portal blood may undergo moderate changes of osmolarity during intestinal absorption (Haberich et al., 1965). Other human tissues are normally bathed in isotonic fluid.

In a variety of diseases, though, extracellular osmolarity may be reduced by hyponatremia (Bichet et al., 1992; McManus & Churchwell, 1994). On the other hand, hyponatremia may be paralleled by isoosmolar or even hyperosmolar states (Bichet et al., 1992), such as hyperglycemia due to uncontrolled diabetes mellitus (Arieff & Carrol, 1972) or ethanol intoxication (Robinson & Loeb, 1971). Obviously, hyponatremia may result from NaCl loss by sweating and replenishment of hypotonic fluid during exercise. As a matter of fact, hyponatremia has been observed in long-distance runners (Nelson et al. 1988, Noakes et al. 1985). During prolonged exhaustive exercise the kidney fails to excrete excess water (Poortmans et al. 1984), presumably due to stimulation of ADH secretion (Zambraski 1990).

Hypernatremia is necessarily paralleled by an increase of extracellular osmolarity (Howard et al., 1992). Accumulation of urea in renal insufficiency (Martinez-Maldonado et al., 1992) enhances both extracellular and intracellular concentrations of urea, which is thus not osmotically active. However, urea may interfere with cell volume regulatory mechanisms and thus alter cell volume (Lang et al., 1998a).

Extracellular Fluid Composition

Cell volume maintenance depends on the presence of electrolyte gradients across the cell membrane (see above). An increase of extracellular K^+ concentration decreases the chemical K^+ gradient and the exit of intracellular K^+, depolarizes the cell membrane, and leads to cellular accumulation of Cl^- (with K^+) and thus to cell swelling. A decrease of extracellular K^+ could lead to cell shrinkage due to cellular loss of KCl (Lang et al., 1998a).

Following an increase of extracellular HCO_3^- concentration, HCO_3^- enters the cells and thus leads to hyperpolarization and cellular retention of K^+. The cellular accumulation of $KHCO_3$ subsequently swells the cells. A decrease of extracellular H^+, e.g., during correction of extracellular acidosis in the course of the treatment of diabetic ketoacidosis, favors cellular extrusion of H^+ through the Na^+/H^+ exchanger. The cellular accumulation of Na^+ then similarly leads to cell swelling (Van der Meulen et al., 1987).

Organic anions such as acetate, lactate, and proprionate swell cells by entry of the nonionized acid, intracellular dissociation, cytosolic acidosis, subsequent stimulation of Na^+/H^+ exchange, and the resulting cellular accumulation of Na^+ with the respective anion (Macknight, 1988).

Energy Depletion

The activity of Na^+/K^+ ATPase is required to establish the ionic gradients across the cell membrane that are important for maintenance of cell volume constancy (Figure 2-2). Inhibition of Na^+/K^+ ATPase, e.g., during ischemia or cooling of the tissue, eventually leads to cell swelling (Lang et al., 1995a, Turner et al., 1995). In cardiac myocytes, however, the swelling is preceded by transient cell shrinkage due to an increase of intracellular Ca^{++} and hypercontraction (Askenasy et al., 1995; Chacon et al., 1994; Smith et al., 1993).

Ion Transport Altered by Hormones and Transmitters

A wide variety of hormones and transmitters stimulates transport across the cell membrane and thus modifies cell volume. Hormones reported to swell target cells include insulin, IGF-1, TGF-β, growth hormone, glucocorticoids, mineralocorticoids, estrogens, progesterone, testosterone, gonadotropin, somatotropin, angiotensin, interleukin, glutamate, and aspartate (Lang et al., 1998a). Hormones reported to shrink target cells include glucagon, VIP, somatoliberin, atriopeptin, nitroxide, ATP, bradykinin, histamine, thrombin, serotonin, prostaglandin E_2, fMLP, and corticostatic peptides. Depending on the type of target cell and the experimental conditions, some hormones and transmitters, e.g., ADH, adenosine, adrenaline, and acetylcholine, may swell or shrink cells.

Insulin and growth factors increase cell volume by stimulation of Na^+/H^+ exchange and, in some cases, of $Na^+,K^+,2Cl^-$ cotransport (Ritter & Woell, 1996). The increase of cell volume participates in the hormonal effects on metabolism and cell proliferation (Lang et al., 1998a).

The stimulation of transepithelial transport by secretagogues (e.g., adrenaline, acetylcholine, or bradykinin) involves activation of ion transport systems at the luminal and basolateral side of the epithelial cell. Depending on the prevailing effect, the secretagogue may either swell or shrink the cell (Lang et al. 1998a, Schultz, 1989)

Activation of Na^+ channels or nonselective cation channels by excitatory neurotransmitters such as glutamate and aspartate swells neurons, whereas activation of K^+ channels or anion channels by inhibitory neurotransmitters such as GABA shrinks neurons (Lang et al., 1998a).

Similar to the respective hormones and transmitters, second messengers swell (cAMP, cGMP, PKC, arachidonic acid, Ras, superoxides) or shrink (cAMP, cGMP, Ca^{++}) cells (Lang et al., 1998a).

Substrate Transport

Cellular accumulation of osmotically active substrates such as amino acids leads to cell swelling. Owing to the steep electrochemical gradient for Na^+, Na^+-coupled transport processes can generate large chemical gradients across the cell membrane. At an extracellular glutamine concentration of 3 mmol/L, for instance, cellular glutamine can increase by more than 30 mmol/L (Häussinger et al., 1990c). Other substrates shown to swell cells include glucose and bile acids.

Metabolism

Degradation of proteins to amino acids, glycogen to glucose phosphate, or triglycerides to glycerol and fatty acids is expected to enhance intracellular osmolarity. However, very little is known about the influence of metabolism on cell volume.

The accumulation of lactate in muscle cells during exercise increases cell volume (Saltin et al., 1987). Besides the osmotic effects of lactate itself, intracellular acidosis leads to cell swelling by activation of the Na^+/H^+ exchanger (see above).

Diabetic ketoacidosis has been reported to cause cell swelling (Brizzolara et al., 1996; Young & Bradley, 1967) due to cellular uptake of acids and enhanced Na^+/H^+ exchange activity. Moreover, the inadequate cellular formation and accumulation of sorbitol from excessive glucose by the action of aldose reductase may lead to cell swelling (Burg & Kador, 1988). On the other hand, hyperglycemia may osmotically shrink cells (Demerdash et al., 1996).

Others

In addition to hormones, a great number of drugs and toxins lead to cell swelling or cell shrinkage. Cell swelling has been reported following exposure to vinblastine, endotoxin, ethanol, and mercurials; cell shrinkage can be caused by H_2O_2, thapsigargin, okadaic acid, and urea. Some drugs, such as ouabain, colchicine, and cytochalasin B, either swell or shrink cells (Lang et al., 1998a).

MECHANISMS OF CELL VOLUME REGULATION

Cells utilize a wide diversity of cell volume regulatory mechanisms. Any given cell may choose only those mechanisms that are most compatible with its particular function. Thus, species and tissue differences are encountered depending on the individual transport systems or osmolytes employed. A description of cell volume regulatory mechanisms that are tissue specific has been given elsewhere [Lang et al., 1998b] and is beyond the scope of this review. It should further be pointed out that much of the knowledge gained on cell volume regulation has been obtained from cell culture experiments that cannot *a priori* be extrapolated to the *in vivo* situation without caution. Nevertheless, ample evidence clearly indicates that the cell volume regulatory mechanisms described below do operate similarly and the described metabolic pathways are similarly sensitive to cell volume in the *in vivo* situation as in cultured cells.

Ion Transport

Ion transport across the cell membrane is the most rapid means of altering cellular osmolarity. If swollen, cells extrude ions to cause a regulatory cell-volume decrease (RVD) (Figure 2-3); if shrunken, cells accumulate ions to cause a regulatory cell-volume increase (RVI) (Figure 2-4).

Regulatory cell-volume decrease (RVD). In most cells swelling leads to activation of separate K^+ and anion channels. The anion channels allow the passage of Cl^-, HCO_3^- and, in part, organic anions and neutral organic osmolytes (Jackson & Strange, 1993; Roy & Banderali, 1994; Weiss & Lang, 1992). Several of the cell volume regulatory ion

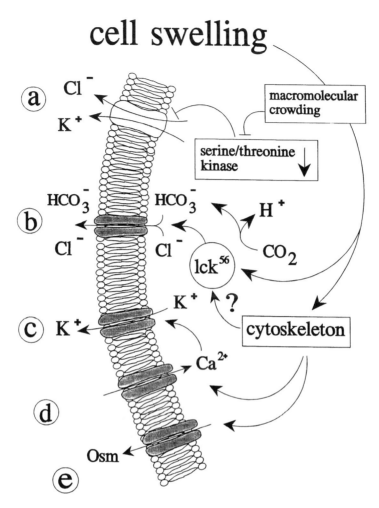

cell swelling

FIGURE 2-3. *Mechanisms of regulatory cell volume decrease.* Upon cell swelling, the cells decrease their osmolarity by release of ions and organic osmolytes as well as by inhibiting ion uptake. The most widely employed mechanisms include activation of K^+ (c), anion (b) and unspecific cation (d) channels, activation of KCl cotransport (a), and release of osmolytes, such as sorbitol, inositol, taurine, and betaine (e); the anion channels are activated by the src-like kinase Lck_{56}.

channels have been cloned, such as the K^+ channels Kv1.3 (n-type K^+ channel) (Deutsch & Chen, 1993), Kv1.5 (Felipe et al., 1993), and minK (Busch et al., 1992) and the Cl^- channel ClC-2 (Gründer et al., 1992; Jentsch, 1996).

The putative roles of brain-derived voltage-dependent anion channel 1 (BR1-VDAC) (Dermietzel et al., 1994), the I_{Cln} chloride channel

cell shrinkage

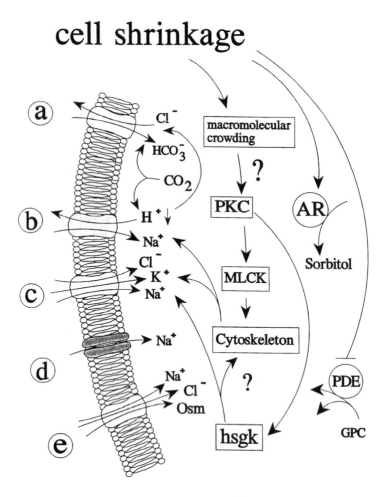

FIGURE 2-4. *Mechanisms of regulatory cell volume increase.* Upon cell shrinkage, the cells accumulate ions and organic osmolytes and decrease electrolyte loss. The most widely used mechanisms include parallel activation of Na^+/H^+ exchange (b) and Cl^-/HCO_3^- exchange (a), $Na^+,K^+,2Cl^-$ cotransport (c), Na^+ channels (d), Na^+ coupled accumulation of inositol, taurine and betaine (e); cellular accumulation of sorbitol by activation of aldosereductase (f) as well as cellular accumulation of glycerophosphorylcholine by inhibition of phosphodiesterase (g).

(Paulmichl et al., 1992), and the P-glycoprotein (or MDR protein) (Valverde et al., 1992, 1996) in cell volume regulation have been issues of considerable controversy (Lang et al., 1998a,b). In addition to ion channels, cells frequently employ electroneutral KCl cotransport for electrolyte release during cell swelling (Lauf, 1988; Perry & O'Neill, 1993).

Some cells release KCl by activation of K^+/H^+ exchange in parallel to Cl^-/HCO_3^- exchange (Cala, 1985). The H^+ and HCO_3^- that are exchanged for KCl produce CO_2, which then diffuses out of the cell and is not osmotically relevant.

In a number of cells, swelling activates nonselective cation channels (Sachs, 1991; Sackin, 1994). The channels allow the passage of Ca^{++}, which then enters the cells and activates Ca^{++} sensitive K^+ channels (Christensen, 1987; Taniguchi & Guggino, 1989; Ubl et al., 1988).

Regulatory cell-volume increase (RVI). The most important transport systems accomplishing electrolyte accumulation in shrunken cells are the $Na^+,K^+,2Cl^-$ cotransporter (Dunham et al., 1990; Geck & Pfeiffer, 1985) and the Na^+/H^+ exchanger (Grinstein et al., 1983). The latter operates in parallel to the Cl^-/HCO_3^- exchanger. The H^+ and HCO_3^- exchanged for NaCl by the Na^+/H^+ exchanger and the Cl^-/HCO_3^- exchanger are replenished from CO_2, which is highly permeable and thus osmotically not relevant. In muscle cells, NaCl cotransport is apparently utilized for NaCl uptake (Dorup & Clausen, 1996). In some cells electrolyte accumulation during RVI is achieved by Na^+ channels and/or nonselective cation channels (Chan & Nelson, 1992; Wehner et al., 1995), leading to depolarization and subsequent cellular Cl^- accumulation. Several of the volume regulatory $Na^+,K^+,2Cl^-$ cotransporters have been cloned (Delpire et al., 1994; Gamba et al., 1994; Payne & Forbush, 1994, 1995; Xu et al., 1994). Among the cloned Na^+/H^+ exchangers, NHE-1 (Demaurex & Grinstein, 1994), NHE-2 (Demaurex & Grinstein, 1994), and NHE-4 (Bookstein et al., 1994) are stimulated, whereas NHE-3 (Bianchini et al., 1995; Demaurex & Grinstein, 1994) is inhibited by cell shrinkage. The cloned anion exchanger AE2, but not AE1, presumably participates in RVI (Jiang et al., 1997). Besides its effect on electrolyte uptake, cell shrinkage inhibits K^+ and Cl^- channels to prevent cellular electrolyte loss (Lang et al., 1998b). Both Na^+/H^+ exchange and $Na^+,K^+,2Cl^-$ cotransport are inhibited by increasing intracellular Cl^- concentration. Upon cell shrinkage, intracellular Cl^- activity increases and may thus impair regulatory cell volume increase.

Osmolytes

High concentrations of ions interfere with structure and function of macromolecules, including proteins (Clark et al., 1981; Iyer et al., 1994; Yancey, 1994); thus, cell volume regulation by cellular accumulation of electrolytes during cell shrinkage is limited. Moreover, altered intracellular ion concentrations would be expected to modify cellular function. To circumvent these effects, cells utilize organic osmolytes in addition to inorganic ions to generate intracellular osmolarity (Burg, 1994; Garcia-

Perez & Burg, 1991; Gerlsma, 1968; Handler & Kwon, 1993; Kinne, 1993; Kinne et al., 1993; Law, 1991). Even at high concentrations organic osmolytes are compatible with normal macromolecular function (Brown & Simpson, 1972). Moreover, they counteract the destabilizing effects of inorganic ions and, in part, of urea (Arakawa & Timasheff, 1985; Flock et al., 1995). The osmolytes most widely used in mammalian cells include polyalcohols, such as sorbitol and inositol, methylamines, such as glycerophosphorylcholine and betaine, amino acids, and amino acid derivatives such as glycine, glutamine, glutamate, aspartate, and taurine (Burg, 1994; Garcia-Perez & Burg, 1991; Kinne, 1993; Kinne et al., 1993; Law, 1991). Osmolytes are specifically important for survival of cells in the renal medulla (Beck et al., 1992; Burg, 1994; Gullans et al., 1988; Wirthensohn et al., 1989) but are utilized in virtually all cells examined thus far.

During cell shrinkage, osmolytes are accumulated by stimulated uptake (myoinositol, betaine, and taurine), enhanced formation (sorbitol), or decreased degradation (glycerophosphorylcholine). These mechanisms are mediated by altered gene expression and thus require days to be fully effective. During cell swelling, osmolytes are rapidly degraded or released.

Glycerophosphorylcholine (GPC) is formed by deacylation of phosphatidylcholine and degraded to glycerol-phosphate and choline by the GPC:choline phosphodiesterase (Garcia-Perez & Burg, 1991; Ullrich, 1959). An increased concentration of extracellular NaCl or urea inhibits the phosphodiesterase and thus leads to accumulation of GPC.

Sorbitol is formed from glucose by aldose reductase (Bedford et al., 1987; Ferraris et al., 1994), which is upregulated by enhanced expression during osmotic cell shrinkage or when intracellular ionic strength increases (Smardo et al., 1992; Uchida et al., 1989).

Myoinositol (inositol) (Kwon & Handler, 1995; Yamauchi et al., 1996), betaine (Takenaka et al., 1995; Yamauchi et al., 1991, 1992), and taurine (Uchida et al., 1992) are taken up into shrunken cells by Na^+-coupled transporters. The respective transporters SMIT (sodium/myoinositol transporter) (Kwon et al., 1992), BGT (betaine/GABA transporter) (Yamauchi et al., 1992), and NCT (Na^+/Cl^- taurine transporter) (Uchida et al., 1992) have been cloned (Kwon, 1994; Kwon & Handler, 1995).

Cell volume modifies the cellular concentration of several amino acids and amino acid metabolites, including glutamine, glutamate, glycine, proline serine, threonine, ß-alanine, (n-acetyl) aspartate, and GABA (Chen & Kempson, 1995). The intracellular concentrations of individual amino acids are rather low. However, the combined osmotic effect of all amino acids is substantial (Law, 1991). Cell shrinkage stimulates Na^+-coupled transport of neutral amino acids (Chen et al., 1994;

Dall'Asta et al., 1994; Gazzola et al., 1991) and proteolysis (Häussinger et al., 1991; Petronini et al., 1992), and it inhibits protein synthesis (Stoll et al., 1992). Thus, cell shrinkage leads to an increase of intracellular amino acid concentration. Cell swelling decreases intracellular amino acid concentration by it effects on inhibition of proteolysis and stimulation of protein synthesis (Häussinger et al., 1990a, 1991; Petronini et al., 1992; Stoll et al., 1992), degradation of glutamine and glycine (Häussinger & Lang, 1990; Häussinger et al., 1993a), and cellular release of amino acids (Hoffmann & Hendil, 1976).

Mechanisms Triggering Volume Regulatory Mechanisms

For cell volume regulation to occur, alterations of cell volume have to be sensed, and the "sensor" must trigger cellular transducing mechanisms that mediate the activation of cell volume regulatory mechanisms.

Among the "sensors" are altered concentration of macromolecules such as proteins (macromolecular crowding) and mechanical stretch on cell membrane or cytoskeleton (Figures 2-3, 2-4).

Macromolecular Crowding. The function of intracellular proteins such as enzymes is critically dependent on their "packing density" or macromolecular crowding (Garner & Burg, 1994; Minton, 1993; Parker, 1993). It is believed that among the enzymes sensitive to ambient protein concentration is a serine/threonine kinase that is inactivated by protein dilution during cell swelling and activated by protein crowding during cell shrinkage (Minton, 1994). The kinase is thought to inhibit volume-regulatory KCl cotransport, and its inactivation during cell swelling is considered to disinhibit volume-regulatory KCl efflux.

Cell Membrane Stretch. Cell swelling increases the tension of the cell membrane (Sachs, 1991; Sackin, 1994), which activates some cell volume-regulatory ion channels (Sackin, 1994). Stretch-activated channels may be selective for K^+ or anions and thus directly serve cell volume regulation (Morris, 1990; Sackin, 1994). Many of those channels are nonselective cation channels, allowing the passage of several cations, including Ca^{++}. The Ca^{++} entering the cells through those channels activates Ca^{++}-sensitive K^+ channels (Christensen, 1987; Taniguchi & Guggino, 1989; Ubl et al., 1988). In contrast to other cells, cells secreting ADH express unselective cation channels, which are inactivated by cell membrane stretch (Oliet & Bourque, 1993). The channels are activated by a decrease of cell membrane tension during cell shrinkage; the subsequent depolarization of the cell membrane then triggers ADH release (Oliet & Bourque, 1993).

Cytoskeleton. Obviously, alterations of cell volume affect the architecture of the cytoskeleton, which in turn influences the expression of cytoskeletal proteins (Häussinger et al., 1994b; Theodoropoulos et al.,

1992). The cytoskeleton is believed to sense alterations of cell volume and mediate activation of some cell volume-regulatory mechanisms (Busch et al., 1994; Häussinger et al., 1993b).

Among the mechanisms linking the sensors to the cell volume-regulatory mechanisms are Ca^{++}, eicosanoids, and kinases. Moreover, alterations of intracellular and vesicular pH may participate in cell volume regulation. As discussed in a subsequent section, alterations of cell volume influence the expression of a variety of genes, which thus alter cell volume regulation and other functions of the cell.

Ca^{++}. Most cells respond to swelling with an increased activity of intracellular Ca^{++}, which is released from 1,4,5-inositol-trisphosphate-sensitive intracellular stores and/or enters the cell via Ca^{++} channels in the plasma membrane (McCarty & O'Neil, 1992). The increase of intracellular Ca^{++} activates some cell volume-regulatory ion channels (see above).

Protein Phosphorylation. Cell swelling and cell shrinkage lead to phosphorylation of distinct proteins. Kinases activated by cell swelling include tyrosine kinases, protein kinase C, adenylate cyclase, MAP kinase, Jun-kinase, and focal adhesion kinase (p121[FAK]) (Hoffmann & Dunham, 1995). The Src-like tyrosine kinase Lck[56] accounts for the activation of lymphocyte cell volume-regulatory Cl^- channels (Lepple-Wienhues et al., 1998). Osmotic cell shrinkage activates protein kinase C and myosin light chain kinase and increases the expression of the serine/threonine kinase h-sgk (human serum and glucocorticoid dependent kinase) (Waldegger et al., 1997). The targets of this latter kinase have remained elusive. Evidence suggests that serine/threonine kinases are involved in the regulation of $Na^+,K^+,2Cl^-$ cotransport and KCl symport (Hoffmann & Dunham, 1995).

Eicosanoids. Cell swelling activates phospholipase A_2, with subsequent formation of the 15-lipoxygenase product hepoxilin A_3 and the 5-lipoxygenase product leukotriene LTD_4 (Hoffmann & Dunham, 1995). In Ehrlich cells, those eicosanoids activate cell volume-regulatory K^+ and/or Cl^- channels and volume regulatory taurine release. The enhanced formation of leukotrienes may lead to decreased formation of PGE_2, which deactivates PGE_2-sensitive Na^+ channels. On the other hand, PGE_2 can activate volume-regulatory K^+ channels in other cells (Lang et al., 1998a).

Cytosolic and Vesicular pH. Cell swelling leads to cytosolic acidification, in part due to HCO_3^- loss through cell volume-regulatory anion channels. Cell shrinkage alkalinizes the cytosol, in part, by stimulation of cell volume-regulatory Na^+/H^+ exchange. Moreover, cell swelling increases and cell shrinkage decreases the pH in acidic cellular compartments (Busch et al., 1994; Lang et al., 1994; Völkl et al., 1993), an effect presumably important for altered proteolysis (see below).

INFLUENCE OF CELL VOLUME ON CELLULAR METABOLISM AND GENE EXPRESSION

Metabolism

Cell volume changes modify a wide variety of metabolic functions.

Macromolecule Metabolism. Most importantly, cell shrinkage stimulates the breakdown of proteins and of glycogen to amino acids and glucose-phosphate, respectively, and inhibits protein and glycogen synthesis (Figure 2-5). Because the monomers are osmotically more active than are the macromolecules, these effects are prone to enhance cellular osmolarity. Cell swelling stimulates protein and glycogen synthesis and inhibits proteolysis and glycogenolysis, thus decreasing intracellular osmolarity by incorporation of the monomers into the osmotically less active macromolecules (Baquet et al., 1990; Häussinger et al., 1990a,1991,1993a; Hallbrucker et al., 1991c; Lang et al., 1989; Low et al., 1996; Meijer et al., 1992; Peak et al., 1992).

Cell Volume as a Second Message in Anabolism and Catabolism. Presumably, the anabolic effect of cell swelling and the catabolic effect of cell shrinkage were among the first mechanisms utilized during evolution to counteract changes of cell volume. As illustrated in Figure 2-4, hormones such as insulin and glucagon exploit these "archaic" mechanisms to modify cellular metabolism. For example, insulin activates the Na^+/H^+ exchanger and the $Na^+,K^+,2Cl^-$ cotransporter to swell hepatocytes and thus impair degradation of macromolecules (Agius et al., 1994; Hallbrucker et al., 1991a; Peak et al., 1992). Also, glucagon shrinks hepatocytes, presumably by activation of ion channels, and thus stimulates the breakdown of macromolecules (Hallbrucker et al., 1991b; Vom Dahl et al., 1991a,b). As illustrated in Figure 2-4, the effect of the hormones on cell volume fully accounts for their effect on proteolysis, i.e., the effect is fully mimicked by the respective osmotic alterations of cell volume and is abolished following phamacological or osmotic reversal of hormone-induced changes in cell volume (Hallbrucker et al., 1991a; Vom Dahl et al., 1991a,b). Similar to insulin, tumor-growth-factor β (TGFβ) inhibits proteolysis and stimulates protein synthesis at least in part by increasing cell volume (Ling et al., 1995a,b; and unpublished observations). Moreover, several amino acids inhibit proteolysis by tiggering cell swelling. In hypercatabolic states, such as burns, acute pancreatitis, severe injury, and liver carcinoma, muscle cell volume is well correlated with urea excretion as an indicator of protein breakdown, again highlighting the interaction of cell volume and protein metabolism (Häussinger et al., 1993a).

Hypercatabolism can be counteracted by glutamine, which modifies

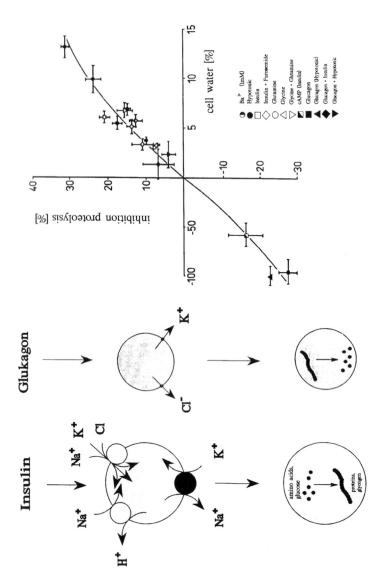

FIGURE 2-5. *Influence of cell volume on hepatic proteolysis.* Effect of insulin and glucagon. Insulin swells cells by KCl uptake via activation of Na^+/H^+ exchange, $Na^+K^+2Cl^-$ cotransport and Na^+/K^+ ATPase activity. Glucagon shrinks cells by activation of K^+ channels and anion channels. The cell volume changes participate in the signaling of hormone action. For instance, the antiproteolytic effect of insulin and the proteolytic effect of glucagon completely depend on the hormone-induced alterations of cell volume.

hepatic proteolysis by inducing cell swelling (Häussinger et al., 1990c). Synthesis of proteoglycans and proteins by osteoblasts or chondrocytes is stimulated by mechanical or osmotic deformation (Breur et al., 1991; Kim et al., 1994; Urban et al., 1993), and bone growth has been correlated with chondrocyte volume (Kuhn et al., 1996). Mechanisms linking cell volume to macromolecule metabolism are still poorly understood. The influence of cell volume on proteolyis may in part be due to the effect of cell volume on lysosomal pH (Lang et al., 1994) because lysosomal proteases are known to have acidic pH optima, and lysosomal alkalinization is known to inhibit proteolysis (Mortimore & Pösö, 1987).

Further Metabolic Pathways. Besides macromolecule formation or breakdown, several metabolic pathways are sensitive to cell volume. Cell swelling inhibits glycolysis and enhances flux through the pentose phosphate pathway, NADPH production (Saha et al., 1992,1993), glutathione (GSH) formation and efflux into blood (Häussinger et al., 1990b), glycine oxidation (Häussinger et al., 1992), glutamine breakdown (Häussinger et al., 1990c), formation of NH_4^+ and urea from amino acids (Häussinger & Lang, 1990), ketoisocaproate oxidation (Häussinger et al., 1992), and lipogenesis from glucose (Baquet et al., 1991). Cell swelling inhibits expression of phosphoenolpyruvate carboxykinase, a key enzyme for gluconeogenesis (Häussinger et al., 1994a). Cell shrinkage exerts the opposite effects on those metabolic functions.

Peroxide Metabolism. The effect of cell volume on pentose phosphate pathway and NADPH generation (Saha et al., 1992) modifies the availability of NADPH for the glutathione reductase to produce GSH. Thus, cell swelling enhances GSH and strengthens the protective mechanisms against peroxides (Saha et al., 1992). On the other hand, cell swelling favors generation of reactive oxygen species by NADPH oxidase, which is inhibited by high osmolarity (Takahashi et al., 1994) and stimulated through formation of arachidonic acid during cell swelling (Henderson et al., 1989). As a result, osmotic cell swelling increases peroxide generation in neutrophils (Kataoka & Fujita, 1991), and osmotic cell shrinkage decreases it (Kataoka & Fujita, 1991; Kuchkina et al., 1993; Manara et al., 1991; Matsumoto et al., 1991).

Gene Expression

Alterations of cell volume exert profound effects on the expression of a wide variety of genes, which in turn alter cellular function (Figure 2-6). Following are examples of genes governed by cell volume.

Cell Swelling. Cell swelling stimulates the expression of the cytoskeletal elements ß-actin (Theodoropoulos et al., 1992) and tubulin (Häussinger et al, 1994b), the extracellular signal-regulated kinases ERK-1 and ERK-2 (Sadoshima et al., 1996), the Jun-kinase JNK (Sa-

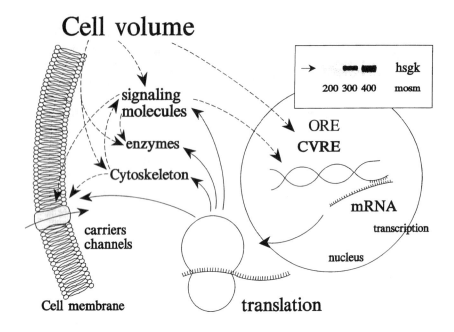

FIGURE 2-6. *Regulation of gene expression by alterations of cell volume.* Cell volume influences the expression of a variety of genes. It does so in part through osmoresponsive (ORE) or cell volume responsive (CVRE) elements. Genes sensitive to cell volume encode for carriers, cytoskeletal elements, enzymes and signaling molecules. The insert demonstrates the upregulation of the serine/threonine kinase h-sgk by increase of medium osmolarity.

doshima et al., 1996), the transcription factors c-Jun (Finkenzeller et al., 1994) and c-Fos (Sadoshima et al., 1996), the enzyme ornithine decarboxylase (Benis & Lundgren, 1993; Lovkvist-Wallstrom et al., 1995; Poulin et al., 1991; Tohyama et al., 1991), and the tumor necrosis factor TNF((Zhang et al., 1996a).

Cell Shrinkage. Osmotic cell shrinkage stimulates the expression of aldose reductase (Garcia-Perez et al., 1989; Smardo et al., 1992) and the Na^+-coupled transport systems for inositol (Burg, 1994; Kwon et al., 1992; Warskulat et al., 1997a), betaine (Ferraris et al., 1996a; Nakanishi et al., 1990; Warskulat et al., 1995; Yamauchi et al., 1991; Zhang et al., 1996b), taurine (Uchida et al., 1991; Warskulat et al., 1997b), osmolytes (Wasserman et al., 1994), and amino acids (Chen et al., 1994; Gazzola et al., 1991; Soler et al., 1993; Yamauchi et al., 1994), i.e., of enzymes and transporters serving cellular accumulation of osmolytes (Burg et al., 1996). Beyond that, cell shrinkage stimulates the expression of heat-shock proteins (Alfieri et al., 1996; Cohen et al., 1991; Sheik-Hamad et al., 1994; Tanaka et al., 1988), which stabilize proteins and thus counteract the destabilizing effects of increased ion concentrations. Osmotic and isotonic cell shrinkage upregulates the expression of the cell volume-regulated kinase, h-sgk, which presumably participates in the signaling of cell volume regulation (Waldegger et al., 1997). Moreover, cell shrinkage stimulates expression of the transport proteins P-glycoprotein (Wei & Roepe, 1994), ClC-K1 (Uchida et al., 1993b) and Na^+/K^+ ATPase a_1 subunit (Ferrer-Martinez et al., 1996), the signaling molecules cyclooxygenase-2 (Zhang et al., 1995), a_1 chimaerin (GTPase activating protein for Rac) (Dong & Lim, 1996), the immediate early gene-transcription factors Egr-1 (Cohen et al., 1994) and c-Fos (Cohen et al., 1991; Giovannelli et al., 1992; Wollnik et al., 1993), the hormone vasopressin (Murphy & Carter, 1990), the enzymes phosphoenolpyruvate carboxykinase (PEPCK) (Lavoinne et al., 1996; Newsome et al., 1994; Warskulat et al., 1996), tyrosine aminotransferase (Warskulat et al., 1996), tyrosine hydroxylase (Kilbourne et al., 1991), dopamine ß hydroxylase (Kilbourne et al., 1991), tissue plasminogen activator (Levin et al., 1993), and matrix metalloproteinase 9 (Rougier et al., 1997), as well as some matrix proteins (Dasgupta et al., 1992; Katayama et al., 1991; Urban et al., 1993).

Mechanisms Linking Cell Volume to Gene Expression. Little information is available on the mechanisms accounting for altered gene expression (Vanden Broeck et al., 1992). Some evidence points to the involvement of the cytoskeleton (Ben-Ze´ev, 1991). The expression of aldose reductase is governed by an osmolarity responsive element (ORE) (Ferraris et al., 1994, 1996b, Ruepp et al., 1996), and the expression of osmolyte transporters by a tonicity responsive element TonE (Takenaka et al., 1994). The stimulation of c-fos expression by swelling of cardiac myocytes depends on tyrosine phosphorylation (Sadoshima et al., 1996), whereas the c-jun transcription following swelling of hepatocytes depends on MAP kinase activation, followed by phosphorylation of c-Jun (Finkenzeller et al., 1994; Noe et al., 1996; Schliess et al., 1995; Tilly et al., 1993). Cell volume influences phosphorylation of a histone-like nuclear protein (Santell et al., 1993), and hypertonicity alters the karyotype (Uchida et al., 1987).

PUTATIVE ROLE OF CELL VOLUME IN PHYSICAL PERFORMANCE

Mechanisms Modifying Cell Volume During Exercise

Extracellular Osmolarity. Obviously, exercise may lead to excessive metabolic formation of osmotically active products as well as to enhanced loss of fluid and may thus influence extracellular osmolarity (Figure 2-7). There are reports of an increased osmolarity in venous effluent from exercising muscle (Raynaud et al., 1986) and an increase of plasma osmolarity during exercise without fluid replenishment (Ashkenazi et al., 1992; Candas et al., 1986; Douguet et al., 1988; Gore et al., 1992; Klein et al., 1980; Nielsen, 1974). The respiratory epithelia are specifically prone to undergo osmotic cell shrinkage during exercise. The increased ventilation leads to evaporation, which then leaves an enhanced osmolarity of airway surface fluid behind (Anderson, 1984, 1985, 1996; Anderson & Daviskas, 1992; Anderson et al., 1989, 1996; Brusasco & Crimi, 1994; Kay, 1989; Sheppard & Eschenbacher, 1984).

Extracellular Fluid Composition. Exercise may enhance extracellular K^+ and lactate concentration and lead to acidosis (McKelvie et al., 1997; Smith et al., 1997; Williams et al., 1985). An increase of extracellular K^+ depolarizes the cell and is expected to favor Cl^- entry and cell swelling (see above). Acidosis stimulates Na^+/H^+ exchange, again leading to cell swelling. As a matter of fact, erythrocyte swelling during exercise (Smith et al., 1997) can be mimicked by enhancement of extracellular K^+ concentration and lactacidosis (Weiss & Evanson, 1997). Upon recovery from exercise, erythrocyte volume decreases (Smith et al., 1995).

Ion Channel Activity. Muscle contraction is triggered and paralleled by activation of ion channels. The activation of Na^+ channels depolarizes the cell membrane and thus stimulates entry of Cl^-. The cellular accumulation of NaCl is expected to swell muscle cells. On the other hand, activation of K^+ channels and the respective hyperpolarization leads to cell shrinkage.

Metabolism. The degradation of glycogen eventually may lead to cellular accumulation of glucose-phosphate and lactate. The intracellular generation of H^+ stimulates the Na^+/H^+ exchanger and thus favors cellular accumulation of Na^+. As a result, cell swelling may occur. Energy depletion impedes the Na^+/K^+-ATPase; the cellular loss of K^+ decreases the K^+ equilibrium potential, which depolarizes the cell membrane and eventually leads to cell swelling (see above).

Hormones, Mediators. Exercise is paralleled by altered release of a number of hormones and mediators such as ADH, ANF, ACTH, glucocorticoids, renin, aldosterone, epinephrine, prostaglandins, histamine, and kinins (Brandenberger et al., 1986,1989; Gilli et al., 1984, Wade & Freund 1990), all of which are known to alter cell volume (see above). However, no firm information is available on the role of hormones in altered cell-volume regulation during exercise.

During exercise, the above mechanisms may be expected to partially counteract each other, i.e., their compounded influence may eventually lead to either cell swelling or cell shrinkage. Little experimental information is available on the function of cell volume-regulatory mechanisms during and after different various types of exercise. To the extent

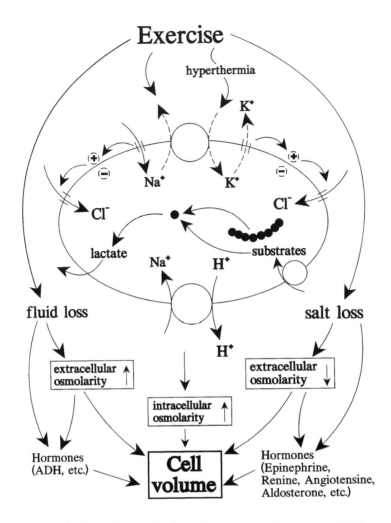

FIGURE 2-7. *Mechanisms altering cell volume during exercise.* Tentative model illustrating cellular and extracellular mechanisms leading to cell swelling or cell shrinkage. During exercise, some cells, including skeletal muscle cells, may swell, while others may shrink. Moreover, the volume of any particular cell may either increase or decrease, depending on the type or duration of physical challenge.

that acidosis prevails, as in brief exhaustive exercise, cells are likely to swell, whereas dehydration during prolonged exercise should lead to cell shrinkage. Preliminary experiments in our laboratory [Lang, Dickhut, Waldegger] indicate that strenuous exercise for 2 h without fluid replacement markedly upregulates the cell volume-regulated kinase h-sgk, pointing to substantial cell shrinkage.

Cell Volume-Sensitive Functions During Exercise

As indicated above, both ion transport and metabolism are sensitive to alterations of cell volume.

Excitability and Contraction. Ion channel activity and thus excitability is highly sensitive to alterations of cell volume. Swelling of cardiac cells activates volume-sensitive Cl^- currents, leading to depolarization of the cell membrane (Vandenberg et al., 1994; Zhang et al., 1993), enhancement of excitability, and shortening of the action potential (Sorota, 1992). Similarly, osmotic cell swelling depolarizes vascular smooth muscle cells, leading to opening of voltage-gated Ca^{++} channels, increase of intracellular Ca^{++} activity, and vasoconstriction (Lang et al., 1995b). Osmolar cell shrinkage results in vasodilation (Sergeev et al., 1992; Steenbergen & Bohlen, 1993). Increased plasma osmolarity decreases, and reduced plasma osmolarity increases, the susceptibility to epileptic seizures (Andrew, 1991; Osehobo & Andrew, 1993), effects which may be explained by respective changes of neuronal cell volume and subsequent alterations of neuronal ion channel activity and release of transmitters.

Beyond their influence on ion channels, alterations of cell volume may interfere with the interaction of contractile elements. Presumably due to such an interaction, moderate osmotic shrinkage of cardiac cells exerts a positive inotropic effect (Ben Haim et al., 1992; Groeneveld et al., 1992). On the other hand, increased ionic strength destabilizes the actinomyosin complex and decreases the Ca^{++}-activated force (Bagni et al., 1994; Godt et al., 1993).

Metabolism. As outlined above, cell swelling increases protein and glycogen synthesis and inhibits proteolysis and glycogenolysis. Thus, anabolism prevails during cell swelling, and catabolism prevails during cell shrinkage. Even though the relation of cell volume and metabolism is best documented for the liver, evidence is accumulating that the same holds true for muscle cells (Häussinger et al., 1993a, Low et al., 1996).

Erythrocyte Deformability. The deformability of erythrocytes is impaired by cell swelling that occurs during an increase of extracellular K^+ concentration and lactacidosis during exercise (Weiss & Evanson, 1997).

Release of Mediators and Hormones. Alterations of extracellular osmolarity and ion composition may modify cell volumes of hormone-secreting cells and thus affect hormone release. Indeed, the release of a wide variety of hormones is sensitive to cell volume. Osmotic cell swelling stimulates the release of insulin (Blackard et al., 1975; Lund et al., 1992), prolactin (Wang et al., 1993), gonadotropin releasing hormone (Inukai et al., 1992), luteinizing hormone (Greer et al., 1983), thyrotropin (Greer et al., 1990; Sato et al., 1991), aldosterone (Hayama et al., 1995;

Schneider et al., 1984), and renin (Frederiksen et al., 1975; Jensen & Skott, 1993; Kurtz, 1990; Skott, 1986). Atrial natriuretic factor (ANF) is released from cardiac myocytes in response to mechanical stretch (Schiebinger & Linden, 1986) and osmotic cell swelling (Greenwald et al., 1989). On the other hand, ANF release has been postulated to be stimulated by cell shrinkage (Zongazo et al., 1991,1992). Osmotic cell shrinkage stimulates the release of ADH (Oliet & Bourque, 1993), of nitric oxide (NO) (Steenbergen & Bohlen, 1993), of the putative hormones ouabain or ouabain-like factors (Blaustein, 1993; Lichtstein et al., 1992), of histamine, 15 hydroxyeicosatetraenoic acid, prostaglandins and leukotriene B_4 from macrophages and basophil granulocytes (Souques et al., 1995; Nielsen et al., 1992), and of substance P from C-fiber neurons (Garland et al., 1995). Osmotic cell shrinkage inhibits the release of prolactin (Sato et al., 1991) and endothelin-1 (Kohan & Padilla, 1993).

Airway Resistance. The increased osmolarity following evaporation during forced ventilation (see above) can trigger the degranulation of macrophages, with the subsequent release of histamine (Nielsen et al., 1992), 15 hydroxyeicosatetraenoic acid, prostaglandins, and leukotriene B_4 (Kay, 1988; Souques et al., 1995; Tan & Spector, 1998). As a result, bronchoconstriction and enhanced fluid secretion occur (Dwyer & Farley, 1997) and can lead to exercise-induced asthma in susceptible individuals.

Performance. While it is clear that dehydration compromises performance (Coyle & Hamilton, 1990; Greenleaf, 1990; Sawka & Pandolf, 1990) and accelerates fatigue (Ladell, 1955), the contribution of altered cell volume during exercise is not clear at this time.

SUMMARY

Ample evidence indicates that exercise is paralleled by alterations of extracellular osmolarity and cell volume (Figure 2-7). In view of the many functions highly sensitive to alterations of cell volume, it is unlikely that these changes leave the physical performance unaffected. Most importantly, the metabolic effects of cell volume would predict anabolic effects of muscle cell swelling and catabolic effects of muscle cell shrinkage. Thus, it appears appropriate to systematically explore the role of altered cell volume and of factors influencing cell volume on physical performance.

ACKNOWLEDGEMENT

Research in the author's laboratory has been supported by the DFG (La 315/4-3).

Agius, L., M. Peak, G. Beresford, M. Al-habori, and T.H. Thomas (1994). The role of ion content and cell volume in insulin action. *Biochem. Soc. Trans.* 22:516–522.

Alfieri, R., P.G. Petronini, S. Urbani, and A.F. Borghetti (1996). Activation of heat shock transcription factor 1 by hypertonic shock in 3T3 cells. *Biochem. J.* 319:601–606.

Anderson, S.D. (1996). Challenge tests to assess airway hyperresponisveness and efficacy of drugs used in the treatment of asthma. *J. Aerosol Med. Depos. Clear. Effects Lung* 9:95–109.

Anderson, S.D. (1985). Issues in exercise-induced asthma. *J. Allergy Clin. Immunol.* 76:763–772.

Anderson, S.D. (1984). Is there a unifying hypothesis for exercise-induced asthma? *J. Allergy Clin. Immunol.* 73:660–665.

Anderson, S.D., and E. Daviskas (1992). The airway microvasculature and exercise induced asthma. *Thorax* 47:748–752.

Anderson, S.D., E. Daviskas, and C.M. Smith (1989). Exercise-induced asthma: a difference in opinion regarding the stimulus. *Allergy Proc.* 10:215–226.

Anderson, S.D., L.T. Rodwell, E. Daviskas, and J. Du toit (1996). The protective effect of nedocromil sodium and other drugs on airway narrowing provoked by hyperosmolar stimuli: A role for the airway epithelium? *J. Allergy Clin. Immunol.* 98:S124–S134.

Andrew, R.D. (1991). Seizure and acute osmotic change: clinical and neurophysiological aspects. *J. Neurol. Sci.* 101:7–18.

Arakawa, T., and S.N. Timasheff (1985). The stabilization of proteins by osmolytes. *Biophys. J.* 47:411–414.

Arieff, A.I., and H.J. Carroll (1972). Nonketotic hyperosmolar coma with hyperglycemia: Clinical features, pathophysiology, renal function, acid-base balance, plasma cerebrospinal fluid equilibria and the effects of therapy in 37 cases. *Medicine* (Baltimore) 51:73–94.

Ashkenazi, I., S. Melamed, and M. Blumenthal (1992). The effect of continuous strenuous exercise on intraocular pressure. *Invest. Ophthalmol. Vis. Sci.* 33:2874–2877.

Askenasy, N., M. Tassini, A. Vivi, and G. Navon (1995). Intracellular volume measurement and detection of edema: multinuclear NMR studies of intact rat hearts during normothermic ischemia. *Magn. Reson. Med.* 33:515–520.

Bagni, M.A., G. Cecchi, P.J. Griffiths, Y. Maeda, G. Rapp, and C.C. Ashley (1994). Lattice spacing changes accompanying isometric tension development in intact single muscle fibers. *Biophys. J.* 67:1965–1975.

Baquet, A., A. Lavoinne, and L. Hue (1991). Comparison of the effects of various amino acids on glycogen synthesis, lipogenesis and ketogenesis in isolated rat hepatocytes. *Biochem. J.* 273:57–62.

Baquet, A., L. Hue, A.J. Meijer, G.M. Van Woerkum, and P.J.A.M. Plomp (1990). Swelling of rat hepatocytes stimulates glycogen synthesis by insulin. *J. Biol. Chem.* 265:955–959.

Beck, F.-X., A. Dörge, and K. Thurau (1988). Cellular osmoregulation in renal medulla. *Renal Physiol. Biochem.* 11:174–186.

Beck, F.-X., M. Schmolke, W.G. Guder, A. Dörge, and K. Thurau (1992). Osmolytes in renal medulla during rapid changes in papillary tonicity. *Am. J. Physiol.* 262:F849–F856.

Bedford, J.J., S.M. Bagnasco, P.F. Kador, H.W. Harris, jr., and M.B. Burg (1987). Characterization and purification of a mammalian osmoregulatory protein, aldose reductase, induced in renal medullary cells by high extracellular NaCl. *J. Biol. Chem.* 262:14255–14259.

Ben Haim, S.A., Y. Edoute, G. Hayam, and O.S. Better (1992). Sodium modulates inotropic response to hyperosmolarity in isolated working rat heart. *Am. J. Physiol.* 263:H1154–H1160.

Benis, R.C., and D.W. Lundgren (1993). Sodium-dependent co-transported analogues of glucose stimulate ornithine decarboxylase mRNA expression in LLC-PK1 cells. *Biochem. J.* 289:751–756.

Ben-Ze'ev, A. (1991). Animal cell shape changes and gene expression. *BioEssays* 13:207–212.

Bianchini, L., A. Kapus, G. Lukacs, S. Wasan, S. Wakabayashi, J. Pouyssegur, F.H. Yu, J. Orlowski, and S. Grintstein (1995). Responsiveness of mutants of NHE-1 isoform of the Na+/H+ antiport to osmotic stress. *Am. J. Physiol.* 269:C998–C1007.

Bichet, D.G., R. Kluge, R.L. Howard, and R.W. Schrier (1992). Hyponatremic states. In: D.W. Seldin and G. Giebisch (eds.) *The Kidney: Physiology and Pathophysiology.* New York: Raven Press, pp. 1727–1751.

Blackard, W.G., M. Kikuchi, A. Rabinovitch, and A.E. Renold (1975). An effect of hyposmolarity on insulin release in vitro. *Am. J. Physiol.* 228:706–713.

Blaustein, M.P. (1993). Physiological effects of endogenous ouabain: control of intracellular Ca2+ stores and cell responsiveness. *Am. J. Physiol.* 264:C1367–C1387.

Bookstein, C., M.W. Musch, A. Depaoli, Y. Xie, M. Villereal, M.C. Rao, and E.B. Chang (1994). A unique sodium-hydrogen exchange isoform (NHE-4) of the inner medulla of the rat kidney is induced by hyperosmolarity. *J. Biol. Chem.* 269:29704–29709.

Brandenberger, G., V. Candas, M. Follenius, and J.M. Kahn (1989). The influence of the initial state of hydration on endocrine responses to exercise in the heat. *Eur. J. Appl. Physiol.* 58:674–679.

Brandenberger, G., V. Candas, M. Follenius, J.P. Libert, and J.M. Kahn (1986). Vascular fluid shifts and endocrine responses to exercise in the heat. Effect of rehydration. *Eur. J. Appl. Physiol.* 55:123–129.

Breur, G.J., B.A. Vanenkevort, C.E. Farnum, and N.J. Wilsman (1991). Linear relationship between the volume of hypertrophic chondrocytes and the rate of longitudinal bone growth in growth plates. *J. Orthop. Res.* 9:348–359.

Brizzolara, A., M.P. Barbieri, L. Adezati, and G.L. Viviani (1996). Water distribution in insulin dependent diabetes mellitus in various states of metabolic control. *Eur. J. Endocrinol.* 135:609–615.

Brown, A.D., and J.R. Simpson (1972). Water relations of sugar-tolerant yeasts: the role of intracellular polyols. *J. Gen. Microbiol.* 72:589–591.

Brusasco, V., and E. Crimi (1994). Allergy and sports: exercise-induced asthma. *Int. J. Sports Med.* 15:S184–S186.

Burg, M.B. (1994). Molecular basis for osmoregulation of organic osmolytes in renal medullary cells. *J. Exp. Zool.* 268:171–175.

Burg, M.B., and P.F. Kador (1988). Sorbitol, osmoregulation, and the complications of diabetes. *J. Clin. Invest.* 81:635–640.

Burg, M.B., E.D. Kwon, and D. Kueltz (1996). Osmotic regulation of gene expression. *FASEB J.* 10:1598–1606.

Busch, G.L., R. Schreiber, P.C. Dartsch, H. Völkl, S. Vom Dahl, D. Häussinger, and F. Lang (1994). Involvement of microtubules in the link between cell volume and pH of acidic cellular compartments. *Proc. Natl. Acad. Sci.* 91:9165–9169.

Busch, A.E., M. Varnum, J.P. Adelman, and R.A. North (1992). Hypotonic solution increases the slowly activating potassium current I_sK expressed in Xenopus oocytes. *Biochem. Biophys. Res. Commun.* 184:804–810.

Cala, P.M. (1985). Volume regulation by Amphiuma red blood cells: characteristics of volume-sensitive K/H and Na/H exchange. *Mol. Physiol.* 8:199–214.

Candas, V., J.P. Libert, G. Brandenberger, J.C. Sagot, C. Amoros, and J.M. Kahn (1986). Hydration during exercise. Effects on thermal and cardiovascular adjustments. *Eur. J. Appl. Physiol.* 55:113–122.

Chacon, E., J.M. Reece, A.L. Nieminen, G. Zahrebelski, B. Herman, and J.J. Lemasters (1994). Distribution of electrical potential, pH, free Ca2+, and volume inside cultured adult rabbit cardiac myocytes during chemical hypoxia: a multi-parameter digitized confocal microscopic study. *Biophys. J.* 66:942–952.

Chan, H.C., and D.J. Nelson (1992). Chloride-dependent cation conductance activated during cellular shrinkage. *Science.* 257:669–671.

Chen, J.G. and S.A. Kempson (1995). Osmoregulation of neutral amino acid transport. *Proc. Soc. Exp. Biol. Med.* 210:1–6.

Chen, J.G., L.R. Klus, D.K. Steenbergen, and S.A. Kempson (1994). Hypertonic upregulation of amino acid transport system A in vascular smooth muscle cells. *Am. J. Physiol.* 267:C529–C536.

Christensen, O. (1987). Mediation of cell volume regulation by Ca^{2+} influx through stretch-activated channels. *Nature* 330:66–68.

Clark, M.E., J.A.M. Hinke, and M.E. Todd (1981). Studies on water in barnacle muscle fibres. II. Role of ions and organic solutes in swelling of chemically-skinned fibres. *J. Exp. Biol.* 90:43–63.

Cohen, D.M., W.W. Chin, and S.R. Gullans (1994). Hyperosmotic urea increases transcription and synthesis of Egr-1 in murine inner medullary collecting duct (mIMCD3) cells. *J. Biol. Chem.* 269:25865–25870.

Cohen, D.M., J.C. Wasserman, and S.R. Gullans (1991). Immediate early gene and HSP70 expression in hyperosmotic stress in MDCK cells. *Am. J. Physiol.* 261:C594–C601.

Coyle, E.F., and M. Hamilton (1990). Fluid Replacement during Exercise: Effects on Physiological Homeostasis and Performance. In: C.V. Gisolfi and D.R. Lamb (eds.) *Fluid Homeostasis During Exercise. Perspecives in Exercise Science and Sports Medicine.* USA: Cooper Publishing Group, pp. 281–308.

Dall'Asta, V., P.A. Rossi, O. Bussolati, and G.C. Gazzola (1994). Response of human fibroblasts to hypertonic stress. Cell shrinkage is counteracted by an enhanced active transport of neutral amino acids. *J. Biol. Chem.* 269:10485–10491.

Dasgupta, S., T.C. Hohman, and D. Carper (1992). Hypertonic stress induces alpha B-crystallin expression. *Exp. Eye. Res.* 54:461–470.

Delpire, E., M.I. Rauchmann, D.R. Beier, S.C. Hebert, and S.R. Gullans (1994). Molecular cloning and chromosome localization of a putative basolateral Na^+-K^+-$2Cl^-$ cotransporter from mouse inner medullary collecting duct (mIMCD-3) cells. *J. Biol. Chem.* 269:25677–25683.

Demaurex, N., and S. Grinstein (1994). Na^+/H^+ antiport: modulation by ATP and role in cell volume regulation. *J. Exp. Biol.* 196:389–404.

Demerdash, T.M., N. Seyrek, M. Smogorzewski, W. Marcinkowski, S. Nassermoadelli, and S.G. Massry (1996). Pathways through which glucose induces a rise in $[Ca^{2+}]_i$ of polymorphonuclear leukocytes of rats. *Kidney Int.* 50:2032–2040.

Dermietzel, R., T.K. Hwang, R. Buettner, A. Hofer, E. Dotzler, M. Kremer, R. Deutzmann, F.P. Thinnes, G.I. Fishman, D.C. Spray, and D. Siemen (1994). Cloning and in situ localization of a brain derived porin that constitutes a large conductance anion channel in astrocytic plasma membranes. *Proc. Natl. Acad. Sci. USA* 91:499–503.

Deutsch, C., and L.Q. Chen (1993). Heterologous expression of specific K⁺ channels in T lymphocytes: functional consequences for volume regulation. *Proc. Natl. Acad. Sci. USA* 90:10036–10040.

Dong, J.M., and L. Lim (1996). Selective up regulation of alpha 1 chimaerin mRNA in SK N SH neuroblastoma by K+ induced depolarisation. *Eur. J. Biochem.* 236:820–826.

Dorup, I., and T. Clausen (1996). Characterization of bumetanide sensitive Na⁺ and K⁺ transport in rat skeletal muscle. *Acta Physiol. Scand.* 158:119–127.

Douguet, D., J. Raynaud, A. Capderou, C. Pannier, G. Reiss, and J. Durand (1988). Muscular venous blood metabolites during rhythmic forearm exercise while breathing air or normoxic helium and argon gas mixtures. *Clin. Physiol.* 8:367–378.

Dunham, P.B., F. Jessen, and E.K. Hoffmann (1990). Inhibition of Na-K-Cl cotransport in Ehrlich ascites cells by antiserum against purified proteins of the cotransporter. *Proc. Natl. Acad. Sci. USA* 87:6828–6832.

Dwyer, T.M., and J.M. Farley (1997). Mucus glycoconjugate secretion in cool and hypertonic solutions. *Am. J. Physiol.* 272:L1121–L1125.

Felipe, A., D.J. Snyders, K.K. Deal, and M.M. Tamkun (1993). Influence of cloned voltage-gated K⁺ channel expression on alanine transport, Rb⁺ uptake, and cell volume. *Am. J. Physiol.* 265:C1230–C1238.

Ferraris, J.D., M.B. Burg, C.K. Williams, E.M. Peters, and A. Garcia-Perez (1996a). Betaine transporter cDNA cloning and effect of osmolytes on its mRNA induction. *Am. J. Physiol.* 270:C650–C654.

Ferraris, J.D., C.K. Williams, K.Y. Jung, J.J. Bedford, M.B. Burg, and A. Garcia-Perez (1996b). ORE, a eukaryotic minimal essential osmotic response element. The aldose reductase gene in hyperosmotic stress. *J. Biol. Chem.* 271:18318–18321.

Ferraris, J.D., C.K. Williams, B.M. Martin, M.B. Burg, and A. Garcia-Perez (1994). Cloning, genomic organization, and osmotic response of the aldose reductase gene. *Proc. Natl. Acad. Sci. USA* 91:10742–10746.

Ferrer-Martinez, A., F.J. Casado, A. Felipe, and M. Pastoranglada (1996). Regulation of Na+, K+ ATPase and the Na+/K+/Cl cotransporter in the renal epithelial cell line NBL 1 under osmotic stress. *Biochem. J.* 319:337–342.

Finkenzeller, G., W. Newsome, F. Lang, and D. Häussinger (1994). Increase of c-jun mRNA upon hypoosmotic cell swelling of rat hepatoma cells. *FEBS Lett.* 340:163–166.

Flock, S., R. Labarbe, and C. Houssier (1995). Osmotic effectors and DNA structure: effect of glycine on precipitation of DNA by multivalent cations. *J. Biomol. Struct. Dyn.* 13:87–102.

Frederiksen, O., P.P. Leyssac, and S.L. Skinner (1975). Sensitive osmometer function of juxtaglomerular cells in vitro. *J. Physiol. Lond.* 252:669–679.

Gamba, G., A. Miyanoshita, M. Lombardi, J. Lytton, W.-S. Lee, M.A. Hediger, and S.C. Hebert (1994). Molecular cloning, primary structure and characterization of two members of the mammalian electroneutral sodium-(potassium)-chloride cotransporter family expressed in kidney. *J. Biol. Chem.* 269:17713–17722.

Garcia-Perez, A., and M.B. Burg (1991). Renal medullary organic osmolytes. *Physiol. Rev.* 71:1081–1115.

Garcia-Perez, A., B. Martin, H.R. Murphy, S. Uchida, H. Murer, B.D. Cowley, J.S. Handler, and M.B. Burg (1989). Molecular cloning of cDNA coding for kidney aldose reductase: Regulation of specific mRNA accumulation by NaCl-mediated osmotic stress. *J. Biol. Chem.* 264:16815–16821.

Garland, A., J.E. Jordan, J. Necheles, L.E. Alger, M.M. Scully, R.J. Miller, D.W. Ray, S.R. White, and J. Solway (1995). Hypertonicity, but not hyperthermia, elicits substance P release from rat fiber neurons in primary culture. *J. Clin. Invest.* 95:2359–2366.

Garner, M.M., and M.B. Burg (1994). Macromolecular crowding and confinement in cells exposed to hypertonicity. *Am. J. Physiol.* 266:C877–C892.

Gazzola, G.C., V. Dall'Asta, F.A. Nucci, P.A. Rossi, O. Bussolati, E.K. Hoffmann, and G.G. Guidotti (1991). Role of amino acid transport system A in the control of cell volume in cultured human fibroblasts. *Cell. Physiol. Biochem.* 1:131–142.

Geck, P., and B. Pfeiffer (1985). Na+K+2Cl- cotransport in animal cells—its role in volume regulation. *Ann. N.Y. Acad. Sci.* 456:166–182.

Gerlsma, S.Y. (1968). Reversible denaturation of ribonuclease in aqueous solutions as influenced by polyhydric alcohols and some other additives. *J. Biol. Chem.* 243:957–961.

Gilli, P., E. Depaoli-Vitali, G. Tarannni, and A. Farinelli (1984). Exercise-induced urinary abnormalities in long-distance runners. *Int. J. Sports Med.* 5:237–240.

Giovannelli, L., P.J. Shiromani, G.F. Jirikowski, and F.E. Bloom (1992). Expression of c-fos protein by immunohistochemically identified oxytocin neurons in the rat hypothalamus upon osmotic stimulation. *Brain. Res.* 588:41–48.

Godt, R.E., R.T. Fogaca, M.A. Andrews, and T.M. Nosek (1993). Influence of ionic strength on contractile force and energy consumption of skinned fibers from mammalian and crustacean striated muscle. *Adv. Exp. Med. Biol.* 332:763–774.

Gore, C.J., G.C. Scroop, J.D. Marker, and P.G. Catcheside (1992). Plasma volume, osmolarity, total protein and electrolytes during treadmill running and cycle ergometer exercise. *Eur. J. Appl. Physiol.* 65:302–310.

Greenleaf, J.E. (1990). Importance of fluid homeostasis for optimal adaptation to exercise and environmental stress: acceleration. In: C.V. Gisolfi and D.R. Lamb (eds.) *Fluid Homeostasis During Exercise. Perspecives in Exercise Science and Sports Medicine.* USA: Cooper Publishing Group, pp. 309–346.

Greenwald, J.E., M. Apkon, K.A. Hruska, and P. Needleman (1989). Stretch-induced atriopeptin secretion in the isolated rat myocyte and its negative modulation by calcium. *J. Clin. Invest.* 83:1061–1065.

Greer, M.A., S.E. Greer, and S. Maruta (1990). Hyposmolar stimulation of secretion of thyrotropin, prolactin, and luteinizing hormone does not require extracellular calcium and is not inhibited by colchicine, cytochalasin B, ouabain, or tetrodotoxin. *Proc. Soc. Exp. Biol. Med.* 193:203–209.

Greer, M.A., S.E. Greer, Z. Opsahl, L. McCafferty, and S. Maruta (1983). Hyposmolar stimulation of in vitro pituitary secretion of luteinizing hormone: A potential clue to the secretory process. *Endocrinology* 113:1531–1533.

Grinstein, S., C.A. Clarke, and A. Rothstein (1983). Activation of Na+/H+ exchange in lymphocytes by osmotically induced volume changes and by cytoplasmic acidification. *J. Gen. Physiol.* 82:619–638.

Groeneveld, A.B., A.A. Van-Lambalgen, G.C. Van-den-Bos, J.J. Nauta, and L.G. Thijs (1992). Metabolic vasodilatation with glucose-insulin-potassium does not change the heterogeneous distribution of coronary blood flow in the dog. *Cardiovasc. Res.* 26:757–764.

Gründer, S., A. Thiemann, M. Pusch, and T.J. Jentsch (1992). Regions involved in the opening of the ClC-2 chloride channel by voltage and cell volume. *Nature* (London) 360:759–762.

Gullans, S.R., J.D. Blumenfeld, J.A. Balschi, M. Kaleta, R.M. Brenner, C.W. Heilig, and S.C. Hebert (1988). Accumulation of major organic osmolytes in renal inner medulla in dehydration. *Am. J. Physiol.* 255:F626–F634.

Haberich, F.J., O. Aziz, and P.E. Nowacki (1965). Über einen osmoreceptorisch tätigen Mechanismus in der Leber. *Pflügers Arch.* 285:73–89.

Hallbrucker, C., S. Vom Dahl, F. Lang, W. Gerok, and D. Häussinger (1991a). Inhibition of hepatic proteolysis by insulin. Role of hormone-induced alterations of the cellular K⁺ balance. *Eur. J. Biochem.* 199:467–474.

Hallbrucker, C., S. Vom Dahl, F. Lang, W. Gerok, and D. Häussinger (1991). Modification of liver cell volume by insulin and glucagon. *Pflügers Arch.* 418:519–521.

Hallbrucker, C., S. Vom Dahl, F. Lang, and D. Häussinger (1991c). Control of hepatic proteolysis by amino acids: the role of cell volume. *Eur. J. Biochem.* 197:717–724.

Handler, J.S., and H.M. Kwon (1993). Regulation of renal cell organic osmolyte transport by tonicity. *Am. J. Physiol.* 265:C1449–C1455.

Häussinger, D., and F. Lang (1990). Exposure of perfused liver to hypotonic conditions modifies cellular nitrogen metabolism. *J. Cell. Biochem.* 43: 355–361.

Häussinger, D., C. Hallbrucker, S. Vom Dahl, S. Decker, U. Schweizer, F. Lang, and W. Gerok (1991). Cell volume is a major determinant of proteolysis control in liver. *FEBS Lett.* 283:70–72.

Häussinger, D., C. Hallbrucker, S. Vom Dahl, F. Lang, and W. Gerok (1990a). Cell swelling inhibits proteolysis in perfused rat liver. *Biochem. J.* 272:239–242.

Häussinger D., F. Lang, K. Bauers, and W. Gerok (1990b). Control of hepatic nitrogen metabolism and gluthatione release by cell volume regulatory mechanisms. *Eur. J. Biochem.* 193:891–898.

Häussinger, D., F. Lang, K. Bauers, and W. Gerok (1990c). Interactions between glutamine metabolism and cell volume regulation in perfused rat liver. *Eur. J. Biochem.* 188:689–695.

Häussinger, D., W. Newsome, S. Vom Dahl, B. Stoll, B. Noe, R. Schreiber, M. Wettstein, and F. Lang (1994a). Control of liver cell function by the hydration state. *Biochem. Soc. Trans.* 22:497–502.

Häussinger, D., E. Roth, F. Lang, and W. Gerok (1993a). Cellular hydration state: an important determinant of protein catabolism in health and disease. *Lancet* 341:1330–1332.

Häussinger, D., N. Saha, C. Hallbrucker, F. Lang, and W. Gerok (1993b). Involvement of microtubules in the swelling-induced stimulation of transcellular taurocholate transport in perfused rat liver. *Biochem. J.* 291:355–360.

Häussinger, D., B. Stoll, Y. Morimoto, F. Lang, and W. Gerok (1992). Anisoosmotic liver perfusion: redox shifts and modulation of (-ketoisocaproate and glycine metabolism. *Biol. Chem. Hoppe- Seyler* 373:723–734.

Häussinger, D., B. Stoll, S. Vom Dahl, P.A. Theodoropoulos, E. Markogiannakis, A. Gravanis, F. Lang, and C. Stournaras (1994b). Effect of hepatocyte swelling on microtubule stability and tubulin mRNA levels. Biochem. *Cell. Biol.* 72:12–19.

Hayama, N., W. Wang, and E.G. Schneider (1995). Osmolality-induced changes in aldosterone secretion involve a chloride-dependent process. *Am. J. Physiol.* 268:R8–R13.

Henderson, L.M., J.B. Chappell, and O.T. Jones (1989). Superoxide generation is inhibited by phospholipase A2 inhibitors. Role for phospholipase A2 in the activation of the NADPH oxidase. *Biochem. J.* 264:249–255.

Hoffmann, E.K., and P.B. Dunham (1995). Membrane mechanisms and intracellular signalling in cell volume regulation. *Int. Rev. Cytology* 161:173–262.

CHANGES IN CELLULAR HYDRATION   **79**

Hoffmann, E.K., and K.B. Hendil (1976). The role of amino acids and taurine in isosmotic intracellular regulation in Ehrlich ascites mouse tumour cells. *J. Comp. Physiol.* 108:279–286.

Howard, R.L., D.G. Bichet, and R.W. Schrier (1992). Hypernatremic and polyuric states. In: D.W. Seldin and G. Giebisch (eds.) *The Kidney: Physiology and Pathophysiology.* New York: Raven Press, pp. 1753–1778.

Inukai, T., X. Wang, S.E. Greer, and M.A. Greer (1992). Cell swelling induced by medium hyposmolarity or isosmolar urea stimulates gonadotropin-releasing hormone secretion from perifused rat median eminence. *Brain Res.* 599:161–164.

Iyer, S.S., D.W. Pearson, W.M. Nauseef, and R.A. Clark (1994). Evidence for a readily dissociable complex of p47phox and p67phox in cytosol of unstimulated human neutrophils. *J. Biol. Chem.* 269:22405–22411.

Jackson, P.S., and K. Strange (1993). Volume-sensitive anion channels mediate swelling-activated inositol and taurine efflux. *Am. J. Physiol.* 265:C1489–C1500.

Jensen, B.L., and O. Skøtt (1993). Osmotically sensitive renin release from permeabilized juxtaglomerular cells. *Am. J. Physiol.* 265:F87–F95.

Jentsch, T.J. (1996). Chloride channels: a molecular perspective. *Curr. Opin. Neurobiol.* 6:303–310.

Jiang, L.W., M.N. Chernova, and S.L. Alper (1997). Secondary regulatory volume increase conferred in xenopus oocytes by expression of AE2 anion exchanger. *Am. J. Physiol.* 41:C191–C202.

Kataoka, S., and Y. Fujita (1991). Basal experiments of active oxygen generation in urinary polymorphonuclear leukocytes. *Nippon. Hinyokika. Gakkai. Zasshi.* 82:16–23.

Katayama, S., M. Abe, K. Tanaka, A. Omoto, K. Negishi, A. Itabashi, and J. Ishii (1991). High glucose concentration suppresses mesangial laminin B2 gene expression. *J. Diabet. Comp.* 5:118–120.

Kay, A.B. (1989). Inflammatory cells in bronchial asthma. *J. Asthma* 26:335–344.

Kay, A.B. (1988). Leucocytes in asthma. *Immunol. Invest.* 17:679–705.

Kilbourne, E.J., A. McMahon, and E.L. Sabban (1991). Membrane depolarization by isotonic or hypertonic KCl: differential effects on mRNA levels of tyrosine hydroxylase and dopamine beta-hydroxylase mRNA in PC12 cells. *J. Neurosci. Methods* 40:193–202.

Kim, Y.-J., R.L.Y. Sah, A.J. Grodzinsky, A.H.K. Plaas, and J.D. Sandy (1994). Mechanical regulation of cartilage bio-synthetic behavior: physical stimuli. *Arch. Biochem. Biophys.* 311:1–12.

Kinne, R.K.H. (1993). The role of organic osmolytes in osmore-gulation: From bacteria to mammals. *J. Exp. Zool.* 265:346–355.

Kinne, R.K.H., R.-P. Czekay, J.M. Grunewald, F.C. Mooren, and E. Kinne-Saffran (1993). Hypotonicity-evoked release of organic osmolytes from distal renal cells: Systems, signals, and sidedness. *Renal Physiol. Biochem.* 16:66–78.

Klein, J.P., H.V. Forster, R.D. Stewart, and A. Wu (1980). Hemoglobin affinity for oxygen during short-term exhaustive exercise. *J. Appl. Physiol.* 48:236–242.

Kohan, D.E., and E. Padilla (1993). Osmolar regulation of endothelin-1 production by rat inner medullary collecting duct. *J. Clin. Invest.* 91:1235–1240.

Kuchkina, N.V., S.N. Orlov, N.I. Pokudin, and A.G. Chuchalin (1993). Volume-dependent regulation of the respiratory burst of activated human neutrophils. *Experientia* 49:995–997.

Kuhn, J.L., J.H. Delacy, and E.E. Leenellett (1996). Relationship between bone growth rate and hypertrophic chondrocyte volume in New Zealand white rabbits of varying ages. *J. Orthopaed. Res.* 14:706–711.

Kurtz, A. (1990). Do calcium-activated chloride channels control renin secretion? *News Physiol. Sci.* 5:43–46.

Kwon, H.M. (1994). Osmoregulation of Na-coupled organic osmolyte transporters. *Renal Physiol. Biochem.* 17:205–207.

Kwon, H.M., and J.S. Handler (1995). Cell volume regulated transporters of compatible osmolytes. *Curr. Opin. Cell Biol.* 7:465–471.

Kwon, H.M., A. Yamauchi, S. Uchida, A.S. Preston, A. Garcia-Perez, M.B. Burg, and J.S. Handler (1992). Cloning of the cDNA for a Na+/myo-Inositol cotransporter, a hypertonicity stress protein. *J. Biol. Chem.* 267:6297–6301.

Ladell, W.S.S. (1955). The effects of water and salt intake upon the performance of men working in hot and humid environments. *J. Physiol.* (Lond.) 127:11–46.

Lang, F., G.L. Busch, and E. Gulbins (1995a). Physiology of cell survival and cell death: Implications for organ conservation. *Nephrol. Dial. Transplant* 10:1551–1555.

Lang, F., G.L. Busch, M. Ritter, H. Völkl, S. Waldegger, E. Gulbins, and D. Häussinger (1998a). The functional significance of cell volume regulatory mechanisms. *Physiol. Rev.* 78:247–306.

Lang, F., G.L. Busch, and H. Völkl (1998b). The diversity of volume regulatory mechanisms. *Cell. Physiol. Biochem.* 8:1–45.

Lang, F., G.L. Busch, H. Völkl, and D. Häussinger (1994). Lysosomal pH—a link between cell volume and metabolism. *Biochem. Soc. Trans.* 22:502–504.

Lang, F., G.L. Busch, G. Zempel, J. Ditlevsen, M. Hoch, U. Emerich, D. Axel, J. Fingerle, S. Meierkord, H. Apfel, P. Krippeit-Drews, and H. Heinle (1995b). Ca^{2+} entry and vasoconstriction during osmotic swelling of vascular smooth muscle cells. *Pflügers Arch.* 431:253–258.

Lang, F., T. Stehle, and D. Häussinger (1989). Water, K$^+$,H$^+$, lactate and glucose fluxes during cell volume regulation in perfused rat liver. *Pflügers Arch.* 413:209–216.

Lauf, P.K. (1988). K:Cl cotransport: Emerging molecular aspects of a ouabain-resistant, volume-responsive transport system in red blood cells. *Renal Physiol. Biochem.* 11:248–259.

Lavoinne, A., A. Husson, M. Quillard, A. Chedeville, and A. Fairand (1996). Glutamine inhibits the lowering effect of glucose on the level of phosphoenolpyruvate carboxykinase mRNA in isolated rat hepatocytes. *Eur. J. Biochem.* 242:537–543.

Law, R.O. (1991). Amino acids as volume-regulatory osmolytes in mammalian cells. *Comp. Biochem. Physiol.* 99:263–277.

Lepple-Wienhues, A., T. Laun, N.K. Kaba, I. Szabo, E. Gulbins, and F. Lang (1998). The tyrosine kinase p56^{lck} mediates activation of swelling-induced chloride channels in lymphocytes. *J. Cell Biol.* 141:281–286.

Levin, E.G., L. Santell, and F. Saljooque (1993). Hyperosmotic stress stimulates tissue plasminogen activator expression by a PKC-independent pathway. *Am. J. Physiol.* 265:C387–C396.

Lichtstein, D., I. Gati, E. Haver, and U. Katz (1992). Digitalis-like compounds in the toad Bufo viridis: tissue and plasma levels and significance in osmotic stress. *Life Sci.* 51:119–128.

Ling, H., S. Vamvakas, G.L. Busch, P. Kulzer, L. Schramm, M. Teschner, F. Lang, and A. Heidland (1995a). Suppressing role of transforming growth factor-b1 on cathepsin activity in cultured tubule cells. *Am. J. Physiol.* 269:F911–F917.

Ling, H., S. Vamvakas, M. Gekle, L. Schaefer, M. Teschner, R.M. Schaefer, and A. Heidland (1995b). Role of lysosomal cathepsin activites in cellular hypertrophy induced by NH$_4$Cl in cultured tubule cells. *J. Am. Soc. Nephrol.* 6:1021.

Lovkvist-Wallstrom, E., L. Stjernborg-Ulvsback, I.E. Scheffler, and L. Persson (1995). Regulation of mammalian ornithine decarboxylase. Studies on the induction of the enzyme by hypotonic stress. *Eur. J. Biochem.* 231:40–44.

Low, S.Y., M.J. Rennie, and P.M. Taylor (1996). Modulation of glycogen synthesis in rat skeletal muscle by changes in cell volume. *J. Physiol. Lond.* 495:299–303.

Lund, P.E., A. Berts, and B. Hellman (1992). Stimulation of insulin release by isosmolar addition of permeant molecules. *Mol. Cell. Biochem.* 109:77–81.

Macknight, A.D. (1988). Principles of cell volume regulation. *Renal Physiol. Biochem.* 11:114–141.

Manara, F.S., J. Chin, and D.L. Schneider (1991). Role of degranulation in activation of the respiratory burst in human neutrophils. *J. Leukoc. Biol.* 79:489–496.

Martinez-Maldonado, M., J.E. Benabe, and H.R. Cordova (1992). Chronic clinical intrinsic renal failure. In: D.W. Seldin and G. Giebisch (eds.) *The Kidney: Physiology and Pathophysiology.* New York: Raven Press, pp. 3227–3288.

Matsumoto, T., P. Van der Auwera, Y. Watanabe, M. Tanaka, N. Ogata, S. Naito, and J. Kumazawa (1991). Neutrophil function in hyperosmotic NaCl is preserved by phosphoenol pyruvate. *Urol. Res.* 19:223–227.

McCarty, N.A. and R.G. O'Neil (1992). Calcium signaling in cell volume regulation. *Physiol. Rev.* 72:1037–1061.

McKelvie, R.S., N.L. Jones, and G.J.F. Heigenhauser (1997). Effect of progressive incremental exercise and beta-adrenergic blockade on erythrocyte ion concentrations. *Can. J. Physiol. Pharmacol.* 75:19–25.

McManus, M.L., and K.B. Churchwell (1994). Clinical significance of cellular osmoregulation. In: K. Strange (ed.) *Cellular and Molecular Physiology of Cell Volume Regulation.* Boca Raton, FL: CRC Press, pp. 63–77.

Meijer, A.J., A. Baquet, L. Gustafson, G.M. Van Woerkom, and L. Hue (1992). Mechanism of activation of liver glycogen synthase by swelling. *J. Biol. Chem.* 267:5823–5828.

Minton, A.P. (1994). Influence of macromolecular crowding on intracellular association reactions: Possible role in volume regulation. In: K. Strange (ed.) *Cellular and Molecular Physiology of Cell Volume Regulation.* Boca Raton, FL: CRC Press, pp. 181–190.

Minton, A.P. (1993). Macromolecular crowding and molecular recognition. *J. Mol. Recognit.* 6:211–214.

Morris, C.E. (1990). Mechanosensitive ion channels. *J. Membr. Biol.* 113:93–107.

Mortimore, G.E, and A.R. Pösö (1987). Intracellular protein cata-bolism and its control during nutrient deprivation and supply. *Ann. Rev. Nutr.* 7:539–564.

Murphy, D., and D. Carter (1990). Vasopressin gene expression in the rodent hypothalamus: transcriptional and posttranscriptional responses to physiological stimulation. *Mol. Endocrinol.* 4:1051–1059.

Nakanishi, T., R.J. Turner, and M.B. Burg (1990). Osmoregulation of betaine transport in mammalian renal medullary cells. *Am. J. Physiol.* 258:F1061–F1067.

Nelson, P.B., A.G. Robinson, W. Kapoor, and J. Rinaldo (1988). Hyponatremia in a marathoner. *Phys. Sportsmed.* 16:78–88.

Newsome, W.P., U. Warskulat, B. Noe, M. Wettstein, B. Stoll, W. Gerok, and D. Häussinger (1994). Modulation of phosphoenolpyruvate carboxykinase mRNA levels by the hepatocellular hydration state. *Biochem. J.* 304:555–560.

Nielsen, B. (1974). Effects of changes in plasma volume and osmolarity on thermoregulation during exercise. *Acta Physiol. Scand.* 90:725–730.

Nielsen, B.W., T. Bjerke, T.M. Damsgaard, T. Herlin, K. ThestrupPedersen, and P.O. Schiotz (1992). Hyperosmolarity selec-tively enhances IgEreceptormediated histamine release from human basophils. *Agents Actions* 35:170–178.

Noakes, T.D., N. Goodwin, B.L. Rayner, T. Branken, and R.K.N. Taylor (1985). Water intoxication: A possible complication during endurance exercise. *Med. Sci. Sport Exer.* 17:370–375.

Noe, B., F. Schliess, M. Wettstein, S. Heinrich, and D. Häussinger (1996). Regulation of taurocholate excretion by a hypoosmolarity-activated signal transduction pathway in rat liver. *Gastroenterology* 110:858–865.

Oliet, S.H., and C.W. Bourque (1993). Mechanosensitive channels transduce osmosensitivity in supraoptic neurons. *Nature* 364:341–343.

Osehobo, E.P., and R.D. Andrew (1993). Osmotic effects upon the theta rhythm, a natural brain oscillation in the hippocampal slice. *Exp. Neurol.* 124:192–199.

Parker, J.C. (1993). In defense of cell volume? *Am. J. Physiol.* 265:C1191–C1200.

Paulmichl, M., Y. Li, K. Wickman, M. Ackerman, E. Peralta, and D. Clapham (1992). New mammalian chloride channel identified by expression cloning. *Nature* 356:238–241.

Payne, J.A., and B. Forbush III (1994). Alternatively spliced isoforms of the putative renal Na-K-Cl cotransporter are differentially distributed within the rabbit kidney. *Proc. Natl. Acad. Sci.* USA 91:4544–4548.

Payne, J.A., and B. Forbush III (1995). Molecular characterization of the epithelial Na-K-Cl cotransporter isoforms. *Curr. Opin. Cell Biol.* 7:493–503.

Peak, M., M. Al-Habouri, and L. Agius (1992). Regulation of glycogen synthesis and glycolysis by insulin, pH and cell volume. *Biochem. J.* 282:797–805.

Perry, P.B., and W.C. O'Neill (1993). Swelling-activated K fluxes in vascular endothelial cells: volume regulation via K-Cl cotransport and K channels. *Am. J. Physiol.* 265:C763–C769.

Petronini, P.G., E.M. De-Angelis, P. Borghetti, A.F. Borghetti, and K.P. Wheeler (1992). Modulation by betaine of cellular responses to osmotic stress. *Biochem. J.* 282:69–73.

Poortmans, J.R. (1984). Exercise and renal function. *Sports Med.* 1:125–153.

Poulin, R., R.S. Wechter, and A.E. Pegg (1991). An early enlargement of the putrescine pool is required for growth in L1210 mouse leukemia cells under hypoosmotic stress. *J. Biol. Chem.* 266:6142–6151.

Raynaud, J., D. Douguet, P. Legros, A. Capderou, B. Raffestin, and J. Durand (1986). Time course of muscular blood metabolites during forearm rhythmic exercise in hypoxia. *J. Appl. Physiol.* 60:1203–1208.

Ritter, M., and E. Wöll (1996). Modification of cellular ion transport by the Ha-ras oncogene: steps towards malignant transformation. *Cell. Physiol. Biochem.* 6:245–270.

Robinson, A.G., and J.N. Loeb (1971). Ethanol ingestion- commonest cause of elevated plasma osmolality? *N. Engl. J. Med.* 284:1253–1255.

Rougier, J.P., P. Moullier, R. Piedagnel, and P.M. Ronco (1997). Hyperosmolality suppresses but TGF beta 1 increases MMP9 in human peritoneal mesothelial cells. *Kidney Int.* 51:337–347.

Roy, G., and U. Banderali (1994). Channels for ions and amino acids in kidney cultured cells (MDCK) during volume regulation. *J. Exp. Zool.* 268:121–126.

Ruepp, B., K.M. Bohren, and K.H. Gabbay (1996). Characterization of the osmotic response element of the human aldose reductase gene promoter. *Proc. Natl. Acad. Sci. U.S.A.* 93:8624–8629.

Sachs, F. (1991). Mechanical transduction by membrane ion channels: A mini review. *Mol. Cell. Biochem.* 104:57–60.

Sackin, H. (1994). Stretch-activated ion channels. In: K. Strange (ed.) *Cellular and Molecular Physiology of Cell Volume Regulation.* Boca Raton, FL: CRC Press, pp. 215–240.

Sadoshima, J., Z.H. Qui, J.P. Morgan, and S. Izumo (1996). Tyrosine kinase activation is an immediate and essential step in hypotonic cell swelling induced ERK activation and c-fos gene expression in cardiac myocytes. *EMBO J.* 15:5535–5546.

Saha, N., R. Schreiber, S. Vom Dahl, F. Lang, W. Gerok, and D. Häussinger (1993). Endogenous hydroperoxide formation, cell volume and cellular K^+ balance in perfused rat liver. *Biochem. J.* 296:701–707.

Saha, N., B. Stoll, F. Lang, and D. Häussinger (1992). Effect of anisotonic cell-volume modulation on glutathione-S-conjugate release, t-butylhydroperoxide metabolism and the pentose-phosphate shunt in perfused rat liver. *Eur. J. Biochem.* 209:437–444.

Saltin, B., G. Sjögaard, S. Strange, and C. Juel (1987). Redistribution of K+ in the human body during muscular exercise; its role to maintain whole body homeostasis. In: K. Shiraki and M.K. Yousef (eds.) *Man in Stressful Environments: Thermal and Work Physiology.* Springfield, IL: Thomas, pp. 247–267.

Santell, L., R.L. Rubin, and E.G. Levin (1993). Enhanced phosphorylation and dephosphorylation of a histone-like protein in response to hyperosmotic and hypoosmotic conditions. *J. Biol. Chem.* 268:21443–21447.

Sato, N., X. Wang, and M.A. Greer (1991). Medium hyperosmolarity depresses thyrotropin-releasing hormone-induced Ca2+ influx and prolactin secretion in GH4C1 cells. *Mol. Cell. Endocrinol.* 77:193–198.

Sawaka, M.N., and K.B. Pandolf (1990). Effects of body water loss on physiological function and exercise performance. In: C.V. Gisolfi and D.R. Lamb (eds.) *Fluid Homeostasis During Exercise. Perspecives in Exercise Science and Sports Medicine.* USA: Cooper Publishing Group, pp. 1–38.

Schiebinger, R.J., and J. Linden (1986). The influence of resting tension on immunoreactive atrial natriuretic peptide secretion by rat atria superfused in vitro. *Circ. Res.* 59:105–109.

Schliess, F., R. Schreiber, and D. Häussinger (1995). Activation of extracellular signal-regulated kinases Erk-1 and Erk-2 by cell swelling in H4IIE hepatoma cells. *Biochem. J.* 309:13–17.

Schneider, E.G., R.E. Taylor, Jr, K.J. Radke, and P.G. Davis (1984). Effect of sodium concentration on aldosterone secretion by isolated perfused canine adrenal glands. *Endocrinol.* 115:2195–2204.

Schultz, S.G. (1989). Volume preservation: then and now. *News Physiol. Sci.* 4:169–172.

Sergeev, I.I.U., O.S. Tarasova, and N.A. Medvedeva (1992). An analysis of the components of the hyperosmotic vasomotor effect. *Fiziol. Zh.* 38:36–42.

Sheik-Hamad, D., A. Garcia-Perez, J.D. Ferraris, E.M. Peters, and M.B. Burg (1994). Induction of gene expression by heat shock versus osmotic stress. *Am. J. Physiol.* 267:F28–F34.

Sheppard, D., and W.L. Eschenbacher (1984). Respiratory water loss as a stimulus to exercise-induced bronchoconstriction. *J. Allergy Clin. Immunol.* 73:640–642.

Skott, O. (1986). Calcium and osmotic stimulation in renin release from isolated rat glomeruli. *Pflügers Arch.* 406:485–491.

Smardo, F.L., M.B. Burg, and A. García-Pérez (1992). Kidney aldose reductase gene transcription is osmotically regulated. *Am. J. Physiol.* 262:C776–C782.

Smith, J.A., M. Kolbuch-Braddon, I. Gillam, R.D. Telford, and M.J. Weidemann (1995). Changes in the susceptibility of red blood cells to oxidative and osmotic stress following submaximal exercise. *Eur. J. Appl. Physiol.* 70:427–436.

Smith, T.W., R.L. Rasmusson, L.A. Lobaugh, and M. Lieberman (1993). Na+/K+ pump inhibition induces cell shrinkage in cultured chick cardiac myocytes. *Basic Res. Cardiol.* 88:411–420.

Smith, J.A., R.D. Telford, M. Kolbuch-Braddon, and M.J. Weidemann (1997). Lactate/H+ uptake by red blood cells during exercise alters their physical properties. *Eur. J. Appl. Physiol.* 75:54–61.

Soler, C., A. Felipe, F.J. Casado, J.D. McGivan, and M. Pastor-Anglada (1993). Hyperosmolarity leads to an increase in derepressed system A activity in the renal epithelial cell line NBL-1. *Biochem. J.* 289:653–658.

Sorota, S. (1992). Swelling-induced chloride-sensitive current in canine atrial cells revealed by whole-cell patch-clamp method. *Circ. Res.* 70:679–687.

Souques, F., L. Crampette, M. Mondain, A.M. Vignola, P. Chanez, J. Bousquet, and A.M. Campbell (1995). Stimulation of dispersed nasal polyp cells by hyperosmolar solutions. *J. Allerg Clin. Immunol.* 96:980–985.

Steenbergen, J.M., and H.G. Bohlen (1993). Sodium hyperosmolarity of intestinal lymph causes arteriolar vasodilation in part mediated by EDRF. *Am. J. Physiol.* 265:H323–H328.

Stoll, B., W. Gerok, F. Lang, and D. Häussinger (1992). Liver cell volume and protein synthesis. *Biochem. J.* 287:217–222.

Takahashi, K., T. Matsumoto, S. Kubo, M. Haraoka, M. Tanaka, and J. Kumazawa (1994). Influence of hyperosmotic environment comparable to the renal medulla upon membrane NADPH oxidase of human polymorphonuclear leukocytes. *J. Urol.* 152:1622–1625.

Takenaka, M., S.M. Bagnasco, A.S. Preston, S. Uchida, A. Yamauchi, H.M. Kwon, and J.S. Handler (1995). The canine betaine gamma-amino-n-butyric acid transporter gene: diverse mRNA isoforms are regulated by hypertonicity and are expressed in a tissue-specific manner. *Proc. Natl. Acad. Sci. USA* 92:1072–1076.

Takenaka, M., A.S. Preston, H.M. Kwon, and J.S. Handler (1994). The tonicitysensitive element that mediates increased transcription of the betaine transporter gene in response to hypertonic stress. *J. Biol. Chem.* 269:29379–29381.

Tan, R.A., and S.L. Spector (1998). Exercise-induced asthma. *Sports Med.* 25:1–6.

Tanaka, K., G. Jay, and K.J. Isselbacher (1988). Expression of heat-shock and glucose-regulated genes: differential effects of glucose starvation and hypertonicity. *Biochim. Biophys. Acta* 950:138–146.

Taniguchi, J., and W.B. Guggino (1989). Membrane stretch: a physiological stimulator of Ca2+-activated K+ channels in thick ascending limb. *Am. J. Physiol.* 257:F347–F352.

Theodoropoulos, P.A., C. Stournaras, B. Stoll, E. Markogiannakis, F. Lang, A. Gravanis, and D. Häussinger (1992). Hepatocyte swelling leads to rapid decrease of the G-/total actin ratio and increases actin mRNA levels. *FEBS Lett.* 311:241–245.

Tilly, B.C., N. Van den Berghe, L.G.J. Tertoolen, M.J. Edixhoven, and H.R. De Jonge (1993). Protein tyrosine phosphorylation is involved in osmoregulation of ionic conductances. *J. Biol. Chem.* 268:19919–19922.

Tohyama, Y., T. Kameji, and S. Hayashi (1991). Mechanisms of dramatic fluctuations of ornithine decarboxylase activity upon tonicity changes in primary cultured rat hepatocytes. *Eur. J. Biochem.* 202:1327–1331.

Turner, D.A., P.G. Aitken, and G.G. Somjen (1995). Optical mapping of translucence changes in rat hippocampal slices during hypoxia. *Neurosci. Lett.* 195:209–213.

Ubl, J., H. Murer, and H.-A. Kolb (1988). Ion channels activated by osmotic and mechanical stress in membranes of opossum kidney cells. *J. Membr. Biol.* 104:223–232.

Uchida, S., A. Garcia-Perez, H. Murphy, and M.B. Burg (1989). Signal for induction of aldose reductase in renal medullary cells by high external NaCl. *Am. J. Physiol.* 256:C614–C620.

Uchida, S., N. Green, H. Coon, T. Triche, S. Mims, and M.B. Burg (1987). High NaCl induces stable changes in phenotype and karyotype of renal cells in culture. *Am. J. Physiol.* 253:C230–C242.

Uchida, S., H.M. Kwon, A.S. Preston, and J.S. Handler (1991). Expression of Madin-Darby canine kidney cell Na+- and Cl−-dependent taurine transporter in Xenopus laevis oocytes. *J. Biol. Chem.* 266:9605–9609.

Uchida, S., H.M. Kwon, A. Yamauchi, A.S. Preston, F. Marumo, and J.S. Handler (1992). Molecular cloning of the cDNA for an MDCK cell Na(+) and Cl(−)-dependent taurine transporter that is regulated by hypertonicity. *Proc. Natl. Acad. Sci. USA* 89:8230–8234.

Uchida, S., S. Sasaki, T. Furukawa, M. Hiraoka, T. Imai, Y. Hirata, and F. Marumo (1993). Molecular cloning of a chloride channel that is regulated by dehydration and expressed predominantly in kidney medulla. *J. Biol. Chem.* 268:3821–3824.

Ullrich, K.J. (1959). Glycerylphosphorylcholinumsatz und Glyceryl-phosphorylcholindiesterase in der Säugetier-Niere. *Biochem. Z.* 331:98–102.

Urban, J.P.G., A.C. Hall, and K.A. Gehl (1993). Regulation of matrix synthesis rates by the ionic and osmotic environment of articular chondrocytes. *J. Cell. Physiol.* 154:262–270.

Valverde, M.A., T.D. Bond, S.P. Hardy, J.C. Taylor, C.F. Higgins, J. Altamirano, and F.J. Alvarez-Leefmans (1996). The multidrug resistance P glycoprotein modulates cell regulatory volume decrease. *EMBO J.* 15:4460–4468.

Valverde, M.A., M. Diaz, F.V. Sepúlveda, D.R. Gill, S.C. Hyde, and C.F. Higgins (1992). Volume-regulated chloride channel associated with the human multidrug-resistant P-glycoprotein. *Nature* 355:830–833.

Van der Meulen, J.A., A. Klip, and S. Grinstein (1987). Possible mechanism for cerebral edema in diabetic ketoacidosis. *Lancet* 2:306–308.

Vanden Broeck, J., A. De Loof, and P. Callaerts (1992). Electrical-ionic control of gene expression. *Int. J. Biochem.* 24:1907–1916.

Vandenberg, J.I., A. Yoshida, K. Kirk, and T. Powell (1994). Swelling-activated and isoprenaline-activated chloride currents in guinea pig cardiac myocytes have distinct electrophysiology and pharmacology. *J. Gen. Physiol.* 104:997–1017.

Völkl, H., W. Rehwald, W. Waitz, D. Häussinger, and F. Lang (1993). Acridine orange fluorescence in renal proximal tubules: effects of NH_3/NH_4^+ and cell volume. *Cell. Physiol. Biochem.* 3:28–33.

Vom Dahl, S., C. Hallbrucker, F. Lang, W. Gerok, and D. Häussinger (1991a). Regulation of liver cell volume and proteolysis by glucagon and insulin. *Biochem. J.* 278:771–777.

Vom Dahl, S., C. Hallbrucker, F. Lang, and D. Häussinger (1991b). Regulation of cell volume in the perfused rat liver by hormones. *Biochem. J.* 280:105–109.

Wade, C.E., and B.J. Freund (1990). Hormonal control of blood volume during and following exercise. In: C.V. Gisolfi and D.R. Lamb (eds.) *Fluid Homeostasis During Exercise. Perspecives in Exercise Science and Sports Medicine.* USA: Cooper Publishing Group, pp. 207–246.

Waldegger, S., P. Barth, G. Raber, F. Lang (1997). Cloning and characterization of a putative human serine/theonine protein kinase transcriptionally modified during anisotonic and isotonic alterations of cell volume. *Proc. Natl. Acad. Sci. USA* 94:4440–4445.

Wang, X., C.L., Chik, A.K. Ho, N. Sato, and M.A. Greer (1993). Cyclic adenosine monophosphate is not part of the transduction chain by which cell-swelling induces secretion in either normal or tumor-derived GH4C1 pituitary cells. *Metabolism* 42:435–439.

Warskulat, U., W.P. Newsome, B. Noe, B. Stoll, and D. Häussinger (1996). Anisoosmotic regulation of hepatic gene expression. *Biol. Chem. Hoppe Seyler* 377:57–65.

Warskulat, U., C. Weik, and D. Häussinger (1997a). Myo-inositol is an osmolyte in rat liver macrophages (Kupffer cells) but not in RAW 264.7 mouse macrophages. *Biochem. J.* 326:289–295.

Warskulat, U., M. Wettstein, and D. Häussinger (1995). Betaine is an osmolyte in RAW 264.7 mouse macrophages. *FEBS Lett.* 377:47–50.

Warskulat, U., M. Wettstein, and D. Häussinger (1997b). Osmoregulated taurine transport in H4IIE hepatoma cells and perfused rat liver. *Biochem. J.* 321:683–690.

Wasserman, J.C., E. Delpire, W. Tonidandel, R. Kojima, and S.R. Gullans (1994). Molecular characterization of ROSIT, a renal osmotic stress-induced Na(+)- Cl(−)-organic solute cotransporter. *Am. J. Physiol.* 267:F688–F694.

Wehner, F., H. Sauer, and R.K.H. Kinne (1995). Hypertonic stress increases the Na+ conductance of rat hepatocytes in primary culture. *J. Gen. Physiol.* 105:507–535.

Wei, L.-Y., and P.D. Roepe (1994). Low external pH and osmotic shock increase the expression of human MDR protein. *Biochemistry* 33:7229–7238.

Weiss, D.J., and O.A. Evanson (1997). Effect of sodium and potassium concentrations and pH on equine erythrocyte volume and deformability. *Comp. Haematol. Int.* 7:37–41.

Weiss, H., and F. Lang (1992). Ion channels activated by swelling of Madin Darby canine kidney (MDCK) cells. *J. Membr. Biol.* 126:109–114.

Williams, C.A., J.G. Mudd, and A.R. Lind (1985). Sympathetic control of the forearm blood flow in man during brief isometric contractions. *Eur. J. Appl. Physiol.* 54:156–162.

Wirthensohn, G., S. Lefrank, M. Schmolke, and W.G. Guder (1989). Regulation of organic osmolyte concentrations in tubules from rat renal inner medulla. *Am. J. Physiol.* 256:F128–F135.

Wollnik, B., C. Kubisch, A. Maass, H. Vetter, and L. Neyses (1993). Hyperosmotic stress induces immediate-early gene expression in ventricular adult cardiomyocytes. *Biochem. Biophys. Res. Commun.* 194:642–646.

Xu, J.-C., C. Lytle, T.T. Zhu, J.A. Payne, E. Benz Jr, and B. Forbush III (1994). Molecular cloning and functional expression of the bumetanide-sensitive Na-K-Cl cotransporter. *Proc. Natl. Acad. Sci. USA* 91:2201–2205.

Yamauchi, A., H.M. Kwon, S. Uchida, A.S. Preston, and J.S. Handler (1991). Myo-inositol and betaine transporters regulated by tonicity are basolateral in MDCK cells. *Am. J. Physiol.* 261:F197–F202.

Yamauchi, A., A. Miyai, K. Yokoyama, T. Itoh, T. Kamada, N. Ueda, and Y. Fujiwara (1994). Response to osmotic stimuli in mesangial cells: role of system A transporter. *Am. J. Physiol.* 267:C1493–C1500.

Yamauchi, A., T. Sugiura, T. Ito, A. Miyai, M. Horio, E. Imai, and T. Kamada (1996). Na+/myo-inositol transport is regulated by basolateral tonicity in Madin-Darby canine kidney cells. *J. Clin. Invest.* 97:263–267.

Yamauchi, A., S. Uchida, H.M. Kwon, A.S. Preston, R.B. Robey, A. GarciaPerez, M.B. Burg, and J.S. Handler (1992). Cloning of a Na(+)- and Cl(⁻)-dependent betaine transporter that is regulated by hypertonicity. *J. Biol. Chem.* 267:649–652.

Yancey, P.H. (1994). Compatible and contracting solutes. In: K. Strange (ed.) *Cellular and Molecular Physiology of Cell Volume Regulation.* Boca Raton, FL: CRC Press, pp. 81–109.

Young, E., and R.F. Bradley (1967). Cerebral edema with irreversible coma in severe diabetic ketoacidosis. *N. Engl. J. Med.* 276:665–669.

Zambraski, E.J. (1990). Renal regulation of fluid homeostasis during exercise. In: C.V. Gisolfi and D.R. Lamb (eds.) USA: Cooper Publishing Group, pp. 247–280.

Zhang, J., R.L. Rasmusson, S.K. Hall, and M. Lieberman (1993). A chloride current associated with swelling of cultured chick heart cells. *J. Physiol.* 472:801–820.

Zhang, F., U. Warskulat, and D. Häussinger (1996a). Modulation of tumor necrosis factor alpha release by anisoosmolarity and betaine in rat liver macrophages (Kupffer cells). *FEBS Lett.* 391:293–296.

Zhang, F., U. Warskulat, M. Wettstein, and D. Häussinger (1996b). Identification of betaine as an osmolyte in rat liver macrophages (Kupffer cells). *Gastroenterology* 110:1543–1552.

Zhang, F., M. Wettstein, U. Warskulat, R. Schreiber, P. Henninger, K. Decker, and D. Häussinger (1995). Hyperosmolarity stimulates prostaglandin synthesis and cyclooxygenase-2 expression in activated rat liver macrophages. *Biochem. J.* 312:135–143.

Zongazo, M.A., A. Carayon, F. Masson, R. Isnard, J. Eurin, G. Maistre, C. Barthelemy, A.C. Prost, and J.C. Legrand (1992). Atrial natriuretic peptide during water deprivation or hemorrhage in rats. Relationship with arginine vasopressin and osmolarity. *J. Physiol.* 86:167–175.

Zongazo, M.A., A. Carayon, F. Masson, G. Maistre, E. Noe, J. Eurin, C. Barthelemy, M. Komajda, and J.C. Legrand (1991). Effects of arginine vasopressin and extracellular osmolarity on atrial natriuretic peptide release by superfused rat atria. *Eur. J. Pharmacol.* 209:45–55.

DISCUSSION

NADEL: The consensus is that skeletal muscle cells accumulate fluid during exercise, but because the body loses a lot of water during exercise, parts of the intracellular fluid compartment lose fluid. So, exercise presents a particularly complex series of problems; during exercise, some cells are swelling and some are shrinking. Skeletal muscle cells apparently are swelling, promoting glycogen and protein synthesis after exercise, but during exercise, when glycogenolysis occurs, cell swelling would appear to be contrary to the cell's needs, according to your model. Could you comment on that?

LANG: If I or any cell physiologist extrapolates his thoughts to the real world, you have to take that with a grain of salt. Nevertheless, I think the cell swelling during exercise is counterproductive for glycogenolysis. So one would actually like the muscle cells to shrink during exercise and to swell thereafter because afterwards you want the cells to produce as much protein and as many enzymes and as much glycogen as possible.

HEIGENHAUSER: How do you differentiate between the cell volume changes and the pH changes? Most of the mechanisms that were described are related to pH effects, but they also have volume effects. In very severe exercise pH drops from 7 to 6.3, with up to 10–15% changes in cell volume in the muscle occurring in very short periods of time. So a lot of these mechanisms have to occur very rapidly and in sequential order to be effective in maintaining homeostasis. Will you comment on this?

LANG: It is very clear that the effects of cell volume on proteolysis and glycogenolysis are not due to cytosolic pH. If you swell the cell, then it becomes acidic, and if you add insulin, it becomes alkaline; yet, in both instances, you have inhibition of proteolysis, and in both instances, the vesicles become alkaline. So, it is not the cytosolic pH but, rather, the lysosomal pH that matters. Lysosomal pH is correlated with cell volume, but cytosolic pH is not.

FEBBRAIO: Most of the data that you presented in your chapter deal with hepatic cells, but you mention briefly in the chapter that it appears that the mechanisms that regulate cell size are similar in muscle cells. Hepatic cells have much higher concentrations of glycerol kinase, they have many more gluconeogenic precursors, and, therefore, the synthesis of glycogen is different compared with glycogen synthesis in a muscle cell. Could you elaborate on the data in muscle cells and whether or not they are entirely consistent with those in hepatic cells?

LANG: We have performed most of our studies in hepatic cells, although I have to say that many of our observations have been reproduced in other cells. I would be very surprised if the basic mechanisms would be different in skeletal muscle. According to indirect evidence, they are the same. For instance, insulin stimulates Na+/H+ exchange in skeletal muscle and hepatic cells in a similar way. We should now look at skeletal muscle and see how much of what we know from other cells applies to muscle.

TIPTON: Are you telling us that one cellular mechanism serves all tissues?

LANG: No, but I think that the basic behavior of cells in different tissues is amazingly similar. We have recently tried to clone the sgk-kinase from the shark on Mount Desert Island, and, surprisingly enough, the shark kinase is structurally and functionally almost identical to the kinase in humans. That indicates that these volume regulatory mechanisms are very well conserved. Different cell types are very similar in activation of cell volume regulatory mechanisms. To be on the safe side, one should study cell volume-sensitive mechanisms in skeletal muscle, but, for the time being, I would be surprised if the major mechanisms would be different.

TIPTON: Many years ago Costill followed the time course of exercise-induced changes in the water content of muscle tissue. Although his measures were crude, both increases and decreases occurred during the experimental period. Have you followed the time course of cellular volume responses in hypertonic and hypotonic mediums?

LANG: We have infused liver first with hypotonic and then with hypertonic solutions or vice versa. If you change from hypotonic to isotonic solution, they behave exactly the same as if you put them into a hypertonic solution. Cell volume-regulatory ion transport is a very fast event. The change of metabolism takes more time. Osmolyte accumulation may require expression of some genes, e.g., those for the osmolyte transporters, and this may take more than half a day. We have one set of preliminary experiments showing that during exercise one osmolyte transporter is upregulated already within 2 h, so *in vivo* genomic regulation may be even faster than under cell culture conditions.

SPRIET: Is it possible that the events that occur in skeletal muscle cells at rest with respect to anabolism or catabolism might be overridden during an exercise situation when there are many additional powerful signals? Also, if cells swell during exercise, is it possible that the body simply allows the swelling to occur and maintains the cell volume at this new size? There are numerous examples of homeostatic mechanisms, e.g., those controlling mean arterial pressure or body temperature, in which the body regulates a variable at a new set point during very stressful situations. During exercise, the metabolic rate is much higher in skeletal muscle cells than in any of the other cells that you have been studying.

LANG: That's a very important point. The same actually applies to proliferating cells. They increase size by 40%, which stimulates protein synthesis. The cells then regulate their volume at this new level. To the extent that the same holds true in exercise, i.e., that swelling of muscle cells stimulates protein synthesis, the respective increase of macromolecule crowding would result in an increase of the cell volume regulatory set point. On the other hand, shrinking the cell causes degradation of the cell's proteins, and consequent to the degradation of the proteins, the set point of cell volume decreases as well.

HEIGENHAUSER: There are many cases in which metabolic change may occur before ion regulation, e.g., during hyperventilation. Red blood cells adapt very rapidly by increasing lactate production in order to counteract the alkalosis. This also occurs in Rainbow Trout when they face rapid changes in water alkalinization. The first thing they do to regulate pH is to upregulate lactate production by downregulating pyruvate dehydrogenase activity. Later, ionic changes occur in the gill where chloride channels are upregulated to transport chloride from the water across the gill. Thereafter, lactate is metabolized, and pH regulation occurs by exchange of electrolytes across the gill. So how these various mechanisms interact depends on what species and tissues are being considered.

LANG: you are perfectly right that the Rainbow Trout upregulates the gill transport systems. However, if you expose these gills to sudden osmotic stress, they almost immediately activate the cell volume-regulatory ion channels. What you are referring to is the adaptation to high or low osmolarity. For that adaptation they need gene expression, and that requires time. Activation of cell volume-regulatory ion channels requires less than a minute. The early genes are generated within 30 min; the kinase appears 30 min following shrinkage. Many genes require much more time for expression.

GISOLFI: What role do water channels play in regulating cell volume?

LANG: There is some preliminary indication that during shrinkage of cells the water channels within the cell membrane are internalized. In general, the water permeability is not the limiting factor for cell swelling or cell shrinkage because cells have abundant water channels. Even if you were to remove 90% of the water channels, they still would swell or shrink. Nevertheless, it may be that cells indeed regulate water channels in response to alterations of cell volume. Removal of water channels is a possibility. It may be the last line of defense in order to cope with extracellular anisotonicity.

GISOLFI: Is it your opinion that all cells have water channels?

LANG: Well, most cells have water channels.

GISOLFI: To my knowledge they have not been found in intestinal epithelia.

LANG: You are right. I would be very surprised if they had no water channels, but I have been surprised many times in my life.

MAUGHAN: When I read about macromolecular crowding, I think of a series of electron micrographs that Eric Hultman published in 1967. He showed a massive increase of glycogen in muscle that was glycogen loaded. There was so much glycogen that the myofilaments were effectively displaced. How does the cell accommodate that amount of glycogen without an increase in hydrostatic pressure?

LANG: Glycogen has osmotic activity that is relatively small as compared to the monomers. An interesting question is whether or not large volumes not filled with free water are sensed by the cell. Possibly in the long run, the cells forget about the water and regulate their volumes according to the macromolecular crowding. Erythrocytes loaded with different concentrations of proteins regulated their volume according to protein content. That is the most convincing evidence that it is indeed the protein concentration that is defended.

ARAGON: In physiological systems (multicellular organisms), whenever you need to maintain homeostasis for any particular variable, there is usually a regulatory center that orchestrates all the different response mechanisms. When cell volume must be regulated, there are so many different factors involved that serve primarily other purposes that it seems even more necessary to have such a regulatory center. Is there any evidence of anything like a volume-regulatory center in the cell? Or is the cell basically left to randomly compensate for all these changes that are happening?

LANG: Indeed, a wide variety of factors do modify cell volume. For instance, insulin or certain amino acids swell hepatocytes by some 10%. If you alter cell volume by changing extracellular osmolarity, the cell senses volume changes of as little 1%, according to evidence of altered ion channel activity. What is known about the cell volume regulatory machinery is the nature of the ion channels involved and the transporters involved, but much less is known about the signaling molecules. As to sensors, it becomes even more of a problem, but I think the most likely sensors are macromolecular crowding and deformation of the cytoskeleton.

ARAGON: I am going to ask you to take a big leap from your field to some practical issues. Some sports drinks include ingredients such as taurine. In light of its role as an osmolyte, do you think it makes sense to add this substance or any other osmolytes to a sports drink?

LANG: I have experienced so many times that reality was more complicated than life in the test tube, so I must refrain from giving advice on this point. Nobody knows the answer.

HARGREAVES: If a muscle cell swells during heavy resistance exercise and over the time it increases its total protein content and increases its size, are the cell volume-regulatory mechanisms maintained? You mentioned a possible change in set point.

LANG: Yes, I think that this is exactly the case. An increased cellular protein content would shift the cell volume-regulatory set point. If you supply the cell with creatine, and let us assume for a moment that creatine is indeed accumulated in the cell, that would stimulate protein synthesis, and the increased protein contents would then make the cells volume regulate at a higher level. On the next day, they would presumably swell again by uptake of creatine, and then they would again respond with protein synthesis. The repetitive cell swelling would then eventually lead to hypertrophied muscle cells that would volume regulate against swelling or shrinking at a higher level.

HARGREAVES: What ultimately regulates the maximal cell volume? Is it an oxygen diffusion distance or is it some of the mechanisms that you have studied that ultimately set the upper limit for cell volume?

LANG: I don't know about an upper limit. Obviously, there is an upper limit in oxygen diffusion, but from the cell volume regulation point of view, there is no real upper limit.

WAGENMAKERS: Regarding the increase in protein synthesis that results from cell swelling, is that for all the proteins, or may it also be for specific proteins with a specific function in the muscle?

LANG: It does not work for all proteins. If you look at transcription in general, then you have an increase of protein synthesis in swollen cells. However, if you make a differential display, you find proteins that are downregulated and proteins that are upregulated upon cell swelling. So not all proteins are uniformly increased. It would be exciting to find out what molecules relevant for performance are upregulated by cell swelling, i.e., what proteins are upregulated by exercise, and to determine the contribution of cell swelling to the upregulation of those proteins.

HEIGENHAUSER: In the animal kingdom, when certain species of toads freeze, changes in osmolytes occur that prevent crystallization of intracellular water. Are there any adaptations that occur in osmolytes of mammalians that sweat and have large changes in fluid volume when they are working in hot temperatures?

LANG: Nobody has studied it, but it is true that osmolytes not only serve to create osmolarity but also to stabilize proteins. That is why they are used in some animals for protection against excessive temperatures. It is amazing that cells throw out the osmolytes just before DNA fragmentation. It may be that this osmolyte loss adds to the destabilization of the cell. It is striking that if you trigger the CD95-receptor in a lymphocyte, it takes about 60 min until the cell shrinks. In 60 min, all kinds of things happen, and after these 60 min, they throw out the osmolytes; a few minutes later, they undergo DNA fragmentation. If you decrease the temperature, then you have no osmolyte release and you have no DNA fragmentation. As soon as you increase the temperature again, then immediately the osmolytes come out, and the DNA fragmentation occurs. This circumstantial evidence suggests that osmolytes serve more functions than just creating osmolarity. I think that getting rid of osmolytes means getting rid of stabilizing molecules.

TARNOPOLSKY: Your work raises some interesting questions about the practical application of creatine and its relationship to protein synthesis. In 1974 and 1976 Joan Ingwall showed that if creatine is added to muscle fibers in culture, there is an increase in actin and myosin synthesis. In 1994, some of your fellow countrymen cloned and sequenced a human creatine transporter that shared strong homology with taurine and betaine and GABA transporters. Thus, it may be that cell swelling is related to the previous observations of increased protein synthesis that we see in culture.

LANG: Yes, I agree.

TARNOPOLSKY: The creatine transporter is down-regulated by large concentrations of exogenous creatine. Perhaps the muscle cell can initially take up creatine to an intracellular concentration of about 160 mM, but there is a subsequent down-regulation of the mRNA for the creatine transporter. Thus, the body appears to adapt to the creatine supply. Otherwise, if one kept taking supplements, one's muscles would theoretically continue to undergo further hypertrophy forever, which clearly is not the case.

LANG: Yes, of course the carrier is regulated. Let us assume that creatine is an osmolyte as well. It is not one of the typical osmolytes, but it is an osmolyte for the skeletal muscle, so if the cell shrinks, it will possibly express the transporter, accumulating creatine by extracting it from the extracellular fluid. If there is no creatine outside, it won't help the cell to express the transporter, and the cell will remain shrunken. Thus, creatine availability may become a limiting factor for cell swelling or reswelling and for the stimulation of anabolism. On the other hand, if you overload the cell with creatine, or if you swell it beyond its set point, you can't force the muscle to take it up because it down-regulates the transporter. We started to examine osmolyte transporter expression in skeletal muscle during exercise and after exercise to see whether osmolytes are available in extracellular fluid. If they are abundant in extracellular fluid, it doesn't make sense to add them, but if they are not available in extracellular fluid, yet the transporters are sitting there, then, and only then, would I expect a beneficial effect of adding the osmolytes.

MONTAIN: When heat stress is applied to a cell, the cell makes stress proteins and is less perturbed the next time it is exposed to heat stress. Could the same kind of phenomenon happen with cell swelling or cell shrinkage? For example, with cell swelling, the cell's cytoskeleton is stressed; perhaps the cell senses the tension change, makes the proteins it needs, and incorporates them into the cytoskeleton so that in a later exposure the same stress will not stimulate protein synthesis because the cytoskeletal strain is less.

LANG: I would say it the other way around. If the cell prepares for the stress by expressing heat shock proteins, and osmolyte transporters, it is better prepared for a second hit by the same stress. The molecules need not to be expressed anymore, but they need to be activated only, which is much faster. Thus, any stress, such as osmotic stress, heat shock, or hypoxia, will have less deleterious effects when applied for the second time.

WILLIS: When creatine in muscle is depleted and replaced by beta GPA, the total osmolytes don't change, yet we see cell shrinkage. Are there effective and ineffective osmolytes for promoting protein synthesis?

LANG: To the extent that they are both osmolytes, they should be equally effective. There are some amino acids, however, which have an additional effect on protein synthesis that cannot be accounted for by their effect on cell volume.

WILLIS: What is the relationship of this scheme for regulating cell volume to the regulation of the volume of intracellular organelles?

LANG: With osmotic cell swelling, both cells and organelles swell. This is not so if you swell the cells isosmotically. For instance, glucagon swells mitochondria at the same time it shrinks the cells; however, the proteolysis parallels the cell volume and not the mitochondria volume. But with any given effect, you have to think about whether it is due to swelling of the organelles rather than to swelling of the cell. The effects I have described are all due to swelling of the cell and not to swelling of the organelles.

FEBBRAIO: In your cell preparation, at what temperature do you conduct your experiments?

LANG: At 37°C.

FEBBRAIO: If you increase the temperature to 43 degrees, are the mechanisms for regulating cell volume consistent with the results that you see at 37°C?

LANG: We have not done those experiments, but we have reduced the temperature. At room temperature, osmolyte release in lymphoctyes treated with CDg5 is completely abolished.

3

Metabolic Responses to Carbohydrate Ingestion: Effects on Exercise Performance

MARK HARGREAVES, PH.D.

INTRODUCTION

Because the endogenous carbohydrate reserves in skeletal muscle, the liver, and the blood are relatively small and there is a heavy reliance on carbohydrate during strenuous exercise, carbohydrate depletion is often correlated with fatigue. One strategy for delaying the onset of carbohydrate depletion is to ingest carbohydrate before, during, and/or after exercise to increase carbohydrate availability and oxidation during exercise and to enhance restoration of endogenous carbohydrate reserves during the postexercise period. The ultimate aim of these dietary manipulations is to enhance exercise performance. This chapter reviews the metabolic and performance responses to carbohydrate ingestion before, during, and after exercise.

CARBOHYDRATE DEPLETION AND FATIGUE

The importance of carbohydrate availability for endurance exercise performance has been recognized since the early part of this century. In the 1920s, hypoglycemia, with the associated neuroglucopenia, was proposed as a cause of fatigue during marathon running because prevention of hypoglycemia—by increasing carbohydrate availability during exercise—was associated with improved exercise performance (Gordon et al., 1925; Levine et al., 1924). Similar observations were made on exercising dogs in the Harvard Fatigue Laboratory (Dill et al., 1932). Perhaps the most cited of the early papers are those of Christensen and Hansen in the late 1930s that clearly demonstrated the importance of carbohydrate ingestion for exercise performance (Christensen & Hansen, 1939a, 1939b). Most of the early studies emphasized the effects of reduced carbohydrate availability on the central nervous system, although Dill et al. (1932) did suggest that fuel availability might be important. The use of invasive procedures in the late 1960s confirmed the importance of carbohydrate and specifically identified intramuscular glycogen availability as a key determinant of endurance exercise capacity (Bergstrom & Hultman, 1967; Bergstrom et al., 1967; Hermansen et al., 1967). Since these pioneering studies, numerous investigations have verified the association between fatigue and glycogen depletion, either in samples of mixed muscle fiber types or in specific fiber types, during prolonged, strenuous exercise (Constantin-Teodosiu et al., 1992; Coyle et al., 1986; Sahlin et al., 1990, 1997; Tsintzas et al., 1996a). Fewer studies have attempted to understand the causal relationship between carbohydrate depletion and fatigue, with most attention focused on either effects of blood glucose availability on central nervous system function or on peripheral fatigue mechanisms related to substrate availability.

Central Mechanisms

The early studies examining the potential involvement of carbohydrate availability in the etiology of fatigue during prolonged exercise focused on the consequences of hypoglycemia and associated neuroglucopenia. These effects included "asthenia, pallor, nervous irritability and prostration" (Levine et al., 1924), which presumably contributed to the impaired exercise performance. In the studies of Christensen and Hansen (1939b), the enhanced exercise capacity observed with glucose ingestion late in exercise was not accompanied by significant increases in estimated carbohydrate oxidation, suggesting that hypoglycemia affected the central nervous system rather than muscle metabolism. The clinical symptoms associated with hypoglycemia, which could impair exercise performance, can occur at blood glucose levels often seen during prolonged strenuous exercise (Mitrakou et al., 1991; Schwartz et al., 1987).

Notwithstanding the difficulties in studying central fatigue mechanisms, especially in human subjects, there is now more information on the potential mechanisms underlying central fatigue during exercise (Davis & Bailey, 1997). It has been suggested that glucose availability may directly influence brain energy metabolism and, by implication, exercise performance (M.L. Burgess et al., 1991). In addition, carbohydrate ingestion may exert indirect effects on central fatigue by blunting the exercise-induced increase of free tryptophan in plasma (Davis et al., 1992). The inhibition of lipolysis by carbohydrate ingestion reduces displacement of tryptophan from albumin by free fatty acids (FFA). The lower concentration of free tryptophan in plasma is thought to reduce tryptophan uptake by the brain and to attenuate the production of serotonin, which is believed to be involved in the development of central fatigue (Davis & Bailey, 1997; Davis et al., 1992). The exact links among substrate availability, brain neurotransmitter levels, and fatigue during prolonged exercise remain to be fully elucidated. Nevertheless, the central nervous system may be an important site of action of increased blood glucose availability.

Peripheral Mechanisms

The association between carbohydrate depletion and fatigue during prolonged, strenuous exercise may be related to impaired rates of ATP resynthesis; the diminished supply of ATP would theoretically limit cross-bridge cycling and/or other cellular processes responsible for muscle contraction. The difficulty with this hypothesis is that intramuscular ATP concentration is reasonably well maintained during exercise, even at the point of fatigue (Sahlin et al., 1990, 1997; Spencer et al., 1991; Tsintzas et al., 1996a). This does not exclude the possibility that fatigue may be a function of the ATP concentration in the immediate vicinity of the cellular ATPases and structures involved in excitation-contraction coupling and force generation. Indeed, reduced localized concentrations of glycogen and ATP have been implicated in the failure of calcium release during repetitive stimulation in single skeletal muscle fibers (Allen et al., 1997; Chin & Allen, 1997; Owen et al., 1996). In addition, increases in the intramuscular concentrations of IMP and hypoxanthine, products of ATP breakdown (Norman et al. 1987, 1988; Sahlin et al., 1990; Spencer et al., 1991), and decreases in creatine phosphate levels (Sahlin et al., 1997) have been observed when muscle glycogen availability is reduced, suggesting an imbalance between rates of ATP degradation and resynthesis. Under such conditions, a reduced concentration of ATP and/or increased concentrations of ADP and P_i could contribute to impaired force generation (Sahlin et al., 1997). Of note, carbohydrate ingestion resulted in a blunting of the increase in muscle IMP levels during prolonged exercise (Spencer et al., 1991).

Reduced availability of intramuscular carbohydrate could limit oxidative ATP production due to a decline in pyruvate levels late in exercise (Sahlin et al., 1990); however, despite markedly reduced muscle glycogen levels, activity of the pyruvate dehydrogenase complex and availability of acetyl CoA remained high during the latter stages of prolonged exercise (Constantin-Teodosiu et al., 1992). An alternate hypothesis is that a reduction in pyruvate, secondary to carbohydrate depletion, reduces flux through anaplerotic reactions that are essential for the maintenance of tricarboxylic acid cycle (TCA) intermediates and flux through the TCA cycle (Sahlin et al., 1990). Consistent with this hypothesis, increased carbohydrate availability during exercise resulted in higher levels of TCA cycle intermediates in muscle and an attenuation of IMP accumulation (Spencer et al., 1991). On the other hand, changes in the levels of TCA cycle intermediates may not always predict flux through the TCA cycle (Gibala et al., 1997). The intracellular mechanisms linking carbohydrate depletion with reduced force and power output require further investigation. Irrespective of the underlying mechanisms, there is clear evidence that increased carbohydrate availability improves exercise performance.

CARBOHYDRATE FEEDINGS BEFORE EXERCISE

The goals of consuming carbohydrate before exercise are to enhance the availability of glycogen in muscle and liver and glucose in blood. Increased dietary carbohydrate intake, in combination with reduced training intensity and/or volume, in the days before competition will increase intramuscular glycogen availability (Bergstrom et al., 1967; Sherman et al., 1981). If precompetition nutritional preparation has been less than optimal, if there has been a moderate period of fasting (8-12 h), or if access to carbohydrate during competition is restricted or impossible, ingestion of carbohydrate in the hours before competition may benefit performance. Research on pre-exercise carbohydrate ingestion has generally focused on two time periods: 3–4 h and 30–60 min before exercise. In both cases, the goal of carbohydrate intake is to enhance glucose availability while minimizing gastrointestinal discomfort and the potential adverse metabolic effects of hyperinsulinemia in susceptible individuals.

Carbohydrate Ingestion 3-4 Hours Before Exercise

Ingestion of a carbohydrate-rich meal (containing roughly 140–330 g carbohydrate) 3–4 h before exercise increases glycogen levels in muscle (and presumably liver) (Chryssanthopoulos et al., 1997; Coyle et al., 1985) and enhances exercise performance (Neufer et al., 1987; Sherman et al., 1989; Wright et al., 1991). The increase in pre-exercise muscle glycogen is one explanation for the enhanced performance. In addition, because liver glycogen levels can be substantially reduced after an overnight fast, ingestion of carbohydrate may increase these reserves and contribute, together with any ongoing absorption of the ingested carbohydrate, to the maintenance of blood glucose levels during the subsequent exercise bout.

Despite plasma glucose and insulin returning to basal levels, ingestion of carbohydrate in the hours before exercise often results in a transient fall in glucose with the onset of exercise (Coyle et al., 1985; Sherman et al., 1989). Indeed, the metabolic perturbations associated with pre-exercise carbohydrate ingestion, including a fall in blood glucose, increased carbohydrate oxidation, and a blunting of the rise in plasma FFA due to inhibition of adipose tissue lipolysis, can persist for up to 6 h following carbohydrate ingestion (Montain et al., 1991). These metabolic effects do not appear to be detrimental to exercise performance, with an increased carbohydrate availability compensating for the greater carbohydrate utilization. No differences in exercise performance were observed following ingestion of meals that produced marked differences in plasma glucose and insulin levels (Wee et al., 1998). The effects of a carbohydrate-rich meal 3–4 h before exercise on subsequent performance may be equivalent to those observed with carbohydrate ingestion during exercise (Chryssanthopoulos et al., 1994), although this is not always the case (Wright et al., 1991). In addition, the combination of a pre-exercise carbohydrate meal and carbohydrate ingestion during exercise may further enhance exercise performance (Chryssanthopoulos & Williams, 1997; Wright et al., 1991). From a practical perspective, if access to carbohydrate during exercise is limited or non-existent, ingestion of 200–300 g carbohydrate 3–4 h before exercise may be an effective strategy for enhancing carbohydrate availability during the subsequent exercise period.

Carbohydrate Ingestion 30-60 Minutes Before Exercise

The ingestion of carbohydrate in the hour before exercise causes a large increase in plasma glucose and insulin. However, as shown in Figure 3-1, at the onset of exercise there is a rapid fall in blood glucose as a consequence of the combined stimulatory effects of hyperinsulinemia and contractile activity on muscle glucose uptake (Ahlborg & Björkman, 1987; Ahlborg & Felig, 1977; Marmy-Conus et al., 1996) and inhibition of the exercise-induced rise in the output of glucose from the liver (Marmy-Conus et al., 1996), despite ongoing intestinal absorption of the ingested carbohydrate.

An enhanced uptake and oxidation of blood glucose by skeletal muscle may account for the increased carbohydrate oxidation often observed following pre-exercise carbohydrate ingestion (Costill et al., 1977; Coyle et al., 1997; Febbraio & Stewart, 1996; Horowitz et al., 1997). An increase in muscle glycogen degradation has also been seen in some (Costill et al., 1977; Hargreaves et al., 1985), but not all studies (Febbraio & Stewart, 1996; Fielding et al., 1987; Hargreaves et al., 1987; Koivisto et al., 1985; Levine et al., 1983). Activation of the pyruvate dehydrogenase complex following carbohydrate ingestion also contributes to enhanced carbohydrate oxidation during exercise (Tsintzas et al., 1998). The increase in plasma FFA with exercise is attenuated following pre-exercise ingestion of carbohydrate (Ahlborg & Felig, 1977; Horowitz et al., 1997; Marmy-Conus et al., 1996) as a consequence of insulin-mediated inhibition of lipolysis (Horowitz et al., 1997). Total fat oxidation is reduced, not only because the availability of plasma FFA is lower (Coyle et al., 1997; Horowitz et al., 1997), but also because intramuscular lipid oxidation is inhibited. This latter point is supported by the fact that restora-

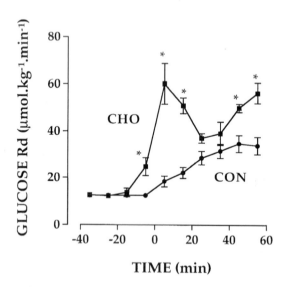

FIGURE 3-1: *Tracer-determined glucose uptake (glucose Rd) before and during exercise at 71 ± 1% peak $\dot{V}O_2$ after ingestion of either 75 g glucose (CHO) or sweet placebo (CON) 30 min before exercise. Values are means ± SEM (n = 6). * Denotes different from CON, P<0.05. Redrawn from Marmy-Conus et al. (1996) with permission.*

tion of plasma FFA availability by Intralipid® and heparin infusion did not completely return fat oxidation to rates seen during exercise in the fasted state (Horowitz et al., 1997). The potential site of regulation is entry of long-chain fatty acids into the mitochondria, catalyzed by carntine palmitoyltransferase, because while oleate oxidation was reduced by pre-exercise ingestion of carbohydrate, oxidation of octanoate, a medium-chain fatty acid, was not (Coyle et al., 1997). A decreased FFA supply to muscle is also consistent with the observations of lower concentrations of acetylcarnitine and citrate in muscle after exercise following carbohydrate ingestion (Tsintzas et al., 1998).

Because the above-mentioned metabolic effects of pre-exercise ingestion of carbohydrate are a consequence of hyperglycemia and hyperinsulinemia, there has been interest in strategies that minimize the changes in plasma glucose and insulin before exercise. These have included the ingestion of fructose (Fielding et al., 1987; Hargreaves et al., 1987; Horowitz et al., 1997; Koivisto et al., 1981, 1985; Levine et al., 1983; Okano et al., 1988), ingestion of carbohydrate types with differing glycemic indices (Febbraio & Stewart, 1996; Goodpaster et al., 1996; Kirwan et al., 1998; Sparks et al., 1998; Thomas et al., 1991, 1994), varying the carbohydrate load (Seifert et al., 1994; Sherman et al., 1991), varying the feeding schedule (Short et al., 1997), the addition of fat (Horowitz & Coyle, 1993), or including warm-up exercise in the pre-exercise period (Brouns et al., 1989). In general, whereas these various interventions do modify the metabolic response to exercise, there appears to be no great advantage for exercise performance in blunting the pre-exercise glycemic and insulinemic responses (see below). For example, pre-exercise fructose ingestion does not inhibit fat oxidation as much as does glucose ingestion (Horowitz et al., 1997), but fructose is less available for oxidation than is glucose (Guezennec et al., 1989).

In recent years there has been interest in the potential application of the glycemic index (GI) concept to pre-exercise carbohydrate nutrition. Foods with a low GI have been proposed to offer an advantage over other carbohydrate sources before exercise (Thomas et al., 1991) because they result in more stable blood glucose and higher plasma FFA levels during subsequent exercise (Thomas et al., 1991; 1994). Indeed, in their first study, Thomas et al. (1991) observed an increase in exercise endurance following ingestion of a low-GI carbohydrate meal; however, pre-exercise ingestion of glucose did not significantly impair exercise performance, and in subsequent studies the GI of the pre-exercise carbohydrate feeding, while influencing the metabolic response to exercise, had no impact on exercise performance (Febbraio & Stewart, 1996; Sparks et al., 1998; Thomas et al., 1994). In addition, ingestion of glucose, a high-GI carbohydrate, before exercise has been shown to enhance performance (see below). Finally, when carbohydrate is consumed during prolonged exercise, the GI of pre-exercise carbohydrate feedings has no effect on metabolism and performance (Burke et al., 1998). The glycemic responses during exercise preceded by carbohydrate ingestion will be determined by a number of factors that include the combined stimulatory effects of insulin and contractile activity on muscle glucose uptake, the balance of inhibitory and stimulatory effects of insulin and catecholamines, respectively, on liver glucose output, and the magnitude of ongoing intestinal absorption of glucose from the ingested carbohydrate. Furthermore, the inhibition of lipolysis and fat oxidation occurs with only small increases in plasma insulin, e.g., following fructose (low GI) ingestion (Horowitz et al., 1997). Thus, it could be argued that if pre-exercise carbohydrate ingestion is the only mechanism by which athletes can increase carbohydrate availability *during* exercise, they would be well advised to ingest as much carbohydrate as possible, without undue gastrointestinal distress, so as to compensate for the reduced fat oxidation and to provide a pool of glucose that becomes available for use during the later stages of exercise.

The metabolic alterations associated with ingestion of carbohydrate in the 30–60 min before exercise have the potential to influence exercise performance. Costill et al. (1977) postulated that the increase in muscle glycogenolysis following carbohydrate ingestion before exercise would result in an earlier onset of fatigue during exercise, and this was suggested in a subsequent study (Foster et al., 1979). In contrast, every study since has shown either unchanged (Chryssanthopoulos et al., 1994a; Devlin et al., 1986; Febbraio & Stewart, 1996; Hargreaves et al., 1987; McMurray et al., 1983; Sparks et al., 1998; Thomas et al., 1994) or enhanced (Gleeson et al., 1986; Goodpaster et al., 1996; Kirwan et al., 1998; Okano et al., 1988; Sherman et al., 1991; Thomas et al., 1991) performance of endurance exercise following ingestion of carbohydrate in the hour before exercise. Thus, notwithstanding the well-documented metabolic effects of pre-exercise ingestion of carbohydrate and the possibility of negative consequences in certain susceptible individuals, there appears to be little evidence to support the practice of avoiding carbohydrate ingestion in the hour before exercise. Individual practice must be determined on the basis of individual experience with various pre-exercise carbohydrate ingestion protocols.

CARBOHYDRATE INGESTION DURING EXERCISE

Perhaps one of the most studied areas in sports nutrition has been the metabolic and performance responses to carbohydrate ingestion during exercise. Ingestion of carbohydrate during prolonged, strenuous exercise enhances performance, measured either by an ability to maintain or increase work output during exercise (Coggan & Coyle, 1988; Ivy et al., 1979; Mitchell et al., 1989; Murray et al., 1991; Neufer et al., 1987; Tsintzas et al., 1993; Williams et al., 1990) or by an increased exercise time to fatigue (Björkman et al., 1984; Coggan & Coyle, 1987, 1989; Coyle et al., 1983, 1986; Davis et al., 1992; Sasaki et al., 1987; Spencer et al., 1991; Tsintzas et al., 1996a,b; Wilber & Moffatt, 1992). These increases in exercise performance are generally believed to be due to maintenance of a high rate of carbohydrate oxidation late in exercise as a consequence of increased availability of blood glucose (Coggan & Coyle, 1987; Coyle et al., 1986) and/or muscle glycogen (Bosch et al., 1996; Tsintzas et al., 1996a). As mentioned earlier, effects on the central nervous system function may also play a role (Davis et al., 1992). Interestingly, carbohydrate ingestion sometimes improves performance of relatively short-duration high-intensity exercise and intermittent exercise when, under normal circumstances, carbohydrate availability is not thought to be limiting (Anantaraman et al., 1995; Ball et al., 1995; Below et al., 1995; Davis et al., 1997; Jeukendrup et al., 1997; Nicholas et al., 1995). The mechanisms underlying the ergogenic benefit of carbohydrate ingestion under these circumstances remain to be determined, but they may involve small increases in intramuscular carbohydrate availability under conditions of high carbohydrate utilization. It should be noted that performance in relatively brief exercise is not always improved by carbohydrate ingestion. For example, carbohydrate feedings did not affect performance in a 20-km cycle time trial that lasted about 30 min (Palmer et al., 1998).

Metabolic Responses to Carbohydrate Ingestion During Exercise

Ingestion of carbohydrate during prolonged, strenuous exercise increases blood glucose levels and rates of carbohydrate oxidation late in exercise (Coggan & Coyle, 1987; Coyle et al., 1986). Liver glucose output is reduced by carbohydrate ingestion (Figure 3-2; Bosch et al., 1994; McConell et al., 1994) due to direct effects of glucose on the liver and possibly also to a blunting of the exercise-induced increases in plasma adrenaline and glucagon (McConell et al., 1994). Although the tracer method used cannot distinguish between liver glycogenolysis and gluconeogenesis, it is likely that there is a significant conservation of liver glycogen after carbohydrate ingestion. In addition, a reduction in splanchnic uptake of gluconeogenic precursors and a decrease in oxygen uptake during prolonged, low-intensity exercise following carbohydrate ingestion suggests a lower rate of gluconeogenesis (Ahlborg & Felig, 1976).

McConell et al. (1994) showed that muscle glucose uptake during exercise, as measured by tracer-determined glucose Rd, is increased by

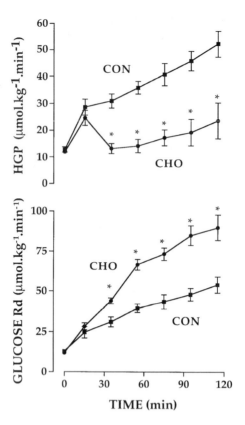

FIGURE 3-2: *Tracer-determined liver glucose output (HGP) and glucose uptake (glucose Rd) during 2 h of exercise at 69 ± 1% V̇O₂ peak with ingestion of either a 10% glucose solution (CHO) or sweet placebo (CON).* Values are means ± SEM (n = 6). * Denotes different from CON, P<0.05. Redrawn from McConell et al. (1994) with permission.

carbohydrate ingestion (Figure 3-2). This is consistent with previous observations that enhanced availability of blood glucose increases the uptake of glucose by leg muscles during low-intensity exercise (Ahlborg & Felig, 1976) and increases the rates of glucose disposal and oxidation during strenuous exercise (Bosch et al., 1994; Coggan et al., 1991; Coyle et al., 1991; Hawley et al., 1994; Howlett et al., 1998). Glucose uptake by skeletal muscle during exercise occurs by facilitated diffusion, mediated by the GLUT-4 glucose transporter that is translocated to the sarcolemma during exercise (Kristiansen et al., 1997). Hyperglycemia enhances the diffusion gradient and may also stimulate GLUT-4 translocation (Galante et al., 1995). Since metabolic clearance rate (glucose Rd/[glucose]) during exercise was increased with carbohydrate ingestion (McConell et al., 1994), higher plasma insulin levels are also important in enhancing muscle glucose uptake under these conditions. The effects of insulin and contraction on glucose transport and GLUT-4 translocation are additive in rat skeletal muscle (Gao et al., 1994). In humans, synergistic effects of insulin and exercise on glucose uptake have also been observed (DeFronzo et al., 1981; Wasserman et al., 1991). Finally, although there are different results on the effects of alterations in plasma FFA concentration on leg glucose uptake during exercise (Hargreaves et al., 1991; Odland et al., 1998), it is possible that a reduction in plasma FFA contributes to the greater glucose uptake during exercise when carbohydrate is ingested.

Because glycogen phosphorylase activity may be inhibited by glucose and glucose-6-P (Johnson, 1992), a higher concentration of glucose in muscles following carbohydrate ingestion (Spencer et al., 1991) has the potential to alter muscle glycogen metabolism. Conflicting reports exist on the effects of carbohydrate ingestion on muscle glycogen degradation during exercise. Most studies utilizing prolonged strenuous, continuous cycling exercise have observed no effect of increased blood glucose availability on net muscle glycogen utilization (Bosch et al., 1994; Coyle et al., 1986, 1991; Fielding et al., 1985; Flynn et al., 1987; Hargreaves & Briggs, 1988; Mitchell et al., 1989; Widrick et al., 1993). However, decreases in glycogen use during cycling have been reported (Erikson et al., 1987) during the latter stages of prolonged exercise (Bosch et al., 1996), when the increase in blood glucose is great (Bergstrom & Hultman, 1967), and during intermittent exercise protocols (Hargreaves et al., 1984; Yaspelkis et al., 1993). In two of these studies (Erikson et al., 1987; Hargreaves et al., 1984), the results were potentially confounded by higher pre-exercise muscle glycogen levels in the control trial that could have accelerated the subsequent rate of glycogen degradation during exercise (Hargreaves et al., 1995). It is possible that during exercise with intermittent periods of rest or low-intensity exercise, carbohydrate ingestion may stimulate glycogen synthesis (Kuipers et al., 1987) and a reduction in net muscle glycogen use. On balance, however, the effects of carbohydrate ingestion on muscle glycogen use during prolonged, strenuous cycling exercise appear small.

In contrast, studies during treadmill running indicate that carbohydrate ingestion reduces net muscle glycogen use, specifically in the type I fibers (Tsintzas et al., 1995; 1996a), and that the increase in muscle glycogen availability late in exercise contributed to the enhanced endurance capacity that was observed (Tsintzas et al., 1996a). Unlike the majority of cycling studies, fatigue following prolonged running exercise is typically not associated with a large fall in blood glucose levels and decreased rates of carbohydrate oxidation (Tsintzas et al., 1993,

1996a; Williams et al., 1990). It is possible that there is a difference in the relative importance of blood glucose versus muscle glycogen as carbohydrate fuel sources during running and cycling and that this can explain the differences in glycogen use with carbohydrate ingestion. Differences in active muscle mass, recruitment patterns, and/or contraction dynamics between running and cycling may also play a role.

The ingestion of carbohydrate reduces plasma FFA levels during prolonged exercise (Coyle et al., 1983, 1986; Davis et al., 1992; Murray et al., 1989a,b, 1991; Tsintzas et al., 1996a). The effects of carbohydrate ingestion during exercise on fat oxidation do not appear to be as great as those observed with pre-exercise carbohydrate ingestion, most likely as a consequence of the smaller increases in plasma insulin levels which, while still blunting lipolysis, may cause a smaller initial increase in muscle glucose uptake and a relatively lesser inhibition of intramuscular lipid oxidation (Horowitz et al., 1998).

Increased blood glucose availability following carbohydrate ingestion also inhibits leucine oxidation (Davies et al., 1982), an effect that may be by a reduced activity of the branched-chain oxoacid dehydrogenase in skeletal muscle (Wagenmakers et al., 1991). Consistent with an inhibitory effect of increased glucose availability on amino-acid catabolism in muscle, we have observed lower accumulations of ammonia in muscle and plasma during exercise when carbohydrate was ingested (Snow et al., 1998).

Type, Amount and Timing of Carbohydrate Ingestion During Exercise

There appear to be relatively few, if any, differences between glucose, sucrose, and maltodextrins in their effects on metabolism and performance when ingested during exercise (Hawley et al., 1992; Massicotte et al., 1989; Murray et al., 1989a; Wagenmakers et al., 1993). In contrast, fructose is not as readily oxidized as other carbohydrate sources (Massicotte et al., 1989) due to its slower rate of absorption, which may cause gastrointestinal distress and impaired performance (Murray et al., 1989a). Galactose is also less available for oxidation when ingested during exercise (Leijssen et al., 1995). Soluble cornstarch is oxidized to a greater extent during exercise than is insoluble starch, due to its higher amylopectin/amylose ratio (Saris et al., 1993). The physical form of the ingested carbohydrate does not exert a major influence because liquid and solid carbohydrate supplements elicit similar metabolic responses during exercise (Lugo et al., 1993; Mason et al., 1993).

There is not a clear dose-response relationship between the amount of carbohydrate ingested during exercise and subsequent exercise performance (Mitchell et al., 1989; Murray et al., 1989b, 1991). Ingestion of carbohydrate at a rate of 13 g·h^{-1} is insufficient to alter either the glucoregulatory hormone response to prolonged exercise or time to fatigue (W.A. Burgess et al., 1991), whereas carbohydrate ingestion at 26 and 78 g·h^{-1} increased 4.8 km cycle performance to a similar extent, following 2 h of exercise at 65–75% V̇O$_2$peak (Murray et al., 1991). No differences in physiological responses to exercise were observed between ingestion of 6%, 8% and 10% sucrose solutions, but performance was enhanced only with 6% (Murray et al., 1989b). There is likely to be little benefit in ingesting carbohydrate solutions more concentrated than 6–8% because this does not cause increased rates of exogenous glucose oxidation (Wagenmakers et al., 1993). Obviously, the important goal of carbohydrate replacement is to provide sufficient carbohydrate to maintain blood glucose and carbohydrate oxidation without causing gastrointestinal distress and impaired fluid delivery. Ingesting carbohydrate at a rate of 30–60 g·h^{-1} has been repeatedly shown to improve exercise performance. This carbohydrate intake can be achieved by ingesting commercially available sports drinks, at a rate of 600–1200 ml·h^{-1}, with the added benefit of preventing performance decrements due to dehydration (ACSM Position Stand, 1996; Coyle & Montain, 1992).

The beneficial effects of carbohydrate ingestion are likely to be most evident during the latter stages of prolonged exercise when endogenous carbohydrate reserves are depleted. Indeed, ingestion of carbohydrate late in exercise, approximately 30 min before the point of fatigue, produced increases in exercise time to fatigue similar in magnitude to those seen with ingestion of carbohydrate early or throughout exercise or with intravenous infusion of glucose at the point of fatigue (Coggan & Coyle, 1989, 1991; Tsintzas et al., 1996b). In contrast, ingestion of carbohydrate at the point of fatigue is not as effective in enhancing endurance capacity (Coggan & Coyle, 1987, 1991); however, delaying carbohydrate intake until late in exercise, despite increasing blood glucose availability and carbohydrate oxidation, does not always enhance exercise performance (McConell et al., 1996). From a practical perspective, because athletes are unable to assess the level of their carbohydrate reserves and their likely point of fatigue, carbohydrate (and fluid) replacement should commence early and continue throughout exercise.

Limitations to Oxidation of Exogenous Carbohydrate

It appears that the peak rates of glucose uptake and/or oxidation late in exercise when carbohydrate is supplied are in the order of 1.0–1.2 g·min^{-1} (Coggan & Coyle, 1987; Coggan et al., 1991; McConell et al., 1994; Wagenmakers et al., 1993). Furthermore, Wagenmakers et al. (1993) observed a plateau in oxidation of exogenous carbohydrate during prolonged exercise, despite the fact that the subjects ingested increased amounts of carbohydrate (Figure 3-3). These authors suggested that there was "accumulation of exogenous carbohydrate in the gastrointestinal tract and/or in unidentified endogenous pools."

An important question is: What limits exogenous carbohydrate oxidation? Theoretically, the site of limitation may be intake, gastric emptying, intestinal absorption, and/or the ability of the muscle to take up and oxidize glucose. Trained skeletal muscle has a remarkable ability to take up and oxidize glucose under conditions of hyperglycemia and hyperinsulinemia during exercise (Coyle et al., 1991; Hawley et al., 1994). This is likely to be related to factors such as greater capillary density, enhanced GLUT-4 levels, and increased maximal activities of hexokinase and the oxidative enzymes responsible for glucose oxidation. Furthermore, with progressive muscle glycogen depletion there may be a greater capacity for glucose uptake and disposal, although this has not been directly proven. Manipulation of muscle glycogen levels before exercise has not increased rates of glucose uptake and oxidation during exercise (Hargreaves et al., 1995; Jeukendrup et al., 1996; Ravussin et al., 1979), perhaps as a consequence of the higher plasma FFA levels and fat oxidation that accompany the dietary manipulations often used to modify muscle glycogen availability. Although it is possible that high rates of muscle glycogenolysis might limit glucose uptake early in exercise (Katz et al., 1991) or during more intense exercise (Pirnay et al., 1995),

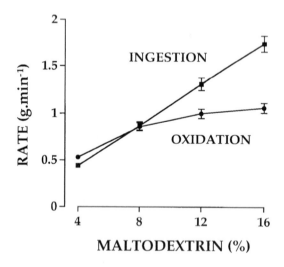

FIGURE 3-3: *Rates of exogenous carbohydrate ingestion and oxidation during the latter stages of exercise at 65% W_{max} with increasing carbohydrate concentration in beverages ingested.* Values are means ± SEM (n = 6). Data from Wagenamakers et al. (1993).

we have observed that hyperglycemia is still effective in increasing glucose Rd under such conditions (Howlett et al., 1998; McConell et al., 1994).

In practice, because voluntary fluid intake is often less than the losses of fluid in sweat (and by implication carbohydrate intake may be less than optimal), laboratory studies employ carbohydrate feeding schedules to ensure that carbohydrate intake is more than adequate. It has been suggested that gastric emptying and intestinal absorption do not limit carbohydrate (and fluid) delivery (Duchman et al., 1997; Rehrer et al., 1992). Rates of gastric emptying and intestinal absorption of glucose from a 6% glucose-electrolyte solution have been measured at 1.2 and 1.3 g·min^{-1}, respectively, under resting conditions (Duchman et al., 1997), values very similar to those for exogenous carbohydrate oxidation. In our own studies, albeit with a 10% glucose solution, tracer-determined glucose Rd late in exercise was higher than the rate of appearance of ingested glucose from the gut, suggesting either a potential gastrointestinal limitation or retention of labeled glucose within the splanchnic bed (McConell et al., 1994). Interestingly, co-ingestion of glucose and fructose, which are absorbed from the intestine by different mechanisms, resulted in greater oxidation of exogenous carbohydrate than did the ingestion of similar amounts of glucose or fructose alone (Adopo et al., 1994). This is also seen with fluid absorption from rehydration beverages containing more than one form of carbohydrate (Shi et al., 1995). These studies suggest that the potential site of limitation of exogenous carbohydrate oxidation may lie in the delivery of ingested carbohydrate from the gastrointestinal tract to the contracting skeletal muscle. Indeed, higher rates of oxidation of exogenous glucose (Hawley et al., 1994) and higher rates of glucose diposal (Coyle et al., 1991) are observed when hyperglycemia is produced by intravenous glucose infusion. However, even under these conditions, a large proportion of the exogenous carbohydrate cannot be accounted for by oxidation, suggesting that there may be an upper limit to muscle glucose uptake and oxidation and/or that other metabolic fates of glucose remain to be determined. It is also possible that the liver plays an active role in regulating the peripheral appearance of ingested glucose, regulating its own glucose uptake and output in relation to the portal delivery of ingested glucose.

CARBOHYDRATE INGESTION AFTER EXERCISE

During the postexercise period, restoration of muscle glycogen reserves is an important metabolic process and is crucial for the recovery of exercise capacity. The complete restoration of muscle glycogen can occur within 24 h (Casey et al., 1995; Keizer et al., 1986; Kochan et al., 1979; MacDougall et al., 1977), depending upon the extent of glycogen depletion and the amount of carbohydrate ingested. In the absence of carbohydrate ingestion, there is a minimal increase in muscle glycogen levels following endurance exercise (Mæhlum & Hermansen, 1978). Following intense exercise that increases muscle and blood lactate levels, glycogenesis from lactate may occur, but it is thought to make a small contribution to overall muscle glycogen resynthesis (Bangsbo et al., 1997). Interestingly, an active recovery from intense exercise, which presumably causes oxidation of lactate, slows the increase in muscle glycogen during the first hour of recovery (Choi et al., 1994). Glucose remains the major precursor for glycogenesis and must be supplied in the postexercise period to facilitate muscle glycogen resynthesis.

There is preferential restoration of muscle glycogen reserves following exercise due to enhanced muscle glucose uptake and greater splanchnic escape of glucose absorbed from the gastrointestinal tract (Hamilton et al., 1996; Mæhlum et al., 1978). The increases in plasma glucose and insulin following ingestion of carbohydrate in the postexercise period have an important role in enhancing glycogen resynthesis (Doyle et al., 1993). In addition, enhanced sarcolemmal glucose transport and activation of glycogen synthase by glycogen-lowering exercise are crucial.

The functional consequences of optimizing postexercise muscle glycogen resynthesis are likely to be important. Increasing dietary carbohydrate intake in the postexercise period enhances recovery of endurance capacity (Brewer et al., 1988; Fallowfield et al., 1993) and intermittent running capacity (Nicholas et al., 1997), with relatively less impact on maximal physical capacity (Keizer et al., 1986) and power output during treadmill sprinting (Nevill et al., 1993). Although not proven, it is possible that the beneficial effects of increased dietary carbohydrate intake are partly related to enhanced muscle glycogen availability. There may be additional benefits of carbohydrate ingestion in the postexercise period. For example, it has been demonstrated recently that carbohydrate supplementation during recovery from resistance exercise decreases the breakdown of myofibrillar protein (Roy et al., 1997).

Determinants of Muscle Glycogen Storage after Exercise

The biochemical mechanisms underlying glycogen synthesis appear to be quite complex. There is evidence that glycogen synthesis may be initiated by the construction of maltosaccharide chains on a protein primer that has been termed glycogenin (Alonso et al., 1995). Glycogenin adds UDP-glucose to its Tyrosine-194 and, following addition of another seven glucose residues, is fully glycosylated and primed for synthesis of glycogen (Alonso et al., 1995). This priming step occurs via an intermediate termed proglycogen, due to the action of a form of glycogen synthase (proglycogen synthase). This enzyme is distinct from the glycogen synthase usually associated with glycogen synthesis which takes proglycogen to macroglycogen (Alonso et al., 1995). Both proglycogen and macroglycogen have been measured in human skeletal muscle (Adamo & Graham, 1998), and proglycogen seems to be the major form of glycogen stored in the early period of recovery from exercise, whereas the increased muscle glycogen storage following a high carbohydrate diet is associated with an increase in the macroglycogen pool (Adamo et al., 1998). The importance of these glycogen pools in the overall regulation of muscle glycogenolysis and glycogenesis during and after exercise remains to be fully elucidated.

The important steps in the resynthesis of glycogen are transport of glucose across the sarcolemma, which is mediated by the GLUT-4 isoform, and activation of glycogen synthase (Figure 3-4). Storage of muscle glycogen after exercise is correlated with both muscle GLUT-4 content (Hickner et al., 1997; McCoy et al., 1996) and glycogen synthase activity (McCoy et al., 1996). Higher muscle GLUT-4 levels and greater glycogen synthase activity may partly explain the faster rates of glycogen synthesis in trained subjects (Hickner et al., 1997) and in type I fibers in the early postexercise period (Casey et al., 1995). Overexpression of GLUT-4 in transgenic mice enhances insulin-stimulated glycogen synthesis (Hansen et al., 1995), and an increase in skeletal muscle GLUT-4 following severe exercise in rats was thought to partly account for the greater ability of these animals to replenish their muscle glycogen stores, compared with non-exercised rats (Ren et al., 1994).

A reduction in skeletal muscle GLUT-4 following eccentric exercise (Asp et al., 1995) may contribute to the impaired muscle glycogen resynthesis rates observed following such exercise (Costill et al., 1990; Doyle et al., 1993; O'Reilly et al., 1987). Overexpression of glycogen synthase in skeletal muscle also results in enhanced glycogen storage (Manchester et al., 1996). In the early postexercise period, initial synthesis of muscle glycogen is insulin-independent (Price et al., 1994) and most likely the result of residual GLUT-4 in the sarcolemma and activation of glycogen synthase by glycogen depletion (see below). With higher plasma insulin levels following carbohydrate ingestion, there will be insulin-stimulated GLUT-4 translocation and further increases in glycogen synthase activity.

Glycogen synthase converts UDP-glucose to glycogen, and its activity is controlled by covalent phosphorylation. Dephosphorylation, by specific phosphatases, results in activation of glycogen synthase and a form (I form) of the enzyme that is less dependent upon glucose-6-P. In contrast, phosphorylation by a protein kinase produces a less active en-

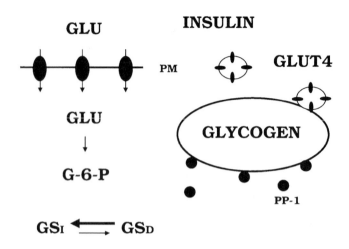

FIGURE 3-4: *Intramuscular factors influencing postexercise glycogen storage.* Depletion of muscle glycogen is associated with increased activity of protein phosphatase-1 (PP1) (which converts the D form of glycogen to the I form) and greater sarcolemmal GLUT-4 content. Increased plasma insulin following carbohydrate ingestion further stimulates GLUT-4 translocation and muscle glucose uptake. Glucose-6-P is an activator of glycogen synthase.

zyme that is more dependent upon glucose-6-P (D form). There may also be a number of intermediate forms with different activities and sensitivities to glucose-6-P (Kochan et al., 1979).

The increase in glycogen synthase activity following exercise is related to the degree of muscle glycogen depletion (Yan et al., 1992; Zachwieja et al., 1991), which may be due to enhanced phosphatase activity and dephosphorylation when glycogen is reduced (Bak & Pedersen, 1990; Yan et al., 1992). Reversal of this process may partly explain the reduction in rates of muscle glycogen synthesis with increasing muscle glycogen levels during recovery (Casey et al., 1995; Zachwieja et al., 1991).

Finally, the plasma glucose and insulin responses following carbohydrate ingestion can account for a large proportion of the variance in postexercise glycogen storage (see Doyle et al., 1993) and will be largely determined by the type and amount of carbohydrate ingested during recovery.

Type, Amount, and Timing of Carbohydrate Ingestion after Exercise

The ability of various carbohydrate substrates to elicit different plasma glucose and insulin responses following their ingestion has led investigators to examine their effects on postexercise muscle glycogen storage. During a 6-h period following exercise, glucose and sucrose ingestion caused greater muscle glycogen storage than did ingestion of fructose (Blom et al., 1987). Ingestion of resistant starch (which contains 100% amylose) resulted in less muscle glycogen storage over a 24-h period than did waxy starch (100% amylopectin), glucose, or maltodextrins (Jozsi et al., 1996). These findings are consistent with the observation that carbohydrate foods with a high GI promote greater muscle glycogen storage than do those with a low GI (Burke et al., 1993). While differences in plasma glucose and insulin responses are likely to contribute to the different rates of glycogen storage, manipulation of the feeding schedule of high-GI carbohydrate foods to alter the glycemic and insulinemic responses did not significantly alter the magnitude of muscle glycogen storage (Burke et al., 1996). Addition of protein to a carbohydrate supplement purportedly enhances the rate of glycogen storage over 4 h of recovery (Zawadzki et al., 1992); however, in two studies where total energy intake was matched, there appeared to be no effect of the addition of protein and fat (Roy & Tarnopolsky, 1998; Tarnopolsky et al., 1997), although in the latter study the protein and fat may have slightly reduced the postingestion glycemic and insulinemic responses. Over a 24-h period, we have observed similar rates of muscle glycogen storage between diets with different macronutrient composition but with equal absolute carbohydrate contents (Burke et al., 1995). No differences in postexercise muscle glycogen storage have been observed between liquid and solid carbohydrate meals (Keizer et al., 1986; Reed et al., 1989).

Over a 4–6 h recovery period following exercise, ingestion of carbohydrate at a rate of $0.7–1.0$ $g \cdot kg^{-1} \cdot 2$ h^{-1} stimulated synthesis of muscle glycogen at rates of $5–8$ $mmol \cdot kg^{-1} \cdot h^{-1}$ (Blom et al., 1987; Ivy et al., 1988a,b). Increasing carbohydrate intake above this value did not enhance glycogen storage in these studies. In contrast, ingestion of carbohydrate at 0.4 $g \cdot kg^{-1}$ every 15 min (1.6 $g \cdot kg^{-1} \cdot h^{-1}$) over a 4-h period produced an average rate of muscle glycogen synthesis of about 10 $mmol \cdot kg^{-1} \cdot h^{-1}$ (Doyle et al., 1993). Over a 24-h period, there may not be much benefit in consuming more than $500–600$ g carbohydrate (Costill et al., 1981). In our own studies, increasing 24-h carbohydrate intake from about 520 g (7 $g \cdot kg^{-1}$) to 870 g (11.8 $g \cdot kg^{-1}$) did not cause additional storage of muscle glycogen (Burke et al., 1995). The addition of fat and protein to the lower-carbohydrate intake did not affect glycogen storage.

Ingestion of carbohydrate immediately after cessation of exercise enhances muscle glycogen resynthesis over a 4-h recovery period (Ivy et al., 1988a). Over a longer recovery period (8–24 h), delaying the ingestion of carbohydrate does not impair overall muscle glycogen storage (Parkin et al., 1997). Nevertheless, if recovery time is reduced due to

multiple training sessions or busy competitive schedules, early ingestion of carbohydrate during recovery is recommended. Frequent ingestion of carbohydrate during 4 h of recovery enhances the rate of muscle
glycogen resynthesis (Doyle et al., 1993). Over 24 h, the frequency of carbohydrate ingestion does not influence glycogen storage, provided the
total carbohydrate intake is adequate (Burke et al., 1996; Costill et al.,
1981).

DIRECTIONS FOR FUTURE RESEARCH

Although it is generally believed that the ergogenic effects of carbohydrate ingestion are mediated by increased carbohydrate availability
to contracting skeletal muscle, there is a need to further investigate the
intracellular mechanisms that may be involved. Recent studies in isolated, single fibers have implicated excitation-contraction coupling as a
key process. In addition, the importance of effects on the central nervous
system requires further investigation. Beneficial effects of carbohydrate
ingestion have sometimes been observed during intense exercise, for
which carbohydrate availability is not normally limiting, but the underlying mechanisms are unknown, and further study is required. Finally,
there is no clear dose-response relationship between carbohydrate ingestion and subsequent effects on exercise metabolism and performance. Further studies should identify the minimal amount of carbohydrate that needs to be ingested to enhance performance under a range of
exercise conditions.

SUMMARY

The depletion of glycogen stores in liver and muscle and lowered
blood glucose availability cause reduced rates of carbohydrate oxidation
and are associated with fatigue during prolonged, strenuous exercise.
Ingestion of carbohydrate before, during, and/or after exercise is an effective strategy for maintaining carbohydrate availability and high rates
of carbohydrate oxidation and for enhancing exercise performance and
recovery. In all situations, carbohydrate ingestion results in enhanced
glucose uptake by skeletal muscle, which is directed either to oxidation
during exercise or to the resynthesis of muscle glycogen in the postexercise recovery period. Although pre-exercise carbohydrate ingestion is
associated with theoretically adverse changes in the metabolic responses
to subsequent exercise, these do not appear to have detrimental effects
on exercise performance. During exercise, the ingestion of carbohydrate
at the rate of 30–60 $g \cdot h^{-1}$ will maintain carbohydrate availability and oxidation and will enhance endurance performance. In the postexercise

period, carbohydrate foods having moderate-to-high glycemic indices should be ingested to facilitate muscle glycogen storage. If the recovery period is short (4–6 h), carbohydrate should be ingested soon after exercise, frequently, and at rates as high as 1–1.6 g·kg^{-1}·h^{-1} to facilitate rapid resynthesis of muscle glycogen. Over a 24-h period, ingestion of 500–600 g is usually sufficient for restoration of muscle glycogen stores.

ACKNOWLEDGMENT

The author has been supported by the National Health & Medical Research Council of Australia, Diabetes Australia, the Gatorade Sports Science Institute, and Ross Australia.

BIBLIOGRAPHY

Adamo, K.B., and T.E. Graham (1998). Comparison of traditional measurements with macroglycogen and proglycogen analysis of muscle glycogen. *J. Appl. Physiol.* 84:908–913.

Adamo, K.B., M.A. Tarnopolsky, and T.E. Graham (1998). Dietary carbohydrate and postexercise synthesis of proglycogen and macroglycogen in human skeletal muscle. *Am. J. Physiol.* 275:E229–E234.

Adopo, E., F. Péronnet, D. Massicotte, G.R. Brisson, and C. Hillaire-Marcel (1994). Respective oxidation of exogenous glucose and fructose given in the same drink during exercise. *J. Appl. Physiol.* 76:1014–1019.

Ahlborg, G., and O. Björkman (1987). Carbohydrate utilization by exercising muscle following pre-exercise glucose ingestion. *Clin. Physiol.* 7:181–195.

Ahlborg, G., and P. Felig (1976). Influence of glucose ingestion on fuel-hormone response during prolonged exercise. *J. Appl. Physiol.* 41:683–688.

Ahlborg, G., and P. Felig (1977). Substrate utilization during prolonged exercise preceded by ingestion of glucose. *Am. J. Physiol.* 233:E188–E194.

Allen, D.G., J. Lännergren, and H. Westerblad (1997). The role of ATP in the regulation of intracellular Ca^{2+} release in single fibres of mouse skeletal muscle. *J. Physiol.* 498:587–600.

Alonso, M.D., J. Lomako, W.M. Lomako, and W.J. Whelan (1995). A new look at the biogenesis of glycogen. *FASEB J.* 9:1126–1137.

American College of Sports Medicine Position Stand (1996). Exercise and fluid replacement. *Med. Sci. Sports Exerc.* 28: i–vii.

Anantaraman, R., A.A. Carmines, G.A. Gaesser, and A. Weltman (1995). Effects of carbohydrate supplementation on performance during 1 hour of high-intensity exercise. *Int. J. Sports Med.* 16:461–465.

Asp, S., J.R. Daugaard, and E.A. Richter (1995). Eccentric exercise decreases glucose transporter GLUT4 protein in human skeletal muscle. *J. Physiol.* 482:705–712.

Bak, J.F., and O. Pedersen (1990). Exercise-enhanced activation of glycogen synthase in human skeletal muscle. *Am. J. Physiol.* 258:E957–E963.

Ball, T.C., S.A. Headley, P.M. Vanderburgh, and J.C. Smith (1995). Periodic carbohydrate replacement during 50 min of high-intensity cycling improves subsequent sprint performance. *Int. J. Sport Nutr.* 5:151–158.

Bangsbo, J., K. Madsen, B. Kiens, and E.A. Richter (1997). Muscle glycogen synthesis in recovery from intense exercise in humans. *Am. J. Physiol.* 273:E416–E424.

Below, P.R., R. Mora-Rodríguez, J. González-Alonso, and E.F. Coyle (1995). Fluid and carbohydrate ingestion independently improve performance during 1 h of intense exercise. *Med. Sci. Sports Exerc.* 27:200–210.

Bergstrom, J., and E. Hultman (1967). A study of the glycogen metabolism during exercise in man. *Scand. J. Clin. Lab. Invest.* 19:218–228.

Bergstrom, J., L. Hermansen, E. Hultman, and B. Saltin (1967). Diet, muscle glycogen and physical performance. *Acta Physiol. Scand.* 71:140–150.

Björkman, O., K. Sahlin, L. Hagenfeldt, and J. Wahren (1984). Influence of glucose and fructose ingestion on the capacity for long-term exercise in well-trained men. *Clin. Physiol.* 4: 483–494.

Blom, P.C.S., A.T. Høstmark, O. Vaage, K.R. Kardel, and S. Mæhlum (1987). Effect of different post-exercise sugar diets on the rate on muscle glycogen synthesis. *Med. Sci. Sports Exerc.* 19:491–496.

Bosch, A.N., S.C. Dennis, and T.D. Noakes (1994). Influence of carbohydrate ingestion on fuel substrate turnover and oxidation during prolonged exercise. *J. Appl. Physiol.* 76: 2364–2372.

Bosch, A.N., S.M. Weltan, S.C. Dennis, and T.D. Noakes (1996). Fuel substrate turnover and oxidation and glycogen sparing with carbohydrate ingestion in non-carbohydrate loaded cyclists. *Pflügers Arch.* 432:1003–1010.

Brewer, J., C. Williams, and A. Patton (1988). The influence of high carbohydrate diets on endurance running performance. *Eur. J. Appl. Physiol.* 57:698–706.

Brouns, F., N.J. Rehrer, W.H.M. Saris, E. Beckers, P. Menheere, and F. ten Hoor (1989). Effect of carbohydrate intake during warming-up on the regulation of blood glucose during exercise. *Int. J. Sports Med.* 10:S68–S75.

Burgess, M.L., R.J. Robertson, J.M. Davis, and J.M. Norris (1991). RPE, blood glucose, and carbohydrate oxidation during exercise: effects of glucose feedings. *Med. Sci. Sports Exerc.* 23:353–359.

Burgess, W.A., J.M. Davis, W.P. Bartoli, and J.A. Woods (1991). Failure of low dose carbohydrate feeding to attenuate glucoregulatory hormone responses and improve endurance performance. *Int. J. Sport Nutr.* 1:338–352.

Burke, L.M., A. Claassen, J.A. Hawley, and T.D. Noakes (1998). Carbohydrate intake during prolonged cycling minimizes effect of plycemic index of preexercise meal. *J. Appl. Physiol.* 85:2220–2226.

Burke, L., G.R. Collier, S.K. Beasley, P.G. Davis, P.A. Fricker, P. Heeley, and M. Hargreaves (1995). Effect of co-ingestion of fat and protein with carbohydrate feedings on muscle glycogen storage. *J. Appl. Physiol.* 78:2187–2192.

Burke, L.M., G.R. Collier, P.G. Davis, P.A. Fricker, A.J. Sanigorski, and M. Hargreaves (1996). Muscle glycogen storage following prolonged exercise: effect of the frequency of carbohydrate feedings. *Am. J. Clin. Nutr.* 64:115–119.

Burke, L.M., G.R. Collier, and M. Hargreaves (1993). Muscle glycogen storage following prolonged exercise: effect of the glycemic index of carbohydrate feedings. *J. Appl. Physiol.* 75:1019–1023.

Casey, A., A.H. Short, E. Hultman, and P.L. Greenhaff (1995). Glycogen resynthesis in human muscle fibre types following exercise-induced glycogen depletion. *J. Physiol.* 483:265–271.

Chin, E., and D.G. Allen (1997). Effects of reduced muscle glycogen concentration on force, Ca^{2+} release and contractile protein function in intact mouse skeletal muscle. *J. Physiol.* 498:17–29.

Choi, D., K.J. Cole, B.H. Goodpaster, W.J. Fink, and D.L. Costill (1994). Effect of passive and active recovery on the resynthesis of muscle glycogen. *Med. Sci. Sports Exerc.* 26:992–996.

Christensen, E.H., and O. Hansen (1939a). III. Arbeitsfähigkeit und Ernährung. *Skand. Arch. Physiol.* 81:160–171.

Christensen, E.H., and O. Hansen (1939b). IV. Hypoglykämie, Arbeitsfähigkeit und Ermüdung. *Skand. Arch. Physiol.* 81:172–179.

Chryssanthopoulos, C., and C. Williams (1997). Pre-exercise carbohydrate meal and endurance running capacity when carbohydrates are ingested during exercise. *Int. J. Sports Med.* 18:543–548.

Chryssanthopoulos, C., L.C.M. Hennessy, and C. Williams (1994a). The influence of pre-exercise glucose ingestion on endurance running capacity. *Br. J. Sports Med.* 28:105–109.

Chryssanthopoulos, C., C. Williams, A. Nowitz, and G. Bogdanis (1997). Influence of a high carbohydrate meal on skeletal muscle glycogen concentration (Abstract). *Proc. E.C.S.S.* 600–601.

Chryssanthopoulos, C., C. Williams, W. Wilson, L. Asher, and L. Hearne (1994b). Comparison between carbohydrate feedings before and during exercise on running performance during a 30–km treadmill time trial. *Int. J. Sport Nutr.* 4:374–386.

Coggan, A.R., and E.F. Coyle (1991). Carbohydrate ingestion during prolonged exercise: effects on metabolism and performance. *Exerc. Sports Sci. Rev.* 19:1–40.

Coggan, A.R., and E.F. Coyle (1988). Effect of carbohydrate feedings during high-intensity exercise. *J. Appl. Physiol.* 65:1703–1709.

Coggan, A.R., and E.F. Coyle (1989). Metabolism and performance following carbohydrate ingestion late in exercise. *Med. Sci. Sports Exerc.* 21:59–65.

Coggan, A.R., and E.F. Coyle (1987). Reversal of fatigue during prolonged exercise by carbohydrate infusion or ingestion. *J. Appl. Physiol.* 63:2388–2395.

Coggan, A.R., R.J. Spina, W.M. Kohrt, D.M. Bier, and J.O. Holloszy (1991). Plasma glucose kinetics in a well-trained cyclist fed glucose throughout exercise. *Int. J. Sport Nutr.* 1:279–288.

Constantin-Teodosiu, D., G. Cederblad, and E. Hultman (1992). Pyruvate dehydrogenase complex activity and acetyl group accumulation in skeletal muscle during prolonged exercise. *J. Appl. Physiol.* 73:2403–2407.

Costill, D.L., E. Coyle, G. Dalsky, W. Evans, W. Fink, and D. Hoopes (1977). Effects of elevated plasma FFA and insulin on muscle glycogen usage during exercise. *J. Appl. Physiol.* 43:695–699.

Costill, D.L., D.D. Pascoe, W.J. Fink, R.A. Robergs, S.I. Barr, and D.R. Pearson (1990). Impaired muscle glycogen resynthesis after eccentric exercise. *J. Appl. Physiol.* 69:46–50.

Costill, D.L., W.M. Sherman, W.J. Fink, C. Maresh, M. Witten, and J.M. Miller (1981). The role of dietary carbohydrates in muscle glycogen resynthesis after strenuous running. *Am. J. Clin. Nutr.* 34:1831–1836.

Coyle, E.F., and S.J. Montain (1992). Benefits of fluid replacement with carbohydrate during exercise. *Med. Sci. Sports Exerc.* 24:S324–S330.

Coyle, E.F., A.R. Coggan, M.K. Hemmert, and J.L. Ivy (1986). Muscle glycogen utilization during prolonged strenuous exercise when fed carbohydrate. *J. Appl. Physiol.* 61:165–172.

Coyle, E.F., A.R. Coggan, M. K. Hemmert, R.C. Lowe, and T.J. Walters (1985). Substrate usage during prolonged exercise following a preexercise meal. *J. Appl. Physiol.* 59:429–433.

Coyle, E.F., J.M. Hagberg, B.F. Hurley, W.H. Martin, A.A. Ehsani, and J.O. Holloszy (1983). Carbohydrate feeding during prolonged strenuous exercise can delay fatigue. *J. Appl. Physiol.* 55:230–235.

Coyle, E.F., M.T. Hamilton, J. Gonzalez-Alonso, S.J. Montain, and J.L. Ivy (1991). Carbohydrate metabolism during intense exercise when hyperglycemic. *J. Appl. Physiol.* 70:834–840.

Coyle, E.F., A.E. Jeukendrup, A.J.M. Wagenmakers, and W.H.M. Saris (1997). Fatty acid oxidation is directly regulated by carbohydrate metabolism during exercise. *Am. J. Physiol.* 273:E268–E275.

Davies, C.T.M., D. Halliday, D.J. Millward, M.J. Rennie, and J.R. Sutton (1982). Glucose inhibits CO_2 production from leucine during whole-body exercise in man (Abstract). *J. Physiol.* 332:40P–41P.

Davis, J.M., and S.P. Bailey (1997). Possible mechanisms of central nervous system fatigue during exercise. *Med. Sci. Sports Exerc.* 29:45–57.

Davis, J.M., S.P. Bailey, J.A. Woods, F.J. Galiano, M.T. Hamilton, and W.P. Bartoli (1992). Effects of carbohydrate feedings on plasma free tryptophan and branched-chain amino acids during prolonged cycling. *Eur. J. Appl. Physiol.* 65:513–519.

Davis, J.M., D.A. Jackson, M.S. Broadwell, J.L. Queary, and C.L. Lambert (1997). Carbohydrate drinks delay fatigue during intermittent, high-intensity cycling in active men and women. *Int. J. Sport Nutr.* 7:261–273.

DeFronzo, R.A., E. Ferrannini, Y. Sato, and J. Wahren (1981). Synergistic interaction between exercise and insulin on peripheral glucose uptake. *J. Clin. Invest.* 68:1468–1474.

Devlin, J.T., J. Calles-Escandon, and E.S. Horton (1986). Effects of preexercise snack feeding on endurance cycle exercise. *J. Appl. Physiol.* 60:980–985.

Dill, D.B., H.T. Edwards, and J.H. Talbott (1932). Studies in muscular activity. VII. Factors limiting the capacity for work. *J. Physiol.* 77:49–62.

Doyle, J.A., W.M. Sherman, and R.L. Strauss (1993). Effects of eccentric and concentric exercise on muscle glycogen replenishment. *J. Appl. Physiol.* 74:1848–1855.

Duchman, S.M., A.J. Ryan, H.P. Schedl, R.W. Summers, T.L. Bleiler, and C.V. Gisolfi (1997). Upper limit for intestinal absorption of a dilute glucose solution in men at rest. *Med. Sci. Sports Exerc.* 29:482–488.

Erikson, M.A., R.J. Schwarzkopf, and R.D. McKenzie (1987). Effects of caffeine, fructose, and glucose ingestion on muscle glycogen utilization during exercise. *Med. Sci. Sports Exerc.* 19:579–583.

Fallowfield, J.L., and C. Williams (1993). Carbohydrate intake and recovery from prolonged exercise. *Int. J. Sport Nutr.* 3:150–164.

Febbraio, M.A., and K.L. Stewart (1996). CHO feeding before prolonged exercise: effect of glycemic index on muscle glycogenloysis and exercise performance. *J. Appl. Physiol.* 81:1115–1120.

Fielding, R.A., D.L. Costill, W.J. Fink, D.S. King, M. Hargreaves, and J.E. Kovaleski (1985). Effect of carbohydrate feeding frequencies and dosage on muscle glycogen use during exercise. *Med. Sci. Sports Exerc.* 17:472–476.

Fielding, R.A., D.L. Costill, W.J. Fink, D.S. King, J.E. Kovaleski, and J.P. Kirwan (1987). Effects of pre-exercise carbohydrate feedings on muscle glycogen use during exercise in well-trained runners. *Eur. J. Appl. Physiol.* 56:225–229.

Flynn, M.G., D.L. Costill, J.A. Hawley, W.J. Fink, P.D. Neufer, R.A. Fielding, and M.D. Sleeper (1987). Influence of selected carbohydrate drinks on cycling performance and glycogen use. *Med. Sci. Sports Exerc.* 19:37–40.

Foster, C., D.L. Costill, and W.J. Fink (1979). Effects of pre-exercise feedings on endurance performance. *Med. Sci. Sports.* 11:1–5.

Galante, P., L. Mosthaf, M. Kellerer, L. Berti, S. Tippmer, B. Bossenmaier, T. Fujiwara, A. Okuno, H. Horikoshi, and H.U. Häring (1995). Acute hyperglycemia provides an insulin-independent inducer for GLUT4 translocation in C2C12 myotubes and rat skeletal muscle. *Diabetes.* 44:646–651.

Gao, J., J-M. Ren, E.A. Gulve, and J.O. Holloszy (1994). Additive effect of contractions and insulin on GLUT-4 translocation into the sarcolemma. *J. Appl. Physiol.* 77:1597–1601.

Gibala, M.J., M.A. Tarnopolsky, and T.E. Graham (1997). Tricarboxylic acid cycle intermediates in human muscle at rest and during prolonged cycling. *Am. J. Physiol.* 272:E239–E244.

Gleeson, M., R.J. Maughan, and P.L. Greenhaff (1986). Comparison of the effects of pre-exercise feeding of glucose, glycerol and placebo on endurance performance and fuel homeostasis in man. *Eur. J. Appl. Physiol.* 55:645–653.

Goodpaster, B.H., D.L. Costill, W.J. Fink, T.A. Trappe, A.C. Jozsi, R.D. Starling, and S.W. Trappe (1996). The effects of pre-exercise starch ingestion on endurance performance. *Int. J. Sports Med.* 17:366–372.

Gordon, B., L.A. Kohn, S.A. Levine, M. Matton, W. de M. Scriver, and W.B. Whiting (1925). Sugar content of the blood in runners following a marathon race. With especial reference to the prevention of hypoglycemia: further observations. *J.A.M.A.* 85:508–509.

Guezennec, C.Y., P. Satabin, F. Duforez, D. Merino, F. Peronnet, and J. Koziet (1989). Oxidation of corn starch, glucose, and fructose ingested before exercise. *Med. Sci. Sports Exerc.* 21:45–50.

Hamilton, K.S., F.K. Gibbons, D.P. Bracy, D.B. Lacy, A.D. Cherrington, and D.H. Wasserman (1996). Effect of prior exercise on the partitioning of an intestinal glucose load between splanchnic bed and skeletal muscle. *J. Clin. Invest.* 98:125–135.

Hansen, P.A., E.A. Gulve, B.A. Marshall, J. Gao, J.E. Pessin, J.O. Holloszy, and M.E. Mueckler (1995). Skeletal muscle glucose transport and metabolism are enhanced in transgenic mice overexpressing the GLUT-4 transporter. *J. Biol. Chem.* 270:1679–1684.

Hargreaves, M., and C.A. Briggs (1988). Effect of carbohydrate ingestion on exercise metabolism. *J. Appl. Physiol.* 65:1553–1555.

Hargreaves, M., D.L. Costill, A. Coggan, W.J. Fink, and I. Nishibata (1984). Effect of carbohydrate feedings on muscle glycogen utilization and exercise performance. *Med. Sci. Sports Exerc.* 16:219–222.

Hargreaves, M., D.L. Costill, W.J. Fink, D.S. King, and R.A. Fielding (1987). Effect of pre-exercise carbohydrate feedings on endurance cycling performance. *Med. Sci. Sports Exerc.* 19:33–36.

Hargreaves, M., D.L. Costill, A. Katz, and W.J. Fink (1985). Effect of fructose ingestion on muscle glycogen usage during exercise. *Med. Sci. Sports Exerc.* 17:360–363.

Hargreaves, M., B. Kiens, and E.A. Richter (1991). Effect of increased plasma free fatty acid concentrations on muscle metabolism in exercising men. *J. Appl. Physiol.* 70:194–201.

Hargreaves, M., G.K. McConell and J. Proietto (1995). Influence of muscle glycogen on glycogenolysis and glucose uptake during exercise. *J. Appl. Physiol.* 78:288–292.

Hawley, J.A., A.N. Bosch, S.M. Weltan, S.C. Dennis, and T.D. Noakes (1994). Glucose kinetics during prolonged exercise in euglycemic and hyperglycemic subjects. *Pflügers Arch.* 426:378–386.

Hawley, J.A., S.C. Dennis, and T.D. Noakes (1992). Oxidation of carbohydrate ingested during prolonged endurance exercise. *Sports Med.* 14:27–42.

Hermansen, L., E. Hultman, and B. Saltin (1967). Muscle glycogen during prolonged severe exercise. *Acta Physiol. Scand.* 71:129–139.

Hickner, R.C., J.S. Fisher, P.A. Hansen, S.B. Racette, C.M. Mier, M.J. Turner, and J.O. Holloszy (1997). Muscle glycogen accumulation after endurance exercise in trained and untrained individuals. *J. Appl. Physiol.* 83:897–903.

Horowitz, J.F., and E.F. Coyle (1993). Metabolic responses to preexercise meals containing various carbohydrates and fat. *Am. J. Clin. Nutr.* 58:235–241.

Horowitz, J.F., R. Mora-Rodríguez, L.O. Byerley, and E.F. Coyle (1997). Lipolytic suppression following carbohydrate ingestion limits fat oxidation. *Am. J. Physiol.* 273:E768–E775.

Horowitz, J.F., R. Mora-Rodríguez, L.O. Byerley, and E.F. Coyle (1998). Carbohydrate ingestion during exercise reduces fat oxidation when glucose uptake increases. *FASEB J.* 10:A143.

Howlett, K., D. Angus, J. Proietto, and M. Hargreaves (1998). Effect of increased blood glucose availability on glucose kinetics during exercise. *J. Appl. Physiol.* 84:1413–1417.

Ivy, J.L., D.L. Costill, W.J. Fink, and R.W. Lower (1979). Influence of caffeine and carbohydrate feedings on endurance performance. *Med. Sci. Sports.* 11:6–11.

Ivy, J.L., A.L. Katz, C.L. Cutler, W.M. Sherman, and E.F. Coyle (1988a). Muscle glycogen synthesis after exercise: effect of time of carbohydrate ingestion. *J. Appl. Physiol.* 64:1480–1485.

Ivy, J.L., M.C. Lee, J.T. Brozinick, and M.J. Reed (1988b). Muscle glycogen storage after different amounts of carbohydrate ingestion. *J. Appl. Physiol.* 65:2018–2023.

Jeukendrup, A.E., L.B. Borghouts, W.H.M. Saris, and A.J.M. Wagenmakers (1996). Reduced oxidation rates of ingested glucose during prolonged exercise with low endogenous CHO availability. *J. Appl. Physiol.* 81:1952–1957.

Jeukendrup, A., F. Brouns, A.J.M. Wagenmakers, and W.H.M. Saris (1997). Carbohydrate-electrolyte feedings improve 1h time trial cycling performance. *Int. J. Sports Med.* 18:125–129.

Johnson, L.N. (1992). Glycogen phosphorylase: control by phosphorylation and allosteric effectors. *FASEB J.* 6:2274–2282.

Jozsi, A.C., T.A. Trappe, R.D. Starling, B. Goodpaster, S.W. Trappe, W.J. Fink, and D.L. Costill (1996). The influence of starch structure on glycogen resynthesis and subsequent cycling performance. *Int. J. Sports Med.* 17:373–378.

Katz, A., K. Sahlin, and S. Broberg (1991). Regulation of glucose utilization in human skeletal muscle during moderate dynamic exercise. *Am. J. Physiol.* 260:E411–E415.

Keizer, H.A., H. Kuipers, G. Van Kranenburg, and P. Guerten (1986). Influence of liquid and solid meals on muscle glycogen resynthesis, plasma fuel hormone response, and maximal physical working capacity. *Int. J. Sports Med.* 8:99–104.

Kirwan, J.P., D. O'Gorman, and W.J. Evans (1998). A moderate glycemic meal before endurance exercise can enhance performance. *J. Appl. Physiol.* 84:53–59.

Kochan, R.G., D.R. Lamb, S.A. Lutz, C.V. Perrill, E.M. Reimann, and K.K. Schlender (1979). Glycogen synthase activation in human skeletal muscle: effects of diet and exercise. *Am. J. Physiol.* 236:E660–E666.

Koivisto, V.A., M. Härkönen, S-L. Karonen, P.H. Groop, R. Elovainio, E. Ferrannini, L. Sacca, and R.A. DeFronzo (1985). Glycogen depletion during prolonged exercise: influence of glucose, fructose and placebo. *J. Appl. Physiol.* 58:731–737.

Koivisto, V.A., S-L. Karonen, and E.A. Nikkilä (1981). Carbohydrate ingestion before exercise: comparison of glucose, fructose, and sweet placebo. *J. Appl. Physiol.* 51:783–787.

Kristiansen, S., M. Hargreaves, and E.A. Richter (1997). Progressive increase in glucose transport and GLUT4 in human sarcolemmal vesicles during moderate exercise. *Am. J. Physiol.* 272:E385–E389.

Kuipers, H., H.A. Keizer, F. Brouns, and W.H.M. Saris (1987). Carbohydrate feeding and glycogen synthesis during exercise in man. *Pflügers Arch.* 410:652–656.

Leijssen, D.P.C., W.H.M. Saris, A.E. Jeukendrup, and A.J.M. Wagenamakers (1995). Oxidation of exogenous [^{13}C]galactose and [^{13}C]glucose during exercise. *J. Appl. Physiol.* 79:720–725.

Levine, L., W.J. Evans, B.S. Cadarette, E.C. Fisher, and B.A. Bullen (1983). Fructose and glucose ingestion and muscle glycogen use during submaximal exercise. *J. Appl. Physiol.* 55:1767–1771.

Levine, S.A., B. Gordon, and C.L. Derick (1924). Some changes in the chemical constituents of the blood following a marathon race. With special reference to the development of hypoglycemia. *J.A.M.A.* 82:1778–1779.

Lugo, M., W.M. Sherman, G.S. Wimer, and K. Garleb (1993). Metabolic responses when different forms of carbohydrate energy are consumed during cycling. *Int. J. Sport Nutr.* 3:398–407.

MacDougall, J.D., G.R. Ward, D.G. Sale, and J.R. Sutton (1977). Muscle glycogen repletion after high-intensity intermittent exercise. *J. Appl. Physiol.* 42:129–132.

Mæhlum, S., P. Felig, and J. Wahren (1978). Splanchnic glucose and muscle glycogen metabolism after glucose feeding during postexercise recovery. *Am. J. Physiol.* 235:E255–E260.

Mæhlum, S., and L. Hermansen (1978). Muscle glycogen concentration during recovery after prolonged severe exercise in fasting subjects. *Scand. J. Clin. Lab. Invest.* 38:557–560.

Manchester, J., A.V. Skurat, P. Roach, S.D. Hauschka, and J.C. Lawrence (1996). Increased glycogen accumulation in transgenic mice overexpressing glycogen synthase in skeletal muscle. *Proc. Natl. Acad. Sci.* 93:10707–10711.

Marmy-Conus, N., S. Fabris, J. Proietto, and M. Hargreaves (1996). Pre-exercise glucose ingestion and glucose kinetics during exercise. *J. Appl. Physiol.* 81:853–857.

Mason, W.L., G. McConell, and M. Hargreaves (1993). Carbohydrate ingestion during exercise: liquid vs. solid feedings. *Med. Sci. Sports Exerc.* 25:966–969.

Massicotte, D., F. Péronnet, G. Brisson, K. Bakkouch, and C. Hillaire-Marcel (1989). Oxidation of a glucose polymer during exercise: comparison with glucose and fructose. J. Appl. Physiol. 66:179–183.

McConell, G.K., S. Fabris, J. Proietto, and M. Hargreaves (1994). Effect of carbohydrate ingestion on glucose kinetics during exercise. *J. Appl. Physiol.* 77:1537–1541.

McConell, G., K. Kloot, and M. Hargreaves (1996). Effect of timing of carbohydrate ingestion on endurance exercise performance. *Med. Sci. Sports Exerc.* 28:1300–1304.

McCoy, M., J. Proietto, and M. Hargreaves (1996). Skeletal muscle GLUT-4 and post-exercise muscle glycogen storage in humans. *J. Appl. Physiol.* 80:411–415.

McMurray, R.G., J.R. Wilson, and B.S. Kitchell (1983). The effects of fructose and glucose on high-intensity endurance performance. *Res. Quart. Ex. Sport.* 54:156–162.

Mitchell, J.B., D.L. Costill, J.A. Houmard, W.J. Fink, D.D. Pascoe, and D.R. Pearson (1989). Influence of carbohydrate dosage on exercise performance and glycogen metabolism. *J. Appl. Physiol.* 67:1843–1849.

Mitrakou, A., C. Ryan, T. Veneman, M. Mokan, J. Jenssen, I. Kiss, J. Durrant, P. Cryer, and J.E. Gerich (1991). Heirarchy of glycemic thresholds for counterregulatory hormone secretion, symptoms and cerebral dysfunction. *Am. J. Physiol.* 260:E67–E74.

Montain, S.J., M.K. Hopper, A.R. Coggan, and E.F. Coyle (1991). Exercise metabolism at different time intervals after a meal. *J. Appl. Physiol.* 70:882–888.

Murray, R., G.L. Paul, J.G. Seifert, and D.E. Eddy (1991). Responses to varying rates of carbohydrate ingestion during exercise. *Med. Sci. Sports Exerc.* 23:713–718.

Murray, R.,G.L. Paul, J.G. Seifert, D.E. Eddy, and G.A. Halaby (1989a). The effects of glucose, fructose, and sucrose ingestion during exercise. *Med. Sci. Sports Exerc.* 21:275–282.

Murray, R., J.G. Seifert, D.E. Eddy, G.L. Paul, and G.A. Halaby (1989b). Carbohydrate feeding and exercise: effect of beverage carbohydrate content. *Eur. J. Appl. Physiol.* 59:152–158.

Neufer, P.D., D.L. Costill, M.G. Flynn, J.P. Kirwan, J.B. Mitchell, and J. Houmard (1987). Improvements in exercise performance: effects of carbohydrate feedings and diet. *J. Appl. Physiol.* 62:983–988.

Nevill, M.E., C. Williams, D. Roper, C. Slater, and A.M. Nevill (1993). Effect of diet on performance during recovery from intermittent sprint exercise. *J. Sports Sci.* 11:119–126.

Nicholas, C.W., P.A. Green, R.D. Hawkins, and C. Williams (1997). Carbohydrate intake and recovery of intermittent running capacity. *Int. J. Sport Nutr.* 7:251–260.

Nicholas, C.W., C. Williams, H.K.A. Lakomy, G. Phillips, and A. Nowitz (1995). Influence of ingesting a carbohydrate-electrolyte solution on endurance capacity during intermittent, high intensity shuttle running. *J. Sports Sci.* 13:283–290.

Norman, B., A. Sollevi, and E. Jansson (1988). Increased IMP content in glycogen-depleted muscle fibres during submaximal exercise in man. *Acta Physiol. Scand.* 133:97–100.

Norman, B., A. Sollevi, L. Kaijser, and E. Jansson (1987). ATP breakdown products in human skeletal muscle during prolonged exercise to exhaustion. *Clin. Physiol.* 7:503–509.

Odland, L.M., G.J.F. Heigenhauser, D. Wong, M.G. Hollidge-Horvath, and L.L. Spriet (1998). Effects of increased fat availability on fat-carbohydrate interaction during prolonged exercise in men. *Am. J. Physiol.* 274:R894–R902, 1998.

Okano, G., H. Takeda, I. Morita, M. Katoh, Z. Mu, and S. Miyake (1988). Effect of pre-exercise fructose ingestion on endurance performance in fed men. *Med. Sci. Sports Exerc.* 20:105–109.

O'Reilly, K.P., M.J. Warhol, R.A. Fielding, W.R. Frontera, C.N. Meredith, and W.J. Evans (1987). Eccentric exercise-induced muscle damage impairs muscle glycogen repletion. *J. Appl. Physiol.* 63:252–256.

Owen, V.J., G.D. Lamb, and D.G. Stephenson (1996). Effect of low [ATP] on depolartization-induced Ca^{2+} release in skeletal muscle fibres of the toad. *J. Physiol.* 493:309–315.

Palmer, G.S., M.C. Clancy, J.A. Hawley, I.M. Rodger, L.M. Burke, and T.D. Noakes (1998). Carbohydrate ingestion immediately before exercise does not improve 20 km time trial performance in well trained cyclists. *Int. J. Sports Med.* 19:415–418, 1998.

Parkin, J.M., M.F. Carey, I.K. Martin, L. Stojanovska, and M.A. Febbraio (1997). Muscle glycogen storage following prolonged exercise: effect of timing of ingestion of high glycemic index food. *Med. Sci. Sports Exerc.* 29:220–224.

Pirnay, F., A.J. Scheen, J.F. Gautier, M. Lacroix, F. Mosora, and P.J. Lefebvre (1995). Exogenous glucose oxidation during exercise in relation to the power output. *Int. J. Sports Med.* 16:456–460.

Price, T.B., D.L. Rothman, R. Taylor, M.J. Avison, G.I. Shulman, and R.G. Shulman (1994). Human muscle glycogen resynthesis after exercise: insulin-dependent and –independent phases. *J. Appl. Physiol.* 76:104–111.

Ravussin, E., P. Pahud, A. Dörner, M.J. Arnaud, and E. Jéquier (1979). Substrate utilization during prolonged exercise preceded by ingestion of ^{13}C-glucose in glycogen depleted and control subjects. *Pflügers Arch.* 382:197–202.

Reed, M.J., J.T. Brozinick, M.C. Lee, and J.L. Ivy (1989). Muscle glycogen storage postexercise: effect of mode of carbohydrate administration. *J. Appl. Physiol.* 66:720–726.

Rehrer, N.J., A.J.M. Wagenmakers, E.J. Beckers, D. Halliday, J.B. Leiper, F. Brouns, R.J. Maughan, K. Westerterp, and W.H.M. Saris (1992). Gastric emptying, absorption, and carbohydrate oxidation during prolonged exercise. *J. Appl. Physiol.* 72:468–475.

Ren, J-M., C.F. Semenkovich, E.A. Gulve, J. Gao, and J.O. Holloszy (1994). Exercise induces rapid increases in GLUT-4 expression, glucose transport and insulin-stimulated glycogen storage in muscle. *J. Biol. Chem.* 269:14396–14401.

Roy, B.D., and M.A. Tarnopolsky (1998). Influence of differing macronutrient intakes on muscle glycogen resynthesis after resistance exercise. *J. Appl. Physiol.* 84:890–896.

Roy, B.D., M.A. Tarnopolsky, J.D. MacDougall, J. Fowles, and K.E. Yarasheski (1997). Effect of glucose supplement timing on protein metabolism after resistance training. *J. Appl. Physiol.* 82:1882–1888.

Sahlin, K., A. Katz, and S. Broberg (1990). Tricarboxylic acid cycle intermediates in human muscle during prolonged exercise. *Am. J. Physiol.* 259:C834–C841.

Sahlin, K., K. Soderlund, M. Tonkonogi, and K. Hirakoba (1997). Phosphocreatine content in single fibres of human muscle after sustained submaximal exercise. *Am. J. Physiol.* 273:C172–C178.

Saris, W.H.M., B.H. Goodpaster, A.E. Jeukendrup, F. Brouns, D. Halliday, and A.J.M. Wagenmakers (1993). Exogenous carbohydrate oxidation from different carbohydrate sources during exercise. *J. Appl. Physiol.* 75:2168–2172.

Sasaki, H., J. Maeda, S. Usui, and T. Ishiko (1987). Effect of sucrose and caffeine ingestion on performance of prolonged strenuous running. *Int. J. Sports Med.* 8:261–265.

Schwartz, N.S., W.E. Clutter, S.D. Shah, and P.E. Cryer (1987). Glycemic thresholds for activation of counterregulatory systems are higher than the threshold for symptoms. *J. Clin. Invest.* 79:777–781.

Seifert, J.G., G.L. Paul, D.E. Eddy, and R. Murray (1994). Glycemic and insulinemic response to preexercise carbohydrate feedings. *Int. J. Sport Nutr.* 4:46–53.

Sherman, W.M., G. Brodowicz, D.A. Wright, W.K. Allen, J. Simonsen, and A. Dernbach (1989). Effects of 4 h preexercise carbohydrate feedings on cycling performance. *Med. Sci. Sports Exerc.* 21:598–604.

Sherman, W.M., D.L. Costill, W.J. Fink, and J.M. Miller (1981). Effect of diet-exercise manipulation on muscle glycogen and its subsequent utilization during performance. *Int. J. Sports Med.* 2:114–118.

Sherman, W.M., M.C. Peden, and D.A. Wright (1991). Carbohydrate feedings 1 h before exercise improve cycling performance. *Am. J. Clin. Nutr.* 54:866–870.

Shi, X., R.W. Summers, H.P. Schedl, S.W. Flanagan, R. Chang, and C.V. Gisolfi (1995). Effects of carbohydrate type and concentration and solution osmolality on water absorption. *Med. Sci. Sports Exerc.* 27:1607–1615.

Short, K.R., M. Sheffield-Moore, and D.L. Costill (1997). Glycemic and insulinemic responses to multiple preexercise carbohydrate feedings. *Int. J. Sport Nutr.* 7:128–137.

Snow, R.J., M.F. Carey, C.G. Stathis, M.A. Febbraio, and M. Hargreaves (1998). Effect of carbohydrate ingestion on ammonia metabolism during exercise. Submitted.

Sparks, M.J., S.E. Selig, and M.A. Febbraio (1998). Pre-exercise carbohydrate ingestion: effect of the glycemic index on endurance exercise performance. *Med. Sci. Sports Exerc.* 30:844–849.

Spencer, M.K., Z. Yan, and A. Katz (1991). Carbohydrate supplementation attenuates IMP accumulation in human muscle during prolonged exercise. *Am. J. Physiol.* 261:C71–C76.

Tarnopolsky, M.A., M. Bosman, J.R. MacDonald, D. Vandeputte, J. Martin, and B.D. Roy (1997). Postexercise protein-carbohydrate supplements increase muscle glycogen in men and women. *J. Appl. Physiol.* 83:1877–1883.

Thomas, D.E., J.R. Brotherhood, and J.C. Brand (1991). Carbohydrate feeding before exercise: effect of glycemic index. *Int. J. Sports Med.* 12:180–186.

Thomas, D.E., J.R. Brotherhood, and J. Brand Miller (1994). Plasma glucose levels after prolonged strenuous exercise correlate inversely with glycemic response to food consumed before exercise. *Int. J. Sports Nutr.* 4:361–373.

Tsintzas, K., R. Liu, C. Williams, I. Campbell, and G. Gaitanos (1993). The effect of carbohydrate ingestion on performance during a 30-km race. *Int. J. Sport Nutr.* 3:127–139.

Tsintzas, O.K., C. Williams, L. Boobis, and P. Greenhaff (1995). Carbohydrate ingestion and glycogen utilization in different muscle fibre types in man. *J. Physiol.* 489:242–250.

Tsintzas, O.K., C. Williams, L. Boobis, and P. Greenhaff (1996a). Carbohydrate ingestion and single muscle fibre glycogen metabolism during prolonged running in men. *J. Appl. Physiol.* 81:801–809.

Tsintzas, K., C. Williams, D. Constantin-Teodosiu, E. Hultman, L. Boobis, and P.L. Greenhaff (1998). Dual effect of carbohydrate feeding on skeletal muscle substrate utilization during exercise in man (Abstract). *J. Physiol.* 506:101P.

Tsintzas, O-K., C. Williams, W. Wilson, and J. Burrin (1996b). Influence of carbohydrate supplementation early in exercise on endurance running capacity. *Med. Sci. Sports Exerc.* 28:1373–1379.

Wagenmakers, A.J.M., E.J. Beckers, F. Brouns, H. Kuipers, P.B. Soeters, G.J. Van der Vusse, and W.H.M. Saris (1991). Carbohydrate supplementation, glycogen depletion, and amino acid metabolism during exercise. *Am. J. Physiol.* 260:E883–E890.

Wagenmakers, A.J.M., F. Brouns, W.H.M. Saris, and D. Halliday (1993). Oxidation rates of orally ingested carbohydrates during prolonged exercise in men. *J. Appl. Physiol.* 75:2774–2780.

Wasserman, D.H., R.J. Geer, D.E. Rice, D. Bracy, P.J. Flakoll, L.L. Brown, J.O. Hill, and N.N. Abumrad (1991). Interaction of exercise and insulin action in humans. *Am. J. Physiol.* 260:E37–E45.

Wee, S-L., C. Williams, S. Gray, and J. Horabin (1999). Influence of high and low glycemic index meals on endurance running capacity. Med. Sci. Sports Exerc. In press.

Widrick, J.J., D.L. Costill, W.J. Fink, M.S. Hickey, G.K. McConell, and H. Tanaka (1993). Carbohydrate feedings and exercise performance: effect of initial muscle glycogen concentration. *J. Appl. Physiol.* 74:2998–3005.

Wilber, R.L., and R.J. Moffatt (1992). Influence of carbohydrdate ingestion on blood glucose and performance in runners. *Int. J. Sport Nutr.* 2:317–327.

Williams, C., M.G. Nute, L. Broadbank, and S. Vinall (1990). Influence of fluid intake on endurance running performance. *Eur. J. Appl. Physiol.* 60:112–119.

Wright, D.A., W.M. Sherman, and A.R. Dernbach (1991). Carbohydrate feedings before, during, or in combination improve cycling endurance performance. *J. Appl. Physiol.* 71:1082–1088.

Yan, Z., M.K. Spencer, and A. Katz (1992). Effect of low glycogen on glycogen synthase in human muscle during and after exercise. *Acta Physiol. Scand.* 145:345–352.

Yaspelkis, B.B., J.G. Patterson, P.A. Anderla, Z. Ding, and J.L. Ivy (1993). Carbohydrate supplementation spares muscle glycogen during variable-intensity exercise. *J. Appl. Physiol.* 75:1477–1485.

Zachwieja, J.J., D.L. Costill, D.D. Pascoe, R.A. Roberds, and W.J. Fink (1991). Influence of muscle glycogen depletion on the rate of resynthesis. *Med. Sci. Sports Exerc.* 23:44–48.

Zawadzki, K.M., B.B. Yaspelkis, and J.L. Ivy (1992). Carbohydrate-protein complex increases the rate of muscle glycogen storage after exercise. *J. Appl. Physiol.* 72:1854–1859.

DISCUSSION

LAMB: When dietary carbohydrate is increased, fat supply and fat utilization are simultaneously decreased. Has there been sufficient testing of the hypothesis that it is the reduction in fat metabolism, not the increase in carbohydrate metabolism, that is responsible for the improvements in performance that are associated with carbohydrate feedings?

HARGREAVES: I think the performance improvement is more related to the carbohydrate intake and the acute insulin changes that have a powerful effect on inhibiting fat metabolism.

MAUGHAN: You quoted the recommendation that people should consume about 30–60 g of carbohydrate/h, and you pointed out that this is very close to the maximum reported rate of exogenous carbohydrate oxidation of about 1 g/min. However, several studies showed that to get to 1 g/min, people had to ingest carbohydrate at much more than that rate. If you ingest less than 1 g/min, you are never going to achieve the maximum rate of exogenous oxidation. Should we really be recommending such small levels of carbohydrate intake if the capacity for oxidation of exogenous carbohydrate is reached only when one consumes carbohydrate at a rate exceeding 1 g/min?

HARGREAVES: There is no good evidence of a clear dose-response relationship between the amount of carbohydrate ingested and the extent of improved performance. We need to find out how much carbohydrate should be consumed to increase carbohydrate oxidation and improve performance and whether or not the increase in carbohydrate oxidation from exogenous glucose accounts for the ergogenic effect.

MAUGHAN: In other words, we should determine the minimum amount of carbohydrate that will be effective in improving performance?

HARGREAVES: I think so. Only one or two reports have systematically examined carbohydrate dosage at the lower end. In both studies, 26 g/h was as effective as 70 g/h.

SPRIET: I have a question about the glucose ingestion studies wherein glucose is given 30–60 min before exercise. Am I correct in assuming that most of those studies were done in an overnight fasted state?

HARGREAVES: Yes, most of the subjects were fasted.

SPRIET: This has some relevance to preparation for endurance exercise. When subjects come to the lab in the fasted state, especially overnight fasted, they will already be predisposed to fat metabolism. When you feed carbohydrate in this situation, the down-regulation of fat metabolism consequent to the glucose ingestion will be greater than if subjects arrived in a well-fed state. How dramatic do you think the down-regulation of fat would be if subjects had already eaten a carbohydrate-rich meal 3 h before a subsequent carbohydrate feeding closer to the start of exercise?

HARGREAVES: I don't think the reduction in fat catabolism following the feeding 30 min before exercise would be as great if the athlete ate a carbohydrate-rich meal 3 h previously. Ed Coyle has shown that the inhibitory effect of ingesting carbohydrate lasts at least 4-6 h and maybe up to 8 h.

SPRIET: So, for a well-fed individual, there is no downside to taking extra carbohydrate just prior to exercise with respect to the fat utilization question because in the well-fed state you are already using more carbohydrate and less fat?

HARGREAVES: On balance, even in the fasted state, most studies suggest that carbohydrate ingestion has no negative effect on performance. It may have a significant positive effect compared to no carbohydrate ingestion before exercise.

FEBBRAIO: In one study from our laboratory we fed subjects 4 h before a subsequent carbohydrate feeding 30 min before exercise. In a similar study, we did not feed the subjects 4 h before exercise. The glycemic and insulinemic responses to ingesting carbohydrate 30 min before exercise were more severe in the fed state, but the metabolic disturbance was transient in both studies. After 40–60 min of exercise, the blood glucose concentration had essentially returned to baseline resting values in both studies. Pre-exercise carbohydrate ingestion does not seem to have a persistent effect on metabolism. In both studies, there was no effect of CHO feeding 30 min before exercise on exercise performance.

WILLIAMS: We found that subjects in a well-fed state use less muscle glycogen during the first hour of running at 70% $\dot{V}O_2$max than they do if they start the exercise in a fasted state. So having a high-carbohydrate meal 3 h before exercise does show a glycogen sparing effect during the first hour of exercise. Also, there is some evidence that providing carbohydrate immediately before exercise decreases the transport of fatty acids in the mitochondria.

COYLE: Athletes normally eat carbohydrate 2-6 h before exercise, and if they do this, it is important that they eat enough carbohydrate. Probably the worst thing they could do is eat less than 50 g of carbohydrate several hours before exercise because then they would be suppressing fat oxidation to a greater extent than they would be replacing the fat-derived energy with carbohydrate-derived energy. As a result, muscle glycogen would be depleted more rapidly. We must get the message across that athletes need to eat plenty of carbohydrate.

MONTAIN: Sometimes there is a beneficial effect of carbohydrate feeding on performance with no evidence that that particular type of exercise (usually 60 min or less) is associated with any carbohydrate deficit. Is there any evidence in your studies of a beneficial effect of CHO feeding on perception of effort that might explain the positive effect on performance?

HARGREAVES: In our research we did not measure perception of effort. However, we did not have any feedback from the subjects that they found one trial any harder than the other.

BAR-OR: We found that healthy adolescents who exercised for 2 h rated this effort about two units higher on the Borg scale of perceived exertion when they drank water during exercise than when they drank a 6% carbohydrate-electrolyte beverage. This occurred even though there were only minimal difference in blood glucose. Conversely, adolescents with insulin-dependent diabetes mellitus had similar ratings of perceived exertion when drinking water or 6% carbohydrate, even though their blood glucose dropped considerably while drinking water. This suggests a dissociation between the level of blood glucose and the way young people rate their effort during exercise.

TARNOPOLSKY: As I recall, Wim Saris' group had subjects warm up in the hour before exercise to provoke an increase in counter-regulatory hormones that prevented the hypoglycemia typically observed when carbohydrate is ingested shortly before exercise. Would you recommend such a warm-up period as a practical suggestion?

HARGREAVES: That has been one of the strategies used to blunt the hypoglycemic response. Certainly, there are many advantages to warm up over and above any effect it may have on metabolic responses. The practical recommendation I would make is for athletes to experiment individually to discover how they respond to pre-exercise carbohydrate ingestion.

SHERMAN: How important is an adaptive response of the glucose transport system in producing the beneficial effects of carbohydrate feedings on performance?

HARGREAVES: Increased skeletal muscle GLUT4 transporters would contribute to the ability of trained athletes to take up and oxidize glucose at high rates when ingesting carbohydrate. Most carbohydrate ingestion studies have been performed in trained subjects. It is possible that lower muscle GLUT4 levels in untrained subjects could limit their ability to oxidize ingested carbohydrate.

SHERMAN: How well established is the relationship between recovery of muscle glycogen after exercise and the recovery of muscle function?

HARGREAVES: I do not think that recovery of muscle glycogen will always increase muscle function. In those studies that have demonstrated enhanced postexercise recovery with carbohydrate ingestion, muscle glycogen has not always been measured.

MAUGHAN: In performance trials we normally measure time to voluntary exhaustion, and from a simplistic perspective, the literature suggests that ratings of perceived exertion increase in more or less a straight line; when the athlete reaches a certain threshold, that is presumably the point of exhaustion. But fatigue isn't like that; it comes on more like a series of waves, and those waves get progressively higher and closer together. So the perception of fatigue changes; it is not a progressive linear increase. This is difficult to reconcile with the metabolic changes during exercise because most of them seem to be more or less linearly progressive. That says to me that central fatigue involves cyclical changes in the way in which we perceive metabolic signals.

HEIGENHAUSER: We just completed a study in which subjects were placed on a diet for 6 d, during which time their diets consisted of 3% carbohydrate and the remainder fat and protein. Compared to the control diet with more carbohydrate, during 30 min of exercise they had similar glucose levels and higher FFA and ketone levels. They also had an increase in ratings of perceived exertion when they were on the fat diet, particularly at the onset of exercise and near the end of the exercise. There was a paradoxical effect in the relationship between their ventilation and their ratings of perceived exertion, namely, the ratings of perceived exertion were higher at slightly lower CO_2 outputs, rather than the other way around. I don't know what the mechanisms underlying this effect might be.

MURRAY: An increasing number of studies show performance benefits with carbohydrate feeding during intermittent exercise of relatively short total duration. How do those data fit with proposed mechanisms by which carbohydrate boosts performance?

HARGREAVES: The challenge here is to identify the potential mechanisms because carbohydrate availability, at least as measured by blood glucose and carbohydrate oxidation, was not limiting. We recently examined muscle glycogen utilization during 60 min of intermittent exercise (1 min 100% $\dot{V}O_2$ peak, 2-min rest) with and without carbohydrate ingestion. Relative to placebo, there was no difference in net muscle glycogen use, measured in mixed muscle, when subjects ingested a 6% carbohydrate beverage; likewise, plasma glucose levels were not different between trials.

DAVIS: It is important to consider the likelihood that glycogen depletion in Type IIA fibers may be the mechanism of fatigue in this model and that carbohydrate feedings may decrease glycogen depletion specifically in these fibers.

WILLIAMS: We have tried to simulate the intermittent activity pattern that might occur over 90 min in a soccer match. We found that when we gave the soccer players a carbohydrate-electrolyte solution, they improved their endurance capacity late in the game. When we followed that up with a biopsy study, we found that those who drank the sports drink used less glycogen in the 90 min. Furthermore, we found that after the match, those on the carbohydrate-electrolyte solution retained their muscle function to a greater degree than did those who were on a placebo. When we analyzed individual muscle fibers, we found glycogen sparing in the type II fiber population when the sports drink was consumed.

BAR-OR: How does consumption of combination of fructose and glucose yield a higher oxidation of exogenous carbohydrate than consumption of glucose alone?

HARGREAVES: Once the glucose transport process in the intestine is saturated, or close to maximal, the absorption of fructose can apparently provide additional carbohydrate for oxidation. Whether this effect results in enhanced exercise performance relative to glucose alone remains to be seen.

4

Protein Metabolism in Strength and Endurance Activities

MARK TARNOPOLSKY, M.D., PH.D., F.R.C.P.(C)

INTRODUCTION

The majority of the energy for both resistance and endurance exercise is derived from the oxidation of lipid and carbohydrate (Table 4-1) (see also Chapter 1). Human skeletal muscle also has the capacity to oxidize certain amino acids for energy. However, it is not of phylogenetic advantage for an organism to oxidize substrates that serve a structural function (e.g., myofibrillar proteins) or regulatory (e.g., succinate dehydrogenase, phosphorylase) function. Therefore, it is not surprising that humans have evolved such that amino acid oxidation is rather minimal but can increase under periods of metabolic stress. During the metabolic stress of endurance exercise, amino acid oxidation accounts for only about 2-5% of the total energy cost (Table 4-1). As discussed further in a subsequent section, this proportion is lower in females as compared to males (Table 4-1). The proportional oxidation of amino acids is increased with higher exercise intensities (Lemon et al., 1982), longer exercise durations (Haralambie & Berg, 1976), and when carbohydrate stores are depleted (Lemon & Mullin, 1980; Wagenmakers et al., 1991).

Given that amino acids can be utilized as a metabolic substrate, the question arises as to whether or not this may have an impact upon dietary protein requirements. This is certainly a difficult question because the potential for increased protein requirements is dependent upon a variety of factors, including, but not restricted to, habitual protein and energy intakes, dietary carbohydrate as a proportion of energy intake, gender, age, the training status of an individual, and the type, intensity, frequency, and duration of exercise. For example, if a 55-kg female ran for 1.5 h at 70% $\dot{V}O_2$peak and protein accounted for 5% of the total energy, she would oxidize about 11 g of protein. If her basal protein requirements were 0.86 $g \cdot kg^{-1} \cdot d^{-1}$ (47.3 $g \cdot d^{-1}$), this would represent a 23% increase in her daily protein requirement. Fortunately, most athletes habitually consume in excess of this amount on a daily basis.

This paper will review some of the basic aspects of amino acid and protein metabolism to provide a framework from which to discuss the impact of acute and habitual exercise on protein metabolism. I also hope

TABLE 4-1. *Energy and substrate utilization from four studies in the same laboratory.*

Reference	Participants	kcal/h	% $\dot{V}O_2$ Peak	CHO (%)	FAT (%)	protein (%)
Tarnopolsky, et al., 1990	N = 6 male	797	63	81	10	9
	N = 6 female	620		61	41	0
Phillips, et al., 1993	N = 6 male	729	65	47	49	3
	N = 6 female	590		35	61	2
Tarnopolsky, et al., 1995	N = 7 male	1019	75	83	8	6
	N = 8 female	666		72	24	1
Tarnopolsky, et al., 1997	N = 8 male	806	72	75	23	2
	N = 8 female	616		68	29	3

to provide to athletes some practical nutritional advice based upon the current available literature. A complete review of all aspects of protein metabolism is outside the scope of this chapter. The reader is referred to other chapters and monographs (Booth & Watson, 1985; Lemon, 1987, 1989, 1996; Paul, 1989; Smith & Rennie, 1990; Tarnopolsky, 1993).

PROTEIN METABOLISM

Amino Acid Metabolism

There are 20 amino acids present in the human body, both as free amino acids and as part of structural and functional proteins. Of these amino acids, nine are considered indispensable or essential: histidine, isoleucine, leucine, lysine, methionine, phenylalanine, threonine, tryptophan, valine (Pellett, 1990). The only sources of indispensable amino acids for the body are dietary intake (I) or protein degradation/breakdown (B). All of the tissues in the body are in a constant state of flux (Q), with proteins being broken down to amino acids (B) and amino acids being incorporated into proteins, i.e., protein synthesis (S). In addition to synthesis, another route for amino acid removal is via oxidation (O). Thus, one may simplistically describe protein turnover or flux as: $Q = B + I = S + O$ (Tarnopolsky et al., 1991). The overall flux is markedly varied among tissues, with terminally differentiated tissues such as muscle and brain having long half lives, and more labile tissues such as lymphocytes having shorter half lives. The endogenous processes of synthesis, degradation, and oxidation are tightly regulated and include redundant control sites to maintain cellular homeostasis (Figure 4-1).

Physiological stressors such as starvation, exercise, and sepsis can alter protein turnover and result in whole-body protein loss. Under the combined influences of nutritional deprivation, sepsis, and surgical stress the losses of body protein are large (Carli et al., 1990; Willmore, 1991). These stressors are associated with cachectic states such as those seen in patients with carcinoma. At the other extreme is the state of myofibrillar proliferation that is a desired outcome in persons partaking in resistance exercise for bodybuilding and weight-lifting. This spectrum of protein states obviously spans a continuum of complex metabolic interactions.

Young and Bier (1987) described a conceptual framework to categorize the protein status of a body, including nutritional protein deficiency (e.g., starvation), accommodation (homeostasis in protein turnover achieved at the expense of the optimal functioning of a physiologically relevant process), adaptation (protein turnover homeostasis achieved with ample amino acid reserve to support growth, brief periods of nutrient deficiency, and other physiological stressors), and protein excess

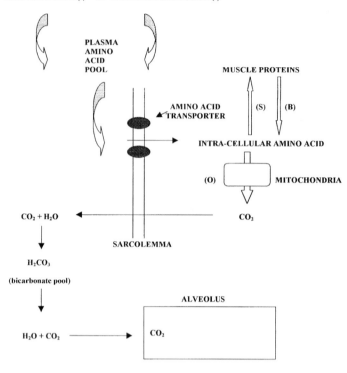

DIETARY INTAKE (I)   +/- INTRAVENOUS INFUSION (I)

PLASMA AMINO ACID POOL

MUSCLE PROTEINS

AMINO ACID TRANSPORTER   (S)   (B)

INTRA-CELLULAR AMINO ACID

(O)   MITOCHONDRIA

$CO_2 + H_2O$ CO_2

SARCOLEMMA

H_2CO_3

(bicarbonate pool)

ALVEOLUS

$H_2O + CO_2$ CO_2

FIGURE 4-1. *Schematic to show the kinetics of amino acids in the plasma and muscle.* I = intake; S = synthesis; B = breakdown; O = oxidation.

(protein intake far in excess of requirements, with amino acids oxidized or converted to other substrates and a substantial excretion of protein metabolic end-products). Ideally, the athlete should be in a state of adaptation; however, there are certain athletes who may be in a state of either nutrient excess or deficiency. The latter extremes may be easily identified. For example, I have heard of a football player who consumed 80 egg whites + 4 L of milk + 250 g protein powder per day (nutrient excess), and many are familiar with the severe energy restriction seen in ballet, combative sports, and gymnastics (nutritional deficiency). As will be elucidated in this chapter, the identification of the optimal protein intake for the physiological stress of exercise is difficult.

An understanding of the impact of exercise upon protein metabolism is very important not only for athletics but also for therapeutic medicine. For example, in Ontario, CANADA (pop. ~ 10,000,000) there are about 60,000 total joint replacements performed each year (Van

Walvern et al., 1996). An important part of the therapeutic regimen following such procedures is therapeutic resistance exercise to improve muscle strength and to facilitate ambulation. An appropriately timed nutritional intervention that hastened the recovery of muscle strength by only one day would result in annual heath-care savings of about $43,500,000 in Ontario alone!

Protein Synthesis

Protein synthesis starts with a signal that induces the expression of a specific gene. A detailed discussion of gene expression is beyond the scope of this chapter, but I will review some of the basic principles. Essentially, a signal (hormone, growth factor, stretch, cytokine, etc.) is transduced to promoters that induce the transcription of a primary RNA transcript. This primary transcript is processed and eventually exported from the nucleus as a mRNA (Booth & Watson, 1985). The mRNA ultimately directs the synthesis of a protein through the process of translation via ribosomes that are free in the cytosol and bound to membranes as rough endoplasmic reticulum. This process also requires transfer RNAs (tRNA) that are specific for each of the amino acids (e.g., leucyl-tRNA, alanyl-tRNA). Prior to translation, the amino acid and its respective tRNA are combined by specific tRNA synthases. The translation process involves the "reading" of the mRNA codons by the specific tRNAs, using the ribosome machinery to physically juxtapose them. The process of translation requires three distinct steps: initiation (tRNA/mRNA union on the ribosome), elongation (mRNA is "read" by specific tRNA, and the amino acid chain elongates), and termination (the completed polypeptide is released from the ribosome).

In general, these processes leading to protein synthesis can be divided into transcriptional (e.g., promoter-region binding), post-transcriptional (e.g., mRNA stability, poly adenylation), translational (e.g., tRNA charging; speed and efficiency of translation), and posttranslational (e.g., nascent protein stability, glycosylation, degradation). Clearly, there are temporal sequences to these processes after a given stimulatory signal such that the predominance of one over another will vary with the timing and duration of the measurement. Additionally, there are tissue- and protein-specific differences in the importance and timing of these processes. For example, the amount of mRNA for heat-shock protein 70 (HSP-70) is elevated within the first 4 min following acute exercise (pretranslational control), whereas α-actin mRNA is not increased at 17 and 41 h after exercise (Wong & Booth, 1990). Furthermore, we found that an acute bout of resistance exercise increased mixed-muscle fractional protein synthetic rate (mixed FSR-see below) at 4 and 24 h following exercise, but there were no changes in total muscle

RNA (Chesley et al., 1992). Taken together, these results suggest that the *acute* increase in FSR for mixed muscle is due to translational and/or posttranslational mechanisms for the myofibrillar protein component, and at least some of the increase contributed by non-myofibrillar proteins such as HSP-70 is transcriptionally regulated.

Temporal changes in mRNA levels in response to a more chronic alteration in contractile activity are evident from observations of increased myosin mRNA and carnitine palmitoyl transferase (CPT II) mRNA following 5 d (Morgan & Loughna, 1989) and 14 d (Yan et al., 1995) of increased contractile activity, respectively. These results suggest that increases in both myofibrillar (myosin) and regulatory (CPT II) proteins following exercise have some pretranslational (transcriptional?) control at some point along a temporal continuum. With the model of immobilization, synthesis of actin protein is reduced within 6 h, yet the mRNA levels are not reduced until 6 d (Watson et al., 1984). This is consistent with the idea that alterations in contractile activity may be associated with rapid changes in protein synthesis and that the locus of control shows temporal changes.

As will be discussed below, an enhancement of protein synthesis is a key process that should be targeted by nutritional strategies designed to facilitate net protein accumulation.

During and After Endurance Exercise. Some studies have reported an attenuation of whole-body protein synthesis during endurance exercise (Evans et al., 1983; Hagg et al., 1982; Knapik et al., 1991; Rennie et al., 1981; Wolfe et al., 1982). This may be due to a false elevation in oxidation rates and a resultant decrease in calculated whole-body protein synthesis if one does not account for the bicarbonate retention factor during studies using stable isotopes (Phillips et al., 1993). We found that whole-body protein synthesis rates did not change in males or females during 90 min of endurance exercise at 65% $\dot{V}O_2$peak when the bicarbonate retention factor was accounted for (Phillips et al., 1993). Carraro and colleagues also found that endurance exercise in humans (40% $\dot{V}O_2$peak) altered neither whole-body (Carraro et al., 1990a) nor mixed-muscle FSR (Carraro et al., 1990b). There may be some differences in the interpretation of the effect of exercise on protein synthetic rates, depending upon which protein is being measured. For example, acute exercise increases FSR for fibronectin but not for albumin nor fibrinogen (Carraro et al., 1990a). Taken together, these data indicate that the FSR for whole-body proteins and for many specific proteins is not acutely altered during low-to-moderate intensity endurance exercise. It may be that at higher intensities of exercise there is an attenuation of protein synthesis due to a more significant alteration in the ratios of ATP/ADP and phosphocreatine/creatine (Bylund-Fellenius et al., 1984).

Fewer studies of protein synthesis following endurance exercise have been reported. However, it appears that mixed- muscle FSR is elevated by 26% in males (Carraro et al., 1990b). This same group reported that endurance exercise did not elevate FSR after endurance exercise in young females, although they found a trend towards an increase (42%)(Tipton et al., 1996). The latter results were not statistically significant due to variability in the determination of FSR. Whole-body protein synthesis does not appear to be elevated acutely following moderate endurance exercise (Carraro et al., 1990a).

Following chronic endurance-exercise training, there is an increase in whole-body protein synthesis at rest (Evans et al., 1983; Lamont et al., 1990), and this directional change is maintained during acute endurance exercise (Evans et al., 1983).

During and After Resistance Exercise. A single study has examined whole-body protein synthesis during and up to 2 h after resistance exercise; there was no acute effect of 60 min of circuit weight training (Tarnopolsky et al., 1991). This contrasts with the consistent finding of an acute stimulatory effect of resistance exercise on mixed-muscle FSR (Biolo et al., 1995c; Chesley et al., 1992; Phillips et al., 1997). An acute bout of resistance exercise elevates FSR for 36–48 h (MacDougall et al., 1995; Phillips et al., 1997). The lone study on females failed to find an acute effect of resistance exercise on FSR (Tipton et al., 1996). This implied that there may be a gender-specific response to exercise-induced FSR increases. However, subsequent work from this same group found no gender-specific differences in FSR elevation following acute resistance exercise (Phillips et al., 1997).

In response to long-term (weeks) resistance exercise stimuli, similar increases in FSR have been observed in both young and elderly subjects (Welle et al., 1995; Yarasheski et al., 1993). We have also found that basal whole-body protein synthesis is greater in well-trained athletes as compared to sedentary controls (Tarnopolsky et al., 1992).

Most of the data have indicated that muscle FSR is increased during recovery from resistance exercise. Therefore, the postexercise period is likely to be key in the planning the timing of nutrient delivery.

Amino Acid Oxidation and Protein Degradation

Amino Acid Oxidation. Human skeletal muscle can oxidize at least seven amino acids, i.e., alanine, asparagine, aspartate, glutamate, isoleucine, leucine, and valine (Goldberg & Chang, 1978). It is possible that some lysine is also oxidized by skeletal muscle (Wolfe et al., 1984). During exercise and other catabolic situations, it appears that the branched-chain amino acids (BCAA), i.e., isoleucine, leucine, and valine, are preferentially oxidized (Goldberg & Chang, 1974; MacLean et al., 1991). In humans, the oxidation of leucine is threefold greater than that of lysine (Wolfe et al., 1984).

Given the importance of the oxidation of the BCAA during exercise, it is important to understand the regulation of this pathway. The BCAA are first transaminated to their keto-acid analogues by a cytosolic enzyme, branched-chain aminotransferase (BCAAT), and the resultant keto-acids are oxidized by a mitochondrial branched-chain keto-acid dehydrogenase enzyme (BCKAD)(Boyer & Odessey, 1991; Khatra et al., 1977). In the cytosol, the resultant amino group is usually transaminated with α-ketoglutarate to form glutamate, which is subsequently transaminated with pyruvate to form alanine (Wolfe et al., 1984) or aminated by glutamine synthase to form glutamine. A lesser amount of the amino-N may end up as free ammonia released from muscle (MacLean et al., 1991; Wagenmakers et al., 1991).

The BCKAD enzyme is inactivated by phosphorylation and activated by dephosphorylation and appears to be rate limiting for BCAA oxidation (Boyer & Odessey, 1991; Khatra et al., 1977). Acute exercise stimulates BCKAD activation (the percent of the enzyme in the active form usually increases from about 5–8% at rest to 20–25% during exercise (Kasperek, 1989; Shimomura et al., 1990; Wagenmakers et al., 1989). This activation is thought to be related to a decrease in the ATP/ADP ratio, an increase in intramuscular acidity, and a depletion of muscle glycogen (Kasperek, 1989; Shimomura, 1990; Wagenmakers et al., 1991). The finding of an inverse correlation between percent activation of BCKAD and muscle glycogen concentration (Shimomura et al. 1990; Wagenmakers et al., 1989, 1991) is very interesting because it provides a theoretical basis for carbohydrate loading and for ingesting carbohydrate replacement drinks during exercise to attenuate BCKAD-mediated amino acid oxidation.

Rodents have been used in only a few studies of the effects of chronic endurance training on amino acid oxidation, and those studies show conflicting results (Dohm et al., 1977; Henderson et al., 1985; Hood & Terjung, 1987). Two studies found that the muscle from trained rodents oxidized more leucine than did muscle from untrained animals (Dohm et al., 1977; Henderson et al., 1985). In another study, using a perfused rodent hindlimb model, Hood and Terjung (1987) found that endurance training reduced the relative contribution of leucine to total energy consumption. It is problematic to extrapolate these results to humans. Furthermore, the quantification of relative exercise intensity in studies of muscle from trained as compared to untrained organisms is difficult even in humans.

We designed a study to examine the progressive adaptations of BCKAD activation to endurance training in six men and six women

(McKenzie et al., 1998). We measured the percent active form of BCKAD before and after endurance exercise at 65% $\dot{V}O_2$peak prior to and following a 30-d endurance training program. Following training, we tested subjects at both the same relative and same absolute exercise intensities. We found that acute exercise increased the fraction of BCKAD in the active form in the untrained state from 8% to 25% and that the percent active form was lower in females. More importantly, we found significant 11% and 13% attenuations of the postexercise activation of BCKAD following training for males and females at both the absolute and relative intensities (McKenzie et al., 1998). These findings are consistent with the hypothesis that the human body has evolved mechanisms that confer phylogenetic advantages under periods of metabolic stress such as exercise; i.e., when the organism is repeatedly stressed, it is of advantage to spare the oxidation of structural and regulatory proteins.

Protein Degradation. Protein degradation in muscle is an important contributor to the intracellular free amino acid pool. The derived amino acids may enter the plasma and be transported to distant tissues, be directly oxidized (see above), or be re-incorporated into tissue protein (synthesis). An understanding of protein degradation is important because the balance between synthesis and degradation is critical to determining whether muscle will be in a net positive or negative protein balance. There are several potential scenarios under which net protein balance may be positive, including increased synthesis with no change in degradation, decreased degradation with no change in synthesis, and a greater increase in synthesis relative to a simultaneous increase in degradation.

There are several pathways for protein degradation in human skeletal muscle, including the lysosomal and non-lysosomal pathways. The lysosomal pathways are important in the degradation of endocytosed proteins and some cytosolic proteins and in the hydrolysis of hormones and immune modulators in plasma (Mitch & Goldberg, 1996). In human skeletal muscle, this pathway is thought to be relatively insignificant, except perhaps under periods of extensive damage following eccentric exercise (Tidball, 1995), and the lysosomal pathway may degrade some non-myofibrillar proteins (Kasperek et al., 1992). The two major non-lysosomal pathways in human skeletal muscle are the ATP-dependent-ubiquitin-pathway (ADUP)(Mitch & Goldberg, 1996), and the calcium-activated neutral protease (CANP) or calpain pathway (Belcastro, 1993; Kameyama & Etlinger, 1979; Zeman et al., 1985).

The CANP pathways are thought to be significant contributors to skeletal muscle proteolysis under the stress of exercise (Belcastro, 1993) and passive muscle stretch (Kameyama & Etlinger, 1979). Intracellular calcium concentration rises during muscle contraction when calcium is released from the sarcoplasmic reticulum (SR) upon activation of ryanodine receptors. Further increases of intracellular calcium may result from an attenuation of Ca^{++} re-uptake from the SR (Byrd et al., 1989) and from the extra-cellular fluid secondary to sarcolemmal disruption (Evans & Cannon, 1991).

The ADUP pathway has apparently not been examined under the stress of exercise. However, this ATP-dependent pathway is a very strong candidate for involvement in exercise-induced proteolysis. This pathway is initiated after the targeting of proteins for degradation (i.e., oxidative modification). Following targeting, ubiquitin molecules are linked to lysine residues through a series of pathways catalysed by three enzymes termed E1, E2, and E3. The polyubiquinated protein is then degraded by the 26S proteosome into peptides, which can be further degraded by exopeptidases (Mitch & Goldberg, 1996). This pathway is activated during starvation and muscle atrophy (Medina et al., 1995) and also during insulin deficiency (Price et al., 1996).

Clearly, there is much work to be done in identifying the quantitative importance of the aforementioned pathways in the degradation of specific skeletal muscle proteins consequent to exercise.

During and After Endurance Exercise. Many studies indicate that acute endurance exercise increases the oxidation of the indispensable amino acid, leucine (Dohm et al., 1985b; Evans et al., 1983; Hagg et al., 1982; Lemon et al., 1982; Phillips et al., 1993; Rennie et al., 1981; Wolfe et al., 1982, 1984). As described above, this appears to be due to an activation of BCKAD. Furthermore, the oxidation of amino acids during endurance exercise shows an expected positive correlation with the relative exercise intensity (Lemon et al., 1982). Following exercise at 65% VO_2peak the rate of leucine oxidation rapidly returns towards baseline (Phillips et al., 1993). After eccentric exercise that induces muscle damage, there is a slight increase in leucine oxidation that persists for up to 10 d (Fielding et al., 1991).

To date, no published reports have determined if endurance exercise training attenuates leucine oxidation in humans, but we are currently completing such a study. At the same absolute exercise intensity, we expect that leucine oxidation will be lower following training because the relative exercise intensity should be lower, causing less activity of BCKAD. It is interesting to note that in a previous study (Phillips et al., 1993), we found that leucine oxidation was lower in women than in men, and our recent study found that this pattern was predictable from the BCKAD data (McKenzie et al., 1998). A single study has described leucine turnover in rested trained and untrained humans; the untrained subjects diverted a greater proportion of total leucine turnover to oxidative pathways when compared to the trained (Lamont et al., 1990).

With respect to protein degradation, it appears that non-myofibrillar protein degradation is increased following exercise, whereas myofibrillar protein degradation is not (Calles-Escandon et al., 1984; Dohm et al., 1985a; Kasperek et al., 1992; Rennie et al., 1981). Following eccentric exercise, however, there may be an increase in myofibrillar protein degradation (Fielding et al., 1991). Whole-body protein degradation is reported to be relatively unchanged (Evans et al., 1983) or slightly increased (Phillips et al., 1993; Rennie et al., 1981; Wolfe et al., 1982, 1984) during endurance exercise in humans. However, this depends upon which amino acid is used for the calculation of degradation; Wolfe and colleagues (1984) found that exercise reduced protein catabolism if they used a lysine tracer and increased it if they used a leucine tracer. Following endurance exercise training, there is a modest increase in whole-body protein degradation (Lamont et al., 1990). However, this occurs simultaneously with an increased synthesis, and it appears that the body protein metabolism is 're-set' at a higher flux rate (see below).

At the whole-body level, there is evidence that that gut proteins are much more labile than expected during exercise and contribute significantly to whole-body proteolysis (Halseth et al., 1997). Alternatively, blood amino acids originating from the gut may also come from a suppression of gut protein synthesis (Nakshabendi et al., 1995). Either of these mechanisms would provide amino acids for muscle uptake and synthesis (Williams et al., 1996).

During and After Resistance Exercise. Only a single study has examined whole-body protein degradation and leucine oxidation during and after resistance exercise (Tarnopolsky et al., 1991). This study found that acute resistance exercise did not affect leucine oxidation during nor for 2 h after a 60-min circuit weightlifting bout (Tarnopolsky et al., 1991). There was also no effect of this exercise on whole-body proteolysis during and after exercise (Tarnopolsky et al., 1991). Furthermore, the absolute rates of whole-body protein synthesis and degradation are greater in well-trained resistance athletes as compared to sedentary controls (Tarnopolsky et al., 1992).

There has been some controversy as to whether resistance exercise induces an increase (Dohm et al., 1982; Pivarnik et al., 1989) or no change (Hickson et al., 1986; Phillips et al., 1997) in myofibrillar protein breakdown. Part of this controversy arises from the fact that myofibrillar protein degradation has been determined using the urinary excretion of 3-methylhistidine (3-MH)(Young & Munro, 1978; Rathmacher et al., 1995). This method requires accurate urinary collections and assumes that most of the 3-MH arises from myofibrillar proteolysis in skeletal muscle and that the proportional contribution from other sources relative to muscle remains constant under varying physiological situations

(Young & Munro, 1978). In addition, it is probably not feasible to accurately measure 3-MH excretion for periods of less than 6 h.

Unfortunately, because there are no suitable methods for the accurate determination of myofibrillar protein degradation, the magnitude and temporal pattern of any exercise-induced myofibrillar proteolysis will remain controversial. Recently, it has become possible to measure the mixed-muscle fractional breakdown rate (FBR) using a method whereby the infusion is stopped and the dilutional decay-kinetics are used in the calculation (Phillips et al., 1997). This method has demonstrated that FBR is elevated following resistance exercise for at least 24 h (Phillips et al., 1997). This has also been confirmed using an arteriovenous isotopic method at 3 h following resistance exercise (Biolo et al., 1995a). Data from 3-MH studies suggest that most of this FBR originates from non-myofibrillar proteins (Hickson et al., 1986; Phillips et al., 1997), but until more accurate myofibrillar FBR measurements can be made, this remains speculative. Myofibrillar FSR can now be determined using stable isotopic tracer incorporation in combination with SDS-PAGE separation of the component proteins (Balagopal et al., 1997).

A few directional changes in FSR and FBR appear to be relatively well established. First, resistance exercise elevates mixed-muscle FSR by 50–100%, and this can persist for up to 48 h after exercise (Biolo et al., 1995c; Chesley et al., 1992; MacDougall et al., 1995; Phillips et al., 1997). Second, following resistance exercise, FBR increases in parallel with FSR, but to a slightly lesser degree (Biolo et al., 1995c; Phillips et al., 1997). In the fasted state, net protein balance is negative and becomes directionally more positive (but still negative) following resistance exercise (Biolo et al., 1995c; Phillips et al., 1997). Finally, there appears to be a directional 'link' between FSR and FBR, i.e., there is an increased turnover.

Future studies need to address the temporal course and magnitude of change in myofibrillar FSR and FBR following resistance exercise. Strategies to enhance FSR and attenuate FBR will be of critical importance to athletes and patients with muscle-wasting conditions. This will be the focus of a subsequent section.

NUTRITIONAL REGULATION OF PROTEIN SYNTHESIS AND DEGRADATION

Carbohydrate (Insulin) Availability

It has been known for some time that there are positive effects of dietary carbohydrate on protein balance (Lemon & Mullin, 1980; Welle et al., 1989; Krempf et al., 1993). For example, carbohydrate loading markedly attenuates exercise-induced accumulation of urea in plasma and excretion of urea in sweat (Lemon & Mullin, 1980), and carbohydrate supplementation increases whole-body protein synthesis (Welle et al., 1989) and attenuates proteolysis (Krempf et al., 1993). These effects are likely due to an attenuation of BCKAD activation (Wagenmakers et al., 1991) and an effect of insulin (see below), respectively. Positive effects of carbohydrate on net protein balance are likely caused by an insulin-mediated stimulation of protein synthesis and attenuation of degradation. The simplicity and relative inexpense of carbohydrate supplementation make this an attractive strategy to favorably alter net protein balance.

Insulin is well known to potentiate glucose uptake and glycogen synthesis (Hayashi et al., 1997). With respect to protein turnover, insulin is generally considered to have a stimulatory effect upon net protein synthesis in muscle (Bennet et al., 1990). The effect of insulin *per se* is a reduction in muscle proteolysis (Bennett et al., 1990; Castellino et al., 1987; Fukagawa et al., 1985; Moller-Loswick et al., 1994; Newman et al., 1994; Tessari et al., 1987;) with no increase in muscle protein synthesis (Castellino et al., 1987; McNurlan et al., 1994; Moller-Loswick et al., 1994; Tessari et al., 1987). It is likely that the insulin-induced hypoaminoacidemia inhibits the potentially stimulatory effect of insulin on protein synthesis because when amino acids and insulin are provided simultaneously, most studies have reported a stimulation of protein synthesis (Bennet et al., 1990; Castellino et al., 1987; Moller-Loswick et al., 1994; Newman et al., 1994; Tessari et al., 1987). Other studies have found that hyperinsulinemia stimulates both muscle FSR and transport of amino acids (leucine, lysine, alanine)(Biolo et al., 1995b). It is possible that under some circumstances, an increase in reutilization of intracellular amino acids may provide substrate for protein synthesis (Svanberg et al., 1996). From the proteolysis standpoint, it appears that insulin is most potent in its attenuation of the proteolysis of globular as compared to myofibrillar proteins (Moller-Loswick et al., 1994).

Amino Acid Availability

Several studies have demonstrated a stimulatory effect of amino acid infusion on muscle protein synthesis (Biolo et al., 1997; Castellino et al., 1987; Garlick & Grant, 1988; Svanberg et al. 1996; Tessari et al., 1987). This effect is seen even with an insulin clamp technique, suggesting that there is an effect of hyperaminoacidemia *per se* (Castellino et al., 1987). It appears that the essential and branched-chain amino acids do increase the sensitivity of the muscle to the effects of insulin on net protein synthesis (Garlick & Grant, 1988). The stimulatory effect of hyperaminoacidemia has been employed to attenuate the postsurgical fall in muscle protein synthesis in patients (Hammarqvist et al., 1989; Willmore, 1991).

The effects of amino acids on protein degradation are contradictory, with some investigations finding an attenuation (Castellinao et al., 1987), others finding no effect (Tessari et al., 1987), and still others finding an attenuation of proteolysis for globular proteins, but not myofibrillar proteins (Svanberg et al., 1996).

In addition to the net stimulatory effect of insulin on protein synthesis in resting skeletal muscle, it appears that there is a potentiation of amino acid transport into muscle after an acute bout of exercise (Davis & Karl, 1986; Zorzano et al., 1986). This is similar to the enhancement of glucose uptake and glycogen synthesis following exercise (Richter et al., 1989; Zawadski et al., 1992). Following resistance exercise, the stimulatory effects of hyperaminoacidemia on amino acid transport and muscle protein synthesis are accentuated (Biolo et al., 1997). The fact that both glucose and amino acids are rapidly transported into muscle following exercise indicates that the immediate postexercise period is a critical time for the ingestion of amino acids and carbohydrate to promote a more positive protein balance. Essentially, this combination of exercise and nutrition provides the stimulus (exercise), the hormonal milieu (insulin), and the substrate (amino acids) for optimal protein anabolism.

From a practical standpoint for both patients and athletes, we need to determine whether oral carbohydrate (CHO) and carbohydrate/protein (CHO/PRO) supplements stimulate synthesis and attenuate degradation of muscle proteins. To this end we performed two studies to examine whether the oral provision of CHO and CHO/PRO supplements improved indices of protein balance following resistance exercise in young males. In the first study of eight men we examined the effect of CHO supplementation (1 g/kg body weight) immediately and 1 h after resistance exercise as compared to the same supplement given with breakfast (Roy et al., 1997). The provision of the CHO supplement in the postexercise period resulted in a more positive nitrogen balance and an attenuation of 3-MH excretion (myofibrillar proteolysis), with no significant increase in FSR (34%), as compared to the trial in which the subjects consumed the supplement several hours prior to exercise (Roy et al., 1997).

We have subsequently completed a nearly identical study with the exception that the subjects were given three different isoenergetic supplements—placebo, CHO (1 g/kg), and CHO/PRO—following resistance exercise (Roy et al., 1998). There was a significant increase in whole-body protein synthesis and proteolysis over the 4 h after exercise for the two supplement trials as compared to placebo, and leucine oxidation was higher for the CHO/PRO supplement (Roy et al., 1998). The increased leucine oxidation observed for the CHO/PRO supplement was likely due to a stimulatory effect of the BCAA component on BCKAD activity (Aftring et al., 1986). Unfortunately, we did not measure FSR or FBS in the latter study, and these measurements are clearly needed. The results of these two studies indicate that the provision of CHO or CHO/PRO supplements shortly after resistance exercise causes favorable alterations in net protein balance. Similar studies should be performed with patients who are participating in rehabilitative exercise.

Testosterone/Growth Hormone

In addition to the anabolic effects of insulin, it is well known that both growth hormone (GH) (Butterfield, 1987; Cameron et al., 1988; Cuneo et al., 1991; Fryburg et al., 1991) and testosterone (Florini, 1987; Griggs et al., 1989) have stimulatory effects on protein synthesis. Furthermore, growth hormone may attenuate oxidative damage in atrophied skeletal muscle (Carmelli et al., 1993). Given that oxidatively modified proteins are targeted for proteolysis via the ubiquitin-proteosome pathway (see above), this may be a mechanism by which GH can attenuate proteolysis.

We are all familiar with the unethical use of GH and testosterone in sports, but for a complete discussion of the metabolic effects and other issues surrounding this, we would require a dedicated chapter. Although there are important therapeutic implications for patients from the pharmacological administration of testosterone (Griggs et al., 1989) and GH (Cuneo et al., 1991; Rudman et al., 1990), I shall limit my discussion to exercise and nutritional strategies that may increase either testosterone or GH.

Testosterone concentration in blood plasma increases acutely following resistance exercise (Kraemer et al., 1990; Volek et al., 1997). Therefore, the postexercise period may be an ideal time for the ingestion of amino acids to promote protein synthesis. To date this hypothesis has not been directly investigated. A somewhat paradoxical finding, and perhaps an important reason for resistance-trained athletes to not overload on protein (see below), is the significant negative correlation between serum testosterone and percent dietary protein intake ($P = -0.71$)(Volek et al., 1997).

Further support for postexercise CHO/PRO supplementation comes from a report that GH is elevated several hours after resistance exercise only after such supplementation (Chandler et al., 1994). Furthermore, the postexercise elevation in plasma GH concentration may be greatest with a resistance exercise regimen that includes more repetitions, relatively lighter loads, and shorter rest periods, i.e., a bodybuilder type of workout (Kraemer et al., 1990).

From a practical standpoint, the most effective natural method to elevate GH and testosterone is to perform muscular contractions. Postexercise CHO and CHO/PRO supplements may slightly enhance the GH response, but high-protein diets may attenuate basal testosterone concentrations.

PROTEIN NUTRITION DURING RESISTANCE AND ENDURANCE EXERCISE

It is important to answer several questions before concluding that protein requirements are elevated by habitual exercise. First, is there a theoretical basis for hypothesizing that exercise may alter protein metabolism in such a way as to warrant an elevated dietary protein requirement? Second, what are the estimates of protein requirements in different athletic groups? Finally, what are the habitual protein intakes of athletes, and are some groups likely to be deficient? To a large extent the first question has already been answered in previous sections of this chapter. I will address the last question first.

Habitual Protein Intakes Among Athletes

I will broadly divide sporting events into two distinct categories, namely, endurance and resistance-type sports. Over the years, I have seen examples of athletes who consumed diets grossly excessive in nutrients and, conversely, grossly deficient in nutrients. There is concern for both of these extremes from both financial and health standpoints. I have seen young male teenagers who have been convinced to consume large amounts of dietary protein supplements at a cost of $20–$30/d and young female runners who have been running > 80 km/wk and consuming only 1,500–1,700 kcal/d.

With extreme protein deficiency one may ultimately see a compromise in function and structure of bodily proteins. This is clearly evident in the extreme cases of anorexia nervosa, critical-illness cachexia, and protein-energy malnutrition. On the other hand, one may see the converse with gross excesses of dietary protein intake. Aside from obesity and the financial cost of producing protein (as compared to CHO or fat), it is unclear whether there are long-term negative health consequences from the excessive consumption of protein (Brenner, 1982; Zaragosa et al., 1987). Fortunately, most athletes fall into the more modest categories of dietary intake, and as seen below, most athletes consume enough dietary protein to easily cover any training-induced elevations in protein requirements (Tables 4-2 and 4-3).

On average, male and female endurance athletes obtain about 14% of their dietary energy from protein. This is about 1.8 and 1.2 g pro-

TABLE 4-2. *Habitual protein intakes among male and female endurance athletes.*

Reference	Participants	Protein	
		$g \cdot kg^{-1} \cdot d^{-1}$	% E_{IN}
Tarnopolsky, et al., 1997	N = 8 male	1.9 (1.2)	17 (6)
	N = 8 female	1.2 (0.3)	14 (2)
Tarnopolsky, et al., 1995	N = 7 male	1.8 (0.4)	15 (5)
	N = 8 female	1.0 (0.2)	12 (1)
Phillips, et al., 1993	N = 6 male	1.9 (0.2)	15 (2)
	N = 6 female	1.0 (0.1)	13 (3)
Schultz, et al., 1992	N = 9 female	1.4 (0.4)	13 (3)
Tarnopolsky, et al., 1990	N = 6 male	1.2 (0.3)	12 (2)
	N = 6 female	1.7 (0.3)	13 (2)
Saris, et al., 1989	N = 5 male	2.2 (0.5)	15 (2)
Deuster, et al., 1986	N = 51 female	1.6 (0.6)	13 (5)
Nelson, et al., 1986	N = 17 EUM*	1.0 (0.4)	15 (4)
	N = 11 AMEN*	0.7 (0.4)	15 (4)
Marcus, et al., 1985	N = 6 EUM*	1.3 (0.4)	17 (3)
	N = 11 AMEN*	1.0 (0.5)	15 (6)
Drinkwater, et al., 1984	N = 13 EUM*	1.1 (0.5)	13 (5)
	N = 14 AMEN*	1.2 (0.5)	16 (6)
Approx. mean	male	1.8 (0.4)	14 (2)
	female	1.2 (0.3)	14 (2)

Values are mean (SD). * EUM = eumenorrheic; AMEN = amenorrheic females.

TABLE 4-3. *Habitual protein intakes among male resistance athletes.*

Reference	Participants	Protein	
		$g \cdot kg^{-1} \cdot d^{-1}$	% E_{IN}
Roy, et al., 1998	N = 10 male (trained*)	1.6 (0.2)	18 (3)
Tarnopolsky, et al., 1992	N = 7 male (football)	1.8 (0.4)	16 (3)
Lemon, et al., 1992	N = 12 male (bodybuilder)	1.4 (0.2)	14 (2)
Chelsey, et al., 1992	N = 12 male (bodybuilder)	1.6 (0.5)	17 (4)
Tarnopolsky, et al., 1988	N = 6 male (bodybuilder)	2.7 (0.5)	17 (3)
Faber, et al., 1986	N = 76 male (bodybuilder)	2.4 (0.6)	22 (5)
Short and Short, 1983	N = 30 male (football)	2.5 (0.8)	18 (5)
	N = 6 male (bodybuilder)	2.3 (0.7)	20 (6)
Approx. mean		2.0 (0.5)	18 (2)

Vales are mean (SD). * trained = weight trained 4X/wk. for > 2 years

tein$\cdot kg^{-1} \cdot d^{-1}$ for males and females, respectively. Males who participate in resistance exercise consume more protein (2.0 g protein$\cdot kg^{-1} \cdot d^{-1}$), which represents a larger proportion of daily energy intake (18%).

Certain groups of athletes who consume too little energy may be at risk for suboptimal protein intakes. The four main groups appear to be amenorrheic female runners (Drinkwater et al., 1984; Marcus et al., 1985; Nelson et al., 1986), male wrestlers (Brownell et al., 1987; Tarnopolsky et al., 1996), male and female gymnasts, (Short & Short, 1983) and female dancers (Brownell et al., 1987; Short & Short, 1983). Some of these groups may be identified from close examination of the reported nutrient intakes for athletes. For example, the mean energy and protein intakes for male gymnasts in one study were fairly adequate at 2080 kcal and 1.1 $g \cdot kg^{-1} \cdot d^{-1}$ respectively; however, some athletes consumed as little as 568 kcal/d and 0.16 g protein$\cdot kg^{-1} \cdot d^{-1}$ (Short & Short, 1983). Similarly, in a study of female runners, Deuster and colleagues (1986) reported acceptable mean energy and protein intakes of 2397 kcal/d and 1.56 $g \cdot kg^{-1} \cdot d^{-1}$, respectively, yet the lowest intakes were 1067 kcal/d and 0.53 g protein$\cdot kg^{-1} \cdot d^{-1}$.

In summary, the majority of strength and endurance athletes consume more protein than the Canadian and U.S. recommended intakes. Even when one takes into account the modest increases required by certain athletes (see below), most athletes are still above these levels. There are some groups of athletes that may not be attaining the recommended intake levels, including wrestlers, gymnasts, amenorrheic female runners, and dancers. Conversely, some male athletes participating in resistance sports consume very high protein intakes. Each athlete must be considered individually in determining the adequacy of protein and energy intakes. Identification of groups at risk for dietary restriction may be helpful for those who counsel athletes about nutrition. Early intervention into unsafe dietary practices at both intake extremes may help to prevent future negative health consequences.

Methods of Determining Protein Requirements

If one were given a large group of willing participants, it would be possible to determine the protein requirement for 'optimal' physiological functioning by measuring relevant outcomes such as muscle mass, resistance to infections, and recovery from other physiological stressors in persons fed different protein intakes over long periods of time. For example, the optimal protein intake for a bodybuilder would be the minimal intake that would support maximal muscle mass accretion. From a practical standpoint, however, this is not feasible, and other methods have been developed.

The traditional method of measuring protein requirements is the nitrogen balance (NBAL) method (Elwyn, 1990; Pellett, 1990). Essentially, this method involves the measurement of all nitrogen entering (N_{IN}) and exiting (N_{OUT}) the body over a given period of time while the subject consumes a given amount of protein. Sources of N_{IN} include diet and intravenous sources (e.g., in patients), whereas sources of N_{OUT} include urine, feces, sweat, and miscellaneous (e.g., menstrual loss, hair, semen, skin). A positive NBAL is indicative of net protein accretion, whereas a negative NBAL is indicative of net protein loss. This technique is most informative when individuals in a group have NBAL determined while consuming progressively greater amounts of protein. From the regression analysis of the protein intake versus NBAL, one can determine the mean protein intake required for zero NBAL and the standard deviation of that mean, which is used to recommend the protein intake that will place 97% of the population at zero NBAL. In practice, the recommended intake values for protein include an allowance for the biological value of the proteins in a mixed diet (Pellett, 1990).

Of relevance to athletes, it is known that carbohydrate and total energy intake can positively affect NBAL (Chiang & Huang, 1988; Elwyn, 1990, Pellett, 1990). Thus, persons with low carbohydrate and energy intakes may require more absolute protein than those with adequate carbohydrate and energy intakes. These dietary interactions may have implications for those athletes who habitually consume low energy diets (e.g., some dancers, amenorrheic runners, wrestlers, and gymnasts).

There have been concerns that the NBAL estimates of protein requirements may underestimate the requirement for 'optimal' functioning. This concern arises from the fact that as protein intakes decrease there is an increase in the efficiency of amino acid reutilization and a lower overall amino acid flux (Meredith et al., 1989; Pellett, 1990; Tarnopolsky et al., 1992). It is felt that zero NBAL can be achieved from a decrease in a physiologically relevant process, i.e., accommodation (Bier, 1989; Young & Bier, 1987). Furthermore, the NBAL method does not provide insight into the amino acid kinetics that are required to achieve NBAL (Bier, 1989) nor the loci for the adaptive changes (Zhang et al., 1998). For example, a resistance athlete may achieve NBAL by attenuating protein synthesis (Tarnopolsky et al., 1992), which is clearly not the optimal physiological status for such an athlete! To address concerns about the validity of the NBAL technique for determining protein requirements, investigators have suggested that amino acid tracers can be useful in providing physiologically relevant information (Bier, 1989; Young & Bier, 1987). As mentioned above, the concepts of nutrient deficiency, accommodation, adaptation, and nutrient excess may be determined using stable isotope tracers in humans (Young & Bier, 1987; Tarnopolsky, 1992).

By determining the responses of protein synthesis and oxidation to different protein intakes, one can determine the optimal protein requirement (adaptation), which would be the protein intake at the point where a plateau occurs in the curve relating synthesis to intake and at the point of upward inflection of the curve relating oxidation to intake(Figure 4-2). Protein intakes in excess of requirements are determined by the plateau in synthesis and the oxidation of excessive amino acids for energy (nutrient excess). Accommodation could be determined by the finding of a relative reduction in protein synthesis (versus adaptation) while a subject was in NBAL. A nutrient deficiency would be defined by a negative NBAL and a further reduction in protein synthesis (Figure 4-2).

Currently, there are no specific allowances for a potential effect of physical exercise upon protein requirements in either Canada or the United States (Food and Nutrition Board/NRC, 1989). This is due partly

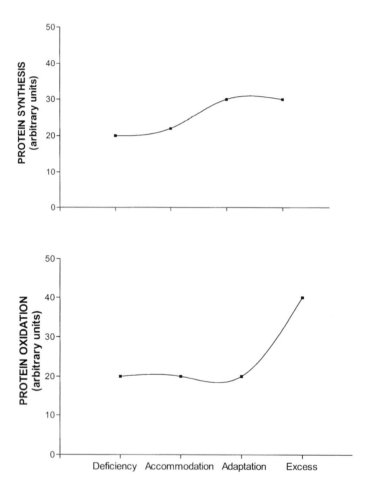

FIGURE 4-2. *Theoretical response curves to varied protein intakes.* The terms *deficiency, accommodation, adaptation* and *excess* are defined in text.

to the fact that most individuals consume enough protein on a habitual basis and partly to the fact that with low-to-moderate exercise, there does not appear to be an increased protein requirement (Butterfield & Calloway, 1984; Campbell et al., 1995). However, with more strenuous activities, the optimal protein intake may exceed the current recommended protein intake (approximately $0.83–0.86$ g protein·kg^{-1}·d^{-1})(see discussion below). Knowledge of the magnitude of such an increase may be helpful in determining the adequacy of a diet in a given athlete. For example, an individual who is performing regular strenuous activity while consuming an energy restrictive diet may wish to know the minimal protein intake for optimal functional status (adaptation). Below, I shall discuss several recent studies that have used NBAL and tracers to examine whether or not physical activity alters dietary protein requirements.

Protein Requirements During Endurance Exercise Training

Endurance exercise results in an increase in amino acid oxidation that usually represents $3–6\%$ of the total energy expenditure (see above). This oxidation may cause an increase in dietary protein requirements if the efficiency of other pathways does not increase and/or the oxidation in other tissues does not decrease. Several studies have used NBAL to determine the protein requirements of humans performing endurance exercise.

Two studies by Gontzea and colleagues were performed in the mid 1970's to determine NBAL following the initiation of an endurance exercise program (Gontzea et al., 1975) and with consumption of two different protein intakes (Gontzea et al., 1974). This group found that 1.5 g protein·kg^{-1}·d^{-1} was adequate for individuals performing endurance exercise (Gontzea et al., 1974) and, perhaps more importantly, that the subjects adapted to the moderate exercise program by improving NBAL over the course of about 1 wk (Gontzea et al., 1975). This raised the possibility that perhaps the increased protein requirement was only at the initiation of an endurance exercise program. Another study at about the same time found that males required about 1.4 g protein·kg^{-1}·d^{-1}, even after a 40-d period of adaptation to the fairly rigorous circuit-training program (Consolazio et al., 1975).

With more moderate intensity endurance exercise ($< 50\%$ $\dot{V}O_2$peak), there does not appear to be a significant increase in protein requirements (Butterfield & Calloway, 1984; Todd et al., 1984). In fact, at these modest exercise intensities, it appears that protein utilization is improved (Butterfield & Calloway, 1984) and energy deficits are better tolerated (Todd et al., 1984). An excellent study using a combined tracer and N excretion method found that 1 g protein·kg^{-1}·d^{-1} was adequate for males performing endurance exercise at 46% $\dot{V}O_2$peak (El-Khoury et al., 1997). These results are not too surprising, given the ability of the body to maintain homeostasis and the phylogenetic advantage conferred by conserving protein in the face of energy deficiency. However, as exercise intensities increase and individuals perform longer and more frequent exercise bouts, there may be a negative impact upon protein homeostasis and NBAL.

For individuals who are well trained, but not elite, there does appear to be a slight increase in dietary protein requirements (Meredith et al., 1989). This group used NBAL to determine the protein requirements in a group of trained young (27 y; $\dot{V}O_2$peak = 65 mL·kg^{-1}·d^{-1}) and middle-aged (52 y; $\dot{V}O_2$peak = 55 mL·kg^{-1}·d^{-1}) males during their habitual training regimen (Meredith et al., 1989). They found that 0.94 g protein·kg^{-1}·d^{-1} was required for NBAL and that whole-body protein synthesis increased with increasing protein intakes (0.61 → 0.92 → 1.21 g·kg^{-1}·d^{-1}). When accounting for individual variability by including two standard deviations to the zero NBAL intercept (as is done for protein requirements), the estimated protein requirement in these males was about 1.28 g protein·kg^{-1}·d^{-1} (Meredith et al., 1989). Another study found that both male ($\dot{V}O_2$peak = 59 mL·kg^{-1}·d^{-1}) and female ($\dot{V}O_2$peak = 55 mL·kg^{-1}·d^{-1}) endurance athletes were in negative NBAL while consuming diets providing protein close to the Canadian Recommended Nutritional Intake (males = 0.94 g·kg^{-1}·d^{-1}; females = 0.80 g·kg^{-1}·d^{-1}) (Phillips et al., 1993). Very interesting findings in this study were the facts that the females were in a less negative NBAL and that their basal leucine oxidation was also lower than for the males (Phillips et al., 1993). These observations are consistent with the lower BCKAD activation that we have recently found for females as compared to males (McKenzie et al., 1998). They also support earlier work by our group that found urea excretion to be increased consequent to exercise for males, but not females (Tarnopolsky et al., 1990).

Three experiments have used NBAL to examine the protein requirements of extremely well-trained endurance athletes. We performed an NBAL experiment in six elite male endurance athletes ($\dot{V}O_2$peak = 76.2 mL·kg^{-1}·d^{-1}) who were training more than 12 h/wk to determine what we considered to be the upper limit of protein requirements for endurance athletes (Tarnopolsky et al., 1988). From NABL experiments at two different protein intakes, we determined the 'safe' protein intake to be 1.6 g protein·kg^{-1}·d^{-1} (Tarnopolsky et al., 1988). We also included a sedentary control group to further strengthen the validity of our measurements and calculated their protein requirement to be 0.86 g protein·kg^{-1}·d^{-1}, which was very close to Canadian and US recommendations (Tarnopolsky et al., 1988). In a simulated Tour de France cycling study it was determined that the protein requirement for NBAL was in the range of 1.5–1.8 g protein·kg^{-1}·d^{-1} (Brouns et al., 1989). Another study determined that the protein requirement for five well-trained runners ($\dot{V}O_2$peak) were about 1.49 g protein·kg^{-1}·d^{-1} (Friedman & Lemon, 1989).

Because the subjects in the above studies were highly trained and the overall intensity and duration of the training regimens were also high, these protein intake values (1.5–1.7 g protein·kg^{-1}·d^{-1}) represent the highest protein requirements that are likely to be needed by elite endurance athletes. Fortunately, the habitual energy intake is usually so high in these athletes (> 3,500 kcal/d) that protein deficiency is not a concern (Table 4-2). Protein requirements in these athletes are elevated probably because the rate of essential amino acid oxidation is high due to the large volume of training (> 12 h/wk) at high intensities (70–75% $\dot{V}O_2$peak). It is interesting that the habitual protein intakes are usually just above the maximal estimated needs for endurance athletes (Table 4-2), which may indicate a homeostatic feedback from some tissue that regulates protein intake.

I have also done a regression analysis from three studies where NBAL data could be determined with accuracy (Friedman & Lemon, 1989; Meredith et al., 1989; Tarnopolsky et al., 1988). This analysis provided 58 data points, and the calculated protein intake for zero NBAL was 1.09 g protein·kg^{-1}·d^{-1}. Including a factor to account for an intake to cover 95% of the 'population', the value was 1.16 g protein·kg^{-1}·d^{-1} (Figure 4-3).

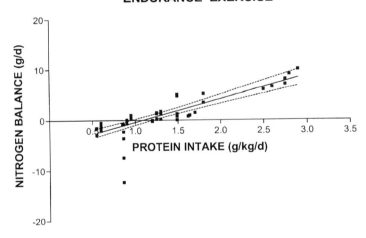

FIGURE 4-3. *Regression analysis of three NBAL studies with endurance athletes.*

Protein Requirements During Resistance Exercise Training

If the protein requirement for resistance athletes is increased, it is based upon a fundamentally different mechanism than that seen in endurance athletes. Resistance-exercise training causes muscle hypertrophy (Lemon et al., 1992; Sale et al., 1987) and not an increase in amino acid oxidation (Tarnopolsky et al., 1991). If there are no changes in efficiency of amino acid retention, there must, at some point, be a protein intake in excess of basal requirements to provide the amino acids required for anabolism. However, some individuals have erroneously concluded that protein requirements are massively increased, and this has been used to perpetuate the myth that the relationship between protein intake and muscle mass accretion is infinitely linear. These ideas have fueled a multibillion dollar industry in protein and amino acid supplements.

Early work from Vernon Young's lab studied the effect of isometric exercise and protein intake upon NBAL and lean body mass (^{40}K counting) (Torun et al., 1977). They found that 1.0 g protein·kg^{-1}·d^{-1} (egg-white and milk) was required to maintain positive NBAL and lean mass accretion in males performing isometric exercise for 75 min/d (Torun et al., 1977). This amounts to about 1.2 g·kg^{-1}·d^{-1} with a mixed protein source.

Similar to the effects of endurance exercise, modest programs of resistance exercise can increase the efficiency of nitrogen utilization at intakes close to the US and Canadian recommendations (Campbell et al., 1995). The adaptive improvements in efficiency during resistance training at intakes around 0.8 g protein·kg^{-1}·d^{-1} have also been observed by others (Hickson et al., 1988). It may be argued that an enhanced ability to achieve NBAL (increased N utilization efficiency) with modest resistance exercise is indicative of adequacy of the intake (Campbell et al., 1995). However, at lower protein intakes (0.8 g·kg^{-1}·d^{-1}) this may be accompanied by a reduction in whole-body protein synthesis, as compared to an intake of 1.6 g·kg^{-1}·d^{-1} (Campbell et al., 1995). This is another example of the utility of leucine kinetics for providing information about the physiological adequacy of a given intake.

In an early study by our group, we determined that the recommended protein intake for six elite bodybuilders was only 1.2 g protein·kg^{-1}·d^{-1}, in spite of their habitual consumption of 2.7 g protein·kg^{-1}·d^{-1}! (Tarnopolsky, 1988). We have argued that this modest increase in requirements is due to an increased overall protein turnover and not to continued accretion of myofibrillar protein (Lemon, et al., 1992; Tarnopolsky et al. 1988, 1992). Given the well-known fact that most of the myofibrillar protein accretion occurs within the first several months of initiating a resistance-exercise program, we sought to determine the 'maximal' protein requirements during exercise initiation (Lemon et al., 1992) and during a combination of weight training and high-intensity sprinting and power activities (i.e., football and rugby)(Tarnopolsky et al., 1992).

In one study we determined NBAL, muscle mass, and strength in 12 men initiating a very rigorous training program (6 d/wk, 2 h/d, 70–85% of one repetition maximum) over a 2-mo period (Lemon et al., 1992). We found that the estimated protein requirements during this period were ~ 1.65 g protein·kg^{-1}·d^{-1} (Lemon et al., 1992). Gains in strength and muscle density consequent to training were not different when subjects consumed 1.44 g as compared to 2.6 g protein·kg^{-1}·d^{-1} (Lemon et al., 1992).

In a second study we investigated both NBAL and leucine kinetics in a group of varsity-level football and rugby players at the peak of the training season (Tarnopolsky et al., 1992). The participants were randomly assigned to receive each of three protein intakes (0.7, 1.4, and 2.8 g protein·kg^{-1}·d^{-1}), and they were compared to an age-matched sedentary control group. The estimated safe protein intake was 0.89 for the sedentary group and 1.76 g protein·kg^{-1}·d^{-1} for the varsity athletes (Tarnopolsky et al., 1992). As expected, overall protein synthesis was greater for the athletes as compared to the sedentary controls at all protein intakes. More importantly, however, was the fact that the athletes' average value for whole-body protein synthesis was lower when consuming 0.7 g than it was when they consumed 1.4 and 2.8 g protein·kg^{-1}·d^{-1}. Protein synthesis appeared to plateau at about 1.4 g protein·kg^{-1}·d^{-1}. At 2.8 g protein·kg^{-1}·d^{-1}, the leucine oxidation nearly doubled, which provided evidence that protein intake above the physiological requirement is merely oxidized for energy (Tarnopolsky et al., 1992).

I have also done a regression analysis from four studies where NBAL data could be determined with accuracy (Campbell, et al., 1995; Lemon et al., 1992; Tarnopolsky et al., 1988, 1992). This analysis provided 101 data points, and the calculated protein intake for zero NBAL was 1.26 g protein·kg^{-1}·d^{-1}. After extrapolating to include 95% of the 'population,' the value was 1.38 g protein·kg^{-1}·d^{-1} (Figure 4-4).

We have also provided evidence that the timing of nutrient ingestion can affect NBAL (Roy et al., 1997). In eight male resistance-trained athletes, we compared the effect of a high-carbohydrate drink consumed immediately following a resistance exercise bout to that of consuming the same drink with breakfast. In spite of the fact that the total energy content and macronutrient distribution were identical for both trials, when the carbohydrate drink was provided immediately after exercise, there was lower urinary urea excretion (more positive NBAL), and 3-MH excretion decreased (Roy et al., 1997), i.e., evidence that the timing of carbohydrate supplements can influence net protein balance in resis-

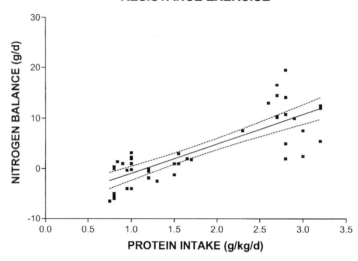

RESISTANCE EXERCISE

FIGURE 4-4. *Regression analysis of four studies with resistance athletes.*

tance sports. Furthermore, the provision of carbohydrate and carbohy-drate-protein supplements immediately following resistance exercise can also hasten muscle glycogen recovery (Roy et al., 1998). A high car-bohydrate diet may also provide for increased muscular endurance in resistance athletes (Walberg et al., 1988).

Therefore, maximal estimated protein intakes for males beginning a very rigorous resistance training program and for those who are per-forming both weight training and high-intensity sprinting types of ac-tivities (i.e., football and rugby) are about 1.6–1.7 $g \cdot kg^{-1} \cdot d^{-1}$. For the bodybuilder in 'steady state' (i.e., habitual training) the requirements are about 1.2 g protein $\cdot kg^{-1} \cdot d^{-1}$. With more modest resistance-exercise programs, dietary protein requirements are not significantly increased and are likely to result in a greater net myofibrillar protein gain than for the non-exercising individual (Torun et al., 1977; Campbell et al., 1995). As with endurance exercise, there are important interactions with both the carbohydrate content and the timing of carbohydrates.

DIRECTIONS FOR FUTURE RESEARCH

Future research should explore the effects of carbohydrate loading and of carbohydrate supplementation before and during exercise upon protein turnover and protein requirements in endurance sports. The potential link(s) following exercise among carbohydrate intake, insulin, and ubiquitin should be explored to determine a potential mechanism for attenuated myofibrillar proteolysis when carbohydrates are provided following exercise. We need to examine the effects of chronic endurance exercise training upon amino acid kinetics and protein requirements. It is also important to more accurately determine protein kinetics and protein requirements for female athletes, particularly in sports that require great strength. We should continue our efforts to educate athletes, many of whom still feel that huge protein intakes are required for optimal muscle mass accretion. Perhaps most importantly, studies should examine the potential benefits of therapeutic resistance exercise and nutritional supplementation in patients with muscle wasting conditions.

SUMMARY

Protein oxidation may provide for 3–6% of the energy cost of endurance exercise. Chronic endurance training in humans appears to attenuate the activation of protein oxidation (BCKAD activity). Females do not oxidize as much protein for energy as do males during endurance exercise. This may be due to a sparing of muscle glycogen and/or a lower BCKAD activity at rest. In spite of the expected attempt by the body to compensate for the physiological stress of chronic exercise, some endurance athletes may train with a high enough intensity and/or volume to impact negatively upon protein requirements. Maximal protein requirements are not likely to exceed 1.6 $g \cdot kg^{-1} \cdot d^{-1}$ under even the most extreme of conditions (Table 4-4). The majority of endurance athletes consume ample protein to cover an elevated need. However, there are some high-risk groups who may consume inadequate energy (e.g., dancers, amenorrheic female runners, and wrestlers).

TABLE 4-4. *Estimated protein requirements for athletes.*

Target Population	Protein Requirement
Sedentary males and females	0.84 $g \cdot kg^{-1} \cdot d^{-1}$
Elite male endurance athletes	1.6 $g \cdot kg^{-1} \cdot d^{-1}$
Moderate intensity endurance athletes[*]	1.2 $g \cdot kg^{-1} \cdot d^{-1}$
Recreational endurance athletes[+]	0.84 $g \cdot kg^{-1} \cdot d^{-1}$
Resistance athletes (early training and football/rugby)	1.7 $g \cdot kg^{-1} \cdot d^{-1}$
Resistance athletes (steady state)	1.2 $g \cdot kg^{-1} \cdot d^{-1}$
Recreational and therapeutic resistance exercise	0.84 $g \cdot kg^{-1} \cdot d^{-1}$
Female athletes	~ 25% lower than male athletes

[*]—exercising ~ 4–5 X/wk for 45–60 min.
[+]—exercising 4– 5 X/wk for 30 min at < 55 % $\dot{V}O_2peak$

Acute resistance exercise does not increase the oxidation of essential amino acids. Both muscle protein synthesis and muscle protein degradation are elevated following an acute bout of resistance exercise; however, net protein balance is more positive. The provision of an immediate nutritional supplement with carbohydrates and some protein will result in an attenuation of protein degradation and a more positive NBAL. This strategy is likely to be helpful in both resistance training and in the care of patients with diseases that result in muscle wasting. Males who acutely initiate a rigorous resistance exercise training program and those who simultaneously perform resistance exercise and sprint/power activities (e.g., football or rugby) require a daily protein intake of about 1.6–1.7 $g\cdot kg^{-1}\cdot d^{-1}$. Athletes who have been habitually performing resistance exercise require a protein intake of about 1.2 $g\cdot kg^{-1}\cdot d^{-1}$ (Table 4-4). As with endurance athletes, most athletes consume at least this amount of protein, and some resistance athletes consume vastly more than this.

BIBLIOGRAPHY

Aftring, R.P, K.P. Block, and M.G. Buse (1986). Leucine and isoleucine activate skeletal muscle branched-chain α-keto acid dehydrogenase in vivo. *Am. J. Physiol.* 250(*Endocrinol. Metab.* 13): E599–E604.

Balagopal, P., O. Ljungqvist, and K.S. Nair (1997). Skeletal muscle myosin heavy-chain rate in healthy subjects. *Am. J. Physiol.* 272(*Endocrinol. Metab.* 35):E45–E50.

Belcastro, A.N. (1993). Skeletal muscle calciumactivated neutral protease (calpain) with exercise. *J. Appl. Physiol.* 74: 1381.

Bier, D.M. (1989). Intrinsically difficult problems: The kinetics of body proteins and amino acids in man. *Diabetes/Metabol. Rev.* 5(2):111–132.

Biolo, G., D. Fleming, S.P. Maggi, and R.R. Wolfe (1995a). Transmembrane transport and intracellular kinetics of amino acids in human skeletal muscle. *Am. J. Physiol.* 268:E75–E84.

Biolo, G., R.Y.D. Fleming, and R.R. Wolfe (1995b). Physiological hyperinsulinemia stimulates protein synthesis and enhances transport of selected amino acids in human skeletal muscle. *J. Clin. Invest.* 95:811–819.

Biolo, G., S.P. Maggi, B.D. Williams, K.D. Tipton, and R.R. Wolfe (1995c). Increased rates of muscle protein turnover and amino acid transport after resistance exercise in humans. *Am. J. of Physiol.* 268:E514–E520.

Biolo, G., K.D. Tipton, S. Klein, and R.R. Wolfe (1997). An abundant supply of amino acids enhances the metabolic effect of exercise on muscle protein. *Amer. J. Physiol.* 273:E122–E129.

Biolo, G., X. Zhang, and R.R. Wolfe (1995d). Role of membrane transport in interorgan amino acid flow between muscle and small intestine. *Metab. Clin. Exper.* 44:719.

Booth, F.W., and P.A. Watson (1985). Control of adaptations in protein levels in response to exercise. *Fed. Proc.* 44:2293–2300.

Boyer, B., and R. Odessey (1991). Kinetic characterization of branched chain ketoacid dehydrogenase. *Arch. Biochem. Biophys.* 285:1.

Brouns, F., S.J. Stroecken, B.R. Thijssen, N.J. Rehrer, and F.ten Hoor. (1989). Eating, drinking and cycling. A Controlled Tour de France simulation study, Part II. Effect of diet manipulation. *Int. J. Sports Med.* 10:S41–S48.

Butterfield, G.E. (1987). Whole body protein utilization in humans. *Med. Sci. Sports Exerc.* 19(Suppl.):157–165.

Butterfield, G.E., and D.H. Calloway (1984). Physical activity improves protein utilization in young men. *Br. J. Nutr.* 51:171–184.

Bylund-Fellenius, A.-C., K.M. Ojamaa, K.E. Flaim, J.B. Li, S.J. Wassner, and L.S. Jefferson. (1984). Protein synthesis versus energy state in contracting muscle of perfused rat hindlimb. *Amer. J. Physiol.* 246:E297–E305.

Byrd, S.K., L.J. McCutcheon, D.R. Hodgson, and P.D. Gollnick (1989). Altered sarcoplasmic reticulum function after high-intensity exercise. *J. Appl. Physiol.* 68:2072.

Calles-Escandon, J., J.J. Cunningham, P. Snyder, R. Jacob, G. Huszar, J. Loke, and P. Felig (1984). Influence of exercise on urea, creatinine, and 3–methylhistidine excretion in normal human subjects. *Am. J. Physiol.* 246(*Endocrinol. Metab.* 9):E334–E338.

Cameron, C.M., J.L. Kostyp, N.A. Adamafio, P. Roos, A. Skottner, A. Forsman, and B. Skoog (1988). The acute effects of growth hormone on amino acid transport and protein synthesis are due to its insulin-like action. *Endocrinol.* 122:471–474.

Campbell, W. W., M.C. Crim, V.R. Young, L.J. Joseph, and W.J. Evans (1995). Effects of resistance training and dietary protein intake on protein metabolism in older adults, *Amer. J. Physiol.* 268:E1143–E1153.

Carli, F., J. Webster. V. Ramachandra, M. Pearson, M. Read, G.C. Ford, S. McArthur. V.R. Preed,. and D. Halliday (1990). Aspects of protein metabolism after elective surgery in patients receiving constant nutritional support. *Clin. Sci.* 78:621–628.

Carmelli, E., Z. Hochberg, E. Livne, I. Lichtenstein, C. Kestelboim, M. Silbermann, and A.Z. Reznick (1993). Effect of growth hormone on gastrocnemius muscle of aged rats after immobilization: biochemistry and morphology. *J. Appl. Physiol.* 75(4):1529–1535.

Carraro, F., W.H. Hartl, C.A. Stuart, D.K. Layman, F. Jahoor, and R.R. Wolfe (1990a). Whole body and plasma protein synthesis in exercise and recovery in human subjects. *Am. J. Physiol.* 258(*Endocrinol. Metab.* 21):E821–E829.

Carraro, F., C.A. Stuart, W.H. Hartl, J. Rosenblatt, and R.R. Wolfe (1990b). Effect of exercise and recovery on muscle protein synthesis in human subjects. *Am. J. Physiol.* 259(*Endocrinol. Metab.* 22):E479–E486.

Castellino, P., L. Luzi, D.C. Simonson, M. Haymond, and R.A. DeFronzo (1987). Effect of insulin and plasma amino acid concentrations on leucine metabolism in man. *J. Clin. Invest.* 80:1784–1793.

Chandler, R.M., H.K. Byrne, J.G. Patterson, and J.L. Ivy (1994). Dietary supplements affect the anabolic hormones after weight training exercise. *J. Appl. Physiol.* 76(2):839–845.

Chesley, A., J.D. MacDougall, M.A. Tarnopolsky, S.A. Atkinson, and K. Smith (1992). Changes in human muscle protein synthesis after resistance exercise. *J. Appl. Physiol.* 73:1383–1388.

Chiang, A.N., and P-C. Huang (1988). Excess energy and nitrogen balance at protein intakes above the requirement level in young men. *Am. J. Clin. Nutr.* 48:1015–1022.

Consolazio, C.F., H.L. Johnson, R.A. Nelson, J.G. Dramise, and J.H. Skala (1975). Protein metabolism during intensive physical training in the young adult. *Am. J. Clin. Nutr.* 28:29–35.

Cuneo, R.C., F. Solomon, C.M. Wiles, R. Hesp, and P.H. Sonksen (1991). Growth hormone treatment in growth hormone-deficient adults. I. Effects on muscle mass and strength. *J. Appl. Physiol.* 70(2):688–694.

Davis, T.A., and I.E. Karl (1986). Response of muscle protein turnover to insulin after acute exercise and training. *Biochem. J.* 240:651–657.

Deuster, P.A., S.B. Kyle, P.B. Moser, R.A. Vigersky, A. Singh, and E.B. Schoomaker (1986). Nutritional survey of highly trained women runners. *Am. J. Clin. Nutr.* 45:954–962.

Dohm, G.L., G.R. Beecher. R.Q. Warren, and R.T. Williams (1982). The influence of exercise on free amino acid concentrations in rat tissues. *J. Appl. Physiol.* 50:41.

Dohm, G.L., A.L. Hecker, W.E. Brown, G.J. Klain, F.R. Puente, E.W. Askew, and G.R. Beecher (1977). Adaptation of protein metabolism to endurance training. *Biochem. J.* 164:705–708.

Dohm, G.L., R.G. Israel, R.L. Breedlove, R.T. Williams, and E.W. Askew (1985a). Biphasic changes in 3methylhistdine excretion in humans after exercise. *Am. J. Physiol.* 248:E588.

Dohm, G.L., G.J. Kasperek, E.B. Tapscott, and H.A. Barakat. (1985b). Protein metabolism during endurance exercise. *Fed. Proc.* 44:348–352.

Dohm, G.L., R.T. Williams, G.J. Kasperek, and A.M. van Rij (1982). Increased excretion of urea and N-methylhistidine by rats and humans after a bout of exercise. *J. Appl. Physiol.* 52:27–32.

Drinkwater, B.L., K. Nilson, C.H. Chestnut III, W.J. Bremner, S. Shainholtz, and M.B. Southworth (1984). Bone mineral content of amenorrheic and eumenorrheic athletes. *N. Engl. J. Med.* 311:277.

El-Khoury, A.E., A. Forslund, R. Olsson, S. Branth, A. Sjödin, A. Andersson, A. Atkinson, A. Selvaraj, L. Hambraeus, and V.R. Young (1997). Moderate exercise at energy balance does not affect 24-h leucine oxidation or nitrogen retention in healthy men. *Am. J. Physiol.* 273:E394.

Elwyn, D.H. (1990). New concepts in nitrogen balance. *Can. J. Gastroenterol.* 4(SA):9A-12A.

Evans, W.J., and J.G. Cannon (1991). The metabolic effects of exercise-induced muscle damage. In: J.O. Holloszy (ed.) *Exercise and Sport Sciences Reviews*, Vol.19. Baltimore, MD: Williams and Wilkins, pp. 99–125.

Evans, W., E.C. Fisher, R.A. Hoerr, and V.R. Young (1983). Protein metabolism and endurance exercise. *Phys. Sportsmed.* 11:63–72.

Fielding, R.A., C.N. Meredith, K.P. O'Reilly, W.R. Frontera, J.G. Cannon, and W.J. Evans (1991). Enhanced protein breakdown after eccentric exercise in young and older men. *J. Appl. Physiol.* 71:674.

Florini, J.R. (1987). Hormonal control of muscle growth. *Muscle and Nerve.* 10:577–598.

Food and Agriculture Organization/World Health Organization/United Nations University (1985)

Energy and protein requirements. *WHO technical report series no.74.* Geneva: World Health Organization.

Food and Nutrition Board/Commission on Life Sciences/National Research Council (1989): *Recommended Daily Allowances.* Washington: National Academy Press, vol. 10, pp. 52–77.

Friedman, J.E., and P.W.R. Lemon (1989). Effect of chronic endurance exercise on retention of dietary protein. *Int. J. Sports. Med.* 10:118–123.

Fryburg, D.A., R.A. Gelfund, and E.J. Barrett (1991). Growth hormone acutely stimulates forearm muscle protein synthesis in normal humans. *Am. J. Physiol.* 260 (*Endocrinol. Metab.* 23):E499–E504.

Garlick, P.J., and I. Grant (1988). Amino acid infusion increases the sensitivity of muscle protein synthesis *in vivo* to insulin. *Biochem. J.* 254, 579–584.

Goldberg, A.L., and T.W. Chang (1978). Regulation and significance of amino acid metabolism in skeletal muscle. *Fed. Proc.* 37:2301.

Gontzea, I., P. Sutezescu, and S. Dumitrache (1975). The influence of adaptation to physical effort on nitrogen balance in man. *Nutr. Reports Int.* 22:231–236.

Gontzea, T., P. Sutezescu, and S. Dumitrache (1974). The influence of muscular activity on nitrogen balance and on the need of man for proteins. *Nutr. Reports Int.* 10:35–41.

Griggs, R.C., W. Kingston, R.F. Jozefowicz, B.E. Herr, G. Forbes, and D. Halliday (1989). Effect of testosterone on muscle mass and muscle protein synthesis. *J. Appl. Physiol.* 66(1):498–503.

Hagg, S.A., Morse, E.L., and S.A. Adibi (1982). Effect of exercise on rates of oxidation, turnover, and plasma clearance of leucine in human subjects. Am. J. Physiol. 242(*Endocrinol. Metab.* 5):E407–E410.

Halseth, A.E., P.J. Flakoll, E.K. Reed, A.B. Messina, M.G. Krishna, D.B. Lacy, P.E. Williams, and D.H. Wasserman (1997). Effect of physical activity and fasting on gut and liver proteolysis in the dog. *Am. J. Physiol.* 36(6):E1073–E1082.

Hammarquist, F., J. Wernerman, R. Ali, A. Von der Deccken, and E. Vinnars (1989). Addition of glutamine to total parental nutrition after elective surgery spares free glutamine in muscle, counteracts the fall in muscle protein synthesis, and improves nitrogen balance. *Ann. Surg.* 209(4):455–461.

Haralambie, G., and A. Berg (1976). Serum urea and amino nitrogen changes with exercise duration. *Eur. J. Appl. Physiol.* 36:39.

Hayachi, T., J.F.P. Wojtaszewski, and L.J. Goodyear (1997). Exercise regulation of glucose transport in skeletal muscle. *Am. J. Physiol.* 36(6):E1039–E1051.

Henderson, S.A., A.L. Black and G.A. Brooks (1985). Leucine turnover and oxidation in trained rats during exercise. *Am. J. Physiol.* 249:E137–E144.

Hickson, J.F., K. Hinkelmann, and D.L. Bredle (1988). Protein intake level and introductory weight training exercise on urinary total nitrogen excretions from untrained men. *Nutr. Res.* 8:725–731.

Hickson, J.F., I. Wolinsky, G.P. Rodriguez, J.M. Avaarnnik, M.C. Kent, and N.W. Shier (1986). Failure of weight training to affect urinary indices of protein metabolism in men. *Med. Sci. Sports Exerc.* 18:563–567.

Hood, D.A., and R.L. Terjung (1987). Effect of endurance training on leucine metabolism in perfused rat skeletal muscle. *Amer. J. Physiol.* 253:E648.

Kameyama, T., and J.D. Etlinger (1979). Calcium-dependent regulation of protein synthesis and degradation in muscle. *Nature* 279:344–346.

Kasperek, G.J. (1989). Regulation of branched-chain 2–oxo acid dehydrogenase activity during exercise. *Am. J.Physiol.* 256 (*Endocrinol. Metab.* 19):E186–E190.

Kasperek, G.J., G.R. Conway, D.S. Krayeski, and J.J. Lohne (1992).A reexamination of the effect of exercise on rate of muscle protein degradation. *Am. J. Physiol.* 263:E1144–E1150.

Kharta, B.S., R.K. Chawla, C.W. Sewell, and D. Rudman (1977). Distribution of branched-chain α-keto acid dehydrogenases in primate tissues. *J. Clin. Invest.* 59:558–564.

Knapik, J., C. Merideth, B. Jones, R. Fielding, V. Young, and W. Evans (1991). Leucine metabolism during fasting and exercise. *J. Appl. Physiol.* 70(1):43–47.

Kraemer, W.J., L. Marchitelli, S.E. Gordon, E. Harman, J.E. Dziados, R. Mello, P. Frykman, D. McCurry, and S.J. Fleck (1990). Hormonal and growth factor responses to heavy resistance exercise protocols. *J. Appl. Physiol.* 69(4):1442–1450.

Krempf, M., R.A. Hoerr, V.A. Pelletier, L.M. Marks, R. Gleason, and V.R. Young (1993). An isotopic study of the effect of dietary carbohydrate on the metabolic fate of dietary leucine and phenylalanine. *Am. J. Clin. Nutr.* 57:161–169.

Lamont, L.S., D.G. Patel, and S.C. Kalhan (1990). Leucine kinetics in endurance-trained humans. *J. Appl. Physiol.* 69(1):1–6.

Lemon, P.W.R. (1996). Is increased dietary protein necessary or beneficial for individuals with a physically active lifestyle? *Nutr. Rev.* 54(4):S169–S175.

Lemon, P.W.R. (1989). Nutrition for muscular development of young athletes. In: C.V. Gisolfi and D.R. Lamb (eds.) *Perspectives in Exercise Science and Sports Medicine* Vol. 2. Youth, Exercise, and Sport. Indianapolis, IN: Benchmark Press, pp. 369–400.

Lemon, P.W.R. (1987). Protein and exercise: update 1987. *Med. Sci. Sports Exerc.* 19(5):S179–S190.

Lemon, P.W.R., and J.P. Mullin (1980). The effect of initial muscle glycogen levels on protein catabolism during exercise. *J. Appl. Physiol.* 48:624–629.

Lemon, P.W.R., F.J. Nagle, J.P. Mullin, and N.J. Benevenga (1982). In vivo leucine oxidation at rest and during two intensities of exercise. *J. Appl. Physiol.* 53(4):947–954.

Lemon, P., M.A. Tarnopolsky, J.D. MacDougall, and S. Atkinson (1992). Protein requirements and muscle mass/strength changes in novice bodybuiders. *J. Appl. Physiol.* 73(2):767–775.

MacDougall, J.D., M.J. Gibala, M.A. Tarnopolsky, J.R. MacDonald, S.A. Interisano, and K.E. Yarasheski (1995). The time course for elevated muscle protein synthesis following heavy resistance exercise. *Can. J. Appl. Physiol.* 20:480–486.

MacLean, D.A., L.L. Spriet, E. Hultman, and T.E. Graham (1991). Plasma and muscle amino acid and ammonia responses during prolonged exercise in humans. *J. Appl. Physiol.* 70(5):2095–2103.

Marcus, R.C., C.P. Madvig, J. Minkoff, M. Goddard, M. Bayer, M. Martin, L. Gaudiani, W. Haskell, and H. Genant (1985). Menstrual function and bone mass in elite women distance runners. *Ann. Int. Med.* 102:158.

McKenzie, S., S.L. Carter, S.M. Phillips, M.J. Gibala, and M.A. Tarnopolsky. (1998). Effect of endurance training on branched-chain oxoacid dehydrogenase (BCOAD) activity in untrained males and females. *The FASEB J.* 12(4):A365.

McNurlan, M.A., P. Essen, A. Thorell, A.G. Calder, S.E. Anderson, O. Ljungqvist, A. Sandgren, I. Grant, I. Tjader, P.E. Ballmer, J. Wernerman, and P.J. Garlick (1994). Response of protein synthesis in human skeletal muscle to insulin: an investigation with L-[2H5] phenylalanine. Am. J. Phsiol. 267:E102–E108.

Meredith, C.N., M.J. Zackin, W.R. Frontera, and W.J. Evans (1989). Dietary protein requirements and body protein metabolism in endurance-trained men. *J. Appl. Physiol.* 66(6):2850–2856.

Mitch, W.E., and A.L. Goldberg (1996). Mechanisms of muscle wasting. *New Eng. J. Med.* 335:1897–1905.

Moller-Loswick, A.C., H. Zachrisson, A. Hyltander, U. Korner, D.E. Matthews, and K. Lundholm (1994). Insulin selectively attenuates breakdown of nonmyofibrillar proteins in peripheral tissues of normal men. *Am. J. Physiol.* 266: E645–E652.

Morgan, M.J., and P.T. Loghna (1989). Work overload induced changes in fast and slow skeletal muscle myosin heavy chain gene expression. *FEBS Lett.* 255(2):427–430.

Nakshabendi, I.M., W. Obeidat, R.I. Russel, S. Downie, K. Smith, and M.J. Rennie (1995). Gut mucosal protein synthesis measured using intravenous and intragastric delivery of stable tracer amino acids. *Am. J. Physiol.* 269:E996.

Nelson, M.E., E.C. Fisher, P.D. Catsos, C.N. Meredith, R.N. Turksoy, and W.J. Evans (1986). Diet and bone status in ammenorheaic runners. *Am. J. Clin. Nutr.* 43:910–916.

Newman, E., M.J. Heslin, R.F. Wolf, P.W.T. Pisters, and M.F. Brennan (1994). The effect of systemic hyperinsulinemia with concomitant amino acid infusion on skeletal muscle protein turnover in the human forearm. *Metabol.* 43(1):70–78. in isolated rabbit muscles. *Biochem. J.* 214:1011–1014.

Paul, G.L. (1989). Dietary protein requirements of physically active individuals. *Sports Med.* 8(3):154–176.

Pellett, P.L. (1990). Protein requirements in humans. *Am. J. Clin. Nutr.* 51:723–737.

Phillips, S.M., S.A. Atkinson, M.A. Tarnopolsky, and J.D. MacDougall (1993). Gender differences in leucine kinetics and nitrogen balance in endurance athletes. *J. Appl. Physiol.* 75(5):2134–2141.

Phillips, S.M., K.D. Tipton, A. Aarsland, S.E. Wolf, and R.R. Wolfe (1997). Mixed muscle protein synthesis and breakdown following resistance exercise in humans, *Amer. J. Physiol.* 273: E99–E107.

Pivarnik, J.M., J.F. Hickson, and I. Wolinsky (1989). Urinary 3-methylhistidine excretion increases with repeated weight training exercise. *Med .Sci. Sports Exerc.* 21:283.

Rathmacher, J.A., P.J. Flakoli, and S.L. Nissen (1995). A compartmental model of 3-methylhistidine metabolism in humans. *Am. J. Physiol.* 269:(Endocrinol. Metab.32) E193–E198.

Rennie, M.J., R.H.T. Edwards, S. Krywawych, C.T.M. Davies, D. Halliday, J.C. Waterlow, and D.J. Millward (1981). Effect of exercise on protein turnover in man. *Clin. Sci.* 61:627–639.

Richter, E.A., K.J. Mikines, H. Galbo, and B. Kiens (1989). Effect of exercise on insulin action in skeletal muscle. *J. Appl. Physiol.* 66(2):876–885.

Roy, B.D., and M.A. Tarnopolsky (1998). Influence of differing macronutrient intakes on muscle glycogen resynthesis after resistance exercise. *J. Appl. Physiol.* 84(3):890–896.

Roy, B.D., M.A. Tarnopolsky, J.D. MacDougall, J. Fowles, and K.E. Yarasheski (1997). Effect of glucose supplement timing on protein metabolism after resistance training. *J. Appl. Physiol.* 82(6): 1822–1888.

Rudman, D., A.G. Feller, H.S. Nagraj, G.A. Gergans, P.Y. Lalitha, A.F. Goldberg, R.A. Schlenker, L. Cohn, I.W. Rudman, and D.E. Mattson (1990). Effects of growth hormone in men over 69 years old. *N. Eng. J. Med.* 323(1):1–6.

Sale, D.G., J.D. MacDougall, S.E. Alway, and J.R. Sutton (1987). Voluntary strength and muscle characteristics in untrained men and women and male bodybuilders. *J. Appl. Physiol.* 62:1786.

Shimomura, Y., T. Suzuki, S. Saitoh, Y. Tasaki, R.A. Harris, and M. Suzuki (1990). Activation of branched-chain α-keto acid dehydrogenase complex by exercise: effect of high-fat diet intake. *J. Appl. Physiol.* 68(1):161–165.

Short, S.H., and W.R. Short (1983). Four-year study of university athletes' dietary intake. *J. Am. Diet Assoc.* 82(6):632–645.

Smith, K., and M.J. Rennie (1990). Protein turnover and amino acid metabolism in human skeletal muscle. *Baill. Clin. Endocr. Met.* 4(3):461–498.

Svanberg, E., A.C. Möller-Loswick, D.E. Matthews, U. Körner, M. Andersson, and K. Lundholm (1996). Effects of amino acids on synthesis and degradation of skeletal muscle proteins in humans. *Amer. J. Physiol.* 271:E718–E724.

Tarnopolsky, M.A. (1993). Protein, caffeine and sports: guidelines for active people. Phys. Sportmed. 21(3):137–149.

Tarnopolsky, M.A., S.A. Atkinson, J.D. MacDougall, A. Chesley, S.Phillips, and H. Schwarcz (1992). Evaluation of protein requirements for trained strength athletes. *J. Appl. Physiol.* 73(5):1986–1995.

Tarnopolsky, M.A., S.A. Atkinson, J.D. MacDougall, B.B. Senor, P.W.R. Lemon, and H.P. Schwarcz (1991). Whole body leucine metabolism during and after resistance exercise in fed humans. *Med. Sci. Sports Exerc.* 23(3):326–333.

Tarnopolsky, M.A., S.A. Atkinson, S.M. Phillips, and J.D. MacDougall (1995). Carbohydrate loading and metabolism during exercise in men and women. *J. Appl. Physiol.* 78:1360–1368.

Tarnopolsky, M.A., N. Cipriano, C. Woodcroft, W.J. Pulkkinen, D.C. Robinson, J.M. Henderson, and J.D. MacDougall. Effect of rapid weight loss and wrestling on muscle glycogen concentration. *Clin. J. Sport Med.* 6(2):78–84.

Tarnopolsky, M.A., J.D. MacDougall, and S.A. Atkinson (1988). Influence of protein intake and training status on nitrogen balance and lean body mass. *J. Appl. Physiol.* 64:187–193.

Tarnopolsky, M.A., L.J. MacDougall, S.A. Atkinson, and J.R. Sutton (1990). Gender differences in substrate for exercise. *J. Appl. Phsiol.* 68(1):302–308.

Tarnopolsky, M.A., B.D. Roy, and J.R. MacDonald (1997). A randomized, controlled trial of creatine monohydrate in patients with mitochondrial cytopathies. *Muscle and Nerve.* 1–8.

Tessari, P., S. Inchiostro, G. Biolo, R. Trevisan, G. Fantin, M.C. Marescotti, E. Iori, A. Tiengo, and G. Crepaldi (1987). Differential effects of hyperinsulinemia and hyperaminoacidemia on leucine-carbon metabolism in vivo. *J. Clin. Invest.* 79:1062–1069.

Tidball, J.G. (1995). Inflammatory cell response to acute muscle injury. *Med. Sci. Sport Exerc.* 27:1022.

Tipton, K.D., A.A. Ferrando, B.D. Williams, and R.R. Wolfe (1996). Muscle protein metabolism in female swimmers after a combination of resistance and endurance exercise. *J. Appl. Physiol.* 81(5): 2034–2038.

Todd, K.S., G.E. Butterfield, and D.H. Calloway (1984). Nitrogen balance in men with adequate and deficient energy intake at three levels of work. *J. Nutr.* 114:2107–2118.

Torun, B., N.S. Scrimshaw, and V.R. Young (1977). Effect of isometric exercises on body potassium and dietary protein requirements of young men. *Am. J. Clin. Nutr.* 30:1983–1993.

Van Walern, C., J.M. Paterson, M. Kapral, B. Chan, M. Bell, G. Hawker, J. Gollish, J. Schatzker, J.I. Williams, and C. Naylor (1996). Appropriateness of total hip and knee replacements in regions of Ontario with high and low utilization rates. *Can. Med. Assoc. J.* 155(6):697–706.

Volek, J.S., W.J. Kraemer, J.A. Bush, T. Incledon, and M. Boetes. (1997). Testosterone and cortisol in relationship to dietary nutrients and resistance exercise. *J. Appl. Physiol.* 82(1):49–54.

Wagenmakers, A.J., E.J. Beckers, F. Brouns, H. Kuipers, P.B. Soeters, G.J. van der Vusse, and W.H. Saris (1991). Carbohydrate supplementation, glycogen depletion, and amino acid metabolism during exercise. *Am. J. Physiol.* 260:E883–E890.

Wagenmakers, A.J.M., J.H. Brookes, J.H. Coakley, T. Reilly, and R.H.T. Edwards (1989). Exercise-induced activation of the branched-chain 2–oxo acid dehydrogenase in human muscle. *Eur. J. Appl. Physiol.* 59:159–167.

Walberg, J.L., M.K. Leidy, D.J. Sturgill, D.E. Hinkle, S.J. Ritchey, and D.R. Sebolt (1988). Macronutrient content of a hypoenergy diet affects nitrogen retention and muscle function in weight lifters. *Int. J. Sports Med.* 9:261–266.

Watson, P.A., Stein, J.P., and F.W. Booth (1984). Changes in actin synthesis and (-actin-mRNA content in rat muscle during immobilization. *Am. J. Physiol.* 247 *(Cell Physiol.*16):C39–C44.

Welle, S., D.E. Matthews, R.G. Campbell, and K.S. Nair (1989). Stimulation of protein turnover by carbohydrate overfeeding in men. *Am. J. Physiol. (Endocrinol. Metab. 20)*:E413–E417.

Welle, S., C. Thornton, R. Jozefowicz, and M. Statt (1995). Myofibrillar protein synthesis in young and old men. *Am. J. Physiol.* 264:E693–E698.

Williams, B.D., R.R. Wolfe., D.P. Bracy, and D.H. Wasserman (1996). Gut proteolysis contributes essential amino acids during exercise. *Am. J. Physiol.* 270:E85.

Willmore, D.W. (1991). Catabolic illness. *N.Eng. J. Med.* 325 (10):695–702.

Wolfe, R.R., R.D. Goodenough, M.H. Wolfe, G.T. Royle, and E.R. Nadel (1982). Isotopic analysis of leucine and urea metabolism in exercising humans. *J. Appl. Physiol.* 52(2):458–466.

Wolfe, R.R., M.H. Wolfe, E.R. Nadel, and J.H.F. Shaw (1984). Isotopic determination of amino acid-urea interactions in exercise in humans. *Am. J. Physiol.* 56(1):221–229.

Wong, T.S., and F.W. Booth (1990). Protein metabolism in rat gastrocnemius muscle after stimulated chronic concentric exercise. *J. Appl. Physiol.* 69(5):1709–1717.

Yan, Z., Salmons, S., Jarvis, J., and F.W. Booth (1995). Increased muscle carnitine palmitoyltransferase II mRNA after increased contractile activity. *Am. J. Physiol.* 268 *(Endocrinol. Metab.* 31):E277–E281.

Yarasheski, K.E., J.F. Zachwieja, and D.M. Bier. (1993). Acute effects of resistance exercise on muscle protein synthesis rate in young and elderly men and women. *Am. J. Physiol.* 265:E210–E214.

Young, V.R., and D.M. Bier (1987). A kinetic approach to the determination of human amino acid requirements. *Nutr. Rev.* 45(10):289–298.

Young, V.R., and H.N. Munro (1978). N-Methylhistidine (3-methylhistidine) and muscle protein turnover: an overview. *Fed. Proc.* 37:2291–2300.

Young, V.R., C. Gulcap, W.M. Rand, D.E. Matthews, and D.M. Bier (1986). Leucine kinetics during three weeks at submaintenance-to-maintenance intakes of leucine in men: Adaptation and accommodation. *Human Nutrition: Clin. Nutr.*41C:1–18.

Zaragosa, R., J. Renau-Piqueras, and M. Portoles (1987). Rats fed prolonged high protein diets show an increase in nitrogen metabolism and liver megamitochondria. *Arch. Biochem. Biophys.* 258:426–435.

Zorzano, A., T.W. Balon, M.N. Goodman, and N.B. Ruderman (1986). Additive effects of prior exercise and insulin on glucose and AIB uptake by rat muscle. *Am. J. Physiol.* 251(Endocrinol. Metab. 14):E21–E26

Zawadski, K.M., B.B. Yaspelkis III, and J.L. Ivy (1992). Carbohydrate-protein complex increases the rate of muscle glycogen storage after exercise. *J. Appl. Physiol.* 72(5):1854–1859.

Zemen, R.J., T. Kameyama, K. Matsumoto, P. Bernstein, and J.D. Etlinger (1985). Regulation of protein degradation in muscle by calcium. *J. Biol. Chem.* 260(25):13619–13624.

Zhang, X., D.L. Chinkes, Y. Sakurai, and R.R. Wolfe (1998). An isotopic method for measurement of muscle protein fractional breakdown rate in vivo. *Am. J. Physiol.* 270:E759.

DISCUSSION

FEBBRAIO: Isn't it important to distinguish between endurance exercise that is weight bearing and non-weight bearing? If one compares exercises that are biased toward eccentric versus concentric muscle actions, the former should produce more muscle damage and protein degradation. If you tease out the mode of exercise, are there differences in the protein requirements or protein degradation figures?

TARNOPOLSKY: The greatest protein requirement that we have attained was with highly fit runners and cross-country skiers, i.e., weight bearing activities, and it may be that the eccentric contractions associated with running down hills, etc., elevated the protein requirements. We have also done some studies with cycling; the protein requirements were somewhat less, but they were less well trained as well. The short answer is that at this time we can't say that protein requirements for a power lifter are different from those of a bodybuilder, etc.

HORSWILL: Is the resistance training protocol used to produce a steady state for isotope studies relevant to the true weight lifter? The isotope studies require a steady state to examine acute effects on protein breakdown, but a bodybuilder striving for hypertrophy would lift more strenuously, i.e., in a non-steady-state manner.

TARNOPOLSKY: The way our studies were performed was to collect expired gas into a very large Douglas bag every 20 min while an individual did circuit weight training. There is no way of determining changes in protein metabolism during the 10 s of a particular lift, but it is more important from a protein requirement standpoint to measure metabolism over a long period. Therefore, 24-h studies of protein turnover such as what Vernon Young is now doing or the 24-h excretion of 3-methylhistidine or nitrogen balance techniques are required. With current tracer technology we cannot determine metabolic changes during an acute contraction, but from a practical standpoint, I don't think it really matters.

HORSWILL: Based on the differences in acute metabolism, i.e., leucine oxidation increasing during endurance training but no change during resistance training, combined with what appears to be a greater daily protein requirement in endurance-trained versus resistance-trained athletes, do you conclude that endurance training reduces the efficiency of protein metabolism, whereas resistance training enhances the efficiency of overall protein metabolism?

TARNOPOLSKY: The body does tend to increase its efficiency, whatever activity is performed, based on our data on the activity of branched-chain keto acid dehydrogenase. I think that under both types of stress the organism tends towards adaptation. Efficiency is a difficult variable to quantify, but I think the body becomes more efficient with both types of activity.

WAGENMAKERS: I want to raise some doubts on your conclusion that protein oxidation is increased during exercise. We did a study last year in Maastricht in which we asked subjects to perform 6 h of exercise; we used three tracers—leucine, phenylalanine, and urea—to follow protein metabolism. Subjects were highly trained, and they ingested carbohydrates during exercise. With leucine there was an increase in oxidation during exercise, but with phenylalanine and urea there was no increase. So we are beginning to doubt whether leucine is a good tracer to follow protein metabolism during exercise. Leucine oxidation may follow the fate of the free amino acid pool but perhaps not the fate of the protein pools in the body.

TARNOPOLSKY: It is well known that urea oxidation doesn't follow leucine oxidation. Bob Wolfe also has had experiences similar to yours.

WAGENMAKERS: There are some suggestions in the literature that urea oxidation does not follow protein oxidation, but our data suggest that it does.

TARNOPOLSKY: Clearly, leucine appears to be preferentially oxidized. Others have used lysine tracers as well as leucine and showed that lysine doesn't track what leucine is doing. I'm not implying that leucine oxidation has a direct relevance to protein requirements, but the tracers can be used if you map out the synthesis and oxidation responses to a particular protein intake. That can be helpful in determining requirement. However, the nitrogen balance technique, which is a marker of overall protein turnover, also tells us something about protein requirements.

WAGENMAKERS: You have shown some differences between males and females and between trained and untrained subjects. One of the major determinants of protein oxidation is protein intake, so my question is, in all these studies was the daily protein intake in g/kg the same for the groups that were compared? Trained active subjects, of course, tend to have a higher daily protein intake in g/kg.

TARNOPOLSKY: Usually, the typical daily protein intake for a trained male endurance athlete is 1.6-1.8 g protein/kg body weight; for females, the value is about 1.2 g protein/kg body weight. That is what most of our male and female athletes consume. The reason we don't match them in terms of protein/kg is that we would have to either bring the females up to a non-habitual intake or drop the males down to a non-habitual intake. That gets in to all the problems of adaptation to a new protein intake; they would need quite a period of time to become adapted to the new diet. In the studies that we did with Stu Phillips in 1993, we moved both males and females from their habitual daily intakes and dropped them down to the Canadian Recommended Nutritional Intake, which is approximately 0.84 g/kg body weight for males and females. So the leucine oxidation data in our study comparing males and females were recorded with subjects at the same dietary protein intakes.

NADEL: Can phenylalanine be used as a tracer in exercise studies?

TARNOPOLSKY: Phenylalanine is not oxidized by skeletal muscle.

NADEL: But phenylalanine can be incorporated into other proteins following exercise.

TARNOPOLSKY: It is not synthesized *de novo* nor is it oxidized by skeletal muscle, but it can be used as a tracer for determining synthesis in turnover rates.

NADEL: Sarcopenia, or muscle wasting, in older people is very common. What is the relative importance of protein intake and physical activity in older people to attenuate sarcopenia with advancing age?

TARNOPOLSKY: Data from S. Nair's lab show that the elderly compared to young individuals had reductions in the fractional synthetic rate of myosin. Thus, the overall rates of protein synthesis seem to be reduced, and that may be contributing to sarcopenia. Wayne Campbell published a study in 1995 in which elderly subjects trained for one month and daily consumed 0.84 g or 1.6 g protein/kg. Their conclusion was that 0.84 g was equivalent to 1.6 g for adapting to the weight training program. These individuals were performing relatively modest resistance activity, 3 times/week at about 70% of the one repetition maximum. The investigators did not study the same individuals at different rates of protein intake. Rather, they studied one group at one protein intake and a second group at another protein intake and did a regression analysis, which is not really valid for quantifying protein requirements. I think that the study needs to be repeated with a single group of subjects trained for longer periods on different dietary intakes to get a proper regression analysis.

WILLIS: When you regress your data for nitrogen balance against daily protein intake, it is a linear relationship right up through about 3.5 g protein/kg. What, then, constitutes excessive protein intake?

TARNOPOLSKY: That is the real problem in nitrogen balance studies. If an individual consumes a very high protein diet, it appears that N balance is more positive, but that doesn't mean there is a net accretion of protein. There are various theories as to uncollected losses and other factors on the very high protein intakes that may account for that. It is generally felt that there is a good chance of error when one is at either extreme of the protein intake continuum. What should be done is to produce a good estimate of what the protein requirement is and have subjects consume various protein intakes on either side of the estimate. That is why in our studies we tried to get the intake close to what we estimated the requirement to be. The protein oxidation data are very helpful to show that when we go from 1.6 g protein/kg, which should be adequate, to 2.4, which is what most of the body builders are taking and which we feel is excessive, that there is no increase in synthesis, but only an increase in oxidation. This suggests that they are just wasting protein and are producing expensive urine. Unfortunately, the whole-body data do not give you the whole picture. Muscle synthetic rate is only 25% of the whole-body rate, so we may be missing some of the data by not doing fractional synthetic rate.

SPRIET: In your training study, did you see any change in total activity of the branched-chain amino acid dehydrogenase enzyme?

TARNOPOLSKY: Yes, we did. The total activity is increased with training and parallels quite nicely the measurements of citrate synthase and complex 1-3 activity, but the percent that was in the active form was attenuated. It wasn't significantly down at rest, but it was markedly attenuated after training when tested at both absolute and relative exercise intensities.

SPRIET: But if the percent in the active form went down and the total activity went up, the actual in-vivo activity may have been the same in the trained versus untrained.

TARNOPOLSKY: That is true, and that is why we combined these data with leucine oxidation data. We used the stable-isotope tracers to show that prior to training, an acute 90-min bout of cycling at 65% $\dot{V}O_2$max caused a 100% increase in leucine oxidation, but there was no increase at the same absolute intensity following training, and about a 12–13% increase at the same relative intensity. There was a very nice correlation between the percent of the dehydrogenase in the active form and leucine oxidation.

SPRIET: Do you have any idea why the maximal catalytic activity of this enzyme is so high, and yet you never see the active form increase above 25%? Also, when you train, the maximum catalytic activity increases further. It seems very wasteful to have all of that enzyme if it never is used.

TARNOPOLSKY: Perhaps the increased synthesis of the enzyme protein simply accompanies the proliferation of the mitochondria, and there is no specific downregulation of the enzyme protein synthesis. There is downregulation of the activity of the enzyme, which may be caused by changes in metabolites, but the mRNA for the BCKAD may increase in concert with the increased proliferation of mitochondria.

TIPTON: What is the scientific evidence concerning renal pathology in athletes who consume excessive protein? Is it a serious problem?

TARNOPOLSKY: There is little evidence that a high protein intake has a negative impact on the human body. Many earlier reviews referred to work by Brenner et al., in a 1982 article from the *New England Journal of Medicine*. These authors found that high protein intakes resulted in increased formation of urea and creatinine by the kidney, but their subjects already had compromised renal function. In a healthy athlete there really are no good data showing that daily consumption of 3 or 4 g protein/kg body weight would have deleterious effects. There is some anecdotal evidence that individuals who have been body builders for many years do not appear to have any deleterious effects. My only caution is that we do not have good data and we don't always know who is predisposed to renal disease. Type II diabetes is very common in North American society and it can cause early renal dysfunction (e.g., proteinuria). The problem of protein supplementation as I see it is almost one of health fraud. When I was a medical student, I had some experience in sports medicine and saw a number of young men, 17–18 years old, who were spending \$20–\$30/week on protein powder supplements. This seems to be a horrible waste of money. From a societal standpoint, protein is much more expensive to produce per pound than are grains and various other carbohydrates.

BAR-OR: In general, growing children and adolescents need more protein than do adults on a body-weight basis. Do you have any data on protein requirements for child or adolescent athletes?

TARNOPOLSKY: To my knowledge, no one has done the proper nitrogen balance experiments in young athletes. Keep in mind that I'm not suggesting that everybody needs to use protein supplements. In fact, the majority of people who are doing endurance types of activity, e.g., 30 min a few times per week, do not need increased protein compared to sedentary people. Likewise, the majority of people who lift weights 20 min/d, 3 d/wk, do not need increased protein. It is only a few intensely training athletes who might need protein supplementation. I doubt that many children would actually get to those extremes.

COGGAN: After an overnight fast, muscle is clearly in a catabolic state.

Yet day in and day out, when we eat a normal diet, our lean body mass remains about the same. Without any more sophisticated information, we know that food intake must have an anabolic effect. Are you aware of any evidence that various amino acid supplements and carbohydrate supplements are any better than regular food for inducing protein accretion? Similarly, do you know of any data differentiating between the effects on protein accretion of the energy provided by carbohydrate or protein intake versus specific effects on protein accretion of carbohydrate-induced insulin secretion or protein intake providing amino acids?

TARNOPOLSKY: Both energy and carbohydrate intake have favorable effects on nitrogen balance. One may be able to get away with a slightly lower protein intake if one has a very high carbohydrate intake or a high energy intake. However, to my knowledge, there are no published reports of experiments that have systematically studied the effects of energy versus specific effects of carbohydrate or protein diets with regard to protein accretion.

ARAGON: You have pointed out that carbohydrate ingestion during exercise has been promoted as a way to favor positive protein balance, at least during endurance exercise. But do you know of any data supporting the ingestion of amino acids during exercise to spare muscle protein from being degraded during exercise?

TARNOPOLSKY: It is an interesting hypothesis that if you provided exogenous branched-chain amino acids that you may downregulate leucine oxidation. I think there is no real reason to do so because a high-carbohydrate diet can attenuate leucine oxidation and have favorable effects on endurance performance. So it seems to me to make a lot more sense to use carbohydrates rather than more expensive branched-chain amino acids to provide an inexpensive improvement of glycogen stores and improvement of endurance performance. There are equivocal data as to whether amino acids enhance endurance exercise performance. Now the caveat to that would be that in the immediate post-resistance-exercise period, carbohydrate intake alone may provoke a hyperinsulemic response, which theoretically could attenuate the increase in protein synthesis. If that is true, consuming combinations of amino acids with carbohydrates in the immediate post-resistance-exercise could theoretically be beneficial.

LUKASKI: All of the data used to estimate human protein requirements are based on the nitrogen balance technique. Isn't there a problem with using three-day balance periods when you consider the variability in gastrointestinal transient time?

TARNOPOLSKY: We use a carmine red-dye marker to measure the fecal excretion from the beginning to the end of our experiments. A three-day balance period is clearly inadequate if you are acutely changing protein diets. In all of our experiments we have individuals adapted for a minimum of seven days if we are not significantly changing the protein intake or for at least 10 days if we are changing their protein intakes. We provide the subjects with pre-packaged food for 10 days even before we do the three-day nitrogen balance.

LUKASKI: We know that athletes or physically active people do not have the highest quality of protein intake. Would you comment on how that would impact you data?

TARNOPOLSKY: In most of our studies, the biological value of our protein is about 0.7–0.8, so we have a typical mixed diet. A high-quality egg and milk protein diet doesn't have much relevance for the general population because most of us don't get all of our protein from egg whites and milk, but rather from a wide range of foods.

WAGENMAKERS: Shouldn't we do more research on the timing of the protein intake? The main aim of endurance exercise is to increase the concentration of the oxidative enzymes, and the main aim of strength training is to increase myofibrillar protein. The period of major adaptation leading to an increase in these proteins may only be 5 or 6 h. You may require a high protein intake in order to deliver amino acid precursors just for that brief period. I think we should do more research on that issue before we give advice for a general increase of daily protein intake. Maybe we can limit increased protein intake only to a brief adaptation period.

TARNOPOLSKY: I agree that we need to fine-tune the timing and the composition of nutrient supplements

REYES: I am concerned with the negative nitrogen balance that develops in athletes or patients who are subjected to prolonged immobilization or bed rest. Are there sufficient data to show that protein supplementation in this group of people could hasten recovery and, therefore, perhaps speed up the return to athletic competition of those athletes who get injured?

TARNOPOLSKY: In theory, a combination of high protein intake, growth factors, etc., may attenuate the negative nitrogen balance, but to date, there has not been a single study showing that either growth factors or high protein diets can change one to a positive nitrogen balance under periods of catabolic stress. Perhaps following surgery, it may be advantageous during rehabilitation with resistance exercise to have the athlete consume carbohydrate and amino acids, but this is hypothetical.

GISOLFI: Are there gender differences in sweat urea production? Is urea in sweat a function of sweat rate? What happens to sweat urea when you go on a high protein diet?

TARNOPOLSKY: There are no systematic studies that address those questions. Exercise clearly increases sweat urea, but the gender and diet effects are unclear.

5

Influence of Dietary Fat and Carbohydrate on Exercise Metabolism and Performance

EDWARD F. COYLE, PH.D.
BRADLEY J. HODGKINSON, M.A.

INTRODUCTION

The typical diet consumed by North Americans contains an energy percentage of approximately 45–50% carbohydrate and 35–40% fat, with approximately 15% derived from protein (Grandjean, 1989; Mc-Dowell, 1994). Interestingly, athletes typically eat diets that are similar to those of non-athletes (Grandjean, 1989; McDowell, 1994), although endurance athletes tend to eat slightly more carbohydrate per day due to their greater overall energy intake (Burke & Read, 1987; Burke et al., 1991; Coetzer et al., 1993; Short & Short, 1983). It is generally recommended that normally active people as well as athletes derive 60% or more of their energy from carbohydrate and approximately 25% from fat, and it appears that some segments of the population achieve these goals (Burke & Read, 1987; Short & Short, 1983).

This paper will review what is known and unknown regarding the effects on metabolism and athletic performance of diets that are relatively high in carbohydrate compared to those relatively high in fat. High-protein diets will also be briefly discussed because they have become popular. However, to maintain the focus upon the interplay between carbohydrate and fat, studies that maintained protein at approximately 10–15% of total energy will first be reviewed. Given this constant proportion of protein, a high-carbohydrate diet will be low in fat and *vice versa*. For the purposes of this review, a high-carbohydrate diet will be one that contains more than 65% carbohydrate and less than 20% fat. A high-fat diet is defined as a diet containing more than 40% fat and less than 45% carbohydrate. It should be noted that high-fat diets, by this classification, still contain sufficient carbohydrate to prevent severe ketosis. Therefore, a third diet to be discussed is one that is extremely low in carbohydrate, i.e., less than 10% carbohydrate, relatively high in fat and protein, and thus ketogenic.

Because the topic of this chapter is the effect of "chronic diets," dietary periods of at least 3 d and as long as 1 mo will be considered. Various adaptations to a given diet may require different lengths of time. For example, alterations in substrate supply may occur relatively quickly, whereas enzymatic adaptations in muscle may require longer periods. Performance in exercise and in sport is influenced by both substrate stores and by muscle metabolism; therefore, alterations in metabolism will likely be complex, depending upon the various interactions of substrate supply and metabolism.

It is difficult to control diet in freely-living people for long periods of time, especially when attempting to simultaneously control exercise training. Therefore, animal studies have obvious advantages. However, species differences sometimes make questionable the applicability of animal results to humans. For example, rats improve endurance when fasted for prolonged periods, yet people clearly demonstrate impaired performance after fasting (Dohm et al., 1983; Loy et al., 1986), probably due to species differences in the relative importance of blood glucose and muscle glycogen for supplying carbohydrate energy. In addition, dogs, but not humans, can train intensely on a high-fat diet, probably due to differences in the abilities of muscle to oxidize fat. Although this review focuses upon human responses, data from other species will be discussed, recognizing possible constraints in interpretation and applicability to people.

EARLY STUDIES OF PERFORMANCE, FUEL OXIDATION, AND MUSCLE GLYCOGEN

The link between adequate dietary carbohydrate and exercise tolerance was established early in this century. Krogh and Lindhard (1920) observed that a high-fat diet reduced the respiratory exchange ratio (RER) and increased perceived exertion, whereas Levine et al. (1924) demonstrated an association between the concentration of glucose in the blood and the physical condition of runners at the end of the Boston marathon and suggested that "adequate ingestion of carbohydrate before and during any prolonged and violent muscular effort would be of considerable benefit in preventing the hypoglycemia and accompanying development of the symptoms of exhaustion."

In a well-controlled and classic study, Christensen and Hansen (1939) reported that a high-carbohydrate diet (83% carbohydrate) enabled subjects to exercise for 210 min, whereas a high-fat diet (94% fat and probably ketogenic) reduced performance to 88 min. As shown in Table 5-1, numerous studies have since confirmed these observations. In general, it appears that the duration of exercise at an intensity of approximately 70% $\dot{V}O_2$max is reduced by more than 50% after short-term consumption of a high-fat diet, as compared to a high-carbohydrate diet. It has long been known that this performance decrement is associated with a reduced RER, indicative of reduced carbohydrate oxidation (Christensen & Hansen, 1939; Krogh & Lindhard, 1920). The classic studies of Bergstrom et al. (1967) indicated that a high-fat diet reduces muscle glycogen at the start of exercise—to a level that is only one-fifth of that achieved on a high-carbohydrate diet—and decreases endurance time to exhaustion, thus establishing the link between muscle glycogen and endurance performance. Subsequent studies have found similar results, i.e., high-fat diets reduced muscle glycogen concentrations to levels that were only 30–40% of those observed with high-carbohydrate diets (Galbo et al., 1979; Gollnick et al., 1972; Martin et al., 1978).

In the studies discussed above and outlined in Table 5-1, the high-fat diets contained less than 10% of total energy as carbohydrate, and the diets were followed for only 3–7 d. It is reasonable to ask if the effect of the high-fat diet on reducing performance would have been so severe if the high-fat diets had contained 20–40% carbohydrate, thus attenuating or preventing ketosis and the potential disturbance of acid-base balance, as discussed below. Furthermore, it has been postulated that adaptation to high-fat diets as well as to ketogenic diets requires 14 d or more (Conlee et al., 1990; Miller et al., 1984; Phinney, 1983a,b). Therefore, the responses to longer-term diets, as well as to those high-fat diets that are less ketogenic, are discussed later after a review of the metabolic responses to high-fat and high-carbohydrate diets lasting 5–7 d.

METABOLIC RESPONSES TO SHORT-TERM DIETS HIGH IN CARBOHYDRATE OR HIGH IN FAT

Substrate Availability

Muscle glycogen. As shown by the RER values in Table 5-1, oxidation of carbohydrate is high and that of fat is low for high-carbohydrate diets, and the converse is true for high-fat diets. Evidence clearly indicates that these effects are associated with muscle glycogen concentrations that are high in subjects who consume high-carbohydrate diets and low in those who consume high-fat diets (Hargreaves et al., 1995; Richter & Galbo, 1986; Sherman et al., 1993).

Blood Glucose. In addition to muscle glycogen, blood glucose is the other major source of carbohydrate energy during exercise. During prolonged exercise at approximately 70% $\dot{V}O_2$max, muscle glycogen is the predominant source of carbohydrate in the early stages of exercise, but as glycogen stores decline, blood glucose utilization by muscle increases and becomes the predominant source of carbohydrate fuel after approximately 2 h of exercise (Coyle, 1995).

The effect of exercise on blood glucose uptake and oxidation is clear, but that of diet is less so. In the resting state, high-fat diets do not appear to alter insulin-stimulated blood glucose disposal by the tissue, although the fate of the disposed glucose is affected (Cutler et al., 1995). After a high-carbohydrate diet, more of the glucose taken up by tissues

TABLE 5-1. *Early studies of diet effects on muscle glycogen, respiratory exchange ratio (RER), and exercise performance.*

Study	year	subjects	dietary composition % CHO / FAT / PRO	diet duration	mode	exercise test	glycogen content (mmol/kg ww) pre	post	RER	performance	% performance difference
Christensen & Hansen	1939	--	4/94/6 83/3/14	3 to 7 days	cycling	176 W to exhaustion	-- --	-- --	--	88 min 210 min	-58%
Bergstrom & Hultman	1967	PE students	0/46/54 82/0/18	3 days	cycling	75% $\dot{V}O_2$max to exhaustion	35 184	11 24	0.795 0.918	57 min 167 min	-66%
Gollnick	1972	students	3/46/51 57/--/--	3 days	cycling	30 min at 74% $\dot{V}O_2$max	43 144	-- --	0.89 0.98	----	--
Martin	1978	2 trained, 2 untrained	<10/--/-- >75/--/--	3 days	walking	70% $\dot{V}O_2$max to exhaustion	43 144	6 77	0.81* 0.91	33 min* 78 min	-58%*
Galbo	1979	moderately trained	10/76/14 77/10/14	4 days	running	70% $\dot{V}O_2$max to exhaustion (30 min run/ 10 min rest)	~45 ~110	~35 ~70	~0.84* ~0.95	64 min* 106 min	-39%*

CHO = carbohydrate; PRO = protein; pre = before exercise; post = after exercise; ww = wet weight; ~ indicates values estimated from graphs; -- indicates no value reported; * statistically significant difference between higher-fat and lower-fat diets.

is oxidized rather than stored (presumably as glycogen), whereas the opposite is the case after a high-fat diet. How these resting studies using insulin to stimulate glucose uptake apply to exercise-induced glucose uptake is not certain.

In an early study of four subjects, Martin et al. (1978) showed that as dietary carbohydrate increased from less than 10% to roughly 50% to greater than 75% of energy intake the arteriovenous difference of blood glucose in the leg after 30 min of treadmill exercise increased from 0.25 mM to 0.34 mM to 0.52 mM. Furthermore, exercise time to exhaustion was closely correlated with the fractional usage of carbohydrates for energy (r = 0.86). This suggests that the high-fat intake reduced blood glucose use, whereas high-carbohydrate intake increased it. When blood glucose uptake was measured with stable-isotope tracers, the rate of glucose uptake during consumption of a diet containing 66% of energy as carbohydrate was three times greater than after a eucaloric ketogenic diet containing less than 10% of energy as carbohydrate (Phinney et al., 1983a,b). Accordingly, blood glucose oxidation provided 28% of total energy expenditure for the high-carbohydrate diet but only 9% of energy expenditure for the ketogenic condition.

On the contrary, Jansson and Kaijser (1982b) reported that after 6 min of exercise, glucose extraction by the exercising legs (65% $\dot{V}O_2$max) was not different on a high-carbohydrate, compared to a high-fat, diet. In another study of 20 subjects, Jansson and Kaijser (1982a) also failed to observe significant differences in glucose extraction by legs muscles exercised for 25 min after the two dietary regimens (Figure 5-1).

Helge et al. (1996) concluded that blood glucose utilization was decreased after 7 wk of consumption of a high-fat diet because RER was lower and the rate of muscle glycogen utilization (calculated from preexercise and postexercise muscle biopsies and total exercise time) was similar, regardless of whether subjects had consumed a high-fat or high-carbohydrate diet. However, because exercise duration differed significantly (65 min versus 102 min) and the rate of glycogen utilization decreases as glycogen stores become depleted (Hargreaves et al., 1995; Richter & Galbo, 1986), calculation of the rate of muscle glycogen utilization is questionable in this instance. Conversely, when both dietary groups were fed a high-carbohydrate diet for another week, glucose clearance appeared to be impaired. In this case, for both groups RER and total glycogen use were identical. However, because exercise duration was reduced in subjects who adapted to a high-fat diet and then were exposed to a high-carbohydrate diet for 1 wk, the rate of muscle glycogen utilization must have been equal to or greater than the rate of glycogen use in subjects fed only the high-carbohydrate diet. As RER was identical throughout the trial, blood glucose oxidation in the high-fat

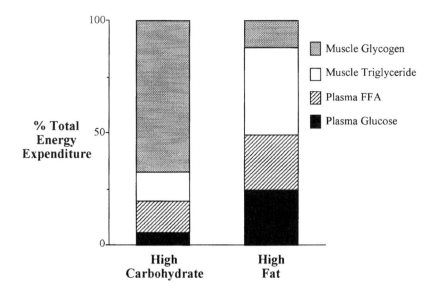

FIGURE 5-1. *The effects of consuming either a high-carbohydrate or a high-fat diet for 5 d on estimated percentage contribution of muscle glycogen, intramuscular triglycerides, plasma FFA, and plasma glucose to total caloric expenditure in 10 subjects after 23 min of exercise at 65% VO_2max.* Data were calculated from leg oxygen extraction, respiratory exchange ratio, gross extraction of FFA, and arterial-femoral venous difference for glucose. Total oxygen extraction from the leg was 4% greater after the high-fat diet. Redrawn from Figure 6 of Jannson and Kaijser (1982a).

group must have been less than or equal to glucose oxidation in the high-carbohydrate group. Blood glucose concentration was also elevated in the subjects who were fed a high-fat diet followed by 1 wk of high-carbohydrate ingestion, suggestive of reduced blood glucose clearance. Research using more direct measures is required to clarify these issues.

Gollnick et al. (1981) and Hargreaves et al. (1992) suggested that muscle glucose uptake and glycogen concentration are inversely related, and this has led to the hypothesis that the lower muscle glycogen content characteristic of high-fat diets might somehow increase glucose uptake. In isolated rat muscle, basal (Hespel & Richter, 1990; Jensen et al., 1997), insulin-stimulated (Jensen et al., 1997), and contraction-stimulated (Hespel & Richter, 1990) glucose uptakes have been inversely correlated with glycogen concentration. However, Hargreaves et al. (1995) observed that in exercising humans, the rate of whole-body glucose uptake (presumably by exercising muscle) is not influenced when muscle glycogen is reduced from 96.2 to 53.7 mmol/kg wet weight. Weltan et al.

(1998) also found that the rate of glucose oxidation, determined by radiolabeled tracer analysis, was unaffected by reducing pre-exercise muscle glycogen concentration from 134 to 80 mmol/kg wet weight when euglycemia was maintained. However, concentrations of circulating hormones and free fatty acids were not controlled in these human studies, and these variables differed significantly in the low- and high-glycogen trials (Hargreaves et al., 1995; Weltan et al., 1998); these differences may have had an impact on glucose uptake, masking the independent effects of glycogen concentration on muscle glucose uptake and oxidation. Notwithstanding the limitations of the experiments discussed above, there is no evidence that dietary-induced alterations of in-vivo muscle glycogen concentration in humans exert much of an influence on muscle glucose uptake during exercise.

High-fat diets also lower liver glycogen concentrations, and this will reduce the availability of blood glucose for energy unless gluconeogenesis is greatly increased to compensate for the reduction in glycogen. Nilsson and Hultman (1973) found that liver glycogen content was reduced from overnight-fasted values by more than 80% when six subjects consumed a very low-carbohydrate diet (6 g/d) for 4–10 d, whereas eating a subsequent high-carbohydrate diet (>400 g/d) for 2–3 d more than doubled liver glycogen content when compared to the overnight-fasted values.

It would seem advantageous for high-fat diets to inhibit blood glucose uptake by muscle during exercise in an attempt to better match the reduction in liver glucose output and thus prevent hypoglycemia. Compared to people, rats rely very heavily upon blood glucose for carbohydrate energy during exercise and also have a remarkable ability for gluconeogenesis (Torgan et al., 1990). As discussed below, in rats, prolonged fasting or a high-fat diet clearly reduces liver glycogen use and increases endurance (Miller et al., 1984). This is probably due to marked increases in gluconeogenesis. Because people appear to have much less ability to increase gluconeogenesis with fasting or with high-fat diets and because people rely more upon muscle glycogen for energy during exercise, fasting markedly impairs exercise performance, and the benefits of high-fat diets are not obvious in humans.

Plasma Free Fatty Acids. The two substrates for fat oxidation are triglyceride stored in adipocytes and that stored in lipid droplets directly inside the muscle fibers (intramuscular triglyceride, IMTG). Adipocyte triglyceride is hydrolyzed to free fatty acids (FFA), which are mobilized in the circulation by binding to albumin in plasma. The release of FFA from adipocytes into the blood is largely influenced by hormonal factors, with catecholamines stimulating lipolysis (Fain & Garcia-Sainz, 1983) and insulin inhibiting lipolysis (Hales et al., 1978).

Numerous experiments have demonstrated higher plasma FFA concentrations at rest and during exercise following consumption of a low-carbohydrate, fat-rich diet (Galbo et al., 1979; Jansson & Kaijser, 1982a; Martin et al., 1978; Maughan et al., 1978; Phinney et al., 1983a,b; Starling et al., 1997). Because the uptake and oxidation of plasma fatty acids largely depend on plasma FFA concentration and metabolic rate (Hagenfeldt & Wahren, 1968; Havel et al., 1967a, 1967b), plasma fatty acid oxidation during exercise would be expected to increase with a diet-induced increased concentration of plasma FFA. Jansson and Kaijser (1982a) measured an 82% greater extraction of plasma FFA during exercise after subjects had consumed for 5 d a high-fat diet compared to high-carbohydrate diet. About 30% of the total increase in fat oxidation after the high-fat diet could be explained by the increase in FFA extraction, with the remainder presumably explained by increased IMTG oxidation (Figure 5-1).

However, the extent to which the fatty acids that are taken up by muscle are either oxidized or reesterified is not clear. The higher concentrations of plasma glycerol observed during exercise after a high-fat diet (Galbo et al. 1979; Maughan et al., 1978) suggest that lipolysis is increased in response to high-fat diets. Therefore, it seems reasonable to expect that oxidation of plasma FFA is increased on a high-fat diet compared to high-carbohydrate diet and that this is responsible for a significant fraction of the increase in total fat oxidation.

Intramuscular Triglyceride. It has long been recognized that plasma FFA uptake provides only one-third to two-thirds of the total fatty acids for oxidation during exercise; thus, intramuscular triglyceride stores must be an important substrate for oxidation (Carlson et al., 1971; Costill et al., 1973; Essen, 1977; Froberg & Mossfeldt, 1971; Paul, 1970). Unfortunately, it is technically difficult to measure IMTG concentration. Furthermore, a lack of change in IMTG before and after exercise does not indicate a lack of IMTG hydrolysis because there can be simultaneous IMTG synthesis from plasma FFA while IMTG hydrolysis is occurring (Guo & Jensen, 1998).

Abumrad et al. (1978) found an almost threefold greater IMTG content in the diaphragms of rats fed lard for 10–11 d, as compared to rats fed a high-carbohydrate diet. Interestingly, this excess fat appeared to be clustered around the mitochondria. Jansson and Kaijser (1982a) reported that intramuscular triglyceride concentration before exercise was approximately twofold greater after a high-fat diet compared to high-carbohydrate diet. However, they were unable to detect a significant decline in IMTG concentration during exercise. However, IMTG use, when calculated from leg RQ and FFA uptake, was threefold greater after the high-fat diet. Therefore, because the increase in fat oxidation is greater than what can be accounted for by the increase in plasma FFA uptake, it seems reasonable to expect that oxidation of IMTG would increase after a high-fat diet.

Conlee et al (1990) found a 53% reduction in IMTG after about 110 min of treadmill running in rats adapted to a diet without carbohydrates, whereas rats fed a high-carbohydrate diet displayed no net degradation of IMTG during exercise. Initial IMTG stores were more than double (5.4 versus 2.5 (mol/g) in the fat-adapted rats.

In addition to increased triglyceride storage, reduced stores of muscle glycogen may drive part of the increase in fat oxidation following a high-fat diet. Starling et al. (1997) examined endurance athletes who were fed either a high-carbohydrate or high-fat diets for 12 h after exhaustive cycling exercise. Muscle glycogen was not restored to pre-exercise levels, but, surprisingly, IMTG stores were greatly elevated on the high-fat diet (44.7 and 27.5 mmol/kg dry weight for high-fat and high-carbohydrate diets, respectively). The high-fat diet increased fat oxidation during an ensuing 1600 kJ time trial, possibly by enhancing lipolysis, because plasma glycerol was elevated throughout exercise. However, after the high-fat diet, subjects were unable to exercise at the intensities achieved after the high-carbohydrate diet, with the largest discrepancies occurring late in the time trial. Apparently, the increase in triglyceride availability in the muscle was unable to compensate for the reduced muscle glycogen; thus, performance was impaired (139.9 min and 117.1 min for high-fat and high-carbohydrate diets, respectively).

Overall Metabolic Stress

Phosphorylation State. Larson et al. (1994) used ^{31}P-magnetic resonance spectroscopy to examine the metabolic state of the quadriceps during incremental exercise to exhaustion after 5 d of a high-carbohydrate diet or high-fat diet. Exercise duration was reduced on the high-fat diet. With the technique used, metabolic stress was assessed by the change in PCr/P_I, the ratio of the concentrations of phosphocreatine (PCr) and inorganic phosphate (P_i), for a given increase in $\dot{V}O_2$. The high-fat diet was associated with a greater fall in PCr/P_i as $\dot{V}O_2$ increased. This is indicative of increased metabolic stress and greater disturbance of cellular homeostasis after the high-fat diet, presumably due to reduced glycolytic flux as a result of a low concentration of muscle glycogen. It is also possible that a reduced ability to oxidize pyruvate limits ATP production, as discussed below. Therefore, high-fat diets in people appear to impair intracellular phosphorylation potential; thus, exercise at a given $\dot{V}O_2$ becomes more metabolically stressful.

Although the stimulus for mitochondrial biogenesis in response to exercise training is not exactly clear, it may be related to the intracellular phosphorylation state of muscle (Williams & Neufer, 1996). If this is the case, high-fat diets might be expected to induce greater increases in mitochondrial content, compared to high-carbohydrate diets, in response to exercise training performed at a given absolute $\dot{V}O_2$. However, high-carbohydrate diets allow exercise to be performed at a higher absolute $\dot{V}O_2$, which also would be effective in stimulating mitochondrial biogenesis. Therefore, it is doubtful that the stimulus for mitochondrial biogenesis would be greater on a high-fat diet than on a high-carbohydrate diet.

Pyruvate Dehydrogenase Activity. Pyruvate dehydrogenase activity increases acutely during exercise in response to increased oxidative metabolism and increased glycolytic flux (Putman et al., 1993). During exercise after a high-fat diet, the activity of this enzyme increases at a lower rate, compared to a high-carbohydrate diet. In association with this observation, muscle acetyl-CoA and acetylcarnitine content and the acetyl-CoA-to-CoASH ratio decreased after the high-fat diet but increased in the high-carbohydrate diet (Putman et al., 1993). The decline in muscle acetyl-CoA and acetylcarnitine content after the high-fat diet is indicative of suboptimal flux of substrate into the mitochondria from both the glycolytic pathway and from fatty acid metabolism. This pattern is indicative of greater metabolic stress after a high-fat diet and is consistent with the ^{31}P-magnetic resonance spectroscopy evidence of impaired phosphorylation potential. This also agrees with the report of Jansson and Kaijser (1984), who noted greater pyruvate release during exercise after a high-fat diet, in spite of a smaller lactate release. They interpreted their results to indicate a decreased activity of pyruvate dehydrogenase and/or a decreased NADH:NAD ratio after a high-fat diet.

Diet Effects on Hormonal Responses to Exercise

Galbo et al. (1979) measured hormonal responses during treadmill running at 70% of $\dot{V}O_2$max after subjects consumed either a high-fat diet or a high-carbohydrate diet. Time to exhaustion was longer for the high-carbohydrate treatment (106 vs. 64 min). Plasma norepinephrine increased and insulin decreased similarly in the high-fat and high-carbohydrate conditions. However, the increases in glucagon, epinephrine, growth hormone, and cortisol, all hormones that stimulate liver glucose output and/or gluconeogenesis, were greater after the high-fat diets. These hormonal responses are also reported in resting individuals who have undergone prolonged fasting (Boyle et al., 1989; Cryer 1996).

Jansson and Kaijser (1982c) examined diet-induced changes in sympathoadrenal activity during submaximal exercise after 5 d on a high-fat and carbohydrate-poor diet (5% carbohydrate, 72% fat, and 23% protein) or after 5 d on a high-carbohydrate diet (78% carbohydrate, 8% fat, and 14% protein). Surprisingly, $\dot{V}O_2$, heart rate, and plasma norepinephrine concentrations during exercise were higher on the high-fat diet. It is not clear how much of the increase in plasma norepinephrine was mediated by the diet *per se* or by the dietary-induced increase in $\dot{V}O_2$.

Diet Effects on Muscle Enzymes

Mitochondrial Enzymes of the Tricarboxcylic Acid Cycle. In addition to provoking changes in substrate availability, increased dietary fat has been hypothesized to produce changes in activities of skeletal muscle enzymes that promote the oxidation of fat at rest and during exercise as a result of increased flux through specific enzymatic pathways (Fitch & Chaikoff, 1960). Whether or not a high-fat diet induces increases in the activities of tricarboxylic-acid-cycle enzymes in the mitochondria of skeletal muscle is not clear. Some investigators have claimed increased $\dot{V}O_2$max, presumably as a result of an increased mitochondrial content in the contracting muscles, to be a result of fat-adaptation (Langfort et al., 1996; Muoio et al., 1994; Simi et al., 1991). However, direct evidence for a high-fat diet-induced increase in mitochondria is limited. Simi et al. (1991) observed in rats that 12 wk of a high-fat diet in the absence of physical training increased citrate synthase activity in the soleus and red quadriceps, increased $\dot{V}O_2$max by 13%, and improved submaximal running endurance by 64%. When training was performed in conjunction with the high-fat diet, further improvements in the oxidative capacity of red muscle, $\dot{V}O_2$max, and endurance were seen (Simi et al., 1991).

Cheng et al. (1997) found in rats no increase in citrate synthase activity after 4 wk of training on either a high-fat diet or a high-carbohydrate diet. After an additional 2 wk of increased training volume, citrate synthase activity increased in the red portion of the vastus lateralis, but not in the soleus, on the high-fat diet only (Cheng et al., 1997). Miller et al. (1984) found inconsistent changes in citrate synthase activity after both 1 and 5 wk of diet involving high fat consumption without training, whereas time to exhaustion was increased at both time points.

Evidence that high-fat diets induce increases in the mitochondrial content of human skeletal muscle is lacking. Untrained humans undergoing 7 wk of endurance training increased citrate synthase activity to the same extent (17–18%), whether fed a high-fat or a high-carbohydrate diet (Helge & Kiens, 1997) (Figure 5-2). In contrast to the typical increase in citrate synthase activity resulting solely from a fat-rich diet in animals, citrate synthase activity was not increased in human subjects not undergoing training, regardless of diet (Helge & Kiens, 1997) (Figure 5-2). In

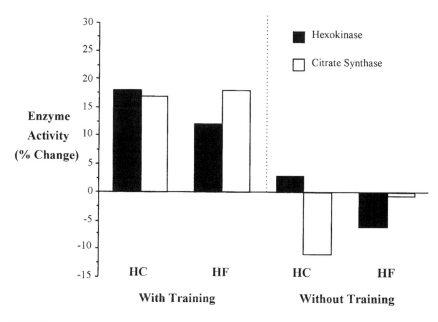

FIGURE 5-2. *Percent change in activities of hexokinase and citrate synthase measured in samples from vastus lateralis muscle of trained and control groups after 7 wk of adaptation to endurance training and a high-fat (HF) or a high-carbohydrate (HC) diet.* Citrate synthase and hexokinase activities increased in the pooled trained groups (HF and HC with training; P<0.05) but not in the pooled untrained groups (HF and HC without training). The increase in citrate synthase and hexokinase activities was not significantly different between the pooled HC diet groups and the pooled HF diet groups. Data from Helge and Kiens (1997).

humans, training, but not diet alone, seems able to induce increases in the mitochondrial content of skeletal muscle (Figure 5-2).

Enzymes of Beta-Oxidation. After only a 1-wk adaptation to a high-fat diet, Miller et al. (1984) observed 35% and 51% increases in β-hydroxyacyl-CoA-dehydrogenase (HAD) activity in the soleus and red vastus lateralis muscle, respectively, of untrained rats, with increases of 98% in the soleus and 77% in the red vastus lateralis observed after 5 wk of training. In agreement, Simi et al. (1991) reported in sedentary rats a roughly 75% greater HAD activity after 12 wk of a high-fat diet compared to a high-carbohydrate diet. Training of the animals on the high-fat diet induced a 100% increase in HAD, and training with a high-carbohydrate diet induced a 30% increase in HAD. These increases in fat oxidative capacity could be induced by greater metabolic stress during training due to low carbohydrate availability and, therefore, might not occur in conditions of voluntary training in which intensity is most often determined by perceived exertion. However, even when rats were trained only by voluntary wheel running, HAD and carnitine palmitoyl transferase I activity levels in the soleus were greater after 2 wk of consumption of a high-fat diet (Cheng et al., 1997). Rats fed a high-fat diet tended to run further than did rats on a high-carbohydrate diet. Therefore, it seems that a high-fat diet, by itself, can bring about increases in fat oxidative capacity, and training in combination with a high-fat diet can enhance this response.

Increases in the activities of β-oxidation enzymes as an adaptation to fat-rich diets may occur, but perhaps to a lesser extent in humans than in rats. Carnitine palmitoyl transferase I activity increased 35% when moderately trained men switched from their habitual diets to a eucaloric, ketogenic diet for 4 wk, without altering their training (Fisher et al., 1983). Conversely, Kiens et al. (1987) found no changes in the HAD activity of trained men subjected to a high-fat diet. Helge and Kiens (1997) found a 25% increase in HAD in untrained humans following 7 wk of adaptation to a high-fat diet, irrespective of whether or not subjects underwent training during this period (Figure 5-3). Helge and Kiens (1997) suggested that the increase in fat oxidative enzymes and fat oxidation normally observed after endurance training is the result of insufficient carbohydrate stores and a consequent increased flux through fat oxidative pathways. Although not always observed, it seems likely that a high-fat diet alone induces increases in HAD activity, and, at least in rats, a high-fat diet in combination with training induces further adaptation in fat oxidative capacity. However, whether or not the increased capacity to oxidize fatty acids induced by high-fat diets confers metabolic performance advantages during exercise is unknown. Helge et al. (1996) have shown that even after restoration of muscle glycogen stores by a 7-d carbohydrate loading period, subjects who had previously adapted to a high-fat diet had inferior performance when compared to subjects who had consumed a high-carbohydrate diet for the entire 8 wk.

ADAPTATIONS OF EXERCISE PERFORMANCE TO HIGH-CARBOHYDRATE OR HIGH-FAT DIETS

Endurance-Trained Subjects

Benefits of a High-Carbohydrate Diet. Investigators in several studies have altered dietary fat and carbohydrate intake in an attempt to increase endurance exercise performance in endurance-trained subjects during a period of maintained or increased training intensity. The interaction of diet and training seems most important because a major goal of

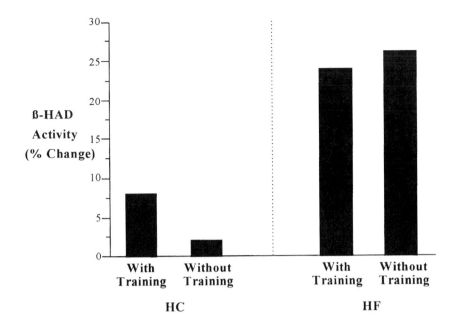

FIGURE 5-3. *Percent change in maximal activity of β-hydroxyacyl-CoA-dehydrogenase (β-HAD) measured in samples from vastus lateralis muscle of trained and control groups after 7 wk of adaptation to training and a high-fat diet (HF) or a high-carbohydrate diet (HC).* The increase in β-HAD activity was significantly greater for the pooled HF diet groups than for the pooled HC diet groups. No differences were detected when the pooled trained groups were compared with the pooled untrained groups. Data from Helge and Kiens (1997).

an optimal diet is to promote increases in training intensity, a prerequisite to improved performance.

Simonsen et al. (1991) conducted a well-controlled study of competitive rowers during the early portion of their season. Four weeks of intense training in combination with a high-carbohydrate diet (70% carbohydrate, 10 g·kg^{-1}·d^{-1}) systematically increased muscle glycogen content each week, whereas glycogen was maintained at baseline levels in subjects on a 43% fat diet (42% carbohydrate, 5 g·kg^{-1}·d^{-1}) (Figure 5-4). Power outputs in 2500-m rowing time trials were recorded three times weekly during the experiment. Although performance throughout the experiment was usually somewhat better for subjects consuming the high-carbohydrate diet, only for the final test after 4 wk of training was a significant effect of diet detected. At that time, power output was increased 10.7% on the high-carbohydrate diet, whereas on the moderate-carbohydrate diet mean power output increased only 1.6% (Simonsen et al., 1991). As shown in Figure 5-4, performance was somewhat variable, especially in the moderate-carbohydrate group. Although subjects in both diet groups were able to complete their daily training, the differences in time-trial performance tended to become more pronounced the longer the diet and training regimens were continued. In this experiment, chronic adaptations in muscle glycogen and in performance were more apparent in subjects who consumed the high-carbohydrate diet.

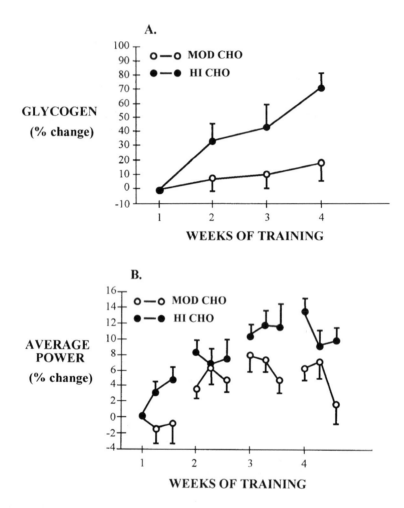

FIGURE 5-4. *Panel A. Percent change in muscle glycogen from day 1 for MOD CHO (5 g carbohydrate· kg body mass^{-1}· d^{-1}) and HI CHO (10 g carbohydrate· kg body mass^{-1}· d^{-1}) groups during 4 wk of intense twice-daily rowing training. Panel B. Overall average power on a rowing ergometer expressed as percent change from performance on day 1. Power output for three 2,500–m time trials was averaged and expressed as percent change from the overall average power output on day 1 of training. Redrawn from Simonsen et al. (1991).*

In an early study, Pruett (1970) observed performance decrements in moderately trained men who consumed a 26% carbohydrate, 69% fat diet (i.e., a high-fat diet) when compared to a high-carbohydrate diet (82% carbohydrate, 9% fat diet) (Table 5-2). After 14 d of diet manipulation and training to maintain aerobic capacity, subjects on the high-fat diet were able to exercise at 70% $\dot{V}O_2$max for only 164 min, whereas subjects on the high-carbohydrate diet could continue for 193 min (Pruett, 1970).

Moderate changes in dietary fat and carbohydrate consumption for about 1 wk do not seem to affect exercise performance in tests lasting about 1 h. For example, in both runners and cyclists Sherman et al. (1993) observed no difference in time to exhaustion at 80% $\dot{V}O_2$max following 60 min of submaximal exercise and 5 1-min sprints between groups of subjects who consumed either 42% or 84% carbohydrate for 1 wk (Table 5-2). In another study, a 40% carbohydrate diet for 7 d did not adversely affect 10-km running performance when compared to a diet containing 55–70% carbohydrate, (Pitsiladis et al., 1996) (Table 5-2). No differences were found in plasma concentrations of lactate, glucose, glycerol, or free fatty acids throughout exercise, although total carbohydrate oxidation was significantly greater in the high-carbohydrate group (171 g vs. 131 g), implying that muscle glycogen content and oxidation were greater in the high-carbohydrate trial.

Experiments that elevate muscle glycogen stores with 3-d carbohydrate-loading diets have observed no performance benefit for endurance athletes in events lasting 60–90 min (Hawley et al., 1997; Madsen et al., 1990). This raises the possibility that high-carbohydrate diets are of little benefit to athletes who compete in events lasting 60–90 min, possibly because muscle glycogen does not limit performance in such events. Perhaps longer durations (14–28 d) of dietary manipulation (Pruett, 1970; Simonsen et al., 1991) are required to produce significant adaptations in exercise performance lasting about 60–90 min.

Putative Benefits of a High-Fat Diet. In contrast to the experiments cited above, Muoio et al. (1994) claimed improved exercise time to exhaustion when dietary fat intake was increased from 15% to 38% in collegiate runners. Time to fatigue at 75–80% $\dot{V}O_2$max increased from 75.8 min to 91.2 min after a test of $\dot{V}O_2$max and 30 min of running at 85% $\dot{V}O_2$max (Muoio et al., 1994). They also claimed that 7 d of adaptation to the increased dietary fat improved $\dot{V}O_2$max (66.4 ml·kg^{-1}·min^{-1} on the increased fat diet vs. 59.6 ml·kg^{-1}·min^{-1} on the reduced fat diet), which they speculated was a result of a higher oxygen cost of ATP production from fat oxidation. Although improbable, it is theoretically possible that only 7 d of increased dietary fat induced enhancement of the activities of the enzymes involved in β-oxidation of fatty acids and in the tricarboxylic acid cycle, resulting in a greater maximal respiratory capacity of

TABLE 5-2. *Adaptations of exercise performance to manipulations of diets lasting 7–28 d in endurance-trained subjects.*

Study	year	subjects	dietary composition % CHO/FAT/PRO	diet duration	mode	exercise test	glycogen content (mmol/kg ww) pre	glycogen content (mmol/kg ww) post	RER	performance	% performance difference
Simonsen	1991	trained collegiate rowers	42/43/15 70/17/13	28 days	rowing	2500 meter time trial (mean work output)	124 155	-- --	-- --	192 W mean work output 207 W mean work output	-7%*
Pruett	1970	moderately trained	26/69/10 59/31/10 82/9/9	14 days	cycling and running	70% V̇O₂max to exhaustion (alternating running and cycling every 45 minutes with 15 min rest periods)	-- -- --	-- -- --	-- -- --	164 min 187 min 193 min	-15%
Sherman	1993	trained runners and cyclists	42/--/-- 84/--/--	7 days	running or cycling	80% V̇O₂max to exhaustion after 60 min at 75% V̇O₂max and 5 one minute sprints at 100% V̇O₂max	~90 ~138	-- --	-- --	cyclists: 550s; runners: 613s; cyclists: 560s; runners: 613s	no difference
Pitsiladis	1996	trained runners	40/44/14 55/--/-- 2d, then 70/--/--3d	7 days	running	10 km time trial	-- -- --	-- -- --	0.87 0.92	48.6 min 48.8 min	0%
Muoio	1994	collegiate runners	50/38/12 61/24/14 73/15/12	7 days	running	30 min @ 85% V̇O₂max, then 75–80% V̇O₂max to exhaustion	-- -- --	-- -- --	~0.92 ~0.92 ~0.92	91.2 min* 69.3 min 75.8 min	+20%*

CHO = carbohydrate; PRO = protein; pre = before exercise; post = after exercise; RER = respiratory exchange ratio; ww = wet weight; ~ indicates values estimated from graphs; -- indicates no value reported; * statistically significant difference between higher-fat and lower-fat diets.

the mitochondria in muscle; such a phenomenon has been postulated to occur in rats (Simi et al., 1991). Although Muoio et al. (1994) concluded that low-fat diets are detrimental to endurance performance, their finding that endurance time to exhaustion was enhanced by consumption of increased amounts of dietary fat is puzzling because they detected no difference in fat oxidation between trials; furthermore, plasma glycerol concentration, a rough indicator of lipolysis, was lower after consumption of the fat-rich diet. Interpretation of the results of this study should be tempered by the fact that the trials were not randomized, and it is well known that training intensity varies greatly throughout the season in collegiate runners.

Untrained Subjects

In rats, a high-fat diet can induce adaptations that increase the capacity of skeletal muscle to oxidize fat (Miller et al., 1984; Simi et al., 1991), and the effects of endurance training seem to be additive to the beneficial enzymatic adaptations derived from a high-fat diet alone (Simi et al., 1991). Therefore, Helge et al. (1996) determined whether or not humans who performed endurance training for 7 wk while consuming a high-fat diet would enhance their capacity to oxidize fat and thus improve endurance performance more than a group trained on a high-carbohydrate diet (Table 5-3). Consumption of a 62% fat diet increased skeletal muscle HAD activity, regardless of whether subjects were trained or not (Figure 5-3), and training increased citrate synthase and hexokinase activities (Figure 5-2), regardless of diet (Helge & Kiens, 1997). Fat oxidation during exercise was enhanced by the high-fat diet. Training 3–4 times weekly for 60–75 min at 50–85% $\dot{V}O_2$max for 7 wk resulted in 11% increases in $\dot{V}O_2$max in both dietary groups (Helge et al., 1996). However, subjects trained and fed a high-fat diet for 7 wk had lower resting muscle glycogen contents and had 34% lower performance times to exhaustion at 81% of pre-training $\dot{V}O_2$max than did subjects trained and fed a high-carbohydrate diet (Figure 5-5, Table 5-3).

The sub-optimal performance improvements in the high-fat group did not appear to be due to acute lack of carbohydrate; restoration of glycogen stores did not equalize performance. During the eighth week of the experiment, glycogen levels for the high-fat subjects were raised (to levels higher than those in subjects fed high-carbohydrate diets for 7 wk) by having them switch to a high-carbohydrate diet. Still, following this increase in glycogen, although RER during exercise was identical in the two groups, performance remained 25% lower in the original high-fat group (Figure 5-5). It was concluded that ingestion of a high-fat diet during training induces sub-optimal adaptations in response to training. Apparently, the increases in oxidative capacity for fat that were induced

TABLE 5-3. Effects of manipulations of diets for 28–56 d on muscle glycogen, respiratory exchange ratio (RER), and exercise performance in untrained subjects.

Study	year	subjects	dietary composition % CHO/FAT/PRO	diet duration	mode	exercise test	glycogen content (mmol/kg ww) pre	post	RER	performance	% performance difference
Untrained Subjects											
Helge	1996	untrained	22/62/16 65/20/15	49 days (diet and training)	cycling	81% pretraining VO_2max to exhaustion	128 152	77 74	~0.81 ~0.88	65 min* 102 min	−36%*
			then both groups: 65/20/15 (1 wk)	56 days total (diet and training)	cycling	81% pretraining VO_2max to exhaustion	185 140	116 73	~0.87 ~0.87	77 min* 102 min	−25%*
Helge	1998	untrained	21/62/18 64/21/15	28 days (diet and training)	cycling	80% pretraining VO_2max to exhaustion	131 186	-- --	~0.84* ~0.94	79.3min 78.5min	1%
			21/62/18 64/21/15	42 days (diet and training)	cycling	80% pretraining VO_2max to exhaustion	-- --	-- --	-- --	~79 min ~120 min	−34%*

CHO = carbohydrate; PRO = protein; pre = before exercise; post = after exercise; ww = wet weight; ~ indicates values estimated from graphs; -- indicates no value reported; * statistically significant difference between higher-fat and lower-fat diets. Data from Helge et al. (1996) and Helge et al. (1998).

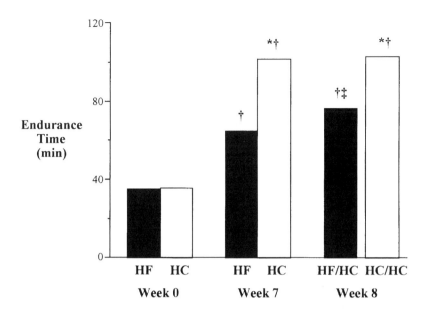

FIGURE 5-5. *Effects of Diet on Time to exhaustion at 81% of pretraining $\dot{V}O_2max$*. Measurements were made before training (Week 0) and after 7 and 8 wk of training while consuming either a high-fat diet (HF) or a high-carbohydrate diet (HC). During the 8th week, the HF group switched to the HC diet (HF/HC), while the HC group continued consuming the HC diet (HC/HC). *P<0.05 between HF and HC; †P<0.05 between week 0 and week 7 values; ‡P<0.05 between week 7 and week 8 values. Data from Helge et al. (1996).

by the high-fat diet (Helge and Kiens, 1997) did not influence exercise metabolism when glycogen content was restored (Helge et al., 1996).

In a later study with a similar protocol, Helge et al. (1998) observed no difference in $\dot{V}O_2max$ nor in submaximal endurance performance after 4 wk of training in combination with a high-fat diet, compared to training with a high-carbohydrate diet. It is likely that when subjects are initially untrained, performance improvements are largely due to the general cardiovascular and metabolic adaptations that occur robustly on either diet. However, when four subjects continued the training and diet regimen for an additional 2 wk, those consuming a high-carbohydrate diet continued to improve their endurance at 81% $\dot{V}O_2max$, whereas those consuming a high-fat diet did not improve further. Helge et al. (1998) suggested that an increased activity of the sympathetic nervous system seen after 6 wk of training on a high-fat diet, but not after only 4 wk, may have produced a detrimental effect of the fat-rich diet. Together, these studies cast much doubt on the hypothesis that a fat-rich diet is beneficial to performance of untrained subjects.

LOW-CARBOHYDRATE KETOGENIC DIETS

Long-Term Diets and Performance

Phinney et al. (1983a,b) conducted a unique study in which endurance-trained cyclists were asked to maintain their normal training for 1 wk while consuming a "normal" diet containing 1.75 g protein·kg^{-1}·d^{-1}, with 66% of the remaining energy as carbohydrate and 33% as fat, followed by 4 wk of training while consuming a eucaloric ketogenic diet that contained the same amount of protein but less than 20 g of carbohydrate per day (Table 5-4). The diets maintained body weight over the 5-wk period. Endurance performance in these well-trained cyclists was assessed as time to fatigue during cycling exercise at 62–64% $\dot{V}O_2$max.

Mean performance times were comparable on the normal and ketogenic diets (147 vs. 151 min), although there was great variability in performance, with individual changes in performance following the high-fat diet ranging from a 57% improvement to a 36% decrement. Other research has shown that well-trained cyclists can exercise for 180 min at intensities greater than 62–64% $\dot{V}O_2$max and that fatigue is associated with very low muscle glycogen concentrations (i.e., less than 30 mmol/kg wet weight), hypoglycemia, and a precipitous decline in RER (Coggan & Coyle, 1991). It is possible that the well-trained cyclists of Phinney et al. (1983a,b) were not truly exhausted after 147 min of exercise on the normal diet. Consistent with this hypothesis are the facts that, on average, the duration of their exercise was relatively brief, they apparently did not exhibit hypoglycemia (plasma glucose = 4.43 mM), and they had a relatively high concentration of muscle glycogen (53 mmol/kg wet weight) at fatigue.

The most remarkable finding of Phinney et al. (1983a,b) was the low RER values, i.e., 0.72 and 0.83 for high-fat and normal diets, respectively (Table 5-4). For the high-fat diet, the low RER values were associated with high plasma FFA concentrations and low initial muscle glycogen concentrations (76 mmol/kg wet weight), both of which would favor fat oxidation over carbohydrate oxidation. It is not clear how much of this shift in substrate oxidation was due simply to altered substrate availability or to enzymatic and other adaptations in the muscle that led to increased fat oxidation. Also, RER and the calculated rate of carbohydrate oxidation may have been underestimated in the ketogenic diet trial because both ketogenesis and gluconeogenesis from amino acids probably contributed to a lower whole body RER (Schutz & Ravussin, 1980).

It should be noted that Phinney commented in a personal communication that cyclists fed the ketogenic diet were limited in their ability

TABLE 5-4. *Effects of low-carbohydrate, ketogenic diets on muscle glycogen, respiratory exchange ratio (RER), and exercise performance.*

Study	year	subjects	dietary composition % CHO/FAT/PRO	diet duration	mode	exercise test	glycogen content (mmol/kg ww) pre	post	RER	performance	% performance difference
Phinney	1983	well trained	--/90/--	28 days	cycling	63% V̇O₂max	76	56	0.72*	151 min	+3%
			66/--/--	7 days		to exhaustion	143	53	0.85	141 min	
Lambert	1994	trained	7/67/26	14 days	cycling	90% V̇O₂max	68.1	--	1.07	8.3 min	-34%
			74/12/14			to exhaustion	120.6	--	1.15	12.5 min	
					cycling	60% V̇O₂max	32	--	0.87*	80 min*	+86%*
						to fatigue	76	--	0.92	43 min	

CHO = carbohydrate; PRO = protein; pre = before exercise; post = after exercise; ww = wet weight; -- indicates no value reported; * statistically significant difference between higher-fat and lower-fat diets.

to exercise more intensely than 64% V̇O₂max; thus, actual racing performance would certainly have been hampered in that condition. This reduced capacity for high-intensity exercise is probably caused by an inability to generate sufficient substrate for oxidative metabolism, either due to inadequate glycogen stores or to limitations in PDH activity so that insufficient acetyl-CoA is produced (Putman et al., 1993). Phinney also noted in a personal communication that a single feeding of carbohydrate for cyclists on the ketogenic diet seemed to reduce their ability to maintain an exercise intensity of 70% V̇O₂max, probably because the carbohydrate feeding reduced the rate of fat oxidation without compensating sufficiently by increasing glycogen stores and carbohydrate oxidation.

In a long-term manipulation of the diets of cyclists who were maintaining their endurance training, Lambert et al. (1994) compared the performance effects of 2 wk of adaptation to a high-fat diet (7% carbohydrate, 67% fat, 26% protein) or a high-carbohydrate diet (74% carbohydrate, 12% fat, 14% protein). Although low in carbohydrate, the high-fat diet was not ketotic because β-hydroxybutyrate concentrations were similar for both diets and at all times. Surprisingly, the high-fat diet did not impair the performance of high-intensity exercise (90% V̇O₂max or >100% V̇O₂max), and subsequent endurance time to exhaustion at 60% V̇O₂max was dramatically improved; subjects cycled 79.7 min in the high-fat trial and only 42.5 min in the high-carbohydrate trial. The relatively poor endurance at this low exercise intensity may be explained by low concentrations of muscle glycogen at the beginning of the cycling trial in both dietary conditions. Still, initial muscle glycogen stores were much greater in the high-carbohydrate than in the high-fat condition. The authors suggested that exercise at this low intensity (60%V0₂max) in a glycogen-depleted state can be extended by chronic adaptation to a high-fat diet. Whether or not such an adaptation enhances the capacity for exercise at a higher intensity when initial glycogen stores are normal is not known.

Acid-Base Balance and Performance of High-Intensity Exercise

Low-carbohydrate diets acutely induce metabolic acidosis during exercise. It is primarily the high dietary content of protein and fat that is responsible for the changes in acid-base status (Maughan et al., 1997). It is now recognized that diet can also affect the performance of high-intensity exercise of brief (2–7 min) duration. A low-carbohydrate diet (< 5% of total energy) causes a 10–30% decline in the cycling power that can be maintained for about 5 min (Maughan et al., 1997). The same effect is observed if exercise is preceded by a 24-h fast (Maughan et al., 1997). Maughan and colleagues (1997) proposed that muscular acidosis may be responsible for reduced high-intensity exercise performance, possibly due to a reduced rate of efflux of lactate and hydrogen ions from the working muscles. It is also possible that reduced substrate flux through the PDH complex may reduce aerobic energy supply during high-intensity exercise and accelerate the onset of fatigue (Maughan et al., 1997; Putman et al., 1993).

Because sodium bicarbonate can reduce diet-induced metabolic acidosis, acute ingestion of sodium bicarbonate has been used to attempt to reverse the acidosis caused by low-carbohydrate diets. However, this treatment does not appear to restore high-intensity exercise capacity, suggesting that acidosis from the consumption of a low-carbohydrate diet is not the cause of fatigue observed during high-intensity exercise (Ball et al., 1996; Ball & Maughan, 1997).

CHRONIC HIGH-FAT DIETS FOLLOWED BY ACUTE HIGH-CARBOHYDRATE DIETS

If high-fat diets do induce persistent adaptations in skeletal muscle that promote fat oxidation and true glycogen sparing during exercise when pre-exercise glycogen concentration is normal, a period of adaptation to a high-fat diet, followed by acute carbohydrate loading, might theoretically increase pre-exercise glycogen stores without proportionally increasing the rate of glycogen utilization during exercise. Improvements in endurance performance capacity would then be expected. Indeed, after 3–8 wk of adaptation to a diet of 0–25% carbohydrate, followed by 3 d of 70% carbohydrate diet, muscle and liver glycogen levels in rats were restored to levels comparable to (Conlee et al., 1990, Saitoh et al., 1996) or greater than (Lapachet et al., 1996) those in rats uniformly fed a high-carbohydrate diet. In addition, intramuscular triglyceride concentration was maintained at higher levels than those found in the rats fed high-carbohydrate, which may promote fat oxidation during exercise (Saitoh et al., 1996). Consequently, performance time to exhaustion is increased in fat-adapted, carbohydrate-loaded rats, when compared to rats fed consistently either high-fat or high-carbohydrate diets (Conlee et al., 1990; Lapachet et al., 1996).

A similar response to a high-fat diet followed by acute carbohydrate loading may occur in humans. Van Zyl et al. (1994) compared 20-km cycling performance after a high-fat diet (15% carbohydrate, 65% fat, 20% protein) or the subjects' habitual diets (53% carbohydrate, 29% fat, 18% protein) for 10 d, followed by 3 d of carbohydrate loading with a 65% carbohydrate diet. During 150 min of cycling at 70% $\dot{V}O_2$max and a subsequent simulated 20-km time trial, subjects ingested an energy drink containing 10% carbohydrate and 4.3% medium-chain triglyceride.

Adaptation to the high-fat diet and acute carbohydrate loading, in association with ingestion of the energy drink during exercise, decreased muscle glycogen oxidation and improved the performance of a 20-km time trial by 80 s. Whether or not a high-fat diet followed by acute carbohydrate loading improves endurance capacity requires further systematic study using a variety of experimental designs to definitively identify the potential effects on exercise performance.

POPULAR DIETS

The Zone Diet

The Zone diet, popularized by the *New York Times* best seller *The Zone* (Sears, 1995), has been recommended by the author for optimal athletic performance and health. The Zone diet is low in carbohydrates and low in total energy, supposedly to maximize fat oxidation. A typical 75-kg endurance athlete, exercising 2 h daily, expends 4200 kcal/d. The Zone diet would allow this athlete to consume only 2000 kcal/d and only 2.7 g of carbohydrate/kg body weight. Although Sears cites experiments in which endurance performance was not impaired (Phinney et al., 1983a,b) or was improved (Muoio et al., 1994) on diets containing a high percentage of fat, the amount of total energy and carbohydrate deprivation advocated by Sears would severely limit muscle glycogen repletion and endurance exercise performance (Loy et al., 1986). Sears also recommends that athletes who have reached their ideal body fat consume a modified "Zone" diet, in which additional fat is consumed to maintain balance between energy expenditure and energy intake. On this diet, the typical endurance athlete described above would consume 66% of total energy 17% as carbohydrate, and 17% as protein. This modified Zone diet is very similar to the diet containing 22% carbohydrate, 62% fat, and 16% protein that produced inferior endurance performance improvements, when compared to a high-carbohydrate diet, over 6 wk (Helge et al., 1998) and 7 wk (Helge et al., 1996) (Table 5-3).

40/30/30 Diet

Another popular diet recommended for endurance athletes advocates consumption of 40% carbohydrate, 30% fat, and 30% protein. Although this diet provides adequate energy and moderately high amounts of carbohydrate for a typical endurance athlete, protein intake is extremely high (4.2 g/kg), which may have deleterious consequences for health (Allen et al., 1979). The typically recommended diet for endurance athletes (60% carbohydrate, 25% fat, 15% protein) seems to have greater potential to maximize endurance performance than does either the Zone diet or the 40/30/30 diet.

RELEVANCE OF ANIMAL STUDIES TO HUMANS

Rats Versus Humans

The applicability to human metabolism of research using rats as subjects is questionable because rat metabolism differs substantially from normal human metabolism. First, resting muscle glycogen concentration in people is typically more than 4-fold greater than that in the rat (i.e., 125 vs. 30 mmol/kg wet weight). Furthermore, rats rely much more heavily upon liver glycogen and gluconeogenesis for carbohydrate fuel when compared to humans (Torgan et al., 1990). Torgan et al. (1990) (Figure 5-6) showed that when rats exercise at 75% $\dot{V}O_2$max, their RER values, and thus their relative rates of oxidation of fat and carbohydrate, are similar to those of humans (Coggan & Coyle, 1991). Although both rats and humans appear to depend on carbohydrate, rats rely very heavily upon blood glucose supplied from liver glycogenolysis and gluconeogenesis, whereas humans rely more heavily upon muscle glycogen.

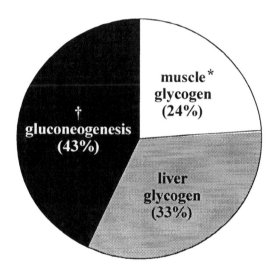

* maximal estimate
† minimal estimate

FIGURE 5-6. *Sources of carbohydrate oxidation in running rats as estimated from the decline in liver glycogen concentration, muscle glycogen concentration, and total carbohydrate oxidation (calculated from $\dot{V}O_2$ and RER).* Muscle glycogen contribution is the maximal estimate, assuming activation of a large muscle mass. The contribution of gluconeogenesis is the minimal estimate and is calculated from the difference between total carbohydrate oxidation and the use of glycogen by liver and muscle. Estimates are based upon the calculations of Torgan et al. (1990).

Therefore, if various diets or fasting were to markedly increase gluco-neogenesis in rats, it might be expected to improve endurance by increasing carbohydrate availability in the rats. However, an increase in gluconeogenesis of the same proportion in humans may have little effect on overall metabolism.

When compared with a diet of normal rat chow, rats that undergo fasting either maintain (Koubi et al., 1991) or improve their endurance capacity (Dohm et al., 1983), whereas performance in humans is clearly impaired by fasting before exercise (Gleeson et al.,1988; Loy et al., 1986; Zinker et al., 1990). Muscle glycogen in humans is not significantly reduced after fasting for between 24 h and 84 h (Knapik et al., 1988; Loy et al., 1986; Maughan & Williams, 1982; Nieman et al., 1987), and the rate of muscle glycogen utilization is not affected (Knapik et al., 1988; Loy et al., 1986; Nieman et al., 1987). However, fasted rats have a lower muscle glycogen content and a very low rate of glycogen breakdown (Dohm, et al., 1983). Liver glycogen content is compromised in both humans and rats after a fast. Fat oxidation is enhanced in humans after a fast (Knapik et al., 1988; Loy et al., 1986; Nieman et al., 1987). In rats, fasting may enhance fat oxidation because of a lower rate of muscle glycogen utilization, but actual carbohydrate and fat oxidation have apparently never been reported. It is possible that fasting might not markedly reduce carbohydrate oxidation in rats if gluconeogenesis were increased sufficiently to maintain blood glucose delivery to the exercising muscle.

After a short-term fast, both rats and humans have increased sympathetic activation and higher plasma concentrations of FFA (Dohm et al., 1983, 1986; Galbo et al., 1981). However, rats may be able to increase gluconeogenesis to a greater extent than can humans during ketogenesis, and rats may be able to spare liver glycogen, thus delaying the development of hypoglycemia, which has been associated with fatigue in endurance exercise (Coggan & Coyle, 1991). Thus, part of the observed discrepancy in performance between rats and humans after a high-fat diet may be explained by differences in ability to maintain blood glucose concentrations through gluconeogenesis.

Dogs Versus Humans

Dogs are a highly aerobic species (Roberts et al., 1996), and it is commonly thought that their endurance performance is improved in response to a high-fat diet. Much of the impetus for feeding dogs a high-fat diet comes from a report by Kronfeld et al. (1973) of a poorly performing sled dog team that had been fed a high-carbohydrate diet. When Kronfeld et al. (1973) altered the diet to include more fat and protein, the performance of the dog team increased in step-wise manner. Unfortunately, the investigators were unable to manipulate the diets of these dogs further, and little systematic analysis of the effects of diet on performance in dogs has been conducted.

A high-fat diet increases FFA availability during exercise in dogs (Hammell et al., 1977; Reynolds et al., 1994) just as in humans, although the plasma FFA levels achieved may be greater in dogs than in less aerobic species (McClelland et al., 1995). McClelland et al. (1994) claim that in dogs albumin binds much more fatty acid than does the albumin of less aerobic species, potentially increasing the delivery of fatty acids originating in adipose tissue to exercising musculature. The aerobic capacity of the dog is remarkably high compared to other mammals, and maximal rates of fat oxidation are proportionally higher (Roberts et al., 1996). A smaller fraction of total fat oxidation can be accounted for by plasma FFA supply in dogs than in less aerobic species (Weber, et al., 1996), indicating that intramuscular triglycerides must be quantitatively more important in dogs.

Reynolds et al. (1995) found that although muscle glycogen content was 30% higher in dogs fed a high-carbohydrate diet, the rate of glycogenolysis was increased to a greater extent during a high-intensity exercise bout than it was in dogs fed a normal diet. These investigators concluded that during running with intense anaerobic periods, e.g., in a sled-dog race, dogs fed high-carbohydrate diets would probably deplete their muscle glycogen stores sooner than would dogs fed a normal diet.

Horses Versus Humans

Horses are also highly aerobic and seem to benefit more from a high-fat diet than do humans. Just as in humans, fatigue in horses is associated with glycogen depletion (Hodgson et al., 1983), and a high initial muscle glycogen concentration has been associated with improved 600-m and 1600-m performance in horses (Harkin et al., 1992; Oldham et al., 1990). However, horses normally have very high concentrations of glycogen in their muscles (170–200 mmol/kg wet weight) (Snow, 1993) with their normal diets, and attempts at carbohydrate loading have not always been successful (Davies et al., 1994; Snow, 1993). Snow (1992) concluded that repletion of glycogen is not greatly accelerated with carbohydrate intake. Furthermore, because they are ruminants, high-carbohydrate diets in horses can lead to excess rapid fermentation in the bowel, to founder, and to colic (Clarke et al., 1990; Sprouse et al., 1987; White et al., 1993). Undigested fiber in the digestive system and the associated water retention may lead to performance decrements.

Several groups of investigators that have supplemented the diets of horses with excess fat have observed performance improvements (Harkin et al., 1992; Oldham et al., 1990; Slade et al., 1975; Webb et al., 1987). Added fat leads to less muscle glycogen use in trained horses

(Griewe et al., 1989) as well as to an increased lactate threshold (Custalow et al., 1993). Pagan et al. (1993) reported that fat feeding decreased blood lactate concentration during intense exercise. Although the exercise performance of both dogs and horses seems to benefit from increased dietary fat, it is unclear if these results have any applicability to highly trained humans.

DIRECTIONS FOR FUTURE RESEARCH

Although a significant amount of work has described the effects on exercise performance of eating carbohydrate and fat during the days and weeks prior to an endurance event, much remains to be determined regarding the potential benefits of diets that include moderate amounts of fat and alternate between periods of high and low amounts of carbohydrate. The major advantage of a high-carbohydrate diet is that it appears to allow more intense training, which is prerequisite to optimal improvements in endurance performance. However, it is not advantageous for athletes to train intensely day after day; thus, there may not be a need to stress a high-carbohydrate diet every day. Future studies should consider periodizing diet to match training. The best approach to this issue is not simple because it may involve doing more than simply eating relatively more carbohydrate during the 24-h period prior to intense training.

SUMMARY

It has long been recognized that diets comprised predominantly of carbohydrate allow people to exercise at 60–80% $\dot{V}O_2max$ longer before fatiguing, compared to diets that contain very little carbohydrate. This effect appears to be largely a result of low muscle glycogen concentration when dietary carbohydrate is inadequate. Although high-fat diets do increase fat oxidation, apparently by increasing the use of both plasma FFA and intramuscular triglyceride, it appears that people are very dependent upon carbohydrate from muscle glycogen to power exercise at 60–80% $\dot{V}O_2max$. Diets with inadequate carbohydrate, i.e., high-fat diets, increase metabolic stress in muscles during exercise at a given intensity and even appear to induce greater mitochondrial enzyme adaptations in exercising rats, but apparently not in humans. Furthermore, increased metabolic stress can always be accomplished by increasing exercise intensity. This would seem to be a more performance-specific method for increasing mitochondrial enzymes and enhancing endurance performance.

BIBLIOGRAPHY

Abumrad, N.A., S.B. Stearns, H.M. Tepperman, and J. Tepperman (1978). Studies on serum lipids, insulin, and glucagon and on muscle triglyceride in rats adapted to high-fat and high-carbohydrate diets. *J. Lipid Res.* 19:423–32.

Allen, L.H., E.A. Oddoye, and S. Morgan (1979). Protein induced hypercalciuria: A longer term study. *Am. J. Clin. Nutr.* 32:741–749.

Ball, D., and R.L. Maughan (1997). The effect of sodium citrate ingestion on the metabolic response to intense exercise following diet manipulation in man. *Exp. Physiol.* 82:1041–56.

Ball, D., P.L. Greenhaff, and R.L. Maughan (1996). The acute reversal of a diet-induced metabolic acidosis does not restore endurance capacity during high-intensity exercise in man. *Eur. J. Appl. Physiol.* 73:105–12.

Bergstrom, J., L. Hermansen, E. Hultman, and B. Saltin (1967). Diet, muscle glycogen and physical performance. *Acta Physiol. Scand.* 71:140–150.

Boyle, P.J., S.D. Shah, and P.E. Cryer (1989). Insulin, glucagon, and catecholamines in prevention of hypoglycemia during fasting. *Am. J. Physiol.* 256:E651–E661.

Burke, L.M., and R.S.D. Read (1987). Diet patterns of elite Australian male triathletes. *Phys. Sportsmed.* 15:140–155.

Burke, L.M., R.A. Gollan, and R.S.D. Read (1991). Dietary intakes and food use of groups of elite male athletes. *Int. J. Sports Nutr.* 1:378–394.

Carlson, L.A., L.G. Ekelund, and S.O. Froberg (1971). Concentration of triglycerides, phospholipids and of free fatty acids and □-hydroxybutyric acid in blood in man in response to exercise. *Eur. J. Clin. Inv.* 1:248–254.

Cheng, B., O. Karamizrak, T.D. Noakes, S.C. Dennis, and E.V. Lambert (1997). Time course of the effects of a high-fat diet and voluntary exercise on muscle enzyme activity in Long-Evans rats. *Physiol. Behav.* 61:701–5.

Christensen, E.H., and O. Hansen (1939). Arbeitsfahigkeit und ernahrung. *Scand. Arch. Physiol.* 81:160–171.

Clark, L.L., M.C. Roberts, and R.A. Argenzio (1990). Feeding and digestive problems in horses: Physiological responses to a concentrated meal. *Vet. Clin. North Am.* 6:433–450.

Coetzer, P., T.D. Noakes, B. Sanders, M.I. Lambert, A.N. Bosch, T. Wiggins, and S.C. Dennis (1993). Superior fatigue resistance of elite black South African distance runners. *J. Appl. Physiol.* 75:1822–27.

Coggan, A.R., and E.F. Coyle (1991). Carbohydrate ingestion during prolonged exercise: effects on metabolism and performance. *Med. Sport Sci. Rev.* 16:1–40.

Conlee, R.K., R.L. Hammer, W.W. Winder, M.L. Bracken, A.G. Nelson, and D.W. Barnett (1990). Glycogen repletion and exercise endurance in rats adapted to a high fat diet. *Metabol.* 39:289–294.

Costill, D.L., A. Bennett, G. Branam, and D. Eddy (1973). Glucose ingestion at rest and during prolonged exercsise. *J. Appl. Physiol.* 34:764–769.

Coyle, E.F (1995). Substrate utilization during exercise in active people. *Am. J. Clin. Nutr.* 61:968–979.

Cryer, P.E. (1996). Role of growth hormone in glucose counterregulation. *Hormone Res.* 46:192–194.

Custalow, S.E., P.L. Ferrante, L.E. Taylor, H.D. Moll, T.N. Meacham, D.S. Kronfeld and W. Tiegs (1993). Lactate and glucose responses to exercise in horse are affected by training and dietary fat. *Proc. Equine Nutr. Physiol. Soc.* 13:179–184.

Cutler, D.L., C.G. Gray, S.W. Park, M.G. Hickman, J.M. Bell, and O.G. Kolterman (1995). Low-carbohydrate diet alters intracellular glucose metabolism but not overall glucose disposal in exercise-trained subjects. *Metabol.* 44:1264–70.

Davies, A.J., D.L. Evans, D.R. Hodgson, and R.J. Rose (1994). Effects of an oral glucose polymer on muscle glycogen resynthesis in standard bred horses. *J. Nutr.* 124:2740S–2741S.

Dohm, G.L., R.T. Beeker, R.G. Israel, and E.B. Tapscott (1986). Metabolic responses after fasting. *J. Appl. Physiol.* 61:1363–1368.

Dohm, G.L., E.B. Tapscott, H.A. Barakat, and G.J. Kasperek (1983). Influence of fasting on glycogen depletion in rats during exercise. *J. Appl. Physiol.* 55:830–833.

Essen, B. (1977). Intramuscular substrate utilization during prolonged exercise. In: P. Milvey (ed.) *Ann. NY Acad. Sci.* New York: New York Academy of Sciences, pp. 30–44.

Fain, J.N., J.A. Garcia-Sainz (1983). Adrenergic regulation of adipocyte metabolism. *J. Lipid Res.* 24:945–966.

Fisher, E.C., W.J. Evans, S.D. Phinney, G.L. Blackburn, B.R. Bistrian, and V.R. Young (1983). Changes in skeletal muscle metabolism induced by a eucaloric ketogenic diet. In: H.G. Knuttgen, J.A. Vogel and J. Poortmans (eds.) *Biochemistry of Exercise,* edited. Champaign: Human Kinetics Publishers Inc., pp. 497–507.

Fitch, W.M., and I.L. Chaikoff (1960). Extent and patterns of adaptation of enzyme activities in livers of normal rats fed diets high in glucose and fructose. *J. Biol. Chem.* 253:554–557.

EXERCISE METABOLISM AND PERFORMANCE **195**

Galbo, H., N.J. Christensen, K.J. Mikines, B. Sonne, J. Hilsted, C. Hagen, and J. Fahrenkrug (1981). The effect of fasting on the homonal response to graded exercise. *J. Clin. Endocrinol. Metalbol.* 52:1106–1112.

Galbo, H., J.J. Holst, and N.J. Christensen (1979). The effect of different diets and of insulin on the hormonal response to prolonged exercise. *Acta Physiol. Scand.* 107:19–32.

Gleeson, M., P.L. Greenhaff, and R.J. Maughan (1988). Influence of a 24 h fast on high intensity cycle exercise performance in man. *Eur. J. Appl. Physiol.* 57:653–659.

Gollnick, P.D., B. Pernow, B. Essen, E. Jansson, and B. Saltin (1981). Availability of glycogen and plasma FFA for substrate utilization in leg muscle of man during exercise. *Clin. Physiol.* 1:27–42.

Gollnick, P.D., K. Piehl, C.W. Saubert 4th, R.B. Armstrong, and B. Saltin (1972). Diet, exercise, and glycogen changes in human muscle fibers. *J. Appl. Physiol.* 33:421–5.

Grandjean, A.C. (1989). Macronutrient intake of US athletes compared with the general population and recommendations made for athletes. *Am. J. Clin. Nutr.* 49:1070–6.

Griewe, K.M., T.N. Meacham, and J.P. Fontenot (1989). Effect of added fat on exercising horses. *Proc. Equine Nutr. Physiol. Soc.* 11:101–106.

Guo, Z., and M.D. Jensen (1998). Intramuscular fatty acid metabolism evaluated with stable isotope tracers. *J. Appl. Physiol.* 84:1674–1679.

Hagenfeldt, L., and J. Wahren (1968). Human forearm muscle metabolism during exercise. II. Uptake, release and oxidation of individual FFA and glycerol. *Scand. J. Clin. Lab. Invest.* 21:263–276.

Hales, C.N., J.P. Luzio, and K. Liddle (1978). Hormonal control of adipose tissue lipolysis. *Biochem. Soc. Symp.* 43: 97–135.

Hammel, E.P., D.S. Kronfeld, V.K. Ganjam, and H.L. Dunlap (1977). Metabolic responses to exhaustive exercise in racing sledge dogs fed diets containing medium, low or zero carbohydrate. *Am. J. Clin. Nutr.* 30:409–418.

Hargreaves, M., G. McConell, and J. Proietto (1995). Influence of muscle glycogen on glycogenolysis and glucose uptake during exercise in humans. *J. Appl. Physiol.* 78:288–292.

Hargreaves, M., I. Meredith, and G.L. Jennings (1992). Muscle glycogen and glucose uptake during exercise in humans. *Exp. Physiol.* 77:641–644.

Havel, R.J, L.G. Ekelund, and A. Holmgren (1967a). Kinetic analysis of the oxidation of palmitate-1-14C in man during prolonged heavy muscular exercise. *J. Lipid Res.* 8:366–373.

Havel, R.J., B. Pernow, and N.L. Jones (1967b). Uptake and release of free fatty acids and other metabolites in the legs of exercising men. *J. Appl. Physiol.* 23:90–99.

Hawley, J.A., G.S. Palmer, T.D. Noakes (1997). Effects of 3 days of carbohydrate supplementation on muscle glycogen content and utilisation during a 1-h cycling performance. *Eur. J. Appl. Physiol.* 75:407–12.

Helge, J.W., and B. Kiens (1997). Muscle enzyme activity in man: Role of substrate availability and training. *Am. J. Physiol.* 41:R1620–R1624.

Helge, J.W., E.A. Richter, and B. Kiens (1996). Interaction of training and diet on metabolism and endurance during exercise in man. *J. Physiol.* 1:293–306.

Helge, J.W., B. Wulff, and B. Kiens (1998). Impact of a fat-rich diet on endurnce in man: role of the dietary period. *Med. Sci. Sports Exerc.* 30:456–461.

Hespel, P., and E.A. Richter (1990). Glucose uptake and transport in contracting, perfused rat muscle with different pre-contraction glycogen concentrations. *J. Physiol.* 427:347–59.

Hodgson, D.R., R.J. Rose, J.R. Allen (1983). Muscle glycogen depletion and repletion patterns in horses performing various distances of endurance exercise. In: D.H. Snow, S.G.B. Persson, and R.J. Rose (eds.) *Equine Exercise Physiology I.* Cambridge, England: Granta Editions, pp. 229–235.

Jansson, E., and L. Kaijser (1982a). Effect of diet on the utilization of blood-borne and intramuscular substrates during exercise in man. *Acta Physiol. Scand.* 115:19–30.

Jansson, E., and L. Kaijser (1982b). Effect of diet on muscle glycogen and blood glucose utilization during a short-term exercise in man. *Acta Physiol. Scand.* 115:341–347.

Jansson, E., and L. Kaijser (1982c). Diet-induced changes in sympatho-adrenal activity during submaximal exercise in relation to substrate utilization in man. *Acta Physiol. Scand.* 114:171–178.

Jansson, E., and L. Kaijser (1984). Leg citrate metabolism at rest and during exercise in relation to diet and substrate utilization in man. *Acta Physiol. Scand.* 122:145–153.

Jensen, J., R. Aslesen, J.L. Ivy, and O. Brors (1997). Role of glycogen concentration and epinephrine on glucose uptake in rate epitrochlearis muscle. *Am. J. Physiol.* 272:E649–E655.

Kiens, B., B. Essen-Gustavsson, P. Gad, and H. Lithell (1987). Lipoprotein lipase activity and intramuscular triglyceride stores after long-term high-fat and high-carbohydrate diets in physically trained men. *Clin. Physiol.* 7:1–9.

Knapik, J.J., C.N. Meredith, B.H. Jones, L. Suek, V.R. Young, and W.J. Evans (1988). Influence of fasting on carbohydrate and fat metabolism during rest and exercise in men. *J. Appl. Physiol.* 64:1923–1929.

Koubi, H.E., D. Desplanches, C. Gabrielle, J.M. Cottet-Emard, B. Sempore, and R.J. Favier (1991). Exercise endurance and fuel utilization: a reevaluation of the effects of fasting. *J. Appl. Physiol.* 70:1337–1343.

Krogh, A., and J. Lindhard (1920). The relative value of fat and carbohydrate as sources of muscular energy. *Bioch. J.* 14:290–363.

Kronfeld, D.S. (1973). Diet and the performance of racing sled dogs. *J. Am. Vet. Med. Assoc.* 162:470–473.

Lambert, E.V., D.P. Speechly, S.C. Dennis, and T.D. Noakes (1994). Enhanced endurance in trained cyclists during moderate intensity exercise following 2 weeks adaptation to a high fat diet. *Eur. J. Appl. Physiol.* 69:287–293.

Langfort, J., W. Pilis, R. Zarzeczny, K. Nazar, and H. Kaciuba-Uscilko (1996). Effects of low-carbohydrate-ketogenic diet on metabolic and hormonal responses to graded exercise in men. *J. Physiol. Pharmacol.* 47:361–71.

Lapachet, R.A.B., W.C. Miller, and D.A. Arnall (1996). Body fat and exercise endurance in trained rats adapted to a high-fat and/or high-carbohydrate diet. *J. Appl. Physiol.* 80:1173–1179.

Larson, D.E., R.L. Hesslink, M.I. Hrovat, R.S. Fishman, and D.M. Systrom (1994). Dietary effects on exercising muscle metabolism and performance by 31P-MRS. *J. Appl. Physiol.* 77: 1108–15.

Levine, S.A., B. Gordon, and C.L. Derick (1924). Some changes in chemical constituents of blood following a marathon race. *JAMA* 82:1778–1779.

Loy, S.F., R.K. Conlee, W.W. Winder, A.G. Nelson, D.A. Arnall, and A.G. Fisher (1986). Effect of 24-hour fast on cycling endurance time at two different intensities. *J. Appl. Physiol.* 61:654–659.

Madsen, K., P.K. Pedersen, P. Rose et al. (1990). Carbohydrate supercompensation and muscle glycogen utilization during exhaustive running in highly trained athletes. *Eur. J. Appl. Physiol.* 61:467–472.

Martin, B., S. Robinson, and D.M. Robertshaw (1978). Influence of diet on leg uptake of glucose during heavy exercise. *Am. J. Clin. Nutr.* 31:62–67.

Maughan, R.J., and C. Williams (1982). Muscle citrate content and the regulation of metabolism in fed and fasted human skeletal muscle. *Clin. Physiol.* 2:21–7.

Maughan, R.J., P.L. Greenhaff, J.B. Leiper, D. Ball, C.P. Lambert, and M. Gleeson (1997). Diet composition and the performance of high-intensity exercise. *J. Sports Sci.* 15:265–275.

Maughan, R.J., C. Williams, D.M. Campbell, and D. Hepburn (1978). Fat and carbohydrate metabolism during low intensity exercise: effects of the availability of muscle glycogen. *Eur. J. Appl. Physiol.* 39:7–16.

McClelland, G., G. Zwingelstein, C.R. Taylor, and J.M. Weber (1995). Effects of exercise on the plasma nonesterfied fatty acid composition of dogs and goats: species with different aerobic capacities and diets. *Lipids* 30:147–53.

McClelland, G., G. Zwingelstein, C.R. Taylor, and J.M. Weber (1994). Increased capacity for circulatory fatty acid transport in a highly aerobic mammal. *Am. J. Physiol.* 266: R1280–6.

McDowell, M.A. (1994). The NHANES III supplemental nutrition survey of older Americans. *Am. J. Clin. Nutr.* 59:224S-226S.

Miller, W.C., R. Bryce, and R.K. Conlee (1984). Adaptation to a high-fat diet that increase exercise endurance in male rats. *J. Appl. Physiol.* 56:78–83.

Muoio, D.M., J.J. Leddy, P.J. Horvath, A.B. Awad, and D.R. Pndergast (1994). Effect of dietary fat on metabolic adjustments to maximal VO$_2$ and endurance in runners. *Med. Sci. Sports Exerc.* 26:81–88.

Nieman, D.C., K.A. Carlson, M.E. Brandstater, R.T. Naegele, and J.W. Blankenship (1987). Running endurance in 27-h-fasted humans. *J. Appl. Physiol.* 63:2502–9.

Nilsson, L.H., and E. Hultman (1973). Liver glycogen in man – the effect of total starvation or a carbohydrate-poor diet followed by carbohydrate refeeding. *Scand. J. Clin. Lab. Invest.* 32:325–330.

Oldham, S.L., G.D. Potter, J.W. Evans, S.B. Smith, T.S. Taylor, and S.W. Barnes (1990). Storage and mobilization of muscle glycogen in racehorsesfed a control and high-fat diet. In: *Proc. 11th Equine Nutr. Physiol Symp.* Stillwater: Oklahoma State University, pp. 57–62.

Pagan, J.D., W. Tiegs, S.G. Jackson, and H.Q. Murphy (1993). The effects of different fat sources on exercise performance in Thoroughbred racing horses. In: *Proc. 13th Equine Nutr. Physiol. Symp.* Gainesville: University of Florida, pp. 125–129.

Paul, P. (1970). FFA metabolism of normal dogs during steady-state exercise at different work loads. *J. Appl. Physiol.* 28:127–132.

Phinney, S.D., B.R. Bistrian, W.J. Evans, E. Gervino, and G.L. Blackburn (1983a). The human metabolic response to chronic ketosis without caloric restriction: preservation of submaximal exercise capability with reduced carbohydrate oxidation. *Metabol.* 32:769–776.

Phinney, S.D., B.R. Bistrain, R.R. Wolfe, and G.L. Blackburn (1983b). The human metabolic response to chronic ketosis without caloric restriction: physical and biochemical adaptation. *Metabol.* 32:757–768.

Pitsiladis, Y.P., C. Duignan, and R.J. Maughan (1996). Effects of alterations in dietary carbohydrate intake on running performance during a 10 km treadmill time trial. *Br. J. Sports Med.* 30:226–231.

Pruett, E.D.R. (1970). Glucose and insulin during prolonged work stress in men living on different diets. *J. Appl. Physiol.* 28:199–208.

Putman, C.T., L.L. Spriet, E. Hultman, M.I. Lindinger, L.C. Lands, R.S. McKelvie, G. Cederblad, N.L. Jones, and G.J.F. Heigenhauser (1993). Pyruvate dehydrogenase activity and acetyl group accumulation during exercise after different diets. *Am. J. Physiol.* 265:E752–E760.

Reynolds, A.J., L. Fuhrer, H.L. Dunlap, M.D. Finke, and F.A. Kallfelz (1994). Lipid metabolite responses to diet and training in sled dogs. *J. Nutr.* 124:2754S-2759S.

Reynolds, A.J., L. Fuhrer, H.L. Dunlap, M. Finke, and F.A. Kallfelz (1995). Effect of diet and training on muscle glycogen storage and utilization in sled dogs. *J. Appl. Physiol.* 79:1601–1607.

Richter, E.A., and H. Galbo (1986). High glycogen levels enhance glycogen breakdown in isolated contracting skeletal muscle. *J. Appl. Physiol.* 61:827–831.

Roberts, T.J., J.M. Weber, H. Hoppeler, E.R. Weibel, and C.R. Taylor (1996). Design of the oxygen and substrate pathways: II. Defining the upper limits of carbohydrate and fat oxidation. *J. Exp. Biol.* 199:1651–1658.

Saitoh, S., T. Matsuo, K. Tagami, H. Chang, K. Tokuyama, and M. Suzuki (1996). Effect of short-term dietary change from fat to high carbohydrate diets on the storage and utilization of glycogen and triacylglycerol in untrained rats. *Eur. J. Appl. Physiol.* 74:13–22.

Schutz, Y., and E. Ravussin (1980). Respiratory quotients lower than 0.70 in ketogenic diets [letter]. *Am. J. Clin. Nutr..* 33:1317–9.

Sears, B. (1995). *The Zone.* New York: Harper Collins.

Sherman, W.M., J.A. Doyle, D.R. Lamb, and R.H. Strauss (1993). Dietary carbohydrate, muscle glycogen, and exercise performance during 7 d of training. *Am. J. Clin. Nutr.* 57:27–31.

Short, S.H., and W.R. Short (1983). Four-year study of university athletes' dietary intake. *J. Am. Diet. Assn.* 82:632–45.

Simi, B., B. Sempore, M.-H. Mayet, and R.J. Favier (1991). Additive effects of training and high-fat diet on energy metabolism during exercise. *J. Appl. Physiol.* 71:197–203.

Simonsen, J.C., W.M. Sherman, D.R. Lamb, A.R. Dernbach, J.A. Doyle, and R. Strauss (1991). Dietary carbohydrate, muscle glycogen, and power output during rowing training. *J. Appl. Physiol.* 70:1500–1505.

Slade, L.M., L.D. Lewis, and C.R. Quinn (1975). Nutritional adaptation of horses for endurance type performance. In: *Proc. 4th Equine Nutr. Physiol.Symp.* Pomona: California State Polytechnical University, pp. 114–128.

Snow, D.H. (1992). A review of nutritional aids to energy production for athletic performance. *Equine Athlete* 5: 6–9.

Snow, D.H. (1993). A review of nutritional aids to energy production for athletic performance. In: J. Foreman (ed.) *Proc. 11th Ann. Assn. Equine Sports Med.* Santa Barbara: Veterinary Practice Publishing Company, pp. 91–95.

Sprouse, R.F., H.E. Garner, and E.M. Green (1987). Plasma endotoxin levels in horses subjected to carbohydrate induced laminitis. *Equine Vet. J.* 19:25–28.

Starling, R.D., T.A. Trappe, A.C. Parcell, C.G. Kerr, W.J. Fink, and D.L. Costill (1997). Effects of diet on muscle triglyceride and endurance performance. *J. Appl. Physiol.* 82: 1185–1189.

Torgan, C.E., J.T. Brozinick, M.E. Willems, and J.L. Ivy (1990). Substrate utilization during acute exercise in obese Zucker rats. *J. Appl. Physiol.* 69:1987–1991.

van Zyl, C., K. Murphy, E.V. Lambert, T.D. Noakes, and S.C. Dennis (1994). Effects of a low carbohydrate, high fat diet prior to carbohydrate loading on endurance cycling performance. *Clin. Science* 87:32–33.

Webb, S.P., G.D. Potter, and J.W. Evans (1987). Physiologic and metabolic response of race and cutting horses to added dietary fat. *Proc. 10th Equine Nutr. Physiol. Symp.* Fort Collins: Colorado State University, pp. 115–120.

Weber, J.M., G. Brichon, G. Zwingelstein, G. McClelland, C. Saucedo, E.R. Weibel, and C.R. Taylor (1996). Design of the oxygen and substrate pathways: IV. Partitioning energy provision from fatty acids. *J. Exp. Biol.* 199:1667–1674.

Weltan, S.M., A.N. Bosch, S.C. Dennis, and T.D. Noakes (1998). Influence of muscle glycogen content on metabolic regulation. *Am. J. Physiol.* 274:E72–E82.

White, N.A., M.K. Tinker, and P. Lessard (1993). Equine colic risk assessment on horse farms: A prospective study. In: *Proc. Am. Assn. Equine Pract.,* pp. 97.

Williams, R.S., and P.D. Neufer (1996). Regulation of gene expression in skeletal muscle by contractile activity. In: L.B. Rowell and J.T. Shepherd (eds.) *Handbook of Physiology, Section 12: Exercise: Regulation and Integration of Multiple Systems.* New York: Oxford University Press, pp. 1124–1150.

Zinker, B.A., K. Britz, and G.A. Brooks (1990). Effects of a 36-hour fast on human endurance and substrate utilization. *J. Appl. Physiol.* 69:1849–1855.

DISCUSSION

WALBERG-RANKIN: What are some of your ideas on the periodization approach to diet to go along with a periodization of training?

COYLE: Athletes need to first structure their training. Typically, they design programs that include two or three days a week of hard training, which is most important. They need to make sure they rest before these days and that they eat enough carbohydrate and maybe even an adequate amount of fat for raising muscle triglycerides so they can do high-quality workouts. In some cases they may simply need to eat a sufficient amount of carbohydrate, perhaps 500 g/d or 7 g/kg body weight per day for the 24–36 h before the hard training session, and to get adequate rest. On days when they are not planning a high-intensity workout, they may not have to be as focused on eating so much carbohydrate. They can slack off and try to get other nutrients into their bodies. So I don't think they have to be focused all the time on some of these dietary carbohydrate recommendations.

WALBERG-RANKIN: So the volume and intensity of exercise would be the primary factors that should influence the diet recommendations for the athlete?

COYLE: Yes. Keep in mind that most athletes train with interval workouts for less than 90 min. It's easy for us to discuss marathon runners who run for 2–3 h/d and deplete their muscle glycogen stores, but we often forget that athletes performing interval training can also deplete their muscle glycogen levels. These athletes also need to recover and plan their diets in preparation for the next workout. This applies to soccer and to many other team sports. We should begin to recognize the stresses of intermittent exercise training and come up with appropriate dietary strategies to optimize that training.

WALBERG-RANKIN: In your discussion of the 40/30/30 diet plan, you used the example of an athlete who consumed 4200 kcal. Female athletes often consume closer to 2500 kcal/d, so the carbohydrate intake with the 40/30/30 plan would be much lower than what we recommend for maintenance of muscle glycogen.

COYLE: Which is why we should provide recommendations for dietary carbohydrate as g/kg body weight per day.

MAUGHAN: You highlighted very clearly the difficulties in translating the rat data to the human. One additional bit of evidence you didn't refer to is the fact that if one feeds glycerol to a rat, its endurance performance is improved, but glycerol feedings are ineffective in humans, probably because of the differences in the gluconeogenic capacity of the liver in the two species.

COYLE: I agree.

EICHNER: I think we should even be stronger in calling the Zone diet a "Zany" diet because the more scientists hesitate to issue practical guidelines, the more it enables pseudoscientists to capture the stage, make a fortune, and impair the public health. A high-protein diet may not necessarily impair renal function over the years, but it is a risk factor for gout and possible renal stones. It's also a risk factor for osteoporosis because it enhances urinary calcium loss. It may also raise blood pressure. So, it seems imprudent to exceed the protein intake recommended by Dr. Tarnopolsky.

COYLE: For endurance athletes who are training very intensely, the Zone diet is a "zany" diet because it will not allow them to train intensely. That certainly is true of the men's swimming team at the University of Texas; they tried the Zone diet and came to that conclusion on their own. Much of the support for the Zone diet has been based on testimonials from athletes, and one should seek their motivation for making these testimonies. In Sears book on the "Zone," he implies that the success of the Stanford swim team is due partly to their use of the Zone diet. His reasoning is that the women's team at the University of Texas had been the NCAA national champions for years, but when Stanford University began using the Zone diet, they started winning the national championships. He failed to mention that another variable that had changed at the same time was that the head swimming coach from Texas moved to Stanford. The consistent variable is that the same coach won all of those championships all those years. Many of the athletes who were supposedly following the Zone diet have gone on record as saying they were not following it.

COGGAN: Just to reinforce that point, I know a fellow who was on the Stanford swim team, and he stated that the swimmers were simply issued guidelines with suggestions that "maybe you want to try this." So the extent to which they were actually consuming that diet is not known.

FEBBRAIO: It has been suggested that beta-oxidation is not the rate-limiting step in oxidative phosphorylation. Rather, the limitation is the rate of entry of fat into the cell and then into the mitochondria. What do we know about the effects of chronic high-fat diets on fatty-acid binding proteins and the carnitine palmitoyl transferase enzymes?

WAGENMAKERS: There are clear results of studies from Glatz and Veerkamp that a high-fat diet increases the cytosolic fatty-acid binding protein in muscles of rats. As far as I know, this has not been shown in man.

COYLE: I wonder what role fatty-acid binding proteins really play in limiting fat oxidation, especially oxidation of plasma fatty acids. VanderVusse, in his review article in the *Handbook of Physiology*, speculates that fatty-acid binding proteins probably don't limit fat oxidation in people.

WAGENMAKERS: That is an important point. We don't understand the physiological roles of the fatty-acid binding proteins; any change in their content doesn't necessarily tell us anything about the oxidative capacity of the muscle.

COYLE: Endurance training in people may increase the fatty-acid bonding proteins, but the oxidation of plasma fatty acids is reduced during exercise at a given absolute intensity. So these adaptations seem to go in opposite directions. Intramuscular triglyceride seems to be more important than plasma fatty acids as a source of fat for oxidation during exercise, and intramuscular triglyceride is clearly the source of fat that adapts to endurance training.

COGGAN: Fatty-acid binding proteins are really multiple proteins. There is the 15 kD intracellular fatty-acid binding protein, the 40 kD plasma membrane fatty-acid binding protein, the so-called fatty acid transporter of 70 kD, etc. They play different roles and adapt differently to training. Therefore, I don't think we should make blanket statements as to how important they may or may not be. Another factor to keep in mind is the limitation imposed by the tools that have been used to try to answer these questions in vivo, specifically the comparison of medium-chain and long-chain fatty acid metabolism. It is often assumed that they differ only in how they get across the mitochondrial membrane. However, medium-chain fatty acids don't have to dissociate from albumin; they cross the plasma membrane and they diffuse through the cytosol without having to use any transporters. I don't think we should over-interpret the data and conclude absolutely that the activity of carnitine palmitoyl transferase is a limiting factor, simply because of the differential response between medium-chain and long-chain fatty acids.

Finally, to reinforce the point Ed Coyle made, although plasma membrane fatty-acid binding proteins are increased with endurance training, utilization of plasma fatty acids at the same absolute intensity goes down. This shows very nicely how dangerous it is to make conclusions about how metabolism and physiology actually function on the basis of anatomical-type measurements. The place to begin is to adequately describe the metabolic response and then search for the biochemical and molecular mechanisms. However, if one begins at the molecular level and extrapolates to higher levels, one can arrive at a completely wrong conclusion as to how metabolism actually works.

TARNOPOLSKY: The increase in fatty-acid binding protein that is seen with endurance training is not necessarily at odds with the observation of decreased oxidation of plasma free fatty acids because as a cytosolic chaperone, the binding protein may actually be chaperoning the free fatty acids from intramuscular triglyceride hydrolysis. Now that people have cloned and sequenced two of the sarcolemmal transport proteins, it is possible that they may actually be downregulated as opposed to the cytosolic binding protein going up. That is going to be exciting work in the future.

COYLE: I am not fully convinced that fatty-acid binding proteins are needed for transport of fatty acids from intramuscular triglycerides, which are in physical contact with the mitochondria.

SPRIET: Recently George Heigenhauser and I had people eat an extremely low-carbohydrate, high-fat diet for 6 d to examine some biochemical mechanisms. Surprisingly, there was no increase the activities of carnitine palmitoyl transferase, β-HAD, or citrate synthase activity after the 6-d diet. However, pyruvate dehydrogenase kinase, which is acutely involved in the activation of PDH, changed very dramatically within 3 d, suggesting that at least in this dietary paradigm, it is the carbohydrate pathways that seem to be more sensitive to alterations in diet than are the fat pathways. It could be that switching to the 40/30/30 diet might upregulate that enzymes of fat metabolism more slowly than it changes enzymes for carbohydrate metabolism. Of course, the implication with the PDH kinase is that if its activity is increased during exercise, it may downregulate the activation of PDH. In another study we found that the downregulation of PDH by PDH kinase can be overridden by having high levels of glycogen. Therefore, no matter how long one has been on a high-fat diet that has increased PDH kinase activity, if one can restore the glycogen levels to normal values, the availability of the carbohydrate seems to override the inhibition by PDH kinase during the exercise period. We adapt rather quickly to changes in carbohydrate intake.

HEIGENHAUSER: Precautions need to be taken when one follows a high-fat, low-carbohydrate diet. For example, in our studies of diets that contained 3% carbohydrate, within 48 h the subjects became glucose intolerant.

COYLE: Low-carbohydrate diets that are ketogenic are metabolically stressing and have been implicated in impaired glucose disposal, which is why some of the more popular low-carbohydrate, high-protein diets, such as the Stillman diet, need to be monitored very carefully. The Stillman diet was first popularized in the 1970s and has reemerged.

FREY: Athletics are big business at large universities. Does each sport have its own specific diet during and outside of the competitive season?

COYLE: Outside the season, probably not; inside the season, yes. The nutritional needs of weight lifters are certainly different from those of endurance athletes. One challenge for us as scientists and practitioners is to work together to arrive at better sport-specific dietary recommendations. If we simply make general recommendations, e.g., that athletes should eat 60% carbohydrate, we are selling the athletes short. We should develop paradigms that emphasize what the critical dietary periods are for each sport.

MONTAIN: My interpretation of the data is that whenever we go to extremes, we run into trouble. If athletes' diets fall within the RDA recommendations for percent of calories from carbohydrate, fat, and protein, their performances will not suffer. We may decide to change the timing of food intake to optimize synthesis of proteins, but day in and day out, we probably don't have to modify athletes' diets very much at all.

COYLE: Despite our recommendations, athletes do not eat diets that are very different from those of most people in the American population. Is that simply because the typical diet is most readily available and they just choose to eat like everybody else, despite potential benefits of eating more carbohydrates? Athletes can eat less carbohydrate and can still train and show training-induced improvements, but they are not optimal improvements. I think they can benefit, for example, by increasing their carbohydrate on a fairly routine basis, but not necessarily every day of every week.

GISOLFI: Are there any effects of diet manipulation on temperature regulation, especially in a warm environment, given the potential for these manipulations to influence fluid balance?

COYLE: I would like to direct that question to Ron Maughan, who completed some of the early studies showing that low-carbohydrate, high-fat diets impaired performance. It is unclear what the mechanism is to explain the impaired performance. According to their recent bicarbonate-infusion studies, the problem doesn't appear to be entirely a function of the acidosis. Whether it is a problem with temperature regulation or whether it is an effect on the brain remains to be seen.

MAUGHAN: We recently did a study in which we fed people high-carbohydrate versus moderately low-carbohydrate diets for a few days prior to an exercise test, once in the cold, and once in the heat. We did not expect the high-carbohydrate diet to improve performance in the heat because we were reasonably sure that glycogen depletion was not the limiting factor in the heat; the subjects reach exhaustion before glycogen is severely depleted. Nevertheless, the high-carbohydrate diet did improve performance in these subjects who were exercising at 32 °C. This result suggests very clearly that the high-carbohydrate diet may well be beneficial in the heat, probably for some reason having nothing to do with glycogen stores. We thought at the time that the metabolic acidosis that accompanies a low-carbohydrate, high-fat, high-protein diet was important, but it is now clear that correcting the acidosis clearly does not restore performance. I believe that there are important effects on brain transmitters, but we still do not have evidence on this matter.

FEBBRAIO: A study published in the 1980s in rats demonstrated that a high-carbohydrate diet reduced thermoregulatory capacity. It was suggested that this occurred because glycogen deposition in the muscle cells drained water from the extravascular space and transferred it to the intracellular compartment. However, it was followed by a study in 1990 by a group in South Africa who demonstrated quite clearly that a high-carbohydrate diet had no effect on thermoregulatory capacity during exercise in humans. So from a practical point, humans preparing for exercise in the heat should not be fearful of carbohydrate loading because it doesn't appear to have any negative effects on the thermoregulatory capacity or on performance.

COGGAN: Along the same line, there are data showing that humans who consume extremely low-carbohydrate diets exhibit greater reductions of splanchnic blood flow during exercise than is normal. Whether that applies to skin blood flow or thermoregulation as well, I don't know. With extreme diets, the detrimental effect on thermoregulation that Dr. Gisolfi suggested may exist.

COYLE: I agree. I would caution athletes going into an endurance event with potential heat stress that they should not eat a diet that is too low in carbohydrate because that will likely lead to beginning the event with a low store of muscle glycogen. Sandy Weltan and colleagues showed that when athletes started exercising with low muscle glycogen stores, even if blood glucose levels were maintained constant by glucose infusion, the athletes exhibited higher concentrations of plasma catecholamines. This might reduce heat dissipation and cause hyperthermia. When we infused glucose intravenously in people during prolonged exercise in the heat, we found that concentrations of plasma catecholamines were reduced and that subjects stayed cooler during exercise compared to when we maintained a saline infusion that provided the same amount of fluid. In that situation, acute glucose infusion and carbohydrate administration improved thermoregulation. It is possible that people who have very low availability of carbohydrate, particularly when they are hypoglycemic and have high circulating concentrations of catecholamines, will experience reduced skin blood flow and will risk heat illness. We should caution people about eating too little carbohydrate in the days before competing in an endurance event.

O'CONNOR: Is it more difficult for athletes, particularly those in sports requiring great skill, to acquire those skills in the training program when they consume low-carbohydrate, high-fat diets?

COGGAN: Requirements of the central nervous system for glucose are estimated to be about 150 g/d; as the carbohydrate supply drops below 150 g, that is when ketosis begins.

SHI: What type or combination of carbohydrates should be recommended for the carbohydrate diet?

COYLE: A person should ingest carbohydrates with a high glycemic index during the first 12 h or so following exercise. Whether one should maintain high glycemia throughout the rest of the period is not clear. Therefore, when focusing on muscle glycogen resynthesis, consuming carbohydrate sources with high glycemic indexes is important. During other periods, if athletes aren't focusing on restoring muscle glycogen, they should attempt to maintain adequate carbohydrate intake for health, to provide other nutrients, and for fiber.

HORSWILL: A preliminary report from Brechtel's lab showed that after a 6-wk treatment of the Zone diet versus a control diet (the control diet supplying about 52% of total calories as carbohydrate), that endurance time at 70% peak oxygen uptake was reduced by 10%, regardless of being on the Zone diet or the control diet. Both diets contained the same low energy content. It is possible that acute dehydration is induced by the Zone diet with high protein intake and low carbohydrate intake; this diet can lead to increased excretion of ketones, urea, and water.

COYLE: I think you are exactly right. The Zone diet, if followed as outlined in the book, is a low calorie diet. It is low in energy whether it contains 50% carbohydrate or 40% carbohydrate. Percent carbohydrate has relatively minor effects if the total amount of carbohydrate and the total amount of energy are low.

6

Nutritional Supplements: Effects on Exercise Performance and Metabolism

Anton J.M. Wagenmakers, Ph.D.

INTRODUCTION

Athletes often search for means beyond training techniques that will give them a significant additional advantage over their competitors. Even small positive effects are considered to be important because the time difference separating number one and two in competition in many cases is minimal, whereas the social and material consequences of such differences, especially for elite athletes, can be very great and often out of proportion when compared to other disciplines and professions. Such means to improve performance in sport are generally known as ergogenic aids. The term *ergogenic* means "work generating" and is derived from the Greek word *ergo* meaning "work." Ergogenic aids can be classified into different categories (Williams, 1992): mechanical aids (e.g., lighter sports equipment or clothing or equipment that leads to improved aerodynamics, such as the clap-skate, which led to a breakthrough in speed skating during the last winter Olympic games (Van Ingen-Schenau et al., 1996); psychological aids (e.g., stress and anxiety control); pharmacological aids (e.g., caffeine, anabolic steroids, erythropoietin); physiological aids (e.g., sodium bicarbonate, blood infusion); and nutritional aids (e.g., carbohydrates, vitamins, carnitine, creatine, special amino acids, and fatty acids).

Most pharmacological and physiological aids, when taken in abnormal quantities, meet the definition of doping and, therefore, are included in the International Olympic Committee (IOC) list of banned substances. This, however, is not the case with nutritional supplements, which by definition are naturally occurring compounds in our diets. Therefore, the use of nutritional supplements that are suspected of having a performance-enhancing effect has become very popular and widespread. A main problem with many of these substances is that it is nearly impossible to unequivocally show that they have the effects on performance claimed in the product information.

The aim of this chapter is to give a critical scientific overview on selected nutritional supplements that are available commercially and are used by athletes in sport practice today. The compounds chosen are creatine, carnitine, branched-chain amino acids, medium-chain fatty acids, and lactate in various chemical forms. First a description will be given of the occurrence of these compounds in the normal diet and the endogenous synthesis rate in the human body, if applicable. Then the role of the compound in human metabolism and the rationale for its use as an ergogenic aid will be summarized. Finally, the effect of nutritional supplementation, i.e., greater than normal intake, on exercise performance and metabolism will be reviewed. Each section will end with a conclusion about whether or not the respective nutritional supplement has a statistically significant effect on performance during exercise in the laboratory setting.

Performance studies should have a double-blind crossover or a double-blind placebo-controlled design to exclude training effects and to avoid selection biases. The reader should keep in mind that positive and negative effects of less than 0.5% can never be unequivocally shown to exist even in the best laboratory under the best-controlled conditions. However, a difference of 0.5 % in running time during a marathon may make the difference between finishing first and finishing fifth. This point is sometimes raised by commercial suppliers of nutritional supplements as a weakness of experimental scientific research. However, it seems reasonable to avoid compounds that have not been unequivocally shown to enhance performance because an ergolytic effect, i.e., a reduction of performance, of 0.5% also cannot be shown to exist, but such and ergolytic effect may be the consequence of using nutritional supplements that have no proven effect on human metabolism and performance.

CREATINE

Among the nutritional substances that are suspected of having an ergogenic effect, creatine has recently become extremely popular. Creatine use is widespread by many elite athletes, particularly in track sprinting events (100–800 m) and by short-distance swimmers. It also is used by competitors in team sports characterized by intermittent exertion of high-intensity, e.g., soccer and tennis, by body builders and strength athletes, and by many recreational athletes.

Currently, the International Olympic Committee does not prohibit the use of creatine supplements, and there appear to be no harmful effects when creatine is used in quantities needed to produce an ergogenic effect in laboratory conditions. However, it is not yet fully clear in which disciplines and conditions athletes should be advised to use creatine. The effects of the long-term use of creatine in combination with strength and endurance training are just beginning to be clarified. Sport practice in this respect precedes a proper scientific evaluation, and in some conditions the use of creatine may well turn out to be meaningless or even ergolytic. For instance, the increase in body weight that is observed in many consumers may well be disadvantageous for marathon runners (Balsom et al., 1993b) or for athletes in in sports where part of the energy output is required to counteract gravitational forces (long jump, high jump, cycling, and running in hills or mountains). Here we will briefly describe the major conclusions from the literature on the role of creatine in human metabolism and on the effects of nutritional supplementation on creatine concentration in muscle, on exercise metabolism, and on performance. For a more complete literature overview and a more exhaustive list of references see earlier reviews (Greenhaff, 1997; Maughan, 1995; Mujika & Padilla, 1997).

Dietary Intake, Biosynthesis and Distribution in Tissues

Creatine, or methylguanidinoacetate, is a naturally occurring compound. The main sources are dietary intake—especially of meat products—and endogenous biosynthesis in the human body. In normal healthy individuals, diet and oral ingestion together provide approximately 2 g of creatine per day, which is equal to the amount broken down to creatinine and excreted in the urine.

Oral ingestion of creatine suppresses its biosynthesis. Absence of creatine from the diet results in a low urinary excretion of creatine and creatinine. Creatinine is the sole end product of creatine degradation and is formed non-enzymatically in an irreversible reaction. Because skeletal muscle is the major store of the bodily creatine pool (see below), muscle is also the major site of creatinine production. Once generated, creatinine enters the circulation by simple diffusion and is excreted in the urine after filtration in the glomeruli of the kidney. The daily urinary creatinine excretion is relatively constant in an individual but can vary among individuals, being dependent on total muscle mass and habitual diet.

As reviewed by Greenhaff (1997), early nutrition studies showed that following a period without dietary creatine, creatine retention is augmented during a subsequent period of dietary creatine supplementation. This seemed to suggest that endogenous biosynthesis did not lead to maximal storage of creatine in muscle.

Creatine is synthesized in the human body in a two step reaction. In the first reaction the guanidino group of arginine is transferred to glycine to produce guanidinoacetate. In the second reaction creatine is formed via transfer of a methylgroup from S-adenosylmethionine to guanidinoacetate. The majority of creatine synthesis in man occurs in liver and kidney.

In a 70-kg man, the total bodily creatine pool is approximately 120 g, 95% of which is found in muscle. Creatine is also found in small quantities in brain, liver, kidney, and testes. Creatine synthesized in the liver and kidneys and absorbed from the gut is transported via the blood to the muscle. All types of muscle take creatine up against a concentration gradient by a sodium-dependent saturable active transport process. The entrapment of creatine in muscle in the form of creatine phosphate, which is unable to pass through the plasma membrane because of its polarity, also helps to create the very high gradient for total creatine, i.e., 30–40 mM in skeletal muscle, with 60–70% being in the form of creatine phosphate.

Functions of Creatine Phosphate in Muscle Metabolism

High Intensity Exercise. Creatine phosphate is present in resting muscle in a concentration that is three to four times that of adenosine triphosphate (ATP), the immediate energy source for muscle contraction. When the ATP concentration in whole muscle falls by 25–30% in humans, fatigue will occur (Hultman et al., 1991; Karlsson & Saltin, 1970). It is important to regenerate ATP at a rate close to that of ATP hydrolysis, thus maintaining the ATP concentration at close to resting levels, if fatigue is to be delayed during high-intensity exercise. An important function of creatine phosphate in muscle is to provide the high-energy phosphate group for ATP regeneration during the first seconds of high-intensity exercise, thus allowing time for glycogen breakdown and glycolysis (the other main process generating cytosolic ATP during high-intensity exercise) to achieve the required rate of ATP production. Transfer of the phosphate group from creatine phosphate to adenosine diphosphate (ADP) is catalyzed by the enzyme creatine kinase, resulting in regeneration of ATP and release of free creatine. The net reactions occurring during the first seconds of high-intensity muscle contractions (Hultman et al., 1991; Karlsson & Saltin, 1970) are as follows:

$$ATP \rightarrow ADP + P_i$$
$$\text{Creatine phosphate} + ADP + H^+ \rightarrow \text{Creatine} + ATP$$

During a 100-m sprint (running), 22 g of ATP are broken down per second or about 50% of the ATP content per kg active muscle per second. Because fatigue occurs in human muscle when the whole-muscle ATP concentration falls by about 30%, the need for rephosphorylation of the ADP formed during contraction is obvious. The creatine kinase reaction is very rapid and increases further during high-intensity exercise because the enzyme is activated by the decrease in muscle pH (due to high rates of glycolysis and lactate formation).

Net breakdown of creatine phosphate makes a significant contribution to the energy supply during the first seconds of high-intensity exercise (Hultman et al., 1991; Karlsson & Saltin, 1970). However, the creatine phosphate store in muscle is finite and can fall to almost zero within 4–5 s of maximal sprinting. Therefore, nutritional manipulations that lead to an increase of the creatine phosphate content of muscle ought to allow a greater amount of work to be done using this energy source and ought to lead to a better or more prolonged maintenance of the ATP concentration that would, from a theoretical point of view, improve performance during intense maximal exercise.

When a larger proportion of ATP regeneration is accounted for by net consumption of creatine phosphate, then, during a 100-m sprint, less ATP will have to be generated by glycogen breakdown and a high rate of glycolysis with lactate and hydrogen ion formation. As lactate and the hydrogen ions formed during high-intensity exercise have been implicated in the fatigue process (Fitts, 1994), this could be a second mechanism by which an increased creatine phosphate availability could lead to improved performance. Furthermore, the creatine kinase reaction also functions to buffer the intracellular pH because a hydrogen ion is used during ATP regeneration (see above). Thus, an increased buffering capacity in the presence of a higher concentration of muscle creatine phosphate is a third mechanism that could explain a positive effect of creatine supplementation on high-intensity exercise performance. However, it is extremely difficult to predict on theoretical grounds how important these effects could be from a quantitative point of view.

Creatine phosphate is rapidly resynthesized following a bout of high-intensity exercise. This occurs via reversal of the creatine kinase reaction, using ATP generated by oxidative metabolism in the mitochondria. Several studies (see Greenhaff, 1997) have shown that the extent of creatine phosphate resynthesis during recovery following a single bout of maximal exercise is positively correlated with exercise performance during a subsequent bout of maximal exercise. The amount of creatine phosphate left during the previous bout of exercise may well be larger, and the recovery rate of creatine phosphate from a theoretical point is expected to be faster, in a muscle containing a higher total creatine content. Therefore, nutritional manipulations leading to increases in total muscle creatine and creatine phosphate content might be expected to have an ergogenic effect on performance in sport events involving repeated bouts of maximal exercise.

Endurance Exercise. In endurance exercise, when ATP is primarily or entirely generated by oxidative phosphorylation in the mitochondria, net creatine phosphate breakdown and the net contribution of creatine phosphate to energy production are minimal. However, creatine and creatine phosphate in that case might provide a shuttle system for the transfer of high-energy phosphate groups from the ATP production site (the mitochondria) to the ATP consumption site (the contracting myofibrils (Bessman & Geiger, 1981; Meyer et al. (1984)) (Figure 6-1). When the diffusion rate of high-energy phosphates would be limited in endurance exercise by the availability of creatine and creatine phosphate (not known at this time), then an increase of the muscle creatine pool with nutritional supplements could conceivably improve aerobic energy supply during prolonged exercise and thus have an ergogenic effect. However, scientists currently do not agree on the potential importance of the creatine shuttle in endurance exercise.

Creatine Supplementation and Concentrations of Total Creatine and Creatine Phosphate in Muscle

Harris and colleages (1992) were the first to observe that creatine supplementation in athletes in amounts of 20 g/d for 6 d increased the muscle total creatine concentration by about 20–25 mmol/kg dry muscle mass (about 5–6 mmol/kg wet muscle) with a range of 2–40 mmol/kg dry muscle. This increase corresponded to about 20% of the basal total creatine concentration of about 125 mmol/kg dry muscle. This has been confirmed in many other laboratories (Greenhaff, 1997; Mujika & Padilla, 1997).

Hultman et al. (1996) investigated a number of creatine supplementation procedures in men. Ingestion of creatine at a rate of 20 g/d for 6 d leads to an increase in total creatine concentration in muscle that confirmed the work of Harris et al. (1992) (Figure 6-2, procedures A and B). A subsequent dose of 2 g/d was enough to maintain the high concentration total creatine for 35 d (procedure B), whereas stopping creatine supplementation after 6 d caused a slow gradual loss (procedure A). When creatine was ingested at a dose of 3 g/d, the rate of increase in muscle creatine was correspondingly lower (procedure C), but after 28 d on 3 g/d the total creatine concentration was similar in procedure B and C (Figure 6-2). Therefore, a loading dose of 20 g/d for 6 d followed by a maintenance dose of 2–3 g/d is advised if athletes want to increase muscle creatine to maximal levels quickly, whereas a continuous dose of 3 g/d leads to the same maximal concentration in about 1 mo. The increase in muscle creatine phosphate concentration was about 30–40% of the increase in total creatine concentration in all of the loading procedures.

For reasons not known, there is considerable variation among sub-

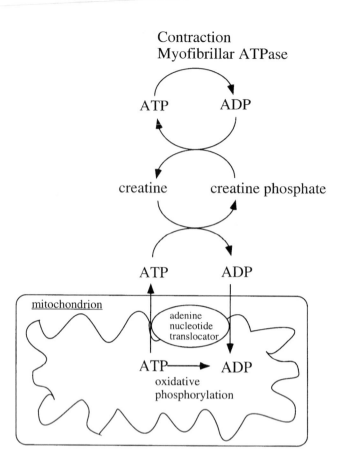

Contraction
Myofibrillar ATPase

ATP   ADP

creatine   creatine phosphate

ATP   ADP

mitochondrion

adenine
nucleotide
translocator

ATP $\longrightarrow$ ADP
oxidative
phosphorylation

FIGURE 6-1. *Hypothetical effect of creatine supplementation on aerobic energy supply endurance exercise.* During prolonged exercise, if there were no creatine phosphate present, ATP would diffuse only slowly from the site of synthesis in the mitochondria to the site of consumption in the contracting myofibrils. High concentrations of creatine phosphate in muscle apparently provide a shuttle system for the rapid transfer of high-energy phosphate groups from the ATP-production pool to the ATP-consumption pool (Bessman & Geiger, 1981; Meyer et al., 1984). There is no evidence that this shuttle system is limited by the availability of creatine and creatine phosphate, but if it were, an increase of the muscle creatine pool with creatine supplements could improve aerobic energy supply during prolonged exercise.

jects in the baseline concentration of total creatine in muscle (possibly related to habitual diet) and in the accumulation of muscle creatine that can be achieved with creatine supplementation (Geenhaff, 1997; Greenhaff et al., 1994; Harris et al., 1992). The largest increase in muscle is seen in those subjects with the lowest initial creatine concentration. A creatine concentration of 160 mmol/kg dry muscle appears to be the maximal creatine concentration achievable as a result of creatine supplementation. This concentration is reached in about 20% of subjects who ingest creatine doses of 20 g/d for 5–6 d. On the other hand, about 20–30% of subjects do not respond to creatine ingestion, i.e., they demonstrate a total creatine increase of < 10 mmol/kg dry muscle. Total creatine in muscle can be increased by a further 40–60% (mean increase = 30–40 mmol/kg dry muscle) when creatine (20 g/d for 5 d) is ingested in a solution containing simple carbohydrates (Green et al., 1996a,b). In that case the muscle total creatine concentration was increased in most subjects to values close to the upper limit of 160 mmol/kg dry muscle. Green et al. (1996a,b) assumed that carbohydrate ingestion stimulated muscle creatine uptake via an insulin-dependent mechanism. Insulin may stimulate the Na^+/K^+-pump activity and thereby the Na^+-dependent creatine transporter in muscle.

Most of the creatine supplementation studies did not use highly trained athletes. The possibility should be investigated that training per se maximizes the total creatine content of muscle and that creatine supplementation leads to smaller increases in highly trained athletes. This would imply that highly trained athletes experience a reduced benefit (see below).

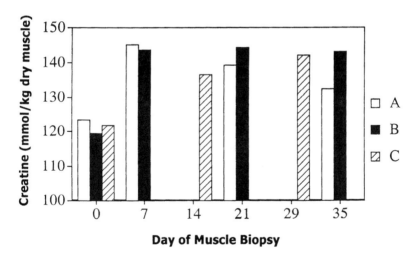

FIGURE 6-2. *Effect of creatine loading on total creatine concentration in muscle.* A: 20 g of creatine was ingested for 6 d and then supplementation was stopped. B: 20 g of creatine was ingested for 6 d and then a maintenance dose of 2 g/d was provided. C: 3 g of creatine was ingested for 28 d. Muscle biopsies were obtained before supplementation began (day 0) and on the indicated days after supplementation was initiated. Data adapted from Hultman et al., 1996.

Creatine Ingestion, Body Weight, and Cell Swelling

Increases in the total creatine concentration in muscle following creatine feeding for 5–6 d at a rate of 20 g/d have been reported to be accompanied by increases in body weight of 0.5–1 kg (Balsom et al., 1993a,b; Greenhaff et al., 1994). A 1.7 kg increase in body mass was observed after 28 d of creatine ingestion at a rate of 20 g/d (Earnest et al., 1995). Hultman et al. (1996) observed a temporary decline in urine production during the first days on creatine ingestion (20 g/d) and suggested that this indicated that water was retained in the body. Because the decrease in urine production exactly paralleled the time course of the increase in muscle creatine concentration documented by Harris et al. (1992), it seems possible that the water was retained in skeletal muscle cells due to an increase of the cellular osmolarity of the muscle fibers and to subsequent cell swelling. Cell swelling has been reported to act as a universal anabolic signal, causing an increase of protein synthesis and net protein deposition (Häussinger et al., 1994; Lang et al., 1998). In line with this hypothesis, Ingwall (1976) reported that addition of creatine to the culture medium stimulated the incorporation of a radioactive leucine tracer into myosin heavy chains and into actin, more so than into other proteins, in short-term cultures of embryonic chicken breast muscle and fetal rat hearts. Moreover, creatine supplementation in a group of patients with gyrate atrophy (a condition in which creatine biosynthesis is impaired) reversed the type II muscle fiber atrophy that is associated with this disease (Sipila et al., 1981). Animals fed with the creatine analogue β-guanidinopropionic acid, which induces a depletion of intramuscular creatine, suffer a loss of myofibrils and atrophy of type II muscle fibers (Laskowski et al., 1981; Van Deursen et al., 1994). Therefore, the possibility should be considered that the increase in total creatine concentration in muscle during creatine supplementation increases the cellular osmolarity and cell swelling of muscle fibers and thereby acts as an anabolic signal in muscle, perhaps especially when prolonged creatine supplementation is combined with strength training and/or endurance training (see below).

Effect of Short-Term Creatine Supplementation on Performance

Repeated Bouts of Maximal Exercise in Normal Healthy Individuals. In most studies investigating the potential ergogenic effect of creatine supplementation, 20 g (4 doses of 5 g) were given daily to healthy normal volunteers for 5–6 d. Performance was measured in placebo-controlled laboratory experiments. In many, but not all, studies (see Greenhaff, 1997; Mujika & Padilla, 1997) creatine supplementation significantly increased the amount of work performed during repeated bouts of brief high-intensity exercise. The rationale behind this clear ergogenic effect of creatine during repetitive exercise has been investigated by Greenhaff et al. (1994). They showed that creatine supplementation facilitated resynthesis of creatine phosphate during recovery from maximal intensity exercise, but only in subjects who demonstrated an increase in muscle creatine of at least 20 mmol/kg dry muscle during creatine supplementation. The higher the initial increase in total creatine in the muscle, the greater the increase in work output during repetitive high-intensity exercise (Greenhaff, 1997). In some of the studies showing no mean effect of creatine, the increase in total creatine in muscle was not measured, and one of the reasons for the lack of an effect may be that several of the subjects had high initial creatine concentrations.

Single Bouts of Competition-Like Maximal Exercise in Highly Trained Athletes. Mujika and Padilla (1997) raised the point that the benefit of creatine supplementation often reported in untrained subjects in experimental laboratory conditions during repeated bouts of maximal exercise has not been observed in highly trained athletes performing single competition-like exercise tasks.

Burke et al. (1996) and Mujika et al. (1996) studied the effect of creatine supplementation versus placebo on 25-m, 50-m and 100-m performance in elite swimmers performing their best strokes. Both studies failed to show an ergogenic effect of creatine supplementation. However, Rossiter et al. (1996) observed an ergogenic effect of creatine versus placebo supplementation on the 1000-m performance of competitive rowers. Furthermore, Bosco et al. (1997) investigated the effect of creatine versus placebo supplementation in qualified sprinters and jumpers. They found that creatine supplementation increased by 13% the time that the athletes were able to maintain a speed of 20 km/h during an all-out run on the treadmill (inclination 5 degrees, duration about 60 s). The also investigated jumping performance during a 45-s maximal continuous jumping exercise. The average rise of the center of gravity was increased significantly during the first and second 15 s, but no difference was seen with the placebo supplementation from 30–45 s. The results were taken to show that creatine supplementation helps to prolong the time during which the maximal rate of power output could be maintained, entirely in line with the theoretical role of creatine phosphate in muscle metabolism.

Grindstaff et al. (1997) found a decrease in swim time in junior competitive swimmers in the first and second heat (not in the third) of three subsequent 100-m freestyle sprint swims after 9 d on 21 g/d of creatine. The conclusion, therefore, is that well-trained athletes also may benefit from creatine supplementation in single competition-like maximal exercise bouts after 5–9 d of creatine supplementation (about 20 g/d). However, many studies have failed to show an effect on single bouts of maximal exercise either in well-trained athletes or in untrained subjects, probably indicating that the effect of creatine supplementation is more profound during repetitive efforts (two potential advantages, i.e., a higher initial store of creatine phosphate and a faster rate of creatine phosphate resynthesis) than during brief single bouts of maximal exercise (only one potential advantage, i.e., a higher initial concentration of creatine phosphate). Nevertheless, from a theoretical point of view, an advantage also should be present during single bouts of maximal exercise, though it may be far from easy to measure these effects, especially in exercise bouts lasting less than 10 s.

Harris et al. (1992) observed in untrained subjects that when submaximal exercise was performed during the first 5 d of supplementation, the increase in total creatine in muscle could be enhanced by another 10%. The mechanism behind this exercise- induced increase of the efficiency of creatine loading is not known. However, the existence of such a mechanism opens the possibility that highly trained athletes already have higher muscle total creatine concentrations on their habitual diets, which contain some creatine, especially when meat or fish is included, than do sedentary and untrained subjects. From this point of view, Mujika and Padilla (1997) may be right that fewer highly trained athletes may benefit from creatine supplementation. To clarify this point, researchers should measure creatine concentrations in various groups of athletes before and after creatine supplementation. Most of the current knowledge regarding the efficiency of creatine loading has been obtained in untrained individuals.

Endurance Exercise. Theoretically, an increase of the total creatine and creatine phosphate pools in muscle by acute creatine supplementation also could produce advantages for performance of endurance exercise. Creatine phosphate and creatine may be involved in a shuttle system to transport the energy-rich phosphate group of ATP from the mitochondria to the myofibrils. If this shuttle would work more efficiently after creatine supplementation, then the cytosolic energy disturbance during exercise could be smaller, leading to less activation of glycogen breakdown and glycolysis, with less lactate production and more aerobic ATP production (more oxygen consumption during exercise).

Balsom et al. (1993b) investigated the effect of creatine supplementation for 6 d on endurance exercise performance in well-trained runners. There was no effect during a high-intensity treadmill run to exhaustion in the laboratory, and they observed a significant decrease in performance during a 6-km run over varying terrain. The fact that subjects showed an increase in body weight of 0.5–1.0 kg may have explained the negative result during the outdoor run. Also, Stroud and colleagues (1994) showed that 5 d of creatine supplementation had no influence on oxygen uptake, respiratory gas exchange, and blood lactate concentration during submaximal incremental treadmill exercise and recovery. Thus, the data on endurance exercise seem to suggest that creatine and creatine phosphate are not rate limiting for the diffusion of energy-rich phosphate groups through the cytosol and that creatine supplementation, therefore, does not have an effect on muscle metabolism in endurance exercise.

Effects of Prolonged Creatine Supplementation on Muscle Performance and Metabolism

Vandenberghe et al. (1997) investigated the effect of creatine loading (4 d of 20 g/d followed by 10 wk of 5 g/d) on muscle creatine phosphate concentration (measured by nuclear magnetic resonance), muscle strength, and body composition in young sedentary female volunteers during a 10-wk resistance training program. Compared with placebo, creatine supplementation was associated with 20–25% greater increases in maximal strength for three of the six resistance-exercise tests employed, 11–25% greater torque production by the arm flexors during intermittent exercise, and greater increases in fat-free body mass (5.8% gain vs. 3.7% gain). These effects were statistically significant (P< 0.05).

Kreider et al. (1998) administered an electrolyte drink containing glucose and taurine or the same drink supplemented with creatine (15.8 g/d) for 28 d in well-trained American-style football players. Dependent variables included performance of 12 repeated 6-s cycling sprints, weightlifting volume (load x total repetitions), and estimated fat-and-bone-free body mass during resistance and agility training. Gains in fat-and-bone-free body mass (2.43 ± 1.4 vs. 1.33 ± 1.1 kg) and the total work performed during the first five (but not the last seven) 6-s sprints were significantly greater in the group ingesting creatine, as were gains in lifting volume in the bench-press (but not in the squat or power clean). These studies by Vandenberghe et al. (1997) and Kreider et al. (1998) suggest that the combination of strength training and creatine ingestion can have significant advantages above strength training alone, both in sedentary subjects and in highly trained athletes.

A long-term study in rats (Brannon et al., 1997) that combined creatine ingestion (3.3 mg per g diet) with high-intensity run training seems to contain important messages for future creatine research on humans. Creatine and creatine phosphate concentrations increased in both the slow soleus and fast plantaris muscles in response to creatine supplementation. Citrate synthase activity (a mitochondrial enzyme used as marker for the muscle oxidative capacity) was increased in both the soleus and plantaris muscles following training. Creatine ingestion caused a significant 15% further increase in the citrate synthase activity of the plantaris, but not of the soleus, of the trained rats. However, in a sedentary control group creatine ingestion increased the citrate synthase activity in the soleus, but not in the plantaris, to the level observed in the trained rats. There were no significant changes in either creatine kinase activity or in the distribution of myosin heavy chain isoforms following training in the two muscles, regardless of diet. Creatine ingestion for 10 d increased running performance at 60 m/min up a 15% grade, which typically exhausts a sedentary rat in less than 2 min, and improved interval running performance at same speed and grade when 30-s runs alternated with 30-s recovery periods. No further change was observed when creatine ingestion was continued in the sedentary animals for 4 wk. High-intensity interval training caused a major improvement in running performance during both continuous and interval run tests, and the combination of high-intensity interval training and creatine ingestion caused by far the largest increase in running performance. For example, the numbers of completed 30-s repetitions during interval running were 8, 10, 16, and 24 in sedentary, sedentary + creatine, trained, and trained + creatine groups, respectively. Brannon et al. (1997) concluded that the gains in high-intensity running performance following creatine loading were a combined result of increased capacities for ATP generation aerobically, as indicated by greater activity of citrate synthase, and anaerobically, as indicated by greater stores of creatine and phosphocreatine.

These data suggest that a new era in creatine supplementation research may emerge. Future research in humans should focus on the combined effects of creatine supplementation with 1) endurance training, 2) high-intensity aerobic training and 3) anaerobic and strength training. It is possible that training with a higher intramuscular creatine content enables the athletes to perform more repetitions at a greater speed or workload and provides an anabolic signal to muscle that leads to improved adaptation and thus to improved sprint performance, muscle strength, and high-intensity endurance performance. Obviously, much more research is needed in this area before definitive conclusions can be made.

CARNITINE

In the overnight fasted state and during exercise of low-to- moderate intensity, long-chain fatty acids are the main energy sources of the human body in general and of the contracting skeletal muscles in particular (Romijn et al., 1993). Since the beginning of this century it has been known that human and animal muscles contain high concentrations (4–5 μmol/g wet weight) of L-carnitine. The primary function of L-carnitine is to transport long-chain fatty acids across the mitochondrial inner membrane, which is otherwise impermeable both to long-chain fatty acids and to fatty acyl-CoA esters (Bremer, 1983). The use of supplementary carnitine by athletes to improve performance during endurance events such as marathons and long-distance cycling has become widespread. Anecdotes have been circulating that carnitine supplementation helped the Italian national soccer team become world-champions in 1982 (Editorial, 1982).

The original idea behind carnitine supplementation in endurance sports was that carnitine would increase the rate of fatty acid oxidation by the exercising muscles and would thus reduce the rate of glycogen breakdown and thereby postpone fatigue. Moreover, supplementation of the diet with carnitine was hypothesized to increase maximal oxygen consumption ($\dot{V}O_2max$) and reduce lactate production during high-intensity exercise (Heinonen, 1996; Wagenmakers, 1991). Products containing carnitine can be found on the shelves of sports and health food shops. Claims have also been made that carnitine can increase fatty acid oxidation under resting conditions and thus can help reduce body fat stores and can accelerate weight loss.

In this section, the role of carnitine in human metabolism, the rationale behind carnitine supplementation, and the effects of carnitine supplementation on exercise performance and metabolism will be critically reviewed. Readers who want to gain more detailed insight into the metabolic aspects of L-carnitine and the hypothesized effects on athletic performance should consult earlier reviews on the biochemistry of L-carnitine and its role in physiology (Bremer, 1983) and pathophysiology (Borum, 1986). A more exhaustive list of references on the effects of carnitine supplementation on performance can be found in earlier reviews (Heinonen, 1996; Wagenmakers, 1991). Only key papers with controlled scientific designs will be mentioned here.

Dietary Intake, Biosynthesis, and Distribution in Tissues

The main sources of L-carnitine are red meats and dairy products in the diet and endogenous biosynthesis. When the diet contains no carnitine, healthy humans still are assumed to produce enough carnitine to maintain normal bodily function. For this reason, carnitine is not regarded as a vitamin, but as a vitamin-like substance. L-Carnitine is synthesized in mammals from trimethyllysine. Specific lysine residues in some intracellular proteins are methylated to form trimethyllysine in a reaction that also requires methionine as methyl donor. Trimethyllysine is released by protein degradation and is then metabolized to L-carnitine in four enzymatic steps. The first three steps can occur in all tissues of the human body. In humans the final reaction occurs in liver and kidney, tissues which together contain only 1.6% of the whole-body carnitine store of 140 mmol or 27 g. About 98% of the carnitine of the human body is present in skeletal muscle and heart, tissues which, therefore, are dependent upon transport of L-carnitine through the circulation. About 0.5% of whole-body carnitine circulates in the blood. Muscle takes up L-carnitine against a concentration gradient (plasma carnitine ~ 40–60 μM; muscle carnitine ~ 4–5 mM) by a saturable active transport process. Carnitine is an end product of human metabolism and is lost from the body only via excretion in urine and stool. Minor daily losses of about 60 mg/d are reduced to less than 20 mg/d on diets free of meat and carnitine (Bremer, 1983). This implies that the rate of endogenous biosynthesis needed to maintain adequate bodily stores of carnitine is also only 20 mg/d. The amounts of carnitine lost in the stool are negligible except after ingestion of oral supplements.

Effect of Exercise on Total, Acylated and Free Carnitine

In tissues and physiological fluids, carnitine is present in the free form and in esterified forms as short- and long-chain acylcarnitines, i.e., carnitine bound to short- and long-chain fatty acids. The predominant short-chain acyl-carnitine is the water-soluble acetyl-carnitine. Also, there are some branched-chain acyl-carnitines, which are products of the

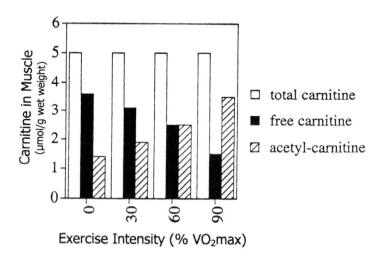

FIGURE 6-3. The concentration of *free carnitine in muscle declines during exercise due to an intensity-dependent increase in acetylcarnitine.* Data from Constantin-Teodosiu et al. (1991).

branched-chain amino acids. In man at rest, acyl-carnitine esters account for 10–40% of total carnitine in blood plasma and for 20–30% of total carnitine in muscle. The indicated proportions vary considerably with nutritional status. During exercise the total carnitine concentration in muscle does not change (Heinonen, 1996; Wagenmakers, 1991). However, the free carnitine concentration falls in proportion to the exercise intensity, whereas the concentration of acetyl-carnitine simultaneously rises (Constantin-Teodosiu et al., 1991; Figure 6-3). During high-intensity exercise (90% $\dot{V}O_2$max) the free carnitine concentration in muscle may fall to values as low as 0.5–1 µmol/g wet weight (Constantin-Teodosiu et al., 1991; Harris et al., 1987) without any change in total carnitine concentration.

Main Functions of Carnitine in Muscle Metabolism

Transport of Long-Chain Fatty Acyl CoA into Mitochondria. In all cells of the human body, carnitine functions to transport long-chain fatty acids across the mitochondrial inner membrane so that the fatty acids can be subjected to β-oxidation and used for ATP production (Figure 6-4). The mitochondrial outer membrane is permeable for most charged molecules and, therefore, also for fatty acids in the unesterified form, long-chain acyl-CoA esters, and carnitine and its esters. However, the inner membrane forms an impermeable barrier and, therefore, is filled with specific transporters for many charged molecules. There is no transporter, though, for long-chain fatty acyl-CoA compounds or for fatty acids. Therefore, carnitine is needed as substrate for carnitine acyltransferase I (CAT I; Figure 6-4) to first convert long-chain acyl-CoA compounds into long-chain acylcarnitines. The long-chain acylcarnitines are then transported across the mitochondrial membrane in exchange for free carnitine out of the mitochondrial matrix in a reaction catalysed by carnitine acylcarnitine translocase. On the matrix side, long-chain acyl-CoA is then regenerated by the action of CAT II and subsequently undergoes β-oxidation.

Modulation of the Acetyl-CoA/CoA Ratio and the Size of the Free CoA Pool. Acetyl-CoA, when generated in muscle in excessive amounts, e.g., when pyruvate dehydrogenase is activated during exercise or ischemia, is converted to acetyl-carnitine in the following reaction:

$$acetyl\text{-}CoA + carnitine \leftrightarrow acetyl\text{-}carnitine + CoA$$

(Constantin-Teodosiu et al., 1991). This is a reversible reaction catalyzed by the enzyme carnitine acetyltransferase, and the reaction has an equilibrium constant of 0.6–0.7 (Bremer, 1983). Human muscle contains only about 0.015 µmol/g wet weight of total CoA (free CoA + acetyl-CoA)

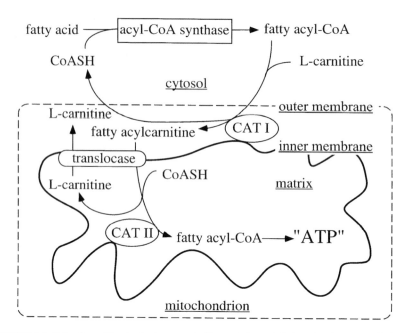

FIGURE 6-4. *Role of carnitine in the transport of long-chain acyl CoA molecules across the inner membrane of the mitochondrion.* CAT = carnitine acyltransferase. Translocase = carnitine acylcarnitine translocase. (See text for full discussion.)

and 4–5 μmol/g wet weight of total carnitine. This implies that a micromolar increase in the acetyl-CoA concentration, as is observed during high-intensity exercise, leads to a millimolar accumulation of acetyl groups in the form of acetyl-carnitine (Constantin-Teodosiu et al., 1991). The availability of free CoA for muscle metabolism, e.g., for activation of fatty acids, for the pyruvate dehydrogenase reaction, and for the α-ketoglutarate dehydrogenase reaction, increases by this temporary storage of acetyl groups in the form of acetylcarnitine. In other words, the carnitine pool in muscle helps store excess acetyl groups and keeps free CoA available for muscle metabolism. The in-vitro addition of carnitine to incubated mitochondria stimulates pyruvate oxidation and the rate of cycling (flux) in the tricarboxylic acid cycle (Wagenmakers, 1991).

Rationale for Carnitine Supplementation as a Slimming Agent

The rationale for carnitine supplementation as a slimming agent for obese and non-obese subjects and athletes is based on one assumption and one overly simplistic thought. The assumption is that regular oral ingestion of carnitine will increase the muscle carnitine concentration. The simplistic thought is that an increase in the muscle free carnitine concentration would increase the rate of fatty acid oxidation in muscle and would thus lead to a gradual loss of the body fat stores. In several careful investigations (Barnett et al., 1994; Vukovich et al., 1994) it has been shown clearly that oral carnitine ingestion (up to 6 g/d for 14 d) does not change the muscle carnitine concentration. Furthermore, it is quite clear that carnitine ingestion does not change (and from a theoretical point of view it cannot change) the in-vivo rate of fat oxidation in humans under resting conditions. The K_m (concentration at which the enzyme has 50% of maximal activity) of carnitine acyltransferase I for carnitine is between 250 and 450 μM (Bremer, 1983), which implies that in muscle in resting conditions more than enough free carnitine (4000–5000 μM) is available to allow the enzyme to function at maximal activity.

Rationale for Carnitine Supplementation to Improve Exercise Performance

Endurance Exercise. During prolonged exercise muscle glycogen, blood glucose, plasma free fatty acids, and intramuscular triacylglycerol are the main fuels used by the contracting muscles (Romijn et al., 1993). With increasing exercise intensity the rate at which muscle glycogen is broken down increases rapidly, and, therefore, muscle glycogen becomes the most important fuel at intensities of 60% $\dot{V}O_2$max and higher. When the muscle glycogen stores have been emptied, fatigue will occur, and the exercise intensity (pace) must be reduced to 50% $\dot{V}O_2$max or lower.

The idea that carnitine supplementation would be useful for athletes to improve endurance performance is based on the following assumptions: 1) the carnitine concentration present in muscle without supplementation is too low to allow CAT I (Figure 6-4) to function at a high velocity and to support the increased rate of fat oxidation during exercise; 2) oral ingestion of carnitine leads to an increase of the total carnitine concentration in muscle; 3) carnitine supplementation, therefore, increases the rate of oxidation of plasma fatty acids and intramuscular triacylglycerol during exercise and thereby reduces glycogen breakdown and postpones fatigue.

The first assumption may well be correct during exercise of relatively high intensities. As indicated above, the free carnitine concentration in muscle is reduced with increasing exercise intensity to values as low as 0.5–1 $\mu mol/g$ wet weight after 3–4 min at 90% $\dot{V}O_2$max (Constantin-Teodosiu et al., 1991; Harris et al., 1987). These values approach the K_m of CAT I for carnitine (250–450 μM) measured in vitro (Bremer, 1983). The fall in muscle free carnitine at high exercise intensities, which is a a consequence of high rates of glycolysis, activation of pyruvate dehydrogenase, and excessive formation of acetyl groups (Constantin-Teodosiu et al., 1991; Figure 6-5) may, in fact, be the cause of the decrease in oxidation of plasma fatty acids and intramuscular triacylglycerol that is observed when the exercise intensity is increased from 60% to 85% VO₂max (Romijn et al., 1993).

However, the second assumption is clearly not valid. Direct measurements in muscle after 14 d of 4–6 g/d of carnitine failed to show increases in the muscle carnitine concentration (Barnett et al., 1994; Vukovich et al., 1994). This implies that carnitine supplementation cannot increase fat oxidation during exercise (the third assumption) and improve performance in human beings by the proposed mechanism. It indeed has been confirmed in many investigations that carnitine supplementation does not increase fat oxidation and reduce glycogen breakdown and does not improve performance during prolonged cycling and

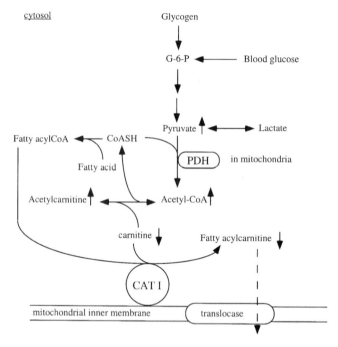

FIGURE 6-5. *Proposed mechanism for the reduction of the oxidation rate of fatty acids in muscle during exercise at ≥ 65% VO₂max.* During exercise, the rates of muscle glycogen breakdown and glycolysis are increased, causing an increase in pyruvate concentration and activation of pyruvate dehydrogenase (PDH). As a consequence, the acetyl-CoA concentration will rise, and by the action of carnitine acetyltransferase (CATI), acetylcarnitine is formed. A micromolar increase in the acetyl-CoA concentration, as is observed during high-intensity exercise, leads to a millimolar accumulation of acetyl groups in the form of acetylcarnitine (Constantin-Teodosiu et al., 1991). Therefore, the free carnitine concentration will decline (Figure 6-3). This decline in free carnitine concentration may limit the activity of CAT I and reduce the rate of fatty oxidation in muscle.

running exercise in man (Heinonen, 1996; Vukovich et al., 1994; Wagenmakers, 1991)

Simi and colleagues (1990) succeeded in increasing the muscle carnitine concentration in rats by about 40% after carnitine supplementation, but they did not observe an effect on the exercise capacity or on the rate of muscle glycogen degradation, suggesting that the increase in fat oxidation during exercise can be adequately supported by the basal carnitine levels.

High-Intensity Exercise. As indicated above, carnitine may function to increase the availability of free CoA for several steps in muscle metabolism not related to fat metabolism. This function of carnitine is of special relevance for brief high intensity exercise such as competitive short- and middle-distance running or swimming for 50–400 m. If carnitine supplementation would increase muscle carnitine concentration and thereby increase CoA availability in these conditions, the flux through pyruvate dehydrogenase could be increased, and less lactate would be produced (Figure 6-5). This could delay fatigue and improve performance by increasing the ability to maintain the highest possible speed for a longer period. Carnitine supplementation in that case also could lead to a greater VO_2max because an increased CoA availability would support a greater maximal flux through the tricarboxylic acid cycle.

However, we now know that carnitine supplementation does not increase the muscle carnitine concentration; therefore, carnitine supplementation cannot have an effect on muscle metabolism during any form of exercise. In agreement with this conclusion, most controlled original investigations employing high-intensity exercise in various laboratories have failed to show effects of carnitine supplementation on VO_2max, on performance, and on lactate accumulation (Barnett et al., 1994; Heinonen, 1996; Trappe et al., 1994; Wagenmakers, 1991).

BRANCHED-CHAIN AMINO ACIDS (BCAA)

A voluntary muscle contraction is the final step in a command chain that extends from the higher centers of the central nervous system to the actin and myosin filaments in the muscle; it involves electrical, metabolic, and mechanical events. Consequently, many sites and mechanisms are potentially implicated in the fatigue process (Fitts, 1994). A distinction is usually made between central fatigue, in which the impairment is in the central nervous system, and peripheral fatigue, in which the impairment is in peripheral nerves or contracting muscles.

In well-motivated subjects a substantial component of fatigue can be attributed to events in the muscle leading to a loss of contractility. Glycogen depletion, a decrease of the resting membrane potential as a consequence of potassium losses, failure of the calcium pump in the sarcoplasmic reticulum, an increase in free ADP and P_i concentration, and failure of the neuromuscular transmission have all been associated with muscle fatigue during prolonged exercise (Fitts, 1994). However, it is also possible that dysfunction of the central nervous system and psychological factors such as motivation and mood may contribute to an eventual decrement in certain types of endurance performance.

The branched-chain amino acids (BCAA)—leucine, isoleucine, and valine—are three of the nine essential amino acids in humans; thus, we depend on dietary protein consumption for an adequate source of these compounds. Hypothetically, the BCAA might be involved with fatigue mechanisms both in the central nervous system and in skeletal muscle. Both proposed interactions will be described here in detail, and a review will be given of performance trials and experimental research with BCAA and tryptophan supplements in order to judge 1) whether BCAA supplements influence performance and 2) the extent to which experimental evidence supports the proposed involvement of BCAA in the mechanism of fatigue.

Branched-Chain Amino Acids as a Fuel

Beginning in the late 1970s it was suggested that BCAA were the third most important fuel for skeletal muscle, after carbohydrate and fatty acids (Goldberg & Chang, 1978; Wagenmakers, 1998). This conclusion was based on the measurement of enzyme activities involved in BCAA metabolism and the large size of the muscle compartment (accounting for 40 to 50% of the total body mass of a lean 70-kg subject). In isolated rat diaphragms leucine oxidation accounted for over 10% of the resting energy expenditure (Goldberg & Chang, 1978). However, in the early 1980s the activity of the branched-chain α-keto-acid dehydrogenase complex (BCKADH), the enzyme that is rate-determining for BCAA oxidation in muscle, was shown to be regulated by a phosphorylation/dephosphorylation cycle, with dephosphorylation causing inactivation. During incubation of isolated rat diaphragms, spontaneous activation of the BCKADH-complex was observed (Wagenmakers et al., 1984), implying that in-vitro measurements of BCAA oxidation far exceeded in-vivo oxidation rates.

In human skeletal muscle only 4–6% of the enzyme was active at rest (Wagenmakers et al., 1989, 1991). Exercise on a cycle ergometer after overnight fasting caused activation of the BCKAD-complex to about 20% active enzyme (Wagenmakers et al., 1989, 1991). With stable isotope methodology ($^{13}CO_2$ production from L-[1-^{13}C]leucine), it was also shown that BCAA oxidation increased 4-fold to 5-fold during exercise in the overnight-fasted state (Knapik et al., 1991; Wolfe et al., 1982). Meanwhile, it has become clear that the nutritional state of the subjects (Knapik et al., 1991; Wagenmakers et al., 1991) and the glycogen content of the muscle (Van Hall et al., 1996; Wagenmakers et al., 1991) influence the activation of the BCKADH-complex by exercise.

Many endurance athletes practice carbohydrate loading the day before competition and also ingest carbohydrate during the competition; however, this dietary regimen prevented activation of the BCKADH-complex in trained subjects who cycled for 2 h at 70–75% of their maximal workloads (Wagenmakers et al., 1991). Carbohydrate ingestion also dramatically reduces the $^{13}CO_2$ production from L-[1-^{13}C]leucine during exercise. This implies that the oxidation of BCAA increases very little during 2 h of competitive exercise at intensities of $\leq$ 75% $\dot{V}O_2$max compared to rest. Because the total energy expenditure increases up to 20-fold at such intensities, due to increased oxidation of carbohydrates and fat, this suggests that the contribution of BCAA oxidation to total energy expenditure is reduced during exercise to less than 1%. Therefore, BCAA do not seem to play a significant role as a fuel during exercise of light, moderate, and high intensity; thus, there seems to be no solid rationale for supplementation of BCAA during exercise.

Branched-Chain Amino Acids and Central Fatigue

In 1987 the "central fatigue" hypothesis was proposed as an important mechanism contributing to the development of fatigue during prolonged moderate-intensity exercise (Newsholme et al., 1987). During exercise, free fatty acids (FFA) are mobilized from adipose tissue and are transported via the blood to muscle to serve as fuel. As the blood FFA concentration rises during exercise, the FFA compete with the amino acid tryptophan for binding sites on albumin, and the FFA displace some of the tryptophan molecules from the albumin; therefore, the free tryptophan concentration in the blood increases. Simultaneously, the increased oxidation of BCAA in muscle (Wagenmakers et al., 1989, 1991) reduces the concentration of the BCAA in the blood. Thus, as the plasma concentration of tryptophan increases and that of BCAA falls, the ratio of free tryptophan to BCAA increases substantially. The increase in this ratio leads to increased tryptophan transport across the blood-brain barrier because BCAA and tryptophan compete for carrier-mediated entry into the central nervous system by the large-neutral-amino-acid transporter (Chaoulofff et al., 1986; Hargreaves & Pardridge, 1988). Once taken up by the brain, tryptophan is converted to serotonin (5-hydroxytryptamine), resulting in a local increase of this neurotransmitter in the brain (Figure 6-4; Chaouloff et al., 1986).

Such an exercise-induced increase in serotonin has been found in certain brain areas in the rat, but it has not been established that it also occurs in man. According to the "central fatigue" hypothesis, the increase in serotonergic activity would subsequently lead to central fatigue, forcing athletes to stop exercise or to reduce running or cycling speed. In neurobiology it has been established that serotonin plays a role in the onset of sleep and that it is a determinant of mood and aggression. It is uncertain, though, that it also plays a role in the experience of fatigue during prolonged exercise.

One of the implications of the "central fatigue" hypothesis is that ingestion of BCAA, which compete with tryptophan for transport into the brain (Hargreaves & Pardridge, 1988), could reduce the exercise-induced increase of brain tryptophan uptake and thus delay fatigue and give athletes the ability to continue longer, even when peripheral fatigue mechanisms come into operation. In other words, BCAA would theoretically be ergogenic, and ingestion of tryptophan prior to exercise would be ergolytic.

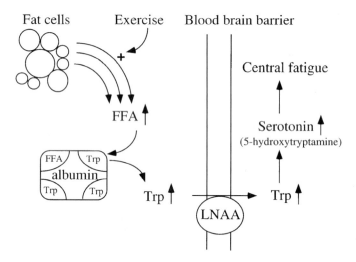

FIGURE 6-6. *Schematic presentation of the "central fatigue" hypothesis of Newsholme et al., 1987.* According to this hypothesis, any factor that changes the rate of tryptophan (Trp) transport via the large-neutral-amino-acid carrier (LNAA) from the blood into the brain can change the concentration of serotonin in the brain. If serotonin is increased, fatigue occurs earlier; if serotonin is decreased, fatigue is delayed. Exercise-induced increases in free fatty acids (FFA) displace tryptophan from binding sites on plasma albumin, resulting in greater concentrations of free tryptophan in the blood, increased transport of tryptophan across the blood-brain barrier, increased serotonin production in the brain, and earlier fatigue. Increasing the plasma concentration of branched-chain amino acids (BCAA) with BCAA supplements has been hypothesized to delay fatigue because the BCAA would compete with tryptophan for binding sites on LNAA. This decreases transport of tryptophan into the brain and reduces serotonin production. See text for full explanation.

Interaction of the BCAA-Aminotransferase Reaction with the Tricarboxylic Acid Cycle in Muscle

The rate of ATP turnover in skeletal muscle is determined partly by the carbon flux through the tricarboxylic (TCA) cycle. One possibility for achieving an increase in TCA-cycle activity in the transition from rest to exercise (to meet the increased energy demand of exercise) is to increase the concentration of the TCA-cycle intermediates in muscle such that more substrate is available for the individual enzymatic reactions. This increase in concentration has been observed for the most abundant TCA-cycle intermediates early during exercise (Essen & Kaijser, 1978; Gibala et al., 1997; Sahlin et al., 1990) and is achieved by rapid conversion of the muscle glutamate pool into α-ketoglutarate (Sahlin et al., 1990; Van Hall et al., 1995b). The reaction used to achieve that increase is the near-equilibrium alanine aminotransferase reaction (Figure 6-7). The increase in muscle pyruvate concentration that occurs at the start of exercise (due to an acceleration of glycolysis) serves as substrate for the alanine aminotransferase reaction and automatically leads to the production of alanine and α-ketoglutarate and to the consumption of glutamate. After the early increases in concentrations of TCA-cycle intermediates, their concentrations subsequently decrease gradually in human subjects exercising to exhaustion at 75% $\dot{V}O_2$max (Gibala et al., 1997; Sahlin et al., 1990).

We have hypothesized that increased oxidation of BCAA plays an important role in the gradual decrease in the concentrations of the TCA-cycle intermediates in endurance exercise (Wagenmakers, 1998). The BCKADH-complex is increasingly activated during prolonged exercise that results in glycogen depletion (Wagenmakers et al., 1989, 1991), and an increase in BCAA oxidation will increase the flux through the preliminary BCAA aminotransferase reaction that produces the branched-chain □-keto acid (Figure 6-8).

In the case of leucine, this BCAA aminotransferase reaction will put a net carbon drain on the TCA-cycle as □-ketoglutarate is removed and is not replaced with other TCA-cycle intermediates (Figure 6-8). On the other hand, increased oxidation of valine and isoleucine will not lead to net removal of TCA-cycle intermediates because the carbon skeleton of valine is oxidized to succinyl-CoA and that of isoleucine to succinyl-CoA and acetyl-CoA, both of which can be used in the TCA cycle.

Net removal of α-ketoglutarate from the TCA cycle via leucine transamination can be compensated for by the alanine aminotransferase reaction (Figure 6-7) as long as muscle glycogen is available and the muscle pyruvate concentration is kept high. However, as activation of the BCKAD-complex is greatest in glycogen-depleted muscle, this

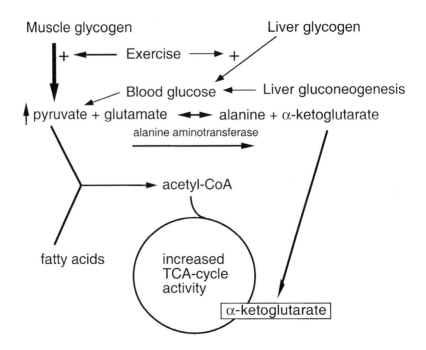

FIGURE 6-7. *The role of the alanine aminotransferase reaction in providing metabolic intermediates for the tricarboxylic acid (TCA) cycle in muscle.* High rates of glycogen breakdown and glycolysis in muscle and the subsequent mass action effect of the increasing concentration of pyruvate on the alanine aminotransferase reaction feeds carbon (□-ketoglutarate) into the TCA cycle during the first minutes of exercise. During more prolonged exercise, glucose released from the liver may provide another source of pyruvate to serve as driving force for synthesis of TCA-cycle intermediates via the alanine aminotransferase reaction.

mechanism eventually is expected to lead to a decrease in the concentration of TCA-cycle intermediates, a reduced TCA-cycle activity, and a reduction of ATP production (Fitts, 1994).

The leg muscles rapidly extract the BCAA after they are ingested, and this is accompanied by activation of the BCKADH-complex at rest and even greater activation during exercise (Van Hall et al., 1996). This could suggest that the indicated carbon drain on the TCA-cycle is larger after BCAA ingestion and that BCAA ingestion could cause premature fatigue during prolonged exercise that is associated with glycogen depletion.

In the previous paragraphs, two hypotheses have been proposed by which BCAA may interact with metabolism in both the central nervous system and in the muscles. One of the interactions predicts that BCAA supplementation would be ergogenic, whereas the other predicts that it would lead to premature fatigue. In the next section, performance trials will be reviewed to help judge whether or not there is sufficient experimental evidence to support one of these hypothetical interactions or whether they have only theoretical rather than practical relevance.

Effect Of Ingestion or Infusion of Branched-Chain Amino Acids on Endurance Performance

The effect of BCAA ingestion on physical performance was investigated for the first time in a field test by Blomstrand et al. (1991). Male runners (n = 193) were studied during a marathon in Stockholm. Subjects were randomly (without matching) divided into an experimental group receiving 16 g of BCAA in plain water during the race and a placebo group receiving flavored water. The subjects additionally had *ad-libitum* access to carbohydrate-containing drinks. No difference was observed in the marathon time of the two groups. However, when the subjects were arbitrarily divided into groups of faster and slower run-

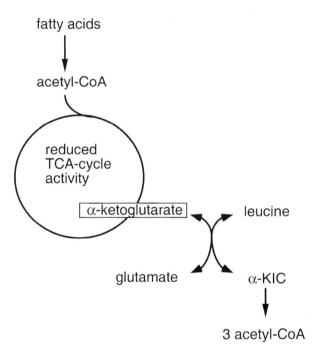

FIGURE 6-8. *Increased rates of leucine transamination remove α-ketoglutarate from the TCA cycle during prolonged exercise.* The subsequent decrease in the concentration of TCA-cycle intermediates reduces the TCA-cycle flux and limits the maximal rate of fat oxidation in glycogen-depleted muscles.

ners, a small but significant reduction in marathon time for the BCAA treatment was observed in the slower runners only. This first study has been the only one claiming a positive effect of BCAA ingestion during exercise. However, three main criticisms can be raised against the design of this experiment: 1) in a performance test investigating a potentially ergogenic effect, subjects in the two groups should have been matched for performance ability; 2) carbohydrate intake and nutritional status should have been controlled and matched in the two groups; and 3) division of subjects into groups of faster and slower runners, taking an arbitrary marathon time as selection criterion, is not in accordance with accepted scientific methods. Each of these points may have biased the data obtained by Blomstrand et al. (1991).

Varnier et al. (1994) investigated six moderately trained subjects after glycogen-depleting exercise followed by overnight fasting. The subjects were investigated the morning after the fast during graded incremental exercise to exhaustion. They received an intravenous infusion of BCAA (260 mg·kg^{-1}·h^{-1} for 70 min) or saline only. No significant BCAA effects on total work performed were detected.

In a laboratory experiment, Blomstrand et al. (1995) investigated performance in five endurance-trained men during exhaustive exercise on a cycle ergometer at 75% $\dot{V}O_2$max after prior reduction of their muscle glycogen stores. During exercise, the subjects were given in random order a 6% carbohydrate solution containing 7 g·L^{-1} of BCAA, a 6% carbohydrate solution, or flavored water. There were no performance differences between the carbohydrate + BCAA and the carbohydrate-only treatments. Blomstrand et al. (1997) also compared flavored water with a solution of BCAA in seven trained endurance cyclists and did not find an effect on total work performed during a 20 min cycling time trial following 1 h of exercise at 70% $\dot{V}O_2$max.

Madsen and colleagues (1996) investigated performance in nine trained cyclists in a 100-km time trial in the laboratory. Subjects used their own bikes at a freely chosen power output, simulating field conditions, and were studied while ingesting flavored water only (placebo), a 5% carbohydrate solution (66 g of carbohydrate per hour), and carbohydrate (66 g/h) plus BCAA (6.8 g/h). There was no difference among treatments in the 100-km finish time.

Mittleman et al. (1998) compared the effects of drinking a solution containing BCAA or a placebo drink during cycling at 40% $\dot{V}O_2$max on time to exhaustion during heat stress. Cycling endurance increased during BCAA ingestion in a mixed group of six women and seven men (153.1 ± 13.3 versus 137.0 ± 12.2 min). Regretfully, there was no carbohydrate treatment or carbohydrate-plus-BCAA treatment in this study; thus, the practical relevance of this isolated observation is not clear.

Van Hall and colleagues (1995a) designed a randomized, double-blind experiment to simultaneously test both the hypothesis that BCAA ingestion would improve performance and the hypothesis that tryptophan ingestion would impair performance. Ten endurance-trained male athletes were studied during cycling exercise at 70–75% of their maximal work rates while ingesting drinks that contained 6% sucrose (control) or 6% sucrose supplemented with 1) tryptophan (3 $g \cdot L^{-1}$), 2) a low dose of BCAA (6 $g \cdot L^{-1}$), or 3) a high dose of BCAA (18 $g \cdot L^{-1}$). These treatments greatly increased the plasma concentration of the respective amino acids to values well outside the normal physiological range. Because they measured the concentrations of all amino acids competing for transport by the large-neutral-amino-acid carrier, Van Hall et al. (1995a) were able to calculate the rate of unidirectional influx of circulating plasma tryptophan into the brain, using kinetic parameters of transport of human brain capillaries reported by Hargreaves and Pardridge (1988). These calculations showed that the BCAA treatments reduced tryptophan transport at exhaustion by only 8–12%, whereas tryptophan ingestion caused an increase of 600–1900%, depending on the use of free or total tryptophan concentration in the calculations. Despite these massive differences in tryptophan transport, the time to exhaustion was not different among the four treatments. Therefore, Van Hall and colleagues concluded that either manipulation of tryptophan supply to the brain by ingestion of BCAA and tryptophan in drinks containing carbohydrate did not change the serotonin concentration in relevant local areas in the brain or any such change in serotonergic activity during prolonged exercise contributed little to the mechanisms of fatigue.

Wagenmakers et al. (1990) investigated the effect of BCAA ingestion (20 g) 30 min prior to graded incremental exercise in two patients with McArdle's disease (muscle glycogen phosphorylase deficiency). Due to the enzyme defect, these patients cannot break muscle glycogen down during exercise and, therefore, have a limited exercise capacity. These patients are an ideal 'experiment of nature' to investigate muscle metabolism in conditions of zero glycogen availability. Ingestion of BCAA reduced the maximal power output that was reached during the tests by about 20%, and heart rate and perceived exertion were higher at the same workload. Ingestion of the keto acids of the BCAA (without the amino group) improved performance in the patients. Ingestion of BCAA increases ammonia production by muscle and increased plasma ammonia concentration during exercise both in patients (Wagenmakers et al., 1990) and in healthy controls (Madsen et al., 1996; MacLean et al., 1996; Van Hall et al., 1995a). Accumulation of ammonia has been hypothesized to have adverse effects on motor function (Bannister & Cameron, 1990).

MEDIUM-CHAIN TRIACYLGLYCEROL (MCT)

Over the past century, research has clearly shown that the point of fatigue in endurance exercise coincides with very low concentrations of muscle glycogen (Fitts, 1994). Carbohydrate ingestion improves performance by maintaining normal glucose concentrations and high carbohydrate-oxidation rates, but carbohydrate ingestion typically does not spare muscle glycogen utilization (Coggan & Coyle, 1991). In contrast, when both emulsions of fat (triacylglycerol) and heparin have been infused intravenously to increase the circulating FFA concentrations, rates of muscle glycogen utilization were decreased (Costill et al., 1977; Vukovich et al., 1993). From these results, it seems that by increasing the rate of fatty acid oxidation during exercise one can reduce muscle glycogen breakdown and, therefore, improve endurance performance. In fact, the success of the trained versus the untrained endurance athlete has been attributed to the ability of the trained athlete to oxidize more fat and less glycogen at the same absolute exercise intensity (Jeukendrup et al., 1998a,b). Because intravenous triacylglycerol emulsions and heparin cannot be applied in sports practice, various other means have been tried to increase plasma FFA availability and fat oxidation during exercise.

Part of the ergogenic effect of caffeine could theoretically lie in its ability to increase lipolysis in adipocytes and in muscle and thus increase fat oxidation in muscle, especially during the first 15 min of exercise (Spriet et al., 1992). High-fat diets have also been used to raise fatty acid concentrations in the blood, but the effects of this manipulation on performance are conflicting (Jeukendrup et al., 1998c). The main problem appears to be that the reduction of carbohydrate intake, which is the consequence of the increase in fat intake, leads to insufficient glycogen stores at the start of exercise. Accordingly, although the objective of shifting more fat and less carbohydrate fuel to oxidation in the mitochondria may be achieved, because the initial glycogen store is lower than normal, the time at which the glycogen concentration falls below a critical level is not postponed, and performance is not improved.

Effects of Orally Ingested Long-Chain Triacylglycerol on Metabolism and Performance

Another approach to increasing the rate of fat oxidation in muscle during exercise is to ingest meals containing triacylglycerol either a few hours before exercise or fat supplements during exercise. However, the use of long-chain triacylglycerol (LCT), containing fatty acids with more than 16 carbon atoms, has disadvantages during exercise. Gastric emptying is reduced considerably by the presence of LCT in the stomach and may lead to gastrointestinal problems and a limited availability of the ingested nutrients. Furthermore, LCT ingested immediately before and during exercise is not immediately available after ingestion. Gastric emptying may take hours, and after digestion and absorption in the gut, the LCT are reassembled in the enterocytes and incorporated into chylomicrons. The chylomicrons are transported via the lymph into the circulation, and the fatty acids are then transported to various tissues and endogenous pools of fat before they are available for oxidation. Tracer experiments have shown that these processes can require more than 2 h (Binnert et al., 1998).

Furthermore, the combined use of glucose and LCT is not very useful for increasing fat oxidation because glucose increases insulin concentration, which reduces lipolysis and blood FFA concentrations and increases deposition of the ingested LCT in endogenous triacylglycerol pools. Moreover, glucose may have a direct inhibiting effect on oxidation of long-chain FFA in muscle, most probably via a mechanism involving inhibition of carnitine palmitoyl transferase I either by malonyl-CoA or by a reduced carnitine availability (see Figure 6-5) (Coyle et al., 1997; Sidossis & Wolfe, 1996). Therefore, it is not surprising that oral ingestion of LCT before and during prolonged exercise does not have an ergogenic effect comparable to that of glucose ingestion (Jeukendrup et al., 1998c). Also, attempts to improve performance by the ingestion of glucose plus LCT, compared to glucose alone, have been negative. Thus, in subsequent research has studied the effects of the ingestion of medium-chain triacylglycerol (MCT) on exercise metabolism and performance.

Rationale for MCT Ingestion

Medium-chain triacylglycerol (MCT) contains fatty acids with chain lengths of six, eight, or ten carbon atoms. In some vegetable oils, e.g., olive oil, MCT is present in high concentrations. In contrast to LCT, Beckers et al. (1992) showed that the addition of MCT to carbohydrate-containing drinks did not reduce the rate of gastric emptying. Isocaloric solutions of a mixture of MCT and carbohydrate actually emptied faster than carbohydrate alone. In contrast to LCT, MCTs are rapidly absorbed after digestion and are transported as medium-chain FFA via the portal vein directly to the liver. If they escape being metabolized by the liver, they are transported via the systemic circulation to other tissues, including muscle. Medium-chain FFA dissolve easily in water and, therefore, bypass the chylomicron-lymph route that has to be taken by long-chain fatty acids after intestinal absorption. Therefore, MCT is a much faster source of plasma FFA than is LCT.

It has also been suggested that medium-chain FFA can be oxidized in the mitochondria independent of the carnitine transport system (Figure 6-4; Bremer, 1983). However, that observation was made in mito-chondria incubated in vitro with very high concentrations of octanoate (C_8-medium-chain fatty acid) that are unlikely to occur in vivo. In contrast to this claim, others have shown that octanoate oxidation in incubated mitochondria from rat skeletal muscle is much higher in the presence of carnitine than in its absence (Groot & Hülsmann, 1973). Furthermore, most tissues, including skeletal muscle, contain carnitine octanoyltransferase (COT), a specific enzyme for conversion of medium-chain fatty acyl-CoA into medium-chain fatty acyl-carnitine (similar to CAT in Figure 6-4, but it acts on medium-chain fatty acyl-CoA only). COT and CAT are both inhibited by malonyl-CoA, but the inhibition of CAT is more complete and occurs at lower concentrations of malonyl-CoA (Saggersen & Carpenter, 1981).

Several studies have shown that glucose ingestion (Coyle et al., 1997) and infusion (Sidossis & Wolfe, 1996) reduce the oxidation of an infused palmitate tracer but not the oxidation of an infused octanoate tracer. This suggests that the oxidation of MCT, in contrast to that of LCT, will not be inhibited when a glucose-triacylglycerol mixture is consumed during exercise. In summary, from a theoretical point of view, MCT is a better FFA source than is LCT, and MCT is better suited for oral ingestion in combination with glucose because MCT, in contrast to LCT: 1) does not reduce gastric emptying; 2) is rapidly absorbed directly into the portal vein; 3) is not reduced by glucose ingestion during exercise; and 4) dissolves better in aqueous solutions and, therefore, is better suited for oral ingestion as a drink (see below).

Metabolism and Oxidation of Orally Ingested MCT during Exercise

Studies with stable isotope (^{13}C)-labelled MCT have shown that rapid and nearly complete oxidation of the MCT occurs both at rest (Binnert et al., 1998; Metges & Wolfram, 1991) and during exercise (Decombaz et al., 1983; Jeukendrup et al., 1995; Massicotte et al., 1992). This nearly complete oxidation occurs both for MCT ingested before (Decombaz et al., 1983; Massicotte et al., 1992) and during exercise (Jeukendrup et al., 1995) in amounts between 30 and 50 g. It is not clear whether the MCT is oxidized in the liver or in other tissues such as muscle. The rationale for use of a combined MCT-glucose supplement is that the addition of the MCT would increase plasma FFA concentration and, therefore, plasma FFA oxidation in muscle and reduce muscle glycogen breakdown.

In studies in which comparisons were made between ingestion of carbohydrate only and an equivalent dose of carbohydrate plus MCT (a maximum of 86 g in 2 h), plasma total FFA concentrations, including

medium-chain FFA, did not increase significantly following MCT ingestion (Jeukendrup et al., 1995; 1996b; 1998d; Van Zyl et al., 1996). This indicates that metabolism of most of the medium-chain FFA absorbed in
the portal vein took place in the liver, which can either fully oxidize the
MCT or convert them to ketone bodies (partial oxidation products).
Three of the four indicated studies (Jeukendrup et al., 1995, 1996b; Van
Zyl et al., 1996) detected significantly higher ketone body concentrations
after carbohydrate + MCT ingestion than after carbohydrate ingestion,
suggesting that at least part of the ingested MCT was converted to ketone bodies in the liver. In the study of Jeukendrup et al. (1998d) ketone
bodies did not increase in a 2-h period after consumption of 85 g of MCT
in a 10% carbohydrate drink, in comparison to carbohydrate only, indicating that larger amounts of MCT may lead to gastrointestinal problems and poor absorption (see below).

Jeukendrup et al. (1995) observed that coingestion of MCT with carbohydrate, in comparison with MCT ingestion alone, accelerated MCT
oxidation during the first 90 min of exercise and caused a higher blood
concentration of ketone bodies in that time. The most likely explanation
for this finding is that the carbohydrate improves the stability of MCT
suspensions and thereby increases the intestinal absorption of the MCT.

The ketone bodies formed in the liver after oral MCT ingestion will
subsequently be oxidized in other tissues. During exercise, it is quite
likely that a major part of that oxidation occurs in muscle; in this way,
MCT ingestion could indirectly supply an additional fuel to the exercising muscle and spare muscle glycogen. From a theoretical point of view,
direct oxidation of the ingested MCT in the liver also could spare liver
glycogen breakdown and thus be of advantage in endurance exercise.
However, Ivy et al. (1980) showed that adding 30 g of MCT to a breakfast cereal had no effect on the rate of total carbohydrate oxidation during 1 h of cycling at 70% $\dot{V}O_2$max. Furthermore, Jeukendrup et al.
(1996b) had subjects ingest 29 g MCT plus 214 g of carbohydrate during
3 h of exercise at 57% $\dot{V}O_2$max and found that MCT ingestion had no effect on total carbohydrate oxidation, on oxidation of the ingested carbohydrate, or on the oxidation of the endogenous carbohydrate, i.e., the
sum of muscle and liver glycogen and liver gluconeogenesis. Direct
biopsy measurements of muscle glycogen also showed no sparing of
muscle glycogen utilization by MCT-carbohydrate coingestion. The conclusion from this study was that most of the ingested MCT was oxidized
during the exercise period (Jeukendrup et al., 1995), but the contribution
of MCT to energy expenditure during exercise (3–7%) was too small to
lead to significant sparing of muscle glycogen or other endogenous carbohydrates (Jeukendrup et al., 1996b).

Van Zyl et al. (1996) added 86 g of MCT to 200 g of carbohydrate and observed significant reductions in total carbohydrate oxidation and muscle glycogen oxidation assessed indirectly with tracer methodology. However, in a recent study from our laboratory, the addition of 85 g of MCT to 170 g of glucose ingested during 2 h of exercise at 60% $\dot{V}O_2$max did not reduce total carbohydrate oxidation and did not spare endogenous carbohydrate (Jeukendrup et al., 1998d). Total carbohydrate oxidation and total fat oxidation were not different between the carbohydrate and carbohydrate + MCT treatment, indicating that the main effect of MCT ingestion was a reduction of the oxidation of the endogenous fat stores. The main difference between Van Zyl et al. (1996) and Jeukendrup et al. (1998d) may be that the subjects in the latter study experienced gastrointestinal problems as a consequence of the large dose of MCT, which may have delayed the emptying of the drinks (see below). Surprisingly, Jeukendrup et al. (1998d) did not find a significant increase in blood ketone bodies in the carbohydrate-plus-MCT trial in comparison with carbohydrate only, whereas in the earlier study (Jeukendrup et al., 1996b), there was a clear increase in ketone bodies with a much smaller MCT dose. This discrepancy remains unresolved.

Effects of Oral MCT Ingestion on Endurance Performance

Only a few studies have investigated the effect of MCT ingestion on exercise performance. Satabin et al. (1987) studied the effect of 45 g of MCT ingested before exercise and compared it with an isocaloric dose of glucose; they did not find a difference in time to fatigue at 60% $\dot{V}O_2$max.

Van Zyl et al. (1996) compared three supplements given in small repeated boluses during 2 h of cycling exercise at 60% $\dot{V}O_2$max: 1) 86 g of MCT in an aqueous emulsion; 2) 200 g of carbohydrate; and 3) 200 g of carbohydrate plus 86 g of MCT. After the 2 h of exercise, subjects performed a simulated 40-km time trial. By far the slowest time (5.3 min slower than in carbohydrate only) was seen when subjects ingested only MCT, but with the carbohydrate-plus-MCT treatment, the time was 1.8 min faster (P<0.05) than with carbohydrate only. In the same study, the carbohydrate-plus-MCT treatment reduced total carbohydrate oxidation and spared muscle glycogen, thus providing a mechanism for the observed ergogenic effect.

Using a similar preliminary exercise protocol (2 h cycling at 60% $\dot{V}O_2$max), Jeukendrup et al. (1998d) then had subjects perform a 15-min time trial at a much higher intensity than the time trial employed by Van Zyl et al. (1996). Jeukendrup et al. (1998d) administered four supplements: 1) an artificially sweetened water placebo; 2) 85 g MCT; 3) 170 g glucose, or 4) 170 g glucose plus 85 g MCT. Neither the carbohydrate supplement nor the carbohydrate-plus-MCT supplement affected performance, when compared with placebo, whereas MCT only impaired performance considerably, similar to the effect observed by Van Zyl et al. (1996). Addition of MCT to the carbohydrate did not reduce total carbohydrate oxidation or oxidation of the endogenous carbohydrate stores during 2 h of rest before the performance test. Therefore, at the start of the exercise test, the muscle glycogen stores must have been unaffected by the MCT, thus explaining the lack of a performance effect.

In pilot studies, Jeukendrup et al. (1998d) observed severe gastrointestinal problems when a 1-h time trial followed the 2 h of preliminary exercise both for the MCT treatment and for the carbohydrate-plus-MCT treatment. For that reason a 15-min time trial was chosen. In the 15-min time trial serious gastrointestinal cramping was observed again in the MCT-only trial, and this explained the reduced performance in that test in comparison with placebo. However, gastrointestinal discomfort was also observed during the first 2 h of exercise and during the time trial in the carbohydrate-plus-MCT trial. This may not only have reduced gastric emptying of the MCT but may also have interfered with the outcome of the performance tests. Similar gastrointestinal complaints were expressed during exercise after 30 g of MCT was added to a breakfast cereal in the study by Ivy et al. (1980).

LACTATE SALTS, POLYLACTATE, AND POLY L-LACTATE™

In 1986, Brooks reviewed the literature indicating that most of the lactate that appears in the blood during moderate-intensity exercise was oxidized by the active type I and type IIa muscle fibers. Lactate is also a good fuel for the human heart, and the rates of lactate clearance and oxidation exceed those rates achieved by glucose. Brooks (1986) suggested that the lactate molecule could serve as a shuttle for transport of glucose-derived carbon moieties between various organs and cells, e.g., from the exercising muscle to the heart, from type II fibers in an active muscle to the neighboring type I fibers in the same muscle, or to the type I fibers of another active muscle.

Based on these findings, several studies have investigated whether or not lactic acid and lactate in various chemical forms could be used as nutritional supplements to improve exercise performance.

Mineral Salts of Lactate

One way to provide lactate to subjects is as a mineral salt. Free lactic acid, because of its low pH and unpleasant taste, is not tolerated by the human gastrointestinal tract in amounts exceeding 2.5 g in 100 ml of solution (Brouns et al., unpublished). Because sport nutrition companies had claimed that regular lactate intake improved lactate clearance and, therefore, could improve performance during events leading to accumulation of lactate, Brouns et al. (1995) investigated the effect of mineral lactate taken twice daily during a 3-wk period on blood lactate concentrations during various exercise tests and recovery from exercise. Subjects were administered 10 g of mineral lactate [8.2 g calcium lactate powder, 6.25 ml sodium lactate solution (60% sodium lactate), 2.05 ml potassium lactate solution (60% potassium lactate), diluted to 100 ml with water]. This dose was chosen because more concentrated solutions and increased amounts caused nausea in all subjects and abdominal cramps and diarrhea in some. This indicates that the amount of lactate that can be given orally as a potential fuel during exercise is minimal in comparison with solutions of glucose and of maltodextrins. The blood lactate concentration did not increase following ingestion of the lactate, indicating that the lactate is mainly metabolized in gut and/or liver and is not available as a substrate for muscle.

One of the probable reasons for the limited gastrointestinal tolerance of solutions of mineral salts of lactate is that the osmolality is much higher for the same amount of oxidizable fuel (a 7% solution has 3–4 times greater osmolality than 7% glucose). Another possibility is that the high local lactate concentration in the gut has a direct effect on gut motility and transit time via unknown mechanisms. It also cannot be excluded that the high mineral load, e.g., 1.5 g of calcium, 1 g sodium, and 0.5 g potassium for each 10 g of mineral lactate, can lead to gastrointestinal symptoms via local effects and may have undesirable systemic effects during exercise.

The direct effect of ingesting mineral salts of lactate on performance has not been investigated, but given the amount of carbohydrate that is normally needed to achieve a performance effect, the expectation is that there will not be an ergogenic effect.

Polylactate

When the lactic acid concentration in an aqueous solution surpasses about 50%, spontaneous chemical dimerization occurs, especially at temperatures above 50°C (Benninga, 1990):

$$2\ CH_3\text{-}CH(OH)\text{-}COOH \rightarrow CH_3\text{-}CH(OH)\text{-}COO\text{-}CH(CH_3)\text{-}COOH + H_2O$$

The reaction does not stop at this stage but continues, forming progressively longer chains or lactate polymers, i.e., polylactate or polylactic acid or polylactide (Benninga, 1990). The general structure of polylactate is:

$$CH_3\text{-}CH(OH)\text{-}CO[O\text{-}CH(CH_3\text{-}CO]n\text{-}OCH(CH_3)\text{-}COOH$$

Polylactate also can be made by controlled chemical synthesis. If polylactate dissolved in water were quickly hydrolyzed in the gastrointestinal tract of humans, it could theoretically be an excellent chemical form of lactate that could be ingested in large enough amounts to be useful as a substrate during exercise. If the osmolality of polylactate could be kept within reasonable limits, such that no problems would presumably occur with water absorption, tolerance in the gastrointestinal tract would be better. However, polylactate is the product of a chemical reaction and does not normally occur in food products. The human body, as far as we know, does not contain enzymes to degrade polylactate rapidly. For that reason the bioavailablity and the intestinal absorption of orally ingested polylactate would probably approach zero.

In fact, polylactate is a solid material that does not dissolve in water. Furthermore, because it is degraded so slowly, it is used by orthopedic and dental surgeons to replace steel plates for the fixation of broken bones. As such, polylactate in the true chemical sense cannot function to generate lactic acid at a high rate and cannot function as a nutritional ergogenic aid during exercise.

Poly L-Lactate™ (Amino Acid Salts of Lactate)

Two groups (Fahey et al., 1991; Swensen et al., 1994) suggest in the titles of their scientific papers that they have investigated the performance effects of polylactate. However, they both appear to have investigated the effects of a commercial product called Poly L-Lactate™ (Champion Nutrition, Concord, CA, USA). The supplement is said to contain molecules of lactate that are ionically bound to amino acids (i.e., amino acid salts of lactate). The principal amino acids used are arginine and others with more than two nitrogen groups because of their ability to bind more than one lactate molecule. Because the molecular weights of amino acids, and especially of arginine, far exceed that of lactate, this indicates that Poly L-Lactate™ contains less than 50% lactate. In other words, a solution of 7% Poly L-Lactate™ may contain only 3.5% lactate or less, with an unspecified amount of arginine and other amino acids. In our experience, when drinks containing arginine in concentrations of 2% and greater are consumed at a rate of 1 L/h, most subjects experience severe gastric intestinal distress, nausea and diarrhea.

Swensen et al. (1994) also observed severe gastrointestinal distress (abdominal cramping, diarrhea, and vomiting) when Poly L-Lactate™ was used in concentrations of 5%. The arginine and other amino acids present in Poly L-Lactate™ may lead to these gastrointestinal symptoms, but a high osmolality may also play a role. In order to prevent gastric distress Swensen et al. (1994) added only 0.75% Poly L-Lactate™ to a

6.25% glucose polymer solution and compared that with a 7% glucose polymer solution. As expected, given the fact that the energy content of the drinks was similar, there was no difference in time to exhaustion during exercise at 70% $\dot{V}O_2$max.

Fahey et al. (1991) used 7% Poly L-Lactate™ solutions in their subjects during 3 h of cycling at 50% $\dot{V}O_2$max and did not report gastrointestinal problems. They also did not report any effect on performance, so there is no claim in the scientific literature that Poly L-Lactate™ has an ergogenic effect. Because of the undesirable gastrointestinal effects of Poly L-Lactate™ and other chemical forms of lactate, it seems wise to avoid the use of these supplements. For a full evaluation of Poly L-Lactate™, the exact amino acid composition should be specified in the product information because amino acids may have positive or negative performance effects independent of any lactate effect.

PRACTICAL ISSUES

Are Nutritional Supplements Necessary for Optimal Performance?

Most nutritional supplements are not necessary for optimal performance. Carbohydrate loading, for example, can easily be achieved with a diet containing normal foodstuffs. The advantage of obtaining a specific nutrient in a diet of normal foods is that such a diet is often cheaper, provides more nutrients, and has a better taste. The disadvantage is that the athlete must be continually aware of the composition of the regular foods being consumed and should have a detailed knowledge of nutrition and dietetics. In rare cases, e.g., for creatine loading, it would be difficult to obtain sufficient intake of the nutrient in a normal diet, and nutritional supplements may be necessary to optimize performance.

Is the Use of Nutritional Supplements Ethical?

In their endeavor to perform better, athletes use new training techniques, improved sport equipment, and advanced psychological preparation. If these approaches are deemed ethical, surely optimal nutritional preparation for a competition is also ethical. As long as all athletes have equal access to nutritional supplements and to the scientific information related to their ergogenicity, they should be allowed to choose whatever nutritional regimen they think is best for them. For example, creatine loading may help an optimally trained body to perform marginally better. Creatine is a natural compound ingested in the habitual diets of most athletes; there appears to be little or no risk to the athlete's health; it is widely available; and there is a reasonable amount of well-publicized reputable scientific information on the consequences of creatine loading. National sport committees have formed opinions on its potential efficacy, and some advise their athletes to use this supplement. Thus, athletes should be allowed to judge for themselves whether or not they want to use creatine in their attempts to improve their performances.

What is not ethical is the commercial marketing of thousands of different products that make unproven claims about ergogenicity. Product marketing should be based on reputable scientific evidence that justifies any performance claims, and this evidence should be available in the public domain. There also should be product information on the safety of short-term and long-term use of the product and on potential side effects (e.g., gastrointestinal dysfunction in the case of MCT-containing products). Many commercial nutritional products currently being marketed may contain substances harmful to health and to performance, but these products will stay on the shelves as long as they sell; this is totally unacceptable and unethical. This laissez-faire governmental approach to commerce encourages corporations to restrict the availability of product information, and this diminishes the ability of athletes and coaches to make rational decisions on optimal nutritional preparation. Sport review and advisory boards and national sport committees have the moral and ethical duty to guide and advise athletes in their choice of nutritional supplements.

DIRECTIONS FOR FUTURE RESEARCH

Future creatine research should focus on measuring the advantages of long-term creatine loading on sprint performance, strength, and endurance performance. The ability during training sessions to perform more repetitions at a higher workload may have advantages in many sport disciplines. A higher creatine content of the muscle also cause enzymatic adaptations that lead to anabolism and increases in strength and or endurance independent of any additional training stimulus. More information is also needed on the advantages of creatine loading during sports of intermittent high-intensity exercise (e.g., soccer or tennis). From a theoretical view, it can be predicted that there will be an advantage, but the hard evidence is missing from the literature, partly due to the fact that proper tests for measurement of this type of performance are rare.

Research on the potential ergogenicity of carnitine should come to an end because it has been conclusively shown that carnitine supplementation does not increase the concentration of carnitine in the muscles. Likewise, there seems to be little or no future for continued research on the ergogenicity of lactate ingestion, which causes gastrointestinal dysfunction, or of BCAA. BCAA ingestion in solutions containing carbohydrate does not postpone fatigue via central mechanisms; therefore, the practical relevance for athletes is non-existent. However, the interaction between BCAA metabolism and the tricarboxylic acid cycle during exercise will continue to provide information on muscular fatigue mechanisms and on metabolic adaptations in glycogen-depleted muscle.

Future scientific research should employ various nutritional manipulations to help determine the relative importance of central versus peripheral fatigue as a determinant of endurance performance. If central fatigue is important, research should determine which neurotransmitters are involved. Local changes in serotonin concentration probably represent only part of a complex interplay between various neuronal cells that use a variety of neurotransmitters. Any research on pharmacological modulation of neurotransmitters should be performed solely as a means to learn about the control mechanisms—not to support the use of drugs as ergogenic aids.

The next logical study of MCT would involve athletes who can tolerate large amounts of MCT in carbohydrate-containing solutions without experiencing gastrointestinal distress. The protocol of van Zyl et al. (1996) should be repeated with these MCT-tolerant athletes to confirm that the observed advantage indeed exists.

SUMMARY

Creatine

Oral creatine supplementation (20 g/d for 5–6 d) apparently increases the total intramuscular creatine content in the majority of men by about 20%, and 30–40% of this increase is creatine phosphate. A subsequent daily dose of 2 g is enough for maintenance of this increased concentration. A daily supplement of 3 g creatine for 1 mo leads to a similar end result. When the creatine is ingested in solutions containing carbohydrate, the increase in muscle total creatine is about 60% greater.

Creatine loading increased the amount of work performed during repeated bouts of brief high-intensity exercise in many, but not all, studies. The mechanisms behind this effect may include a decreased accumulation of hydrogen ions, i.e., an attenuated rate of glycolysis, a faster ATP turnover due to the greater initial concentration of creatine phosphate, and a faster rate of resynthesis of creatine phosphate during recovery between exercise bouts. Fewer studies have shown an ergogenic effect during single bouts of maximal exercise in highly trained athletes.

No studies have shown an ergogenic effect on endurance performance. The increase in body mass often seen in athletes may adversely affect endurance performance.

The few studies that have investigated the combined effects of long-term creatine ingestion and strength or high-intensity running training show impressive improvements of performance, perhaps greater than those seen after short-term supplementation. This may be explained both by the possibility that the higher intramuscular creatine content enables the athletes to do more repetitions during training at a higher speed or workload and by the possibility that creatine exerts a direct anabolic effect on the muscles, leading to improved adaptation and thus improved performance. However, more research is needed on the combination of long-term creatine supplementation and training before these suggestions can be regarded as conclusive.

Carnitine

Oral carnitine supplementation in humans for periods of 2–3 wk does not increase the carnitine concentration in muscle and, therefore, cannot have an effect on muscle metabolism at rest or during exercise. Carnitine supplementation does not help one to lose weight or reduce body fat mass. Moreover, carnitine supplementation neither increases fat oxidation nor reduces glycogen breakdown during prolonged cycling or running. Carnitine supplementation does not increase $\dot{V}O_2$max and does not reduce lactate accumulation during high-intensity exercise.

Branched-Chain Amino Acids (BCAA)

Performance studies indicate that neither BCAA ingestion nor tryptophan ingestion in drinks containing carbohydrates has an important effect on endurance performance in healthy subjects. This suggests that the performance studies do not provide sufficient experimental support for the "central fatigue" hypothesis of Newsholme and colleagues nor for the proposed interaction of BCAA with the TCA-cycle in skeletal muscle proposed by Wagenmakers and colleagues. The data obtained in patients with McArdle's disease seem to contain the message that BCAA ingestion may be disadvantageous when there is no coingestion of carbohydrate and when the glycogen stores of the body have simultaneously been emptied. Because ammonia accumulation theoretically can lead to central fatigue and loss of motor-coordination (Bannister & Cameron, 1990), one should be very skeptical about the use of BCAA supplements in sport activities where performance critically depends on motor coordination (e.g., tennis and soccer).

Given the likelihood that there will be no positive effects of BCAA supplementation on performance, athletes are advised to avoid the unnecessary risks associated with BCAA supplementation. BCAA supplements should never be taken instead of carbohydrate supplements. The advantages of the latter have been clearly demonstrated during prolonged exercise at intensities of 50–80% $\dot{V}O_2$max (e.g., Coggan & Coyle, 1991).

Medium-Chain Triacylglycerol

In theory, an increase in plasma FFA availability and greater plasma FFA oxidation by muscle during prolonged exercise should spare muscle glycogen from breakdown and thus improve performance. For various reasons, e.g., reduced gastric emptying, slow absorption, and/or inhibition of long-chain fatty acid oxidation by glucose ingestion, this theory is not supported by studies that have combined the ingestion of carbohydrate and LCT immediately before and during exercise. In contrast to LCT, MCT ingested orally immediately before and during exercise does not usually reduce gastric emptying or decrease the availability of any coingested carbohydrate. The MCT is rapidly absorbed as medium-chain FFA directly into the portal vein and oxidized.

Only one study (Van Zyl et al., 1996) observed muscle glycogen sparing and a positive effect on time trial performance when MCT was added to a carbohydrate drink and ingested during exercise. Several other studies failed to find such positive effects of MCT ingestion, and in several of these studies, ingestion of MCT alone or in combination with carbohydrate caused severe gastrointestinal distress and impaired exercise performance. In all studies, ingestion of only MCT had no effect or had a negative effect on performance, often as a consequence of gastrointestinal distress.

In sports practice, MCT should never be used during competition without ample previous experience during training sessions. Athletes should determine in advance whether or not their digestive systems can tolerate the ingestion of MCT in combination with carbohydrate. Those athletes who can tolerate the MCT in practice may experience a small benefit during prolonged exercise.

Lactate Salts, Polylactate and Poly L-Lactate™

Solutions of mineral salts of lactate can be taken in maximal bolus amounts of about 10 g without causing gastrointestinal problems. The performance effects of these amounts have not been investigated but are expected to be non-existent, given the amount of carbohydrate needed for performance improvement. Long-term ingestion of lactate boluses twice daily does not change blood lactate concentrations during exercise and recovery and, therefore, is not expected to have a performance effect. Polylactate, i.e., an actual polymer of lactate, is degraded very slowly in the human body and cannot function as an ergogenic aid. Poly L-Lactate™ is a commercial supplement and consists of an unspecified mixture of amino acid salts of lactate. There are no studies showing an ergogenic effect of Poly L-Lactate™, and solutions containing ≥ 2.5% concentrations of the product can cause severe gastrointestinal problems. The main problem with lactate supplements, in each of the available forms, is that the gastrointestinal tract cannot tolerate amounts that would be sufficient to exert any beneficial effects on exercise performance.

ACKNOWLEDGEMENT

I thank Paul Greenhaff (University of Nottingham) and my former PhD students Gerrit van Hall (Copenhagen Muscle Research Centre) and Asker Jeukendrup (University of Birmingham) for helpful discussions and critical reading of the manuscript. I thank my wife Marijke and my children, Margreet and Martijn for having patience during the preparation of this chapter and the endless list of papers, reviews and grant applications.

BIBLIOGRAPHY

Balsom, P.D., B. Ekblom, K. Söderlund, B. Sjödin, and E. Hultman (1993a). Creatine supplementation and dynamic high-intensity intermittent exercise. *Scand. J. Med. Sci. Sports* 3:143–149.
Balsom, P.D., S.D.R. Harridge, K. Söderlund, B. Sjödin, and E. Hultman (1993b). Creatine supplementation per se does not enhance endurance exercise performance. *Acta Physiol. Scand.* 149:521–523.
Banister, E.W., and B.J.C. Cameron (1990). Exercise-induced hyperammonemia: Peripheral and central effects. *Int. J. Sports Med.* 11:S129–S142.
Barnett, C., D.L. Costill, M.D. Vukovich, K.J. Cole, B.H. Goodpaster, S.W. Trappe, and W.J. Fink (1994). Effect of L-carnitine supplementation on muscle and blood carnitine content and lactate accumulation during high-intensity sprint cycling. *Int. J. Sport Nutr.* 4: 280–288.
Beckers, E.J., A.E. Jeukendrup, F. Brouns, A.J.M. Wagenmakers, and W.H.M. Saris (1992). Gastric emptying of carbohydrate-medium chain triglyceride suspensions at rest. *Int. J. Sports Med.* 13:581–584.
Benninga, H. (1990). *A History of Lactic Acid Making*. Dordrecht, The Netherlands: Kluwer Academic Publishers, pp. 203–204.
Bessman, S.P., and P.J. Geiger (1981). Transport of energy in muscle: The phosphorylcreatine shuttle. *Science* 211:448–452.
Binnert, C., C. Pachiaudi, M. Beylot, D. Hans, J. van der Mander, P. Chantre, J.P. Riou, and M. Lavalle (1998). Influence of human obesity on the metabolic fate of dietary long- and medium-chain triacylglycerols. *Am. J. Clin. Nutr.* 67:595–601.
Blomstrand, E., S. Andersson, P. Hassmén, B. Ekblom, and E.A. Newsholme (1995). Effect of branched-chain amino acid and carbohydrate supplementation on the exercise induced change in plasma and muscle concentration of amino acids in human subjects. *Acta Physiol. Scand.* 153:87–96.
Blomstrand, E., P. Hassmén, B. Ekblom, and E.A. Newsholme (1991). Administration of branched-chain amino acids during sustained exercise-effects on performance and on plasma concentration of some amino acids. *Eur. J. Appl. Physiol. Occup. Physiol.* 63:83–88.
Blomstrand, E., P. Hassmén, S. Ek, B. Ekblom, and E.A. Newsholme (1997). Influence of ingesting a solution of branched-chain amino acids on perceived exertion during exercise. *Acta Physiol. Scand.* 159:41–49.
Borum, P.B. (1986). Clinical Aspects of *Human Carnitine Deficiency*. Oxford: Pergamon Press.
Bosco, C., J. Tihanyi, J. Pucspk, I. Kovacs, A. Gabossy, R. Colli, G. Pulvirenti, C. Tranquilli, C. Foti, M. Viru, and A. Viru (1997). Effect of oral creatine supplementation on jumping and running performance. *Int. J. Sports Med.* 18:369–372.
Brannon, T.A., G.R. Adams, C.L. Conniff, and K.M. Baldwin (1997). Effects of creatine loading and training on running performance and biochemical properties of rat skeletal muscle. *Med. Sci. Sports Ex.* 29:489–495.
Bremer, J. (1983). Carnitine—Metabolism and functions. *Physiol. Rev.* 63:1421–1466.

Brooks, G.A. (1986). The lactate shuttle during exercise and recovery. *Med. Sci. Sports Ex.* 18:360–368.

Brouns, F., M. Fogelholm, G. van Hall, A.J.M. Wagenmakers, and W.H.M. Saris (1995). Chronic oral lactate supplementation does not affect lactate disappearance from blood after exercise. *Int. J. Sports Nut.* 5:117–124.

Burke, L.M., D.B. Pyne, and R.D. Telford (1996). Effect of oral creatine supplementation on single effort sprint performance in elite swimmers. *Int. J. Sport Nutr.* 6:222–233.

Chaouloff, F., G.A. Kennett, B. Serrurrier, D. Merino, and G. Curzon (1986). Amino acid analysis demonstrates that increased plasma free tryptophan causes the increase of brain tryptophan during exercise in the rat. *J. Neurochem.* 46:1647–1650.

Coggan, A.R., and E.F. Coyle (1991). Carbohydrate ingestion during prolonged exercise: Effects on metabolism and performance. In: J.O. Holloszy (ed.) *Ex. Sport Sci. Rev.,* Baltimore, USA: Williams and Wilkins, vol 19:1–40.

Constantin-Teodosiu, D., J.I. Carlin, G. Cederblad, R.C. Harris, and E. Hultman (1991). Acetyl group accumulation and pyruvate dehydrogenase activity in human muscle during incremental exercise. *Acta Physiol. Scand.* 143:367–372.

Costill, D.L., E.F. Coyle, G. Dalsky, W. Evans, W.J. Fink, and D. Hoopes (1977). Effects of elevated plasma FFA and insulin on muscle glycogen usage during exercise. *J. Appl. Physiol.* 43:695–699.

Coyle, E.F., A.E. Jeukendrup, A.J.M. Wagenmakers and W.H.M. Saris (1997). Fatty acid oxidation in man is directly regulated by carbohydrate metabolism. *Am. J. Physiol.* 273:E268–E255.

Decombaz, J., M.J. Arnaud, H. Milan, H. Moesch, G. Philippossian, A.L. Thelin, and H. Howald (1983). Energy metabolism of medium-chain trigylcerides versus carbohydrates during exercise. *Eur. J. Appl. Physiol. Occup. Physiol.* 52:9–14.

Earnest, C.P., P.G. Snell, R. Rodriguez, A.L. Almada, and T.L. Mitchell (1995). The effect of creatine monohydrate ingestion on anaerobic power indices, muscular strength and body composition. *Acta Physiol. Scand.* 153:207–209.

Editorial (1982). *Münich Med. Wochenschr.* 124: 9.

Essen, B., and L. Kaijser (1978). Regulation of glycolysis in intermittent exercise in man. *J. Physiol.* 281:499–511.

Fahey, T.D., J.D. Larsen, G.A. Brooks, W. Colvin, S. Henderson, and D. Lary (1991). The effects of ingesting polylactate or glucose polymer drinks during prolonged exercise. *Int. J. Sport Nutr.* 1:249–256.

Fitts, R.H. (1994). Cellular mechanisms of muscle fatigue. *Physiol. Rev.* 74:49–94.

Gibala, M.J., M.A. Tarnapolski, and T.E. Graham (1997). Tricarboxylic acid cycle intermediates in human muscle at rest and during prolonged cycling. *Am. J. Physiol.* 272:E239–E244.

Goldberg, A.L., and T.W. Chang (1978). Regulation and significance of amino acid metabolism in skeletal muscle. *Federation Proc.* 37:2301–2307.

Green, A.L., E. Hultman, I.A. Macdonald, D.A. Sewell, and P.L. Greenhaff (1996a). Carbohydrate ingestion augments skeletal muscle creatine accumulation during creatine supplementation in man. *Am. J. Physiol.* 271:E281–E826.

Green, A.L., E.J. Simpson, J.J. Littlewood, I.A. Macdonald, and P.L. Greenhaff (1996b). Carbohydrate ingestion augments creatine retention during creatine feeding in man. *Acta Physiol. Scand.* 158: 195–202.

Greenhaff, P.L. (1997). The nutritional biochemistry of creatine. *Nut. Biochem.* 11:610–618.

Greenhaff, P.L., K. Bodin, K. Söderlund, and E. Hultman (1994). The effect of oral creatine supplementation on skeletal muscle phosphocreatine resynthesis. *Am. J. Physiol.* 266: E725–E730, 1994.

Greenhaff, P.L., A. Casey, A.H. Short, R. Harris, K. Söderlund, and E. Hultman (1993). Influence of oral creatine supplementation on muscle torque during repeated bouts of maximal voluntary exercise in man. *Clin. Sci.* 84:565–571.

Grindstaff, P.D., R. Kreider, R. Bishop, M. Wilson, L. Wood, C. Alexander, and A. Almada (1997). Effects of creatine supplementation on repetitive sprint performance and body composition in competitive swimmers. *Int. J. Sports Nutr.* 7:330–346.

Groot, P.H.E., and W.C. Hülsman (1973). The activation and oxidation of octanaoate and palmitate by rat skeletal muscle mitochondria. *Biochim. Biophys.* Acta 316:124–135.

Hargreaves, K.M., and W.M. Pardridge (1988). Neutral amino acid transport at the human blood-brain barrier. *J. Biol. Chem.* 263:19392–19397.

Harris, R.C., C.V. Foster, and E. Hültman (1987). Acetylcarnitine formation during intense muscular contraction in humans. *J. Appl. Physiol.* 63:440–442.

Harris, R.C., K. Söderlund, and E. Hültman (1992). Elevation of creatine in resting and exercised muscle of normal subjects by creatine supplementation. *Clin. Sci.* 83:367–374.

Häussinger, D., F. Lang, and W. Gerok (1994). Regulation of cell function by the cellular hydration state. *Am.J. Physiol.* 267:E343–E355.

Heinonen, O.J. (1996). Carnitine and physical exercise. *Sports Med.* 22:109–132.

Hültman, E., P.L. Greenhaff, J-M. Ren, and K. Söderlund (1991). Energy metabolism and fatigue during intense muscle contraction. *Biochem. Soc. Trans.* 19:347–353.

Hültman, E., K. Söderlund, J.A. Timmons, G. Cederblad, and P.L. Greenhaff (1996). Muscle creatine loading in men. *J. Appl. Physiol.* 81: 232–237.

Ingwall, J.S. (1976). Creatine and the control of muscle-specific protein synthesis in cardiac and skeletal muscle. *Circ. Res.* 38:115–122.

Ivy, J.L., D.L. Costill, W.J. Fink, and E. Maglischo (1980). Contribution of medium and long-chain triglyceride intake to energy metabolism during prolonged exercise. *Int. J. Soprts Med.* 1:15–20.

Jeukendrup, A.E., W.H.M. Saris, P. Schrauwen, F. Brouns and A.J.M. Wagenmakers (1995). Metabolic availability of oral medium chain triacylglycerols coingested with carbohydrates during prolonged exercise. *J. Appl. Physiol.* 79:756–762.

Jeukendrup, A.E., W.H.M. Saris, R. van Diesen, F. Brouns and A.J.M. Wagenmakers (1996a). Effect of endogenous carbohydrate availability on oral medium-chain triglyceride oxidation during prolonged exercise. *J. Appl. Physiol.* 80:949–954.

Jeukendrup, A.E., W.H.M. Saris, and A.J.M. Wagenmakers (1998a). Fat metabolism during exercise: a review. Part I: Fatty acid mobilization and muscle metabolism. *Int. J. Sport Med.* 19: In Press.

Jeukendrup, A.E., W.H.M. Saris, and A.J.M. Wagenmakers (1998b). Fat metabolism during exercise: a review. Part II: Regulation of metabolism and effects of training. *Int. J. Sport Med.* 19: In Press.

Jeukendrup, A.E., W.H.M. Saris, and A.J.M. Wagenmakers (1998c). Fat metabolism during exercise: a review. Part III: The effects of nutritional interventions. *Int. J. Sport Med.* 19: In Press.

Jeukendrup, A.E., J.J.H.C. Thielen, A.J.M. Wagenmakers, F. Brouns, and W.H.M. Saris (1998d). Effect of medium-chain triacylglycerol and carbohydrate ingestion during exercise on substrate utilization and subsequent cycling performance. *Am. J. Clin. Nutr.* 67:397–404.

Jeukendrup, A.E., A.J.M. Wagenmakers, F. Brouns, D. Halliday and W.H.M. Saris (1996b). Effect of carbohydrate (carbohydrate) and fat supplementation on carbohydrate metabolism during prolonged exercise. *Metabolism* 45:915–921.

Karlsson, J., and B. Saltin (1970). Adenosine triphosphate and creatine phosphate in working muscles during exhaustive exercise in man. *J. Appl. Physiol.* 29:598–602.

Knapik, J., C. Meredith, B. Jones, R. Fielding, V. Young, and W. Evans (1991). Leucine metabolism during fasting and exercise. *J. Appl. Physiol.* 70:43–47.

Kreider, R.B., M. Ferreira, M. Wilson, P. Grindstaff, S. Plisk, J. Reinardy, E. Cantler, and A.L. Almada (1998). Effects of creatine supplementation on body composition, strength, and sprint performance. *Med. Sci. Sports Ex.* 30:73–82.

Lang, F., G.L. Busch, M. Ritter, H. Volkl, S. Waldegger, E. Gulbins, and D. Häussinger (1998). Functional significance of cell volume regulatory mechanisms. *Physiol. Rev.* 78:247–306.

Laskowski, M.B., R. Chevli, and C.D. Fitch (1981). Biochemical and ultrastructural changes in skeletal muscle induced by a creatine antagonist. *Metabolism* 30:1080–1085.

MacLean, D.A., T.E. Graham, and B. Saltin (1996). Stimulation of muscle ammonia production during exercise following branched-chain amino acid supplementation in humans. *J. Physiol.* 493:909–922.

Madsen, K., D.A. MacLean, B. Kiens, and D. Christensen (1996). Effects of glucose, glucose plus branched-chain amino acids or placebo on bike performance over 100 km. *J. Appl. Physiol.* 81: 2644–2650.

Massicotte, D., F. Peronnet, G.R. Brisson, C. Hillaire-Marcel (1992). Oxidation of exogenous medium-chain free fatty acids during prolonged exercise—comparison with glucose. *J. Appl. Physiol.* 73: 1334–1339.

Maughan, R.J. (1995). Creatine supplementation and exercise performance. *Int. J. Sport Nut.* 5:94–101.

Metges, C.C., and G. Wolfram (1991). Medium- and long-chain triglycerides labeled with 13C: comparison of oxidation after oral or parenteral administration in humans. *J. Nutr.* 121:31–36.

Meyer, R.A., H.L. Sweeney, and M.J. Kushmerick (1984). A simple analysis of the 'phosphocreatine shuttle'. *Am. J. Physiol.* 246:C365–C377.

Mittleman, K.D., M.R. Ricci, and S.P. Bailey (1998) Branched-chain amino acids prolong exercise during heat stress in men and women. *Med. Sci. Sports Exerc.* 30:83–91.

Mujika, I., and S. Padilla (1997). Creatine supplementation as an ergogenic aid for sports performance in highly trained athletes: A critical review. *Int. J. Sports Med.* 18:491–496.

Mujika, I., J.-C. Chatard, L. Lacoste, F. Barale, and A. Geysant (1996). Creatine supplementation does not improve sprint performance in competitive swimmers. *Med. Sci. Sports Ex.* 28:1435–1441.

Newsholme, E.A., I.N. Acworth, and E. Blomstrand (1987). Amino acids, brain neurotransmitters and a functional link between muscle and brain that is important in sustained exercise. In: G. Benzi (ed.) *Advances in Myochemistry.* London: John Libby Eurotext, pp. 127–138.

Romijn, J.A., E.F. Coyle, L. Sidossis, A. Gastaldelli, J.F. Horowitz, E. Endert, and R.R. Wolfe (1993). Regulation of endogenous fat and carbohydrate metabolism in relation to exercise intensity. *Am. J. Physiol.* 265:E380–E391.

Rossiter, H.B., E.R. Cannell, and P.M. Jakeman (1996). The effect of oral creatine supplementation on the 1000-m performance of competitive rowers. *J. Sports Sci.* 14:175–179.

Saggerson, E.D., and C.A. Carpenter (1981). Carnitine palmitoyltransferase and carnitine octanoyltransferase activities in liver, kidney cortex, adipocyte, lactating mammary gland, skeletal muscle and heart. Relative activities, latency and effect of malonylCoA. *FEBS Lett.* 129:229–232.

Sahlin, K., A. Katz, and S. Broberg (1990). Tricarboxylic acid cycle intermediates in human muscle during prolonged exercise. *Am. J. Physiol.* 269:C834–841.

Satabin, P., P. Portero, G. Defer, J. Bricout, and C.Y. Guezennec (1987). Metabolic and hormonal responses to lipid and carbohydrate diets during exercise in man. *Med. Sci. Sports Ex.* 19:218–223.

Sidossis, L.S., and R.R. Wolfe (1996). Glucose and insulin-induced inhibition of fatty acid oxidation: the glucose-fatty acid cycle reversed. *Am. J. Physiol.* 270:E733–E738.

Simi, B., M.H. Mayet, B. Sempore, and R. Favier (1990). Large variations in skeletal muscle carnitine level fail to modify energy metabolism in exercising rats. *Comp. Biochem. Physiol.* A 97:543–549.

Sipila, I., J. Rapola, O. Simell, and A. Vannas (1981). Supplementary creatine as a treatment for gyrate atrophy of the choroid and retina. *New Eng. J. Med.* 304:867–870.

Spriet, L.L., D.A. MacLean, D.J. Dyck, E. Hultman, G. Cederblad and T.E. Graham (1992). Caffeine ingestion and muscle metabolism during prolonged exercise in humans. *Am. J. Physiol.* 262:E891–E898.

Stroud, M.A., D. Holliman, D. Bell, A. Green, I.A. Macdonald, and P.L. Greenhaff (1994). Effect of oral creatine supplementation on respiratory gas exchange and blood lactate accumulation during steady-state incremental treadmill exercise and recovery. *Clin Sci.* 87:707–710.

Swensen, T., G. Crater, D.R. Bassett, and E.T. Howley (1994). Adding polylactate to a glucose polymer solution does not improve endurance. *Int. J. Sports Med.* 15: 30–435.

Trappe, S.W., D.L. Costill, B. Goodpaster, M.D. Vukovich, and W.J. Fink (1994). The effects of L-carnitine supplementation on performance during interval swimming. *Int. J. Sports Med.* 15:181–185.

Vandenberghe, K., M. Goris, P. van Hecke, M. van Leemputte, L. van Gerven, and P. Hespel (1997). Long-term creatine intake is beneficial to muscle performance during resistance training. *J. Appl. Physiol.* 83:2055–2063.

Van Deursen, J., P. Jap, A. Heerschap, H. ter Laak, W. Ruitenbeek, and B. Wieringa (1994). Effects of the creatine analogue β-guanidinopropionic acid on skeletal muscles of mice deficient in muscle creatine kinase. *Biochim. Biophys. Acta* 1185:327–335.

Van Hall, G., D.A. MacLean, B. Saltin, and A.J.M. Wagenmakers (1996). Mechanisms of activation of muscle branched-chain α-keto acid dehydrogenase during exercise in man. *J. Physiol.* 494:899–905.

Van Hall, G., J.S.H. Raaymakers, W.H.M. Saris, and A.J.M. Wagenmakers (1995a). Ingestion of branched-chain amino acids and tryptophan during sustained exercise—Failure to affect performance. *J. Physiol.* 486:789–794.

Van Hall, G., B. Saltin, G.J. van der Vusse, K. Söderlund, and A.J.M. Wagenmakers (1995b). Deamination of amino acids as a source for ammonia production in human skeletal muscle during prolonged exercise. *J. Physiol.* 489:251–261.

Van Ingen-Schenau, G.J. (1996). A new skate allowing powerful plantar flexions improves performance. *Med. Sci. Sports Ex.* 28:531–535.

Van Zyl, C.G., E.V. Lambert, J.A. Hawley, T.D. Noakes, and S.C. Dennis (1996). Effects of medium-chain triglyceride ingestion on fuel metabolism and cycling performance. *J. Appl. Physiol.* 80:2217–2225.

Varnier, M., P. Sarto, D. Martines, L. Lora, F. Carmignoto, G.P. Lees, and R. Naccarato (1994). Effect of infusing branched-chain amino acids during incremental exercise with reduced muscle glycogen content. *Eur. J. Appl. Physiol. Occup. Physiol.* 69:26–31.

Vukovich, M.D., D.L. Costill, and W.J. Fink (1994). Carnitine supplementation: effect on muscle carnitine and glycogen content during exercise. *Med. Sci. Sports Exerc.* 26:1122–1129.

Vukovich, M.D., D.L. Costill, M.S. Hickey, S.W. Trappe, K.J. Cole, and W.J. Fink (1993). Effect of fat emulsion infusion and fat feeding on muscle glycogen utilization during cycle exercise. *J. Appl. Physiol.* 75:1513-1518.

Wagenmakers, A.J.M. (1991). L-carnitine supplementation and performance in man. In: F. Brouns (ed.) *Advances in Nutrition and Topsport.,* Med Sport Sci. Basel: Karger, vol 32: pp. 110–117.

Wagenmakers, A.J.M. (1998). Muscle amino acid metabolism at rest and during exercise: Role in human physiology and metabolism. In: J.O. Holloszy (ed.) *Ex. Sport Sci. Rev.* Baltimore, USA: Williams and Wilkins, vol 26: chapter 11.

Wagenmakers, A.J.M., E.J. Beckers, F. Brouns, H. Kuipers, P.B.Soeters, G.J. van der Vusse, and W.H.M. Saris (1991). Carbohydrate supplementation, glycogen depletion, and amino acid metabolism during exercise. *Am. J. Physiol.* 260:E883–890.

Wagenmakers, A.J.M., J.H. Brookes, J.H. Coakley, T. Reilly, R.H.T. Edwards (1989). Exercise-induced activation of the branched-chain 2-oxo acid dehydrogenase in human muscle. *Eur. J. Appl. Physiol. Occup. Physiol.* 59:159–167.

Wagenmakers, A.J.M., J.H. Coakley, and R.H.T. Edwards (1990). Metabolism of branched-chain amino acids and ammonia durig exercise: Clues from McArdle's disease. *Int. J. Sports Med.* 11:S101–S113.

Wagenmakers, A.J.M., J.T.G. Schepens, and J.H. Veerkamp (1984). Increase of the activity state and loss of total activity of the branched-chain 2-oxo acid dehydrogenase complex in rat diaphragm during incubation. *Biochem. J.* 224:491–496.

Williams, M.H. (1992). Ergogenic and ergolytic substances. *Med. Sci. Sports Ex.* 24:S344–S348.

Wolfe, R.R., R.D. Goodenough, M.H. Wolf, G.T. Royle, and E.R. Nadel (1982). Isotopic analysis of leucine and urea metabolism in exercising humans. *J. Appl. Physiol.* 52:458–466.

DISCUSSION

LAMB: In the paper by Balsom's group in which the subjects did 10 by 6-s cycling bouts with 30-s rest intervals, the results were reported as pedal revolutions per minute. The effect of creatine was detected in only the last 2 s of the last few bouts. Apparently, there was no significant overall effect of creatine on the performance of the 10 by 6-s sprints and no effect on a single 6-s bout. Thus, I do not consider these results very compelling in terms of a performance effect of creatine. Also, in the report by Bosco's lab, the mean power output in the 45-s jump test was the same in both creatine-supplemented and placebo groups. The investigators did not control the rate of jumping; although the creatine-supplemented group jumped a bit higher on average, they jumped fewer times in 45 s. Also, the matching of subjects appeared to be inadequate because, although they found a significant improvement running on the treadmill compared to baseline treadmill in the creatine group, the data were about the same for the control group and the creatine group at the end of the experiment. Finally, in the Kreider study, there was a rather atypical finding with the interval cycling test; the significant performance benefit occurred early rather than late as Balsom and others have reported.

WAGENMAKERS: I agree that some of the studies I have cited are not perfect. In my conclusions about the relative efficacy of various supplements on improving exercise performance, I have tried to distinguish those supplements, such as creatine, for which there are many studies showing positive results from supplements such as carnitine, for which I found only a single study that claims positive effects on performance. Furthermore, there is a logical theoretical rationale behind the creatine effect, whereas I can find no biochemical rationale for using carnitine. I think there is a reason to believe ergogenic claims for creatine. We certainly need to do more research, but in certain cases we know enough to advise some athletes about potential positive effects of creatine in sport. Of course, scientists do not decide whether supplements are used in sports practice; athletes and trainers do.

KENNEY: I don't think there is any doubt that muscle fibers swell and increase their hydration with creatine loading. Does this intracellular hydration occur at the expense of the interstitial fluid spaces or perhaps of the intravascular fluid?

WAGENMAKERS: I cannot see a reason for a decrease in the volume of the interstitial or the intravascular spaces. Why would such changes occur?

KENNEY: Fluid being retained in intracellular space ultimately comes from the interstitial and intravascular spaces. If total body water increases proportionally, then concentration gradients stay the same, and there is no net fluid flux. But if total body water doesn't increase, perhaps due to inadequate fluid intake, and more fluid moves inside the cell, it has to come at the expense of another fluid compartment.

WAGENMAKERS: But total body water should increase, shouldn't it? There are very well-designed control mechanisms for maintaining the volumes of the interstitial and intravascular spaces.

KENNEY: It should if athletes consume enough fluids. But wrestlers and other athletes may not, and this might lead to a relative dehydration of the interstitial and/or intravascular compartments. Conceivably, this might contribute to muscle cramps that have been reported by many athletes who use creatine supplements.

WAGENMAKERS: We completed a study of total body water before and after creatine supplementation in trained rowers. We saw an increase in the creatine concentration of the muscle, but we did not find an increase in body weight in our subjects. We are still puzzled about this. Hultman et al. (1996) convincingly showed that there is decreased urine production in the first days of creatine loading, suggesting that there is fluid retention. When you couple this observation with the increase in the creatine concentration in the muscle, it seems likely that there is an expansion of the muscle fiber volume, but more research should be done to be certain about it. Creatine loading from this perspective may be very important in patients with muscle wasting due to disease, disuse, inactivity, and aging.

TARNOPOLSKY: We have done a number of studies of creatine loading. In particular, we have been interested in the possibility of differences in creatine-supplementation effects between males and females. In one study, 15 males and 15 females were randomized to creatine or placebo for 5 d at 20 g/d. We were one of the few studies that did a randomized crossover design for each individual after a 6-wk washout period. With those 30 individuals, we detected a small but significant attenuation of fatigue during plantar dorsiflexion in the creatine-loaded subjects.

Later, we did a calculation of the sample size needed to detect a performance change as small as this had we used separate groups of subjects rather than a crossover design. The plantar flexion test we used to test performance has relatively low variability compared to other tests used in the literature. Nevertheless, we calculated that we would have needed a sample size of about 100 individuals to detect a difference of the magnitude we found in our crossover study. In my opinion, further creatine studies with only a half-dozen subjects are a complete waste of time because of their low statistical power. Further studies should use crossover designs and should employ adequate numbers of subjects and appropriate outcome measures.

I believe that creatine supplementation by body builders may not be justified. They are probably already consuming enough dietary creatine in the large amount of meat they consume so that they have maximized their muscle creatine stores. However, patients with neuromuscular diseases may profit greatly from creatine supplementation. In our clinic we have seen strength improvements of about 20–25% in creatine-supplemented patients afflicted with a variety of neuromuscular disorders, including muscular dystrophy, inflammatory myopathy, and MELAS syndrome. Each of these diseases is characterized by abnormally low stores of phosphocreatine.

Finally, Flint Beal at Harvard provided rats with a chemical called 3-nitropropionic acid, which caused a severe energy defect in the brain and caused lesions in their brains, very much like Huntington's disease. When rats were first supplemented with 1% creatine, the creatine seemed to provide complete protection against the lesions when the 3-nitropropionic acid was then administered. I think the potential for the use of creatine in clinical therapy is much greater than in bodybuilding.

WALBERG-RANKIN: Is there concrete evidence that the amounts of ammonia accumulated in the blood following BCAA consumption affect motor coordination?

WAGENMAKERS: That is entirely theoretical; few labs are able to do controlled coordination studies.

DAVIS: There is evidence of neurological impairments in patients who have liver disease characterized by ammonia levels similar to those observed following supplementation with high doses of BCAA during exercise. I believe that motor control abnormalities in athletic situations would also occur.

WALBERG-RANKIN: People are taking creatine for months and even years. Some athletes take creatine while they are consuming an energy-restricted diet. Do you think there are any health consequences of taking creatine during energy restriction? Three U.S. wrestlers died in 1997 while attempting to lose body weight. Some people have implied that creatine might have been involved in these deaths.

WAGENMAKERS: I do not know the details on the wrestlers, so I cannot comment on it. However, it is very important that if athletes use creatine, they stick to the maintenance dose of 2 g/d, which has been shown to optimize creatine stores in the muscles. Why use more? It doesn't make sense. A dose of 2 g/d will be close to the normal dietary intake, so there will be no risk of unwanted effects on health.

CLARKSON: Newspaper accounts did link the deaths of the three wrestlers last fall to creatine. However, the Centers for Disease Control and the Food and Drug Administration investigated the deaths and did not determine that creatine was a contributing factor. At this point there is no confirmation that creatine was involved in any of the three wrestlers' deaths. However, if creatine causes an increase in body weight through increased cell hydration, then wrestlers may try to cut additional body weight through acute dehydration to compensate for the weight gain due to creatine. Conceivably, this could be a potential problem for other wrestlers who are taking creatine.

HORSWILL: In a recent study in the *European Journal of Applied Physiology* by Oopik et al., athletes lost 3–4% of their body weights while either loading with creatine or taking a placebo. There was a tendency for plasma volume to be reduced to a greater extent with athletes on the creatine: a 4% reduction in plasma volume for the creatine group versus a 2% for the placebo. That is a small change in plasma volume, but it is also small reduction in total body weight. In competition, athletes may lose 8% to 12% of body weight. Do you think plasma volume is reduced to a greater extent in creatine-loaded athletes during heat stress and dehydration? Maybe this precipitates the cramping and heat illnesses that have been associated with creatine loading.

WAGENMAKERS: It is impossible to answer your question with experimental evidence. My opinion is that the normal regulatory mechanisms will come into action and prevent the fluid shifts you are talking about. The human body is not so defenseless that it cannot cope with an increase in creatine content of 30 mmol/kg dry muscle. Some people, in fact, already have very high creatine concentrations, and they can apparently easily deal with these high concentrations without getting into difficulty. Suggestions have also been made that top athletes have high creatine concentrations before supplementation starts. I do not see a reason to worry about unwanted fluid shifts.

SATTERWHITE: We know that there are limits to creatine absorption. If wrestlers or other athletes consume more than can be absorbed in the gastrointestinal tract, is there a subsequent osmotic effect that could lead to dehydration?

WAGENMAKERS: If athletes ingest so much creatine that it cannot be absorbed from the gut, it is certainly possible for them to become somewhat dehydrated through diarrhea.

SPRIET: It would be rather simple with a muscle biopsy to measure the wet:dry weight ratio. Muscle biopsies sampled before and after creatine supplementation at rest may give some information as to the distribution of the additional water that has been taken on.

LANG: You need only a few percent cell volume increase to inhibit proteolysis and to stimulate protein synthesis. The hypothesis is that if one supplements the diet with creatine, there will be a slight increase in the muscular cell volume that stimulates protein synthesis. That would activate the mechanisms regulating extracellular fluid volume such as increasing the output of vasopressin, renin-angiotensin, and aldosterone. Through thirst and reduced renal output, these mechanisms should rapidly restore extracellular fluid volume.

We are not talking about a rapid shift of large volumes of water at a given time, but about a small percentage increase of muscle cell volume, which then triggers protein synthesis. The next day there is another 3% swelling. That again stimulates protein synthesis, and the muscle may increase by 10% or 16% volume, but at a given time there is only a small shift of water, and the extracellular fluid volume is always regulated in the interim. Thus, it is probably not much of a problem for extracellular fluid homeostasis.

TARNOPOLSKY: The amount of total water retained by carbohydrate loading is much larger than that retained during creatine loading, yet we do not seem concerned with dehydration in athletes undergoing carbohydrate loading. Also, we found no effect whatsoever on blood pressure during acute creatine supplementation of 20 g/d for 5 d in males and females. Finally, the evidence that the water retained with creatine loading is within the muscle cell is not strong. There are no direct measurements proving that the water is within the myofibril per se. I think we have to be cautious about that.

WAGENMAKERS: I agree.

SPRIET: You cited a study from the Greenhaff group in which subjects consumed carbohydrate along with the ingested creatine and further increased the creatine uptake in the muscle by 60%. One thing that has to be stressed is the large amount of carbohydrate that was taken four times a day to achieve this. I do not think that is something we want to encourage athletes to do; it appears that they would be getting over 50% of their daily intake of energy from just the carbohydrate supplement.

I also think you have overemphasized one of the potential reasons that creatine supplementation might enhance metabolism. You state that the phosphocreatine shuttle system is the way in which energy is transduced in the cell, but as far as I know, there is no evidence in skeletal muscle that we need the phosphocreatine shuttle. In fact, studies in rat skeletal muscle in which creatine stores were depleted by feeding the rats ß-guanidino propionic acid (GPA), a creatine analogue, showed that energy transduction was not affected.

WAGENMAKERS: Energy production and exercise performance were impaired in those animals. Meyer et al. (1984) concluded from their experiments that direct diffusion of high-energy phosphates between mitochondria and myofibrils was almost entirely due to diffusion of creatine phosphate and creatine.

FEBBRAIO: When the total creatine content fell after supplementation with GPA in the rat studies of Terjung et al., mitochondrial enzymes were upregulated. In Balsom's study that showed a negative effect of creatine supplementation on endurance exercise performance, the negative effect was attributed to an increase in body weight. However, if decreasing creatine content upregulates mitochondrial enzymes, maybe increasing creatine causes a downregulation of those enzymes, which would decrease the capacity for aerobic energy production. I don't think we have done enough work looking at what effect raising total creatine content in muscle has on metabolism, particular during prolonged exercise. It is quite possible that it has a negative effect.

WAGENMAKERS: I would not expect that an increase in creatine content would downregulate mitochondrial enzymes. In a rat study of long-term creatine supplementation combined with high-intensity endurance training, there was a larger increase in citrate synthase activity in the rats that ingested creatine, and their endurance performance increased dramatically (Brannon et al. 1997). The reason for the upregulation of mitochondria in the rat model with GPA is that GPA stresses metabolism, which causes increased mitogenesis in an attempt to make more ATP by the oxidative pathways. However, there is no reason to expect that an increase in creatine will lead to downregulation of the mitochondrial content. In fact, I think the rat literature convincingly shows that the opposite is the case when creatine ingestion is combined with training.

HEIGENHAUSER: With regard to lactate supplementation, I agree with your premise that the amount of lactate that can be provided is not significant from the standpoint of energy production, but I think that sodium lactate is a very good vehicle for changing acid-base balance because it is a good way to deliver sodium. In the horseracing industry, sodium lactate is often used to enhance performance. When sodium lactate is administered, lactate is metabolized, and the remaining sodium cation increases the bicarbonate concentration. I would not write off sodium lactate as an ergogenic aid because bicarbonate loading has been shown to increase equine performance.

Bicarbonate loading in horses is illegal, but the same effect can be achieved with sodium acetate or magnesium hydroxide. A very good way to slowly change the acid-base balance is to administer sodium lactate. Ten grams of sodium lactate is equivalent to about half the dose found to be ergogenic in studies of bicarbonate loading in humans.

WAGENMAKERS: Are you talking about intravenous administration?

HEIGENHAUSER: No. In humans, it is taken orally with 500–1,000 ml of water. In the horse, it is delivered to the gut through an esophageal tube.

WAGENMAKERS: That is not a very practical way to give it to an athlete.

HEIGENHAUSER: It might not be a practical way, but there is anecdotal evidence that it does improve performance. In the laboratory we certainly can see changes in performance in humans if the individuals are exercising at fairly high intensities.

WAGENMAKERS: I'll stick to my conclusion that there is no reason to advise athletes to add lactate to carbohydrate drinks.

HEIGENHAUSER: But you are basing your conclusion only on the metabolism of lactate, not on its effects on acid-base balance.

WAGENMAKERS: My advice is based primarily on the practical consequences of severe gastrointestinal problems.

HEIGENHAUSER: But if you give it with enough water, you do not get those problems.

7

Vitamin and Mineral Metabolism and Exercise Performance

Henry C. Lukaski, Ph.D.

INTRODUCTION

There is an intensified effort to compel the public to increase physical activity and to improve the nutritional quality of the diet as a practical and cost effective means to promote health and well being in the population (National Research Council, 1989a). This emphasis on the synergy between diet and physical activity rejuvenates interest in the fundamental roles of nutrients in enhancing biological function while promoting health. The adoption of these healthful behaviors prompts speculation about the need to supplement the diet with additional amounts of micronutrients, vitamins, and minerals, particularly among physically active individuals.

Recreational and competitive athletes are conspicuous targets of advertisements for nutritional supplements. Claims for the ability of nutritional supplements to enhance performance, delay fatigue during competition, speed recovery after heavy training sessions, and enhance vigor fill sports magazines and the popular press. Advertisements for nutritional supplements are effective, based on surveys of athletes. Among almost 3000 high school and collegiate athletes, 44 and 13% took vitamin and mineral supplements, respectively (Parr et al., 1984). Similarly, 31% of 80 Australian Olympic athletes (Steel, 1970) and 29% of 347 non-elite marathon runners reported taking some form of nutritional supplement (Nieman et al., 1989). Additional reports confirm significant use of nutritional supplements, including 75% of female runners (Barr, 1986), 92% of world class amateur and professional athletes (Grandjean, 1983), and 100% of female body builders (Lamar-Hildebrand et al., 1989).

A survey of football players, gymnasts, and runners indicates that more than 40% of the competitive athletes consume nutritional supplements (Sobal & Marquart, 1994). Thus, the use of nutritional supplements is quite pervasive among physically active individuals.

The impetus for this extensive use of supplements originates from some questionable perceptions. One impression is that most physically active individuals, as compared to their less active counterparts, fail to consume a diet that contains adequate amounts of vitamins and mineral elements and that this failure may lead to marginal nutrient deficiency, substandard training and performance, and, eventually, adverse health consequences. Another perception is that physical activity promotes excessive losses of micronutrients because of increased catabolism and excretion. These opinions fuel the use of vitamin and mineral supplements to improve physical performance, although scientific evidence to support the generalized use of nutritional supplements to augment physical performance is lacking (Singh et al., 1992; Tellford et al., 1992a; Weight et al., 1988a). With the exception of a few situations of well-described nutritional deficiency, there is little experimental evidence to support these claims.

Some other factors contribute to the widespread use of nutritional supplements among physically active individuals. One consideration is the lack of nutrition knowledge among coaches, trainers, and athletes. In a review of the literature, Marquart et al. (1998) found that coaches and athletes, including elite, collegiate, recreational, and childhood athletes, reported a lack of knowledge of basic nutritional principles and nutritional guidelines for physically active individuals. Although there was a general awareness of the roles of the macronutrients, there was a dearth of awareness of the importance and need for vitamins and minerals by physically active people. A second concern is the widely held view that existing dietary guidelines (National Research Council, 1989b) are based on data derived from individuals who were not involved in physical training or athletic competition. Thus, speculation and lack of well-researched dietary recommendations, along with aggressive promotion of supplements, contribute to the extensive use of vitamin and mineral supplements among physically active people.

This chapter examines the interaction between micronutrient metabolism and physical performance. It addresses the issues of nutrient functions, effects of diet on absorption and utilization, and the role that physical activity plays in nutrient excretion. Emphasis is placed on integration of newer techniques for monitoring nutrient metabolism and status with traditional approaches of nutritional assessment. The objective is to increase awareness of the effect of physical activity on micronutrient homeostasis and metabolism and to determine the need, if appropriate, for micronutrient supplementation in response to increased physical activity among healthy individuals.

BIOLOGICAL FUNCTIONS OF MICRONUTRIENTS AS RELATED TO PHYSICAL ACTIVITY

Micronutrients, as compared to macronutrients, are consumed in small amounts and participate in distinct biological functions. On the average, a moderately active adult may consume daily more than 3 kg of water, more than 500 g of carbohydrate, 70–100 g of protein, and perhaps 50 g or more of fat (Clark, 1997). Consumption of some macrominerals (calcium, phosphorus, and sodium) may reach a gram or more, whereas intakes of trace and ultratrace mineral elements and vitamins are very small fractions of a gram (Figure 7-1). These differences in nutrient intake apparently reflect turnover rates in the body (Figure 7-2). For example, water and carbohydrate turn over rapidly because of their immediate biological roles in temperature regulation and as a fuel substrate. Fat

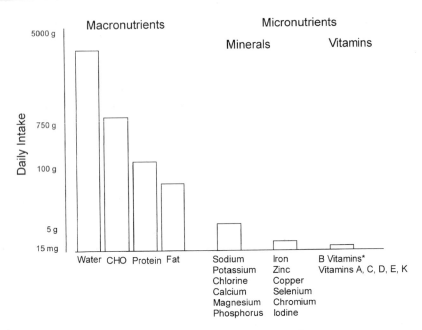

FIGURE 7-1. *Ranges of daily macronutrient and micronutrient intakes.*

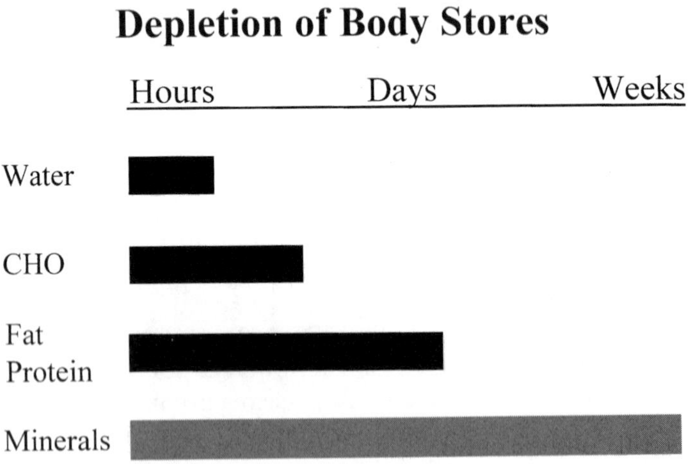

Depletion of Body Stores

FIGURE 7-2. *Estimated daily turnover of nutrients.*

and protein have slower turnover rates because of relatively large storage depots. In contrast, vitamins and minerals are conserved in the body because of their roles as components of enzymes and cofactors; they thus serve as facilitators of energy metabolism and metabolic processes.

Because of their broad and well-defined roles in supporting various biological functions, vitamins and minerals are designated as essential for humans. Many of these established roles serve to promote physical performance.

Vitamins

Vitamins are organic compounds that are found in small amounts in foods and are essential nutrients because they cannot be synthesized by the body. They act as catalysts for biochemical reactions involved in physiological processes that are essential for health and optimal function; vitamins are not direct sources of energy. Because the activities of these metabolic processes increase during exercise, there is a need for an adequate supply of vitamins to promote physical performance. There are two broad classifications of vitamins based on their solubility in either water or fat.

Water Soluble Vitamins. This classification includes the B complex vitamins and vitamin C (ascorbic acid). In general, the B vitamins (thiamin, riboflavin, niacin, pyridoxine, biotin, folic acid, and pantothenic acid) regulate energy metabolism by modulating the synthesis and degradation of carbohydrate, fat, and protein (Table 7-1). Vitamin B_{12}, however, is required for hemoglobin synthesis. In contrast, vitamin C acts as an antioxidant rather than as a promoter of energy metabolism.

The water-soluble vitamins are not stored in large quantities in the body and, thus, must be consumed on a regular basis. The quantity of individual vitamins stored is variable. For example, consumption of a diet deficient in most B vitamins can result in symptoms within 3–7 d (Keith, 1994). Vitamin B_{12}, however, is the exception because it can be stored in the liver for a year or longer (Armstrong et al., 1974). A diet deficient in vitamin C provokes signs of deficiency with a few weeks and results in scurvy in about 6 mo (Irwin & Hutchins, 1976).

Fat Soluble Vitamins. This category comprises vitamins A, D, E, and K, which can be stored in adipose tissue in substantial amounts. Because the fat-soluble vitamins have no direct role in regulating energy metabolism, they function in roles supportive of energy utilization. For example, vitamin E and beta carotene, a precursor of vitamin A, act as antioxidants in reducing muscle damage and enhancing recovery from exercise (Kanter, 1994). Vitamin D, which promotes calcium utilization in bone formation, and Vitamin K, which is needed for proper coagulation, apparently play no role in exercise performance (Keith, 1994).

TABLE 7-1. *Biological Functions of Some Vitamins, with Reference to Exercise.*

	Function	Recommended Intake	Deficiency Sign or Symptom
Water Soluble			
Thiamin (B_1)	Carbohydrate metabolism	1.5 mg*	Weakness, decreased endurance, muscle wasting
Riboflavin (B_2)	Oxidative metabolism, electron transport system	1.7 mg*	Altered skin and mucous membrane and nervous system function
Niacin	Oxidative metabolism, electron transport system	20 mg*	Irritability, diarrhea
Pyridoxine (B_6)	Gluconeogenesis	2.0 mg*	Dermatitis, convulsions
Cyanocobalamin (B_{12})	Hemoglobin formation	6.0 μg*	Anemia, neurological symptoms
Folic acid	Hemoglobin and nucleic acid formation	400 μg*	Anemia, fatigue
Ascorbic acid (Vit C)	Antioxidant	60 mg**	Fatigue, loss of appetite
Fat Soluble			
Retinol (Vit A)	Antioxidant	5000 IU**	Appetite loss, prone to infections
Tocopherol (Vit E)	Antioxidant	30 IU**	Nerve and muscle damage

* Institute of Medicine, 1998
** National Research Council, 1989b

Minerals

Twelve minerals are designated as essential nutrients, and dietary recommendations or estimated safe and adequate daily dietary intakes have been established for them (National Research Council, 1989b). Four of these minerals have biochemical functions that have the potential to impact physical performance; they include magnesium, iron, zinc, and chromium. (Table 7-2)

These mineral elements exert diverse biological effects by serving as components of enzymes that regulate a variety of metabolic processes. These processes include energy transduction at the cellular level, gas transport, antioxidant protection, membrane receptor functions, second messenger systems, and integration of physiological systems. Mineral elements, therefore, regulate the utilization of macronutrients in energy metabolism.

MICRONUTRIENT METABOLISM

Vitamins and minerals are absorbed from the gastrointestinal tract, transported by the blood, and then taken into cells. These nutrients are incorporated into proteins and function as cofactors or components of

TABLE 7-2. *Exercise-Related Functions of Selected Mineral Elements.*

	Function	Recommended Intake	Deficiency Sign or Symptom
Magnesium	Energy metabolism, nerve conduction, muscle contraction	280 mg*(F[#]) 359 mg*(M)	Muscle weakness, nausea irritability
Iron	Hemoglobin synthesis	15 mg**(F) 12 mg**(M)	Anemia, cognitive impairment, immune abnormalities
Zinc	Nucleic acid synthesis, glycolysis, carbon dioxide removal	12 mg**(F) 15 mg**(M)	Loss of appetite, growth retardation, immune abnormalities
Chromium	Glucose metabolism	50-200 µg**	Glucose intolerance

*Institute of Medicine, 1998
**National Research Council, 1989b
[#]F = female, M = male

biologically active compounds. The processes by which micronutrients are absorbed, redistributed in the body, and excreted are termed *metabolism*. The primary aspects of micronutrient metabolism are presented in Figure 7-3. Only a fraction of ingested micronutrients is absorbed; the vast majority of dietary vitamins and minerals is excreted in the feces. The relatively small amount of absorbed micronutrients is lost from the body in urine, menses, and sweat. The processes of absorption and excretion are influenced by the nutritional status of the individual. The balance between intake and losses of a nutrient reflects body retention of the nutrient. Homeostatic adaptations regulate the absorption and excretion of nutrients to preserve physiological functions and well being.

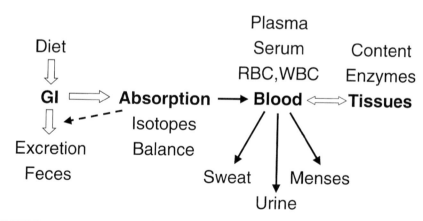

FIGURE 7-3. *Outline of micronutrient metabolism.*

Generally, investigations into the interactions between diet and physical activity have related various indices of micronutrient status (e.g., circulating concentrations of micronutrients) and measures of performance. Observations from these studies provide some basic insight into relationships between diet and performance. However, to understand the impact of exercise on nutrient metabolism and, conversely, the effect of graded dietary intake of nutrients on exercise performance, studies of nutrient absorption, transport and distribution, breakdown, and excretion are needed.

Stages of Nutrient Deficiency

The impact of a nutritional deficit on an individual depends on the magnitude and duration of the nutrient deficiency. There are four general stages of nutritional deficiency (Table 7-3). The preliminary stage of deficiency refers to the consumption of an inadequate amount or poor availability of the nutrient in the diet. An example is the dramatic change in the type of diet consumed (e.g., change from a meat-containing diet to a meat-free diet) or a change in the individual's physiological state (e.g., pregnancy or lactation). The second stage is characterized as biochemical deficiency. The body pool of the nutrient is decreased by inadequate dietary intake or by increased loss from the body. This stage may be identified by a chemical analysis of blood or urine. Physiological deficiency is the third stage and is associated with nonspecific signs or symptoms such as loss of appetite, muscle weakness, or physical fatigue. These first three stages of nutritional deficiency are designated marginal or subclinical deficiency. Whether or not these stages impact physical performance depends on the energy requirements of the activity and the biochemical role of the limiting nutrient. Muscular weakness and fatigue will have a negative impact on physical performance. The final stage of nutritional deficiency is clinically manifest malnutrition; it is identified with specific clinical signs of illness. A common example is anemia. Delineation of the nutritional etiology includes assessment of iron, copper, folic acid, and

TABLE 7-3. *Stages of Nutrient Deficiency.*

Stage	Description	Characteristics
Preliminary	Inadequate intake or bioavailability	Dramatic change in diet composition or physiological state
Biochemical	Decreased body pool because of inadequate intake or increased losses	Decreased circulating nutrient or enzyme activity
Physiological	Appearance of non-specific symptoms	General malaise
Clinical	Appearance of specific symptoms	Clinical signs or symptoms of illness

vitamin B_{12} status. Both physical performance and health are adversely impacted by clinical nutritional deficiency.

VITAMIN METABOLISM AND PERFORMANCE

Information regarding the interactions between vitamin metabolism and physical performance is very limited because research designs have not been as comprehensive as necessary to form reasonable conclusions. For example, measurements of vitamin intake, variations in vitamin intake, biochemical assessments of vitamin status, and determinations of physical performance are required. Only a few studies have provided such information.

This section will discuss the interaction between the metabolism of some vitamins (thiamin, riboflavin, niacin, pyridoxine, folate, cobalamin, ascorbic acid, vitamins A, and E) and physical activity. Other vitamins (biotin, pantothenic acid, and vitamins D and K) will not be discussed because of the lack of information relating their metabolism with exercise.

Water Soluble Vitamins

Vitamin B_1 (Thiamin). Thiamin plays a key role in carbohydrate and protein metabolism. As the compound thiamin pyrophosphate, it acts as a coenzyme in the conversion of pyruvate to acetyl CoA and α-ketoglutarate to succinyl CoA, and it participates in the decarboxylation of branched-chain amino acids. Thus, thiamin has been suggested to be a potential limiting nutrient in physical performance.

Ingested thiamin is fairly well absorbed, rapidly converted to the physiologically active forms, poorly stored, and excreted in the urine. The small intestine absorbs thiamin by either active transport or passive diffusion. In humans, single oral doses greater than 2.5–5 mg are unabsorbed (Rindi & Ventura, 1972; Thomson & Leevy, 1972). Thiamin is transported by the portal blood to the liver. Circulating thiamin is found in erythrocytes and is bound mainly to albumin. Thiamin and its metabolites are excreted in the urine, with negligible amounts of thiamin excreted in the bile.

Substances with antithiamin activity occur naturally in some foods. This activity is termed thiaminase, and two types of thiaminase have been reported (Somogyi, 1966). Thiaminase has been found in fresh- and salt-water fish and more recently in some plant sources, including tea, coffee, blueberries, Brussel sprouts, and red cabbage. Heating or cooking destroys thiaminase activity.

The suggested intake for thiamin ranges from 1.1–1.2 mg/d for women and men, respectively. Because the thiamin requirement depends on energy intake, the RDA is 0.5 mg/1000 kcal (Institute of Medicine, 1998). Physically active individuals who consume large energy intakes should consume proportionally more thiamin. Studies have found adequate thiamin intakes in different groups of athletes (Peifer, 1997).

However, thiamin intake may be a problem for some groups of athletes. For example, individuals who consume low-energy diets for participation in athletic events that feature weight classes or physical appearance may have less than adequate thiamin intakes. Also, athletes who consume diets that emphasize foods low in nutrients (e.g., sodas or candy) may be prone to low thiamin intakes. Some examples of athletes with low dietary thiamin include competitive female gymnasts (Benson et al., 1985; Loosli et al., 1986) and collegiate wrestlers (Short & Short, 1983; Steen & McKinney, 1986).

Controlled human studies have found no significant effects of graded dietary thiamin intakes on physiological function. Keys et al. (1943) observed no change in cardiovascular function, intermediary metabolism (plasma glucose, lactate and pyruvate concentrations), muscle strength, or performance during treadmill exercise of young men who consumed diets containing 0.23, 0.33, 0.53, and 0.63 mg thiamin per 1000 kcal for 12-wk periods. Urinary thiamin excretion, expressed as a percentage of total daily intake, demonstrated an adaptation; it decreased when dietary thiamin was reduced. In a double-blind study of partial thiamin depletion, Wood et al. (1980) fed young men 0.5 and 5 mg thiamin for 4–5 wk periods in a cross-over design and found no change in endurance on the ergocycle and no change in nerve conduction velocity in the presence of biochemical evidence of thiamin depletion (i.e., urinary thiamin and erythrocyte transketolase activity decreased, and thiamin pyrophosphate increased). Thus, thiamin restriction for brief periods apparently does not have an adverse impact on physical performance. Short-term thiamin insufficiency, however, may be manifest with pyruvate accumulation and increased circulating lactate during exercise, which may promote fatigue and impair training (Chen et. al., 1989).

Vitamin B$_2$ (Riboflavin). Riboflavin functions in electron transport systems for energy transduction as the coenzymes flavin mononucleotide (FMN) and flavin adenine dinucleotide (FAD); it is needed for oxidative energy metabolism. Because riboflavin is found in a variety of foods, including dairy products, meat, vegetables, and cereals, riboflavin deficiency is uncommon in Western countries. Evidence is available, however, that riboflavin deficiency may be more common in athletes in developing countries where food availability may be limited (Chen et. al., 1989).

Because dietary sources of riboflavin are largely in the form of coenzyme derivatives, hydrolysis is needed before absorption can occur. The absorptive process occurs in the upper small intestine by a saturable transport system; absorption is proportional to the intake and reaches a maximum at 25 mg (Jusko & Levy, 1975). The capacity of the human gastrointestinal tract to absorb riboflavin is limited to 20 mg in a single dose. Bile salts facilitate absorption of riboflavin. Diets containing psyllium gum apparently decrease the rate of riboflavin absorption, whereas wheat bran has no effect (Roe et al., 1988). Antacids, such as aluminum hydroxide and magnesium hydroxide, apparently decrease riboflavin absorption (Feldman & Hedrick, 1983). Alcohol also interferes with riboflavin absorption (Pinto et al., 1987). In general, the presence of food in the intestine increases riboflavin absorption, presumably by decreasing the rate of gastric emptying and intestinal transit. Several metals (copper, iron and zinc) and drugs (caffeine, theophylline, and saccharine) chelate with riboflavin and may affect its bioavailability (Jusko & Levy, 1975). Boric acid also binds with riboflavin, as well as with glucose and ascorbic acid (Pinto et al., 1978; Roe et al, 1972). The clinical significance of this binding is not known in most cases. Riboflavin is loosely associated with albumin, although significant amounts are complexed with other proteins.

Recommendations for riboflavin intake are based on energy intake. It is suggested that an intake of 0.6 mg/1000 kcal will meet the needs of most healthy adults (Institute of Medicine, 1998). The current RDA is 1.1 and 1.3 mg/d for women and men, respectively (Institute of Medicine, 1998).

Biochemical assessment of riboflavin status involves the measurement of the activity of glutathione reductase, for which FAD is a cofactor. Determination of the activity of glutathione reductase in erythrocytes (EGR) is a reliable assessment tool for riboflavin status in humans. An activity coefficient (EGRAC), or the ratio the enzyme activity with and without added FAD, is used to monitor riboflavin nutritional status.

Surveys indicate that most athletes consume adequate amounts of riboflavin (Short, 1994). However, some groups of athletes, particularly those individuals with concerns about body weight, may be at risk of riboflavin depletion. Female collegiate gymnasts have low self-reported dietary riboflavin (Kirchner et al., 1995).

Initiation of increased physical activity, such as an exercise program, apparently has an adverse impact on riboflavin nutriture. Sedentary young women consuming 2.15 mg riboflavin/d experienced a significant increase in EGRAC, indicative of decreased riboflavin status, within 4 d of starting an endurance exercise program, with a concomitant increase in urinary riboflavin excretion (Belko et al., 1983). Women, aged 50–67 y, fed low (90 µg/1000 kcal), as compared to adequate (600 µg/1000 kcal), amounts of riboflavin had decreased riboflavin status (significantly increased ERGAC and decreased urinary riboflavin) after 4 wk of endurance training (Trebler Winters et al., 1992). Differences in dietary riboflavin, however, did not affect the magnitude of the changes in peak oxygen uptake and anaerobic threshold after training. Men with mild riboflavin depletion experienced a deterioration in riboflavin status (ERGAC from 1.36 to 1.57; urinary riboflavin from 273 to 232 µg/d) at the start of physical training, but these changes did not affect the energy cost of treadmill walking (Soares et al., 1993). Thus, biochemical evidence of altered riboflavin status may reflect changes in riboflavin retention or utilization in response to exercise training without adverse effects on physical performance. These findings suggest that functional consequences of decreased riboflavin nutriture may require longer duration to become manifest than do biochemical indices of impaired riboflavin status.

Niacin. This term refers to two compounds, nicotinic acid and nicotinamide. Nicotinamide is a precursor of nicotinamide adenine nucleotide (NAD) and nicotinamide adenine dinucleotide phosphate (NADP), which serve as electron and proton acceptors, respectively. Thus, they function in energy metabolism: NAD as an electron carrier in many oxidative reactions and NADPH as a hydrogen donor in the pentose phosphate shunt.

Nicotinic acid and nicotinamide are rapidly absorbed from the stomach and the small intestine (Bechgaard & Jespersen, 1977). At low concentrations, absorption occurs by facilitated diffusion, but at higher concentrations passive diffusion predominates. Three to four grams of niacin given orally can be almost completely absorbed. Nicotinamide is the major form in the blood and results from enzymatic hydrolysis of NAD in the intestinal mucosa and liver (Mrocheck et al., 1976). Excess niacin is methylated in the liver and excreted in the urine.

The RDA for niacin is 14 and 16 mg/d for women and men, respectively (Institute of Medicine, 1998). To calculate the adequacy of a diet as a source of niacin, a factor is calculated for the contribution of tryptophan to meeting the niacin need. The quantity of tryptophan required to produce the same biological effect as 1 mg of niacin is 60 mg. Thus, 60 mg tryptophan is biologically equivalent to 1 mg niacin (National Research Council, 1989b).

Niacin intake by various groups of athletes seems to be adequate (Short, 1994). Athletes who generally restrict food consumption, e.g., ballet dancers and gymnasts, tend to have decreased niacin intakes (Short, 1994).

Biochemical assessment of niacin status is limited by the lack of a reliable marker. The ratio of two urinary metabolites of niacin has been used. No reliable data for comparisons of niacin nutriture among groups of athletes or between control and athletic groups are available.

Studies to evaluate the role of dietary or supplemental niacin or nicotinic acid on metabolic responses during acute exercise or physical training provide limited information. As summarized by Keith (1994), the impetus for research on niacin and performance is based on the potentially adverse effect of niacin on fatty acid utilization and, thus, the influence of accelerated depletion of glycogen stores on measures of performance. Heath et al. (1993) used pharmacological doses of nicotinic acid (1 g before submaximal exercise, then 3 g/d for 21 d). Compared to tests without nicotinic acid supplements, the acute effect of 1 g nicotinic acid was to decrease circulating free fatty acid (FFA) concentration and to increase respiratory exchange ratio (RER), which suggests a reduced mobilization and utilization of fat. The effect on RER was diminished after 11 d of treatment, which implies that an adaptation to nicotinic acid supplementation had occurred.

Murray et al. (1995) determined the effect on performance of consuming nicotinic acid (330 and 521 mg for women and men, respectively) along with a glucose-electrolyte beverage. It was speculated that the mixture of nicotinic acid and glucose would reduce FFA concentrations and increase dependence on glucose from the beverage, which hypothetically might attenuate the use of muscle glycogen. The supplemental nicotinic acid diminished the anticipated increase in FFA concentration. Performance, however, was not different in the subjects who consumed the carbohydrate-electrolyte beverage and nicotinic acid supplement as compared to the placebo-treated volunteers.

Vitamin B$_6$. This term is generic for all biologically active forms of vitamin B$_6$. The forms include pyridoxine, pyridoxal, pyridoxamine, pyridoxine phosphate, pyridoxal phosphate, and pyridoxamine phosphate (Leklem, 1990). Pyridoxine, pyridoxal, and pyridoxamine are the forms most common in foods. Vitamin B$_6$, in the form of pyridoxal phosphate, acts as a cofactor for transferases, transaminases, decarboxylases, and cleavage enzymes used in transformations of amino acids. During exercise, pyridoxal phosphate is needed for gluconeogenesis. Another important function is glycogenolysis, in which pyridoxine phosphate is a cofactor for glycogen phosphorylase (Leklem, 1990).

There is limited information about absorption of the vitamin B$_6$ vitamers in humans. Based on animal data, it is concluded that pyridoxine and the major forms of vitamin B$_6$ are absorbed by a nonsaturable, passive process in the intestine (Leklem, 1991). Vitamin B$_6$ is transported in the blood both in the plasma and in erythrocytes. The primary forms of vitamin B$_6$ are readily and efficiently absorbed, but the glucoside form is not (Leklem, 1986). The bioavailability of vitamin B$_6$ is generally >75% for most foods (Kabir et al., 1983; Kies et al., 1984; Leklem et al., 1980; Lindberg et al., 1983). Other factors that may limit the bioavailability include food processing, fiber content, and the presence of other forms of vitamin B_6 (Gregory & Ink, 1986). The RDA for vitamin B_6 is 1.5 and 1.7 mg/d for women and men, respectively (Institute of Medicine, 1998). In general, male and female athletes consume adequate amounts of this vitamin (Manore, 1994). When athletes fail to ingest adequate vitamin B_6, it is explained by low energy intake, particularly among athletes attempting to maintain low body weights, which also may be related to poor food choices (Manore, 1994).

Assessment of vitamin B_6 status in humans requires measurement of the concentrations of pyridoxal phosphate and vitamin B_6 in plasma and 4-pyridoxic acid in urine (National Research Council, 1989b). Another biochemical measure of vitamin B_6 status is erythrocyte aminotransferase activity (Leklem, 1990).

Few studies have examined the vitamin B_6 status of physically active people. Three surveys reported that 40–60% of athletes have reduced vitamin B_6 based on the test of erythrocyte aminotransferase activity (Guilland et al, 1989; Tellford et al, 1992b; Fogelholm et al., 1993). Only one study (Guilland et al., 1989) reported more than one indicator of B_6 nutriture, and it found less (17–35%) deficiency among the athletes than when only one indicator of B_6 status was used. This finding indicates the need to use independent biochemical measures of nutritional status as well as of dietary B_6 intakes to assess the interaction between diet and performance.

Coburn et al. (1991) examined the influence of dietary B_6 on vitamers of B_6 in blood and on B_6 in muscle. The male subjects received a B_6 depletion diet (1.8 μmols pyridoxine HCl per day) for 6 wk followed by a self-selected diet supplemented with 980 μmols/d pyridoxine HCl for 6 wk. Depletion resulted in a significant decrease in plasma pyridoxal and pyridoxal phosphate concentrations and a significant increase in erythrocyte aminotransferase activity. Muscle pyridoxal phosphate was unaffected by dietary B_6. These findings indicate that despite alterations in dietary B_6, skeletal muscle concentrations of B_6 are constant and that plasma B_6 concentration is not a good indicator of tissue stores.

Folate. This vitamin functions in the synthesis of purines and pyrimidines that are needed for DNA production and erythropoiesis. A deficiency of folate causes abnormal cell replication, particularly in the erythropoietic system, and results in megaloblastic anemia. This type of anemia also is caused by vitamin B_{12} deficiency. Supplemental folate in the presence of B_{12} deficiency can correct megaloblastic anemia, but not the B_{12} deficiency (National Research Council, 1989b). Thus, folate supplementation can hinder the detection of B_{12} depletion if the screening variable is anemia.

Folic acid in food is present as polyglutamate complexes; specific conjugase enzymes cleave the excess glutamates before folate is absorbed in the intestine. The bioavailability of folate in food depends on the degree of binding with glutamate. Folate monoglutamate has a greater bioavailability than does folate polyglutamate (90 vs. 50%) because of the requirement for hydrolysis of the latter (Halstad, 1990). Glucose and galactose increase absorption of monoglutamyl folate by active transport mechanisms. Undefined factors in food (e.g., folate hydrolase inhibitors and binders) that impair active transport clearly reduce bioavailability of folate (Halstad,1990). Folate is transported in the blood as either the free form or in association with low- or high-affinity binders (proteins). Folate is excreted in the urine and bile in metabolically active and inactive forms.

The RDA for folate is 400 µg/d for women and men; it increases to 600 and 500 µg/d during pregnancy and lactation, respectively (Institute of Medicine, 1998). Surveys of athletes prior to 1989 indicated that a significant percentage of female athletes and adolescent ballet dancers and gymnasts did not consume at least two-thirds of the RDA (180 µg/d) for folate (McMartin, 1997). Studies after 1989 did not find a high proportion of athletes consuming low dietary folate. These differences may be attributed to the change in RDA for folate from 400 to 180 µg/d in 1989 (National Research Council, 1989b). Unfortunately, the more recent surveys did not include athletic groups at risk for folate deficiency. With the recent increase in the RDA for folate to 400 µg/d (Institute of Medicine, 1998), nutritional surveys of athletes may find dietary folate inadequacy.

There are limited data that assess blood biochemical measures of folate status in physically active individuals. Singh et al. (1993) found adequate serum folate concentration in ultra marathoners.

Folate supplementation of folate-deficient athletes did not improve physical performance (Matter et al., 1987). Female marathoners with low serum folate concentrations (< 4.5 ng/ml) supplemented with folate (5 mg/d for 10 wk) did not experience a significant change in treadmill performance, cardiorespiratory function, or metabolic response during exercise as compared to placebo-treated, folate-depleted controls (Matter et al., 1987). The lack of a physiological benefit of supplementation contrasted with a significant increase in serum folate. Thus, changes in circulating folate may not reflect changes in the status of tissue or cellular folate.

Vitamin B_{12} (Cobalamin). The term vitamin B_{12} has two meanings. To a chemist, it means cyanocobalamin, the vitamin with a cyanide group. To a nutritionist, it is the cobalamin molecule without the cyanide group. The biologically active form of the vitamin contains the cobalamin moiety with or without the cyanide group.

This vitamin is found only in animal food products; it is required for normal erythrocyte production because of its role in folate metabolism and for proper function of the nervous system (Institute of Medicine, 1998). Interest in vitamin B_{12} among physically active individuals stems from its vital role in erythropoiesis.

This vitamin, which is found in polypeptide linkages in foods, must be hydrolyzed and then complexed with a specific glycoprotein (intrinsic factor) in the lumen of the small intestine for absorption (Herbert & Das, 1994). Vitamin B_{12} also is reabsorbed from the bile via the enterohepatic circulation. The principal cause of vitamin B_{12} deficiency is inadequate intake, particularly among strict vegetarians and alcoholics (Herbert & Das, 1994). An inhibitor of vitamin B_{12} absorption is excessive vitamin C supplementation. Megadoses (500 mg) of vitamin C adversely affect vitamin B_{12} availability from food; individuals consuming even greater doses of ascorbic acid (1000 mg) may develop vitamin B_{12} deficiency (Herbert et al., 1978). High doses of vitamin C, in the presence of iron, inactivate vitamin B_{12} and destroy intrinsic factor (Herbert et al., 1994; Shaw et al., 1990).

The RDA for vitamin B_{12} is 2.4 µg/d for adults (Institute of Medicine, 1998). Surveys of nutrient intakes by groups of athletes suggest that certain groups may not be consuming adequate amounts of this vitamin, based on the previous RDA of 2 µg/d (National Research Council, 1989b). Athletes on energy-restrictive diets (Benson et al., 1985; Loosli et al., 1986; Welch et al., 1987) and strict vegetarians (Janelle & Barr, 1995) are at risk for vitamin B_{12} depletion.

Vitamin B_{12} status is assessed by using blood or urine concentrations. Based on the limited data available, athletes have adequate B_{12} status (McMartin, 1998). Normal B_{12} concentrations were found in endurance athletes (Weight et al, 1988b).

Vitamin B_{12} supplementation apparently has no beneficial effect on performance. Montoye et al. (1955) provided 50 µg cyanocobalamin daily to adolescent boys and found no improvement in the half mile run or Harvard step test scores after 7 wk, as compared to the nonsupplemented control group. Similarly, parenteral B_{12} administered to nonanemic men failed to elicit improvements in endurance capacity, muscle strength, and performance (Tin-May-Than et al., 1978). Thus, supplemental B_{12} does not benefit performance unless a nutritional deficit is present.

Vitamin C (Ascorbic acid). Vitamin C has many biological functions that can be influential in physical performance (Davies et al., 1991). It is necessary for normal collagen synthesis and thus plays a prominent role in development and maintenance of cartilage, ligaments, and tendons. It also plays a role in the synthesis of carnitine, which transports long-chain fatty acids into mitochondria, and the catecholamines, epinephrine and norepinephrine. Ascorbic acid facilitates the transport and uptake of nonheme iron at the mucosa, the reduction of folic acid intermediates, and the synthesis of cortisol. Recent evidence indicates that vitamin C is a potent antioxidant that serves to regenerate vitamin E from its oxidized by-product (Sen & Hanninen, 1994).

Ascorbic acid is absorbed in the human intestine with an energy-dependent active process that is saturable and dose-dependent. At low doses (< 30 mg/d), ascorbic acid absorption is nearly 100%; at usual dietary intakes (30–180 mg/d), absorption is 70–90% (Kubler & Gehler, 1970). Absorption, however, decreases to 50% with a dose of 1500 mg and to 16% with a 12,000 mg dose (Kubler & Gehler, 1970). Maximal ascorbic acid absorption is attained by ingestion of several spaced doses of less than 1000 mg throughout the day rather than ingestion of one megadose (Kallner et al., 1977). There are no data for bioavailability of vitamin C from foods or administered with compounds found in foods.

Vitamin C depletion, theoretically, may adversely impact various aspects of physical performance (Keith, 1997). These detrimental effects range from nonspecific responses, e.g., fatigue and muscle weakness, to anemia. They also have clear impacts, including decreased ability to train (because of recurrent injuries to connective tissues) and decrements in endurance performance as a result of anemia. Historical reports indicate that sailors and soldiers with scurvy (vitamin C deficiency) experienced shortness of breath during physical exertion and reduced energy and endurance during work (Carpenter, 1986).

The recommendation for vitamin C intake is 60 mg/d, which is adequate to maintain tissue concentrations and to prevent scurvy in most individuals (National Research Council, 1989b). Physiological stressors, such as infection, cigarette smoking, altitude, and extreme environmental temperatures, increase vitamin C requirements (National Research Council, 1989b). Exercise is another physiological stressor that may increase vitamin C needs.

On the average, physically active adults consume adequate amounts of vitamin C (Keith, 1997). Male athletes have a range of vitamin C intake of 95–520 mg/d whereas females have intakes ranging from 55–230 mg/d, as compared to the RDA of 60 mg/d. However, some athletic groups have suboptimal intakes. Among male athletes, 23% of wrestlers (Steen & McKinney, 1986) and 20% of football players (Hickson et al., 1987) consumed less than 70% of the RDA. Female athletes show a similar pattern, with 13 and 22% of basketball players and gymnasts (Hickson et al., 1986), 25% cyclists (Keith et al., 1994), and 10% of collegiate gymnasts (Loosli et al., 1986) ingesting less than 70% of the RDA. Increased dietary vitamin C intake may be indicated to meet the RDA in some groups of athletes.

Athletes generally display plasma vitamin C concentrations in the range of normal values (Keith, 1997). Some surveys, however, report a small fraction (12%) of athletes with values less than the lower limit (Tellford et al., 1992a) and all values at the lower end of the range (Duthie et al., 1990). Caution should be used when interpreting plasma ascorbic acid values because physical activity within the previous 24 hr can increase plasma vitamin C concentrations (Duthie et al., 1990).

Physical activity may affect vitamin C homeostasis. Among professional soccer players, a strenuous training session resulted in a 50% decrease in ascorbic acid in leukocytes (Boddy et al., 1974). Urinary vitamin C excretion was inconsistently impacted by physical training. Comparisons between trained and sedentary men show equivocal findings. Physically active men have either reductions in urinary ascorbic acid or no difference as compared to sedentary men (Fishbaine & Butterfield, 1984). However, when dietary vitamin C was controlled (315 mg /d), trained and sedentary men had a similar urinary output of vitamin C (Fishbaine & Butterfield, 1984).

Vitamin C may indirectly affect physical performance by enhancing physiological functions. Men supplemented daily with 250 or 500 mg vitamin C or placebo for 10 d and exposed to controlled exercise in the heat had a decreased body temperature as compared to the men treated with placebo (Kotze et al., 1977). The mechanism of this apparent adaptation was not described.

Vitamin C supplements have been reported to enhance immune function. Male runners, with a dietary vitamin C intake of 500 mg/d, received either 600 mg vitamin C or placebo for 21 d and then ran in a marathon race. During the 14 d after the race, the runners supplemented with vitamin C had less upper respiratory tract infections than did the men receiving the placebo (33 vs. 68%) (Peters et al., 1993). Additional studies are needed to define the immune function that may be beneficially impacted by vitamin C.

Clear evidence of a beneficial effect of vitamin C supplementation on physical performance is lacking (Keith, 1997). Vitamin C, however, may exert permissive effects on physiological functions (i.e., antioxidant, immunocompetence, and collagen repair) that facilitate recovery from intense training.

Fat Soluble Vitamins

Vitamin A. Vitamin A includes a group of compounds including retinol, retinaldehyde and retinoic acid. Another source of vitamin A is the group of chemicals termed carotenoids, principally β-carotene, which are precursors of vitamin A and are present in plant foods. Humans can meet the requirement for vitamin A by consuming various retinoids with vitamin A activity; these compounds are widespread in animal products (National Research Council, 1989b). Vitamin A serves many functions, including the maintenance of epithelial cells, facilitating vision, and promotion of cell growth and immune function (National Research Council, 1989b).

Preformed vitamin A in foods is found principally as retinyl ester. Proteolytic digestion in the stomach releases retinyl ester and provitamin A carotenoids from foods and makes them available for aggregation with other lipids. Together with carotenoids, retinol and carotenols are transported in micellar form into the circulation (Olson, 1996). The absorption and utilization of vitamin A are facilitated by dietary fat, vitamin E, and protein and are reduced by the presence of oxidized fat and oxidizing agents in food. Among healthy people who ingest at least 10 g of fat daily, vitamin A is absorbed with an efficiency exceeding 80%. Dietary carotenoids in the range of 1–3 mg/d are about 40% absorbed. As the amount of carotenoids in the diet increases, the absorptive efficiency decreases (Brubacher & Weiser, 1985). The absorption of carotenoids is more dependent on the presence of bile acids than on the absorption of vitamin A (Olson, 1994). Protein, zinc, and iron deficiencies adversely affect vitamin A transport, storage, and utilization (Underwood, 1984).

The requirement for vitamin A is expressed as retinol equivalents (RE). One RE equals 1 μg retinol or 6 μg β-carotene. The RDA for vitamin A is 800 RE for women and 1000 RE for men (National Research Council, 1989b). In contrast to the water-soluble vitamins, very large intakes of vitamin A are toxic and can result in significant metabolic perturbations, including anorexia, hair loss, and kidney and liver damage (Aronson, 1986). Carotenoids, however, even at large intakes, apparently are not usually dangerous to health (National Research Council, 1986b). However, high doses of supplemental β-carotene unexpectedly increased the incidence of lung cancer and heart disease among men who were at increased risk because of a history of smoking, alcohol use, or exposure to asbestos (Omenn et al., 1996). The finding of increased morbidity among smokers who consumed supplemental β-carotene suggests that this compound acts as a pro-oxidant under conditions produced by smoking.

Groups of athletes generally report vitamin A intakes in excess of the RDA. Surveys of endurance runners (Peters et al., 1986), professional ballet dancers (Cohen et al., 1985), female collegiate athletes (Welch et al., 1987), male collegiate athletes (Guilland et al., 1989), female collegiate heavyweight rowers (Nelson Steen et al., 1995), and male cross country runners (Niekamp et al., 1995) indicate adequate dietary vitamin A. Adolescents and young adults participating in wrestling (Steen & McKinney, 1986), ballet (Benson et al., 1985), and gymnastics (Loosli et al., 1986) tend to consume less than 2/3 of the RDA for vitamin A.

Although one may speculate that food restriction may explain the diminished vitamin A among these athletes, food selection may also be important. For example, young women beginning an exercise program reported a decrease in vitamin A intake unrelated to any decrease in dietary energy (Johnson et al., 1972). This decrease was related to a relatively high fat intake (>40% of dietary energy) and very low consumption of fruits and vegetables. Therefore, food selection as well as reduced food intake may contribute to reduced vitamin A intakes among certain groups of athletes.

Vitamin A status can be assessed by measuring blood retinol, which provides an index of bodily stores of vitamin A. For example, when liver stores of vitamin A are low, plasma retinol decreases (Olson, 1996). Guilland et al. (1989) found that despite low self-reported intakes of vitamin A among athletes, biochemical measures of retinol were normal. Similarly, Weight et al. (1988b) measured blood retinol and found normal stores of vitamin A in highly trained athletes.

A survey of elite German athletes (Rokitzki et al., 1989) found that plasma retinol concentrations were within the range of normal values (49–93 µg/dl), but there was considerable variability in β-carotene (14–123 µg/dl). The results from the 24 athletes from four sports (marathon runners, weight lifters, swimmers, and cyclists) were similar to values obtained from 150 blood donors for retinol (60 ± 14 µg/dl) and β-carotene (38 ± 25 µg/dl). These data for elite athletes indicate an adequate intake of vitamin A but a varied, although not extremely low, intake of β-carotene.

The importance of diet in maintaining the blood content of vitamin A and β-carotene is emphasized among other groups of active adults. For example, physically active, older Dutch women (60–80 y) had dietary vitamin A similar to that of sedentary controls (1.1 vs. 1.0 mg/d) (Voorrips et al., 1991). The active women consumed more fruits and vegetables, whereas the sedentary women had greater intakes of meat and milk. This dietary pattern increased serum β-carotene concentrations relatively more in the active women (0.99 ± 0.59 vs. 0.67 ± 0.22 mmol/L), whereas serum retinol concentrations were similar (1.99 ± 0.41 vs. 2.02 ± 0.39 mmol/L) among the active as compared to the sedentary women. Similar findings have been reported for older men in the U.S. (Kazi et al., 1995). Thus, circulating vitamin A reflects bodily stores of vitamin A, which apparently are stable and maintained because they are large, whereas β-carotene is more variable, probably because of fluctuations in carotenoid intake.

Vitamin A and β-carotene concentrations exhibit transient changes after exercise. Various reports indicate a consistent increase (18–40%) in vitamin A and a lesser decrease (10%) in β-carotene following repeated bouts of exercise or after endurance exercise (Hillman & Rosner, 1958; James et al., 1953). It is unclear if the increase in retinol is related to hemoconcentration or to mobilization of retinol from stores in the liver.

The role of β-carotene as a facilitator of performance has been examined. The effects of ingestion of a single dose of β-carotene 2 h prior to ergocycle exercise to exhaustion on stress-hormone production has been examined (Hosegawa, 1993). Men treated with placebo experienced increases in corticotropin-releasing hormone, adrenocorticotrophic hormone, epinephrine, and norepinephrine. This stress-hormone response was progressively diminished with increasing doses of β-carotene and was completely suppressed in the men who ingested 30 mg. The rapid biological response to a single dose of β-carotene is surprising and should be confirmed in studies in which each subject serves as his/her own control.

There is limited information describing the effects of dietary vitamin A on performance. Running performance did not change in men maintained on a diet deficient in vitamin A for 6 mo and subsequently supplemented with vitamin A for 6 wk (Wald et al., 1942). This finding may be explained by the large vitamin A intake (75,000 IU) prior to the start of the depletion phase, which probably increased bodily stores of vitamin A.

Although a small percentage of athletes selects diets that are inadequate in vitamin A, there is no evidence that these athletes have biochemical deficiencies or that exercise increases vitamin A needs. Whether or not β-carotene provides any beneficial effect on performance remains to be determined.

Vitamin E. Vitamin E is a generic term for eight naturally occurring compounds in two classes designated as α-tocopherols and γ-tocopherols; the two classes have different biological activities (Meydani, 1995). The most active and well known of these compounds is RRR-α-tocopherol, formerly known as d-α-tocopherol. Vitamin E supplements contain either the natural or synthetic form of α-tocopherol. The natural form of vitamin E, RRR-α-tocopherol and its acetate or succinate esters, are more bioavailable than are the synthetic forms (Acuff et al., 1994). The principal sources of dietary vitamin E include vegetables, seed oils, sunflower seeds, nuts, whole grains, and wheat germ oil; animal products are generally poor sources of vitamin E (National Research Council, 1989b).

Dietary vitamin E is primarily composed of α- and γ-tocopherol, of which 20–50% is normally absorbed. Vitamin E is absorbed in a manner similar to that for dietary fat (Kayden & Traber, 1993). Thus, any impairment in bile production and secretion, pancreatic function, and chylomicron metabolism will impair vitamin E absorption and utilization. As the intake of polyunsaturated fatty acids increases, the vitamin E requirement increases (Horwitt, 1974). Among common vegetable oils in the U.S., the vitamin E content parallels the content of polyunsaturated fat in the oil.

The biological role of vitamin E is to serve as an antioxidant of polyunsaturated fatty acids in cell membranes and subcellular structures (Machlin & Benedich, 1987). It also influences cellular responses to oxidative stress through modulation of signal transduction pathways (Azzi et al., 1992). Vitamin E deficiency is associated with neurological damage and hemolysis.

Vitamin E may play a differential role in oxidative metabolism in different muscle fibers. Human skeletal muscle consists of two major fibers, Type I (slow-twitch) and Type II (fast-twitch). Type I fibers contain plenty of myoglobin and mitochondrial enzymes, and they replenish phosphocreatine more efficiently via oxidative phosphorylation than do Type II fibers (Pette & Spamer, 1986). Type I, as compared to Type II, fibers also have greater catalase activity to eliminate reactive oxygen species produced from an increased oxidative metabolism (Lammi-Keefe et al., 1980). Thus, Type I fibers may also use more vitamin E than do Type II fibers. Muscles composed of mainly Type I fibers have been reported to contain greater (-tocopherol concentrations than do muscles composed principally of Type II fibers (Fry et al., 1993). Thus, it may be hypothesized that vitamin E is a key nutrient in supporting physical performance.

Vitamin E deficiency adversely affects skeletal muscle; it can lead to muscular tissue degradation in animals (Chan & Hegarty, 1977) and humans (Neville et al., 1983). In addition, vitamin E deficiency may promote transformation of Type I to Type II fibers (Neville et al., 1983; Pillai et al., 1994). The mechanism by which these actions occur is unknown, but it apparently is related to free-radical damage. Thus, severe vitamin E deficiency increases oxidative stress in skeletal muscles, alters muscle fiber types, and causes degradation and inflammatory processes that lead to dystrophic conditions. Most of the experimental data are from animal studies; there is only limited evidence from research on humans. Thus, it is necessary to determine if dietary restriction of vitamin E in humans actually is associated with severe skeletal muscle derangements as described in experimental animal models.

The RDA for vitamin E is 8 and 10 mg of α-tocopherol for women and men, respectively (National Research Council, 1989b). This estimate is based on maintenance of normal physiological function and protection of tissues from extensive lipid peroxidation. Factors such as increasing dietary polyunsaturated fatty acids and the degree of unsaturation of fatty acids in the diet increase the vitamin E need of an individual. Vitamin E is relatively nontoxic at intakes up to 800 mg/d (National Research Council, 1989b).

According to the NHANES II nutrition study, the vitamin E content of the diets of the majority of the U.S. population is slightly less than the

RDA, and the diets of 20% of men and 32% of women contain less than 50% of the RDA (Murphy et al., 1990). Although a summary of 22 dietary intake surveys of endurance and power athletes indicated that they consumed vitamin E in amounts commensurate with the RDA, a majority of the athletes ingested vitamin/mineral supplements (Economos et al., 1993). In contrast, other surveys reported that only 53% of college athletes (Guilland et al., 1989), 50% of adolescent gymnasts (Loosli et al., 1986), and 38% of ballerinas (Benson et al., 1985) consumed more than 70% of the RDA. Interestingly, Guilland et al. (1989) found that the mean intake of vitamin E for athletes was 77% of the RDA, as compared to only 60% among sedentary controls. Thus, vitamin E intake is less than recommended and is similar among physically active and inactive groups. Finally, athletes who restrict food intake tend to consume inadequate amounts of vitamin E.

Because exercise causes a dramatic increase in oxidative metabolism, there is growing interest in the effect of exercise and vitamin E on metabolism and performance. Vitamin E supplementation (400 mg α-tocopherol daily for 6 wk) did not affect performance during standard fitness tests, including a 1-mile run, bench step tests, 400-m swim test, and motor fitness tests of male adolescent swimmers (Sharman et al., 1971). Likewise, work capacity and muscle strength were unaffected in collegiate male swimmers given 1200 IU vitamin E for 85 d (Shephard et al., 1974), and peak oxygen uptake was not changed in ice hockey players given 1200 IU daily for 50 d (Watt et al., 1974). Similarly, swimming endurance and blood lactate response was not altered in competitive swimmers given 900 IU of vitamin E daily for 6 mo (Lawrence et al., 1975). Finally, motor fitness tests, cardiorespiratory function during ergocycle tests, and 400-m swim times were not affected in male and female trained swimmers given 400 mg of vitamin E daily for 6 wk (Sharman et al., 1976). Thus, generalized supplementation with vitamin E apparently does not enhance performance.

Beneficial effects of vitamin E supplementation may impact physiological responses to free-radical assault during exercise. Young men receiving 300 mg of α-tocopherol daily for 4 wk had reduced leakage of enzymes and a lower malonaldehyde (MDA) concentration in the blood after strenuous exercise, as compared to unsupplemented controls (Sumida et al., 1989). Similarly, Goldfarb et al. (1989) supplemented men with 800 IU of vitamin E daily for 4 wk and found decreased lipid peroxides (chemical markers of lipid peroxidation) and MDA in the blood of men. Urinary excretion of lipid peroxides was reduced in young and old men supplemented with 800 mg α-tocopherol, as compared to unsupplemented controls, 12 d after the exercise bout (Meydani et al., 1993).

Vitamin E deficiency probably is rare among athletes consuming balanced diets. Evidence for a beneficial effect of vitamin E supplementation on physical performance is lacking. Although vitamin E apparently acts in the prevention of damage associated with lipid peroxidation, results are equivocal in studies of vitamin E effects on exercise-induced muscle damage in humans. The generalized use of large doses of supplemental vitamin E is not encouraged because vitamin E may attenuate protein degradation, and some protein degradation seems to be required to stimulate postexercise muscle protein synthesis (Booth, 1989). Additional human studies are needed to examine the relationships between vitamin E intake, objective measures of exercise-induced muscle soreness and damage, and skeletal muscle protein turnover.

MINERAL METABOLISM AND PERFORMANCE

In contrast to the vitamins, there are burgeoning data describing the interaction between mineral metabolism and physical activity. Investigations that include assessments of intake, excretion, and in some cases retention, as related to various measures of performance, will be described.

Iron

Iron is a key trace element that is required for optimal energy production. It serves as a functional component of iron-containing proteins including hemoglobin, myoglobin, cytochromes, and specific iron-containing enzymes. Thus, iron plays a critical role in the delivery of oxygen to tissues and facilitates the use of oxygen at the cellular and subcellular levels. It is apparent that iron status can impact physical performance.

The recommended intake of iron is 15 and 10 mg/d for women and men, respectively (National Research Council, 1989b). Sources of iron in the diet are classified into two groups, heme and nonheme iron. Heme iron is found in meat as myoglobin. Nonheme iron comes from vegetables and grains. The ability of the body to absorb and utilize dietary iron is influenced by the chemical form of the iron. Heme iron is absorbed with greater efficiency (5–35%) than is nonheme iron (2–20%; National Research Council, 1989b) from single meals. Men absorb an average of 6% of total dietary iron; women of childbearing age absorb 13% on average (Charlton & Bothwell, 1983).

Many factors influence dietary iron absorption and utilization. Vitamin C enhances nonheme iron absorption from a single, but not repeated, meals (Hunt et al., 1994). Components of meat, including heme iron (Cook & Monsen, 1976) and perhaps stearic acid (Lukaski, in press), enhance nonheme iron absorption and utilization. Some dietary inhibitors of nonheme iron absorption include bran, phytic acid, calcium phosphate, and polyphenols (Charlton & Bothwell, 1983; Skikne & Baynes, 1994). Coffee may also inhibit iron absorption, but the active component has not been identified (Morck et al., 1983).

Haymes (1998) has reviewed the adequacy of dietary iron among various groups of physically active people, including competitive athletes. Male athletes generally consume at least the RDA for iron, but female athletes tend to consume somewhat less than the recommended 15 mg/d. A primary cause of iron deficiency among women is inadequate iron intake. It is estimated that approximately half of all girls and women over the age of 12 y in the U.S. consume 10 mg or less of iron daily (National Research Council, 1989b), and only 25% of women of childbearing age consume the RDA for iron (Centers for Disease Control and Prevention, 1998). Women runners consume about 12–15 mg of iron daily (Haymes & Spillman, 1989; Manore et al., 1989; Pate et al., 1993). These runners have low intakes of meat; they also have high intakes of fiber, which reduce the bioavailability of iron to about 10% (Haymes, 1998). When this low amount of available iron (i.e., 1.5 mg) is contrasted with menstrual iron losses of about 0.9 mg and postulated sweat iron of about 0.3 to 0.5 mg, iron balance may be compromised.

The effect of chronic iron losses that exceed iron intake is reduced iron status. This process is thought to occur in stages characterized by depletion of bodily iron stores, decreased erythropoiesis, and then depletion of functional iron, leading to anemia. Assessment of tissue iron depletion may be performed by measurements of serum ferritin, which are closely correlated with bone-marrow iron content. As iron stores are depleted, iron absorption increases with concomitant increases in transferrin concentration in the blood. If the quantity of iron in the blood does not increase (e.g., as a result of increased iron absorption), transferrin saturation decreases; this response will impair erythropoiesis. The final stage is decreased hemoglobin concentration.

Alterations in iron status among various groups of athletes have been summarized by Haymes (1998). Low ferritin concentrations (<12 μg/L) have been reported in male and female runners. Iron deficiency, defined as ferritin concentration <12 μg/L and transferrin saturation <16%, has been observed among women competing in field hockey, cross-country skiing, crew, basketball, and softball. Anemia also has been found, principally in female runners and skiers. The prevalence of these disturbances is similar to that found in the general population. Depleted stores of iron in tissues are seen in about 20–25% of girls and women in the U.S. (Centers for Disease Control and Prevention, 1998), which is consistent with most surveys of female runners (Haymes, 1998). However, some youth and adult female runners have a greater prevalence of tissue iron depletion (25–44%). Male runners and skiers have more tissue iron depletion (4–13%) than is expected from population standards (2%). Iron-deficiency erythropoiesis also is increased among some athletic groups, although this apparently is limited to girl runners (20–34%). Anemia, however, is as common among male and female athletes as it is in general population.

Studies in humans verify the importance of iron to work performance. Gardner et al. (1975, 1977) found that iron-deficient workers treated with iron supplements had decreased blood lactate concentration and increased oxygen uptake during standardized testing. The workers with the lowest hemoglobin concentrations also had the shortest performance time to exhaustion. Edgerton et al. (1981) found that work decrements in iron-deficient anemic workers reflected the level of anemia rather than nonhemoglobin-related biochemical changes. After transfusion, the work capacity of the transfused workers was the same as that measured in other workers with the same (normal) hemoglobin concentrations. These findings illustrate the importance of hemoglobin-associated iron to aerobic work performance, in which delivery of oxygen to muscles is limiting at high-intensity workloads.

Identification of the effects of iron deficiency without anemia on work performance is challenging. Iron-deficient anemic rats transfused with erythrocytes still had deficits in endurance capacity in comparison to nonanemic rats (Davies, 1984). However, when anemic rats are injected with iron dextran and then tested within 18 h of treatment, a significant increase in submaximal endurance was found (Willis et al., 1990). This finding suggests that non-heme iron acts as a cofactor in regulating the enzymes of oxidative metabolism and thus plays an important role in submaximal endurance performance.

The effects of iron supplementation on blood biochemical measures of iron status are clear. Among iron-deficient anemic women, iron supplementation not only improves iron status, it also increases work capacity and reduces heart rate and lactate concentration during exercise (Gardner et al., 1975).

Several studies have examined changes in the iron nutriture of athletes supplemented with various doses of iron during training (Table 7-4). When iron supplements were 18 mg/d and the athletes were not anemic (Cooter & Mowbray, 1978; Haymes & Spillman, 1989), no significant changes in iron status were noted. When supplements that equaled or exceeded 50 mg/d were given to iron-deficient athletes, significant improvements in iron status were observed.

TABLE 7-4. *Efficacy of Iron Supplementation in Athletes.*

Source	Activity	Iron Dose mg/d	Hemoglobin Change	Ferritin Change
Cooter & Mowbray, 1978	Basketball	18	No	–
Haymes et al, 1986	Skiing	18	No	No
Pate et al., 1979	Varied	50	No	–
Matter et al., 1987	Running	50	No	Yes
Nickerson & Tripp, 1983	Running	60	Yes	No
Yoshida et al., 1990	Running	60	No	Yes
Lamanca & Haymes, 1993	Endurance	100	Yes	Yes
Newhouse et al., 1989	Running	100	No	Yes
Klingshirn et al., 1992	Running	100	No	Yes
Fogelholm et al., 1992b	Varied	100	No	Yes
Clement et al., 1986	Running	100	No	Yes
Running		200	Yes	Yes
Schoene et al., 1983	Varied	270	No	Yes
Rowland et al., 1988	Running	300	No	Yes

When iron supplements were given to iron-deficient non-anemic athletes, performance effects were equivocal. Matter et al. (1987) noted changes in serum ferritin without any benefit on peak oxygen uptake or blood lactate concentrations in female marathoners. Other studies also have not reported performance changes in iron-deficient non-anemic athletes supplemented with iron (Newhouse et al., 1989; Schoene et al., 1983). In contrast, Rowland et al., (1988) found an improvement in endurance in adolescent, non-anemic female runners supplemented with iron.

A practical question is the influence of raising serum ferritin concentrations in women without overt anemia on the metabolic response during work capacity tests. Two controlled studies (Newhouse & Clement, 1995; Lukaski et al., 1991) reported decreases in blood lactate concentrations without a change in peak oxygen uptake when serum ferritin concentrations were increased to levels $>12 \mu g/L$. These findings indicate an increased reliance on glycolytic metabolism when tissue iron stores are depleted in the absence of anemia.

Some athletes, particularly females, show evidence of iron deficiency, but the prevalence of anemia is similar to other women in the population. Iron deficiency without anemia apparently does not affect peak aerobic performance, but anemia decreases aerobic performance. Although the data are inconsistent, endurance performance does not seem to be enhanced by iron supplementation in adults with iron deficiency without anemia.

Magnesium

Magnesium is required in a wide variety of fundamental cellular activities that support diverse physiological systems. Magnesium is involved in more than 300 enzymatic reactions in which food is metabolized and new products are formed (Shils, 1994). Some of these enzyme reactions are involved in glycolysis, fat and protein metabolism, hydrolysis of adenosine triphosphate (ATP), and the second messenger system. Magnesium also serves as a physiological regulator of membrane stability and neuromuscular, cardiovascular, immune, and hormonal functions. Thus, magnesium may be considered a potentially limiting element for human performance.

The absorption and retention of magnesium are critical for maintaining homeostasis of this essential mineral. The amount of magnesium in the diet and, to a variable extent, the presence of enhancing and inhibiting dietary components regulate the percentage of dietary magnesium absorbed by healthy individuals. As dietary magnesium increases, fractional absorption decreases. At low dietary intakes (7–36 mg/d), absorption ranged from 65–77%. With greater intakes (960–1000 mg/d), absorption decreased to 11 to 14% (Fine et al., 1991; Roth & Werner, 1979). Magnesium absorption occurs both in the small and large intestine (Brannan et al., 1976). Renal conservation of magnesium is a key regulator of body magnesium homeostasis (Shils, 1969).

The recommended intake of magnesium is 320 and 420 mg/d for women and men, respectively (Institute of Medicine, 1997). Dietary sources of magnesium include green, leafy vegetables and unprocessed grains. Some sources of water may also be good sources of magnesium (Lukaski, 1995).

Dietary surveys of athletes found an important pattern of magnesium intakes. In general, magnesium intakes for male athletes equaled or exceeded the previous RDA of 350 mg/d (National Research Council, 1989b), but those of female athletes tended to be 60–65% of the recommendation of 280 mg/d (Lukaski, 1995). Regardless of gender, athletes participating in sports that require weight classifications (e.g., wrestling) or have an aesthetic component included in the competition (e.g., ballet or gymnastics) tended to consume inadequate amounts of dietary magnesium, i.e., 30–55% of the 1989 RDA (Hickson et al., 1986).

Not all cross-sectional studies of athletes have found inadequate dietary magnesium. Comparisons of magnesium intakes among male and female cross-country skiers and control subjects reported magnesium intakes of 170–185% of the 1989 RDA (290 and 350 mg/d for women and men, respectively) for the athletes, as compared to 108–116% for the age- and gender-matched control subjects (Fogelholm et al., 1992a).

Redistribution and increased loss of magnesium from the body have been observed during and immediately after acute exercise. Intense exercise, such as a competitive ski race, results in a transient decrease in serum magnesium followed by a return to pre-exercise concentrations with 24–48 h (Refsum et al., 1973). As compared to pre-exercise conditions, a bout of intense exercise is associated with a shift in magnesium from the plasma into the erythrocytes (Deuster et al., 1987). The direction and magnitude of this shift depend on the intensity of the exercise; the more anaerobic the exercise, the greater the movement of magnesium from the plasma into erythrocytes. In addition, urinary magnesium losses increased 21% on the day of exercise, as compared to control or nonexercise conditions, and returned to nonexercise levels on the day following the exercise (Deuster et al., 1987; Stendig-Lindberg et al., 1987). These findings indicate a transient increase in magnesium loss that returns to equilibrium in subsequent days if no additional strenuous exercise is performed. The amount of urinary magnesium was related to the degree of exercise-induced anaerobiosis, indexed by postexercise oxygen consumption and plasma lactate concentration (Deuster et al., 1987). This relationship has been interpreted to suggest an increased need for magnesium when glycolytic metabolism is dominant.

Sweat losses of magnesium increase during exercise (Consolazio et al., 1963). Men exercising in the heat (100°F) lost 15–18 mg of magnesium daily in sweat. This output represented 10–15% of total daily magnesium losses (feces, urine, and sweat) and only 4–5% of dietary magnesium intake.

Magnesium deficiency impairs physical performance. Clear evidence was provided when muscle spasms in a tennis player were associated with a decrease in serum magnesium concentration to 0.65 mmol /L; the normal range is 0.8–1.2 mmol/L (Liu et al., 1983). Daily treatment with 500 mg/d of magnesium gluconate relieved the muscle spasms within a few days.

Supplementation of diets of competitive athletes with magnesium salts has been reported to improve cellular function (Golf et al., 1993). Among competitive female athletes with plasma magnesium concentrations at the low end of the range of normal values, serum total creatine kinase and creatine kinase isoenzyme MB decreased after training in the women supplemented with 360 mg magnesium as magnesium aspartate daily for 3 wk, as compared to the women receiving placebo (Golf et al., 1983). Serum lactate concentration and oxygen uptake during an exhaustive rowing-ergometer test decreased in male competitive rowers supplemented with magnesium (360 mg/d) for 4 wk, as compared to the rowers receiving placebo (Golf et al., 1993).

Supplemental magnesium also has been reported to increase muscle strength and power (Brilla & Haley, 1992). Young men participating in a strength-training program received either a placebo or a magnesium supplement to reach a daily magnesium intake of 8 mg/kg body weight. Daily magnesium intakes were estimated as 250 and 507 mg/d for the placebo and supplement groups, respectively. The 7-wk training program was performed at 70% of maximal effort for leg extension and leg press exercises to strengthen quadriceps muscles. Although strength increased in both treatment groups, peak knee-extension torque increased more in the men taking magnesium supplements. This observation indicates that strength gain occurs with dietary magnesium intakes of 250 mg/d, but further increases in strength are achieved with intakes of 500 mg/d, which exceed the current RDA of 420 mg/d (Institute of Medicine, 1997). It also suggests a key role for magnesium in activities that require glycolytic metabolism.

The effects of diet-induced magnesium depletion and repletion on biochemical measures of magnesium metabolism and exercise performance have been determined in postmenopausal women (Lukaski et al., 1997). Magnesium intake was 320 mg/d for the first 35 d (control); it decreased to 180 mg/d for the next 91 d (depletion) and then increased to 380 mg/d for 49 d (repletion). Although total serum magnesium concentration did not change in response to dietary magnesium, ionized magnesium, expressed as a percentage of total serum magnesium, significantly increased during depletion, indicating a mobilization of magnesium from bodily stores. Low dietary magnesium caused negative magnesium balance or net magnesium loss, as compared to positive values when dietary magnesium was 320 mg or more, and it decreased skeletal muscle magnesium concentration, as compared to when dietary magnesium was not restricted. Magnesium depletion increased oxygen uptake (12%) and heart rate (10 bpm) during progressive ergocycle exercise. These results indicate that dietary magnesium deprivation induces magnesium loss from the body, depletes skeletal muscle magnesium stores, and decreases muscular efficiency during submaximal work in women.

The findings of Lukaski et al. (1997) confirm the observation of Golf et al. (1983) of increased oxygen requirement during steady-state submaximal work when magnesium status was low, and indicate that the adverse effects of magnesium depletion are independent of training status. The biological mechanism of decreased energy efficiency during magnesium restriction, however, is unknown. Possible mechanisms include a decrease in magnesium-dependent ATPase activity or a reduction in myoneural function resulting in an increased recruitment of antagonistic muscles to accommodate the increasing work during the exercise tests (Rayssiguier et al., 1990). These intriguing hypotheses require additional investigation to delineate the role of magnesium in work performance.

Marathon runners with adequate magnesium status did not benefit from supplemental magnesium. Terblanche et al. (1992) found that magnesium supplementation (magnesium aspartate hydrochloride, 365 mg/d for 6 wk), as compared to placebo, elicited no beneficial effects on running performance, resistance to muscle damage, muscle magnesium concentration, and skeletal muscle function in trained runners.

These findings confirm that magnesium supplementation per se does not elicit beneficial effect on physiological function or performance when magnesium status is normal.

Zinc

This mineral element is required for the structure and activity of more than 300 enzymes from many species (Vallee & Auld, 1990). The biological importance of zinc is reflected by the numerous functions and activities over which it exerts a regulatory role (Vallee & Falchuk, 1993). Zinc is required for nucleic acid and protein synthesis as well as for cellular differentiation and replication. It also is needed for glucose utilization and insulin secretion. Because of its role in glucose homeostasis, zinc also impacts lipid metabolism. Zinc exerts regulatory actions in various aspects of hormone metabolism, including the production, storage and secretion of hormones, as well as regulating hormone-receptor interactions and end-organ responsiveness. Adequate zinc is needed for the integration of many physiological systems such as immunocompetence, reproduction, taste, wound healing, skeletal development, behavior, and gastrointestinal function. The vast array of functions influenced by zinc status suggests that zinc should be a key regulatory nutrient in exercise performance.

Because of its association with various proteins, zinc in food must be hydrolyzed before it can be absorbed. Homeostatic control of zinc metabolism involves a balance between absorption of dietary zinc and endogenous zinc secretion through adaptive regulation that is influenced by zinc intake (Solomons & Cousins, 1984). Intestinal zinc absorption is regulated by the mucosal cells; when dietary intake is low, it is up regulated, and endogenous secretion is decreased (Taylor et al., 1991). Zinc absorption involves saturable and nonsaturable components (Cousins, 1985).

Dietary components impact zinc absorption (Sandstrom & Lonnerdal, 1989). Inhibition of gastric acid secretion may reduce zinc absorption in humans (Sturniolo et al., 1991). Phytic acid, histidine and cysteine form complexes with zinc in the intestine and decrease its absorption (Cousins, 1985). Inorganic iron in high doses and cadmium compete with zinc to attach to mucosal binding sites in the intestine and thus reduce zinc absorption (Solomons & Cousins, 1984). Folic acid (800 μg) impairs zinc absorption in men and women when dietary zinc is low (10 mg), but not when it is high (> 13 mg), and when plasma zinc is low (77 vs. 81 μg/dl) (Milne, 1989).

Zinc is transported in the circulation in association with specific proteins and amino acids. Although up to 12 plasma proteins bind zinc in vitro, albumin and α-macroglobulin contain the majority of zinc in the plasma (70% and 20–40%, respectively) and permit exchanges of zinc between cells and plasma (Cousins, 1989).

Based on self-reported food and beverage consumption (Lukaski, 1997), athletes generally consume zinc in amounts exceeding the RDA of 12 and 15 mg/d, respectively, for women and men (National Research Council, 1989b). However, a significant proportion of participants in some activities, including long-distance running and gymnastics, may consume less than 10 mg/d. Among athletes who restrict their food intakes, marginal intake of zinc is more prevalent in females than in males (Benson et al., 1985; Deuster et al., 1989; Loosli et al., 1986).

Attention to zinc status as a potential factor affecting physical performance came with the report of decreased serum zinc concentrations among some endurance runners (Dressendorfer & Sockolow, 1980). About 25% of 76 competitive male runners had serum zinc values less than the lower limit designated for the range of normal values. Importantly, serum zinc was significantly correlated with weekly training distance. The investigators postulated that dietary habits, specifically the avoidance of animal products and consumption of low-zinc, high-carbohydrate foods along with increased losses of zinc, may have caused the low serum zinc concentrations in some of the runners.

There are inconsistent reports of low circulating zinc concentrations in physically active adults. Elite German athletes had serum zinc values similar to those of gender-matched nonathletes (Haralambie, 1981). Low serum zinc, however, was found in about 25% of the athletes, as compared to only 13% of the nonathletes. Serum zinc values also were low in a group of female marathon runners, with 22% having values that would be considered low (Deuster et al., 1989; Singh et al., 1990). In contrast, no differences in plasma zinc concentrations were found in comparisons of female and male collegiate athletes and gender-matched controls (Lukaski et al., 1983, 1990). One plausible explanation for these findings is that dietary zinc may have been inadequate in the athletes with the decreased circulating zinc; indeed, they had zinc intakes less than the RDA (Deuster et al., 1989; Lukaski et al., 1990). The relationship between dietary zinc and plasma zinc concentration indicates that when athletes consume at least 70% of the RDA, plasma zinc concentrations are within the range of normal values (Lukaski, 1997).

There are limited data on how zinc status may affect physical performance. Preliminary observations indicate that zinc enhances muscle contraction in vitro (Issacson & Sandow, 1963; Richardson & Drake, 1979). Krotkiewski et al. (1982) supplemented 16 middle-aged women with zinc (135 mg/d) and a placebo in a double-blind, cross-over study. Isokinetic muscle strength (torque at constant velocities of 60°, 120°, and 180° per s) and endurance (percent decline in peak torque of 50 maximal isokinetic contractions at 180°/s) as well as isometric endurance (duration of time a subject could maintain 50% isokinetic strength at a 60° angle of knee flexion) were measured with a one-leg exercise test on a standardized dynamometer. The investigators tested performance before and after 14 d of treatment with a 14-d washout period between each treatment phase. No measures of strength or endurance changed after placebo treatment, but zinc supplementation increased isokinetic strength at 180°/s and isometric endurance. Because these muscle functions rely on recruitment of fast-twitch, glycolytic muscle fibers, one might hypothesize that zinc supplementation enhanced the activity of lactate dehydrogenase, a zinc-dependent enzyme. Interpretation of the significance of these findings is confounded by the very large dose of the zinc supplement (more than 10 times the RDA for women), which suggests that any biological effect on performance was a pharmacological response. Furthermore, there is a concern about the limited duration of the supplementation period and the ability of the body to utilize the administered zinc.

Another zinc-containing enzyme may play a role in facilitating physical performance. Carbonic anhydrase, which regulates the elimination of carbon dioxide from cells, is a zinc-dependent enzyme (Vallee & Falchuk, 1993). Preliminary data indicate that the activity of this enzyme in red blood cells responds to dietary zinc (Canfield et al., 1984). In a study of physically active young men (Lukaski, 1996), oxygen utilization during constant-load ergocycle work was decreased when dietary zinc was 4, as compared to, 17 mg/d. Furthermore, carbon dioxide elimination rate was decreased when zinc intake was low. Measurements of total activity of erythrocyte carbonic anhydrase decreased in response to restricted zinc intake. However, because respiratory quotient increased with zinc restriction, it may be speculated that lactate dehydrogenase activity also was adversely impacted. These findings provide some of the first evidence of impaired metabolic response during exercise when dietary zinc is suboptimal.

Chromium

Chromium is an essential mineral element that functions broadly in the regulation of glucose, lipid, and protein metabolism by potentiating the action of insulin at the cellular level (Mertz, 1993). The mechanism of this interaction between biologically active chromium and insulin, however, remains undefined (Anderson, 1997; Nielsen, 1996). Physiologically active forms of chromium facilitate insulin action, which results in a reduced need for insulin (Mertz, 1993). This fundamental role of chromium, together with the knowledge that the general public may consume diets low in chromium (Anderson & Kozlovsky, 1985) and the recognition of high rates of utilization of carbohydrate during various types of physical activity, have prompted physically active individuals to consider chromium as a potentially important nutrient for physical fitness and health.

Although chromium can exist in a number of valence states, the 3^+ state is the most biologically stable (Mertz, 1969). Small amounts of hexavalent chromium can be reduced to the trivalent state in the stomach (Mertz, 1969).

Intestinal absorption of trivalent chromium is quite low. Two men consuming an average of 37 µg chromium per day had a mean chromium absorption of 1.8% (Offenbacher et al., 1986). Because of the analytical problems associated with measurement of actual chromium absorption, urinary excretion has been used as an indicator of absorption. Adults receiving a supplement of 200 µg of chromium daily excreted an average of 0.4% (Anderson et al., 1983). Chromium absorption was 2% when intake was low (10 µg); it decreased to 0.4–0.5% when intake was increased to 40 µg (Anderson & Kozlovsky, 1985).

The majority of the information regarding the influence of dietary components on chromium absorption comes from studies of rats. Amino acids (Dowling et al., 1990), starch as compared to glucose, fructose, and sucrose (Seaborn & Stoecker, 1989), ascorbic acid (Seaborn & Stoecker, 1992), and zinc deficiency (Hahn & Evans, 1975) increase chromium absorption. Ascorbic acid (100 mg) also increased serum chromium in women supplemented with 1000 µg chromium (Offenbacher, 1994).

Although chromium is considered an essential nutrient, there is no RDA for chromium. The estimated safe and adequate daily dietary intake (ESADDI) for chromium is 50–200 µg/d (National Research Council, 1989b). Few diets, however, contain even the minimum threshold of the ESADDI at 50 µg. The mean daily intake of men consuming a typical Western diet is 33 µg/d, and for women it is 25 µg/d (Anderson & Kozlovsky, 1985).

Routine assessment of dietary chromium for an individual is problematic. The chromium concentration of food is very low, and contamination of samples can be a difficulty. There is a reliance on limited food composition data. It has been estimated that the nutrient density of chromium in the typical Western diet ranges from 5–24 µg/1000 kcal with an average intake of 15 µg/1000 kcal (Anderson, 1997). Foods contain variable amounts of chromium; fruits, whole grains, and vegetables are primary contributors of chromium in the diet (Miller-Ihli, 1996).

There is little evidence that chromium excretion increases after exercise. Acute exercise in trained male runners increased the excretion of urinary chromium from 0.09 to 0.36 ng/mg creatinine (Anderson et al., 1982). In this study, chromium excretion immediately after a 6-mi run was minimal, i.e., about 2% of total daily excretion. However, it almost doubled on the day of the run as compared to the urinary losses on the day before the run (300 vs. 160 ng/d). In another study (Anderson et al., 1984), serum chromium concentration increased significantly at the end of a timed run (3.3 nmol/L) and remained elevated for 2 h after the completion of the run (3.7 nmol/L), as compared to pre-exercise values (2 nmol/L). Urinary chromium losses also were increased on the day of the run (7.1 vs. 3.8 nmol/d).

Because dietary chromium can affect circulating and urinary chromium, additional studies were initiated. Trained and untrained men consumed a controlled diet containing 9 µg chromium per 1000 kcal for 7 d, during which time a standardized exercise test was performed (Anderson et al., 1988). The test included a brief warm up followed by intermittent bouts of high-intensity running (30 s at 90% peak oxygen uptake with 30-s rest periods) until exhaustion. Serum chromium was similar between groups and did not change immediately after the exercise test. Two hours after the test, however, serum chromium concentration almost doubled in the trained men, whereas the untrained men showed no apparent change; these differences between trained and untrained subjects were not statistically significant. The trained men, as compared to the untrained, excreted significantly more chromium in urine (from 1.7–2.3 nmol) than did the untrained men, who had no significant change in urinary chromium loss. Because the trained men performed more exercise at a greater absolute intensity, these findings indicate that high-intensity exercise can increase the urinary loss of small amounts of chromium.

Based on the findings of a potentially low dietary chromium and slightly increased chromium losses during exercise, chromium supplementation has been proposed to enhance physical performance because of its purported anabolic actions (Evans, 1989). The principal chemical form of chromium used to evaluate the efficacy of chromium supplements on performance has been chromium picolinate, an organic compound that is considered to enhance the bioavailability of chromium (Evans & Pouchnik, 1993).

The effect of supplemental chromium (200 µg/d as chromium picolinate) and resistance training on body composition was studied in young men (Evans, 1989). In the first trial, 10 young men received either the chromium supplement or a placebo for 40 d while participating in a weight-training program. Chromium supplementation was associated with a significant weight gain (2.2 kg) and lean body mass gain (1.6 kg) and a slight gain in fat, as determined with anthropometry. A second study included male football players who participated in a more intensive strength-training regimen for 42 d. The 16 men who received the chromium supplement had significant changes in body composition after 14 d (body fatness decreased 2.7%, and lean body mass increased 1.8 kg); no significant changes were seen in the men receiving the placebo. After 42 d, the men receiving the chromium lost body weight (1.2 kg) and fat (3.4 kg) and gained lean body weight (2.6 kg), whereas the placebo-treated men also lost fat (1.8 kg) and gained lean body weight (1.8 kg). It was concluded that chromium supplementation significantly increases lean body mass gain.

Kaats et al. (1996) evaluated the effects of graded chromium supplementation (0, 100 and 200 µg) on body composition changes of adults. The supplement was provided in a protein-carbohydrate drink that was consumed in at least two servings daily for 72 d. Consumption of either 200 or 400 µg of chromium daily was associated with a significantly more positive index of body composition change (gain of fat-free mass and loss of body fat), when compared to no chromium supplementation.

Other studies have not confirmed these findings. Hasten et al. (1990) found that chromium supplementation (200 µg/d as chromium picolinate) of male and female students who were beginning weight training had no effect on anthropometric measurements or strength gain. Body weight gain was significantly greater in the women than the men. Similarly, compared to a placebo group, chromium supplementation (400 µg/d for 16 wk) of active-duty U.S. Navy personnel participating in individualized fitness programs did not significantly enhance the reduction in body weight or body fat or increase fat-free mass determined by anthropometry (Trent et al., 1995).

Other studies of chromium supplementation and resistance training have not found beneficial effects of chromium. Compared to men treated with a placebo, both collegiate football players (Clancy et al., 1994) and untrained men (Hallmark et al., 1996) provided with 200 µg of chromium daily for durations of 9 and 12 wk, respectively, did not experience a significant increase in fat-free mass, a decrease in body fat (determined with densitometry), or an increase in strength. Chromium picolinate (200 µg chromium daily) also was ineffective in promoting decreases in body fat or increases in muscle mass and bone mass or density in young men participating in strength training (Lukaski et al., 1996).

The effect of chromium supplementation on weight loss and glucose metabolism in mildly obese women has been examined (Grant et al., 1997). Young women were randomly assigned to receive chromium picolinate with and without exercise training, placebo with exercise, or chromium nicotinate with exercise. Chromium supplements contained 200 µg/capsule, and the women consumed two capsules daily for 9 wk. Chromium supplementation, regardless of chemical form, had no significant effect on body fat loss. Chromium nicotinate, as compared to chromium picolinate, reduced the insulin response to an oral glucose load.

Although most diets may not provide adequate chromium, the use of chromium supplements apparently provides no beneficial effect on body composition or function. Additional research is needed to identify individuals who might benefit from supplemental chromium to enhance biological function.

GENERALIZED SUPPLEMENTATION: BENEFITS AND CAUTION

The increased interest in physical activity and diet to promote health and well being may prompt some individuals to consume vitamin and mineral supplements. Experimental findings indicate that clinical vitamin and mineral deficiencies are rare in the general population when a balanced diet is consumed. However, some individuals who seek to enhance performance may opt for nutritional supplements.

The general use of nutritional supplements is not recommended unless under the supervision of a physician or a registered dietitian. This guideline is presented because indiscriminate use of some vitamin and mineral supplements may lead to adverse nutritional and health effects that are dependent upon the amount of the supplement and the duration of the use.

Supplementation with B vitamins does not usually pose a significant problem because the body excretes these water-soluble vitamins when they are presented in amounts exceeding the need of the body. However, vitamin C consumed in excessive doses can increase circulating oxalate concentrations and thus promote kidney stones (National Research Council, 1989b). Also, high doses of supplemental vitamin C can adversely affect vitamin B_{12} status (Herbert et al., 1978). When ingested in very high doses, either acutely or chronically, vitamin A can cause toxic manifestations such as headache, vomiting, hair loss, bone deformities, and liver damage. Signs of toxicity occur with sustained daily intakes, including food and supplements, exceeding 15,000 µg retinol (50,000 IU) in adults. Compared to vitamin A, vitamin E is relatively safe, with oral doses of 100–800 mg/d tolerated without physical signs or biochemical evidence of toxicity.

Excessive intakes of certain mineral elements can cause metabolic disturbances. Magnesium supplements exceeding 500 mg/d often cause gastrointestinal disturbances, including diarrhea in some individuals, and may exert a negative effect on phosphate balance (Spencer, 1986). Excessive supplemental zinc can inhibit copper absorption, can cause copper deficiency at doses of 50 mg/d, and may induce microcytic anemia (Fisher et al., 1984). Similarly, ingestion of 50 mg of zinc for 12 d decreases erythrocyte superoxide dismutase activity in healthy women (Abdallah & Samman, 1993). Supplemental zinc at doses of 160 mg/d, taken for prolonged periods, can decrease high-density lipoprotein (HDL) cholesterol (Hooper et al., 1980). Zinc supplements ranging from 15–50 mg/d have been suggested to attenuate the exercise-induced increase in HDL-cholesterol concentration (Goodwin et al., 1985). Iron supplements in large amounts can be problematic because of induced gastrointestinal problems, although amounts of 25–75 mg/d are well tolerated by many people (Finch & Monsen, 1972). The principal concern with iron supplementation is the potential for excessive iron accumulation in men with the genetic tendency for iron overload (Cartwright et al., 1979). The use of single-nutrient supplements (vitamin and mineral), therefore, is not always innocuous.

The use of single-nutrient supplements generally may be hazardous without proper medical supervision. An interesting example is the generalized use of zinc supplements to protect against oxidative damage. Ingestion of supplemental zinc (50 mg/d for 4 wk in a cross-over designed experiment) had no beneficial effect on low-density lipoprotein oxidation in men with normal serum zinc concentrations (Gatto & Samman, 1995). In contrast, diabetic men with decreased serum zinc concentrations experienced a reduction in blood biochemical markers of lipid peroxidation after zinc supplementation (30 mg/d for 3 mo) (Faure et al., 1995). Therefore, the use of nutrient supplements will not be useful in ameliorating biological impairments when nutritional status is adequate.

The use of generalized vitamin and mineral supplementation has not been propitious on nutritional status and physical performance of trained athletes. Studies of elite, male and female athletes supplemented with a balanced vitamin and mineral preparation while training for participation in a wide variety of competitive sports have not shown any beneficial effects on biochemical measures of nutritional status or sports performance (Singh et al., 1992; Tellford et al., 1992a,b; Weight et al., 1988a,b).

Two professional organizations provide advice to physically active individuals who seek to use nutritional supplements. Both the American Dietetic Association (1996) and the American College of Sports Medicine

(1998) indicate that the proper nutritional strategy to promote optimal health and performance is to obtain adequate nutrients from a wide variety of foods. Vitamin and mineral supplementation is appropriate when scientific evidence supports safety and effectiveness. Because some groups of physically active people (e.g., young athletes, participants in sports that require weight standards for competition, and overweight individuals beginning an exercise program) may be at increased risk of nutrient depletion, the use of a balanced vitamin and mineral supplement, not exceeding the recommended or safe and adequate daily intake, may be consumed as a preventive measure.

DIRECTIONS FOR FUTURE RESEARCH

Although a variety of diverse biochemical functions are well established for vitamins and minerals, there is a paucity of evidence that inadequate vitamin and mineral nutriture adversely impacts physical performance. The principal limitation in evaluating previous studies attempting to examine the interaction between diet (vitamin or mineral intake) and performance is the use of incomplete research designs. Future studies examining this important interaction should determine nutrient intake, blood biochemical indicators of nutritional status and nutrient losses, and functional measures of performance. There is a need for information delineating the mechanisms of altered physiologic function associated with restricted vitamin or mineral intake; this includes description of changes in nutrient-dependent enzymatic activity and regulation of gene expression in skeletal muscle. Novel approaches using isotopic tracer methods may be used to study adaptations in micronutrient absorption, utilization, and redistribution in response to variations in diet and physical activity. Determinations of synergistic, and potentially antagonistic, interactions between physical activity and diet are needed to serve as a basis for recommendations for vitamin and mineral intakes to promote health and optimal biological function for active people.

SUMMARY

Because of growing interest in optimizing health, enhancing training, and maximizing physical performance, physically active individuals may embrace the use of vitamin and mineral supplements. These individuals should recognize these important facts.
- Evidence of inadequate dietary vitamin and mineral intakes among physically active individuals is generally lacking. Some vigorous individuals, particularly adolescent ballerinas, gymnasts, long-distance

runners, and wrestlers may not consume adequate amounts of micronutrients because they limit food intake to meet weight restrictions for competition or aesthetic requirements.

- Physically active individuals should consume a diet that contains a variety of foods to maximize intakes of vitamins and minerals, as well as other nutrients, and thus to eliminate the need for nutritional supplements.
- Performance will not be improved if individuals consuming nutritionally-adequate diets use nutritional supplements.
- Only individuals with a defined nutrient deficiency or deficiencies will benefit from supplementation of the limiting nutrient(s).
- A licensed, registered dietitian who is experienced in counseling physically active people should address questions and concerns about the quality of an individual's diet.
- Use of megadoses of vitamins and minerals is not recommended because of potential toxicity or other adverse interactions among vitamins and minerals.
- Physically active individuals who intermittently consume a balanced vitamin and mineral supplement should not exceed the recommended intakes for essential nutrients.

BIBLIOGRAPHY

Abdallah, S.M., and S. Samman (1993). The effect of increasing dietary zinc on the activity of superoxide dismutase and zinc concentration in erythrocytes of healthy female subjects. *Eur. J. Clin. Nutr.* 47:327–332.

Acuff, R.V., S.S. Thedford, N.N. Hidiroglou, A.M. Papas, and T.A.J. Odom (1994). Relative bioavailability of RRR- and all-rac-α-tocopherol acetate in humans: studies using deuterated compounds. *Am. J. Clin. Nutr.* 60:397–402.

American College of Sports Medicine (1998). Current Comment: Vitamin and Mineral Supplements and Exercise. Indianapolis, IN: *American College of Sports Medicine.*

American Dietetic Association (1996). Position of The American Dietetic Association: Vitamin and mineral supplementation. *J. Am. Diet. Assoc.* 96:73–77.

Anderson, R.A. (1997). Chromium as an essential nutrient or humans. *Regul. Toxicol. Pharmacol.* 26:S35-S41.

Anderson, R.A., and A.S. Kozlovsky (1985). Chromium intake, absorption and excretion in subjects consuming self-selected diets. *Am. J. Clin. Nutr.* 41:175–199.

Anderson, R.A., N.A. Bryden, M.M. Polansky, and P.A. Deuster (1988). Exercise effects on chromium excretion of trained and untrained men consuming a constant diet. *J. Appl. Physiol.* 64:249–252.

Anderson, R.A., M.M. Polansky, and N.A. Bryden (1984). Strenuous running: acute effects on chromium, copper, zinc and selected clinical variables in urine and serum of male runners. *Biol. Trace Elem. Res.* 6:32–36.

Anderson, R.A., M.M. Polansky, N.A. Bryden, K.Y. Patterson, C. Veillon, and W.H. Glinsmann (1983). Effects of chromium supplementation on urinary chromium excretion of human subjects and correlation of chromium excretion with selected clinical variables. *J. Nutr.* 113:276–281.

Anderson, R.A., M.M. Polansky, N.A. Bryden, E.E. Roginski, K.Y. Patterson, and D.C. Reamer (1982). Effect of exercise (running) on serum glucose, insulin, glucagon and chromium excretion. *Diabetes* 31:212–216

Armstrong, B.K., R.E. Davis, D.J. Nicol, A.J. van Merwyk, and C.J. Larwood (1974). Hematological, vitamin B_{12}, and folate studies on Seventh Day Adventist vegetarians. *Am. J. Clin. Nutr.* 27:712–718.

Aronson, V. (1986). Vitamins and minerals as ergogenic aids. *Phys. Sportsmed.* 14:209–212.

Azzi, A., D. Boscobonik, and C. Hensey (1992). The protein kinase C family. *Eur. J. Biochem.* 208:547–557.

Barr, S.I. (1986). Nutritional knowledge and selected nutritional practices of female recreational athletes. *J. Nutr. Educ.* 18:167–174.

Bechgaard, H., and S. Jespersen (1977). GI absorption of niacin in humans. *J. Pharm. Sci.* 66:871–872.

Belko, A.Z., E. Obarzanek, H.J. Kalkwarf, M.A. Rotter, S. Bogusz, D. Miller, J.D. Haas, and D.A. Roe (1983). Effects of exercise on riboflavin requirements of young women. *Am. J. Clin. Nutr.* 37:509–517.

Benson, J., D.M. Gillien, K. Bourdet, and A.R. Loosli (1985). Inadequate nutrition and chronic calorie restriction in adolescent ballerinas. *Phys. Sportsmed.* 13: 79–90.

Boddy, K., R. Hume, P.C. King, E. Weyers, and T. Rowan (1974). Total body, plasma, and erythrocyte potassium and leukocyte ascorbic acid in ultrafit subjects. *Clin. Sci. Mol. Med.* 46:449–456.

Booth, F.W. (1989). Application of molecular biology to exercise physiology. *Exerc. Sports Sci. Rev.* 17:1–27.

Brannan, P.G., P. Vergne-Marini, C.Y.C. Pak, A.R. Hull, and J.S. Fordtran (1976). Magnesium absorption in the human small intestine: results in normal subjects, patients with chronic renal disease, and in patients with absorptive hypercalcemia. *J. Clin. Invest.* 57:1412–1418.

Brilla, L.R., and T.F. Haley (1992). Effect of magnesium supplementation on strength training in humans. *J. Am. Coll. Nutr.* 11:326–329.

Brubacher, G., and H. Weiser (1985). The vitamin A activity of beta-carotene. *Int. J. Vitam. Nutr. Res.* 55:5–15.

Canfield, W.K., W.T. Johnson, C. Drain, L.K. Johnson, and L.M. Klevay (1984). Changes in red cell carbonic anhydrase activity in men consuming diets of different zinc content. *Clin. Res.* 32:783A (abstract).

Carpenter, K.J. (1986). The History of Scurvy and Vitamin C. London: Cambridge University Press.

Cartwright, G.E., C.Q. Edwards, K. Kravitz, M. Slotnick, D.B. Amos, A. Johnson, and L. Buskjaer (1979). Hereditary hemochromatosis: phenotypic expression of the disease. *N. Engl. J. Med.* 301:175–179

Centers for Disease Control and Prevention (1998). Recommendations to Prevent and Control Iron Deficiency in the United States. *MMWR* 47 (No. RR-3):1–29.

Chan, A.C., and P.V.J. Hegarty (1977). Morphological changes in skeletal muscles in vitamin E-deficient and refed rabbits. *Br. J. Nutr.* 38:361–369.

Charlton, R.W., and T.H. Bothwell (1983). Iron absorption. *Ann. Rev. Med.* 34:55–68.

Chen, J.D., J.F. Wang, K.J. Li, Y.W. Zhao, S.W. Wang, Y. Jiao, and X.Y. Hou (1989). Nutritional problems and measures in elite and amateur athletes. *Am. J. Clin. Nutr.* 49:1084–1089.

Clancy, S.P., P.M. Clarkson, M.E. DeCheke, K. Nosaka, P.S. Freederson, J.J. Cunningham, and B. Valentine (1994). Effects of chromium supplementation on body composition, strength and urinary chromium loss in football players. *Int. J. Sports Nutr.* 4:142–153.

Clark, N. (1997). *Sports Nutrition Guidebook*, 2nd edition. Champaign, IL: Human Kinetics.

Clement, D.B., J.E. Taunton, D.C. McKenzie, L.L. Sawchuk, and J.P. Wiley (1986). High- and low-dose iron supplementation in iron-deficient endurance trained females. In: F.I. Katch (ed.) *Sport, Health and Nutrition*, Champaign, IL: Human Kinetics, pp. 75–81.

Coburn, S.P., P.J. Ziegler, D.L. Costill, J.D. Mahuren, W.J. Fink, W.E. Schaltenbrand, T.A. Pauly, D.R. Pearson, P.S. Conn, and T.R. Guilarte (1991). Response of vitamin B_6 content of muscle to changes in vitamin B_6 intake in men. *Am. J. Clin. Nutr.* 53:1436–1442.

Cohen, J.L., L. Potosnak, O. Frank, and H. Baker (1985). A nutritional and hematological assessment of elite ballet dancers. *Phys. Sportsmed.* 13:43–54.

Consolazio, C.F., L.O. Matoush, R.A. Nelson, R.S. Harding, and J.E. Canham (1963). Excretion of sodium, potassium, magnesium, and iron in human sweat and the relation of each to balance and requirements. *J. Nutr.* 79:407–415.

Cook, J.D., and E.R. Monsen (1976). Food iron absorption in human subjects. III. Comparison of the effect of animal protein on nonheme absorption. *Am. J. Clin. Nutr.* 29:859–867.

Cooter, G.R., and K. Mowbray (1978). Effects of iron supplementation and activity on serum iron depletion and hemoglobin levels in female athletes. *Res. Quart.* 49:114–117.

Cousins, R.J. (1985). Absorption, transport and hepatic metabolism of copper and zinc: special reference to metallothionein and ceruloplasmin. *Physiol. Rev.* 65:238–309.

Cousins, R.J. (1989). Systematic transport of zinc, In: C.F. Mills (ed.) *Zinc in Human Biology*. New York: Springer-Verlag, pp. 79–93.

Davies, M.B., J. Austin, and D.A. Pantridge (1991). *Vitamin C: Its Chemistry and Biochemistry.* Cambridge, England: The Royal Society of Chemistry.

Deuster, P.A., B.A. Day, A. Singh, L. Douglass, and P.B. Moser-Vellon (1989). Zinc status of highly trained women runners and untrained women. *Am. J. Clin. Nutr.* 49:1295–1301.

Deuster, P.A., E. Dolev, S.B. Kyle, R.A. Anderson, and E.B. Schoonmaker (1987). Magnesium homeostasis during high intensity anaerobic exercise in men. *J. Appl. Physiol.* 62:545–550.

Dowling, H.J., E.G. Offenbacher, and F.X. Pi-Sunyer (1990). Effects of amino acids on the absorption of trivalent chromium and its retention by regions of the small intestine. *Nutr. Res.* 10:1261–1271.

Dressendorfer, R.H., and R. Sockolov (1980). Hypozincemia in runners. *Phys. Sports Med.* 8:97–100.

Duthie, G.G., J.D. Robertson, R.J. Maughan, and P.C. Morrice (1990). Blood antioxidant status and erythrocyte lipid peroxidation following distance running. *Arch. Biochem. Biophys.* 282:78–83.

Economos, C.D., S.S. Bortz, and M.E. Nelson (1993). Nutritional practices of elite athletes: recommendations. *Sports Med.* 16:381–399.

Edgerton, V.R., Y. Ohira, J. Hettiarachchi, B. Senewirante, G.W. Gardner, and R.J. Barnard (1981). Elevation of hemoglobin and work tolerance in iron-deficient subjects (1981). *J. Nutr. Sci. Vitaminol.* 27:77–86.

Evans, G.W. (1989). The effect of chromium picolinate on insulin-controlled parameters in humans. *Int. J. Biosoc. Med. Res.* 11:163–180.

Evans, G.W., and D.J. Pouchnik (1993). Composition and biological activity of chromium-pyridine carboxylate complexes. *J. Inorg. Chem.* 49:177–187.

Faure, P., P.Y. Benhamou, A. Perard, S. Halimi, and A.M. Roussel (1995). Lipid peroxidation in insulin-dependent diabetic patients with early retina degenerative lesions: effects of an oral zinc supplement. *Eur. J. Clin. Nutr.* 49:282–288.

Feldman, S., and W. Hedrick (1983). Antacid effects on the gastrointestinal absorption of riboflavin. *J. Pharm. Sci.* 72:121–123.

Finch, C.A., and E.R. Monsen (1972). Iron nutrition and the fortification of food with iron. *J. Am. Med. Assoc.* 219:1462–1465.

Fine, K.D., C.A. Santa Ana, J.L. Porter, and J.S. Fordtran (1991). Intestinal absorption of magnesium from food and supplements. *J. Clin. Invest.* 88:396–402.

Fischer, P.W.F., A. Giroux, and M.R. L'Abbe (1984). Effect of zinc supplementation on copper status in adult man. *Am. J. Clin. Nutr.* 40:743–746.

Fishbaine, B., and G. Butterfield (1984). Ascorbic acid status of running and sedentary men. *Int. J. Vit. Nutr. Res.* 54: 273–277.

Fogelholm, M., J.-J. Himberg, K. Alopaeus, C.-J. Gref, J.T. Laakso, J. Lehto, and H. Mussalo-Ruahamaa (1992a). Dietary and biochemical indices of nutritional status in male and female athletes and controls. *J. Am. Coll. Nutr.* 11:181–191.

Fogelholm, M.J., I. Jaakkola, and T. Lammpisjarvi (1992b). Effect of iron supplementation in female athletes with low serum ferritin concentrations. *Int. J. Sports Med.* 13:158–162.

Fogelholm, M., I. Ruokonen, J.T. Laakso, T. Vuorimaa, and J.J. Himberg (1993). Lack of association between indices of vitamin B_1, B_2 and B_6 status and exercise-induced blood lactate in young adults. *Int. J. Sports Nutr.* 3:165–176.

Fry, J.M., G.M. Smith, and E.J. Speijers (1993). Plasma and tissue concentrations of alpha-tocopherol during vitamin E depletion in sheep. *Br. J. Nutr.* 69:225–232.

Gardner, G.W., V.R. Edgerton, R.J. Barnard, and E.H. Bernauer (1975). Cardiorespiratory, hematological and physical performance responses of anemic subjects to iron treatment. *Am. J. Clin. Nutr.* 28:982–988.

Gardner, G.W., V.R. Edgerton, B. Senewiratne, R. Barnard, and Y. Ohira (1977). Physical work capacity and metabolic stress in subjects with iron deficiency anemia. *Am. J. Clin. Nutr.* 30:910–917.

Gatto, L.M., and S. Samman (1995). The effect of zinc supplementation on plasma lipids and low-density lipoprotein oxidation in males. *Free Rad. Biol. Med.* 19:517–521.

Goldfarb, A.H., M.K. Todd, B.T. Boyer, H.M. Alessio, and R.G. Cutler (1989). Effect of vitamin E on lipid peroxidation at 80% VO_2 max. *Med. Sci. Sports Exerc.* 21:S16.

Golf, S., V. Graef, H.-J. Gerlach, and K.E. Seim (1983). Changes in serum creatine kinase and serum creatine kinase MB activities during training and magnesium supplementation in elite female athletes. *Magnesium Bull.* 2:43–46.

Golf, S.W., D. Bohmer, and P.E. Nowacki (1993). Is magnesium a limiting factor in competitive exercise? A summary of relevant scientific data. In: S. Golf, D. Dralle, and L. Vecchiet (eds.) *Magnesium 1993.* London: John Libbey & Co., pp. 209–220.

Goodwin, J.S., W.C. Hunt, P. Hooper, and P.J. Garry (1985). Relationship between zinc intake, physical activity, and blood levels of high-density lipoprotein cholesterol in a healthy elderly population. *Metabolism* 34:519–523.

Grandjean, A.C. (1983). Vitamins, diet and the athlete. *Clin. Sports Med.* 2:105–114.

Grant, K.E., R.M. Chandler, A.L. Castle, and J.L. Ivy (1997). Chromium and exercise training: effect on obese women. *Med. Sci. Sports Exerc.* 29:992–998.

Gregory, J.F., and S.L. Ink (1986). The bioavailability of vitamin B-6. In: R.D. Reynolds and J.E. Leklem (eds.) *Vitamin B-6: Its Role in Health and Disease.* New York: Liss, pp. 3–23.

Guilland, J.C., T. Penarand, C. Gallet, V. Boggio, F. Fuchs, and J. Klepping (1989). Vitamin status of young athletes including the effects of supplementation. *Med. Sci. Sports Exerc.* 21:441–449.

Hallmark, M.A., T.H. Reynolds, C.A. DeSouza, C.O. Dotson, R.A. Anderson, and M.A. Rodgers (1996). Effects of chromium and resistive training on muscle strength and body composition. *Med. Sci. Sports Exerc.* 28:139–144.

Halstad, C.H. (1990). Intestinal absorption of dietary folates. In: M.F. Picciano, E.L.R. Stokstad, and J.F. Gregory (eds.) *Folic Acid Metabolism in Health and Disease,* New York: Wiley-Liss, pp. 23–45.

Haralambie, G. (1981). Serum zinc in athletes during training. *Int. J. Sports Med.* 2:135–138.

Hasten, D.L., E.P. Rome, D.B. Franks, and M. Hegsted (1990). Effects of chromium picolinate on beginning weight training students. *Int. J. Sports Nutr.* 2:343–350.

Haymes, E.M. (1998). Trace minerals and exercise. In: I. Wolinsky (ed.) *Nutrition in Exercise and Sport*, 3rd ed. Boca Raton, FL: CRC Press, pp. 197–218.

Haymes, E.M., and D.M. Spillman (1989). Iron status of women distance runners. *Int. J. Sports Med.* 10:430–435.

Haymes, E.M., J.L. Puhl, and T.E. Temples (1986). Training for cross-country skiing and iron status. *Med. Sci. Sports Exerc.* 18:162–167.

Heath, E.M., A.R. Wilcox, and C.M. Quinn (1993). Effects of nicotinic acid on respiratory exchange ratio and substrate levels during exercise. *Med. Sci. Sports Exerc.* 25:1018–1023.

Herbert, V., and K.C. Das (1994). Folic acid and vitamin B_{12}. In: M.E. Shils, J.A. Olson, and M. Shike (eds.) *Modern Nutrition in Health and Disease*, 8th ed., Philadelphia, PA: Lea & Febiger, pp. 402–425.

Herbert, V., E. Jacob, K.-T. J. Wong, J. Scott, and R.D. Pfeffer (1978). Low serum vitamin B-12 levels in patients receiving ascorbic acid in megadoses: studies concerning the effect of ascorbate on radioisotope vitamin B-12 assay. *Am. J. Clin. Nutr.* 31:253–258.

Herbert, V., S. Shaw, E. Jayatilleke, and T.S. Kasdan (1994). Most free radical injury is iron-related: it is promoted by iron, hemin, holoferritin, and vitamin C, and inhibited by desferoxamine and apoferritin. *Stem Cells* 12:289–303.

Hickson, J.F., J.W. Schrader, J.M. Pivarnik, and J.E. Stockton (1987). Nutritional intake from food sources of soccer athletes during two stages of training. *Nutr. Rep. Int.* 34:85–90.

Hickson, J.F., J. Schrader, and L.C. Trischler (1986). Dietary intakes of female basketball and gymnastics athletes. *J. Am. Diet. Assoc.* 86:251–253.

Hillman, R.W., and M.C. Rosner (1958). Effects of exercise on blood (plasma) concentrations of vitamin A, carotene and tocopherols. *J. Nutr.* 64:605–613.

Hooper, P.L., L. Visconti, P.J. Garry, and G.E. Johnson (1980). Zinc lowers high-density lipoprotein cholesterol levels. *J. Am. Med. Assoc.* 244:1960–1961.

Horwitz, M.K. (1974). Status of human requirements of vitamin E. *Am. J. Clin. Nutr.* 27:1182–1193.

Hosegawa, T. (1993). Anit-stress effect of β-carotene. *Ann. N.Y. Acad. Sci.* 691:281–288.

Hunt, J.R., S.K. Gallagher, and L.K. Johnson (1994). Effect of ascorbic acid on apparent iron absorption by women with low iron stores. *Am. J. Clin. Nutr.* 59:1381–1385.

Institute of Medicine, Food and Nutrition Board (1997). Dietary Reference Intakes for Calcium, Phosphorus, Magnesium, Vitamin D, and Fluoride. Washington, D.C.: National Academy Press.

Institute of Medicine, Food and Nutrition Board (1998). Dietary Reference Intakes for Thiamin, Riboflavin, Niacin, Vitamin B-6, Folate, Vitamin B-12, Pantothenic Acid, Biotin, and Choline. Washington, D.C.: National Academy Press.

Irwin, M.I., and Hutchins, B.K. (1976). A conspectus of research on Vitamin C requirements of man. *J. Nutr.* 106:821–897.

Issacson, A., and A. Sandow (1963). Effect of zinc on responses of skeletal muscle. *J. Gen. Physiol.* 46:655–677.

James, W.H., and I.M. El Gindi (1953). Effects of strenuous physical activity on blood vitamin A and carotene in young men. *Science* 118:629–631.

Janelle, K.C., and S.I. Barr (1995). Nutrient intakes and eating behavior of vegetarian and nonvegetarian women. *J. Am. Diet. Assoc.* 95:180–189.

Johnson, R.E., J.A. Mastropaolo, and M.A. Wharton (1972). Exercise, dietary intake and body composition. *J. Am. Diet. Assoc.* 60:399–403.

Jusko, W.J., and G. Levy (1975). Absorption, protein binding and elimination of riboflavin. In: R.S. Rivlin (ed.) *Riboflavin*. New York: Plenum Press, pp. 92–152.

Kaats, G.B., K. Blum, J.A. Fisher, and J.A. Adelman (1996). Effects of chromium picolinate supplementation on body composition: a randomized, double-masked, placebo-controlled study. *Curr. Ther. Res.* 57:747–756.

Kabir, H., J.E. Leklem, and L.T. Miller (1983). Comparative bioavailability of vitamin B-6 from tuna, whole wheat bread, and peanut butter in humans. *J. Nutr.* 113:2412–2420.

Kallner, A., D. Hartmann, and D. Horning (1977). On the absorption of ascorbic acid in man. *Int. J. Vit. Nutr. Res.* 47:383–388.

Kanter, M.M. (1994). Free radicals, exercise and antioxidant supplementation. *Int. J. Sports Nutr.* 4:205–220.

Kayden, H.J., and M.G. Traber (1993). Absorption, lipoprotein transport, and regulation of plasma concentrations of vitamin E in humans. *J. Lipid Res.* 34:343–358.

Kazi, N., P.A. Murphy, E.S. Connor, P.E. Bowen, M. Stacewicz-Sapuntzakis, and F.L. Iber (1995). Serum antioxidant and retinol levels in physically active vs physically inactive elderly veterans. In: W.E. Langbein, D.J. Wyman, and A. Osis (eds.) *National Veterans Golden Age Games Research Monograph*. Hines, IL: Edward Hines, Jr. Veterans Administration Hospital, pp. 50–65.

Keith, R.E. (1997). Ascorbic acid. In: I.Wolinsky and J.A. Driskell (eds.) *Sports Nutrition: Vitamins and Trace Elements*. Boca Raton, FL: CRC Press, pp. 29–45.

Keith, R.E. (1994). Vitamins in sport and exercise. In: J.F. Hickson and I. Wolinsky (eds.) *Nutrition in Exercise and Sport*, 2nd ed. Boca Raton, FL: CRC Press, pp. 159–183.

Keys, A., A.F. Henschel, O. Michelsen, and J.M. Brozek (1943). The performance of normal young men on controlled thiamin intakes. *J. Nutr.* 26:399–415.

Kies, C., S. Kan, and H.M. Fox (1984). Vitamin B-6availability from wheat, rice, corn brans for humans. *Nutr. Rep. Int.* 30:483–491.

Kirchner, E.M., R.D. Lewis, and P.J. O'Connor (1995). Bone mineral density and dietary intake of female college gymnasts. *Med. Sci. Sports Exerc.* 27:542–549.

Klingshirn, L.A., R.R. Pate, S.P. Bourque, J.M. Davis, and R.G. Sargent (1992). Effect of iron supplementation on endurance capacity in iron-depleted female runners. *Med. Sci. Sports Exerc.* 24:819–824.

Kotze, H.F., W.H. van der Walt, B.B. Rogers, and N.B. Strydom (1977). Effects of plasma ascorbic acid levels on heat acclimatization in man. *J. Appl. Physiol.* 42:711–716.

Krotkiewski, M., P. Gudmundsson, P. Backstrom, and K. Mandroukas (1982). Zinc and muscle strength and endurance. *Acta Physiol. Scand.* 116:309–311.

Kubler, W., and J. Gehler (1970). Zur kinetik der enteralen ascorbinsaure-resorption. Ein beitrag zur berechnung nicht dosisproptionaler resorptionsvorgange. *Int. J. Vit. Nutr. Res.* 40:442–453.

Lamanca, J.J., and E.M. Haymes (1993). Effects of iron repletion on VO2max, endurance and blood lactate. *Med. Sci. Sports Exerc.* 25:1386–1392.

Lamar-Hildebrand, N., L. Saldanha, and J. Endres (1989). Dietary and exercise practices of college-aged female body builders. *J. Am. Diet. Assoc.* 89:1308–1310.

Lawrence, J.D., R.C. Bower, W.P Reihl, and J.L. Smith (1975). Effects of alpha-tocopherol acetate on the swimming endurance of trained swimmers. *Am. J. Clin. Nutr.* 28:205–208.

Leklem, J.E. (1986). Bioavailability of vitamins: applications of human nutrition. In: A.R. Doberrz, J.A. Miller, and B.S. Schweigert (eds.) *Food and Agricultural Opportunities Research Opportunities to Improve Human Nutrition*, Newark, DE: University of Delaware, pp. A56–A73.

Leklem, J.E. (1990) Vitamin B₆: a status report. *J.Nutr.*120:1503–1507.

Leklem, J.E. (1991). Vitamin B-6. In: L.J. Machlin (ed.) *Handbook of Vitamins*, 2ⁿᵈ ed. New York: Dekker, pp. 341–392.

Leklem, J.E., L.T. Miller, A.D. Perera, and D.E. Peffers (1980). Bioavailability of vitamin B-6 from wheat bread in humans. *J. Nutr.* 110:1819–1828.

Lindberg, A.S., J.E. Leklem, and L.T. Miller (1983). The effect of wheat bran on the bioavailability of vitamin B-6 in young men. *J. Nutr.* 113:2578–2586.

Liu, L., G. Borowski, and L.I. Rose (1983). Hypomagnesemia in a tennis player. *Phys. Sportsmed.* 11:79–80.

Loosli, A.R., J. Benson, D.M. Gillien, and K. Bourdet (1986). Nutritional habits and knowledge in competitive adolescent female gymnasts. *Phys. Sportsmed.* 14:118–121.

Lukaski, H.C. (In press). Dietary fatty acids and minerals, In: C.K. Chow (ed.) *Dietary Fatty Acids in Foods and Their Health Implications*, 2ⁿᵈ ed. New York: Marcel Dekker.

Lukaski, H.C. (1996). Functional effects of dietary zinc and copper restriction in humans. *Abstracts of F.A.S.E.B. Conference on Trace Elements*, pp. 11–14.

Lukaski, H.C. (1995). Prevention and treatment of magnesium deficiency in athletes. In: *Magnesium and Physical Activity*, L. Vecchiet (ed.) London: Parthenon Publishing, pp. 211–225.

Lukaski, H.C. (1997). Zinc. In: I. Wolinsky and J.A. Driskell, (eds.) *Sports Nutrition: Vitamins and Trace Elements*. Boca Raton, FL: CRC Press, pp. 157–173.

Lukaski, H.C., W.W. Bolonchuk, L.M. Klevay, D.B. Milne, and H.H. Sandstead (1983). Maximal oxygen consumption as related to magnesium, copper and zinc nutriture. *Am. J. Clin. Nutr.* 37:407–415.

Lukaski, H.C., W.W. Bolonchuk, W.A. Siders, and C.B. Hall (1996). Chromium supplementation and resistance training: effects on body composition, strength and trace element status of men. *Am. J. Clin. Nutr.* 63:954–965.

Lukaski, H.C., C.B. Hall, and W.A. Siders (1991). Altered metabolic response of iron-deficient women during graded maximal exercise testing. *Eur. J. Appl. Physiol.* 63:140–145.

Lukaski, H.C., B.S. Hoverson, S.K. Gallagher, and W.W. Bolonchuk (1990). Physical training and copper, iron and zinc status of swimmers. *Am. J. Clin. Nutr.* 53:1093–1099.

Lukaski, H.C., D.B. Milne, and F.H. Nielsen (1997). Decreased efficiency during exercise among postmenopausal women fed low magnesium diet. *F.A.S.E.B. J.* 11:A147.

Machlin, L.J., and A. Bendich (1987). Free radical tissue damage: protective role of antioxidant nutrients. *F.A.S.E.B. J.* 1:441–445.

Manore, M.M. (1994). Vitamin B₆ and exercise. *Int. J. Sports Nutr.* 4:89–103.

Manore, M.M., P.D. Besenfelder, C.L. Wells, S.S. Carroll, and S.P. Hooker (1989). Nutrient intakes and iron status among female runners. *J. Am. Diet. Assoc.* 89:257–259.

Marquart, L.F., E.A. Cohen, and S.H. Short (1998). Nutrition knowledge of athletes and their coaches and surveys, In: I. Wolinsky (ed.) *Nutrition in Exercise and Sport*, 3ʳᵈ ed. Boca Raton, FL: CRC Press, pp. 559–596.

Matter, M., T. Stittfall, J. Graves, K. Myburgh, B. Adams, and T.D. Noakes (1987). The effect of iron and folate therapy on maximal exercise performance in female marathon runners with iron and folate deficiency. *Clin. Sci.* 72:415–422.

McMartin, K. (1997). Folate and B$_{12}$. In: I. Wolinsky and J.A. Driskell (eds.) *Sports Nutrition: Vitamins and Trace Elements*, Boca Raton, FL: CRC Press, pp.85–96.

Mertz, W. (1993). Chromium in human nutrition. *J. Nutr.* 123:626–633.

Mertz, W. (1969). Chromium occurrence and function in biological systems. *Physiol. Rev.* 49:163–239.

Meydani, M. (1995). Antioxidant vitamins. *Front. Clin. Nutr.* 4:7–54.

Meydani, M., W.J. Evans, G. Handleman, L. Biddle, R.A. Fielding, S.N. Meydani, J. Burrill, J. Fiatarone, M.A. Fiatarone, J.B. Blumberg, and J.G. Cannon (1993). Protective effect of vitamin E on exercise-induced oxidative damage in young and older adults. *Am. J. Physiol.* 264:R992-R998.

Miller-Ihli, N.J. (1996). Graphite furnace atomic absorption spectrometry for the determination of the chromium content of selected U.S. foods. *J. Food Comp. Anal.* 9:290–300.

Milne, D.B. (1989). Effects of folic acid supplements on zinc-65 absorption and retention. *J. Trace Elem. Exp. Med.* 2:297–304.

Montoye, H.J., P.J. Spata, V. Pinckney, and L. Barron (1955). Effect of vitamin B$_{12}$ supplementation on physical fitness and growth of boys. *J. Appl. Physiol.* 7:589–592.

Morck, T.A., S.R. Lynch, and J.D. Cook (1983). Inhibition of food iron absorption by coffee. *Am. J. Clin. Nutr.* 37:416–420.

Mrocheck, J.E., R.L. Jolley, D.S. Young, and W.J. Turner (1976). Metabolic responses of humans to ingestion of nicotinic acid and nicotinamide. *Clin. Chem.* 22:1821–1827.

Murphy, S.P., A.F. Subar, and G. Block. (1990). Vitamin E intake and sources in the United States. *Am. J. Clin. Nutr.* 52:361–367.

Murray, R., W.P. Bartoli, D.E. Eddy, and M.K. Horn (1995). Physiological and performance responses to nicotinic acid ingestion during exercise. *Med. Sci. Sports Exerc.* 27:1057–1062.

National Research Council, Committee on Diet and Health, Food and Nutrition Board (1989a). *Diet and Health: Implications for Reducing Chronic Disease Risk*. Washington, D.C.: National Academy Press, pp. 665–710.

National Research Council, Food and Nutrition Board (1989b). *Recommended Dietary Allowances*. Washington, D.C.: National Academy Press.

Nelson Steen, S., K. Mayer, K.D. Brownell, and T.A. Wadden (1995). Dietary intake of female collegiate heavy weight rowers. *Int. J. Sports Nutr.* 5:225–231.

Neville, H.E., S.P. Ringel, M.A. Guggenheim, C.A. Wehling, and J.M. Starcevich (1983). Ultrastructural and histochemical abnormalities of skeletal muscle in patients with chronic vitamin E deficiency. *Neurology* 33:483–488.

Newhouse, I.J., and D.B. Clement (1995). The efficacy of iron supplementation in iron depleted women, In: C.V. Kies and J.A. Driskell (eds.) *Sports Nutrition: Minerals and Electrolytes*. Boca Raton, FL: CRC Press, pp. 47–57.

Newhouse, I.J., D.B. Clement, J.E. Taunton, and D.C. McKenzie (1989). The effects of prelatent/latent iron deficiency on physical work capacity. *Med. Sci. Sports Exerc.* 21:263–268.

Nickerson, H.J., and A.D. Tripp (1983). Iron deficiency in adolescent cross-country skiers. *Phys. Sportsmed.* 11:60–66.

Niekamp, R.A., and J.T. Baer (1995). In-season dietary adequacy of trained male cross-country runners. *Int. J. Sports Nutr.* 5:45–55.

Nielsen, F.H. (1996). Chromium. In: M.E. Shils, J.A. Olson, and M. Shike (eds.) *Modern Nutrition in Health and Disease*, 9th edition. Philadelphia: Lea & Febiger, pp. 264–268.

Nieman, D.C., J. R. Gates, J. V. Butler, L.M. Pollett, S.J. Dietrich, and R. D. Lutz. (1989). Supplementation patterns in marathon runners. *J. Am. Diet. Assoc.* 89:1615–1619.

Offenbacher, E.G. (1994). Promotion of chromium absorption by ascorbic acid. *Trace Elem. Electrolytes* 11:178–181.

Offenbacher, E., H. Spencer, H.J. Dowling, and F.X. Pi-Sunyer (1986). Metabolic chromium balances in men. *Am. J. Clin. Nutr.* 44:77–82.

Olson, J.A. (1994). Absorption, transport and metabolism of carotenoids. *Pure Appl. Chem.* 66:1011–1016.

Olson, J.A. (1996). Vitamin A. In: E.E. Ziegler and L.J. Filer (eds., *Present Knowledge in Nutrition*, 7th ed. Washington, D.C.: International Life Science Institute Press, pp. 109–119.

Omenn, G.S., G.E. Goodman, M.D. Thornquist, J. Balmes, M.R. Cullen, A. Glass, J.P. Keogh, F.L. Meyskens, B. Valanis, J.H. Williams, S. Barnhart, and S. Hammar (1996). Effects of a combination of beat-carotene and vitamin A on lung and cardiovascular disease. *N. Engl. J. Med.* 334:1150–1155.

Parr, R.B., M.A. Porter, and S.C. Hodgson (1984). Nutrition knowledge and practices of coaches, trainers, and athletes. *Phys. Sportsmed.* 12:126–138.

Pate, R.R., M. Maguire, and J. Van Wyk (1979). Dietary supplementation in women athletes. *Phys. Sportsmed.* 7:81–87.

Pate, R.R., B.J. Miller, J.M. Davis, C.A. Slentz, and L.A. Klingshirn (1993). Iron status of female runners. *Int. J. Sports Nutr.* 3:222–228.

Peifer, J.J. (1997). Thiamin. In: I. Wolinsky and J.A. Driskell (eds.) *Sports Nutrition: Vitamins and Trace Elements*. Boca Raton, FL: CRC Press, pp. 47–56.

Peters, A.J., R.H. Dressendorfer, J. Rimar, and C.L. Keen (1986). Diet of endurance runners competing in a 20-day road race. *Phys. Sportsmed.* 14:63–70.

Peters, E.M., J.M. Goetzsche, B. Grobbelaar, and T.D. Noakes (1993). Vitamin C supplementation reduces the incidence of post race symptoms of upper-respiratory infection in ultramarathon runners. *Am. J. Clin. Nutr.* 57:170–174

Pette, D., and C. Spamer (1986). Metabolic properties of muscle fibers. *Fed. Proc.* 45:2910–2914.

Pillai, S.R., M.G. Traber, H.J. Kayden, N.R. Cox, M. Toivio-Kinnucan, J.C. Wright, K.G. Braund, R.D. Whitley, B.C. Gilger, and J.E. Steiss (1994). Concomitant brainstem axonal dystrophy and necrotizing myopathy in vitamin E-deficient rats. *J. Neurol. Sci.* 123:64–73.

Pinto, J.T., Y.P. Huang, and R.S. Rivlin (1987). Mechanisms underlying the differential effects of alcohol upon the bioavailability of riboflavin and flavin adenine dinucleotide. *J. Clin. Invest.* 79:1343–1348.

Pinto, J., Y.P. Huang, R.J. McConnell, and R.S. Rivlin (1978). Increased urinary riboflavin excretion resulting from boric acid ingestion. *J. Lab. Clin. Med.* 92:126–134.

Rayssiguier, Y., C.Y. Guezennec, and J. Durlach (1990). New experimental and clinical data on the relationship between magnesium and sport. *Magnesium Res.* 3:93–102.

Refsum, H.E., H.D. Meen, and S.B. Stromme (1973). Whole blood, serum and erythrocyte magnesium concentrations after repeated heavy exercise of long duration. *Scand. J. Clin. Lab, Invest.* 32:123–127.

Richardson, J.H., and P.D. Drake (1979). The effect of zinc on fatigue of striated muscle. *J. Sports Med. Phys. Fitness* 19:133–134.

Rindi, G., and U. Ventura (1972). Thiamin intestinal transport. *Physiol. Rev.* 52:821–827.

Roe, D.A., H. Kalkwarf, and J. Stevens (1988). Effect of fiber supplements on the apparent absorption of pharmacologic doses of riboflavin. *J. Am. Diet. Assoc.* 88:211–213.

Roe, D.A., D.B. McCormick, and R.T. Lin (1972). Effects of riboflavin on boric acid toxicity. *J. Pharm. Sci.* 61:1081–1085.

Rokitzki, L., A. Berg, and J. Keul (1989). Blood and serum status of water and fat soluble vitamins in athletes and non-athletes. In: P. Walter, G. Brubacher, and H. Stahlein (eds.) *Elevated Dosages of Vitamins.* Lewiston, NY: Hans Huber Publishers, pp.192–212.

Roth, P., and E. Werner (1979). Intestinal absorption of magnesium in man. *Int. J. Appl. Radiat. Isot.* 30:523–526.

Rowland, T.W., M.B. Deisroth, G.M. Green, and J.F. Kelleher (1988). The effect of iron therapy on the exercise capacity of nonanemic iron-deficient adolescent runners. *Am. J. Dis. Child.* 142:165–169.

Sandstrom, B.M., and B. Lonnerdal (1989). Promoters and antagonists of zinc absorption, In: C.F. Mills (ed.) *Zinc in Human Biology.* New York: Springer-Verlag, pp. 57–78.

Schoene, R.B., P. Escaourrou, H.T. Robertson, K.L. Nilson, J.R. Parsons, and N.J. Smith (1983). Iron repletion decreases maximal exercise lactate concentrations in female athletes with minimal iron deficiency anemia. *J. Lab. Clin. Med.* 102:306–312.

Seaborn, C.D., and B.J. Stoecker (1992). Effects of ascorbic acid depletion and chromium status on retention and urinary excretion of 51-chromium. *Nutr. Res.* 12:1229–1234.

Seaborn, C.D., and B.J. Stoecker (1989). Effects of starch, sucrose, fructose, and glucose on chromium absorption and tissue concentrations in lean and obese mice. *J. Nutr.* 119:1444–1451.

Sen, C.K., and O. Hanninen (1994). Physiological antioxidants, In: C.K. Sen, L. Packer, and O. Hanninen (eds.) *Exercise and Oxygen Toxicity.* Amsterdam: Elsevier, pp. 89–126.

Sharman, I.M., M.G. Down, and N.G. Norgan (1976). The effects of vitamin E on physiological function and athletic performance in trained swimmers. *J. Sports Med.* 16:215–220.

Sharman, I.M., M.G. Down, and R.N. Sen (1971). The effects of vitamin E and training on physiological function and athletic performance in adolescent swimmers. *Br. J. Nutr.* 26:265–276.

Shaw, S., V. Herbert, and N. Colman (1990). Effect of ethanol-generated free radicals on gastric intrinsic factor and glutathione. *Alcohol* 7:153–157.

Shephard, R.J., R. Campbell, P. Pimm, D. Stuart, and G.R. Wright (1974). Vitamin E, exercise, and the recovery from physical activity. *Eur. J. Appl. Physiol.* 33:119–126.

Shils, M.E. (1969). Experimental human magnesium deficiency. *Medicine (Baltimore)* 48:61–85.

Shils, M.E. (1994). Magnesium. In: M.E. Shils, J.A. Olson, and M. Shike (eds.) *Modern Nutrition in Health and Disease,* 8th ed. Philadelphia: Lea & Febiger, pp. 164–184.

Short, S.H. (1994). Surveys of dietary intake and nutrition knowledge of athletes and their coaches. In: I. Wolinsky and J.F. Hickson, Jr. (eds.) *Nutrition in Exercise and Sport,* 2nd ed. Boca Raton, FL: CRC Press, pp. 367–416.

Short, S.H., and W.R. Short (1983). Four-year study of university athletes' dietary intake. *J. Am. Diet. Assoc.* 82:632–645.

Singh, A., P.A. Deuster, and P.B. Moser (1990). Zinc and copper status of women by physical activity and menstrual status. *J. Sports Med. Phys. Fitness* 30:29–35.

Singh, A., P. Evans, K.L. Gallagher, and P.A. Deuster (1993). Dietary intakes and biochemical profiles of nutritional status of ultra marathoners. *Med. Sci. Sports Exerc.* 25:328–334.

Singh, A., F.M. Moses, and P.A. Deuster (1992). Chronic multivitamin-mineral supplementation does not enhance physical performance. *Med. Sci. Sports Exerc.* 24:726–732.

Skikne, B., and R.D. Baynes (1994). Iron absorption, In: J.H. Brock, J.W. Halliday, M.J. Pippard, and L.W. Powell (eds.) *Iron Metabolism in Health and Disease*. London: W.B. Saunders, pp. 151–187.

Soares, M.J., K. Satyanarayana, M.S. Bamji, C.M. Jacob, Y. Venkata Ramana, and S. Sudhakar Rao (1993). The effect of exercise on the riboflavin status of adult men. *Brit. J. Nutr.* 69:541–551.

Sobal, J., and L.F. Marquart (1994). Vitamin/mineral supplement use among athletes: a review of the literature. *Int. J. Sports Nutr.* 4:320–327.

Solomons, N.W., and R.J. Cousins (1984). Zinc, In: N.W. Solomons and I.H. Rosenberg (eds.) *Absorption and Malabsorption of Mineral Nutrients*. New York: Alan R. Liss, pp. 125–197.

Somogyi, J.C. (1966). Biochemical aspects of antimetabolites of thiamin. *Bibl. Nutr. Diet.* 8:74–96.

Spencer, H. (1986). Minerals and mineral interactions in human beings. *J. Am. Diet. Assoc.* 86:864–867.

Steel, J.E. (1970). A nutritional study of Australian Olympic athletes. *Med. J. Aust.* 2:119–123.

Steen, S.N., and S. McKinney (1986). Nutritional assessment of college wrestlers. *Phys. Sportsmed.* 14:101–116.

Stendig-Lindberg, G., Y. Shapiro, Y. Epstein, E. Gallum, E. Schonberger, E. Graff, and W.E. Wacker (1987). Changes in serum magnesium concentration after strenuous exercise. *J. Am. Coll. Nutr.* 6:35–40.

Sturniolo, G.C., M.C. Montino, L. Rossetto, A. Martin, R. D'Inca, A. D'Odorico, and R. Naccarato (1991). Inhibition of gastric acid secretion reduces zinc absorption in man. *J. Am. Coll. Nutr.* 10:372–375.

Sumida, S., K. Tanaka, H. Kitao, and F. Nakadomo (1989). Exercise-induced lipid peroxidation and leakage of enzymes before and after vitamin E supplementation. *Int. J. Biochem.* 21:835–838.

Taylor, C.M., J.R. Bacon, P.J. Aggett, and I. Bremner (1991). Homeostatic regulation of zinc absorption and endogenous losses in zinc-deprived men. *Am. J. Clin. Nutr.* 53:755–763.

Tellford, R.D., E.A. Catchpole, V. Deakin, A.G. Hahn, and A.W. Plank (1992a). The effect of 7 to 8 months of vitamin/mineral supplementation on athletic performance. *Int. J. Sports Nutr.* 2:135–153.

Tellford, R.D., E.A. Catchpole, V. Deakin, A.C. McLeay, and A.W. Plank (1992b). The effect of 7 to 8 months of vitamin/mineral supplementation on the vitamin and mineral status of athletes. *Int. J. Sports Nutr.* 2:123–134.

Terblanche, S., T.D. Noakes, S.C. Dennis, D.W. Marais, and M. Eckert (1992). Failure of magnesium supplementation to influence marathon running performance or recovery in magnesium-replete subjects. *Int. J. Sports Nutr.* 2:154–164.

Thomson, A.D., and C.M. Leevy (1972). Observations on the mechanism of thiamin hydrochloride absorption in man. *Clin. Sci.* 43:153–163.

Tin-May-Than, Ma-Win-May, Khin-Sann-Aung, and M.Mya-Tu (1978). Effect of vitamin B_{12} on physical performance capacity. *Brit. J. Nutr.* 40:269–273.

Trebler Winters, L.R., J.-S. Yoon, H.J. Kalkwarf, J.C. Davies, M.G. Berkowitz, J. Haas, and D.A. Roe (1992). Riboflavin requirements and exercise adaptation in older women. *Am. J. Clin. Nutr.* 56:526–532.

Trent, L.K., and D. Thieding-Cancel (1995). Effects of chromium picolinate on body composition. *J. Sports Med. Phys. Fitness* 35:273–280.

Underwood, B.A. (1984). Vitamin A in animal and human nutrition, In: M.B. Sporn, A.B. Roberts, and D.S. Goodman (eds.) *The Retinoids*, vol 1. Orlando, FL: Academic Press, pp. 281–392.

Vallee, B.L., and D.S. Auld (1990). Zinc coordination, function and structure of zinc enzymes and other proteins. *Biochemistry* 29:5647–5659.

Vallee, B.L., and K.H. Falchuk (1993). The biochemical basis of zinc physiology. *Physiol. Rev.* 73:79–118.

Voorrips, L.E., W.A. van Staveren, and J.G.A.J. Hautvaust (1991). Are physically active elderly women in a better nutritional condition that their sedentary peers? *Eur. J. Clin. Nutr.* 45:545–552.

Wald, G., L. Brouha, and R. Johnson (1942). Experimental human vitamin A deficiency and ability to perform muscular exercise. *Am. J. Physiol.* 137:551–554.

Watt, T., T.T. Romet, I. McFarlane, D. McGuey, C. Allen, and R.C. Goode (1974). Vitamin E and oxygen consumption. *Lancet* 2:354–355.

Weight, L.M., K.H. Myburgh, and T.D. Noakes (1988a). Vitamin and mineral supplementation: effect on the running performance of trained athletes. *Am. J. Clin. Nutr.* 47:192–195.

Weight, L.M., T.D. Noakes, D. Labadarios, J. Graves, P. Jacobs, and P.A. Berman (1988b). Vitamin and mineral status of trained athletes including the effects of supplementation. *Am. J. Clin. Nutr.* 47:186–191.

Welch, P.K., K.A. Zager, J. Endres, and S.W. Poon (1987). Nutrition education, body composition and dietary intake of female college athletes. *Phys. Sportsmed.* 15:63–74.

Willis, W.T., K. Gohil, G.A. Brooks, and P.R. Dallman (1990). Iron deficiency: improved exercise performance within 15 hours of iron treatment. *J. Nutr.* 120:909–916.

Wood, B., A. Gijsberg, A. Goode, S. Davis, J. Mulholland, and K. Breen (1980). A study of partial thiamin restriction in human volunteers. *Am. J. Clin. Nutr.* 33:848–861.

Yoshida, T., M. Udo, M. Chida, M. Ichioka, and K. Makiguchi (1990). Dietary iron supplement during severe physical training in competitive distance runners. *Sports Training Med. Rehab.* 1:279–285.

VITAMIN AND MINERAL METABOLISM **307**

DISCUSSION

CLARKSON: I think it is important to understand how absorption, as well as transport, uptake, retention, and other factors that affect bioavailability occur for the various micronutrients. Even though we don't know how these processes change with training, such information provides the foundation to understand some of the potential effects of training.

I have some concerns with the Brilla & Haley (1992) study on magnesium supplementation. Their subjects had been ingesting low levels of magnesium, so in this mineral-deficient state, the magnesium supplement had an ergogenic effect. However, the study has been widely interpreted as showing that magnesium supplementation improves performance in general, which is not true. Another problem with that study is that there were several types of strength measurements made, and supplement effects were detected for only one of those measurements, so I don't think we should conclude generally that magnesium increases strength.

Finally, I have a question. When chromium and other minerals are mobilized into the blood during exercise, they are not reutilized by the tissues; why are they excreted in the urine rather than being reutilized?

LUKASKI: The simple answer is that there is catabolism going on during the exercise. These minerals are released from depots, including muscle, into the blood and then they are simply filtered out to the kidneys. There are very few minerals that can actually be reabsorbed once they are liberated, and chromium is not one of them. Manganese and zinc are the only two of which I am aware.

WAGENMAKERS: Free radicals have been implicated recently in cellular adaptation mechanisms and in the adaptation of muscle to training. This may imply that vitamin E supplementation might attenuate some of the training adaptations that are essential for athletes. Shouldn't we be more careful with vitamin E supplementation because it could have adverse effects on these physiological adaptations to training?

LUKASKI: That's an interesting thought. I am not aware of any studies that have shown that vitamin E supplementation had adverse effects on recovery and/or training. I can't give you a good answer.

WAGENMAKERS: We need long-term studies to test this possibility of an adverse effect of vitamin E supplementation adaptive processes.

LUKASKI: I agree.

MAUGHAN: You seem to be suggesting that routine supplementation with a balanced multivitamin supplement is not harmful but that supplementation with single vitamins may cause problems in some instances. If we think about the case of an athlete who goes for nutritional assessment or nutritional counseling, the usual method of assessing nutritional status is by dietary recall or recording the weights of foods consumed. Based on these data, the nutritional advice is then determined according to the RDA or perhaps the RDA plus a percentage because the athlete is physically active and may have an increased requirement. However, we know there are major problems with the dietary recall method and indeed with 7-day weighed-food-intake method in terms of assessing intake. Is it reasonable to make a recommendation for supplementing with a single vitamin without a biochemical evaluation of nutritional status?

LUKASKI: With the exception of a few specific nutrients, it is very difficult to arrive at a firm nutritional diagnosis with an acceptable degree of validity. Iron is one mineral that can be assessed with biochemical tests. Magnesium and calcium, when measured in the ionized forms that are not routinely assessed in a clinical laboratory, also can be evaluated. I totally agree with you that reliance on dietary history, particularly for mineral elements, is not ideal, but it is a reasonable start. If one examines the relationships between reported dietary intakes and analyzed diets, there is a large discrepancy. The dietary histories generally provide low estimates. It would be wonderful if a dietitian would do a counseling session to get a sense of the food groups the individual is eating, provide an initial assessment of the probable limiting nutrient(s), and then go to the clinic and get a blood biochemical test that might fine-tune that initial assessment. One problem that may be encountered is excessively high biochemical concentrations in blood because of exercise-induced hemoconcentration. We do both the dietary histories and the appropriate blood test, and then we simply recommend altered food selections to overcome the nutrition deficit in question. Alternatively, use of a balanced multivitamin/mineral preparation on a very infrequent basis, perhaps twice a week, may be suggested.

SPRIET: I have a question about the increased energy cost of submaximal cycling you reported when subjects had low magnesium values. Are you sure that there are no other factors occurring in the low-magnesium situations, e.g., poor coordination during exercise? Perhaps the subjects were recruiting more muscle groups or contracting in a less efficient manner, thereby accounting for the extra oxygen cost.

LUKASKI: I can't answer that question absolutely. Our physician does all the exams and looks at motor function. We have no evidence of altered physiological function other than some EEG changes, but we have not looked specifically at alteration in motor coordination.

HORSWILL: Do we completely understand the effect of exercise on increasing urinary losses of trace minerals? Morrison found that when subjects were well fed, the mineral losses were not as great as originally thought. The effects of exercise, feeding, and the interaction between the two on mineral losses needs further clarification.

Finally, please comment on the adverse effects of chromium supplementation, particularly the potential for chromium to become an oxidative agent in the body and cause damage.

LUKASKI: We've published data on resistance training and showed that urinary chromium losses tend to go up in the day after training and then return to baseline levels. The danger is that trivalent chromium is the chemical form of chromium that is provided in all the nutritional supplements, and once in the body, the chromium can undergo auto-oxidation to the hexavalent state, which is potently carcinogenic. There is some evidence that this does occur naturally, but we have no idea whether exercise or increasing dietary chromium will promote it. It is a concern because of an in-vitro study that showed mutagenic capacity of chromium picolinate.

HORSWILL: Specifically, it was the chromium picolinate that produced negative effects. Chromium chloride did not have that adverse effect.

LUKASKI: That's correct; it appeared to be the picolinate that was the promoter of the carcinogenic effect.

WAGENMAKERS: You showed data suggesting that oxygen consumption for the same load was higher in subjects with a lower muscle magnesium concentration. It is very unusual that the metabolic efficiency is reduced during exercise. When the magnesium concentration falls in the muscle, it implies that most of the ATPases reduce their activities, and if there is a reduced function of the ATPases, this will lead to a decrease in contractility and premature fatigue, but I would not expect an increased oxygen demand for a given work load. Can you explain that finding?

LUKASKI: I can't; we did not anticipate that finding. The purpose of the study was to see if we would increase the incidence of premature atrial contractions and compare that with ventricular concentrations in these older women. I suppose that the mechanism would involve the reduced activities of these ATPases. We also noted a slight increase in resting oxygen utilization in these women when they were sitting before we began the exercise.

WAGENMAKERS: But if the ATPases have a reduced function, then this will lead to a loss of contractility and not to a reduced oxygen consumption.

LUKASKI: We have similar data in rats, i.e., an increased oxygen requirement to do low-level work, but we have not pursued this.

WAGENMAKERS: I like the suggestion that the efficiency may have been reduced due to a loss of coordination.

LUKASKI: That seems like a reasonable explanation.

BAR-OR: I would like to suggest that the low magnesium may have led to increased co-contraction of antagonist muscles. We found among groups of children at different maturational stages that the young children have a higher submaximal oxygen uptake coincident with markedly greater co-contraction of antagonists. In other words, the antagonist muscle does not relax when it is supposed to relax. I am not sure if magnesium has anything to do with lack of relaxation of a muscle group, but at least it is a hypothesis.

LANG: I like that hypothesis. Since magnesium deficiency is known to increase neuromuscular excitability, it could well be that in a magnesium-deficient state, the antagonist muscle continues to be active when it should be at rest.

TIPTON: How low must the magnesium concentration in the tissue be before performance is impaired? Is there a threshold percent of normal concentration that must be achieved before we can expect a function to change?

LUKASKI: We don't know. In human studies, too few are willing to provide large enough samples of tissue for absolute determination of mineral status. The assumption is that what is measurable in the blood reflects the tissue level. The reality is that there are various pools of nutrients within the body, particularly pools of minerals. If one begins to exhaust an important pool, for example, in muscle cells, the reserve pool, perhaps in bone or liver, will begin to supply the mineral.

TIPTON: In your magnesium study, did you test for muscle strength? Since you used a whole-body performance test and found no significant group difference, do you think a significant difference would have occurred if you had been more specific in the testing of muscle?

LUKASKI: Perhaps.

GISOLFI: You indicated that with vitamin E deficiency there was increased enzyme leakage into the blood, but there was no performance decrement. Might that be due to the test that was utilized to evaluate performance? Do you know of any dose-response studies wherein the decrease or the deficiency in vitamin E was reduced in stepwise fashion and performance was evaluated? If there is any benefit, how long might someone have to be on vitamin E to achieve any benefit?

LUKASKI: I don't know of any dose-response studies, but all the studies that have used approximately the same dose, 300–800 mg/d, all seem to show enzyme leakage. It doesn't seem to be dose dependent. The duration of vitamin E therapy required is likely to be dependent on the degree of deficit.

GISOLFI: With what form of exercise would you expect to see a decrement in performance with a deficiency in vitamin E? Short-term exercise as opposed to long-term?

LUKASKI: I would presume long-term, but I am not sure that there is sufficient evidence to support my hypothesis.

HEIGENHAUSER: I would like to discuss the effect of depletion of zinc on carbonic anhydrase activity and the decreases in VCO_2. One needs to achieve almost 100% inhibition of carbonic anhydrase activity in order to get decreases in the kinetics of CO_2 excretion. In your studies, carbonic anhydrase activity within the red blood cell is high. Would you speculate on whether the depletion of zinc is affecting some of the other isoenzymes of carbonic anhydrase; alternatively, do you think that zinc has an effect on lactate dehydrogenase activity? Could the effects on CO_2 excretion be caused by a decrease in lactate dehydrogenase activity so that the muscle is unable to produce lactate, thereby causing a shift over to fat metabolism? Under these circumstances, it would not be a decreased ability to excrete CO_2 but, rather, the switch of substrate over to fat that decreases the RER.

LUKASKI: You are correct. This is the key issue. We reported total activity of carbonic anhydrase, but there are two forms in the red blood cell, with one of them being more responsive to zinc. Few published data on dietary zinc, even in animals, suggest a carbonic anhydrase response at rest or at exercise. Your hypothesis that it's an LDH phenomenon is very important; I think that it is probably the most viable explanation for our data.

TARNOPOLSKY: Are there any good studies done in the heat that have examined the effect of heat on absorption of various minerals and increased excretion of those minerals?

LUKASKI: The only data that are even close to what are needed are those of Consolazio, and they suffer because only arm sweat collections were used. He has estimates of mineral balance but no true measurements of absorption. So, the work has not been done.

CHEN: Many athletes take large amounts of supplements, and they might not be aware of the harmful side effects and the nutrient imbalance because of excessive intake of different micronutrients. The amounts of supplementation can be costly, and large doses of some of the micronutrients can be harmful to health. Is it possible to establish an upper limit of some of the micronutrients, beyond which one's health might be jeopardized?

LUKASKI: The National Research Council is now developing ranges of intake, and these are called recommended dietary intakes; there are three or four ranges. The minerals have not yet come under investigation. I believe that is going to come later this fall. The calcium and magnesium data are published, and they do have various levels of intake based on this concept of threshold for toxicity. So the athletes would certainly be at the "highest" level.

EICHNER: The use of zinc supplements is still common in the general population. This fad was started in part by the researcher who did a double-blind control trial in adults and showed that zinc lozenges cut in half the duration of the common cold. Then he was found to be a stockholder in the company making the zinc lozenges. Recently, in the *Journal of the American Medical Association,* he repeated his study in children and adolescents and found no benefit of zinc lozenges for the common cold. It is not widely known that long-term, high-dose zinc supplementation can cause copper deficiency and in turn severe anemia, sideroblastic anemia, which definitely impairs athletic performance. About 15 cases have been reported; it is reversible when they stop taking zinc.

Also, I think you appropriately conclude that iron depletion without anemia does not impair performance, but based on the Rowland study, you say perhaps it may in adolescents. I would soften that because in the Rowland study there was a slight rise in hemoglobin in the iron-supplemented group, and the difference in performance between the two groups was as much because of a puzzling fall in performance in the placebo group as to a rise in the iron group.

LUKASKI: When we feed humans 1 mg zinc for 2 or 3 months to induce zinc deficiency, we do not get functional changes within days as the "zinc" lozenges might infer, even when we do studies of immune function. So we are very dubious about zinc supplements.

WILLIAMS: Could you comment on some of the papers that have suggested that supplementation with vitamin C and vitamin E may decrease the muscle soreness that occurs following unaccustomed exercise? The practical value of the supplementation would be to help athletes during early preseason training. Many athletes during preseason training become so sore that it influences their ability to continue the training.

LUKASKI: I was unable to find studies that used objective measurements of muscle soreness. Soreness is always self-reported. If there were a more objective measure of soreness, I would be much more confident in recommending vitamin C and E for that purpose. The concern I always have about vitamin C supplements is that they promote kidney stones, and we don't know who might be most susceptible. Certainly, an athlete who is restricting his fluid intake and taking megadoses of vitamin C could be a candidate for oxalate buildup in the kidney.

WILLIAMS: Is the only adverse effect of vitamin C supplementation the possibility of kidney stone formation?

LUKASKI: No. Megadoses of vitamin C will impair copper absorption and utilization. In essence, one could promote iron overload.

8

Temperature, Muscle Metabolism and Performance

Mark A. Febbraio, Ph.D.

INTRODUCTION

It is well established that hot environments reduce one's capacity to endure prolonged exercise. This reduction in endurance capacity is primarily caused by the attenuated thermal gradient between the skin and the environment, which causes a reduced rate of body heat dissipation that ultimately leads to greater heat storage. In an effort to delay the onset of acute hyperthermia, a several thermoregulatory and cardiovascular responses are invoked. These responses have been the subject of many comprehensive reviews (Buskirk, 1977; Gisolfi & Wenger, 1984; Hardy, 1961; Nadel, 1985; Rowell, 1974). Fewer studies have examined the combined effect of temperature on exercise metabolism, and it seems likely that the physiological responses to exercise and heat stress, coupled with the resultant changes in many circulating hormones, may influence metabolic processes that take place during exercise. Indeed, most of the literature concerning exercise metabolism has been conducted in comfortable ambient temperatures. Hence, the purpose of this chapter is to examine the effects of alterations in environmental temperature on exercise metabolism and performance and to characterize the underlying mechanisms that may be responsible for any metabolic changes that may take place.

METABOLIC ALTERATIONS DURING EXERCISE AND HEAT STRESS

Substrate Metabolism

It is often assumed that hyperthermia during prolonged exercise causes an increase in the use of intramuscular carbohydrate (CHO). However, a careful examination of the literature reveals that this assumption is controversial. In some reports, intramuscular CHO utilization was augmented when exercise in the heat was compared with that in a cooler environment (Febbraio et al. 1994a; 1994b; Fink et al., 1975; Hargreaves et al., 1996a). In addition, muscle glycogenolytic rate has been shown to be reduced when the rise in body temperature is attenuated by heat acclimation (Febbraio et al., 1994a; King et al., 1995; Kirwan et al., 1987), by providing external cooling (Kozlowski et al., 1985), by preventing dehydration (Gonzalez-Alonso et al., 1997a; Hargreaves et al., 1996b), or by reducing the ambient temperature (Febbraio et al., 1996c; Parkin et al., 1998). In contrast, others (Nielsen et al., 1990; Yaspelkis et al., 1993; Young et al., 1985, 1995) have not observed increased use of intramuscular glycogen during exercise under heat stress. This conflict in the literature is most likely related to methodological differences and is summarized in Table 8-1. It is clear from a careful examination of the literature that ambient temperature does in fact increase the utilization of intramuscular glycogen. However, because exercise by itself causes relative hyperthermia (Febbraio et al., 1996c), the difference in bodily core temperature between experimental conditions must be of sufficient magnitude to cause altered metabolic responses.

Factors such as the magnitude of difference in ambient temperature, the acclimation status of the subject population, and the presence or absence of circulating air will all affect core temperature responses. It is not surprising, therefore, that in the study by Yaspelkis et al. (1993) glycogenolysis was not altered during exercise in the hot trial because the ambient temperature difference between the two experimental conditions was ~10°C, and the subject population was heat acclimatized. Consequently, the largest difference in core temperature at any point in the comparison of the two experimental trials was 0.4°C, a difference unlikely to have major physiological ramifications.

It is also important to note that the rate of glycogenolysis during submaximal exercise is largely influenced by the pre-exercise concentration of muscle glycogen (Chesley et al., 1995; Hargreaves et al., 1995; Hespel & Richter, 1992). This occurs because glycogen can bind to phosphorylase, the enzyme responsible for its breakdown, to increase phosphorylase activity (Johnson, 1982). It is not surprising, therefore, that when pre-exercise glycogen levels were higher before exercise in cooler, relative to warmer, experimental conditions, no differences were observed in intramuscular glycogenolysis (Nielsen et al., 1990; Young et al., 1995).

The increase in glycogen utilization observed during exercise and heat stress appears to involve both anaerobic and aerobic energy pathways. Muscle lactate accumulation is augmented in both humans (Febbraio et al., 1994a, 1994b; Gonzalez-Alonso et al. 1997a; Hargreaves et al., 1996b; Parkin et al., 1998; Young et al., 1985) and dogs (Kozlowski et al., 1985) during exercise and heat stress. In addition, increases in blood lactate accumulation during exercise and thermal stress have been well documented (Brown et al., 1982; Dimri et al., 1980; Dolny & Lemon, 1988; Febbraio et al., 1994a; Fink et al., 1975; Gonzalez-Alonso et al. 1995; MacDougall et al., 1974; Powers et al., 1985; Rowell et al., 1969; Yaspelkis et al., 1993; Young et al., 1985). Although these data suggest that anaerobic glycolysis is augmented during exercise and heat stress, they do not allow for precise measurements of glycolytic rates.

Few studies have examined lactate efflux from contracting skeletal muscle and uptake by other organs and tissues during exercise and heat stress. Nielsen et al. (1990) demonstrated that neither arteriovenous differences in lactate concentration nor lactate release rates from contracting

TABLE 8-1. *Summary of studies that have examined exercise metabolism and heat stress.*

Reference	Methodology	End Exercise difference in Trec (°C)	End Exercise difference in Tmus (°C)	Circulating Air	Acclimation Status	Resting Glycogen	Result
Febbraio et al. 1994a	40 min cycling bout 20°C vs 40°C	1.0	1.3	No	unacclimated	not different	increased glycogenolysis
Febbraio et al. 1994a	40 min cycling bout @ 40°C before vs after heat acclim.	0.5	0.4	No	not applicable	not different	decreased glycogenolysis
Febbraio et al. 1994b	40 min cycling bout 20°C vs 40°C	1.0	1.7	No	unacclimated	not different	increased glycogenolysis
Febbraio et al. 1996c	40 min cycling bout 20°C vs 3°C	1.1	0.6	No	unacclimated	not different	decreased glycogenolysis
Fink et al. 1975	3 x 15 min cycling bouts 9°C vs 41°C	approx. 1.0	not reported	No	unacclimated	not different	increased glycogenolysis
Gonzalez -Alonso et al. 1997a	135 min cycling bout @ 35°C euhydrated vs dehydrated	1.5 (esophageal)	~1.8	Yes	unacclimated	not reported	increased glycogenolysis
Hargreaves et al. 1996a	40 min cycling bout 20°C vs 40°C	0.9	not reported	No	unacclimated	N/A	increased estimated CHO oxidation
Hargreaves et al. 1996b	120 min cycling bout @ 20°C euhydrated vs dehydrated	0.6	0.6	Yes	unacclimated	not different	increased glycogenolysis
King et al. 1985	prolonged intermittent exercise @~40°C before vs after heat acclim.	0.3	not reported	not reported	not applicable	not different	decreased glycogenolysis
Kirwan et al. 1987	60 min cycling @ ~40°C before vs after heat acclim.	not reported	not reported	not reported	not applicable	not different	decreased glycogenolysis

Study	Exercise						
Kozlowski et al. 1985	prolonged treadmill running in dogs until exhaustion @ 20°C without vs with trunk cooling	1.1	1.2	not reported	unacclimated	not different	decreased rate of glycogenolysis
Nielsen et al. 1990	30 min uphill walking @ ~20°C then 60 min uphill walking @40°C	0.9 (esophageal)	1.8	not reported	not reported	higher prior to cooler environment	no temperature effect
Parkin et al. 1998	prolonged cycling to exhaustion 20°C vs 3°C	no difference, exercise duration 30% longer @ 3°C	no difference, exercise duration 30% longer @ 3°C	No	unacclimated glycogenolysis	not different	decreased rate of
Yaspelkis et al. 1993	60 min cycling bout ~24°C vs ~34°C	0.4	not reported	Yes	heat acclimatized	not different	no temperature effect
Young et al. 1985	30 min cycling bout ~21°C vs ~49°C	0.7	not reported	not reported	unacclimated	not different	no temperature effect on glycogen use
Young et al. 1995	60 min cycling immersed in water 20°C vs 3°C	~1.0 on average	no significant	not applicable differences	unacclimated	differences observed	no temperature effect on glycogen use

skeletal muscle were different when exercise in the heat was compared with that in a cooler environment, although these results are difficult to interpret because 60 min of exercise in the heat followed 30 min of exercise in a thermoneutral environment, rendering the experiment non-counterbalanced. When comparing exercise that resulted in dehydration and hyperthermia with similar exercise in a euhydrated state, Gonzalez-Alonso et al. (1997a) observed a higher postexercise muscle lactate content, in the presence of an augmented lactate release, in the hyperthermic condition. In addition, although Rowell et al. (1968) observed a reduced hepatic lactate removal during exercise in the heat, the reduction could not account for the magnitude of the increase in noted in arterial lactate concentration. Taken together, these three studies suggest that exercise in the heat increases the intramuscular production of lactate.

It has been suggested that the increase in glycolysis and lactate accumulation during exercise in the heat may arise from an increased utilization of blood-borne glucose, resulting from an augmented hepatic glucose production (Young, 1990). This hypothesis was based on the observation that intramuscular lactate accumulation can be elevated even when the rate of glycogen utilization is unchanged (Young et al., 1985). Many studies have observed relative hyperglycemia during exercise and heat stress (Febbraio et al. 1994a; Fink et al., 1975; Hargreaves et al., 1996a; Yaspelkis et al., 1993), which reflects an imbalance between glucose production and utilization. Using a dye infusion method, Rowell et al. (1968) showed that hepatic glucose production was augmented in heat-stressed humans. We confirmed these findings using an isotopic tracer dilution technique (Hargreaves et al., 1996a). Of note, however, was our observation that the augmented hepatic glucose production or rate of appearance (Ra) was not accompanied by any change in the rate of glucose uptake or disappearance (Rd) (Figure 8-1). Although one cannot exclude the possibility that increased blood flow to the skin and increased sweat gland activity may have enhanced the uptake of glucose in skin, there are no data on the quantitative importance of skin glucose metabolism during exercise. Hence, the available literature suggests that the increased muscle lactate accumulation is unlikely to be caused by an increased uptake and subsequent oxidation of blood-borne glucose.

An increased respiratory exchange ratio (RER) (Dolny & Lemon, 1988; Febbraio et al. 1994a, 1994b; Hargreaves et al., 1996a; Young et al., 1985) suggests that CHO is also oxidized to a greater extent during exercise and heat stress, possibly at the expense of lipid oxidation. The glucose kinetic data from our previous study (Hargreaves et al., 1996a) support this hypothesis because the Rd of glucose was not different, but CHO oxidation was greater when exercise at 40°C was compared with that at 20°C. If we assume that the glucose removed from the blood was

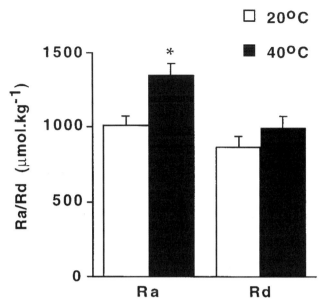

FIGURE 8-1. *Total hepatic glucose production (HGP = R_a) and glucose uptake (R_d) during 40 min of exercise at 70% $\dot{V}O_2peak$ in different environmental conditions.* Values are means ± SEM (n = 6). * P<0.05 vs. 20°C. Data from Hargreaves et al. (1996a)

fully oxidized within contracting skeletal muscle, the calculated oxidation of intramuscular glycogen was higher in the 40°C trial.

Few studies have examined lipid metabolism during exercise and heat stress. Plasma free fatty acid (FFA) concentration is similar during exercise in the heat and in a cooler environment (Fink et al., 1975; Nielsen et al., 1990; Yaspelkis et al., 1993). However, plasma FFA concentration reflects only a balance between whole-body lipolysis and FFA uptake by other tissues and organs during exercise and is, therefore, not a good marker of lipid utilization during exercise. Although Fink et al. (1975) observed similar plasma concentrations of FFA when comparing exercise in the heat with that in a cooler environment, they also demonstrated that intramuscular triacylglycerol utilization was attenuated during exercise in the hotter condition. There have been no subsequent attempts to measure intramuscular triacylglycerol utilization in human skeletal muscle during exercise and heat stress, a fact most likely attributable to the high variability associated with current analytical techniques (Wendling et al., 1996b).

Only two studies have examined the effect of exercise and heat stress on FFA uptake. Nielsen et al. (1990) observed no change in FFA uptake during exercise in the heat when compared with similar exercise in a cooler environment, although, as previously discussed, the non-counterbalanced design adopted by these researchers was likely to have confounded the metabolic measurements. In contrast, Gonzalez-Alonso et al. (1997a) observed a lower FFA uptake during the latter stages of exercise with dehydration-induced hyperthermia, when compared with a euhydrated trial in the heat.

Although plasma glycerol concentration is a better marker of whole-body lipolysis than is FFA concentration (because of the inability of skeletal muscle to take up and subsequently oxidize glycerol) (Stryer, 1988), only one study determined the effect of exercise and heat stress on plasma glycerol concentration. Yaspelkis et al. (1993) observed no difference between exercise in the heat with that in a neutral environment although, as previously discussed, the results from this study must be interpreted with caution because of the minimal differences in thermal stress between the two trials.

Given the current evidence, it appears that exercise and acute heat stress increase the utilization of intramuscular glycogen by both oxidative and non-oxidative energy pathways. The increase in lactate accumulation in both contracting muscle and plasma is likely to be caused by net intramuscular glycogenolysis rather than by increased uptake and oxidation of blood-borne glucose. The relative hyperglycemia that is frequently observed during exercise and heat stress is due to an augmented hepatic glucose production, rather than to a decreased uptake of glucose by muscle. Furthermore, the limited literature suggests that the augmented carbohydrate utilization in the heat causes a substrate shift away from lipid catabolism.

The effect of exercise and heat stress on protein metabolism has not been directly measured, perhaps because the contribution of protein to energy turnover during exercise is minimal, compared with the contribution of CHO and lipid. However, there is indirect evidence suggesting that protein catabolism may be increased during exercise in the heat. An increase in the accumulation of intramuscular ammonia occurs in humans, both untrained (Snow et al., 1993) and endurance-trained (Febbraio et al., 1994b). Although a major pathway for ammonia production during exercise is via the deamination of adenosine 5'-monophosphate (AMP) to form ammonia and inosine 5'-monophosphate (IMP), ammonia can also be formed in skeletal muscle from the oxidation of branched-chain amino acids (BCAA) (Graham et al., 1995). During our more recent study (Febbraio et al., 1994b), the augmented accumulation of ammonia was observed in the absence of any difference in IMP accumulation. In addition, the exercise-induced increase in ammonia during the hotter experimental condition was 5-fold greater than the accumulation of IMP. Hence, these data suggest that protein degradation may be increased during exercise in the heat. However, Dolny and Lemon (1988) concluded that protein degradation, as measured by urea excretion, is attenuated during exercise in the heat. Finally, Mittleman et al. (1998) found that BCAA supplementation during low-intensity exercise increased endurance performance in hot conditions, also suggesting that the protein requirements during exercise in the heat may be increased. Given the paucity of data regarding protein catabolism during exercise and heat stress, coupled with the conflict in the existing literature, further research examining the effect of heat stress on protein degradation is warranted, especially that which uses isotopic tracer dilution techniques.

Energy Metabolism in Muscle

Few studies have examined the effect of whole-body heat stress on energy metabolism in muscle during exercise. A reduction in intramuscular contents of ATP and phosphocreatine (PCr) and increases in the accumulation of adenosine- 5' diphosphate (ADP) and AMP have been observed in dogs during fatiguing submaximal exercise with heat stress (Kozlowski et al., 1985). While PCr degradation is augmented during exercise and heat stress in humans, total adenine nucleotide metabolism, IMP accumulation, and the energy-charge potential of the contracting muscle are unaltered when 40 min of exercise at 40°C is compared with similar exercise at 20°C (Febbraio et al,. 1994b). Although the discrepancy between these two studies may be related to species differences, it may also be explained by the important fact that one protocol required the participants to exercise to exhaustion, whereas the other was non-fatiguing and of fixed duration.

MECHANISMS RESPONSIBLE FOR ALTERATIONS IN SUBSTRATE METABOLISM DURING EXERCISE IN THE HEAT

Several possible mechanisms have been proposed to account for the shift towards increased carbohydrate metabolism in a hot environment. These include: 1) an alteration in neuromuscular recruitment pattern favoring greater use of fast-twitch rather than slow-twitch fibers during exercise (Sawka et al., 1984; Young et al., 1985); 2) a reduction in the supply of oxygen (O_2) and substrate secondary to an attenuated muscle blood flow during exercise in the heat (Rowell, 1974); 30 a direct temperature (Q_{10}) effect on enzyme reaction rates (Kozlowski et al., 1985; Young et al., 1985); and 4) an enhanced sympathoadrenal response (King et al., 1985; Yaspelkis et al., 1993).

Alterations in Neuromuscular Recruitment Patterns

As previously discussed, higher concentrations of lactate in muscle and plasma can occur without any net change in glycogenolysis during exercise in the heat (Yaspelkis et al., 1993, Young et al., 1985). Furthermore, Young et al. (1985) reported a significant correlation between the percentage of fast-twitch fibers and the difference in postexercise accumulation of lactate in muscle when exercise in a hot (49°C) environment was compared with that in a cool (21°C) one. This observation lead these authors to hypothesize that exercise in the heat either causes recruitment of a greater proportion of fast-twitch fibers or that fast-twitch fibers are more sensitive to temperature change than are slow-twitch fibers. We have tested such hypotheses by performing similar correlations and by histochemical analyses of glycogen use in slow and fast fibers after 40 min of exercise in 40°C and 20°C conditions (Febbraio et al., 1994a). In contrast with the findings of Young et al. (1985), we did not observe any correlation between lactate accumulation and fiber type ($r = 0.06$; P>0.05). Furthermore, histochemical analyses suggested that slow-twitch fibers were preferentially recruited, irrespective of environmental temperature (Figure 8-2), a neuromuscular recruitment pattern that is consistent with previous observations during prolonged exercise in thermoneutral conditions (Gollnick et al., 1973).

Reductions in Blood Flow to Contracting Skeletal Muscle

During exercise and heat stress, blood must be distributed to the skin to allow for evaporative cooling. Accordingly, many studies (Brengelmann et al., 1977; Johnson & Park, 1979; Johnson & Rowell, 1975; Nadel et al., 1977, 1979) have observed an increase in skin blood flow during exercise and heat stress. The cutaneous vasodilatation may displace blood volume into cutaneous veins, lower cardiac filling pressure, and reduce cardiac output at a time when the cardiovascular demand is at its greatest (Rowell, 1986).

The increased demand for circulation in the skin during exercise and heat stress is met by an attenuated blood flow to other organs. Reductions in splanchnic (Rowell et al., 1968), hepatic (Rowell et al., 1965), renal (Radigan & Robinson, 1949), and inactive skeletal muscle (Rowell, 1986) blood flow occurs when exercise in the heat is compared with that in a cooler environment. However, many authors (Fink et al., 1975; Kozlowski et al., 1985; Rowell et al., 1996; Young 1990) have also hypothesized that the skin and active muscle "compete" for blood during exercise in the heat because the cardiovascular demand exceeds the pumping capacity of the heart (Rowell et al., 1996). If this were the case, such a cardiovascular alteration could have important effects on meta-

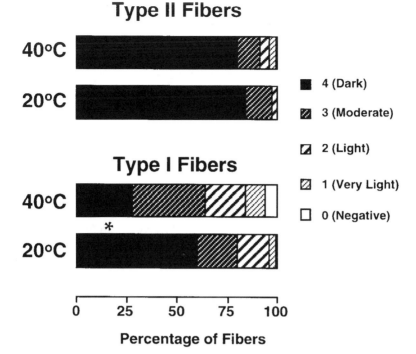

Type II Fibers

40°C

20°C

■ 4 (Dark)

▨ 3 (Moderate)

◪ 2 (Light)

▨ 1 (Very Light)

☐ 0 (Negative)

Type I Fibers

40°C

*

20°C

0   25   50   75   100

Percentage of Fibers

FIGURE 8-2. *Histochemical analyses of glycogen content in muscle stained with periodic acid Schiff (PAS) reagent in type I and type II fibers after 40 min of exercise at 70% $\dot{V}O_2$peak in different environmental conditions.* Values are means ± SEM (n = 6). * P<0.05 for percentage of dark-stained fibers at 40°C vs. 20°C. Data from Febbraio et al. (1994a)

bolic processes because it may reduce O_2 availability and cellular respiration. Whether or not blood flow to contracting skeletal muscle is reduced is the subject of some controversy. In addition, if blood flow is reduced during exercise and heat stress, it is unclear whether this leads to any modification in O_2 extraction. Quantitative measurements of blood flow to contracting muscle using radioactive microspheres have demonstrated a reduced blood flow in heat-stressed, exercising sheep (Bell et al., 1983). However, direct measurements of blood flow to active muscles using a thermodilution technique (Nielsen et al., 1990, 1993; Savard et al., 1988) or plethysmography and Doppler flowmetry (Smolander & Louhevaara, 1992) have revealed unaltered blood flow during exercise and heat stress. While species differences are likely to account for the discrepancy in the literature, it may be possible that in the human studies the degree of thermal circulatory stress was not enough to compromise cardiac pumping capacity.

Gonzalez-Alonso (1997a) observed a reduced blood flow to contracting muscle during exercise with dehydration and hyperthermia, compared with similar exercise when the subjects maintained euhydration. It must be noted, however, that the impairment to cardiovascular function is much greater with the combination of dehydration and hyperthermia compared with hyperthermia alone, when both these experimental conditions are expressed relative to a control trial in a cooler environment (Gonzalez-Alonso et al., 1997b). It appears, therefore, that blood flow to contracting muscle during exercise and heat stress may be reduced if the heat stress is very severe.

Any effect of reductions in blood flow on muscle metabolism may depend upon whether or not a compensatory extraction of O_2 occurs in the muscle. Schumacker et al. (1987) observed an increase in O_2 extraction with hypovolemia during hyperthermic exercise in dogs. This phenomenon has been confirmed in humans during dynamic exercise. Although the combination of dehydration and hyperthermia during leg exercise causes a 1.0 $L \cdot min^{-1}$ decrease in blood flow to contracting muscle when compared with similar exercise in a euhydrated state, leg O_2 consumption is unaffected (Gonzalez-Alonso et al., 1997a). These results were observed in the presence of increased intramuscular glycogen utilization and lactate accumulation. Hence, the data from the limited number of studies suggest that while blood flow to contracting muscle may be compromised during exercise and heat stress, arteriovenous O_2 difference is increased accordingly so that O_2 availability in the leg is not limiting. It appears, therefore, that O_2 availability is not the main factor mediating the augmented glycogenolysis and lactate accumulation during exercise and heat stress.

It is possible, of course, that alterations in metabolism may occur independent of O_2 availability as affected by blood flow to contracting muscle. Recent evidence suggests that functional vascular shunts exist in skeletal muscle such that metabolism is altered via the change in the rate of supply of nutrients and removal of products (For review see Clarke et al. 1995). One should not underestimate, therefore, the influence of reduced blood flow to contracting muscle during exercise and heat stress. Further research is warranted to examine the interaction between blood flow to contracting muscle and intramuscular metabolism during exercise and heat stress.

Direct Effect of Intramuscular Temperature on Metabolism

During exercise, intramuscular temperature (T_{mus}) rises in proportion to the increase in workload (Saltin & Hermansen, 1966). The rise in T_{mus} is, however, often augmented during exercise and thermal stress (Table 8-1). It has been suggested that this rise in T_{mus} *per se* may act upon key glycogenolytic and glycolytic enzymes that will ultimately alter flux rates through these pathways (Kozlowski et al., 1985; Young, 1990). The direct temperature effect on enzyme-mediated reactions is referred to as the Q_{10} effect. The Q_{10} values commonly found for enzyme-mediated reactions are 2.0–3.0, i.e., for every 10°C increase in temperature, a 2-3-fold increase in enzyme reaction rate is observed (Florkin & Stolz, 1968). Given that T_{mus} can be increased by up to 1.8°C when comparing exercise in the heat with that in a thermoneutral environment, enzyme reaction rates could increase by approximately 30–40% under these circumstances.

Few studies have attempted to directly increase T_{mus} and examine intramuscular metabolism. In 1972 Edwards and co-workers elucidated the effect of elevations in T_{mus} on metabolism during isometric contractions to fatigue. They demonstrated that both intramuscular glycogen utilization and lactate accumulation were augmented during contractions following limb immersion in a water bath at 44°C, compared with water bath temperatures of 12°C and 26°C, respectively. Of note, however, was the observation that limb heating also resulted in an increase in core temperature, whereas it was reduced in the 12°C trial. Because an elevated core temperature increases plasma epinephrine (Febbraio et al., 1994a; Galbo et al., 1979; Hargreaves et al., 1996a; Powers et al., 1982), which may increase glycogenolysis during exercise (Greenhaff et al., 1991; Jannson et al., 1986; Spriet et al., 1988), this may have confounded the results. In addition, because isometric and dynamic exercise differ with respect to energy turnover (Fenn, 1923), the results from Edwards et al. (1972) could not clearly determine whether elevated T_{mus} *per se* plays a regulatory role in metabolic processes during dynamic exercise coupled with thermal stress.

In order to address this question further, we have conducted experiments in which we have used heating pads and water-perfused cuffs wrapped around the quadriceps muscle. These methods have elevated T_{mus} alone prior to and during intense and submaximal, dynamic exercise (Febbraio et al., 1996a; Starkie et al., 1998). Data from our initial study, summarized in Table 8-2, demonstrated that raising muscle temperature increased glycogenolysis and lactate accumulation in the absence of changes in core temperature or plasma catecholamine levels.

It is important to note that the exercise model used in our study (Febbraio et al., 1996a) was of short duration and of very high intensity. In addition to the changes in glycogenolysis and lactate formation, we also observed an augmented decline in the total adenine nucleotide pool (TAN = ATP + ADP + AMP) and increased IMP accumulation. It is likely that the decrease in the TAN pool was due to a Q_{10} effect on the activity of several enzymes, i.e., adenosinetriphosphatases, adenosine

TABLE 8-2. *Muscle (T_{mus})and rectal (T_{rec})temperatures, plasma concentrations of epinephrine (Epi)and norepinephrine (Norepi), and intramuscular concentrations of glycogen (Gly) and lactate (La⁻) before heating (Pre-heat) and before (pre-exercise) and after (postexercise) 2 min of exercise at a workload corresponding to 120% $\dot{V}O_2$max in 20(conditions with (HT) and without (CT) 60 min of pre-exercise heating of the quadriceps femoris muscle group. Data are expressed as means (SEM (n = 7). *P<0.05 vs. CT; †P<0.05 vs. pre-exercise. Data from Febbraio et al. (1996a).*

		Pre-heat	Pre-exercise	Postexercise
T_{mus}	HT	35.1 ± 1.2	37.3 ± 0.4*	37.8 ± 0.2*†
(°C)	CT		35.4 ± 0.1	37.2 ± 0.1†
T_{rec}	HT	37.0 ± 0.1	36.8 ± 0.1	36.9 ± 0.0
(°C)	CT		36.4 ± 0.4	36.5 ± 0.4
Epi	HT	0.18 ± 0.04	0.21 ± 0.02	4.79 ± 0.89†
(nmol·L⁻¹)	CT		0.25 ± 0.05	5.44 ± 1.52†
Norepi	HT	1.83 ± 0.23	1.71 ± 0.18	15.60 ± 2.36†
(nmol·L⁻¹)	CT		1.65 ± 0.30	14.95 ± 3.55†
Gly	HT	434 ± 30	409 ± 24	250 ± 18*†
(mmol·kg⁻¹)	CT		446 ± 23	325 ± 26†
La⁻	HT	5.2 ± 0.7	7.1 ± 0.7	92.4 ± 9.3*†
(mmol·kg⁻¹)	CT		5.0 ± 0.8	73.7 ± 9.7†

5'-monophosphate deaminase, 5'-nucleotidase, and nucleoside phosphorylase. While it was possible that the increase in glycogenolysis and anaerobic glycolysis also resulted from a Q_{10} effect on glycogenolytic and glycolytic processes, one could not rule out the possibility that the decrease in TAN mediated these alterations in carbohydrate metabolism. It has been demonstrated that TAN degradation, especially increased free ADP, causes allosteric activation of key glycogenolytic and glycolytic enzymes, namely phosphofructokinase (PFK) (Uyeda, 1979) and phosphorylase (Ren & Hultman, 1990), thereby increasing flux through glycolysis.

To further address the effect of temperature on metabolic processes, we conducted a study in which we heated one leg and cooled the other for 40 min prior to and 20 min during exercise at 70% $\dot{V}O_2$peak using water-perfused cuffs. A difference in T_{mus} was observed after the 40 min of pre-exercise treatment, and although this difference was reduced during the 20 min of exercise, it was nonetheless still significant at the end of exercise. In addition to the higher T_{mus} observed in the heated leg, we also observed an augmented rate of glycogen use but no differences in metabolism of the high-energy phosphagens in comparison with the cooled leg (Starkie et al., 1998). Therefore, the data suggest that temperature *per se* plays a regulatory role in intramuscular CHO utilization and appears to be responsible, in part, for the frequently observed increase in glycogen utilization during exercise and heat stress.

Effect of the Catecholamines

It is well known that secretion of epinephrine increases during exercise (for review see Galbo, 1983) and that this increase is augmented with heat stress (Febbraio et al., 1994a, 1996c; Galbo et al. 1979; Gonzalez-Alonso et al. 1997a; Hargreaves et al., 1996a, 1996b; Nielsen et al., 1990; Powers et al., 1982). Glycogen phosphorylase activity is enhanced by β-adrenergic stimulation (Richter et al., 1982). Hence, it has been suggested that an increase in epinephrine secretion causes a concomitant increase in utilization of intramuscular glycogen (Galbo, 1983). Although intramuscular glycogen utilization often closely matches the plasma epinephrine response during exercise and heat stress (Febbraio et al., 1994a, 1996c; Gonzalez-Alonso et al. 1997a; Hargreaves et al., 1996b), this is not always the case (Nielsen et al., 1990).

The effect of epinephrine on intramuscular glycogen utilization is a complex phenomenon. Studies conducted using animals have demonstrated that epinephrine infusion increases glycogen utilization, during either voluntary submaximal exercise or electrical stimulation, both in rats (Richter et al., 1981, 1982) and in dogs (Issekutz, 1985). In addition, removal of the adrenal medulla (Hashimoto et al., 1982) or β-adrenergic blockade (Issekutz, 1984) reduces glycogen use in these animals. However, in human subjects, manipulations of plasma epinephrine concentrations via epinephrine infusion have produced conflicting results. Those which have demonstrated that epinephrine enhances muscle glycogen use have infused supraphysiological doses (Jannson et al., 1986; Spriet et al., 1988). In contrast, two studies have demonstrated that glycogenolysis is not increased during intense dynamic (Chesley et al., 1995) or prolonged (Wendling et al. 1996a) exercise when epinephrine is infused to mimic physiological increases during exercise.

It has been suggested that the effect of epinephrine on glycogen phosphorylase is diminished by cellular regulatory mechanisms such as calcium (Ca^{2+}) release, substrate availability, and posttransformational allosteric modulators such as free AMP and free IMP (Chesley et al., 1995; Ren & Hultman, 1990; Wendling et al., 1996a). Although intramuscular energetics were not reported by Wendling et al. (1996a), in the study by Chesley et al. (1995), exercise was conducted at 85% $\dot{V}O_2max$, an intensity that probably activated glycogen phosphorylase irrespective of epinephrine concentration, via local factors such as Ca^{2+} release from the sarcoplasmic reticulum and posttransformational factors such as P_i, and concentrations of free ADP and free AMP. Accordingly, calculated concentrations of P_i, free ADP, and free AMP were markedly increased when an epinephrine infusion was compared with a control trial (Chesley et al., 1995). As previously discussed, however, an increase in glycogen utilization during exercise and heat stress in trained men has been observed in circumstances where there has been little, if any, disruption to the intracellular milieu (Febbraio et al., 1994b). This suggests that epinephrine may play a role in the regulation of carbohydrate metabolism during prolonged exercise. To determine if the augmented increase in circulating epinephrine is a potential regulator of the increase in carbohydrate utilization during exercise and heat stress, we infused epinephrine into subjects at 20°C to mimic the sympathoadrenal response observed at 40°C (Febbraio et al., 1998). The results (Figure 8-3) demonstrate that epinephrine does indeed increase muscle glycogen utilization and lactate formation in trained men exercising at 70% $\dot{V}O_2$peak, a condition that has no effect on the energy charge potential or the ATP/ADP ratio in the contracting muscle, irrespective of the environmental temperature (Febbraio et al., 1994b). Hence, the increase in muscle glycogen utilization that occurs during exercise and heat stress appears to be mediated in part by an enhanced sympathoadrenal response.

Interestingly, RER is increased during exercise and heat stress (Dolny & Lemon, 1988; Febbraio et al. 1994a, 1994b; Hargreaves et al., 1996a; Young et al., 1985) or when epinephrine is infused during exercise (Febbraio et al., 1998; Turner et al., 1995). Notwithstanding the limitations of using pulmonary RER data as a measure of CHO oxidation, these observations raise an important question as to mechanisms that may activate CHO oxidation. Although unclear, the increase in CHO oxidation may be related to activation of the pyruvate dehydrogenase complex. The activity of this complex is dependent upon the balance between the activation of pyruvate dehydrogenase phosphatase and the inhibition of pyruvate dehydrogenase kinase. The phosphatase is activated by increased Ca^{2+} concentration, whereas the kinase is inhibited by increased concentrations of pyruvate and ADP (Putman et al., 1993). Although pyruvate has not been measured during exercise and heat stress or with epinephrine infusion, it is possible that in these circumstances pyruvate formation is increased and subsequently metabolized both aerobically and anaerobically.

The increase in hepatic glucose production observed during exercise and heat stress (Hargreaves et al., 1996a; Rowell et al., 1968) may also be mediated by an augmented sympathoadrenal response. Apart from exercise and heat stress, factors such as hypoxia (Cooper et al., 1986) and increased active muscle mass (Kjær et al., 1991) also are accompanied by a parallel increase in hepatic glucose production and plasma epinephrine. Studies in exercising rats have previously demonstrated a role for epinephrine in the regulation of hepatic glucose metab-

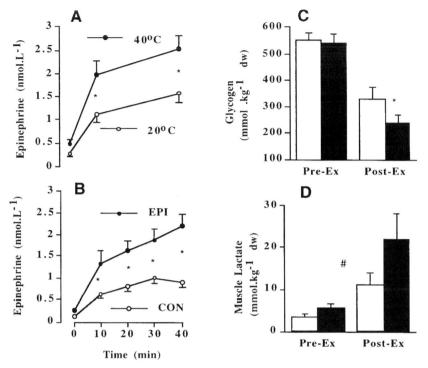

FIGURE 8-3. *Effects of environmental temperature and epinephrine infusion on plasma epineph-rine, muscle glycogen utilization, and muscle lactate accumulation during 40 min of exercise at 70% $\dot{V}O_2peak$.* A. Plasma epinephrine concentrations at 40°C and 20°C. Data from Febbraio et al. 1994a; Hargreaves et al. 1996a. B, C, D: Plasma epinephrine concentration (B), muscle glycogen use (C) and muscle lactate accumulation (D) with (EPI, filled bars) and without (CON, unfilled bars) epinephrine infusion (Data from Febbraio et al. 1998). Data are means (± SEM); n = 20 for A; n = 6 for B,C,D. * P<0.05 vs. corresponding values at the same time point; # Main effect of treatment (P<0.05).

olism (Richter et al., 1981; Sonne et al., 1985). However, few studies have examined the role of sympathoadrenal activity on hepatic glucose production in humans. Kjær et al. (1993) observed that epinephrine infused at physiological concentrations into subjects who underwent local anesthesia of the sympathetic coeliac ganglion, which innervates the liver, the pancreas, and the adrenal medulla, had little effect on hepatic glucose production. In addition, the rise in hepatic glucose production during exercise in liver transplant patients, who lack sympathetic nerve activity to the liver, was not different from that of kidney transplant patients who received immunosuppressive medication similar to that administered to the liver transplant patients (Kjær et al. 1995). These previous studies suggest that epinephrine is not a major stimulus for hepatic glucose production, although one must be cautious extrapolating these data to healthy populations with intact neural activity. In contrast, we have recently demonstrated that epinephrine infused at physiological concentrations into trained men during exercise causes an increase in both circulating glucose and hepatic glucose production (Howlett et al., 1998). Hence, it is possible that the relative hyperglycemia and augmented hepatic glucose production associated with exercise and heat stress is mediated by an increase in epinephrine concentration.

Apart from the well described sympathoadrenal effects, there is also evidence to suggest that muscle sympathetic nerve activity (MSNA) may play a role in both muscle and liver metabolism during exercise and heat stress. Norepinephrine concentrations are often (Febbraio et al., 1996c; Hargreaves et al., 1996a), but not always (Febbraio et al., 1994a), greater during exercise and heat stress than during exercise in temperate environments. Although circulating norepinephrine concentrations do not allow one to determine rates of spillover, the data indicate that sympathetic nerve activity is elevated during exercise and heat stress. It has also been shown that MSNA is augmented during isometric exercise with muscle heating (Ray & Gracey, 1997). Thus, it is evident that MSNA activity is thermosensitive and may also contribute to alterations in metabolism.

MECHANISMS UNDERLYING ALTERATIONS IN INTRAMUSCULAR ENERGY METABOLISM DURING EXERCISE IN THE HEAT

Several possible mechanisms can explain the increased PCr degradation observed during exercise in the heat (Febbraio et al., 1994b; Kozlowski et al., 1985). An increase in T_{mus} may augment ATP utilization by directly enhancing the activity of the ATPases (e.g., myosin, Na^+-K^+, Ca^{2+}) or by altering the rate and/or efficiency of cross-bridge cycling (Edwards et al., 1972). In addition, although increasing T_{mus} does not increase whole-body $\dot{V}O_2$ (Febbraio et al., 1994b; Koga et al., 1997) or leg $\dot{V}O_2$ (Gonzalez-Alonso et al., 1997a), some evidence suggests that an elevation in T_{mus} may impair mitochondrial ATP production.

For example, Brooks et al. (1971) studied the phosphorylative efficiency of *in vitro* isolated mitochondria from rat skeletal muscle by examining the ratio of ADP to oxygen (ADP:O) over a range of temperatures. They observed a constant ADP:O ratio at temperatures ranging from 25–40°C; however, above 40°C the ADP:O ratio decreased linearly with increasing temperature. This suggests that for a given $\dot{V}O_2$, the increase in ADP rephosphorylation was less than the rate of ATP degradation. Similarly, Willis and Jackman (1994), using mitochondria from rat and rabbit skeletal muscle, found a 20% reduction in the ADP:O ratio at 43°C when compared with 37°C and suggested that the rise in muscle temperature with severe exercise increases non-specific proton leakage back across the inner mitochondrial membrane and decreases the ADP:O ratio.

Mills et al. (1996) observed an increase in the plasma concentration of lipid hyperoxides (an indicator of oxidative stress) in hyperthermic horses that exercised to fatigue. This result is also consistent with the hypothesis that the greater degradation of PCr observed during exercise and heat stress results from a temperature-induced perturbation of mitochondrial function. Because muscle lactate accumulation is increased during exercise and heat stress, it is also possible that muscle pH is lower. If so, this may shift the equilibrium of the creatine phosphokinase reaction, favoring greater PCr hydrolysis than rephosphorylation (Harris et al., 1977).

LIMITS TO EXERCISE PERFORMANCE IN THE HEAT

Laboratory Studies Versus Competitive Performance

Numerous laboratory studies have shown that thermal stress reduces exercise capacity (Booth et al., 1997; Brück & Olschewski, 1987; Febbraio et al., 1996b; Galloway & Maughan, 1997; Gonzalez-Alonso et al., 1997a; Hessemer et al., 1984; Kozlowski et al., 1985; Kruk et al., 1985; Lee & Haymes, 1995; MacDougall et al., 1974; Nielsen et al., 1993; Saltin et al., 1972; Schmidt & Brück, 1981). In contrast, although impaired athletic performances during competition in the heat have been documented (Terrados & Maughan, 1995), it must be noted that in some circumstances athletes can perform well in the heat (Maughan et al., 1985; Noakes et al., 1991; Robinson, 1963). This apparent anomaly within the literature can be best reconciled by examining the interaction between the exercise intensity or, more importantly, the degree of endogenous heat production and the exogenous heat load. In general, during many endurance athletic events the exercise intensity is moderate and the exogenous heat load high but not extreme. The athletes, therefore, can adequately regulate their body temperatures and minimize cardiovascular strain. In these circumstances the heat stress is aptly referred to as "compensable heat stress" (Montain et al., 1994; Sawka et al., 1992) and can be overcome. In contrast, during many laboratory experiments, especially those that include minimal opportunity for convective heat loss, the exercise intensity coupled with the magnitude of the exogenous heat load often causes "uncompensable heat stress," a situation in which the body's cardiovascular and thermoregulatory capacities are insufficient to cope with the heat load. In these circumstances core temperature continues to rise, and performance must deteriorate.

Is Fatigue During Exercise in the Heat Substrate Dependent?

During prolonged exercise in comfortable ambient temperatures, fatigue often coincides with glycogen concentrations <150 mmol·kg^{-1} dry muscle weight (Coggan & Coyle, 1987; Constantin-Teodosiu et al., 1992; Coyle et al., 1986; Sahlin et al., 1990). Given that glycogen utilization is augmented during exercise in the heat, it is reasonable to suggest that the reduced endurance performance often observed during exercise and heat stress may be related to substrate availability. It is somewhat paradoxical, therefore, that fatigue during exercise with uncompensable heat stress is not related to carbohydrate availability but appears to be related to hyperthermia. In contrast with studies conducted in comfortable ambient temperatures, glycogen concentration at fatigue during prolonged exercise in the heat is ≥300 mmol·kg^{-1} dry weight in unacclimatized, endurance-trained (Parkin et al., 1988) and non-specifically trained (Nielsen et al., 1990) individuals. Furthermore, CHO feeding during prolonged exercise in the heat, when the heat stress is uncompensable, has no effect on endurance performance (Davis et al., 1988a; Febbraio et al., 1996b; Levine et al., 1991; Millard-Stafford et al., 1990). These studies are in contrast to the well-described ergogenic benefits of carbohydrate supplementation during prolonged exercise in comfortable ambient temperatures (Coyle & Montain, 1992) and when the heat stress is compensable (Below et al., 1995; Davis et al., 1988b; Millard-Stafford et al., 1992; Murray et al., 1987). It appears, therefore, that in severe, but not mild, heat stress, the limit to exercise performance is not related to substrate availability.

The Role of the Central Nervous System

It has been hypothesized that fatigue during exercise and heat stress is related to adverse effects of heat on motor control centers in the brain (Brück & Olschewski, 1987; Nielsen et al., 1990). This hypothesis has not been tested directly, although the concept of a critical core temperature limiting exercise performance is supported by some studies. In 1993, Nielsen et al. (1990) conducted a study in which trained men were heat acclimated by exercising at 60% V̇O$_2$peak to fatigue in a hot environment for 9-12 consecutive days. Although exercise capacity increased from 48 to 80 min, fatigue occurred at the same core temperature every day. Of note, during this study the investigators detected no reduction in blood flow to muscle or skin, no lack of substrate, and no accumulation of lactate or potassium at the point of fatigue when subjects were either unacclimated or acclimated. In addition, no decline in force produced during a maximal voluntary contraction was observed at fatigue in any trial.

Two studies conducted in our laboratory also suggest that fatigue may be associated with the attainment of a critical core temperature leading to a diminished neural drive to exercise. When subjects ingested beverages containing low to moderate concentrations of carbohydrate during exercise to exhaustion at 33°C, endurance performance was unaffected by the drink if the change in plasma volume or the rise in body core temperature was similar to that occurring when the subjects ingested a placebo. In contrast, when a high carbohydrate (14%) beverage was ingested, the plasma volume was less well maintained, the rise in body core temperature was augmented, and performance tended to be diminished. However, in all drink conditions, fatigue coincided with a similar core temperature (Febbraio et al., 1996b).

In another study, we studied the effect of heat stress on a 30-min laboratory time-trial performance in elite road cyclists. Subjects performed two such time-trials at either 32°C or 23°C. Although mean power output was decreased in the hot trial by 6.5%, rectal temperature was remarkably similar for both trials during the entire exercise period (Tatterson et al., 1998). These data suggest that during self-paced exercise in the heat, a power output is selected relative to an upper limit in body core temperature. Unfortunately, we are not sure of the mechanism that may be responsible for such a phenomenon.

Further evidence has emerged regarding a possible role for the central nervous system in the etiology of fatigue during exercise in the heat. According to the central fatigue hypothesis (Newsholme et al., 1987), exercise performance is related to the brain's supply of tryptophan, a precursor of 5-hydroxytryptamine, which is a neurotransmitter linked to endurance exercise performance (Davis & Bailey, 1997). The specific transport mechanism for entry of tryptophan into the brain is shared with the branched-chain amino acids. Therefore, a decrease in the free tryptophan to BCAA ratio, facilitated by BCAA feeding, would theoretically improve exercise performance. However, attempts to alter this ratio by supplementation with BCAA and/or tryptophan has had no effect on exercise performance when the exercise has been conducted in a thermoneutral environment (Madsen et al., 1996; van Hall et al. 1995). In contrast, as previously discussed, Mittleman et al. (1998) found that when BCAA were fed during exercise in a hot environment, performance was improved. Taken together, the available literature suggests a role for the brain in exercise performance in the heat, and further research in this area is indeed warranted.

Temperature-Induced Metabolic Perturbation

Although exercise performance in the heat can be independent of substrate supply and related to core temperature, there may be a temperature-induced perturbation in intramuscular metabolic processes. As previously discussed, the augmented PCr degradation observed during exercise and heat stress (Febbraio et al., 1994b; Kozlowski et al., 1985) may be related to a temperature-induced dysfunction to the mitochondria. During prolonged submaximal exercise, when the rate of ATP turnover can be met via oxidative phosphorylation, glycogen stores within the muscle are lowered, eventually giving rise to reduced glycolytic flux. This reduced flux causes a fall in pyruvate formation (Sahlin et al., 1990) and a reduction in the concentration of intermediate compounds of the tricarboxylic acid cycle (Gibala et al., 1997). Spencer et al. (1992) hypothesized that this reduction in flux through the TCA cycle decreases mitochondrial NADH production and energy turnover via oxidative phosphorylation, leading to ATP generation from alternative pathways. One such pathway, the adenylate kinase reaction, also produces AMP that is rapidly deaminated to IMP. Accordingly, following prolonged exercise, many studies have noted the accumulation of IMP at fatigue in the presence of low intramuscular glycogen stores (Broberg & Sahlin, 1989; Norman et al., 1988; Sahlin et al., 1990; Spencer et al., 1991, 1992); in these studies, IMP was not accumulated earlier during exercise when glycogen stores were adequate (Norman et al., 1988; Sahlin et al., 1990). In contrast, Parkin et al. (1998) showed that IMP concentrations were elevated during exercise and heat stress, even though stores of glycogen in contracting muscle remained adequate at fatigue (Figure 8-4). During exercise at 40°C in this study, fatigue coincided with a T_{mus} >40°C, but during exercise in the other trials, the T_{mus} was <40°C. As previously discussed, mitochondrial dysfunction can occur at temperatures >40°C but not <40°C (Brooks et al., 1971; Willis & Jackman 1994). Hence, although the limit to performance during exercise and heat stress is related to core temperature, one cannot rule out the possibility that dysfunction of metabolic processes within muscle contributes to the genesis of fatigue.

PREPARATION FOR EXERCISE IN THE HEAT

Heat Acclimation

As discussed, exercise performance that causes uncompensable heat stress appears to be largely dependent on the attainment of a critical core temperature (Nielsen et al., 1993). Because heat acclimatization delays attainment of this critical core temperature (Nielsen et al., 1993),

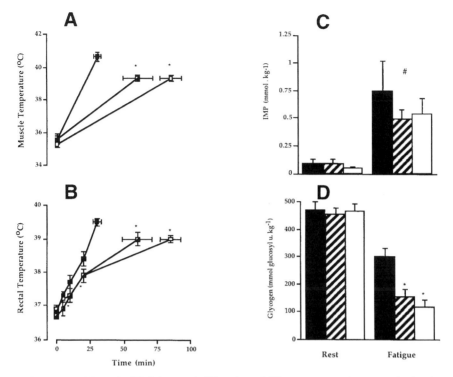

FIGURE 8-4. *Means (± SEM) for muscle (A) and rectal (B) temperatures, intramuscular inosine 5'-monophosphate (IMP) (C), and muscle glycogen content (D) during exercise to fatigue at 70% V̇O₂peak at 40°C (filled squares & bars), 20°C (hatched squares & bars), and 3°C (open squares & bars).* Data from Parkin et al. (1998). N = 8. * P<0.05 vs. 40°C; # Main effect of exercise (P<0.05).

athletes should be advised to adopt a heat acclimatization program prior to competition. Heat acclimatization, a process that involves repeated exercise bouts in a hot environment, invokes adaptations that decrease body core temperature, heart rate, and urinary and sweat electrolyte concentrations and increase total sweat rate and plasma volume (Armstrong & Maresh, 1991). Gisolfi (1987) suggested that heat acclimatization include mild to moderate activity (20–50% V̇O₂max) for a duration of 90 min for a period of 7-14 d. Since the major physiological adaptations reach a plateau by day 14 of the heat acclimatization regime (Armstrong & Maresh, 1991), extending the program beyond this time presumably will not produce any additional benefit. It must be noted, however, that athletes who perform better during competition in the heat often reside in hot environments. It is likely, therefore, that chronic adaptations may take place.

In addition to the beneficial cardiovascular and thermoregulatory adaptations associated with heat acclimation, this process also reduces muscle glycogen utilization and lactate accumulation (King et al., 1985; Kirwan et al., 1987; Febbraio et al., 1994a). In fact, in the studies of King et al.(1985) and Kirwan et al. (1987) the glycogen use during exercise after acclimation was attenuated by approximately 40%. This adaptation, although often overlooked in assessing the benefits of heat acclimation, is nonetheless very important. When heat stress is compensable, performance is likely to be limited by substrate availability; therefore, an attenuation of glycogen use should improve exercise performance. The metabolic adaptations associated with heat acclimation are likely to be mediated by the lower T_{mus} and sympathoadrenal response that results from heat acclimation (Febbraio et al., 1994a).

Despite the fact that heat acclimation or acclimatization enhances endurance performance, athletes who undertake a heat acclimatization program prior to competition should ensure that their diets contain sufficient CHO. This is important because even though heat acclimatization reduces net muscle glycogen utilization during exercise and heat stress, postacclimatization glycogenolysis remains somewhat higher than that observed during exercise in cooler conditions (Febbraio et al., 1994a). Although a high CHO diet reduces thermoregulatory capacity in rats (Francesconi & Hubbard, 1986), there is no evidence that this occurs in humans (Schwellnus et al., 1990). Therefore, athletes should not be fearful that such a diet will negate the effects of a heat acclimatization regime.

Fluid Availability

One needs to carefully monitor fluid intake when preparing for exercise in the heat. During heat acclimatization, there is an increased requirement for fluid intake because of the enhanced sweating response (Greenleaf et al., 1983). Exercise-induced dehydration is associated with an increase in core temperature (Hamilton et al., 1991; Montain & Coyle, 1992), reduced cardiovascular function (Hamilton et al., 1991; Montain & Coyle, 1992), and impaired exercise performance (Walsh et al., 1994). These deleterious physiological effects are attenuated, if not prevented, by fluid ingestion (Candas et al., 1986; Costill et al., 1970; Hamilton et al., 1991; Montain & Coyle, 1992), which also improves exercise performance (Maughan et al., 1989; McConell et al., 1997; Walsh et al., 1994). Dehydration during exercise increases T_{mus}, exacerbates the sympathoadrenal response, and increases glycogen utilization (Gonzalez- Alonso et al., 1997a; Hargreaves et al., 1996b). Therefore, if athletes become dehydrated, they also increase their likelihood of depleting their intramuscular CHO stores.

WHAT IS THE BEST NUTRITIONAL PREPARATION FOR EXERCISE IN A HOT ENVIRONMENT?

It is clear that both CHO and fluid are very important components of the diets of those exercising in the heat. Apart from maintaining a diet rich in CHO and remaining euhydrated in the days leading up to exercise, there are several strategies that could be employed during exercise, particularly that which lasts for longer than 60 min. It would be advisable to ingest a CHO/electrolyte beverage frequently during exercise. Since the relative importance of fluid delivery is increased during exercise in the heat, one may be tempted to ingest water in these circumstances. However, the ingestion of a CHO/electrolyte beverage empties from the gut at the same rate as water (Francis, 1979; Owen et al., 1986; Ryan et al., 1989), but can spare muscle glycogen when compared to water (Yaspelkis & Ivy, 1991). In addition, the relative importance of electrolyte intake is increased during exercise in the heat. It has been suggested that sodium be included in rehydration beverages to replace sodium losses in sweat, to prevent hyponatremia, to promote the maintenance of plasma volume, and to enhance intestinal absorption of glucose and fluid (Maughan, 1994). Although the addition of sodium to a beverage has little effect on glucose or fluid bioavailability during exercise (Hargreaves et al., 1994), such an addition will maintain the drive for drinking, minimize urinary fluid loss during recovery from exercise, and maintain the extracellular fluid volume space (Maughan & Leiper, 1995; Nose et al., 1988; Takamata et al., 1995).

The amount of CHO within a fluid beverage ingested during exercise in the heat appears to have little effect on fluid availability or exercise performance, provided the CHO is not too concentrated. The changes in plasma volume and exercise performance in the heat are similar when beverages containing 0%, 4.2%, or 7% CHO are ingested. However, when a 14% CHO solution is ingested during exercise in the heat, the maintenance of plasma volume is reduced, the rise in rectal temperature tends to be augmented, and exercise performance tends to fall (Figure 8-5) (Febbraio et al., 1996b). It is important, therefore, to keep the concentration of CHO within a fluid beverage <~10% during exercise in the heat. A practical recommendation for athletes is to consume CHO/electrolyte beverages every 15 min during the exercise and to attempt to replace as much of the sweat lost as possible, i.e., up 400 ml every 15 min because the rate of fluid loss during exercise in the heat is ~1.6 L. h^{-1} (Febbraio unpublished observations). The CHO/electrolyte beverage should also be ingested during recovery to help replenish intramuscular glycogen stores and promote rehydration, especially during repeated exercise sessions in a hot environment (Terrados & Maughan, 1995).

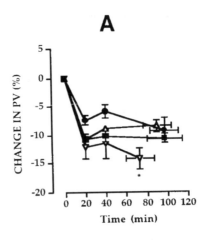

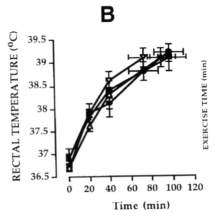

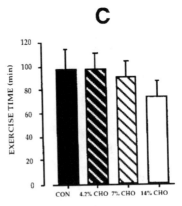

FIGURE 8-5. *Mean (± SEM) changes in plasma volume (A), rectal temperature (B) and time to exhaustion (C), while consuming placebo (CON, -■-), 4.2% carbohydrate (LCHO, -●-), 7% carbohydrate (-Δ-) or 14% carbohydrate (HCHO, -∇-) during fatiguing exercise at 70% $\dot{V}O_2max$ in 33°C conditions. * P<0.05 vs. other trials. Data from Febbraio et al. (1996b).*

Because there is some evidence that protein catabolism is increased during exercise in the heat (Febbraio et al., 1994b; Mittleman et al., 1998; Snow et al., 1993), it might be tempting to recommend that protein intake be increased prior to and during such exercise. However, there is little research on protein requirements during exercise in the heat, and more is required before definitive recommendations can be made.

Likewise, there is some evidence to suggest that oxyradical generation may be increased via the combination of exercise and heat stress (Mills et al., 1996), and it is possible that there could be some benefit in consuming antioxidants such as alpha-tocopherol (vitamin E) and ascorbic acid (vitamin C). This recommendation is speculative, however, because the hypothesis that such supplementation is advantageous during exercise in the heat is yet to be experimentally investigated.

Glycerol Hyperhydration

Because there are deleterious effects of dehydration during exercise, especially that which is conducted in a hot environment, it would seem to be desirable to hyperhydrate prior to exercise. Accordingly, there are some reports that pre-exercise ingestion of beverages containing glycerol increases fluid retention, reduces sweat rate, and enhances thermoregulatory capacity (Freund et al., 1995; Koenigsberg et al. 1991; Lyons et al., 1990, Montner et al., 1996), especially during exercise in a hot environment (Lyons et al., 1990). It must be noted, however, that only one study demonstrated lower core temperature with glycerol hyperhydration (Lyons et al. 1990), and others have not detected any substantial benefit to glycerol feedings (Latzka et al., 1997; Murray et al., 1991).

Any effectiveness of glycerol hyperhydration that may occur is not clearly understood, but if may be related to an attenuated rate of free-water clearance and/or an increase in the kidney's medullary concentration gradient resulting in increased glomerular reabsorption (Freund et al., 1995). There are no reports of the effect of glycerol hyperhydration on intramuscular metabolism. More data are required, therefore, before definitive recommendations regarding this practice can be made. Finally, because most of the excess water that may be accumulated during pre-exercise hyperhydration may be lost 2-3 h after ingestion, athletes may need to urinate during prolonged athletic events. Competitive athletes should thoroughly test the practice of glycerol hyperhydration in training prior to competition.

During exercise in the heat a balance between preventing hyperthermia and maintaining adequate fuel supply to fuel muscle contraction must be maintained. In order to achieve this balance, athletes need to closely monitor hydration levels and carbohydrate intake leading up to exercise. Daily monitoring of body weight and ensuring that urine is pallid will provide a guide to hydration status, and athletes should strive to consume sufficient carbohydrate energy before, during, and after exercise.

DIRECTIONS FOR FUTURE RESEARCH

Although it is clear that substrate metabolism is altered during exercise and heat stress, there are some key areas that warrant further research. No studies have examined the time-course for metabolic responses that take place during exercise and heat stress. In addition, it would be of interest to examine the effect of heat stress on the pyruvate dehydrogenase complex during exercise because both carbohydrate oxidation and lactate accumulation appear to be augmented in these circumstances.

It is also clear that the ingestion of ~6% CHO beverage will provide some ergogenic benefit during exercise in the heat by attenuating dehydration and providing some exogenous carbohydrate. However, while other dietary practices such as pre-exercise glycerol hyperhydration and supplementation with BCAA and antioxidants might confer some benefit during exercise in the heat, further research into such practices is needed before definitive recommendations can be made.

SUMMARY

Apart from the major cardiovascular and thermoregulatory responses that take place during acute exercise and heat stress, a number of metabolic alterations may have an impact on exercise performance. Both intramuscular glycogen use and glycolysis are augmented, whereas lipid utilization appears to decrease during exercise and heat stress. In addition, high-energy phosphagen metabolism and protein catabolism may, in some circumstances, be increased during exercise in the heat. Apart from changes that take place within the contracting muscle, liver glucose production is also increased during exercise and heat stress, although this change is not accompanied by any increase in peripheral glucose uptake. As a consequence, circulating glucose is higher during exercise and thermal stress. These changes appear to be mediated by muscle temperature *per se* and by an augmented sympathoadrenal response. In contrast, there is no evidence to suggest that exercise and heat stress affect either fiber-type recruitment patterns or V_{02} in contracting muscle.

In contrast with submaximal exercise in comfortable ambient temperatures, exercise in the heat does not appear to be limited by CHO availability when the heat stress is uncompensable. Rather, the limitation to performance during exercise and uncompensable heat stress is related to the attainment of a critical core temperature. However, there is a possibility that metabolic dysfunction plays a role in the etiology of fatigue because there is some evidence to suggest that metabolic function is impaired when the cellular temperature is greater than 40°C. In contrast, during compensable heat stress, it is likely that CHO availability is of critical importance.

In practical terms, athletes should be advised to 1) adopt a heat acclimatization program, 2) consume a diet rich in CHO, and 3) maintain adequate hydration levels when preparing for competition in hot environments. Despite the fact that substrate availability does not always appear to be a major limitation to exercise performance, it is prudent to ingest a 4–8% CHO beverage throughout exercise because such a beverage empties from the gastrointestinal tract as fast as water but also provides extra glucose and electrolytes that may be required. Importantly, drinking such a beverage may increase *ad libitum* fluid consumption because of increased palatability.

ACKNOWLEDGEMENT

This chapter is dedicated to the late Ethan R. Nadel, Ph.D., an inspiration to all who study the physiology of thermoregulation.

The collaborations with Professor Mark Hargreaves, Associate Professor Michael Carey, and Dr. Rod Snow have been fundamental to my research activity over the last six years and are gratefully acknowledged. The author also thanks graduate students Damien Angus, Kirsten Howlett, Donna Lambert, Phillip Murton, Jo Ann Parkin, Rebecca Starkie, and Abbey Tatterson for their intellectual and technical contributions. The author is also grateful for the constructive comments provided by Dr. Ethan Nadel and Dr. Scott Montain in the preparation of this chapter. Financial support for specific projects has been received from the Australian Research Council, The Australian Sports Commission, Cadbury Schweppes, and Ross Australia.

BIBLIOGRAPHY

Armstrong L.E., and C.M. Maresh (1991). The induction and decay of heat acclimatization in trained athletes. *Sports Med.* 12:302–312.

Below, P.R., R. Mora-Rodriguez, J. Gonzalez-Alonso, and E.F. Coyle (1995). Fluid and carbohydrate ingestion independently improve performance during 1 hr of intense exercise. *Med. Sci. Sports Exerc.* 27:200–210.

Booth, J., F. Marino, and J.J. Ward (1997). Improved running performance in hot humid conditions following whole body precooling. *Med. Sci. Sports Exerc.* 29:943–949.

Brengelmann, G.L., J.M. Johnson, L. Hermansen, and L.B. Rowell (1977). Altered control of skin blood flow during exercise at high internal temperatures *J. Appl. Physiol.* 43:790–794.

Broberg, S., and K. Sahlin (1989). Adenine nucleotide degradation in human skeletal muscle during prolonged exercise. *J. Appl. Physiol.* 67:116–122.

Brooks, G.A., K.J. Hittelman, J.A. Faulkner, and R.E. Beyer (1971). Temperature, skeletal muscle mitochondrial functions, and oxygen debt. *Am. J. Physiol.* 220:1053–1059.

Brown, N.J., L.A. Stephenson, G. Lister, and E.R. Nadel. (1982). Relative anaerobiosis during heavy exercise in the heat. *Fed. Proc.* 41:1677–1682.

Brück, K., and H. Olschewski (1987). Body temperature related factors diminishing the drive to exercise. *Can. J. Physiol. Pharmacol.* 65:1274–1280.

Buskirk, E.R. (1977). Temperature regulation with exercise. *Exerc. Sports Sci. Rev.* 5:45–88.

Candas, V., J.P. Libert, G. Brandenberger, J.C. Sagot, C. Amaros, and J.M Kahn (1986). Hydration during exercise: effects on thermal and cardiovascular adjustments. *Eur. J. Appl. Physiol.* 55:113–122.

Chesley, A., E. Hultman, and L.L. Spriet (1995). Effects of epinephrine infusion on muscle glycogenolysis during intense aerobic exercise. *Am. J. Physiol.* 268:E127–E134.

Clarke, M.G., E.Q. Colqhoun, S. Rattigan, K.A. Dora, T.P.D. Eldershaw, J.L. Hall, and J. Ye (1995). Vascular and endocrine control of muscle metabolism. *Am. J. Physiol.* 268:E797–E812.

Coggan, A.R., and E.F. Coyle (1987). Reversal of fatigue following prolonged exercise by carbohydrate infusion or ingestion. *J. Appl. Physiol.* 63:2388–2395.

Constantin-Teodosiu, D., G. Cederblad, and E. Hultman (1992). PDC activity and acetyl group accumulation in skeletal muscle during prolonged exercise. *J. Appl. Physiol.* 73:2403–2407.

Cooper, D.M., D.W. Wasserman, M. Vranic, and K. Wasserman (1986). Glucose turnover in response to exercise during high- and low FIO$_2$ breathing in man. *Am. J. Physiol.* 251:E209–E214.

Costill, D.L., W.F. Krammer, and A. Fisher (1970). Fluid ingestion during distance running. *Arch. Environ. Health* 21:520–525.

Coyle, E.F., and S.J. Montain (1992). Benefits of fluid replacement with carbohydrate during exercise. *Med. Sci. Sports Exerc.* 24:S324–S330.

Coyle, E.F., A.R. Coggan, M.K. Hemmert, and J.L. Ivy (1986). Muscle glycogen utilisation during prolonged strenuous exercise when fed carbohydrate. *J. Appl. Physiol.* 61:165–172.

Davis, J.M., and S.P. Bailey (1997). Possible mechanisms of central nervous system fatigue during exercise. *Med. Sci. Sports Exerc.* 29:45–57.

Davis, J.M., W.A. Burgess, C.A. Slentz, W.P. Bartoli, and R.R. Pate (1988a). Effects of ingesting 6% and 12% glucose/electrolyte beverages during prolonged intermittent cycling in the heat. *Eur. J. Appl. Physiol.* 57:563–569.

Davis, J.M., D.R. Lamb, R.R. Pate, C.A. Slentz, W.A. Burgess, and W.P. Bartoli (1988b). Carbohydrate-electrolyte drinks: effects on endurance cycling in the heat. *Am. J. Clin. Nutr.* 48:1023–1030.

Dimri, G.P., M.S. Malhotra, J. Sen Gupta, T. Sapath Kumar, and B.S. Arora (1980). Alterations in aerobic-anaerobic proportions of metabolism during work in the heat. *Eur. J. Appl. Physiol.* 45:43–50, 1980.

Dolny, D.G., and P.W.R. Lemon (1988). Effect of ambient temperature on protein breakdown during prolonged exercise. *J. Appl. Physiol* 64:550–555.

Edwards, R.H.T., R.C. Harris, E. Hultman, L. Kaijser, D. Koh, and L-O. Nordesjo (1972). Effect of temperature on muscle energy metabolism and endurance during successive isometric contractions, sustained to fatigue, of the quadriceps muscle in man. *J. Physiol.* 220:335–352.

Febbraio, M.A., M.F. Carey, R.J. Snow, C.G. Stathis, and M. Hargreaves (1996a). Influence of elevated muscle temperature on metabolism during intense, dynamic exercise. *Am. J. Physiol.* 271:R1251–R1255.

Febbraio, M.A., D.L. Lambert, R.L. Starkie, J. Proietto, and M. Hargreaves (1998). Effect of epinephrine on muscle glycogenolysis during exercise in trained men. *J. Appl. Physiol.* 84:465–470.

Febbraio, M.A., P. Murton, S.E. Selig, S.A. Clark, D.L. Lambert, D.J. Angus, and M.F. Carey (1996b). Effect of CHO ingestion on exercise metabolism and performance in different ambient temperatures. *Med. Sci. Sports Exerc.* 28:1380–1387.

Febbraio, M.A., R.J. Snow, M. Hargreaves, C.G. Stathis, I.K. Martin, and M.F. Carey (1994a). Muscle metabolism during exercise and heat stress in trained men: effect of acclimation. *J. Appl. Physiol.* 76:589–597.

Febbraio, M.A., R.J. Snow, C.G. Stathis, M. Hargreaves, and M.F. Carey (1996c). Blunting the rise in body temperature reduces muscle glycogenolysis during exercise in humans. *Exp. Physiol.* 81:685–693.

Febbraio, M.A., R.J. Snow, C.G. Stathis, M. Hargreaves, and M.F. Carey (1994b). Effect of heat stress on muscle energy metabolism during exercise. *J. Appl. Physiol.* 77:2827–2831.

Fenn, W.O. (1923). A quantitative comparison between the energy liberated and the work performed by the isolated sartorius muscle of the frog. *J. Physiol. Lond.* 58:175–203.

Fink, W.J., D.L. Costill, and P.J. Van Handel (1975). Leg muscle metabolism during exercise in the heat and cold. *Eur. J. Appl. Physiol* 34:183–190.

Florkin, M., and E.H. Stoltz (1968). *Comprehensive Biochemistry, No. 12.* New York: Elselvier.

Francesconi, R.P., and R.W. Hubbard (1986). Dietary manipulation and exercise in the heat: thermoregulatory and metabolic effects in rats. *Aviat. Space Environ. Med.* 57:31–35.

Francis, K.T. (1979). Effect of water and electrolyte replacement during exercise in the heat on biochemical indices of stress and performance. *Aviat. Space Environ. Med.* 50:115–119.

Freund, B.J., S.J. Montain, A.J. Young, M.N. Sawka, J. DeLuca, K.B. Pandolf, and C.R. Valeri (1995). Glycerol hyperhydration: hormonal, renal and vascular fluid responses. *J. Appl. Physiol.* 79:2069–2077.

Galbo, H. (1983). *Hormonal and Metabolic Adaptations to Exercise.* New York: Thieme-Stratton Inc.

Galbo, H., M.E. Houston, N.J. Christensen, J.J. Holst, B. Nielsen, E. Nygaard, and J. Suzuki (1979). The effect of water temperature on the hormonal response to prolonged swimming. *Acta Physiol. Scand.* 105:326–337.

Galloway, S.D., and R.J. Maughan (1997). Effects of ambient temperature on the capacity to perform prolonged cycle exercise in man. *Med. Sci. Sports Exerc.* 29:1240–1249.

Gibala, M.J., M.A. Tarnopolsky, and T.E. Graham (1997). Tricarboxylic acid cycle intermediates in human muscle at rest and during prolonged cycling. *Am. J. Physiol.* 272:E239–E244.

Gisolfi, C.V. (1987). Influence of acclimatisation and training on heat tolerance and physical endurance.

In: J.R.S. Hales and D.A.B. Richards (eds.) *Heat Stress: Physical Exertion and the Environment*. Amsterdam: Exerpta Medica.

Gisolfi, C.V., and C.B. Wenger (1984). Temperature regulation during exercise: old concepts, new ideas. *Exerc. Sports Sci. Rev.* 12:339–372.

Gollnick, P.D., R.B. Armstrong, C.W. Saubert IV, W.L. Sembrowich, R.E. Shepherd, and B. Saltin (1973). Glycogen depletion patterns in human skeletal muscle fibres during prolonged work. *Pflüegers Arch.* 344:1–12.

Gonzalez-Alonso, J., J.A.L. Calbert, and B. Nielsen (1997a). Metabolic alterations with dehydration-induced reductions in blood flow in exercising humans. *Proc. 2nd Congress, Eur. Cong. Sports Sci.* 492–493 (Abstract).

Gonzalez-Alonso, J., R. Mora-Rodriguez, P.R. Below, and E.F. Coyle (1995). Dehydration reduces cardiac output and increases systemic and cutaneous vascular resistance during exercise. *J. Appl. Physiol.* 79:1487–1496.

Gonzalez-Alonso, J., R. Mora-Rodriguez, P.R. Below, and E.F. Coyle (1997b). Dehydration markedly impairs cardiovascular function in hyperthermic endurance athletes during exercise. *J. Appl. Physiol.* 82:1229–1236.

Graham, T.E., J.W.E. Rush, and D.A. MacLean (1995). Skeletal muscle amino acid metabolism and ammonia production during exercise. In: M. Hargreaves (ed.) *Exercise Metabolism*. Champaign Illinois: Human Kinetics, pp 131–176.

Greenhaff, P.L., J.-M. Ren, K. Söderlund, and E. Hultman (1991). Energy metabolism in single human muscle fibers during contractions with and without epinephrine infusion. *Am. J. Physiol.* 260:E713–E718.

Greenleaf, J.E., P.J. Brock, L.C. Keil, and J.T. Morse (1983). Drinking and water balance during exercise and heat acclimation. *J. Appl. Physiol.* 54:414–419.

Hamilton, M.T., J. Gonzalez-Alonso, S.J. Montain, and E.F. Coyle (1991). Fluid replacement and glucose infusion during exercise prevent cardiovascular drift. *J. Appl. Physiol.* 71:871–877.

Hardy, J.D. (1961). Physiology of temperature regulation. *Physiol. Rev.* 41:521–606.

Hargreaves, M., D. Angus, K. Howlett, N. Marmy Conus, and M. Febbraio (1996a). Effect of heat stress on glucose kinetics during exercise. *J.Appl. Physiol.* 81:1594–1597.

Hargreaves, M., D. Costill, L. Burke, G. McConell, and M. Febbraio (1994). Influence of sodium on glucose bioavailability during exercise. *Med. Sci. Sports Exerc.* 26:365–368.

Hargreaves, M., P. Dillo, D. Angus, and M. Febbraio (1996b). Effect of fluid ingestion on muscle metabolism during prolonged exercise. *J.Appl. Physiol.* 80:363–366.

Hargreaves, M., G. McConell, and J. Proietto (1995). Influence of muscle glycogen on glycogenolysis and glucose uptake during exercise in humans. *J.Appl. Physiol.* 78:288–292.

Harris, R.C., K. Sahlin, and E. Hultman (1977). Phosphagen and lactate contents of m. quadriceps femoris in man after exercise. *J. Appl. Physiol.* 43:852–857.

Hashimoto I., M.B. Knudson, E.G. Noble, G.A. Klug, and P.D. Gollnick (1982). Exercise-induced glycogenolysis in sympathectomized rats. *Jpn. J. Physiol.* 32:153–160.

Hespel, P., and E.A. Richter (1992). Mechanisms linking glycogen and glycogenolytic rate in perfused contracting rat skeletal muscle. *Biochem. J.* 284:777–780.

Hessemer, V., D. Langush, K. Brük, R. Bodeker, and T. Breidenbach (1984). Effects of slightly lowered body temperatures on endurance performance in humans. *J. Appl. Physiol* 57:1731–1737.

Howlett, K, M.A. Febbraio, and M. Hargreaves (1998). Liver glucose production during strenuous exercise in humans: role of adrenaline. *J. Physiol.* (in press).

Issekutz, B. (1984). Effect of β-adrenergic blockade on lactate turnover in exercising dogs. *J. Appl. Physiol.* 57:1754–1759.

Issekutz, B. (1985). Effect of epinephrine on carbohydrate metabolism in exercising dogs. *Metab.* 34:457–464.

Jansson E., P. Hjemdahl, and L. Kaijser (1986). Epinephrine induced changes in muscle carbohydrate metabolism during exercise in male subjects. *J. Appl. Physiol.* 60:1466–1470.

Johnson, J.M., and M.K. Park (1979) Reflex control of skin blood flow by skin temperature: role of core temperature. *J. Appl. Physiol. Respirat. Environ. Exercise Physiol.* 47:1188–1193.

Johnson, J.M., and L.B. Rowell (1965). Forearm skin and muscle vascular responses to prolonged exercise in man. *J. Appl. Physiol.* 39:920–924.

Johnson, L.N. (1982) Glycogen phosphorylase: control by phosphorylation and allosteric effectors. *FASEB J.* 6:2274–2282.

King, D.S., D.L. Costill, W.J. Fink, M. Hargreaves, and R.A. Fielding. (1985) Muscle metabolism during exercise in the heat in unacclimatized and acclimatized humans *J.Appl. Physiol.* 59:1350–1354.

Kirwan, J.P., D.L. Costill, H. Kuipers, M.J. Burrell, W.J. Fink, J.E. Kovaleski, and R.A. Fielding. (1987). Substrate utilization in leg muscle of men after heat acclimation. *J.Appl. Physiol.* 63:31–35.

Kjær, M., B. Kiens, M. Hargreaves, and E.A. Richter (1991). Influence of active muscle mass on glucose homeostasis during exercise in humans. *J.Appl. Physiol.* 71:552–557.

Kjær, M., S. Keiding, K. Engfred, K. Rasmussen, B. Sonne, P. Kirkrgård, and H. Galbo (1995). Glucose homeostasis during exercise in humans with a liver or kidney transplant. *Am. J. Physiol.* 268:E636–E644.

Kjær, M., K. Engfred, A. Fernandes, N.H Secher, and H. Galbo. (1993) Regulation of hepatic glucose production during exercise in humans: role of sympathoadrenergic activity.*Am. J. Physiol.* 265:E275–E283.

Koenigsberg, P., P.T. Lyons, R. Nagy, and M.L. Riedesel, (1991) 40 hour glycerol-induced hyperhydration. *FASEB J.* 5:A768 (abstract).

Koga, S., T. Shiojiri, N. Kondo, and T.J. Barstow (1997). Effect of increased muscle temperature on oxygen uptake kinetics during exercise. *J. Appl. Physiol.* 83:1333–1338.

Kozlowski, S., Z. Brzezinska, B. Kruk, H Kaciuba-Uscilko, J.E. Greenleaf, and K. Nazar. (1985) Exercise hyperthermia as a factor limiting physical performance: temperature effect on muscle metabolism. *J. Appl. Physiol.* 59:766–773.

Kruk, B., H. Kaciuba-Uscilco, K. Nazar, J.E. Greenleaf, and S. Koslowski (1985). Hypothalamic, rectal, and muscle temperatures in exercising dogs: effect of cooling. *J. Appl. Physiol.* 58:1444–1448.

Latzka, W.A., M.N. Sawka, S.J. Montain, G.R. Skrinar, R.A. Fielding, R.P. Matott, and K.B. Pandolf (1997). Hyperhydration: thermoregulatory effects during compensable exercise-heat stress. *J. Appl. Physiol.* 83:860–866.

Lee, D.T., and E.M. Haymes (1995). Exercise duration and thermoregulatory responses after whole body precooling. *J. Appl. Physiol.* 79:1971–1976.

Levine, L., M.S. Rose, R.P. Francesconi, P.D. Neufer, M.N. Sawka (1991). Fluid replacement during sustained activity in the heat: nutrient solution vs water. *Aviat. Space Environ. Med.* 62:559–564.

Lyons, T.P., M.L. Riedesel, L.E Meuli, and T.W. Chick, (1990). Effects of glycerol-induced hyperhydration prior to exercise in the heat on sweating and core temperature *Med. Sci. Sports Exerc.* 22:477–483.

MacDougall, J.D., W.G. Reddan, C.R. Layton, and J.A. Dempsey (1974). Effects of metabolic hyperthermia on performance during heavy prolonged exercise. *J. Appl. Physiol.* 36:538–554.

Madsen, K., D.A. MacLean, B. Kiens, and D. Christensen (1996). Effects of glucose, glucose plus branched chain amino acids, or placebo on bike performance over 100km. *J. Appl. Physiol.* 81:2644–2650.

Maughan, R.J. (1994). Fluid and electrolyte loss and replacement in Exercise. In M. Harries, C. Williams, W.D. Stanish, and L.J. Micheli (eds.) *Oxford Textbook of Sports Medicine*. New York: Oxford University Press, pp. 82–93.

Maughan, R.J., and J.B. Leiper (1995). Sodium intake and post-exercise rehydration in man. *Eur. J. Appl. Physiol.* 71:311–319.

Maughan, R.J. C.E. Fenn, and J.B. Leiper (1989). Effects of fluid, electrolyte and substrate ingestion on endurance capacity. *Eur. J. Appl. Physiol. Occup. Physiol.* 58:481–486.

Maughan, R.J., J.B. Leiper and J. Thompson (1985). Rectal temperature after marathon running. *Br. J. Sports Med.* 19:192–196.

McConell, C.M. Burge, S.L. Skinner, and M. Hargreaves (1997). Influence of ingested fluid volume on physiological responses during prolonged exercise. *Acta Physiol. Scand.* 160:149–156.

Millard-Stafford, M., P.B. Sparling, L.B. Rosskopf, and L.J. Dicarlo (1992). Carbohydrate-electrolyte replacement improves distance running performance in the heat. *Med. Sci. Sports Exerc.* 24:934–940.

Millard-Stafford, M., P.B. Sparling, L.B. Rosskopf, B.T. Hinson, and L.J. Dicarlo (1990). Carbohydrate-electrolyte replacement during a simulated triathlon in the heat. *Med. Sci. Sports Exerc.* 22:621–628.

Mills, P.C., N.C. Smith, I. Casas, P. Harris, R.C. Harris, and D.J. Marlin (1996). Effects of exercise intensity and environmental stress on indices of oxidative stress and iron homeostasis during exercise in the horse. *Eur. J. Appl. Physiol.* 74:60–66.

Mittleman, K, M. Ricci, and S.P. Bailey (1998). Branched-chain amino acids prolong exercise during heat stress in men and women. *Med Sci. Sports Exerc.* 30:83–91.

Montain, S.J., and E.F. Coyle (1992). Influence of graded dehydration on hyperthermia and cardiovascular drift during exercise. *J. Appl. Physiol.* 73:1340–1350.

Montain, S.J., M.N. Sawka, B.S. Cadarette, M.D. Quigley, and J.M. McKay (1994). Physiological tolerance to uncompensable heat stress: effects of exercise intensity, protective clothing and climate. *J. Appl. Physiol.* 77:216–222.

Montner, P., D. Stark, M.L. Riedelsel, G. Murata, R.A. Robergs, M. Timms, and T.W. Chick (1996). Pre-exercise glycerol hydration improves cycling endurance time. *Int. J. Sports Med.* 17:27–33.

Murray, R., D.E. Eddy, T.W. Murray, J.G. Seifert, G.L. Paul, and G.A. Halaby (1987). The effect of fluid and carbohydrate feedings during intermittent cycling exercise. *Med. Sci. Sports Exerc.* 19:597–604.

Murray, R., D.E. Eddy, G.L. Paul, J.G. Seifert, and G.A. Halaby (1991). Physiological responses to glycerol ingestion during exercise. *J. Appl. Physiol.* 71:144–149.

Nadel, E.R. (1985). Recent advances in temperature regulation during exercise in humans. *Fed. Proc.* 44:2286–2292.

Nadel, E.R., E. Cafarelli, M.F. Roberts, and C.B. Wenger (1979). Circulatory regulation during exercise in different ambient temperatures. *J. Appl. Physiol.* 46:430–437.

Nadel, E.R., C.B. Wenger, M.F. Roberts, J.A.J. Stolwijk, and E. Cafarelli (1977). Physiological defenses against hyperthermia of exercise. *Ann. NY Acad. Sci.* 301:98–109.

Newsholme, E.A., I.N. Acworth, and E. Blomstrand (1987). Amino acids, brain neurotransmitters and a functional link between muscle and brain that is important in sustained exercise. In G. Benzi (ed.) *Advances in Myochemistry*. London: John Libby Eurotext, pp. 127–139.

Nielsen, B., J.R.S. Hales, S. Strange, K. Juel Christensen, J. Warberg, and B. Saltin (1993). Human circulatory and thermoregulatory adaptations with heat acclimation and exercise in a hot, dry environment. *J. Physiol.* 460:467–485.

Nielsen, B., G. Savard, E.A. Richter, M. Hargreaves, and B. Saltin (1990). Muscle blood flow and muscle metabolism during exercise and heat stress *J. Appl. Physiol.* 69:1040–1046.

Noakes, T.D., K.H. Myburgh, J. Du Plessis, L. Lang, M. Lambert, C. Van Der Riet, and R. Schall (1991). Metabolic rate, not percent dehydration, predicts rectal temperature in marathon runners. *Med. Sci. Sports Exerc.* 23:443–449.

Norman, B., A. Sollevi, and E. Jansson (1988). Increased IMP content in glycogen-depleted muscle fibres during submaximal exercise in man. *Acta Physiol. Scand.* 133:97–100.

Nose, H., G.W. Mack, X. Shi, and E.R. Nadel (1988). Role of osmolality and plasma volume during rehydration in humans. *J. Appl. Physiol.* 65:332–336.

Owen, M.D., K.C. Kregel, P.T. Wall, and C.V. Gisolfi (1986). Effects of ingesting carbohydrate beverages during exercise in the heat. *Med. Sci. Sports Exerc.* 18:568–575.

Parkin, J.M., M.F. Carey, S. Zhao, and M.A. Febbraio (1998). Effect of ambient temperature on human skeletal muscle metabolism during fatiguing submaximal exercise. *J. Appl. Physiol.* (in review).

Powers, S.K., E.T. Howley, and R. Cox (1982). A differential catecholamine response during exercise and passive heating. *Med. Sci. Sports Exerc.*. 14:435–439.

Powers, S.K., E.T. Howley, and R. Cox (1985). Blood lactate concentrations during submaximal work under differing environmental conditions. *Int. J. Sports Med.* 25:84–89.

Putman, C.T., L.L. Spriet, E. Hultman, M.I. Lindinger, L.C. Lands, R.S. McKelvie, G. Cederblad, N.L. Jones, and G.J.F. Heigenhauser (1993). Pyruvate dehydrogenase activity and acetyl group accumulation during exercise after different diets. *Am. J. Physiol.* 265:E752–E760.

Radigan, L.R., and S. Robinson (1949) Effect of environmental heat stress and exercise on renal blood flow and filtration rate. *J. Appl. Physiol.* 2:185–191.

Ray, C.A., and K.H. Gracey (1997). Augmentation of exercise-induced muscle sympathetic nerve activity during muscle heating. *J. Appl. Physiol.* 82:1719–1725.

Ren, J-M., and E. Hultman (1990). Regulation of phosphorylase a activity in human skeletal muscle. *J. Appl. Physiol.* 67:919–923.

Richter, E.A., N.B. Ruderman, H. Gavras, E.R. Belur, and H. Galbo (1982). Muscle glycogenolysis during exercise: dual control by epinephrine and contractions. *Am. J. Physiol.* 240:242:E25–E32.

Richter, E.A., B. Sonne, N.J. Christensen, and H. Galbo (1981). Role of epinephrine for muscular glycogenolysis and pancreatic hormone secretion in running rats. *Am. J. Physiol.* E526–E532.

Robinson, S. (1963). Temperature regulation during exercise. *Pediatrics* 32:691–702.

Rowell, L.B. (1974). Human cardiovascular adjustments to exercise and thermal stress. *Physiol. Rev.* 54:75–159.

Rowell, L.B. (1986). *Human Circulation: Regulation during Physical Stress*. New York: Oxford University Press.

Rowell, L.B., G.L. Brengelmann, J.R. Blackmon, R.D. Twiss, and F. Kusumi (1968). Splanchnic blood flow and metabolism in heat stressed man. *J. Appl. Physiol.* 24:475–484.

Rowell, L.B., J.R. Blackmon, R.H. Martin, J.A. Mazzarella, R.A. Bruce (1965). Hepatic clearance of indocyanine green in man under thermal and exercise stresses. *J. Appl. Physiol.* 20:384–394.

Rowell, L.B., J.A. Murray, G.L. Brengelmann, and K.K. Kranning (1969). Human cardiovascular adjustments to rapid changes in skin temperature during exercise. *Circ. Res.* 24:711–724.

Rowell, L.B., D.S. O'Leary, and D.L. Kellogg Jr. (1996) Intergration of cardiovascular control systems in dynamic exercise. In L.B. Rowell, L.B and J.T. Shepherd (eds.) *Handbook of Physiology. Section 12. Exercise: Regulation and Intergration of Multiple Systems*. New York: Oxford University Press.

Ryan, A.J., T.L. Bleiler, J.E. Carter, J.E., and C.V. Gisolfi (1989). Gastric emptying during prolonged cycling exercise in the heat. *Med. Sci. Sports Exerc.* 21:51–58.

Sahlin, K., A. Katz, and S. Broberg (1990). Tricarboxylic acid cycle intermediates in human muscle during prolonged exercise. *Am. J. Physiol.* 259:C834–C841.

Saltin, B., and L. Hermansen (1966). Esophageal, rectal and muscle temperature during exercise. *J. Appl. Physiol.* 21:1757–1762.

Saltin, B., A.P. Gagge, U. Bergh, and J.A.J. Stolwijk (1972). body temperature and sweating during exhaustive exercise. *J. Appl. Physiol.* 32:635–643.

Savard, G.K., B. Nielsen, J. Laszczynska, B.E. Larsen, and B. Saltin (1988). Muscle blood flow is not reduced in humans during moderate exercise and heat stress. *J. Appl. Physiol.* 64:649–657.

Sawka, M.N., A.J. Young, B.S. Caderette, L. Levine, and K.B. Pandolf (1984). Influence of heat stress and acclimation on maximal aerobic power. *Eur. J. Appl. Physiol. Occup. Physiol.* 53:294–298.

TEMPERATURE, MUSCLE METABOLISM **347**

Sawka, M.N., A.J. Young, W.A. Latzka, P.D. Neufer, M.D. Quigley, and K.B. Pandolf (1992). Human tolerance to heat strain during exercise:influence of hydration. *J. Appl. Physiol.* 73:368–375.

Schmidt, V., and K. Brück (1981). Effect of a precooling maneuver on body temperature and exercise performance. *J. Appl. Physiol.: Respirat. Environ. Exercise Physiol.* 50:772–778.

Schumacker, P.T., J. Rowland, S. Saltz, D.P.Nelson, and L.D.H. Wood (1987). Effects of hyperthermia and hypothermia on oxygen extraction by tissues during hypovolemia. *J. Appl. Physiol.* 63:1246–1252.

Schwellnus, M.P., M.F. Gordon, G.G. van Zyl, J.F. Cilliers, H.C. Grobler, J. Kuyl, and H.W. Kohl (1990). Effect of a high carbohydrate diet on core temperature during prolonged exercise. *Brit. J. Sports Med.* 24:99–102.

Smolander, J., and V. Louhevaara (1992). Effects of heat stress on muscle blood flow during dynamic handgrip exercise. *Eur. J. Appl. Physiol.* 65:215–220.

Snow, R.J., M.A. Febbraio, M.F. Carey, and M. Hargreaves (1993). Heat stress increases ammonia accumulation during exercise. *Exp. Physiol.* 78: 847–850.

Sonne, B., K.J. Mikines, E.A. Richter, N.J. Christensen, and H. Galbo (1985). Role of liver nerves and adrenal medulla in glucose turnover in running rats. *J. Appl. Physiol.* 59:1640–1646.

Spencer, M.K., Z. Yan, and A. Katz (1991). Carbohydrate supplementation attenuates IMP accumulation in human muscle during prolonged exercise. *Am. J. Physiol.* 261:C71–C76.

Spencer, M.K., Z. Yan, and A. Katz (1992). Effect of low glycogen on carbohydrate and energy metabolism in human muscle during exercise. *Am. J. Physiol.* 262:C975–C979.

Spriet, L.L., E. Hultman, and Ren, J.M. (1988). Epinephrine enhances muscle glycogenolysis during prolonged electrical stimulation. *J. Appl. Physiol.* 64:1439–1444.

Starkie, R.L., M. Hargreaves, D.L. Lambert, J. Proietto, and M.A. Febbraio (1998). Effect of temperature on muscle metabolism during submaximal exercise. *Exp. Physiol.* (in review).

Stryer, L. (1988). *Biochemistry.* New York: Freeman and Company.

Takamata, A., G.W. Mack, C.M. Gillen, A.C. Jozsi, and E.R. Nadel (1995). Osmoregulatory modulation of thermal sweating in humans: reflex effects of drinking. *Am. J. Physiol.* 268:R414–R422.

Tatterson, A., D.T. Martin, A. Hahn, and M.A. Febbraio (1998). Effect of heat stress on metabolic and thermoregulatory responses during time trial performance in elite cyclists. *J. Appl. Physiol.* (in review).

Terrados, N., and R.J. Maughan (1995). Exercise in the heat: strategies to minimize the adverse effects on performance. *J. Sports Sci.* 13:S55–S62.

Turner, M.J., E.T. Howley, H. Tanaka, M. Ashraf, D.R. Bassett, and D.J. Keefer (1995). Effect of graded epinephrine infusion on blood lactate response to exercise. *J. Appl. Physiol.* 79:1206–1211.

Uyeda, K. (1979) Phosphofructokinase. *Adv. Enzymol. Rel. Areas Mol. Biol.* 48:193–244.

van Hall, G., J.S.H. Raaymakers, W.H.M. Saris, and A.J.M. Wagenmakers (1995). Ingestion of branched-chain amino acids and tryptophan during sustained exercise in man: failure to affect performance. *J. Physiol.* 486:789–794.

Walsh, R.M., T.D. Noakes, J.A. Hawley, and S.C. Dennis (1994). Impaired high-intensity cycling performance time at low levels of dehydration. *Int. J. Sports Med.* 15:392–398.

Wendling, P.S., S.J. Peters, G.J.F. Heigenhauser, and L.L. Spriet (1996a). Epinephrine infusion does not enhance net muscle glycogenolysis during prolonged aerobic exercise. *Can. J. Appl. Physiol.* 21:271–284.

Wendling, P.S., S.J. Peters, G.J.F. Heigenhauser, and L.L. Spriet (1996b). Variability of triacylglecerol content in human skeletal muscle biopsy samples. J. Appl. Physiol. 81:1150–1155.

Willis, W.T. and M.R. Jackman (1994). Mitochondrial function during heavy exercise. *Med. Sci. Sports Exerc.* 26:1347–1354.

Yaspelkis III, B.B., and J.L. Ivy (1991). Effect of carbohydrate supplements and water on exercise metabolism in the heat. *J. Appl. Physiol.* 71:680–687.

Yaspelkis III, B.B., G.C. Scroop, K.M. Wilmore, K.M., and J.L. Ivy (1993). Carbohydrate metabolism during exercise in hot and thermoneutral environments. *Int. J. Sports Med.* 14:13–19.

Young, A.J. (1990). Energy substrate utilization during exercise in extreme environments. *Exer. Sports Sci. Rev.* 18:65–117.

Young, A.J., M.N. Sawka, L. Levine, P.W. Burgoon, W.L. Latzka, R.R. Gonzalez, and K.B. Pandolf (1995). Metabolic and thermal adaptations from endurance training in hot and cold water. *J. Appl. Physiol.* 78:793–801.

Young, A.J., M.N. Sawka, L. Levine, B.S. Cadarette, and K.B. Pandolf (1985). Skeletal muscle metabolism during exercise is influenced by heat acclimation *J. Appl. Physiol.* 59:1929–1935.

DISCUSSION

SPRIET: Is there any information to suggest that calcium concentrations are higher inside the cell during exercise in a hot versus a temperate environment?

FEBBRAIO: There is some evidence from in vitro experiments using rat muscle homogenates that calcium uptake is reduced when the muscle is incubated at high temperatures. In the preparation the calcium assay was conducted with optimal ATP concentrations. This means that there must have been some temperature effect on the structure of either the calcium pump or some other apparatus associated with calcium kinetics. We tried to do the experiment in humans by using our muscle temperature model, but the muscle temperature only rose to approximately 38°C, and we saw no effect on calcium of this small increase in temperature. However, I am sure that calcium is very important.

SPRIET: It seems to me that one thing is still missing in our understanding of whether the heat effect operates primarily at the mitochondria and/or at the level of mobilization of substrates. I think we need to do some experiments that examine the time course of these events. One of these effects could be more predominant at different time points. For instance, the epinephrine effect on substrate mobilization could be a bigger player early in the hot environment; as the muscle temperatures diverge during the control and hot environments, mitochondrial effects might then emerge. Some of the data are only end-point data, i.e., we are only looking at the beginning and the end. I think it could be quite important to examine the energy status of the cell very early in the hot and cool environments.

FEBBRAIO: That is a very important point. We need to make some intermediate measurements to see if the fall in PCr is related to some early metabolic changes and to see if the change in glycogen or the change in phosphorylase activity occurs early or later in exercise.

KENNEY: You made the point that carbohydrate metabolism increases with increased intramuscular temperature. You also made the point that there appears to be no benefit of CHO feeding if prolonged aerobic exercise is done in a situation of uncompensable heat stress. Why do you think that is the case?

FEBBRAIO: When the heat stress is uncompensable, I think fatigue is most closely related to one's perception of how hot one is, and I believe that this perception is not substrate dependent. However, in marathons a runner could get to a point where the convective heat loss is sufficient to allow a plateau in core temperature to be achieved. The runner is still hotter than normal but can cope with the heat. In this case, carbohydrate supplementation would presumably be beneficial.

KENNEY: You indicated that during self-paced exercise in the heat, a power output is selected relative to an upper limit in core temperature. If that is the case, what is the sensed variable? How do we sense the projected upper limit in core temperature in order to self-select an exercise temperature?

FEBBRAIO: That is an easy question to answer—I have no idea. However, I will describe an experiment we recently completed. We tested members of the Australian cycling team in an environmental chamber at 23°C or 33°C. We told them to complete a time trial as fast as possible. In the first 5 min their power outputs fell in the hot compared with the cool environment, and they continued to stay lower for the duration of the experiment. We hypothesized that rectal temperature would be greater in the hot trial, but this was not the case. Between 5 and 30 min of exercise the mean rectal temperature was exactly the same in both environments. So there is some sensory mechanism that directs us to titrate the workload so we don't get too hot. What that mechanism is, I have no idea.

MAUGHAN: The idea that there is a protective mechanism that makes us select a low work load in the heat or stops us when core temperature reaches a limiting point is very attractive, but it is difficult to see how that functions in these situations. The data from the Nielsen studies seem very clear that when you reach a certain temperature you stop. The thing I find difficult to understand in their study is that as the subjects became acclimated, they exercised longer, but the rate of change of temperature was exactly the same. The difference was entirely due to a reduction in the pre-exercise core temperature. Does this mean that all the traditional mechanisms, e.g., the expansion of plasma volume, the increased sweat rate, and the better distribution of sweating, that accompany acclimation are totally ineffective, that they don't change the rate of rise of core temperature?

FEBBRAIO: The data are certainly are consistent with that conclusion. There are interventions we could use to lower pre-exercise core temperature and improve performance. However, the Nielsen study is only one study, so we really need to be cautious about concluding that all of the adaptations that occur with progressive heat acclimatization are redundant, and all you really need to do is lower core temperature. Reducing the body core temperature at rest certainly appears to be what is causing the improved performance in trained people who exercise in the heat.

NADEL: The available human muscle blood flow data are only taken from steady-state analyses and don't show what happens at the onset of exercise, during which time an elevation in carbohydrate oxidation in the heat may occur due to a lag in the muscle blood flow response in the heat. Those experiments have not been done.

FEBBRAIO: We know that at the onset of steady-state exercise oxygen kinetics are not at steady state for a number of minutes. You are correct that we don't know if the oxygen kinetics change at the onset of exercise when comparing exercise in the heat with exercise in the cooler environment.

TARNOPOLSKY: In humans there is a point mutation in the ryanodine receptor that results in malignant hyperthermia. One of the potentially fatal outcomes of this is rhabdomyolysis and damage to the kidneys. Is there any evidence that exercise in the heat results in more muscle damage or a greater increase in serum creatine kinase activity than does exercise in a cool environment?

FEBBRAIO: I'll describe one case of rhabdomyolysis that occurred in a large individual in an 8-km run at a fast pace in the heat. He was leading the race when he collapsed and exhibited severe rhabdomyolysis. His creatine kinase activity went through the roof, and when they fasciotomized the muscle, the muscle was khaki in color and resembled cooked meat. He also had major renal damage and neurologic impairment. In laboratory experiments, there is some evidence to suggest that there is a heat-induced increase in oxidative stress within the muscles.

MAUGHAN: You identified some practical issues in terms of preparing for the heat. Many people might get the impression that when you say "heat," you mean 40°C, and that you don't need to be concerned with acclimatization, fluid ingestion, and other preparation strategies until you are in that very hot environment. Would you suggest the temperature range at which we may have to begin to think about some of those issues? One reason for asking the question is that a recent study of ours showed that performance is already reduced at 20°C compared to 10°C. You are suggesting that mechanisms causing fatigue may be different in the heat as opposed to a cool environment. So we need to look at all the studies that have been done at temperatures of 18°–20°C to consider whether the temperature factor is important in the fatigue process even in moderate conditions.

FEBBRAIO: In all of the experiments conducted at 20°, there is a thermal component; we never see core temperatures remaining at resting levels. They always go up, but because it compensable heat stress, core temperature levels off. There is a thermal component, but those experiments seem to suggest that exercise is substrate dependent.

COYLE: In Marius Nielsen's classic studies in the 1930s, he found that body core temperature is not different when people exercise at moderate intensities, even though environments varied from approximately 5°–30°C. At these environmental temperatures one can dissipate the heat to the environment. Are there differences in muscle temperatures in environments that produce little difference in core temperatures? Would you expect any difference in glycogenolysis when people exercise in environments of 5° up to maybe 30°C?

FEBBRAIO: Yes, I would. We found greater rates of glycogenolysis in subject who completed a fixed amount of work in 40 min at 3° versus 20°. We did see differences in body core temperature. The data from

Nielsen have always confused me somewhat because, at least in our hands, when we drop the ambient temperature and keep the work rate constant, the core temperature, heart rate, muscle temperature, and plasma epinephrine concentration all fall. We see a blunting of glycogenolysis and of lactate production.

HAGERMAN: Where does humidity factor in?

FEBBRAIO: If humidity is high and the environment is hot, it is a major problem. At high humidity, because the gradient between the moisture in the air and the moisture in the skin is minimal, there is no evaporative cooling; therefore, the body loses its ability to thermoregulate.

DAVIS: I like your suggestion that a decrease in central drive may be an important mechanism that stops people from exercising too hard or too long in the heat. The problem, of course, is that we have been unable to come up with physiologic mechanisms to explain changes in the brain that might cause this. I think it could be explained by the elevations in FFA that would result from the higher circulating concentrations of epinephrine and cortisol that occur under hot conditions. There is clear evidence, especially in animals, that elevated circulating FFA leads to increased free tryptophan and increased serotonin metabolism in the brain. It is certainly possible that increased brain serotonin could be a mechanism for a decrease in central drive that causes one to stop exercise. There are potential nutritional strategies that might help in this regard if this is the mechanism.

FEBBRAIO: When we looked at FFA with elevated epinephrine, we didn't see a difference.

DAVIS: There are lots of studies that have shown increased FFA in response to increases in epinephrine.

FEBBRAIO: Perhaps at a lower exercise intensity FFA may be altered when epinephrine rises. Epinephrine may not affect glycolytic processes if the exercise is intense and carbohydrate is the major metabolite.

MAUGHAN: If circulating prolactin concentration is a marker for central serotonergic activity, then several lines of evidence would support the concept of serotonin-related central fatigue. There are much higher serum prolactin levels in the heat, and there is a fairly good linear relationship between rectal temperature and serum prolactin in the heat. If we pre-cool people before exercise and then do a standard exercise test in the heat, the prolactin concentration is lower. If we pre-heat them by water immersion in warm water, prolactin response is higher, and the subjective sensation of fatigue is correspondingly higher.

NADEL: At the limiting body core temperature, many other associated variables may be contributing to fatigue as well, so I think it is naïve to think of body core temperature in and of itself as the only factor rather than as a contributing factor to fatigue. Certainly, at very high core temperatures the body's ability to return blood to the heart also becomes limiting, placing an additional stress on the heart and compromising the heart's ability to deliver oxygen and fuels to the contracting muscles. At a very high body core temperature, I believe that numerous factors contribute to the fatigue.

COGGAN: You seem to argue fairly strongly against the possibility that alterations in muscle blood flow play a role in the heat-induced effects on metabolism. I'm sure you are aware of the distinction that has been proposed between nutritive and non-nutritive flow. Also, your case is made on the fact that limb $\dot{V}O_2$ is maintained, with the implication that a change in oxygen uptake is the only mechanism by which a change in flow could affect metabolism. I don't think you really want to come on quite that strongly.

FEBBRAIO: You are correct; I do not.

HEIGENHAUSER: I would like to suggest a different interpretation of the changes in IMP during heat stress. This might actually be a protective effect rather than a detrimental effect. For an athlete's performance, it is a detrimental effect because it adversely affects performance, but for the well being of the individual, it might be a protective effect. George Brooks showed that heat stress can lead to mitochondrial dysfunction. Were it not for the production of IMP, it is possible that heat stress could eventually lead to denaturation of enzyme proteins. It would be interesting to study the relationships among IMP accumulation in heat stress, uncoupling proteins, and heat shock proteins and how these variables adapt to exercise in the heat.

FEBBRAIO: I agree.

WAGENMAKERS: Is there evidence that in-vivo uncoupling occurs and metabolic efficiency goes down in the extreme heat?

FEBBRAIO: We are not aware of any in-vivo data, but we are doing experiments in which we are looking at mitochondrial ATP production rates in the heat.

WAGENMAKERS: Does the oxygen consumption at a given work load go up in the heat? Might uncoupling explain the increase in glycogen consumption in the heat?

FEBBRAIO: We have observed oxygen consumption to be higher, lower, and unchanged in our various experiments. I don't know how to reconcile the oxygen consumption data. I think we really need to look at it from a cellular perspective.

WAGENMAKERS: With the techniques available today, measurements are done in vitro, but we really want to look at the in-vivo situation.

FEBBRAIO: Your point is well taken.

9

Effects of Gender and Aging on Substrate Metabolism During Exercise in Humans

Andrew R. Coggan, Ph.D.

INTRODUCTION

The metabolic responses to exercise are influenced by a host of factors. Probably the most important of these are the intensity and duration of the exercise bout and the physical fitness, habitual diet, and nutritional state (i.e., fasted vs. fed) of the individual. The mode of exercise and the environmental conditions (e.g., temperature) may also play a major role. The effects of these various factors on substrate metabolism have been reviewed in detail elsewhere (e.g., Coggan & Mendenhall, 1992; Coggan & Williams, 1995; Chapter 8 of this book). The purpose of the present chapter is to consider the potential influence of two additional factors, i.e., a person's gender and/or age, on substrate metabolism during exercise. The focus herein will be on fuel utilization during "aerobic" exercise, i.e., during continuous, dynamic exercise with a large muscle mass that requires an oxygen uptake ($\dot{V}O_2$) less than the individual's peak or maximal $\dot{V}O_2$ ($\dot{V}O_2max$) and which can be sustained for minutes or even hours. For information on the effects of gender and aging on the metabolic responses to short-duration, very high intensity exercise (e.g., weight lifting, sprinting), readers are referred to another recent review (Sale & Spriet, 1995).

EFFECT OF GENDER

Interest in potential gender differences in substrate metabolism during exercise dates back at least 20 y, when the rapidly increasing participation of women in sports made it important to know more about the metabolic effects of exercise in this population. At least in the United States, recent funding initiatives by the federal government and by the military have served to further heighten this interest. Nonetheless, the data in this area are still fragmentary and often contradictory. In part, the latter may reflect various limitations in many of the studies performed to date. However, it probably also simply reflects the inherent difficulty of trying to compare exercise responses in two groups that are, *a priori*, different in important physiological characteristics. Specifically, when compared to the average man, the average woman has a higher percentage of body fat, a smaller fat free mass (FFM), and a lower $\dot{V}O_2max$ (in L/min, mL·min^{-1}·kg^{-1}, or even mL·min^{-1}·kg FFM^{-1}) (Cureton, 1981). Women therefore generally cannot exercise at as high an absolute power output and/or $\dot{V}O_2$ as men, which means that they are not exposed to the same absolute challenge to physiological homeostasis. Different approaches have been used to try to deal with this problem, but unfortunately none is entirely perfect. For example, merely equating the exercise intensity as a percentage of $\dot{V}O_2max$ overlooks the fact that at least some responses to exercise (e.g., activation of the sympathetic nervous system (SNS)) seem to be a function of both the absolute and the relative exercise intensity (Davy et al, 1995; Hagberg et al., 1988; Silverman & Mazzeo, 1996). Matching male and female subjects for $\dot{V}O_2max$ (e.g., Costill et al., 1979; Phillips et al., 1993; Powers et al., 1980; Tarnopolsky et al., 1990) circumvents this problem but may result in the selection of more trained/gifted women because $\dot{V}O_2max$ is typically lower in women, even when normalized to FFM. Indeed, matching of men and women on any characteristic that normally differs between the genders creates a potential risk that the subjects selected for study are no longer representative of the population as a whole. Finally, an additional complication that arises when studying gender differences is that in women substrate utilization during exercise may vary depending on the phase of the menstrual cycle (Hackney et al., 1994; Lavoie et al., 1987; Zderic et al., 1998). While other studies (e.g., Bonen et al., 1983; Kanaley et al., 1992; Nicklas et al., 1989) do not support this conclusion, this possibility nonetheless raises a fundamental question: Does the term "gender difference" refer to a difference that exists regardless of menstrual cycle phase (or status) or one that is present only at certain times during the cycle (in which case it might be better termed a "menstrual difference")? This distinction may seem somewhat arbitrary but could be important in trying to determine the mechanisms accounting for any gender (or menstrual) differences in exercise metabolism. Unfortunately, few if any studies have attempted to address this issue.

The above considerations are not meant to imply that comparing the responses of men and women to exercise cannot be enlightening but merely to emphasize that it is important to keep such issues in mind when considering the discussion that follows.

Substrate Metabolism During Exercise

Costill and colleagues (1979) appear to have been the first to expressly compare substrate metabolism during exercise in men and women. Spurred in part by anecdotal claims that women were better able to utilize fat as a fuel, and thus were better suited for endurance exercise, these investigators obtained biopsy samples of gastrocnemius muscle from 13 male and 12 female distance runners for determination of fiber type distribution and activities of mitochondrial respiratory enzymes. Plasma substrate concentrations and the respiratory exchange ratio (RER) also were measured during 1 h of treadmill exercise at 70% $\dot{V}O_2$max. The two groups were matched on the basis of total training volume and $\dot{V}O_2$max in mL·min^{-1}·kg^{-1} in an attempt to eliminate differences in habitual physical activity/training status as a possible confounding factor. As such, this experimental design may have actually favored the selection of more elite female athletes, as discussed above. Despite this, activities of mitochondrial marker enzymes (i.e., succinate dehydrogenase, carnitine palmitoyl transferase) in muscle, as well as the rate of ^{14}C-palmitoyl CoA oxidation by muscle homogenates, were 30–50% lower in the female runners. The latter data are consistent with other studies suggesting that the respiratory capacity of muscle may be lower in untrained (Borges & Essén-Gustavsson, 1989; Coggan et al., 1992; Green et al., 1984) or trained (Cadefeau et al., 1990; Costill et al., 1976) women, compared to their male counterparts, as will be discussed in more detail later. Perhaps as a consequence, exercise at 70% $\dot{V}O_2$max appeared to be somewhat more stressful for the women, as evidenced by the fact that their plasma lactate concentrations rose more during exercise. Plasma free fatty acid (FFA) and glycerol concentrations, on the other hand, did not differ in the male and female subjects. More importantly, no gender difference was found in RER during exercise, indicating that the net rates of carbohydrate and fat oxidation did not differ in the two groups. Based on these data it was concluded that gender had no significant effect on the overall pattern of substrate metabolism during exercise.

The findings of Costill et al. (1979) were supported by Powers et al. (1980), who reported that four male and four female runners matched on the basis of total training volume and $\dot{V}O_2$max in mL·min^{-1}·kg^{-1} had similar RER values during moderate intensity exercise (i.e., during 90 min of running at 65% $\dot{V}O_2$max). Along the same lines, Helgerud et al. (1990) observed that RER values as well as blood lactate levels did not differ in performance-matched (marathon time ≈ 200 min) male and female athletes (n = 6/group) when they ran at their ventilatory thresholds (i.e., at 8384% $\dot{V}O_2$max) or at their marathon race paces (i.e., at 77-78% $\dot{V}O_2$max). This was true even though the women had trained nearly twice as much in the 2 mo prior to the race, and had a $\dot{V}O_2$max in mL·min^{-1}·kg FFM^{-1} almost 15% higher than that of the men. In contrast, however, Froberg and Pedersen (1984) found that active but untrained women (n = 6) had lower RER values (~0.92 vs. ~0.97) and could cycle longer (54 vs. 37 min) at 80% $\dot{V}O_2$max compared to similarly-active men (n = 7). Blood lactate concentrations also tended to be lower in the women, although this difference only approached statistical significance. Curiously, however, these gender differences were not observed during exercise at a slightly higher intensity (i.e., 90% $\dot{V}O_2$max). A unique aspect of this investigation was that the subjects were all students in the same physical education program, and thus had participated in the same activity classes for ~15 h/wk for almost a year prior to being studied. Consequently, the male and female subjects were presumably well matched in terms of habitual physical activity, even though $\dot{V}O_2$max was 30%, 17%, and 6% lower in the women when expressed in L/min, mL·min^{-1}·kg^{-1}, or in mL·min^{-1}·kg FFM^{-1}, respectively. Also studying untrained subjects, but without such careful control over activity levels, Blatchford et al. (1985) similarly found that women (n = 6) had lower RER values (i.e., ~0.85 vs. ~0.80) than did men (n = 6) during sustained exercise (i.e., during 90 min of walking at 35% $\dot{V}O_2$max). In keeping with this higher rate of fat oxidation, plasma FFA concentrations were significantly higher in the women throughout exercise. Plasma glycerol concentrations, on the other hand, were higher in the women only at the mid-point of the exercise bout. Based on their data, both Froberg and Pedersen (1984) and Blatchford et al. (1985) concluded that women rely more on fat for energy during exercise and speculated that this was due to a greater rate of lipolysis and/or fatty acid mobilization.

Two other reports in the 1980s also concluded that women tended to oxidize more fat than did men during submaximal exercise (Lavoie, 1986; Nygaard, 1986). In contrast, others could not demonstrate such a difference (Graham et al., 1986; Jansson, 1986; Wallace et al., 1980). Unfortunately, essentially no data are provided in these abstracts, and none of these studies has ever been published in the peer-reviewed literature. These investigations are therefore mentioned here mostly because they have often been cited (and miscited) in other publications.

The literature prior to 1990 is thus quite inconsistent, with some studies providing evidence of a gender difference in substrate metabolism during exercise, but others not. These discrepant findings may be related to the small number of subjects studied, their level of training or amount of habitual physical activity, or the different means used to try to equate the male and female groups for the latter factor. As suggested elsewhere (Tarnopolsky et al., 1990), in theory such discrepancies might also be related to the menstrual cycle phase/status of the female subjects, since many studies apparently did not attempt to control for this potentially confounding variable, or for the use of oral contraceptives. Perhaps just as important, in all of the published studies described above, assessment of substrate metabolism was limited to measurement of only respiratory gas exchange and occasionally plasma substrate concentrations. When performed carefully, indirect calorimetry provides a sensitive means of quantifying substrate oxidation; however, it can only provide information about the overall net rates of carbohydrate and fat oxidation, and cannot be used to detect more discrete differences in fuel sources, e.g., differences in the utilization of muscle glycogen vs. plasma glucose. Likewise, determination of plasma substrate concentration alone says little or nothing about the actual rates of mobilization and utilization of that substrate and is, therefore, at best only an indirect predictor of fuel selection.

The limitations of these earlier studies led MacDougall and coworkers to reexamine the influence of gender on substrate metabolism during exercise (Tarnopolsky et al., 1990). Six men and six women, all endurance-trained, were studied during 15.5 km (90–101 min) of treadmill running at 65% $\dot{V}O_2$max. The subjects were matched on the basis of training volume and competition history and on $\dot{V}O_2$max in mL·min^{-1}·kg FFM^{-1}. The female subjects (all eumenorrheic) were studied during the mid-follicular phase of their menstrual cycles and were not taking oral contraceptives. Notably, diet was controlled for 2 d prior to these experiments, with the subjects provided isocaloric rations containing 55% of energy from carbohydrate, 30% of energy from fat, and 15% of energy from protein. Substrate metabolism was assessed via measurement of RER and plasma substrate concentrations as well as via measurement of muscle glycogen utilization (biopsy of the vastus lateralis) and 24-h urinary urea nitrogen excretion. The results supported the concept that women rely less on carbohydrate and more on fat for fuel during exercise: RER values averaged 0.07 units lower (i.e., 0.87 vs. 0.94), whereas glycogen utilization was 20% less in the females, compared to the males. Interestingly, the women also apparently catabolized much less protein, as exercise did not increase 24-h urea nitrogen excretion in this group, whereas exercise caused a ~40% increase in the men. Because plasma FFA and glycerol concentrations were similar in the two groups, it was suggested that, compared to men, women may utilize more intramuscular triglycerides during exercise.

In a follow-up study, Phillips et al. (1993) expanded on the above observations by measuring leucine kinetics and oxidation in men and women during exercise (n = 6 per group). The experimental design was the same as that described above, except that the subjects' diets were controlled for a longer period (12 d) prior to testing (to permit measurement of whole-body nitrogen balance). Consistent with the previous data, both RER and urea nitrogen excretion were significantly lower in the female subjects. This was accompanied by significantly lower rates of whole-body leucine appearance (a measure of protein degradation) and oxidation, even when normalized to FFM. On the other hand, nonoxidative leucine disposal (an index of protein synthesis) did not differ between the two groups. From these data it was estimated that during exercise, protein oxidation provided 2% of total energy in the women versus 3% of total energy in the men.

Subsequently, the same group of investigators examined the influence of carbohydrate "loading" on substrate metabolism during exercise in men and women (Tarnopolsky et al., 1995). The subjects (seven men and eight women) were again matched on the basis of training history/volume, but unlike prior studies, they differed in $\dot{V}O_2$max in mL·min^{-1}·kg FFM^{-1} (the latter being 14% lower in the female subjects). In addition, half of the women were using oral contraceptives. Even so, RER and urea nitrogen excretion were again found to be significantly lower in the female subjects during exercise (1 h of cycling at 75% $\dot{V}O_2$max), on both the normal- and high-carbohydrate diets (55–60% vs. 75% of energy). However, in contrast to their report in 1990, in the 1995 paper muscle glycogen utilization during exercise did not differ in the two groups following the normal diet, and it was greater in the men following the high-carbohydrate diet, seemingly only because they stored more glycogen under this condition. Moreover, plasma glucose concentrations were similar in the two groups during exercise, regardless of diet, whereas it was previously reported to be higher in women (Tarnopolsky et al., 1990). Consistent with previous results, though, no gender differences were observed in plasma FFA or glycerol concentrations, although the latter in particular tended to increase less during exercise in both groups following the high carbohydrate diet.

Finally, in a more recent study Tarnopolsky et al. (1997a) examined the effect of supplementation of carbohydrate or carbohydrate-protein-fat on the rate of postexercise glycogen resynthesis in men and women. In this study, male and female athletes (n = 8 per group) who were matched for training history and $\dot{V}O_2$max (mL·min^{-1}·kg FFM^{-1}) cycled for 90 min at 65% $\dot{V}O_2$max to reduce glycogen levels, after which the rate of glycogen resynthesis was determined. Consistent with previous studies, RER values during this exercise bout were slightly but significantly lower in the women compared to the men (0.88–0.90 vs. 0.90–0.93, depending on the trial). However, there was no gender difference in plasma glucose concentration during exercise, in contrast to what was originally reported by Tarnopolsky et al. (1990). Similarly, there also was no gender difference in urea nitrogen excretion following exercise, in contrast to what had previously been reported by this group (Phillips et al., 1993; Tarnopolsky et al., 1990, 1995). Lastly, there was no gender difference in any of the three trials (placebo, carbohydrate, or carbohydrate-fat-protein) in the rate of muscle glycogen resynthesis during the first 4 h following exercise. Therefore, greater glycogen storage in men versus women following a high-carbohydrate diet (Tarnopolsky et al., 1995) does not seem to be due to a greater ability of men to rapidly synthesize glycogen following exercise.

Thus, although there are many inconsistencies, when taken as a whole the literature suggests that, in comparison to men, women may rely less on carbohydrate (and protein) and more on fat for energy during endurance exercise. This conclusion must be considered tentative, however, because it is based on limited data (almost entirely RER measurements), and even nearly identical studies by the same investigators show important discrepancies (e.g., in glycogen utilization). Indeed, the difficulty of consistently demonstrating a gender difference in substrate metabolism during exercise in and of itself implies that gender must have less of an influence than other factors (e.g., habitual activity and diet). Nonetheless, it appears that gender may exert an independent effect on the overall balance of carbohydrate and fat oxidation during exercise. As discussed below, however, it is still unclear how such an effect might be mediated.

Mechanisms

The mechanisms responsible for the putative gender difference in fuel selection during exercise are obscure. Various authors have speculated that the rate of lipolysis may be greater in women during exercise due to 1) the lipolytic influence of estrogen (estradiol, E_2) (Ruby & Robergs, 1994; Tarnopolsky et al., 1995), 2) regional differences in adipocyte metabolism/hormonal responsiveness (Crampes et al., 1989;

Després et al., 1984; Hellström et al., 1996), or 3) simply a greater adipose tissue mass (Blatchford et al., 1985). Indeed, some investigators have observed that levels of plasma FFA and/or glycerol are higher in women than in men during prolonged exercise (Blatchford et al., 1985; Hellström et al., 1996). In most studies, however, no such differences were found (Costill et al., 1979; Friedmann & Kindermann, 1989; Tarnopolsky et al., 1990, 1995). Of course, it is possible that FFA production and utilization during exercise may differ in men and women, even if the plasma FFA concentration does not. However, in a preliminary study of four men and four women, we found no gender difference in the rates of appearance (R_a) or disappearance (R_d) of FFA per kilogram of FFM during 60 min of cycling at 50% $\dot{V}O_2$max (Mendenhall et al., 1995) (Figure 9-1A). Since the women had approximately twice as much body fat, the R_a of FFA per kilogram of fat mass was actually lower in this group. Similar results were obtained in additional subjects studied during exercise at 75% $\dot{V}O_2$max (unpublished observations). These findings are consistent with previous data showing that in other stressful conditions (i.e., prolonged fasting) the R_a of FFA is proportional to the amount of metabolically active tissue, not to the amount of body fat (Klein et al., 1988). Thus, although lipolysis in adipocytes may be greater in women when studied *in vitro* (Crampes et al., 1989; Després et al., 1984) or *in situ* (Hellström et al., 1996), this does not seem to translate into a greater whole-body FFA R_a during exercise *in vivo*. This in turn implies that E_2, at least at concentrations normally present during the

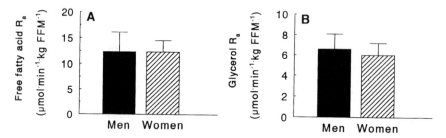

FIGURE 9-1. *Rates of appearance (R_a) of free fatty acids (panel A) and glycerol (panel B) relative to fat free mass (FFM) in untrained men and women during 60 min of cycle ergometer exercise at 50% $\dot{V}O_2$max (n = 4 per group). Free fatty acid and glycerol R_a were determined via infusions of [2,2-^{2}H]palmitate and [1,1,2,3,3-^{2}H]glycerol, respectively, whereas FFM was determined using dual-energy X-ray absorptiometry (DEXA). The women, whose $\dot{V}O_2$max in mL·min^{-1}·kg FFM^{-1} was similar to that of the men, were studied during the mid-follicular phase of their normal menstrual cycles. No significant differences were observed, suggesting that reported gender differences in substrate oxidation during exercise are not due to differences in plasma FFA turnover or in the overall rate of lipolysis. From Mendenhall et al. (1995).*

mid-follicular phase of the menstrual cycle, has no effect on the overall rate of lipolysis in adipose tissue during exercise. In keeping with the latter conclusion, Ruby et al. (1997) found that providing a replacement dose of E_2 (100 µg/d) to amenorrheic, E_2deficient women for up to 6 d had no significant effect on glycerol R_a (a measure of whole-body lipolytic rate) or RER during 90 min of running at 65% $\dot{V}O_2$max. Somewhat along the same lines, Tarnopolsky et al. (1997b) found that giving E_2 to men (100→300 µg/d) for 9 d had no effect on glycerol levels, RER, glycogen utilization, or any other measure of substrate metabolism during 90 min of cycling at 60% $\dot{V}O_2$max. This was true even though this treatment doubled plasma E_2 levels and suppressed testosterone concentrations by >50%. Thus, apparent gender differences in carbohydrate and fat oxidation during exercise do not seem to be related to a greater rate of adipose tissue lipolysis in women, or even to the relatively acute presence of E_2. Of course, this does not rule out the possibility that more prolonged exposure to E_2 (such as normally occurs *in vivo*) can influence the mix of substrates oxidized during exercise.

Since the overall mobilization of adipose tissue triglycerides seems to be similar in men and women during exercise, any gender difference in substrate oxidation must be the result of some other factor or factors. As first suggested by Friedmann and Kindermann (1989), one possibility is that women rely more on intramuscular triglycerides (IMTG) during exercise. Indeed, Forsberg et al. (1991) found that the total lipid content of muscle biopsy samples was more than twice as great in women compared to men. It is unclear, however, whether this represents a difference in IMTG content or merely greater contamination of the biopsy samples with adipose tissue. The latter seems quite possible because a) muscle fat content measured in this manner parallels body fat content, also being higher in older than in younger subjects (Forsberg et al., 1991), and b) based on quantitative electron microscopic analysis, Hoppeler et al. (1985) found that, if anything, intracellular lipid stores tended to be lower, not higher, in women. Perhaps more importantly, greater IMTG lipolysis in women during exercise would presumably be reflected in a higher glycerol R_a, yet we have been unable to detect any gender difference in this measurement during exercise at either 50% or 75% $\dot{V}O_2$max (Figure 9-1B; unpublished observations). However, although the men and women in these studies were similar in terms of their habitual physical activity, they were not specifically matched on this (or on any other) variable. Moreover, the assumption that glycerol R_a accurately reflects the whole-body lipolytic rate has been challenged (Elia et al., 1993; Kurpad et al., 1994). Thus, the possibility that IMTG lipolysis is greater in women than in men during exercise cannot be completely ruled out.

Alternatively, rather than the mobilization and thus utilization of lipid fuels being greater in women during exercise, their mobilization and hence utilization of carbohydrate fuels (e.g., muscle glycogen) could simply be less. Such a difference could potentially result from a gender difference in skeletal muscle characteristics. As indicated earlier, several studies have reported that the activities of succinate dehydrogenase and other enzymes of the tricarboxylic acid cycle (TCA) in muscle are slightly lower in women compared to men (Borges & Essén-Gustavsson, 1989; Coggan et al., 1992; Costill et al., 1976; Green et al., 1984). Other investigations, though, have not found any such difference (Cadefeau et al., 1990; Esbjornsson et al., 1993; Simoneau et al., 1985). A somewhat more robust finding is that activities of muscle glycolytic enzymes (e.g., phosphofructokinase) are lower in women (Cadefeau et al., 1990; Costill et al., 1976; Green et al., 1984; Simoneau et al., 1985), although again this has not always been found (Coggan et al., 1992; Esbjornsson et al., 1993). In general, though, it appears that when compared to men, women have a lower muscle glycogenolytic/glycolytic capacity relative to the capacity for oxidative metabolism. This may due to a gender difference in the fraction of total muscle volume (and thus of a muscle biopsy sample) occupied by type I (slow-twitch) fibers: while muscle fiber-type distribution (i.e., percentage) is similar in men and women (Coggan et al., 1992; Essén-Gustavsson & Borges, 1986; Simoneau et al., 1985), women have 25–40% smaller type II fibers but only 10–25% smaller type I fibers (Coggan et al., 1992; Essén-Gustavsson & Borges, 1986; Simoneau et al., 1985). Consequently, type I fibers account for a greater percentage of muscle area or volume in women (Coggan et al., 1992; Essén-Gustavsson & Borges, 1986; Simoneau et al., 1985). Regardless of the exact cause, however, a gender difference in the relative capacities of the Embden-Meyerhof and Kreb's pathways could in theory help explain why women seemingly depend less on carbohydrate and more on fat for energy during exercise. Such a preferential oxidation of fatty acids might be aided by the fact that although women tend to have slightly lower activities of TCA cycle enzymes, activities of enzymes of β-oxidation (e.g., β-hydroxacyl-CoA dehydrogenase) seem to be similar in men and women (Coggan et al., 1992; Essén-Gustavsson & Borges, 1986; Green et al., 1984; Simoneau et al., 1985). Again, this could theoretically contribute to a selective "channeling" of fatty-acid-derived acetyl CoA into the TCA cycle. It must also be recognized, however, that these differences between men and women in muscle enzyme activities may be the result, and not the cause, of a gender difference in muscle substrate metabolism.

Finally, yet another factor potentially contributing to a gender difference in glycogenolytic flux during exercise is a difference in the hormonal response to exercise. Several studies have reported that plasma epinephrine levels are significantly lower in women than in men exercising at the same relative intensity (Hellström et al., 1996; Mendenhall et al., 1995; Tarnopolsky et al., 1990). This is true even though the overall level of SNS activation seems to be roughly similar, at least judged from plasma norepinephrine levels (Hellström et al., 1996; Mendenhall et al., 1995; Tarnopolsky et al., 1990). Even though epinephrine may be more important in regulating lipid metabolism than carbohydrate metabolism during exercise, lower plasma epinephrine levels in women could at least theoretically contribute to a lesser stimulation of muscle glycogenolysis during exercise. Significant gender differences in the growth hormone response to exercise (higher in women) have also been reported (Bunt et al., 1986). However, whether this might contribute to a gender difference in substrate oxidation during exercise is uncertain. Presumably, if it did, it would do so by affecting lipolysis in adipose tissue, but as previously discussed, the rate of lipolysis does not appear to vary between men and women during exercise. Furthermore, other investigators have reported that growth hormone levels are lower, not higher, in women compared to men during exercise (Tarnopolsky et al., 1990).

EFFECT OF AGING

As with gender, studies of the effects of aging on substrate metabolism during exercise are complicated by between-group differences in $\dot{V}O_2$max, which raise the question of how to best standardize the exercise intensity. Indeed, age-related differences in $\dot{V}O_2$max are often larger than those due to gender: a typical healthy but sedentary 70 y old man, for example, will have a $\dot{V}O_2$max of approximately 25 mL·min^{-1}·kg^{-1}, i.e., roughly half that of a sedentary young man. By comparison, gender-related differences in $\dot{V}O_2$max (in mL·min^{-1}·kg^{-1}) are usually ≤20%. Because of the large decline in $\dot{V}O_2$max with aging, it is difficult, if not impossible, to match subjects of markedly different ages on this basis unless they also differ markedly in terms of their levels of habitual physical activity (e.g., compare untrained young vs. trained older subjects). On the other hand, unlike gender, which is a condition, aging is a process, one fundamental aspect of which is a progressive decrease in $\dot{V}O_2$max. Thus, in the study of age-related changes in exercise metabolism, there is some logic in simply comparing subjects at the same absolute power output or $\dot{V}O_2$, even though this requires that the older subjects exercise at a greater percentage of their $\dot{V}O_2$max.

These two areas of research (i.e., the effects of gender and the effects of aging on exercise metabolism) are similar in another respect: there is an extremely limited amount of information presently available. In the case of aging, this seems to be largely due to the focus of the field of exercise physiology on other areas, e.g., on the effects of aging on the cardiovascular system or on the potential health benefits of regular exercise in older individuals. As will be discussed, though, recent studies have provided more complete data on the effects of aging (and/or inactivity) on fuel utilization during exercise.

Substrate Metabolism During Exercise

Historically, the effects of aging on substrate metabolism have been assessed simply by measuring RER during an incremental exercise test. Over the years, a number of such investigations (e.g., Durnin & Mikulicic, 1956; Julius et al., 1967; Montoye, 1982; Robinson, 1938) have shown that older subjects exhibit higher RER values at a given absolute exercise intensity. For example, Montoye (1982), in a population study of 1,058 healthy men and boys ranging in age from 10 to 69 y, found that RER while walking at 3 mph rose as a function of age, particularly at steep grades. Based on such observations, it has long been believed that aging results in a greater dependence on carbohydrate and a lesser dependence on fat for energy during exercise at a constant intensity. This interpretation is indirectly supported by the observation that blood lactate levels are significantly higher in older subjects under such conditions (Åstrand, 1958; Robinson, 1938; Strandell, 1964).

In some regards, the results described above are entirely predictable: because exercise at a given absolute intensity requires a larger fraction of $\dot{V}O_2$max for older individuals, a greater dependence on carbohydrate for energy would be anticipated. However, other data suggest that a decrease in $\dot{V}O_2$max is not the only factor accounting for age-related changes in substrate metabolism during exercise. For example, in a longitudinal investigation, Gardner et al. (1988) studied 20 middle-aged and older men on two occasions 16 y apart. Over this time period, the men's $\dot{V}O_2$max fell by 14% (i.e., from 2.80 to 2.41 L/min), whereas their RER while cycling for 10 min at 100 W rose from 0.79 to 0.92. The latter, however, was not the result of an increase in relative exercise intensity: because $\dot{V}O_2$ during this submaximal exercise task decreased by 10% (i.e., from 1.78 to 1.61 L/min), the percentage of $\dot{V}O_2$max required (i.e., 64% and 67% $\dot{V}O_2$max) was actually quite similar on the two occasions. Even so, RER rose markedly. Data from retrospective studies such as this one should obviously be viewed with caution. Nonetheless, the results of Gardner et al. (1988) are consistent with other data (discussed subsequently) indicating that alterations in substrate metabolism with aging are not solely the result of the age-related decrease in $\dot{V}O_2$max.

Another factor to consider in interpreting the age-related increase in RER found during graded exercise tests is that the metabolic and physiological responses elicited under such conditions are not necessarily the same as those observed during constant-intensity exercise, especially in older individuals. For example, at rest, concentrations of norepinephrine in plasma tend to be higher in older compared to younger subjects, and this difference usually persists or is even exaggerated during brief, submaximal exercise (Davy et al., 1995; Fleg et al., 1985; Lehman & Keul, 1986). During prolonged exercise, however, norepinephrine levels are the same in younger and older subjects (Hagberg et al., 1988; Sial et al., 1996), or even lower in older persons (Davy et al., 1995), because norepinephrine does not increase as rapidly over time in older individuals. Plasma epinephrine levels (Davy et al., 1995; Hagberg et al., 1988) and rectal temperature (Davy et al., 1995) also increase more slowly in older subjects during prolonged exercise. Because aging may affect the time course as well as the magnitude of various physiological responses to exercise, differences observed during the brief stages of an incremental exercise test must be interpreted carefully. This may be especially true for RER, because aging may cause a slowing of $\dot{V}O_2$ kinetics relative to $\dot{V}CO_2$ kinetics at the onset of exercise (Babcock et al., 1994). A slower rise in $\dot{V}O_2$ compared to $\dot{V}CO_2$ during incremental exercise could theoretically account for a higher RER under such conditions, even in the absence of any changes in substrate oxidation.

Therefore, studies in which older individuals are examined during prolonged bouts of exercise, e.g., walking or cycling, are essential in understanding the effects of aging on substrate metabolism during exercise. Unfortunately, there have been very few such investigations, and even some of those suffer from important limitations. For example, Suominen et al. (1977) used the needle biopsy method to measure muscle glycogen utilization and lactate accumulation in 20 men ages 56–70 during 30–45 min of cycling at 70–80% $\dot{V}O_2$max. Quantitatively, the responses observed were generally similar to those reported for younger individuals; however, the absence of any young control subjects in this study obviously greatly weakens this conclusion. On the other hand, Meredith et al. (1989) stated in their abstract that, when expressed relative to the amount of work accomplished (i.e., per joule), glycogen utilization was greater in older (65 y old) compared to younger (24 y old) subjects during 30 min of exercise at 74–79% $\dot{V}O_2$max. However, the actual data were not presented, and it is therefore not clear if the apparent difference in glycogen utilization was because the older subjects really used more glycogen during exercise, or simply because they exercised at a lower absolute power output and therefore performed less work during the exercise bout. It is thus difficult to draw any definitive conclusions from these studies about the effects of aging on substrate metabolism during exercise.

The state of the literature is such that only a handful of studies appear to have even measured RER values and/or plasma substrate concentrations during prolonged exercise in older persons (Hagberg et al., 1988; Silverman & Mazzeo, 1996; Tankersly et al., 1991). In the most comprehensive such investigation, Hagberg et al. (1988) studied young (20–32 y old) and older (60–70 y old) untrained and trained men (n = 10–13/group) exercising on a treadmill for 1 h at 70% $\dot{V}O_2$max. A number of training- and age-related differences were observed, especially in the hormonal responses to exercise, but, in general, the older subjects appeared to be less stressed when compared to young subjects of the same training status. In particular, the older untrained men had lower RER values and also lower blood lactate levels than did the young untrained men. Therefore, these results suggest that although aging may result in a greater dependence on carbohydrate during exercise at the same absolute intensity, the opposite may be true during exercise at the same relative (and thus a lower absolute) intensity. This interpretation is consistent with data showing that although both $\dot{V}O_2$max and the lactate threshold (or ventilatory threshold) decrease as a function of age, the former apparently declines more rapidly than the latter, such that "threshold" occurs at a higher percentage of $\dot{V}O_2$max in older persons (Cunningham et al., 1985; Posner et al., 1987; Silverman & Mazzeo, 1996). As previously discussed, however, responses observed during incremental exercise tests such as those typically used to determine such thresholds do not necessarily correspond to those observed during more prolonged exercise, at least in older individuals. In fact, Silverman and Mazzeo (1996) found that, when compared to young men (mean age 23 y), older men (mean age 67 y) had higher blood lactate concentrations and RER values during 45 min of cycling at 60–65% $\dot{V}O_2$max, even though their average lactate threshold as measured during an incremental exercise test was significantly higher than that of the young subjects. In contrast, Tankersly et al. (1991) found that young men (mean age 29 y) and "normally fit" older men (mean age 66 y) had similar RER values when exercising at the same relative intensity (i.e., cycling for 20 min at 65–70% $\dot{V}O_2$max). These older men, however, were actually fitter than average, having a $\dot{V}O_2$max of 33 mL·min^{-1}·kg^{-1}. This is about 20% greater than that typically found in sedentary men this age (Hagberg et al., 1988; Kohrt et al., 1991; Ogawa et al., 1992; Silverman & Mazzeo, 1996) and equal to that of such subjects after they have undergone 9–12 mo of endurance training (Kohrt et al., 1991; Sial et al., 1998). This might explain why these authors did not find a higher RER as reported by Silverman and Mazzeo (1996).

Data regarding the effects of aging on substrate metabolism during exercise are thus quite limited and sometimes conflicting. Because of this, we recently examined the metabolic responses to prolonged exercise in six young (mean age 26 y) and six older (mean age 73 y) men and women (Sial et al., 1996). All of the subjects were healthy and normally active, but none exercised on a regular basis. The older subjects were studied during 60 min of cycling at 50% $\dot{V}O_2$max, whereas each of the young control subjects was studied twice—once during exercise at the same absolute intensity (i.e., at the same absolute power output) and once during exercise at the same relative intensity (i.e., at 50% $\dot{V}O_2$max). To facilitate these comparisons, the young and older subjects were individually matched on the basis of gender, height, weight, and lean body mass. Overall rates of carbohydrate and fat oxidation were determined from $\dot{V}O_2$ and RER, whereas the R_a and R_d of glucose, glycerol, and FFA were measured using infusion of stable-isotope tracers.

In keeping with data obtained during incremental exercise tests, during prolonged exercise at the same absolute intensity RER was higher in the older subjects, indicating that they oxidized more carbohydrate and less fat than did their younger counterparts (Figure 9-2A). In particular, the rate of utilization of muscle glycogen appeared to be greater in the older men and women during exercise. These differences might be expected, given that exercise at the same absolute intensity represented a higher relative intensity for the older subjects. However,

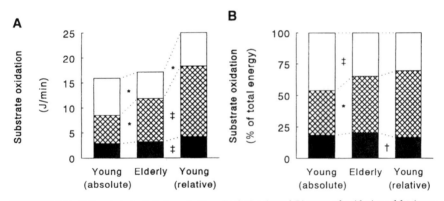

FIGURE 9-2. *Estimated absolute (panel A) and relative (panel B) rates of oxidation of fat (open bars), muscle glycogen (cross-hatched bars), and plasma glucose (solid bars) during 60 min of cycle ergometer exercise in six older men and women and in six gender-matched young subjects.* Overall rates of fat and carbohydrate oxidation were determined from $\dot{V}O_2$ and RER, with the contribution of plasma glucose to carbohydrate oxidation estimated from glucose R_d. The contribution of muscle glycogen was then derived by difference. The older subjects were studied during exercise at 50% $\dot{V}O_2$max, whereas the young subjects were studied twice: once during exercise at the same absolute intensity (i.e., at the same absolute power output) and once during exercise at the same relative intensity (i.e., at 50% $\dot{V}O_2$max) as in the older subjects. Value in older subjects significantly different from that of young subjects: *P<0.05, †P<0.01, ‡P<0.001. From Sial et al. (1996).

glucose R_a and R_d were not increased (Figure 9-3C); normally, an increase on these values accompanies an increase in relative exercise intensity (Coggan, 1991). Moreover, fat oxidation was lower in the older compared to the younger subjects, despite there being no difference in the overall rate of lipolysis (i.e., glycerol R_a; Figure 93A) and there being a higher FFA R_a and R_d in the former group (Figure 9-3B). Thus, the older subjects must have oxidized a smaller percentage of the fatty acids mobilized via lipolysis, with a greater fraction directed to reesterification. The age-related difference in fat oxidation during exercise is even more impressive when differences in FFA availability are taken into account: plasma FFA concentrations averaged 0.48 ± 0.03 mmol/L in the older group vs. 0.28 ± 0.04 mmol/L in the younger group (P<0.001). This elevation in plasma FFA levels was partially due to the higher R_a but was mostly due to a reduced clearance of FFA from plasma (Figure 9-4).

Differences in substrate oxidation between the young and older subjects were less striking when the groups were compared at the same percentage of $\dot{V}O_2$max and the data were normalized to overall energy expenditure (Figure 9-2B). Specifically, the overall balance of carbohydrate and fat oxidation did not differ in the two groups (i.e., RER values were similar). However, in a relative sense the older subjects relied more upon plasma glucose and less upon muscle glycogen for their carbohydrate needs during exercise. Furthermore, although glucose, glycerol, and FFA R_a and R_d were considerably lower in the older men and women (Figure 93), presumably reflecting their lower absolute metabolic rates, plasma FFA levels were still higher in the older compared to the younger group (0.48 ± 0.03 vs.0.40 ± 0.02 mmol/L; P<0.01), due to the older subjects' much lower rate of FFA clearance (Figure 9-4). Thus, although the relative contribution of fat oxidation to energy metabolism was similar in the young and older subjects, FFA utilization was still seemingly impaired in the older group.

Thus, although more studies are clearly needed, the available data indicate that aging is associated with significant alterations in substrate metabolism during exercise, not only at the same absolute intensity, but even at the same relative intensity. Possible mechanisms accounting for these changes are considered in the section below.

Mechanisms

One factor that seems likely to contribute to the changes in substrate metabolism described above is an age-related decline in muscle respiratory capacity. Although initial studies (Borges & Essén-Gustavsson, 1989; Örlander et al., 1978) found no difference, subsequent investigations have consistently shown that the maximal activities of mitochondrial marker enzymes (e.g., citrate synthase) in muscle are 25–40%

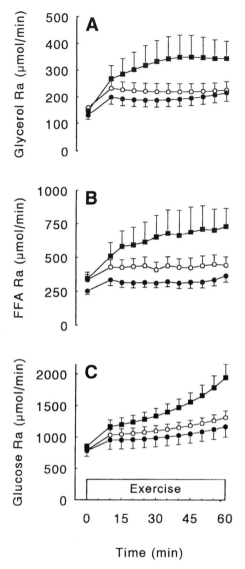

FIGURE 9-3. *Rates of appearance (R_a) of glycerol (panel A), free fatty acids (FFA; panel B), and glucose (panel C) at rest and during exercise in young and older subjects.* The older subjects were studied during exercise at 50% $\dot{V}O_2$max (open circles), whereas the young subjects were studied twice: once during exercise at the same absolute intensity (i.e., at the same absolute power output; closed circles) and once during exercise at the same relative intensity (i.e., at 50% $\dot{V}O_2$max; closed squares) as in the older subjects. During exercise at the same absolute intensity, glucose and glycerol R_a were similar in the two groups, but FFA R_a was significantly higher (P<0.05) in the older men and women. During exercise at the same relative intensity, the R_a of all three substrates was lower (P<0.001) in the older compared to the younger subjects. From Sial et al. (1996).

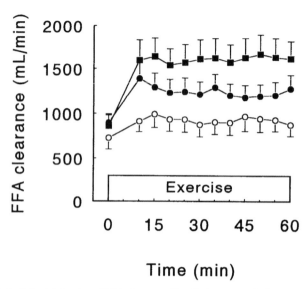

FIGURE 9-4. *Calculated rates of FFA clearance (i.e., R_d/concentration) at rest and during exercise in young and older subjects.* The older subjects were studied during exercise at 50% VO_2max (open circles), whereas the young subjects were studied twice: once during exercise at the same absolute intensity (i.e., at the same absolute power output; closed circles), and once during exercise at the same relative intensity (i.e., at 50% VO_2max; closed squares) as in the older subjects. FFA clearance was significantly lower ($P<0.001$) in the older subjects at either the same absolute or the same relative intensity. From Sial et al. (1996).

lower in healthy but sedentary older subjects when compared to young individuals (Coggan et al., 1992, 1993; McCully et al., 1993; Meredith et al., 1989; Proctor et al., 1995; Rooyackers et al., 1996). This decline in muscle respiratory capacity is probably largely the result of an age-related reduction in total mitochondrial volume (Örlander et al., 1978). There may also, however, be a decrease in respiratory capacity per mitochondrion (Rooyackers et al., 1996; Trounce et al., 1989). In either case, a decrease in the rate of synthesis of mitochondrial proteins (Rooyackers et al., 1996) likely plays a major role in explaining the decrease in respiratory capacity in muscle with aging. However, other factors, such a simultaneous increase in the rate of mitochondrial protein degradation, cannot be ruled out.

Regardless of its cause, the lower respiratory capacity found in muscles of older persons has important implications with respect to the regulation of substrate metabolism. The underlying concepts have been reviewed most recently by Meyer and Foley (1996) and will not be discussed in detail here. Essentially, with fewer respiratory chains per unit of muscle, each respiratory chain must be "turned on" to a greater extent at any given metabolic rate to balance the rate of ATP synthesis with the rate of ATP degradation. Consequently, at the same absolute power output or $\dot{V}O_2$, the steady-state concentrations of ATP and phosophocreatine (PCr) in muscle would be expected to be lower, and those of ADP and P_i would be expected to be higher, in older persons, who have a lower respiratory capacity in their muscles. The higher ADP concentrations in turn would result in higher AMP levels, which would result in higher IMP and NH_4^+ levels. These metabolic alterations would stimulate glycogenolysis and glycolysis, such that the rate of production and utilization of pyruvate would be higher; as a result, the rate of fatty acid utilization would be lower in older individuals.

To determine whether the lower respiratory capacity of muscle in older persons is in fact associated with alterations in muscle metabolism, we used ^{31}P magnetic resonance spectroscopy (^{31}P-MRS) to measure high-energy phosphate levels and pH in the gastrocnemius muscles of healthy young and older men during one-legged plantar flexion exercise (Coggan et al., 1993). In an attempt to differentiate the effects of aging from the effects of sedentary lifestyle, both endurance trained and untrained subjects were studied. As shown in Figure 9-5A, the ratio of P_i to PCr (proportional to free ADP concentration) in the gastrocnemius

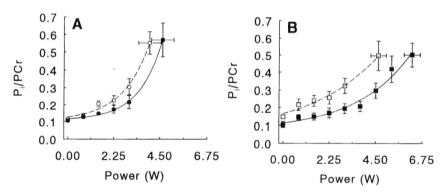

FIGURE 9-5. *Effect of one-legged plantar flexion exercise on the ratio of inorganic phosphate (P_i) to phosphocreatine (PCr) (i.e., P_i/PCr, an index of energetic stress) in the gastrocnemius muscles of young (closed symbols and solid lines) and older (open symbols and dashed lines) untrained (circles; panel A) and endurance-trained (squares; panel B) men (n = 6 per group). Subjects exercised for 3 min at each power output, with steady-state P_i/PCr measured during the last minute of each stage using ^{31}P magnetic resonance spectroscopy. Regardless of their training status, in the older subjects P_i/PCr rose more rapidly as function of power output during exercise. This difference persisted even when power output was expressed relative to peak power or to total plantar flexor muscle area or volume (determined using ^1H magnetic resonance imaging) (data not shown), indicating that the age-related difference in high energy phosphate metabolism was not simply due to the lower exercise capacity or smaller muscles of the older subjects. From Coggan et al. (1993).*

muscle rose more rapidly as a function of power output during exercise in the older untrained men compared to the young untrained men. An even greater age-related difference in the metabolic response to exercise was observed in the older trained men compared to the young trained men (Figure 9-5B). Associated with this more rapid rise in P_i/PCr during exercise was an earlier fall in muscle pH, which is consistent with an earlier and/or greater stimulation of glycogenolysis and thus lactate production. Step-wise multiple regression analysis suggests that these age-related differences in the metabolic response to exercise may be equally due to the ~15% smaller muscle size (determined using ^{1}H magnetic resonance imaging) and ~20% lower respiratory capacity (i.e., citrate synthase activity) in the muscles of the older subjects (multiple r = 0.77; P<0.001). Other factors (e.g., muscle fiber-type distribution, muscle capillarization, $\dot{V}O_2$max) did not contribute significantly to this relationship. When power output was expressed relative to total volume of plantar-flexor muscles to correct for the age-related muscle atrophy, only citrate-synthase activity was significantly correlated with the metabolic response (i.e., with the rate of increase in P_i/PCr during exercise) (r = −0.63; P<0.001). In a very similar study, McCully et al. (1993) also found that muscle P_i/PCr increases more rapidly as a function of power output during exercise in older persons and that this variable was correlated with the lower activity of citrate synthase in the muscles of the older subjects.

A reduction in muscle respiratory capacity with aging therefore almost certainly contributes to the age-related differences in substrate utilization previously discussed. Interestingly, in our study, differences in respiratory capacity and also in metabolism in muscle during exercise were apparent even between young and older endurance athletes, despite the facts that several of the older athletes were competitive on a national or international basis and all trained as much as the young athletes. Thus, although a decrease in habitual physical activity with age undoubtedly plays a major role in causing such changes, some factor or factors related to aging *per se* also seem to be important. It also should be emphasized that the exercise model used in these ^{31}PMRS studies, i.e., one-legged plantar flexion, activates only a very small muscle mass (≤1 kg) and thus represents a minimal challenge to central cardiac function. These studies therefore provide support for the concept that factors independent of the decrease in maximal cardiac output (and thus in $\dot{V}O_2$max) with aging are, at least in part, responsible for the age-related differences in substrate metabolism found during exercise using a large muscle mass (e.g., cycling). This is not to say, however, that changes in the cardiovascular system with aging do not play any role. In fact, there is some evidence that with aging there is a reduction in muscle blood flow during exercise, even at relatively low intensities (Proctor et al., 1998; Wahren et al., 1974). If so, the reduced delivery of O_2 and other substrates (e.g., FFA) could certainly contribute to a shift towards carbohydrate as an energy source. However, other studies (Jasperse et al., 1994; Martin et al., 1991) have reported that aging has no effect on muscle blood flow during submaximal exercise.

In addition to the factors discussed above, numerous other age-related changes could also affect substrate metabolism during exercise. These include, but are certainly not limited to, changes in skeletal muscle characteristics other than respiratory capacity, changes in the hormonal response to exercise, or changes in the plasma or intramuscular availability of substrates. At present, however, solid data linking such factors to alterations in substrate usage during exercise in older persons are still lacking.

PRACTICAL ISSUES

Differences in substrate utilization during exercise between men and women or between young and older persons are interesting from a scientific and physiological perspective, in part because they may help explain differences in exercise capacity between such groups. However, these differences may also have some important practical implications. For example, if women do rely more on fat for energy during exercise, then the optimal diet for athletic performance in women may be lower in carbohydrate content than what has been routinely recommended. In support of this possibility, Tarnopolsky et al. (1995) reported that, unlike male athletes, female athletes did not increase their muscle glycogen stores or their time to fatigue at 85% $\dot{V}O_2$max when their dietary carbohydrate intake was increased from 55–60% to 75% of energy intake for 4 d prior to being tested. In contrast, however, O'Keefe et al. (1989) found that time to fatigue at 80% $\dot{V}O_2$max was greater in 5 out of 7 female cyclists when they consumed 72% of their energy as carbohydrate for a week before being studied, compared to when they consumed 54% of dietary energy as carbohydrate. Although not statistically significant, mean time to fatigue increased by 15%, i.e., from 98 ± 5 min on the moderate carbohydrate diet to 113 ± 10 min on the high carbohydrate diet. Thus, the optimal carbohydrate intake for female athletes and whether or not it differs from that of male athletes remain uncertain.

Converse to the above, an age-related decrease in fat oxidation and corresponding increase in carbohydrate utilization during exercise suggest that active older individuals might benefit from a greater intake of dietary carbohydrate than that normally advocated for young people. More important, however, is the impact such age-related changes in substrate utilization may have on long-term health. Skeletal muscle is a major consumer of fatty acids, accounting for about one-third of FFA disposal at rest and two-thirds or more during exercise; thus, a reduced ability of skeletal muscle to oxidize fatty acids during physical activity could be one factor contributing to the development of obesity in older persons. Moreover, there is growing evidence that an increase in plasma FFA concentration itself plays a key role in the development of "meta-bolic-syndrome" diseases such as non-insulin dependent diabetes mellitus (Boden, 1997; Frayn et al., 1996). Accordingly, a reduction in muscle fatty acid utilization with aging might be one factor accounting for the high incidence of such diseases in older persons.

DIRECTIONS FOR FUTURE RESEARCH

It should be apparent from this review that there are huge gaps in our knowledge about the effects of gender or age on substrate metabolism during exercise. Additional studies using techniques such as muscle biopsy sampling, arteriovenous-balance measurements, isotopic tracer infusion, or microdialysis are clearly needed to further our understanding of the effects (or lack thereof) of these factors on the metabolic responses to exercise. At the same time, it will be important to also identify the mechanisms responsible for any gender- or age-related differences in substrate metabolism during exercise. Finally, additional research is needed to address applied questions that arise as a result of these possible differences, e.g., whether the optimal diet for female athletes differs from that for male athletes, or whether age-related changes in substrate metabolism can be counteracted by interventions such as endurance training. Considerably more research needs to be done before it will be possible to definitively address the topics that form the basis for this chapter.

SUMMARY

Despite considerable interest in the topic over the last two decades, relatively few studies have specifically addressed the question of whether or not substrate utilization differs in men and women during exercise. Those that have done so have yielded conflicting results. Some studies have suggested that, when compared to men, women tend to rely less on carbohydrate and more on fat for energy during exercise. This conclusion has been based almost entirely on measurement of RER during exercise, although in one study muscle glycogen utilization was measured using the biopsy technique. In contrast, other similar studies have failed to provide any evidence for a gender difference in substrate metabolism during exercise. These discrepant findings are probably partly due to various limitations in many of the studies performed to date. However, they also suggest that gender is much less potent than other factors (e.g., habitual activity and diet) in influencing the metabolic responses to exercise. On the whole, though, it appears that gender may play a role in determining the overall balance of carbohydrate and fat oxidation during exercise.

The mechanism responsible for the apparent gender difference in substrate preference during exercise is not known. It has often been suggested that women utilize more fatty acids during exercise as a result of higher rates of lipolysis in adipose tissue and/or muscle. However, preliminary studies have shown no difference between men and women in rate of appearance of FFA or glycerol during exercise. Thus, any gender difference in substrate oxidation during exercise is presumably due to a difference in the fate (i.e., oxidation vs. reesterification) of the fatty acids that are mobilized. In theory, this could be due to a gender difference in skeletal muscle characteristics, with a higher ratio of oxidative to glycolytic enzyme activity in women, which would favor the utilization of fatty acids over carbohydrate. Alternatively or in addition, women could rely less on carbohydrate as a result of a differing hormonal response to exercise (i.e., lower epinephrine levels). At present, however, all of these proposed mechanisms are merely speculative.

As with gender, only a limited amount of information is available regarding the effects of aging on substrate metabolism during exercise. Most studies have relied primarily on the measurement of RER, typically during an incremental exercise test. Based on such data it has long been accepted that older persons depend more on carbohydrate and less on fat when exercising at the same absolute intensity as young individuals. It has been somewhat less clear whether aging affects substrate metabolism when exercise is performed at the same percentage of $\dot{V}O_2$max. However, recent research using stable-isotope tracers indicates that aging affects substrate metabolism not only during exercise at the same absolute intensity but even at the same relative intensity. At the same absolute exercise intensity, older subjects oxidize more carbohydrate (in particular, more muscle glycogen) and less fat, despite higher FFA levels and a higher rate of FFA turnover. Utilization of plasma glucose, on the other hand, is similar to that in young people. At the same relative exercise intensity, the overall balance of carbohydrate and fat oxidation is similar in young and older individuals, but the relative contribution of plasma glucose is higher and that of muscle glycogen is lower in older subjects. Moreover, the utilization of plasma FFA still seems to be impaired, as evidenced by higher FFA levels despite a much lower rate of FFA appearance. These age-related changes in substrate metabolism are probably due in part to a reduction in muscle respiratory capacity with aging. This hypothesis is supported by the results of ^{31}P-MRS studies showing that aging is associated with greater changes in high-energy phosphate levels during exercise. However, many other factors probably also play a role. Additional research is needed to identify these factors, as well as to determine if the changes that have been observed can be ameliorated by interventions such as endurance exercise training.

ACKNOWLEDGMENT

The author's research is supported by National Institutes of Health grant AG-14769.

BIBLIOGRAPHY

Åstrand, I. (1958). The physical work capacity of workers 50–64 years old. *Acta Physiol. Scand.* 42:73–86.

Babcock, M.A., D.H. Paterson, D.A. Cunningham, and J.R. Dickinson (1994). Exercise on-transient gas exchange kinetics are slowed as a funtion of age. *Med. Sci. Sports Exerc.* 26:440–446.

Blatchford, F.K., R.G. Knowlton, and D.A. Schneider (1985). Plasma FFA responses to prolonged walking in untrained men and women. *Eur. J. Appl. Physiol.* 53:343–347.

Boden, G. (1997). Perspectives in Diabetes. Role of fatty acids in pathogenesis of insulin resistance and NIDDM. *Diabetes* 46:3–10.

Bonen, A., F.J. Haynes, W. Watson-Wright, M.M. Sopper, G.N. Pierce, M.P. Low, and T.E. Graham (1983). Effects of menstrual cycle on metabolic responses to exercise. *J. Appl. Physiol.* 55:1506–1513.

Borges, O., and B. Essén-Gustavsson (1989). Enzyme activities in type I and II muscle fibres of human skeletal muscle in relation to age and torque development. *Acta Physiol. Scand.* 136:29–36.

Cadefeau, J., J. Casademont, J.M. Grau, J. Fernandez, A. Balaguer, M. Vernet, R. Cusso, and A. Urbano-Marquez (1990). Biochemical and histochemical adaptation to sprint training in young athletes. *Acta Physiol. Scand.* 140:341–351.

Coggan, A.R. (1991). Plasma glucose metabolism during exercise in humans. *Sports Med.* 11:102–124.

Coggan, A.R., and L.A. Mendenhall (1992). Effect of diet on substrate metabolism during exercise. In: D.R. Lamb and C.V. Gisolfi (eds.) *Perspectives in Exercise Science and Sports Medicine, Vol. 5: Energy Metabolism in Exercise and Sport.* Dubuque, IA: Brown and Benchmark, pp. 435–464.

Coggan, A.R., and B.D. Williams (1995). Metabolic adaptations to endurance training: substrate metabolism during exercise. In: M. Hargreaves (ed.) *Exercise Metabolism.* Champaign, IL: Human Kinetics, pp. 77–210.

Coggan, A.R., A.M. Abduljalil, S.C. Swanson, M.S. Earle, J.W. Farris, L.A. Mendenhall, and P.-M. Robitaille (1993). Muscle metabolism during exercise in young and older untrained and endurance-trained men. *J. Appl. Physiol.* 75:2125–2133.

Coggan, A.R., R.J. Spina, M.A. Rogers, D.S. King, M. Brown, P.M. Nemeth, and J.O. Holloszy (1992). Histochemical and enzymatic comparison of the gastrocnemius muscle of young and elderly men and women. *J. Geront.* 47:B71–B76.

Costill, D.L., J. Daniels, W. Evans, W. Fink, G. Krahenbuhl, and B. Saltin (1976). Skeletal muscle enzymes and fiber composition in male and female track athletes. *J. Appl. Physiol.* 40:149–154.

Costill, D.L., W.J. Fink, L.H. Getchell, J.L. Ivy, and F.A. Witzmann (1979). Lipid metabolism in skeletal muscle of endurance-trained males and females. *J. Appl. Physiol.* 47:781–791.

Crampes, F., D. Riviere, M. Beauville, M. Marceron, and M. Garrigues (1989). Lipolytic response of adipocytes to epinephrine in sedentary and exercise-trained subjects: sex-related differences. *Eur. J. Appl. Physiol.* 59:249–255.

Cunningham, D.A., E.A. Nancekievill, D.H. Paterson, A.P. Donner, and R.A. Rechnitzer (1985). Ventilation threshold and aging. *J. Gerontol.* 40:703–707.

Cureton, K. (1981). Matching of male and female subjects using $\dot{V}O_2$max. *Res. Q. Exerc. Sport* 51:261–268.

Davy, K.P., D.G. Johnson, and D.R. Seals (1995). Cardiovascular, plasma norepinephrine, and thermal adjustments to prolonged exercise in young and older healthy humans. *Clin. Physiol.* 15:169–181.

Després, J.P., C. Bouchard, R. Savard, A. Tremblay, M. Marcotte, and G. Thériault (1984). Effects of exercise-training and detraining on fat cell lipolysis in men and women. *Eur. J. Appl. Physiol.* 53:25–30.

Durnin, J.V.G.A., and V. Mikulicic (1956). The influence of graded exercises on oxygen consumption, pulmonary ventilation and heart rate of young and elderly men. *Q. J. Exper. Physiol.* 41:442–452.

Elia, M., K. Kahn, G. Calder, and A. Kurpad (1993). Glycerol exchange across the human forearm assessed by a combination of tracer and arteriovenous techniques. *Clin. Sci.* 84:99–104.

Esbjornsson, M., C. Sylven, I. Holm, and E. Jansson (1993). Fast twitch fibers may predict anaerobic performance in both females and males. *Int. J. Sports Med.* 14:257–263.

Fleg, J.L., S.P. Tzankoff, and E.G. Lakatta (1985). Age-related augmentation of plasma catecholamines during dynamic exercise in healthy males. *J. Appl. Physiol.* 59:1033–1039.

Forsberg, A.M., E. Nilsson, J. Werneman, J. Bergstron, and E. Hultman (1991). Muscle composition in relation to age and sex. *Clin. Sci.* 81:248–256.

Frayn, K.N., C.M. Williams, and P. Arner (1996). Are increased plasma non-esterified fatty acid concentrations a risk marker for coronary heart disease and other chronic diseases? *Clin. Sci.* 90:243–253.

Friedmann, B., and W. Kindermann (1989). Energy metabolism and regulatory hormones in women and men during endurance exercise. *Eur. J. Appl. Physiol.* 59:1–9.

Froberg, K., and P.K. Pedersen (1984). Sex differences in endurance capacity and metabolic responses to prolonged, heavy exercise. *Eur. J. Appl. Physiol.* 52:446–450.

Gardner, A.W., E.T. Poehlman, D.A. Sedlock, and D.L. Corrigan (1988). A longitudinal study of energy expenditure in males during steady-state exercise. *J. Geront.* 43:B22-B-25.

Green, H.J., I.G. Fraser, and D.A. Ranney (1984). Male and female differences in enzyme activities of energy metabolism in vastus lateralis muscle. *J. Neurol. Sci.* 65:323–331.

Graham, T.E., J.P. Van Dijk, M. Viswanathan, K.A. Giles, A. Bonen, and J.C. George (1986). Exercise metabolic responses in men and eumenorrheic and amenorrheic women. In: B. Saltin (ed). *Biochemistry of Exercise VI.* Champaign, IL: Human Kinetics, pp. 227–228 (abstract).

Hackney, A.C., M.A. McCracken-Compton, and B. Ainsworth (1994). Substrate responses to submaximal exercise in the midfollicular and midluteal phases of the menstrual cycle. *Int. J. Sports Med.* 4:299–308.

Hagberg, J.M., D.R. Seals, J.E. Yerg, J. Gavin, R. Gingrich, B. Premachandra, and J.O. Holloszy (1988). Metabolic responses to exercise in young and older athletes and sedentary men. *J. Appl. Physiol.* 65:900–908.

Helgerud, J., F. Ingjer, and S.B. Strömme (1990). Sex differences in performance-matched marathon runners. *Eur. J. Appl. Physiol.* 61:433–439.

Hellström, L, E. Blaak, and E. Hagström-Toft (1996). Gender differences in adrenergic regualtion of lipid mobilization during exercise. *Int. J. Sports Med.* 17:439–447.

Hoppeler, H., H. Howald, K. Conley, S.L. Lindstedt, H. Classen, P. Vock, and E.R. Weibel (1985). Endurance training in humans: aerobic capacity and structure of skeletal muscle. *J. Appl. Physiol.* 59:320–327.

Jansson, E. (1986). Sex differences in metabolic response to exercise. In: B. Saltin (ed). *Biochemistry of Exercise VI.* Champaign, IL: Human Kinetics, pp. 228–229 (abstract).

Jasperse, J.L., D.R. Seals, and R. Callister (1994). Active forearm blood flow adjustments to handgrip exercise in young and older healthy men. *J. Physiol.* 474:353–360.

Julius, S., A. Amery, L.S. Whitlock, and J. Conway (1967). Influence of age on the hemodynamic response to exercise. *Circulation* 36:222–230.

Kanaley, J.A., R.A. Boileau, J.A. Bahr, J.E. Misner, and R.A. Nelson (1992). Substrate oxidation and GH responses to exercise are independent of menstrual cycle phase and status. *Med. Sci. Sports Exerc.* 24:873–880.

Klein, S., V.R. Young, G.L. Blackburn, B.R. Bistrian, and R.R. Wolfe (1988). The impact of body composition on the regulation of lipolysis during short-term fasting. *J. Am. Coll. Nutr.* 7:77–84.

Kohrt, W.M., M.T. Malley, A.R. Coggan, R.J. Spina, T. Ogawa, A.A. Ehsani, R.E. Bourey, W.H. Martin III, and J.O. Holloszy (1991). Effects of gender, age, and fitness level on response of $\dot{V}O_2$max to training in 61–70 yr olds. *J. Appl. Physiol.* 71:2004–2011.

Kurpad, A., A. Kahn, A.G. Calder, S. Coppack, K. Frayn, I. MacDonald, and M. Elia (1994). Effect of noradrenaline on glycerol turnover and lipolysis in the whole body and subcutaneous adipose tissue in humans *in vivo*. *Clin. Sci.* 86:177–184.

Lavoie, J.-M. (1986). Sex differences in epinephrine and blood glucose response to exercise. In: B. Saltin (ed). *Biochemistry of Exercise VI.* Champaign, IL: Human Kinetics, pp. 229–230 (abstract).

Lavoie, J.-M., N. Dionne, R. Helie, and G.R. Brisson (1987). Menstrual cycle phase dissociation of blood glucose homeostasis during exercise. *J. Appl. Physiol.* 62:1084–1089.

Lehman, M., and J. Keul (1986). Age-associated changes of exercise-induced plasma catecholamine responses. *Eur. J. Appl. Physiol.* 55:302–306.

Martin, W.H. III, T. Ogawa, W.M. Kohrt, M.T. Malley, E. Korte, P.S. Kieffer, and K.B. Schechtman (1991). Effects of aging, gender, and physical training on peripheral vascular function. *Circulation* 84:654–664.

McCully, K.K., R.A. Fielding, W.J. Evans, J.S. Leigh, and J.D. Possner (1993). Relationships between in vivo and in vitro measurements of metabolism in young and old human calf muscles. *J. Appl. Physiol.* 75:813–819.

Mendenhall, L.A., S. Sial, S. Klein, and A.R. Coggan (1995). Gender differences in substrate metabolism during moderate intensity cycling. *Med. Sci. Sports Exerc.* 27:S213 (abstract).

Meredith, C.N., W.R Frontera, E.C. Fisher, V.A. Hughes, J.C. Herland, J. Edwards, and W.J. Evans

(1989). Peripheral effects of endurance training in young and old subjects. *J. Appl. Physiol.* 66:2844–2849.

Meyer, R.A., and J.M. Foley (1996). Cellular processes integrating the metabolic response to exercise. In: L.B. Rowell and J.T. Shepherd (eds). *Handbook of Physiology, Section 12. Exercise: Regulation and Integration of Multiple Systems.* New York: Oxford, pp. 841–869.

Montoye, H.J. (1982). Age and oxygen utilization during submaximal treadmill exercise in males. *J. Gerontol.* 37:396–402.

Nicklas, B.J., A.C. Hackney, and R.L. Sharp (1989). The menstrual cycle and exercise: performance, muscle glycogen, and substrate responses. *Int. J. Sports Med.* 10:264–269.

Nygaard, E. (1986). Sex differences in adaptation to exercise. In: B. Saltin (ed.). *Biochemistry of Exercise VI.* Champaign, IL: Human Kinetics, pp. 230–231 (abstract).

Ogawa, T., R.J. Spina, W.H. Martin III, W.M. Kohrt, K.B. Schechtman, J.O. Holloszy, and A.A. Eshani (1992). Effects of aging, sex, and physical training on the cardiovascular responses to exercise. *Circulation* 86:494–503.

O'Keefe, K.A., R.E. Keith, G.D. Wilson, and D.L. Blessing (1989). Dietary carbohydrate intake and endurance exercise performance of trained female cyclists. *Nutr. Res.* 9:819–830.

Örlander, J., K.-H. Kiessling, J. Karlsson, and J. Aniansson (1978). Skeletal muscle metabolism and ultrastructure in relation to age in sedentary men. *Acta Physiol. Scand.* 104:249–261.

Phillips, S.M., S.A. Atkinson, M.A. Tarnopolsky, and J.D. MacDougall (1993). Gender differences in leucine kinetics and nitrogen balance in endurance athletes. *J. Appl. Physiol.* 75:2134–2141.

Posner, J.D., K.M. Gorman, H.S Klein, and C.J. Cline (1987). Ventilatory threshold: measurement and variation with age. *J. Appl. Physiol.* 63:1519–1525.

Powers, S.K., W. Riley, and E.T. Howley (1980). Comparison of fat metabolism between trained men and women during prolonged aerobic work. *Res. Q. Exerc. Sport* 51:427–431.

Proctor, D.N., P.H. Shen, N.M. Dietz, T.J. Eickhoff, L.A. Lawler, E.J. Ebersold, D.L. Loeffler, and M. Joyner (1998). Reduced leg blood flow during dynamic exercise in older endurance-trained men. *J. Appl. Physiol.* 85:68–75.

Proctor D.N., W.E. Sinning, J.M. Walro, G.C. Sieck, and P.W. Lemon (1995). Oxidative capacity of human muscle fiber types: effects of age and training status. *J. Appl. Physiol.* 78:2033–2038.

Robinson, S. (1938). Experimental studies of physical fitness in relation to age. *Arbeitphysiologie* 10:251–323.

Rooyackers, O.E., D.B. Adey, P.A. Ades, and K.S. Nair (1996). Effect of age on in vivo rates of mitochondrial protein synthesis in human skeletal muscle. *Proc. Natl. Acad. Sci. USA* 93:15364–15369.

Ruby, B.C., and R.A. Roberg (1994). Gender differences in substrate utilization during exercise. *Sports Med.* 17:393–410.

Ruby, B.C., R.A. Roberg, D.L. Waters, M. Burge, C. Mermier, and L. Stolarczyk (1997). Effect of estradiol on substrate turnover during exercise in amenorrheic females. *Med. Sci. Sports Exerc.* 29:1160–1669.

Sale, D.G., and L.L. Spriet (1995). Skeletal muscle function and energy metabolism. In: O. BarOr, D.R. Lamb, and P.M. Clarkson (eds.) *Perspectives in Exercise Science and Sports Medicine, Vol. 9: Exercise and the Female—A Life Span Approach.* Carmel, IN: Cooper Publ., pp. 289–364.

Sial, S., A.R. Coggan, R. Carroll, J.S. Goodwin, and S. Klein (1996). Fat and carbohydrate metabolism during exercise in elderly and young subjects. *Am. J. Physiol.* 271:E983–E989.

Sial, S., A.R. Coggan, R.C. Hickner, and S. Klein (1998). Effect of training on fat and carbohydrate metabolism during exercise in elderly subjects. *Am. J. Physiol.* 274:E785–E790.

Silverman, H.G., and R.S. Mazzeo (1996). Hormonal responses to maximal and submaximal exercise in trained and untrained men of various ages. *J. Geront.: Biol. Sci.* 51A:B30–B37.

Simoneau, J.-A., G. Lortie, M.R. Boulay, M.-C. Thibault, G. Thériault, and C. Bouchard (1985). Skeletal muscle histochemical and biochemical characteristics in sedentary male and female subjects. *Can. J. Physiol. Pharmacol.* 63:30–35.

Souminen, H., E. Heikkinen, H. Liesen, D. Michel, and W. Hollman (1977). Effects of 8 weeks' endurance training on skeletal muscle metabolism in 56–70-year-old sedentary men. *Eur. J. Appl. Physiol.* 37:173–180.

Strandell, T. (1964). Heart rate, arterial lactate concentration and oxygen uptake during exercise in old men compared with young men. *Acta Physiol. Scand.* 60:197–216.

Tankersly, C.G., J. Smolander, W.L. Kenney, and S.M. Fortney (1991). Sweating and skin blood flow: effects of age and maximal oxygen uptake. *J. Appl. Physiol.* 71:236–242.

Tarnopolsky, M.A., S.A. Atkinson, S.M. Phillips, and J.D. MacDougall (1995). Carbohydrate loading and metabolism during exercise in men and women. *J. Appl. Physiol.* 78:1360–1368.

Tarnopolsky, M.A., M. Bosman, J.R. MacDonald, D. Vandeputte, J. Martin, and B.D. Roy (1997a). Postexercise protein-carbohydrate and carbohydrate supplements increase muscle glycogen in men and women. *J. Appl. Physiol.* 83:1877–1883.

Tarnopolsky, M.A., S. Ettinger, J.R. MacDonald, B. Roy, and S. McKenzie (1997b). 17(Estradiol does not affect muscle metabolism in males. *Med Sci. Sports Exerc.* 29:S93 (abstract).

Tarnopolsky, L.J., J.D. MacDougall, S.A. Atkinson, M.A. Tarnopolsky, and J.R. Sutton (1990). Gender differences in substrate for endurance exercise. *J. Appl. Physiol.* 68:302–308.

Trounce, I., E. Byrne, and S. Marzuki (1989). Decline in skeletal muscle respiratory chain function: possible factor in ageing. *Lancet* 8639:636–639.

Wahren, J., B. Saltin, L. Jorfeldt, and B. Pernow (1974). Influence of age on the local circulatory adaptation to leg exercise. *Scand. J. Clin. Lab. Invest.* 33:79–86.

Wallace, J.P., C.L. Hamill, M. Druckenmiller, J.L. Hodgson, J. Mendez, and E.R. Buskirk (1980). Concentrations of metabolic substrates during prolonged exercise in men and women. *Med. Sci. Sports Exerc.* 12:101 (abstract).

Zderic, T.W., A.R. Coggan, B.J. Sharkey, and B.C. Ruby (1998). Glucose kinetics and substrate oxidation during exercise in the follicular and luteal phases. *Med. Sci. Sports Exerc.* 30:S258 (abstract).

DISCUSSION

WAGENMAKERS: I think that if you want to match men and women for training status, you have to match for mitochondrial content of the muscle and for $\dot{V}O_2$max per unit lean body mass. Muscles have the same training status and the same $\dot{V}O_2$max per unit muscle mass when they have the same mitochondrial content.

COGGAN: Are you implying that it is the number of mitochondria that determines one's $\dot{V}O_2$max?

WAGENMAKERS: No, it determines fat or carbohydrate utilization at a given workload.

COGGAN: Ideally, we want to match the subjects on their habitual physical activity. If a man and a woman who have the same genetic propensities to be endurance athletes undergo the same training program relative to what they can actually do, they would be the ideal subjects to compare, whether or not they have the same $\dot{V}O_2$max. If you used subjects such as these, you would probably find that $\dot{V}O_2$max per unit lean body mass would be lower in the women, just as it is in an untrained population. It is less clear whether or not the respiratory capacity of muscle in the trained women would be the same as in the trained men; Costill's study suggests it would be lower in the women, but given the era in which that study was completed, I wonder if those women were training as hard as women of today might be.

WAGENMAKERS: So if you want to make those comparisons, you really should go for top athletes; for such subjects, even body composition is not much different between men and women.

COGGAN: If one tries to match subjects, of course, they are no longer representative of the whole population, and the investigator is addressing a different problem.

FEBBRAIO: If we are trying to study metabolism, matching subjects at the same percentage of $\dot{V}O_2$max is inappropriate because we don't know if the subject being tested maintains metabolic control at that percentage of $\dot{V}O_2$max or not; the metabolic response at 70% $\dot{V}O_2$max for one individual may be very different from that at 70% $\dot{V}O_2$max in another individual. We need to come up with a variable that will normalize for metabolic response to exercise, not necessarily for how high one's $\dot{V}O_2$max is.

COGGAN: I agree completely. Unfortunately, there are two problems encountered in trying to carry this idea beyond the theoretical. One is that %$\dot{V}O_2$max as a concept is very deeply engrained in the literature. The other is that lactate threshold is a fairly crude measure of a person's "metabolic fitness." It may be the best way that we have, but for subjects with a fairly narrow range of lactate thresholds, I'm not sure that adjusting the intensity relative to lactate threshold instead of $\dot{V}O_2$max really helps reduce intersubject variability. There is enough error in determination of lactate threshold that normalizing the exercise intensity to $\dot{V}O_2$max may work just as well in a homogeneous population. Clearly, however, in a heterogeneous group of subjects it makes much more sense to compare metabolic responses when subjects are exercising at the same percentage of lactate threshold, not the at the same percentage of $\dot{V}O_2$max.

FEBBRAIO: Nonetheless, Coyle's data suggests that lactate threshold is a more sensitive measure than is $\dot{V}O_2$max.

COGGAN: Actually Coyle's group didn't compare the subjects at the same percentage of lactate threshold. There was simply the observation that performance varied six-fold in individuals with the same $\dot{V}O_2$max. However, in other studies we have compared individuals at the same percentage of lactate threshold, and when there is a sufficiently heterogeneous group of subjects, normalizing with lactate threshold really helps. In the present context though, we want to know if there any evidence that men and women differ with respect to lactate threshold. I am not aware of any such evidence. So, while on an individual basis it makes a difference whether you exercise subjects at the same percentage of lactate threshold or the same percentage of $\dot{V}O_2$max, I do not think you introduce any systematic bias into a gender comparison by using the traditional %$\dot{V}O_2$max approach.

HEIGENHAUSER: I have a lot of difficulty with gender comparisons in substrate utilization because the method of standardization of body size or muscle mass involved in the exercise may be inappropriate and because the use of RER to measure substrate utilization can be very problematic. For example, body mass is usually standardized per kg, but it might better be scaled to an exponent. Also, very small differences in measurement of RER can produce tremendous differences in calculations of substrate utilization. The very subtle changes in whole-body metabolism between genders that may occur are very difficult to measure. For example, very small differences in the diet consumed prior to exercise can make a tremendous difference in RER.

COGGAN: Your comments should be required reading for any beginning Ph.D. student who is proposing to study subtle gender differences in metabolism. This is a very challenging field. I also agree that although good RER measurements provide a valuable tool, not every investigator makes such measurements with enough care. We need other techniques to verify RER measurements so we can definitively determine if there are gender and age differences in metabolism during exercise.

TARNOPOLSKY: In our studies we find that matching males and females is very difficult. For example, if we want to match six males with six females, we usually have to start with about 30 males and 30 females, and we do dietary analyses, menstrual histories, and tests of $\dot{V}O_2$max and lactate threshold for each of these 60 subjects to get a few subjects well-matched on all of these variables. Also, I suggest that anyone who is doing these studies should use prepackaged meals for the subjects. Another problem with interpreting previous reports in the literature is that there are probably large fiber-type recruitment differences in response to treadmill exercise versus cycle ergometry that may explain some of the different results.

COGGAN: What is your view on the issue of insufficient generalizability of results to the entire population when investigators use elite athletes to match genders appropriately? Is it really appropriate to match in the way you have described?

TARNOPOLSKY: I agree that matching creates problems. There are two approaches that we have taken to try to overcome the matching problems. One is to use untrained males and females and to train them for a defined period of time and then test them at the same relative and absolute intensities. The second approach deals more with the issue of whether or not either estrogen or testosterone influences metabolism. We have used an estrogen patch in males to make their hormonal milieu more like that of females. One problem with our original data is that we could not quite reduce the testosterone levels of the males to levels found in the females nor could we get the males' estrogen up to female levels. But we now have an oral estrogen preparation that will accomplish these two goals.

KENNEY: I would like to weigh in very briefly on this matching issue from the aging perspective. You have said several times that when we match, in this case older and younger subjects on the basis of $\dot{V}O_2$max and other characteristics, we move away from the ability to generalize the subsequent results. I suggest that in many cases, based on the current state of our knowledge in these areas, we need to move away from emphasizing our ability to generalize the results and back toward answering basic mechanistic questions. For instance, if we compare older and younger subjects who have the same $\dot{V}O_2$max, we are trying to determine the potential of aging muscle to minimize age differences or the potentially inevitable consequences of aging because we are comparing "successful agers" with the average young. I think that is a valid approach in studying the aging effects per se.

Another way to make these comparisons is to test very large samples of very heterogeneous subject populations, whether they are males and females or older and younger subjects. Fairly sophisticated multiple-regression techniques are then used to discover which of those independent variables is most important in determining an important dependent variable, e.g., RER or some other measure of substrate utilization. In most of those studies, regardless of the variable of interest, as soon as we enter training status or $\dot{V}O_2$max or heat acclimation into the prediction equations, any significant gender and age effects disappear. Do you agree that this might be the case in the area of substrate metabolism as well?

COGGAN: I agree that the value of the matching approach may vary with the state of knowledge in an area. With respect to the effects of aging on metabolism, I do not think that we are ready to go down the matching path just yet. Still, I agree that there can be distinct advantages to matching when one is investigating basic mechanisms. However, people often misinterpret the results of a matching study. For example, in one study of the aging effects on the sympathetic nervous system response to exercise, the subjects were matched on $\dot{V}O_2$max, and this meant comparing trained master athletes to untrained young men. No differences were found in epinephrine and norepinephrine levels during exercise, and it was concluded that aging has no effect on the sympathetic nervous response to exercise. That interpretation is clearly incorrect. The proper interpretation is that the effects of aging on the response of the sympathetic nervous system to exercise are apparently mediated by the decline in $\dot{V}O_2$max with age.

KENNEY: With respect to exercise metabolism, it seems that much more is known about training effects on substrate utilization than is known about gender effects and aging effects. What I am suggesting is that if learn more about the mechanistic effects of gender and aging using these matching techniques, we may be able to couple that information with what we know about training status, hormonal effects, and other factors to bring the picture into clearer focus.

COGGAN: That is why in our studies of muscle metabolism during exercise, in which we used magnetic resonance spectroscopy, we studied not only young and old untrained men, but also young and old trained men. We did so to try to distinguish the effects of training or habitual physical activity from the effects of aging. **COYLE:** An obvious major gender difference is the amount of body fat. One approach that we've taken was to compare women who varied in body composition from 7%

to 26% body fat and who were matched in other regards, including their training status. They were all trained endurance athletes. We found no difference in any aspect of fat metabolism, despite their body fat differences. Their rates of fat oxidation and their rates of fatty acid appearance were similar, despite three- or four-fold differences in body fat. Furthermore, the fat metabolism of the women on average was not different from that of lean, well-trained men.

BAR-OR: There is another possibility of eliminating some of the confounders that you have alluded to, namely, by testing prepubescent children. By studying children, one can investigate gender-related differences in groups that have similar body mass, height, body composition, aerobic fitness, and hormonal status. Another useful model is longitudinal observation of both sexes during various stages of puberty. The downside of studying children is the ethical constraint that limits the investigator to non-invasive techniques.

SPINA: There may be gender-related differences in regional distribution of blood flow that could affect cardiovascular capacity during exercise. In animal models, estrogen has an important vessel dilatory effect, and that could be a possible mechanism for differences, which could also pertain to the aging issue.

COGGAN: There is a huge gap in our knowledge of the effect of aging on muscle blood flow during exercise. Clearly, this has potential implications with respect to substrate metabolism. In this chapter I avoided reviewing animal studies.

TIPTON: In this field, it seems to me that the best information we have comes from animal studies. I am surprised you did not start your review from what is known from animal studies and then discuss the human data, such as it is.

COGGAN: That would certainly be one approach, but of course one would also have to take into consideration the possibility of species differences.

TARNOPOLSKY: Kendrick's lab studied female rats that were oviarectomized. Ovariectomy caused an increase in glycogen utilization, both in skeletal muscle and heart, and a decrease in lipid utilization. Ellis and also Kendrick's group administered estrogen to male rats and found an increase in lipid oxidation and a sparing of glycogen utilization. They also measured lipoprotein lipase activity both in the periphery and in the muscle. The lipase activity increased markedly in the skeletal muscle and decreased in the adipose tissue.

SPRIET: Many times when we are looking at small differences between carbohydrate and fat metabolism, there is a real problem in quantifying a small difference on the fat side because it is too small to measure with the current techniques that we have. If there were a slightly greater fat utilization in women versus men and you were using a glycerol tracer in an attempt to calculate the extra glycerol in the women that you would predict from the RER differences, could you detect that small amount of additional glycerol?

COGGAN: I think it is a specious calculation because it requires too many assumptions. One would have to assume that a certain percentage of FFA uptake was oxidized, which might vary from 50–80%, and that there is a fixed ratio between FFA R_a and glycerol R_a. Depending on what assumptions one makes, the expected difference in glycerol R_a would vary considerably.

SPRIET: Would it be useful to do tracer measurements across the working limb as opposed to the whole body? If it is a fairly small effect we are looking for and we are convinced that it is intramuscular triglyceride that is providing the difference, would there be merit in moving those measurements to the working muscles?

COGGAN: There would certainly be merit in moving the question down to the working limb. That is what we are now doing with aging and with gender. I think those will be very interesting studies. However, a new methodological concern comes into play, i.e., the variability in measuring muscle blood flow. The coefficient of variation for either dye dilution or thermal dilution is on the order of 5–7%; this affects all of the substrate utilization calculations and limits our ability to detect subtle differences.

EICHNER: I'd like your view on a provocative South African field study which suggests that women can beat men in long races. They matched men and women at the marathon distance and recorded their performances in a 10-km run and in a double marathon. The men tended to win the shorter race, and the women the longer race. Training and running economy were similar, and they did look indirectly at fat use. Only the men seemed to burn more fat during the race. They concluded that the women simply refused to slow down; they ran longer at a higher percentage of their $\dot{V}O_2$max. Does this study show that ultradistance racing is mind over matter and that men can suffer for only 6–7 miles, whereas women can suffer for 6–7 h?

COGGAN: Perhaps there are performance differences related to differences in metabolism, but it gets very speculative to address this issue.

MAUGHAN: Some years ago, Petrofsky showed that muscle temperature was closely related to the thickness of the subcutaneous fat layer. Therefore, the muscle temperature, at least at rest, may be different between males and females because of the population difference in subcutaneous fat thickness, and we know, of course, that muscle temperature has an influence on metabolism and may have some influence on the choice of substrate. Do you know of any evidence to suggest that subcutaneous fat layer thickness might be a factor?

COGGAN: I don't know of any direct evidence. However, the apparent explanation would be that women have a higher muscle temperature, yet they have a slower rate of glycogenolysis. In that regard, the results are paradoxical because as Mark Febbraio has so elegantly shown, increases in muscle temperature per se cause greater glycogen utilization during exercise.

MAUGHAN: That is exactly the point; the subcutaneous fat influence on muscle temperature doesn't seem to fit very well with the other data.

O'CONNOR: Regional fat distribution is very different between males and females. Should that be taken into account?

COGGAN: Deprés' work shows different rates of fat mobilization, depending upon the source. Whether that influences fat utilization or oxidation at the muscle level is a different question. John Miles at the Mayo Clinic has looked at how body fat distribution may influence resting metabolism, but I don't know of any data on the effect of body fat distribution on exercise metabolism. However, since total fat content does not seem to be very important, it is hard to argue that there is an effect of specific fat depots.

WAGENMAKERS: An important consideration that has not yet been raised is the type of exercise testing that is being employed when men and women are being compared. Because women have a greater fat mass, the workload per unit muscle mass will be larger if gravitational forces are involved, e.g., in running, and this may have a major influence on the use of muscle glycogen. Most of the studies have used cycling exercise. Female cyclists with a fairly high body fat content can perform quite well, but there are relatively few top female runners who have much body fat.

Index

Carnitine, acyl-carnitines, 222–223; biosynthesis, 221–222; branched-chain acyl-carnitines, 222–223; described, 220–221; dietary intake, 221–222; exercise effects, 222–223; exercise performance improvement rationale, 225–227; muscle metabolism functions, 223–224; rationale as a slimming agent, 224–225; tissue distribution, 221–222; trimethyllysine release process steps, 221–222

Catabolism, cell volume influences, 67

Catecholamines, effect on substrate metabolism alteration, 329–332

Cell membrane stretch, described, 65

Cell shrinkage, described, 70–71

Cell swelling, creatine ingestion effects, 216; described, 69–70

Cell volume constancy, energy depletion, 58; extracellular fluid composition, 58; extracellular fluid osmolarity, 57–58; gene expression, 69–71; ion transport alteration, 58–59; metabolic pathways, 69; metabolism challenges, 59–60; osmolytes, 63–65; peroxide metabolism, 69; putative role in physical performance, 71–75; regulatory triggering mechanisms, 65–66; substrate transport challenges, 59

Cellular metabolism, cell integrity factors, 54–57; cell swelling by energy depletion, 56; cell volume influence on gene expresion, 67–71; cell volume physical performance role, 71–75; challenges of cell volume constancy, 57–60; gene expression, 69–71; regulation mechanisms, 60–66

Central fatigue hypothesis, BCAA (branched-chain amino acids), 229–230

Central mechanisms, carbohydrate depletion/fatigue, 94–95

Central nervous system, exercise in the heat, 334–335

CHO (carbohydrate), aerobic/anaerobic ATP synthesis role, 6; extramuscular storage in the liver, 4

Chromium, 293–297

Contracting skeletal muscle, blood flow reductions, 324–326

Contraction, cell volume-sensitive functions, 74

Covalent regulation, metabolic pathway enzyme control, 7

Creatine, biosynthesis, 210–211; described, 209–210; dietary intake, 210–211; gyrate atrophy, 216; ingestion effects on body weight/cell swelling, 216; prolonged supplementation effect on performance, 219–220; short-term supplementation effect on performance, 216–219; supplementation procedures, 213–215; tissue distribution process, 210–211; total concentrations in muscle measurements, 213–215

Creatine phosphate, muscle metabolism functions, 211–213; total concentrations in muscle measurements, 213–215

Cytoplasm, fat transfer process, 23

Cytoskeleton, cell volume regulatory triggering mechanism, 65–66

Cytosolic, cell volume regulatory triggering mechanism, 66

Dietary intake, amino acid source, 127

Diets, 40/30/30, 190; animal study relevance to humans, 191–193; carnitine intake guidelines, 221–222; creatine intake guidelines, 210–211; dogs versus humans, 192–193; fuel oxidation studies, 167–168; high-carbohydrate, 166; high-fat, 166; high-fat followed by acute high-carbohydrate effects, 189–190; horses versus humans, 193–194; low-carbohydrate ketogenic, 186–189; muscle glycogen studies, 167–168; performance studies, 167–168; rats versus humans, 191–192; typical North American percentages, 166; Zone, 199

Dogs, diet study revelance to humans, 192–193

Doping, versus nutritional supplements, 208–209

E vitamin, 281–284

Eicosanoids, cell volume regulatory triggering mechanism, 66

Endurance athletes, 40/30/30 diet, 190; Zone diet, 190

Endurance exercise, carnitine supplementation rationale, 225–227; creatine phosphate functions in muscles, 213; ingestion of BCAA effects on performance, 233–235; oral MCT ingestion effects, 240–241; protein degradation during/after, 134–135; protein requirement determination methods, 142–145; protein requirements during, 145–147; protein synthesis processes during/after, 130–131

Endurance-trained subjects high-carbohydrate diet benefits, 178–181; putative benefits of a high-fat diet, 181–183

Energy depletion, cell volume constancy, 58

Energy metabolism in muscle, metabolic alteration and heat stress, 323

Enzymes, near-equilibrium, 7; non-equilibrium, 7

Ergogenic aids, categories, 208; described, 208

Ergogenic, defined, 208

Erythrocyte deformability, described, 74

Estrogen, gender differences, 361

Excitability, cell volume-sensitive functions, 74

Exercise, carbohydrate feedings before, 94–100; carbohydrate ingestion during, 100–107; carnitine supplementation performance rationale, 225–227; cell volume-sensitive functions, 74–75; diet effects on hormonal responses, 175–176; performance limits in the heat, 333–336; postexercise carbohydrate ingestion, 107–112; temperature changes, 315–342; total carnitine concentration effects, 222–223

Exercise in the heat, central nervous system, 334–335; fatigue, 334; fluid availability, 338; glycerol hyperhydration, 341–342; heat acclimation, 336–338; laboratory studies vs competitive performance, 333–334; prepara-

tion, 336–338; temperature induced metabolic perturbation, 336
Exercise intensity, human energy production study, 3–4
Exercise metabolism and heat stress, 318–319
Exercise performance, vitamin/mineral metabolism, 261–213
Exogenous carbohydrates, oxidation during exercise, 105–107
Extracellular fluid composition, described, 58, 72
extracellular fluid osmolarity, described, 57–58; kidney regulation, 55
Extracellular osmolarity, described, 71–72

FABP (fatty acid binding protein), FAA transfer responsibility, 23
Fat free mass (FFM), 356
Fat metabolism, beta-oxidation pathway degradation process, 26; cytoplasmic storage as TGm, 23; mitochondria transport process, 24–26; muscle triacylglycerol metabolism regulation, 23–24; muscle uptake process, 22–23; regulation during physical activity, 22–26
Fat soluble vitamins, A, 278–281; described, 265–266, 278–284; E, 281–284
Fat, coordinate regulation in the carbohydrate metabolism, 26–30; extramuscular storage in adipose tissue, 4; typical North American diet percentage, 166
Fatigue, carbohydrate availability, 94; central mechanisms, 94–95
FFA (free fatty acid), skeletal muscle uptake process, 22–23; substrate metabolism, 321
Fluid intake, carbohydrate ingestion, 107
Fluid, exercise in the heat, 338; loss during exercise in the heat, 339
Folate vitamin, 274–275
Force generation, impaired, 96
40/30/30 diet, described, 190
Free ADP, measurement limitations, 37
Fuel oxidation, early diet studies, 167–168

Galactose, ingestion during exercise, 104
Gender, carbohydrate loading differences, 360; mechanisms for differences, 361
Gender differences, effecting research, 356–357; glycogenolytic flux, 364; growth hormone levels during exercise, 365; plasma epinephrine levels, 365; substrate metabolism during exercise, 356–365
Gene expression, cell volume constancy, 69–71
Glucose, ingestion during exercise, 104; transport process during physical activity, 16–17
Glucose-fatty acid, carbohydrate metabolism cycle, 27
GLUT (glucose transporters), described, 16–17
GLUT-4 glucose transporter, 102, 109
Glutamine, hypercatabolism counteraction process, 67–69
Glycemic index (GI), pre-exercise carbohydrate ingestion, 99–100

Glycerol hyperhydration, nutrition, 341–342
Glycogen content in muscle, substrate metabolism, 325
Glycogen utilization, substrate metabolism, 317
Glycogenolysis, described, 18–20; substrate metabolism, 317
Glycogenolytic flux, gender differemces, 364
Glycolysis, described, 17–18
GPC (glycerophosphorylcholine), described, 64
Growth hormone (GH), protein synthesis effects, 139–140
Growth hormone levels, gender differences during exercises, 365
Gyrate atrophy, described, 216

Heat acclimation, exercise in the heat, 336–338
Heat stress, exercise metabolism, 318–319; metabolic alterations, 316–323; protein metabolism, 322
Hepatic glucose production, substrate metabolism, 321
High intensity exercise, creatine phosphate functions in muscles, 211–212
High-carbohydrate diets, beta-oxidation enzymes, 177–178; blood glucose response, 168–172; defined, 166; diet effects on hormonal responses, 175–176; endurance-trained subject benefits, 178–181; exercise performance adaptations, 178–185; intramuscular triglyceride response, 173–174; muscle enzyme effects, 176–178; muscle glycogen response, 167–168; overall metabolic stress, 174–175; plasma free fatty acids response, 172–173; short-term metabolic responses, 168–178; untrained subject effects, 183–185
High-fat diets, beta-oxidation enzymes, 177–178; blood glucose response, 168–172; defined, 166; diet effects on hormonal responses, 175–176; endurance trained subject benefits, 181–183; exercise performance adaptations, 178–185; followed by acute high-carbohydrate diets, 189–190; intramuscular triglyceride response, 173–174; muscle enzyme effects, 176–178; muscle glycogen response, 167–168; overall metabolic stress, 174–175; plasma free fatty acids response, 172–173; short-term metabolic responses, 168–178; untrained subject effects, 183–185
High-intensity exercise, acid-base balance, 188–189; carnitine supplementation rationale, 227
Hormones, cell volume-sensitive functions, 74; ion transport, 58–59; protein synthesis effects, 139–140; putative role of cell volume in physical performance, 72
Horses, diet study revelance to humans, 193–194
Humans, animal diet studies, 191–193; energy production study, 3–7; increased carbohydrate availability studies, 29–30; increased fat availability studies, 27–28; skeletal muscle malonyl-CoA studies, 28–29
Hypercatabolism, counteracting, 67–69

Muscle triacylglycerol metabolism, regulation process, 23–24
Muscles
  age-related decline in respiratory capacity, 370–375
  postexercise carbohydrate ingestion, 110–112
  skeletal, 109
Myoinositiol (inositol), described, 64

NBAL (nitrogen balance), protein requirement determination method, 142–143
Near-equilibrium enzymes, metabolic pathways, 7
Neuroglucopenia, carbohydrate depletion, 94
Neuromuscular recruitment patterns, substrate metabolism alteration, 324
Niacin vitamin, 272–273
NMR (nuclear magnetic resonance), skeletal muscle metabolism study, 7
Non-equilibrium enzymes, metabolic pathways, 7
Non-lysosomal pathway, protein degradation, 133–134
Norepinephrine, amounts effected by aging, 367
Nutrition, preparation for exercise in the heat, 339–342
Nutritional (ergogenic) aids, types, 208
Nutritional supplements, athlete's search for an advantage, 208; athletes as advertising target, 262–263; BCAA (branched-chain amino acids), 227–235; carnitine, 220–227; creatine, 209–220; ethical issues, 243–244; future research directions, 245–246; lactate salts, 241–242; MCT (medium-chain triacylglyc-erol), 236–241; mineral salts of lactate, 241–242; Poly L-Lactate (amino acid salts of lactate), 243; polylactate, 242–243; practical issues, 243–244; versus doping, 208–209

Oral carbohydrate (CHO) supplements, protein degradation study, 138–139
Osmolytes, cell volume constancy factors, 63–65
Oxidation, amino acid removal process, 127
Oxidative phosphorylation (aerobic metabo-lism), described, 4–5

Performance, cell volume-sensitive functions, 75; early diet studies, 167–168; prolonged creating supplementation effect, 219–220; short-term creatine supplementation effect, 216–219; temperature and muscle metabo-lism, 315–353
Peripheral mechanisms, carbohydrate depletion and fatigue, 95–96
Peroxide metabolism, described, 69
Pharmacological (ergogenic) aids, types, 208
Phosphocreatine, anaerobic ATP degradation process, 30–31
Phosphorylation state, high-fat/high-carbohy-drate diet effects, 174–175
Physical activity, aerobic carbohydrate metabo-lism regulation, 16–21; anaerobic ATP

production regulation methods, 30–37; ATP metabolic signal types, 8–10; ATP utilization, 3; biological functions of micronutrients, 263–266; coordinate regulation of fat, 26–30; exercise intensity, 3–4; fat metabolism regula-tion, 22–26; GLUT (glucose transporters), 16–17; glycogenolysis, 18–20; glycolysis, 17–18; human energy production study, 3–7; metabolic control of enzymes and pathways, 7; metabolic fuel sources, 4; metabolic path-way ATP production rates, 4–6; mitochondr-ial respiration regulation, 10–12; public awareness efforts, 262–263; pyruvate dehy-drogenase, 20–21; skeletal muscle metabolism study methods, 6–7; tricarboxylic acid cycle regulation, 12–15
Physiological stressors, protein metabolism, 127
Plasma epinephrine levels, gender, 365
Plasma free fatty acids, metabolicresponseto-high-fat/high CHO diet, 172–173
Poly L-Lactate (amino acid salts of lactate), de-scribed, 243–244
Polylactate, described, 242–243
Post-transcriptional processes, protein synthe-sis, 129
Post-translational processes, protein synthesis, 129
Postexercise carbohydrate ingestion, 107–112; muscle glycogen storage, 108–110; type/amount/timing, 110
Postexercise glycogen resynthesis, gender differences, 361
Protein degradation, amino acid source, 127; described, 133–134; endurance exercise, 134; pathways, 133–134
Protein excess, described, 127–128
Protein metabolism, amino acid metabolism, 127–128; amino acids as metabolic substrate, 126; exercise impacts, 129–130; future re-search directions, 150–151; heat stress, 322; physiological stressors, 127; protein degrada-tion regulation processes, 136–140; protein nutrition during eudurance exercise, 145–147; protein nutrition during resistance exercise, 148–150; protein synthesis, 129–131; protein synthesis regulation processes, 136–140; strength and endurance activities, 125–151
Protein nutrition, eudurance exercise require-ments, 145–147; requirement determination methods, 142–145; resistance exercise require-ments, 148–150
Protein phosphorylation, described, 66
Protein synthesis, amino acid oxidation process, 131–133; carbohydrate (insulin) availability, 136–137; described, 127, 129–130; endurance exercise, 130–131; growth hormone (GH) ef-fects, 139–140; protein degradation processes, 133–136; resistance exercise, 131; testosterone effects, 139–140
Protein, typical North American diet percent-age, 166
Psychological (ergogenic) aids, types, 208
Pyruvate dehydrogenase activity, described, 20–21; high-fat/high-carbohydrate diet effect, 175

Rats, diet study revelance to humans, 191–192

Resistance exercise, protein degradation during/after, 135–136; protein requirement determination methods, 142–145; protein requirement determination methods, 148–150; protein synthesis processes during/after, 131

Respiratory capacity, muscles, 370–375

RVD, (regulatory cell-volume decrease), ion transport, 60–63

RVI (regulatory cell-volume increase), ion transport, 63

Skeletal muscle, amino acid oxidation capacity, 126–127; amino acid oxidation process, 131–133; ATP synthesis ability, 4–5; BCAA-aminotransferase reaction with TCA-cycle, 231–233; carnitine production/storage processes, 221–222; creatine concentration measurement studies, 213–215; creatine production/storage process, 210–211; fat metabolism regulation process, 22–26; FFA (free fatty acid) uptake process, 22–23; metabolism study methods, 6–7; overexpression of glycogen synyhase, 109; protein degradation pathways, 133–134

Slimming agents, carnitine rationale, 224–225

Sorbitol, described, 64

substrate metabolism, alterations during exercise in heat, 323; ambient temperature, 317; blood flow reductions, 324–326; carbohydrate loading, 360; catecholamines effect on, 329–332; contracting skeletal muscle, 324–326; effects of aging, 365–375; effects of gender and aging, 355–387; fatigue during exercise in the heat, 334; free fatty acid (FFA), 321; gender differences during exercise, 357–361; glycogen utilization, 317; glycogenolysis, 317; hepatic glucose production 321; intramuscular temperature, 326–329; mechanisms of alteration, 323–332; metabolic alterations, 316–323; muscle glycogen, 317; protein metabolism, 322

Substrate phosphorylation (anaerobic ATP production), described, 4–5

Substrate transport, cell volume constancy, 59

Sucrose, ingestion during exercise, 104

Sympathetic nervous system (SNS), 356

Temperature induced metabolic perturbation, 336

Temperature, muscle metabolism and performance, 315–353

Testosterone hormone, protein synthesis effects, 139–140

Thermal stress, labratory verses competitive performance, 333–334

Thiamin (B1) vitamin, 269–270

Timing, carbohydrates taken during exercise, 104–105

Transciptional processes, protein synthesis, 129

Translational processes, protein synthesis, 129

Transmitters, cell volume constancy, 58–59

Tricarboxcylic acid cycle, mitochondrial enzymes, 176–177

tricarboxylic acid cycle, regulation during physical activity, 12–15

Tricarboxylic acid, BCAA-aminotransferase reaction in muscle, 231–233

Trimethyllysine, release process steps, 221–222

Type/amount/timing, carbohydrates taken during exercise, 104–105; postexercise carbohydrate ingestion, 110–112

UDP glucose, converting, 109

Vesicular pH, cell volume regulatory triggering mechanism, 66

Vitamins, A, 278–281; B_1 (thiamin), 269–270; B_2 (riboflavin), 270–272; B_6, 273–274; B_{12} (cobalamin), 275–276; C (asorbic acid), 276–278; described, 265–266; E, 281–284; fat soluble, 265–266, 278–284; folate, 274–275; future research directions, 299; niacin, 272–273; supplementation benefits/cautions, 297–299; water soluble, 265–266; water soluble, 269–278

water soluble vitamins; B_1 (thiamin), 269–270; B_2 (riboflavin), 270–272; B_6, 273–274; B_{12} (cobalamin), 275–276; C (asorbic acid), 276–278; described, 265–266; folate, 274–275; niacin, 272–273

zinc, 291–293

Zone diet, described, 199